The Norton
Introduction to Literature

PORTABLE EDITION

THE NORTON
INTRODUCTION
TO *Literature*

PORTABLE EDITION

ALISON BOOTH
University of Virginia

J. PAUL HUNTER
Emeritus, University of Chicago
University of Virginia

KELLY J. MAYS
University of Nevada, Las Vegas

W. W. Norton & Company
New York, London

W. W. Norton & Company has been independent since its founding in 1923, when William Warder Norton and Mary D. Herter Norton first published lectures delivered at the People's Institute, the adult education division of New York City's Cooper Union. The Nortons soon expanded their program beyond the Institute, publishing books by celebrated academics from America and abroad. By mid-century, the two major pillars of Norton's publishing program—trade books and college texts—were firmly established. In the 1950s, the Norton family transferred control of the company to its employees, and today—with a staff of four hundred and a comparable number of trade, college, and professional titles published each year—W. W. Norton & Company stands as the largest and oldest publishing house owned wholly by its employees.

Editor: Peter Simon
Developmental editor: Michael Fleming
Electronic media editor: Eileen Connell
Editorial assistant: Birgit Larsson
Production manager: Diane O'Connor
Photo research: Stephanie Romeo
Permissions clearance: Katrina Washington
Interior design: Charlotte Staub
Managing editor, College: Marian Johnson

Composition: Binghamton Valley Composition
Manufacturing: Courier Companies

Copyright © 2006 by W. W. Norton & Company, Inc.

ISBN(13): 978-0-393-92856-3 (pbk.)
ISBN(10): 0-393-92856-X (pbk.)

W. W. Norton & Company, Inc., 500 Fifth Avenue, New York, NY 10110
www.wwnorton.com

W. W. Norton & Company Ltd., Castle House, 75/76 Wells Street, London
W1T 3QT

5 6 7 8 9 0

Brief Contents

Fiction

Poetry

Drama

Contents

WEB indicates that a work is featured on *LitWeb*.

Poetry

Reading More Poetry 571

Drama

Biographical Sketches: Playwrights 1113

Writing About Literature 1116

Critical Approaches 1187

Preface for Instructors

Over the past thirty years, *The Norton Introduction to Literature* has helped students learn to read and enjoy literature. This Portable Edition offers in a single, compact volume a complete course in reading and writing about literature. We have shaped it as a teaching anthology focused on the actual tasks, challenges, and questions typically faced by college students and instructors. It offers practical advice to help students transform their first impressions of literary works into fruitful discussions and meaningful critical essays, and it helps students and instructors together tackle the more complex questions at the heart of literary study. We have assembled *The Norton Introduction to Literature* with an eye to providing a book that is as flexible and useful as possible—serving many different teaching styles and individual preferences—and that also conveys the excitement at the heart of literature itself.

Features of *The Norton Introduction to Literature*, Portable Edition

Diverse selections with broad appeal

As in the classroom, the readings remain at the heart of all we do, so we have given high priority to selecting a rich array of representative literary works. Among the 30 stories, 205 poems, and 8 plays in *The Norton Introduction to Literature*, Portable Edition, readers will find selections by well-established and emerging voices alike, representing a wide variety of times, places, cultural perspectives, and styles. The readings are excitingly diverse in terms of subject and style as well as authorship and national origin. In selecting and presenting literary texts, our top priority continues to be quality and pedagogical relevance and usefulness.

Helpful and unobtrusive editorial matter

The editorial material before and after the selections avoids dictating any interpretation or response, but instead highlights essential terms and concepts while providing students with a way into the literature that follows. Questions and writing suggestions help readers apply general concepts to specific readings in order to develop, articulate, and debate their own responses. We have annotated the works, as in all Norton anthologies, with a light hand, seeking to be informative but not interpretive.

An introduction to the study of literature

To introduce students to fiction, poetry, and drama is to open up a complex field of study with a long history. The Introduction addresses many of the questions students may have about this field, concerning not only the nature of literature but also the practice of criticism. By exploring answers to the question "What do we do with literature?" we clear away some of the mystery about matters of method and approach, and we provide motivated students with a sense of the issues and opportunities that lie ahead if they continue their study of literature. The "Critical Approaches" chapter provides an overview of contemporary critical theory and its terminology and is useful as an introduction, a refresher, or a preparation for further study.

Helpful guidance for writing about literature

"Writing about Literature" offers detailed and comprehensive guidance on how to write an essay about literature. As in the book's other sections, the first steps are easy, outlining an essay's basic formal elements—thesis, structure, and so on. Following these steps encourages students to approach the essay both as a distinctive genre with its own specifications and as an accessible form of writing with a clear purpose. From here, we walk students step-by-step through the writing process—how to choose a topic, gather evidence, and develop an argument; we detail the methods of writing a research essay; and we explain the mechanics of effective quotation and responsible citation and documentation. Finally, we include a sample research paper—annotated by the editors to call attention to important features of good student writing.

A Handy Format

The size and design of the Portable Edition make it a joy to read and convenient to carry. Students will bring *this* book to class with them.

Pedagogy

- The chapter introductions in the Portable Edition of *The Norton Introduction to Literature* clearly introduce major terms and concepts.
- In the *Reading, Responding, Writing* and the *Understanding the Text* sections of the book, a question or set of questions follows each piece.
- To encourage students to use the media that accompanies *The Norton Introduction to Literature*, the Portable Edition places [WEB] icons next to the titles of literary works that are featured on on *LitWeb*, the online companion to the anthology.
- Biographical information about the authors whose work is included in the anthology is gathered at the end of each genre section, and almost all biographical sketches are accompanied by a portrait of the author.

Accompanying Media

LITWEB (wwnorton.com/litweb)

This online companion to *The Norton Introduction to Literature* encourages students to think through their responses to literature in three stages: articulating a personal response, rereading creatively and analytically, and researching contextual and scholarly resources on the Web in order to enrich their own interpretive work. LitWeb's features include:

- **In-Depth Literary Workshops.** Featuring 50 works from the text, these workshops guide students through the reading, rereading, and contextual exploration of a work. Author biographies and a set of related links are included.
- **Online Glossary and Glossary Flashcards.** These flashcards allow students to test and reinforce their knowledge of over 200 literary terms.
- *Writing about Literature.* This substantial section from *The Norton Introduction to Literature* is included online in its entirety.
- Self-Grading **Multiple-Choice Quizzes** on the elements of literature.
- Access to **Norton Poets Online** (*nortonpoets.com*), which features interviews with over 60 contemporary poets, dozens of audio recordings of poets reading their work, essays, online poetry workshops, and an e-mail newsletter.

Norton Literature Online

In addition to the book-specific resources available in *LitWeb*, every new copy of *The Norton Introduction to Literature* provides students with *free* access to *Norton Literature Online*, the gateway to all Norton's outstanding online literary resources. You can find more information about *Norton Literature Online* inside the back cover of this book.

Instructor's Resources

Instructor's Manual

Revised by Barbara Bird and Linda Yakle, both of St. Petersburg College, this thorough guide offers in-depth discussions of nearly all the works in the anthology as well as teaching suggestions and tips for the writing intensive literature course.

Teaching Poetry: A Handbook of Exercises for Large and Small Classes (Allan J. Gedalof, University of Western Ontario)

This practical handbook offers a wide variety of innovative in-class exercises to enliven classroom discussion of poetry. Each of these flexible teaching exercises includes straightforward, step-by-step guidelines and suggestions for variation.

Norton Resource Library (wwnorton.com/nrl)

The Norton Resource Library offers teachers an online source of instructional content for use in conventional classrooms, course management systems, or distance education environments.

To obtain any of these instructional resources, please contact your local Norton representative.

Acknowledgments

Our collaboration on this book continually reminds us of why we follow the vocation of teaching literature, which after all is a communal rather than solitary calling. Our own teachers and students as well as our colleagues have shown us how to join private responses to literature with shared learning and interpretation, both in discussion and in writing.

We have many people to thank as this edition reaches publication. Of our colleagues and students, we would like to offer special thanks to Gordon Braden and Victor Luftig for opportunities to teach high school English teachers; to Cindy Wall for being an inspirational colleague who also teaches from this text; to Megan Becker-Leckrone, Joseph Clark, Lotta Lofgren, Chip Tucker, Karen Chase, and John O'Brien for help with sources, both literary and pedagogical; to Ellen Malenas, Jill Rappaport, and Chloe Wigston Smith for their expertise as a teaching team in "Introduction to the Major"; and to Richard Gibson for allowing us to reprint his research essay.

The Norton Introduction to Literature thrives because teachers and students who use it take the time to provide us with valuable feedback and suggestions for improvement. We thank all of you who do so, and especially the following, whose written comments on the Eighth Edition helped us plan the Ninth: Matt Babcock, Brigham Young University—Idaho; Mary Bayer, Grand Rapids Community College; Brad Bowers, Barry University; Paul Bruss, Eastern Michigan University; Donna Campbell, Gonzaga University; Deany M. Cheramie, Xavier University; Dean Cooledge, University of Maryland—Eastern Shore; Frances Secco Davidson, Mercer County Community College; Harry Eiss, Eastern Michigan University; Stephen George, Brigham Young University—Idaho; Jerry Gilbert, Jackson State Community College; Atalissa S. Gilfoyle, J. Sargeant Reynolds Community College; Brian Glover, University of Virginia; Kendall Grant, Brigham Young University—Idaho; Anne C. Halligan, Broome Community College; Jack Harrell, Brigham Young University—Idaho; Peter Hawkes, East Stroudsburg University; Rose Hawkins, Community College of Southern Nevada; Pat Heintzelman, Lamar University; Anne Hendricks, Brigham Young University—Idaho; Cynthia Ho, University of North Carolina—Asheville; Caroline Hunt, College of Charleston; Charles Jimenez, Hillsborough Community College; Linda Karch, Norwich University; Alan Kelly, Millersville University; Mary Ann Klein, Quincy University; Dennis P. Kriewald, Laredo Community College; Shawn Liang, Mohawk Valley Community College; David Lipton, Long Beach City College; Nicholas Mason, Brigham Young University; Arch Mayfield, Wayland University; Michael McKeon, Rutgers University; Michael Minassian, Broward Community College; David Mulry, Longview Community College (Odessa); Nancy Nahra, Champlain College; Kelly Owen, College of Charleston; David Paddy, Whittier College; Daniel G. Payne, State University of New York, Oneonta; Velvet Pearson, Long Beach City College; Robert Peltier, Trinity College; Jahan Ramazani, University of Virginia; Catherine Rodriguez, University of Virginia; Phillip A. Snyder, Brigham Young University; Paula Soper, Brigham Young University—Idaho; Darlene Sybert, University of Missouri; Craig Warren, University of Virginia; Sarah Watson, East Texas Baptist University; Sharon Wynkoop, Grand Rapids Community College; and David Zimmerman, Montgomery College.

The Norton
Introduction to Literature

PORTABLE EDITION

Introduction

Why Literature Matters

In the opening chapters of Charles Dickens's novel *Hard Times* (1854), the Utilitarian politician Thomas Gradgrind warns the teachers and pupils at his "model" school to avoid using their imaginations. "Teach these boys and girls nothing but Facts. Facts alone are wanted in life," exclaims Mr. Gradgrind to the schoolmaster, Mr. M'Choakumchild. To press his point, Mr. Gradgrind asks "girl number twenty," Sissy Jupe, whose father performs in the circus, to define a horse. When she cannot, Gradgrind turns to Bitzer, a pale, lifeless boy who "looked as though, if he were cut, he would bleed white." A "model" student of this "model" school, Bitzer gives exactly the kind of definition to satisfy Mr. Gradgrind:

> "Quadruped. Graminivorous. Forty teeth, namely, twenty-four grinders, four eye-teeth, and twelve incisive. Sheds coat in spring; in marshy countries, sheds hoofs."

Anyone who has any sense of what a horse is rebels against Bitzer's lifeless version of that animal and against the "Gradgrind" view of reality. Like The Grinch Who Stole Christmas, or like Dickens's own Ebenezer Scrooge in *A Christmas Carol*, Gradgrind wants to kill the irrational spirit; he wants to deal only with material things that can be bought and sold and with qualities that can be measured and counted. As these first scenes of *Hard Times* lead us to expect, in the course of the novel the fact-grinding Mr. Gradgrind learns that human beings cannot live on facts alone; that it is dangerous to stunt the faculties of imagination and feeling; that, in the words of one of the novel's more lovable characters, "People must be amused." Through the downfall of an exaggerated enemy of imagination, Dickens reminds us why we like and even *need* to read literature.

Over the ages, people like Gradgrind have dismissed literature as a luxury, a frivolous pastime, or even a sinful indulgence. Pretending to agree with the Grad-grinds of the world, Oscar Wilde asserted that "all art is quite useless"; but by this Wilde was suggesting that beauty and pleasure are the sole aims of the arts, including imaginative literature. Others (including Dickens himself) have argued for a kind of middle ground between the positions of a Gradgrind and a Wilde, insisting that literature should and does instruct as well as entertain.

> *Writing is not literature unless it gives to the reader a pleasure which arises not only from the things said, but from the way in which they are said.*
>
> —STOPFORD BROOKE

Wonderfully, instruction and delight often go hand in hand in our expe-

1

rience of literature: we learn from what delights us or what leads us to appreciate new kinds of delight. The pleasure of reading comes in many varieties, however, and sometimes the best pleasures require an effort that beginners tend to call pain. A lot of the writing that is called *literature* is at first difficult for any reader to grasp. But if we read literature only for pleasure, why would we bother with any piece of writing that requires such effort? One answer is that new kinds of pleasure open up through that effort. As we challenge ourselves to read more difficult literature, we become able to extend ourselves further, much like athletes who train for heavier weights or longer jumps with repeated practice.

Another answer came from Wilde himself, for whom literature is of supreme importance precisely because it frees us from the utilitarian preoccupations and activities of daily life. We value literature (all art, really) for breaking the rules of the ordinary. In some kinds of written entertainment, we find immediate "escape," but even imaginative writing that is more difficult to read and understand than a John Grisham or Patricia Cornwell novel offers escape of a sort: it takes us beyond familiar ways of thinking. A realistic story, poem, or play can satisfy a desire for broader experience, even unpleasant experience; we can learn what it might be like to grow up on a Canadian fox farm, for example, or to clean ashtrays in the Singapore airport. We yearn for such knowledge in a very personal way, as though we can know our own identities and experiences only by leaping over the boundaries that usually separate us from other selves and worlds. As even Wilde might have conceded, literature seems extremely *useful* in this respect.

> *Literature is the human activity that takes the fullest and most precise account of variousness, possibility, complexity, and difficulty.*
> —LIONEL TRILLING

Ultimately, it is impossible to separate knowledge from imagination or instruction from pleasure. For many ages, different peoples have affirmed that while imaginative writing may be like playing, such play is the closest we come to grappling with the complexity of life. Perhaps nothing is more important; perhaps literature is the very thing humanity can least afford to do without. Literature itself provides many examples of characters or even real people who gain a feeling of mastery, meaning, and purpose through learning to read and to write. Take a famous episode in *The Autobiography of Malcolm X* (1964). Malcolm X, in prison, with only an eighth-grade education, realizes he needs to learn standard written and spoken English if he is to succeed as a leader. He begins by copying every word in the dictionary and soon moves to absorbing the books on history and religion in the prison's extensive library. What were the fruits of this labor? "I had never been so truly free in my life. . . . [A] new world opened to me, of being able to read and *understand*." Literacy and a wide knowledge of literature of various kinds can be a sort of franchise, like the vote, and can launch a career.

You may already feel the power and pleasure to be gained from a sustained encounter with challenging reading. Then why not simply enjoy it in solitude, on your own free time? Because reading is only one of the activities involved in gaining a full understanding of literature. Literature has a history, and learning that history makes all the difference in the pleasure you can derive from literature. By studying different kinds of literature, or **genres**, as well as different works from various times in history and from various national traditions—by becoming familiar with the conventions of writing a sonnet in seventeenth-century England or of writing a short story in 1920s America—you can come to appreciate and even love works that you might have disliked if you simply read them on your own. Discussing works with your teachers and other students, and writing about them, will give you practice in analyzing them in greater depth. A clear understanding of the aims and designs of a story, poem, or play never falls like a bolt from the blue. Instead, it emerges from a process that often involves comparing this work with other works of its genre, trying to put into words *how* and *why* this work had such an effect on you, and responding to what others say or write about it.

Yet studying literature involves more than cultivating your own skills and insights. Reading can open worlds and change a person's life, but literature also has the potential for political effects. The international best-seller *Uncle Tom's Cabin* (1852), for example, helped create such strong antislavery sentiments before the U.S. Civil War that Abraham Lincoln reportedly described its author, Harriet Beecher Stowe, as "the little lady who started the big war." The personal and the political effects of literature intertwine. A sense of self and an identity as part of a group or a nationality are shaped and reinforced by respected traditions, and many groups and nations now try to recover and protect their own literary traditions rather than be misrepresented by the writings of others. Margaret Atwood has claimed that when Canadian literature was ignored, for instance, Canada itself seemed to have forgotten its identity. Since the 1970s, Canada and many other former colonies of European countries have recovered and developed thriving literatures of their own. Instead of one **canon**—or a single selective list of the most-recognized or most-esteemed works—there are now many canons of literature written in English.

> *When other people tell your story, it always comes out crooked.*
> —CHIPPEWA ELDER

"The Canon"

As you begin your college-level study of literature, a debate rages all around you about "the canon." Although this debate has many dimensions, it is often reduced to questions about which authors should be included in literature courses and anthologies: why Dryden and Pope but not Aphra Behn; why Ralph Ellison and not Zora Neale Hurston; why Joseph Conrad or Doris Lessing and not V. S. Naipaul or Bessie Head? *Whom* we publish and teach matters, because our choices convey certain messages about the many kinds of people who have made an art of writing. There are many more people who have expressed themselves in writing than you will be able to read in your lifetime, let alone your college career or this semester. Any anthology, any literature course, leaves out far more than it includes. The anthology you hold in your hands represents a diverse array of authors both ancient and modern, but it does not treat an assortment of types of authors as an end in itself. The works included here are *good*—each after its kind is a splendid creation—but of course such a judgment of quality requires some supporting evidence. As you read, you can gather the most telling evidence, identify your own standards for judging texts, define your own approaches to interpreting them, and finally decide for yourself whether these works belong in the book or in your personal "canon."

Debates about the canon and about whom we should include on the list of literary "greats" won't end soon, largely because such arguments are part of a discussion as old as literature itself. And even the notion of "literature" has had an interesting history.

What Is Literature?

Before you opened this book, you probably could guess that it would contain the sorts of stories, poems, and plays you have encountered in English classes or in the literature section of a library or bookstore. The three genres of imaginative writing that we select for *The Norton Introduction to Literature* form the heart of literature as it has been defined in schools and universities for over a century. *The Oxford English Dictionary (OED)* defines literature as "writing which has claim to consideration on the ground of beauty of form or emotional effect." The key elements in this definition may be *writing*—after all, the words *literature* and *letters* have roots in common—and *beauty* and *emotion*. But we sometimes use the word *literature* to refer to writing that has little to do with feelings or artful form, as in "scientific literature"—the articles on a particular subject—or "campaign literature." And at least some of the nonfictional works studied in literature classrooms—Martin Luther King Jr.'s "Letter from Birmingham Jail," for example—were originally intended as "campaign literature" of one sort or another.

Literature is not things but a way to comprehend things.
—NORMAN N. HOLLAND

Could literature, then, include *anything* written? Or could it include works that do not depend on written words, such as staged performances or works recorded on media such as videotape or film? Every society has forms of oral storytelling or poetry, and some peoples do not write down the cherished myths and traditions that are their "literature." If you go on to take more classes in literature or to major in English or another language, you might encounter texts that stretch the concept of literature still further: Web sites or electronic games, for example.

The concept of "literature" as we know it is fairly new. Two hundred years ago, before universities were open to women or people of color, a small male elite studied the ancient classics in Greek and Latin, never dreaming of taking college courses about poetry or fiction or drama written in the modern languages in everyday use. Before modern literature became part of the college curriculum, the word *literature* itself had to be invented. At first, it referred to the cultivation of reading or the practice of writing ("he was a man of much literature"). Only later did it refer to a specialized category of works. Over time, this category narrowed more and more, eventually designating only a special set of imaginative writings, particularly associated with a language and nation (as in "English," "American," or "French" literature). Roughly speaking, by 1900 a college student could take a course in English literature, and the syllabus would exclude most nonfictional forms of writing, from travel writing and journalism to biography, history, or philosophy. Although students at the time would have read widely in these genres of nonfiction, the curriculum in "English literature" had become a walled-in flower garden filled with works of beauty, pleasure, and imagination, and its walls held fast for most of the twentieth century.

But now, as you begin this introduction to literature in the twenty-first century, the walls of that garden are coming down. Literature today generally encompasses oral and even visual forms (film and video being closely related to drama, of course), and it takes in, as it did long ago, writings of diverse design and purpose, including nonfiction. As a twenty-first-century student of literature, you may feel the pleasure *National literature is now rather an unmeaning term; the epoch of world literature is at hand, and everyone must strive to hasten its approach.*
—J. W. GOETHE

of reading the best imaginative writings of the past, hoping with the speaker of Keats's "Ode on Melancholy" to "burst Joy's grape against" your "palate fine"—to test your palate or taste for the beauty of language and form. Obviously, the garden reserved for beautiful poetry, fiction, and drama is flourishing; this anthology is testament to its continued health. But the fields beyond the unwalled garden are wild and inviting as well.

Since there has never been absolute, lasting agreement about *what* counts as literature, we might consider instead *how* and *why* we look at particular forms of expression. A song lyric, a screenplay, a supermarket romance, a novel by Toni Morrison or Thomas Mann, and a poem by Walt Whitman or Katherine Philips—each may be interpreted in *literary ways* that yield insights and pleasures. Honing your skills at this kind of interpretation is the primary purpose of this book and most literature courses. By learning to recognize how a story, poem, or play works—not only how it is beautiful and pleasurable but also how it is *effective*—you should gain interpretative skills that you can take with you when you explore zones outside the garden of literature.

Thinking Critically about Literature

From the start of your first encounter with a literary work, you begin the process of **literary criticism** as you formulate questions about the mode (*is this fiction? is it a novel?*), the manner (*who is the narrator? is the style modern, funny?*), and the aims of the text (*is it satiric? is the reader supposed to sympathize with the main character?*). To read the text well, you need to pick up on signals about the way the text is formed, and almost as soon as you have noticed these signals, you begin to explain what they might mean. Your critical reading of a work could start with a simple catalog of its **elements**: you could name the **characters;** retell the **action;** identify the **meter** and **rhyme scheme.** By writing these observations down, you might find new details to observe in the process. Your reading and writing about a work could advance a step further with the help of literary terms, such as **stanza, narrator, metaphor,** because these terms conveniently and quickly identify specific effects and help to connect them to similar techniques or features of other works. A good reader quickly moves from noticing details of a work to interpreting the significance of the way elements are combined in this particular work. A practiced reader, further, compares this work to others, recognizing the characteristics of, say, realist novels or lyrics about love, and noting how this particular example distinguishes itself from others of its genre. Whenever you read, you make crucial assessments of this sort, perhaps even subconsciously.

If you have made a good mental picture of the work and noted your detailed observations, you have laid the foundation of good critical reading and writing. Yet a description of details is not enough for an essay of literary criticism. As a student in a course on literature, you will be discussing works of literature with your class and writing interpretations of these works, to be read by classmates, your instructor, perhaps a parent or friend. Remember that *your* reader will want to learn something from your essay that is not in plain view on a first reading of the literary work. Criticism, in other words, becomes worthwhile when it expresses something unexpected or debatable about a work. This does not mean that good criticism consists of an extreme interpretation based on your own personal feelings. To be persuasive, your critical writing needs to support your impressions with the sort of evidence—such as the details that you have noted in preparation—that will convince others to share your impressions. You will need to argue a case for your interpretation; often the heart of your argument is that the specific evidence you have put forward is a key to a better understanding of the work. Both discussion and writing will help you become a better reader and literary critic in this way. Very often, you will make the text itself seem all the richer and more complex in the process of showing others how it works: its design and the meanings of its effects. Before you venture into this new territory of making your thoughts about works of literature known to your peers and your teacher, however, it might help to review what it means to approach literature from a critical and analytical perspective.

Methods of literary interpretation, like definitions of literature, have varied over time. We may be amused or amazed at the assumptions that guided literary studies in an earlier age, but we should beware of assuming that our own approach is natural, correct, or inevitable. It is good to remember, for instance, that in the early 1800s, many people decried the seductive dangers of novel-reading, especially for young girls. The warnings back then resemble those we hear now about television, video games, and the Internet. Perhaps your children will live in a time when the digital media of the early twenty-first century receives the kind of careful interpretation and appreciation that we grant to novels today.

Every reader has a theory about literature and how to interpret it, whether articulated or not. Over a century ago, an American professor of English, C. T. Winchester, argued in *Some Principles of Literary Criticism* (1902) that "Literary Criticism" should "determine the essential or intrinsic virtues of literature" and measure each

Literature is language charged with meaning. . . . Literature is news that stays news.

—EZRA POUND

work according to those standards. To Winchester, the student's or critic's task is aesthetic "appreciation" of works that have gained "permanence" because of their "appeal to the emotions"; historical or biographical concerns should be kept subordinate to aesthetic judgment. Winchester's plan looked natural or normal in his day, but today it seems unduly limiting. In the late twentieth century, literary scholars questioned nearly every one of Winchester's (and his generation's) underlying assumptions. These more recent scholars called into question the power of language to refer to reality or to express shared values or feelings, the notion that the author consciously intends all or even most of the meanings that can be found in a work, and the near-sacred status that literature had enjoyed for centuries. In the "Critical Approaches" chapter, we provide sketches of some contemporary theories and methods that encourage various ways of seeing literature and culture generally. Knowing a little about these "schools" of literary criticism or theory may help you to recognize and refine your own critical assumptions and methods, and may save you steps in clarifying your views.

Do you need to know anything specialized about literary criticism as you begin to learn how to interpret and write about literature? Your manner of literary criticism rightly will differ from that of a professional literary critic or theorist, as much as the lab work of a student in biology or chemistry differs from the research conducted by the authors of articles in *Science* or *Nature*. Yet just as the student in a lab should be engaged in hands-on discovery, and sometimes has an opportunity to contribute to a published finding, you will be able to develop original and interesting responses to what you read. To offer another metaphor that is even more appropriate to the arts (which have often been called nourishment for the spirit): most of us have thought a great deal about food, yet few of us are farmers, chefs, or restaurant critics. Dining offers greater pleasure, though, when we know the kinds of ingredients that went into each dish, how it has been prepared, and whether the plate before us presents a good example of gumbo or bouillabaisse.

Often students and even teachers of literature object to systems or theories of literary criticism. Too much information about the writer, the work, or the contexts surrounding them, or too many technical terms, can interfere with an original response. Many students wonder not only about the uses of a systematic critical theory, but also about the aims of thorough interpretation or close reading. Why subject the poor text to such probing and questioning? Did the author ever really intend such deep paradoxes or heavy symbolism? Why not content ourselves with our private, unspoiled impressions, and let the text go about its business?

The problem with this understandable wish for an innocent reading and a pure text is that neither of these exist. Three entities must unite in order to produce any act of reading and interpretation: the source of the text (the **author** and other factors that produce it); the **text** itself; and the receiver of the text (the **reader** and other aspects of reception). Your reading and interpretation will be enhanced if you take each of these components into consideration. The most important thing to realize is that each of these three factors, involving real people and their roles or positions, is surrounded by a **historical context**—by external events, cultural and personal values and beliefs, as well as economic constraints and opportunities—that has partly shaped it.

To illustrate the importance of historical context, let's begin by looking at the person with whom you are most familiar: *you.* You undoubtedly sense your uniqueness, and may even see that your uniqueness is determined in part by your beliefs and values as well as by your personal history. But you may not perceive those beliefs, values, and history as having been shaped in turn by many external forces beyond your own or your friends' and family's control. Now and then you may have wondered about the effects of such forces or have been frustrated by the limits they place on you. (Have you ever wished you were born in a different century, or as a different type of person?) At times, you have probably realized that your perceptions of the world depend on who you are—and that someone figuratively standing in a different place would see things from a different point of view.

Nevertheless, it is difficult to maintain this sort of perspective on ourselves and what influences our responses. As a reader, for example, you may feel that you are just reading a poem neutrally, the way you might read a newspaper report about weather on the other side of the world. In any kind of reading, however, you apply your experience with reading similar texts, drawing on your fluency in the language, your ability to read this and other kinds of texts, as well as the information and assumptions that you have been accumulating since birth. You carry the baggage of someone alive today with your particular cultural and family history, and you have particular skills and preconceptions that frame your reading.

Literature is the one place in any society where, within the secrecy of our own heads, we can hear voices talking about everything in every possible way.

—SALMAN RUSHDIE

Just as you are a unique reader, the story, play, or poem that you read imports its own historical context, and so it actually changes more or less over time. The sequence of words may remain almost identical, from the author's original manuscript to the original published form to the pages of this anthology (although textual scholars would emphasize how much variation there may be between editions). But words in themselves don't create meaning. Think of the puzzlement created by Egyptian hieroglyphs until the Rosetta Stone, found in 1799, provided clues to enable the work of translation. The signs carved in the second century B.C.E. had lost their power to convey meaning until scholars in the 1920s recreated the key, but even then, modern readers could only guess at the nature of the ancient beliefs and practices to which the signs originally referred. Each time we read a text, we become to some extent archeologists or linguists, unearthing and re-creating a sequence of letters, spaces, punctuation marks that has been lying dormant. Most of the literature reprinted here reflects the literary practices and fashions of our own era, yet historical change can be significant over even a few decades, or across different social groups and cultures. When you read, you should be aware of when the work was written and published, since knowing this can help prevent misinterpretations of everything from words that have changed meanings to whether the style was innovative or old-fashioned when the work first came out. Placing a text in its historical and social context can be a rewarding critical method.

If both the reader and the text belong in historical contexts that shape our interpretation, so too does the writer. Contextual issues relating to the author usually concern the career—other works by the same person, relative success and reputation—and what is known about the life. When you read a work in this anthology, the writer's name (or "Anonymous") should be what you notice right after the title. Combined with the publication date, this can provide keys to your reading. The Biographical Sketches following each genre give brief biographies for most of the writers, and you can easily find more information in reference works online or in print, such as *The Dictionary of Literary Biography*. Your instructors may encourage you to read several works by the same author and to learn about the writer's life. Knowing something about the person who wrote the work inevitably shapes interpretation, just as the writer's life was shaped by historical, social, and cultural conditions. Imagine Phillis Wheatley, who had been enslaved as a child in Africa and brought to Boston in 1761, finding time after her housework to write **heroic couplets** with the quill of a bird dipped in homemade ink, by the light of a candle made of animal fat, on paper so expensive that people seldom threw out a "rough draft." Her poetry was of her time, but it was viewed as a curiosity: the first published writing by an African American woman. Most readings of literature draw upon such information about the author's historical context and biography. Yet we cannot return to Boston in the 1770s and interview Wheatley to ask her what she meant in any line of her poetry.

Even when a poet or playwright or fiction writer is still alive, it can be misleading to take his or her word about what the work means. Though critics usually do consider what is known about the writer, they prefer to focus on the text itself rather than the creator's state-

Literature always anticipates life. It does not copy it, but molds it to its purpose.
—OSCAR WILDE

ments about what it means. This is precisely because literary works usually intertwine more implications than anyone could consciously intend, and hence remain open to the varied interpretation of others. Further, critics avoid identifying the actual author with the **speaker** of a poem, the **characters** in a play, or the **narrator** of a fictional story. Even very personal or autobiographical writing is an utterance that has been removed from its source, the real person who might write contradictory things in different moods, or would speak differently when just chatting with a friend. Critics have developed the concept of the **implied author**, the designing personality or value system that guides us in this particular text, in order not to confuse the interpretation with too much concern for the biography and intentions of the real author. The implied author will often seem to ask a reader to stand at a distance from the viewpoint of a narrator or speaker: the blandly decent lawyer in "Bartleby, the Scrivener" or the monomaniacal duke in "My Last Duchess," for instance. It is helpful to set aside biography during reading, and to consider whether we are asked to resist the values or behaviors being shown to us. Should we sympathize with Bartleby's nihilism and reproach the lawyer? What sort of future son-in-law would proudly insinuate that he murdered his previous wife? The speaker in a **dramatic monologue** or the narrator who is also a participant in a story should be regarded as akin to a character in a play, that is, as distinct from the poet or author. Because characters in most plays are created to be performed by actors on stage, audiences seldom confuse characters with the playwright, though there may be lines or speeches that seem close to what the playwright would have been likely to say in person.

And all else is literature.
                          —PAUL VERLAINE

Bearing in mind the various contexts that shape the source, text, and audience will help you develop more persuasive interpretations of literature. You will notice, too, that interpretation is always open to discussion. There will always be a variety of respected approaches—generally concentrating on different aspects of the exchange between source, text, and audience—to the study of texts that reward interpretation. You may become acquainted with the variety of schools of literary criticism and theory that, across the generations, have yielded powerful interpretations of literature. Such diversity of methods might suggest that the discussion is pointless: there is no arguing taste, any interpretation will do as well as another. On the contrary, it is quite easy to judge whether any of the various interpretations is reasonably supported by the evidence in the text—the sorts of aspects of the work that this introduction has advised you to look for. That's when the discussion gets interesting. Because there is no single, straight, paved road to the destination of understanding a text, you can explore some of the blazed trails or less-traveled paths. In sharing your interpretations, tested against your peers' responses and guided by the instructor's or other critics' expertise, you will hone your own critical skills, both in discussion and in writing about literature. After the intricate and interactive process of interpretation, you will find that the work has changed when you read it again. What we do with literature alters what it does to us.

Fiction: Reading, Responding, Writing

Do you remember the first story you ever heard? The most recent story you told? Even if fairy tales and children's books were never a big part of your life, and even if novels and short stories are only a fraction of your entertainment diet now, you are, and have always been, immersed in stories. Jokes, gossip, news items, television shows, and films are some of our culture's most common forms of storytelling, and many popular video games essentially invite us to cooperate in creating stories. Stories also fill and structure our everyday conversations. Of course, these stories tend to begin "You'll never guess what happened . . ." or "So there I was, minding my own business, when . . . ," rather than "Once upon a time . . ." or *Su-num-twee* ("listen to me," as Spokane storytellers say). Yet all of these phrases have a similarly magical effect. They alert us that we are about to enter a story, and they ask us to pay a special kind of attention to both the tale and its teller. For all their wonderful variety, too, the stories that follow such phrases have, at their core, much the same shape and perform many of the same functions. Among other things, stories not only create greater intimacy between teller and listener, but they also indirectly connect us to all those who have—in every age and every corner of the world—gathered together to share stories. Most cultures have or had oral storytellers. Many of the stories that we now regard as among the world's greatest were written down only after they had been sung or recited by generations of storytellers.

Of course, there are some differences between written and oral stories, and also between the experiences of listening and reading. When we tell a story aloud, for instance, we tend to tell it differently each time, adding and subtracting details, giving it a different "spin." The same process occurs on an even greater scale as a tale passes from one teller to another (as anyone who has ever tracked the progress of a rumor knows well). As a result, oral tales tend to have a fluidity that their written counterparts lack. Many exist in multiple versions. And it's often difficult or impossible to trace a story back to a single "author" or creator. In a sense, then, an oral story is the creation of a whole community (or of many communities), just as oral storytelling tends to be a much more communal event than reading is.

Still, the private experience of reading fiction can be shared and enhanced when you talk with others about what you read, or when you write about it. A literature class will enhance your knowledge and skills in the process of interpretation, and give you a chance to practice talking and writing about literature. This chapter and those that follow will, we hope, aid you in that process. As you encounter a diverse array of written fiction and discuss its various elements, you will increase your understanding of the way fiction works and the way readers can make sense of it for themselves and others.

This chapter, in particular, invites you to think further about the shape and function of storytelling—in part by introducing you to a series of stories that themselves explore just these issues. In a way, this chapter aims to save you some steps on your journey into the world of written fiction by showing how far you have already traveled. The techniques of highly skilled authors and readers of literary fiction have much in common with those we deploy every day. Perhaps without knowing it, you are thus in many ways already expert at both telling stories and interpreting them.

For stories are everywhere: human beings live by stories, and we would find it hard to make sense of our experience if we did not create, share, and compare stories about it. Consider a well-known tale, "The Blind Men and the Elephant," a Buddhist story over two thousand years old. Like other oral stories, this one exists in many versions. Here's our own way of telling it:

The Elephant in the Village of the Blind

Once there was a village high in the mountains in which everyone was born blind. One day a traveler arrived from far away with many fine things to sell and many tales to tell. The villagers asked, "How did you travel so far and so high carrying so much?" The traveler said, "On my elephant." "What is an elephant?" the villagers asked, having never even heard of such an animal in their remote mountain village. "See for yourself," the traveler replied.

The elders of the village were a little afraid of the strange-smelling creature that took up so much space in the middle of the village square. They could hear it breathing and munching on hay, and feel its slow, swaying movements disturbing the air around them. First one elder reached out and felt its flapping ear. "An elephant is soft but tough, and flexible, like a leather fan." Another grasped its back leg. "An elephant is a rough, hairy pillar." An old woman took hold of a tusk and gasped, "An elephant is a cool, smooth staff." A young girl seized the tail and declared, "An elephant is a fringed rope." A boy took hold of the trunk and announced, "An elephant is a water pipe." Soon others were stroking its sides, which were furrowed like a dry plowed field, and others determined that its head was an overturned washing tub attached to the water pipe.

At first each villager argued with the others on the definition of the elephant, as the traveler watched in silence. Two elders were about to come to blows about a fan that could not possibly be a pillar. Meanwhile the elephant patiently enjoyed the investigations as the cries of curiosity and angry debate mixed in the afternoon sun. Soon someone suggested that a list could be made of all the parts: the elephant had four pillars, one tub, two fans, a water pipe, and two staffs, and was covered in tough, hairy leather or dried mud. Four young mothers, sitting on a bench and comparing impressions, realized that the elephant was in fact an enormous, gentle ox with a stretched nose. The traveler agreed, adding only that it was also a powerful draft horse and that if they bought some of his wares for a good price he would be sure to come that way again in the new year.

It takes very little to make a story. You need a **narrator** or teller and an **audience** of listeners or readers. (In this story as in many others, you don't need to know exactly who is telling or receiving the story. The narrator and the audience could be anyone.) Of course you also need something to tell about, including characters and a potentially problematic situation—here, a village of blind people. Then you need a **plot**, beginning with some event that destabilizes the original situation. (If everything is balanced, nothing happens.) Often such an event is the arrival of an unfamiliar person or thing, in this case an elephant and a traveler. That event creates a **conflict**—here, the misunderstandings about what an elephant is.

It would be easy to change the components of this simple story. Try it yourself. Changing any aspect of the story will inevitably change how it works and what it means to the listener or reader. For example, most versions of this story feature not an entire village of blind people (as our version does), but a small group of blind men who claim to be wiser than their sighted neighbors. These blind men quarrel endlessly because none of them can see; none can put together all the evidence of all their senses or all the elephant's various parts to create a whole. Such traditional versions of the story criticize people who are too proud of what they think they know, and imply that sighted people would know better what an elephant is. We prefer those versions of the tale that, like ours, are set in an imaginary "country" of the blind. (There is an old adage, "In the country of the blind, the one-eyed man is king.") This changes the emphasis of the story from the errors of a few blind wise men to the value and the insufficiency of *any* one person's perspective. For though it's clear that the various members of the community in this version will never agree entirely on one interpretation of (or story about) the elephant, they do not let themselves get bogged down in endless dispute. Instead they compare and combine their various stories and "readings" in order to form a more satisfying, holistic understanding of the wonder in their midst.

Fiction is not a dream. Nor is it guesswork. It is imagining based on facts, and the facts must be accurate or the work of imagining will not stand up.

—MARGARET CULKIN BANNING

Perhaps the point of this tale is to show you how to get along when you disagree about a story you have read in a literature classroom! From another angle, it illustrates how any one reader grapples with any one story: by observing one part of the story (or elephant) at a time, a reader tries to understand how those parts work together to form a whole. In reading even the shortest of stories, you read word by word, sentence by sentence, receiving new information one piece at a time. You make sense of each new piece by adding it to those you have already gathered, and as you proceed you form **expectations** about what is yet to come. Thus reading is in itself a kind of storytelling: you project the possible futures of the characters much as you project your own future in the "story" of your own life. Conversely, your expectations for a story will be guided not only by its various features, but also by your unique life "story" and point of view. Just as the blind villagers' individual interpretations of the elephant depend on what previous experiences they bring to bear (of pillars, water pipes, oxen, and dried mud, for example), and also on where (quite literally) they stand in relation to the elephant, so, too, will your response to a work of fiction.

The following short short story is a contemporary work, not a version of a traditional tale. Yet here, too, the writer has given us a minimal amount of information to go on, making each word matter. And here, as in "The Elephant in the Village of the Blind," characters have different perceptions or interpretations of things they have never seen before, in this case the places and objects they encounter on a cross-country car trip. As you read the story, pay attention to your expectations, drawing on your experience of life and on the information you get from this specific story's title and first few sentences. When and how does the story begin to challenge and change your initial expectations?

LINDA BREWER

20/20

By the time they reached Indiana, Bill realized that Ruthie, his driving companion, was incapable of theoretical debate. She drove okay, she went halves on gas, etc., but she refused to argue. She didn't seem to know how. Bill was used to East Coast women who disputed everything he said, every step of the way. Ruthie stuck to simple observation, like "Look, cows." He chalked it up to the fact that she was from rural Ohio and thrilled to death to be anywhere else.

She didn't mind driving into the setting sun. The third evening out, Bill rested his eyes while she cruised along making the occasional announcement.

"Indian paintbrush. A golden eagle."

Miles later he frowned. There was no Indian paintbrush, that he knew of, near Chicago.

The next evening, driving, Ruthie said, "I never thought I'd see a Bigfoot in real life." Bill turned and looked at the side of the road streaming innocently out behind them. Two red spots winked back—reflectors nailed to a tree stump.

"Ruthie, I'll drive," he said. She stopped the car and they changed places in the light of the evening star.

"I'm so glad I got to come with you," Ruthie said. Her eyes were big, blue, and capable of seeing wonderful sights. A white buffalo near Fargo.

A UFO above Twin Falls. A handsome genius in the person of Bill himself. This last vision came to her in Spokane and Bill decided to let it ride.

Brewer's title, like all good titles, leads us into the story armed with certain expectations. "20/20" refers to near-perfect eyesight, and it may also remind us of the expression "20/20 hindsight," which suggests that our observations about what has already happened tend to be more accurate than our predictions. (The form of the title "20/20" also reflects the doubleness of the couple's two kinds of vision and of the way they split the driving and expenses.) As a result, the title may initially prepare us for a story that focuses on vision and on the difference between foresight and hindsight, expectation and outcome. This title may alert us to expect the unexpected.

The story itself begins with a potentially difficult situation: two contrasting characters, Bill and Ruthie, alone together for days on a long car trip. Setting is established in a few words: "they reached Indiana." Characters are named, their relationship and different personalities quickly sketched: both are "driving companion[s]," but only one is "incapable of theoretical debate." From our experience of the car trips and relationships that are worth telling about, we expect several possible problems: the car might break down; they might get lost; Bill might begin to hate a woman who refuses to argue with him; Ruthie might be provoked to argue with someone who looks down on easy-going Midwesterners. Then a specific event creates a conflict quite different from (even the opposite of) the one we've been led to expect: Ruthie is driving into the setting sun on the third evening, and she announces that she has seen things that reason and experience tell Bill (and us) she could not have seen in this landscape. The next evening it is worse: she remarks that she just saw a legendary monster, Bigfoot. This must mean that Ruthie is "seeing things" and should not be allowed to drive. But the next phase of the story offers yet another unexpected shift at once comic and romantic: Ruthie's speech and Bill's praise of her eyes show that Bill now admires the imaginative eyesight that leads Ruthie to see him as "a handsome genius." As a result, he will "let it ride," accepting her vision of life because it has endowed the American landscape and Bill himself with mythic grandeur.

Both Bill and Ruthie are telling stories and forming interpretations of what they see and what happened to them on their journey. Ruthie may not argue with Bill, but her statements seem like the beginnings of "tall tales" ("I really saw Bigfoot one evening while I was driving through Nebraska . . ."). We never know what Ruthie privately thinks; what she says and does is reported as Bill would see it, through his point of view. In chapter 2 we will examine the different kinds of narration and point of view used in fiction. The point here is to notice that the development of a fictional story is often a matter of the conflicting stories characters tell. We are all storytellers, just as we are all interpreters of what others tell us. Whenever we report on what we've seen, plan the future, or ponder a personal decision, we are telling stories—forming interpretations, projecting expectations, drawing conclusions. To make sense of experience in these ways, we must also take in and respond to the versions of reality that other people have expressed.

At each point in the story you should both test your initial predictions and formulate new questions or statements about the story, whether in your mind or on paper. This is part of the natural process of hearing stories, as when Bill slowly begins to doubt Ruthie's announcement about Indian paintbrush outside Chicago. He begins to reinterpret her character in light of this new realization: if her observation can't be true, why is she saying it? You may feel it is a very long way from the everyday effort to understand another person to the process of writing an interpretation of a short story for a class. But the steps along that way can be similar and fairly straightforward. Writing a critical essay is just a more committed and systematic way of talking about what you have read.

Thus far we have considered very short forms of storytelling, but in the rest of this and subsequent chapters we turn to longer and more complex fiction. As you proceed you will recognize common qualities and features in the stories, whether long or short. And you will find that all the stories invite you to engage in a similar process of interpretation. In reading most stories, it makes sense to start by responding to the characters and situations almost as if these were real, and to check on your views as the story progresses. In its first few paragraphs, for example, Raymond Carver's "Cathedral" introduces us to three characters: a jealous husband who has a phobia of blind people (and who is also the story's narrator); a wife who likes to write poetry, who has already left one unsatisfying marriage, and who maintains a friendship with a blind man; and a blind man who is sensitive to things the narrator dislikes. Whose side are you on initially? Do you feel sorry for the blind man? Or sorry for the wife, or the husband/narrator? What do you expect to happen? For example, are you worried that the husband will openly insult the blind man?

Answering such questions about the characters and situation can lead you to form a statement about a story, the sort of statement that might eventually become a **thesis** (or debatable claim) in a critical essay. One such statement might be: " 'Cathedral' is a story told by a man who has a problem with sharing feelings who is married to a woman who likes to share her feelings." Until you have read the rest of the story, you don't know if this statement will be true for the whole work, but in most stories such an early, hypothetical statement is a good prediction of what will be important by the end.

Although the design of the story, and the information it provides you should shape your response and expectations, you will also draw on your own knowledge of life and human behavior. You may have unique reasons for reacting more strongly than other readers. You may have lived through similar situations or be related to someone like a character in the story. Everyone is entitled to a personal response, however different it might be from the usual readings of a work. Still, other readers will only be persuaded to share your opinion if you can point to evidence in the text that justifies such a response. The shared interpretation based on the common ground of this particular text is worth the effort of collaboration, as when the villagers try to assemble all the parts of the elephant, or as when generations build a cathedral. Also, like the narrator of Carver's story trying to imagine a cathedral without using the sense of sight, you might in the course of discussing and writing about a story learn something new and change your mind.

As you read, respond, and write about fiction, however, you should draw upon your knowledge of stories (and literature in general) as well as your experience of real life. Your expectations about a particular work of fiction will emerge in great part from knowing that this *is* a work of fiction (and not real life) and that such works

Fiction is like a spider's web, attached ever so slightly perhaps, but still attached to life at all four corners.

—VIRGINIA WOOLF

share certain tendencies. You already know a lot about the customs or conventions of stories. For instance, you know that stories are generally written in the past tense, and very often in the third person. Both "The Elephant in the Village of the Blind" and "20/20" tell what happened in the past to people who are not telling the story themselves. When a story uses the present tense and the first person, as in the beginning of Grace Paley's "A Conversation with My Father," you should notice this and ask why. Is Paley trying to make us feel as if she is speaking directly to us about a personal experience? Does it make the conversation appear to be happening right now? Why are the stories that the narrator tells her father during this "conversation" told in the third person and past tense? The way a story is told affects how close you feel to the tellers, characters, and events. Yet there are no strict rules about the effects of specific ways of narrating. Sherman Alexie's "Flight Patterns," for example, feels very intimate and recent, even though it is in the third person and past tense. Questions about how a story is narrated can help you measure many of its qualities, but especially how close the audience is expected to feel to the narrator.

Yet another principle that you already know is that every detail in a story can offer you clues. This means that an interpretation of any full story can grow out of a question about a single puzzling detail. Titles, as we have already suggested, can provide keys to the whole story. Why is Carver's story called "Cathedral" instead of "The Blind Man"? This might lead you to questions about other details within the story. What difference would it make if the television program they watch were not on cathedrals but on elephants or internal combustion engines? As you notice and interpret such details in the story, you can relate them to characters and actions. Why is it the narrator and not the wife who stays up late and watches TV with the blind man? Does the narrator reveal any handicap in trying to describe the cathedral, the way the blind people do in trying to describe an elephant? Questions about parts of a story help lead you to significant interpretations of the whole.

When reading a story or any kind of literature, you respond to words—that is, to all the choices of wording and sentence structure that make up a **voice** or **style**. This might seem to be one of the more difficult aspects of literature to analyze, and yet if you speak English and the story is written in English you are already attuned to differences of voice or style. Such differences include vocabularies, from plain monosyllables to fancy polysyllables, and manners, from rude to polite. Many modern writers try to capture the patterns of everyday speech of different regions, dialects, or ethnic groups. Grace Paley has commented on the way many writers combine common modes of speech with refined literary style. In an interview at the age of seventy-three (in 1995), Paley claimed that everyone has "two ears. One ear is that literary ear, and it's a good old ear. It's with us when we write in the tradition of English writing, or Western writing that includes Proust and Flaubert. . . . But there is also something else . . . and that is the ear of the language of home, and the language of your street and your own people."[1] This comment also seems fitting for the achievements of both Raymond Carver and Sherman Alexie, who listen closely to the unofficial voices around them and shape these effectively into very artful literary fiction.

You too have ears for different styles. If you were to tell a story about an incident to a friend your own age, to your five-year-old nephew, or to your teacher or parent, you would likely modify the words and the tone you used. Yet your character and behavior would probably come through to each of your listeners. The personality of the narrator in Raymond Carver's "Cathedral" comes through in his speech patterns (we imagine he is speaking to someone he knows as he recalls the visit). "Just amazing. . . . A beard on a blind man! Too much, I say." The voice or writing style conveys a "style" of personality, which makes the reader feel a certain way. It is difficult to describe the precise tone of a style, but by looking closely at words and passages—by quoting selectively as we just did from the narrator of "Cathedral"—you can show how style or voice contributes to the effect of a story.

When you listen to a story you usually wonder about the person who is telling it, based not only on what is told but how it is told, which includes the personality of the teller. A reader readily becomes curious about the author of a published story or the personality that seems to be telling it. Thus your observations about voice and style may lead you to ask questions about the author. Is Raymond Carver like the sarcastic husband in "Cathedral"? You might consult an entry in a biographical dictionary in your library, on the Web, or in the "Biographical Sketches" in this book, and learn that Carver struggled with substance abuse. But does that make the story autobiographical? Did Carver share the narrator's prejudice about blind people? The answers to such questions usually should be sought in the work itself. "Cathedral" exposes the narrator's flaws and shows that his prejudice was wrong.

Students of literature often bring up questions about the author's intentions and the relation of the fiction to the author's life. It is difficult to answer such questions without oversimplifying the meaning of the work (or the life). Nevertheless, some information about the author "behind" the work can provide a useful context, just as information

> *The good ended happily, and the bad unhappily. That is what Fiction means.*
> —OSCAR WILDE

---

1. "Lit Chat: Grace Paley," *Salon* (www.salon.com/11/departments/litchat1.html).

about when and where a work was first published can be key to a convincing interpretation. Sherman Alexie's "Flight Patterns" was published in 2003 in the United States, in a collection called *Ten Little Indians*, and like the protagonist of the story, the author is a Native American. This does not mean that the character William is just a stand-in for Alexie. Nevertheless, the fact that William has some experiences in common with his creator makes a difference in how we respond—how close we feel to William, how authentic or "real" the story seems to us.

Entire essays may be devoted to a story's style, to the author's biography, or to the interaction of both: the voices in the story and the author's personal and social background or historical context. But most of your critical writing will probably concern other matters. When you have read an entire story, you should notice its form or **structure.** Think of form as the blueprint or architectural plan of a story, which provides a general outline of the whole structure as well as details of the design of the parts. Are there any repetitions or patterns that occur throughout the story? Here as elsewhere, you should draw upon your experience of literature and of life to answer such questions. You inevitably have absorbed the standard forms or structures that most stories take. In the stories that follow, we offer some examples of common plans or shapes for stories: the journey to a destination, the return to the past, the shared scene of storytelling. Such structures are effective in fiction because they resemble the forms of storytelling that we know from everyday experience.

One of the most important types of literary knowledge, closely related to form and structure, is the concept of **genre,** or the conventions of different kinds of literature—fiction, poetry, and drama. Your experience of fiction tells you that there are, indeed, different kinds or **subgenres** of fiction, each of which has a slightly different shape. Different kinds of stories have their own conventions: fairy tales begin with "Once upon a time"; in ghost stories and certain other scary stories there is almost always a beautiful young woman threatened by danger; comic stories almost always end happily; and so on. Your expectations as you read a particular story and your sense of how well it worked when it is over are guided by your assumptions about just what kind of story it is.

Obviously, there are many ways to approach both reading stories and writing about them, just as there are many varieties of stories on which to feast. Any good story can feed our intellect and our imagination—those two faculties that are contrasted in the story of Bill and Ruthie in "20/20." Fiction helps us extend our knowledge and understanding of the actual world and it prepares us for the extraordinary and unexpected. Effective fiction often presents familiar conditions in such a way that they become unfamiliar. This effect, called defamiliarization, occurs in everyday life when, for example, you return from a trip and see things in your own room as though they were new or not your own. Usually we perceive what habit and convention have told us is "really there," but at certain times none of it looks obvious or natural. Stories, then, may function the way travel does: by taking us out of our world and into another, they enable us to look at things anew much as his car trip with Ruthie helps Bill to do.

Many of us initially prefer literature that reflects our own time and place to literature of other countries and eras. We may want our tales to be small, familiar, and realistic rather than tall, exotic, and fantastic. Indeed, we must find some way to relate any story to our own lives before we can find it intellectually or emotionally meaningful. No one would deny that one of the many things that fiction may be "for" is learning about ourselves and the world around us, with the advantages of artistic enhancement and defamiliarization. But often the last thing we want is a story about people just like ourselves or about a world just like our own. Fiction has the power to be excitingly strange, like a UFO above Twin Falls or Bigfoot loping through Nebraska. It can take us to other places, times, or ways of life, making the unfamiliar more familiar. And whether it focuses on the actual or the extraordinary, all good fiction takes us out of ourselves, beyond the limited vision of our own eyes. It shows us that there are worlds beyond our own immediate experience, and other ways of looking at those worlds.

RAYMOND CARVER

Cathedral

This blind man, an old friend of my wife's, he was on his way to spend the night. His wife had died. So he was visiting the dead wife's relatives in Connecticut. He called my wife from his in-laws'. Arrangements were made. He would come by train, a five-hour trip, and my wife would meet him at the station. She hadn't seen him since she worked for him one summer in Seattle ten years ago. But she and the blind man had kept in touch. They made tapes and mailed them back and forth. I wasn't enthusiastic about his visit. He was no one I knew. And his being blind bothered me. My idea of blindness came from the movies. In the movies, the blind moved slowly and never laughed. Sometimes they were led by seeing-eye dogs. A blind man in my house was not something I looked forward to.

That summer in Seattle she had needed a job. She didn't have any money. The man she was going to marry at the end of the summer was in officers' training school. He didn't have any money, either. But she was in love with the guy, and he was in love with her, etc. She'd seen something in the paper: HELP WANTED—*Reading to Blind Man*, and a telephone number. She phoned and went over, was hired on the spot. She'd worked with this blind man all summer. She read stuff to him, case studies, reports, that sort of thing. She helped him organize his little office in the county social-service department. They'd become good friends, my wife and the blind man. How do I know these things? She told me. And she told me something else. On her last day in the office, the blind man asked if he could touch her face. She agreed to this. She told me he touched his fingers to every part of her face, her nose—even her neck! She never forgot it. She even tried to write a poem about it. She was always trying to write a poem. She wrote a poem or two every year, usually after something really important had happened to her.

When we first started going out together, she showed me the poem. In the poem, she recalled his fingers and the way they had moved around over her face. In the poem, she talked about what she had felt at the time, about what went through her mind when the blind man touched her nose and lips. I can remember I didn't think much of the poem. Of course, I didn't tell her that. Maybe I just don't understand poetry. I admit it's not the first thing I reach for when I pick up something to read.

Anyway, this man who'd first enjoyed her favors, the officer-to-be, he'd been her childhood sweetheart. So okay. I'm saying that at the end of the summer she let the blind man run his hands over her face, said goodbye to him, married her childhood etc., who was now a commissioned officer, and she moved away from Seattle. But they'd kept in touch, she and the blind man. She made the first contact after a year or so. She called him up one night from an Air Force base in Alabama. She wanted to talk. They talked. He asked her to send him a tape and tell him about her life. She did this. She sent the tape. On the tape, she told the blind man about her husband and about their life together in the military. She told the blind man she loved her husband but she didn't like it where they lived and she didn't like it that he was a part of the military-industrial thing. She told the blind man she'd written a poem and he was in it. She told him that she was writing a poem about what it was like to be an Air Force officer's wife. The poem wasn't finished yet. She was still writing it. The blind man made a tape. He sent her the tape. She made a tape. This went on for years. My wife's officer was posted to one base and then another. She sent tapes from Moody AFB, McGuire, McConnell, and finally Travis, near Sacramento, where one night she got to feeling lonely and cut off from people she kept losing in that moving-around life. She got to feeling she couldn't go it another step. She went in and swallowed all the pills and capsules in the medicine chest and washed them down with a bottle of gin. Then she got into a hot bath and passed out.

5   But instead of dying, she got sick. She threw up. Her officer—why should he have a name? he was the childhood sweetheart, and what more does he want?—came home from somewhere, found her, and called the ambulance. In time, she put it all on a tape and sent the tape to the blind man. Over the years, she put all kinds of stuff on tapes and sent the tapes off lickety-split. Next to writing a poem every year, I think it was her chief means of recreation. On one tape, she told the blind man she'd decided to live away from her officer for a time. On another tape, she told him about her divorce. She and I began going out, and of course she told her blind man about it. She told him everything, or so it seemed to me. Once she asked me if I'd like to hear the latest tape from the blind man. This was a year ago. I was on the tape, she said. So I said okay, I'd listen to it. I got us drinks and we settled down in the living room. We made ready to listen. First she inserted the tape into the player and adjusted a couple of dials.

Then she pushed a lever. The tape squeaked and someone began to talk in this loud voice. She lowered the volume. After a few minutes of harmless chitchat, I heard my own name in the mouth of this stranger, this blind man I didn't even know! And then this: "From all you've said about him, I can only conclude—" But we were interrupted, a knock at the door, something, and we didn't ever get back to the tape. Maybe it was just as well. I'd heard all I wanted to.

Now this same blind man was coming to sleep in my house.

"Maybe I could take him bowling," I said to my wife. She was at the draining board doing scalloped potatoes. She put down the knife she was using and turned around.

"If you love me," she said, "you can do this for me. If you don't love me, okay. But if you had a friend, any friend, and the friend came to visit, I'd make him feel comfortable." She wiped her hands with the dish towel.

"I don't have any blind friends," I said.

"You don't have *any* friends," she said. "Period. Besides," she said, "god- 10 damn it, his wife's just died! Don't you understand that? The man's lost his wife!"

I didn't answer. She'd told me a little about the blind man's wife. Her name was Beulah. Beulah! That's a name for a colored woman.

"Was his wife a Negro?" I asked.

"Are you crazy?" my wife said. "Have you just flipped or something?" She picked up a potato. I saw it hit the floor, then roll under the stove. "What's wrong with you?" she said. "Are you drunk?"

"I'm just asking," I said.

Right then my wife filled me in with more detail than I cared to know. 15 I made a drink and sat at the kitchen table to listen. Pieces of the story began to fall into place.

Beulah had gone to work for the blind man the summer after my wife had stopped working for him. Pretty soon Beulah and the blind man had themselves a church wedding. It was a little wedding—who'd want to go to such a wedding in the first place?—just the two of them, plus the minister and the minister's wife. But it was a church wedding just the same. It was what Beulah had wanted, he'd said. But even then Beulah must have been carrying the cancer in her glands. After they had been inseparable for eight years—my wife's word, *inseparable*—Beulah's health went into a rapid decline. She died in a Seattle hospital room, the blind man sitting beside the bed and holding on to her hand. They'd married, lived and worked together, slept together—had sex, sure—and then the blind man had to bury her. All this without his having ever seen what the goddamned woman looked like. It was beyond my understanding. Hearing this, I felt sorry for the blind man for a little bit. And then I found myself thinking what a pitiful life this woman must have led. Imagine a woman who could never see herself as she was seen in the eyes of her loved one. A woman who could go on day after day and never receive the smallest compliment from her beloved. A woman whose husband could never read the expression on her face, be it misery or something better. Someone who could wear makeup or not—what difference to him? She could, if she wanted, wear green eye-shadow around one eye, a straight pin in her nostril, yellow slacks and purple shoes, no matter. And then to slip off into death, the blind man's hand on her hand, his blind eyes streaming tears—I'm imagining now—her last thought maybe this: that he never even knew what she looked like, and she on an express to the grave. Robert was left with a small insurance policy and half of a twenty-peso Mexican coin. The other half of the coin went into the box with her. Pathetic.

So when the time rolled around, my wife went to the depot to pick him up. With nothing to do but wait—sure, I blamed him for that—I was having a drink and watching the TV when I heard the car pull into the drive. I got up from the sofa with my drink and went to the window to have a look.

I saw my wife laughing as she parked the car. I saw her get out of the car and shut the door. She was still wearing a smile. Just amazing. She went around to the other side of the car to where the blind man was already starting to get out. This blind man, feature this, he was wearing a full beard! A beard on a blind man! Too much, I say. The blind man reached into the back seat and dragged out a suitcase. My wife took his arm, shut the car door, and, talking all the way, moved him down the drive and then up the steps to the front porch. I turned off the TV. I finished my drink, rinsed the glass, dried my hands. Then I went to the door.

My wife said, "I want you to meet Robert. Robert, this is my husband. I've told you all about him." She was beaming. She had this blind man by his coat sleeve.

20   The blind man let go of his suitcase and up came his hand.

I took it. He squeezed hard, held my hand, and then he let it go.

"I feel like we've already met," he boomed.

"Likewise," I said. I didn't know what else to say. Then I said, "Welcome. I've heard a lot about you." We began to move then, a little group, from the porch into the living room, my wife guiding him by the arm. The blind man was carrying his suitcase in his other hand. My wife said things like, "To your left here, Robert. That's right. Now watch it, there's a chair. That's it. Sit down right here. This is the sofa. We just bought this sofa two weeks ago."

I started to say something about the old sofa. I'd liked that old sofa. But I didn't say anything. Then I wanted to say something else, small-talk, about the scenic ride along the Hudson. How going *to* New York, you should sit on the right-hand side of the train, and coming *from* New York, the left-hand side.

25   "Did you have a good train ride?" I said. "Which side of the train did you sit on, by the way?"

"What a question, which side!" my wife said. "What's it matter which side?" she said.

"I just asked," I said.

"Right side," the blind man said. "I hadn't been on a train in nearly forty years. Not since I was a kid. With my folks. That's been a long time. I'd nearly forgotten the sensation. I have winter in my beard now," he said.

"So I've been told, anyway. Do I look distinguished, my dear?" the blind man said to my wife.

"You look distinguished, Robert," she said. "Robert," she said. "Robert, it's just so good to see you."

My wife finally took her eyes off the blind man and looked at me. I had 30 the feeling she didn't like what she saw. I shrugged.

I've never met, or personally known, anyone who was blind. This blind man was late forties, a heavy-set, balding man with stooped shoulders, as if he carried a great weight there. He wore brown slacks, brown shoes, a light-brown shirt, a tie, a sports coat. Spiffy. He also had this full beard. But he didn't use a cane and he didn't wear dark glasses. I'd always thought dark glasses were a must for the blind. Fact was, I wished he had a pair. At first glance, his eyes looked like anyone else's eyes. But if you looked close, there was something different about them. Too much white in the iris, for one thing, and the pupils seemed to move around in the sockets without his knowing it or being able to stop it. Creepy. As I stared at his face, I saw the left pupil turn in toward his nose while the other made an effort to keep in one place. But it was only an effort, for that eye was on the roam without his knowing it or wanting it to be.

I said, "Let me get you a drink. What's your pleasure? We have a little of everything. It's one of our pastimes."

"Bub, I'm a Scotch man myself," he said fast enough in this big voice.

"Right," I said. Bub! "Sure you are. I knew it."

He let his fingers touch his suitcase, which was sitting alongside the 35 sofa. He was taking his bearings. I didn't blame him for that.

"I'll move that up to your room," my wife said.

"No, that's fine," the blind man said loudly. "It can go up when I go up."

"A little water with the Scotch?" I said.

"Very little," he said.

"I knew it," I said. 40

He said, "Just a tad. The Irish actor, Barry Fitzgerald? I'm like that fellow. When I drink water, Fitzgerald said, I drink water. When I drink whiskey, I drink whiskey." My wife laughed. The blind man brought his hand up under his beard. He lifted his beard slowly and let it drop.

I did the drinks, three big glasses of Scotch with a splash of water in each. Then we made ourselves comfortable and talked about Robert's travels. First the long flight from the West Coast to Connecticut, we covered that. Then from Connecticut up here by train. We had another drink concerning that leg of the trip.

I remembered having read somewhere that the blind didn't smoke because, as speculation had it, they couldn't see the smoke they exhaled. I thought I knew that much and that much only about blind people. But this blind man smoked his cigarette down to the nubbin and then lit another one. This blind man filled his ashtray and my wife emptied it.

When we sat down at the table for dinner, we had another drink. My wife heaped Robert's plate with cube steak, scalloped potatoes, green beans.

I buttered him up two slices of bread. I said, "Here's bread and butter for you." I swallowed some of my drink. "Now let us pray," I said, and the blind man lowered his head. My wife looked at me, her mouth agape. "Pray the phone won't ring and the food doesn't get cold," I said.

45   We dug in. We ate everything there was to eat on the table. We ate like there was no tomorrow. We didn't talk. We ate. We scarfed. We grazed that table. We were into serious eating. The blind man had right away located his foods, he knew just where everything was on his plate. I watched with admiration as he used his knife and fork on the meat. He'd cut two pieces of meat, fork the meat into his mouth, and then go all out for the scalloped potatoes, the beans next, and then he'd tear off a hunk of buttered bread and eat that. He'd follow this up with a big drink of milk. It didn't seem to bother him to use his fingers once in a while, either.

We finished everything, including half a strawberry pie. For a few moments, we sat as if stunned. Sweat beaded on our faces. Finally, we got up from the table and left the dirty plates. We didn't look back. We took ourselves into the living room and sank into our places again. Robert and my wife sat on the sofa. I took the big chair. We had us two or three more drinks while they talked about the major things that had come to pass for them in the past ten years. For the most part, I just listened. Now and then I joined in. I didn't want him to think I'd left the room, and I didn't want her to think I was feeling left out. They talked of things that had happened to them—to them!—these past ten years. I waited in vain to hear my name on my wife's sweet lips: "And then my dear husband came into my life"— something like that. But I heard nothing of the sort. More talk of Robert. Robert had done a little of everything, it seemed, a regular blind jack-of-all-trades. But most recently he and his wife had had an Amway distributorship, from which, I gathered, they'd earned their living, such as it was. The blind man was also a ham radio operator. He talked in his loud voice about conversations he'd had with fellow operators in Guam, in the Philippines, in Alaska, and even in Tahiti. He said he'd have a lot of friends there if he ever wanted to go visit those places. From time to time, he'd turn his blind face toward me, put his hand under his beard, ask me something. How long had I been in my present position? (Three years.) Did I like my work? (I didn't.) Was I going to stay with it? (What were the options?) Finally, when I thought he was beginning to run down, I got up and turned on the TV.

My wife looked at me with irritation. She was heading toward a boil. Then she looked at the blind man and said, "Robert, do you have a TV?"

The blind man said, "My dear, I have two TVs. I have a color set and a black-and-white thing, an old relic. It's funny, but if I turn the TV on, and I'm always turning it on, I turn on the color set. It's funny, don't you think?"

I didn't know what to say to that. I had absolutely nothing to say to that. No opinion. So I watched the news program and tried to listen to what the announcer was saying.

50   "This is a color TV," the blind man said. "Don't ask me how, but I can tell."

"We traded up a while ago," I said.

The blind man had another taste of his drink. He lifted his beard, sniffed it, and let it fall. He leaned forward on the sofa. He positioned his ashtray on the coffee table, then put the lighter to his cigarette. He leaned back on the sofa and crossed his legs at the ankles.

My wife covered her mouth, and then she yawned. She stretched. She said, "I think I'll go upstairs and put on my robe. I think I'll change into something else. Robert, you make yourself comfortable," she said.

"I'm comfortable," the blind man said.

"I want you to feel comfortable in this house," she said.   55

"I am comfortable," the blind man said.

After she'd left the room, he and I listened to the weather report and then to the sports roundup. By that time, she'd been gone so long I didn't know if she was going to come back. I thought she might have gone to bed. I wished she'd come back downstairs. I didn't want to be left alone with a blind man. I asked him if he wanted another drink, and he said sure. Then I asked if he wanted to smoke some dope with me. I said I'd just rolled a number. I hadn't, but I planned to do so in about two shakes.

"I'll try some with you," he said.

"Damn right," I said. "That's the stuff."

I got our drinks and sat down on the sofa with him. Then I rolled us   60
two fat numbers. I lit one and passed it. I brought it to his fingers. He took it and inhaled.

"Hold it as long as you can," I said. I could tell he didn't know the first thing.

My wife came back downstairs wearing her pink robe and her pink slippers.

"What do I smell?" she said.

"We thought we'd have us some cannabis," I said.

My wife gave me a savage look. Then she looked at the blind man and   65
said, "Robert, I didn't know you smoked."

He said, "I do now, my dear. There's a first time for everything. But I don't feel anything yet."

"This stuff is pretty mellow," I said. "This stuff is mild. It's dope you can reason with," I said. "It doesn't mess you up."

"Not much it doesn't, bub," he said, and laughed.

My wife sat on the sofa between the blind man and me. I passed her the number. She took it and toked and then passed it back to me. "Which way is this going?" she said. Then she said, "I shouldn't be smoking this. I can hardly keep my eyes open as it is. That dinner did me in. I shouldn't have eaten so much."

"It was the strawberry pie," the blind man said. "That's what did it," he   70
said, and he laughed his big laugh. Then he shook his head.

"There's more strawberry pie," I said.

"Do you want some more, Robert?" my wife said.

"Maybe in a little while," he said.

We gave our attention to the TV. My wife yawned again. She said, "Your bed is made up when you feel like going to bed, Robert. I know you must have had a long day. When you're ready to go to bed, say so." She pulled his arm. "Robert?"

75   He came to and said, "I've had a real nice time. This beats tapes, doesn't it?"

I said, "Coming at you," and I put the number between his fingers. He inhaled, held the smoke, and then let it go. It was like he'd been doing it since he was nine years old.

"Thanks, bub," he said. "But I think this is all for me. I think I'm beginning to feel it," he said. He held the burning roach out for my wife.

"Same here," she said. "Ditto. Me, too." She took the roach and passed it to me. "I may just sit here for a while between you two guys with my eyes closed. But don't let me bother you, okay? Either one of you. If it bothers you, say so. Otherwise, I may just sit here with my eyes closed until you're ready to go to bed," she said. "Your bed's made up, Robert, when you're ready. It's right next to our room at the top of the stairs. We'll show you up when you're ready. You wake me up now, you guys, if I fall asleep." She said that and then she closed her eyes and went to sleep.

The news program ended. I got up and changed the channel. I sat back down on the sofa. I wished my wife hadn't pooped out. Her head lay across the back of the sofa, her mouth open. She'd turned so that her robe had slipped away from her legs, exposing a juicy thigh. I reached to draw her robe back over her, and it was then that I glanced at the blind man. What the hell! I flipped the robe open again.

80   "You say when you want some strawberry pie," I said.

"I will," he said.

I said, "Are you tired? Do you want me to take you up to your bed? Are you ready to hit the hay?"

"Not yet," he said. "No, I'll stay up with you, bub. If that's all right. I'll stay up until you're ready to turn in. We haven't had a chance to talk. Know what I mean? I feel like me and her monopolized the evening." He lifted his beard and he let it fall. He picked up his cigarettes and his lighter.

"That's all right," I said. Then I said, "I'm glad for the company."

85   And I guess I was. Every night I smoked dope and stayed up as long as I could before I fell asleep. My wife and I hardly ever went to bed at the same time. When I did go to sleep, I had these dreams. Sometimes I'd wake up from one of them, my heart going crazy.

Something about the church and the Middle Ages was on the TV. Not your run-of-the-mill TV fare. I wanted to watch something else. I turned to the other channels. But there was nothing on them, either. So I turned back to the first channel and apologized.

"Bub, it's all right," the blind man said. "It's fine with me. Whatever you want to watch is okay. I'm always learning something. Learning never ends. It won't hurt me to learn something tonight. I got ears," he said.

We didn't say anything for a time. He was leaning forward with his head turned at me, his right ear aimed in the direction of the set. Very disconcerting. Now and then his eyelids drooped and then they snapped open again. Now and then he put his fingers into his beard and tugged, like he was thinking about something he was hearing on the television.

On the screen, a group of men wearing cowls was being set upon and tormented by men dressed in skeleton costumes and men dressed as devils. The men dressed as devils wore devil masks, horns, and long tails. This pageant was part of a procession. The Englishman who was narrating the thing said it took place in Spain once a year. I tried to explain to the blind man what was happening.

"Skeletons," he said. "I know about skeletons," he said, and he nodded. 90

The TV showed this one cathedral. Then there was a long, slow look at another one. Finally, the picture switched to the famous one in Paris, with its flying buttresses and its spires reaching up to the clouds. The camera pulled away to show the whole of the cathedral rising above the skyline.

There were times when the Englishman who was telling the thing would shut up, would simply let the camera move around over the cathedrals. Or else the camera would tour the countryside, men in fields walking behind oxen. I waited as long as I could. Then I felt I had to say something. I said, "They're showing the outside of this cathedral now. Gargoyles. Little statues carved to look like monsters. Now I guess they're in Italy. Yeah, they're in Italy. There's paintings on the walls of this one church."

"Are those fresco paintings, bub?" he asked, and he sipped from his drink.

I reached for my glass. But it was empty. I tried to remember what I could remember. "You're asking me are those frescoes?" I said. "That's a good question. I don't know."

The camera moved to a cathedral outside Lisbon. The differences in the 95 Portuguese cathedral compared with the French and Italian were not that great. But they were there. Mostly the interior stuff. Then something occurred to me, and I said, "Something has occurred to me. Do you have any idea what a cathedral is? What they look like, that is? Do you follow me? If somebody says cathedral to you, do you have any notion what they're talking about? Do you know the difference between that and a Baptist church, say?"

He let the smoke dribble from his mouth. "I know they took hundreds of workers fifty or a hundred years to build," he said. "I just heard the man say that, of course. I know generations of the same families worked on a cathedral. I heard him say that, too. The men who began their life's work on them, they never lived to see the completion of their work. In that wise, bub, they're no different from the rest of us, right?" He laughed. Then his eyelids drooped again. His head nodded. He seemed to be snoozing. Maybe he was imagining himself in Portugal. The TV was showing another cathedral now. This one was in Germany. The Englishman's voice droned on. "Cathedrals," the blind man said. He sat up and rolled his head back and forth. "If you want the truth, bub, that's about all I know. What I just said. What I heard him say. But maybe you could describe one to me? I wish you'd do it. I'd like that. If you want to know, I really don't have a good idea."

I stared hard at the shot of the cathedral on the TV. How could I even begin to describe it? But say my life depended on it. Say my life was being threatened by an insane guy who said I had to do it or else.

I stared some more at the cathedral before the picture flipped off into the countryside. There was no use. I turned to the blind man and said, "To begin with, they're very tall." I was looking around the room for clues. "They reach way up. Up and up. Toward the sky. They're so big, some of them, they have to have these supports. To help hold them up, so to speak. These supports are called buttresses. They remind me of viaducts, for some reason. But maybe you don't know viaducts, either? Sometimes the cathedrals have devils and such carved into the front. Sometimes lords and ladies. Don't ask me why this is," I said.

He was nodding. The whole upper part of his body seemed to be moving back and forth.

100   "I'm not doing so good, am I?" I said.

He stopped nodding and leaned forward on the edge of the sofa. As he listened to me, he was running his fingers through his beard. I wasn't getting through to him, I could see that. But he waited for me to go on just the same. He nodded, like he was trying to encourage me. I tried to think what else to say. "They're really big," I said. "They're massive. They're built of stone. Marble, too, sometimes. In those olden days, when they built cathedrals, men wanted to be close to God. In those olden days, God was an important part of everyone's life. You could tell this from their cathedral-building. I'm sorry," I said, "but it looks like that's the best I can do for you. I'm just no good at it."

"That's all right, bub," the blind man said. "Hey, listen. I hope you don't mind my asking you. Can I ask you something? Let me ask you a simple question, yes or no. I'm just curious and there's no offense. You're my host. But let me ask if you are in any way religious? You don't mind my asking?"

I shook my head. He couldn't see that, though. A wink is the same as a nod to a blind man. "I guess I don't believe in it. In anything. Sometimes it's hard. You know what I'm saying?"

"Sure, I do," he said.

105   "Right," I said.

The Englishman was still holding forth. My wife sighed in her sleep. She drew a long breath and went on with her sleeping.

"You'll have to forgive me," I said. "But I can't tell you what a cathedral looks like. It just isn't in me to do it. I can't do any more than I've done."

The blind man sat very still, his head down, as he listened to me.

I said, "The truth is, cathedrals don't mean anything special to me. Nothing. Cathedrals. They're something to look at on late-night TV. That's all they are."

110   It was then that the blind man cleared his throat. He brought something up. He took a handkerchief from his back pocket. Then he said, "I get it, bub. It's okay. It happens. Don't worry about it," he said. "Hey, listen to me. Will you do me a favor? I got an idea. Why don't you find us some heavy paper? And a pen. We'll do something. We'll draw one together. Get us a pen and some heavy paper. Go on, bub, get the stuff," he said.

So I went upstairs. My legs felt like they didn't have any strength in them. They felt like they did after I'd done some running. In my wife's room, I looked around. I found some ballpoints in a little basket on her table. And then I tried to think where to look for the kind of paper he was talking about.

Downstairs, in the kitchen, I found a shopping bag with onion skins in the bottom of the bag. I emptied the bag and shook it. I brought it into the living room and sat down with it near his legs. I moved some things, smoothed the wrinkles from the bag, spread it out on the coffee table.

The blind man got down from the sofa and sat next to me on the carpet.

He ran his fingers over the paper. He went up and down the sides of the paper. The edges, even the edges. He fingered the corners.

"All right," he said. "All right, let's do her." 115

He found my hand, the hand with the pen. He closed his hand over my hand. "Go ahead, bub, draw," he said. "Draw. You'll see. I'll follow along with you. It'll be okay. Just begin now like I'm telling you. You'll see. Draw," the blind man said.

So I began. First I drew a box that looked like a house. It could have been the house I lived in. Then I put a roof on it. At either end of the roof, I drew spires. Crazy.

"Swell," he said. "Terrific. You're doing fine," he said. "Never thought anything like this could happen in your lifetime, did you, bub? Well, it's a strange life, we all know that. Go on now. Keep it up."

I put in windows with arches. I drew flying buttresses. I hung great doors. I couldn't stop. The TV station went off the air. I put down the pen and closed and opened my fingers. The blind man felt around over the paper. He moved the tips of his fingers over the paper, all over what I had drawn, and he nodded.

"Doing fine," the blind man said. 120

I took up the pen again, and he found my hand. I kept at it. I'm no artist. But I kept drawing just the same.

My wife opened up her eyes and gazed at us. She sat up on the sofa, her robe hanging open. She said, "What are you doing? Tell me, I want to know."

I didn't answer her.

The blind man said, "We're drawing a cathedral. Me and him are working on it. Press hard," he said to me. "That's right. That's good," he said. "Sure. You got it, bub. I can tell. You didn't think you could. But you can, can't you? You're cooking with gas now. You know what I'm saying? We're going to really have us something here in a minute. How's the old arm?" he said. "Put some people in there now. What's a cathedral without people?"

My wife said, "What's going on? Robert, what are you doing? What's 125 going on?"

"It's all right," he said to her. "Close your eyes now," the blind man said to me.

I did it. I closed them just like he said.

"Are they closed?" he said. "Don't fudge."

"They're closed," I said.

130   "Keep them that way," he said. He said, "Don't stop now. Draw."

So we kept on with it. His fingers rode my fingers as my hand went over the paper. It was like nothing else in my life up to now.

Then he said, "I think that's it. I think you got it," he said. "Take a look. What do you think?"

But I had my eyes closed. I thought I'd keep them that way for a little longer. I thought it was something I ought to do.

"Well?" he said. "Are you looking?"

135   My eyes were still closed. I was in my house. I knew that. But I didn't feel like I was inside anything.

"It's really something," I said.

                                                                1983

QUESTIONS

1. In the opening sections of "Cathedral," what do the narrator's remarks about himself, his wife, and the blind man suggest about the kind of person he is? How might Raymond Carver intend for the reader to feel about the narrator at first?

2. At what key moments in the story does the narrator's attitude toward the blind man begin to change? How does this change our view of him?

3. What is the importance of drawing the cathedral, both to the narrator and to the story itself?

GRACE PALEY

A Conversation with My Father

My father is eighty-six years old and in bed. His heart, that bloody motor, is equally old and will not do certain jobs any more. It still floods his head with brainy light. But it won't let his legs carry the weight of his body around the house. Despite my metaphors, this muscle failure is not due to his old heart, he says, but to a potassium shortage. Sitting on one pillow, leaning on three, he offers last-minute advice and makes a request.

"I would like you to write a simple story just once more," he says, "the kind de Maupassant wrote, or Chekhov, the kind you used to write. Just recognizable people and then write down what happened to them next."

I say, "Yes, why not? That's possible." I want to please him, though I don't remember writing that way. I *would* like to try to tell such a story, if he means the kind that begins: "There was a woman . . ." followed by plot, the absolute line between two points which I've always despised. Not for literary reasons, but because it takes all hope away. Everyone, real or invented, deserves the open destiny of life.

Finally I thought of a story that had been happening for a couple of years right across the street. I wrote it down, then read it aloud. "Pa," I said, "how about this? Do you mean something like this?"

Once in my time there was a woman and she had a son. They lived 5
nicely, in a small apartment in Manhattan. This boy at about fifteen
became a junkie, which is not unusual in our neighborhood. In order to
maintain her close friendship with him, she became a junkie too. She
said it was part of the youth culture, with which she felt very much at
home. After a while, for a number of reasons, the boy gave it all up and
left the city and his mother in disgust. Hopeless and alone, she grieved.
We all visit her.

"O.K., Pa, that's it," I said, "an unadorned and miserable tale."

"But that's not what I mean," my father said. "You misunderstood me
on purpose. You know there's a lot more to it. You know that. You left
everything out. Turgenev[1] wouldn't do that. Chekhov wouldn't do that.
There are in fact Russian writers you never heard of, you don't have an
inkling of, as good as anyone, who can write a plain ordinary story, who
would not leave out what you have left out. I object not to facts but to
people sitting in trees talking senselessly, voices from who knows where . . ."

"Forget that one, Pa, what have I left out now? In this one?"

"Her looks, for instance."

"Oh. Quite handsome, I think. Yes." 10

"Her hair?"

"Dark, with heavy braids, as though she were a girl or a foreigner."

"What were her parents like, her stock? That she became such a person.
It's interesting, you know."

"From out of town. Professional people. The first to be divorced in their
county. How's that? Enough?" I asked.

"With you, it's all a joke," he said. "What about the boy's father. Why 15
didn't you mention him? Who was he? Or was the boy born out of wedlock?"

"Yes," I said. "He was born out of wedlock."

"For Godsakes, doesn't anyone in your stories get married? Doesn't anyone have the time to run down to City Hall before they jump into bed?"

"No," I said. "In real life, yes. But in my stories, no."

"Why do you answer me like that?"

"Oh, Pa, this is a simple story about a smart woman who came to N.Y.C. 20
full of interest love trust excitement very up to date, and about her son,
what a hard time she had in this world. Married or not, it's of small consequence."

"It is of great consequence," he said.

"O.K.," I said.

"O.K. O.K. yourself," he said, "but listen. I believe you that she's good-
looking, but I don't think she was so smart."

"That's true," I said. "Actually that's the trouble with stories. People start
out fantastic. You think they're extraordinary, but it turns out as the work
goes along, they're just average with a good education. Sometimes the other

---

1. Ivan Sergeyevich Turgenev (1818–1883); his best-known novel, *Fathers and Sons*, deals with the
conflict between generations.

way around, the person's a kind of dumb innocent, but he outwits you and
you can't even think of an ending good enough."

25   "What do you do then?" he asked. He had been a doctor for a couple
of decades and then an artist for a couple of decades and he's still interested
in details, craft, technique.

"Well, you just have to let the story lie around till some agreement can
be reached between you and the stubborn hero."

"Aren't you talking silly, now?" he asked. "Start again," he said. "It so
happens I'm not going out this evening. Tell the story again. See what you
can do this time."

"O.K.," I said. "But it's not a five-minute job." Second attempt:

Once, across the street from us, there was a fine handsome woman,
our neighbor. She had a son whom she loved because she'd known him
since birth (in helpless chubby infancy, and in the wrestling, hugging
ages, seven to ten, as well as earlier and later). This boy, when he fell into
the fist of adolescence, became a junkie. He was not a hopeless one. He
was in fact hopeful, an ideologue and successful converter. With his busy
brilliance, he wrote persuasive articles for his high-school newspaper.
Seeking a wider audience, using important connections, he drummed
into Lower Manhattan newsstand distribution a periodical called *Oh!
Golden Horse!*[2]

30   In order to keep him from feeling guilty (because guilt is the stony
heart of nine tenths of all clinically diagnosed cancers in America today,
she said), and because she had always believed in giving bad habits room
at home where one could keep an eye on them, she too became a junkie.
Her kitchen was famous for a while—a center for intellectual addicts who
knew what they were doing. A few felt artistic like Coleridge[3] and others
were scientific and revolutionary like Leary.[4] Although she was often high
herself, certain good mothering reflexes remained, and she saw to it that
there was lots of orange juice around and honey and milk and vitamin
pills. However, she never cooked anything but chili, and that no more
than once a week. She explained, when we talked to her, seriously, with
neighborly concern, that it was her part in the youth culture and she
would rather be with the young, it was an honor, than with her own
generation.

One week, while nodding through an Antonioni[5] film, this boy was
severely jabbed by the elbow of a stern and proselytizing girl, sitting
beside him. She offered immediate apricots and nuts for his sugar level,
spoke to him sharply, and took him home.

She had heard of him and his work and she herself published, edited,

2. *Horse* is slang for heroin.   3. Samuel Taylor Coleridge (1772–1834), English Romantic poet,
claimed that his poem "Kubla Khan" recorded what he remembered of a dream stimulated by opium.
4. Timothy Leary (1920–1996), American psychologist, promoted the use of psychedelic drugs.
5. Michelangelo Antonioni (b. 1912), Italian film director (*Blow-Up, Zabriskie Point*). *Nodding:* a slang
term referring to the narcotic effect of heroin.

and wrote a competitive journal called *Man Does Live By Bread Alone*. In the organic heat of her continuous presence he could not help but become interested once more in his muscles, his arteries, and nerve connections. In fact he began to love them, treasure them, praise them with funny little songs in *Man Does Live . . .*

> *the fingers of my flesh transcend*
> *my transcendental soul*
> *the tightness in my shoulders end*
> *my teeth have made me whole*

To the mouth of his head (that glory of will and determination) he brought hard apples, nuts, wheat germ, and soybean oil. He said to his old friends, From now on, I guess I'll keep my wits about me. I'm going on the natch. He said he was about to begin a spiritual deep-breathing journey. How about you too, Mom? he asked kindly.

His conversion was so radiant, splendid, that neighborhood kids his age began to say that he had never been a real addict at all, only a journalist along for the smell of the story. The mother tried several times to give up what had become without her son and his friends a lonely habit. This effort only brought it to supportable levels. The boy and his girl took their electronic mimeograph and moved to the bushy edge of another borough. They were very strict. They said they would not see her again until she had been off drugs for sixty days.

At home alone in the evening, weeping, the mother read and reread the seven issues of *Oh! Golden Horse!* They seemed to her as truthful as ever. We often crossed the street to visit and console. But if we mentioned any of our children who were at college or in the hospital or dropouts at home, she would cry out, My baby! My baby! and burst into terrible, face-scarring, time-consuming tears. The End. 35

First my father was silent, then he said, "Number One: You have a nice sense of humor. Number Two: I see you can't tell a plain story. So don't waste time." Then he said sadly, "Number Three: I suppose that means she was alone, she was left like that, his mother. Alone. Probably sick?"

I said, "Yes."

"Poor woman. Poor girl, to be born in a time of fools, to live among fools. The end. The end. You were right to put that down. The end."

I didn't want to argue, but I had to say, "Well, it is not necessarily the end, Pa."

"Yes," he said, "what a tragedy. The end of a person." 40

"No, Pa," I begged him. "It doesn't have to be. She's only about forty. She could be a hundred different things in this world as time goes on. A teacher or a social worker. An ex-junkie! Sometimes it's better than having a master's in education."

"Jokes," he said. "As a writer that's your main trouble. You don't want to recognize it. Tragedy! Plain tragedy! Historical tragedy! No hope. The end."

"Oh, Pa," I said. "She could change."

"In your own life, too, you have to look it in the face." He took a couple of nitroglycerin.[6] "Turn to five," he said, pointing to the dial on the oxygen tank. He inserted the tubes into his nostrils and breathed deep. He closed his eyes and said, "No."

45   I had promised the family to always let him have the last word when arguing, but in this case I had a different responsibility. That woman lives across the street. She's my knowledge and my invention. I'm sorry for her. I'm not going to leave her there in that house crying. (Actually neither would Life, which unlike me has no pity.)

Therefore: She did change. Of course her son never came home again. But right now, she's the receptionist in a storefront community clinic in the East Village. Most of the customers are young people, some old friends. The head doctor said to her, "If we only had three people in this clinic with your experiences . . ."

"The doctor said that?" My father took the oxygen tubes out of his nostrils and said, "Jokes. Jokes again."

"No, Pa, it could really happen that way, it's a funny world nowadays."

"No," he said. "Truth first. She will slide back. A person must have character. She does not."

50   "No, Pa," I said. "That's it. She's got a job. Forget it. She's in that storefront working."

"How long will it be?" he asked. "Tragedy! You too. When will you look it in the face?"

1974

QUESTIONS

1. What different ideas about stories and storytelling do the narrator and her father seem to have in "A Conversation with My Father"? What might account for their different attitudes?
2. In what ways is the narrator's second version of her story an improvement over the first? Why does her father still reject the story?
3. Why does the narrator's father object so strongly to the jokes in the stories, even though he compliments her "nice sense of humor"? Are jokes out of place in a story about someone facing death?

6. Medicine for certain heart conditions.

SHERMAN ALEXIE

Flight Patterns

At 5:05 A.M., Patsy Cline fell loudly to pieces on William's clock radio.[1] He hit the snooze button, silencing lonesome Patsy, and dozed for fifteen more minutes before Donna Fargo bragged about being the happiest girl in the whole USA. William wondered what had ever happened to Donna Fargo, whose birth name was the infinitely more interesting Yvonne Vaughn, and wondered *why* he knew Donna Fargo's birth name. Ah, he was the bemused and slightly embarrassed owner of a twenty-first-century American mind.[2] His intellect was a big comfy couch stuffed with sacred and profane trivia. He knew the names of all nine of Elizabeth Taylor's husbands and could quote from memory the entire Declaration of Independence. William knew Donna Fargo's birth name because he *wanted* to know her birth name. He wanted to know all of the great big and tiny little American details. He didn't want to choose between Ernie Hemingway and the Spokane tribal elders, between Mia Hamm and Crazy Horse, between *The Heart Is a Lonely Hunter* and Chief Dan George. William wanted all of it. Hunger was his crime. As for dear Miss Fargo, William figured she probably played the Indian casino circuit along with the Righteous Brothers, Smokey Robinson, Eddie Money, Pat Benatar, RATT, REO Speedwagon, and dozens of other formerly famous rock- and country-music stars. Many of the Indian casino acts were bad, and most of the rest were pure nostalgic entertainment, but a small number made beautiful and timeless music. William knew the genius Merle Haggard played thirty or forty Indian casinos every year, so long live Haggard and long live tribal economic sovereignty. Who cares about fishing and hunting rights? Who cares about uranium mines and nuclear-waste-dump sites on sacred land? Who cares about the recovery of tribal languages? Give me Freddy Fender singing "Before the Next Teardrop Falls" in English and Spanish to 206 Spokane Indians, William thought, and I will be a happy man.

But William wasn't happy this morning. He'd slept poorly—he always slept poorly—and wondered again if his insomnia was a physical or a mental condition. His doctor had offered him sleeping-pill prescriptions, but William declined for philosophical reasons. He was an Indian who didn't smoke or drink or eat processed sugar. He lifted weights three days a week, ran every day, and competed in four triathlons a year. A two-mile swim, a 150-mile bike ride, and a full marathon. A triathlon was a religious quest. If Saint Francis were still around, he'd be a triathlete. Another exaggeration! Theological hyperbole! Rabid self-justification! Diagnostically speak-

---

1. A reference to country music singer Patsy Cline's recording of "I Fall to Pieces" (1961). *Donna Fargo:* American singer (b. 1949) best known for her recording of "Happiest Girl in the Whole U.S.A." (1972).
2. The story contains many references to American popular culture of the post–World War II era.

ing, William was an obsessive-compulsive workaholic who was afraid of pills. So he suffered sleepless nights and constant daytime fatigue.

This morning, awake and not awake, William turned down the radio, changing Yvonne Vaughn's celebratory anthem into whispered blues, and rolled off the couch onto his hands and knees. His back and legs were sore because he'd slept on the living room couch so the alarm wouldn't disturb his wife and daughter upstairs. Still on his hands and knees, William stretched his spine, using the twelve basic exercises he'd learned from Dr. Adams, that master practitioner of white middle-class chiropractic voodoo. This was all part of William's regular morning ceremony. Other people find God in ornate ritual, but William called out to Geronimo, Jesus Christ, Saint Therese, Buddha, Allah, Billie Holiday, Simon Ortiz, Abe Lincoln, Bessie Smith, Howard Hughes, Leslie Marmon Silko, Joan of Arc and Joan of Collins, John Woo, Wilma Mankiller, and Karl and Groucho Marx while he pumped out fifty push-ups and fifty abdominal crunches. William wasn't particularly religious; he was generally religious. Finished with his morning calisthenics, William showered in the basement, suffering the water that was always too cold down there, and threaded his long black hair into two tight braids—the indigenous businessman's tonsorial special—and dressed in his best travel suit, a navy three-button pinstripe he'd ordered online. He'd worried about the fit, but his tailor was a magician and had only mildly chastised William for such an impulsive purchase. After knotting his blue paisley tie, purchased in person and on sale, William walked upstairs in bare feet and kissed his wife, Marie, good-bye.

"Cancel your flight," she said. "And come back to bed."

5   "You're supposed to be asleep," he said.

She was a small and dark woman who seemed to be smaller and darker at that time of the morning. Her long black hair had once again defeated its braids, but she didn't care. She sometimes went two or three days without brushing it. William was obsessive about his mane, tying and retying his ponytail, knotting and reknotting his braids, experimenting with this shampoo and that conditioner. He greased down his cowlicks (inherited from a cowlicked father and grandfather) with shiny pomade, but Marie's hair was always unkempt, wild, and renegade. William's hair hung around the fort, but Marie's rode on the warpath! She constantly pulled stray strands out of her mouth. William loved her for it. During sex, they spent as much time readjusting her hair as they did readjusting positions. Such were the erotic dangers of loving a Spokane Indian woman.

"Take off your clothes and get in bed," Marie pleaded now.

"I can't do that," William said. "They're counting on me."

"Oh, the plane will be filled with salesmen. Let some other salesman sell what you're selling."

10   "Your breath stinks."

"So do my feet, my pits, and my butt, but you still love me. Come back to bed, and I'll make it worth your while."

William kissed Marie, reached beneath her pajama top, and squeezed her breasts. He thought about reaching inside her pajama bottoms. She wrapped her arms and legs around him and tried to wrestle him into bed. Oh, God, he wanted to climb into bed and make love. He wanted to fornicate, to sex, to breed, to screw, to make the beast with two backs. *Oh, sweetheart, be my little synonym!* He wanted her to be both subject and object. Perhaps it was wrong (and unavoidable) to objectify female strangers, but shouldn't every husband seek to objectify his wife at least once a day? William loved and respected his wife, and delighted in her intelligence, humor, and kindness, but he also loved to watch her lovely ass when she walked, and stare down the front of her loose shirts when she leaned over, and grab her breasts at wildly inappropriate times—during dinner parties and piano recitals and uncontrolled intersections, for instance. He constantly made passes at her, not necessarily expecting to be successful, but to remind her he still desired her and was excited by the thought of her. She was his passive and active.

"Come on," she said. "If you stay home, I'll make you Scooby."

He laughed at the inside joke, created one night while he tried to give her sexual directions and was so aroused that he sounded exactly like Scooby-Doo.

"Stay home, stay home, stay home," she chanted and wrapped herself 15 tighter around him. He was supporting all of her weight, holding her two feet off the bed.

"I'm not strong enough to do this," he said.

"Baby, baby, I'll make you strong," she sang, and it sounded like she was writing a Top 40 hit in the Brill Building, circa 1962. How could he leave a woman who sang like that? He hated to leave, but he loved his work. He was a man, and men needed to work. More sexism! More masculine tunnel vision! More need for gender-sensitivity workshops! He pulled away from her, dropping her back onto the bed, and stepped away.

"Willy Loman," she said, "you must pay attention to me."[3]

"I love you," he said, but she'd already fallen back to sleep—a narcoleptic gift William envied—and he wondered if she would dream about a man who never left her, about some unemployed agoraphobic Indian warrior who liked to cook and wash dishes.

William tiptoed into his daughter's bedroom, expecting to hear her light 20 snore, but she was awake and sitting up in bed, and looked so magical and androgynous with her huge brown eyes and crew-cut hair. She'd wanted to completely shave her head: *I don't want long hair, I don't want short hair, I don't want hair at all, and I don't want to be a girl or a boy, I want to be a yellow and orange leaf some little kid picks up and pastes in his scrapbook.*

"Daddy," she said.

"Grace," he said. "You should be asleep. You have school today."

"I know," she said. "But I wanted to see you before you left."

"Okay," said William as he kissed her forehead, nose, and chin. "You've seen me. Now go back to sleep. I love you and I'm going to miss you."

---

3. A reference to Willy Loman, the protagonist of Arthur Miller's play *Death of a Salesman* (1949); Willy's wife, Linda, says of her husband, "Attention, attention must finally be paid to such a person."

25   She fiercely hugged him.

"Oh," he said. "You're such a lovely, lovely girl."

Preternaturally serious, she took his face in her eyes and studied his eyes. Morally examined by a kindergartner!

"Daddy," she said. "Go be silly for those people far away."

She cried as William left her room. Already quite sure he was only an adequate husband, he wondered, as he often did, if he was a bad father. During these mornings, he felt generic and violent, like some caveman leaving the fire to hunt animals in the cold and dark. Maybe his hands were smooth and clean, but they felt bloody.

30   Downstairs, he put on his socks and shoes and overcoat and listened for his daughter's crying, but she was quiet, having inherited her mother's gift for instant sleep. She had probably fallen back into one of her odd little dreams. While he was gone, she often drew pictures of those dreams, coloring the sky green and the grass blue—everything backward and wrong—and had once sketched a man in a suit crashing an airplane into the bright yellow sun. Ah, the rage, fear, and loneliness of a five-year-old, simple and true! She'd been especially afraid since September 11 of the previous year and constantly quizzed William about what he would do if terrorists hijacked his plane.

"I'd tell them I was your father," he'd said to her before he left for his last business trip. "And they'd stop being bad."

"You're lying," she'd said. "I'm not supposed to listen to liars. If you lie to me, I can't love you."

He couldn't argue with her logic. Maybe she was the most logical person on the planet. Maybe she should be illegally elected president of the United States.

William understood her fear of flying and of his flight. He was afraid of flying, too, but not of terrorists. After the horrible violence of September 11, he figured hijacking was no longer a useful weapon in the terrorist arsenal. These days, a terrorist armed with a box cutter would be torn to pieces by all of the coach-class passengers and fed to the first-class upgrades. However, no matter how much he tried to laugh his fear away, William always scanned the airports and airplanes for little brown guys who reeked of fundamentalism. That meant William was equally afraid of Osama bin Laden and Jerry Falwell wearing the last vestiges of a summer tan. William himself was a little brown guy, so the other travelers were always sniffing around him, but he smelled only of Dove soap, Mennen deodorant, and sarcasm. Still, he understood why people were afraid of him, a brown-skinned man with dark hair and eyes. If Norwegian terrorists had exploded the World Trade Center, then blue-eyed blondes would be viewed with more suspicion. Or so he hoped.

35   Locking the front door behind him, William stepped away from his house, carried his garment bag and briefcase onto the front porch, and waited for his taxi to arrive. It was a cold and foggy October morning. William could smell the saltwater of Elliott Bay and the freshwater of Lake Washington. Surrounded by gray water and gray fog and gray skies and

gray mountains and a gray sun, he'd lived with his family in Seattle for three years and loved it. He couldn't imagine living anywhere else, with any other wife or child, in any other time.

William was tired and happy and romantic and exaggerating the size of his familial devotion so he could justify his departure, so he could survive his departure. He did sometimes think about other women and other possible lives with them. He wondered how his life would have been different if he'd married a white woman and fathered half-white children who grew up to complain and brag about their biracial identities: *Oh, the only box they have for me is Other! I'm not going to check any box! I'm not the Other! I am Tiger Woods!* But William most often fantasized about being single and free to travel as often as he wished—maybe two million miles a year—and how much he'd enjoy the benefits of being a platinum frequent flier. Maybe he'd have one-night stands with a long series of traveling saleswomen, all of them thousands of miles away from husbands and children who kept looking up "feminism" in the dictionary. William knew that was yet another sexist thought. In this capitalistic and democratic culture, talented women should also enjoy the freedom to emotionally and physically abandon their families. After all, talented and educated men have been doing it for generations. Let freedom ring!

Marie had left her job as a corporate accountant to be a full-time mother to Grace. William loved his wife for making the decision, and he tried to do his share of the housework, but he suspected he was an old-fashioned bastard who wanted his wife to stay at home and wait, wait, wait for him.

Marie was always waiting for William to call, to come home, to leave messages saying he was getting on the plane, getting off the plane, checking in to the hotel, going to sleep, waking up, heading for the meeting, catching an earlier or later flight home. He spent one third of his life trying to sleep in uncomfortable beds and one third of his life trying to stay awake in airports. He traveled with thousands of other capitalistic foot soldiers, mostly men but increasing numbers of women, and stayed in the same Ramadas, Holiday Inns, and Radissons. He ate the same room-service meals and ran the same exercise-room treadmills and watched the same pay-per-view porn and stared out the windows at the same strange and lonely cityscapes. Sure, he was an enrolled member of the Spokane Indian tribe, but he was also a fully recognized member of the notebook-computer tribe and the security-checkpoint tribe and the rental-car tribe and the hotel-shuttle-bus tribe and the cell-phone-roaming-charge tribe.

William traveled so often, the Seattle-based flight attendants knew him by first name.

At five minutes to six, the Orange Top taxi pulled into the driveway. The driver, a short and thin black man, stepped out of the cab and waved. William rushed down the stairs and across the pavement. He wanted to get away from the house before he changed his mind about leaving.

"Is that everything, sir?" asked the taxi driver, his accent a colonial cocktail of American English, formal British, and French sibilants added to a base of what must have been North African.

"Yes, it is, sir," said William, self-consciously trying to erase any class differences between them. In Spain the previous summer, an elderly porter had cursed at William when he insisted on carrying his own bags into the hotel. "Perhaps there is something wrong with the caste system, sir," the hotel concierge had explained to William. "But all of us, we want to do our jobs, and we want to do them well."

William didn't want to insult anybody; he wanted the world to be a fair and decent place. At least that was what he wanted to want. More than anything, he wanted to stay home with his fair and decent family. He supposed he wanted the world to be fairer and more decent to his family. We are special, he thought, though he suspected they were just one more family on this block of neighbors, in this city of neighbors, in this country of neighbors, in a world of neighbors. He looked back at his house, at the windows behind which slept his beloved wife and daughter. When he traveled, he had nightmares about strangers breaking into the house and killing and raping Marie and Grace. In other nightmares, he arrived home in time to save his family by beating the intruders and chasing them away. During longer business trips, William's nightmares became more violent as the days and nights passed. If he was gone over a week, he dreamed about mutilating the rapists and eating them alive while his wife and daughter cheered for him.

"Let me take your bags, sir," said the taxi driver.

45   "What?" asked William, momentarily confused.

"Your bags, sir."

William handed him the briefcase but held on to the heavier garment bag. A stupid compromise, thought William, but it's too late to change it now. God, I'm supposed to be some electric aboriginal warrior, but I'm really a wimpy liberal pacifist. *Dear Lord, how much longer should I mourn the death of Jerry Garcia?*

The taxi driver tried to take the garment bag from William.

"I've got this one," said William, then added, "I've got it, sir."

50   The taxi driver hesitated, shrugged, opened the trunk, and set the briefcase inside. William laid the garment bag next to his briefcase. The taxi driver shut the trunk and walked around to open William's door.

"No, sir," said William as he awkwardly stepped in front of the taxi driver, opened the door, and took a seat. "I've got it."

"I'm sorry, sir," said the taxi driver and hurried around to the driver's seat. This strange American was making him uncomfortable, and he wanted to get behind the wheel and drive. Driving comforted him.

"To the airport, sir?" asked the taxi driver as he started the meter.

"Yes," said William. "United Airlines."

55   "Very good, sir."

In silence, they drove along Martin Luther King Jr. Way, the bisector of an African American neighborhood that was rapidly gentrifying. William and his family were Native American gentry! They were the very first Indian family to ever move into a neighborhood and bring up the property values! That was one of William's favorite jokes, self-deprecating and politely racist. White folks could laugh at a joke like that and not feel guilty. But how guilty could white people feel in Seattle? Seattle might be the only city in the country where white people lived comfortably on a street named after Martin Luther King, Jr.

No matter where he lived, William always felt uncomfortable, so he enjoyed other people's discomfort. These days, in the airports, he loved to watch white people enduring random security checks. It was a perverse thrill, to be sure, but William couldn't help himself. He knew those white folks wanted to scream and rage: *Do I look like a terrorist?* And he knew the security officers, most often low-paid brown folks, wanted to scream back: *Define terror, you Anglo bastard!* William figured he'd been pulled over for pat-down searches about 75 percent of the time. Random, my ass! But that was okay! William might have wanted to irritate other people, but he didn't want to scare them. He wanted his fellow travelers to know exactly who and what he was: *I am a Native American and therefore have ten thousand more reasons to terrorize the U.S. than any of those Taliban jerk-offs, but I have chosen instead to become a civic American citizen, so all of you white folks should be celebrating my kindness and moral decency and awesome ability to forgive!* Maybe William should have worn beaded vests when he traveled. Maybe he should have brought a hand drum and sang "Way, ya, way, ya, hey." Maybe he should have thrown casino chips into the crowd.

The taxi driver turned west on Cherry, drove twenty blocks into downtown, took the entrance ramp onto I-5, and headed south for the airport. The freeway was moderately busy for that time of morning.

"Where are you going, sir?" asked the taxi driver.

"I've got business in Chicago," William said. He didn't really want to 60 talk. He needed to meditate in silence. He needed to put his fear of flying inside an imaginary safe deposit box and lock it away. We all have our ceremonies, thought William, our personal narratives. He'd always needed to meditate in the taxi on the way to the airport. Immediately upon arrival at the departure gate, he'd listen to a tape he'd made of rock stars who died in plane crashes. Buddy Holly, Otis Redding, Stevie Ray, "Oh Donna," "Chantilly Lace," "(Sittin' on) The Dock of the Bay." William figured God would never kill a man who listened to such a morbid collection of music. Too easy a target, and plus, God could never justify killing a planeful of innocents to punish one minor sinner.

"What do you do, sir?" asked the taxi driver.

"You know, I'm not sure," said William and laughed. It was true. He worked for a think tank and sold ideas about how to improve other ideas. Two years ago, his company had made a few hundred thousand dollars by designing and selling the idea of a better shopping cart. The CGI prototype was amazing. It looked like a mobile walk-in closet. But it had yet to be manufactured and probably never would be.

"You wear a good suit," said the taxi driver, not sure why William was laughing. "You must be a businessman, no? You must make lots of money."

"I do okay."

"Your house is big and beautiful."

65

"Yes, I suppose it is."

"You are a family man, yes?"

"I have a wife and daughter."

"Are they beautiful?"

70   William was pleasantly surprised to be asked such a question. "Yes," he said. "Their names are Marie and Grace. They're very beautiful. I love them very much."

"You must miss them when you travel."

"I miss them so much I go crazy," said William. "I start thinking I'm going to disappear, you know, just vanish, if I'm not home. Sometimes I worry their love is the only thing that makes me human, you know? I think if they stopped loving me, I might burn up, spontaneously combust, and turn into little pieces of oxygen and hydrogen and carbon. Do you know what I'm saying?"

"Yes sir, I understand love can be so large."

William wondered why he was being honest and poetic with a taxi driver. There is emotional safety in anonymity, he thought.

75   "I have a wife and three sons," said the driver. "But they live in Ethiopia with my mother and father. I have not seen any of them for many years."

For the first time, William looked closely at the driver. He was clear-eyed and handsome, strong of shoulder and arm, maybe fifty years old, maybe older. A thick scar ran from his right ear down his neck and beneath his collar. A black man with a violent history; William thought and immediately reprimanded himself for racially profiling the driver: *Excuse me, sir, but I pulled you over because your scar doesn't belong in this neighborhood.*

"I still think of my children as children," the driver said. "But they are men now. Taller and stronger than me. They are older now than I was when I last saw them."

William did the math and wondered how this driver could function with such fatherly pain. "I bet you can't wait to go home and see them again," he said, following the official handbook of the frightened American male: *When confronted with the mysterious, you can defend yourself by speaking in obvious generalities.*

"I cannot go home," said the taxi driver, "and I fear I will never see them again."

80   William didn't want to be having this conversation. He wondered if his silence would silence the taxi driver. But it was too late for that.

"What are you?" the driver asked.

"What do you mean?"

"I mean, you are not white, your skin, it is dark like mine."

"Not as dark as yours."

85   "No," said the driver and laughed. "Not so dark, but too dark to be white. What are you? Are you Jewish?"

Because they were so often Muslim, taxi drivers all over the world had often asked William if he was Jewish. William was always being confused for something else. He was ambiguously ethnic, living somewhere in the darker section of the Great American Crayola Box, but he was more beige than brown, more mauve than sienna.

"Why do you want to know if I'm Jewish?" William asked.

"Oh, I'm sorry, sir, if I offended you. I am not anti-Semitic. I love all of my brothers and sisters. Jews, Catholics, Buddhists, even the atheists, I love them all. Like you Americans sing, 'Joy to the world and Jeremiah Bullfrog!' "

The taxi driver laughed again, and William laughed with him.

"I'm Indian," William said.   90

"From India?"

"No, not jewel-on-the-forehead Indian," said William. "I'm a bows-and-arrows Indian."

"Oh, you mean ten little, nine little, eight little Indians?"

"Yeah, sort of," said William. "I'm that kind of Indian, but much smarter. I'm a Spokane Indian. We're salmon people."

"In England, they call you Red Indians."   95

"You've been to England?"

"Yes, I studied physics at Oxford."

"Wow," said William, wondering if this man was a liar.

"You are surprised by this, I imagine. Perhaps you think I'm a liar?"

William covered his mouth with one hand. He smiled this way when he   100
was embarrassed.

"Aha, you do think I'm lying. You ask yourself questions about me. How could a physicist drive a taxi? Well, in the United States, I am a cabdriver, but in Ethiopia, I was a jet-fighter pilot."

By coincidence or magic, or as a coincidence that could willfully be interpreted as magic, they drove past Boeing Field at that exact moment.

"Ah, you see," said the taxi driver, "I can fly any of those planes. The prop planes, the jet planes, even the very large passenger planes. I can also fly the experimental ones that don't fly. But I could make them fly because I am the best pilot in the world. Do you believe me?"

"I don't know," said William, very doubtful of this man but fascinated as well. If he was a liar, then he was a magnificent liar.

On both sides of the freeway, blue-collared men and women drove trucks   105
and forklifts, unloaded trains, trucks, and ships, built computers, televisions, and airplanes. Seattle was a city of industry, of hard work, of calluses on the palms of hands. So many men and women working so hard. William worried that his job—his selling of the purely theoretical—wasn't a real job at all. He didn't build anything. He couldn't walk into department and grocery stores and buy what he'd created, manufactured, and shipped. William's life was measured by imaginary numbers: the binary code of computer languages, the amount of money in his bank accounts, the interest rate on his mortgage, and the rise and fall of the stock market. He invested much of his money in socially responsible funds. Imagine that! Imagine choosing to trust your money with companies that supposedly made their millions through ethical means. Imagine the breathtaking privilege of such a choice. All right, so maybe this was an old story for white men. For most of American history, who else but a white man could endure the existential crisis of economic success? But this story was original and aboriginal for William. For thousands of years, Spokane Indians had lived subsistence

lives, using every last part of the salmon and deer because they'd die without every last part, but William only ordered salmon from menus and saw deer on television. Maybe he romanticized the primal—for thousands of years, Indians also died of ear infections—but William wanted his comfortable and safe life to contain more *wilderness*.

"Sir, forgive me for saying this," the taxi driver said, "but you do not look like the Red Indians I have seen before."

"I know," William said. "People usually think I'm a longhaired Mexican."

"What do you say to them when they think such a thing?"

"No habla español. Indio de Norteamericanos."

110   "People think I'm black American. They always want to hip-hop rap to me. 'Are you East Coast or West Coast?' they ask me, and I tell them I am Ivory Coast."

"How have things been since September eleventh?"

"Ah, a good question, sir. It's been interesting. Because people think I'm black, they don't see me as a terrorist, only as a crackhead addict on welfare. So I am a victim of only one misguided idea about who I am."

"We're all trapped by other people's ideas, aren't we?"

"I suppose that is true, sir. How has it been for you?"

115   "It's all backward," William said. "A few days after it happened, I was walking out of my gym downtown, and this big phallic pickup pulled up in front of me in the crosswalk. Yeah, this big truck with big phallic tires and a big phallic flagpole and a big phallic flag flying, and the big phallic symbol inside leaned out of his window and yelled at me, 'Go back to your own country!' "

"Oh, that is sad and funny," the taxi driver said.

"Yeah," William said. "And it wasn't so much a hate crime as it was a crime of irony, right? And I was laughing so hard, the truck was halfway down the block before I could get breath enough to yell back, 'You first!' "

William and the taxi driver laughed and laughed together. Two dark men laughing at dark jokes.

"I had to fly on the first day you could fly," William said. "And I was flying into Baltimore, you know, and D.C. and Baltimore are pretty much the same damn town, so it was like flying into Ground Zero, you know?"

120   "It must have been terrifying."

"It was, it was. I was sitting in the plane here in Seattle, getting ready to take off, and I started looking around for suspicious brown guys. I was scared of little brown guys. So was everybody else. We were all afraid of the same things. I started looking around for big white guys because I figured they'd be undercover cops, right?"

"Imagine wanting to be surrounded by white cops!"

"Exactly! I didn't want to see some pacifist, vegan, whole-wheat, free-range, organic, progressive, gray-ponytail, communist, liberal, draft-dodging, NPR-listening wimp! What are they going to do if somebody tries to hijack the plane? Throw a Birkenstock at him? Offer him some pot?"

"Marijuana might actually stop the violence everywhere in the world," the taxi driver said.

"You're right," William said. "But on that plane, I was hoping for 125
about twenty-five NRA-loving, gun-nut, serial-killing, psychopathic, Ollie
North, Norman Schwarzkopf, right-wing, Agent Orange, post-traumatic-
stress-disorder, CIA, FBI, automatic-weapon, smart-bomb, laser-sighting
bastards!"

"You wouldn't want to invite them for dinner," the taxi driver said. "But
you want them to protect your children, am I correct?"

"Yes, but it doesn't make sense. None of it makes sense. It's all contradictions."

"The contradictions are the story, yes?"

"Yes."

"I have a story about contradictions," said the taxi driver. "Because you 130
are a Red Indian, I think you will understand my pain."

"*Su-num-twee,*" said William.

"What is that? What did you say?"

"*Su-num-twee.* It's Spokane. My language."

"What does it mean?"

"Listen to me."   135

"Ah, yes, that's good. *Su-num-twee, su-num-twee.* So, what is your name?"

"William."

The taxi driver sat high and straight in his seat, like he was going to say
something important. "William, my name is Fekadu. I am Oromo and
Muslim, and I come from Addis Ababa in Ethiopia, and I want you to *su-
num-twee.*"

There was nothing more important than a person's name and the names
of his clan, tribe, city, religion, and country. By the social rules of his tribe,
William should have reciprocated and officially identified himself. He
should have been polite and generous. He was expected to live by so many
rules, he sometimes felt like he was living inside an indigenous version of
an Edith Wharton[4] novel.

"Mr. William," asked Fekadu, "do you want to hear my story? Do you 140
want to *su-num-twee?*"

"Yes, I do, sure, yes, please," said William. He was lying. He was twenty
minutes away from the airport and so close to departure.

"I was not born into an important family," said Fekadu. "But my father
worked for an important family. And this important family worked for the
family of Emperor Haile Selassie.[5] He was a great and good and kind and
terrible man, and he loved his country and killed many of his people. Have
you heard of him?"

"No, I'm sorry, I haven't."

"He was magical. Ruled our country for forty-three years. Imagine that!
We Ethiopians are strong. White people have never conquered us. We won
every war we fought against white people. For all of our history, our emper-

---

4. American novelist (1862–1937) known for her sophisticated depictions of upper-class mores.
5. Haile Selassie (1892–1975), emperor of Ethiopia from 1930 to 1936 and again from 1941 to 1974,
when he was overthrown in a violent military coup.

ors have been strong, and Selassie was the strongest. There has never been
a man capable of such love and destruction."

145   "You fought against him?"

Fekadu breathed in so deeply that William recognized it as a religious
moment, as the first act of a ceremony, and with the second act, an exha-
lation, the ceremony truly began.

"No," Fekadu said. "I was a smart child. A genius. A prodigy. It was
Selassie who sent me to Oxford. And there I studied physics and learned
the math and art of flight. I came back home and flew jets for Selassie's
army."

"Did you fly in wars?" William asked.

"Ask me what you really want to ask me, William. You want to know if
I was a killer, no?"

150   William had a vision of his wife and daughter huddling terrified in their
Seattle basement while military jets screamed overhead. It happened every
August when the U.S. Navy Blue Angels came to entertain the masses with
their aerial acrobatics.

"Do you want to know if I was a killer?" asked Fekadu. "Ask me if I was
a killer."

William wanted to know the terrible answer without asking the terrible
question.

"Will you not ask me what I am?" asked Fekadu.

"I can't."

155   "I dropped bombs on my own people."

In the sky above them, William counted four, five, six jets flying in holding patterns while awaiting permission to land.

"For three years, I killed my own people," said Fekadu. "And then, on
the third of June in 1974, I could not do it anymore. I kissed my wife and
sons good-bye that morning, and I kissed my mother and father, and I lied
to them and told them I would be back that evening. They had no idea
where I was going. But I went to the base, got into my plane, and flew
away."

"You defected?" William asked. How could a man steal a fighter plane?
Was that possible? And if possible, how much courage would it take to
commit such a crime? William was quite sure he could never be that courageous.

"Yes, I defected," said Fekadu. "I flew my plane to France and was almost
shot down when I violated their airspace, but they let me land, and they
arrested me, and soon enough, they gave me asylum. I came to Seattle five
years ago, and I think I will live here the rest of my days."

160   Fekadu took the next exit. They were two minutes away from the airport.
William was surprised to discover that he didn't want this journey to end
so soon. He wondered if he should invite Fekadu for coffee and a sandwich,
for a slice of pie, for brotherhood. William wanted to hear more of this
man's stories and learn from them, whether they were true or not. Perhaps
it didn't matter if any one man's stories were true. Fekadu's autobiography
might have been completely fabricated, but William was convinced that

somewhere in the world, somewhere in Africa or the United States, a man, a jet pilot, wanted to fly away from the war he was supposed to fight. There must be hundreds, maybe thousands, of such men, and how many were courageous enough to fly away? If Fekadu wasn't describing his own true pain and loneliness, then he might have been accidentally describing the pain of a real and lonely man.

"What about your family?" asked William, because he didn't know what else to ask and because he was thinking of his wife and daughter. "Weren't they in danger? Wouldn't Selassie want to hurt them?"

"I could only pray Selassie would leave them be. He had always been good to me, but he saw me as impulsive, so I hoped he would know my family had nothing to do with my flight. I was a coward for staying and a coward for leaving. But none of it mattered, because Selassie was overthrown a few weeks after I defected."

"A coup?"

"Yes, the Derg[6] deposed him, and they slaughtered all of their enemies and their enemies' families. They suffocated Selassie with a pillow the next year. And now I could never return to Ethiopia because Selassie's people would always want to kill me for my betrayal and the Derg would always want to kill me for being Selassie's soldier. Every night and day, I worry that any of them might harm my family. I want to go there and defend them. I want to bring them here. They can sleep on my floor! But even now, after democracy has almost come to Ethiopia, I cannot go back. There is too much history and pain, and I am too afraid."

"How long has it been since you've talked to your family?"   165

"We write letters to each other, and sometimes we receive them. They sent me photos once, but they never arrived for me to see. And for two days, I waited by the telephone because they were going to call, but it never rang."

Fekadu pulled the taxi to a slow stop at the airport curb. "We are here, sir," he said. "United Airlines."

William didn't know how this ceremony was supposed to end. He felt small and powerless against the collected history. "What am I supposed to do now?" he asked.

"Sir, you must pay me thirty-eight dollars for this ride," said Fekadu and laughed. "Plus a very good tip."

"How much is good?"   170

"You see, sometimes I send cash to my family. I wrap it up and try to hide it inside the envelope. I know it gets stolen, but I hope some of it gets through to my family. I hope they buy themselves gifts from me. I hope."

"You pray for this?"

"Yes, William, I pray for this. And I pray for your safety on your trip, and I pray for the safety of your wife and daughter while you are gone."

"Pop the trunk, I'll get my own bags," said William as he gave sixty

---

6. The brutal military junta that overthrew Haile Selassie in 1974 and ruled Ethiopia until the Derg ("Committee") was itself toppled in 1991.

dollars to Fekadu, exited the taxi, took his luggage out of the trunk, and slammed it shut. Then William walked over to the passenger-side window, leaned in, and studied Fekadu's face and the terrible scar on his neck.

175   "Where did you get that?" William asked.

Fekadu ran a finger along the old wound. "Ah," he said. "You must think I got this flying in a war. But no, I got this in a taxicab wreck. William, I am a much better jet pilot than a car driver."

Fekadu laughed loudly and joyously. William wondered how this poor man could be capable of such happiness, however temporary it was.

"Your stories," said William. "I want to believe you."

"Then believe me," said Fekadu.

180   Unsure, afraid, William stepped back.

"Good-bye, William American," Fekadu said and drove away.

Standing at curbside, William couldn't breathe well. He wondered if he was dying. Of course he was dying, a flawed mortal dying day by day, but he felt like he might fall over from a heart attack or stroke right there on the sidewalk. He left his bags and ran inside the terminal. Let a luggage porter think his bags were dangerous! Let a security guard x-ray the bags and find mysterious shapes! Let a bomb-squad cowboy explode the bags as precaution! Let an airport manager shut down the airport and search every possible traveler! Let the FAA president order every airplane to land! Let the American skies be empty of everything with wings! Let the birds stop flying! Let the very air go still and cold! William didn't care. He ran through the terminal, searching for an available pay phone, a landline, something true and connected to the ground, and he finally found one and dropped two quarters into the slot and dialed his home number, and it rang and rang and rang and rang, and William worried that his wife and daughter were harmed, were lying dead on the floor, but then Marie answered.

"Hello, William," she said.

"I'm here," he said.

2003

QUESTIONS

1. In what ways does William represent, and not represent, an "American"? How might William react when Fekadu calls him "William American"?

2. The taxi driver asks William, "The contradictions are the story, yes?" What might this indicate about Sherman Alexie's conception of the reality behind a good story?

3. At the end of "Flight Patterns," does William fully believe Fekadu's story? Does it matter to William whether or not Fekadu's story is factual?

SUGGESTIONS FOR WRITING

1. Citing examples from one or more of the stories in this chapter, write an essay discussing the effects of storytelling on the actions, attitudes, or relationships of the characters.

2. A joke can be ruined if you tell the punchline first. Some stories, however, can begin at the end or interrupt the action to fill in the past. Choose one of the stories in this chapter and look carefully at the order in which events are told. Notice any points that seem out of chronological order or not set in the "present" of the story, and note whether any long periods of time are skipped or summarized. Would another arrangement work just as well? Write an essay in which you show how time and the order of telling are arranged in this story, and explain why this is an effective way to provide what readers or characters need to know at each stage.

3. Write a first-person account of "A Conversation with My [Relative]" in which you try to get along with that relative although you are confronting an issue that you disagree about. Your account may be true or fictitious, and the narrator or speaker may be you or a fictional person. Whether imagined or accurate to your experience, the story should provide details of personality and situation that seem realistic, as if it actually happened.

4. Retell all or part of any story in this chapter in an entirely different way. For example, you might recast "The Elephant in the Village of the Blind" as a newspaper story or retell the after-dinner events of "Cathedral" through the voice of the blind man.

STUDENT WRITING

The essay below was written by a student in response to the following assignment:

> All of the stories in the "Reading, Responding, Writing" chapter seem to be saying something about the act of storytelling. Write a brief essay that compares any two stories in the chapter, showing how their ideas about storytelling are similar or different.

Nina Sullivan's response to this assignment is a respectable short essay, written without reference to sources outside the stories themselves. Notice how Sullivan grounds her argument in concrete details from the texts.

Sullivan 1

Nina Sullivan
Professor Hall
English 301
25 January 2004

The Heart of Storytelling in "A Conversation with My Father" and "Flight Patterns"

At first glance, Grace Paley's "A Conversation with My Father" and Sherman Alexie's "Flight Patterns" seem totally different. One features a white woman and the terminally ill father with whom she is obviously very close. The other focuses on a Native American businessman and a North African cabdriver who are virtual strangers. But if we look closer, the stories start to seem much more alike. Both stories contain stories within stories; in each, one character attempts to tell a story while another attempts to interpret it. In the process, both stories show us that the act of storytelling can lead to illumination. By showing us characters whose perceptions of others are fundamentally altered by the exchange of stories, Paley and Alexie demonstrate the power of stories to influence real lives by opening our minds and our hearts.

In "A Conversation with My Father," the narrator transforms her own and her father's view of a neighbor by turning the woman into a fictional character. At the behest of her father, the narrator tells a story about how the neighbor joined her son in heroin addiction only to be abandoned by him. When the father

---

criticizes this version of the tale, however, calling for more detail, the narrator expands the story. This time, trying to imagine how the neighbor "became such a person" (33; all page references are to the class text, The Norton Introduction to Literature, Portable ed.), she describes both the woman and her son in more positive, sympathetic terms: the mother is "a fine handsome woman" (34) whose "good mothering reflexes remained" despite her drug habit (34); her son is a "hopeful . . . ideologue" who abandons his mother only because he's trying to encourage her to quit heroin (34).

This more detailed version of the story leads the narrator's father to empathize with the neighbor's sad situation: "Poor girl," he says (35); "I suppose that mèans she was alone, she was left like that, his mother" (35). Moved by his response, the narrator insists that there is hope for the woman and that her story need not end in tragedy. Declaring that now she is "sorry for" her neighbor and that this newfound "pity" won't allow her "to leave her [the neighbor] there in that house crying," the narrator hastily concocts a more hopeful ending in which the woman becomes a receptionist in a community clinic (36). Prior to telling the story, the narrator feels no real emotional tie to the anonymous woman across the street, but by meeting her father's demands that she turn the woman into a character with specific traits and a complex, detailed history, the narrator begins to touch both her father's heart and her own.

At the same time, sharing this story also brings both the narrator and her father face to face with the sad facts that his heart, like all hearts, is a mere "bloody motor" bound to fail sooner or later (32), and that, however different our life stories are, they all have precisely the same tragic ending. This seems to be what the father has in mind when he comments on the way the narrator chooses to conclude the second version of her story. "The end. The end. You were right to put that down. The end," he says (35), implicitly reminding his daughter that his own end is near and that she will be left alone like the mother in the story. Perhaps sensing this, the narrator is suddenly compelled to give the story a happy ending—as much for herself, perhaps, as for her fictional character. Still, as her father recognizes, even this final version of the story, though much less flippant and ironic than the original, is less an act of empathy than another evasion of tragedy. "When will you look it in the face?" her father asks her (36). His question (which is also the final line of Paley's story) reminds us that real life is tragic, and so even a smart, funny story like the narrator's is deficient if it ignores life's tragic dimension. The narrator's earlier comment that "Life . . . unlike me has no pity" (34) implies that she does—deep down, reluctantly—acknowledge this truth.

A comparable set of revelations takes place in Alexie's "Flight Patterns" when a cab driver turns his own life into a story that challenges the preconceptions of the protagonist, William. Despite his own experience with racial prejudice and his strong desire that "the world . . . be a fair and decent place" for all (42), William makes a series of racist assumptions immediately upon meeting his driver. When he notices the man's facial scar, for example, William simply assumes that he is "[a] black man with a violent history" (44). Moments later, when the driver asks, "Are you Jewish?" William wonders whether the driver, like so many "taxi drivers all over the world," is a Muslim (44). Perhaps more important, William simply doesn't want to know anything about the driver and doesn't want to talk to him at all. When the driver begins to speak about his family, William feels both annoyed and "frightened." Not "want[ing] to be having this conversation," he tries to end it, first *by speaking in obvious generalities"* and then by retreating into silence, hoping "his silence would silence the taxi driver" (44).

William soon realizes, however, that "it was too late for that" (44). As they make their way to the airport, the taxi driver, Fekadu, tells his story and through it reveals the simplistic and essentially erroneous nature of William's conjectures about him. Rather than the "crackhead addict on welfare" so many people take him to be (46), Fekadu is an Oxford-educated former fighter pilot who defected from Ethiopia when he could no longer tolerate bombing his own people on the government's behalf. Ironically, then, Fekadu does turn out to be the "black man with a violent history" William initially believed him to be. But his complex "story about contradictions" (47) reveals that he was in fact willing to sacrifice everything— home, family, money, security, and status—in order to avoid further violence (48).

Confronted with his false preconceptions, William comes to view Fekadu in a more complex and sympathetic way. Marveling at the courage it would take to do what Fekadu did, and "quite sure he could never be that courageous" himself (48), William suddenly sees Fekadu as an individual as complex as he is and in some ways much more noble. Whereas he once didn't want to talk to Fekadu at all, William is now "surprised to discover" that he actually "want[s] to hear more of this man's stories and learn from them." Not "want[ing] this journey to end," he feels a rush of empathy that makes him want to "invite Fekadu for coffee and a sandwich, for a slice of pie, for brotherhood" (48). Once he learns of Fekadu's personal tragedies and sacrifices, William's initial impression of Fekadu as just another "black man with a violent history" gives way to a sense of brotherhood and camaraderie. Fekadu's story leads William to reexamine its teller, to connect Fekadu's experiences as an outsider with his own, and to feel some hope that listening to strangers' stories might help prevent conflict.

Fekadu's story not only leads William to feel an almost familial connection to its teller but also gives William a better appreciation of his own family and relative good fortune. Moved by the story of how Fekadu became separated from his loved ones, William is filled with a new sense of the preciousness of those he has just left behind. Leaving his bags on the curb, he runs into the airport to call his wife and to assure her "I'm here" (50).

Just as in "A Conversation with My Father," where a woman comes to feel sympathy for her neighbor only after trying to capture the woman's life in story form, in "Flight Patterns" a man comes to see a stranger as a brother only after that stranger turns his life into a story. Both protagonists are jolted into seeing the parallels with their own lives, and they emerge from the experience with a renewed sense of sympathy for, and connection to, other people. In both cases, that sympathy comes out of a keener awareness of the things that all people share—the love of family, the pain of solitude, the fact of death.

Interestingly, both stories suggest that storytelling can have this effect on us regardless of whether we try to tell another person's story or we hear it. They also imply that it ultimately doesn't matter much whether the stories are factual or not. As Paley's narrator admits, the "woman [who] lives across the street" is as much a creature of "invention" as of "knowledge" (36). And though Alexie's William initially wonders whether or not Fekadu "was a liar" (45), he couldn't care less by the time the taxi ride is over, for now he is "convinced" that even if "Fekadu's autobiography . . . [were] completely fabricated," even "[i]f Fekadu wasn't describing his own true pain and loneliness," Fekadu's story nonetheless truthfully describes the pain of thousands of "real and lonely m[e]n" (49). What William comes to see is what both these stories affirm: whether fact or fiction, stories have the power to make us all a little less "lonely," a little more "real," and a lot more sympathetic to each other.

Understanding the Text

1 PLOT

It could be said that the heart of any story is an answer to the question, "What happened?" In some stories the outward events may be very slight: "what happened" is minimal. Other stories are more dramatic, with secrets revealed or roles reversed. But whether the work of fiction deals with subtle thoughts or violent crises, you can discover its **plot**. *Plot* simply means the arrangement of the **action**, which may consist of any kind of event or series of events recounted in the story. The questions you ask about plot, or what is happening as you read, will shape your response to a story. What are the opening and concluding circumstances of the story, and how do the beginning and the ending differ? How did earlier events cause characters to behave in certain ways? Why is the sequence of events in a character's life rearranged out of chronological order as the story itself unfolds? Are there particular actions, objects, or other details that provide clues or comments on what happens because of when they are mentioned or the ways they recur or change? Such questions, in various ways relating to matters of cause and effect and of time, will lead to a clearer understanding of a story.

Most stories rely on a standard plot structure: **conflict**—a struggle of some sort—and resolution. The conflict and its resolution may be mild and comic or it may involve such destructive forces as war or racism and the deadening effects of everyday life. Generally, plot follows a five-part pattern: exposition, rising action, turning point (or climax), falling action, and conclusion. The first part of the action, called the **exposition**, introduces the characters, their situation, and, usually, a time and place. It may be as short as a sentence— "Once there was a village high in the mountains in which everyone was born blind"—or it may extend to lengthy paragraphs that set a scene or describe a typical action before the exceptional events of the story begin. Exposition usually reveals some source of conflict and may blend right away into the second phase of the plot, the **rising action**: destabilizing events that break the routine and intensify the conflict. At this point, stories tend to present a **discriminated occasion**—something distinct that happened "one day last November" or "one afternoon in his sixteenth summer." The middle, or rising action, of many traditional stories presents a series of similar but steadily intensifying incidents. The **turning point** or **climax** of the action is the third part of a story, where the incidents and the conflicts they introduce converge on a decisive moment, realization, or action. The final phase of a story presents the outcome, sometimes separated into the **falling action** and the **conclusion.** Thus, at the climax and resolution of "The Elephant" tale, the villagers unite their conflicting opinions of the elephant, and they come to an understanding with each other and with the traveler. All the actions of the story are fulfilled, and the situation that was destabilized at the beginning of the story either becomes stable once more or is replaced by a new stable situation.

This typical arrangement of the action of a story is a guide to your **expectations** or predictions. Yet it is not praise, of course, to call a story "predictable." The interest or special quality of any story depends on how it deviates from or adds to an expected pattern or structure. The reader needs to have a motive for continuing to read. At each step of the way you ask, "What happens next?" or "Where will this end?" Your wonder about these questions may be more or less urgent. As you read you may experience none of the **suspense** or intense curiosity and doubt provoked by mysteries, thrillers, or fiction with "twists" of plot. Yet expectations can motivate us to read on even when we feel the events are familiar and we already know the outcome. Many great stories—the myth of Oedipus, for example—begin after the outcome is well known to the audience. Detective fiction often begins just before or just after the crime is committed, so that the rest of the story concerns the process of explaining what happened and identifying "who done it." The full effect of the story comes as you think back or reread the sequence of hints or clues that you have been given, including false clues or "red herrings" that make you look in the wrong direction. Even in stories that lack such dramatic actions as murder, the big "con," the chase, or the destruction of a villain who would destroy the world, the full impact of the plot may come as you review the whole work after the end.

The effect of a story depends a great deal on your response to plot, which in turn depends on **structure.** Plot structure concerns not only the connections between causes and effects but also the arrangements of moments in time. Events in everyday life have little apparent structure since they follow each other rapidly and in overwhelming quantity; only our attention can select them, sort them out, and make sense of them. Where is the meaning or pattern in the tick, tick, tick of a clock or in a list of all the details that fill a day or a week? Stories generally try to avoid that feeling of dull monotony by creating a tension between tick and tock or tock and tick, that is, by lending a meaningful pattern to mere chronology.

Rearrangement of chronological order is one of the fundamentals of plot. Many stories are notable for interesting choices about the structure, or the order and interrelation of parts. This can be the key to your interpretation of a story. In life, actions occur one after the other, sequentially. Not all stories, however, describe events chronologically. Even in oral storytelling we often start the main story and then realize we have to back up to explain previous events that have placed people in this situation. In literary fiction, the telling is often out of order to create a sequence of effects on the audience, or to imitate the way a character's memories or responses are developing in the present time of the story. Ask yourself how the story would be different if events in the characters' lives or the paragraphs that you read were rearranged. One reason for altering chronological order is to engage the reader's attention, to make the reader read on.

The difference between chronology and plot resembles the difference between ancient chronicles that list the events of a king's reign and histories that make a meaningful plan out of those events. "The king died and then the queen died," to use one critic's example, is not a plot, for it has not been "tampered with." "The queen died after the king died" includes the same events, but the order in which they are reported has been changed. The reader of the first sentence focuses on the king first; the reader of the second sentence focuses on the queen. Probably there is an additional causal connection between the two events: the queen died *because* her husband had died. While essentially the same thing has been said, the difference in focus and emphasis changes the effect and the meaning. The chronological record has been structured into plot.

The ordering of events, then, provides stories with structure and plot, which shapes our response and interpretation. Like titles, the beginnings of stories are particularly important. Why does a story begin where it does? No event (at least since the Big Bang) is a true beginning; your own life story begins before you were born and even before you were conceived. So to begin a story the author has to select a given point rather than any other. Why does John Cheever's "The Country Husband," in this chapter, open with "To begin at the beginning, the airplane from Minneapolis in which Francis Weed was traveling East ran into heavy weather"? The story could have begun instead with, say, paragraph 11, when the Weeds are preparing to go out on the evening when Francis meets the baby-sitter; or even, with a few adjustments, with paragraph 15, when the baby-sitter opens the door and Francis sees her for the first time, for it is with their encounter that the story truly seems to begin. Yet the brush with death in the crash and Francis's inability to share the experience with anyone he knows provide a context for his brush with the vitality and desire that comprise the rest of the story.

Surely it was time someone invented a new plot, or that the author came out from the bushes.
—VIRGINIA WOOLF

The point at which a story ends is also a critical aspect of its structure. The destabilization or conflict that initiates the story should be resolved. Thus, a typical ending either reestablishes the old order or establishes a new one. Francis Weed's story ends less than two weeks after the beginning, whereas it would have been possible to "fast forward" to his old age or to the collapse of his first real affair a decade later. The author's selection of the appropriate ending governs your conclusions about how to interpret the details that have been selected to represent this character's fictional life. In fiction, the meaningful shape derives from selecting part of life rather than merely recounting the chronicle of events to the end of the individual's existence. Short fiction is a good form for portraying relatively short periods of time and private experiences, rather than entire lifetimes or extended public events. There can be exceptions to the common structures and patterns of time, as well as exceptions to the common beginnings and endings of short stories. The point is that where the author has made selections and placed emphases determines how a story affects us and what we make of it.

In between the beginning and the end, stories often re-order the time sequence within the fictional world. James Baldwin's "Sonny's Blues" begins, "I read about it in the paper . . . ," and that "it" without antecedent is repeated seven times in the first two paragraphs. This unidentified crisis triggers an intense emotional response in the narrator, a high school teacher who is "scared for Sonny." Read those first two paragraphs and stop. If you try at this point to examine what is going on in your mind, you more than likely will find that you are asking yourself what "it" might refer to, and you probably will have framed for yourself several possible answers. This may be part of the reason that Baldwin begins how and where he does, getting you engaged in the story so that you will read on. To do this, Baldwin "tampers" with chronology, reaching back into the characters' past to dramatize a scene that happened before the fictional present. Thus "Sonny's Blues" uses the technique (familiar from the movies) of **flashback.** By the third paragraph, the narrator begins to tell us about Sonny as a boy, still without identifying the bad news he has read about the adult Sonny. Baldwin relies on such movements from the present to remembered scenes, in a series of flashbacks, partly because the story is about the narrator's changing response to the alarming directions his brother's life has taken at various stages.

You may think that the way to write about the plot of a story is to retell the whole thing in fewer words, removing all the details. But a summary of the events without the details would therefore miss too much of the real nature of a story. It would also risk leaving the reader cold, because the characters would not seem alive and the situation would seem too abstract. This is essentially the complaint of the dying father in "A Conversation with My Father" when his daughter tells a very short, flat story without developing the characters or complicating the plot. Some stories deliberately avoid the techniques that create the illusion that the characters, places, and actions are real. When a story defies your expectations that there will be substantial detail, complex characters, and realistic actions of everyday life, you should ask, Is this an intentional effect? The story may be more magical or more philosophical, more about improbable cause and effect or about the questions of what we can know or express about reality, than about the inner experience of people like us.

In order to understand the intended effect of a story, it is a good rule of thumb to be questioning if not suspicious about the slightest matters in it. Descriptions of objects or incidents may turn out to be part of the plot or "what happens." One writer has said that if there is a gun on the wall at the beginning of a story, it must be fired by the end. Usually incidents or details seem less foreboding than a loaded gun, yet a good reading of a story should consider the relevance or significance even of matters that would be left out of a plot summary. In paragraph 9 of "The Country Husband," for example, Francis Weed listens to "the evening sounds of Shady Hill." These include Mr. Nixon's yelling at the squirrels that raid the birdfeeder: "Varmints! Rascals! Avaunt and quit my sight!" And Donald Goslin is playing (badly) Beethoven's *Moonlight Sonata*. These seem like incidental details, yet both sounds reappear in paragraphs 40 and 41. The repetition of such details becomes part of the plot of the story rather than mere decoration of the setting.

As you focus on such details, ask yourself what a particular item adds to the story. What would be lost without it? In what part of the story does the detail appear and is it, or something else like it, repeated elsewhere in the story? Details in fiction can be like colors in a room, a painting, or an outfit of clothes and accessories—hints to make a connection between parts of the whole. As you discuss or write about a story, you may be dazzled by the wide range and complexity of the details contributing to its effect, and even stymied by differing opinions about the significance of any one detail. It may seem strange when classmates ignore details that matter a great deal to you, or notice details that eluded you. These differences of selection and explanation may shed light on why readers respond to, understand, and judge stories differently. That is one of the pleasures of pondering and discussing stories that avoid direct statements of what happened. In order to keep you engaged and alert, a story must make you ask questions about what will happen or what will be revealed next. A good story is a guessing game.

Like all guessing games, from quiz shows to philosophy, the plot game in fiction has certain guidelines. A well-structured plot will play fair with you, offering at appropriate points all the necessary indications or clues to what will happen next, not just springing new and essential information on you at the last minute. It can be a sign of unoriginal or badly made fiction if a story resorts to a sudden rescue, surprise, or twist. Cause and effect, as well as the beginning and ending of the story, should be integrated; the story shouldn't undermine the reader's expectations, as in "Meanwhile, unknown to our hero, the Marines were just on the other side of the hill," or "Susan rolled over in bed and realized the whole thing had been just a dream." Even so, too much uncertainty is frustrating just as knowing too well where it is all heading is wearisome or boring. Readers may expect and want a loaded gun to fire by the last paragraph, but that sort of plot detail can be too predictable. Readers can also be moved and intrigued by changes in feeling that are difficult to express and that lead to no catastrophic action. Many satisfying stories continue to provoke questions long after you have read and reread them. To respond fully to a story you must be alert to its signals and guess along with the author. One way of seeing whether and how your mind is engaged in your reading is to pause at crucial points in the story and consciously explore what you think is coming. Unlike most guessing games, however, the reward in reading short fiction is not for the right guess—anticipating the outcome before the final paragraph—but for the number of guesses, right *and* wrong, that you make, the number of signals you respond to.

As regards plots I find real life no help at all. Real life seems to have no plots.
—IVY COMPTON-BURNETT

Short fiction has a great advantage over novels or other longer works in this regard; rereading a short story is a relatively easy thing to do, and among its layered pleasures is the knowledge that with each attempt, you will arrive at a slightly different answer to the question, "What happened?"

JOHN CHEEVER

The Country Husband

To begin at the beginning, the airplane from Minneapolis in which Francis Weed was traveling East ran into heavy weather. The sky had been a hazy blue, with the clouds below the plane lying so close together that nothing could be seen of the earth. The mist began to form outside the windows, and they flew into a white cloud of such density that it reflected the exhaust fires. The color of the cloud darkened to gray, and the plane began to rock. Francis had been in heavy weather before, but he had never been shaken up so much. The man in the seat beside him pulled a flask out of his pocket and took a drink. Francis smiled at his neighbor, but the man looked away; he wasn't sharing his pain killer with anyone. The plane began to drop and flounder wildly. A child was crying. The air in the cabin was overheated and stale, and Francis' left foot went to sleep. He read a little from a paper book that he had bought at the airport, but the violence of the storm divided his attention. It was black outside the ports. The exhaust fires blazed and shed sparks in the dark, and, inside, the shaded lights, the stuffiness, and the window curtains gave the cabin an atmosphere of intense and misplaced domesticity. Then the light flickered and went out. "You know what I've always wanted to do?" the man beside Francis said suddenly. "I've always wanted to buy a farm in New Hampshire and raise beef cattle." The stewardess announced that they were going to make an emergency landing. All but the children saw in their minds the spreading wings of the Angel of Death. The pilot could be heard singing faintly, "I've got sixpence, jolly, jolly sixpence. I've got sixpence to last me all my life . . ."[1] There was no other sound.

The loud groaning of the hydraulic valves swallowed up the pilot's song, and there was a shrieking high in the air, like automobile brakes, and the plane hit flat on its belly in a cornfield and shook them so violently that an old man up forward howled, "Me kidneys! Me kidneys!" The stewardess flung open the door, and someone opened an emergency door at the back, letting in the sweet noise of their continuing mortality—the idle splash and smell of a heavy rain. Anxious for their lives, they filed out of the doors and scattered over the cornfield in all directions, praying that the thread would hold. It did. Nothing happened. When it was clear that the plane would not burn or explode, the crew and the stewardess gathered the passengers together and led them to the shelter of a barn. They were not far from Philadelphia, and in a little while a string of taxis took them into the

1. Song popular with Allied troops in World War II.

city. "It's just like the Marne,"[2] someone said, but there was surprisingly little relaxation of that suspiciousness with which many Americans regard their fellow travelers.

In Philadelphia, Francis Weed got a train to New York. At the end of that journey, he crossed the city and caught just as it was about to pull out the commuting train that he took five nights a week to his home in Shady Hill.

He sat with Trace Bearden. "You know, I was in that plane that just crashed outside Philadelphia," he said. "We came down in a field..." He had traveled faster than the newspapers or the rain, and the weather in New York was sunny and mild. It was a day in late September, as fragrant and shapely as an apple. Trace listened to the story, but how could he get excited? Francis had no powers that would let him re-create a brush with death—particularly in the atmosphere of a commuting train, journeying through a sunny countryside where already, in the slum gardens, there were signs of harvest. Trace picked up his newspaper, and Francis was left alone with his thoughts. He said good night to Trace on the platform at Shady Hill and drove in his secondhand Volkswagen up to the Blenhollow neighborhood, where he lived.

The Weeds' Dutch Colonial house was larger than it appeared to be 5 from the driveway. The living room was spacious and divided like Gaul,[3] into three parts. Around an ell to the left as one entered from the vestibule was the long table, laid for six, with candles and a bowl of fruit in the center. The sounds and smells that came from the open kitchen door were appetizing, for Julia Weed was a good cook. The largest part of the living room centered on a fireplace. On the right were some bookshelves and a piano. The room was polished and tranquil, and from the windows that opened to the west there was some late-summer sunlight, brilliant and as clear as water. Nothing here was neglected; nothing had not been burnished. It was not the kind of household where, after prying open a stuck cigarette box, you would find an old shirt button and a tarnished nickel. The hearth was swept, the roses on the piano were reflected in the polish of the broad top, and there was an album of Schubert waltzes on the rack. Louisa Weed, a pretty girl of nine, was looking out the western windows. Her young brother Henry was standing beside her. Her still younger brother, Toby, was studying the figures of some tonsured monks drinking beer on the polished brass of the woodbox. Francis, taking off his hat and putting down his paper, was not consciously pleased with the scene; he was not that reflective. It was his element, his creation, and he returned to it with that sense of lightness and strength with which any creature returns to his home. "Hi, everybody," he said. "The plane from Minneapolis..."

Nine times out of ten, Francis would be greeted with affection, but tonight the children are absorbed in their own antagonisms. Francis had

2. On September 8, 1914, over one thousand Paris taxicabs were requisitioned to move troops to the Marne River to halt the encircling Germans.

3. Ancient France (Gaul) is so described by Julius Caesar in *The Gallic War*.

not finished his sentence about the plane crash before Henry plants a kick in Louisa's behind. Louisa swings around, saying, *"Damn you!"* Francis makes the mistake of scolding Louisa for bad language before he punishes Henry. Now Louisa turns on her father and accuses him of favoritism. Henry is always right; she is persecuted and lonely; her lot is hopeless. Francis turns to his son, but the son has justification for the kick—she hit him first; she hit him on the ear, which is dangerous. Louisa agrees with this passionately. She hit him on the ear, and she *meant* to hit him on the ear, because he messed up her china collection. Henry says that this is a lie. Little Toby turns away from the woodbox to throw in some evidence for Louisa. Henry claps his hand over little Toby's mouth. Francis separates the two boys but accidentally pushes Toby into the woodbox. Toby begins to cry. Louisa is already crying. Just then, Julia Weed comes into that part of the room where the table is laid. She is a pretty, intelligent woman, and the white in her hair is premature. She does not seem to notice the fracas. "Hello, darling," she says serenely to Francis. "Wash your hands, everyone. Dinner is ready." She strikes a match and lights the six candles in this vale of tears.[4]

This simple announcement, like the war cries of the Scottish chieftains, only refreshes the ferocity of the combatants. Louisa gives Henry a blow on the shoulder. Henry, although he seldom cries, has pitched nine innings and is tired. He bursts into tears. Little Toby discovers a splinter in his hand and begins to howl. Francis says loudly that he has been in a plane crash and that he is tired. Julia appears again from the kitchen and, still ignoring the chaos, asks Francis to go upstairs and tell Helen that everything is ready. Francis is happy to go; it is like getting back to headquarters company.[5] He is planning to tell his oldest daughter about the airplane crash, but Helen is lying on her bed reading a *True Romance* magazine, and the first thing Francis does is to take the magazine from her hand and remind Helen that he has forbidden her to buy it. She did not buy it, Helen replies. It was given to her by her best friend, Bessie Black. Everybody reads *True Romance*. Bessie Black's father reads *True Romance*. There isn't a girl in Helen's class who doesn't read *True Romance*. Francis expresses his detestation of the magazine and then tells her that dinner is ready—although from the sounds downstairs it doesn't seem so. Helen follows him down the stairs. Julia has seated herself in the candlelight and spread a napkin over her lap. Neither Louisa nor Henry has come to the table. Little Toby is still howling, lying face down on the floor. Francis speaks to him gently: "Daddy was in a plane crash this afternoon, Toby. Don't you want to hear about it?" Toby goes on crying. "If you don't come to the table now, Toby," Francis says, "I'll have to send you to bed without any supper." The little boy rises, gives him a cutting look, flies up the stairs to his bedroom, and

---

4. Common figurative reference to earthly life (vale is valley); allusion to Bible: "Blessed is the man whose help is from thee: in his heart he hath disposed to ascend by steps, in the vale of tears, in the place which he hath set" (Psalms 83.6–7).

5. That is, like escaping from combat to relative safety behind the lines.

slams the door. "Oh, dear," Julia says, and starts to go after him. Francis says that she will spoil him. Julia says that Toby is ten pounds underweight and has to be encouraged to eat. Winter is coming, and he will spend the cold months in bed unless he has his dinner. Julia goes upstairs. Francis sits down at the table with Helen. Helen is suffering from the dismal feeling of having read too intently on a fine day, and she gives her father and the room a jaded look. She doesn't understand about the plane crash, because there wasn't a drop of rain in Shady Hill.

Julia returns with Toby, and they all sit down and are served. "Do I have to look at that big, fat slob?" Henry says, of Louisa. Everybody but Toby enters into this skirmish, and it rages up and down the table for five minutes. Toward the end, Henry puts his napkin over his head and, trying to eat that way, spills spinach all over his shirt. Francis asks Julia if the children couldn't have their dinner earlier. Julia's guns are loaded for this. She can't cook two dinners and lay two tables. She paints with lightning strokes that panorama of drudgery in which her youth, her beauty, and her wit have been lost. Francis says that he must be understood; he was nearly killed in an airplane crash, and he doesn't like to come home every night to a battlefield. Now Julia is deeply concerned. Her voice trembles. He doesn't come home every night to a battlefield. The accusation is stupid and mean. Everything was tranquil until he arrived. She stops speaking, puts down her knife and fork, and looks into her plate as if it is a gulf. She begins to cry. "Poor Mummy!" Toby says, and when Julia gets up from the table, drying her tears with a napkin, Toby goes to her side. "Poor Mummy," he says. "Poor Mummy!" And they climb the stairs together. The other children drift away from the battlefield, and Francis goes into the back garden for a cigarette and some air.

It was a pleasant garden, with walks and flower beds and places to sit. The sunset had nearly burned out, but there was still plenty of light. Put into a thoughtful mood by the crash and the battle, Francis listened to the evening sounds of Shady Hill. "Varmints! Rascals!" old Mr. Nixon shouted to the squirrels in his bird-feeding station. "Avaunt and quit my sight!" A door slammed. Someone was cutting grass. Then Donald Goslin, who lived at the corner, began to play the "Moonlight Sonata."[6] He did this nearly every night. He threw the tempo out the window and played it *rubato*[7] from beginning to end, like an outpouring of tearful petulance, lonesomeness, and self-pity—of everything it was Beethoven's greatness not to know. The music rang up and down the street beneath the trees like an appeal for love, for tenderness, aimed at some lovely housemaid—some fresh-faced, homesick girl from Galway, looking at old snapshots in her third-floor room. "Here, Jupiter, here, Jupiter," Francis called to the Mercers' retriever. Jupiter crashed through the tomato vines with the remains of a felt hat in his mouth.

---

6. Beethoven's *Sonata Quasi una Fantasia* (1802), a famous and frequently sentimentalized piano composition. 7. With intentional deviations from strict tempo.

10   Jupiter was an anomaly. His retrieving instincts and his high spirits were
out of place in Shady Hill. He was as black as coal, with a long, alert,
intelligent, rakehell face. His eyes gleamed with mischief, and he held his
head high. It was the fierce, heavily collared dog's head that appears in
heraldry, in tapestry, and that used to appear on umbrella handles and
walking sticks. Jupiter went where he pleased, ransacking wastebaskets,
clotheslines, garbage pails, and shoe bags. He broke up garden parties and
tennis matches, and got mixed up in the processional at Christ Church on
Sunday, barking at the men in red dresses.[8] He crashed through old Mr.
Nixon's rose garden two or three times a day, cutting a wide swath through
the Condesa de Sastagos,[9] and as soon as Donald Goslin lighted his barbecue fire on Thursday nights, Jupiter would get the scent. Nothing the
Goslins did could drive him away. Sticks and stones and rude commands
only moved him to the edge of the terrace, where he remained, with his
gallant and heraldic muzzle, waiting for Donald Goslin to turn his back
and reach for the salt. Then he would spring onto the terrace, lift the steak
lightly off the fire, and run away with the Goslins' dinner. Jupiter's days
were numbered. The Wrightsons' German gardener or the Farquarsons'
cook would soon poison him. Even old Mr. Nixon might put some arsenic
in the garbage that Jupiter loved. "Here, Jupiter, Jupiter!" Francis called,
but the dog pranced off, shaking the hat in his white teeth. Looking at the
windows of his house, Francis saw that Julia had come down and was
blowing out the candles.
    Julia and Francis Weed went out a great deal. Julia was well liked and
gregarious, and her love of parties sprang from a most natural dread of
chaos and loneliness. She went through the morning mail with real anxiety,
looking for invitations, and she usually found some, but she was insatiable,
and if she had gone out seven nights a week, it would not have cured her
of a reflective look—the look of someone who hears distant music—for she
would always suppose that there was a more brilliant party somewhere else.
Francis limited her to two week-night parties, putting a flexible interpretation on Friday, and rode through the weekend like a dory in a gale. The
day after the airplane crash, the Weeds were to have dinner with the
Farquarsons.
    Francis got home late from town, and Julia got the sitter while he
dressed, and then hurried him out of the house. The party was small and
pleasant, and Francis settled down to enjoy himself. A new maid passed
the drinks. Her hair was dark, and her face was round and pale and seemed
familiar to Francis. He had not developed his memory as a sentimental
faculty. Wood smoke, lilac, and other such perfumes did not stir him, and
his memory was something like his appendix—a vestigial repository. It was
not his limitation at all to be unable to escape the past; it was perhaps his
limitation that he had escaped it so successfully. He might have seen the
maid at other parties, he might have seen her taking a walk on Sunday
afternoons, but in either case he would not be searching his memory now.

8. Probably the choir.   9. Uncommon yellow and red roses, difficult to grow.

Her face was, in a wonderful way, a moon face—Norman or Irish—but it was not beautiful enough to account for his feeling that he had seen her before, in circumstances that he ought to be able to remember. He asked Nellie Farquarson who she was. Nellie said that the maid had come through an agency, and that her home was Trénon, in Normandy—a small place with a church and a restaurant that Nellie had once visited. While Nellie talked on about her travels abroad, Francis realized where he had seen the woman before. It had been at the end of the war. He had left a replacement depot with some other men and taken a three-day pass in Trénon. On their second day, they had walked out to a crossroads to see the public chastisement of a young woman who had lived with the German commandant during the Occupation.

It was a cool morning in the fall. The sky was overcast, and poured down onto the dirt crossroads a very discouraging light. They were on high land and could see how like one another the shapes of the clouds and the hills were as they stretched off toward the sea. The prisoner arrived sitting on a three-legged stool in a farm cart. She stood by the cart while the Mayor read the accusation and the sentence. Her head was bent and her face was set in that empty half smile behind which the whipped soul is suspended. When the Mayor was finished, she undid her hair and let it fall across her back. A little man with a gray mustache cut off her hair with shears and dropped it on the ground. Then, with a bowl of soapy water and a straight razor, he shaved her skull clean. A woman approached and began to undo the fastenings of her clothes, but the prisoner pushed her aside and undressed herself. When she pulled her chemise over her head and threw it on the ground, she was naked. The women jeered; the men were still. There was no change in the falseness or the plaintiveness of the prisoner's smile. The cold wind made her white skin rough and hardened the nipples of her breasts. The jeering ended gradually, put down by the recognition of their common humanity. One woman spat on her, but some inviolable grandeur in her nakedness lasted through the ordeal. When the crowd was quiet, she turned—she had begun to cry—and, with nothing on but a pair of worn black shoes and stockings, walked down the dirt road alone away from the village. The round white face had aged a little, but there was no question but that the maid who passed his cocktails and later served Francis his dinner was the woman who had been punished at the crossroads.

The war seemed now so distant and that world where the cost of partisanship had been death or torture so long ago. Francis had lost track of the men who had been with him in Vésey. He could not count on Julia's discretion. He could not tell anyone. And if he had told the story now, at the dinner table, it would have been a social as well as a human error. The people in the Farquarsons' living room seemed united in their tacit claim that there had been no past, no war—that there was no danger or trouble in the world. In the recorded history of human arrangements, this extraordinary meeting would have fallen into place, but the atmosphere of Shady Hill made the memory unseemly and impolite. The prisoner withdrew after passing the coffee, but the encounter left Francis feeling languid; it had opened his memory and his senses, and left them dilated. Julia went into the house. Francis stayed in the car to take the sitter home.

15   Expecting to see Mrs. Henlein, the old lady who usually stayed with the children, he was surprised when a young girl opened the door and came out onto the lighted stoop. She stayed in the light to count her textbooks. She was frowning and beautiful. Now, the world is full of beautiful young girls, but Francis saw here the difference between beauty and perfection. All those endearing flaws, moles, birthmarks, and healed wounds were missing, and he experienced in his consciousness that moment when music breaks glass, and felt a pang of recognition as strange, deep and wonderful as anything in his life. It hung from her frown, from an impalpable darkness in her face—a look that impressed him as a direct appeal for love. When she had counted her books, she came down the steps and opened the car door. In the light, he saw that her cheeks were wet. She got in and shut the door.

"You're new," Francis said.

"Yes. Mrs. Henlein is sick. I'm Anne Murchison."

"Did the children give you any trouble?"

"Oh, no, no." She turned and smiled at him unhappily in the dim dashboard light. Her light hair caught on the collar of her jacket, and she shook her head to set it loose.

20   "You've been crying."

"Yes."

"I hope it was nothing that happened in our house."

"No, no, it was nothing that happened in your house." Her voice was bleak. "It's no secret. Everybody in the village knows. Daddy's an alcoholic, and he just called me from some saloon and gave me a piece of his mind. He thinks I'm immoral. He called just before Mrs. Weed came back."

"I'm sorry."

25   "Oh, *Lord!*" She gasped and began to cry. She turned toward Francis, and he took her in his arms and let her cry on his shoulder. She shook in his embrace, and this movement accentuated his sense of the fineness of her flesh and bone. The layers of their clothing felt thin, and when her shuddering began to diminish, it was so much like a paroxysm of love that Francis lost his head and pulled her roughly against him. She drew away. "I live on Belleview Avenue," she said. "You go down Lansing Street to the railroad bridge."

"All right." He started the car.

"You turn left at that traffic light. . . . Now you turn right here and go straight on toward the tracks."

The road Francis took brought him out of his own neighborhood, across the tracks, and toward the river, to a street where the near-poor lived, in houses whose peaked gables and trimmings of wooden lace conveyed the purest feelings of pride and romance, although the houses themselves could not have offered much privacy or comfort, they were all so small. The street was dark, and, stirred by the grace and beauty of the troubled girl, he seemed, in turning into it, to have come into the deepest part of some submerged memory. In the distance, he saw a porch light burning. It was the only one, and she said that the house with the light was where she lived. When he stopped the car, he could see beyond the porch light into a dimly lighted hallway with an old-fashioned clothes tree. "Well, here we are," he said, conscious that a young man would have said something different.

She did not move her hands from the books, where they were folded, and she turned and faced him. There were tears of lust in his eyes. Determinedly—not sadly—he opened the door on his side and walked around to open hers. He took her free hand, letting his fingers in between hers, climbed at her side the two concrete steps, and went up a narrow walk through a front garden where dahlias, marigolds, and roses—things that had withstood the light frosts—still bloomed, and made a bittersweet smell in the night air. At the steps, she freed her hand and then turned and kissed him swiftly. Then she crossed the porch and shut the door. The porch light went out, then the light in the hall. A second later, a light went on upstairs at the side of the house, shining into a tree that was still covered with leaves. It took her only a few minutes to undress and get into bed, and then the house was dark.

Julia was asleep when Francis got home. He opened a second window 30 and got into bed to shut his eyes on that night, but as soon as they were shut—as soon as he had dropped off to sleep—the girl entered his mind, moving with perfect freedom through its shut doors and filling chamber after chamber with her light, her perfume, and the music of her voice. He was crossing the Atlantic with her on the old *Mauretania*[1] and, later, living with her in Paris. When he woke from his dream, he got up and smoked a cigarette at the open window. Getting back into bed, he cast around in his mind for something he desired to do that would injure no one, and he thought of skiing. Up through the dimness in his mind rose the image of a mountain deep in snow. It was late in the day. Wherever his eyes looked, he saw broad and heartening things. Over his shoulder, there was a snow-filled valley, rising into wooded hills where the trees dimmed the whiteness like a sparse coat of hair. The cold deadened all sound but the loud, iron clanking of the lift machinery. The light on the trails was blue, and it was harder than it had been a minute or two earlier to pick the turns, harder to judge—now that the snow was all deep blue—the crust, the ice, the bare spots, and the deep piles of dry powder. Down the mountain he swung, matching his speed against the contours of a slope that had been formed in the first ice age, seeking with ardor some simplicity of feeling and circumstance. Night fell then, and he drank a Martini with some old friend in a dirty country bar.

In the morning, Francis' snow-covered mountain was gone, and he was left with his vivid memories of Paris and the *Mauretania*. He had been bitten gravely. He washed his body, shaved his jaws, drank his coffee, and missed

---

1. The original *Mauretania* (1907–35), sister ship of the *Lusitania*, which was sunk by the Germans in 1915, was the most famous transatlantic liner of its day.

the seven-thirty-one. The train pulled out just as he brought his car to the station, and the longing he felt for the coaches as they drew stubbornly away from him reminded him of the humors of love. He waited for the eight-two, on what was now an empty platform. It was a clear morning; the morning seemed thrown like a gleaming bridge of light over his mixed affairs. His spirits were feverish and high. The image of the girl seemed to put him into a relationship to the world that was mysterious and enthralling. Cars were beginning to fill up the parking lot, and he noticed that those that had driven down from the high land above Shady Hill were white with hoarfrost. This first clear sign of autumn thrilled him. An express train—a night train from Buffalo or Albany—came down the tracks between the platforms, and he saw that the roofs of the foremost cars were covered with a skin of ice. Struck by the miraculous physicalness of everything, he smiled at the passengers in the dining car, who could be seen eating eggs and wiping their mouths with napkins as they traveled. The sleeping-car compartments, with their soiled bed linen, trailed through the fresh morning like a string of rooming-house windows. Then he saw an extraordinary thing; at one of the bedroom windows sat an unclothed woman of exceptional beauty, combing her golden hair. She passed like an apparition through Shady Hill, combing and combing her hair, and Francis followed her with his eyes until she was out of sight. Then old Mrs. Wrightson joined him on the platform and began to talk.

"Well, I guess you must be surprised to see me here the third morning in a row," she said, "but because of my window curtains I'm becoming a regular commuter. The curtains I bought on Monday I returned on Tuesday, and the curtains I bought Tuesday I'm returning today. On Monday, I got exactly what I wanted—it's a wool tapestry with roses and birds—but when I got them home, I found they were the wrong length. Well, I exchanged them yesterday, and when I got them home, I found they were still the wrong length. Now I'm praying to high heaven that the decorator will have them in the right length, because you know my house, you *know* my living-room windows, and you can imagine what a problem they present. I don't know what to do with them."

"I know what to do with them," Francis said.

"What?"

35 "Paint them black on the inside, and shut up."

There was a gasp from Mrs. Wrightson, and Francis looked down at her to be sure that she knew he meant to be rude. She turned and walked away from him, so damaged in spirit that she limped. A wonderful feeling enveloped him, as if light were being shaken about him, and he thought again of Venus combing and combing her hair as she drifted through the Bronx. The realization of how many years had passed since he had enjoyed being deliberately impolite sobered him. Among his friends and neighbors, there were brilliant and gifted people—he saw that—but many of them, also, were bores and fools, and he had made the mistake of listening to them all with equal attention. He had confused a lack of discrimination with Christian love, and the confusion seemed general and destructive. He was grateful to the girl for this bracing sensation of independence. Birds were singing—cardinals and the last of the robins. The sky shone like enamel. Even the smell of ink from his morning paper honed his appetite for life, and the world that was spread out around him was plainly a paradise.

If Francis had believed in some hierarchy of love—in spirits armed with hunting bows, in the capriciousness of Venus and Eros[2]—or even in magical potions, philters, and stews, in scapulae and quarters of the moon,[3] it might have explained his susceptibility and his feverish high spirits. The autumnal loves of middle age are well publicized, and he guessed that he was face to face with one of these, but there was not a trace of autumn in what he felt. He wanted to sport in the green woods, scratch where he itched, and drink from the same cup.

His secretary, Miss Rainey, was late that morning—she went to a psychiatrist three mornings a week—and when she came in, Francis wondered what advice a psychiatrist would have for him. But the girl promised to bring back into his life something like the sound of music. The realization that this music might lead him straight to a trial for statutory rape at the country courthouse collapsed his happiness. The photograph of his four children laughing into the camera on the beach at Gay Head reproached him. On the letterhead of his firm there was a drawing of the Laocoön,[4] and the figure of the priest and his sons in the coils of the snake appeared to him to have the deepest meaning.

He had lunch with Pinky Trabert. At a conversational level, the mores of his friends were robust and elastic, but he knew that the moral card house would come down on them all—on Julia and the children as well—if he got caught taking advantage of a baby-sitter. Looking back over the recent history of Shady Hill for some precedent, he found there was none. There was no turpitude; there had not been a divorce since he lived there; there had not even been a breath of scandal. Things seemed arranged with more propriety even than in the Kingdom of Heaven. After leaving Pinky, Francis went to a jeweler's and bought the girl a bracelet. How happy this clandestine purchase made him, how stuffy and comical the jeweler's clerks seemed, how sweet the women who passed at his back smelled! On Fifth Avenue, passing Atlas with his shoulders bent under the weight of the world,[5] Francis thought of the strenuousness of containing his physicalness within the patterns he had chosen.

He did not know when he would see the girl next. He had the bracelet 40

---

2. Roman name for the goddess of love (Greek: *Aphrodite*) and Greek name for her son (Roman: *Cupid*).

3. Love-inducing and predictive magic. *Scapulae:* small Roman Catholic icons that hang from a ribbon worn around the shoulders.

4. Famous Greek statue, now in the Vatican museum; the "meaning" for Weed seems to reside in the physical struggle, not in the legend (in which the priest and his sons were punished for warning the Trojans about the wooden horse).

5. In Greek legend the Titan Atlas supported the heavens on his shoulders, but he has come to be depicted as bearing the globe; the statue is at Rockefeller Center.

in his inside pocket when he got home. Opening the door of his house, he found her in the hall. Her back was to him, and she turned when she heard the door close. Her smile was open and loving. Her perfection stunned him like a fine day—a day after a thunderstorm. He seized her and covered her lips with his, and she struggled but she did not have to struggle for long, because just then little Gertrude Flannery appeared from somewhere and said, "Oh, Mr. Weed . . ."

Gertrude was a stray. She had been born with a taste for exploration, and she did not have it in her to center her life with her affectionate parents. People who did not know the Flannerys concluded from Gertrude's behavior that she was the child of a bitterly divided family, where drunken quarrels were the rule. This was not true. The fact that little Gertrude's clothing was ragged and thin was her own triumph over her mother's struggle to dress her warmly and neatly. Garrulous, skinny, and unwashed, she drifted from house to house around the Blenhollow neighborhood, forming and breaking alliances based on an attachment to babies, animals, children her own age, adolescents, and sometimes adults. Opening your front door in the morning, you would find Gertrude sitting on your stoop. Going into the bathroom to shave, you would find Gertrude using the toilet. Looking into your son's crib, you would find it empty, and, looking further, you would find that Gertrude had pushed him in his baby carriage into the next village. She was helpful, pervasive, honest, hungry, and loyal. She never went home of her own choice. When the time to go arrived, she was indifferent to all its signs. "Go home, Gertrude," people could be heard saying in one house or another, night after night. "Go home, Gertrude. It's time for you to go home now, Gertrude." "You had better go home and get your supper, Gertrude." "I told you to go home twenty minutes ago, Gertrude." "Your mother will be worrying about you, Gertrude." "Go home, Gertrude, go home."

There are times when the lines around the human eye seem like shelves of eroded stone and when the staring eye itself strikes us with such a wilderness of animal feeling that we are at a loss. The look Francis gave the little girl was ugly and queer, and it frightened her. He reached into his pockets—his hands were shaking—and took out a quarter. "Go home, Gertrude, go home, and don't tell anyone, Gertrude. Don't—" He choked and ran into the living room as Julia called down to him from upstairs to hurry and dress.

The thought that he would drive Anne Murchison home later that night ran like a golden thread through the events of the party that Francis and Julia went to, and he laughed uproariously at dull jokes, dried a tear when Mabel Mercer told him about the death of her kitten, and stretched, yawned, sighed, and grunted like any other man with a rendezvous at the back of his mind. The bracelet was in his pocket. As he sat talking, the smell of grass was in his nose, and he was wondering where he would park the car. Nobody lived in the old Parker mansion, and the driveway was used as a lovers' lane. Townsend Street was a dead end, and he could park there, beyond the last house. The old lane that used to connect Elm Street to the riverbanks was overgrown, but he had walked there with his children, and he could drive his car deep enough into the brushwoods to be concealed.

The Weeds were the last to leave the party, and their host and hostess spoke of their own married happiness while they all four stood in the hallway saying good night. "She's my girl," their host said, squeezing his wife. "She's my blue sky. After sixteen years, I still bite her shoulders. She makes me feel like Hannibal crossing the Alps."[6]

The Weeds drove home in silence. Francis brought the car up the driveway and sat still, with the motor running. "You can put the car in the garage," Julia said as she got out. "I told the Murchison girl she could leave at eleven. Someone drove her home." She shut the door, and Francis sat in the dark. He would be spared nothing then, it seemed, that a fool was not spared: ravening lewdness, jealousy, this hurt to his feelings that put tears in his eyes, even scorn—for he could see clearly the image he now presented, his arms spread over the steering wheel and his head buried in them for love.

Francis had been a dedicated Boy Scout when he was young, and, remembering the precepts of his youth, he left his office early the next afternoon and played some round-robin squash, but, with his body toned up by exercise and a shower, he realized that he might better have stayed at his desk. It was a frosty night when he got home. The air smelled sharply of change. When he stepped into the house, he sensed an unusual stir. The children were in their best clothes, and when Julia came down, she was wearing a lavender dress and her diamond sunburst. She explained the stir: Mr. Hubber was coming at seven to take their photograph for the Christmas card. She had put out Francis' blue suit and a tie with some color in it, because the picture was going to be in color this year. Julia was lighthearted at the thought of being photographed for Christmas. It was the kind of ceremony she enjoyed.

Francis went upstairs to change his clothes. He was tired from the day's work and tired with longing, and sitting on the edge of the bed had the effect of deepening his weariness. He thought of Anne Murchison, and the physical need to express himself, instead of being restrained by the pink lamps of Julia's dressing table, engulfed him. He went to Julia's desk, took a piece of writing paper, and began to write on it. "Dear Anne, I love you, I love you, I love you . . ." No one would see the letter, and he used no restraint. He used phrases like "heavenly bliss," and "love nest." He salivated, sighed, and trembled. When Julia called him to come down, the abyss between his fantasy and the practical world opened so wide that he felt it affected the muscles of his heart.

Julia and the children were on the stoop, and the photographer and his assistant had set up a double battery of floodlights to show the family and

---

6. The Carthaginian general (274–183 B.C.E.) attacked the Romans from the rear by crossing the Alps, considered impregnable, with the use of elephants.

the architectural beauty of the entrance to their house. People who had come home on a late train slowed their cars to see the Weeds being photographed for their Christmas card. A few waved and called to the family. It took half an hour of smiling and wetting their lips before Mr. Hubber was satisfied. The heat of the lights made an unfresh smell in the frosty air, and when they were turned off, they lingered on the retina of Francis' eyes.

Later that night, while Francis and Julia were drinking their coffee in the living room, the doorbell rang. Julia answered the door and let in Clayton Thomas. He had come to pay for some theatre tickets that she had given his mother some time ago, and that Helen Thomas had scrupulously insisted on paying for, though Julia had asked her not to. Julia invited him in to have a cup of coffee. "I won't have any coffee," Clayton said, "but I will come in for a minute." He followed her into the living room, said good evening to Francis, and sat awkwardly in a chair.

50   Clayton's father had been killed in the war, and the young man's fatherlessness surrounded him like an element. This may have been conspicuous in Shady Hill because the Thomases were the only family that lacked a piece; all the other marriages were intact and productive. Clayton was in his second or third year of college, and he and his mother lived alone in a large house, which she hoped to sell. Clayton had once made some trouble. Years ago, he had stolen some money and run away; he had got to California before they caught up with him. He was tall and homely, wore horn-rimmed glasses, and spoke in a deep voice.

"When do you go back to college, Clayton?" Francis asked.

"I'm not going back," Clayton said. "Mother doesn't have the money, and there's no sense in all this pretense. I'm going to get a job, and if we sell the house, we'll take an apartment in New York."

"Won't you miss Shady Hill?" Julia asked.

"No," Clayton said. "I don't like it."

55   "Why not?" Francis asked.

"Well, there's a lot here I don't approve of," Clayton said gravely. "Things like the club dances. Last Saturday night, I looked in toward the end and saw Mr. Granner trying to put Mrs. Minot into the trophy case. They were both drunk. I disapprove of so much drinking."

"It was Saturday night," Francis said.

"And all the dovecotes are phony," Clayton said. "And the way people clutter up their lives. I've thought about it a lot, and what seems to me to be really wrong with Shady Hill is that it doesn't have any future. So much energy is spent in perpetuating the place—in keeping out undesirables, and so forth—that the only idea of the future anyone has is just more and more commuting trains and more parties. I don't think that's healthy. I think people ought to be able to dream big dreams about the future. I think people ought to be able to dream great dreams."

"It's too bad you couldn't continue with college," Julia said.

60   "I want to go to divinity school," Clayton said.

"What's your church?" Francis asked.

"Unitarian, Theosophist, Transcendentalist, Humanist,"[7] Clayton said.

"Wasn't Emerson a transcendentalist?" Julia asked.

"I mean the English transcendentalists," Clayton said. "All the American transcendentalists were goops."

"What kind of job do you expect to get?" Francis asked. 65

"Well, I'd like to work for a publisher," Clayton said, "but everyone tells me there's nothing doing. But it's the kind of thing I'm interested in. I'm writing a long verse play about good and evil. Uncle Charlie might get me into a bank, and that would be good for me. I need the discipline. I have a long way to go in forming my character. I have some terrible habits. I talk too much. I think I ought to take vows of silence. I ought to try not to speak for a week, and discipline myself. I've thought of making a retreat at one of the Episcopalian monasteries, but I don't like Trinitarianism."

"Do you have any girl friends?" Francis asked.

"I'm engaged to be married," Clayton said. "Of course, I'm not old enough or rich enough to have my engagement observed or respected or anything, but I bought a simulated emerald for Anne Murchison with the money I made cutting lawns this summer. We're going to be married as soon as she finishes school."

Francis recoiled at the mention of the girl's name. Then a dingy light seemed to emanate from his spirit, showing everything—Julia, the boy, the chairs—in their true colorlessness. It was like a bitter turn of the weather.

"We're going to have a large family," Clayton said. "Her father's a terrible 70 rummy, and I've had my hard times, and we want to have lots of children. Oh, she's wonderful, Mr. and Mrs. Weed, and we have so much in common. We like all the same things. We sent out the same Christmas card last year without planning it, and we both have an allergy to tomatoes, and our eyebrows grow together in the middle. Well, goodnight."

Julia went to the door with him. When she returned, Francis said that Clayton was lazy, irresponsible, affected, and smelly. Julia said that Francis seemed to be getting intolerant; the Thomas boy was young and should be given a chance. Julia had noticed other cases where Francis had been short-tempered. "Mrs. Wrightson has asked everyone in Shady Hill to her anniversary party but us," she said.

"I'm sorry, Julia."

"Do you know why they didn't ask us?"

"Why?"

"Because you insulted Mrs. Wrightson." 75

"Then you know about it?"

"June Masterson told me. She was standing behind you."

Julia walked in front of the sofa with a small step that expressed, Francis knew, a feeling of anger.

---

7. All are deviations from orthodox Christianity and tend to be more human- than God-oriented; the American transcendentalists (see below) tended to change the emphasis from the study of thought to belief in "intuition."

"I did insult Mrs. Wrightson, Julia, and I meant to. I've never liked her parties, and I'm glad she's dropped us."

80 "What about Helen?"

"How does Helen come into this?"

"Mrs. Wrightson's the one who decides who goes to the assemblies."

"You mean she can keep Helen from going to the dances?"

"Yes."

85 "I hadn't thought of that."

"Oh. I knew you hadn't thought of it," Julia cried, thrusting hiltdeep into this chink of his armor. "And it makes me furious to see this kind of stupid thoughtlessness wreck everyone's happiness."

"I don't think I've wrecked anyone's happiness."

"Mrs. Wrightson runs Shady Hill and has run it for the last forty years. I don't know what makes you think that in a community like this you can indulge every impulse you have to be insulting, vulgar, and offensive."

"I have very good manners," Francis said, trying to give the evening a turn toward the light.

90 "Damn you, Francis Weed!" Julia cried, and the spit of her words struck him in the face. "I've worked hard for the social position we enjoy in this place, and I won't stand by and see you wreck it. You must have understood when you settled here that you couldn't expect to live like a bear in a cave."

"I've got to express my likes and dislikes."

"You can conceal your dislikes. You don't have to meet everything head on, like a child. Unless you're anxious to be a social leper. It's no accident that we get asked out a great deal! It's no accident that Helen has so many friends. How would you like to spend your Saturday nights at the movies? How would you like to spend your Sunday raking up dead leaves? How would you like it if your daughter spent the assembly nights sitting at her window, listening to the music from the club? How would you like it—" He did something then that was, after all, not so unaccountable, since her words seemed to raise up between them a wall so deadening that he gagged. He struck her full in the face. She staggered and then, a moment later, seemed composed. She went up the stairs to their room. She didn't slam the door. When Francis followed, a few minutes later, he found her packing a suitcase.

"Julia, I'm very sorry."

"It doesn't matter," she said. She was crying.

95 "Where do you think you're going?"

"I don't know. I just looked at a timetable. There's an eleven-sixteen into New York. I'll take that."

"You can't go, Julia."

"I can't stay. I know that."

"I'm sorry about Mrs. Wrightson, Julia, and I'm—"

100 "It doesn't matter about Mrs. Wrightson. That isn't the trouble."

"What is the trouble?"

"You don't love me."

"I do love you, Julia."

"No, you don't."

"Julia, I do love you, and I would like to be as we were—sweet and bawdy 105
and dark—but now there are so many people."

"You hate me."

"I don't hate you, Julia."

"You have no idea of how much you hate me. I think it's subconscious.
You don't realize the cruel things you've done."

"What cruel things, Julia?"

"The cruel acts your subconscious drives you to in order to express your 110
hatred of me."

"What, Julia?"

"I've never complained."

"Tell me."

"You don't know what you're doing."

"Tell me." 115

"Your clothes."

"What do you mean?"

"I mean the way you leave your dirty clothes around in order to express
your subconscious hatred of me."

"I don't understand."

"I mean your dirty socks and your dirty pajamas and your dirty under- 120
wear and your dirty shirts!" She rose from kneeling by the suitcase and
faced him, her eyes blazing and her voice ringing with emotion. "I'm talking
about the fact that you've never learned to hang up anything. You just leave
your clothes all over the floor where they drop, in order to humiliate me.
You do it on purpose!" She fell on the bed, sobbing.

"Julia, darling!" he said, but when she felt his hand on her shoulder she
got up.

"Leave me alone," she said. "I have to go." She brushed past him to the
closet and came back with a dress. "I'm not taking any of the things you've
given me," she said. "I'm leaving my pearls and the fur jacket."

"Oh, Julia!" Her figure, so helpless in its self-deceptions, bent over the
suitcase made him nearly sick with pity. She did not understand how desolate her life would be without him. She didn't understand the hours that
working women have to keep. She didn't understand that most of her
friendships existed within the framework of their marriage, and that without this she would find herself alone. She didn't understand about travel,
about hotels, about money. "Julia, I can't let you go! What you don't understand, Julia, is that you've come to be dependent on me."

She tossed her head back and covered her face with her hands. "Did you
say that *I* was dependent on *you?*" she asked. "Is that what you said? And
who is it that tells you what time to get up in the morning and when to
go to bed at night? Who is it that prepares your meals and picks up your
dirty clothes and invites your friends to dinner? If it weren't for me, your
neckties would be greasy and your clothing would be full of moth holes.
You were alone when I met you, Francis Weed, and you'll be alone when I
leave. When Mother asked you for a list to send out invitations to our
wedding, how many names did you have to give her? Fourteen!"

"Cleveland wasn't my home, Julia." 125

"And how many of your friends came to the church? Two!"

"Cleveland wasn't my home, Julia."

"Since I'm not taking the fur jacket," she said quietly, "you'd better put it back into storage. There's an insurance policy on the pearls that comes due in January. The name of the laundry and maid's telephone number— all those things are in my desk. I hope you won't drink too much, Francis. I hope that nothing bad will happen to you. If you do get into serious trouble, you can call me."

"Oh, my darling, I can't let you go!" Francis said. "I can't let you go, Julia!" He took her in his arms.

130   "I guess I'd better stay and take care of you for a little while longer," she said.

Riding to work in the morning, Francis saw the girl walk down the aisle of the coach. He was surprised; he hadn't realized that the school she went to was in the city, but she was carrying books, she seemed to be going to school. His surprise delayed his reaction, but then he got up clumsily and stepped into the aisle. Several people had come between them, but he could see her ahead of him, waiting for someone to open the car door, and then, as the train swerved, putting out her hand to support herself as she crossed the platform into the next car. He followed her through that car and half-way through another before calling her name—"Anne! Anne!"—but she didn't turn. He followed her into still another car, and she sat down in an aisle seat. Coming up to her, all his feelings warm and bent in her direction, he put his hand on the back of her seat—even this touch warmed him— and leaning down to speak to her, he saw that it was not Anne. It was an older woman wearing glasses. He went on deliberately into another car, his face red with embarrassment and the much deeper feeling of having his good sense challenged; for if he couldn't tell one person from another, what evidence was there that his life with Julia and the children had as much reality as his dreams of iniquity in Paris or the litter, the grass smell, and the cave-shaped trees in Lovers' Lane.

Late that afternoon, Julia called to remind Francis that they were going out for dinner. A few minutes later, Trace Bearden called. "Look, fellar," Trace said. "I'm calling for Mrs. Thomas. You know? Clayton, that boy of hers, doesn't seem able to get a job, and I wondered if you could help. If you'd call Charlie Bell—I know he's indebted to you—and say a good word for the kid, I think Charlie would—"

"Trace, I hate to say this," Francis said, "but I don't feel that I can do anything for that boy. The kid's worthless. I know it's a harsh thing to say, but it's a fact. Any kindness done for him would backfire in everybody's face. He's just a worthless kid, Trace, and there's nothing else to be done about it. Even if we got him a job, he wouldn't be able to keep it for a week. I know that to be a fact. It's an awful thing, Trace, and I know it is, but instead of recommending that kid, I'd feel obligated to warn people against him—people who knew his father and would naturally want to step in and do something. I'd feel obliged to warn them. He's a thief . . ."

The moment this conversation was finished, Miss Rainey came in and stood by his desk. "I'm not going to be able to work for you any more, Mr. Weed," she said. "I can stay until the seventeenth if you need me, but I've been offered a whirlwind of a job, and I'd like to leave as soon as possible."

She went out, leaving him to face alone the wickedness of what he had done to the Thomas boy. His children in their photograph laughed and laughed, glazed with all the bright colors of summer, and he remembered that they had met a bagpiper on the beach that day and he had paid the piper a dollar to play them a battle song of the Black Watch.[8] The girl would be at the house when he got home. He would spend another evening among his kind neighbors, picking and choosing dead-end streets, cart tracks, and the driveways of abandoned houses. There was nothing to mitigate his feeling—nothing that laughter or a game of softball with the children would change—and, thinking back over the plane crash, the Farquarsons' new maid, and Anne Murchison's difficulties with her drunken father, he wondered how he could have avoided arriving at just where he was. He was in trouble. He had been lost once in his life, coming back from a trout stream in the north woods, and he had now the same bleak realization that no amount of cheerfulness or hopefulness or valor or perseverance could help him find, in the gathering dark, the path that he'd lost. He smelled the forest. The feeling of bleakness was intolerable, and he saw clearly that he had reached the point where he would have to make a choice.

He could go to a psychiatrist, like Miss Rainey; he could go to church and confess his lusts; he could go to a Danish-massage parlor[9] in the West Seventies that had been recommended by a salesman; he could rape the girl or trust that he would somehow be prevented from doing this; or he could get drunk. It was his life, his boat, and, like every other man, he was made to be the father of thousands, and what harm could there be in a tryst that would make them both feel more kindly toward the world? This was the wrong train of thought, and he came back to the first, the psychiatrist. He had the telephone number of Miss Rainey's doctor, and he called and asked for an immediate appointment. He was insistent with the doctor's secretary—it was his manner in business—and when she said that the doctor's schedule was full for the next few weeks, Francis demanded an appointment that day and was told to come at five.

The psychiatrist's office was in a building that was used mostly by doctors and dentists, and the hallways were filled with the candy smell of mouthwash and memories of pain. Francis' character had been formed upon a series of private resolves—resolves about cleanliness, about going off the high diving board or repeating any other feat that challenged his courage, about punctuality, honesty, and virtue. To abdicate the perfect loneliness in which he had made his most vital decisions shattered his concept of character and left him now in a condition that felt like shock. He was stupefied. The scene for his *miserere mei Deus*[1] was, like the waiting

---

8. Originally a British Highland regiment that became a line regiment and distinguished itself in battle.   9. Sometimes fronts for houses of prostitution.
1. "Have mercy upon me, O God"; first words of Psalm 51.

room of so many doctor's offices, a crude token gesture toward the sweets of domestic bliss: a place arranged with antiques, coffee tables, potted plants, and etchings of snow-covered bridges and geese in flight, although there were no children, no marriage bed, no stove, even, in this travesty of a house, where no one had ever spent the night and where the curtained windows looked straight onto a dark air shaft. Francis gave his name and address to a secretary and then saw, at the side of the room, a policeman moving toward him. "Hold it, hold it," the policeman said. "Don't move. Keep your hands where they are."

"I think it's all right, Officer," the secretary began. "I think it will be—"

"Let's make sure," the policeman said, and he began to slap Francis' clothes, looking for what—pistols, knives, an icepick? Finding nothing, he went off and the secretary began a nervous apology: "When you called on the telephone, Mr. Weed, you seemed very excited, and one of the doctor's patients has been threatening his life, and we have to be careful. If you want to go in now?" Francis pushed open a door connected to an electrical chime, and in the doctor's lair sat down heavily, blew his nose into a handkerchief, searched in his pockets for cigarettes, for matches, for something, and said hoarsely, with tears in his eyes, "I'm in love, Dr. Herzog."

140   It is a week or ten days later in Shady Hill. The seven-fourteen has come and gone, and here and there dinner is finished and the dishes are in the dish-washing machine. The village hangs, morally and economically, from a thread; but it hangs by its thread in the evening light. Donald Goslin has begun to worry the "Moonlight Sonata" again. *Marcato ma sempre pianissimo!*[2] He seems to be wringing out a wet bath towel, but the housemaid does not heed him. She is writing a letter to Arthur Godfrey.[3] In the cellar of his house, Francis Weed is building a coffee table. Dr. Herzog recommends woodwork as a therapy, and Francis finds some true consolation in the simple arithmetic involved and in the holy smell of new wood. Francis is happy. Upstairs, little Toby is crying, because he is tired. He puts off his cowboy hat, gloves, and fringed jacket, unbuckles the belt studded with gold and rubies, the silver bullets and holsters, slips off his suspenders, his checked shirt, and Levi's, and sits on the edge of his bed to pull off his high boots. Leaving this equipment in a heap, he goes to the closet and takes his space suit off a nail. It is a struggle for him to get into the long tights, but he succeeds. He loops the magic cape over his shoulders and, climbing onto the footboard of his bed, he spreads his arms and flies the short distance to the floor, landing with a thump that is audible to everyone in the house but himself.

"Go home, Gertrude, go home," Mrs. Masterson says. "I told you to go home an hour ago, Gertrude. It's way past your suppertime, and your mother will be worried. Go home!" A door on the Babcocks' terrace flies open, and out comes Mrs. Babcock without any clothes on, pursued by a

2. Stressed but always very softly.

3. At the time of the story, host of a daytime radio program especially popular with housewives.

naked husband. (Their children are away at boarding school, and their terrace is screened by a hedge.) Over the terrace they go and in at the kitchen door, as passionate and handsome a nymph and satyr as you will find on any wall in Venice. Cutting the last of the roses in her garden, Julia hears old Mr. Nixon shouting at the squirrels in his bird-feeding station. "Rapscallions! Varmints! Avaunt and quit my sight!" A miserable cat wanders into the garden, sunk in spiritual and physical discomfort. Tied to its head is a small straw hat—a doll's hat—and it is securely buttoned into a doll's dress, from the skirts of which protrudes its long, hairy tail. As it walks, it shakes its feet, as if it had fallen into water.

"Here, pussy, pussy, pussy!" Julia calls.

"Here, pussy, here, poor pussy!" But the cat gives her a skeptical look and stumbles away in its skirts. The last to come is Jupiter. He prances through the tomato vines, holding in his generous mouth the remains of an evening slipper. Then it is dark; it is a night where kings in golden suits ride elephants over the mountains.[4]

1958

QUESTIONS

1. Francis Weed commutes by train "five nights a week to his home in Shady Hill," but "The Country Husband" begins on the night his plane makes an emergency landing and he nearly doesn't make it home. How does this interruption of routine help to prepare for the rest of the story? Why is it significant that everyone else acts as if nothing unusual has happened?

2. Francis "had not developed his memory as a sentimental faculty." Why is memory important in this story? What kinds of memories do people try to ignore and what kinds of memories actually do surface in the story?

3. Consider the story's ending: has Francis's ordered life in Shady Hill been reestablished, or has there been a significant and lasting change in his life?

JAMES BALDWIN

WEB

Sonny's Blues

I read about it in the paper, in the subway, on my way to work. I read it, and I couldn't believe it, and I read it again. Then perhaps I just stared at it, at the newsprint spelling out his name, spelling out the story. I stared at it in the swinging lights of the subway car, and in the faces and bodies of the people, and in my own face, trapped in the darkness which roared outside.

It was not to be believed and I kept telling myself that, as I walked from

4. Reference to Hannibal; see note 6, p. 73, above. Also, see Sinclair Lewis, *Main Street* (1920), in which the protagonist finds the small town of Gopher Prairie stifling and leaves with her son for Washington, D.C., where she tells him, " 'We're going to find elephants with golden howdahs from which peep young maharanees with necklaces of rubies. . . .' "

the subway station to the high school. And at the same time I couldn't doubt it. I was scared, scared for Sonny. He became real to me again. A great block of ice got settled in my belly and kept melting there slowly all day long, while I taught my classes algebra. It was a special kind of ice. It kept melting, sending trickles of ice water all up and down my veins, but it never got less. Sometimes it hardened and seemed to expand until I felt my guts were going to come spilling out or that I was going to choke or scream. This would always be at a moment when I was remembering some specific thing Sonny had once said or done.

When he was about as old as the boys in my classes his face had been bright and open, there was a lot of copper in it; and he'd had wonderfully direct brown eyes, and great gentleness and privacy. I wondered what he looked like now. He had been picked up, the evening before, in a raid on an apartment downtown, for peddling and using heroin.

I couldn't believe it: but what I mean by that is that I couldn't find any room for it anywhere inside me. I had kept it outside me for a long time. I hadn't wanted to know. I had had suspicions, but I didn't name them, I kept putting them away. I told myself that Sonny was wild, but he wasn't crazy. And he'd always been a good boy, he hadn't ever turned hard or evil or disrespectful, the way kids can, so quick, so quick, especially in Harlem. I didn't want to believe that I'd ever see my brother going down, coming to nothing, all that light in his face gone out, in the condition I'd already seen so many others. Yet it had happened and here I was, talking about algebra to a lot of boys who might, every one of them for all I knew, be popping off needles every time they went to the head.[1] Maybe it did more for them than algebra could.

5   I was sure that the first time Sonny had ever had horse,[2] he couldn't have been much older than these boys were now. These boys, now, were living as we'd been living then, they were growing up with a rush and their heads bumped abruptly against the low ceiling of their actual possibilities. They were filled with rage. All they really knew were two darknesses, the darkness of their lives, which was now closing in on them, and the darkness of the movies, which had blinded them to that other darkness, and in which they now, vindictively, dreamed, at once more together than they were at any other time, and more alone.

When the last bell rang, the last class ended, I let out my breath. It seemed I'd been holding it for all that time. My clothes were wet—I may have looked as though I'd been sitting in a steam bath, all dressed up, all afternoon. I sat alone in the classroom a long time. I listened to the boys outside, downstairs, shouting and cursing and laughing. Their laughter struck me for perhaps the first time. It was not the joyous laughter which— God knows why—one associates with children. It was mocking and insular, its intent was to denigrate. It was disenchanted, and in this, also, lay the authority of their curses. Perhaps I was listening to them because I was thinking about my brother and in them I heard my brother. And myself.

1. Lavatory.   2. Heroin.

One boy was whistling a tune, at once very complicated and very simple, it seemed to be pouring out of him as though he were a bird, and it sounded very cool and moving through all that harsh, bright air, only just holding its own through all those other sounds.

I stood up and walked over to the window and looked down into the courtyard. It was the beginning of the spring and the sap was rising in the boys. A teacher passed through them every now and again, quickly, as though he or she couldn't wait to get out of that courtyard, to get those boys out of their sight and off their minds. I started collecting my stuff. I thought I'd better get home and talk to Isabel.

The courtyard was almost deserted by the time I got downstairs. I saw this boy standing in the shadow of a doorway, looking just like Sonny. I almost called his name. Then I saw that it wasn't Sonny, but somebody we used to know, a boy from around our block. He'd been Sonny's friend. He'd never been mine, having been too young for me, and, anyway, I'd never liked him. And now, even though he was a grown-up man, he still hung around that block, still spent hours on the street corners, was always high and raggy. I used to run into him from time to time and he'd often work around to asking me for a quarter or fifty cents. He always had some real good excuse, too, and I always gave it to him. I don't know why.

But now, abruptly, I hated him. I couldn't stand the way he looked at 10 me, partly like a dog, partly like a cunning child. I wanted to ask him what the hell he was doing in the school courtyard.

He sort of shuffled over to me, and he said, "I see you got the papers. So you already know about it."

"You mean about Sonny? Yes, I already know about it. How come they didn't get you?"

He grinned. It made him repulsive and it also brought to mind what he'd looked like as a kid. "I wasn't there. I stay away from them people."

"Good for you." I offered him a cigarette and I watched him through the smoke. "You come all the way down here just to tell me about Sonny?"

"That's right." He was sort of shaking his head and his eyes looked 15 strange, as though they were about to cross. The bright sun deadened his damp dark brown skin and it made his eyes look yellow and showed up the dirt in his kinked hair. He smelled funky. I moved a little away from him and I said, "Well, thanks. But I already know about it and I got to get home."

"I'll walk you a little ways," he said. We started walking. There were a couple of kids still loitering in the courtyard and one of them said goodnight to me and looked strangely at the boy beside me.

"What're you going to do?" he asked me. "I mean, about Sonny?"

"Look. I haven't seen Sonny for over a year, I'm not sure I'm going to do anything. Anyway, what the hell *can* I do?"

"That's right," he said quickly, "ain't nothing you can do. Can't much help old Sonny no more, I guess."

It was what I was thinking and so it seemed to me he had no right to 20 say it.

"I'm surprised at Sonny, though," he went on—he had a funny way of talking, he looked straight ahead as though he were talking to himself—"I thought Sonny was a smart boy, I thought he was too smart to get hung."

"I guess he thought so too," I said sharply, "and that's how he got hung. And how about you? You're pretty goddamn smart, I bet."

Then he looked directly at me, just for a minute. "I ain't smart," he said. "If I was smart, I'd have reached for a pistol a long time ago."

"Look. Don't tell *me* your sad story, if it was up to me, I'd give you one." Then I felt guilty—guilty, probably, for never having supposed that the poor bastard *had* a story of his own, much less a sad one, and I asked, quickly, "What's going to happen to him now?"

25   He didn't answer this. He was off by himself some place.

"Funny thing," he said, and from his tone we might have been discussing the quickest way to get to Brooklyn, "when I saw the papers this morning, the first thing I asked myself was if I had anything to do with it. I felt sort of responsible."

I began to listen more carefully. The subway station was on the corner, just before us, and I stopped. He stopped, too. We were in front of a bar and he ducked slightly, peering in, but whoever he was looking for didn't seem to be there. The juke box was blasting away with something black and bouncy and I half watched the barmaid as she danced her way from the juke box to her place behind the bar. And I watched her face as she laughingly responded to something someone said to her, still keeping time to the music. When she smiled one saw the little girl, one sensed the doomed, still-struggling woman beneath the battered face of the semi-whore.

"I never *give* Sonny nothing," the boy said finally, "but a long time ago I come to school high and Sonny asked me how it felt." He paused, I couldn't bear to watch him, I watched the barmaid, and I listened to the music which seemed to be causing the pavement to shake. "I told him it felt great." The music stopped, the barmaid paused and watched the juke box until the music began again. "It did."

All this was carrying me some place I didn't want to go. I certainly didn't want to know how it felt. It filled everything, the people, the houses, the music, the dark, quicksilver barmaid, with menace; and this menace was their reality.

30   "What's going to happen to him now?" I asked again.

"They'll send him away some place and they'll try to cure him." He shook his head. "Maybe he'll even think he's kicked the habit. Then they'll let him loose"—he gestured, throwing his cigarette into the gutter. "That's all."

"What do you mean, that's *all?*"

But I knew what he meant.

"I *mean*, that's *all.*" He turned his head and looked at me, pulling down the corners of his mouth. "Don't you know what I mean?" he asked, softly.

35   "How the hell *would* I know what you mean?" I almost whispered it, I don't know why.

"That's right," he said to the air, "how would *he* know what I mean?"

He turned toward me again, patient and calm, and yet I somehow felt him shaking, shaking as though he were going to fall apart. I felt that ice in my guts again, the dread I'd felt all afternoon; and again I watched the barmaid, moving about the bar, washing glasses, and singing. "Listen. They'll let him out and then it'll just start all over again. That's what I mean."

"You mean—they'll let him out. And then he'll just start working his way back in again. You mean he'll never kick the habit. Is that what you mean?"

"That's right," he said, cheerfully. "*You* see what I mean."

"Tell me," I said at last, "why does he want to die? He must want to die, he's killing himself, why does he want to die?"

He looked at me in surprise. He licked his lips. "He don't want to die. 40 He wants to live. Don't nobody want to die, ever."

Then I wanted to ask him—too many things. He could not have answered, or if he had, I could not have borne the answers. I started walking. "Well, I guess it's none of my business."

"It's going to be rough on old Sonny," he said. We reached the subway station. "This is your station?" he asked. I nodded. I took one step down. "Damn!" he said, suddenly. I looked up at him. He grinned again. "Damn it if I didn't leave all my money home. You ain't got a dollar on you, have you? Just for a couple of days, is all."

All at once something inside gave and threatened to come pouring out of me. I didn't hate him any more. I felt that in another moment I'd start crying like a child.

"Sure," I said. "Don't sweat." I looked in my wallet and didn't have a dollar, I only had a five. "Here," I said. "That hold you?"

He didn't look at it—he didn't want to look at it. A terrible, closed look 45 came over his face, as though he were keeping the number on the bill a secret from him and me. "Thanks," he said, and now he was dying to see me go. "Don't worry about Sonny. Maybe I'll write him or something."

"Sure," I said. "You do that. So long."

"Be seeing you," he said. I went on down the steps.

And I didn't write Sonny or send him anything for a long time. When I finally did, it was just after my little girl died, and he wrote me back a letter which made me feel like a bastard.

Here's what he said:

Dear brother,   50

You don't know how much I needed to hear from you. I wanted to write you many a time but I dug how much I must have hurt you and so I didn't write. But now I feel like a man who's been trying to climb up out of some deep, real deep and funky hole and just saw the sun up there, outside. I got to get outside.

I can't tell you much about how I got here. I mean I don't know how to tell you. I guess I was afraid of something or I was trying to escape from something and you know I have never been very strong in the head (smile). I'm glad Mama and Daddy are dead and can't see what's happened to their son and I swear if I'd known what I was doing I would never have hurt you so, you and a lot of other fine people who were nice to me and who believed in me.

I don't want you to think it had anything to do with me being a musician. It's more than that. Or maybe less than that. I can't get anything straight in my head down here and I try not to think about what's going to happen to me when I get outside again. Sometime I think I'm going to flip and *never* get outside and sometime I think I'll come straight back. I tell you one thing, though, I'd rather blow my brains out than go through this again. But that's what they all say, so they tell me. If I tell you when I'm coming to New York and if you could meet me, I sure would appreciate it. Give my love to Isabel and the kids and I was sure sorry to hear about little Gracie. I wish I could be like Mama and say the Lord's will be done, but I don't know it seems to me that trouble is the one thing that never does get stopped and I don't know what good it does to blame it on the Lord. But maybe it does some good if you believe it.

Your brother,
Sonny

Then I kept in constant touch with him and I sent him whatever I could and I went to meet him when he came back to New York. When I saw him many things I thought I had forgotten came flooding back to me. This was because I had begun, finally, to wonder about Sonny, about the life that Sonny lived inside. This life, whatever it was, had made him older and thinner and it had deepened the distant stillness in which he had always moved. He looked very unlike my baby brother. Yet, when he smiled, when we shook hands, the baby brother I'd never known looked out from the depths of his private life, like an animal waiting to be coaxed into the light.

"How you been keeping?" he asked me.

55 "All right. And you?"

"Just fine." He was smiling all over his face. "It's good to see you again."

"It's good to see you."

The seven years' difference in our ages lay between us like a chasm: I wondered if these years would ever operate between us as a bridge. I was remembering, and it made it hard to catch my breath, that I had been there when he was born; and I had heard the first words he had ever spoken. When he started to walk, he walked from our mother straight to me. I caught him just before he fell when he took the first steps he ever took in this world.

"How's Isabel?"

60 "Just fine. She's dying to see you."

"And the boys?"

"They're fine, too. They're anxious to see their uncle."

"Oh, come on. You know they don't remember me."

"Are you kidding? Of course they remember you."

He grinned again. We got into a taxi. We had a lot to say to each other, 65 far too much to know how to begin.

As the taxi began to move, I asked, "You still want to go to India?"

He laughed. "You still remember that. Hell, no. This place is Indian enough for me."

"It used to belong to them," I said.

And he laughed again. "They damn sure knew what they were doing when they got rid of it."

Years ago, when he was around fourteen, he'd been all hipped on the 70 idea of going to India. He read books about people sitting on rocks, naked, in all kinds of weather, but mostly bad, naturally, and walking barefoot through hot coals and arriving at wisdom. I used to say that it sounded to me as though they were getting away from wisdom as fast as they could. I think he sort of looked down on me for that.

"Do you mind," he asked, "if we have the driver drive alongside the park? On the west side—I haven't seen the city in so long."

"Of course not," I said. I was afraid that I might sound as though I were humoring him, but I hoped he wouldn't take it that way.

So we drove along, between the green of the park and the stony, lifeless elegance of hotels and apartment buildings, toward the vivid, killing streets of our childhood. These streets hadn't changed, though housing projects jutted up out of them now like rocks in the middle of a boiling sea. Most of the houses in which we had grown up had vanished, as had the stores from which we had stolen, the basements in which we had first tried sex, the rooftops from which we had hurled tin cans and bricks. But houses exactly like the houses of our past yet dominated the landscape, boys exactly like the boys we once had been found themselves smothering in these houses, came down into the streets for light and air and found themselves encircled by disaster. Some escaped the trap, most didn't. Those who got out always left something of themselves behind, as some animals amputate a leg and leave it in the trap. It might be said, perhaps, that I had escaped, after all, I was a school teacher; or that Sonny had, he hadn't lived in Harlem for years. Yet, as the cab moved uptown through streets which seemed, with a rush, to darken with dark people, and as I covertly studied Sonny's face, it came to me that what we both were seeking through our separate cab windows was that part of ourselves which had been left behind. It's always at the hour of trouble and confrontation that the missing member aches.

We hit 110th Street and started rolling up Lenox Avenue. And I'd known this avenue all my life, but it seemed to me again, as it had seemed on the day I'd first heard about Sonny's trouble, filled with a hidden menace which was its very breath of life.

"We almost there," said Sonny. 75

"Almost." We were both too nervous to say anything more.

We live in a housing project. It hasn't been up long. A few days after it was up it seemed uninhabitably new, now, of course, it's already rundown.

It looks like a parody of the good, clean, faceless life—God knows the people who live in it do their best to make it a parody. The beat-looking grass lying around isn't enough to make their lives green, the hedges will never hold out the streets, and they know it. The big windows fool no one, they aren't big enough to make space out of no space. They don't bother with the windows, they watch the TV screen instead. The playground is most popular with the children who don't play at jacks, or skip rope, or roller skate, or swing, and they can be found in it after dark. We moved in partly because it's not too far from where I teach, and partly for the kids; but it's really just like the houses in which Sonny and I grew up. The same things happen, they'll have the same things to remember. The moment Sonny and I started into the house I had the feeling that I was simply bringing him back into the danger he had almost died trying to escape.

Sonny has never been talkative. So I don't know why I was sure he'd be dying to talk to me when supper was over the first night. Everything went fine, the oldest boy remembered him, and the youngest boy liked him, and Sonny had remembered to bring something for each of them; and Isabel, who is really much nicer than I am, more open and giving, had gone to a lot of trouble about dinner and was genuinely glad to see him. And she's always been able to tease Sonny in a way that I haven't. It was nice to see her face so vivid again and to hear her laugh and watch her make Sonny laugh. She wasn't, or, anyway, she didn't seem to be, at all uneasy or embarrassed. She chatted as though there were no subject which had to be avoided and she got Sonny past his first, faint stiffness. And thank God she was there, for I was filled with that icy dread again. Everything I did seemed awkward to me, and everything I said sounded freighted with hidden meaning. I was trying to remember everything I'd heard about dope addiction and I couldn't help watching Sonny for signs. I wasn't doing it out of malice. I was trying to find out something about my brother. I was dying to hear him tell me he was safe.

"Safe!" my father grunted, whenever Mama suggested trying to move to a neighborhood which might be safer for children. "Safe, hell! Ain't no place safe for kids, nor nobody."

80   He always went on like this, but he wasn't, ever, really as bad as he sounded, not even on weekends, when he got drunk. As a matter of fact, he was always on the lookout for "something a little better," but he died before he found it. He died suddenly, during a drunken weekend in the middle of the war, when Sonny was fifteen. He and Sonny hadn't ever got on too well. And this was partly because Sonny was the apple of his father's eye. It was because he loved Sonny so much and was frightened for him, that he was always fighting with him. It doesn't do any good to fight with Sonny. Sonny just moves back, inside himself, where he can't be reached. But the principal reason that they never hit it off is that they were so much alike. Daddy was big and rough and loud-talking, just the opposite of Sonny, but they both had—that same privacy.

Mama tried to tell me something about this, just after Daddy died. I was home on leave from the army.

This was the last time I ever saw my mother alive. Just the same, this picture gets all mixed up in my mind with pictures I had of her when she was younger. The way I always see her is the way she used to be on a Sunday afternoon, say, when the old folks were talking after the big Sunday dinner. I always see her wearing pale blue. She'd be sitting on the sofa. And my father would be sitting in the easy chair, not far from her. And the living room would be full of church folks and relatives. There they sit, in chairs all around the living room, and the night is creeping up outside, but nobody knows it yet. You can see the darkness growing against the windowpanes and you hear the street noises every now and again, or maybe the jangling beat of a tambourine from one of the churches close by, but it's real quiet in the room. For a moment nobody's talking, but every face looks darkening, like the sky outside. And my mother rocks a little from the waist, and my father's eyes are closed. Everyone is looking at something a child can't see. For a minute they've forgotten the children. Maybe a kid is lying on the rug, half asleep. Maybe somebody's got a kid in his lap and is absent-mindedly stroking the kid's head. Maybe there's a kid, quiet and big-eyed, curled up in a big chair in the corner. The silence, the darkness coming, and the darkness in the faces frighten the child obscurely. He hopes that the hand which strokes his forehead will never stop—will never die. He hopes that there will never come a time when the old folks won't be sitting around the living room, talking about where they've come from, and what they've seen, and what's happened to them and their kinfolk.

But something deep and watchful in the child knows that this is bound to end, is already ending. In a moment someone will get up and turn on the light. Then the old folks will remember the children and they won't talk any more that day. And when light fills the room, the child is filled with darkness. He knows that every time this happens he's moved just a little closer to that darkness outside. The darkness outside is what the old folks have been talking about. It's what they've come from. It's what they endure. The child knows that they won't talk any more because if he knows too much about what's happened to *them,* he'll know too much too soon, about what's going to happen to *him.*

The last time I talked to my mother, I remember I was restless. I wanted to get out and see Isabel. We weren't married then and we had a lot to straighten out between us.

There Mama sat, in black, by the window. She was humming an old church song, *Lord, you brought me from a long ways off.* Sonny was out somewhere. Mama kept watching the streets. 85

"I don't know," she said, "if I'll ever see you again, after you go off from here. But I hope you'll remember the things I tried to teach you."

"Don't talk like that," I said, and smiled. "You'll be here a long time yet."

She smiled, too, but she said nothing. She was quiet for a long time. And I said, "Mama, don't you worry about nothing. I'll be writing all the time, and you be getting the checks. . . ."

"I want to talk to you about your brother," she said, suddenly. "If anything happens to me he ain't going to have nobody to look out for him."

90   "Mama," I said, "ain't nothing going to happen to you *or* Sonny. Sonny's all right. He's a good boy and he's got good sense."

"It ain't a question of his being a good boy," Mama said, "nor of his having good sense. It ain't only the bad ones, nor yet the dumb ones that gets sucked under." She stopped, looking at me. "Your Daddy once had a brother," she said, and she smiled in a way that made me feel she was in pain. "You didn't never know that, did you?"

"No," I said, "I never knew that," and I watched her face.

"Oh, yes," she said, "your Daddy had a brother." She looked out of the window again. "I know you never saw your Daddy cry. But *I* did—many a time, through all these years."

I asked her, "What happened to his brother? How come nobody's ever talked about him?"

95   This was the first time I ever saw my mother look old.

"His brother got killed," she said, "when he was just a little younger than you are now. I knew him. He was a fine boy. He was maybe a little full of the devil, but he didn't mean nobody no harm."

Then she stopped and the room was silent, exactly as it had sometimes been on those Sunday afternoons. Mama kept looking out into the streets.

"He used to have a job in the mill," she said, "and, like all young folks, he just liked to perform on Saturday nights. Saturday nights, him and your father would drift around to different places, go to dances and things like that, or just sit around with people they knew, and your father's brother would sing, he had a fine voice, and play along with himself on his guitar. Well, this particular Saturday night, him and your father was coming home from some place, and they were both a little drunk and there was a moon that night, it was bright like day. Your father's brother was feeling kind of good, and he was whistling to himself, and he had his guitar slung over his shoulder. They was coming down a hill and beneath them was a road that turned off from the highway. Well, your father's brother, being always kind of frisky, decided to run down this hill, and he did, with that guitar banging and clanging behind him, and he ran across the road, and he was making water behind a tree. And your father was sort of amused at him and he was still coming down the hill, kind of slow. Then he heard a car motor and that same minute his brother stepped from behind the tree, into the road, in the moonlight. And he started to cross the road. And your father started to run down the hill, he says he don't know why. This car was full of white men. They was all drunk, and when they seen your father's brother they let out a great whoop and holler and they aimed the car straight at him. They was having fun, they just wanted to scare him, the way they do sometimes, you know. But they was drunk. And I guess the boy, being drunk, too, and scared, kind of lost his head. By the time he jumped it was too late. Your father says he heard his brother scream when the car rolled over him, and he heard the wood of that guitar when it give, and he heard them strings go flying, and he heard them white men shouting, and the car kept on a-going and it ain't stopped till this day. And, time your father got down the hill, his brother weren't nothing but blood and pulp."

Tears were gleaming on my mother's face. There wasn't anything I could say.

"He never mentioned it," she said, "because I never let him mention it 100 before you children. Your Daddy was like a crazy man that night and for many a night thereafter. He says he never in his life seen anything as dark as that road after the lights of that car had gone away. Weren't nothing, weren't nobody on that road, just your Daddy and his brother and that busted guitar. Oh, yes. Your Daddy never did really get right again. Till the day he died he weren't sure but that every white man he saw was the man that killed his brother."

She stopped and took out her handkerchief and dried her eyes and looked at me.

"I ain't telling you all this," she said, "to make you scared or bitter or to make you hate nobody. I'm telling you this because you got a brother. And the world ain't changed."

I guess I didn't want to believe this. I guess she saw this in my face. She turned away from me, toward the window again, searching those streets.

"But I praise my Redeemer," she said at last, "that He called your Daddy home before me. I ain't saying it to throw no flowers at myself, but, I declare, it keeps me from feeling too cast down to know I helped your father get safely through this world. Your father always acted like he was the roughest, strongest man on earth. And everybody took him to be like that. But if he hadn't had me there—to see his tears!"

She was crying again. Still, I couldn't move. I said, "Lord, Lord, Mama, 105 I didn't know it was like that."

"Oh, honey," she said, "there's a lot that you don't know. But you are going to find out." She stood up from the window and came over to me. "You got to hold on to your brother," she said, "and don't let him fall, no matter what it looks like is happening to him and no matter how evil you gets with him. You going to be evil with him many a time. But don't you forget what I told you, you hear?"

"I won't forget," I said. "Don't you worry, I won't forget. I won't let nothing happen to Sonny."

My mother smiled as though she was amused at something she saw in my face. Then, "You may not be able to stop nothing from happening. But you got to let him know you's *there*."

Two days later I was married, and then I was gone. And I had a lot of things on my mind and I pretty well forgot my promise to Mama until I got shipped home on a special furlough for her funeral.

And, after the funeral, with just Sonny and me alone in the empty 110 kitchen, I tried to find out something about him.

"What do you want to do?" I asked him.

"I'm going to be a musician," he said.

For he had graduated, in the time I had been away, from dancing to the juke box to finding out who was playing what, and what they were doing with it, and he had bought himself a set of drums.

"You mean, you want to be a drummer?" I somehow had the feeling that being a drummer might be all right for other people but not for my brother Sonny.

115   "I don't think," he said, looking at me very gravely, "that I'll ever be a good drummer. But I think I can play a piano."

I frowned. I'd never played the role of the oldest brother quite so seriously before, had scarcely ever, in fact, *asked* Sonny a damn thing. I sensed myself in the presence of something I didn't really know how to handle, didn't understand. So I made my frown a little deeper as I asked: "What kind of musician do you want to be?"

He grinned. "How many kinds do you think there are?"

"Be *serious*," I said.

He laughed, throwing his head back, and then looked at me. "I *am* serious."

120   "Well, then, for Christ's sake, stop kidding around and answer a serious question. I mean, do you want to be a concert pianist, you want to play classical music and all that, or—or what?" Long before I finished he was laughing again. "For Christ's *sake*, Sonny!"

He sobered, but with difficulty. "I'm sorry. But you sound so—*scared!*" and he was off again.

"Well, you may think it's funny now, baby, but it's not going to be so funny when you have to make your living at it, let me tell you *that*." I was furious because I knew he was laughing at me and I didn't know why.

"No," he said, very sober now, and afraid, perhaps, that he'd hurt me, "I don't want to be a classical pianist. That isn't what interests me. I mean"—he paused, looking hard at me, as though his eyes would help me to understand, and then gestured helplessly, as though perhaps his hand would help—"I mean, I'll have a lot of studying to do, and I'll have to study *everything*, but, I mean, I want to play *with*—jazz musicians." He stopped. "I want to play jazz," he said.

Well, the word had never before sounded as heavy, as real, as it sounded that afternoon in Sonny's mouth. I just looked at him and I was probably frowning a real frown by this time. I simply couldn't see why on earth he'd want to spend his time hanging around nightclubs, clowning around on bandstands, while people pushed each other around a dance floor. It seemed—beneath him, somehow. I had never thought about it before, had never been forced to, but I suppose I had always put jazz musicians in a class with what Daddy called "good-time people."

125   "Are you *serious*?"

"Hell, *yes*, I'm serious."

He looked more helpless than ever, and annoyed, and deeply hurt.

I suggested, helpfully: "You mean—like Louis Armstrong?"

His face closed as though I'd struck him. "No. I'm not talking about none of that old-time, down home crap."

130   "Well, look, Sonny, I'm sorry, don't get mad. I just don't altogether get it, that's all. Name somebody—you know, a jazz musician you admire."

"Bird."

"Who?"

"Bird! Charlie Parker![3] Don't they teach you nothing in the goddamn army?"

I lit a cigarette. I was surprised and then a little amused to discover that I was trembling. "I've been out of touch," I said. "You'll have to be patient with me. Now. Who's this Parker character?"

"He's just one of the greatest jazz musicians alive," said Sonny, sullenly, 135 his hands in his pockets, his back to me. "Maybe *the* greatest," he added, bitterly, "that's probably why *you* never heard of him."

"All right," I said, "I'm ignorant. I'm sorry. I'll go out and buy all the cat's records right away, all right?"

"It don't," said Sonny, with dignity, "make any difference to me. I don't care what you listen to. Don't do me no favors."

I was beginning to realize that I'd never seen him so upset before. With another part of my mind I was thinking that this would probably turn out to be one of those things kids go through and that I shouldn't make it seem important by pushing it too hard. Still, I didn't think it would do any harm to ask: "Doesn't all this take a lot of time? Can you make a living at it?"

He turned back to me and half leaned, half sat, on the kitchen table. "Everything takes time," he said, "and—well, yes, sure, I can make a living at it. But what I don't seem to be able to make you understand is that it's the only thing I want to do."

"Well, Sonny," I said gently, "you know people can't always do exactly 140 what they *want* to do—"

"*No,* I don't know that," said Sonny, surprising me. "I think people *ought* to do what they want to do, what else are they alive for?"

"You getting to be a big boy," I said desperately, "it's time you started thinking about your future."

"I'm thinking about my future," said Sonny, grimly. "I think about it all the time."

I gave up. I decided, if he didn't change his mind, that we could always talk about it later. "In the meantime," I said, "you got to finish school." We had already decided that he'd have to move in with Isabel and her folks. I knew this wasn't the ideal arrangement because Isabel's folks are inclined to be dicty[4] and they hadn't especially wanted Isabel to marry me. But I didn't know what else to do. "And we have to get you fixed up at Isabel's."

There was a long silence. He moved from the kitchen table to the win- 145 dow. "That's a terrible idea. You know it yourself."

"Do you have a *better* idea?"

He just walked up and down the kitchen for a minute. He was as tall as I was. He had started to shave. I suddenly had the feeling that I didn't know him at all.

3. Charlie ("Bird") Parker (1920-1955), brilliant saxophonist and jazz innovator; working in New York in the mid-1940s, he developed, with Dizzy Gillespie and others, the style of jazz called "bebop." He was a narcotics addict.   4. Snobbish, bossy.

He stopped at the kitchen table and picked up my cigarettes. Looking at me with a kind of mocking, amused defiance, he put one between his lips. "You mind?"

"You smoking already?"

150   He lit the cigarette and nodded, watching me through the smoke. "I just wanted to see if I'd have the courage to smoke in front of you." He grinned and blew a great cloud of smoke to the ceiling. "It was easy." He looked at my face. "Come on, now. I bet you was smoking at my age, tell the truth."

I didn't say anything but the truth was on my face, and he laughed. But now there was something very strained in his laugh. "Sure. And I bet that ain't all you was doing."

He was frightening me a little. "Cut the crap," I said. "We already decided that you was going to go and live at Isabel's. Now what's got into you all of a sudden?"

"*You* decided it," he pointed out. "*I* didn't decide nothing." He stopped in front of me, leaning against the stove, arms loosely folded. "Look, brother. I don't want to stay in Harlem no more, I really don't." He was very earnest. He looked at me, then over toward the kitchen window. There was something in his eyes I'd never seen before, some thoughtfulness, some worry all his own. He rubbed the muscle of one arm. "It's time I was getting out of here."

"Where do you want to *go*, Sonny?"

155   "I want to join the army. Or the navy, I don't care. If I say I'm old enough, they'll believe me."

Then I got mad. It was because I was so scared. "You must be crazy. You goddamn fool, what the hell do you want to go and join the *army* for?"

"I just told you. To get out of Harlem."

"Sonny, you haven't even finished *school*. And if you really want to be a musician, how do you expect to study if you're in the *army*?"

He looked at me, trapped, and in anguish. "There's ways. I might be able to work out some kind of deal. Anyway, I'll have the G.I. Bill when I come out."

160   "*If* you come out." We stared at each other. "Sonny, please. Be reasonable. I know the setup is far from perfect. But we got to do the best we can."

"I ain't learning nothing in school," he said. "Even when I go." He turned away from me and opened the window and threw his cigarette out into the narrow alley. I watched his back. "At least, I ain't learning nothing you'd want me to learn." He slammed the window so hard I thought the glass would fly out, and turned back to me. "And I'm sick of the stink of these garbage cans!"

"Sonny," I said, "I know how you feel. But if you don't finish school now, you're going to be sorry later that you didn't." I grabbed him by the shoulders. "And you only got another year. It ain't so bad. And I'll come back and I swear I'll help you do *whatever* you want to do. Just try to put up with it till I come back. Will you please do that? For me?"

He didn't answer and he wouldn't look at me.

"Sonny. You hear me?"

He pulled away. "I hear you. But you never hear anything *I* say."   165
I didn't know what to say to that. He looked out of the window and
then back at me. "OK," he said, and sighed. "I'll try."

Then I said, trying to cheer him up a little, "They got a piano at Isabel's.
You can practice on it."

And as a matter of fact, it did cheer him up for a minute. "That's right,"
he said to himself. "I forgot that." His face relaxed a little. But the worry,
the thoughtfulness, played on it still, the way shadows play on a face which
is staring into the fire.

But I thought I'd never hear the end of that piano. At first, Isabel would
write me, saying how nice it was that Sonny was so serious about his music
and how, as soon as he came in from school, or wherever he had been when
he was supposed to be at school, he went straight to that piano and stayed
there until suppertime. And, after supper, he went back to that piano and
stayed there until everybody went to bed. He was at the piano all day
Saturday and all day Sunday. Then he bought a record player and started
playing records. He'd play one record over and over again, all day long
sometimes, and he'd improvise along with it on the piano. Or he'd play
one section of the record, one chord, one change, one progression, then
he'd do it on the piano. Then back to the record. Then back to the piano.

Well, I really don't know how they stood it. Isabel finally confessed that   170
it wasn't like living with a person at all, it was like living with sound. And
the sound didn't make any sense to her, didn't make any sense to any of
them—naturally. They began, in a way, to be afflicted by this presence that
was living in their home. It was as though Sonny were some sort of god,
or monster. He moved in an atmosphere which wasn't like theirs at all.
They fed him and he ate, he washed himself, he walked in and out of their
door; he certainly wasn't nasty or unpleasant or rude, Sonny isn't any of
those things; but it was as though he were all wrapped up in some cloud,
some fire, some vision all his own; and there wasn't any way to reach him.

At the same time, he wasn't really a man yet, he was still a child, and
they had to watch out for him in all kinds of ways. They certainly couldn't
throw him out. Neither did they dare to make a great scene about that
piano because even they dimly sensed, as I sensed, from so many thousands
of miles away, that Sonny was at that piano playing for his life.

But he hadn't been going to school. One day a letter came from the
school board and Isabel's mother got it—there had, apparently, been other
letters but Sonny had torn them up. This day, when Sonny came in, Isabel's
mother showed him the letter and asked where he'd been spending his
time. And she finally got it out of him that he'd been down in Greenwich
Village, with musicians and other characters, in a white girl's apartment.
And this scared her and she started to scream at him and what came up,
once she began—though she denies it to this day—was what sacrifices they
were making to give Sonny a decent home and how little he appreciated
it.

Sonny didn't play the piano that day. By evening, Isabel's mother had calmed down but then there was the old man to deal with, and Isabel herself. Isabel says she did her best to be calm but she broke down and started crying. She says she just watched Sonny's face. She could tell, by watching him, what was happening with him. And what was happening was that they penetrated his cloud, they had reached him. Even if their fingers had been a thousand times more gentle than human fingers ever are, he could hardly help feeling that they had stripped him naked and were spitting on that nakedness. For he also had to see that his presence, that music, which was life or death to him, had been torture for them and that they had endured it, not at all for his sake, but only for mine. And Sonny couldn't take that. He can take it a little better today than he could then but he's still not very good at it and, frankly, I don't know anybody who is.

The silence of the next few days must have been louder than the sound of all the music ever played since time began. One morning, before she went to work, Isabel was in his room for something and she suddenly realized that all of his records were gone. And she knew for certain that he was gone. And he was. He went as far as the navy would carry him. He finally sent me a postcard from some place in Greece and that was the first I knew that Sonny was still alive. I didn't see him any more until we were both back in New York and the war had long been over.

175   He was a man by then, of course, but I wasn't willing to see it. He came by the house from time to time, but we fought almost every time we met. I didn't like the way he carried himself, loose and dreamlike all the time, and I didn't like his friends, and his music seemed to be merely an excuse for the life he led. It sounded just that weird and disordered.

Then we had a fight, a pretty awful fight, and I didn't see him for months. By and by I looked him up, where he was living, in a furnished room in the Village, and I tried to make it up. But there were lots of other people in the room and Sonny just lay on his bed, and he wouldn't come downstairs with me, and he treated these other people as though they were his family and I weren't. So I got mad and then he got mad, and then I told him that he might just as well be dead as live the way he was living. Then he stood up and he told me not to worry about him any more in life, that he *was* dead as far as I was concerned. Then he pushed me to the door and the other people looked on as though nothing were happening, and he slammed the door behind me. I stood in the hallway, staring at the door. I heard somebody laugh in the room and then the tears came to my eyes. I started down the steps, whistling to keep from crying, I kept whistling to myself, *You going to need me, baby, one of these cold, rainy days.*

I read about Sonny's trouble in the spring. Little Grace died in the fall. She was a beautiful little girl. But she only lived a little over two years. She died of polio and she suffered. She had a slight fever for a couple of days, but it didn't seem like anything and we just kept her in bed. And we would certainly have called the doctor, but the fever dropped, she seemed to be all right. So we thought it had just been a cold. Then, one day, she was up, playing, Isabel was in the kitchen fixing lunch for the two boys when they'd come in from school, and she heard Grace fall down in the living room. When you have a lot of children you don't always start running when one of them falls, unless they start screaming or something. And, this time, Gracie was quiet. Yet, Isabel says that when she heard that *thump* and then that silence, something happened to her to make her afraid. And she ran to the living room and there was little Grace on the floor, all twisted up, and the reason she hadn't screamed was that she couldn't get her breath. And when she did scream, it was the worst sound, Isabel says, that she'd ever heard in all her life, and she still hears it sometimes in her dreams. Isabel will sometimes wake me up with a low, moaning, strangling sound and I have to be quick to awaken her and hold her to me and where Isabel is weeping against me seems a mortal wound.

I think I may have written Sonny the very day that little Grace was buried. I was sitting in the living room in the dark, by myself, and I suddenly thought of Sonny. My trouble made his real.

One Saturday afternoon, when Sonny had been living with us, or anyway, been in our house, for nearly two weeks, I found myself wandering aimlessly about the living room, drinking from a can of beer, and trying to work up courage to search Sonny's room. He was out, he was usually out whenever I was home, and Isabel had taken the children to see their grandparents. Suddenly I was standing still in front of the living room window, watching Seventh Avenue. The idea of searching Sonny's room made me still. I scarcely dared to admit to myself what I'd be searching for. I didn't know what I'd do if I found it. Or if I didn't.

On the sidewalk across from me, near the entrance to a barbecue joint, 180 some people were holding an old-fashioned revival meeting. The barbecue cook, wearing a dirty white apron, his conked[5] hair reddish and metallic in the pale sun, and a cigarette between his lips, stood in the doorway, watching them. Kids and older people paused in their errands and stood there, along with some older men and a couple of very tough-looking women who watched everything that happened on the avenue, as though they owned it, or were maybe owned by it. Well, they were watching this, too. The revival was being carried on by three sisters in black, and a brother. All they had were their voices and their Bibles and a tambourine. The brother was testifying[6] and while he testified two of the sisters stood together, seeming to say, amen, and the third sister walked around with the tambourine outstretched and a couple of people dropped coins into it. Then the brother's testimony ended and the sister who had been taking up the collection dumped the coins into her palm and transferred them to the pocket of her long black robe. Then she raised both hands, striking the tambourine against the air, and then against one hand, and she started to sing. And the two other sisters and the brother joined in.

It was strange, suddenly, to watch, though I had been seeing these meetings all my life. So, of course, had everybody else down there. Yet, they paused and watched and listened and I stood still at the window. " 'Tis the

---

5. Processed: straightened and greased.   6. Publicly professing belief.

old ship of Zion," they sang, and the sister with the tambourine kept a steady, jangling beat, *"it has rescued many a thousand!"* Not a soul under the sound of their voices was hearing this song for the first time, not one of them had been rescued. Nor had they seen much in the way of rescue work being done around them. Neither did they especially believe in the holiness of the three sisters and the brother, they knew too much about them, knew where they lived, and how. The woman with the tambourine, whose voice dominated the air, whose face was bright with joy, was divided by very little from the woman who stood watching her, a cigarette between her heavy, chapped lips, her hair a cuckoo's nest, her face scarred and swollen from many beatings, and her black eyes glittering like coal. Perhaps they both knew this, which was why, when, as rarely, they addressed each other, they addressed each other as Sister. As the singing filled the air the watching, listening faces underwent a change, the eyes focusing on something within; the music seemed to soothe a poison out of them; and time seemed, nearly, to fall away from the sullen, belligerent, battered faces, as though they were fleeing back to their first condition, while dreaming of their last. The bar-becue cook half shook his head and smiled, and dropped his cigarette and disappeared into his joint. A man fumbled in his pockets for change and stood holding it in his hand impatiently, as though he had just remem-bered a pressing appointment further up the avenue. He looked furious. Then I saw Sonny, standing on the edge of the crowd. He was carrying a wide, flat notebook with a green cover, and it made him look, from where I was standing, almost like a schoolboy. The coppery sun brought out the copper in his skin, he was very faintly smiling, standing very still. Then the singing stopped, the tambourine turned into a collection plate again. The furious man dropped in his coins and vanished, so did a couple of the women, and Sonny dropped some change in the plate, looking directly at the woman with a little smile. He started across the avenue, toward the house. He has a slow, loping walk, something like the way Harlem hipsters walk, only he's imposed on this his own half-beat. I had never really noticed it before.

I stayed at the window, both relieved and apprehensive. As Sonny dis-appeared from my sight, they began singing again. And they were still singing when his key turned in the lock.

"Hey," he said.

"Hey, yourself. You want some beer?"

185 "No. Well, maybe." But he came up to the window and stood beside me, looking out. "What a warm voice," he said.

They were singing *If I could only hear my mother pray again!*

"Yes," I said, "and she can sure beat that tambourine."

"But what a terrible song," he said, and laughed. He dropped his note-book on the sofa and disappeared into the kitchen. "Where's Isabel and the kids?"

"I think they went to see their grandparents. You hungry?"

190 "No." He came back into the living room with his can of beer. "You want to come some place with me tonight?"

I sensed, I don't know how, that I couldn't possibly say no. "Sure. Where?"

He sat down on the sofa and picked up his notebook and started leafing through it. "I'm going to sit in with some fellows in a joint in the Village."

"You mean, you're going to play, tonight?"

"That's right." He took a swallow of his beer and moved back to the window. He gave me a sidelong look. "If you can stand it."

"I'll try," I said.   195

He smiled to himself and we both watched as the meeting across the way broke up. The three sisters and the brother, heads bowed, were singing *God be with you till we meet again*. The faces around them were very quiet. Then the song ended. The small crowd dispersed. We watched the three women and the lone man walk slowly up the avenue.

"When she was singing before," said Sonny, abruptly, "her voice reminded me for a minute of what heroin feels like sometimes—when it's in your veins. It makes you feel sort of warm and cool at the same time. And distant. And—and sure." He sipped his beer, very deliberately not looking at me. I watched his face. "It makes you feel—in control. Sometimes you've got to have that feeling."

"Do you?" I sat down slowly in the easy chair.

"Sometimes." He went to the sofa and picked up his notebook again. "Some people do."

"In order," I asked, "to play?" And my voice was very ugly, full of contempt and anger.   200

"Well"—he looked at me with great, troubled eyes, as though, in fact, he hoped his eyes would tell me things he could never otherwise say—"they *think* so. And *if* they think so—!"

"And what do *you* think?" I asked.

He sat on the sofa and put his can of beer on the floor. "I don't know," he said, and I couldn't be sure if he were answering my question or pursuing his thoughts. His face didn't tell me. "It's not so much to *play*. It's to *stand* it, to be able to make it at all. On any level." He frowned and smiled: "In order to keep from shaking to pieces."

"But these friends of yours," I said, "they seem to shake themselves to pieces pretty goddamn fast."

"Maybe." He played with the notebook. And something told me that I   205
should curb my tongue, that Sonny was doing his best to talk, that I should listen. "But of course you only know the ones that've gone to pieces. Some don't—or at least they haven't *yet* and that's just about all *any* of us can say." He paused. "And then there are some who just live, really, in hell, and they know it and they see what's happening and they go right on. I don't know." He sighed, dropped the notebook, folded his arms. "Some guys, you can tell from the way they play, they on something *all* the time. And you can see that, well, it makes something real for them. But of course," he picked up his beer from the floor and sipped it and put the can down again, "they *want* to, too, you've got to see that. Even some of them that say they don't—*some*, not all."

"And what about you?" I asked—I couldn't help it. "What about you? Do *you* want to?"

He stood up and walked to the window and I remained silent for a long time. Then he sighed. "Me," he said. Then: "While I was downstairs before, on my way here, listening to that woman sing, it struck me all of a sudden how much suffering she must have had to go through—to sing like that. It's *repulsive* to think you have to suffer that much."

I said: "But there's no way not to suffer—is there, Sonny?"

"I believe not," he said and smiled, "but that's never stopped anyone from trying." He looked at me. "Has it?" I realized, with this mocking look, that there stood between us, forever, beyond the power of time or forgiveness, the fact that I had held silence—so long!—when he had needed human speech to help him. He turned back to the window. "No, there's no way not to suffer. But you try all kinds of ways to keep from drowning in it, to keep on top of it, and to make it seem—well, like *you*. Like you did something, all right, and now you're suffering for it. You know?" I said nothing. "Well you know," he said, impatiently, "why *do* people suffer? Maybe it's better to do something to give it a reason, *any* reason."

210 "But we just agreed," I said, "that there's no way not to suffer. Isn't it better, then, just to—take it?"

"But nobody just takes it," Sonny cried, "that's what I'm telling you! *Everybody* tries not to. You're just hung up on the *way* some people try—it's not *your* way!"

The hair on my face began to itch, my face felt wet. "That's not true," I said, "that's not true. I don't give a damn what other people do, I don't even care how they suffer. I just care how *you* suffer." And he looked at me. "Please believe me," I said, "I don't want to see you—die—trying not to suffer."

"I won't," he said flatly, "die trying not to suffer. At least, not any faster than anybody else."

"But there's no need," I said, trying to laugh, "is there? in killing yourself."

215 I wanted to say more, but I couldn't. I wanted to talk about will power and how life could be—well, beautiful. I wanted to say that it was all within; but was it? or, rather, wasn't that exactly the trouble? And I wanted to promise that I would never fail him again. But it would all have sounded—empty words and lies.

So I made the promise to myself and prayed that I would keep it.

"It's terrible sometimes, inside," he said, "that's what's the trouble. You walk these streets, black and funky and cold, and there's not really a living ass to talk to, and there's nothing shaking, and there's no way of getting it out—that storm inside. You can't talk it and you can't make love with it, and when you finally try to get with it and play it, you realize *nobody's* listening. So *you've* got to listen. You got to find a way to listen."

And then he walked away from the window and sat on the sofa again, as though all the wind had suddenly been knocked out of him. "Sometimes you'll do *anything* to play, even cut your mother's throat." He laughed and looked at me. "Or your brother's." Then he sobered. "Or your own." Then:

"Don't worry. I'm all right now and I think I'll *be* all right. But I can't forget—where I've been. I don't mean just the physical place I've been, I mean where I've *been*. And *what* I've been."

"What have you been, Sonny?" I asked.

He smiled—but sat sideways on the sofa, his elbow resting on the back, 220 his fingers playing with his mouth and chin, not looking at me. "I've been something I didn't recognize, didn't know I could be. Didn't know anybody could be." He stopped, looking inward, looking helplessly young, looking old. "I'm not talking about it now because I feel *guilty* or anything like that—maybe it would be better if I did, I don't know. Anyway, I can't really talk about it. Not to you, not to anybody," and now he turned and faced me. "Sometimes, you know, and it was actually when I was most *out* of the world, I felt that I was in it, that I was *with* it, really, and I could play or I didn't really have to *play*, it just came out of me, it was there. And I don't know how I played, thinking about it now, but I know I did awful things, those times, sometimes, to people. Or it wasn't that I *did* anything to them— it was that they weren't real." He picked up the beer can; it was empty; he rolled it between his palms: "And other times—well, I needed a fix, I needed to find a place to lean, I needed to clear a space to *listen*—and I couldn't find it, and I—went crazy, I did terrible things to *me*, I was terrible *for* me." He began pressing the beer can between his hands, I watched the metal begin to give. It glittered, as he played with it like a knife, and I was afraid he would cut himself, but I said nothing. "Oh well. I can never tell you. I was all by myself at the bottom of something, stinking and sweating and crying and shaking, and I smelled it, you know? *my* stink, and I thought I'd die if I couldn't get away from it and yet, all the same, I knew that everything I was doing was just locking me in with it. And I didn't know," he paused, still flattening the beer can, "I didn't know, I still *don't* know, something kept telling me that maybe it was good to smell your own stink, but I didn't think that *that* was what I'd been trying to do—and—who can stand it?" and he abruptly dropped the ruined beer can, looking at me with a small, still smile, and then rose, walking to the window as though it were the lodestone rock. I watched his face, he watched the avenue. "I couldn't tell you when Mama died—but the reason I wanted to leave Harlem so bad was to get away from drugs. And then, when I ran away, that's what I was running from—really. When I came back, nothing had changed, *I* hadn't changed, I was just—older." And he stopped, drumming with his fingers on the windowpane. The sun had vanished, soon darkness would fall. I watched his face. "It can come again," he said, almost as though speaking to himself. Then he turned to me. "It can come again," he repeated. "I just want you to know that."

"All right," I said, at last. "So it can come again. All right."

He smiled, but the smile was sorrowful. "I had to try to tell you," he said.

"Yes," I said. "I understand that."

"You're my brother," he said, looking straight at me, and not smiling at all.

"Yes," I repeated, "yes. I understand that." 225

He turned back to the window, looking out. "All that hatred down there," he said, "all that hatred and misery and love. It's a wonder it doesn't blow the avenue apart."

We went to the only nightclub on a short, dark street, downtown. We squeezed through the narrow, chattering, jampacked bar to the entrance of the big room, where the bandstand was. And we stood there for a moment, for the lights were very dim in this room and we couldn't see. Then, "Hello, boy," said the voice and an enormous black man, much older than Sonny or myself, erupted out of all that atmospheric lighting and put an arm around Sonny's shoulder. "I been sitting right here," he said, "waiting for you."

He had a big voice, too, and heads in the darkness turned toward us.

Sonny grinned and pulled a little away, and said, "Creole, this is my brother. I told you about him."

230   Creole shook my hand. "I'm glad to meet you, son," he said, and it was clear that he was glad to meet me *there,* for Sonny's sake. And he smiled, "You got a real musician in *your* family," and he took his arm from Sonny's shoulder and slapped him, lightly, affectionately, with the back of his hand.

. "Well. Now I've heard it all," said a voice behind us. This was another musician, and a friend of Sonny's, a coal-black, cheerful-looking man, built close to the ground. He immediately began confiding to me, at the top of his lungs, the most terrible things about Sonny, his teeth gleaming like a lighthouse and his laugh coming up out of him like the beginning of an earthquake. And it turned out that everyone at the bar knew Sonny, or almost everyone; some were musicians, working there, or nearby, or not working, some were simply hangers-on, and some were there to hear Sonny play. I was introduced to all of them and they were all very polite to me. Yet, it was clear that, for them, I was only Sonny's brother. Here, I was in Sonny's world. Or, rather: his kingdom. Here, it was not even a question that his veins bore royal blood.

They were going to play soon and Creole installed me, by myself, at a table in a dark corner. Then I watched them, Creole, and the little black man, and Sonny, and the others, while they horsed around, standing just below the bandstand. The light from the bandstand spilled just a little short of them and, watching them laughing and gesturing and moving about, I had the feeling that they, nevertheless, were being most careful not to step into that circle of light too suddenly; that if they moved into the light too suddenly, without thinking, they would perish in flame. Then, while I watched, one of them, the small black man, moved into the light and crossed the bandstand and started fooling around with his drums. Then—being funny and being, also, extremely ceremonious—Creole took Sonny by the arm and led him to the piano. A woman's voice called Sonny's name and a few hands started clapping. And Sonny, also being funny and being ceremonious, and so touched, I think, that he could have cried, but neither hiding it nor showing it, riding it like a man, grinned, and put both hands to his heart and bowed from the waist.

Creole then went to the bass fiddle and a lean, very bright-skinned brown man jumped up on the bandstand and picked up his horn. So there they were, and the atmosphere on the bandstand and in the room began to change and tighten. Someone stepped up to the microphone and announced them. Then there were all kinds of murmurs. Some people at the bar shushed others. The waitress ran around, frantically getting in the last orders, guys and chicks got closer to each other, and the lights on the bandstand, on the quartet, turned to a kind of indigo. Then they all looked different there. Creole looked about him for the last time, as though he were making certain that all his chickens were in the coop, and then he— jumped and struck the fiddle. And there they were.

All I know about music is that not many people ever really hear it. And even then, on the rare occasions when something opens within, and the music enters, what we mainly hear, or hear corroborated, are personal, private, vanishing evocations. But the man who creates the music is hearing something else, is dealing with the roar rising from the void and imposing order on it as it hits the air. What is evoked in him, then, is of another order, more terrible because it has no words, and triumphant, too, for that same reason. And his triumph, when he triumphs, is ours. I just watched Sonny's face. His face was troubled, he was working hard, but he wasn't with it. And I had the feeling that, in a way, everyone on the bandstand was waiting for him, both waiting for him and pushing him along. But as I began to watch Creole, I realized that it was Creole who held them all back. He had them on a short rein. Up there, keeping the beat with his whole body, wailing on the fiddle, with his eyes half closed, he was listening to everything, but he was listening to Sonny. He was having a dialogue with Sonny. He wanted Sonny to leave the shoreline and strike out for the deep water. He was Sonny's witness that deep water and drowning were not the same thing—he had been there, and he knew. And he wanted Sonny to know. He was waiting for Sonny to do the things on the keys which would let Creole know that Sonny was in the water.

And, while Creole listened, Sonny moved, deep within, exactly like some- one in torment. I had never before thought of how awful the relationship must be between the musician and his instrument. He has to fill it, this instrument, with the breath of life, his own. He has to make it do what he wants it to do. And a piano is just a piano. It's made out of so much wood and wires and little hammers and big ones, and ivory. While there's only so much you can do with it, the only way to find this out is to try; to try and make it do everything.

And Sonny hadn't been near a piano for over a year. And he wasn't on much better terms with his life, not the life that stretched before him now. He and the piano stammered, started one way, got scared, stopped; started another way, panicked, marked time, started again; then seemed to have found a direction, panicked again, got stuck. And the face I saw on Sonny I'd never seen before. Everything had been burned out of it, and, at the same time, things usually hidden were being burned in, by the fire and fury of the battle which was occurring in him up there.

Yet, watching Creole's face as they neared the end of the first set, I had the feeling that something had happened, something I hadn't heard. Then

235

they finished, there was scattered applause, and then, without an instant's warning, Creole started into something else, it was almost sardonic, it was *Am I Blue*.[7] And, as though he commanded, Sonny began to play. Something began to happen. And Creole let out the reins. The dry, low, black man said something awful on the drums, Creole answered, and the drums talked back. Then the horn insisted, sweet and high, slightly detached perhaps, and Creole listened, commenting now and then, dry, and driving, beautiful and calm and old. Then they all came together again, and Sonny was part of the family again. I could tell this from his face. He seemed to have found, right there beneath his fingers, a damn brand-new piano. It seemed that he couldn't get over it. Then, for a while, just being happy with Sonny, they seemed to be agreeing with him that brand-new pianos certainly were a gas.

Then Creole stepped forward to remind them that what they were playing was the blues. He hit something in all of them, he hit something in me, myself, and the music tightened and deepened, apprehension began to beat the air. Creole began to tell us what the blues were all about. They were not about anything very new. He and his boys up there were keeping it new, at the risk of ruin, destruction, madness, and death, in order to find new ways to make us listen. For, while the tale of how we suffer, and how we are delighted, and how we may triumph is never new, it always must be heard. There isn't any other tale to tell, it's the only light we've got in all this darkness.

And this tale, according to that face, that body, those strong hands on those strings, has another aspect in every country, and a new depth in every generation. Listen, Creole seemed to be saying, listen. Now these are Sonny's blues. He made the little black man on the drums know it, and the bright, brown man on the horn. Creole wasn't trying any longer to get Sonny in the water. He was wishing him Godspeed. Then he stepped back, very slowly, filling the air with the immense suggestion that Sonny speak for himself.

240   Then they all gathered around Sonny and Sonny played. Every now and again one of them seemed to say, amen. Sonny's fingers filled the air with life, his life. But that life contained so many others. And Sonny went all the way back, he really began with the spare, flat statement of the opening phrase of the song. Then he began to make it his. It was very beautiful because it wasn't hurried and it was no longer a lament. I seemed to hear with what burning he had made it his, and what burning we had yet to make it ours, how we could cease lamenting. Freedom lurked around us and I understood, at last, that he could help us to be free if we would listen, that he would never be free until we did. Yet, there was no battle in his face now, I heard what he had gone through, and would continue to go through until he came to rest in earth. He had made it his: that long line, of which we knew only Mama and Daddy. And he was giving it back, as everything must be given back, so that, passing through death, it can live forever. I saw my mother's face again, and felt, for the first time, how the

---

7. A favorite jazz standard, brilliantly recorded by Billie Holiday.

stones of the road she had walked on must have bruised her feet. I saw the moonlit road where my father's brother died. And it brought something else back to me, and carried me past it, I saw my little girl again and felt Isabel's tears again, and I felt my own tears begin to rise. And I was yet aware that this was only a moment, that the world waited outside, as hungry as a tiger, and that trouble stretched above us, longer than the sky.

Then it was over. Creole and Sonny let out their breath, both soaking wet, and grinning. There was a lot of applause and some of it was real. In the dark, the girl came by and I asked her to take drinks to the bandstand. There was a long pause, while they talked up there in the indigo light and after awhile I saw the girl put a Scotch and milk on top of the piano for Sonny. He didn't seem to notice it, but just before they started playing again, he sipped from it and looked toward me, and nodded. Then he put it back on top of the piano. For me, then, as they began to play again, it glowed and shook above my brother's head like the very cup of trembling.[8]

1957

QUESTIONS

1. What parts of "Sonny's Blues" correspond to the plot stages of a traditionally told story: exposition, discriminated occasion, rising action, turning point, climax, falling action, conclusion?
2. What is the relationship between the chronology and the plot of "Sonny's Blues"? What does Baldwin gain, or lose, by reordering the events of the story as he does?
3. What is different about the narrative style used to describe the nightclub scene at the story's conclusion? Does this change of style make you reconsider what the story's message might be?

SUGGESTIONS FOR WRITING

1. Write an essay comparing and contrasting the way any two stories in this anthology handle the traditional elements of plot: exposition, rising action, discriminated occasion, climax, falling action, conclusion. Consider especially how plot elements contribute to the overall artistic effect.
2. Many stories depict events that do not occur in a simple chronology. For example, "Sonny's Blues" makes liberal use of flashbacks that rearrange the order of events. Using any story from this anthology, write an essay discussing the way the author has created a plot from a series of discontinuous events.
3. Using the characters, settings, and events of "Sonny's Blues," write a narrative that tells the same story from Sonny's point of view.

---

8. See Isaiah 51.17, 22–23: "Awake, awake, stand up, O Jerusalem, which hast drunk at the hand of the Lord the cup of his fury; thou hast drunken the dregs of the cup of trembling, and wrung them out. . . .Behold, I have taken out of thine hand the cup of trembling, even the dregs of the cup of my fury; thou shalt no more drink it again: But I will put it into the hand of them that afflict thee. . . ."

2 NARRATION AND POINT OF VIEW

When we read fiction, our sense of who is telling us the story is as important as our sense of what happens. Unlike drama, in which events occur before us directly, narrative fiction is always mediated; someone is always *between* us and the events—a viewer, a speaker, or both. The way a story is mediated is a key element of fictional structure. This mediation involves both the angle of vision—the point from which the people, events, and other details are viewed—and the words in which the story is embodied. The viewing aspect is called the **focus**, and the verbal aspect the **voice.** Both are generally considered together in the term **point of view.** The teller of a story or novel—the voice that speaks *all* the words we read in it—is called the **narrator.**

Focus acts much as a camera does, choosing what we can look at and the angle at which we can view it, framing, proportioning, emphasizing—even distorting. Whereas plot is a structure that arranges cause and effect as well as time, focus arranges space and measures the distance or closeness of narrator, characters, and readers.

The choice of a point of view is the initial act of a culture.

—JOSÉ ORTEGA Y GASSET

We must pay careful attention to the focus at any given point in a story. Is it fixed or mobile? Does it stay at more or less the same angle to, and at the same distance from, the characters and action, or does it move around or in and out? When the focus centers on a single individual in the story, or relies on that character's voice or thoughts, we say that the point of view is **limited.** When that person leaves the room, the camera must go too, and if we are to know what happens in the room when the focal character is gone, some means of bringing that information must be devised, such as a letter or a report by another character. When stories or novels have several focal characters, the point of view is said to be **unlimited.** The camera is free not only to pull back from a character but may also follow scenes when that character is absent and record the perceptions and internal voices of new characters. **Third-person narrators** ("he" or "she") with unlimited access to the thoughts of more than one character are often called **omniscient** (meaning "all-knowing").

Identifying the particular kind of narration and point of view an author has chosen for a story is much more than a technical exercise. When you pick up a story or novel, among the first questions you should ask are "Who is telling this?" and "Who sees or knows what?" As you find answers, you begin to locate what makes this story unique. The events in the characters' lives could be presented in a variety of ways, but a different kind of narrator or point of view would change the story utterly.

Point of view may be limited to a **first-person narrator** ("I"), such as

Montresor in Edgar Allan Poe's "The Cask of Amontillado." Sometimes such a narrator addresses an **auditor,** an audience within the fiction whose possible reaction is part of the story. Reading a story told in the first person resembles our everyday efforts to understand what people tell us about themselves. In a story, we can find signals that suggest the right mixture of sympathy and distrust to give the speaker. Often a first-person narrator unintentionally reveals herself—the reader can see her flaws—as she tries to be impressive. Sometimes a first-person narrator gives false or distorted information. Some fictions are narrated by villains, insane people, fools, liars, or hypocrites. When we resist a narrator's point of view and judge his or her flaws or misperceptions, we call that narrator **unreliable.** Successful first-person fictions often leave us undecided about the reliability of their narrators or speakers.

First-person narration isn't the only type that gives us a limited focus on one character, of course. Readers can gain a privileged insight into one character's experiences through third-person narration as well. Many narratives, from novels to short stories to films, focus on a **centered** or **central consciousness,** filtering things, people, and events through an individual character's perceptions and responses. The modern short story, with its tightly controlled range, often centers on one character's changing state of mind in an ordinary situation during a brief period of time. In third-person narratives, a reader may identify, close-up, with a complex personality but also take in the whole picture, with a bit of distance or perspective on that personality.

This is a work of history in fictional form—that is, in personal perspective, which is the only kind of history that exists.
—JOYCE CAROL OATES

In some stories, the point of view shifts—or jumps—from a previously established centered consciousness. The shift may strike us as breaking the rules of the story, or we may need to adjust our understanding of what the story is trying to do. Some stories make a point of asking us to revise our expectations, to bend our rules both for reality and for storytelling. If the narrator refuses to choose what "really" happened, we as readers must think about alternatives; the story may be *about* making choices in stories as well as in life. Discovering the way the rules work in any story is the first big step to understanding its whole effect, and hence its fresh way of making order out of experience.

Much rarer than first- or third person narration is second-person narration, in which "you" do this or that. Some authors—notably Jay McInerney in his novel *Bright Lights, Big City* [1984]—have employed the second-person voice, creating an effect similar to conversational anecdotes. At

There are as many opinions as there are people: each has his own point of view.
—TERENCE

times, you, the flesh-and-blood reader, may identify yourself as the person addressed, even if you have nothing in common with that person. At other times, you may imagine "you" as a character.

To appreciate and enjoy a story, then, you need to find out how it is being

Narrative teases me. I have
little concern in the progress
of events.

—CHARLES LAMB

told and by whom: you should identify the narrator and the point of view. Sometimes the narrator is a character, like Montresor in Poe's story, and sometimes the narrator has a clear personality even if he or she played no part in the events. At other times, readers may answer the question "Who is telling this story?" with the name of the author. This can be misleading, however. In most cases, the narrator should not necessarily be identified with the author, even when there is little to distinguish their personalities or experiences from each other. Of course, we can dig up a few facts about the author's life and read them into the story, or, worse, read the character or detail of the story into the author's life, as if a writer has no freedom to invent different people. It is more prudent, however, especially on the basis of a single story, to speak not of the author but of the author's **persona,** the voice or figure of the author who designs the story and creates the narrator who tells it. This persona may or may not resemble in nature or values the actual person of the author. Mary Anne Evans wrote novels under the name George Eliot; her first-person narrator speaks of "himself." That male authorial persona is close to the voice and focus of the masculine narrator of her novels, and neither should be confused with the brilliant, learned Victorian woman with the rather difficult life and poor health. Most authors create such a persona or representative to "write" their stories, wishing perhaps to keep the questions of their own failings or limitations out of the way.

We say *write* the stories. But just as poets write of singing their songs (their poems), so we often speak of telling a story, and we speak of a narrator, which means a teller. There are stories, usually with first-person narrators, that make much of the convention of oral storytelling, and stories with auditors also have a kind of "oral" feeling. They may remind us of the acts of telling and listening that are so basic to human communities and communication. Children love to hear a story read aloud, even if they have already read it to themselves many times. Older readers, too, enjoy imagining a narrative as a scene of telling. We know that we are only reading words on a page, but we imagine the narrator speaking to us, giving shape, focus, and voice to a particular history.

EDGAR ALLAN POE

The Cask of Amontillado

The thousand injuries of Fortunato I had borne as I best could, but when he ventured upon insult I vowed revenge. You, who so well know the nature of my soul, will not suppose, however, that I gave utterance to a threat. *At length* I would be avenged; this was a point definitively settled—but the very definitiveness with which it was resolved precluded the idea of risk. I must not only punish but punish with impunity. A wrong is unredressed when retribution overtakes its redresser. It is equally unredressed when the avenger fails to make himself felt as such to him who has done the wrong.

It must be understood that neither by word nor deed had I given Fortunato cause to doubt my good will. I continued, as was my wont, to smile in his face, and he did not perceive that my smile *now* was at the thought of his immolation.

He had a weak point—this Fortunato—although in other regards he was a man to be respected and even feared. He prided himself upon his connoisseurship in wine. Few Italians have the true virtuoso spirit. For the most part their enthusiasm is adopted to suit the time and opportunity, to practice imposture upon the British and Austrian *millionaires*. In painting and gemmary, Fortunato, like his countrymen, was a quack, but in the matter of old wines he was sincere. In this respect I did not differ from him materially;—I was skilful in the Italian vintages myself, and bought largely whenever I could.

It was about dusk, one evening during the supreme madness of the carnival season, that I encountered my friend. He accosted me with excessive warmth, for he had been drinking much. The man wore motley. He had on a tight-fitting parti-striped dress,[1] and his head was surmounted by the conical cap and bells. I was so pleased to see him that I should never have done wringing his hand.

I said to him—"My dear Fortunato, you are luckily met. How remarkably 5 well you are looking to-day. But I have received a pipe[2] of what passes for Amontillado, and I have my doubts."

"How?" said he. "Amontillado? A pipe? Impossible! And in the middle of the carnival!"

"I have my doubts," I replied; "and I was silly enough to pay the full Amontillado price without consulting you in the matter. You were not to be found, and I was fearful of losing a bargain."

"Amontillado!"

"I have my doubts."

"Amontillado!"

"And I must satisfy them." 10

"Amontillado!"

"As you are engaged, I am on my way to Luchresi. If any one has a critical turn it is he. He will tell me——"

"Luchresi cannot tell Amontillado from Sherry."

"And yet some fools will have it that his taste is a match for your own." 15

"Come, let us go."

"Whither?"

"To your vaults."

"My friend, no; I will not impose upon your good nature. I perceive you have an engagement. Luchresi——"

"I have no engagement;—come." 20

"My friend, no. It is not the engagement, but the severe cold with which

1. Fortunato wears a jester's costume (i.e., motley), not a woman's dress. 2. A large cask.

I perceive you are afflicted. The vaults are insufferably damp. They are encrusted with nitre."

"Let us go, nevertheless. The cold is merely nothing. Amontillado! You have been imposed upon. And as for Luchresi, he cannot distinguish Sherry from Amontillado."

Thus speaking, Fortunato possessed himself of my arm; and putting on a mask of black silk and drawing a *roquelaire*[3] closely about my person, I suffered him to hurry me to my palazzo.

There were no attendants at home; they had absconded to make merry in honour of the time. I had told them that I should not return until the morning, and had given them explicit orders not to stir from the house. These orders were sufficient, I well knew, to insure their immediate disappearance, one and all, as soon as my back was turned.

25   I took from their sconces two flambeaux,[4] and giving one to Fortunato, bowed him through several suites of rooms to the archway that led into the vaults. I passed down a long and winding staircase, requesting him to be cautious as he followed. We came at length to the foot of the descent, and stood together upon the damp ground of the catacombs of the Montresors.

The gait of my friend was unsteady, and the bells upon his cap jingled as he strode.

"The pipe," said he.

"It is farther on," said I; "but observe the white web-work which gleams from these cavern walls."

He turned towards me, and looked into my eyes with two filmy orbs that distilled the rheum of intoxication.

30   "Nitre[5]?" he asked, at length.

"Nitre," I replied. "How long have you had that cough?"

"Ugh! ugh! ugh!—ugh! ugh! ugh!—ugh! ugh! ugh!—ugh! ugh! ugh!—ugh! ugh! ugh!"

My poor friend found it impossible to reply for many minutes.

"It is nothing," he said, at last.

35   "Come," I said, with decision, "we will go back; your health is precious. You are rich, respected, admired, beloved; you are happy, as once I was. You are a man to be missed. For me it is no matter. We will go back; you will be ill, and I cannot be responsible. Besides, there is Luchresi——"

"Enough," he said; "the cough is a mere nothing; it will not kill me. I shall not die of a cough."

"True—true," I replied; "and, indeed, I had no intention of alarming you unneccessarily—but you should use all proper caution. A draught of this Medoc[6] will defend us from the damps."

Here I knocked off the neck of a bottle which I drew from a long row of its fellows that lay upon the mould.

---

3. Man's heavy, knee-length cloak.   4. That is, two torches from their wall brackets.
5. Potassium nitrate (saltpeter), a white mineral often found on the walls of damp caves, and used in gunpowder.   6. Like De Grâve (below), a French wine.

"Drink," I said, presenting him the wine.

He raised it to his lips with a leer. He paused and nodded to me famil- 40
iarly, while his bells jingled.

"I drink," he said, "to the buried that repose around us."

"And I to your long life."

He again took my arm, and we proceeded.

"These vaults," he said, "are extensive."

"The Montresors," I replied, "were a great and numerous family." 45

"I forget your arms."

"A huge human foot d'or,[7] in a field azure; the foot crushes a serpent
rampant whose fangs are imbedded in the heel."

"And the motto?"

"Nemo me impune lacessit."[8]

"Good!" he said. 50

The wine sparkled in his eyes and the bells jingled. My own fancy grew
warm with the Medoc. We had passed through long walls of piled skeletons,
with casks and puncheons[9] intermingling, into the inmost recesses of the
catacombs. I paused again, and this time I made bold to seize Fortunato
by an arm above the elbow.

"The nitre!" I said; "see, it increases. It hangs like moss upon the vaults.
We are below the river's bed. The drops of moisture trickle among the
bones. Come, we will go back ere it is too late. Your cough——"

"It is nothing," he said; "let us go on. But first, another draught of the
Medoc."

I broke and reached him a flaçon of De Grâve. He emptied it at a breath.
His eyes flashed with a fierce light. He laughed and threw the bottle
upwards with a gesticulation I did not understand.

I looked at him in surprise. He repeated the movement—a grotesque 55
one.

"You do not comprehend?" he said.

"Not I," I replied.

"Then you are not of the brotherhood."

"How?"

"You are not of the masons."[1] 60

"Yes, yes," I said; "yes, yes."

"You? Impossible! A mason?"

"A mason," I replied.

"A sign," he said, "a sign."

"It is this," I answered producing from beneath the folds of my *roquelaire* 65
a trowel.

"You jest," he exclaimed, recoiling a few paces. "But let us proceed to
the Amontillado."

"Be it so," I said, replacing the tool beneath the cloak and again offering

---

7. Of gold.   8. No one provokes me with impunity.   9. Large casks.

1. Masons or Freemasons, an international secret society condemned by the Catholic Church. Montresor means by mason one who builds with stone, brick, etc.

him my arm. He leaned upon it heavily. We continued our route in search of the Amontillado. We passed through a range of low arches, descended, passed on, and descending again, arrived at a deep crypt, in which the foulness of the air caused our flambeaux rather to glow than flame.

At the most remote end of the crypt there appeared another less spacious. Its walls had been lined with human remains, piled to the vault overhead, in the fashion of the great catacombs of Paris. Three sides of this interior crypt were still ornamented in this manner. From the fourth side the bones had been thrown down, and lay promiscuously upon the earth, forming at one point a mound of some size. Within the wall thus exposed by the displacing of the bones, we perceived a still interior crypt or recess, in depth about four feet, in width three, in height six or seven. It seemed to have been constructed for no especial use within itself, but formed merely the interval between two of the colossal supports of the roof of the catacombs, and was backed by one of their circumscribing walls of solid granite.

It was in vain that Fortunato, uplifting his dull torch, endeavoured to pry into the depth of the recess. Its termination the feeble light did not enable us to see.

70   "Proceed," I said; "herein is the Amontillado. As for Luchresi——"

"He is an ignoramus," interrupted my friend, as he stepped unsteadily forward, while I followed immediately at his heels. In an instant he had reached the extremity of the niche, and finding his progress arrested by the rock, stood stupidly bewildered. A moment more and I had fettered him to the granite. In its surface were two iron staples, distant from each other about two feet, horizontally. From one of these depended a short chain, from the other a padlock. Throwing the links about his waist, it was but the work of a few seconds to secure it. He was too much astounded to resist. Withdrawing the key I stepped back from the recess.

"Pass your hand," I said, "over the wall; you cannot help feeling the nitre. Indeed, it is *very* damp. Once more let me *implore* you to return. No? Then I must positively leave you. But I will first render you all the little attentions in my power."

"The Amontillado!" ejaculated my friend, not yet recovered from his astonishment.

"True," I replied; "the Amontillado."

75   As I said these words I busied myself among the pile of bones of which I have before spoken. Throwing them aside, I soon uncovered a quantity of building stone and mortar. With these materials and with the aid of my trowel, I began vigorously to wall up the entrance of the niche.

I had scarcely laid the first tier of the masonry when I discovered that the intoxication of Fortunato had in great measure worn off. The earliest indication I had of this was a low moaning cry from the depth of the recess. It was *not* the cry of a drunken man. There was then a long and obstinate silence. I laid the second tier, and the third, and the fourth; and then I heard the furious vibration of the chain. The noise lasted for several minutes, during which, that I might hearken to it with the more satisfaction, I ceased my labours and sat down upon the bones. When at last the clanking subsided, I resumed the trowel, and finished without interruption the fifth, the sixth, and the seventh tier. The wall was now nearly upon a level with my breast. I again paused, and holding the flambeaux over the mason-work, threw a few feeble rays upon the figure within.

A succession of loud and shrill screams, bursting suddenly from the throat of the chained form, seemed to thrust me violently back. For a brief moment I hesitated, I trembled. Unsheathing my rapier, I began to grope with it about the recess; but the thought of an instant reassured me. I placed my hand upon the solid fabric of the catacombs and felt satisfied. I reapproached the wall. I replied to the yells of him who clamoured. I re-echoed, I aided, I surpassed them in volume and in strength. I did this, and the clamourer grew still.

It was now midnight, and my task was drawing to a close. I had completed the eighth, the ninth and the tenth tier. I had finished a portion of the last and the eleventh; there remained but a single stone to be fitted and plastered in. I struggled with its weight; I placed it partially in its destined position. But now there came from out the niche a low laugh that erected the hairs upon my head. It was succeeded by a sad voice, which I had difficulty in recognizing as that of the noble Fortunato. The voice said—

"Ha! ha! ha!—he! he! he!—a very good joke, indeed—an excellent jest. We will have many a rich laugh about it at the palazzo—he! he! he!—over our wine—he! he! he!"

"The Amontillado!" I said.

"He! he! he!—he! he! he!—yes, the Amontillado. But is it not getting late? Will not they be awaiting us at the palazzo—the Lady Fortunato and the rest? Let us be gone."

"Yes," I said, "let us be gone."

"For the love of God, Montresor!"

"Yes," I said, "for the love of God!"

But to these words I hearkened in vain for a reply. I grew impatient. I called aloud—

"Fortunato!"

No answer. I called again—

"Fortunato!"

No answer still. I thrust a torch through the remaining aperture and let it fall within. There came forth in return only a jingling of the bells. My heart grew sick; it was the dampness of the catacombs that made it so. I hastened to make an end of my labour. I forced the last stone into its position; I plastered it up. Against the new masonry I re-erected the old rampart of bones. For the half of a century no mortal has disturbed them. *In pace requiescat!*[2]

1846

2. May he rest in peace!

QUESTIONS

1. What can the reader infer about Montresor's social position and character from hints in the text? What evidence does the text provide that Montresor is an unreliable narrator?

2. Who is the auditor, the "You," addressed in the first paragraph of "The Cask of Amontillado"? When is the story being told? Why is it being told? How does your knowledge of the auditor and the occasion influence the effect the story has on you?

3. What devices does Poe use to create and heighten the suspense in the story? Is the outcome ever in doubt?

ERNEST HEMINGWAY

Hills Like White Elephants

The hills across the valley of the Ebro[1] were long and white. On this side there was no shade and no trees and the station was between two lines of rails in the sun. Close against the side of the station there was the warm shadow of the building and a curtain, made of strings of bamboo beads, hung across the open door into the bar, to keep out flies. The American and the girl with him sat at a table in the shade, outside the building. It was very hot and the express from Barcelona would come in forty minutes. It stopped at this junction for two minutes and went on to Madrid.

"What should we drink?" the girl asked. She had taken off her hat and put it on the table.

"It's pretty hot," the man said.

"Let's drink beer."

5   "Dos cervezas," the man said into the curtain.

"Big ones?" a woman asked from the doorway.

"Yes. Two big ones."

The woman brought two glasses of beer and two felt pads. She put the felt pads and the beer glasses on the table and looked at the man and the girl. The girl was looking off at the line of hills. They were white in the sun and the country was brown and dry.

"They look like white elephants," she said.

10   "I've never seen one," the man drank his beer.

"No, you wouldn't have."

"I might have," the man said. "Just because you say I wouldn't have doesn't prove anything."

The girl looked at the bead curtain. "They've painted something on it," she said. "What does it say?"

"Anis del Toro. It's a drink."

15   "Could we try it?"

---

1. River in northern Spain.

The man called "Listen" through the curtain. The woman came out from the bar.

"Four reales."[2]

"We want two Anis del Toro."

"With water?"

"Do you want it with water?"   20

"I don't know," the girl said. "Is it good with water?"

"It's all right."

"You want them with water?" asked the woman.

"Yes, with water."

"It tastes like licorice," the girl said and put the glass down.   25

"That's the way with everything."

"Yes," said the girl. "Everything tastes of licorice. Especially all the things you've waited so long for, like absinthe."

"Oh, cut it out."

"You started it," the girl said. "I was being amused. I was having a fine time."

"Well, let's try and have a fine time."   30

"All right. I was trying. I said the mountains looked like white elephants. Wasn't that bright?"

"That was bright."

"I wanted to try this new drink. That's all we do, isn't it—look at things and try new drinks?"

"I guess so."

The girl looked across at the hills.   35

"They're lovely hills," she said. "They don't really look like white elephants. I just meant the coloring of their skin through the trees."

"Should we have another drink?"

"All right."

The warm wind blew the bead curtain against the table.

"The beer's nice and cool," the man said.   40

"It's lovely," the girl said.

"It's really an awfully simple operation, Jig," the man said. "It's not really an operation at all."

The girl looked at the ground the table legs rested on.

"I know you wouldn't mind it, Jig. It's really not anything. It's just to let the air in."

The girl did not say anything.   45

"I'll go with you and I'll stay with you all the time. They just let the air in and then it's all perfectly natural."

"Then what will we do afterward?"

"We'll be fine afterward. Just like we were before."

"What makes you think so?"

"That's the only thing that bothers us. It's the only thing that's made   50
us unhappy."

---

2. Spanish coins.

The girl looked at the bead curtain, put her hand out and took hold of two of the strings of beads.

"And you think then we'll be all right and be happy."

"I know we will. You don't have to be afraid. I've known lots of people that have done it."

"So have I," said the girl. "And afterward they were all so happy."

55 "Well," the man said, "if you don't want to you don't have to. I wouldn't have you do it if you didn't want to. But I know it's perfectly simple."

"And you really want to?"

"I think it's the best thing to do. But I don't want you to do it if you don't really want to."

"And if I do it you'll be happy and things will be like they were and you'll love me?"

"I love you now. You know I love you."

60 "I know. But if I do it, then it will be nice again if I say things are like white elephants, and you'll like it?"

"I'll love it. I love it now but I just can't think about it. You know how I get when I worry."

"If I do it you won't ever worry?"

"I won't worry about that because it's perfectly simple."

"Then I'll do it. Because I don't care about me."

65 "What do you mean?"

"I don't care about me."

"Well, I care about you."

"Oh, yes. But I don't care about me. And I'll do it and then everything will be fine."

"I don't want you to do it if you feel that way."

70 The girl stood up and walked to the end of the station. Across, on the other side, were fields of grain and trees along the banks of the Ebro. Far away, beyond the river, were mountains. The shadow of a cloud moved across the field of grain and she saw the river through the trees.

"And we could have all this," she said. "And we could have everything and every day we make it more impossible."

"What did you say?"

"I said we could have everything."

"We can have everything."

75 "No, we can't."

"We can have the whole world."

"No, we can't."

"We can go everywhere."

"No, we can't. It isn't ours any more."

80 "It's ours."

"No, it isn't. And once they take it away, you never get it back."

"But they haven't taken it away."

"We'll wait and see."

"Come on back in the shade," he said. "You mustn't feel that way."

85 "I don't feel any way," the girl said. "I just know things."

"I don't want you to do anything that you don't want to do—"

"Nor that isn't good for me," she said. "I know. Could we have another beer?"

"All right. But you've got to realize—"

"I realize," the girl said. "Can't we maybe stop talking?"

They sat down at the table and the girl looked across at the hills on the 90
dry side of the valley and the man looked at her and at the table.

"You've got to realize," he said, "that I don't want you to do it if you don't want to. I'm perfectly willing to go through with it if it means anything to you."

"Doesn't it mean anything to you? We could get along."

"Of course it does. But I don't want anybody but you. I don't want any one else. And I know it's perfectly simple."

"Yes, you know it's perfectly simple."

"It's all right for you to say that, but I do know it." 95

"Would you do something for me now?"

"I'd do anything for you."

"Would you please please please please please please please stop talking?"

He did not say anything but looked at the bags against the wall of the station. There were labels on them from all the hotels where they had spent nights.

"But I don't want you to," he said, "I don't care anything about it." 100

"I'll scream," the girl said.

The woman came out through the curtains with two glasses of beer and put them down on the damp felt pads. "The train comes in five minutes," she said.

"What did she say?" asked the girl.

"That the train is coming in five minutes."

The girl smiled brightly at the woman, to thank her. 105

"I'd better take the bags over to the other side of the station," the man said. She smiled at him.

"All right. Then come back and we'll finish the beer."

He picked up the two heavy bags and carried them around the station to the other tracks. He looked up the tracks but could not see the train. Coming back, he walked through the barroom, where people waiting for the train were drinking. He drank an Anis at the bar and looked at the people. They were all waiting reasonably for the train. He went out through the bead curtain. She was sitting at the table and smiled at him.

"Do you feel better?" he asked.

"I feel fine," she said. "There's nothing wrong with me. I feel fine." 110

1927

QUESTIONS

1. Find the first indication in "Hills Like White Elephants" that the two main characters are not getting along. What is the first clue about the exact nature of their conflict? Why are they going to Madrid? Why do the characters (and the author) refrain from speaking about it explicitly?

2. Point of view includes what characters see. Notice each use of the word "look." What does each person in the story look at, and what does each person seem to understand or feel? Is there anything in the story that none of these people would be able to see or know? How do the different kinds of observation add to the effect of the story?

3. Research the phrase "white elephant." What is the significance of this phrase in the story's title?

SUGGESTIONS FOR WRITING

1. Write a parody of "The Cask of Amontillado" set in modern times, perhaps on a college campus ("A Barrel of Bud"?).

2. Hemingway's "Hills Like White Elephants" offers a detached perspective on relationships between men and women. Write an essay on the story in which you show how the voice (style and tone) of the narration and the point of view help to convey the text's perspective on sexual relationships.

3. Carry a notebook or tape recorder for a day or two, and note any stories you tell or hear, such as in daydreams, in conversation, on the phone, through e-mail or instant messaging. Consider what makes stories. Your transcripts may be short and may consist of memories, observations about your own character or those of people around you, plans, or predictions about the future. Choose two of your notes and modify them into plot summaries (no more than a paragraph each), using the first or the third person, the present or the past tense. Add a note about whether a full version of each story should give the inner thoughts of one or more characters, and why.

3 CHARACTER

Reading most short stories, your first thoughts may concern *who* as much as *what* and *how*. Character inevitably is a focus of your response to fiction, even if the story goes out of its way to avoid creating the illusion of real people acting in a real world. Stories almost always concern human beings (there may be fables about animals, geometric shapes, flowers), and we are all experts, from our own social experience, at attributing personalities to someone or something with a name and a certain role in the action. As in our assessments of plot, in our response to character we are guided by expectations based on our reading as well as our experience.

A **character** is someone who acts, appears, or is referred to as playing a part in a literary work, usually fiction or drama. **Characterization**—the art and technique of representing fictional personages—depends upon action or plot as well as narration and point of view. Many stories present characters through the medium of a narrator who is offstage, without a body or a personality, a past or a future, who is simply a voice and style and medium for the story. In other stories, the narrator both tells us the story and plays the central role in the action. Still other stories are narrated in the first person by characters who play an important part in the action, but who serve as witnesses to the experience of the main, title characters. In still another variation, the observing narrator is present in the events in the story but can scarcely be distinguished as a separate personality. In short, there can be various combinations of narration and characterization that guide how we perceive the story about the main characters.

The most common term for the character with the leading male role is **hero,** the "good guy," who opposes the **villain,** or "bad guy." The leading female character is the **heroine.** Heroes and heroines are usually larger than life, stronger or *The sum of tendencies to act in a certain way.* —T. H. HUXLEY

better than most human beings, sometimes almost godlike. In most modern fiction, however, the leading character is much more ordinary, more like the rest of us. Such a character is sometimes called an **antihero,** not because he opposes the hero but because he is not heroic in stature or perfection, is not so clearly or simply a "good guy." An older and more neutral term than *hero* for the leading character, a term that does not imply either the presence or the absence of outstanding virtue (and that has the added advantage of referring equally to male and female characters), is **protagonist,** whose opponent is the **antagonist.** You might get into long and pointless arguments by calling Francis Weed (in John Cheever's "The Country Husband") or Montresor (in "A Cask of Amontillado") a hero, but most would agree that each is his story's protagonist. Some stories, however, leave open to debate the question of which character most deserves to be called the *protagonist*.

The **major** or **main characters** are those we see more of over a longer period of time; we learn more about them, and we think of them as more complex and, therefore, frequently more "realistic" than the **minor characters**, the figures who fill out the story. These major characters can grow and change too, sometimes even contradicting expectations.

Yet while minor characters may be less prominent and less complex, they are ultimately just as indispensable to a story as major characters. A very good first question when you set out to write about a character is, "How would this story be different without this character?" Minor characters often play a key role in shaping our interpretations of, and attitudes toward, the major characters, and also in precipitating the changes that major characters undergo. In Herman Melville's "Bartleby, the Scrivener," for example, "flighty" Turkey and "fiery" Nippers help us, as well as the story's narrator, to recognize the uniqueness of the "singularly sedate" Bartleby. Like many a minor character, then, Turkey and Nippers might be described as **foils** to this major character in the sense that they serve as contrasts to the protagonist. "Bartleby the Scrivener" would not absolutely *need* Turkey and Nippers, but these foils to the main character help to bring out what is exceptional about him, his unchanging lack of appetite.

Characters that change, develop, or act from conflicting motives are said to be **round characters;** they can "surprise convincingly," as one critic puts it. Simple characters that, like Turkey and Nippers, behave in unchanging or unsurprising ways are called **flat.** But we must be careful not to let terms like *flat* and *round* or *major* and *minor* turn into value judgments. Because flat characters are less complex than round ones, it is easy to assume they are artistically inferior; however, we need only to think of the characters of Charles Dickens, almost all of whom are flat, to realize that this is not always true.

Characterization can cause the greatest disagreements about the meaning or quality of a story. Discussion can get wrapped up in whether you liked or disliked so-and-so, or whether you trusted her motives or would have done the same thing in her place. Your teacher will probably warn you not to confuse characters with real people. After all, these are imaginary beings created out of words for certain effects. Yet if a story asks us to suppose the reality of the persons in it, how can we avoid applying our real-life judgments of personality? And don't our opinions about people differ widely in real life?

The very term *character*, when it refers not to a fictional personage but to a combination of qualities in a human being, is somewhat ambiguous. It usually has moral overtones, often favorable (a man of character); it is sometimes neutral but evaluative (character reference). Judgment about character usually involves moral terms like *good* and *bad* and *strong* and *weak*. And individuals and cultures have held conflicting views of what produces character, whether innate factors such as genes or environmental factors such as upbringing. Views differ as well as to whether character is simply a matter of fate, something determined and unchanging, or whether it can change through experience, conversion, or an act of will. Thus the representation of people in fiction can provoke debates that concern the most fundamental values about human nature and varieties of personality—and no one is likely to win such debates any time soon.

Nevertheless, such debates can indeed be meaningful, even if irresolvable, insofar as they are provoked by the story that you have read. You can also come to more definite conclusions by focusing more closely upon the characters in a particular story and by remembering that the whole work is an imaginary world—more or less like our own—with its own rules. Rather than asking whether the protagonist is a good or bad person, likable or not, or true to life or not, you should consider whether the characterization is good or bad, whether it is effective in the story's own terms. Just as an actor receives a Best Actor award for playing a character well rather than for playing a good character, so an author may be recognized for good characterization even if we do not like or admire the character the author has created. Often the "bad" or at least morally complex characters interest and teach us the most. Although we should remember that characters exist only in the context of the story, we may learn about real people from characters in fiction or learn to understand fictional characters in part from what we know about real people. Part of the pleasure of many stories is that they afford us an opportunity of seeming to inhabit another person's mind. Even our closest friends would find it hard to convey to us the kinds of intimate details that fiction can express imaginatively.

Character is that which reveals moral purpose, exposing the class of things a man chooses or avoids.
—ARISTOTLE

Such better-than-lifelike understanding can be one benefit of interpreting character in fiction. But as we have suggested, some stories and some characters are designed for different effects. Flat or opaque characterization has its place, and so do **stereotypes**: characters based on conscious or unconscious cultural assumptions about what a person's sex, age, ethnicity, nationality, occupation, marital status, and so on will tell us about that person's traits, actions, even values. Any character belongs more or less to a type. One of the chief ways we have of describing or defining is by placing the thing to be defined in a category or class and then distinguishing it from the other members of that class. Characters are almost inevitably identified by category—by sex, age, nationality, occupation, or other characteristics. We learn that the narrator of "Why I Live at the P.O." is a white woman, relatively young, who lives in a small town in Mississippi. The humor of her story may depend on readers' expectations about poor, Southern, uneducated families, and some might object that those expectations are prejudiced. Yet in some stories, characterization exaggerates the conflicts between and among types in order to raise issues about the way people judge and treat each other as types.

It seems that the analysis of character is the highest human entertainment. And literature does it, unlike gossip, without mentioning real names.
—ISAAC BASHEVIS SINGER

Excellent fiction can emerge from the surprises or conflicts created by stereotypical categories. In spite of our best intentions, we function in everyday life by quickly assessing the people we meet, and inevitably categorizing them. It can be wonderful—and it is often a story worth telling to our friends—to discover that a person of a type you really dislike (perhaps a "loser," "bully," "weirdo," or other objectionable type) actually has an individual character and something to say or do that you appreciate. The difference between a stereotype and observed behavior can create a round character, one who can surprise convincingly.

The usual sources of such classifications of people are observations of physical characteristics, which are the stock in trade of narrators of fiction: well-selected, closely observed details of appearance. In most stories we not only see what characters look like, but also see what they do and hear what they say; we sometimes learn what they think, and what other people think or say about them; we often know what kind of clothes they wear, what and how much they own, treasure, or covet; we may be told about their childhood, parents, or some parts of their past. And all of this information combines to shape our sense of the characters. With the new information of later events or observations, characters may change in our perceptions as well as in their own right.

What we don't know about a character can be as significant and revealing as what we do know. What, for example, is the effect of the fact that we never learn the narrator's name in "Bartleby, the Scrivener"? Or that we know only the nicknames of Nippers and Turkey? As you consider the characterization within a story, pay close attention to the many sorts of things that you are not explicitly told about the characters.

The identification of characters by action or behavior, and thus plot, is even more important than the appearance of characters in guiding your response. As always, it is misleading to isolate the elements of fiction except for purposes of analysis. Throughout a story, plot (or incident) and character are fused. As novelist Henry James wrote,

> What is character but the determination of incident? What is incident but the illustration of character? . . . It is an incident for a woman to stand up with her hand resting on a table and look at you in a certain way; or if it is not an incident I think it will be hard to say what it is. At the same time it is an expression of character. If you say you don't see it, . . . this is exactly what the artist who has reasons of his own for thinking he *does* see it undertakes to show you.

Character is destiny.
—GEORGE ELIOT

Though characterization is gradual, taking place sequentially through the story, it is not, as it may seem natural to assume, entirely cumulative. We do not begin with an empty space called "Bartleby" and fill it in gradually by adding physical traits, habitual actions, ways of speaking, and so on. Our imagination does not work that way. Rather, just as at each point in the action we project some sort of configuration of how the story will come out or what the world of the story will be like or mean, so we project a more or less complete image of each character at the point at which he or she is first mentioned or appears. The image is based on the initial reference in the text, our reading, and our life experiences and associations. The next time the character appears, we continue to project an image of a complete personality that we might eventually get to know, though we are still only slightly acquainted with this character. Just as in the plot we project a new series of developments and a new outcome at each stage, in characterization we are prepared to be surprised by the traits or qualities that emerge in the course of the action. In other words, rather than assembling a character the way a child attaches the eyes, ears, or hat to a Mr. Potato Head, we overlay a series of impressions of a complete, existing person. Though the final image may be the most enduring, the early images do not all disappear: our view of the character is multidimensional, flickering, like a time-lapse photograph.

Perhaps that is why it is rare that any actor in a film based on a novel or story matches the way we imagined that character if we have read the book or story first—our imagination has not one image but rather a sequence of images associated with that character. It is also why some of us feel that seeing the film before reading the book hobbles the imagination. A particular character's physical attributes, for example, may not be described in a novel until after that character has been involved in some incident; the reader may then need to adjust his or her earlier vision of that character, which is not an option for the viewer of a film. It is thus the reader, rather than a casting director, who finalizes a character in his or her own imagination. Indeed, you may consider yourself a collaborator with the writer in *realizing* the appearance, manner, and personality of the characters described on the page, as the words leave so much to the imagination. For we are all artists representing reality to ourselves. If we study the art of characterization and think about the way we interpret fictional characters, we may become better artists, able to enrich our reading both of fictional texts and of real people and situations.

EUDORA WELTY

Why I Live at the P.O.

I was getting along fine with Mama, Papa-Daddy, and Uncle Rondo until my sister Stella-Rondo just separated from her husband and came back home again. Mr. Whitaker! Of course I went with Mr. Whitaker first, when he first appeared here in China Grove, taking "Pose Yourself" photos, and Stella-Rondo broke us up. Told him I was one-sided. Bigger on one side than the other, which is a deliberate, calculated falsehood: I'm the same. Stella-Rondo is exactly twelve months to the day younger than I am and for that reason she's spoiled.

She's always had anything in the world she wanted and then she'd throw it away. Papa-Daddy give her this gorgeous Add-a-Pearl necklace when she was eight years old and she threw it away playing baseball when she was nine, with only two pearls.

So as soon as she got married and moved away from home the first thing she did was separate! From Mr. Whitaker! This photographer with the popeyes she said she trusted. Came home from one of those towns up in Illinois and to our complete surprise brought this child of two.

Mama said she like to make her drop dead for a second. "Here you had this marvelous blonde child and never so much as wrote your mother a word about it," says Mama. "I'm thoroughly ashamed of you." But of course she wasn't.

5 Stella-Rondo just calmly takes off this *hat*, I wish you could see it. She says, "Why, Mama, Shirley-T.'s adopted, I can prove it."

"How?" says Mama, but all I says was, "H'm!" There I was over the hot stove, trying to stretch two chickens over five people and a completely unexpected child into the bargain without one moment's notice.

"What do you mean—'H'm'?" says Stella-Rondo, and Mama says, "I heard that, Sister."

I said that oh, I didn't mean a thing, only that whoever Shirley-T. was, she was the spit-image of Papa-Daddy if he'd cut off his beard, which of course he'd never do in the world. Papa-Daddy's Mama's papa and sulks.

Stella-Rondo got furious! She said, "Sister, I don't need to tell you you got a lot of nerve and always did have and I'll thank you to make no future reference to my adopted child whatsoever."

10 "Very well," I said. "Very well, very well. Of course I noticed at once she looks like Mr. Whitaker's side too. That frown. She looks like a cross between Mr. Whitaker and Papa-Daddy."

"Well, all I can say is she isn't."

"She looks exactly like Shirley Temple to me," says Mama, but Shirley-T. just ran away from her.

So the first thing Stella-Rondo did at the table was turn Papa-Daddy against me.

"Papa-Daddy," she says. He was trying to cut up his meat. "Papa-Daddy!" I was taken completely by surprise. Papa-Daddy is about a million years old and's got this long-long beard. "Papa-Daddy, Sister says she fails to understand why you don't cut off your beard."

15 So Papa-Daddy l-a-y-s down his knife and fork! He's real rich. Mama says he is, he says he isn't. So he says, "Have I heard correctly? You don't understand why I don't cut off my beard?"

"Why," I says, "Papa-Daddy, of course I understand, I did not say any such a thing, the idea!"

He says, "Hussy!"

I says, "Papa-Daddy, you know I wouldn't any more want you to cut off your beard than the man in the moon. It was the farthest thing from my mind! Stella-Rondo sat there and made that up while she was eating breast of chicken."

But he says, "So the postmistress fails to understand why I don't cut off my beard. Which job I got you through my influence with the government. 'Bird's nest'—is that what you call it?"

20 Not that it isn't the next to smallest P.O. in the entire state of Mississippi.

I says, "Oh, Papa-Daddy," I says, "I didn't say any such a thing, I never dreamed it was a bird's nest, I have always been grateful though this is the next to smallest P.O. in the state of Mississippi, and I do not enjoy being referred to as a hussy by my own grandfather."

But Stella-Rondo says, "Yes, you did say it too. Anybody in the world could of heard you, that had ears."

"Stop right there," says Mama, looking at *me*.

So I pulled my napkin straight back through the napkin ring and left the table.

As soon as I was out of the room Mama says, "Call her back, or she'll 25 starve to death," but Papa-Daddy says, "This is the beard I started growing on the Coast when I was fifteen years old." He would of gone on till nightfall if Shirley-T. hadn't lost the Milky Way she ate in Cairo.

So Papa-Daddy says, "I am going out and lie in the hammock, and you can all sit here and remember my words: I'll never cut off my beard as long as I live, even one inch, and I don't appreciate it in you at all." Passed right by me in the hall and went straight out and got in the hammock.

It would be a holiday. It wasn't five minutes before Uncle Rondo suddenly appeared in the hall in one of Stella-Rondo's flesh-colored kimonos, all cut on the bias, like something Mr. Whitaker probably thought was gorgeous.

"Uncle Rondo!" I says. "I didn't know who that was! Where are you going?"

"Sister," he says, "get out of my way, I'm poisoned."

"If you're poisoned stay away from Papa-Daddy," I says. "Keep out of 30 the hammock. Papa-Daddy will certainly beat you on the head if you come within forty miles of him. He thinks I deliberately said he ought to cut off his beard after he got me the P.O., and I've told him and told him and told him, and he acts like he just don't hear me. Papa-Daddy must of gone stone deaf."

"He picked a fine day to do it then," says Uncle Rondo, and before you could say "Jack Robinson" flew out in the yard.

What he'd really done, he'd drunk another bottle of that prescription. He does it every single Fourth of July as sure as shooting, and it's horribly expensive. Then he falls over in the hammock and snores. So he insisted on zigzagging right on out to the hammock, looking like a half-wit.

Papa-Daddy woke with this horrible yell and right there without moving an inch he tried to turn Uncle Rondo against me. I heard every word he said. Oh, he told Uncle Rondo I didn't learn to read till I was eight years old and he didn't see how in the world I ever got the mail put up at the P.O., much less read it all, and he said if Uncle Rondo could only fathom the lengths he had gone to get me that job! And he said on the other hand he thought Stella-Rondo had a brilliant mind and deserved credit for getting out of town. All the time he was just lying there swinging as pretty as you please and looping out his beard, and poor Uncle Rondo was *pleading* with him to slow down the hammock, it was making him as dizzy as a witch to watch it. But that's what Papa-Daddy likes about a hammock. So

Uncle Rondo was too dizzy to get turned against me for the time being. He's Mama's only brother and is a good case of a one-track mind. Ask anybody. A certified pharmacist.

Just then I heard Stella-Rondo raising the upstairs window. While she was married she got this peculiar idea that it's cooler with the windows shut and locked. So she has to raise the window before she can make a soul hear her outdoors.

35   So she raises the window and says, "*Oh!*" You would have thought she was mortally wounded.

Uncle Rondo and Papa-Daddy didn't even look up, but kept right on with what they were doing. I had to laugh.

I flew up the stairs and threw the door open! I says, "What in the wide world's the matter, Stella-Rondo? You mortally wounded?"

"No," she says, "I am not mortally wounded but I wish you would do me the favor of looking out that window there and telling me what you see."

So I shade my eyes and look out the window.

40   "I see the front yard," I says.

"Don't you see any human beings?"

"I see Uncle Rondo trying to run Papa-Daddy out of the hammock," I says. "Nothing more. Naturally, it's so suffocating-hot in the house, with all the windows shut and locked, everybody who cares to stay in their right mind will have to go out and get in the hammock before the Fourth of July is over."

"Don't you notice anything different about Uncle Rondo?" asks Stella-Rondo.

"Why, no, except he's got on some terrible-looking flesh-colored contraption I wouldn't be found dead in, is all I can see," I says.

45   "Never mind, you won't be found dead in it, because it happens to be part of my trousseau, and Mr. Whitaker took several dozen photographs of me in it," says Stella-Rondo. "What on earth could uncle Rondo *mean* by wearing part of my trousseau out in the broad open daylight without saying so much as 'Kiss my foot,' *knowing* I only got home this morning after my separation and hung my negligee up on the bathroom door, just as nervous as I could be?"

"I'm sure I don't know, and what do you expect me to do about it?" I says. "Jump out the window?"

"No, I expect nothing of the kind. I simply declare that Uncle Rondo looks like a fool in it, that's all," she says. "It makes me sick to my stomach."

"Well, he looks as good as he can," I says. "As good as anybody in reason could." I stood up for Uncle Rondo, please remember. And I said to Stella-Rondo, "I think I would do well not to criticize so freely if I were you and came home with a two-year-old child I had never said a word about, and no explanation whatever about my separation."

"I asked you the instant I entered this house not to refer one more time to my adopted child, and you gave me your word of honor you would not," was all Stella-Rondo would say, and started pulling out every one of her eyebrows with some cheap Kress tweezers.

So I merely slammed the door behind me and went down and made 50
some green-tomato pickle. Somebody had to do it. Of course Mama had
turned both the Negroes loose; she always said no earthly power could
hold one anyway on the Fourth of July, so she wouldn't even try. It turned
out that Jaypan fell in the lake and came within a very narrow limit of
drowning.

So Mama trots in. Lifts up the lid and says, "H'm! Not very good for
your Uncle Rondo in his precarious condition, I must say. Or poor little
adopted Shirley-T. Shame on you!"

That made me tired. I says, "Well, Stella-Rondo had better thank her
lucky stars it was her instead of me came trotting in with that very peculiar-
looking child. Now if it had been me that trotted in from Illinois and
brought a peculiar-looking child or two, I shudder to think of the reception
I'd of got, much less controlled the diet of an entire family."

"But you must remember, Sister, that you were never married to Mr.
Whitaker in the first place and didn't go up to Illinois to live," says Mama,
shaking a spoon in my face. "If you had I would of been just as overjoyed
to see you and your little adopted girl as I was to see Stella-Rondo, when
you wound up with your separation and came on back home."

"You would not," I says.

"Don't contradict me, I would," says Mama. 55

But I said she couldn't convince me though she talked till she was blue
in the face. Then I said, "Besides, you know as well as I do that that child
is not adopted."

"She most certainly is adopted," says Mama, stiff as a poker.

I says, "Why, Mama, Stella-Rondo had her just as sure as anything in
this world, and just too stuck up to admit it."

"Why, Sister," said Mama. "Here I thought we were going to have a
pleasant Fourth of July, and you start right out not believing a word your
own baby sister tells you!"

"Just like Cousin Annie Flo. Went to her grave denying the facts of life," 60
I reminded Mama.

"I told you if you ever mentioned Annie Flo's name I'd slap your face,"
says Mama, and slaps my face.

"All right, you wait and see," I says.

"I," says Mama, "*I* prefer to take my children's word for anything when
it's humanly possible." You ought to see Mama, she weighs two hundred
pounds and has real tiny feet.

Just then something perfectly horrible occurred to me.

"Mama," I says, "can that child talk?" I simply had to whisper! "Mama, 65
I wonder if that child can be—you know—in any way? Do you realize?" I
says, "that she hasn't spoke one single, solitary word to a human being up
to this minute? This is the way she looks," I says, and I looked like this.

Well, Mama and I just stood there and stared at each other. It was
horrible!

"I remember well that Joe Whitaker frequently drank like a fish," says
Mama. "I believed to my soul he drank *chemicals*." And without another
word she marches to the foot of the stairs and calls Stella-Rondo.

"Stella-Rondo? O-o-o-o-o! Stella-Rondo!"

"What?" says Stella-Rondo from upstairs. Not even the grace to get up off the bed.

70 "Can that child of yours talk?" asks Mama.

Stella-Rondo says, "Can she what?"

"Talk! Talk!" says Mama. "Burdyburdyburdyburdy!"

So Stella-Rondo yells back, "Who says she can't talk?"

"Sister says so," says Mama.

75 "You didn't have to tell me, I know whose word of honor don't mean a thing in this house," says Stella-Rondo.

And in a minute the loudest Yankee voice I ever heard in my life yells out, "OE'm Pop-OE the Sailor-r-r Ma-a-an!" and then somebody jumps up and down in the upstairs hall. In another second the house would of fallen down.

"Not only talks, she can tap-dance!" calls Stella-Rondo. "Which is more than some people I won't name can do."

"Why, the little precious darling thing!" Mama says, so surprised. "Just as smart as she can be!" Starts talking baby talk right there. Then she turns on me. "Sister, you ought to be thoroughly ashamed! Run upstairs this instant and apologize to Stella-Rondo and Shirley-T."

"Apologize for what?" I says. "I merely wondered if the child was normal, that's all. Now that she's proved she is, why, I have nothing further to say."

80 But Mama just turned on her heel and flew out, furious. She ran right upstairs and hugged the baby. She believed it was adopted. Stella-Rondo hadn't done a thing but turn her against me from upstairs while I stood there helpless over the hot stove. So that made Mama, Papa-Daddy, and the baby all on Stella-Rondo's side.

Next, Uncle Rondo.

I must say that Uncle Rondo has been marvelous to me at various times in the past and I was completely unprepared to be made to jump out of my skin, the way it turned out. Once Stella-Rondo did something perfectly horrible to him—broke a chain letter from Flanders Field—and he took the radio back he had given her and gave it to me. Stella-Rondo was furious! For six months we all had to call her Stella instead of Stella-Rondo, or she wouldn't answer. I always thought Uncle Rondo had all the brains of the entire family. Another time he sent me to Mammoth Cave with all expenses paid.

But this would be the day he was drinking that prescription, the Fourth of July.

So at supper Stella-Rondo speaks up and says she thinks Uncle Rondo ought to try to eat a little something. So finally Uncle Rondo said he would try a little cold biscuits and ketchup, but that was all. So *she* brought it to him.

85 "Do you think it wise to disport with ketchup in Stella-Rondo's flesh-colored kimono?" I says. Trying to be considerate! If Stella-Rondo couldn't watch out for her trousseau, somebody had to.

"Any objections?" asks Uncle Rondo, just about to pour out all of the ketchup.

"Don't mind what she says, Uncle Rondo," says Stella-Rondo. "Sister has been devoting this solid afternoon to sneering out my bedroom window at the way you look."

"What's that?" says Uncle Rondo. Uncle Rondo has got the most terrible temper in the world. Anything is liable to make him tear the house down if it comes at the wrong time.

So Stella-Rondo says, "Sister says, 'Uncle Rondo certainly does look like a fool in that pink kimono!'"

Do you remember who it was really said that?   90

Uncle Rondo spills out all the ketchup and jumps out of his chair and tears off the kimono and throws it down on the dirty floor and puts his foot on it. It had to be sent all the way to Jackson to the cleaners and re-pleated.

"So that's your opinion of your Uncle Rondo, is it?" he says. "I look like a fool, do I? Well, that's the last straw. A whole day in this house with nothing to do, and then to hear you come out with a remark like that behind my back!"

"I didn't say any such of a thing, Uncle Rondo," I says, "and I'm not saying who did, either. Why, I think you look all right. Just try to take care of yourself and not talk and eat at the same time," I says. "I think you better go lie down."

"Lie down my foot," says Uncle Rondo. I ought to of known by that he was fixing to do something perfectly horrible.

So he didn't do anything that night in the precarious state he was in—   95
just played Casino with Mama and Stella-Rondo and Shirley-T. and gave Shirley-T. a nickel with a head on both sides. It tickled her nearly to death, and she called him "Papa." But at 6:30 A.M. the next morning, he threw a whole five-cent package of some unsold one-inch firecrackers from the store as hard as he could into my bedroom and they every one went off. Not one bad one in the string. Anybody else, there'd be one that wouldn't go off.

Well, I'm just terribly susceptible to noise of any kind, the doctor has always told me I was the most sensitive person he had ever seen in his whole life, and I was simply prostrated. I couldn't eat! People tell me they heard it as far as the cemetery, and old Aunt Jep Patterson, that had been holding her own so good, thought it was Judgment Day and she was going to meet her whole family. It's usually so quiet here.

And I'll tell you it didn't take me any longer than a minute to make up my mind what to do. There I was with the whole entire house on Stella-Rondo's side and turned against me. If I have anything at all I have pride.

So I just decided I'd go straight down to the P.O. There's plenty of room there in the back, I says to myself.

Well! I made no bones about letting the family catch on to what I was up to. I didn't try to conceal it.

The first thing they knew, I marched in where they were all playing Old   100
Maid and pulled the electric oscillating fan out by the plug, and everything got real hot. Next I snatched the pillow I'd done the needlepoint on right

off the davenport from behind Papa-Daddy. He went "Ugh!" I beat Stella-Rondo up the stairs and finally found my charm bracelet in her bureau drawer under a picture of Nelson Eddy.[1]

"So that's the way the land lies," says Uncle Rondo. There he was, piecing on the ham. "Well, Sister, I'll be glad to donate my army cot if you got any place to set it up, providing you'll leave right this minute and let me get some peace." Uncle Rondo was in France.

"Thank you kindly for the cot and 'peace' is hardly the word I would select if I had to resort to firecrackers at 6:30 A.M. in a young girl's bedroom," I says to him. "And as to where I intend to go, you seem to forget my position as postmistress of China Grove, Mississippi," I says. "I've always got the P.O."

Well, that made them all sit up and take notice.

I went out front and started digging up some four-o'clocks to plant around the P.O.

105   "Ah-ah-ah!" says Mama, raising the window. "Those happen to be my four-o'clocks. Everything planted in that star is mine. I've never known you to make anything grow in your life."

"Very well," I says. "But I take the fern. Even you, Mama, can't stand there and deny that I'm the one watered that fern. And I happen to know where I can send in a box top and get a packet of one thousand mixed seeds, no two the same kind, free."

"Oh, where?" Mama wants to know.

But I says, "Too late. You 'tend to your house, and I'll 'tend to mine. You hear things like that all the time if you know how to listen to the radio. Perfectly marvelous offers. Get anything you want free."

So I hope to tell you I marched in and got that radio, and they could of all bit a nail in two, especially Stella-Rondo, that it used to belong to, and she well knew she couldn't get it back, I'd sue for it like a shot. And I very politely took the sewing-machine motor I helped pay the most on to give Mama for Christmas back in 1929, and a good big calendar, with the first-aid remedies on it. The thermometer and the Hawaiian ukulele certainly were rightfully mine, and I stood on the step-ladder and got all my watermelon-rind preserves and every fruit and vegetable I'd put up, every jar. Then I began to pull the tacks out of the bluebird wall vases on the archway to the dining room.

110   "Who told you you could have those, Miss Priss?" says Mama, fanning as hard as she could.

"I bought 'em and I'll keep track of 'em," I says. "I'll tack 'em up one on each side of the post-office window, and you can see 'em when you come to ask me for your mail, if you're so dead to see 'em."

"Not I! I'll never darken the door to that post office again if I live to be

---

1. Opera singer (1901–1967) who enjoyed phenomenal popularity in the 1930s and 1940s when he costarred in numerous film musicals with Jeanette MacDonald. The two were known as "America's Singing Sweethearts."

a hundred," Mama says. "Ungrateful child! After all the money we spent on you at the Normal."[2]

"Me either," says Stella-Rondo. "You can just let my mail lie there and *rot*, for all I care. I'll never come and relieve you of a single, solitary piece."

"I should worry," I says. "And who you think's going to sit down and write you all those big fat letters and postcards, by the way? Mr. Whitaker? Just because he was the only man ever dropped down in China Grove and you got him—unfairly—is he going to sit down and write you a lengthy correspondence after you come home giving no rhyme nor reason whatsoever for your separation and no explanation for the presence of that child? I may not have your brilliant mind, but I fail to see it."

So Mama says, "Sister, I've told you a thousand times that Stella-Rondo simply got homesick, and this child is far too big to be hers," and she says, "Now, why don't you just sit down and play Casino?"

Then Shirley-T. sticks out her tongue at me in this perfectly horrible way. She has no more manners than the man in the moon. I told her she was going to cross her eyes like that some day and they'd stick.

"It's too late to stop me now," I says. "You should have tried that yesterday. I'm going to the P.O. and the only way you can possibly see me is to visit me there."

So Papa-Daddy says, "You'll never catch me setting foot in that post office, even if I should take a notion into my head to write a letter some place." He says, "I won't have you reachin' out of that little old window with a pair of shears and cuttin' off any beard of mine. I'm too smart for you!"

"We all are," says Stella-Rondo.

But I said, "If you're so smart, where's Mr. Whitaker?"

So then Uncle Rondo says, "I'll thank you from now on to stop reading all the orders I get on postcards and telling everybody in China Grove what you think is the matter with them," but I says, "I draw my own conclusions and will continue in the future to draw them." I says, "If people want to write their innermost secrets on penny postcards, there's nothing in the wide world you can do about it, Uncle Rondo."

"And if you think we'll ever *write* another postcard you're sadly mistaken," says Mama.

"Cutting off your nose to spite your face then," I says. "But if you're all determined to have no more to do with the U.S. mail, think of this: What will Stella-Rondo do now, if she wants to tell Mr. Whitaker to come after her?"

"Wah!" says Stella-Rondo. I knew she'd cry. She had a conniption fit right there in the kitchen.

"It will be interesting to see how long she holds out," I says. "And now—I am leaving."

"Good-bye," says Uncle Rondo.

"Oh, I declare," says Mama, "to think that a family of mine should

---

2. That is, normal school (teachers' college).

quarrel on the Fourth of July, or the day after, over Stella-Rondo leaving old Mr. Whitaker and having the sweetest little adopted child! It looks like we'd all be glad!"

"Wah!" says Stella-Rondo, and has a fresh conniption fit.

"He left *her*—you mark my words," I says. "That's Mr. Whitaker. I know Mr. Whitaker. After all, I knew him first. I said from the beginning he'd up and leave her. I foretold every single thing that's happened."

130   "Where did he go?" asks Mama.

"Probably to the North Pole, if he knows what's good for him," I says.

But Stella-Rondo just bawled and wouldn't say another word. She flew to her room and slammed the door.

"Now look what you've gone and done, Sister," says Mama. "You go apologize."

"I haven't the time, I'm leaving," I says.

135   "Well, what are you waiting around for?" asks Uncle Rondo.

So I just picked up the kitchen clock and marched off, without saying, "Kiss my foot," or anything, and never did tell Stella-Rondo good-bye.

There was a girl going along on a little wagon right in front.

"Girl," I says, "come help me haul these things down the hill, I'm going to live in the post office."

Took her nine trips in her express wagon. Uncle Rondo came out on the porch and threw her a nickel.

140   And that's the last I've laid eyes on any of my family or my family laid eyes on me for five solid days and nights. Stella-Rondo may be telling the most horrible tales in the world about Mr. Whitaker, but I haven't heard them. As I tell everybody, I draw my own conclusions.

But oh, I like it here. It's ideal, as I've been saying. You see, I've got everything cater-cornered, the way I like it. Hear the radio? All the war news. Radio, sewing machine, book ends, ironing board and that great big piano lamp—peace, that's what I like. Butter-bean vines planted all along the front where the strings are.

Of course, there's not much mail. My family are naturally the main people in China Grove, and if they prefer to vanish from the face of the earth, for all the mail they get or the mail they write, why, I'm not going to open my mouth. Some of the folks here in town are taking up for me and some turned against me. I know which is which. There are always people who will quit buying stamps just to get on the right side of Papa-Daddy.

But here I am, and here I'll stay. I want the world to know I'm happy.

And if Stella-Rondo should come to me this minute, on bended knees, and *attempt* to explain the incidents of her life with Mr. Whitaker, I'd simply put my fingers in both my ears and refuse to listen.

1941

QUESTIONS

1. What is your initial impression of Sister, the story's narrator? At what points in the story do you find yourself reassessing this character? Why?
2. How would you characterize the other members of Sister's family? Which of them (Stella-Rondo, Mama, Papa-Daddy, Uncle Rondo) seem most fully fleshed out, and which seem flat?
3. Is there a realistic way to account for the melodrama of Sister's family life, or is Welty merely exaggerating for comic effect? What clues in the text make "Why I Live at the P.O." believable or unbelievable?

HERMAN MELVILLE

Bartleby, the Scrivener

A Story of Wall Street

I am a rather elderly man. The nature of my avocations for the last thirty years has brought me into more than ordinary contact with what would seem an interesting and somewhat singular set of men, of whom as yet nothing that I know of has ever been written:—I mean the law-copyists or scriveners. I have known very many of them, professionally and privately, and if I pleased, could relate divers histories, at which good-natured gentlemen might smile, and sentimental souls might weep. But I waive the biographies of all other scriveners for a few passages in the life of Bartleby, who was a scrivener the strangest I ever saw or heard of. While of other law-copyists I might write the complete life, of Bartleby nothing of that sort can be done. I believe that no materials exist for a full and satisfactory biography of this man. It is an irreparable loss to literature. Bartleby was one of those beings of whom nothing is ascertainable, except from the original sources, and in his case those are very small. What my own astonished eyes saw of Bartleby, *that* is all I know of him, except, indeed, one vague report which will appear in the sequel.[1]

Ere introducing the scrivener, as he first appeared to me, it is fit I make some mention of myself, my *employées,* my business, my chambers, and general surroundings; because some such description is indispensable to an adequate understanding of the chief character about to be presented.

Imprimis:[2] I am a man who, from his youth upwards, has been filled with a profound conviction that the easiest way of life is the best. Hence, though I belong to a profession proverbially energetic and nervous, even to turbulence, at times, yet nothing of that sort have I ever suffered to invade my peace. I am one of those unambitious lawyers who never addresses a jury, or in any way draws down public applause; but in the cool tranquillity of a snug retreat, do a snug business among rich men's bonds

---

1. That is, in the following story.   2. In the first place.

and mortgages and title-deeds. All who know me, consider me an eminently *safe* man. The late John Jacob Astor,[3] a personage little given to poetic enthusiasm, had no hesitation in pronouncing my first grand point to be prudence; my next, method. I do not speak it in vanity, but simply record the fact, that I was not unemployed in my profession by the late John Jacob Astor; a name which, I admit, I love to repeat, for it hath a rounded and orbicular sound to it, and rings like unto bullion. I will freely add that I was not insensible to the late John Jacob Astor's good opinion.

Some time prior to the period at which this little history begins, my avocations had been largely increased. The good old office, now extinct in the State of New York, of a Master in Chancery[4] had been conferred upon me. It was not a very arduous office, but very pleasantly remunerative. I seldom lose my temper; much more seldom indulge in dangerous indignation at wrongs and outrages; but I must be permitted to be rash here and declare, that I consider the sudden and violent abrogation of the office of Master in Chancery, by the new Constitution, as a—premature act; inasmuch as I had counted upon a life-lease of the profits, whereas I only received those of a few short years. But this is by the way.

5   My chambers were up stairs at No. —— Wall Street. At one end they looked upon the white wall of the interior of a spacious skylight shaft, penetrating the building from top to bottom. This view might have been considered rather tame than otherwise, deficient in what landscape painters call "life." But if so, the view from the other end of my chambers offered, at least, a contrast, if nothing more. In that direction my windows commanded an unobstructed view of a lofty brick wall, black by age and everlasting shade; which wall required no spyglass to bring out its lurking beauties, but for the benefit of all near-sighted spectators, was pushed up to within ten feet of my window panes. Owing to the great height of the surrounding buildings, and my chambers being on the second floor, the interval between this wall and mine not a little resembled a huge square cistern.

At the period just preceding the advent of Bartleby, I had two persons as copyists in my employment, and a promising lad as an office-boy. First, Turkey; second, Nippers, third, Ginger Nut. These may seem names the like of which are not usually found in the Directory.[5] In truth they were nicknames, mutually conferred upon each other by my three clerks, and were deemed expressive of their respective persons or characters. Turkey was a short, pursy[6] Englishman of about my own age, that is, somewhere not far from sixty. In the morning, one might say, his face was of a fine florid hue, but after twelve o'clock, meridian—his dinner hour—it blazed like a grate full of Christmas coals; and continued blazing—but, as it were,

---

3. New York fur merchant and landowner (1763–1848) who died the richest man in the United States.

4. A court of chancery can temper the law, applying "dictates of conscience" or "the principles of natural justice"; the office of Master was abolished in 1847.

5. Post Office Directory.   6. Fat, short-winded.

with a gradual wane—till 6 o'clock, P.M. or thereabouts, after which I saw no more of the proprietor of the face, which gaining its meridian with the sun, seemed to set with it, to rise, culminate, and decline the following day, with the like regularity and undiminished glory. There are many singular coincidences I have known in the course of my life, not the least among which was the fact, that exactly when Turkey displayed his fullest beams from his red and radiant countenance, just then, too, at that critical moment, began the daily period when I considered his business capacities as seriously disturbed for the remainder of the twenty-four hours. Not that he was absolutely idle, or averse to business then; far from it. The difficulty was, he was apt to be altogether too energetic. There was a strange, inflamed, flurried, flighty recklessness of activity about him. He would be incautious in dipping his pen into his inkstand. All his blots upon my documents were dropped there after twelve o'clock, meridian. Indeed, not only would he be reckless and sadly given to making blots in the afternoon, but some days he went further, and was rather noisy. At such times, too, his face flamed with augmented blazonry, as if cannel coal had been heaped on anthracite.[7] He made an unpleasant racket with his chair; spilled his sand-box; in mending his pens, impatiently split them all to pieces, and threw them on the floor in a sudden passion; stood up and leaned over his table, boxing his papers about in a most indecorous manner, very sad to behold in an elderly man like him. Nevertheless, as he was in many ways a most valuable person to me, and all the time before twelve o'clock, merid-ian, was the quickest, steadiest creature too, accomplishing a great deal of work in a style not easy to be matched—for these reasons, I was willing to overlook his eccentricities, though indeed, occasionally, I remonstrated with him. I did this very gently, however, because, though the civilest, nay, the blandest and most reverential of men in the morning, yet in the after-noon he was disposed, upon provocation, to be slightly rash with his tongue, in fact, insolent. Now, valuing his morning services as I did, and resolved not to lose them; yet, at the same time made uncomfortable by his inflamed ways after twelve o'clock; and being a man of peace, unwilling by my admonitions to call forth unseemly retorts from him; I took upon me, one Saturday noon (he was always worse on Saturdays), to hint to him, very kindly, that perhaps now that he was growing old, it might be well to abridge his labors; in short, he need not come to my chambers after twelve o'clock, but, dinner over, had best go home to his lodgings and rest himself till tea-time. But no; he insisted upon his afternoon devotions. His coun-tenance became intolerably fervid, as he oratorically assured me—gesticu-lating with a long ruler at the other end of the room—that if his services in the morning were useful, how indispensable, then, in the afternoon?

"With submission, sir," said Turkey on this occasion, "I consider myself your right-hand man. In the morning I but marshal and deploy my col-umns; but in the afternoon I put myself at their head, and gallantly charge the foe, thus!"—and he made a violent thrust with the ruler.

---

7. A fast, bright-burning coal heaped on slow-burning, barely glowing coal.

"But the blots, Turkey," intimated I.

"True,—but, with submission, sir, behold these hairs! I am getting old. Surely, sir, a blot or two of a warm afternoon is not to be severely urged against gray hairs. Old age—even if it blot the page—is honorable. With submission, sir, we *both* are getting old."

This appeal to my fellow-feeling was hardly to be resisted. At all events, I saw that go he would not. So I made up my mind to let him stay, resolving, nevertheless, to see to it, that during the afternoon he had to do with my less important papers.

Nippers, the second on my list, was a whiskered, sallow, and, upon the whole, rather piratical-looking young man of about five and twenty. I always deemed him the victim of two evil powers—ambition and indigestion. The ambition was evinced by a certain impatience of the duties of a mere copyist, an unwarrantable usurpation of strictly professional affairs, such as the original drawing up of legal documents. The indigestion seemed betokened in an occasional nervous testiness and grinning irritability, causing the teeth to audibly grind together over mistakes committed in copying; unnecessary maledictions, hissed, rather than spoken, in the heat of business; and especially by a continual discontent with the height of the table where he worked. Though of a very ingenious mechanical turn, Nippers could never get this table to suit him. He put chips under it, blocks of various sorts, bits of pasteboard, and at last went so far as to attempt an exquisite adjustment by final pieces of folded blotting-paper. But no invention would answer. If, for the sake of easing his back, he brought the table lid at a sharp angle well up towards his chin, and wrote there like a man using the steep roof of a Dutch house for his desk:—then he declared that it stopped the circulation in his arms. If now he lowered the table to his waistbands, and stooped over it in writing, then there was a sore aching in his back. In short, the truth of the matter was, Nippers knew not what he wanted. Or, if he wanted any thing, it was to be rid of a scrivener's table altogether. Among the manifestations of his diseased ambition was a fondness he had for receiving visits from certain ambiguous-looking fellows in seedy coats, whom he called his clients. Indeed I was aware that not only was he, at times, considerable of a ward-politician, but he occasionally did a little business at the Justices' courts, and was not unknown on the steps of the Tombs.[8] I have good reason to believe, however, that one individual who called upon him at my chambers, and who, with a grand air, he insisted was his client, was no other than a dun,[9] and the alleged title-deed, a bill. But with all his failings, and the annoyances he caused me, Nippers, like his compatriot Turkey, was a very useful man to me; wrote a neat, swift hand; and, when he chose, was not deficient in a gentlemanly sort of deportment. Added to this, he always dressed in a gentlemanly sort of way: and so, incidentally, reflected credit upon my chambers. Whereas with respect to Turkey, I had much ado to keep him from being a reproach to me. His clothes were apt to look oily and smell of eating-houses. He wore

8. Prison in New York City.   9. Bill collector.

his pantaloons very loose and baggy in summer. His coats were execrable; his hat not to be handled. But while the hat was a thing of indifference to me, inasmuch as his natural civility and deference, as a dependent Englishman, always led him to doff it the moment he entered the room, yet his coat was another matter. Concerning his coats, I reasoned with him; but with no effect. The truth was, I suppose, that a man with so small an income, could not afford to sport such a lustrous face and a lustrous coat at one and the same time. As Nippers once observed, Turkey's money went chiefly for red ink. One winter day I presented Turkey with a highly-respectable looking coat of my own, a padded gray coat, of a most comfortable warmth, and which buttoned straight up from the knee to the neck. I thought Turkey would appreciate the favor, and abate his rashness and obstreperousness of afternoons. But no. I verily believe that buttoning himself up in so downy and blanket-like a coat had a pernicious effect upon him; upon the same principle that too much oats are bad for horses. In fact, precisely as a rash, restive horse is said to feel his oats, so Turkey felt his coat. It made him insolent. He was a man whom prosperity harmed.

Though concerning the self-indulgent habits of Turkey I had my own private surmises, yet touching Nippers I was well persuaded that whatever might be his faults in other respects, he was, at least, a temperate young man. But indeed, nature herself seemed to have been his vintner,[1] and at his birth charged him so thoroughly with an irritable, brandy-like disposition, that all subsequent potations were needless. When I consider how, amid the stillness of my chambers, Nippers would sometimes impatiently rise from his seat, and stooping over his table, spread his arms wide apart, seize the whole desk, and move it, and jerk it, with a grim, grinding motion on the floor, as if the table were a perverse voluntary agent, intent on thwarting and vexing him; I plainly perceive that for Nippers, brandy and water were altogether superfluous.

It was fortunate for me that, owing to its peculiar cause—indigestion—the irritability and consequent nervousness of Nippers, were mainly observable in the morning, while in the afternoon he was comparatively mild. So that Turkey's paroxysms only coming on about twelve o'clock, I never had to do with their eccentricities at one time. Their fits relieved each other like guards. When Nippers' was on, Turkey's was off; and *vice versa*. This was a good natural arrangement under the circumstances.

Ginger Nut, the third on my list, was a lad some twelve years old. His father was a carman,[2] ambitious of seeing his son on the bench instead of a cart, before he died. So he sent him to my office as student at law, errand boy, and cleaner and sweeper, at the rate of one dollar a week. He had a little desk to himself, but he did not use it much. Upon inspection, the drawer exhibited a great array of the shells of various sorts of nuts. Indeed, to this quick-witted youth the whole noble science of the law was contained in a nutshell. Not the least among the employments of Ginger Nut, as well as one which he discharged with the most alacrity, was his duty as cake

---

1. Wine seller. 2. Driver of wagon or cart that hauls goods.

and apple purveyor for Turkey and Nippers. Copying law papers being proverbially a dry, husky sort of business, my two scriveners were fain to moisten their mouths very often with Spitzenbergs[3] to be had at the numerous stalls nigh the Custom House and Post Office. Also, they sent Ginger Nut very frequently for that peculiar cake—small, flat, round, and very spicy—after which he had been named by them. Of a cold morning when business was but dull, Turkey would gobble up scores of these cakes, as if they were mere wafers—indeed they sell them at the rate of six or eight for a penny—the scrape of his pen blending with the crunching of the crisp particles in his mouth. Of all the fiery afternoon blunders and flurried rashnesses of Turkey, was his once moistening a ginger-cake between his lips, and clapping it on to a mortgage for a seal. I came within an ace of dismissing him then. But he mollified me by making an oriental bow, and saying—"With submission, sir, it was generous of me to find you in[4] stationery on my own account."

15   Now my original business—that of a conveyancer and title hunter,[5] and drawer-up of recondite documents of all sorts—was considerably increased by receiving the master's office. There was now great work for scriveners. Not only must I push the clerks already with me, but I must have additional help. In answer to my advertisement, a motionless young man one morning stood upon my office threshold, the door being open, for it was summer. I can see that figure now—pallidly neat, pitiably respectable, incurably forlorn! It was Bartleby.

After a few words touching his qualifications, I engaged him, glad to have among my corps of copyists a man of so singularly sedate an aspect, which I thought might operate beneficially upon the flighty temper of Turkey, and the fiery one of Nippers.

I should have stated before that ground glass folding-doors divided my premises into two parts, one of which was occupied by my scriveners, the other by myself. According to my humor I threw open these doors, or closed them. I resolved to assign Bartleby a corner by the folding-doors, but on my side of them, so as to have this quiet man within easy call, in case any trifling thing was to be done. I placed his desk close up to a small side-window in that part of the room, a window which originally had afforded a lateral view of certain grimy backyards and bricks, but which, owing to subsequent erections, commanded at present no view at all, though it gave some light. Within three feet of the panes was a wall, and the light came down from far above, between two lofty buildings, as from a very small opening in a dome. Still further to a satisfactory arrangement, I procured a high green folding screen, which might entirely isolate Bartleby from my sight, though not remove him from my voice. And thus, in a manner, privacy and society were conjoined.

At first Bartleby did an extraordinary quantity of writing. As if long

---

3. Red-and-yellow American apple.   4. Supply you with.

5. Lawyer who draws up deeds for transferring property, and one who searches out legal control of title deeds.

famishing for something to copy, he seemed to gorge himself on my documents. There was no pause for digestion. He ran a day and night line, copying by sunlight and by candlelight. I should have been quite delighted with his application, had he been cheerfully industrious. But he wrote on silently, palely, mechanically.

It is, of course, an indispensable part of a scrivener's business to verify the accuracy of his copy, word by word. Where there are two or more scriveners in an office, they assist each other in this examination, one reading from the copy, the other holding the original. It is a very dull, wearisome, and lethargic affair. I can readily imagine that to some sanguine temperaments it would be altogether intolerable. For example, I cannot credit that the mettlesome poet Byron would have contentedly sat down with Bartleby to examine a law document of, say, five hundred pages, closely written in a crimpy hand.

Now and then, in the haste of business, it had been my habit to assist 20 in comparing some brief document myself, calling Turkey or Nippers for this purpose. One object I had in placing Bartleby so handy to me behind the screen, was to avail myself of his services on such trivial occasions. It was on the third day, I think, of his being with me, and before any necessity had arisen for having his own writing examined, that, being much hurried to complete a small affair I had in hand, I abruptly called to Bartleby. In my haste and natural expectancy of instant compliance, I sat with my head bent over the original on my desk, and my right hand sideways, and somewhat nervously extended with the copy, so that immediately upon emerging from his retreat, Bartleby might snatch it and proceed to business without the least delay.

In this very attitude did I sit when I called to him, rapidly stating what it was I wanted him to do—namely, to examine a small paper with me. Imagine my surprise, nay, my consternation, when without moving from his privacy, Bartleby, in a singularly mild, firm voice, replied, "I would prefer not to."

I sat awhile in perfect silence, rallying my stunned faculties. Immediately it occurred to me that my ears had deceived me, or Bartleby had entirely misunderstood my meaning. I repeated my request in the clearest tone I could assume. But in quite as clear a one came the previous reply, "I would prefer not to."

"Prefer not to," echoed I, rising in high excitement, and crossing the room with a stride. "What do you mean? Are you moon-struck?[6] I want you to help me compare this sheet here—take it," and I thrust it towards him.

"I would prefer not to," said he.

I looked at him steadfastly. His face was leanly composed; his gray eye 25 dimly calm. Not a wrinkle of agitation rippled him. Had there been the least uneasiness, anger, impatience or impertinence in his manner; in other words, had there been anything ordinarily human about him, doubtless I

6. Crazy.

should have violently dismissed him from the premises. But as it was, I should have as soon thought of turning my pale plaster-of-paris bust of Cicero[7] out-of-doors. I stood gazing at him awhile, as he went on with his own writing, and then reseated myself at my desk. This is very strange, thought I. What had one best do? But my business hurried me. I concluded to forget the matter for the present, reserving it for my future leisure. So calling Nippers from the other room, the paper was speedily examined.

A few days after this, Bartleby concluded four lengthy documents, being quadruplicates of a week's testimony taken before me in my High Court of Chancery. It became necessary to examine them. It was an important suit, and great accuracy was imperative. Having all things arranged I called Turkey, Nippers and Ginger Nut from the next room, meaning to place the four copies in the hands of my four clerks, while I should read from the original. Accordingly Turkey, Nippers and Ginger Nut had taken their seats in a row, each with his document in hand, when I called to Bartleby to join this interesting group.

"Bartleby! quick, I am waiting."

I heard a slow scrape of his chair legs on the uncarpeted floor, and soon he appeared standing at the entrance of his hermitage.

"What is wanted?" said he mildly.

"The copies, the copies," said I hurriedly. "We are going to examine them. There"—and I held towards him the fourth quadruplicate.

"I would prefer not to," he said, and gently disappeared behind the screen.

For a few moments I was turned into a pillar of salt,[8] standing at the head of my seated column of clerks. Recovering myself, I advanced towards the screen, and demanded the reason for such extraordinary conduct.

"*Why* do you refuse?"

"I would prefer not to."

With any other man I should have flown outright into a dreadful passion, scorned all further words, and thrust him ignominiously from my presence. But there was something about Bartleby that not only strangely disarmed me, but in a wonderful manner touched and disconcerted me. I began to reason with him.

"These are your own copies we are about to examine. It is labor saving to you, because one examination will answer for your four papers. It is common usage. Every copyist is bound to help examine his copy. Is it not so? Will you not speak? Answer!"

"I prefer not to," he replied in a flute-like tone. It seemed to me that while I had been addressing him, he carefully revolved every statement that I made; fully comprehended the meaning; could not gainsay the irresistible

---

7. Marcus Tullius Cicero (106–43 B.C.E.), pro-republican Roman statesman, barrister, writer, and orator.

8. Struck dumb; in Genesis 19.26, Lot's wife, defying God's command, "looked back from behind him, and she became a pillar of salt."

conclusion; but, at the same time, some paramount consideration prevailed with him to reply as he did.

"You are decided, then, not to comply with my request—a request made according to common usage and common sense?"

He briefly gave me to understand that on that point my judgment was sound. Yes: his decision was irreversible.

It is not seldom the case that when a man is browbeaten in some unprec- 40 edented and violently unreasonable way, he begins to stagger in his own plainest faith. He begins, as it were, vaguely to surmise that, wonderful as it may be, all the justice and all the reason is on the other side. Accordingly, if any disinterested persons are present, he turns to them for some rein-forcement for his own faltering mind.

"Turkey," said I, "what do you think of this? Am I not right?"

"With submission, sir," said Turkey, with his blandest tone, "I think that you are."

"Nippers," said I, "what do *you* think of it?"

"I think I should kick him out of the office."

(The reader of nice perceptions will here perceive that, it being morning, 45 Turkey's answer is couched in polite and tranquil terms, but Nippers replies in ill-tempered ones. Or, to repeat a previous sentence, Nippers's ugly mood was on duty, and Turkey's off.)

"Ginger Nut," said I, willing to enlist the smallest suffrage[9] in my behalf, "what do *you* think of it?"

"I think, sir, he's a little *luny*," replied Ginger Nut, with a grin.

"You hear what they say," said I, turning towards the screen, "come forth and do your duty."

But he vouchsafed no reply. I pondered a moment in sore perplexity. But once more business hurried me. I determined again to postpone the consideration of this dilemma to my future leisure. With a little trouble we made out to examine the papers without Bartleby, though at every page or two, Turkey deferentially dropped his opinion that this proceeding was quite out of the common; while Nippers, twitching in his chair with a dyspeptic nervousness, ground out between his set teeth occasional hissing maledictions against the stubborn oaf behind the screen. And for his (Nip-pers's) part, this was the first and the last time he would do another man's business without pay.

Meanwhile Bartleby sat in his hermitage, oblivious to everything but his 50 own peculiar business there.

Some days passed, the scrivener being employed upon another lengthy work. His late remarkable conduct led me to regard his ways narrowly. I observed that he never went to dinner; indeed that he never went anywhere. As yet I had never of my personal knowledge known him to be outside of my office. He was a perpetual sentry in the corner. At about eleven o'clock though, in the morning, I noticed that Ginger Nut would advance toward the opening in Bartleby's screen, as if silently beckoned thither by a gesture

9. Favorable vote.

invisible to me where I sat. The boy would then leave the office jingling a few pence, and reappear with a handful of ginger-nuts which he delivered in the hermitage, receiving two of the cakes for his trouble.

He lives, then, on ginger-nuts, thought I; never eats a dinner, properly speaking; he must be a vegetarian then; but no; he never eats even vegetables, he eats nothing but ginger-nuts. My mind then ran on in reveries concerning the probable effects upon the human constitution of living entirely on ginger-nuts. Ginger-nuts are so called because they contain ginger as one of their peculiar constituents, and the final flavoring one. Now what was ginger? A hot, spicy thing. Was Bartleby hot and spicy? Not at all. Ginger, then, had no effect upon Bartleby. Probably he preferred it should have none.

Nothing so aggravates an earnest person as a passive resistance. If the individual so resisted be of a not inhumane temper, and the resisting one perfectly harmless in his passivity; then, in the better moods of the former, he will endeavor charitably to construe to his imagination what proves impossible to be solved by his judgment. Even so, for the most part, I regarded Bartleby and his ways. Poor fellow! thought I, he means no mischief; it is plain he intends no insolence; his aspect sufficiently evinces that his eccentricities are involuntary. He is useful to me. I can get along with him. If I turn him away, the chances are he will fall in with some less indulgent employer, and then he will be rudely treated, and perhaps driven forth miserably to starve. Yes. Here I can cheaply purchase a delicious self-approval. To befriend Bartleby; to humor him in his strange wilfulness, will cost me little or nothing, while I lay up in my soul what will eventually prove a sweet morsel for my conscience. But this mood was not invariable with me. The passiveness of Bartleby sometimes irritated me. I felt strangely goaded on to encounter him in new opposition, to elicit some angry spark from him answerable to my own. But indeed I might as well have essayed to strike fire with my knuckles against a bit of Windsor soap.[1] But one afternoon the evil impulse in me mastered me, and the following little scene ensued:

"Bartleby," said I, "when those papers are all copied, I will compare them with you."

55   "I would prefer not to."

"How? Surely you do not mean to persist in that mulish vagary?"

No answer.

I threw open the folding-doors near by, and turning upon Turkey and Nippers, exclaimed in an excited manner—

"He says, a second time, he won't examine his papers. What do you think of it, Turkey?"

60   It was afternoon, be it remembered. Turkey sat glowing like a brass boiler, his bald head steaming, his hands reeling among his blotted papers.

"Think of it?" roared Turkey; "I think I'll just step behind his screen, and black his eyes for him!"

So saying, Turkey rose to his feet and threw his arms into a pugilistic

---

1. Scented soap, usually brown.

position. He was hurrying away to make good his promise, when I detained him, alarmed at the effect of incautiously rousing Turkey's combativeness after dinner.

"Sit down, Turkey," said I, "and hear what Nippers has to say. What do you think of it, Nippers? Would I not be justified in immediately dismissing Bartleby?"

"Excuse me, that is for you to decide, sir. I think his conduct quite unusual, and indeed unjust, as regards Turkey and myself. But it may only be a passing whim."

"Ah," exclaimed I, "you have strangely changed your mind then—you speak very gently of him now." 65

"All beer," cried Turkey; "gentleness is effects of beer—Nippers and I dined together today. You see how gentle *I* am, sir. Shall I go and black his eyes?"

"You refer to Bartleby, I suppose. No, not today, Turkey," I replied; "pray, put up your fists."

I closed the doors, and again advanced towards Bartleby. I felt additional incentives tempting me to my fate. I burned to be rebelled against again. I remembered that Bartleby never left the office.

"Bartleby," said I, "Ginger Nut is away; just step round to the Post Office, won't you? (it was but a three minutes' walk,) and see if there is anything for me."

"I would prefer not to." 70

"You *will* not?"

"I *prefer* not."

I staggered to my desk, and sat there in a deep study. My blind inveteracy returned. Was there any other thing in which I could procure myself to be ignominiously repulsed by this lean, penniless wight?—my hired clerk? What added thing is there, perfectly reasonable, that he will be sure to refuse to do?

"Bartleby!"

No answer. 75

"Bartleby," in a louder tone.

No answer.

"Bartleby," I roared.

Like a very ghost, agreeably to the laws of magical invocation, at the third summons, he appeared at the entrance of his hermitage.

"Go to the next room, and tell Nippers to come to me." 80

"I prefer not to," he respectfully and slowly said, and mildly disappeared.

"Very good, Bartleby," said I, in a quiet sort of serenely severe self-possessed tone, intimating the unalterable purpose of some terrible retribution very close at hand. At the moment I half intended something of the kind. But upon the whole, as it was drawing towards my dinner-hour, I thought it best to put on my hat and walk home for the day, suffering much from perplexity and distress of mind.

Shall I acknowledge it? The conclusion of this whole business was, that it soon became a fixed fact of my chambers, that a pale young scrivener, by the name of Bartleby, had a desk there; that he copied for me at the

usual rate of four cents a folio (one hundred words); but he was permanently exempt from examining the work done by him, that duty being
transferred to Turkey and Nippers, one of compliment doubtless to their
superior acuteness; moreover, said Bartleby was never on any account to
be dispatched on the most trivial errand of any sort; and that even if
entreated to take upon him such a matter, it was generally understood that
he would prefer not to—in other words, that he would refuse point-blank.

As days passed on, I became considerably reconciled to Bartleby. His
steadiness, his freedom from all dissipation, his incessant industry (except
when he chose to throw himself into a standing revery behind his screen),
his great stillness, his unalterableness of demeanor under all circumstances,
made him a valuable acquisition. One prime thing was this,—*he was always
there;*—first in the morning, continually through the day, and the last at
night. I had a singular confidence in his honesty. I felt my most precious
papers perfectly safe in his hands. Sometimes to be sure I could not, for
the very soul of me, avoid falling into sudden spasmodic passions with
him. For it was exceeding difficult to bear in mind all the time those strange
peculiarities, privileges, and unheard of exemptions, forming the tacit stip-
ulations on Bartleby's part under which he remained in my office. Now
and then, in the eagerness of dispatching pressing business, I would inad-
vertently summon Bartleby, in a short, rapid tone, to put his finger, say,
on the incipient tie of a bit of red tape with which I was about compressing
some papers. Of course, from behind the screen the usual answer, "I prefer
not to," was sure to come; and then, how could a human creature with the
common infirmities of our nature, refrain from bitterly exclaiming upon
such perverseness—such unreasonableness? However, every added repulse
of this sort which I received only tended to lessen the probability of my
repeating the inadvertence.

85   Here it must be said, that according to the custom of most legal gentlemen occupying chambers in densely-populated law buildings, there were
several keys to my door. One was kept by a woman residing in the attic,
which person weekly scrubbed and daily swept and dusted my apartments.
Another was kept by Turkey for convenience sake. The third I sometimes
carried in my own pocket. The fourth I knew not who had.

Now, one Sunday morning I happened to go to Trinity Church, to hear
a celebrated preacher, and finding myself rather early on the ground, I
thought I would walk round to my chambers for a while. Luckily I had my
key with me; but upon applying it to the lock, I found it resisted by something inserted from the inside. Quite surprised, I called out; when to my
consternation a key was turned from within; and thrusting his lean visage
at me, and holding the door ajar, the apparition of Bartleby appeared, in
his shirt sleeves, and otherwise in a strangely tattered dishabille, saying
quietly that he was sorry, but he was deeply engaged just then, and—preferred not admitting me at present. In a brief word or two, he moreover
added, that perhaps I had better walk round the block two or three times,
and by that time he would probably have concluded his affairs.

Now, the utterly unsurmised appearance of Bartleby, tenanting my law-
chambers of a Sunday morning, with his cadaverously gentlemanly *noncha-*

lance, yet withal firm and self-possessed, had such a strange effect upon me, that incontinently I slunk away from my own door, and did as desired. But not without sundry twinges of impotent rebellion against the mild effrontery of this unaccountable scrivener. Indeed, it was his wonderful mildness, chiefly, which not only disarmed me, but unmanned me, as it were. For I consider that one, for the time, is sort of unmanned when he tranquilly permits his hired clerk to dictate to him, and order him away from his own premises. Furthermore, I was full of uneasiness as to what Bartleby could possibly be doing in my office in his shirt sleeves, and in an otherwise dismantled condition of a Sunday morning. Was anything amiss going on? Nay, that was out of the question. It was not to be thought of for a moment that Bartleby was an immoral person. But what could he be doing there?—copying? Nay again, whatever might be his eccentricities, Bartleby was an eminently decorous person. He would be the last man to sit down to his desk in any state approaching to nudity. Besides, it was Sunday; and there was something about Bartleby that forbade the supposition that he would by any secular occupation violate the proprieties of the day.

Nevertheless, my mind was not pacified; and full of a restless curiosity, at last I returned to the door. Without hindrance I inserted my key, opened it, and entered. Bartleby was not to be seen. I looked round anxiously, peeped behind his screen; but it was very plain that he was gone. Upon more closely examining the place, I surmised that for an indefinite period Bartleby must have ate, dressed, and slept in my office, and that too without plate, mirror, or bed. The cushioned seat of a ricketty old sofa in one corner bore the faint impress of a lean, reclining form. Rolled away under his desk, I found a blanket under the empty grate, a blacking box[2] and brush; on a chair, a tin basin, with soap and a ragged towel; in a newspaper a few crumbs of ginger-nuts and a morsel of cheese. Yes, thought I, it is evident enough that Bartleby has been making his home here, keeping bachelor's hall all by himself. Immediately then the thought came sweeping across me, What miserable friendlessness and loneliness are here revealed! His poverty is great; but his solitude, how horrible! Think of it. Of a Sunday, Wall Street is deserted as Petra;[3] and every night of every day it is an emptiness. This building too, which of weekdays hums with industry and life, at nightfall echoes with sheer vacancy, and all through Sunday is forlorn. And here Bartleby makes his home; sole spectator of a solitude which he has seen all populous—a sort of innocent and transformed Marius brooding among the ruins of Carthage![4]

For the first time in my life a feeling of overpowering stinging melan-

---

2. Box of black shoe polish.   3. Once a flourishing Middle Eastern trade center, long in ruins.
4. Gaius (or Caius) Marius (157–86 B.C.E.), Roman consul and general, expelled from Rome in 88 B.C.E. by Sulla; when an officer of Sextilius, the governor, forbade him to land in Africa, Marius replied, "Go tell him that you have seen Caius Marius sitting in exile among the ruins of Carthage," applying the example of the fortune of that city to the change of his own condition. The image was so common that a few years after "Bartleby," Dickens apologizes for using it: "like that lumbering Marius among the ruins of Carthage, who has sat heavy on a thousand millions of similes" ("The Calais Night-Mail," in *The Uncommercial Traveler*).

choly seized me. Before, I had never experienced aught but a not-unpleasing sadness. The bond of a common humanity now drew me irresistibly to gloom. A fraternal melancholy! For both I and Bartleby were sons of Adam. I remembered the bright silks and sparkling faces I had seen that day, in gala trim, swan-like sailing down the Mississippi of Broadway; and I contrasted them with the pallid copyist, and thought to myself, Ah, happiness courts the light, so we deem the world is gay; but misery hides aloof, so we deem that misery there is none. These sad fancyings—chimeras, doubtless, of a sick and silly brain—led on to other and more special thoughts, concerning the eccentricities of Bartleby. Presentiments of strange discoveries hovered round me. The scrivener's pale form appeared to me laid out, among uncaring strangers, in its shivering winding sheet.

90   Suddenly I was attracted by Bartleby's closed desk, the key in open sight left in the lock.

I mean no mischief, seek the gratification of no heartless curiosity, thought I; besides, the desk is mine, and its contents too, so I will make bold to look within. Everything was methodically arranged, the papers smoothly placed. The pigeonholes were deep, and removing the files of documents, I groped into their recesses. Presently I felt something there, and dragged it out. It was an old bandanna handkerchief, heavy and knotted. I opened it, and saw it was a savings' bank.

I now recalled all the quiet mysteries which I had noted in the man. I remembered that he never spoke but to answer; that though at intervals he had considerable time to himself, yet I had never seen him reading—no, not even a newspaper; that for long periods he would stand looking out, at his pale window behind the screen, upon the dead brick wall; I was quite sure he never visited any refectory or eating house; while his pale face clearly indicated that he never drank beer like Turkey, or tea and coffee even, like other men; that he never went anywhere in particular that I could learn; never went out for a walk, unless indeed that was the case at present; that he had declined telling who he was, or whence he came, or whether he had any relatives in the world; that though so thin and pale, he never complained of ill health. And more than all, I remembered a certain unconscious air of pallid—how shall I call it?—of pallid haughtiness, say, or rather an austere reserve about him, which had positively awed me into my tame compliance with his eccentricities, when I had feared to ask him to do the slightest incidental thing for me, even though I might know, from his long-continued motionlessness, that behind his screen he must be standing in one of those dead-wall reveries of his.

Revolving all these things, and coupling them with the recently discovered fact that he made my office his constant abiding place and home, and not forgetful of his morbid moodiness; revolving all these things, a prudential feeling began to steal over me. My first emotions had been those of pure melancholy and sincerest pity; but just in proportion as the forlornness of Bartleby grew and grew to my imagination, did that same melancholy merge into fear, that pity into repulsion. So true it is, and so terrible too, that up to a certain point the thought or sight of misery enlists our best affections; but, in certain special cases, beyond that point it does not. They err who would assert that invariably this is owing to the inherent selfishness of the human heart. It rather proceeds from a certain hopelessness of remedying excessive and organic ill. To a sensitive being, pity is not seldom pain. And when at last it is perceived that such pity cannot lead to effectual succor, common sense bids the soul be rid of it. What I saw that morning persuaded me that the scrivener was the victim of innate and incurable disorder. I might give alms to his body; but his body did not pain him; it was his soul that suffered, and his soul I could not reach.

I did not accomplish the purpose of going to Trinity Church that morning. Somehow, the things I had seen disqualified me for the time from churchgoing. I walked homeward, thinking what I would do with Bartleby. Finally, I resolved upon this;—I would put certain calm questions to him the next morning, touching his history, &c., and if he declined to answer them openly and unreservedly (and I supposed he would prefer not), then to give him a twenty-dollar bill over and above whatever I might owe him, and tell him his services were no longer required; but that if in any other way I could assist him, I would be happy to do so, especially if he desired to return to his native place, wherever that might be, I would willingly help to defray the expenses. Moreover, if, after reaching home, he found himself at any time in want of aid, a letter from him would be sure of a reply.

The next morning came. 95

"Bartleby," said I, gently calling to him behind his screen.

No reply.

"Bartleby," said I, in a still gentler tone, "come here; I am not going to ask you to do anything you would prefer not to do—I simply wish to speak to you."

Upon this he noiselessly slid into view.

"Will you tell me, Bartleby, where you were born?" 100

"I would prefer not to."

"Will you tell me *anything* about yourself?"

"I would prefer not to."

"But what reasonable objection can you have to speak to me? I feel friendly towards you."

He did not look at me while I spoke, but kept his glance fixed upon my 105 bust of Cicero, which as I then sat, was directly behind me, some six inches above my head.

"What is your answer, Bartleby?" said I, after waiting a considerable time for a reply, during which his countenance remained immovable, only there was the faintest conceivable tremor of the white attenuated mouth.

"At present I prefer to give no answer," he said, and retired into his hermitage.

It was rather weak in me I confess, but his manner on this occasion nettled me. Not only did there seem to lurk in it a certain calm disdain, but his perverseness seemed ungrateful, considering the undeniable good usage and indulgence he had received from me.

Again I sat ruminating what I should do. Mortified as I was at his behavior, and resolved as I had been to dismiss him when I entered my office, nevertheless I strangely felt something superstitious knocking at my heart, and forbidding me to carry out my purpose, and denouncing me for a villain if I dared to breathe one bitter word against this forlornest of mankind. At last, familiarly drawing my chair behind his screen, I sat down and said: "Bartleby, never mind then about revealing your history; but let me entreat you, as a friend, to comply as far as may be with the usages of this office. Say now you will help to examine papers tomorrow or next day: in short, say now that in a day or two you will begin to be a little reasonable: —say so, Bartleby."

110   "At present I would prefer not to be a little reasonable," was his mildly cadaverous reply.

Just then the folding-doors opened, and Nippers approached. He seemed suffering from an unusually bad night's rest, induced by severer indigestion than common. He overheard those final words of Bartleby.

"*Prefer not*, eh?" gritted Nippers—"I'd *prefer* him, if I were you, sir," addressing me—"I'd *prefer* him; I'd give him preferences, the stubborn mule! What is it, sir, pray, that he *prefers* not to do now?"

Bartleby moved not a limb.

"Mr. Nippers," said I, "I'd prefer that you would withdraw for the present."

115   Somehow, of late I had got into the way of involuntarily using this word "prefer" upon all sorts of not exactly suitable occasions. And I trembled to think that my contact with the scrivener had already and seriously affected me in a mental way. And what further and deeper aberration might it not yet produce? This apprehension had not been without efficacy in determining me to summary means.

As Nippers, looking very sour and sulky, was departing, Turkey blandly and deferentially approached.

"With submission, sir," said he, "yesterday I was thinking about Bartleby here, and I think that if he would but prefer to take a quart of good ale every day, it would do much towards mending him and enabling him to assist in examining his papers."

"So you have got the word too," said I, slightly excited.

"With submission, what word, sir?" asked Turkey, respectfully crowding himself into the contracted space behind the screen, and by so doing making me jostle the scrivener. "What word, sir?"

120   "I would prefer to be left alone here," said Bartleby, as if offended at being mobbed in his privacy.

"*That's* the word, Turkey," said I—"*that's* it."

"Oh, *prefer*? oh yes—queer word. I never use it myself. But, sir, as I was saying, if he would but prefer—"

"Turkey," interrupted I, "you will please withdraw."

"Oh certainly, sir, if you prefer that I should."

125   As he opened the folding-door to retire, Nippers at his desk caught a glimpse of me, and asked whether I would prefer to have a certain paper copied on blue paper or white. He did not in the least roguishly accent the

word *prefer*. It was plain that it involuntarily rolled from his tongue. I thought to myself, surely I must get rid of a demented man, who already has in some degree turned the tongues, if not the heads of myself and clerks. But I thought it prudent not to break the dismission at once.

The next day I noticed that Bartleby did nothing but stand at his window in his dead-wall revery. Upon asking him why he did not write, he said that he had decided upon doing no more writing.

"Why, how now? what next?" exclaimed I, "do no more writing?"

"No more."

"And what is the reason?"

"Do you not see the reason for yourself," he indifferently replied.   130

I looked steadfastly at him, and perceived that his eyes looked dull and glazed. Instantly it occurred to me, that his unexampled diligence in copying by his dim window for the first few weeks of his stay with me might have temporarily impaired his vision.

I was touched. I said something in condolence with him. I hinted that of course he did wisely in abstaining from writing for a while; and urged him to embrace that opportunity of taking wholesome exercise in the open air. This, however, he did not do. A few days after this, my other clerks being absent, and being in a great hurry to dispatch certain letters by the mail, I thought that, having nothing else earthly to do, Bartleby would surely be less inflexible than usual, and carry these letters to the post office. But he blankly declined. So, much to my inconvenience, I went myself.

Still added days went by. Whether Bartleby's eyes improved or not, I could not say. To all appearance, I thought they did. But when I asked him if they did, he vouchsafed no answer. At all events, he would do no copying. At last, in reply to my urgings, he informed me that he had permanently given up copying.

"What!" exclaimed I; "suppose your eyes should get entirely well—better than ever before—would you not copy then?"

"I have given up copying," he answered, and slid aside.   135

He remained, as ever, a fixture in my chamber. Nay—if that were possible—he became still more of a fixture than before. What was to be done? He would do nothing in the office: why should he stay there? In plain fact, he had now become a millstone[5] to me, not only useless as a necklace, but afflictive to bear. Yet I was sorry for him. I speak less than truth when I say that, on his own account, he occasioned me uneasiness. If he would but have named a single relative or friend, I would instantly have written, and urged their taking the poor fellow away to some convenient retreat. But he seemed alone, absolutely alone in the universe. A bit of wreck in the mid-Atlantic. At length, necessities connected with my business tyrannized over all other considerations. Decently as I could, I told Bartleby that in six days' time he must unconditionally leave the office. I warned him to

---

5. Heavy stone for grinding grain. See Matthew 18.6: "But whoso shall offend one of these little ones which believe in me, it were better for him that a millstone were hanged about his neck, and that he were drowned in the depth of the sea."

take measures, in the interval, for procuring some other abode. I offered to assist him in this endeavor, if he himself would but take the first step towards a removal. "And when you finally quit me, Bartleby," added I, "I shall see that you go not away entirely unprovided. Six days from this hour, remember."

At the expiration of that period, I peeped behind the screen, and lo! Bartleby was there.

I buttoned up my coat, balanced myself; advanced slowly towards him, touched his shoulder, and said, "The time has come; you must quit this place; I am sorry for you; here is money; but you must go."

"I would prefer not," he replied, with his back still towards me.

"You *must*."

He remained silent.

Now I had an unbounded confidence in this man's common honesty. He had frequently restored to me sixpences and shillings[6] carelessly dropped upon the floor, for I am apt to be very reckless in such shirt-button affairs. The proceeding then which followed will not be deemed extraordinary.

"Bartleby," said I, "I owe you twelve dollars on account; here are thirty-two; the odd twenty are yours.—Will you take it?" and I handed the bills towards him.

But he made no motion.

"I will leave them here then," putting them under a weight on the table. Then taking my hat and cane and going to the door I tranquilly turned and added—"After you have removed your things from these offices, Bartleby, you will of course lock the door—since everyone is now gone for the day but you—and if you please, slip your key underneath the mat, so that I may have it in the morning. I shall not see you again; so good-bye to you. If hereafter in your new place of abode I can be of any service to you, do not fail to advise me by letter. Good-bye, Bartleby, and fare you well."

But he answered not a word; like the last column of some ruined temple, he remained standing mute and solitary in the middle of the otherwise deserted room.

As I walked home in a pensive mood, my vanity got the better of my pity. I could not but highly plume myself on my masterly management in getting rid of Bartleby. Masterly I call it, and such it must appear to any dispassionate thinker. The beauty of my procedure seemed to consist in its perfect quietness. There was no vulgar bullying, no bravado of any sort, no choleric hectoring, and striding to and fro across the apartment, jerking out vehement commands for Bartleby to bundle himself off with his beggarly traps.[7] Nothing of the kind. Without loudly bidding Bartleby depart—as an inferior genius might have done—I *assumed* the ground that depart he must; and upon that assumption built all I had to say. The more I thought over my procedure, the more I was charmed with it. Nevertheless, next morning, upon awakening, I had my doubts,—I had somehow slept

---

6. Coins.   7. Personal belongings, luggage.

off the fumes of vanity. One of the coolest and wisest hours a man has is just after he awakes in the morning. My procedure seemed as sagacious as ever,—but only in theory. How it would prove in practice—there was the rub. It was truly a beautiful thought to have assumed Bartleby's departure; but, after all, that assumption was simply my own, and none of Bartleby's. The great point was, not whether I had assumed that he would quit me, but whether he would prefer so to do. He was more a man of preferences than assumptions.

After breakfast, I walked downtown, arguing the probabilities *pro* and *con*. One moment I thought it would prove a miserable failure, and Bartleby would be found all alive at my office as usual; the next moment it seemed certain that I should see his chair empty. And so I kept veering about. At the corner of Broadway and Canal Street, I saw quite an excited group of people standing in earnest conversation.

"I'll take odds he doesn't," said a voice as I passed.

"Doesn't go?—done!" said I, "put up your money." 150

I was instinctively putting my hand in my pocket to produce my own, when I remembered that this was an election day. The words I had overheard bore no reference to Bartleby, but to the success or non-success of some candidate for the mayoralty. In my intent frame of mind, I had, as it were, imagined that all Broadway shared in my excitement, and were debating the same question with me. I passed on, very thankful that the uproar of the street screened my momentary absent-mindedness.

As I had intended, I was earlier than usual at my office door. I stood listening for a moment. All was still. He must be gone. I tried the knob. The door was locked. Yes, my procedure had worked to a charm; he indeed must be vanished. Yet a certain melancholy mixed with this: I was almost sorry for my brilliant success. I was fumbling under the door mat for the key, which Bartleby was to have left there for me, when accidentally my knee knocked against a panel, producing a summoning sound, and in response a voice came to me from within—"Not yet; I am occupied."

It was Bartleby.

I was thunderstruck. For an instant I stood like the man who, pipe in mouth, was killed one cloudless afternoon long ago in Virginia, by summer lightning; at his own warm open window he was killed, and remained leaning out there upon the dreamy afternoon, till some one touched him, when he fell.

"Not gone!" I murmured at last. But again obeying that wondrous ascen- 155 dancy which the inscrutable scrivener had over me, and from which ascendency, for all my chafing, I could not completely escape, I slowly went downstairs and out into the street, and while walking round the block, considered what I should next do in this unheard-of perplexity. Turn the man out by an actual thrusting I could not; to drive him away by calling him hard names would not do; calling in the police was an unpleasant idea; and yet, permit him to enjoy his cadaverous triumph over me,—this too I could not think of. What was to be done? or, if nothing could be done, was there anything further that I could *assume* in the matter? Yes, as before

I had prospectively assumed that Bartleby would depart, so now I might retrospectively assume that departed he was. In the legitimate carrying out of this assumption, I might enter my office in a great hurry, and pretending not to see Bartleby at all, walk straight against him as if he were air. Such a proceeding would in a singular degree have the appearance of a home-thrust.[8] It was hardly possible that Bartleby could withstand such an application of the doctrine of assumptions. But upon second thoughts the success of the plan seemed rather dubious. I resolved to argue the matter over with him again.

"Bartleby," said I, entering the office, with a quietly severe expression, "I am seriously displeased. I am pained, Bartleby. I had thought better of you. I had imagined you of such a gentlemanly organization, that in any delicate dilemma a slight hint would suffice—in short, an assumption. But it appears I am deceived. Why," I added, unaffectedly starting, "you have not even touched that money yet," pointing to it, just where I had left it the evening previous.

He answered nothing.

"Will you, or will you not, quit me?" I now demanded in a sudden passion, advancing close to him.

"I would prefer *not* to quit you," he replied, gently emphasizing the *not*.

160 "What earthly right have you to stay here? Do you pay any rent? Do you pay my taxes? Or is this property yours?"

He answered nothing.

"Are you ready to go on and write now? Are your eyes recovered? Could you copy a small paper for me this morning? or help examine a few lines? or step round to the post office? In a word, will you do anything at all, to give a coloring to your refusal to depart the premises?"

He silently retired into his hermitage.

I was now in such a state of nervous resentment that I thought it but prudent to check myself at present from further demonstrations. Bartleby and I were alone. I remembered the tragedy of the unfortunate Adams and the still more unfortunate Colt in the solitary office of the latter;[9] and how poor Colt, being dreadfully incensed by Adams, and imprudently permitting himself to get wildly excited, was at unawares hurried into his fatal act—an act which certainly no man could possibly deplore more than the actor himself. Often it had occurred to me in my ponderings upon the subject, that had that altercation taken place in the public street, or at a private residence, it would not have terminated as it did. It was the circumstance of being alone in a solitary office, up stairs, of a building entirely unhallowed by humanizing domestic associations—an uncarpeted office, doubtless, of a dusty, haggard sort of appearance;—this it must have been, which greatly helped to enhance the irritable desperation of the hapless Colt.

---

8. In fencing, a successful thrust to the opponent's body.
9. In 1841, John C. Colt, brother of the famous gunmaker, unintentionally killed Samuel Adams, a printer, when he hit him on the head during a fight.

But when this old Adam[1] of resentment rose in me and tempted me 165
concerning Bartleby, I grappled him and threw him. How? Why, simply by
recalling the divine injunction: "A new commandment[2] give I unto you,
that ye love one another." Yes, this it was that saved me. Aside from higher
considerations, charity often operates as a vastly wise and prudent principle—a great safeguard to its possessor. Men have committed murder for
jealousy's sake, and anger's sake, and hatred's sake, and selfishness' sake,
and spiritual pride's sake; but no man that ever I heard of, ever committed
a diabolical murder for sweet charity's sake. Mere self-interest, then, if no
better motive can be enlisted, should, especially with high-tempered men,
prompt all beings to charity and philanthropy. At any rate, upon the occasion in question, I strove to drown my exasperated feelings towards the
scrivener by benevolently construing his conduct. Poor fellow, poor fellow!
thought I, he don't mean anything; and besides, he has seen hard times,
and ought to be indulged.

I endeavored also immediately to occupy myself, and at the same time
to comfort my despondency. I tried to fancy that in the course of the
morning, at such time as might prove agreeable to him, Bartleby, of his
own free accord, would emerge from his hermitage, and take up some
decided line of march in the direction of the door. But no. Half-past twelve
o'clock came; Turkey began to glow in the face, overturn his inkstand, and
become generally obstreperous; Nippers abated down into quietude and
courtesy; Ginger Nut munched his noon apple; and Bartleby remained
standing at his window in one of his profoundest dead-wall reveries. Will
it be credited? Ought I to acknowledge it? That afternoon I left the office
without saying one further word to him.

Some days now passed, during which, at leisure intervals I looked a little
into "Edwards on the Will," and "Priestley on Necessity."[3] Under the circumstances, those books induced a salutary feeling. Gradually I slid into
the persuasion that these troubles of mine touching the scrivener, had been
all predestinated from eternity, and Bartleby was billeted upon me for some
mysterious purpose of an all-wise Providence, which it was not for a mere
mortal like me to fathom. Yes, Bartleby, stay there behind your screen,
thought I; I shall persecute you no more; you are harmless and noiseless
as any of these old chairs; in short, I never feel so private as when I know
you are here. At least I see it, I feel it; I penetrate to the predestinated

---

1. Sinful element in human nature, see e.g., "Invocation of Blessing on the Child," in the *Book of
Common Prayer:* "Grant that the old Adam in this child may be so buried, that the new man may
be raised up in him." Christ is sometimes called the "new Adam."
2. In John 13.34, where, however, the phrasing is "I give unto . . ."
3. Jonathan Edwards (1703–1758), New England Calvinist theologian and revivalist, in *The Freedom
of the Will* (1754), argued that human beings are not in fact free, for though they choose according
to the way they see things, that way is predetermined (by biography, environment, and character),
and they act out of personality rather than by will. Joseph Priestley (1733–1804), dissenting preacher,
scientist, grammarian, and philosopher, in *The Doctrine of Philosophical Necessity* (1777), argued that
free will is theologically objectionable, metaphysically incomprehensible, and morally undesirable.

purpose of my life. I am content. Others may have loftier parts to enact; but my mission in this world, Bartleby, is to furnish you with office-room for such period as you may see fit to remain.

I believe that this wise and blessed frame of mind would have continued with me, had it not been for the unsolicited and uncharitable remarks obtruded upon me by my professional friends who visited the rooms. But thus it often is, that the constant friction of illiberal minds wears out at last the best resolves of the more generous. Though to be sure, when I reflected upon it, it was not strange that people entering my office should be struck by the peculiar aspect of the unaccountable Bartleby, and so be tempted to throw out some sinister observations concerning him. Sometimes an attorney having business with me, and calling at my office, and finding no one but the scrivener there, would undertake to obtain some sort of precise information from him touching my whereabouts; but without heeding his idle talk, Bartleby would remain standing immovable in the middle of the room. So after contemplating him in that position for a time, the attorney would depart, no wiser than he came.

Also, when a Reference[4] was going on, and the room full of lawyers and witnesses and business was driving fast; some deeply occupied legal gentleman present, seeing Bartleby wholly unemployed, would request him to run round to his (the legal gentleman's) office and fetch some papers for him. Thereupon, Bartleby would tranquilly decline, and yet remain idle as before. Then the lawyer would give a great stare, and turn to me. And what could I say? At last I was made aware that all through the circle of my professional acquaintance, a whisper of wonder was running round, having reference to the strange creature I kept at my office. This worried me very much. And as the idea came upon me of his possibly turning out a long-lived man, and keep occupying my chambers, and denying my authority; and perplexing my visitors; and scandalizing my professional reputation; and casting a general gloom over the premises; keeping soul and body together to the last upon his savings (for doubtless he spent but half a dime a day), and in the end perhaps outlive me, and claim possession of my office by right of his perpetual occupancy: as all these dark anticipations crowded upon me more and more, and my friends continually intruded their relentless remarks upon the apparition in my room; a great change was wrought in me. I resolved to gather all my faculties together, and forever rid me of this intolerable incubus.[5]

170   Ere revolving any complicated project, however, adapted to this end, I first simply suggested to Bartleby the propriety of his permanent departure. In a calm and serious tone, I commended the idea to his careful and mature consideration. But having taken three days to meditate upon it, he apprised me that his original determination remained the same; in short, that he still preferred to abide with me.

What shall I do? I now said to myself, buttoning up my coat to the last button. What shall I do? what ought I to do? what does conscience say I

4. Consultation or committee meeting.   5. Evil spirit.

should do with this man, or rather ghost. Rid myself of him, I must; go, he shall. But how? You will not thrust him, the poor, pale, passive mortal,—you will not thrust such a helpless creature out of your door? you will not dishonor yourself by such cruelty? No, I will not, I cannot do that. Rather would I let him live and die here, and then mason up his remains in the wall. What then will you do? For all your coaxing, he will not budge. Bribes he leaves under your own paperweight on your table; in short, it is quite plain that he prefers to cling to you.

Then something severe, something unusual must be done. What! surely you will not have him collared by a constable, and commit his innocent pallor to the common jail? And upon what ground could you procure such a thing to be done?—a vagrant, is he? What! he a vagrant, a wanderer, who refuses to budge? It is because he will *not* be a vagrant, then, that you seek to count him *as* a vagrant. That is too absurd. No visible means of support: there I have him. Wrong again: for indubitably he *does* support himself, and that is the only unanswerable proof that any man can show of his possessing the means so to do. No more then. Since he will not quit me, I must quit him. I will change my offices; I will move elsewhere; and give him fair notice, that if I find him on my new premises I will then proceed against him as a common trespasser.

Acting accordingly, next day I thus addressed him: "I find these chambers too far from the City Hall; the air is unwholesome. In a word, I propose to remove my offices next week, and shall no longer require your services. I tell you this now, in order that you may seek another place."

He made no reply, and nothing more was said.

On the appointed day I engaged carts and men, proceeded to my chambers, and having but little furniture, everything was removed in a few hours. Throughout, the scrivener remained standing behind the screen, which I directed to be removed the last thing. It was withdrawn; and being folded up like a huge folio, left him the motionless occupant of a naked room. I stood in the entry watching him a moment, while something from within me upbraided me.

I re-entered, with my hand in my pocket—and—and my heart in my mouth.

"Good-bye, Bartleby; I am going—good-bye, and God some way bless you; and take that," slipping something in his hand. But it dropped upon the floor, and then,—strange to say—I tore myself from him whom I had so longed to be rid of.

Established in my new quarters, for a day or two I kept the door locked, and started at every footfall in the passages. When I returned to my rooms after any little absence, I would pause at the threshold for an instant, and attentively listen, ere applying my key. But these fears were needless. Bartleby never came nigh me.

I thought all was going well, when a perturbed-looking stranger visited me, inquiring whether I was the person who had recently occupied rooms at No. —— Wall Street.

Full of forebodings, I replied that I was.

"Then sir," said the stranger, who proved a lawyer, "you are responsible for the man you left there. He refuses to do any copying; he refuses to do anything; he says he prefers not to; and he refuses to quit the premises."

"I am very sorry, sir," said I, with assumed tranquillity, but an inward tremor, "but, really, the man you allude to is nothing to me—he is no relation or apprentice of mine, that you should hold me responsible for him."

"In mercy's name, who is he?"

"I certainly cannot inform you. I know nothing about him. Formerly I employed him as a copyist; but he has done nothing for me now for some time past."

185   "I shall settle him then,—good morning, sir."

Several days passed, and I heard nothing more; and though I often felt a charitable prompting to call at the place and see poor Bartleby, yet a certain squeamishness of I know not what withheld me.

All is over with him, by this time, thought I at last, when through another week no further intelligence reached me. But coming to my room the day after, I found several persons waiting at my door in a high state of nervous excitement.

"That's the man—here he comes," cried the foremost one, whom I recognized as the lawyer who had previously called upon me alone.

"You must take him away, sir, at once," cried a portly person among them, advancing upon me, and whom I knew to be the landlord of No. —— Wall Street. "These gentlemen, my tenants, cannot stand it any longer; Mr. B——" pointing to the lawyer, "has turned him out of his room, and he now persists in haunting the building generally, sitting upon the banisters of the stairs by day, and sleeping in the entry by night. Everybody is concerned; clients are leaving the offices; some fears are entertained of a mob; something you must do, and that without delay."

190   Aghast at this torrent, I fell back before it, and would fain have locked myself in my new quarters. In vain I persisted that Bartleby was nothing to me—no more than to anyone else. In vain:—I was the last person known to have anything to do with him, and they held me to the terrible account. Fearful then of being exposed in the papers (as one person present obscurely threatened) I considered the matter, and at length said, that if the lawyer would give me a confidential interview with the scrivener, in his (the lawyer's) own room, I would that afternoon strive my best to rid them of the nuisance they complained of.

Going upstairs to my old haunt, there was Bartleby silently sitting upon the banister at the landing.

"What are you doing here, Bartleby?" said I.

"Sitting upon the banister," he mildly replied.

I motioned him into the lawyer's room, who then left us.

195   "Bartleby," said I, "are you aware that you are the cause of great tribulation to me, by persisting in occupying the entry after being dismissed from the office?"

No answer.

"Now one of two things must take place. Either you must do something, or something must be done to you. Now what sort of business would you like to engage in? Would you like to re-engage in copying for someone?"

"No; I would prefer not to make any change."

"Would you like a clerkship in a drygoods store?"

"There is too much confinement about that. No, I would not like a 200 clerkship; but I am not particular."

"Too much confinement," I cried, "why you keep yourself confined all the time!"

"I would prefer not to take a clerkship," he rejoined, as if to settle that little item at once.

"How would a bartender's business suit you? There is no trying of the eyesight in that."

"I would not like it at all; though, as I said before, I am not particular."

His unwonted wordiness inspirited me. I returned to the charge. 205

"Well then, would you like to travel through the country collecting bills for the merchants? That would improve your health."

"No, I would prefer to be doing something else."

"How then would going as a companion to Europe, to entertain some young gentleman with your conversation,—how would that suit you?"

"Not at all. It does not strike me that there is anything definite about that. I like to be stationary. But I am not particular."

"Stationary you shall be then," I cried, now losing all patience, and for 210 the first time in all my exasperating connection with him fairly flying into a passion. "If you do not go away from these premises before night, I shall feel bound—indeed I *am* bound—to—to—to quit the premises myself!" I rather absurdly concluded, knowing not with what possible threat to try to frighten his immobility into compliance. Despairing of all further efforts, I was precipitately leaving him, when a final thought occurred to me—one which had not been wholly unindulged before.

"Bartleby," said I, in the kindest tone I could assume under such exciting circumstances, "will you go home with me now—not to my office, but my dwelling—and remain there till we can conclude upon some convenient arrangement for you at our leisure? Come, let us start now, right away."

"No: at present I would prefer not to make any change at all."

I answered nothing; but effectually dodging everyone by the suddenness and rapidity of my flight, rushed from the building, ran up Wall Street toward Broadway, and jumping into the first omnibus was soon removed from pursuit. As soon as tranquillity returned I distinctly perceived that I had now done all that I possibly could, both in respect to the demands of the landlord and his tenants, and with regard to my own desire and sense of duty, to benefit Bartleby, and shield him from rude persecution. I now strove to be entirely carefree and quiescent; and my conscience justified me in the attempt; though indeed it was not so successful as I could have wished. So fearful was I of being again hunted out by the incensed landlord and his exasperated tenants, that, surrendering my business to Nippers, for a few days I drove about the upper part of the town and through the suburbs, in my rockaway;[6] crossed over to Jersey City and Hoboken, and paid fugitive visits to Manhattanville and Astoria. In fact I almost lived in my rockaway for the time.

When again I entered my office, lo, a note from the landlord lay upon the desk. I opened it with trembling hands. It informed me that the writer had sent to the police, and had Bartleby removed to the Tombs as a vagrant. Moreover, since I knew more about him than anyone else, he wished me to appear at that place, and make a suitable statement of the facts. These tidings had a conflicting effect upon me. At first I was indignant; but at last almost approved. The landlord's energetic, summary disposition had led him to adopt a procedure which I do not think I would have decided upon myself; and yet as a last resort, under such peculiar circumstances, it seemed the only plan.

215   As I afterwards learned, the poor scrivener, when told that he must be conducted to the Tombs, offered not the slightest obstacle, but in his pale unmoving way, silently acquiesced.

Some of the compassionate and curious bystanders joined the party; and headed by one of the constables arm in arm with Bartleby, the silent procession filed its way through all the noise, and heat, and joy of the roaring thoroughfares at noon.

The same day I received the note I went to the Tombs, or to speak more properly, the Halls of Justice. Seeking the right officer, I stated the purpose of my call, and was informed that the individual I described was indeed within. I then assured the functionary that Bartleby was a perfectly honest man, and greatly to be compassionated, however unaccountably eccentric. I narrated all I knew, and closed by suggesting the idea of letting him remain in as indulgent confinement as possible till something less harsh might be done—though indeed I hardly knew what. At all events, if nothing else could be decided upon, the alms-house must receive him. I then begged to have an interview.

Being under no disgraceful charge, and quite serene and harmless in all his ways, they had permitted him freely to wander about the prison, and especially in the inclosed grass-platted yards thereof. And so I found him there, standing all alone in the quietest of the yards, his face towards a high wall, while all around, from the narrow slits of the jail windows, I thought I saw peering out upon him the eyes of murderers and thieves.

"Bartleby!"

220   "I know you," he said, without looking round,—"and I want nothing to say to you."

"It was not I that brought you here, Bartleby," said I, keenly pained at his implied suspicion. "And to you, this should not be so vile a place. Nothing reproachful attaches to you by being here. And see, it is not so sad a place as one might think. Look, there is the sky, and here is the grass."

"I know where I am," he replied, but would say nothing more, and so I left him.

6. A light, four-wheeled carriage.

As I entered the corridor again, a broad meat-like man, in an apron, accosted me, and jerking his thumb over his shoulder said—"Is that your friend?"

"Yes."

"Does he want to starve? If he does, let him live on the prison fare, that's all." 225

"Who are you?" asked I, not knowing what to make of such an unofficially-speaking person in such a place.

"I am the grub-man. Such gentlemen as have friends here, hire me to provide them with something good to eat."

"Is this so?" said I, turning to the turnkey.

He said it was.

"Well then," said I, slipping some silver into the grub-man's hands (for 230 so they called him). "I want you to give particular attention to my friend there; let him have the best dinner you can get. And you must be as polite to him as possible."

"Introduce me, will you?" said the grub-man, looking at me with an expression which seemed to say he was all impatience for an opportunity to give a specimen of his breeding.

Thinking it would prove of benefit to the scrivener, I acquiesced; and asking the grub-man his name, went up with him to Bartleby.

"Bartleby, this is Mr. Cutlets; you will find him very useful to you."

"Your sarvant, sir, your sarvant," said the grub-man, making a low salutation behind his apron. "Hope you find it pleasant here, sir;—spacious grounds—cool apartments, sir—hope you'll stay with us some time—try to make it agreeable. May Mrs. Cutlets and I have the pleasure of your company to dinner, sir, in Mrs. Cutlets' private room?"

"I prefer not to dine today," said Bartleby, turning away. "It would dis- 235 agree with me; I am unused to dinners." So saying he slowly moved to the other side of the inclosure, and took up a position fronting the dead-wall.

"How's this?" said the grub-man, addressing me with a stare of astonishment. "He's odd, ain't he?"

"I think he is a little deranged," said I, sadly.

"Deranged? deranged is it? Well now, upon my word, I thought that friend of yourn was a gentleman forger; they are always pale and genteel-like, them forgers. I can't help pity 'em—can't help it, sir. Did you know Monroe Edwards?"[7] he added touchingly, and paused. Then laying his hand pityingly on my shoulder, sighed, "he died of consumption at Sing Sing. So you weren't acquainted with Monroe?"

"No, I was never socially acquainted with any forgers. But I cannot stop longer. Look to my friend yonder. You will not lose by it. I will see you again."

Some few days after this, I again obtained admission to the Tombs, and 240 went through the corridors in quest of Bartleby; but without finding him.

---

7. Famously flamboyant swindler and forger (1808–1847) who died in Sing Sing prison, north of New York City.

"I saw him coming from his cell not long ago," said a turnkey, "may be he's gone to loiter in the yards."

So I went in that direction.

"Are you looking for the silent man?" said another turnkey passing me. "Yonder he lies—sleeping in the yard there. 'Tis not twenty minutes since I saw him lie down."

The yard was entirely quiet. It was not accessible to the common prisoners. The surrounding walls, of amazing thickness, kept off all sounds behind them. The Egyptian character of the masonry weighed upon me with its gloom. But a soft imprisoned turf grew under foot. The heart of the eternal pyramids, it seemed, wherein, by some strange magic, through the clefts, grass seed, dropped by birds, had sprung.

245   Strangely huddled at the base of the wall, his knees drawn up, and lying on his side, his head touching the cold stones, I saw the wasted Bartleby. But nothing stirred. I paused; then went close up to him; stooped over, and saw that his dim eyes were open; otherwise he seemed profoundly sleeping. Something prompted me to touch him. I felt his hand, when a tingling shiver ran up my arm and down my spine to my feet.

The round face of the grub-man peered upon me now. "His dinner is ready. Won't he dine today, either? Or does he live without dining?"

"Lives without dining," said I, and closed the eyes.

"Eh!—He's asleep, ain't he?"

"With kings and counsellors,"[8] murmured I.

250   There would seem little need for proceeding further in this history. Imagination will readily supply the meager recital of poor Bartleby's interment. But ere parting with the reader, let me say, that if this little narrative has sufficiently interested him, to awaken curiosity as to who Bartleby was, and what manner of life he led prior to the present narrator's making his acquaintance, I can only reply, that in such curiosity I fully share, but am wholly unable to gratify it. Yet here I hardly know whether I should divulge one little item of rumor, which came to my ear a few months after the scrivener's decease. Upon what basis it rested, I could never ascertain; and hence, how true it is I cannot now tell. But inasmuch as this vague report has not been without a certain strange suggestive interest to me, however sad, it may prove the same with some others; and so I will briefly mention it. The report was this: that Bartleby had been a subordinate clerk in the Dead Letter Office at Washington, from which he had been suddenly removed by a change in the administration. When I think over this rumor, I cannot adequately express the emotions which seize me. Dead letters! does it not sound like dead men? Conceive a man by nature and misfortune prone to a pallid hopelessness, can any business seem more fitted to heighten it than that of continually handling these dead letters, and assorting them for the flames? For by the cartload they are annually burned. Sometimes from out the folded paper the pale clerk takes a ring:—the finger

8. I.e., dead. See Job 3.13–14: "then had I been at rest, With kings and counsellors of the earth, which built desolate places for themselves."

it was meant for, perhaps, molders in the grave; a banknote sent in swiftest charity:—he whom it would relieve, nor eats nor hungers any more; pardon for those who died despairing; hope for those who died unhoping; good tidings for those who died stifled by unrelieved calamities. On errands of life, these letters speed to death.
   Ah Bartleby! Ah humanity!

1853

QUESTIONS

1. By the end of "Bartleby, the Scrivener," what does the reader know for certain about Bartleby? Why do you think Melville provides so little explicit information about this character?
2. The narrator tells us that his clerks' nicknames are "expressive of their respective persons or characters," but he explains only Turkey's nickname in this regard. How would you explain the appropriateness of Nipper's nickname? of Ginger Nut's?
3. One of the few words Bartleby utters is *prefer,* and the other characters find themselves using this "queer word." What can we learn about Bartleby and the others by the ways in which they use the word *prefer*?

SUGGESTIONS FOR WRITING

1. Write a first-person narrative in the manner of "Why I Live at the P.O." that makes free use of dialect and exaggeration for comic effect.
2. Write an essay analyzing the character of Bartleby the scrivener. Is Bartleby fully rounded or flat? Does his character change or remain static? Is he best understood as a realistically depicted individual or as a representative of some type or some idea?
3. Write an essay discussing the author's method of characterization in any story you've read so far in this book. How does this method serve the author's storytelling purposes? Are the characters in the story round or flat, individual or stereotypical, distinctly or vaguely depicted, etc.?

STUDENT WRITING

The following is a first-draft analysis of character and narration in Raymond Carver's "Cathedral." Read this paper as you would one of your peers' papers, looking for opportunities for the writer to improve her presentation. Is the language consistently appropriate for academic writing? Does the essay maintain its focus? Does it demonstrate a steady progression of well-supported arguments toward a strong, well-earned conclusion? Is there any redundant or otherwise unnecessary material? Are there ideas that need to be developed further?

Bethany Qualls
Professor Netherton
English 301
23 September 2004

Character and Narration in "Cathedral"

A reader in search of an exciting plot will be pretty disappointed by Raymond Carver's "Cathedral" because the truth is nothing much happens. A suburban husband and wife receive a visit from her former boss, who is blind. After the wife falls asleep, the two men watch a TV program about cathedrals and eventually try to draw one. Along the way the three characters down a few cocktails and smoke a little pot. But that's about as far as the action goes. Instead of focusing on plot, then, the story really asks us to focus on the characters, especially the husband who narrates the story. Through his words even more than his actions the narrator unwittingly shows us why nothing much happens to him by continually demonstrating his utter inability to connect with others or to understand himself.

The narrator's isolation is most evident in the distanced way he introduces his own story and the people in it. He does not name the other characters or himself, referring to them only by using labels such as "[t]his blind man," "[h]is wife," "my wife" (21; all page references are to the class text, <u>The Norton Introduction to Literature</u>, Portable ed.) and "[t]he man [my wife] was going to marry" (21). Even after the narrator's wife starts referring to their visitor as "Robert," the narrator keeps calling him "the blind man" (23). These labels distance him from the other characters and also leave readers with very little connection to them.

At least three times the narrator himself notices that this habit of not naming or really acknowledging people is significant. Referring to his wife's "officer," he asks, "why should he have a name? he was the childhood sweetheart, and what more does he want?" (22). Moments later he describes how freaked out he was when he listened to a tape the blind man had sent his wife and "heard [his] own name in the mouth of this . . . blind man . . . [he] didn't even know!" (23). Yet once the blind man arrives and begins to talk with the wife, the narrator finds himself "wait[ing] in vain to hear [his] name on [his] wife's sweet lips" and disappointed to hear "nothing of the sort" (26). Simply using someone's name suggests a kind of intimacy that the narrator avoids and yet secretly yearns for.

Also reinforcing the narrator's isolation and dissatisfaction with it are the awkward euphemisms and clichés he uses, which emphasize how disconnected he is from his own feelings and how uncomfortable he is with other people's. Referring to his wife's first husband, the narrator says it was he "who'd first enjoyed her favors" (22), an antiquated expression even in 1983, the year the story was published. Such language reinforces our sense that the narrator is unable to speak in language that is meaningful or heartfelt, especially when he actually tries to talk about emotions. He describes his wife's feelings for her first husband, for example, by using generic language and then just trailing off entirely: "she was in love with the guy, and he was in love with her, etc." (21). When he refers to the blind man and his wife as "inseparable," he points out that this is, in fact, his "wife's word," not one that he's come up with (23). And even when he admits that he would like to hear his wife talk about him (26), he speaks in language that seems to come from books or movies rather than the heart.

Once the visit actually begins, the narrator's interactions and conversations with the other characters are even more awkward. His discomfort with the very idea of the visit is obvious to his wife and to the reader. As he says in his usual deadpan manner, "I wasn't enthusiastic about his visit" (21). During the visit he sits silent when his wife and Robert are talking and then answers Robert's questions about his life and feelings with the shortest possible phrases: "How long had I been in my present position? (Three years.) Did I like my work? (I didn't.)" (26). Finally, he tries to escape even that much involvement by simply turning on the TV and tuning Robert out (26).

Despite Robert's best attempt to make a connection with the narrator, the narrator resorts to a label again, saying that he "didn't want to be left alone with a blind man" (27). Robert, merely "a blind man," remains a category, not a person, and the narrator can initially relate to Robert only by invoking the stereotypes about that category that he has learned "from the movies" (21). He confides to the reader that he believes that blind people always wear dark glasses, that they never smoke (25), and that a beard on a blind man is "[t]oo much" (24). It follows that the narrator is amazed about the connection his wife and Robert have because he is unable to see Robert as a person like any other. "[W]ho'd want to go to such a wedding in the first place?" (23) he asks rhetorically about Robert's wedding to his wife, Beulah.

Misconceptions continue as the narrator assumes Beulah would "never receive the smallest compliment from her beloved" since the compliments he is thinking about are physical ones (23). Interestingly, when faced with a name that is specific (Beulah), the narrator immediately assumes that he knows what the person with that name must be like ("a colored woman"[23]), even though she is not in the room or known to him. Words fail or mislead the narrator in both directions, as he's using them and as he hears them.

There is hope for the narrator at the end as he gains some empathy and forges a bond with Robert over the drawing of a cathedral. That process seems to begin when the narrator admits to himself, the reader, and Robert that he is "glad for the [Robert's] company" (28) and, for the first time, comes close to disclosing the literally nightmarish loneliness of his life. It culminates in a moment of physical and emotional intimacy that the narrator admits is "like nothing else in my life up to now" (32)—a moment in which discomfort with the very idea of blindness gives way to an attempt to actually experience blindness from the inside. Because the narrator has used words to distance himself from the world, it seems totally right that all this happens only when the narrator *stops* using words. They have a tendency to blind him.

However, even at the very end it isn't completely clear just whether or how the narrator has really changed. He does not completely interact with Robert but has to be prodded into action by him. By choosing to keep his eyes closed, he not only temporarily experiences blindness but also shuts out the rest of the world, since he "didn't feel like [he] was inside anything" (32). Perhaps most important, he remains unable to describe his experience meaningfully, making it difficult for readers to decide whether or not he has really changed. For example, he says, "It was like nothing else in my life up to now" (32), but he doesn't explain why this is true. Is it because he is doing something for someone else? Because he is thinking about the world from another's perspective? Because he feels connected to Robert? Because he is drawing a picture while probably drunk and high? There is no way of knowing.

It's possible that not feeling "inside anything" (32) could be a feeling of freedom from his own habits of guardedness and insensitivity, his emotional "blindness." But even with this final hope for connection, for the majority of the story the narrator is a closed, judgmental man who isolates himself and cannot connect with others. The narrator's view of the world is one filled with misconceptions that the visit from Robert starts to slowly change, yet it is not clear what those changes are, how far they will go, or whether they will last. So a reader is left wondering how much really happens in this story.

4 SETTING

All stories, like all individuals, are embedded in a context or **setting**—a time and place. The time can be contemporary, as in Sherman Alexie's "Flight Patterns," or historical, as in Edgar Allan Poe's "The Cask of Amontillado." A story may be set in a mythical past, as in "The Elephant in the Village of the Blind," or an indeterminate future. Setting can be very limited, recounting the actions of only a few hours (Raymond Carver's "Cathedral"), or it may span several years (James Baldwin's "Sonny's Blues"). The place can be interior and unremarkable (Grace Paley's "A Conversation with My Father"), or it can be a historic and memorable site. Although short stories seldom cover as much "ground" in time or space as many novels do, the setting may include several locations, or express the sensations of a particular class in a distinct region, as in the American suburbia of John Cheever's "The Country Husband," the rural South of Eudora Welty's "Why I Live at the P.O.," or Harlem during the mid-twentieth century as portrayed in "Sonny's Blues." Other stories convey impressions of locales that are foreign to the reader, where climate, language, and customs create wonder or uneasiness. Just as character and plot are so closely interrelated as to be ultimately indistinguishable, so too are character, plot, and setting. The individuals in the stories are embedded in the specific context, and the more we know of the setting, and of the relationship of the characters to the setting, the more likely we are to understand the characters and the story. Often the setting is a key to discovering interpretations of the story beyond the experience of individual characters and connecting it to traditions, phases of history, and social issues.

In stories that you have already read as well as in those in this chapter, various settings provide historical and social contexts for the characters' experiences. Thus John Cheever's "The Country Husband" is set in suburban New York not long after World War II; the Weeds and their neighbors are typical of middle-class families in that period, the wife raising Baby-Boomer children, the husband commuting to an office job in the city. While many readers recognize this version of the American Dream from their experience or from movies and television, Cheever's story shows that the suburban setting is less familiar and conflict-free than it seems. Other stories are set at a greater distance from most readers, whether in remote times or foreign countries. "A Cask of Amontillado" might seem improbable if Poe had set it in the Baltimore of his own lifetime, whereas a cruel plot of revenge seems more suited to Renaissance Italy; the characters and plot are Machiavellian, char-

> *Fiction depends for its life on place. Place is the crossroads of circumstance, the proving ground of, What happened? Who's here? Who's coming?*
> —EUDORA WELTY

acterized by the unscrupulous cunning described by the Italian Renaissance politician and writer Niccolò Machiavelli (1469–1527). Ernest Hemingway's "Hills Like White Elephants" presents a realistic setting in modern Spain, and a situation that at first seems commonplace. Yet something feels very alien about the episode, not only because readers may never have been to Spain. Because they are so sparse, details of the landscape and the bar at the station are magnified in their significance, as if setting alone tells most of the story.

The stories that follow rely on setting in differing ways and to different degrees, but you will see in each of them a revealing portrait of a time and place. Just as our own memories of important experiences include complex impressions of when and where they occurred—the weather, the shape of the room, the music that was playing, even the fashions or the events in the news back then—so stories rely on setting to give substance to the other elements of fiction.

AMY TAN

[WEB]

A Pair of Tickets

The minute our train leaves the Hong Kong border and enters Shenzhen, China, I feel different. I can feel the skin on my forehead tingling, my blood rushing through a new course, my bones aching with a familiar old pain. And I think, My mother was right. I am becoming Chinese.

"Cannot be helped," my mother said when I was fifteen and had vigorously denied that I had any Chinese whatsoever below my skin. I was a sophomore at Galileo High in San Francisco, and all my Caucasian friends agreed: I was about as Chinese as they were. But my mother had studied at a famous nursing school in Shanghai, and she said she knew all about genetics. So there was no doubt in her mind, whether I agreed or not: Once you are born Chinese, you cannot help but feel and think Chinese.

"Someday you will see," said my mother. "It's in your blood, waiting to be let go."

And when she said this, I saw myself transforming like a werewolf, a mutant tag of DNA suddenly triggered, replicating itself insidiously into a *syndrome,* a cluster of telltale Chinese behaviors, all those things my mother did to embarrass me—haggling with store owners, pecking her mouth with a toothpick in public, being color-blind to the fact that lemon yellow and pale pink are not good combinations for winter clothes.

5   But today I realize I've never really known what it means to be Chinese. I am thirty-six years old. My mother is dead and I am on a train, carrying with me her dreams of coming home. I am going to China.

We are going to Guangzhou, my seventy-two-year-old father, Canning Woo, and I, where we will visit his aunt, whom he has not seen since he was ten years old. And I don't know whether it's the prospect of seeing his aunt or if it's because he's back in China, but now he looks like he's a young boy, so innocent and happy I want to button his sweater and pat his head. We are sitting across from each other, separated by a little table with two cold cups of tea. For the first time I can ever remember, my father has tears in his eyes, and all he is seeing out the train window is a sectioned field of yellow, green, and brown, a narrow canal flanking the tracks, low rising hills, and three people in blue jackets riding an ox-driven cart on this early October morning. And I can't help myself. I also have misty eyes, as if I had seen this a long, long time ago, and had almost forgotten.

In less than three hours, we will be in Guangzhou, which my guidebook tells me is how one properly refers to Canton these days. It seems all the cities I have heard of, except Shanghai, have changed their spellings. I think they are saying China has changed in other ways as well. Chungking is Chongqing. And Kweilin is Guilin. I have looked these names up, because after we see my father's aunt in Guangzhou, we will catch a plane to Shanghai, where I will meet my two half-sisters for the first time.

They are my mother's twin daughters from her first marriage, little babies she was forced to abandon on a road as she was fleeing Kweilin for Chungking in 1944. That was all my mother had told me about these daughters, so they had remained babies in my mind, all these years, sitting on the side of a road, listening to bombs whistling in the distance while sucking their patient red thumbs.

And it was only this year that someone found them and wrote with this joyful news. A letter came from Shanghai, addressed to my mother. When I first heard about this, that they were alive, I imagined my identical sisters transforming from little babies into six-year-old girls. In my mind, they were seated next to each other at a table, taking turns with the fountain pen. One would write a neat row of characters: *Dearest Mama. We are alive.* She would brush back her wispy bangs and hand the other sister the pen, and she would write: *Come get us. Please hurry.*

Of course they could not know that my mother had died three months 10 before, suddenly, when a blood vessel in her brain burst. One minute she was talking to my father, complaining about the tenants upstairs, scheming how to evict them under the pretense that relatives from China were moving in. The next minute she was holding her head, her eyes squeezed shut, groping for the sofa, and then crumpling softly to the floor with fluttering hands.

So my father had been the first one to open the letter, a long letter it turned out. And they did call her Mama. They said they always revered her as their true mother. They kept a framed picture of her. They told her about their life, from the time my mother last saw them on the road leaving Kweilin to when they were finally found.

And the letter had broken my father's heart so much—these daughters calling my mother from another life he never knew—that he gave the letter to my mother's old friend Auntie Lindo and asked her to write back and tell my sisters, in the gentlest way possible, that my mother was dead.

But instead Auntie Lindo took the letter to the Joy Luck Club and discussed with Auntie Ying and Auntie An-mei what should be done, because they had known for many years about my mother's search for her twin daughters, her endless hope. Auntie Lindo and the others cried over this double tragedy, of losing my mother three months before, and now again. And so they couldn't help but think of some miracle, some possible way of reviving her from the dead, so my mother could fulfill her dream.

So this is what they wrote to my sisters in Shanghai: "Dearest Daughters, I too have never forgotten you in my memory or in my heart. I never gave up hope that we would see each other again in a joyous reunion. I am only sorry it has been too long. I want to tell you everything about my life since I last saw you. I want to tell you this when our family comes to see you in China. . . ." They signed it with my mother's name.

15   It wasn't until all this had been done that they first told me about my sisters, the letter they received, the one they wrote back.

"They'll think she's coming, then," I murmured. And I had imagined my sisters now being ten or eleven, jumping up and down, holding hands, their pigtails bouncing, excited that their mother—*their* mother—was coming, whereas my mother was dead.

"How can you say she is not coming in a letter?" said Auntie Lindo. "She is their mother. She is your mother. You must be the one to tell them. All these years, they have been dreaming of her." And I thought she was right.

But then I started dreaming, too, of my mother and my sisters and how it would be if I arrived in Shanghai. All these years, while they waited to be found, I had lived with my mother and then had lost her. I imagined seeing my sisters at the airport. They would be standing on their tiptoes, looking anxiously, scanning from one dark head to another as we got off the plane. And I would recognize them instantly, their faces with the identical worried look.

"*Jyejye, Jyejye.* Sister, Sister. We are here," I saw myself saying in my poor version of Chinese.

20   "Where is Mama?" they would say, and look around, still smiling, two flushed and eager faces. "Is she hiding?" And this would have been like my mother, to stand behind just a bit, to tease a little and make people's patience pull a little on their hearts. I would shake my head and tell my sisters she was not hiding.

"Oh, that must be Mama, no?" one of my sisters would whisper excitedly, pointing to another small woman completely engulfed in a tower of presents. And that, too, would have been like my mother, to bring mountains of gifts, food, and toys for children—all bought on sale—shunning thanks, saying the gifts were nothing, and later turning the labels over to show my sisters, "Calvin Klein, 100% wool."

I imagined myself starting to say, "Sisters, I am sorry, I have come alone . . ." and before I could tell them—they could see it in my face—they were wailing, pulling their hair, their lips twisted in pain, as they ran away from me. And then I saw myself getting back on the plane and coming home.

After I had dreamed this scene many times—watching their despair turn from horror into anger—I begged Auntie Lindo to write another letter. And at first she refused.

"How can I say she is dead? I cannot write this," said Auntie Lindo with a stubborn look.

"But it's cruel to have them believe she's coming on the plane," I said. 25 "When they see it's just me, they'll hate me."

"Hate you? Cannot be." She was scowling. "You are their own sister, their only family."

"You don't understand," I protested.

"What I don't understand?" she said.

And I whispered, "They'll think I'm responsible, that she died because I didn't appreciate her."

And Auntie Lindo looked satisfied and sad at the same time, as if this 30 were true and I had finally realized it. She sat down for an hour, and when she stood up she handed me a two-page letter. She had tears in her eyes. I realized that the very thing I had feared, she had done. So even if she had written the news of my mother's death in English, I wouldn't have had the heart to read it.

"Thank you," I whispered.

The landscape has become gray, filled with low flat cement buildings, old factories, and then tracks and more tracks filled with trains like ours passing by in the opposite direction. I see platforms crowded with people wearing drab Western clothes, with spots of bright colors: little children wearing pink and yellow, red and peach. And there are soldiers in olive green and red, and old ladies in gray tops and pants that stop mid-calf. We are in Guangzhou.

Before the train even comes to a stop, people are bringing down their belongings from above their seats. For a moment there is a dangerous shower of heavy suitcases laden with gifts to relatives, half-broken boxes wrapped in miles of string to keep the contents from spilling out, plastic bags filled with yarn and vegetables and packages of dried mushrooms, and camera cases. And then we are caught in a stream of people rushing, shoving, pushing us along, until we find ourselves in one of a dozen lines waiting to go through customs. I feel as if I were getting on a number 30 Stockton bus in San Francisco. I am in China, I remind myself. And somehow the crowds don't bother me. It feels right. I start pushing too.

I take out the declaration forms and my passport. "Woo," it says at the top, and below that, "June May," who was born in "California, U.S.A.," in 1951. I wonder if the customs people will question whether I'm the same person as in the passport photo. In this picture, my chin-length hair is swept back and artfully styled. I am wearing false eyelashes, eye shadow, and lip liner. My cheeks are hollowed out by bronze blusher. But I had not expected the heat in October. And now my hair hangs limp with the humidity. I wear no makeup; in Hong Kong my mascara had melted into dark circles and everything else had felt like layers of grease. So today my face is plain, unadorned except for a thin mist of shiny sweat on my forehead and nose.

35   Even without makeup, I could never pass for true Chinese. I stand five-foot-six, and my head pokes above the crowd so that I am eye level only with other tourists. My mother once told me my height came from my grandfather, who was a northerner, and may have even had some Mongol blood. "This is what your grandmother once told me," explained my mother. "But now it is too late to ask her. They are all dead, your grandparents, your uncles, and their wives and children, all killed in the war, when a bomb fell on our house. So many generations in one instant."

She had said this so matter-of-factly that I thought she had long since gotten over any grief she had. And then I wondered how she knew they were all dead.

"Maybe they left the house before the bomb fell," I suggested.

"No," said my mother. "Our whole family is gone. It is just you and I."

"But how do you know? Some of them could have escaped."

40   "Cannot be," said my mother, this time almost angrily. And then her frown was washed over by a puzzled blank look, and she began to talk as if she were trying to remember where she had misplaced something. "I went back to that house. I kept looking up to where the house used to be. And it wasn't a house, just the sky. And below, underneath my feet, were four stories of burnt bricks and wood, all the life of our house. Then off to the side I saw things blown into the yard, nothing valuable. There was a bed someone used to sleep in, really just a metal frame twisted up at one corner. And a book, I don't know what kind, because every page had turned black. And I saw a teacup which was unbroken but filled with ashes. And then I found my doll, with her hands and legs broken, her hair burned off. . . . When I was a little girl, I had cried for that doll, seeing it all alone in the store window, and my mother had bought it for me. It was an American doll with yellow hair. It could turn its legs and arms. The eyes moved up and down. And when I married and left my family home, I gave the doll to my youngest niece, because she was like me. She cried if that doll was not with her always. Do you see? If she was in the house with that doll, her parents were there, and so everybody was there, waiting together, because that's how our family was."

The woman in the customs booth stares at my documents, then glances at me briefly, and with two quick movements stamps everything and sternly nods me along. And soon my father and I find ourselves in a large area filled with thousands of people and suitcases. I feel lost and my father looks helpless.

"Excuse me," I say to a man who looks like an American. "Can you tell me where I can get a taxi?" He mumbles something that sounds Swedish or Dutch.

"Syau Yen! Syau Yen!" I hear a piercing voice shout from behind me. An old woman in a yellow knit beret is holding up a pink plastic bag filled with wrapped trinkets. I guess she is trying to sell us something. But my father is staring down at this tiny sparrow of a woman, squinting into her eyes. And then his eyes widen, his face opens up and he smiles like a pleased little boy.

"*Aiyi! Aiyi!*"—Auntie Auntie!—he says softly.

"Syau Yen!" coos my great-aunt. I think it's funny she has just called 45 my father "Little Wild Goose." It must be his baby milk name, the name used to discourage ghosts from stealing children.

They clasp each other's hands—they do not hug—and hold on like this, taking turns saying, "Look at you! You are so old. Look how old you've become!" They are both crying openly, laughing at the same time, and I bite my lip, trying not to cry. I'm afraid to feel their joy. Because I am thinking how different our arrival in Shanghai will be tomorrow, how awkward it will feel.

Now Aiyi beams and points to a Polaroid picture of my father. My father had wisely sent pictures when he wrote and said we were coming. See how smart she was, she seems to intone as she compares the picture to my father. In the letter, my father had said we would call her from the hotel once we arrived, so this is a surprise, that they've come to meet us. I wonder if my sisters will be at the airport.

It is only then that I remember the camera. I had meant to take a picture of my father and his aunt the moment they met. It's not too late.

"Here, stand together over here," I say, holding up the Polaroid. The camera flashes and I hand them the snapshot. Aiyi and my father still stand close together, each of them holding a corner of the picture, watching as their images begin to form. They are almost reverentially quiet. Aiyi is only five years older than my father, which makes her around seventy-seven. But she looks ancient, shrunken, a mummified relic. Her thin hair is pure white, her teeth are brown with decay. So much for stories of Chinese women looking young forever, I think to myself.

Now Aiyi is crooning to me: "*Jandale.*" So big already. She looks up at 50 me, at my full height, and then peers into her pink plastic bag—her gifts to us, I have figured out—as if she is wondering what she will give to me, now that I am so old and big. And then she grabs my elbow with her sharp pincerlike grasp and turns me around. A man and a woman in their fifties are shaking hands with my father, everybody smiling and saying, "Ah! Ah!" They are Aiyi's oldest son and his wife, and standing next to them are four other people, around my age, and a little girl who's around ten. The introductions go by so fast, all I know is that one of them is Aiyi's grandson, with his wife, and the other is her granddaughter, with her husband. And the little girl is Lili, Aiyi's great-granddaughter.

Aiyi and my father speak the Mandarin dialect from their childhood, but the rest of the family speaks only the Cantonese of their village. I understand only Mandarin but can't speak it that well. So Aiyi and my father gossip unrestrained in Mandarin, exchanging news about people from their old village. And they stop only occasionally to talk to the rest of us, sometimes in Cantonese, sometimes in English.

"Oh, it is as I suspected," says my father, turning to me. "He died last summer." And I already understood this. I just don't know who this person, Li Gong, is. I feel as if I were in the United Nations and the translators had run amok.

"Hello," I say to the little girl. "My name is Jing-mei." But the little girl squirms to look away, causing her parents to laugh with embarrassment. I try to think of Cantonese words I can say to her, stuff I learned from friends in Chinatown, but all I can think of are swear words, terms for bodily functions, and short phrases like "tastes good," "tastes like garbage," and "she's really ugly." And then I have another plan: I hold up the Polaroid camera, beckoning Lili with my finger. She immediately jumps forward, places one hand on her hip in the manner of a fashion model, juts out her chest, and flashes me a toothy smile. As soon as I take the picture she is standing next to me, jumping and giggling every few seconds as she watches herself appear on the greenish film.

By the time we hail taxis for the ride to the hotel, Lili is holding tight onto my hand, pulling me along.

55   In the taxi, Aiyi talks nonstop, so I have no chance to ask her about the different sights we are passing by.

"You wrote and said you would come only for one day," says Aiyi to my father in an agitated tone. "One day! How can you see your family in one day! Toishan is many hours' drive from Guangzhou. And this idea to call us when you arrive. This is nonsense. We have no telephone."

My heart races a little. I wonder if Auntie Lindo told my sisters we would call from the hotel in Shanghai?

Aiyi continues to scold my father. "I was so beside myself, ask my son, almost turned heaven and earth upside down trying to think of a way! So we decided the best was for us to take the bus from Toishan and come into Guangzhou—meet you right from the start."

And now I am holding my breath as the taxi driver dodges between trucks and buses, honking his horn constantly. We seem to be on some sort of long freeway overpass, like a bridge above the city. I can see row after row of apartments, each floor cluttered with laundry hanging out to dry on the balcony. We pass a public bus, with people jammed in so tight their faces are nearly wedged against the window. Then I see the skyline of what must be downtown Guangzhou. From a distance, it looks like a major American city, with highrises and construction going on everywhere. As we slow down in the more congested part of the city, I see scores of little shops, dark inside, lined with counters and shelves. And then there is a building, its front laced with scaffolding made of bamboo poles held together with plastic strips. Men and women are standing on narrow platforms, scraping the sides, working without safety straps or helmets. Oh, would OSHA[1] have a field day here, I think.

60   Aiyi's shrill voice rises up again: "So it is a shame you can't see our village, our house. My sons have been quite successful, selling our vegetables in

---

1. The Occupational Safety and Health Administration, a division of the U.S. Department of Labor.

the free market. We had enough these last few years to build a big house, three stories, all of new brick, big enough for our whole family and then some. And every year, the money is even better. You Americans aren't the only ones who know how to get rich!"

The taxi stops and I assume we've arrived, but then I peer out at what looks like a grander version of the Hyatt Regency. "This is communist China?" I wonder out loud. And then I shake my head toward my father. "This must be the wrong hotel." I quickly pull out our itinerary, travel tickets, and reservations. I had explicitly instructed my travel agent to choose something inexpensive, in the thirty-to-forty-dollar range. I'm sure of this. And there it says on our itinerary: Garden Hotel, Huanshi Dong Lu. Well, our travel agent had better be prepared to eat the extra, that's all I have to say.

The hotel is magnificent. A bellboy complete with uniform and sharp-creased cap jumps forward and begins to carry our bags into the lobby. Inside, the hotel looks like an orgy of shopping arcades and restaurants all encased in granite and glass. And rather than be impressed, I am worried about the expense, as well as the appearance it must give Aiyi, that we rich Americans cannot be without our luxuries even for one night.

But when I step up to the reservation desk, ready to haggle over this booking mistake, it is confirmed. Our rooms are prepaid, thirty-four dollars each. I feel sheepish, and Aiyi and the others seem delighted by our temporary surroundings. Lili is looking wide-eyed at an arcade filled with video games.

Our whole family crowds into one elevator, and the bellboy waves, saying he will meet us on the eighteenth floor. As soon as the elevator door shuts, everybody becomes very quiet, and when the door finally opens again, everybody talks at once in what sounds like relieved voices. I have the feeling Aiyi and the others have never been on such a long elevator ride.

Our rooms are next to each other and are identical. The rugs, drapes, 65 bedspreads are all in shades of taupe. There's a color television with remote-control panels built into the lamp table between the two twin beds. The bathroom has marble walls and floors. I find a built-in wet bar with a small refrigerator stocked with Heineken beer, Coke Classic, and Seven-Up, mini-bottles of Johnnie Walker Red, Bacardi rum, and Smirnoff vodka, and packets of M & M's, honey-roasted cashews, and Cadbury chocolate bars. And again I say out loud, "This is communist China?"

My father comes into my room. "They decided we should just stay here and visit," he says, shrugging his shoulders. "They say, Less trouble that way. More time to talk."

"What about dinner?" I ask. I have been envisioning my first real Chinese feast for many days already, a big banquet with one of those soups steaming out of a carved winter melon, chicken wrapped in clay, Peking duck, the works.

My father walks over and picks up a room service book next to a *Travel & Leisure* magazine. He flips through the pages quickly and then points to the menu. "This is what they want," says my father.

So it's decided. We are going to dine tonight in our rooms, with our family, sharing hamburgers, french fries, and apple pie à la mode.

70 Aiyi and her family are browsing the shops while we clean up. After a hot ride on the train, I'm eager for a shower and cooler clothes.

The hotel has provided little packets of shampoo which, upon opening, I discover is the consistency and color of hoisin sauce.[2] This is more like it, I think. This is China. And I rub some in my damp hair.

Standing in the shower, I realize this is the first time I've been by myself in what seems like days. But instead of feeling relieved, I feel forlorn. I think about what my mother said, about activating my genes and becoming Chinese. And I wonder what she meant.

Right after my mother died, I asked myself a lot of things, things that couldn't be answered, to force myself to grieve more. It seemed as if I wanted to sustain my grief, to assure myself that I had cared deeply enough.

But now I ask the questions mostly because I want to know the answers. What was that pork stuff she used to make that had the texture of sawdust? What were the names of the uncles who died in Shanghai? What had she dreamt all these years about her other daughters? All the times when she got mad at me, was she really thinking about them? Did she wish I were they? Did she regret that I wasn't?

———————————

75 At one o'clock in the morning, I awake to tapping sounds on the window. I must have dozed off and now I feel my body uncramping itself. I'm sitting on the floor, leaning against one of the twin beds. Lili is lying next to me. The others are asleep, too, sprawled out on the beds and floor. Aiyi is seated at a little table, looking very sleepy. And my father is staring out the window, tapping his fingers on the glass. The last time I listened my father was telling Aiyi about his life since he last saw her. How he had gone to Yenching University, later got a post with a newspaper in Chungking, met my mother there, a young widow. How they later fled together to Shanghai to try to find my mother's family house, but there was nothing there. And then they traveled eventually to Canton and then to Hong Kong, then Haiphong and finally to San Francisco. . . .

"Suyuan didn't tell me she was trying all these years to find her daughters," he is now saying in a quiet voice. "Naturally, I did not discuss her daughters with her. I thought she was ashamed she had left them behind."

"Where did she leave them?" asks Aiyi. "How were they found?"

I am wide awake now. Although I have heard parts of this story from my mother's friends.

"It happened when the Japanese took over Kweilin," says my father.

80 "Japanese in Kweilin?" says Aiyi. "That was never the case. Couldn't be. The Japanese never came to Kweilin."

———————————

2. Sweet brownish-red sauce made from soybeans, sugar, water, spices, garlic, and chili.

"Yes, that is what the newspapers reported. I know this because I was working for the news bureau at the time. The Kuomintang[3] often told us what we could say and could not say. But we knew the Japanese had come into Kwangsi Province. We had sources who told us how they had captured the Wuchang-Canton railway. How they were coming overland, making very fast progress, marching toward the provincial capital."

Aiyi looks astonished. "If people did not know this, how could Suyuan know the Japanese were coming?"

"An officer of the Kuomintang secretly warned her," explains my father. "Suyuan's husband also was an officer and everybody knew that officers and their families would be the first to be killed. So she gathered a few possessions and, in the middle of the night, she picked up her daughters and fled on foot. The babies were not even one year old."

"How could she give up those babies!" sighs Aiyi. "Twin girls. We have never had such luck in our family." And then she yawns again.

"What were they named?" she asks. I listen carefully. I had been planning 85 on using just the familiar "Sister" to address them both. But now I want to know how to pronounce their names.

"They have their father's surname, Wang," says my father. "And their given names are Chwun Yu and Chwun Hwa."

"What do the names mean?" I ask.

"Ah." My father draws imaginary characters on the window. "One means 'Spring Rain,' the other 'Spring Flower,'" he explains in English, "because they born in the spring, and of course rain come before flower, same order these girls are born. Your mother like a poet, don't you think?"

I nod my head. I see Aiyi nod her head forward, too. But it falls forward and stays there. She is breathing deeply, noisily. She is asleep.

"And what does Ma's name mean?" I whisper. 90

"'Suyuan,'" he says, writing more invisible characters on the glass. "The way she write it in Chinese, it mean 'Long-Cherished Wish.' Quite a fancy name, not so ordinary like flower name. See this first character, it mean something like 'Forever Never Forgotten.' But there is another way to write 'Suyuan.' Sound exactly the same, but the meaning is opposite." His finger creates the brushstrokes of another character. "The first part look the same: 'Never Forgotten.' But the last part add to first part make the whole word mean 'Long-Held Grudge.' Your mother get angry with me, I tell her her name should be Grudge."

My father is looking at me, moist-eyed. "See, I pretty clever, too, hah?"

I nod, wishing I could find some way to comfort him. "And what about my name," I ask, "what does 'Jing-mei' mean?"

"Your name also special," he says. I wonder if any name in Chinese is not something special. "'Jing' like excellent *jing*. Not just good, it's something pure, essential, the best quality. *Jing* is good leftover stuff when you

3. National People's Party, led by Generalissimo Chiang Kai-shek (1887–1975), which fought successfully against the Japanese occupation before being defeated militarily in 1949 by the Chinese Communist Party, led by Mao Zedong (1893–1976).

take impurities out of something like gold, or rice, or salt. So what is left—just pure essence. And 'Mei,' this is common *mei*, as in *meimei*, 'younger sister.'"

95   I think about this. My mother's long-cherished wish. Me, the younger sister who was supposed to be the essence of the others. I feed myself with the old grief, wondering how disappointed my mother must have been. Tiny Aiyi stirs suddenly, her head rolls and then falls back, her mouth opens as if to answer my question. She grunts in her sleep, tucking her body more closely into the chair.

    "So why did she abandon those babies on the road?" I need to know, because now I feel abandoned too.

    "Long time I wondered this myself," says my father. "But then I read that letter from her daughters in Shanghai now, and I talk to Auntie Lindo, all the others. And then I knew. No shame in what she done. None."

    "What happened?"

    "Your mother running away—" begins my father.

100   "No, tell me in Chinese," I interrupt. "Really, I can understand."

    He begins to talk, still standing at the window, looking into the night.

After fleeing Kweilin, your mother walked for several days trying to find a main road. Her thought was to catch a ride on a truck or wagon, to catch enough rides until she reached Chungking, where her husband was stationed.

    She had sewn money and jewelry into the lining of her dress, enough, she thought, to barter rides all the way. If I am lucky, she thought, I will not have to trade the heavy gold bracelet and jade ring. These were things from her mother, your grandmother.

    By the third day, she had traded nothing. The roads were filled with people, everybody running and begging for rides from passing trucks. The trucks rushed by, afraid to stop. So your mother found no rides, only the start of dysentery pains in her stomach.

105   Her shoulders ached from the two babies swinging from scarf slings. Blisters grew on the palms from holding two leather suitcases. And then the blisters burst and began to bleed. After a while, she left the suitcases behind, keeping only the food and a few clothes. And later she also dropped the bags of wheat flour and rice and kept walking like this for many miles, singing songs to her little girls, until she was delirious with pain and fever.

    Finally, there was not one more step left in her body. She didn't have the strength to carry those babies any farther. She slumped to the ground. She knew she would die of her sickness, or perhaps from thirst, from starvation, or from the Japanese, who she was sure were marching right behind her.

    She took the babies out of the slings and sat them on the side of the road, then lay down next to them. You babies are so good, she said, so quiet. They smiled back, reaching their chubby hands for her, wanting to be picked up again. And then she knew she could not bear to watch her babies die with her.

She saw a family with three young children in a cart going by. "Take my babies, I beg you," she cried to them. But they stared back with empty eyes and never stopped.

She saw another person pass and called out again. This time a man turned around, and he had such a terrible expression—your mother said it looked like death itself—she shivered and looked away.

When the road grew quiet, she tore open the lining of her dress, and 110 stuffed jewelry under the shirt of one baby and money under the other. She reached into her pocket and drew out the photos of her family, the picture of her father and mother, the picture of herself and her husband on their wedding day. And she wrote on the back of each the names of the babies and this same message: "Please care for these babies with the money and valuables provided. When it is safe to come, if you bring them to Shanghai, 9 Weichang Lu, the Li family will be glad to give you a generous reward. Li Suyuan and Wang Fuchi."

And then she touched each baby's cheek and told her not to cry. She would go down the road to find them some food and would be back. And without looking back, she walked down the road, stumbling and crying, thinking only of this one last hope, that her daughters would be found by a kindhearted person who would care for them. She would not allow herself to imagine anything else.

She did not remember how far she walked, which direction she went, when she fainted, or how she was found. When she awoke, she was in the back of a bouncing truck with several other sick people, all moaning. And she began to scream, thinking she was now on a journey to Buddhist hell. But the face of an American missionary lady bent over her and smiled, talking to her in a soothing language she did not understand. And yet she could somehow understand. She had been saved for no good reason, and it was now too late to go back and save her babies.

When she arrived in Chungking, she learned her husband had died two weeks before. She told me later she laughed when the officers told her this news, she was so delirious with madness and disease. To come so far, to lose so much and to find nothing.

I met her in a hospital. She was lying on a cot, hardly able to move, her dysentery had drained her so thin. I had come in for my foot, my missing toe, which was cut off by a piece of falling rubble. She was talking to herself, mumbling.

"Look at these clothes," she said, and I saw she had on a rather unusual 115 dress for wartime. It was silk satin, quite dirty, but there was no doubt it was a beautiful dress.

"Look at this face," she said, and I saw her dusty face and hollow cheeks, her eyes shining black. "Do you see my foolish hope?"

"I thought I had lost everything, except these two things," she murmured. "And I wondered which I would lose next. Clothes or hope? Hope or clothes?"

"But now, see here, look what is happening," she said, laughing, as if all her prayers had been answered. And she was pulling hair out of her head as easily as one lifts new wheat from wet soil.

It was an old peasant woman who found them. "How could I resist?" the peasant woman later told your sisters when they were older. They were still sitting obediently near where your mother had left them, looking like little fairy queens waiting for their sedan to arrive.

120   The woman, Mei Ching, and her husband, Mei Han, lived in a stone cave. There were thousands of hidden caves like that in and around Kweilin so secret that the people remained hidden even after the war ended. The Meis would come out of their cave every few days and forage for food supplies left on the road, and sometimes they would see something that they both agreed was a tragedy to leave behind. So one day they took back to their cave a delicately painted set of rice bowls, another day a little footstool with a velvet cushion and two new wedding blankets. And once, it was your sisters.

They were pious people, Muslims, who believed the twin babies were a sign of double luck, and they were sure of this when, later in the evening, they discovered how valuable the babies were. She and her husband had never seen rings and bracelets like those. And while they admired the pictures, knowing the babies came from a good family, neither of them could read or write. It was not until many months later that Mei Ching found someone who could read the writing on the back. By then, she loved these baby girls like her own.

In 1952 Mei Han, the husband, died. The twins were already eight years old, and Mei Ching now decided it was time to find your sisters' true family.

She showed the girls the picture of their mother and told them they had been born into a great family and she would take them back to see their true mother and grandparents. Mei Ching told them about the reward, but she swore she would refuse it. She loved these girls so much, she only wanted them to have what they were entitled to—a better life, a fine house, educated ways. Maybe the family would let her stay on as the girls' amah. Yes, she was certain they would insist.

Of course, when she found the place at 9 Weichang Lu, in the old French Concession, it was something completely different. It was the site of a factory building, recently constructed, and none of the workers knew what had become of the family whose house had burned down on that spot.

125   Mei Ching could not have known, of course, that your mother and I, her new husband, had already returned to that same place in 1945 in hopes of finding both her family and her daughters.

Your mother and I stayed in China until 1947. We went to many different cities—back to Kweilin, to Changsha, as far south as Kunming. She was always looking out of one corner of her eye for twin babies, then little girls. Later we went to Hong Kong, and when we finally left in 1949 for the United States, I think she was even looking for them on the boat. But when we arrived, she no longer talked about them. I thought, At last, they have died in her heart.

When letters could be openly exchanged between China and the United States, she wrote immediately to old friends in Shanghai and Kweilin. I did not know she did this. Auntie Lindo told me. But of course, by then, all the street names had changed. Some people had died, others had moved away. So it took many years to find a contact. And when she did find an old schoolmate's address and wrote asking her to look for her daughters, her friend wrote back and said this was impossible, like looking for a needle on the bottom of the ocean. How did she know her daughters were in Shanghai and not somewhere else in China? The friend, of course, did not ask, How do you know your daughters are still alive?

So her schoolmate did not look. Finding babies lost during the war was a matter of foolish imagination, and she had no time for that.

But every year, your mother wrote to different people. And this last year, I think she got a big idea in her head, to go to China and find them herself. I remember she told me, "Canning, we should go, before it is too late, before we are too old." And I told her we were already too old, it was already too late.

I just thought she wanted to be a tourist! I didn't know she wanted to go and look for her daughters. So when I said it was too late, that must have put a terrible thought in her head that her daughters might be dead. And I think this possibility grew bigger and bigger in her head, until it killed her.

Maybe it was your mother's dead spirit who guided her Shanghai schoolmate to find her daughters. Because after your mother died, the schoolmate saw your sisters, by chance, while shopping for shoes at the Number One Department Store on Nanjing Dong Road. She said it was like a dream, seeing these two women who looked so much alike, moving down the stairs together. There was something about their facial expressions that reminded the schoolmate of your mother.

She quickly walked over to them and called their names, which of course, they did not recognize at first, because Mei Ching had changed their names. But your mother's friend was so sure, she persisted. "Are you not Wang Chwun Yu and Wang Chwun Hwa?" she asked them. And then these double-image women became very excited, because they remembered the names written on the back of an old photo, a photo of a young man and woman they still honored, as their much-loved first parents, who had died and become spirit ghosts still roaming the earth looking for them.

At the airport, I am exhausted. I could not sleep last night. Aiyi had followed me into my room at three in the morning, and she instantly fell asleep on one of the twin beds, snoring with the might of a lumberjack. I lay awake thinking about my mother's story, realizing how much I have never known about her, grieving that my sisters and I had both lost her.

And now at the airport, after shaking hands with everybody, waving good-bye, I think about all the different ways we leave people in this world. Cheerily waving good-bye to some at airports, knowing we'll never see each other again. Leaving others on the side of the road, hoping that we will. Finding my mother in my father's story and saying good-bye before I have a chance to know her better.

135   Aiyi smiles at me as we wait for our gate to be called. She is so old. I put one arm around her and one arm around Lili. They are the same size, it seems. And then it's time. As we wave good-bye one more time and enter the waiting area, I get the sense I am going from one funeral to another. In my hand I'm clutching a pair of tickets to Shanghai. In two hours we'll be there.

The plane takes off. I close my eyes. How can I describe to them in my broken Chinese about our mother's life? Where should I begin?

"Wake up, we're here," says my father. And I awake with my heart pounding in my throat. I look out the window and we're already on the runway. It's gray outside.

And now I'm walking down the steps of the plane, onto the tarmac and toward the building. If only, I think, if only my mother had lived long enough to be the one walking toward them. I am so nervous I cannot even feel my feet. I am just moving somehow.

Somebody shouts, "She's arrived!" And then I see her. Her short hair. Her small body. And that same look on her face. She has the back of her hand pressed hard against her mouth. She is crying as though she had gone through a terrible ordeal and were happy it is over.

140   And I know it's not my mother, yet it is the same look she had when I was five and had disappeared all afternoon, for such a long time, that she was convinced I was dead. And when I miraculously appeared, sleepy-eyed, crawling from underneath my bed, she wept and laughed, biting the back of her hand to make sure it was true.

And now I see her again, two of her, waving, and in one hand there is a photo, the Polaroid I sent them. As soon as I get beyond the gate, we run toward each other, all three of us embracing, all hesitations and expectations forgotten.

"Mama, Mama," we all murmur, as if she is among us.

My sisters look at me, proudly. *"Meimei jandale,"* says one sister proudly to the other. "Little Sister has grown up." I look at their faces again and I see no trace of my mother in them. Yet they still look familiar. And now I also see what part of me is Chinese. It is so obvious. It is my family. It is in our blood. After all these years, it can finally be let go.

My sisters and I stand, arms around each other, laughing and wiping the tears from each other's eyes. The flash of the Polaroid goes off and my father hands me the snapshot. My sisters and I watch quietly together, eager to see what develops.

145   The gray-green surface changes to the bright colors of our three images, sharpening and deepening all at once. And although we don't speak, I know we all see it: Together we look like our mother. Her same eyes, her same mouth, open in surprise to see, at last, her long-cherished wish.

1989

QUESTIONS

1. Why is the opening scene of "A Pair of Tickets"—the train journey from Hong Kong to Guangzhou—an appropriate setting for June May's remark that she is "becoming Chinese"?
2. When June May arrives in Guangzhou, what are some details that seem familiar to her, and what are some that seem exotic? Why is she so preoccupied with comparing China to America?
3. June May says that "she could never pass for true Chinese," yet by the end of the story she has discovered "the part of me that is Chinese." How does the meaning of "Chinese" evolve throughout the story?

ANTON CHEKHOV

The Lady with the Dog[1]

I

It was said that a new person had appeared on the sea-front: a lady with a little dog. Dmitri Dmitritch Gurov, who had by then been a fortnight at Yalta,[2] and so was fairly at home there, had begun to take an interest in new arrivals. Sitting in Verney's pavilion, he saw, walking on the sea-front, a fair-haired young lady of medium height, wearing a *béret*; a white Pomeranian dog was running behind her.

And afterwards he met her in the public gardens and in the square several times a day. She was walking alone, always wearing the same *béret*, and always with the same white dog; no one knew who she was, and every one called her simply "the lady with the dog."

"If she is here alone without a husband or friends, it wouldn't be amiss to make her acquaintance," Gurov reflected.

He was under forty, but he had a daughter already twelve years old, and two sons at school. He had been married young, when he was a student in his second year, and by now his wife seemed half as old again as he. She was a tall, erect woman with dark eyebrows, staid and dignified, and, as she said of herself, intellectual. She read a great deal, used phonetic spelling, called her husband, not Dmitri, but Dimitri, and he secretly considered her unintelligent, narrow, inelegant, was afraid of her, and did not like to be at home. He had begun being unfaithful to her long ago—had been unfaithful to her often, and, probably on that account, almost always spoke ill of women, and when they were talked about in his presence, used to call them "the lower race."

It seemed to him that he had been so schooled by bitter experience that he might call them what he liked, and yet he could not get on for two days together without "the lower race." In the society of men he was bored and not himself, with them he was cold and uncommunicative; but when he 5

---

1. Translated by Constance Garnett.   2. Russian city on the Black Sea; a resort.

was in the company of women he felt free, and knew what to say to them and how to behave; and he was at ease with them even when he was silent. In his appearance, in his character, in his whole nature, there was something attractive and elusive which allured women and disposed them in his favour; he knew that, and some force seemed to draw him, too, to them.

Experience often repeated, truly bitter experience, had taught him long ago that with decent people, especially Moscow people—always slow to move and irresolute—every intimacy, which at first so agreeably diversifies life and appears a light and charming adventure, inevitably grows into a regular problem of extreme intricacy, and in the long run the situation becomes unbearable. But at every fresh meeting with an interesting woman this experience seemed to slip out of his memory, and he was eager for life, and everything seemed simple and amusing.

One evening he was dining in the gardens, and the lady in the *béret* came up slowly to take the next table. Her expression, her gait, her dress, and the way she did her hair told him that she was a lady, that she was married, that she was in Yalta for the first time and alone, and that she was dull there. . . . The stories told of the immorality in such places as Yalta are to a great extent untrue; he despised them, and knew that such stories were for the most part made up by persons who would themselves have been glad to sin if they had been able; but when the lady sat down at the next table three paces from him, he remembered these tales of easy conquests, of trips to the mountains, and the tempting thought of a swift, fleeting love affair, a romance with an unknown woman, whose name he did not know, suddenly took possession of him.

He beckoned coaxingly to the Pomeranian, and when the dog came up to him he shook his finger at it. The Pomeranian growled: Gurov shook his finger at it again.

The lady looked at him and at once dropped her eyes.

10   "He doesn't bite," she said, and blushed.

"May I give him a bone?" he asked; and when she nodded he asked courteously, "Have you been long in Yalta?"

"Five days."

"And I have already dragged out a fortnight here."

There was a brief silence.

15   "Time goes fast, and yet it is so dull here!" she said, not looking at him.

"That's only the fashion to say it is dull here. A provincial will live in Belyov or Zhidra and not be dull, and when he comes here it's 'Oh, the dulness! Oh, the dust!' One would think he came from Grenada."[3]

She laughed. Then both continued eating in silence, like strangers, but after dinner they walked side by side; and there sprang up between them the light jesting conversation of people who are free and satisfied, to whom it does not matter where they go or what they talk about. They walked and talked of the strange light on the sea: the water was of a soft warm lilac hue, and there was a golden streak from the moon upon it. They talked of

3. Romantic city in southern Spain.

how sultry it was after a hot day. Gurov told her that he came from Moscow, that he had taken his degree in Arts, but had a post in a bank; that he had trained as an opera-singer, but had given it up, that he owned two houses in Moscow. . . . And from her he learnt that she had grown up in Petersburg, but had lived in S— since her marriage two years before, that she was staying another month in Yalta, and that her husband, who needed a holiday too, might perhaps come and fetch her. She was not sure whether her husband had a post in a Crown Department or under the Provincial Council[4]—and was amused by her own ignorance. And Gurov learnt, too, that she was called Anna Sergeyevna.

Afterwards he thought about her in his room at the hotel—thought she would certainly meet him next day; it would be sure to happen. As he got into bed he thought how lately she had been a girl at school, doing lessons like his own daughter; he recalled the diffidence, the angularity, that was still manifest in her laugh and her manner of talking with a stranger. This must have been the first time in her life she had been alone in surroundings in which she was followed, looked at, and spoken to merely from a secret motive which she could hardly fail to guess. He recalled her slender, delicate neck, her lovely grey eyes.

"There's something pathetic about her, anyway," he thought, and fell asleep.

II

A week had passed since they had made acquaintance. It was a holiday. It was sultry indoors, while in the street the wind whirled the dust round and round, and blew people's hats off. It was a thirsty day, and Gurov often went into the pavilion, and pressed Anna Sergeyevna to have syrup and water or an ice. One did not know what to do with oneself.

In the evening when the wind had dropped a little, they went out on the groyne to see the steamer come in. There were a great many people walking about the harbour; they had gathered to welcome some one, bringing bouquets. And two peculiarities of a well-dressed Yalta crowd were very conspicuous: the elderly ladies were dressed like young ones, and there were great numbers of generals.

Owing to the roughness of the sea, the steamer arrived late, after the sun had set, and it was a long time turning about before it reached the groyne. Anna Sergeyevna looked through her lorgnette at the steamer and the passengers as though looking for acquaintances, and when she turned to Gurov her eyes were shining. She talked a great deal and asked disconnected questions, forgetting next moment what she had asked; then she dropped her lorgnette in the crush.

The festive crowd began to disperse; it was too dark to see people's faces. The wind had completely dropped, but Gurov and Anna Sergeyevna still stood as though waiting to see some one else come from the steamer. Anna

20

---

4. That is, a post in a national department, appointed by the czar, or a post in an elective local council.

Sergeyevna was silent now, and sniffed the flowers without looking at Gurov.

"The weather is better this evening," he said. "Where shall we go now? Shall we drive somewhere?"

25   She made no answer.

Then he looked at her intently, and all at once put his arm round her and kissed her on the lips, and breathed in the moisture and the fragrance of the flowers; and he immediately looked round him, anxiously wondering whether any one had seen them.

"Let us go to your hotel," he said softly. And both walked quickly.

The room was close and smelt of the scent she had bought at the Japanese shop. Gurov looked at her and thought: "What different people one meets in the world!" From the past he preserved memories of careless, good-natured women, who loved cheerfully and were grateful to him for the happiness he gave them, however brief it might be; and of women like his wife who loved without any genuine feeling, with superfluous phrases, affectedly, hysterically, with an expression that suggested that it was not love nor passion, but something more significant; and of two or three others, very beautiful, cold women, on whose faces he had caught a glimpse of a rapacious expression—an obstinate desire to snatch from life more than it could give, and these were capricious, unreflecting, domineering, unintelligent women not in their first youth, and when Gurov grew cold to them their beauty excited his hatred, and the lace on their linen seemed to him like scales.

But in this case there was still the diffidence, the angularity of inexperienced youth, an awkward feeling; and there was a sense of consternation as though some one had suddenly knocked at the door. The attitude of Anna Sergeyevna—"the lady with the dog"—to what had happened was somehow peculiar, very grave, as though it were her fall—so it seemed, and it was strange and inappropriate. Her face dropped and faded, and on both sides of it her long hair hung down mournfully; she mused in a dejected attitude like "the woman who was a sinner" in an old-fashioned picture.

30   "It's wrong," she said. "You will be the first to despise me now."

There was a water-melon on the table. Gurov cut himself a slice and began eating it without haste. There followed at least half an hour of silence.

Anna Sergeyevna was touching; there was about her the purity of a good, simple woman who had seen little of life. The solitary candle burning on the table threw a faint light on her face, yet it was clear that she was very unhappy.

"How could I despise you?" asked Gurov. "You don't know what you are saying."

"God forgive me," she said, and her eyes filled with tears. "It's awful."

35   "You seem to feel you need to be forgiven."

"Forgiven? No. I am a bad, low woman; I despise myself and don't attempt to justify myself. It's not my husband but myself I have deceived. And not only just now; I have been deceiving myself for a long time. My husband may be a good, honest man, but he is a flunkey! I don't know what he does there, what his work is, but I know he is a flunkey! I was twenty when I was married to him. I have been tormented by curiosity; I wanted something better. 'There must be a different sort of life,' I said to myself. I wanted to live! To live, to live! . . . I was fired by curiosity . . . you don't understand it, but, I swear to God, I could not control myself; something happened to me: I could not be restrained. I told my husband I was ill, and came here. . . . And here I have been walking about as though I were dazed, like a mad creature; . . . and now I have become a vulgar, contemptible woman whom any one may despise."

Gurov felt bored already, listening to her. He was irritated by the naïve tone, by this remorse, so unexpected and inopportune; but for the tears in her eyes, he might have thought she was jesting or playing a part.

"I don't understand," he said softly. "What is it you want?"

She hid her face on his breast and pressed close to him.

"Believe me, believe me, I beseech you . . ." she said. "I love a pure, honest 40 life, and sin is loathsome to me. I don't know what I am doing. Simple people say: 'The Evil One has beguiled me.' And I may say of myself now that the Evil One has beguiled me."

"Hush, hush! . . ." he muttered.

He looked at her fixed, scared eyes, kissed her, talked softly and affectionately, and by degrees she was comforted, and her gaiety returned; they both began laughing.

Afterwards when they went out there was not a soul on the sea-front. The town with its cypresses had quite a deathlike air, but the sea still broke noisily on the shore; a single barge was rocking on the waves, and a lantern was blinking sleepily on it.

They found a cab and drove to Oreanda.

"I found out your surname in the hall just now: it was written on the 45 board—Von Diderits," said Gurov. "Is your husband a German?"

"No; I believe his grandfather was a German, but he is an Orthodox Russian himself."

At Oreanda they sat on a seat not far from the church, looked down at the sea, and were silent. Yalta was hardly visible through the morning mist; white clouds stood motionless on the mountain-tops. The leaves did not stir on the trees, grasshoppers chirruped, and the monotonous hollow sound of the sea rising up from below, spoke of the peace, of the eternal sleep awaiting us. So it must have sounded when there was no Yalta, no Oreanda here; so it sounds now, and it will sound as indifferently and monotonously when we are all no more. And in this constancy, in this complete indifference to the life and death of each of us, there lies hid, perhaps, a pledge of our eternal salvation, of the unceasing movement of life upon earth, of unceasing progress towards perfection. Sitting beside a young woman who in the dawn seemed so lovely, soothed and spellbound in these magical surroundings—the sea, mountains, clouds, the open sky— Gurov thought how in reality everything is beautiful in this world when one reflects: everything except what we think or do ourselves when we forget our human dignity and the higher aims of our existence.

A man walked up to them—probably a keeper—looked at them and walked away. And this detail seemed mysterious and beautiful, too. They saw a steamer come from Theodosia, with its lights out in the glow of dawn.

"There is dew on the grass," said Anna Sergeyevna, after a silence.

50   "Yes. It's time to go home."

They went back to the town.

Then they met every day at twelve o'clock on the sea-front, lunched and dined together, went for walks, admired the sea. She complained that she slept badly, that her heart throbbed violently; asked the same questions, troubled now by jealousy and now by the fear that he did not respect her sufficiently. And often in the square or gardens, when there was no one near them, he suddenly drew her to him and kissed her passionately. Complete idleness, these kisses in broad daylight while he looked round in dread of some one's seeing them, the heat, the smell of the sea, and the continual passing to and fro before him of idle, well-dressed, well-fed people, made a new man of him; he told Anna Sergeyevna how beautiful she was, how fascinating. He was impatiently passionate, he would not move a step away from her, while she was often pensive and continually urged him to confess that he did not respect her, did not love her in the least, and thought of her as nothing but a common woman. Rather late almost every evening they drove somewhere out of town, to Oreanda or to the waterfall; and the expedition was always a success, the scenery invariably impressed them as grand and beautiful.

They were expecting her husband to come, but a letter came from him, saying that there was something wrong with his eyes, and he entreated his wife to come home as quickly as possible. Anna Sergeyevna made haste to go.

"It's a good thing I am going away," she said to Gurov. "It's the finger of destiny!"

55   She went by coach and he went with her. They were driving the whole day. When she had got into a compartment of the express, and when the second bell had rung, she said:

"Let me look at you once more . . . look at you once again. That's right."

She did not shed tears, but was so sad that she seemed ill, and her face was quivering.

"I shall remember you . . . think of you," she said. "God be with you; be happy. Don't remember evil against me. We are parting forever—it must be so, for we ought never to have met. Well, God be with you."

The train moved off rapidly, its lights soon vanished from sight, and a minute later there was no sound of it, as though everything had conspired together to end as quickly as possible that sweet delirium, that madness. Left alone on the platform, and gazing into the dark distance, Gurov listened to the chirrup of the grasshoppers and the hum of the telegraph wires, feeling as though he had only just waked up. And he thought, musing, that there had been another episode or adventure in his life, and it, too, was at an end, and nothing was left of it but a memory. . . . He was moved, sad, and conscious of a slight remorse. This young woman whom he would never meet again had not been happy with him; he was genuinely warm and affectionate with her, but yet in his manner, his tone, and his caresses there had been a shade of light irony, the coarse condescension of a happy man who was, besides, almost twice her age. All the time she had called him kind, exceptional, lofty; obviously he had seemed to her different from what he really was, so he had unintentionally deceived her. . . .

Here at the station was already a scent of autumn; it was a cold evening. 60

"It's time for me to go north," thought Gurov as he left the platform. "High time!"

III

At home in Moscow everything was in its winter routine; the stoves were heated, and in the morning it was still dark when the children were having breakfast and getting ready for school, and the nurse would light the lamp for a short time. The frosts had begun already. When the first snow has fallen, on the first day of sledge-driving it is pleasant to see the white earth, the white roofs, to draw soft, delicious breath, and the season brings back the days of one's youth. The old limes and birches, white with hoar-frost, have a good-natured expression; they are nearer to one's heart than cypresses and palms, and near them one doesn't want to be thinking of the sea and the mountains.

Gurov was Moscow born; he arrived in Moscow on a fine frosty day, and when he put on his fur coat and warm gloves, and walked along Petrovka, and when on Saturday evening he heard the ringing of the bells, his recent trip and the places he had seen lost all charm for him. Little by little he became absorbed in Moscow life, greedily read three newspapers a day, and declared he did not read the Moscow papers on principle! He already felt a longing to go to restaurants, clubs, dinner-parties, anniversary celebrations, and he felt flattered at entertaining distinguished lawyers and artists, and at playing cards with a professor at the doctors' club. He could already eat a whole plateful of salt fish and cabbage. . . .

In another month, he fancied, the image of Anna Sergeyevna would be shrouded in a mist in his memory, and only from time to time would visit him in his dreams with a touching smile as others did. But more than a month passed, real winter had come, and everything was still clear in his memory as though he had parted with Anna Sergeyevna only the day before. And his memories glowed more and more vividly. When in the evening stillness he heard from his study the voices of his children, preparing their lessons, or when he listened to a song or the organ at the restaurant, or the storm howled in the chimney, suddenly everything would rise up in his memory: what had happened on the groyne, and the early morning with the mist on the mountains, and the steamer coming from Theodosia, and the kisses. He would pace a long time about his room, remembering it all and smiling; then his memories passed into dreams, and in his fancy the past was mingled with what was to come. Anna Sergeyevna did not visit him in dreams, but followed him about everywhere like a shadow and haunted him. When he shut his eyes he saw her as though she were living before him, and she seemed to him lovelier, younger, tenderer than she was; and he imagined himself finer than he had been in Yalta. In the evenings she peeped out at him from the bookcase, from the fireplace, from the corner—he heard her breathing, the caressing rustle of her dress. In the street he watched the women, looking for some one like her.

65   He was tormented by an intense desire to confide his memories to some one. But in his home it was impossible to talk of his love, and he had no one outside; he could not talk to his tenants nor to any one at the bank. And what had he to talk of? Had he been in love, then? Had there been anything beautiful, poetical, or edifying or simply interesting in his relations with Anna Sergeyevna? And there was nothing for him but to talk vaguely of love, of woman, and no one guessed what it meant; only his wife twitched her black eyebrows, and said: "The part of a lady-killer does not suit you at all, Dimitri."

One evening, coming out of the doctors' club with an official with whom he had been playing cards, he could not resist saying:

"If only you knew what a fascinating woman I made the acquaintance of in Yalta!"

The official got into his sledge and was driving away, but turned suddenly and shouted:

"Dmitri Dmitritch!"

70   "What?"

"You were right this evening: the sturgeon was a bit too strong!"

These words, so ordinary, for some reason moved Gurov to indignation, and struck him as degrading and unclean. What savage manners, what people! What senseless nights, what uninteresting, uneventful days! The rage for card-playing, the gluttony, the drunkenness, the continual talk always about the same thing. Useless pursuits and conversations always about the same things absorb the better part of one's time, the better part of one's strength, and in the end there is left a life grovelling and curtailed, worthless and trivial, and there is no escaping or getting away from it— just as though one were in a madhouse or a prison.

Gurov did not sleep all night, and was filled with indignation. And he had a headache all next day. And the next night he slept badly; he sat up in bed, thinking, or paced up and down his room. He was sick of his children, sick of the bank; he had no desire to go anywhere or to talk of anything.

In the holidays in December he prepared for a journey, and told his wife he was going to Petersburg to do something in the interests of a young friend—and he set off for S——. What for? He did not very well know himself. He wanted to see Anna Sergeyevna and to talk with her—to arrange a meeting, if possible.

75   He reached S—— in the morning, and took the best room at the hotel, in which the floor was covered with grey army cloth, and on the table was an inkstand, grey with dust and adorned with a figure on horseback, with its hat in its hand and its head broken off. The hotel porter gave him the necessary information; Von Diderits lived in a house of his own in Old

Gontcharny Street—it was not far from the hotel: he was rich and lived in good style, and had his own horses; every one in the town knew him. The porter pronounced the name "Dridirits."

Gurov went without haste to Old Gontcharny Street and found the house. Just opposite the house stretched a long grey fence adorned with nails.

"One would run away from a fence like that," thought Gurov, looking from the fence to the windows of the house and back again.

He considered: to-day was a holiday, and the husband would probably be at home. And in any case it would be tactless to go into the house and upset her. If he were to send her a note it might fall into her husband's hands, and then it might ruin everything. The best thing was to trust to chance. And he kept walking up and down the street by the fence, waiting for the chance. He saw a beggar go in at the gate and dogs fly at him; then an hour later he heard a piano, and the sounds were faint and indistinct. Probably it was Anna Sergeyevna playing. The front door suddenly opened, and an old woman came out, followed by the familiar white Pomeranian. Gurov was on the point of calling to the dog, but his heart began beating violently, and in his excitement he could not remember the dog's name.

He walked up and down, and loathed the grey fence more and more, and by now he thought irritably that Anna Sergeyevna had forgotten him, and was perhaps already amusing herself with some one else, and that that was very natural in a young woman who had nothing to look at from morning till night but that confounded fence. He went back to his hotel room and sat for a long while on the sofa, not knowing what to do, then he had dinner and a long nap.

"How stupid and worrying it is!" he thought when he woke and looked at the dark windows: it was already evening. "Here I've had a good sleep for some reason. What shall I do in the night?" 80

He sat on the bed, which was covered by a cheap grey blanket, such as one sees in hospitals, and he taunted himself in his vexation:

"So much for the lady with the dog . . . so much for the adventure. . . . You're in a nice fix. . . ."

That morning at the station a poster in large letters had caught his eye. "The Geisha"[5] was to be performed for the first time. He thought of this and went to the theatre.

"It's quite possible she may go to the first performance," he thought.

The theatre was full. As in all provincial theatres, there was a fog above the chandelier, the gallery was noisy and restless; in the front row the local dandies were standing up before the beginning of the performance, with their hands behind them; in the Governor's box the Governor's daughter, wearing a boa, was sitting in the front seat, while the Governor himself lurked modestly behind the curtain with only his hands visible; the orchestra was a long time tuning up; the stage curtain swayed. All the time the 85

5. Operetta by Sidney Jones (1861–1946) that toured eastern Europe in 1898–99.

audience were coming in and taking their seats Gurov looked at them eagerly.

Anna Sergeyevna, too, came in. She sat down in the third row, and when Gurov looked at her his heart contracted, and he understood clearly that for him there was in the whole world no creature so near, so precious, and so important to him; she, this little woman, in no way remarkable, lost in a provincial crowd, with a vulgar lorgnette in her hand, filled his whole life now, was his sorrow and his joy, the one happiness that he now desired for himself, and to the sounds of the inferior orchestra, of the wretched provincial violins, he thought how lovely she was. He thought and dreamed.

A young man with small side-whiskers, tall and stooping, came in with Anna Sergeyevna and sat down beside her; he bent his head at every step and seemed to be continually bowing. Most likely this was the husband whom at Yalta, in a rush of bitter feeling, she had called a flunkey. And there really was in his long figure, his side-whiskers, and the small bald patch on his head, something of the flunkey's obsequiousness; his smile was sugary, and in his buttonhole there was some badge of distinction like the number on a waiter.

During the first interval the husband went away to smoke; she remained alone in her stall. Gurov, who was sitting in the stalls, too, went up to her and said in a trembling voice, with a forced smile:

"Good-evening."

90   She glanced at him and turned pale, then glanced again with horror, unable to believe her eyes, and tightly gripped the fan and the lorgnette in her hands, evidently struggling with herself not to faint. Both were silent. She was sitting, he was standing, frightened by her confusion and not venturing to sit down beside her. The violins and the flute began tuning up. He felt suddenly frightened; it seemed as though all the people in the boxes were looking at them. She got up and went quickly to the door; he followed her, and both walked senselessly along passages, and up and down stairs, and figures in legal, scholastic, and civil service uniforms, all wearing badges, flitted before their eyes. They caught glimpses of ladies, of fur coats hanging on pegs; the draughts blew on them, bringing a smell of stale tobacco. And Gurov, whose heart was beating violently, thought:

"Oh, heavens! Why are these people here and this orchestra! . . ."

And at that instant he recalled how when he had seen Anna Sergeyevna off at the station he had thought that everything was over and they would never meet again. But how far they were still from the end!

On the narrow, gloomy staircase over which was written "To the Amphitheatre," she stopped.

"How you have frightened me!" she said, breathing hard, still pale and overwhelmed. "Oh, how you have frightened me! I am half dead. Why have you come? Why?"

95   "But do understand, Anna, do understand . . ." he said hastily in a low voice. "I entreat you to understand. . . ."

She looked at him with dread, with entreaty, with love; she looked at him intently, to keep his features more distinctly in her memory.

"I am so unhappy," she went on, not heeding him. "I have thought of nothing but you all the time; I live only in the thought of you. And I wanted to forget, to forget you; but why, oh, why, have you come?"

On the landing above them two schoolboys were smoking and looking down, but that was nothing to Gurov; he drew Anna Sergeyevna to him, and began kissing her face, her cheeks, and her hands.

"What are you doing, what are you doing!" she cried in horror, pushing him away. "We are mad. Go away to-day; go away at once.... I beseech you by all that is sacred, I implore you.... There are people coming this way!"

Some one was coming up the stairs. 100

"You must go away," Anna Sergeyevna went on in a whisper. "Do you hear, Dmitri Dmitritch? I will come and see you in Moscow. I have never been happy; I am miserable now, and I never, never shall be happy, never! Don't make me suffer still more! I swear I'll come to Moscow. But now let us part. My precious, good, dear one, we must part!"

She pressed his hand and began rapidly going downstairs, looking round at him, and from her eyes he could see that she really was unhappy. Gurov stood for a little while, listened, then, when all sound had died away, he found his coat and left the theatre.

IV

And Anna Sergeyevna began coming to see him in Moscow. Once in two or three months she left S——, telling her husband that she was going to consult a doctor about an internal complaint—and her husband believed her, and did not believe her. In Moscow she stayed at the Slaviansky Bazaar hotel, and at once sent a man in a red cap to Gurov. Gurov went to see her, and no one in Moscow knew of it.

Once he was going to see her in this way on a winter morning (the messenger had come the evening before when he was out). With him walked his daughter, whom he wanted to take to school: it was on the way. Snow was falling in big wet flakes.

"It's three degrees above freezing-point, and yet it is snowing," said 105 Gurov to his daughter. "The thaw is only on the surface of the earth; there is quite a different temperature at a greater height in the atmosphere."

"And why are there no thunderstorms in the winter, father?"

He explained that, too. He talked, thinking all the while that he was going to see *her*, and no living soul knew of it, and probably never would know. He had two lives: one, open, seen and known by all who cared to know, full of relative truth and of relative falsehood, exactly like the lives of his friends and acquaintances; and another life running its course in secret. And through some strange, perhaps accidental, conjunction of circumstances, everything that was essential, of interest and of value to him, everything in which he was sincere and did not deceive himself, everything that made the kernel of his life, was hidden from other people; and all that was false in him, the sheath in which he hid himself to conceal the truth—such, for instance, as his work in the bank, his discussions at the club, his "lower race," his presence with his wife at anniversary festivities—all that was open. And he judged of others by himself, not believing in what he saw, and always believing that every man had his real, most interesting life under the cover of secrecy and under the cover of night. All personal life rested on secrecy, and possibly it was partly on that account that civilised man was so nervously anxious that personal privacy should be respected.

After leaving his daughter at school, Gurov went on to the Slaviansky Bazaar. He took off his fur coat below, went upstairs, and softly knocked at the door. Anna Sergeyevna, wearing his favourite grey dress, exhausted by the journey and the suspense, had been expecting him since the evening before. She was pale; she looked at him, and did not smile, and he had hardly come in when she fell on his breast. Their kiss was slow and prolonged, as though they had not met for two years.

"Well, how are you getting on there?" he asked. "What news?"

110 "Wait; I'll tell you directly. . . . I can't talk."

She could not speak; she was crying. She turned away from him, and pressed her handkerchief to her eyes.

"Let her have her cry out. I'll sit down and wait," he thought, and he sat down in an arm-chair.

Then he rang and asked for tea to be brought him, and while he drank his tea she remained standing at the window with her back to him. She was crying from emotion, from the miserable consciousness that their life was so hard for them; they could only meet in secret, hiding themselves from people, like thieves! Was not their life shattered?

"Come, do stop!" he said.

115 It was evident to him that this love of theirs would not soon be over, that he could not see the end of it. Anna Sergeyevna grew more and more attached to him. She adored him, and it was unthinkable to say to her that it was bound to have an end some day; besides, she would not have believed it!

He went up to her and took her by the shoulders to say something affectionate and cheering, and at that moment he saw himself in the looking-glass.

His hair was already beginning to turn grey. And it seemed strange to him that he had grown so much older, so much plainer during the last few years. The shoulders on which his hands rested were warm and quivering. He felt compassion for this life, still so warm and lovely, but probably already not far from beginning to fade and wither like his own. Why did she love him so much? He always seemed to women different from what he was, and they loved in him not himself, but the man created by their imagination, whom they had been eagerly seeking all their lives; and afterwards, when they noticed their mistake, they loved him all the same. And not one of them had been happy with him. Time passed, he had made their acquaintance, got on with them, parted, but he had never once loved; it was anything you like, but not love.

And only now when his head was grey he had fallen properly, really in love—for the first time in his life.

Anna Sergeyevna and he loved each other like people very close and akin, like husband and wife, like tender friends; it seemed to them that fate itself had meant them for one another, and they could not understand why he had a wife and she a husband; and it was as though they were a pair of birds of passage, caught and forced to live in different cages. They forgave each other for what they were ashamed of in their past, they forgave everything in the present, and felt that this love of theirs had changed them both.

In moments of depression in the past he had comforted himself with   120 any arguments that came into his mind, but now he no longer cared for arguments; he felt profound compassion, he wanted to be sincere and tender. . . .

"Don't cry, my darling," he said. "You've had your cry; that's enough. . . . Let us talk now, let us think of some plan."

Then they spent a long while taking counsel together, talked of how to avoid the necessity for secrecy, for deception, for living in different towns and not seeing each other for long at a time. How could they be free from this intolerable bondage?

"How? How?" he asked, clutching his head. "How?"

And it seemed as though in a little while the solution would be found, and then a new and splendid life would begin; and it was clear to both of them that they had still a long, long road before them, and that the most complicated and difficult part of it was only just beginning.

1899

QUESTIONS

1. When Gurov and Anna take their first walk together, they discuss "the strange light of the sea: the water was of a soft warm lilac hue, and there was a golden streak from the moon upon it." Why do you think Chekhov waits until this moment to provide descriptive details of the story's setting in Yalta?
2. How do the weather and season described in each section relate to the action in that section?
3. What is Gurov's attitude toward his affair with Anna at the outset? What is Anna's attitude? What are some indications that both Gurov and Anna are unprepared for the relationship that develops between them?

––––

SUGGESTIONS FOR WRITING

1. In "A Pair of Tickets," Amy Tan provides detailed descriptions of June May's journeys to Guangzhou and Shanghai. In his account of his wife's escape from Kweilin, June May's father says little about the landscape. Write an essay in which you compare and contrast the two very different storytelling techniques used in this story.
2. In both of the stories in this chapter, a place encountered for the first time by a traveler is described with great vividness: both the city of Guangzhou in "A Pair of Tickets," and the city of Yalta in "The Lady with the Dog." Citing

examples from these stories, write an essay in which you discuss the effect of new surroundings on our perceptions, emotions, and memories.

3. Write an essay in which you compare and contrast the use of setting in any two stories in this book. You might compare the re-creation of two similar settings, such as landscapes far from home, foreign cities, or stifling suburbs; or you might contrast the treatment of different kinds of settings. Be sure to consider not only the authors' descriptive techniques but also the way the authors use setting to shape plot, point of view, and character.

4. Write a fifth section for "The Lady with the Dog."

5 SYMBOL

One of the aspects of literature that can puzzle both beginners and experts is the use of **figures of speech** or **figurative** language—language that creates imaginative connections between our ideas and our senses or that reveals striking similarities between things we had never associated before. Reading and interpreting a short story does not require that you correctly name its figures of speech, but your skill and appreciation will grow when you learn to recognize the common varieties of figurative language.

When a figure is expressed as an explicit comparison, often signaled by *like* or *as*, it is called a **simile**: "eyes as blue as the sky," for example. An implicit comparison or identification of one thing with another unlike itself, without a verbal signal but just seeming to say "A *is* B," is called a **metaphor**: for example, "His intellect was a big comfy couch" ("Flight Patterns"). Some stories employ an **extended metaphor**—a detailed and complex metaphor that stretches through most of a work—to underscore the work's themes.

Another term of figurative language that you have probably encountered is **symbol**. Like other figures of speech, a **symbol** compares or puts together two things that are in some ways *unlike*. In general, you may think of a symbol as a metaphor multiplied. A symbol is a metaphor that has been in use by many people for a long time, or that otherwise has a magnified or many-layered significance. A writer using a symbol expects the audience to recognize it and to have deep or complex associations with what it means, even if this meaning cannot be expressed in words. A symbol usually conveys an abstraction or cluster of abstractions, from the ideal to the imperceptible or the irrational, in a more concrete form. The "stars and stripes"—a descriptive figure of speech for the U.S. flag—stands for the United States; the consensus on what the flag refers to, and the many meanings associated with the vast country it represents, contribute to its richness as a symbol. Other symbols may be more flexible or ambiguous than a flag. A rose can be a symbol of godly love, of romantic desire, of female beauty, of a husband's appreciation for his wife, of the gardens and innocence associated with England or Ireland, of mortality (because the flower wilts) or of hidden cruelty (because it has thorns). The many meanings of a rose throughout civilization are familiar enough to make any mention of a rose in literature or art symbolic. A few symbolic character types, plots, objects, or settings—for example the trickster, the quest, the garden—have become so pervasive and have recurred in so many cultures that they are considered **archetypes** (literary elements that recur in cultural and cross-cultural myth). It is true that literature often invents fresh symbols. If the representative object or concept does not have a familiar association with what it represents, the work must provide clues to its significance. The context of an entire story or poem can guide you in how far to push your own "translation" of what the figure of speech means and whether a metaphor has the deeper significance of a symbol.

But why speak of anything in terms of something else? Why should snakes commonly be symbolic of evil? Sure, some snakes are poisonous, but for some people so are bees, and a lot of snakes are not only harmless but actually helpful ecologically. (In Rudyard Kipling's *The Jungle Book,* the python Ka, while frightening, is on the side of law and order.) The answer is simply that through repeated use over the centuries, the snake has become a traditional symbol of evil—not just danger, sneakiness, and repulsiveness, but absolute spiritual evil. In Nathaniel Hawthorne's "Young Goodman Brown," you will encounter a walking stick carved in the image of a snake, and the context of the rest of the story will support the idea that this is a symbolic reference to the temptation of Adam and Eve by the snake, or Satan, in Paradise. Not only the meaningful names of characters but many other details in the story appear to carry double figurative meanings, and in case there is any doubt, just before the stranger with the walking stick appears, Brown says, "What if the devil himself should be at my very elbow!"

A story isn't any good unless it successfully resists paraphrase, unless it hangs on and expands in the mind.
—FLANNERY O'CONNOR

However, a single item—even something as traditionally fraught with significance as a snake or a rose—becomes a symbol only when its potentially symbolic meaning is confirmed by something else in the story, just as a point needs a second point to define a line. It is best to read the entire story and note any and all of the potential symbols before you try to assess the significance of any one of them. Most often, a symbol is a focal point in a story, a single object or situation that draws the attention of one or more characters.

An **allegory** can be regarded as an "extended" symbol that encompasses a whole work. In an allegory, the widely recognized association of one idea with a more concrete or perceptible thing (country and flag, love and rose) is extended, possibly with a variety of other symbols, across a narrative with at least two distinct levels of meaning. *The Pilgrim's Progress* is probably the most famous prose allegory in English; its central character is named Christian; he was born in the City of Destruction and sets out for the Celestial City, passes through the Slough of Despond and Vanity Fair, meets men named Pliable and Obstinate, and so on. Because an allegory sets up series of correspondences rather than using a single well-known symbol, allegories usually help the reader translate these correspondences—*this equals that*—as the obvious names above suggest. The point of an allegory is not to make us hunt for disguised meanings, but to let us enjoy an invented world where everything is especially meaningful, everything corresponds to something else according to a moral or otherwise "correct" plan.

When an entire story, like "Young Goodman Brown" or "A Hunger Artist," is allegorical or symbolic, it is sometimes called a **myth.** *Myth* originally meant a story of communal origin that provided an explanation or religious interpretation of man, nature, the universe, or the relation between them.

When members of one culture call the stories of another culture "myths," the word usually implies that the stories are false: we speak of classical myths, but Christians do not speak of Christian myth. Sometimes we apply the term *myth* to stories by individual modern authors in order to suggest that these stories express experiences or truths that are shared by a community or that extend beyond any one culture or time, whereas a symbolic story may be more personal or private.

Symbols do not exist solely for the transmission of a meaning we can paraphrase. Like other figures of speech, they are most effective when they cannot be neatly translated into an abstract phrase: when the "something else" that the "something" stands for remains elusive. A good symbol cannot be extracted from the story in which it serves, but it leaves a lasting image of what the story is about. The ultimate unparaphrasable nature of most symbolic images or stories is not vagueness but richness, not disorder but complexity.

NATHANIEL HAWTHORNE

Young Goodman Brown

Young goodman Brown came forth, at sunset, into the street of Salem village,[1] but put his head back, after crossing the threshold, to exchange a parting kiss with his young wife. And Faith, as the wife was aptly named, thrust her own pretty head into the street, letting the wind play with the pink ribbons of her cap, while she called to goodman Brown.

"Dearest heart," whispered she, softly and rather sadly, when her lips were close to his ear, "pr'y thee, put off your journey until sunrise, and sleep in your own bed to-night. A lone woman is troubled with such dreams and such thoughts, that she's afeard of herself, sometimes. Pray, tarry with me this night, dear husband, of all nights in the year!"

"My love and my Faith," replied young goodman Brown, "of all nights in the year, this one night must I tarry away from thee. My journey, as thou callest it, forth and back again, must needs be done 'twixt now and sunrise. What, my sweet, pretty wife, dost thou doubt me already, and we but three months married!"

"Then, God bless you!" said Faith, with the pink ribbons, "and may you find all well, when you come back."

"Amen!" cried goodman Brown. "Say thy prayers, dear Faith, and go to bed at dusk, and no harm will come to thee." 5

So they parted; and the young man pursued his way, until, being about to turn the corner by the meeting-house, he looked back, and saw the head

---

1. Salem, Massachusetts, Hawthorne's birthplace (1804), was the scene of the famous witch trials of 1692. Hawthorne's own ancestors were involved in the persecution of witches and Quakers. Hawthorne wrote, "I take shame upon myself for their sakes and pray that any curse incurred by them . . . may be now and henceforth removed." *Goodman:* husband, master of household.

of Faith still peeping after him, with a melancholy air, in spite of her pink ribbons.

"Poor little Faith!" thought he, for his heart smote him. "What a wretch am I, to leave her on such an errand! She talks of dreams, too. Methought, as she spoke, there was trouble in her face, as if a dream had warned her what work is to be done to-night. But, no, no! 't would kill her to think it. Well; she's a blessed angel on earth; and after this one night, I'll cling to her skirts and follow her to Heaven."

With this excellent resolve for the future, goodman Brown felt himself justified in making more haste on his present evil purpose. He had taken a dreary road, darkened by all the gloomiest trees of the forest, which barely stood aside to let the narrow path creep through, and closed immediately behind. It was all as lonely as could be; and there is this peculiarity in such a solitude, that the traveler knows not who may be concealed by the innumerable trunks and the thick boughs overhead; so that, with lonely footsteps, he may yet be passing through an unseen multitude.

"There may be a devilish Indian behind every tree," said goodman Brown, to himself; and he glanced fearfully behind him, as he added, "What if the devil himself should be at my very elbow!"

10   His head being turned back, he passed a crook of the road, and looking forward again, beheld the figure of a man, in grave and decent attire, seated at the foot of an old tree. He arose, at goodman Brown's approach, and walked onward, side by side with him.

"You are late, goodman Brown," said he. "The clock of the Old South was striking as I came through Boston; and that is full fifteen minutes agone."

"Faith kept me back awhile," replied the young man, with a tremor in his voice, caused by the sudden appearance of his companion, though not wholly unexpected.

It was now deep dusk in the forest, and deepest in that part of it where these two were journeying. As nearly as could be discerned, the second traveler was about fifty years old, apparently in the same rank of life as goodman Brown, and bearing a considerable resemblance to him, though perhaps more in expression than features. Still, they might have been taken for father and son. And yet, though the elder person was as simply clad as the younger, and as simple in manner too, he had an indescribable air of one who knew the world, and would not have felt abashed at the governor's dinner-table, or in king William's[2] court, were it possible that his affairs should call him thither. But the only thing about him, that could be fixed upon as remarkable, was his staff, which bore the likeness of a great black snake, so curiously wrought, that it might almost be seen to twist and wriggle itself, like a living serpent. This, of course, must have been an ocular deception, assisted by the uncertain light.

"Come, goodman Brown!" cried his fellow-traveler, "this is a dull pace for the beginning of a journey. Take my staff, if you are so soon weary."

2. William III (1650–1702), ruler of England from 1689 to 1702.

"Friend," said the other, exchanging his slow pace for a full stop, "having 15 kept covenant by meeting thee here, it is my purpose now to return whence I came. I have scruples, touching the matter thou wot'st of."

"Sayest thou so?" replied he of the serpent, smiling apart. "Let us walk on, nevertheless, reasoning as we go, and if I convince thee not, thou shalt turn back. We are but a little way in the forest, yet."

"Too far, too far!" exclaimed the goodman, unconsciously resuming his walk. "My father never went into the woods on such an errand, nor his father before him. We have been a race of honest men and good Christians, since the days of the martyrs. And shall I be the first of the name of Brown, that ever took this path, and kept"—

"Such company, thou wouldst say," observed the elder person, interpreting his pause. "Good, goodman Brown! I have been as well acquainted with your family as with ever a one among the Puritans; and that's no trifle to say. I helped your grandfather, the constable, when he lashed the Quaker woman so smartly through the streets of Salem. And it was I that brought your father a pitch-pine knot, kindled at my own hearth, to set fire to an Indian village, in king Philip's[3] war. They were my good friends, both; and many a pleasant walk have we had along this path, and returned merrily after midnight. I would fain be friends with you, for their sake."

"If it be as thou sayest," replied goodman Brown, "I marvel they never spoke of these matters. Or, verily, I marvel not, seeing that the least rumor of the sort would have driven them from New-England. We are a people of prayer, and good works, to boot, and abide no such wickedness."

"Wickedness or not," said the traveler with the twisted staff, "I have a 20 very general acquaintance here in New-England. The deacons of many a church have drunk the communion wine with me; the selectmen, of divers towns, make me their chairman; and a majority of the Great and General Court are firm supporters of my interest. The governor and I, too—but these are state-secrets."

"Can this be so!" cried goodman Brown, with a stare of amazement at his undisturbed companion. "Howbeit, I have nothing to do with the governor and council; they have their own ways, and are no rule for a simple husbandman, like me. But, were I to go on with thee, how should I meet the eye of that good old man, our minister, at Salem village? Oh, his voice would make me tremble, both Sabbath-day and lecture-day!"[4]

Thus far, the elder traveler had listened with due gravity, but now burst into a fit of irrepressible mirth, shaking himself so violently, that his snake-like staff actually seemed to wriggle in sympathy.

"Ha! ha! ha!" shouted he, again and again; then composing himself, "Well, go on, goodman Brown, go on; but, pr'y thee, don't kill me with laughing!"

"Well, then, to end the matter at once," said goodman Brown, consid-

---

3. Metacom or Metacomet, chief of the Wampanoag Indians, known as King Philip, led a war against the New England colonists in 1675–76 that devastated many frontier communities.

4. The day for an informal sermon; in the New England colonies, this was usually a Thursday.

erably nettled, "there is my wife, Faith. It would break her dear little heart; and I'd rather break my own!"

25   "Nay, if that be the case," answered the other, "e'en[5] go thy ways, goodman Brown. I would not, for twenty old women like the one hobbling before us, that Faith should come to any harm."

As he spoke, he pointed his staff at a female figure on the path, in whom goodman Brown recognized a very pious and exemplary dame, who had taught him his catechism, in youth, and was still his moral and spiritual adviser, jointly with the minister and deacon Gookin.

"A marvel, truly, that goody[6] Cloyse should be so far in the wilderness, at night-fall!" said he. "But, with your leave, friend, I shall take a cut through the woods, until we have left this Christian woman behind. Being a stranger to you, she might ask whom I was consorting with, and whither I was going."

"Be it so," said his fellow-traveler. "Betake you to the woods, and let me keep the path."

Accordingly, the young man turned aside, but took care to watch his companion, who advanced softly along the road, until he had come within a staff's length of the old dame. She, meanwhile, was making the best of her way, with singular speed for so aged a woman, and mumbling some indistinct words, a prayer, doubtless, as she went. The traveler put forth his staff, and touched her withered neck with what seemed the serpent's tail.

30   "The devil!" screamed the pious old lady.

"Then goody Cloyse knows her old friend?" observed the traveler, confronting her, and leaning on his writhing stick.

"Ah, forsooth, and is it your worship, indeed?" cried the good dame. "Yea, truly is it, and in the very image of my old gossip, goodman Brown, the grandfather of the silly fellow that now is. But, would your worship believe it? my broomstick hath strangely disappeared, stolen, as I suspect, by that unhanged witch, goody Cory, and that, too, when I was all anointed with the juice of smallage and cinque-foil and wolf's-bane"[7] —

"Mingled with fine wheat and the fat of a new-born babe," said the shape of old goodman Brown.

"Ah, your worship knows the receipt," cried the old lady, cackling aloud. "So, as I was saying, being all ready for the meeting, and no horse to ride on, I made up my mind to foot it; for they tell me, there is a nice young man to be taken into communion to-night. But now your good worship will lend me your arm, and we shall be there in a twinkling."

35   "That can hardly be," answered her friend. "I may not spare you my arm, goody Cloyse, but here is my staff, if you will."

So saying, he threw it down at her feet, where, perhaps, it assumed life, being one of the rods which its owner had formerly lent to the Egyptian

---

5. Just.   6. Short for "goodwife" or housewife.   7. Plants traditionally associated with witchcraft.

Magi.[8] Of this fact, however, goodman Brown could not take cognizance. He had cast up his eyes in astonishment, and looking down again, beheld neither goody Cloyse nor the serpentine staff, but his fellow-traveler alone, who waited for him as calmly as if nothing had happened.

"That old woman taught me my catechism!" said the young man; and there was a world of meaning in this simple comment.

They continued to walk onward, while the elder traveler exhorted his companion to make good speed and persevere in the path, discoursing so aptly, that his arguments seemed rather to spring up in the bosom of his auditor, than to be suggested by himself. As they went, he plucked a branch of maple, to serve for a walking-stick, and began to strip it of the twigs and little boughs, which were wet with evening dew. The moment his fingers touched them, they became strangely withered and dried up, as with a week's sunshine. Thus the pair proceeded, at a good free pace, until suddenly, in a gloomy hollow of the road, goodman Brown sat himself down on the stump of a tree, and refused to go any farther.

"Friend," said he, stubbornly, "my mind is made up. Not another step will I budge on this errand. What if a wretched old woman do choose to go to the devil, when I thought she was going to Heaven! Is that any reason why I should quit my dear Faith, and go after her?"

"You will think better of this, by-and-by," said his acquaintance, composedly. "Sit here and rest yourself awhile; and when you feel like moving again, there is my staff to help you along."

Without more words, he threw his companion the maple stick, and was as speedily out of sight, as if he had vanished into the deepening gloom. The young man sat a few moments, by the roadside, applauding himself greatly, and thinking with how clear a conscience he should meet the minister, in his morning-walk, nor shrink from the eye of good old deacon Gookin. And what calm sleep would be his, that very night, which was to have been spent so wickedly, but purely and sweetly now, in the arms of Faith! Amidst these pleasant and praiseworthy meditations, goodman Brown heard the tramp of horses along the road, and deemed it advisable to conceal himself within the verge of the forest, conscious of the guilty purpose that had brought him thither, though now so happily turned from it.

On came the hoof-tramps and the voices of the riders, two grave old voices, conversing soberly as they drew near. These mingled sounds appeared to pass along the road, within a few yards of the young man's hiding-place; but owing, doubtless, to the depth of the gloom, at that particular spot, neither the travelers nor their steeds were visible. Though their figures brushed the small boughs by the way-side, it could not be seen that they intercepted, even for a moment, the faint gleam from the strip of

40

---

8. In Exodus 7.8–12, the Lord instructs Moses to have his brother Aaron, high priest of the Hebrews, throw down his rod before the pharaoh, whereupon it will be turned into a serpent. The pharaoh has his magicians (magi) do likewise, "but Aaron's rod swallowed up their rods."

bright sky, athwart which they must have passed. Goodman Brown alternately crouched and stood on tip-toe, pulling aside the branches, and thrusting forth his head as far as he durst, without discerning so much as a shadow. It vexed him the more, because he could have sworn, were such a thing possible, that he recognized the voices of the minister and deacon Gookin, jogging along quietly, as they were wont to do, when bound to some ordination or ecclesiastical council. While yet within hearing, one of the riders stopped to pluck a switch.

"Of the two, reverend Sir," said the voice like the deacon's, "I had rather miss an ordination-dinner than to-night's meeting. They tell me that some of our community are to be here from Falmouth[9] and beyond, and others from Connecticut and Rhode-Island; besides several of the Indian powows, who, after their fashion, know almost as much deviltry as the best of us. Moreover, there is a goodly young woman to be taken into communion."

"Mighty well, deacon Gookin!" replied the solemn old tones of the minister. "Spur up, or we shall be late. Nothing can be done, you know, until I get on the ground."

45   The hoofs clattered again, and the voices, talking so strangely in the empty air, passed on through the forest, where no church had ever been gathered, nor solitary Christian prayed. Whither, then, could these holy men be journeying, so deep into the heathen wilderness? Young goodman Brown caught hold of a tree, for support, being ready to sink down on the ground, faint and overburthened with the heavy sickness of his heart. He looked up to the sky, doubting whether there really was a Heaven above him. Yet, there was the blue arch, and the stars brightening in it.

"With Heaven above, and Faith below, I will yet stand firm against the devil!" cried goodman Brown.

While he still gazed upward, into the deep arch of the firmament, and had lifted his hands to pray, a cloud, though no wind was stirring, hurried across the zenith, and hid the brightening stars. The blue sky was still visible, except directly overhead, where this black mass of cloud was sweeping swiftly northward. Aloft in the air, as if from the depths of the cloud, came a confused and doubtful sound of voices. Once, the listener fancied that he could distinguish the accents of town's-people of his own, men and women, both pious and ungodly, many of whom he had met at the communion-table, and had seen others rioting at the tavern. The next moment, so indistinct were the sounds, he doubted whether he had heard aught but the murmur of the old forest, whispering without a wind. Then came a stronger swell of those familiar tones, heard daily in the sunshine, at Salem village, but never, until now, from a cloud of night. There was one voice, of a young woman, uttering lamentations, yet with an uncertain sorrow, and entreating for some favor, which, perhaps, it would grieve her to obtain. And all the unseen multitude, both saints and sinners, seemed to encourage her onward.

---

9. A port in southern Massachusetts; Salem is in northern Massachusetts.

"Faith!" shouted goodman Brown, in a voice of agony and desperation; and the echoes of the forest mocked him, crying—"Faith! Faith!" as if bewildered wretches were seeking her, all through the wilderness.

The cry of grief, rage, and terror, was yet piercing the night, when the unhappy husband held his breath for a response. There was a scream, drowned immediately in a louder murmur of voices, fading into far-off laughter, as the dark cloud swept away, leaving the clear and silent sky above goodman Brown. But something fluttered lightly down through the air, and caught on the branch of a tree. The young man seized it, and beheld a pink ribbon.

"My Faith is gone!" cried he, after one stupefied moment. "There is no good on earth; and sin is but a name. Come, devil! for to thee is this world given."

And maddened with despair, so that he laughed loud and long, did goodman Brown grasp his staff and set forth again, at such a rate, that he seemed to fly along the forest-path, rather than to walk or run. The road grew wilder and drearier, and more faintly traced, and vanished at length, leaving him in the heart of the dark wilderness, still rushing onward, with the instinct that guides mortal man to evil. The whole forest was peopled with frightful sounds; the creaking of the trees, the howling of wild beasts, and the yell of Indians; while, sometimes, the wind tolled like a distant church-bell, and sometimes gave a broad roar around the traveler, as if all Nature were laughing him to scorn. But he was himself the chief horror of the scene, and shrank not from its other horrors.

"Ha! ha! ha!" roared goodman Brown, when the wind laughed at him. "Let us hear which will laugh loudest! Think not to frighten me with your deviltry! Come witch, come wizard, come Indian powow, come devil himself! and here come goodman Brown. You may as well fear him as he fear you!"

In truth, all through the haunted forest, there could be nothing more frightful than the figure of goodman Brown. On he flew, among the black pines, brandishing his staff with frenzied gestures, now giving vent to an inspiration of horrid blasphemy, and now shouting forth such laughter, as set all the echoes of the forest laughing like demons around him. The fiend in his own shape is less hideous, than when he rages in the breast of man. Thus sped the demoniac on his course, until, quivering among the trees, he saw a red light before him, as when the felled trunks and branches of a clearing have been set on fire, and throw up their lurid blaze against the sky, at the hour of midnight. He paused, in a lull of the tempest that had driven him onward, and heard the swell of what seemed a hymn, rolling solemnly from a distance, with the weight of many voices. He knew the tune; it was a familiar one in the choir of the village meeting-house. The verse died heavily away, and was lengthened by a chorus, not of human voices, but of all the sounds of the benighted wilderness, pealing in awful harmony together. Goodman Brown cried out; and his cry was lost to his own ear, by its unison with the cry of the desert.

In the interval of silence, he stole forward, until the light glared full upon his eyes. At one extremity of an open space, hemmed in by the dark wall of the forest, arose a rock, bearing some rude, natural resemblance either to an altar or a pulpit, and surrounded by four blazing pines, their tops aflame, their stems untouched, like candles at an evening meeting. The mass of foliage, that had overgrown the summit of the rock, was all on fire, blazing high into the night, and fitfully illuminating the whole field. Each pendent twig and leafy festoon was in a blaze. As the red light arose and fell, a numerous congregation alternately shone forth, then disappeared in shadow, and again grew, as it were, out of the darkness, peopling the heart of the solitary woods at once.

55   "A grave and dark-clad company!" quoth goodman Brown.

In truth, they were such. Among them, quivering to-and-fro, between gloom and splendor, appeared faces that would be seen, next day, at the council-board of the province, and others which, Sabbath after Sabbath, looked devoutly heavenward, and benignantly over the crowded pews, from the holiest pulpits in the land. Some affirm, that the lady of the governor was there. At least, there were high dames well known to her, and wives of honored husbands, and widows, a great multitude, and ancient maidens, all of excellent repute, and fair young girls, who trembled, lest their mothers should espy them. Either the sudden gleams of light, flashing over the obscure field, bedazzled goodman Brown, or he recognized a score of the church-members of Salem village, famous for their especial sanctity. Good old deacon Gookin had arrived, and waited at the skirts of that venerable saint, his revered pastor. But, irreverently consorting with these grave, reputable, and pious people, these elders of the church, these chaste dames and dewy virgins, there were men of dissolute lives and women of spotted fame, wretches given over to all mean and filthy vice, and suspected even of horrid crimes. It was strange to see, that the good shrank not from the wicked, nor were the sinners abashed by the saints. Scattered, also, among their pale-faced enemies, were the Indian priests, or powows, who had often scared their native forest with more hideous incantations than any known to English witchcraft.

"But, where is Faith?" thought goodman Brown; and, as hope came into his heart, he trembled.

Another verse of the hymn arose, a slow and solemn strain, such as the pious love, but joined to words which expressed all that our nature can conceive of sin, and darkly hinted at far more. Unfathomable to mere mortals is the lore of fiends. Verse after verse was sung, and still the chorus of the desert swelled between, like the deepest tone of a mighty organ. And, with the final peal of that dreadful anthem, there came a sound, as if the roaring wind, the rushing streams, the howling beasts, and every other voice of the unconverted wilderness, were mingling and according with the voice of guilty man, in homage to the prince of all. The four blazing pines threw up a loftier flame, and obscurely discovered shapes and visages of horror on the smoke-wreaths, above the impious assembly. At the same moment, the fire on the rock shot redly forth, and formed a glowing arch above its base, where now appeared a figure. With reverence be it spoken, the apparition bore no slight similitude, both in garb and manner, to some grave divine of the New-England churches.

"Bring forth the converts!" cried a voice, that echoed through the field and rolled into the forest.

At the word, goodman Brown stept forth from the shadow of the trees, and approached the congregation, with whom he felt a loathful brotherhood, by the sympathy of all that was wicked in his heart. He could have well nigh sworn, that the shape of his own dead father beckoned him to advance, looking downward from a smoke-wreath, while a woman, with dim features of despair, threw out her hand to warn him back. Was it his mother? But he had no power to retreat one step, nor to resist, even in thought, when the minister and good old deacon Gookin, seized his arms, and led him to the blazing rock. Thither came also the slender form of a veiled female, led between goody Cloyse, that pious teacher of the catechism, and Martha Carrier, who had received the devil's promise to be queen of hell. A rampant hag was she! And there stood the proselytes, beneath the canopy of fire.

"Welcome, my children," said the dark figure, "to the communion of your race! Ye have found, thus young, your nature and your destiny. My children, look behind you!"

They turned; and flashing forth, as it were, in a sheet of flame, the fiend-worshippers were seen; the smile of welcome gleamed darkly on every visage.

"There," resumed the sable form, "are all whom ye have reverenced from youth. Ye deemed them holier than yourselves, and shrank from your own sin, contrasting it with their lives of righteousness, and prayerful aspirations heavenward. Yet, here are they all, in my worshipping assembly! This night it shall be granted you to know their secret deeds; how hoary-bearded elders of the church have whispered wanton words to the young maids of their households; how many a woman, eager for widow's weeds, has given her husband a drink at bed-time, and let him sleep his last sleep in her bosom; how beardless youths have made haste to inherit their fathers' wealth; and how fair damsels—blush not, sweet ones!—have dug little graves in the garden, and bidden me, the sole guest, to an infant's funeral. By the sympathy of your human hearts for sin, ye shall scent out all the places—whether in church, bed-chamber, street, field, or forest—where crime has been committed, and shall exult to behold the whole earth one stain of guilt, one mighty blood-spot. Far more than this! It shall be yours to penetrate, in every bosom, the deep mystery of sin, the fountain of all wicked arts, and which, inexhaustibly supplies more evil impulses than human power—than my power, at its utmost!—can make manifest in deeds. And now, my children, look upon each other."

They did so; and, by the blaze of the hell-kindled torches, the wretched man beheld his Faith, and the wife her husband, trembling before that unhallowed altar.

"Lo! there ye stand, my children," said the figure, in a deep and solemn tone, almost sad, with its despairing awfulness, as if his once angelic nature could yet mourn for our miserable race. "Depending upon one another's hearts, ye had still hoped, that virtue were not all a dream. Now are ye undeceived! Evil is the nature of mankind. Evil must be your only happiness. Welcome, again, my children, to the communion of your race!"

"Welcome!" repeated the fiend-worshippers, in one cry of despair and triumph.

And there they stood, the only pair, as it seemed, who were yet hesitating on the verge of wickedness, in this dark world. A basin was hollowed, naturally, in the rock. Did it contain water, reddened by the lurid light? or was it blood? or, perchance, a liquid flame? Herein did the Shape of Evil dip his hand, and prepare to lay the mark of baptism upon their foreheads, that they might be partakers of the mystery of sin, more conscious of the secret guilt of others, both in deed and thought, than they could now be of their own. The husband cast one look at his pale wife, and Faith at him. What polluted wretches would the next glance shew them to each other, shuddering alike at what they disclosed and what they saw!

"Faith! Faith!" cried the husband. "Look up to Heaven, and resist the Wicked One!"

Whether Faith obeyed, he knew not. Hardly had he spoken, when he found himself amid calm night and solitude, listening to a roar of the wind, which died heavily away through the forest. He staggered against the rock and felt it chill and damp, while a hanging twig, that had been all on fire, besprinkled his cheek with the coldest dew.

70   The next morning, young goodman Brown came slowly into the street of Salem village, staring around him like a bewildered man. The good old minister was taking a walk along the graveyard, to get an appetite for breakfast and meditate his sermon, and bestowed a blessing, as he passed, on goodman Brown. He shrank from the venerable saint, as if to avoid an anathema. Old deacon Gookin was at domestic worship, and the holy words of his prayer were heard through the open window. "What God doth the wizard pray to?" quoth goodman Brown. Goody Cloyse, that excellent old Christian, stood in the early sunshine, at her own lattice, catechising a little girl, who had brought her a pint of morning's milk. Goodman Brown snatched away the child, as from the grasp of the fiend himself. Turning the corner by the meeting-house, he spied the head of Faith, with the pink ribbons, gazing anxiously forth, and bursting into such joy at sight of him, that she skipt along the street, and almost kissed her husband before the whole village. But, goodman Brown looked sternly and sadly into her face, and passed on without a greeting.

Had goodman Brown fallen asleep in the forest, and only dreamed a wild dream of a witch-meeting?

Be it so, if you will. But, alas! it was a dream of evil omen for young goodman Brown. A stern, a sad, a darkly meditative, a distrustful, if not a desperate man, did he become, from the night of that fearful dream. On the Sabbath-day, when the congregation were singing a holy psalm, he could not listen, because an anthem of sin rushed loudly upon his ear, and drowned all the blessed strain. When the minister spoke from the pulpit, with power and fervid eloquence, and, with his hand on the open bible, of the sacred truths of our religion, and of saint-like lives and triumphant deaths, and of future bliss or misery unutterable, then did goodman Brown turn pale, dreading, lest the roof should thunder down upon the gray blasphemer and his hearers. Often, awakening suddenly at midnight, he shrank from the bosom of Faith, and at morning or eventide, when the family knelt down at prayer, he scowled, and muttered to himself, and gazed sternly at his wife, and turned away. And when he had lived long, and was borne to his grave, a hoary corpse, followed by Faith, an aged woman, and children and grandchildren, a goodly procession, besides neighbors, not a few, they carved no hopeful verse upon his tomb-stone; for his dying hour was gloom.

1835

QUESTIONS

1. Why does goodman Brown go into the forest? Why is he surprised to find other people he knows already there?
2. What are some aspects of "Young Goodman Brown" that seem allegorical, and what are some that seem symbolic? Are there images or occurrences in the story that defy such analysis? Why?
3. If there is a "lesson" to be learned from "Young Goodman Brown," what do you think it is? Why do you think that, many years after the main action described in the story, goodman Brown's "dying hour was gloom"?

FRANZ KAFKA

A Hunger Artist[1]

During these last decades the interest in professional fasting has markedly diminished. It used to pay very well to stage such great performances under one's own management, but today that is quite impossible. We live in a different world now. At one time the whole town took a lively interest in the hunger artist; from day to day of his fast the excitement mounted; everybody wanted to see him at least once a day; there were people who bought season tickets for the last few days and sat from morning till night in front of his small barred cage; even in the nighttime there were visiting hours, when the whole effect was heightened by torch flares; on fine days the cage was set out in the open air, and then it was the children's special treat to see the hunger artist; for their elders he was often just a joke that happened to be in fashion, but the children stood open-mouthed, holding each other's hands for greater security, marveling at him as he sat there pallid in black tights, with his ribs sticking out so prominently, not even on a seat but down among straw on the ground, sometimes giving a courteous nod, answering questions with a constrained smile, or perhaps

---

1. Translated by Edwin and Willa Muir.

stretching an arm through the bars so that one might feel how thin it was, and then again withdrawing deep into himself, paying no attention to anyone or anything, not even to the all-important striking of the clock that was the only piece of furniture in his cage, but merely staring into vacancy with half shut eyes, now and then taking a sip from a tiny glass of water to moisten his lips.

Besides casual onlookers there were also relays of permanent watchers selected by the public, usually butchers, strangely enough, and it was their task to watch the hunger artist day and night, three of them at a time, in case he should have some secret recourse to nourishment. This was nothing but a formality, instituted to reassure the masses, for the initiates knew well enough that during his fast the artist would never in any circumstances, not even under forcible compulsion, swallow the smallest morsel of food: the honor of his profession forbade it. Not every watcher, of course, was capable of understanding this, there were often groups of night watchers who were very lax in carrying out their duties and deliberately huddled together in a retired corner to play cards with great absorption, obviously intending to give the hunger artist the chance of a little refreshment, which they supposed he could draw from some private hoard. Nothing annoyed the artist more than such watchers; they made him miserable; they made his fast seem unendurable; sometimes he mastered his feebleness sufficiently to sing during their watch for as long as he could keep going, to show them how unjust their suspicions were. But that was of little use; they only wondered at his cleverness in being able to fill his mouth even while singing. Much more to his taste were the watchers who sat close up to the bars, who were not content with the dim night lighting of the hall but focused him in the full glare of the electric pocket torch[2] given them by the impresario. The harsh light did not trouble him at all, in any case he could never sleep properly, and he could always drowse a little, whatever the light, at any hour, even when the hall was thronged with noisy onlookers. He was quite happy at the prospect of spending a sleepless night with such watchers; he was ready to exchange jokes with them, to tell them stories out of his nomadic life, anything at all to keep them awake and demonstrate to them again that he had no eatables in his cage and that he was fasting as not one of them could fast. But his happiest moment was when the morning came and an enormous breakfast was brought them, at his expense, on which they flung themselves with the keen appetite of healthy men after a weary night of wakefulness. Of course there were people who argued that this breakfast was an unfair attempt to bribe the watchers, but that was going rather too far, and when they were invited to take on a night's vigil without a breakfast, merely for the sake of the cause, they made themselves scarce, although they stuck stubbornly to their suspicions.

Such suspicions, anyhow, were a necessary accompaniment to the profession of fasting. No one could possibly watch the hunger artist contin-

2. Flashlight.

uously, day and night, and so no one could produce first-hand evidence that the fast had really been rigorous and continuous; only the artist himself could know that, he was therefore bound to be the sole completely satisfied spectator of his own fast. Yet for other reasons he was never satisfied; it was not perhaps mere fasting that had brought him to such skeleton thinness that many people had regretfully to keep away from his exhibitions, because the sight of him was too much for them, perhaps it was dissatisfaction with himself that had worn him down. For he alone knew, what no other initiate knew, how easy it was to fast. It was the easiest thing in the world. He made no secret of this, yet people did not believe him, at the best they set him down as modest; most of them, however, thought he was out for publicity or else was some kind of cheat who found it easy to fast because he had discovered a way of making it easy, and then had the impudence to admit the fact, more or less. He had to put up with all that, and in the course of time had got used to it, but his inner dissatisfaction always rankled, and never yet, after any term of fasting—this must be granted to his credit—had he left the cage of his own free will. The longest period of fasting was fixed by his impresario at forty days,[3] beyond that term he was not allowed to go, not even in great cities, and there was good reason for it, too. Experience had proved that for about forty days the interest of the public could be stimulated by a steadily increasing pressure of advertisement, but after that the town began to lose interest, sympathetic support began notably to fall off; there were of course local variations as between one town and another or one country and another, but as a general rule forty days marked the limit. So on the fortieth day the flower-bedecked cage was opened, enthusiastic spectators filled the hall, a military band played, two doctors entered the cage to measure the results of the fast, which were announced through a megaphone, and finally two young ladies appeared, blissful at having been selected for the honor, to help the hunger artist down the few steps leading to a small table on which was spread a carefully chosen invalid repast. And at this very moment the artist always turned stubborn. True, he would entrust his bony arms to the outstretched helping hands of the ladies bending over him, but stand up he would not. Why stop fasting at this particular moment, after forty days of it? He had held out for a long time, an illimitably long time; why stop now, when he was in his best fasting form, or rather, not yet quite in his best fasting form? Why should he be cheated of the fame he would get for fasting longer, for being not only the record hunger artist of all time, which presumably he was already, but for beating his own record by a performance beyond human imagination, since he felt that there were no limits to his capacity for fasting? His public pretended to admire him so much, why should it have so little patience with him; if he could endure fasting longer, why shouldn't the public endure it? Besides, he was tired, he was comfortable sitting in the straw, and now he was supposed to lift himself

---

3. A common biblical length of time; in the New Testament, Jesus fasts for forty days in the desert and has visions of both God and the devil.

to his full height and go down to a meal the very thought of which gave him a nausea that only the presence of the ladies kept him from betraying, and even that with an effort. And he looked up into the eyes of the ladies who were apparently so friendly and in reality so cruel, and shook his head, which felt too heavy on its strengthless neck. But then there happened yet again what always happened. The impresario came forward, without a word—for the band made speech impossible—lifted his arms in the air above the artist, as if inviting Heaven to look down upon its creature here in the straw, this suffering martyr, which indeed he was, although in quite another sense; grasped him round the emaciated waist, with exaggerated caution, so that the frail condition he was in might be appreciated; and committed him to the care of the blenching ladies, not without secretly giving him a shaking so that his legs and body tottered and swayed. The artist now submitted completely; his head lolled on his breast as if it had landed there by chance; his body was hollowed out; his legs in a spasm of self-preservation clung close to each other at the knees, yet scraped on the ground as if it were not really solid ground, as if they were only trying to find solid ground; and the whole weight of his body, a feather-weight after all, relapsed onto one of the ladies, who, looking round for help and panting a little—this post of honor was not at all what she had expected it to be—first stretched her neck as far as she could to keep her face at least free from contact with the artist, when finding this impossible, and her more fortunate companion not coming to her aid but merely holding extended on her own trembling hand the little bunch of knucklebones that was the artist's, to the great delight of the spectators burst into tears and had to be replaced by an attendant who had long been stationed in readiness. Then came the food, a little of which the impresario managed to get between the artist's lips, while he sat in a kind of half-fainting trance, to the accompaniment of cheerful patter designed to distract the public's attention from the artist's condition; after that, a toast was drunk to the public, supposedly prompted by a whisper from the artist in the impresario's ear; the band confirmed it with a mighty flourish, the spectators melted away, and no one had any cause to be dissatisfied with the proceedings, no one except the hunger artist himself, he only, as always.

So he lived for many years, with small regular intervals of recuperation, in visible glory, honored by the world, yet in spite of that troubled in spirit, and all the more troubled because no one would take his trouble seriously. What comfort could he possibly need? What more could he possibly wish for? And if some good-natured person, feeling sorry for him, tried to console him by pointing out that his melancholy was probably caused by fasting, it could happen, especially when he had been fasting for some time, that he reacted with an outburst of fury and to the general alarm began to shake the bars of his cage like a wild animal. Yet the impresario had a way of punishing these outbreaks which he rather enjoyed putting into operation. He would apologize publicly for the artist's behavior, which was only to be excused, he admitted, because of the irritability caused by fasting, a condition hardly to be understood by well-fed people; then by natural transition he went on to mention the artist's equally incomprehensible boast that he could fast for much longer than he was doing; he praised the high ambition, the good will, the great self-denial undoubtedly implicit in such a statement; and then quite simply countered it by bringing out photographs, which were also on sale to the public, showing the artist on the fortieth day of a fast lying in bed almost dead from exhaustion. This perversion of the truth, familiar to the artist though it was, always unnerved him afresh and proved too much for him. What was a consequence of the premature ending of his fast was here presented as the cause of it! To fight against this lack of understanding, against a whole world of non-understanding, was impossible. Time and again in good faith he stood by the bars listening to the impresario, but as soon as the photographs appeared he always let go and sank with a groan back on to his straw, and the reassured public could once more come close and gaze at him.

A few years later when the witnesses of such scenes called them to mind, they often failed to understand themselves at all. For meanwhile the aforementioned change in public interest had set in; it seemed to happen almost overnight; there may have been profound causes for it, but who was going to bother about that; at any rate the pampered hunger artist suddenly found himself deserted one fine day by the amusement seekers, who went streaming past him to other more favored attractions. For the last time the impresario hurried him over half Europe to discover whether the old interest might still survive here and there; all in vain; everywhere, as if by secret agreement, a positive revulsion from professional fasting was in evidence. Of course it could not really have sprung up so suddenly as all that, and many premonitory symptoms which had not been sufficiently remarked or suppressed during the rush and glitter of success now came retrospectively to mind, but it was now too late to take any countermeasures. Fasting would surely come into fashion again at some future date, yet that was no comfort for those living in the present. What, then, was the hunger artist to do? He had been applauded by thousands in his time and could hardly come down to showing himself in a street booth at village fairs, and as for adopting another profession, he was not only too old for that but too fanatically devoted to fasting. So he took leave of the impresario, his partner in an unparalleled career, and hired himself to a large circus; in order to spare his own feelings he avoided reading the conditions of his contract.

A large circus with its enormous traffic in replacing and recruiting men, animals and apparatus can always find a use for people at any time, even for a hunger artist, provided of course that he does not ask too much, and in this particular case anyhow it was not only the artist who was taken on but his famous and long-known name as well, indeed considering the peculiar nature of his performance, which was not impaired by advancing age, it could not be objected that here was an artist past his prime, no longer at the height of his professional skill, seeking a refuge in some quiet corner of a circus; on the contrary, the hunger artist averred that he could fast as well as ever, which was entirely credible, he even alleged that if he were allowed to fast as he liked, and this was at once promised him without more ado, he could astound the world by establishing a record never yet achieved, a statement which certainly provoked a smile among the other professionals, since it left out of account the change in public opinion, which the hunger artist in his zeal conveniently forgot.

He had not, however, actually lost his sense of the real situation and took it as a matter of course that he and his cage should be stationed, not in the middle of the ring as a main attraction, but outside, near the animal cages, on a site that was after all easily accessible. Large and gaily painted placards made a frame for the cage and announced what was to be seen inside it. When the public came thronging out in the intervals to see the animals, they could hardly avoid passing the hunger artist's cage and stopping there for a moment, perhaps they might even have stayed longer had not those pressing behind them in the narrow gangway, who did not understand why they should be held up on their way toward the excitements of the menagerie, made it impossible for anyone to stand gazing quietly for any length of time. And that was the reason why the hunger artist, who had of course been looking forward to these visiting hours as the main achievement of his life, began instead to shrink from them. At first he could hardly wait for the intervals; it was exhilarating to watch the crowds come streaming his way, until only too soon—not even the most obstinate self-deception, clung to almost consciously, could hold out against the fact—the conviction was borne in upon him that these people, most of them, to judge from their actions, again and again, without exception, were all on their way to the menagerie. And the first sight of them from the distance remained the best. For when they reached his cage he was at once deafened by the storm of shouting and abuse that arose from the two contending factions, which renewed themselves continuously, of those who wanted to stop and stare at him—he soon began to dislike them more than the others—not out of real interest but only out of obstinate self-assertiveness, and those who wanted to go straight on to the animals. When the first great rush was past, the stragglers came along, and these, whom nothing could have prevented from stopping to look at him as long as they had breath, raced past with long strides, hardly even glancing at him, in their haste to get to the menagerie in time. And all too rarely did it happen that he had a stroke of luck, when some father of a family fetched up before him with his children, pointed a finger at the hunger artist and explained at length what the phenomenon meant, telling stories of earlier years when he himself had watched similar but much more thrilling performances, and the children, still rather uncomprehending, since neither inside nor outside school had they been sufficiently prepared for this lesson—what did they care about fasting?—yet showed by the brightness of their intent eyes that new and better times might be coming. Perhaps, said the hunger artist to himself many a time, things would be a little better if his cage were set not quite so near the menagerie. That made it too easy for people to make their choice, to say nothing of what he suffered from the stench of the menagerie, the animals' restlessness by night, the carrying past of raw lumps of flesh for the beasts of prey, the roaring at feeding times, which depressed him continually. But he did not dare to lodge a complaint with the management; after all, he had the animals to thank for the troops of people who passed his cage, among whom there might always be one here and there to take an interest in him, and who could tell where they might seclude him if he called attention to his existence and thereby to the fact that, strictly speaking, he was only an impediment on the way to the menagerie.

A small impediment, to be sure, one that grew steadily less. People grew familiar with the strange idea that they could be expected, in times like these, to take an interest in a hunger artist, and with this familiarity the verdict went out against him. He might fast as much as he could, and he did so; but nothing could save him now, people passed him by. Just try to explain to anyone the art of fasting! Anyone who has no feeling for it cannot be made to understand it. The fine placards grew dirty and illegible, they were torn down; the little notice board telling the number of fast days achieved, which at first was changed carefully every day, had long stayed at the same figure, for after the first few weeks even this small task seemed pointless to the staff; and so the artist simply fasted on and on, as he had once dreamed of doing, and it was no trouble to him, just as he had always foretold, but no one counted the days, no one, not even the artist himself, knew what records he was already breaking, and his heart grew heavy. And when once in a time some leisurely passer-by stopped, made merry over the old figure on the board and spoke of swindling, that was in its way the stupidest lie ever invented by indifference and inborn malice, since it was not the hunger artist who was cheating; he was working honestly, but the world was cheating him of his reward.

Many more days went by, however, and that too came to an end. An overseer's eye fell on the cage one day and he asked the attendants why this perfectly good cage should be left standing there unused with dirty straw inside it; nobody knew, until one man, helped out by the notice board, remembered about the hunger artist. They poked into the straw with sticks and found him in it. "Are you still fasting?" asked the overseer. "When on earth do you mean to stop?" "Forgive me, everybody," whispered the hunger artist; only the overseer, who had his ear to the bars, understood him. "Of course," said the overseer, and tapped his forehead with a finger to let the attendants know what state the man was in, "we forgive you." "I always wanted you to admire my fasting," said the hunger artist. "We do admire it," said the overseer, affably. "But you shouldn't admire it," said the hunger artist. "Well, then we don't admire it," said the overseer, "but why shouldn't we admire it?" "Because I have to fast, I can't help it," said the hunger artist. "What a fellow you are," said the overseer, "and why can't you help it?" "Because," said the hunger artist, lifting his head a little and speaking, with his lips pursed, as if for a kiss, right into the overseer's ear, so that no syllable might be lost, "because I couldn't find the food I liked. If I had found it, believe me, I should have made no fuss and stuffed myself like you or anyone else." These were his last words, but in his dimming eyes remained the firm though no longer proud persuasion that he was still continuing to fast.

10   "Well, clear this out now!" said the overseer, and they buried the hunger artist, straw and all. Into the cage they put a young panther. Even the most insensitive felt it refreshing to see this wild creature leaping around the cage that had so long been dreary. The panther was all right. The food he liked was brought him without hesitation by the attendants; he seemed not even to miss his freedom; his noble body, furnished almost to the bursting point with all that it needed, seemed to carry freedom around with it too; somewhere in his jaws it seemed to lurk; and the joy of life streamed with such ardent passion from his throat that for the onlookers it was not easy to stand the shock of it. But they braced themselves, crowded round the cage, and did not want ever to move away.

1924

QUESTIONS

1. What are some possible symbolic interpretations of the hunger artist? the impresario? How do you interpret the panther that replaces the dead artist at the end of "A Hunger Artist"?
2. Why is fasting such a powerful symbolic art form? What are some of the "hungers" that it might represent?
3. Shortly before he dies, the hunger artist declares that his art shouldn't be admired. Why not? What do you make of his explanation that he simply couldn't find the food that he liked? What "food" might have satisfied him?

_____

SUGGESTIONS FOR WRITING

1. Write an essay in which you argue that "Young Goodman Brown" is either an allegory in which a more or less "correct" interpretation is possible or a symbolic tale that cannot be "decoded" with any certainty. Be sure to use specific details from the story.
2. Write an analysis of the symbolism in either "The Country Husband," or "Bartleby, the Scrivener."
3. Write an essay that explores the parallels between specific details in "A Hunger Artist" and art in general.
4. Write a parody of any of the stories in this chapter. See if you can make the symbolism deliberately heavy-handed and obvious, or perhaps obscure and puzzling.

6 THEME

If you ask what a story is about, an author might answer by telling you the subject. Indeed, a story often announces its subject in the title: "An Occurrence at Owl Creek Bridge." A friend might answer with a short statement: "a man's thoughts as he faces execution for spying during the Civil War." You might answer with a written summary of the plot. A teacher might answer by stating the story's **theme**—its central idea, its thesis, its message— "war destroys dreams." Notice that the theme is far more general than the subject, and consider too that not everyone will agree on a story's theme. While you can usually state a subject and summarize the action after one reading, it sometimes takes several readings to puzzle out a story's theme— deciphering the theme requires paying attention to all the elements of literature: setting, character, plot, symbols, point of view, and language.

Classroom discussions of literature may seem to suggest that we read a work only to figure out its theme. But most themes reflect common wisdom and, stated baldly, they may seem unoriginal. Thus, while we might say that " 'Young Goodman Brown' is about a young husband who finds everyone he thought good and pure attending a witches' meeting," the story's *theme* may be stated: "Everyone partakes of evil." Such a thematic statement is far from the end point of reading and interpretation. Instead, it should be a first step toward understanding the work to notice the way each element supports the theme and, perhaps most important, complicates it.

Themes are most powerful when they somehow draw on common experience and knowledge. This is not to say that only people who have been directly involved in a war can appreciate the theme of "An Occurrence at Owl Creek Bridge." *Ideas are to literature what light is to painting.* —PAUL BOURGET

Nor is it necessary to have been a starving artist to admire and pity the hunger artist and resent the way he is exploited. To be sure, some familiarity with the historical and cultural context of a story can assist readers in recognizing its theme or themes, and the significance of any story is modified to some extent by the reader's experience of books and life. Yet stories can be an enrichment of experience, inviting readers to travel out of their own immediate circumstances to imagine others. We are able to recognize the common ground of a general theme through the uncommon aspects of experiences different from our own.

Stories, novels, and films often capture our imaginations because they depict ways of life we have never experienced. Since the earliest times, human beings have longed to hear about other lands and other peoples. Although today such forms of nonfiction as ethnography, history, and travel writing can satisfy this longing, fiction remains a uniquely effective way to convey the subtleties of interaction among different people and cultures. When, for example, a person from one country visits another, there are likely to be the kinds of conflicts and revelations that make for a good story. The stories in this chapter emphasize cultural and social differences, while at the same time pondering estrangement or loss within families or between lovers. Each story conveys both a powerful sense of place and also the great distances between cultures; in each case this is what gives rise to the story's theme.

The meaning of a story has to be embodied in it, has to be made concrete in it. A story is a way to say something that can't be said any other way, and it takes every word in the story to say what the meaning is.

—FLANNERY O'CONNOR

In distinctive ways, these stories explore failures to bridge cultural gaps, each story addressing this theme through a subtle use of the elements of fiction. A simple paraphrase or summary of the story would miss what is distinctive about its handling of the idea of cultural differences. Each story has its own specific context in a country with its own history and religious traditions. Aided by footnotes, perhaps, you may interpret the **allusions**—references to history, religion, cultural practices, and so on. You may observe particular metaphors or actions that enhance the meaning of the story and enrich your own restatement of the theme. As always, the title is a key to the rest of the details in a story. In "A Souvenir of Japan," for example, the narrator is a tall, blond, blue-eyed woman who recalls a time when she lived with a younger Japanese man in a Japanese city. From the first half of the first sentence ("When I went outside to see if he was coming home"), we expect a frustrated love story. But the title and the second half of the first sentence turn the reader's attention to the customs of the country, as if offering souvenirs of a tour. The unusual mixture of travelogue and love story calls our attention to the story's theme about the incompatibility of the lovers and their cultures. In "The Management of Grief," the title calls attention to a businesslike way of dealing with death. In this story, a terrorist bombing of an airliner eliminates the family of Mukherjee's narrator, Shaila Bhave, who must serve as go-between and translator as she tries to rebuild a life in a new world, Canada.

Misunderstandings across great cultural divides—and the self-deceiving stories people tell—are themes in these stories. Yet even with their interrelated themes, these stories differ in substance, form, and effect. To locate each theme is not to "close the case," but rather to begin a more searching investigation of the details that make each story vivid and unique. Remember, the theme is an incomplete abstraction from the story; the story and its details do not disappear or lose significance once distilled into theme, nor could you reconstruct a story merely from a statement of its theme. Indeed, theme and story are fused, inseparable. Often difficult to put into words, themes are the common ground that helps you recognize and care about a story, though it seems to be about lives and experiences very different from your own.

ANGELA CARTER

A Souvenir of Japan

When I went outside to see if he was coming home, some children dressed ready for bed in cotton nightgowns were playing with sparklers in the vacant lot on the corner. When the sparks fell down in beards of stars, the smiling children cooed softly. Their pleasure was very pure because it was so restrained. An old woman said: "And so they pestered their father until he bought them fireworks." In their language, fireworks are called *hannabi*, which means "flower fire." All through summer, every evening, you can see all kinds of fireworks, from the humblest to the most elaborate, and once we rode the train out of Shinjuku for an hour to watch one of the public displays which are held over rivers so that the dark water multiplies the reflections.

By the time we arrived at our destination, night had already fallen. We were in the suburbs. Many families were on their way to enjoy the fireworks. Their mothers had scrubbed and dressed up the smallest children to celebrate the treat. The little girls were especially immaculate in pink and white cotton kimonos tied with fluffy sashes like swatches of candy floss. Their hair had been most beautifully brushed, arranged in sleek, twin bunches and decorated with twists of gold and silver thread. These children were all on their best behavior, because they were staying up late, and held their parents' hands with a charming propriety. We followed the family parties until we came to some fields by the river and saw, high in the air, fireworks already opening out like variegated parasols. They were visible from far away and, as we took the path that led through the fields towards their source, they seemed to occupy more and more of the sky.

Along the path were stalls where shirtless cooks with sweatbands round their heads roasted corncobs and cuttlefish over charcoal. We bought cuttlefish on skewers and ate them as we walked along. They had been basted with soy sauce and were very good. There were also stalls selling goldfish in plastic bags and others for big balloons with rabbit ears. It was like a fairground—but such a well-ordered fair! Even the patrolling policemen carried colored paper lanterns instead of torches.[1] Everything was altogether quietly festive. Ice-cream sellers wandered among the crowd, ringing handbells. Their boxes of wares smoked with cold and they called out in plaintive voices, "Icy, icy, icy cream!" When young lovers dispersed discreetly down the tracks in the sedge, the shadowy, indefatigable salesmen pursued them with bells, lamps and mournful cries.

By now, a great many people were walking towards the fireworks but their steps fell so softly and they chatted in such gentle voices there was no more noise than a warm, continual, murmurous humming, the cozy sound of shared happiness, and the night filled with a muted, bourgeois

---

1. Flashlights (British).

yet authentic magic. Above our heads, the fireworks hung dissolving earrings on the night. Soon we lay down in a stubbled field to watch the
fireworks. But, as I expected, he very quickly grew restive.

5   "Are you happy?" he asked. "Are you sure you're happy?" I was watching
the fireworks and did not reply at first although I knew how bored he was
and, if he was himself enjoying anything, it was only the idea of my pleasure—or, rather, the idea that he enjoyed my pleasure, since this would be
a proof of love. I became guilty and suggested we return to the heart of
the city. We fought a silent battle of self-abnegation and I won it, for I had
the stronger character. Yet the last thing in the world that I wanted was to
leave the scintillating river and the gentle crowd. But I knew his real desire
was to return and so return we did, although I do not know if it was worth
my small victory of selflessness to bear his remorse at cutting short my
pleasure, even if to engineer this remorse had, at some subterranean level,
been the whole object of the outing.

But usually I found myself waiting for him to come home knowing,

Nevertheless, as the slow train nosed back into the thickets of neon, his
natural liveliness returned. He could not lose his old habit of walking
through the streets with a sense of expectation, as if a fateful encounter
might be just around the corner, for, the longer one stayed out, the longer
something remarkable might happen and, even if nothing ever did, the
chance of it appeased the sweet ache of his boredom for a little while.
Besides, his duty by me was done. He had taken me out for the evening
and now he wanted to be rid of me. Or so I saw it. The word for wife,
okusan, means the person who occupies the inner room and rarely, if ever,
comes out of it. Since I often appeared to be his wife, I was frequently
subjected to this treatment, though I fought against it bitterly.

But I usually found myself waiting for him to come home knowing,
with a certain resentment, that he would not; and that he would not even
telephone me to tell me he would be late, either, for he was far too guilty
to do so. I had nothing better to do than to watch the neighborhood
children light their sparklers and giggle; the old woman stood beside me
and I knew she disapproved of me. The entire street politely disapproved
of me. Perhaps they thought I was contributing to the delinquency of a
juvenile for he was obviously younger than I. The old woman's back was
bowed almost to a circle from carrying, when he was a baby, the father who
now supervised the domestic fireworks in his evening *déshabillé* of loose,
white, crepe drawers, naked to the waist. Her face had the seamed reserve
of the old in this country. It was a neighborhood poignantly rich in old
ladies.

At the corner shop, they put an old lady outside on an upturned beer
crate each morning, to air. I think she must have been the household grandmother. She was so old she had lapsed almost entirely into a somnolent
plant life. She was of neither more nor less significance to herself or to the
world than the pot of morning glories which blossomed beside her and
perhaps she had less significance than the flowers, which would fade before
lunch was ready. They kept her very clean. They covered her pale cotton
kimono with a spotless pinafore trimmed with coarse lace and she never

dirtied it because she did not move. Now and then, a child came out to comb her hair. Her consciousness was quite beclouded by time and, when I passed by, her rheumy eyes settled upon me always with the same, vague, disinterested wonder, like that of an Eskimo watching a train. When she whispered, *Irrasyaimase,* the shopkeeper's word of welcome, in the ghostliest of whispers, like the rustle of a paper bag, I saw her teeth were rimmed with gold.

The children lit sparklers under a mouse-colored sky and, because of the pollution in the atmosphere, the moon was mauve. The cicadas throbbed and shrieked in the backyards. When I think of this city, I shall always remember the cicadas who whirr relentlessly all through the summer nights, rising to a piercing crescendo in the subfusc dawn. I have heard cicadas even in the busiest streets, though they thrive best in the back alleys, where they ceaselessly emit that scarcely tolerable susurration which is like a shrill intensification of extreme heat.

A year before, on such a throbbing, voluptuous, platitudinous, subtrop- 10
ical night, we had been walking down one of these shady streets together, in and out of the shadows of the willow trees, looking for somewhere to make love. Morning glories climbed the lattices which screened the low, wooden houses, but the darkness hid the tender colors of these flowers, which the Japanese prize because they fade so quickly. He soon found a hotel, for the city is hospitable to lovers. We were shown into a room like a paper box. It contained nothing but a mattress spread on the floor. We lay down immediately and began to kiss one another. Then a maid soundlessly opened the sliding door and, stepping out of her slippers, crept in on stockinged feet, breathing apologies. She carried a tray which contained two cups of tea and a plate of candies. She put the tray down on the matted floor beside us and backed, bowing and apologizing, from the room while our uninterrupted kiss continued. He started to unfasten my shirt and then she came back again. This time, she carried an armful of towels. I was stripped stark naked when she returned for a third time to bring the receipt for his money. She was clearly a most respectable woman and, if she was embarrassed, she did not show it by a single word or gesture.

I learned his name was Taro. In a toy store, I saw one of those books for children with pictures which are cunningly made of paper cut-outs so that, when you turn the page, the picture springs up in the three stylized dimensions of a backdrop in Kabuki. It was the story of Momotaro, who was born from a peach. Before my eyes, the paper peach split open and there was the baby, where the stone should have been. He, too, had the inhuman sweetness of a child born from something other than a mother, a passive, cruel sweetness I did not immediately understand, for it was that of the repressed masochism which, in my country, is usually confined to women.

Sometimes he seemed to possess a curiously unearthly quality when he perched upon the mattress with his knees drawn up beneath his chin in the attitude of a pixie on a doorknocker. At these times, his face seemed somehow both too flat and too large for his elegant body which had such curious, androgynous grace with its svelte, elongated spine, wide shoulders and unusually well developed pectorals, almost like the breasts of a girl approaching puberty. There was a subtle lack of alignment between face and body and he seemed almost goblin, as if he might have borrowed another person's head, as Japanese goblins do, in order to perform some devious trick. These impressions of a weird visitor were fleeting yet haunting. Sometimes, it was possible for me to believe he had practiced an enchantment upon me, as foxes in this country may, for, here, a fox can masquerade as human and at the best of times the high cheekbones gave to his face the aspect of a mask.

His hair was so heavy his neck drooped under its weight and was of a black so deep it turned purple in sunlight. His mouth also was purplish and his blunt, bee-stung lips those of Gauguin's Tahitians. The touch of his skin was as smooth as water as it flows through the fingers. His eyelids were retractable, like those of a cat, and sometimes disappeared completely. I should have liked to have had him embalmed and been able to keep him beside me in a glass coffin, so that I could watch him all the time and he would not have been able to get away from me.

As they say, Japan is a man's country. When I first came to Tokyo, cloth carps fluttered from poles in the gardens of the families fortunate enough to have borne boy children, for it was the time of the annual festival, Boys Day. At least they do not disguise the situation. At least one knows where one is. Our polarity was publicly acknowledged and socially sanctioned. As an example of the use of the word *dewa*, which occasionally means, as far as I can gather, "in," I once found in a textbook a sentence which, when translated, read: "In a society where men dominate, they value women only as the object of men's passions." If the only conjunction possible to us was that of the death-defying double-somersault of love, it is, perhaps, a better thing to be valued only as an object of passion than never to be valued at all. I had never been so absolutely the mysterious other. I had become a kind of phoenix, a fabulous beast; I was an outlandish jewel. He found me, I think, inexpressibly exotic. But I often felt like a female impersonator in Japan.

15   In the department store there was a rack of dresses labeled: "For Young and Cute Girls Only." When I looked at them, I felt as gross as Glumdalclitch.[2] I wore men's sandals because they were the only kind that fitted me and, even so, I had to take the largest size. My pink cheeks, blue eyes and blatant yellow hair made of me, in the visual orchestration of this city in which all heads were dark, eyes brown and skin monotone, an instrument which played upon an alien scale. In a sober harmony of subtle plucked instruments and wistful flutes, I blared. I proclaimed myself like in a perpetual fanfare. He was so delicately put together that I thought his skeleton must have the airy elegance of a bird's and I was sometimes afraid

2. In Jonathan Swift's *Gulliver's Travels*, Glumdalclitch is a giantess of Brobdingnag. She is Gulliver's nurse and, though only nine years old, is nearly forty feet tall.

that I might smash him. He told me that when he was in bed with me, he felt like a small boat upon a wide, stormy sea.

We pitched our tent in the most unlikely surroundings. We were living in a room furnished only by passion amongst homes of the most astounding respectability. The sounds around us were the swish of brooms upon *tatami* matting and the clatter of demotic Japanese. On all the window ledges, prim flowers bloomed in pots. Every morning, the washing came out on the balconies at seven. Early one morning, I saw a man washing the leaves of his tree. Quilts and mattresses went out to air at eight. The sunlight lay thick enough on these unpaved alleys to lay the dust and somebody always seemed to be practicing Chopin in one or another of the flimsy houses, so lightly glued together from plywood it seemed they were sustained only by willpower. Once I was at home, however, it was as if I occupied the inner room and he did not expect me to go out of it, although it was I who paid the rent.

Yet, when he was away from me, he spent much of the time savoring the most annihilating remorse. But this remorse or regret was the stuff of life to him and out he would go again the next night, or, if I had been particularly angry, he would wait until the night after that. And, even if he fully intended to come back early and had promised me he would do so, circumstances always somehow denied him and once more he would contrive to miss the last train. He and his friends spent their nights in a desultory progression from coffee shop to bar to *pachinko* parlor to coffee shop again, with the radiant aimlessness of the pure existential hero. They were connoisseurs of boredom. They savored the various bouquets of the subtly differentiated boredoms which rose from the long, wasted hours at the dead end of night. When it was time for the first train in the morning, he would go back to the mysteriously deserted, Piranesi[3] perspectives of the station, discolored by dawn, exquisitely tortured by the notion—which probably contained within it a damped-down spark of hope—that, this time, he might have done something irreparable.

I speak as if he had no secrets from me. Well, then, you must realize that I was suffering from love and I knew him as intimately as I knew my own image in a mirror. In other words, I knew him only in relation to myself. Yet, on those terms, I knew him perfectly. At times, I thought I was inventing him as I went along, however, so you will have to take my word for it that we existed. But I do not want to paint our circumstantial portraits so that we both emerge with enough well-rounded, spuriously detailed actuality that you are forced to believe in us. I do not want to practice such sleight of hand. You must be content only with glimpses of our outlines, as if you had caught sight of our reflections in the lookingglass of somebody else's house as you passed by the window. His name was not Taro. I only called him Taro so that I could use the conceit of the peach boy, because it seemed appropriate.

---

3. Giambattista Piranesi (1720–1778), Italian architect, painter, and engraver famous for exaggerated (oversized), dramatic, mysterious, almost dreamlike prints of Roman architecture and ruins.

Speaking of mirrors, the Japanese have a great respect for them and, in old-fashioned inns, one often finds them hooded with fabric covers when not in use. He said: "Mirrors make a room uncozy." I am sure there is more to it than that although they love to be cozy. One must love coziness if one is to live so close together. But, as if in celebration of the thing they feared, they seemed to have made the entire city into a cold hall of mirrors which continually proliferated whole galleries of constantly changing appearances, all marvelous but none tangible. If they did not lock up the real looking-glasses, it would be hard to tell what was real and what was not. Even buildings one had taken for substantial had a trick of disappearing overnight. One morning, we woke to find the house next door reduced to nothing but a heap of sticks and a pile of newspapers neatly tied with string, left out for the garbage collector.

20   I would not say that he seemed to me to possess the same kind of insubstantiality although his departure usually seemed imminent, until I realized he was as erratic but as inevitable as the weather. If you plan to come and live in Japan, you must be sure you are stoical enough to endure the weather. No, it was not insubstantiality; it was a rhetoric valid only on its own terms. When I listened to his protestations, I was prepared to believe he believed in them, although I knew perfectly well they meant nothing. And that isn't fair. When he made them, he believed in them implicitly. Then, he was utterly consumed by conviction. But his dedication was primarily to the idea of himself in love. This idea seemed to him magnificent, even sublime. He was prepared to die for it, as one of Baudelaire's dandies[4] might have been prepared to kill himself in order to preserve himself in the condition of a work of art, for he wanted to make this experience a masterpiece of experience which absolutely transcended the everyday. And this would annihilate the effects of the cruel drug, boredom, to which he was addicted although, perhaps, the element of boredom which is implicit in an affair so isolated from the real world was its principal appeal for him. But I had no means of knowing how far his conviction would take him. And I used to turn over in my mind from time to time the question: how far does a pretense of feeling, maintained with absolute conviction, become authentic?

This country has elevated hypocrisy to the level of the highest style. To look at a samurai, you would not know him for a murderer, or a geisha for a whore. The magnificence of such objects hardly pertains to the human. They live only in a world of icons and there they participate in rituals which transmute life itself to a series of grand gestures, as moving as they are absurd. It was as if they all thought, if we believe in something hard enough, it will come true and, lo and behold! they had and it did. Our street was in essence a slum but, in appearance, it was a little enclave of harmonious quiet and, *mirabile dictu,* it was the appearance which was

---

4. Charles Baudelaire (1821–1867), French writer who lived a life of excess and debauchery and who depicted this lifestyle, that of a "dandy," in his infamous poetic work *Les fleurs du mal* (*The Flowers of Evil*) (1857).

the reality, because they all behaved so well, kept everything so clean and lived with such rigorous civility. What terrible discipline it takes to live harmoniously. They had crushed all their vigor in order to live harmoniously and now they had the wistful beauty of flowers pressed dry in an enormous book.

But repression does not necessarily give birth only to severe beauties. In its programmed interstices, monstrous passions bloom. They torture trees to make them look more like the formal notion of a tree. They paint amazing pictures on their skins with awl and gouge, sponging away the blood as they go; a tattooed man is a walking masterpiece of remembered pain. They boast the most passionate puppets in the world who mimic love suicides in a stylized fashion, for here there is no such comfortable formula as "happy ever after." And, when I remembered the finale of the puppet tragedies, how the wooden lovers cut their throats together, I felt the beginnings of unease, as if the hieratic imagery of the country might overwhelm me, for his boredom had reached such a degree that he was insulated against everything except the irritation of anguish. If he valued me as an object of passion, he had reduced the word to its root, which derives from the Latin, *patior*, I suffer. He valued me as an instrument which would cause him pain.

So we lived under a disoriented moon which was as angry a purple as if the sky had bruised its eye, and, if we made certain genuine intersections, these only took place in darkness. His contagious conviction that our love was unique and desperate infected me with an anxious sickness; soon we would learn to treat one another with the circumspect tenderness of comrades who are amputees, for we were surrounded by the most moving images of evanescence, fireworks, morning glories, the old, children. But the most moving of these images were the intangible reflections of ourselves we saw in one another's eyes, reflections of nothing but appearances, in a city dedicated to seeming, and, try as we might to possess the essence of each other's otherness, we would inevitably fail.

1974

QUESTIONS

1. How does the narrator's use of pronouns like "he" and "we" in the opening paragraphs serve to immerse the reader in "A Souvenir of Japan"? How does this use of unreferenced pronouns mirror the situation of an outsider plunged into an alien culture?

2. In what ways does this story present a "souvenir of Japan" to an English-speaking outsider? What does the word "souvenir" imply about the narrator's feelings toward Japan and the story she has to tell?

3. How does Angela Carter's use of the word "reflections" at the end of the opening paragraph prefigure many of the images that make up her portrait of Japanese culture? When she uses the same word, "reflections," twice in the final sentence of the story, what additional layers of meaning and thematic significance has the word acquired?

BHARATI MUKHERJEE

The Management of Grief

A woman I don't know is boiling tea the Indian way in my kitchen. There are a lot of women I don't know in my kitchen, whispering, and moving tactfully. They open doors, rummage through the pantry, and try not to ask me where things are kept. They remind me of when my sons were small, on Mother's Day or when Vikram and I were tired, and they would make big, sloppy omelets. I would lie in bed pretending I didn't hear them.

Dr. Sharma, the treasurer of the Indo-Canada Society, pulls me into the hallway. He wants to know if I am worried about money. His wife, who has just come up from the basement with a tray of empty cups and glasses, scolds him. "Don't bother Mrs. Bhave with mundane details." She looks so monstrously pregnant her baby must be days overdue. I tell her she shouldn't be carrying heavy things. "Shaila," she says, smiling, "this is the fifth." Then she grabs a teenager by his shirttails. He slips his Walkman off his head. He has to be one of her four children, they have the same domed and dented foreheads. "What's the official word now?" she demands. The boy slips the headphones back on. "They're acting evasive, Ma. They're saying it could be an accident or a terrorist bomb."

All morning, the boys have been muttering, Sikh Bomb, Sikh Bomb. The men, not using the word, bow their heads in agreement. Mrs. Sharma touches her forehead at such a word. At least they've stopped talking about space debris and Russian lasers.

Two radios are going in the dining room. They are tuned to different stations. Someone must have brought the radios down from my boys' bedrooms. I haven't gone into their rooms since Kusum came running across the front lawn in her bathrobe. She looked so funny, I was laughing when I opened the door.

5   The big TV in the den is being whizzed through American networks and cable channels.

"Damn!" some man swears bitterly. "How can these preachers carry on like nothing's happened?" I want to tell him we're not that important. You look at the audience, and at the preacher in his blue robe with his beautiful white hair, the potted palm trees under a blue sky, and you know they care about nothing.

The phone rings and rings. Dr. Sharma's taken charge. "We're with her," he keeps saying. "Yes, yes, the doctor has given calming pills. Yes, yes, pills are having necessary effect." I wonder if pills alone explain this calm. Not peace, just a deadening quiet. I was always controlled, but never repressed. Sound can reach me, but my body is tensed, ready to scream. I hear their voices all around me. I hear my boys and Vikram cry, "Mommy, Shaila!" and their screams insulate me, like headphones.

The woman boiling water tells her story again and again. "I got the news first. My cousin called from Halifax before six A.M., can you imagine? He'd gotten up for prayers and his son was studying for medical exams and he heard on a rock channel that something had happened to a plane. They said first it had disappeared from the radar, like a giant eraser just reached out. His father called me, so I said to him, what do you mean, 'something bad'? You mean a hijacking? And he said, *behn,*[1] there is no confirmation of anything yet, but check with your neighbors because a lot of them must be on that plane. So I called poor Kusum straightaway. I knew Kusum's husband and daughter were booked to go yesterday."

Kusum lives across the street from me. She and Satish had moved in less than a month ago. They said they needed a bigger place. All these people, the Sharmas and friends from the Indo-Canada Society had been there for the housewarming. Satish and Kusum made homemade tandoori on their big gas grill and even the white neighbors piled their plates high with that luridly red, charred, juicy chicken. Their younger daughter had danced, and even our boys had broken away from the Stanley Cup telecast to put in a reluctant appearance. Everyone took pictures for their albums and for the community newspapers—another of our families had made it big in Toronto—and now I wonder how many of those happy faces are gone. "Why does God give us so much if all along He intends to take it away?" Kusum asks me.

I nod. We sit on carpeted stairs, holding hands like children. "I never once told him that I loved him," I say. I was too much the well brought up woman. I was so well brought up I never felt comfortable calling my husband by his first name.

"It's all right," Kusum says. "He knew. My husband knew. They felt it. Modern young girls have to say it because what they feel is fake."

Kusum's daughter, Pam, runs in with an overnight case. Pam's in her McDonald's uniform. "Mummy! You have to get dressed!" Panic makes her cranky. "A reporter's on his way here."

"Why?"

"You want to talk to him in your bathrobe?" She starts to brush her mother's long hair. She's the daughter who's always in trouble. She dates Canadian boys and hangs out in the mall, shopping for tight sweaters. The younger one, the goody-goody one according to Pam, the one with a voice so sweet that when she sang *bhajans*[2] for Ethiopian relief even a frugal man like my husband wrote out a hundred dollar check, *she* was on that plane. *She* was going to spend July and August with grandparents because Pam wouldn't go. Pam said she'd rather waitress at McDonald's. "If it's a choice between Bombay and Wonderland, I'm picking Wonderland," she'd said.

"Leave me alone," Kusum yells. "You know what I want to do? If I didn't have to look after you now, I'd hang myself."

Pam's young face goes blotchy with pain. "Thanks," she says, "don't let me stop you."

"Hush," pregnant Mrs. Sharma scolds Pam. "Leave your mother alone.

1. No.   2. Hymns.

Mr. Sharma will tackle the reporters and fill out the forms. He'll say what has to be said."

Pam stands her ground. "You think I don't know what Mummy's thinking? *Why her?* that's what. That's sick! Mummy wishes my little sister were alive and I were dead."

Kusum's hand in mine is trembly hot. We continue to sit on the stairs.

20 She calls before she arrives, wondering if there's anything I need. Her name is Judith Templeton and she's an appointee of the provincial government. "Multiculturalism?" I ask, and she says, "partially," but that her mandate is bigger. "I've been told you knew many of the people on the flight," she says. "Perhaps if you'd agree to help us reach the others . . . ?"

She gives me time at least to put on tea water and pick up the mess in the front room. I have a few *samosas*[3] from Kusum's housewarming that I could fry up, but then I think, why prolong this visit?

Judith Templeton is much younger than she sounded. She wears a blue suit with a white blouse and a polka dot tie. Her blond hair is cut short, her only jewelry is pearl drop earrings. Her briefcase is new and expensive looking, a gleaming cordovan leather. She sits with it across her lap. When she looks out the front windows onto the street, her contact lenses seem to float in front of her light blue eyes.

"What sort of help do you want from me?" I ask. She has refused the tea, out of politeness, but I insist, along with some slightly stale biscuits.[4]

"I have no experience," she admits. "That is, I have an MSW and I've worked in liaison with accident victims, but I mean I have no experience with a tragedy of this scale—"

25 "Who could?" I ask.

"—and with the complications of culture, language, and customs. Someone mentioned that Mrs. Bhave is a pillar—because you've taken it more calmly."

At this, perhaps, I frown, for she reaches forward, almost to take my hand. "I hope you understand my meaning, Mrs. Bhave. There are hundreds of people in Metro directly affected, like you, and some of them speak no English. There are some widows who've never handled money or gone on a bus, and there are old parents who still haven't eaten or gone outside their bedrooms. Some houses and apartments have been looted. Some wives are still hysterical. Some husbands are in shock and profound depression. We want to help, but our hands are tied in so many ways. We have to distribute money to some people, and there are legal documents—these things can be done. We have interpreters, but we don't always have the human touch, or maybe the right human touch. We don't want to make mistakes, Mrs. Bhave, and that's why we'd like to ask you to help us."

"More mistakes, you mean," I say.

"Police matters are not in my hands," she answers.

---

3. Fried turnovers filled with finely chopped meat or vegetables.   4. Cookies.

"Nothing I can do will make any difference," I say. "We must all grieve 30
in our own way."

"But you are coping very well. All the people said, Mrs. Bhave is the
strongest person of all. Perhaps if the others could see you, talk with you,
it would help them."

"By the standards of the people you call hysterical, I am behaving very
oddly and very badly, Miss Templeton." I want to say to her, *I wish I could
scream, starve, walk into Lake Ontario, jump from a bridge*. "They would not
see me as a model. I do not see myself as a model."

I am a freak. No one who has ever known me would think of me reacting
this way. This terrible calm will not go away.

She asks me if she may call again, after I get back from a long trip that
we all must make. "Of course," I say. "Feel free to call, anytime."

Four days later, I find Kusum squatting on a rock overlooking a bay in 35
Ireland. It isn't a big rock, but it juts sharply out over water. This is as close
as we'll ever get to them. June breezes balloon out her sari and unpin her
knee-length hair. She has the bewildered look of a sea creature whom the
tides have stranded.

It's been one hundred hours since Kusum came stumbling and screaming across my lawn. Waiting around the hospital, we've heard many stories.
The police, the diplomats, they tell us things thinking that we're strong,
that knowledge is helpful to the grieving, and maybe it is. Some, I know,
prefer ignorance, or their own versions. The plane broke into two, they say.
Unconsciousness was instantaneous. No one suffered. My boys must have
just finished their breakfasts. They loved eating on planes, they loved the
smallness of plates, knives, and forks. Last year they saved the airline salt
and pepper shakers. Half an hour more and they would have made it to
Heathrow.

Kusum says that we can't escape our fate. She says that all those people—
our husbands, my boys, her girl with the nightingale voice, all those Hin-
dus, Christians, Sikhs, Muslims, Parsis, and atheists on that plane—were
fated to die together off this beautiful bay. She learned this from a swami
in Toronto.

I have my Valium.

Six of us "relatives"—two widows and four widowers—choose to spend
the day today by the waters instead of sitting in a hospital room and scanning photographs of the dead. That's what they call us now: relatives. I've
looked through twenty-seven photos in two days. They're very kind to us,
the Irish are very understanding. Sometimes understanding means freeing
a tourist bus for this trip to the bay, so we can pretend to spy our loved
ones through the glassiness of waves or in sunspeckled cloud shapes.

I could die here, too, and be content. 40

"What is that, out there?" She's standing and flapping her hands and
for a moment I see a head shape bobbing in the waves. She's standing in
the water, I, on the boulder. The tide is low, and a round, black, headsized
rock has just risen from the waves. She returns, her sari end dripping and

ruined and her face is a twisted remnant of hope, the way mine was a hundred hours ago, still laughing but inwardly knowing that nothing but the ultimate tragedy could bring two women together at six o'clock on a Sunday morning. I watch her face sag into blankness.

"That water felt warm, Shaila," she says at length.

"You can't," I say. "We have to wait for our turn to come."

I haven't eaten in four days, haven't brushed my teeth.

45   "I know," she says. "I tell myself I have no right to grieve. They are in a better place than we are. My swami says I should be thrilled for them. My swami says depression is a sign of our selfishness."

Maybe I'm selfish. Selfishly I break away from Kusum and run, sandals slapping against stones, to the water's edge. What if my boys aren't lying pinned under the debris? What if they aren't stuck a mile below that innocent blue chop? What if, given the strong currents. . . .

Now I've ruined my sari, one of my best. Kusum has joined me, knee-deep in water that feels to me like a swimming pool. I could settle in the water, and my husband would take my hand and the boys would slap water in my face just to see me scream.

"Do you remember what good swimmers my boys were, Kusum?"

"I saw the medals," she says.

50   One of the widowers, Dr. Ranganathan from Montreal, walks out to us, carrying his shoes in one hand. He's an electrical engineer. Someone at the hotel mentioned his work is famous around the world, something about the place where physics and electricity come together. He has lost a huge family, something indescribable. "With some luck," Dr. Ranganathan suggests to me, "a good swimmer could make it safely to some island. It is quite possible that there may be many, many microscopic islets scattered around."

"You're not just saying that?" I tell Dr. Ranganathan about Vinod, my elder son. Last year he took diving as well.

"It's a parent's duty to hope," he says. "It is foolish to rule out possibilities that have not been tested. I myself have not surrendered hope."

Kusum is sobbing once again. "Dear lady," he says, laying his free hand on her arm, and she calms down.

"Vinod is how old?" he asks me. He's very careful, as we all are. *Is,* not *was.*

55   "Fourteen. Yesterday he was fourteen. His father and uncle were going to take him down to the Taj and give him a big birthday party. I couldn't go with them because I couldn't get two weeks off from my stupid job in June." I process bills for a travel agent. June is a big travel month.

Dr. Ranganathan whips the pockets of his suit jacked inside out. Squashed roses, in darkening shades of pink, float on the water. He tore the roses off creepers in somebody's garden. He didn't ask anyone if he could pluck the roses, but now there's been an article about it in the local papers. When you see an Indian person, it says, please give him or her flowers.

"A strong youth of fourteen," he says, "can very likely pull to safety a younger one."

My sons, though four years apart, were very close. Vinod wouldn't let Mithun drown. *Electrical engineering*, I think, foolishly perhaps: this man knows important secrets of the universe, things closed to me. Relief spins me lightheaded. No wonder my boys' photographs haven't turned up in the gallery of photos of the recovered dead. "Such pretty roses," I say.

"My wife loved pink roses. Every Friday I had to bring a bunch home. I used to say, why? After twenty-odd years of marriage you're still needing proof positive of my love?" He has identified his wife and three of his children. Then others from Montreal, the lucky ones, intact families with no survivors. He chuckles as he wades back to shore. Then he swings around to ask me a question. "Mrs. Bhave, you are wanting to throw in some roses for your loved ones? I have two big ones left."

But I have other things to float: Vinod's pocket calculator; a half-painted   60 model B-52 for my Mithun. They'd want them on their island. And for my husband? For him I let fall into the calm, glassy waters a poem I wrote in the hospital yesterday. Finally he'll know my feelings for him.

"Don't tumble, the rocks are slippery," Dr. Ranganathan cautions. He holds out a hand for me to grab.

Then it's time to get back on the bus, time to rush back to our waiting posts on hospital benches.

Kusum is one of the lucky ones. The lucky ones flew here, identified in multiplicate their loved ones, then will fly to India with the bodies for proper ceremonies. Satish is one of the few males who surfaced. The photos of faces we saw on the walls in an office at Heathrow and here in the hospital are mostly of women. Women have more body fat, a nun said to me matter-of-factly. They float better. Today I was stopped by a young sailor on the street. He had loaded bodies, he'd gone into the water when—he checks my face for signs of strength—when the sharks were first spotted. I don't blush, and he breaks down. "It's all right," I say. "Thank you." I had heard about the sharks from Dr. Ranganathan. In his orderly mind, science brings understanding, it holds no terror. It is the shark's duty. For every deer there is a hunter, for every fish a fisherman.

The Irish are not shy; they rush to me and give me hugs and some are crying. I cannot imagine reactions like that on the streets of Toronto. Just strangers, and I am touched. Some carry flowers with them and give them to any Indian they see.

After lunch, a policeman I have gotten to know quite well catches hold   65 of me. He says he thinks he has a match for Vinod. I explain what a good swimmer Vinod is.

"You want me with you when you look at photos?" Dr. Ranganathan walks ahead of me into the picture gallery. In these matters, he is a scientist, and I am grateful. It is a new perspective. "They have performed miracles," he says. "We are indebted to them."

The first day or two the policemen showed us relatives only one picture at a time; now they're in a hurry, they're eager to lay out the possibles, and even the probables.

The face on the photo is of a boy much like Vinod; the same intelligent eyes, the same thick brows dipping into a V. But this boy's features, even his cheeks, are puffier, wider, mushier.

"No." My gaze is pulled by other pictures. There are five other boys who look like Vinod.

70   The nun assigned to console me rubs the first picture with a fingertip. "When they've been in the water for a while, love, they look a little heavier." The bones under the skin are broken, they said on the first day—try to adjust your memories. It's important.

"It's not him. I'm his mother. I'd know."

"I know this one!" Dr. Ranganathan cries out suddenly from the back of the gallery. "And this one!" I think he senses that I don't want to find my boys. "They are the Kutty brothers. They were also from Montreal." I don't mean to be crying. On the contrary, I am ecstatic. My suitcase in the hotel is packed heavy with dry clothes for my boys.

The policeman starts to cry. "I am so sorry, I am so sorry, ma'am. I really thought we had a match."

With the nun ahead of us and the policeman behind, we, the unlucky ones without our children's bodies, file out of the makeshift gallery.

75   From Ireland most of us go on to India. Kusum and I take the same direct flight to Bombay, so I can help her clear customs quickly. But we have to argue with a man in uniform. He has large boils on his face. The boils swell and glow with sweat as we argue with him. He wants Kusum to wait in line and he refuses to take authority because his boss is on a tea break. But Kusum won't let her coffins out of sight, and I shan't desert her though I know that my parents, elderly and diabetic, must be waiting in a stuffy car in a scorching lot.

"You bastard!" I scream at the man with the popping boils. Other passengers press closer. "You think we're smuggling contraband in those coffins!"

Once upon a time we were well brought up women; we were dutiful wives who kept our heads veiled, our voices shy and sweet.

In India, I become, once again, an only child of rich, ailing parents. Old friends of the family come to pay their respects. Some are Sikh, and inwardly, involuntarily, I cringe. My parents are progressive people; they do not blame communities for a few individuals.

In Canada it is a different story now.

80   "Stay longer," my mother pleads. "Canada is a cold place. Why would you want to be all by yourself?" I stay.

Three months pass. Then another.

"Vikram wouldn't have wanted you to give up things!" they protest. They call my husband by the name he was born with. In Toronto he'd changed to Vik so the men he worked with at his office would find his name as easy as Rod or Chris. "You know, the dead aren't cut off from us!"

My grandmother, the spoiled daughter of a rich *zamindar,*[5] shaved her

---

5. Landowner.

head with rusty razor blades when she was widowed at sixteen. My grand-father died of childhood diabetes when he was nineteen, and she saw herself as the harbinger of bad luck. My mother grew up without parents, raised indifferently by an uncle, while her true mother slept in a hut behind the main estate house and took her food with the servants. She grew up a rationalist. My parents abhor mindless mortification.

The zamindar's daughter kept stubborn faith in Vedic rituals; my par-ents rebelled. I am trapped between two modes of knowledge. At thirty-six, I am too old to start over and too young to give up. Like my husband's spirit, I flutter between worlds.

Courting aphasia, we travel. We travel with our phalanx of servants and 85
poor relatives. To hill stations and to beach resorts. We play contract bridge in dusty gymkhana clubs. We ride stubby ponies up crumbly mountain trails. At tea dances, we let ourselves be twirled twice round the ballroom. We hit the holy spots we hadn't made time for before. In Varanasi, Kalighat, Rishikesh, Hardwar, astrologers and palmists seek me out and for a fee offer me cosmic consolations.

Already the widowers among us are being shown new bride candidates. They cannot resist the call of custom, the authority of their parents and older brothers. They must marry; it is the duty of a man to look after a wife. The new wives will be young widows with children, destitute but of good family. They will make loving wives, but the men will shun them. I've had calls from the men over crackling Indian telephone lines. "Save me," they say, these substantial, educated, successful men of forty. "My parents are arranging a marriage for me." In a month they will have buried one family and returned to Canada with a new bride and partial family.

I am comparatively lucky. No one here thinks of arranging a husband for an unlucky widow.

Then, on the third day of the sixth month into this odyssey, in an aban-doned temple in a tiny Himalayan village, as I make my offering of flowers and sweetmeats to the god of a tribe of animists, my husband descends to me. He is squatting next to a scrawny *sadhu*[6] in moth-eaten robes. Vikram wears the vanilla suit he wore the last time I hugged him. The *sadhu* tosses petals on a butter-fed flame, reciting Sanskrit mantras and sweeps his face of flies. My husband takes my hands in his.

You're beautiful, he starts. Then, *What are you doing here?*

Shall I stay? I ask. He only smiles, but already the image is fading. *You* 90
must finish alone what we started together. No seaweed wreathes his mouth. He speaks too fast just as he used to when we were an envied family in our pink split-level. He is gone.

In the windowless altar room, smoky with joss sticks and clarified butter lamps, a sweaty hand gropes for my blouse. I do not shriek. The *sadhu* arranges his robe. The lamps hiss and sputter out.

When we come out of the temple, my mother says, "Did you feel some-thing weird in there?"

6. Hindu holy man.

My mother has no patience with ghosts, prophetic dreams, holy men, and cults.

"No," I lie. "Nothing."

95   But she knows that she's lost me. She knows that in days I shall be leaving.

Kusum's put her house up for sale. She wants to live in an ashram in Hardwar. Moving to Hardwar was her swami's idea. Her swami runs two ashrams, the one in Hardwar and another here in Toronto.

"Don't run away," I tell her.

"I'm not running away," she says. "I'm pursuing inner peace. You think you or that Ranganathan fellow are better off?"

Pam's left for California. She wants to do some modelling, she says. She says when she comes into her share of the insurance money she'll open a yoga-cum-aerobics studio in Hollywood. She sends me postcards so naughty I daren't leave them on the coffee table. Her mother has withdrawn from her and the world.

100   The rest of us don't lose touch, that's the point. Talk is all we have, says Dr. Ranganathan, who has also resisted his relatives and returned to Montreal and to his job, alone. He says, whom better to talk with than other relatives? We've been melted down and recast as a new tribe.

He calls me twice a week from Montreal. Every Wednesday night and every Saturday afternoon. He is changing jobs, going to Ottawa. But Ottawa is over a hundred miles away, and he is forced to drive two hundred and twenty miles a day. He can't bring himself to sell his house. The house is a temple, he says; the king-sized bed in the master bedroom is a shrine. He sleeps on a folding cot. A devotee.

There are still some hysterical relatives. Judith Templeton's list of those needing help and those who've "accepted" is in nearly perfect balance. Acceptance means you speak of your family in the past tense and you make active plans for moving ahead with your life. There are courses at Seneca and Ryerson[7] we could be taking. Her gleaming leather briefcase is full of college catalogues and lists of cultural societies that need our help. She has done impressive work, I tell her.

"In the textbooks on grief management," she replies—I am her confidante, I realize, one of the few whose grief has not sprung bizarre obsessions—"there are stages to pass through: rejection, depression, acceptance, reconstruction." She has compiled a chart and finds that six months after the tragedy, none of us still reject reality, but only a handful are reconstructing. "Depressed Acceptance" is the plateau we've reached. Remarriage is a major step in reconstruction (though she's a little surprised, even shocked, over *how* quickly some of the men have taken on new families). Selling one's house and changing jobs and cities is healthy.

---

7. Seneca College of Applied Arts and Technology, in Willowdale; Ryerson Polytechnical Institute, Toronto.

How do I tell Judith Templeton that my family surrounds me, and that like creatures in epics, they've changed shapes? She sees me as calm and accepting but worries that I have no job, no career. My closest friends are worse off than I. I cannot tell her my days, even my nights, are thrilling.

She asks me to help with families she can't reach at all. An elderly couple 105 in Agincourt whose sons were killed just weeks after they had brought their parents over from a village in Punjab. From their names, I know they are Sikh. Judith Templeton and a translator have visited them twice with offers of money for air fare to Ireland, with bank forms, power-of-attorney forms, but they have refused to sign, or to leave their tiny apartment. Their sons' money is frozen in the bank. Their sons' investment apartments have been trashed by tenants, the furnishings sold off. The parents fear that anything they sign or any money they receive will end the company's or the country's obligations to them. They fear they are selling their sons for two airline tickets to a place they've never seen.

The high-rise apartment is a tower of Indians and West Indians, with a sprinkling of Orientals. The nearest bus stop kiosk is lined with women in saris. Boys practice cricket in the parking lot. Inside the building, even I wince a bit from the ferocity of onion fumes, the distinctive and immediate Indianness of frying *ghee,* but Judith Templeton maintains a steady flow of information. These poor old people are in imminent danger of losing their place and all their services.

I say to her, "They are Sikh. They will not open up to a Hindu woman." And what I want to add is, as much as I try not to, I stiffen now at the sight of beards and turbans. I remember a time when we all trusted each other in this new country, it was only the new country we worried about.

The two rooms are dark and stuffy. The lights are off, and an oil lamp sputters on the coffee table. The bent old lady has let us in, and her husband is wrapping a white turban over his oiled, hip-length hair. She immediately goes to the kitchen, and I hear the most familiar sound of an Indian home, tap water hitting and filling a teapot.

They have not paid their utility bills, out of fear and the inability to write a check. The telephone is gone; electricity and gas and water are soon to follow. They have told Judith their sons will provide. They are good boys, and they have always earned and looked after their parents.

We converse a bit in Hindi. They do not ask about the crash and I 110 wonder if I should bring it up. If they think I am here merely as a translator, then they may feel insulted. There are thousands of Punjabi-speakers, Sikhs, in Toronto to do a better job. And so I say to the old lady, "I too have lost my sons, and my husband, in the crash."

Her eyes immediately fill with tears. The man mutters a few words which sound like a blessing. "God provides and God takes away," he says.

I want to say, but only men destroy and give back nothing. "My boys and my husband are not coming back," I say. "We have to understand that."

Now the old woman responds. "But who is to say? Man alone does not decide these things." To this her husband adds his agreement.

Judith asks about the bank papers, the release forms. With a stroke of the pen, they will have a provincial trustee to pay their bills, invest their money, send them a monthly pension.

115   "Do you know this woman?" I ask them.

The man raises his hand from the table, turns it over and seems to regard each finger separately before he answers. "This young lady is always coming here, we make tea for her and she leaves papers for us to sign." His eyes scan a pile of papers in the corner of the room. "Soon we will be out of tea, then will she go away?"

The old lady adds, "I have asked my neighbors and no one else gets angrezi[8] visitors. What have we done?"

"It's her job," I try to explain. "The government is worried. Soon you will have no place to stay, no lights, no gas, no water."

"Government will get its money. Tell her not to worry, we are honorable people."

120   I try to explain the government wishes to give money, not take. He raises his hand. "Let them take," he says. "We are accustomed to that. That is no problem."

"We are strong people," says the wife. "Tell her that."

"Who needs all this machinery?" demands the husband. "It is unhealthy, the bright lights, the cold air on a hot day, the cold food, the four gas rings. God will provide, not government."

"When our boys return," the mother says. Her husband sucks his teeth. "Enough talk," he says.

Judith breaks in. "Have you convinced them?" The snaps on her cordovan briefcase go off like firecrackers in that quiet apartment. She lays the sheaf of legal papers on the coffee table. "If they can't write their names, an X will do—I've told them that."

125   Now the old lady has shuffled to the kitchen and soon emerges with a pot of tea and two cups. "I think my bladder will go first on a job like this," Judith says to me, smiling. "If only there was some way of reaching them. Please thank her for the tea. Tell her she's very kind."

I nod in Judith's direction and tell them in Hindi, "She thanks you for the tea. She thinks you are being very hospitable but she doesn't have the slightest idea what it means."

I want to say, humor her. I want to say, my boys and my husband are with me too, more than ever. I look in the old man's eyes and I can read his stubborn, peasant's message: *I have protected this woman as best I can. She is the only person I have left. Give to me or take from me what you will, but I will not sign for it. I will not pretend that I accept.*

In the car, Judith says, "You see what I'm up against? I'm sure they're lovely people, but their stubbornness and ignorance are driving me crazy. They think signing a paper is signing their sons' death warrants, don't they?"

I am looking out the window. I want to say, *In our culture, it is a parent's duty to hope.*

8. English, Anglo.

"Now Shaila, this next woman is a real mess. She cries day and night, 130
and she refuses all medical help. We may have to—"

"—Let me out at the subway," I say.

"I beg your pardon?" I can feel those blue eyes staring at me.

It would not be like her to disobey. She merely disapproves, and slows
at a corner to let me out. Her voice is plaintive. "Is there anything I said?
Anything I did?"

I could answer her suddenly in a dozen ways, but I choose not to.
"Shaila? Let's talk about it," I hear, then slam the door.

A wife and mother begins her new life in a new country, and that life is 135
cut short. Yet her husband tells her: Complete what we have started. We,
who stayed out of politics and came halfway around the world to avoid
religious and political feuding have been the first in the New World to die
from it. I no longer know what we started, nor how to complete it. I write
letters to the editors of local papers and to members of Parliament. Now
at least they admit it was a bomb. One MP answers back, with sympathy,
but with a challenge. You want to make a difference? Work on a campaign.
Work on mine. Politicize the Indian voter.

My husband's old lawyer helps me set up a trust. Vikram was a saver
and a careful investor. He had saved the boys' boarding school and college
fees. I sell the pink house at four times what we paid for it and take a small
apartment downtown. I am looking for a charity to support.

We are deep in the Toronto winter, gray skies, icy pavements. I stay
indoors, watching television. I have tried to assess my situation, how best
to live my life, to complete what we began so many years ago. Kusum has
written me from Hardwar that her life is now serene. She has seen Satish
and has heard her daughter sing again. Kusum was on a pilgrimage, passing
through a village when she heard a young girl's voice, singing one of her
daughter's favorite *bhajans*. She followed the music through the squalor of
a Himalayan village, to a hut where a young girl, an exact replica of her
daughter, was fanning coals under the kitchen fire. When she appeared,
the girl cried out, "Ma!" and ran away. What did I think of that?

I think I can only envy her.

Pam didn't make it to California, but writes me from Vancouver. She
works in a department store, giving make-up hints to Indian and Oriental
girls. Dr. Ranganathan has given up his commute, given up his house and
job, and accepted an academic position in Texas where no one knows his
story and he has vowed not to tell it. He calls me now once a week.

I wait, I listen, and I pray, but Vikram has not returned to me. The voices 140
and the shapes and the nights filled with visions ended abruptly several
weeks ago.

I take it as a sign.

One rare, beautiful, sunny day last week, returning from a small errand
on Yonge Street, I was walking through the park from the subway to my
apartment. I live equidistant from the Ontario Houses of Parliament and
the University of Toronto. The day was not cold, but something in the bare

trees caught my attention. I looked up from the gravel, into the branches and the clear blue sky beyond. I thought I heard the rustling of larger forms, and I waited a moment for voices. Nothing.

"What?" I asked.

Then as I stood in the path looking north to Queen's Park and west to the university, I heard the voices of my family one last time. *Your time has come,* they said. *Go, be brave.*

I do not know where this voyage I have begun will end. I do not know which direction I will take. I dropped the package on a park bench and started walking.

1988

QUESTIONS

1. What words and images in the opening paragraphs of "The Management of Grief" provide the reader with clues to the story's underlying themes of cultural dislocation and the mixing of cultures?

2. Throughout the story Bharati Mukherjee pays close attention to the significance of words and the ways that words express, or fail to express, emotional truths. Find some examples of words and phrases that the narrator and other characters notice as having special significance. Can you think of words in one culture that defy translation into the language of another?

3. Air travel, of course, has greatly increased communication—and, sometimes, friction—between cultures. What is the thematic significance of this story's central event, a plane disaster?

SUGGESTIONS FOR WRITING

1. In any one story in this book find five words that have special thematic significance, and write an essay discussing the way each relates to the story as a whole.

2. Sometimes the theme in a work of literature can be expressed as a strong, clear statement: "A always follows from B," or "An X can never be a Y." More often, though, especially in modern literature, authors offer subtler, often ambiguous themes that deliberately undermine our faith in simple absolutes: "A doesn't necessarily always follow B," or "There are times when an X can be a Y." Write an essay in which you argue that one of the stories in this book has an "always" or "never" kind of theme, and contrast it to the more indeterminate theme in another story.

3. The great twentieth-century painter Pablo Picasso once said, "One does a whole painting for one peach and people think just the opposite—that that particular peach is but a detail." Is a work of art "about" the details of its surface, or "about" its underlying themes? Write an essay exploring the relationship between details and theme in one or more of the stories in this anthology.

7 THE WHOLE TEXT

Plot, point of view, character, setting, symbol, and theme are useful concepts. But they do not really exist as discrete parts of a finished work. Analyzing a story means thinking about issues smaller than the whole story—focusing on certain particulars before trying to consider the story as a whole. Our analysis may be enhanced by discussing a story in terms of its "elements," but we must remember both the arbitrariness of those distinctions and the integrity of the story as a whole. As you read the stories that follow in this chapter, apply all that you

For the fiction writer ... the whole story is the meaning, because it is an experience, not an abstraction.

—FLANNERY O'CONNOR

have learned about the history, the structure, and the elements of fiction, but be especially alert to how the various elements interact. Notice how, after taking a story apart in order to analyze it, we can put it back together.

JOSEPH CONRAD

The Secret Sharer

I

On my right hand there were lines of fishing-stakes resembling a mysterious system of half-submerged bamboo fences, incomprehensible in its division of the domain of tropical fishes, and crazy[1] of aspect as if abandoned for ever by some nomad tribe of fishermen now gone to the other end of the ocean; for there was no sign of human habitation as far as the eye could reach. To the left a group of barren islets, suggesting ruins of stone walls, towers, and blockhouses, had its foundations set in a blue sea that itself looked solid, so still and stable did it lie below my feet; even the track of light from the westering sun shone smoothly, without that animated glitter which tells of an imperceptible ripple. And when I turned my head to take a parting glance at the tug which had just left us anchored outside the bar, I saw the straight line of the flat shore joined to the stable sea, edge to edge, with a perfect and unmarked closeness, in one leveled floor half brown, half blue under the enormous dome of the sky. Corresponding in their insignificance to the islets of the sea, two small clumps of trees, one on each side of the only fault in the impeccable joint, marked the mouth

1. Irregular, rickety.

of the river Meinam[2] we had just left on the first preparatory stage of our homeward journey; and, far back on the inland level, a larger and loftier mass, the grove surrounding the great Paknam pagoda, was the only thing on which the eye could rest from the vain task of exploring the monotonous sweep of the horizon. Here and there gleams as of a few scattered pieces of silver marked the windings of the great river; and on the nearest of them, just within the bar, the tug steaming right into the land became lost to my sight, hull and funnel and masts, as though the impassive earth had swallowed her up without an effort, without a tremor. My eye followed the light cloud of her smoke, now here, now there, above the plain, according to the devious curves of the stream, but always fainter and farther away, till I lost it at last behind the mitre-shaped hill of the great pagoda. And then I was left alone with my ship, anchored at the head of the Gulf of Siam.

She floated at the starting-point of a long journey, very still in an immense stillness, the shadows of her spars flung far to the eastward by the setting sun. At that moment I was alone on her decks. There was not a sound in her—and around us nothing moved, nothing lived, not a canoe on the water, not a bird in the air, not a cloud in the sky. In this breathless pause at the threshold of a long passage we seemed to be measuring our fitness for a long and arduous enterprise, the appointed task of both our existences to be carried out, far from all human eyes, with only sky and sea for spectators and for judges.

There must have been some glare in the air to interfere with one's sight, because it was only just before the sun left us that my roaming eyes made out beyond the highest ridge of the principal islet of the group something which did away with the solemnity of perfect solitude. The tide of darkness flowed on swiftly; and with tropical suddenness a swarm of stars came out above the shadowy earth, while I lingered yet, my hand resting lightly on my ship's rail as if on the shoulder of a trusted friend. But, with all that multitude of celestial bodies staring down at one, the comfort of quiet communion with her was gone for good. And there were also disturbing sounds by this time—voices, footsteps forward; the steward flitted along the main deck, a busily ministering spirit; a hand-bell tinkled urgently under the poop deck. . . .

I found my two officers waiting for me near the supper table, in the lighted cuddy.[3] We sat down at once, and as I helped the chief mate, I said:

5 "Are you aware that there is a ship anchored inside the islands? I saw her mast-heads above the ridge as the sun went down."

He raised sharply his simple face, overcharged by a terrible growth of whisker, and emitted his usual ejaculations, "Bless my soul, sir! You don't say so!"

My second mate was a round-cheeked, silent young man, grave beyond his years, I thought; but as our eyes happened to meet I detected a slight

2. The Menan (Chao Phraya) runs through Bangkok, Thailand, into the Gulf of Siam. The Paknam Pagoda stands at the mouth of the river.
3. A small cabin, adjacent to the captain's quarters, beneath the poop deck.

quiver on his lips. I looked down at once. It was not my part to encourage sneering on board my ship. It must be said, too, that I knew very little of my officers. In consequence of certain events of no particular significance, except to myself, I had been appointed to the command only a fortnight before. Neither did I know much of the hands forward. All these people had been together for eighteen months or so, and my position was that of the only stranger on board. I mention this because it has some bearing on what is to follow. But what I felt most was my being a stranger to the ship; and if all the truth must be told, I was somewhat of a stranger to myself. The youngest man on board (barring the second mate), and untried as yet by a position of the fullest responsibility, I was willing to take the adequacy of the others for granted. They had simply to be equal to their tasks; but I wondered how far I should turn out faithful to that ideal conception of one's own personality every man sets up for himself secretly.

Meantime the chief mate, with an almost visible effect of collaboration on the part of his round eyes and frightful whiskers, was trying to evolve a theory of the anchored ship. His dominant trait was to take all things into earnest consideration. He was of a painstaking turn of mind. As he used to say, he "liked to account to himself" for practically everything that came in his way, down to a miserable scorpion he had found in his cabin a week before. The why and the wherefore of that scorpion—how it got on board and came to select his room rather than the pantry (which was a dark place and more what a scorpion would be partial to), and how on earth it managed to drown itself in the inkwell of his writing-desk—had exercised him infinitely. The ship within the islands was much more easily accounted for; and just as we were about to rise from table he made his pronouncement. She was, he doubted not, a ship from home lately arrived. Probably she drew too much water to cross the bar except at the top of spring tides. Therefore she went into that natural harbor to wait for a few days in preference to remaining in an open roadstead.

"That's so," confirmed the second mate suddenly, in his slightly hoarse voice. "She draws over twenty feet. She's the Liverpool ship *Sephora* with a cargo of coal. Hundred and twenty-three days from Cardiff."

We looked at him in surprise.

"The tugboat skipper told me when he come on board for your letters, sir," explained the young man. "He expects to take her up the river the day after tomorrow."

After thus overwhelming us with the extent of his information he slipped out of the cabin. The mate observed regretfully that he "could not account for that young fellow's whims." What prevented him telling us all about it at once, he wanted to know.

I detained him as he was making a move. For the last two days the crew had had plenty of hard work, and the night before they had very little sleep. I felt painfully that I—a stranger—was doing something unusual when I directed him to let all hands turn in without setting an anchor-watch.[4] I

10

---

4. A detachment of seamen kept on deck while the ship lies at anchor.

proposed to keep on deck myself till one o'clock or thereabouts. I would get the second mate to relieve me at that hour.

"He will turn out the cook and the steward at four," I concluded, "and then give you a call. Of course at the slightest sign of any sort of wind we'll have the hands up and make a start at once."

15   He concealed his astonishment. "Very well, sir." Outside the cuddy he put his head in the second mate's door to inform him of my unheard-of caprice to take a five hours' anchor-watch on myself. I heard the other raise his voice incredulously—"What? The captain himself?" Then a few more murmurs, a door closed, then another. A few moments later I went on deck.

My strangeness, which had made me sleepless, had prompted that unconventional arrangement, as if I had expected in those solitary hours of the night to get on terms with the ship of which I knew nothing, manned by men of whom I knew very little more. Fast alongside a wharf, littered like any ship in port with a tangle of unrelated things, invaded by unrelated shore people, I had hardly seen her yet properly. Now, as she lay cleared for sea, the stretch of her main deck seemed to me very fine under the stars. Very fine, very roomy for her size, and very inviting. I descended the poop and paced the waist, my mind picturing to myself the coming passage through the Malay Archipelago, down the Indian Ocean, and up the Atlantic. All its phases were familiar enough to me, every characteristic, all the alternatives which were likely to face me on the high seas—everything! . . . except the novel responsibility of command. But I took heart from the reasonable thought that the ship was like other ships, the men like other men, and that the sea was not likely to keep any special surprises expressly for my discomfiture.

Arrived at that comforting conclusion, I bethought myself of a cigar and went below to get it. All was still down there. Everybody at the after end of the ship was sleeping profoundly. I came out again on the quarter-deck, agreeably at ease in my sleeping suit on that warm, breathless night, barefooted, a glowing cigar in my teeth, and, going forward, I was met by the profound silence of the fore end of the ship. Only as I passed the door of the forecastle I heard a deep, quiet, trustful sigh of some sleeper inside. And suddenly I rejoiced in the great security of the sea as compared with the unrest of the land, in my choice of that untempted life presenting no disquieting problems, invested with an elementary moral beauty by the absolute straightforwardness of its appeal and by the singleness of its purpose.

The riding-light[5] in the fore-rigging burned with a clear, untroubled, as if symbolic, flame, confident and bright in the mysterious shades of the night. Passing on my way aft along the other side of the ship, I observed that the rope side-ladder, put over, no doubt, for the master of the tug when he came to fetch away our letters, had not been hauled in as it should have been. I became annoyed at this, for exactitude in small matters is the

---

5. Special light displayed by a ship while ("riding") at anchor.

very soul of discipline. Then I reflected that I had myself peremptorily dismissed my officers from duty, and by my own act had prevented the anchor-watch being formally set and things properly attended to. I asked myself whether it was wise ever to interfere with the established routine of duties even from the kindest of motives. My action might have made me appear eccentric. Goodness only knew how that absurdly whiskered mate would "account" for my conduct, and what the whole ship thought of that informality of their new captain. I was vexed with myself.

Not from compunction certainly, but, as it were mechanically, I proceeded to get the ladder in myself. Now a side-ladder of that sort is a light affair and comes in easily, yet my vigorous tug, which should have brought it flying on board, merely recoiled upon my body in a totally unexpected jerk. What the devil! . . . I was so astounded by the immovableness of that ladder that I remained stockstill, trying to account for it to myself like that imbecile mate of mine. In the end, of course, I put my head over the rail.

The side of the ship made an opaque belt of shadow on the darkling 20 glassy shimmer of the sea. But I saw at once something elongated and pale floating very close to the ladder. Before I could form a guess a faint flash of phosphorescent light,[6] which seemed to issue suddenly from the naked body of a man, flickered in the sleeping water with the elusive, silent play of summer lightning in a night sky. With a gasp I saw revealed to my stare a pair of feet, the long legs, a broad livid back immersed right up to the neck in a greenish cadaverous glow. One hand, awash, clutched the bottom rung of the ladder. He was complete but for the head. A headless corpse! The cigar dropped out of my gaping mouth with a tiny plop and a short hiss quite audible in the absolute stillness of all things under heaven. At that I suppose he raised up his face, a dimly pale oval in the shadow of the ship's side. But even then I could only barely make out down there the shape of his black-haired head. However, it was enough for the horrid, frost-bound sensation which had gripped me about the chest to pass off. The moment of vain exclamations was past too. I only climbed on the spare spar and leaned over the rail as far as I could, to bring my eyes nearer to that mystery floating alongside.

As he hung by the ladder, like a resting swimmer, the sea-lightning played about his limbs at every stir; and he appeared in it ghastly, silvery, fish-like. He remained as mute as a fish, too. He made no motion to get out of the water, either. It was inconceivable that he should not attempt to come on board, and strangely troubling to suspect that perhaps he did not want to. And my first words were prompted by just that troubled incertitude.

"What's the matter?" I asked in my ordinary tone, speaking down to the face upturned exactly under mine.

"Cramp," it answered, no louder. Then slightly anxious, "I say, no need to call any one."

"I was not going to," I said.

6. Light emitted by microscopic plankton; same as "sea lightning," below.

25   "Are you alone on deck?"

"Yes."

I had somehow the impression that he was on the point of letting go the ladder to swim away beyond my ken—mysterious as he came. But, for the moment, this being appearing as if he had risen from the bottom of the sea (it was certainly the nearest land to the ship) wanted only to know the time. I told him. And he, down there, tentatively:

"I suppose your captain's turned in?"

"I am sure he isn't," I said.

30   He seemed to struggle with himself, for I heard something like the low, bitter murmur of doubt. "What's the good?" His next words came out with a hesitating effort.

"Look here, my man. Could you call him out quietly?"

I thought the time had come to declare myself.

"*I* am the captain."

I heard a "By Jove!" whispered at the level of the water. The phosphorescence flashed in the swirl of the water all about his limbs, his other hand seized the ladder.

35   "My name's Leggatt."

The voice was calm and resolute. A good voice. The self-possession of that man had somehow induced a corresponding state in myself. It was very quietly that I remarked:

"You must be a good swimmer."

"Yes. I've been in the water practically since nine o'clock. The question for me now is whether I am to let go this ladder and go on swimming till I sink from exhaustion or—to come on board here."

I felt this was no mere formula of desperate speech, but a real alternative in the view of a strong soul. I should have gathered from this that he was young; indeed, it is only the young who are ever confronted by such clear issues. But at the time it was pure intuition on my part. A mysterious communication was established already between us two—in the face of that silent, darkened tropical sea. I was young, too; young enough to make no comment. The man in the water began suddenly to climb up the ladder, and I hastened away from the rail to fetch some clothes.

40   Before entering the cabin I stood still, listening in the lobby at the foot of the stairs. A faint snore came through the closed door of the chief mate's room. The second mate's door was on the hook, but the darkness in there was absolutely soundless. He, too, was young and could sleep like a stone. Remained the steward, but he was not likely to wake up before he was called. I got a sleeping suit out of my room, and, coming back on deck, saw the naked man from the sea sitting on the main-hatch, glimmering white in the darkness, his elbows on his knees and his head in his hands. In a moment he had concealed his damp body in a sleeping suit of the same gray-stripe pattern as the one I was wearing, and followed me like my double on the poop. Together we moved right aft, barefooted, silent.

"What is it?" I asked in a deadened voice, taking the lighted lamp out of the binnacle, and raising it to his face.

"An ugly business."

He had rather regular features; a good mouth; light eyes under some-what heavy, dark eyebrows; a smooth, square forehead; no growth on his cheeks; a small, brown mustache, and a well-shaped, round chin. His expression was concentrated, meditative, under the inspecting light of the lamp I held up to his face; such as a man thinking hard in solitude might wear. My sleeping suit was just right for his size. A well-knit young fellow of twenty-five at most. He caught his lower lip with the edge of white, even teeth.

"Yes," I said, replacing the lamp in the binnacle. The warm, heavy trop-ical night closed upon his head again.

"There's a ship over there," he murmured.   45

"Yes, I know. The *Sephora*. Did you know of us?"

"Hadn't the slightest idea. I am the mate of her—" He paused and cor-rected himself. "I should say I *was*."

"Aha! Something wrong?"

"Yes. Very wrong indeed. I've killed a man."

"What do you mean? Just now?"   50

"No, on the passage. Weeks ago. Thirty-nine south. When I say a man—"

"Fit of temper," I suggested confidently.

The shadowy, dark head, like mine, seemed to nod imperceptibly above the ghostly gray of my sleeping suit. It was, in the night, as though I had been faced by my own reflection in the depths of a sombre and immense mirror.

"A pretty thing to have to own up to for a Conway[7] boy," murmured my double distinctly.

"You're a Conway boy?"   55

"I am," he said, as if startled. Then, slowly . . . "Perhaps you too . . ."

It was so; but being a couple of years older I had left before he joined. After a quick interchange of dates a silence fell; and I thought suddenly of my absurd mate with his terrific whiskers and the "Bless my soul—you don't say so" type of intellect. My double gave me an inkling of his thoughts by saying:

"My father's a parson in Norfolk. Do you see me before a judge and jury on that charge? For myself I can't see the necessity. There are fellows that an angel from heaven—And I am not that. He was one of those creatures that are just simmering all the time with a silly sort of wickedness. Mis-erable devils that have no business to live at all. He wouldn't do his duty and wouldn't let anybody else do theirs. But what's the good of talking! You know well enough the sort of ill-conditioned snarling cur . . ."

He appealed to me as if our experiences had been as identical as our clothes. And I knew well enough the pestiferous danger of such a character where there are no means of legal repression. And I knew well enough also that my double there was no homicidal ruffian. I did not think of asking

---

7. The wooden battleship *Conway* was used to train young officers for the Royal Navy and merchant service.

him for details, and he told me the story roughly in brusque, disconnected sentences. I needed no more. I saw it all going on as though I were myself inside that other sleeping suit.

60   "It happened while we were setting a reefed foresail,[8] at dusk. Reefed foresail! You understand the sort of weather. The only sail we had left to keep the ship running; so you may guess what it had been like for days. Anxious sort of job, that. He gave me some of his cursed insolence at the sheet.[9] I tell you I was overdone with this terrific weather that seemed to have no end to it. Terrific, I tell you—and a deep ship. I believe the fellow himself was half crazed with funk. It was no time for gentlemanly reproof, so I turned round and felled him like an ox. He up and at me. We closed just as an awful sea made for the ship. All hands saw it coming and took to the rigging, but I had him by the throat, and went on shaking him like a rat, the men above us yelling. 'Look out! Look out!' Then a crash as if the sky had fallen on my head. They say that for over ten minutes hardly anything was to be seen of the ship—just the three masts and a bit of the forecastle head and of the poop all awash driving along in a smother of foam. It was a miracle that they found us, jammed together behind the forebits. It's clear that I meant business, because I was holding him by the throat still when they picked us up. He was black in the face. It was too much for them. It seems they rushed us aft together, gripped as we were, screaming 'Murder!' like a lot of lunatics, and broke into the cuddy. And the ship running for her life, touch and go all the time, any minute her last in a sea fit to turn your hair gray only a-looking at it. I understand that the skipper, too, started raving like the rest of them. The man had been deprived of sleep for more than a week, and to have this spring on him at the height of a furious gale nearly drove him out of his mind. I wonder they didn't fling me overboard after getting the carcass of their precious shipmate out of my fingers. They had rather a job to separate us, I've been told. A sufficiently fierce story to make an old judge and a respectable jury sit up a bit. The first thing I heard when I came to myself was the maddening howling of that endless gale, and on that the voice of the old man. He was hanging on to my bunk, staring into my face out of his sou'wester.

"'Mr. Leggatt, you have killed a man. You can act no longer as chief mate of this ship.'"

His care to subdue his voice made it sound monotonous. He rested a hand on the end of the skylight to steady himself with, and all that time did not stir a limb, so far as I could see. "Nice little tale for a quiet tea party," he concluded in the same tone.

One of my hands, too, rested on the end of the skylight; neither did I stir a limb, so far as I knew. We stood less than a foot from each other. It occurred to me that if old "Bless my soul—you don't say so" were to put his head up the companion and catch sight of us, he would think he was

8. In severe weather, sails are reduced in size ("reefed") by folding and tying.
9. Rope used to secure the lower corner of a sail.

seeing double, or imagine himself come upon a scene of weird witchcraft:
the strange captain having a quiet confabulation by the wheel with his own
gray ghost. I became very much concerned to prevent anything of the sort.
I heard the other's soothing undertone:

"My father's a parson in Norfolk," it said. Evidently he had forgotten
he had told me this important fact before. Truly a nice little tale.

"You had better slip down into my stateroom now," I said, moving off 65
stealthily. My double followed my movements; our bare feet made no
sound; I let him in, closed the door with care, and, after giving a call to
the second mate, returned on deck for my relief.

"Not much sign of any wind yet," I remarked when he approached.

"No, sir. Not much," he assented sleepily in his hoarse voice, with just
enough deference, no more, and barely suppressing a yawn.

"Well, that's all you have to look out for. You have got your orders."

"Yes, sir."

I paced a turn or two on the poop and saw him take up his position 70
face forward with his elbow in the ratlines of the mizzen-rigging before I
went below. The mate's faint snoring was still going on peacefully. The
cuddy lamp was burning over the table on which stood a vase with flowers,
a polite attention from the ship's provision merchant—the last flowers we
should see for the next three months at the very least. Two bunches of
bananas hung from the beam symmetrically, one on each side of the
rudder-casing. Everything was as before in the ship—except that two of her
captain's sleeping suits were simultaneously in use, one motionless in the
cuddy, the other keeping very still in the captain's stateroom.

It must be explained here that my cabin had the form of the capital
letter L, the door being within the angle and opening into the short part
of the letter. A couch was to the left, the bedplace to the right; my writing-
desk and the chronometers' table faced the door. But any one opening it,
unless he stepped right inside, had no view of what I call the long (or
vertical) part of the letter. It contained some lockers surmounted by a
bookcase; and a few clothes, a thick jacket or two, caps, oilskin coat, and
such-like, hung on hooks. There was at the bottom of that part a door
opening into my bathroom, which could be entered also directly from the
saloon. But that way was never used.

The mysterious arrival had discovered the advantage of this particular
shape. Entering my room, lighted strongly by a big bulkhead lamp swung
on gimbals above my writing-desk, I did not see him anywhere till he
stepped out quietly from behind the coats hung in the recessed part.

"I heard somebody moving about, and went in there at once," he whispered.

I, too, spoke under my breath.

"Nobody is likely to come in here without knocking and getting per- 75
mission."

He nodded. His face was thin and the sunburn faded, as though he had
been ill. And no wonder. He had been, I heard presently, kept under arrest
in his cabin for nearly nine weeks. But there was nothing sickly in his eyes

or in his expression. He was not a bit like me, really; yet, as we stood leaning over my bed-place, whispering side by side, with our dark heads together and our backs to the door, anybody bold enough to open it stealthily would have been treated to the uncanny sight of a double captain busy talking in whispers with his other self.

"But all this doesn't tell me how you came to hang on to our side-ladder," I inquired, in the hardly audible murmurs we used, after he had told me something more of the proceedings on board the *Sephora* once the bad weather was over.

"When we sighted Java Head[1] I had had time to think all those matters out several times over. I had six weeks of doing nothing else, and with only an hour or so every evening for a tramp on the quarterdeck."

He whispered, his arms folded on the side of my bedplace, staring through the open port. And I could imagine perfectly the manner of this thinking out—a stubborn if not a steadfast operation; something of which I should have been perfectly incapable.

80   "I reckoned it would be dark before we closed with the land," he continued, so low that I had to strain my hearing, near as we were to each other, shoulder touching shoulder almost. "So I asked to speak to the old man. He always seemed very sick when he came to see me—as if he could not look me in the face. You know, that foresail saved the ship. She was too deep to have run long under bare poles. And it was I that managed to set it for him. Anyway, he came. When I had him in my cabin—he stood by the door looking at me as if I had the halter round my neck already—I asked him right away to leave my cabin door unlocked at night while the ship was going through Sunda Straits. There would be the Java coast within two or three miles, off Anjer Point. I wanted nothing more. I've had a prize for swimming my second year in the Conway."

"I can believe it," I breathed out.

"God only knows why they locked me in every night. To see some of their faces you'd have thought they were afraid I'd go about at night strangling people. Am I a murdering brute? Do I look it? By Jove! if I had been he wouldn't have trusted himself like that into my room. You'll say I might have chucked him aside and bolted out, there and then—it was dark already. Well, no. And for the same reason I wouldn't think of trying to smash the door. There would have been a rush to stop me at the noise, and I did not mean to get into a confounded scrimmage. Somebody else might have got killed—for I would not have broken out only to get chucked back, and I did not want any more of that work. He refused, looking more sick than ever. He was afraid of the men, and also of that old second mate of his who had been sailing with him for years—a gray-headed old humbug; and his steward, too, had been with him devil knows how long—seventeen years or more—a dogmatic sort of loafer who hated me like poison, just

---

1. A famous landmark for clipper ships engaged in the China trade on the western end of Java, the southern entrance to the Sunda Straits mentioned below; the killing thus took place some fifteen hundred miles south of the present scene.

because I was the chief mate. No chief mate ever made more than one voyage in the *Sephora*, you know. Those two old chaps ran the ship. Devil only knows what the skipper wasn't afraid of (all his nerve went to pieces altogether in that hellish spell of bad weather we had)—of what the law would do to him—of his wife, perhaps. Oh yes! she's on board. Though I don't think she would have meddled. She would have been only too glad to have me out of the ship in any way. The 'brand of Cain'[2] business, don't you see? That's all right. I was ready enough to go off wandering on the face of the earth—and that was price enough to pay for an Abel of that sort. Anyhow, he wouldn't listen to me. 'This thing must take its course. I represent the law here.' He was shaking like a leaf. 'So you won't?' 'No!' 'Then I hope you will be able to sleep on that," I said, and turned my back on him. 'I wonder that *you* can,' cries he, and locks the door.

"Well, after that, I couldn't. Not very well. That was three weeks ago. We have had a slow passage through the Java Sea; drifted about Carimata[3] for ten days. When we anchored here they thought, I suppose, it was all right. The nearest land (and that's five miles) is the ship's destination; the consul would soon set about catching me; and there would have been no object in bolting to these islets there. I don't suppose there's a drop of water on them. I don't know how it was, but tonight that steward, after bringing me my supper, went out to let me eat it, and left the door unlocked. And I ate it—all there was, too. After I had finished I strolled out on the quarterdeck. I don't know that I meant to do anything. A breath of fresh air was all I wanted, I believe. Then a sudden temptation came over me. I kicked off my slippers and was in the water before I had made up my mind fairly. Somebody heard the splash and they raised an awful hullabaloo. "He's gone! Lower the boats! He's committed suicide! No, he's swimming.' Certainly I was swimming. It's not easy for a swimmer like me to commit suicide by drowning. I landed on the nearest islet before the boat left the ship's side. I heard them pulling about in the dark, hailing, and so on, but after a bit they gave up. Everything quieted down and the anchorage became as still as death. I sat down on a stone and began to think. I felt certain they would start searching for me at daylight. There was no place to hide on those stony things—and if there had been, what would have been the good? But now I was clear of that ship I was not going back. So after a while I took off all my clothes, tied them up in a bundle with a stone inside, and dropped them in the deep water on the outer side of that islet. That was suicide enough for me. Let them think what they liked, but I didn't mean to drown myself. I meant to swim till I sank—but that's not the same thing. I struck out for another of these little islands, and it was from that one that I first saw your riding-light. Something to swim for. I went on easily, and on the way I came upon a flat rock a foot or two above water. In the daytime, I dare say, you might make it out with

---

2. Genesis 4.15.

3. The Karimata Islands in the straits between Borneo and Sumatra, some three hundred miles northeast of the Sunda Straits.

a glass from your poop. I scrambled up on it and rested myself for a bit. Then I made another start. That last spell must have been over a mile."

His whisper was getting fainter and fainter, and all the time he stared straight out through the porthole, in which there was not even a star to be seen. I had not interrupted him. There was something that made comment impossible, in his narrative, or perhaps in himself; a sort of feeling, a quality, which I can't find a name for. And when he ceased, all I found was a futile whisper, "So you swam for our light?"

85   "Yes—straight for it. It was something to swim for. I couldn't see any stars low down because the coast was in the way, and I couldn't see the land, either. The water was like glass. One might have been swimming in a confounded thousand feet deep cistern with no place for scrambling out anywhere; but what I didn't like was the notion of swimming round and round like a crazed bullock before I gave out; and as I didn't mean to go back . . . No. Do you see me being hauled back, stark naked, off one of these little islands by the scruff of the neck and fighting like a wild beast? Somebody would have got killed for certain, and I did not want any of that. So I went on. Then your ladder—"

"Why didn't you hail the ship?" I asked, a little louder.

He touched my shoulder lightly. Lazy footsteps came right over our heads and stopped. The second mate had crossed from the other side of the poop and might have been hanging over the rail, for all we knew.

"He couldn't hear us talking—could he?" My double breathed into my very ear anxiously.

His anxiety was an answer, a sufficient answer, to the question I had put to him. An answer containing all the difficulty of that situation. I closed the porthole quietly, to make sure. A louder word might have been overheard.

90   "Who's that?" he whispered then.

"My second mate. But I don't know much more of the fellow than you do."

And I told him a little about myself. I had been appointed to take charge while I least expected anything of the sort, not quite a fortnight ago. I didn't know either the ship or the people. Hadn't had the time in port to look about me or size anybody up. And as to the crew, all they knew was that I was appointed to take the ship home. For the rest, I was almost as much of a stranger on board as himself, I said. And at the moment I felt it most acutely. I felt that it would take very little to make me a suspect person in the eyes of the ship's company.

He had turned about meantime; and we, the two strangers in the ship, faced each other in identical attitudes.

"Your ladder—" he murmured, after a silence. "Who'd have thought of finding a ladder hanging over at night in a ship anchored out here! I felt just then a very unpleasant faintness. After the life I've been leading for nine weeks, anybody would have got out of condition. I wasn't capable of swimming round as far as your rudder-chains. And, lo and behold! there was a ladder to get hold of. After I gripped it I said to myself, "What's the good?' When I saw a man's head looking over I thought I would swim away presently and leave him shouting—in whatever language it was. I didn't mind being looked at. I—I liked it. And then you speaking to me so quietly—as if you had expected me—made me hold on a little longer. It had been a confounded lonely time—I don't mean while swimming. I was glad to talk a little to somebody that didn't belong to the *Sephora*. As to asking for the captain, that was a mere impulse. It could have been no use, with all the ship knowing about me and the other people pretty certain to be round here in the morning. I don't know—I wanted to be seen, to talk with somebody, before I went on. I don't know what I would have said. . . . 'Fine night, isn't it?' or something of the sort."

"Do you think they will be round here presently?" I asked, with some 95 incredulity.

"Quite likely," he said faintly.

He looked extremely haggard all of a sudden. His head rolled on his shoulders.

"H'm. We shall see then. Meantime get into that bed," I whispered. "Want help? There."

It was a rather high bedplace with a set of drawers underneath. This amazing swimmer really needed the lift I gave him by seizing his leg. He tumbled in, rolled over on his back, and flung one arm across his eyes. And then, with his face nearly hidden, he must have looked exactly as I used to look in that bed. I gazed upon my other self for a while before drawing across carefully the two green serge curtains which ran on a brass rod. I thought for a moment of pinning them together for greater safety, but I sat down on the couch, and once there I felt unwilling to rise and hunt for a pin. I would do it in a moment. I was extremely tired, in a peculiarly intimate way, by the strain of stealthiness, by the effort of whispering, and the general secrecy of this excitement. It was three o'clock by now, and I had been on my feet since nine, but I was not sleepy; I could not have gone to sleep. I sat there, fagged out,[4] looking at the curtains, trying to clear my mind of the confused sensation of being in two places at once, and greatly bothered by an exasperating knocking in my head. It was a relief to discover suddenly that it was not in my head at all, but on the outside of the door. Before I could collect myself, the words "Come in" were out of my mouth, and the steward entered with a tray, bringing in my morning coffee. I had slept, after all, and I was so frightened that I shouted, "This way! I am here, steward," as though he had been miles away. He put down the tray on the table next the couch and only then said, very quietly, "I can see you are here, sir." I felt him give me a keen look, but I dared not meet his eyes just then. He must have wondered why I had drawn the curtains of my bed before going to sleep on the couch. He went out, hooking the door open as usual.

I heard the crew washing decks above me. I knew I would have been told 100 at once if there had been any wind. Calm, I thought, and I was doubly

4. Exhausted.

vexed. Indeed, I felt dual more than ever. The steward reappeared suddenly in the doorway. I jumped up from the couch so quickly that he gave a start.

"What do you want here?"

"Close your port, sir—they are washing decks."

"It is closed," I said, reddening.

"Very well, sir." But he did not move from the doorway and returned my stare in an extraordinary, equivocal manner for a time. Then his eyes, wavered, all his expression changed, and in a voice unusually gentle, almost coaxingly.

105   "May I come in to take the empty cup away, sir?"

"Of course!" I turned my back on him while he popped in and out. Then I unhooked and closed the door and even pushed the bolt. This sort of thing could not go on very long. The cabin was as hot as an oven, too. I took a peep at my double, and discovered that he had not moved; his arm was still over his eyes; but his chest heaved, his hair was wet, his chin glistened with perspiration. I reached over him and opened the port.

"I must show myself on deck," I reflected.

Of course, theoretically, I could do what I liked, with no one to say nay to me within the whole circle of the horizon; but to lock my cabin door and take the key away I did not dare. Directly I put my head out of the companion I saw the group of my two officers, the second mate barefooted, the chief mate in long india-rubber boots, near the break of the poop, and the steward half-way down the poop ladder talking to them eagerly. He happened to catch sight of me and dived, the second ran down on the main deck shouting some order or other, and the chief mate came to meet me, touching his cap.

There was a sort of curiosity in his eye that I did not like. I don't know whether the steward had told them that I was "queer" only, or downright drunk, but I know the man meant to have a good look at me. I watched him coming with a smile which, as he got into point-blank range, took effect and froze his very whiskers. I did not give him time to open his lips.

110   "Square the yards by lifts and braces[5] before the hands go to breakfast."

It was the first particular order I had given on board that ship; and I stayed on deck to see it executed too. I had felt the need of asserting myself without loss of time. That sneering young cub got taken down a peg or two on that occasion, and I also seized the opportunity of having a good look at the face of every foremast man as they filed past me to go to the after braces. At breakfast time, eating nothing myself, I presided with such frigid dignity that the two mates were only too glad to escape from the cabin as soon as decency permitted; and all the time the dual working of my mind distracted me almost to the point of insanity. I was constantly watching myself, my secret self, as dependent on my actions as my own personality, sleeping in that bed, behind that door which faced me as I sat at the head of the table. It was very much like being mad, only it was worse, because one was aware of it.

5. Ropes that adjust the position of the yardarms, vertically (lifts) and horizontally (braces).

I had to shake him for a solid minute, but when at last he opened his eyes it was in the full possession of his senses, with an inquiring look.

"All's well so far," I whispered. "Now you must vanish into the bathroom."

He did so, as noiseless as a ghost, and I then rang for the steward, and facing him boldly, directed him to tidy up my stateroom while I was having my bath—"and be quick about it." As my tone admitted of no excuses, he said, "Yes, sir," and ran off to fetch his dustpan and brushes. I took a bath and did most of my dressing, splashing, and whistling softly for the steward's edification, while the secret sharer of my life stood drawn bolt upright in that little space, his face looking very sunken in daylight, his eyelids lowered under the stern, dark line of his eyebrows drawn together by a slight frown.

When I left him there to go back to my room the steward was finishing dusting. I sent for the mate and engaged him in some insignificant conversation. It was, as it were, trifling with the terrific character of his whiskers; but my object was to give him an opportunity for a good look at my cabin. And then I could at last shut, with a clear conscience, the door of my stateroom and get my double back into the recessed part. There was nothing else for it. He had to sit still on a small folding stool, half smothered by the heavy coats hanging there. We listened to the steward going into the bathroom out of the saloon, filling the water-bottles there, scrubbing the bath, setting things to rights, whisk, bang, clatter—out again into the saloon—turn the key—click. Such was my scheme for keeping my second self invisible. Nothing better could be contrived under the circumstances. And there we sat: I at my writing-desk ready to appear busy with some papers, he behind me, out of sight of the door. It would not have been prudent to talk in daytime; and I could not have stood the excitement of that queer sense of whispering to myself. Now and then, glancing over my shoulder, I saw him far back there, sitting rigidly on the low stool, his bare feet close together, his arms folded, his head hanging on his breast— and perfectly still. Anybody would have taken him for me.

I was fascinated by it myself. Every moment I had to glance over my shoulder. I was looking at him when a voice outside the door said:

"Beg pardon, sir."

"Well!" . . . I kept my eyes on him, and so when the voice outside the door announced, "There's a ship's boat coming our way, sir," I saw him give a start—the first movement he had made for hours. But he did not raise his bowed head.

"All right. Get the ladder over."

I hesitated. Should I whisper something to him? But what? His immobility seemed to have been never disturbed. What could I tell him he did not know already? . . . Finally I went on deck.

II

The skipper of the *Sephora* had a thin, red whisker all round his face, and the sort of complexion that goes with hair of that color; also the particular, rather smeary shade of blue in the eyes. He was not exactly a showy figure; his shoulders were high, his stature but middling—one leg slightly more bandy than the other. He shook hands, looking vaguely around. A spiritless tenacity was his main characteristic, I judged. I behaved with a politeness which seemed to disconcert him. Perhaps he was shy. He mumbled to me as if he were ashamed of what he was saying; gave his name (it was something like Archbold—but at this distance of years I hardly am sure), his ship's name, and a few other particulars of that sort, in the manner of a criminal making a reluctant and doleful confession. He had had terrible weather on the passage out—terrible—terrible—wife aboard, too.

By this time we were seated in the cabin and the steward brought in a tray with a bottle and glasses. "Thanks! No." Never took liquor. Would have some water, though. He drank two tumblerfuls. Terrible thirsty work. Ever since daylight had been exploring the islands round his ship.

"What was that for—fun?" I asked with an appearance of polite interest.

"No!" He sighed. "Painful duty."

125   As he persisted in his mumbling and I wanted my double to hear every word, I hit upon the notion of informing him that I regretted to say I was hard of hearing.

"Such a young man too!" he nodded, keeping his smeary, blue, unintelligent eyes fastened upon me. "What was the cause of it—some disease?" he inquired, without the least sympathy and as if he thought that, if so, I'd got no more than I deserved.

"Yes; disease," I admitted in a cheerful tone which seemed to shock him. But my point was gained, because he had to raise his voice to give me his tale. It is not worth while to record that version. It was just over two months since all this had happened, and he had thought so much about it that he seemed completely muddled as to its bearings, but still immensely impressed.

"What would you think of such a thing happening on board your own ship? I've had the *Sephora* for these fifteen years. I am a well-known shipmaster."

He was densely distressed—and perhaps I should have sympathized with him if I had been able to detach my mental vision from the unsuspected sharer of my cabin as though he were my second self. There he was on the other side of the bulkhead, four or five feet from us, no more, as we sat in the saloon. I looked politely at Captain Archbold (if that was his name), but it was the other I saw, in a gray sleeping suit, seated on a low stool, his bare feet close together, his arms folded, and every word said between us falling into the ears of his dark head bowed on his chest.

130   "I have been at sea now, man and boy, for seven and thirty years, and I've never heard of such a thing happening in an English ship. And that it should be my ship. Wife on board, too."

I was hardly listening to him.

"Don't you think," I said, "that the heavy sea which, you told me, came aboard just then might have killed the man? I have seen the sheer weight of a sea kill a man very neatly, by simply breaking his neck."

"Good God!" he uttered impressively, fixing his smeary blue eyes on me. "The sea! No man killed by the sea ever looked like that." He seemed positively scandalized at my suggestion. And as I gazed at him, certainly not prepared for anything original on his part, he advanced his head close to mine and thrust his tongue out at me so suddenly that I couldn't help starting back.

After scoring over my calmness in this graphic way he nodded wisely. If I had seen the sight, he assured me, I would never forget it as long as I lived. The weather was too bad to give the corpse a proper sea burial. So next day at dawn they took it up on the poop, covering its face with a bit of bunting; he read a short prayer, and then, just as it was, in its oilskins and long boots, they launched it amongst those mountainous seas that seemed ready every moment to swallow up the ship herself and the terrified lives on board of her.

"That reefed foresail saved you," I threw in.   135

"Under God—it did," he exclaimed fervently. "It was by a special mercy, I firmly believe, that it stood some of those hurricane squalls."

"It was the setting of that sail which—" I began.

"God's own hand in it," he interrupted me. "Nothing less could have done it. I don't mind telling you that I hardly dared give the order. It seemed impossible that we could touch anything without losing it, and then our last hope would have been gone."

The terror of that gale was on him yet. I let him go on for a bit, then said casually—as if returning to a minor subject:

"You were very anxious to give up your mate to the shore people, I   140
believe?"

He was. To the law. His obscure tenacity on that point had in it something incomprehensible and a little awful; something, as it were, mystical, quite apart from his anxiety that he should not be suspected of "countenancing any doings of that sort." Seven and thirty virtuous years at sea, of which over twenty of immaculate command, and the last fifteen in the *Sephora,* seemed to have laid him under some pitiless obligation.

"And you know," he went on, groping shamefacedly amongst his feelings, "I did not engage that young fellow. His people had some interest with my owners. I was in a way forced to take him on. He looked very smart, very gentlemanly, and all that. But do you know—I never liked him, somehow. I am a plain man. You see, he wasn't exactly the sort for the chief mate of a ship like the *Sephora.*"

I had become so connected in thoughts and impressions with the secret sharer of my cabin that I felt as if I, personally, were being given to understand that I, too, was not the sort that would have done for the chief mate of a ship like the *Sephora.* I had no doubt of it in my mind.

"Not at all the style of man. You understand," he insisted superfluously, looking hard at me.

I smiled urbanely. He seemed at a loss for a while.   145

"I suppose I must report a suicide."

"Beg pardon?"

"Sui-cide! That's what I'll have to write to my owners directly I get in."

"Unless you manage to recover him before tomorrow," I assented dispassionately.... "I mean, alive."

150 He mumbled something which I really did not catch, and I turned my ear to him in a puzzled manner. He fairly bawled:

"The land—I say, the mainland is at least seven miles off my anchorage."

"About that."

My lack of excitement, of curiosity, of surprise, of any sort of pronounced interest, began to arouse his distrust. But except for the felicitous pretense of deafness I had not tried to pretend anything. I had felt utterly incapable of playing the part of ignorance properly, and therefore was afraid to try. It is also certain that he had brought some ready-made suspicions with him, and that he viewed my politeness as a strange and unnatural phenomenon. And yet how else could I have received him? Not heartily! That was impossible for psychological reasons, which I need not state here. My only object was to keep off his inquiries. Surlily? Yes, but surliness might have provoked a point-blank question. From its novelty to him and from its nature, punctilious courtesy was the manner best calculated to restrain the man. But there was the danger of his breaking through my defense bluntly. I could not, I think, have met him by a direct lie, also for psychological (not moral) reasons. If he had only known how afraid I was of his putting my feeling of identity with the other to the test! But, strangely enough (I thought of it only afterward), I believe that he was not a little disconcerted by the reverse side of that weird situation, by something in me that reminded him of the man he was seeking—suggested a mysterious similitude to the young fellow he had distrusted and disliked from the first.

However that might have been the silence was not very prolonged. He took another oblique step.

155 "I reckon I had no more than a two-mile pull to your ship. Not a bit more."

"And quite enough, too, in this awful heat," I said.

Another pause full of mistrust followed. Necessity, they say, is mother of invention, but fear, too, is not barren of ingenious suggestions. And I was afraid he would ask me point-blank for news of my other self.

"Nice little saloon, isn't it?" I remarked, as if noticing for the first time the way his eyes roamed from one closed door to the other. "And very well fitted out, too. Here, for instance," I continued, reaching over the back of my seat negligently and flinging the door open, "is my bathroom."

He made an eager movement, but hardly gave it a glance. I got up, shut the door of the bathroom, and invited him to have a look round, as if I were very proud of my accommodation. He had to rise and be shown round, but he went through the business without any raptures whatever.

160 "And now we'll have a look at my stateroom," I declared, in a voice as loud as I dared to make it, crossing the cabin to the starboard side with purposely heavy steps.

He followed me in and gazed around. My intelligent double had vanished. I played my part.

"Very convenient—isn't it?"

"Very nice. Very comf . . ." He didn't finish, and went out brusquely as if to escape from some unrighteous wiles of mine. But it was not to be. I had been too frightened not to feel vengeful; I felt I had him on the run, and I meant to keep him on the run. My polite insistence must have had something menacing in it, because he gave in suddenly. And I did not let him off a single item: mates' rooms, pantry, storerooms, the very sail-locker, which was also under the poop—he had to look into them all. When at last I showed him out on the quarter-deck he drew a long, spiritless sigh, and mumbled dismally that he must really be going back to his ship now. I desired my mate, who had joined us, to see to the captain's boat.

The man of whiskers gave a blast on the whistle which he used to wear hanging round his neck, and yelled, "*Sephora's* away!" My double down there in my cabin must have heard, and certainly could not feel more relieved than I. Four fellows came running out from somewhere forward and went over the side, while my own men, appearing on deck too, lined the rail. I escorted my visitor to the gangway ceremoniously, and nearly overdid it. He was a tenacious beast. On the very ladder he lingered, and in that unique, guiltily conscientious manner of sticking to the point:

"I say . . . you . . . you don't think that—"   165

I covered his voice loudly.

"Certainly not. . . . I am delighted. Goodbye."

I had an idea of what he meant to say, and just saved myself by the privilege of defective hearing. He was too shaken generally to insist, but my mate, close witness of that parting, looked mystified and his face took on a thoughtful cast. As I did not want to appear as if I wished to avoid all communication with my officers, he had the opportunity to address me.

"Seems a very nice man. His boat's crew told our chaps a very extraordinary story, if what I am told by the steward is true. I suppose you had it from the captain, sir?"

"Yes. I had a story from the captain."   170

"A very horrible affair—isn't it, sir?"

"It is."

"Beats all these tales we hear about murders in Yankee ships."

"I don't think it beats them. I don't think it resembles them in the least."

"Bless my soul—you don't say so! But of course I've no acquaintance   175
whatever with American ships, not I, so I couldn't go against your knowledge. It's horrible enough for me. . . . But the queerest part is that those fellows seemed to have some idea the man was hidden aboard here. They had really. Did you ever hear of such a thing?"

"Preposterous—isn't it?"

We were walking to and fro athwart the quarter-deck. No one of the crew forward could be seen (the day was Sunday), and the mate pursued:

"There was some little dispute about it. Our chaps took offense. 'As if we would harbor a thing like that,' they said. 'Wouldn't you like to look for him in our coal-hole?' Quite a tiff. But they made it up in the end. I suppose he did drown himself. Don't you, sir?"

"I don't suppose anything."

180   "You have no doubt in the matter, sir?"

"None whatever."

I left him suddenly. I felt I was producing a bad impression, but with my double down there it was most trying to be on deck. And it was almost as trying to be below. Altogether a nerve-trying situation. But on the whole I felt less torn in two when I was with him. There was no one in the whole ship whom I dared take into my confidence. Since the hands had got to know his story, it would have been impossible to pass him off for any one else, and an accidental discovery was to be dreaded now more than ever. . . .

The steward being engaged in laying the table for dinner, we could talk only with our eyes when I first went down. Later in the afternoon we had a cautious try at whispering. The Sunday quietness of the ship was against us; the stillness of air and water around her was against us; the elements, the men were against us—everything was against us in our secret partnership; time itself—for this could not go on for ever. The very trust in Providence was, I supposed, denied to his guilt. Shall I confess that this thought cast me down very much? And as to the chapter of accidents which counts for so much in the book of success, I could only hope that it was closed. For what favorable accident could be expected?

"Did you hear everything?" were my first words as soon as we took up our position side by side, leaning over my bedplace.

185   He had. And the proof of it was his earnest whisper, "The man told you he hardly dared to give the order."

I understood the reference to be to that saving foresail.

"Yes. He was afraid of it being lost in the setting."

"I assure you he never gave the order. He may think he did, but he never gave it. He stood there with me on the break of the poop after the main-topsail blew away, and whimpered about our last hope—positively whimpered about it and nothing else—and the night coming on! To hear one's skipper go on like that in such weather was enough to drive any fellow out of his mind. It worked me up into a sort of desperation. I just took it into my own hands and went away from him, boiling, and—But what's the use telling you? *You* know! . . . Do you think that if I had not been pretty fierce with them I should have got the men to do anything? Not it! The boss'en[6] perhaps? Perhaps! It wasn't a heavy sea—it was a sea gone mad! I suppose the end of the world will be something like that; and a man may have the heart to see it coming once and be done with it—but to have to face it day after day . . . I don't blame anybody. I was precious little better than the rest. Only—I was an officer of that old coal-wagon, anyhow. . . ."

"I quite understand," I conveyed that sincere assurance into his ear. He was out of breath with whispering; I could hear him pant slightly. It was all very simple. The same strung-up force which had given twenty-four men a chance, at least, for their lives had, in a sort of recoil, crushed an unworthy mutinous existence.

6. *Bosun* or *boatswain:* a petty officer in charge of the deck crew and of the rigging.

But I had no leisure to weigh the merits of the matter—footsteps in the 190
saloon, a heavy knock. "There's enough wind to get under way with, sir."
Here was the call of a new claim upon my thoughts and even upon my
feelings.

"Turn the hands up," I cried through the door. "I'll be on deck directly."

I was going out to make the acquaintance of my ship. Before I left the
cabin our eyes met—the eyes of the only two strangers on board. I pointed
to the recessed part where the little camp-stool awaited him and laid my
finger on my lips. He made a gesture—somewhat vague—a little mysterious,
accompanied by a faint smile, as if of regret.

This is not the place to enlarge upon the sensations of a man who feels
for the first time a ship move under his feet to his own independent word.
In my case they were not unalloyed. I was not wholly alone with my command; for there was that stranger in my cabin. Or, rather, I was not completely and wholly with her. Part of me was absent. That mental feeling of
being in two places at once affected me physically as if the mood of secrecy
had penetrated my very soul. Before an hour had elapsed since the ship
had begun to move, having occasion to ask the mate (he stood by my side)
to take a compass bearing of the Pagoda, I caught myself reaching up to
his ear in whispers. I say I caught myself, but enough had escaped to startle
the man. I can't describe it otherwise than by saying that he shied. A grave,
preoccupied manner, as though he were in possession of some perplexing
intelligence, did not leave him henceforth. A little later I moved away from
the rail to look at the compass with such a stealthy gait that the helmsman
noticed it—and I could not help noticing the unusual roundness of his
eyes. These are trifling instances, though it's to no commander's advantage
to be suspected of ludicrous eccentricities. But I was also more seriously
affected. There are to a seaman certain words, gestures, that should in given
conditions come as naturally, as instinctively, as the winking of a menaced
eye. A certain order should spring on to his lips without thinking; a certain
sign should get itself made, so to speak, without reflection. But all unconscious alertness had abandoned me. I had to make an effort of will to recall
myself back (from the cabin) to the conditions of the moment. I felt that
I was appearing an irresolute commander to those people who were watching me more or less critically.

And, besides, there were the scares. On the second day out, for instance,
coming off the deck in the afternoon (I had straw slippers on my bare feet)
I stopped at the open pantry door and spoke to the steward. He was doing
something there with his back to me. At the sound of my voice he nearly
jumped out of his skin, as the saying is, and incidentally broke a cup.

"What on earth's the matter with you?" I asked, astonished. 195

He was extremely confused. "Beg your pardon, sir. I made sure you were
in your cabin."

"You see I wasn't."

"No, sir. I could have sworn I had heard you moving in there not a
moment ago. It's most extraordinary . . . very sorry, sir."

I passed on with an inward shudder. I was so identified with my secret double that I did not even mention the fact in those scanty, fearful whispers we exchanged. I suppose he had made some slight noise of some kind or other. It would have been miraculous if he hadn't at one time or another. And yet, haggard as he appeared, he looked always perfectly self-controlled, more than calm—almost invulnerable. On my suggestion he remained almost entirely in the bathroom, which, upon the whole, was the safest place. There could be really no shadow of an excuse for any one ever wanting to go in there, once the steward had done with it. It was a very tiny place. Sometimes he reclined on the floor, his legs bent, his head sustained on one elbow. At others I would find him on the camp-stool, sitting in his gray sleeping suit and with his cropped dark hair like a patient, unmoved convict. At night I would smuggle him into my bedplace, and we would whisper together, with the regular footfalls of the officer of the watch passing and repassing over our heads. It was an infinitely miserable time. It was lucky that some tins of fine preserves were stowed in a locker in my stateroom; hard bread I could always get hold of; and so he lived on stewed chicken, pâté de foie gras, asparagus, cooked oysters, sardines—on all sorts of abominable sham-delicacies out of tins. My early morning coffee he always drank; and it was all I dared do for him in that respect.

200   Every day there was the horrible maneuvering to go through so that my room and then the bathroom should be done in the usual way. I came to hate the sight of the steward, to abhor the voice of that harmless man. I felt that it was he who would bring on the disaster of discovery. It hung like a sword over our heads.

The fourth day out, I think (we were then working down the east side of the Gulf of Siam, tack for tack,[7] in light winds and smooth water)—the fourth day, I say, of this miserable juggling with the unavoidable, as we sat at our evening meal, that man, whose slightest movement I dreaded, after putting down the dishes ran up on deck busily. This could not be dangerous. Presently he came down again; and then it appeared that he had remembered a coat of mine which I had thrown over a rail to dry after having been wetted in a shower which had passed over the ship in the afternoon. Sitting stolidly at the head of the table I became terrified at the sight of the garment on his arm. Of course he made for my door. There was no time to lose.

"Steward!" I thundered. My nerves were so shaken that I could not govern my voice and conceal my agitation. This was the sort of thing that made my terrifically whiskered mate tap his forehead with his forefinger. I had detected him using that gesture while talking on deck with a confidential air to the carpenter. It was too far to hear a word, but I had no doubt that this pantomime could only refer to the strange new captain.

"Yes, sir," the pale-faced steward turned resignedly to me. It was this maddening course of being shouted at, checked without rhyme or reason, arbitrarily chased out of my cabin, suddenly called into it, sent flying out

_____

7. By following a zigzag course into the wind.

of his pantry on incomprehensible errands, that accounted for the growing wretchedness of his expression.

"Where are you going with that coat?"

"To your room, sir."   205

"Is there another shower coming?"

"I'm sure I don't know, sir. Shall I go up again and see, sir?"

"No! never mind."

My object was attained, as of course my other self in there would have heard everything that passed. During this interlude my two officers never raised their eyes off their respective plates; but the lip of that confounded cub, the second mate, quivered visibly.

I expected the steward to hook my coat on and come out at once. He   210 was very slow about it; but I dominated my nervousness sufficiently not to shout after him. Suddenly I became aware (it could be heard plainly enough) that the fellow for some reason or other was opening the door of the bathroom. It was the end. The place was literally not big enough to swing a cat in. My voice died in my throat and I went stony all over. I expected to hear a yell of surprise and terror, and made a movement, but had not the strength to get on my legs. Everything remained still. Had my second self taken the poor wretch by the throat? I don't know what I could have done next moment if I had not seen the steward come out of my room, close the door, and then stand quietly by the sideboard.

"Saved," I thought. "But, no! Lost! Gone! He was gone!"

I laid my knife and fork down and leaned back in my chair. My head swam. After a while, when sufficiently recovered to speak in a steady voice, I instructed my mate to put the ship round at eight o'clock himself.

"I won't come on deck," I went on. "I think I'll turn in, and unless the wind shifts I don't want to be disturbed before midnight. I feel a bit seedy."

"You did look middling bad a little while ago," the chief mate remarked without showing any great concern.

They both went out, and I stared at the steward clearing the table. There   215 was nothing to be read on that wretched man's face. But why did he avoid my eyes? I asked myself. Then I thought I should like to hear the sound of his voice.

"Steward!"

"Sir!" Startled as usual.

"Where did you hang up that coat?"

"In the bathroom, sir." The usual anxious tone. "It's not quite dry yet, sir."

For some time longer I sat in the cuddy. Had my double vanished as he   220 had come? But of his coming there was an explanation, whereas his disappearance would be inexplicable.... I went slowly into my dark room, shut the door, lighted the lamp, and for a time dared not turn round. When at last I did I saw him standing bolt upright in the narrow recessed part. It would not be true to say I had a shock, but an irresistible doubt of his bodily existence flitted through my mind. Can it be, I asked myself, that he is not visible to other eyes than mine? It was like being haunted.

Motionless, with a grave face, he raised his hands slightly at me in a gesture which meant clearly, "Heavens! what a narrow escape!" Narrow indeed. I think I had come creeping quietly as near insanity as any man who has not actually gone over the border. That gesture restrained me, so to speak.

The mate with the terrific whiskers was now putting the ship on the other tack. In the moment of profound silence which follows upon the hands going to their stations I heard on the poop his raised voice: "Hard alee!"[8] and the distant shout of the order repeated on the main deck. The sails, in that light breeze, made but a faint fluttering noise. It ceased. The ship was coming round slowly; I held my breath in the renewed stillness of expectation; one wouldn't have thought that there was a single living soul on her decks. A sudden brisk shout, "Mainsail haul!" broke the spell, and in the noisy cries and rush overhead of the men running away with the main brace we two, down in my cabin, came together in our usual position by the bedplace.

He did not wait for my question. "I heard him fumbling here and just managed to squat myself down in the bath," he whispered to me. "The fellow only opened the door and put his arm in to hang the coat up. All the same...."

"I never thought of that," I whispered back, even more appalled than before at the closeness of the shave, and marveling at that something unyielding in his character which was carrying him through so finely. There was no agitation in his whisper. Whoever was being driven distracted, it was not he. He was sane. And the proof of his sanity was continued when he took up the whispering again.

"It would never do for me to come to life again."

225   It was something that a ghost might have said. But what he was alluding to was his old captain's reluctant admission of the theory of suicide. It would obviously serve his turn—if I had understood at all the view which seemed to govern the unalterable purpose of his action.

"You must maroon me as soon as ever you can get amongst these islands off the Cambodje[9] shore," he went on.

"Maroon you! We are not living in a boy's adventure tale," I protested. His scornful whispering took me up.

"We aren't indeed! There's nothing of a boy's tale in this. But there's nothing else for it. I want no more. You don't suppose I am afraid of what can be done to me? Prison or gallows or whatever they may please. But you don't see me coming back to explain such things to an old fellow in a wig and twelve respectable tradesmen, do you? What can they know whether I am guilty or not—or of *what* I am guilty, either? That's my affair. What does the Bible say? 'Driven off the face of the earth.'[1] Very well. I am off the face of the earth now. As I came at night so I shall go."

"Impossible!" I murmured. "You can't."

230   "Can't?.... Not naked like a soul on the Day of Judgment. I shall freeze

8. That is, put the helm all the way over to the side away from the wind.   9. Cambodian.
1. Genesis 4.14.

on to this sleeping suit. The Last Day is not yet—and . . . you have understood thoroughly. Didn't you?"

I felt suddenly ashamed of myself. I may say truly that I understood—and my hesitation in letting that man swim away from my ship's side had been a mere sham sentiment, a sort of cowardice.

"It can't be done now till next night," I breathed out. "The ship is on the offshore tack and the wind may fail us."

"As long as I know that you understand," he whispered. "But of course you do. It's a great satisfaction to have got somebody to understand. You seem to have been there on purpose." And in the same whisper, as if we two whenever we talked had to say things to each other which were not fit for the world to hear, he added, "It's very wonderful."

We remained side by side talking in our secret way—but sometimes silent or just exchanging a whispered word or two at long intervals. And as usual he stared through the port. A breath of wind came now and again into our faces. The ship might have been moored in dock, so gently and on an even keel she slipped through the water, that did not murmur even at our passage, shadowy and silent like a phantom sea.

At midnight I went on deck, and to my mate's great surprise put the ship round on the other tack. His terrible whiskers flitted round me in silent criticism. I certainly should not have done it if it had been only a question of getting out of that sleepy gulf as quickly as possible. I believe he told the second mate, who relieved him, that it was a great want of judgment. The other only yawned. That intolerable cub shuffled about so sleepily and lolled against the rails in such a slack, improper fashion that I came down on him sharply.

"Aren't you properly awake yet?"

"Yes, sir! I am awake."

"Well, then, be good enough to hold yourself as if you were. And keep a look out. If there's any current we'll be closing with some islands long before daylight."

The east side of the gulf is fringed with islands, some solitary, others in groups. On the blue background of the high coast they seem to float on silvery patches of calm water, arid and gray, or dark green and rounded like clumps of evergreen bushes, with the larger ones, a mile or two long, showing the outlines of ridges, ribs of gray rock under the dank mantle of matted leafage. Unknown to trade, to travel, almost to geography, the manner of life they harbor is an unsolved secret. There must be villages—settlements of fishermen at least—on the largest of them, and some communication with the world is probably kept up by native craft. But all that forenoon, as we headed for them, fanned along by the faintest of breezes, I saw no sign of man or canoe in the field of the telescope I kept on pointing at the scattered group.

At noon I gave no orders for a change of course, and the mate's whiskers became much concerned and seemed to be offering themselves unduly to my notice. At last I said:

"I am going to stand right in. Quite in—as far as I can take her."

235

240

The stare of extreme surprise imparted an air of ferocity also to his eyes, and he looked truly terrific for a moment.

"We're not doing well in the middle of the gulf," I continued casually. "I am going to look for the land breezes tonight."

"Bless my soul! Do you mean, sir, in the dark amongst the lot of all them islands and reefs and shoals?"

245   "Well, if there are any regular land breezes at all on this coast one must get close inshore to find them—mustn't one?"

"Bless my soul!" he exclaimed again under his breath. All that afternoon he wore a dreamy, comtemplative appearance which in him was a mark of perplexity. After dinner I went into my stateroom as if I meant to take some rest. There we two bent our dark heads over a half-unrolled chart lying on my bed.

"There," I said. "It's got to be Koh-ring.² I've been looking at it ever since sunrise. It has got two hills and a low point. It must be inhabited. And on the coast opposite there is what looks like the mouth of a biggish river—with some town, no doubt, not far up. It's the best chance for you that I can see."

"Anything. Koh-ring let it be."

He looked thoughtfully at the chart as if surveying chances and distances from a lofty height—and following with his eyes his own figure wandering on the blank land of Cochin-China, and then passing off that piece of paper clean out of sight into uncharted regions. And it was as if the ship had two captains to plan her course for her. I had been so worried and restless running up and down that I had not had the patience to dress that day. I had remained in my sleeping suit, with straw slippers and a soft floppy hat. The closeness of the heat in the gulf had been most oppressive, and the crew were used to see me wandering in that airy attire.

250   "She will clear the south point as she heads now," I whispered into his ear. "Goodness only knows when, though—but certainly after dark. I'll edge her in to half a mile, as far as I may be able to judge in the dark . . ."

"Be careful," he murmured warningly—and I realized suddenly that all my future, the only future for which I was fit, would perhaps go irretrievably to pieces in any mishap to my first command.

I could not stop a moment longer in the room. I motioned him to get out of sight and made my way on the poop. That unplayful cub had the watch. I walked up and down for a while thinking things out, then beckoned him over.

"Send a couple of hands to open the two quarter-deck ports," I said mildly.

He actually had the impudence, or else so forgot himself in his wonder at such an incomprehensible order, as to repeat:

255   "Open the quarter-deck ports! What for, sir?"

---

2. Conrad's name for one of a large number of islands at the head of the Gulf of Siam; *Koh* or *Ko* means *island*.

"The only reason you need concern yourself about is because I tell you to do so. Have them opened wide and fastened properly."

He reddened and went off, but I believe made some jeering remark to the carpenter as to the sensible practice of ventilating a ship's quarter-deck. I know he popped into the mate's cabin to impart the fact to him, because the whiskers came on deck, as it were by chance, and stole glances at me from below—for signs of lunacy or drunkenness, I suppose.

A little before supper, feeling more restless than ever, I rejoined, for a moment, my second self. And to find him sitting so quietly was surprising, like something against nature, inhuman.

I developed my plan in a hurried whisper.

"I shall stand in as close as I dare and then put her round. I shall pres- ently find means to smuggle you out of here into the sail-locker, which communicates with the lobby. But there is an opening, a sort of square for hauling the sails out, which gives straight on the quarterdeck and which is never closed in fine weather, so as to give air to the sails. When the ship's way is deadened in stays[3] and all the hands are aft at the main braces you shall have a clear road to slip out and get overboard through the open quarter-deck port. I've had them both fastened up. Use a rope's end to lower yourself into the water so as to avoid a splash—you know. It could be heard and cause some beastly complication."

He kept silent for a while, then whispered, "I understand."

"I won't be there to see you go," I began with an effort. "The rest . . . I only hope I have understood too."

"You have. From first to last"—and for the first time there seemed to be a faltering, something strained in his whisper. He caught hold of my arm, but the ringing of the supper bell made me start. He didn't though; he only released his grip.

After supper I didn't come below again till well past eight o'clock. The faint, steady breeze was loaded with dew; and the wet, darkened sails held all there was of propelling power in it. The night, clear and starry, sparkled darkly, and the opaque, lightless patches shifting slowly amongst the low stars were the drifting islets. On the port bow there was a big one more distant and shadowily imposing by the great space of sky it eclipsed.

On opening the door I had a back view of my very own self looking at a chart. He had come out of the recess and was standing near the table.

"Quite dark enough," I whispered.

He stepped back and leaned against my bed with a level, quiet glance. I sat on the couch. We had nothing to say to each other. Over our heads the officer of the watch moved here and there. Then I heard him move quickly. I knew what that meant. He was making for the companion; and presently his voice was outside my door.

"We are drawing in pretty fast, sir. Land looks rather close."

"Very well," I answered. "I am coming on deck directly."

3. When the ship's forward progress is slowed or stopped while tacking (changing course) into the wind.

270   I waited till he was gone out of the cuddy, then rose. My double moved too. The time had come to exchange our last whispers, for neither of us was ever to hear each other's natural voice.

"Look here!" I opened a drawer and took out three sovereigns. "Take this, anyhow. I've got six and I'd give you the lot, only I must keep a little money to buy some fruit and vegetables for the crew from native boats as we go through Sunda Straits."

He shook his head.

"Take it," I urged him, whispering desperately. "No one can tell what . . ."

He smiled and slapped meaningly the only pocket of the sleeping jacket. It was not safe, certainly. But I produced a large old silk handkerchief of mine, and tying the three pieces of gold in a corner, pressed it on him. He was touched, I suppose, because he took it at last and tied it quickly round his waist under the jacket, on his bare skin.

275   Our eyes met; several seconds elapsed, till, our glances still mingled, I extended my hand and turned the lamp out. Then I passed through the cuddy, leaving the door of my room wide open. . . . "Steward!"

He was still lingering in the pantry in the greatness of his zeal, giving a rub-up to a plated cruet stand the last thing before going to bed. Being careful not to wake up the mate, whose room was opposite, I spoke in an undertone.

He looked round anxiously. "Sir!"

"Can you get me a little hot water from the galley?"

"I am afraid, sir, the galley fire's been out for some time now."

280   "Go and see."

He fled up the stairs.

"Now," I whispered loudly into the saloon—too loudly, perhaps, but I was afraid I couldn't make a sound. He was by my side in an instant—the double captain slipped past the stairs—through a tiny dark passage . . . a sliding door. We were in the sail-locker, scrambling on our knees over the sails. A sudden thought struck me. I saw myself wandering barefooted, bareheaded, the sun beating on my dark poll. I snatched off my floppy hat and tried hurriedly in the dark to ram it on my other self. He dodged and fended off silently. I wonder what he thought had come to me before he understood and suddenly desisted. Our hands met gropingly, lingered united in a steady, motionless clasp for a second. . . . No word was breathed by either of us when they separated.

I was standing quietly by the pantry door when the steward returned.

"Sorry, sir. Kettle barely warm. Shall I light the spirit-lamp?"

285   "Never mind."

I came out on deck slowly. It was now a matter of conscience to shave the land as close as possible—for now he must go overboard whenever the ship was put in stays. Must! There could be no going back for him. After a moment I walked over to leeward and my heart flew into my mouth at the nearness of the land on the bow. Under any other circumstances I would not have held on a minute longer. The second mate had followed me anxiously.

I looked on till I felt I could command my voice.

"She will weather," I said then in a quiet tone.

"Are you going to try that, sir?" he stammered out incredulously.

I took no notice of him and raised my tone just enough to be heard by the helmsman. 290

"Keep her good full."[4]

"Good full, sir."

The wind fanned my cheek, the sails slept, the world was silent. The strain of watching the dark loom of the land grow bigger and denser was too much for me. I had to shut my eyes—because the ship must go closer. She must! The stillness was intolerable. Were we standing still?

When I opened my eyes the second view started my heart with a thump. The black southern hill of Koh-ring seemed to hang right over the ship like a towering fragment of the everlasting night. On that enormous mass of blackness there was not a gleam to be seen, not a sound to be heard. It was gliding irresistibly towards us and yet seemed already within reach of the hand. I saw the vague figures of the watch grouped in the waist, gazing in awed silence.

"Are you going on, sir?" inquired an unsteady voice at my elbow. 295

I ignored it. I had to go on.

"Keep her full. Don't check her way. That won't do now," I said warningly.

"I can't see the sails very well," the helmsman answered me, in strange, quavering tones.

Was she close enough? Already she was, I won't say in the shadow of the land, but in the very blackness of it, already swallowed up as it were, gone too close to be recalled, gone from me altogether.

"Give the mate a call," I said to the young man who stood at my elbow 300 as still as death. "And turn all hands up."

My tone had a borrowed loudness reverberated from the height of the land. Several voices cried out together, "We are all on deck, sir."

Then stillness again, with the great shadow gliding closer, towering higher, without a light, without a sound. Such a hush had fallen on the ship that she might have been a bark of the dead floating in slowly under the very gate of Erebus.[5]

"My God! Where are we?"

It was the mate moaning at my elbow. He was thunderstruck, and as it were deprived of the moral support of his whiskers. He clapped his hands and absolutely cried out, "Lost!"

"Be quiet," I said sternly. 305

He lowered his tone, but I saw the shadowy gesture of his despair. "What are we doing here?"

"Looking for the land wind."

He made as if to tear his hair, and addressed me recklessly.

4. That is, keep the ship's sails filled with wind.

5. In Greek mythology, a place of darkness in the underworld.

"She will never get out. You have done it, sir. I knew it'd end in something like this. She will never weather, and you are too close now to stay.
She'll drift ashore before she's round. O my God!"

310 I caught his arm as he was raising it to batter his poor devoted head,
and shook it violently.

"She's ashore already," he wailed, trying to tear himself away.

"Is she? . . . Keep good full there!"

"Good full, sir," cried the helmsman in a frightened, thin, childlike voice.

I hadn't let go the mate's arm and went on shaking it. "Ready about,[6]
do you hear? You go forward"—shake—"and stop there"—shake—"and hold
your noise"—shake—"and see these head-sheets properly overhauled"—
shake, shake—shake.

315 And all the time I dared not look towards the land lest my heart should
fail me. I released my grip at last and he ran forward as if fleeing for dear
life.

I wondered what my double there in the sail-locker thought of this
commotion. He was able to hear everything—and perhaps he was able to
understand why, on my conscience, it had to be thus close—no less. My
first order "Hard alee!" re-echoed ominously under the towering shadow
of Koh-ring as if I had shouted in a mountain gorge. And then I watched
the land intently. In that smooth water and light wind it was impossible
to feel the ship coming-to.[7] No! I could not feel her. And my second self
was making now ready to slip out and lower himself overboard. Perhaps
he was gone already . . . ?

The great black mass brooding over our very mast-heads began to pivot
away from the ship's side silently. And now I forgot the secret stranger
ready to depart, and remembered only that I was a total stranger to the
ship. I did not know her. Would she do it? How was she to be handled?

I swung the mainyard and waited helplessly. She was perhaps stopped,
and her very fate hung in the balance, with the black mass of Koh-ring like
the gate of the everlasting night towering over her taffrail. What would she
do now? Had she way on her[8] yet? I stepped to the side swiftly, and on the
shadowy water I could see nothing except a faint phosphorescent flash
revealing the glassy smoothness of the sleeping surface. It was impossible
to tell—and I had not learned yet the feel of my ship. Was she moving?
What I needed was something easily seen, a piece of paper, which I could
throw overboard and watch. I had nothing on me. To run down for it I
didn't dare. There was no time. All at once my strained, yearning stare
distinguished a white object floating within a yard of the ship's side—white,
on the black water. A phosphorescent flash passed under it. What was that
thing? . . . I recognized my own floppy hat. It must have fallen off his head
. . . and he didn't bother. Now I had what I wanted—the saving mark for
my eyes. But I hardly thought of my other self, now gone from the ship,

---

6. That is, be ready to change the ship's direction by shifting the helm and adjusting the set of the
sails; *see these head-sheets properly overhauled:* slacken the ropes that secure the sails of the foremast.
7. Coming to a standstill.   8. Was she moving?

to be hidden for ever from all friendly faces, to be a fugitive and a vagabond on the earth, with no brand of the curse on his sane forehead to stay a slaying hand . . . too proud to explain.

And I watched the hat—the expression of my sudden pity for his mere flesh. It had been meant to save his homeless head from the dangers of the sun. And now—behold—it was saving the ship, by serving me for a mark to help out the ignorance of my strangeness. Ha! It was drifting forward, warning me just in time that the ship had gathered sternway.[9]

"Shift the helm," I said in a low voice to the seaman standing still like a statue.   320

The man's eyes glistened wildly in the binnacle light as he jumped round to the other side and spun round the wheel.

I walked to the break of the poop. On the overshadowed deck all hands stood by the forebraces waiting for my order. The stars ahead seemed to be gliding from right to left. And all was so still in the world that I heard the quiet remark, "She's round," passed in a tone of intense relief between two seamen.

"Let go and haul."

The foreyards ran round with a great noise, amidst cheery cries. And now the frightful whiskers made themselves heard giving various orders. Already the ship was drawing ahead. And I was alone with her. Nothing! no one in the world should stand now between us, throwing a shadow on the way of silent knowledge and mute affection; the perfect communion of a seaman with his first command.

Walking to the taffrail, I was in time to make out, on the very edge of a darkness thrown by a towering black mass like the very gateway of Ere-bus—yes, I was in time to catch an evanescent glimpse of my white hat left behind to mark the spot where the secret sharer of my cabin and of my thoughts, as though he were my second self, had lowered himself into the water to take his punishment: a free man, a proud swimmer striking out for a new destiny.   325

1912

QUESTIONS

1. How does the second paragraph of "The Secret Sharer" help to establish setting? Which words in this paragraph might have figurative significance, or should be read as having meaning for the characterization, plot, and theme of the story? Are there words—or details of the setting—in this paragraph that reappear in other parts of the story?

2. How does paragraph 7 contribute to the characterization of the second mate and the narrator, and how does it reveal the relations among people on board the ship? Does this paragraph add to your expectations for the plot? What words or ideas in the narrator's account catch your attention as warnings, rationalizations, or excuses?

9. That is, that the ship had begun moving backward.

3. How does the "unconventional arrangement" of the narrator-captain's standing the first anchor-watch relate to his character? to the plot? to the theme(s)?

4. When the narrator notices that the rope side-ladder has not been hauled in, he blames himself for having disturbed the ship's routine and conjectures about how his conduct will be "accounted" for by the chief mate and members of the crew. It is just then that "the secret sharer" appears at the very end of that same ladder, as "something elongated and pale" (paragraph 20). What other words in paragraphs 20 and 21 convey the narrator's perception of this strange personage? How do these descriptions, which include significant adjectives ("silvery"), metaphors ("corpse"), and similes ("mute as a fish"), contribute to the tone and effect of the story? What is the connection between the captain's worries about managing the ship and his reaction to the apparition?

5. When Leggatt tells his story, there is a shift in the focus and voice. How does this story within a story function in the plot of "The Secret Sharer"? How does it help define the character of Leggatt? How does it relate to the theme of "the double" in the larger story?

6. The captain of the *Sephora* tells his version of Leggatt's crime, but the narrator says, "It is not worth while to record that version. It was just over two months since all this had happened, and . . . he seemed completely muddled" (paragraph 127). Why do you think the narrator seems so eager to discount Captain Archbold's version of what had happened aboard the *Sephora*?

7. Captain Archbold believes Leggatt was too gentlemanly to be chief mate of the *Sephora*, and the narrator, now so identified with Leggatt, thinks Archbold would not consider the narrator himself a suitable chief mate (much less captain). How central to the story is this issue of fitness to lead? What role does Leggatt play in initiating the narrator into leadership or captaincy?

8. There seems to be a turn in the story after Archbold leaves: ironically, Leggatt seems more of a burden to the narrator, who now becomes more aware of his role as captain: "I was not wholly alone with my command; for there was that stranger in my cabin. . . . Part of me was absent" (paragraph 193). What is the effect of this feeling of split identity on the plot? How does it relate to focus?

9. How does the captain's giving Leggatt his hat figure in the plot? What does it suggest about the narrator's character and feelings? Of what, if anything, might it be a symbol?

The story that follows is funnier than "The Secret Sharer," but no less meaningful. It is the title story, or chapter, of a work that calls itself a novel but can also be seen as a collection of related but separable stories (indeed, many of the chapters were first published separately as stories, and an expanded edition of *Love Medicine* adds four new stories or chapters and rearranges the original sequence). The experiences of a Native American reservation and the healing power of "touch" are likely to seem unfamiliar to most readers. Stop reading after paragraph 18, look at the first of the Questions on page 285, and get your bearings.

LOUISE ERDRICH

Love Medicine

I never really done much with my life, I suppose. I never had a television. Grandma Kashpaw had one inside her apartment at the Senior Citizens, so I used to go there and watch my favorite shows. For a while she used to call me the biggest waste on the reservation and hark back to how she saved me from my own mother, who wanted to tie me in a potato sack and throw me in a slough. Sure, I was grateful to Grandma Kashpaw for saving me like that, for raising me, but gratitude gets old. After a while, stale. I had to stop thanking her. One day I told her I had paid her back in full by staying at her beck and call. I'd do anything for Grandma. She knew that. Besides, I took care of Grandpa like nobody else could, on account of what a handful he'd gotten to be.

But that was nothing. I know the tricks of mind and body inside out without ever having trained for it, because I got the touch. It's a thing you got to be born with. I got secrets in my hands that nobody ever knew to ask. Take Grandma Kashpaw with her tired veins all knotted up in her legs like clumps of blue snails. I take my fingers and I snap them on the knots. The medicine flows out of me. The touch. I run my fingers up the maps of those rivers of veins or I knock very gentle above their hearts or I make a circling motion on their stomachs, and it helps them. They feel much better. Some women pay me five dollars.

I couldn't do the touch for Grandpa, though. He was a hard nut. You know, some people fall right through the hole in their lives. It's invisible, but they come to it after time, never knowing where. There is this woman here, Lulu Lamartine, who always had a thing for Grandpa. She loved him since she was a girl and always said he was a genius. Now she says that his mind got so full it exploded.

How can I doubt that? I know the feeling when your mental power builds up too far. I always used to say that's why the Indians got drunk. Even statistically we're the smartest people on the earth. Anyhow with Grandpa I couldn't hardly believe it, because all my youth he stood out as a hero to me. When he started getting toward second childhood he went through different moods. He would stand in the woods and cry at the top of his shirt. It scared me, scared everyone, Grandma worst of all.

Yet he was so smart—do you believe it?—that he *knew* he was getting 5 foolish.

He said so. He told me that December I failed school and come back on the train to Hoopdance. I didn't have nowhere else to go. He picked me up there and he said it straight out: "I'm getting into my second childhood." And then he said something else I still remember: "I been chosen for it. I couldn't say no." So I figure that a man so smart all his life—tribal chairman and the star of movies and even pictured in the statehouse and on cans of snuff—would know what he's doing by saying yes. I think he was called to second childhood like anybody else gets a call for the priest-hood or the army or whatever. So I really did not listen too hard when the doctor said this was some kind of disease old people got eating too much sugar. You just can't tell me that a man who went to Washington and gave them bureaucrats what for could lose his mind from eating too much Milky Way. No, he put second childhood on himself.

Behind those songs he sings out in the middle of Mass, and back of those stories that everybody knows by heart, Grandpa is thinking hard about life. I know the feeling. Sometimes I'll throw up a smokescreen to think behind. I'll hitch up to Winnipeg and play the Space Invaders for six hours, but all the time there and back I will be thinking some fairly deep thoughts that surprise even me, and I'm used to it. As for him, if it was just the thoughts there wouldn't be no problem. Smokescreen is what irritates the social structure, see, and Grandpa has done things that just distract people to the point they want to throw him in the cookie jar where they keep the mentally insane. He's far from that, I know for sure, but even Grandma had trouble keeping her patience once he started sneaking off to Lamartine's place. He's not supposed to have his candy, and Lulu feeds it to him. That's *one* of the reasons why he goes.

Grandma tried to get me to put the touch on Grandpa soon after he began stepping out. I didn't want to, but before Grandma started telling me again what a bad state my bare behind was in when she first took me home, I thought I should at least pretend.

I put my hands on either side of Grandpa's head. You wouldn't look at him and say he was crazy. He's a fine figure of a man, as Lamartine would say, with all his hair and half his teeth, a beak like a hawk, and cheeks like the blades of a hatchet. They put his picture on all the tourist guides to North Dakota and even copied his face for artistic paintings. I guess you could call him a monument all of himself. He started grinning when I put my hands on his templates, and I knew right then he knew how come I touched him. I knew the smokescreen was going to fall.

10   And I was right: just for a moment it fell.

"Let's pitch whoopee," he said across my shoulder to Grandma.

They don't use that expression much around here anymore, but for damn sure it must have meant something. It got her goat right quick.

She threw my hands off his head herself and stood in front of him, overmatching him pound for pound, and taller too, for she had a growth spurt in middle age while he had shrunk, so now the length and breadth of her surpassed him. She glared and spoke her piece into his face about how he was off at all hours tomcatting and chasing Lamartine again and making a damn old fool of himself.

"And you got no more whoopee to pitch anymore anyhow!" she yelled at last, surprising me so my jaw just dropped, for us kids all had pretended for so long that those rustling sounds we heard from their side of the room at night never happened. She sure had pretended it, up till now, anyway. I saw that tears were in her eyes. And that's when I saw how much grief and love she felt for him. And it gave me a real shock to the system. You see I thought love got easier over the years so it didn't hurt so bad when it hurt, or feel so good when it felt good. I thought it smoothed out and old people hardly noticed it. I thought it curled up and died, I guess. Now I saw it rear up like a whip and lash.

She loved him. She was jealous. She mourned him like the dead. 15

And he just smiled into the air, trapped in the seams of his mind.

So I didn't know what to do. I was in a laundry then. They was like parents to me, the way they had took me home and reared me. I could see her point for wanting to get him back the way he was so at least she could argue with him, sleep with him, not be shamed out by Lamartine. She'd always love him. That hit me like a ton of bricks. For one whole day I felt this odd feeling that cramped my hands. When you have the touch, that's where longing gets you. I never loved like that. It made me feel all inspired to see them fight, and I wanted to go out and find a woman who I would love until one of us died or went crazy. But I'm not like that really. From time to time I heal a person all up good inside, however when it comes to the long shot I doubt that I got staying power.

And you need that, staying power, going out to love somebody. I knew this quality was not going to jump on me with no effort. So I turned my thoughts back to Grandma and Grandpa. I felt her side of it with my hands and my tangled guts, and I felt his side of it within the stretch of my mentality. He had gone out to lunch one day and never came back. He was fishing in the middle of Matchimanito. And there was big thoughts on his line, and he kept throwing them back for even bigger ones that would explain to him, say, the meaning of how we got here and why we have to leave so soon. All in all, I could not see myself treating Grandpa with the touch, bringing him back, when the real part of him had chose to be off thinking somewhere. It was only the rest of him that stayed around causing trouble, after all, and we could handle most of it without any problem.

Besides, it was hard to argue with his reasons for doing some things. Take Holy Mass. I used to go there just every so often, when I got frustrated mostly, because even though I know the Higher Power dwells everyplace, there's something very calming about the cool greenish inside of our mission. Or so I thought, anyway. Grandpa was the one who stripped off my delusions in this matter, for it was he who busted right through what Father calls the sacred serenity of the place.

We filed in that time. Me and Grandpa. We sat down in our pews. Then 20 the rosary got started up pre-Mass and that's when Grandpa filled up his chest and opened his mouth and belted out them words.

HAIL MARIE FULL OF GRACE.

He had a powerful set of lungs.

And he kept on like that. He did not let up. He hollered and he yelled them prayers, and I guess people was used to him by now, because they only muttered theirs and did not quit and gawk like I did. I was getting red-faced, I admit. I give him the elbow once or twice, but that wasn't nothing to him. He kept on. He shrieked to heaven and he pleaded like a movie actor and he pounded his chest like Tarzan in the Lord I Am Not

Worthies. I thought he might hurt himself. Then after a while I guess I got used to it, and that's when I wondered: how come?

So afterwards I out and asked him. "How come? How come you yelled?"

25 "God don't hear me otherwise," said Grandpa Kashpaw.

I sweat. I broke right into a little cold sweat at my hairline because I knew this was perfectly right and for years not one damn other person had noticed it. God's been going deaf. Since the Old Testament, God's been deafening up on us. I read, see. Besides the dictionary, which I'm constantly in use of, I had this Bible once. I read it. I found there was discrepancies between then and now. It struck me. Here God used to raineth bread from clouds, smite the Phillipines, sling fire down on red-light districts where people got stabbed. He even appeared in person every once in a while. God used to pay attention, is what I'm saying.

Now there's your God in the Old Testament and there is Chippewa Gods as well. Indian Gods, good and bad, like tricky Nanabozho or the water monster, Missepeshu, who lives over in Matchimanito. That water monster was the last God I ever heard to appear. It had a weakness for young girls and grabbed one of the Pillagers off her rowboat. She got to shore all right, but only after this monster had its way with her. She's an old lady now. Old Lady Pillager. She still doesn't like to see her family fish that lake.

Our Gods aren't perfect, is what I'm saying, but at least they come around. They'll do a favor if you ask them right. You don't have to yell. But you do have to know, like I said, how to ask in the right way. That makes problems, because to ask proper was an art that was lost to the Chippewas once the Catholics gained ground. Even now, I have to wonder if Higher Power turned it back, if we got to yell, or if we just don't speak its language.

I looked around me. How else could I explain what all I had seen in my short life—King smashing his fist in things, Gordie drinking himself down to the Bismarck hospitals, or Aunt June left by a white man to wander off in the snow. How else to explain the times my touch don't work, and farther back, to the oldtime Indians who was swept away in the outright germ warfare and dirty-dog killing of the whites. In those times, us Indians was so much kindlier than now.

30 We took them in.

Oh yes, I'm bitter as an old cutworm just thinking of how they done to us and doing still.

So Grandpa Kashpaw just opened my eyes a little there. Was there any sense relying on a God whose ears was stopped? Just like the government? I says then, right off, maybe we got nothing but ourselves. And that's not much, just personally speaking. I know I don't got the cold hard potatoes it takes to understand everything. Still, there's things I'd like to do. For instance, I'd like to help some people like my Grandpa and Grandma Kashpaw get back some happiness within the tail ends of their lives.

I told you once before I couldn't see my way clear to putting the direct touch on Grandpa's mind, and I kept my moral there, but something soon happened to make me think a little bit of mental adjustment wouldn't do him and the rest of us no harm.

It was after we saw him one afternoon in the sunshine courtyard of the Senior Citizens with Lulu Lamartine. Grandpa used to like to dig there. He had his little dandelion fork out, and he was prying up them dandelions right and left while Lamartine watched him.

"He's scratching up the dirt, all right," said Grandma, watching Lamartine watch Grandpa out the window. 35

Now Lamartine was about half the considerable size of Grandma, but you would never think of sizes anyway. They were different in an even more noticeable way. It was the difference between a house fixed up with paint and picky fence, and a house left to weather away into the soft earth, is what I'm saying. Lamartine was jacked up, latticed, shuttered, and vinyl sided, while Grandma sagged and bulged on her slipped foundations and let her hair go the silver gray of rain-dried lumber. Right now, she eyed the Lamartine's pert flowery dress with such a look it despaired me. I knew what this could lead to with Grandma. Alternating tongue storms and rock-hard silences was hard on a man, even one who didn't notice, like Grandpa. So I went fetching him.

But he was gone when I popped through the little screen door that led out on the courtyard. There was nobody out there either, to point which way they went. Just the dandelion fork quibbling upright in the ground. That gave me an idea. I snookered over to the Lamartine's door and I listened in first, then knocked. But nobody. So I went walking through the lounges and around the card tables. Still nobody. Finally it was my touch that led me to the laundry room. I cracked the door. I went in. There they were. And he was really loving her up good, boy, and she was going hell for leather. Sheets was flapping on the lines above, and washcloths, pillowcases, shirts was also flying through the air, for they was trying to clear out a place for themselves in a high-heaped but shallow laundry cart. The washers and dryers was all on, chock-full of quarters, shaking and moaning. I couldn't hear what Grandpa and the Lamartine was billing and cooing, and they couldn't hear me.

I didn't know what to do, so I went inside and shut the door.

The Lamartine wore a big curly light-brown wig. Looked like one of them squeaky little white-people dogs. Poodles they call them. Anyway, that wig is what saved us from the worse. For I could hardly shout and tell them I was in there, no more could I try and grab him. I was trapped where I was. There was nothing I could really do but hold the door shut. I was scared of somebody else upsetting in and really getting an eyeful. Turned out though, in the heat of the clinch, as I was trying to avert my eyes you see, the Lamartine's curly wig jumped off her head. And if you ever been in the midst of something and had a big change like that occur in the someone, you can't help know how it devastates your basic urges. Not only that, but her wig was almost with a life of its own. Grandpa's eyes were bugging at the change already, and swear to God if the thing didn't rear up and pop him in the face like it was going to start something. He scrambled up, Grandpa did, and the Lamartine jumped up after him all addled looking. They just stared at each other, huffing and puffing, with quizzical expression. The surprise seemed to drive all sense completely out of Grandpa's mind.

40   "The letter was what started the fire," he said. "I never would have done it."

"What letter?" said the Lamartine. She was stiff-necked now, and elegant, even bald, like some alien queen. I gave her back the wig. The Lamartine replaced it on her head, and whenever I saw her after that, I couldn't help thinking of her bald, with special powers, as if from another planet.

"That was a close call," I said to Grandpa after she had left.

But I think he had already forgot the incident. He just stood there all quiet and thoughtful. You really wouldn't think he was crazy. He looked like he was just about to say something important, explaining himself. He said something, all right, but it didn't have nothing to do with anything that made sense.

He wondered where the heck he put his dandelion fork. That's when I decided about the mental adjustment.

45   Now what was mostly our problem was not so much that he was not all there, but that what was there of him often hankered after Lamartine. If we could put a stop to that, I thought, we might be getting someplace. But here, see, my touch was of no use. For what could I snap my fingers at to make him faithful to Grandma? Like the quality of staying power, this faithfulness was invisible. I know it's something that you got to acquire, but I never known where from. Maybe there's no rhyme or reason to it, like my getting the touch, and then again maybe it's a kind of magic.

It was Grandma Kashpaw who thought of it in the end. She knows things. Although she will not admit she has a scrap of Indian blood in her, there's no doubt in my mind she's got some Chippewa. How else would you explain the way she'll be sitting there, in front of her TV story, rocking in her armchair and suddenly she turns on me, her brown eyes hard as lake-bed flint.

"Lipsha Morrissey," she'll say, "you went out last night and got drunk." How did she know that? I'll hardly remember it myself. Then she'll say she just had a feeling or ache in the scar of her hand or a creak in her shoulder. She is constantly being told things by little aggravations in her joints or by her household appliances. One time she told Gordie never to ride with a crazy Lamartine boy. She had seen something in the polished-up tin of her bread toaster. So he didn't. Sure enough, the time came we heard how Lyman and Henry went out of control in their car, ending up in the river. Lyman swam to the top, but Henry never made it.

Thanks to Grandma's toaster, Gordie was probably spared.

50   Someplace in the blood Grandma Kashpaw knows things. She also remembers things, I found. She keeps things filed away. She's got a memory like them video games that don't forget your score. One reason she remem-

bers so many details about the trouble I gave her in early life is so she can flash back her total when she needs to.

Like now. Take the love medicine. I don't know where she remembered that from. It came tumbling from her mind like an asteroid off the corner of the screen.

Of course she starts out by mentioning the time I had this accident in church and did she leave me there with wet overhalls? No she didn't. And ain't I glad? Yes I am. Now what you want now, Grandma?

But when she mentions them love medicines, I feel my back prickle at the danger. These love medicines is something of an old Chippewa specialty. No other tribe has got them down so well. But love medicines is not for the layman to handle. You don't just go out and get one without paying for it. Before you get one, even, you should go through one hell of a lot of mental condensation. You got to think it over. Choose the right one. You could really mess up your life grinding up the wrong little thing.

So anyhow, I said to Grandma I'd give this love medicine some thought. I knew the best thing was to go ask a specialist like Old Lady Pillager, who lives up in a tangle of bush and never shows herself. But the truth is I was afraid of her, like everyone else. She was known for putting the twisted mouth on people, seizing up their hearts. Old Lady Pillager was serious business, and I have always thought it best to steer clear of that whenever I could. That's why I took the powers in my own hands. That's why I did what I could.

I put my whole mentality to it, nothing held back. After a while I started to remember things I'd heard gossiped over. 55

I heard of this person once who carried a charm of seeds that looked like baby pearls. They was attracted to a metal knife, which made them powerful. But I didn't know where them seeds grew. Another love charm I heard about I couldn't go along with, because how was I suppose to catch frogs in the act, which it required. Them little creatures is slippery and fast. And then the powerfullest of all, the most extreme, involved nail clips and such. I wasn't anywhere near asking Grandma to provide me all the little body bits that this last love recipe called for. I went walking around for days just trying to think up something that would work.

Well I got it. If it hadn't been the early fall of the year, I never would have got it. But I was sitting underneath a tree one day down near the school just watching people's feet go by when something tells me, look up! Look up! So I look up, and I see two honkers, Canada geese, the kind with little masks on their faces, a bird what mates for life. I see them flying right over my head naturally preparing to land in some slough on the reservation, which they certainly won't get off of alive.

It hits me, anyway. Them geese, they mate for life. And I think to myself, just what if I went out and got a pair? And just what if I fed some part— say the goose heart—of the female to Grandma and Grandpa ate the other heart? Wouldn't that work? Maybe it's all invisible, and then maybe again it's magic. Love is a stony road. We know that for sure. If it's true that the higher feelings of devotion get lodged in the heart like people say, then we'd be home free. If not, eating goose heart couldn't harm nobody anyway. I thought it was worth my effort, and Grandma Kashpaw thought so, too. She had always known a good idea when she heard one. She borrowed me Grandpa's gun.

So I went out to this particular slough, maybe the exact same slough I never got thrown in by my mother, thanks to Grandma Kashpaw, and I hunched down in a good comfortable pile of rushes. I got my gun loaded up. I ate a few of these soft baloney sandwiches Grandma made me for lunch. And then I waited. The cattails blown back and forth above my head. Them stringy blue herons was spearing up their prey. The thing I know how to do best in this world, the thing I been training for all my life, is to wait. Sitting there and sitting there was no hardship on me. I got to thinking about some funny things that happened. There was this one time that Lulu Lamartine's little blue tweety bird, a paraclete, I guess you'd call it, flown up inside her dress and got lost within there. I recalled her running out into the hallway trying to yell something, shaking. She was doing a right good jig there, cutting the rug for sure, and the thing is it *never* flown out. To this day people speculate where it went. They fear she might perhaps of crushed it in her corsets. It sure hasn't ever yet been seen alive. I thought of funny things for a while, but then I used them up, and strange things that happened started weaseling their way into my mind.

60   I got to thinking quite naturally of the Lamartine's cousin named Wristwatch. I never knew what his real name was. They called him Wristwatch because he got his father's broken wristwatch as a young boy when his father passed on. Never in his whole life did Wristwatch take his father's watch off. He didn't care if it worked, although after a while he got sensitive when people asked what time it was, teasing him. He often put it to his ear like he was listening to the tick. But it was broken for good and forever, people said so, at least that's what they thought.

Well I saw Wristwatch smoking in his pickup one afternoon and by nine that evening he was dead.

He died sitting at the Lamartine's table, too. As she told it, Wristwatch had just eaten himself a good-size dinner and she said would he take seconds on the hot dish when he fell over to the floor. They turnt him over. He was gone. But here's the strange thing: when the Senior Citizen's orderly took the pulse he noticed that the wristwatch Wristwatch wore was now working. The moment he died the wristwatch started keeping perfect time. They buried him with the watch still ticking on his arm.

I got to thinking. What if some gravediggers dug up Wristwatch's casket in two hundred years and that watch was still going? I thought what question they would ask and it was this: Whose hand wound it?

I started shaking like a piece of grass at just the thought.

65   Not to get off the subject or nothing. I was still hunkered in the slough. It was passing late into the afternoon and still no honkers had touched down. Now I don't need to tell you that the waiting did not get to me, it was the chill. The rushes was very soft, but damp. I was getting cold and debating to leave, when they landed. Two geese swimming here and there as big as life, looking deep into each other's little pinhole eyes. Just the

ones I was looking for. So I lifted Grandpa's gun to my shoulder and I aimed perfectly, and *blam! Blam!* I delivered two accurate shots. But the thing is, them shots missed. I couldn't hardly believe it. Whether it was that the stock had warped or the barrel got bent someways, I don't quite know, but anyway them geese flown off into the dim sky, and Lipsha Morrissey was left there in the rushes with evening fallen and his two cold hands empty. He had before him just the prospect of another day of bone-cracking chill in them rushes, and the thought of it got him depressed.

Now it isn't my style, in no way, to get depressed.

So I said to myself, Lipsha Morrissey, you're a happy S.O.B. who could be covered up with weeds by now down at the bottom of this slough, but instead you're alive to tell the tale. You might have problems in life, but you still got the touch. You got the power, Lipsha Morrissey. Can't argue that. So put your mind to it and figure out how not to be depressed.

I took my advice. I put my mind to it. But I never saw at the time how my thoughts led me astray toward a tragic outcome none could have known. I ignored all the danger, all the limits, for I was tired of sitting in the slough and my feet were numb. My face was aching. I was chilled, so I played with fire. I told myself love medicine was simple. I told myself the old superstitions was just that—strange beliefs. I told myself to take the ten dollars Mary MacDonald had paid me for putting the touch on her arthritis joint, and the other five I hadn't spent yet from winning bingo last Thursday. I told myself to go down to the Red Owl store.

And here is what I did that made the medicine backfire. I took an evil shortcut. I looked at birds that was dead and froze.

All right. So now I guess you will say, "Slap a malpractice suit on Lipsha 70 Morrissey."

I heard of those suits. I used to think it was a color clothing quack doctors had to wear so you could tell them from the good ones. Now I know better that it's law.

As I walked back from the Red Owl with the rock-hard, heavy turkeys, I argued to myself about malpractice. I thought of faith. I thought to myself that faith could be called belief against the odds and whether or not there's any proof. How does that sound? I thought how we might have to yell to be heard by Higher Power, but that's not saying it's not *there*. And that is faith for you. It's belief even when the goods don't deliver. Higher Power makes promises we all know they can't back up, but anybody ever go and slap an old malpractice suit on God? Or the U.S. government? No they don't. Faith might be stupid, but it gets us through. So what I'm heading at is this. I finally convinced myself that the real actual power to the love medicine was not the goose heart itself but the faith in the cure.

I didn't believe it, I knew it was wrong, but by then I had waded so far into my lie I was stuck there. And then I went one step further.

The next day, I cleaned the hearts away from the paper packages of gizzards inside the turkeys. Then I wrapped them hearts with a clean hankie and brung them both to get blessed up at the mission. I wanted to get official blessings from the priest, but when Father answered the door to the rectory, wiping his hands on a little towel, I could tell he was a busy man.

75   "Booshoo,[1] Father," I said. "I got a slight request to make of you this afternoon."

"What is it?" he said.

"Would you bless this package?" I held out the hankie with the hearts tied inside it.

He looked at the package, questioning it.

"It's turkey hearts," I honestly had to reply.

80   A look of annoyance crossed his face.

"Why don't you bring this matter over to Sister Martin," he said. "I have duties."

And so, although the blessing wouldn't be as powerful, I went over to the Sisters with the package.

I rung the bell, and they brought Sister Martin to the door. I had her as a music teacher, but I was always so shy then. I never talked out loud. Now, I had grown taller than Sister Martin. Looking down, I saw that she was not feeling up to snuff. Brown circles hung under her eyes.

"What's the matter?" she said, not noticing who I was.

85   "Remember me, Sister?"

She squinted up at me.

"Oh yes," she said after a moment. "I'm sorry, you're the youngest of the Kashpaws. Gordie's brother."

Her face warmed up.

"Lipsha," I said, "that's my name."

90   "Well, Lipsha," she said, smiling broad at me now, "what can I do for you?"

They always said she was the kindest-hearted of the Sisters up the hill, and she was. She brought me back into their own kitchen and made me take a big yellow wedge of cake and a glass of milk.

"Now tell me," she said, nodding at my package. "What have you got wrapped up so carefully in those handkerchiefs?"

Like before, I answered honestly.

"Ah," said Sister Martin. "Turkey hearts." She waited.

95   "I hoped you could bless them."

She waited some more, smiling with her eyes. Kindhearted though she was, I began to sweat. A person could not pull the wool down over Sister Martin. I stumbled through my mind for an explanation, quick, that wouldn't scare her off.

"They're a present," I said, "for Saint Kateri's statue."[2]

---

1. *Bonjour,* French for "good day" or "hello."
2. Kateri Kekakwitha (1656–1680), "Lily of the Mohawk," born in what is now upstate New York to a Mohawk father and an Algonquin mother who was a devout Christian. Following the deaths of her parents, Kateri moved to a Jesuit mission near Montreal to spend the rest of her short life in prayer and chastity. Miracles were attributed to her after her death; she was beatified in 1980 and canonized in 1991.

"She's not a saint yet."

"I know," I stuttered on. "In the hopes they will crown her."

"Lipsha," she said, "I never heard of such a thing."   100

So I told her. "Well the truth is," I said, "it's a kind of medicine."

"For what?"

"Love."

"Oh Lipsha," she said after a moment, "you don't need any medicine. I'm sure any girl would like you exactly the way you are."

I just sat there. I felt miserable, caught in my pack of lies.   105

"Tell you what," she said, seeing how bad I felt, "my blessing won't make any difference anyway. But there is something you can do."

I looked up at her, hopeless.

"Just be yourself."

I looked down at my plate. I knew I wasn't much to brag about right then, and I shortly became even less. For as I walked out the door I stuck my fingers in the cup of holy water that was sacred from their touches. I put my fingers in and blessed the hearts, quick, with my own hand.

I went back to Grandma and sat down in her little kitchen at the Senior   110 Citizens. I unwrapped them hearts on the table, and her hard agate eyes went soft. She said she wasn't even going to cook those hearts up but eat them raw so their power would go down strong as possible.

I couldn't hardly watch when she munched hers. Now that's true love. I was worried about how she would get Grandpa to eat his, but she told me she'd think of something and don't worry. So I did not. I was supposed to hide off in her bedroom while she put dinner on a plate for Grandpa and fixed up the heart so he'd eat it. I caught a glint of the plate she was making for him. She put that heart smack on a piece of lettuce like in a restaurant and then attached to it a little heap of boiled peas.

He sat down. I was listening in the next room.

She said, "Why don't you have some mash potato?" So he had some mash potato. Then she gave him a little piece of boiled meat. He ate that. Then she said, "Why you didn't never touch your salad yet. See that heart? I'm feeding you it because the doctor said your blood needs building up."

I couldn't help it, at that point I peeked through a crack in the door.

I saw Grandpa picking at that heart on his plate with a certain look. He   115 didn't look appetized at all, is what I'm saying. I doubted our plan was going to work. Grandma was getting worried, too. She told him one more time, loudly, that he had to eat that heart.

"Swallow it down," she said. "You'll hardly notice it."

He just looked at her straight on. The way he looked at her made me think I was going to see the smokescreen drop a second time, and sure enough it happened.

"What you want me to eat this for so bad?" he asked her uncannily.

Now Grandma knew the jig was up. She knew that he knew she was working medicine. He put his fork down. He rolled the heart around his saucer plate.

120   "I don't want to eat this," he said to Grandma. "It don't look good."

"Why it's fresh grade-A," she told him. "One hundred percent."

He didn't ask percent what, but his eyes took on an even more warier look.

"Just go on and try it," she said, taking the salt shaker up in her hand. She was getting annoyed. "Not tasty enough? You want me to salt it for you?" She waved the shaker over his plate.

"All right, skinny white girl!" She had got Grandpa mad. Oopsy-daisy, he popped the heart into his mouth. I was about to yawn loudly and come out of the bedroom. I was about ready for this crash of wills to be over, when I saw he was still up to his old tricks. First he rolled it into one side of his cheek. "Mmmmm," he said. Then he rolled it into the other side of his cheek. "Mmmmmmm," again. Then he stuck his tongue out with the heart on it and put it back, and there was no time to react. He had pulled Grandma's leg once too far. Her goat was got. She was so mad she hopped up quick as a wink and slugged him between the shoulderblades to make him swallow.

125   Only thing is, he choked.

He choked real bad. A person can choke to death. You ever sit down at a restaurant table and up above you there is a list of instructions what to do if something slides down the wrong pipe? It sure makes you chew slow, that's for damn sure. When Grandpa fell off his chair better believe me that little graphic illustrated poster fled into my mind. I jumped out the bedroom. I done everything within my power that I could do to unlodge what was choking him. I squeezed underneath his rib cage. I socked him in the back. I was desperate. But here's the factor of decision: he wasn't choking on the heart alone. There was more to it than that. It was other things that choked him as well. It didn't seem like he wanted to struggle or fight. Death came and tapped his chest, so he went just like that. I'm sorry all through my body at what I done to him with that heart, and there's those who will say Lipsha Morrissey is just excusing himself off the hook by giving song and dance about how Grandpa gave up.

Maybe I can't admit what I did. My touch had gone worthless, that is true. But here is what I seen while he lay in my arms.

You hear a person's life will flash before their eyes when they're in danger. It was him in danger, not me, but it was *his* life come over me. I saw him dying, and it was like someone pulled the shade down in a room. His eyes clouded over and squeezed shut, but just before that I looked in. He was still fishing in the middle of Matchimanito. Big thoughts was on his line and he had half a case of beer in the boat. He waved at me, grinned, and then the bobber went under.

Grandma had gone out of the room crying for help. I bunched my force up in my hands and I held him. I was so wound up I couldn't even breathe. All the moments he had spent with me, all the times he had hoisted me on his shoulders or pointed into the leaves was concentrated in that moment. Time was flashing back and forth like a pinball machine. Lights blinked and balls hopped and rubber bands chirped, until suddenly I realized the last ball had gone down the drain and there was nothing. I felt his force leaving him, flowing out of Grandpa never to return. I felt his mind weakening. The bobber going under in the lake. And I felt the touch retreat back into the darkness inside my body, from where it came.

One time, long ago, both of us were fishing together. We caught a big old snapper what started towing us around like it was a motor. "This here fishline is pretty damn good," Grandpa said. "Let's keep this turtle on and see where he takes us." So we rode along behind that turtle, watching as from time to time it surfaced. The thing was just about the size of a washtub. It took us all around the lake twice, and as it was traveling, Grandpa said something as a joke. "Lipsha," he said, "we are glad your mother didn't want you because we was always looking for a boy like you who would tow us around the lake."

"I ain't no snapper. Snappers is so stupid they stay alive when their head's chopped off," I said.

"That ain't stupidity," said Grandpa. "Their brain's just in their heart, like yours is."

When I looked up, I knew the fuse had blown between my heart and my mind and that a terrible understanding was to be given.

Grandma got back into the room and I saw her stumble. And then she went down too. It was like a house you can't hardly believe has stood so long, through years of record weather, suddenly goes down in the worst yet. It makes sense, is what I'm saying, but you still can't hardly believe it. You think a person you know has got through death and illness and being broke and living on commodity rice will get through anything. Then they fold and you see how fragile were the stones that underpinned them. You see how instantly the ground can shift you thought was solid. You see the stop signs and the yellow dividing markers of roads you traveled and all the instructions you had played according to vanish. You see how all the everyday things you counted on was just a dream you had been having by which you run your whole life. She had been over me, like a sheer overhang of rock dividing Lipsha Morrissey from outer space. And now she went underneath. It was as though the banks gave way on the shores of Matchimanito, and where Grandpa's passing was just the bobber swallowed under by his biggest thought, her fall was the house and the rock under it sliding after, sending half the lake splashing up to the clouds.

Where there was nothing.

You play them games never knowing what you see. When I fell into the dream alongside of both of them I saw that the dominions I had defended myself from anciently was but delusions of the screen. Blips of light. And I was scot-free now, whistling through space.

I don't know how I come back. I don't know from where. They was slapping my face when I arrived back at Senior Citizens and they was oxygenating her. I saw her chest move, almost unwilling. She sighed the way she would when somebody bothered her in the middle of a row of beads she was counting. I think it irritated her to no end that they brought her back. I knew from the way she looked after they took the mask off, she was not going to forgive them disturbing her restful peace. Nor was she forgiving Lipsha Morrissey. She had been stepping out onto the road of death, she told the children later at the funeral. I asked was there any stop signs or dividing markers on that road, but she clamped her lips in a vise the way she always done when she was mad.

Which didn't bother me. I knew when things had cleared out she wouldn't have no choice. I was not going to speculate where the blame was put for Grandpa's death. We was in it together. She had slugged him between the shoulders. My touch had failed him, never to return.

All the blood children and the took-ins, like me, came home from Minneapolis and Chicago, where they had relocated years ago. They stayed with friends on the reservation or with Aurelia or slept on Grandma's floor. They were struck down with grief and bereavement to be sure, every one of them. At the funeral I sat down in the back of the church with Albertine. She had gotten all skinny and ragged haired from cramming all her years of study into two or three. She had decided that to be a nurse was not enough for her so she was going to be a doctor. But the way she was straining her mind didn't look too hopeful. Her eyes were bloodshot from driving and crying. She took my hand. From the back we watched all the children and the mourners as they hunched over their prayers, their hands stuffed full of Kleenex. It was someplace in that long sad service that my vision shifted. I began to see things different, more clear. The family kneeling down turned to rocks in a field. It struck me how strong and reliable grief was, and death. Until the end of time, death would be our rock.

140 So I had perspective on it all, for death gives you that. All the Kashpaw children had done various things to me in their lives—shared their folks with me, loaned me cash, beat me up in secret—and I decided, because of death, then and there I'd call it quits. If I ever saw King again, I'd shake his hand. Forgiving somebody else made the whole thing easier to bear.

Everybody saw Grandpa off into the next world. And then the Kashpaws had to get back to their jobs, which was numerous and impressive. I had a few beers with them and I went back to Grandma, who had sort of got lost in the shuffle of everybody being sad about Grandpa and glad to see one another.

Zelda had sat beside her the whole time and was sitting with her now. I wanted to talk to Grandma, say how sorry I was, that it wasn't her fault, but only mine. I would have, but Zelda gave me one of her looks of strict warning as if to say, "I'll take care of Grandma. Don't horn in on the women."

If only Zelda knew, I thought, the sad realities would change her. But of course I couldn't tell the dark truth.

It was evening, late. Grandma's light was on underneath a crack in the door. About a week had passed since we buried Grandpa. I knocked first but there wasn't no answer, so I went right in. The door was unlocked. She was there but she didn't notice me at first. Her hands were tied up in her rosary, and her gaze was fully absorbed in the easy chair opposite her, the one that had always been Grandpa's favorite. I stood there, staring with her, at the little green nubs in the cloth and plastic armrest covers and the sad little hair-tonic stain he had made on the white doily where he laid his head. For the life of me I couldn't figure what she was staring at. Thin space. Then she turned.

"He ain't gone yet," she said.   145

Remember that chill I luckily didn't get from waiting in the slough? I got it now. I felt it start from the very center of me, where fear hides, waiting to attack. It spiraled outward so that in minutes my fingers and teeth were shaking and clattering. I knew she told the truth. She seen Grandpa. Whether or not he had been there is not the point. She had *seen* him, and that meant anybody else could see him, too. Not only that but, as is usually the case with these here ghosts, he had a certain uneasy reason to come back. And of course Grandma Kashpaw had scanned it out.

I sat down. We sat together on the couch watching his chair out of the corner of our eyes. She had found him sitting in his chair when she walked in the door.

"It's the love medicine, my Lipsha," she said. "It was stronger than we thought. He came back even after death to claim me to his side."

I was afraid. "We shouldn't have tampered with it," I said. She agreed. For a while we sat still. I don't know what she thought, but my head felt screwed on backward. I couldn't accurately consider the situation, so I told Grandma to go to bed. I would sleep on the couch keeping my eye on Grandpa's chair. Maybe he would come back and maybe he wouldn't. I guess I feared the one as much as the other, but I got to thinking, see, as I lay there in darkness, that perhaps even through my terrible mistakes some good might come. If Grandpa did come back, I thought he'd return in his right mind. I could talk with him. I could tell him it was all my fault for playing with power I did not understand. Maybe he'd forgive me and rest in peace. I hoped this. I calmed myself and waited for him all night.

He fooled me though. He knew what I was waiting for, and it wasn't   150 what he was looking to hear. Come dawn I heard a blood-splitting cry from the bedroom and I rushed in there. Grandma turnt the lights on. She was sitting on the edge of the bed and her face looked harsh, pinched-up, gray.

"He was here," she said. "He came and laid down next to me in bed. And he touched me."

Her heart broke down. She cried. His touch was so cold. She laid back in bed after a while, as it was morning, and I went to the couch. As I lay there, falling asleep, I suddenly felt Grandpa's presence and the barrier between us like a swollen river. I felt how I had wronged him. How awful was the place where I had sent him. Behind the wall of death, he'd watched the living eat and cry and get drunk. He was lonesome, but I understood he meant no harm.

"Go back," I said to the dark, afraid and yet full of pity. "You got to be with your own kind now," I said. I felt him retreating, like a sigh, growing less. I felt his spirit as it shrunk back through the walls, the blinds, the

brick courtyard of Senior Citizens. "Look up Aunt June," I whispered as he
left.

I slept late the next morning, a good hard sleep allowing the sun to rise
and warm the earth. It was past noon when I awoke. There is nothing, to
my mind, like a long sleep to make those hard decisions that you neglect
under stress of wakefulness. Soon as I woke up that morning, I saw exactly
what I'd say to Grandma. I had gotten humble in the past week, not just
losing the touch but getting jolted into the understanding that would prey
on me from here on out. Your life feels different on you, once you greet
death and understand your heart's position. You wear your life like a garment from the mission bundle sale ever after—lightly because you realize
you never paid nothing for it, cherishing because you know you won't ever
come by such a bargain again. Also you have the feeling someone wore it
before you and someone will after. I can't explain that, not yet, but I'm
putting my mind to it.

155   "Grandma," I said, "I got to be honest about the love medicine."
    She listened. I knew from then on she would be listening to me the way
I had listened to her before. I told her about the turkey hearts and how I
had them blessed. I told her what I used as love medicine was purely a fake,
and then I said to her what my understanding brought me.
    "Love medicine ain't what brings him back to you, Grandma. No, it's
something else. He loved you over time and distance, but he went off so
quick he never got the chance to tell you how he loves you, how he doesn't
blame you, how he understands. It's true feeling, not no magic. No supermarket heart could have brung him back."
    She looked at me. She was seeing the years and days I had no way of
knowing, and she didn't believe me. I could tell this. Yet a look came on
her face. It was like the look of mothers drinking sweetness from their
children's eyes. It was tenderness.
    "Lipsha," she said, "you was always my favorite."
160   She took the beads off the bedpost, where she kept them to say at night,
and she told me to put out my hand. When I did this, she shut the beads
inside of my fist and held them there a long minute, tight, so my hand
hurt. I almost cried when she did this. I don't really know why. Tears shot
up behind my eyelids, and yet it was nothing. I didn't understand, except
her hand was so strong, squeezing mine.

The earth was full of life and there were dandelions growing out the window, thick as thieves, already seeded, fat as big yellow plungers. She let my
hand go. I got up. "I'll go out and dig a few dandelions," I told her.
    Outside, the sun was hot and heavy as a hand on my back. I felt it flow
down my arms, out my fingers, arrowing through the ends of the fork into
the earth. With every root I prized up there was return, as if I was kin to
its secret lesson. The touch got stronger as I worked through the grassy
afternoon. Uncurling from me like a seed out of the blackness where I was
lost, the touch spread. The spiked leaves full of bitter mother's milk. A

buried root. A nuisance people dig up and throw in the sun to wither. A globe of frail seeds that's indestructible.

1982

QUESTIONS

1. In the first dramatized scene, Lipsha, the narrator, at Grandma Kashpaw's request, tries to "put the touch" on Grandpa. By this time, some seventeen or eighteen paragraphs into the story, focus and voice and the setting and situation have been established. What is your initial impression of Lipsha's character? Given what you have observed of the structure and elements of the story so far, what do you expect to happen?

2. How is "love medicine" related to the plot? to Grandma's and Lipsha's characters? to theme? In what way(s) may it be considered a symbol?

3. When Lipsha thinks of Wristwatch's grave being dug up in two hundred years, the watch still running, and the diggers asking, "Whose hand wound it?" he says he "started shaking like a piece of grass at just the thought" (paragraph 64). Is he shaking with awe and fear or with laughter? Do you find it awesome or funny?

4. Lipsha tells the stories of Lulu's "tweety bird" that disappeared up her dress and of Wristwatch, whose broken watch started keeping time after its owner dropped dead. He then says, "Not to get off the subject or nothing" (paragraph 65). Are these stories off the subject? How do they arouse expectations? How do they function in the plot? What do they tell you of Lipsha's character? of the nature of the people on the reservation? Are they related to the theme? If so, how?

5. Where in the story is there a difference between how you feel and how you believe Lipsha feels? What is the effect? What is the relationship of this difference to plot, character, voice, and the other elements of the story?

6. Lipsha counsels himself to "put your mind to it and figure out how not to be depressed," but then he adds, "I never saw at the time how my thoughts led me astray toward a tragic outcome none could have known" (paragraph 68). There is a death involved. Is it "tragic"? How do you respond to it?

7. Lipsha says he took "an evil shortcut" in practicing love medicine: does that mean that he has discovered that the old beliefs are not "superstitions" or "strange," as he thought at the time?

8. In the final two paragraphs of the story, has Lipsha's "voice" changed? How do you think he has changed in the course of the story?

"The Open Boat" is a very different kind of story. It engages, from the very beginning, a powerful sense of fear and impending tragedy; the story's major effects arise from suspense over whether the four men in a boat can survive their battle with the raging seas. As in "Love Medicine," the effects depend heavily on the narrative point of view, on our knowing events from the "inside" as they happen rather than from a larger, or longer, perspective. As in both "The Secret Sharer" and "Love Medicine," in "The Open Boat" the narrative voice is striking and unusual. Each word seems specially chosen, in these stories, to contribute to a feeling or mood as well as to reveal the attitudes of the narrator. Yet in Stephen Crane's story the narrator is not quite a character in the action, since it is told in the third person. Thinking about the elements of a story—plot, character, setting, symbol, and theme as well as point of view—can be very helpful here in sorting out how the story generates its strong sense of anxiety and potential doom. The plot is, in one sense, very simple—four men in a boat try to get to shore safely after a shipwreck—and the theme can also be phrased simply and in several different ways: *nature is ultimately indifferent to humanity*, for example, or *human beings are capable of noble sacrifice and heroism, even if fate foils them.* And from the first words, the setting—the stormy sea off the coast of Florida—is presented in the bleakest terms. Setting or location, here, *is* fate, or we might say it determines plot and reveals character. (Notice, too, that the setting seems to have a character or personality of its own, through various descriptions that personify nature.) The accident of being in the wrong place at the wrong time, of having to struggle to stay alive, becomes a relentless test of character and a suspension of outcome. The way the waves threaten the small boat from constantly shifting angles seems to symbolize the life-or-death predicament the men must face. Although the necessary basic knowledge about each literary element is presented within the opening paragraphs, take note, as you read, of how details accumulate to enrich and complicate each of the elements as the story proceeds.

STEPHEN CRANE

The Open Boat

A Tale Intended to Be after the Fact:[1] Being the Experience of Four Men from the Sunk Steamer Commodore

I

None of them knew the color of the sky. Their eyes glanced level and were fastened upon the waves that swept toward them. These waves were of the hue of slate, save for the tops, which were of foaming white, and all of the men knew the colors of the sea. The horizon narrowed and widened, and dipped and rose, and at all times its edge was jagged with waves that seemed thrust up in points like rocks.

Many a man ought to have a bathtub larger than the boat which here rode upon the sea. These waves were most wrongfully and barbarously abrupt and tall, and each froth-top was a problem in small-boat navigation.

The cook squatted in the bottom, and looked with both eyes at the six inches of gunwale which separated him from the ocean. His sleeves were rolled over his fat forearms, and the two flaps of his unbuttoned vest dangled as he bent to bail out the boat. Often he said, "Gawd! that was a

---

1. Crane had an experience very like the one here re-created in fiction. His autobiographical account of his adventure at sea was published in the New York *Press* on January 7, 1897.

narrow clip." As he remarked it he invariably gazed eastward over the broken sea.

The oiler, steering with one of the two oars in the boat, sometimes raised himself suddenly to keep clear of water that swirled in over the stern. It was a thin little oar, and it seemed often ready to snap.

The correspondent, pulling at the other oar, watched the waves and 5 wondered why he was there.

The injured captain, lying in the bow, was at this time buried in that profound dejection and indifference which comes, temporarily at least, to even the bravest and most enduring when, willy-nilly, the firm fails, the army loses, the ship goes down. The mind of the master of a vessel is rooted deep in the timbers of her, though he command for a day or a decade; and this captain had on him the stern impression of a scene in the grays of dawn of seven turned faces, and later a stump of a topmast with a white ball on it, that slashed to and fro at the waves, went low and lower, and down. Thereafter there was something strange in his voice. Although steady, it was deep with mourning, and of a quality beyond oration or tears.

"Keep 'er a little more south, Billie," said he.

"A little more south, sir," said the oiler in the stern.

A seat in his boat was not unlike a seat upon a bucking broncho, and by the same token a broncho is not much smaller. The craft pranced and reared and plunged like an animal. As each wave came, and she rose for it, she seemed like a horse making at a fence outrageously high. The manner of her scramble over these walls of water is a mystic thing, and, moreover, at the top of them were ordinarily these problems in white water, the foam racing down from the summit of each wave requiring a new leap, and a leap from the air. Then, after scornfully bumping a crest, she would slide and race and splash down a long incline, and arrive bobbing and nodding in front of the next menace.

A singular disadvantage of the sea lies in the fact that after successfully 10 surmounting one wave you discover that there is another behind it just as important and just as nervously anxious to do something effective in the way of swamping boats. In a ten-foot dinghy one can get an idea of the resources of the sea in the line of waves that is not probable to the average experience, which is never at sea in a dinghy. As each slaty wall of water approached, it shut all else from the view of the men in the boat, and it was not difficult to imagine that this particular wave was the final outburst of the ocean, the last effort of the grim water. There was a terrible grace in the move of the waves, and they came in silence, save for the snarling of the crests.

In the wan light the faces of the men must have been gray. Their eyes must have glinted in strange ways as they gazed steadily astern. Viewed from a balcony, the whole thing would, doubtless, have been weirdly picturesque. But the men in the boat had no time to see it, and if they had had leisure, there were other things to occupy their minds. The sun swung steadily up the sky, and they knew it was broad day because the color of the sea changed from slate to emerald-green streaked with amber lights, and the foam was like tumbling snow. The process of the breaking day was unknown to them. They were aware only of this effect upon the color of the waves that rolled toward them.

In disjointed sentences the cook and the correspondent argued as to the difference between a life-saving station and a house of refuge. The cook had said: "There's a house of refuge just north of the Mosquito Inlet Light, and as soon as they see us they'll come off in their boat and pick us up."

"As soon as who see us?" said the correspondent.

"The crew," said the cook.

15 "Houses of refuge don't have crews," said the correspondent. "As I understand them, they are only places where clothes and grub are stored for the benefit of shipwrecked people. They don't carry crews."

"Oh, yes, they do," said the cook.

"No, they don't," said the correspondent.

"Well, we're not there yet, anyhow," said the oiler, in the stern.

"Well," said the cook, "perhaps it's not a house of refuge that I'm thinking of as being near Mosquito Inlet Light; perhaps it's a life-saving station."

20 "We're not there yet," said the oiler in the stern.

II

As the boat bounced from the top of each wave the wind tore through the hair of the hatless men, and as the craft plopped her stern down again the spray slashed past them. The crest of each of these waves was a hill, from the top of which the men surveyed for a moment a broad tumultuous expanse, shining and wind-riven. It was probably splendid, it was probably glorious, this play of the free sea, wild with lights of emerald and white and amber.

"Bully good thing it's an on-shore wind," said the cook. "If not, where would we be? Wouldn't have a show."

"That's right," said the correspondent.

The busy oiler nodded his assent.

25 Then the captain, in the bow, chuckled in a way that expressed humor, contempt, tragedy, all in one. "Do you think we've got much of a show now, boys?" said he.

Whereupon the three were silent, save for a trifle of hemming and hawing. To express any particular optimism at this time they felt to be childish and stupid, but they all doubtless possessed this sense of the situation in their minds. A young man thinks doggedly at such times. On the other hand, the ethics of their condition was decidedly against any open suggestion of hopelessness. So they were silent.

"Oh, well," said the captain, soothing his children, "we'll get ashore all right."

But there was that in his tone which made them think; so the oiler quoth, "Yes! if this wind holds."

The cook was bailing. "Yes! if we don't catch hell in the surf."

30 Canton-flannel[2] gulls flew near and far. Sometimes they sat down on

---

2. A plain-weave cotton fabric.

the sea, near patches of brown seaweed that rolled over the waves with a movement like carpets on a line in a gale. The birds sat comfortably in groups, and they were envied by some in the dinghy, for the wrath of the sea was no more to them than it was to a covey of prairie chickens a thousand miles inland. Often they came very close and stared at the men with black bead-like eyes. At these times they were uncanny and sinister in their unblinking scrutiny, and the men hooted angrily at them, telling them to be gone. One came, and evidently decided to alight on the top of the captain's head. The bird flew parallel to the boat and did not circle, but made short sidelong jumps in the air in chicken fashion. His black eyes were wistfully fixed upon the captain's head. "Ugly brute," said the oiler to the bird. "You look as if you were made with a jackknife." The cook and the correspondent swore darkly at the creature. The captain naturally wished to knock it away with the end of the heavy painter,[3] but he did not dare do it, because anything resembling an emphatic gesture would have capsized this freighted boat; and so, with his open hand, the captain gently and carefully waved the gull away. After it had been discouraged from the pursuit the captain breathed easier on account of his hair, and others breathed easier because the bird struck their minds at this time as being somehow gruesome and ominous.

In the meantime the oiler and the correspondent rowed; and also they rowed. They sat together in the same seat, and each rowed an oar. Then the oiler took both oars; then the correspondent took both oars, then the oiler; then the correspondent. They rowed and they rowed. The very ticklish part of the business was when the time came for the reclining one in the stern to take his turn at the oars. By the very last star of truth, it is easier to steal eggs from under a hen than it was to change seats in the dinghy. First the man in the stern slid his hand along the thwart and moved with care, as if he were of Sèvres.[4] Then the man in the rowing-seat slid his hand along the other thwart. It was all done with the most extraordinary care. As the two sidled past each other, the whole party kept watchful eyes on the coming wave, and the captain cried: "Look out, now! Steady, there!"

The brown mats of seaweed that appeared from time to time were like islands, bits of earth. They were travelling, apparently, neither one way nor the other. They were, to all intents, stationary. They informed the men in the boat that it was making progress slowly toward the land.

The captain, rearing cautiously in the bow after the dinghy soared on a great swell, said that he had seen the lighthouse at Mosquito Inlet. Presently the cook remarked that he had seen it. The correspondent was at the oars then, and for some reason he too wished to look at the lighthouse; but his back was toward the far shore, and the waves were important, and for some time he could not seize an opportunity to turn his head. But at last there came a wave more gentle than the others, and when at the crest of it he swiftly scoured the western horizon.

"See it?" said the captain.

"No," said the correspondent, slowly; "I didn't see anything."   35

---

3. A mooring rope attached to the bow of a boat.   4. A type of fine china.

"Look again," said the captain. He pointed. "It's exactly in that direction."

At the top of another wave the correspondent did as he was bid, and this time his eyes chanced on a small, still thing on the edge of the swaying horizon. It was precisely like the point of a pin. It took an anxious eye to find a lighthouse so tiny.

"Think we'll make it, Captain?"

"If this wind holds and the boat don't swamp, we can't do much else," said the captain.

40   The little boat, lifted by each towering sea and splashed viciously by the crests, made progress that in the absence of seaweed was not apparent to those in her. She seemed just a wee thing wallowing, miraculously top up, at the mercy of five oceans. Occasionally a great spread of water, like white flames, swarmed into her.

"Bail her, cook," said the captain, serenely.

"All right, Captain," said the cheerful cook.

III

It would be difficult to describe the subtle brotherhood of men that was here established on the seas. No one said that it was so. No one mentioned it. But it dwelt in the boat, and each man felt it warm him. They were a captain, an oiler, a cook, and a correspondent, and they were friends—friends in a more curiously iron-bound degree than may be common. The hurt captain, lying against the water jar in the bow, spoke always in a low voice and calmly; but he could never command a more ready and swiftly obedient crew than the motley three of the dinghy. It was more than a mere recognition of what was best for the common safety. There was surely in it a quality that was personal and heart-felt. And after this devotion to the commander of the boat, there was this comradeship, that the correspondent, for instance, who had been taught to be cynical of men, knew even at the time was the best experience of his life. But no one said that it was so. No one mentioned it.

"I wish we had a sail," remarked the captain. "We might try my overcoat on the end of an oar, and give you two boys a chance to rest." So the cook and the correspondent held the mast and spread wide the overcoat; the oiler steered; and the little boat made good way with her new rig. Sometimes the oiler had to scull sharply to keep a sea from breaking into the boat, but otherwise sailing was a success.

45   Meanwhile the lighthouse had been growing slowly larger. It had now almost assumed color, and appeared like a little gray shadow on the sky. The man at the oars could not be prevented from turning his head rather often to try for a glimpse of this little gray shadow.

At last, from the top of each wave, the men in the tossing boat could see land. Even as the lighthouse was an upright shadow on the sky, this land seemed but a long black shadow on the sea. It certainly was thinner than paper. "We must be about opposite New Smyrna,"[5] said the cook, who

5. Town on the Florida coast.

had coasted this shore often in schooners. "Captain, by the way, I believe they abandoned that life-saving station there about a year ago."

"Did they?" said the captain.

The wind slowly died away. The cook and the correspondent were not now obliged to slave in order to hold high the oar. But the waves continued their old impetuous swooping at the dinghy, and the little craft, no longer underway, struggled woundily over them. The oiler or the correspondent took the oars again.

Shipwrecks are *apropos* of nothing. If men could only train for them and have them occur when the men had reached pink condition, there would be less drowning at sea. Of the four in the dinghy none had slept any time worth mentioning for two days and two nights previous to embarking in the dinghy, and in the excitement of clambering about the deck of a foundering ship they had also forgotten to eat heartily.

For these reasons, and for others, neither the oiler nor the correspondent   50 was fond of rowing at this time. The correspondent wondered ingenuously how in the name of all that was sane could there be people who thought it amusing to row a boat. It was not an amusement; it was a diabolical punishment, and even a genius of mental aberrations could never conclude that it was anything but a horror to the muscles and a crime against the back. He mentioned to the boat in general how the amusement of rowing struck him, and the weary-faced oiler smiled in full sympathy. Previously to the foundering, by the way, the oiler had worked a double watch in the engine-room of the ship.

"Take her easy, now, boys," said the captain. "Don't spend yourselves. If we have to run a surf you'll need all your strength, because we'll sure have to swim for it. Take your time."

Slowly the land arose from the sea. From a black line it became a line of black and a line of white—trees and sand. Finally the captain said that he could make out a house on the shore. "That's the house of refuge, sure," said the cook. "They'll see us before long, and come out after us."

The distant lighthouse reared high. "The keeper ought to be able to make us out now, if he's looking through a glass," said the captain. "He'll notify the life-saving people."

"None of those other boats could have got ashore to give word of the wreck," said the oiler, in a low voice, "else the life-boat would be out hunting us."

Slowly and beautifully the land loomed out of the sea. The wind came   55 again. It had veered from the northeast to the southeast. Finally a new sound struck the ears of the men in the boat. It was the low thunder of the surf on the shore. "We'll never be able to make the lighthouse now," said the captain. "Swing her head a little more north, Billie."

"A little more north, sir," said the oiler.

Whereupon the little boat turned her nose once more down the wind, and all but the oarsman watched the shore grow. Under the influence of this expansion doubt and direful apprehension were leaving the minds of the men. The management of the boat was still most absorbing, but it could not prevent a quiet cheerfulness. In an hour, perhaps, they would be ashore.

Their backbones had become thoroughly used to balancing in the boat, and they now rode this wild colt of a dinghy like circus men. The correspondent thought that he had been drenched to the skin, but happening to feel in the top pocket of his coat, he found therein eight cigars. Four of them were soaked with sea-water; four were perfectly scatheless. After a search, somebody produced three dry matches; and thereupon the four waifs rode impudently in their little boat and, with an assurance of an impending rescue shining in their eyes, puffed at the big cigars, and judged well and ill of all men. Everybody took a drink of water.

IV

"Cook," remarked the captain, "there don't seem to be any signs of life about your house of refuge."

60   "No," replied the cook. "Funny they don't see us!"

A broad stretch of lowly coast lay before the eyes of the men. It was of low dunes topped with dark vegetation. The roar of the surf was plain, and sometimes they could see the white lip of a wave as it spun up the beach. A tiny house was blocked out black upon the sky. Southward, the slim lighthouse lifted its little gray length.

Tide, wind, and waves were swinging the dinghy northward. "Funny they don't see us," said the men.

The surf's roar was here dulled, but its tone was nevertheless thunderous and and mighty. As the boat swam over the great rollers the men sat listening to this roar. "We'll swamp sure," said everybody.

It is fair to say here that there was not a life-saving station within twenty miles in either direction; but the men did not know this fact, and in consequence they made dark and opprobrious remarks concerning the eyesight of the nation's life-savers. Four scowling men sat in the dinghy and surpassed records in the invention of epithets.

65   "Funny they don't see us."

The light-heartedness of a former time had completely faded. To their sharpened minds it was easy to conjure pictures of all kinds of incompetency and blindness and, indeed, cowardice. There was the shore of the populous land, and it was bitter and bitter to them that from it came no sign.

"Well," said the captain, ultimately, "I suppose we'll have to make a try for ourselves. If we stay out here too long, we'll none of us have strength left to swim after the boat swamps."

And so the oiler, who was at the oars, turned the boat straight for the shore. There was a sudden tightening of muscles. There was some thinking.

"If we don't all get ashore," said the captain—"if we don't all get ashore, I suppose you fellows know where to send news of my finish?"

70   They then briefly exchanged some addresses and admonitions. As for the reflections of the men, there was a great deal of rage in them. Perchance they might be formulated thus: "If I am going to be drowned—if I am

going to be drowned—if I am going to be drowned, why, in the name of the seven mad gods who rule the sea, was I allowed to come thus far and contemplate sand and trees? Was I brought here merely to have my nose dragged away as I was about to nibble the sacred cheese of life? It is preposterous. If this old ninny-woman, Fate, cannot do better than this, she should be deprived of the management of men's fortunes. She is an old hen who knows not her intention. If she has decided to drown me, why did she not do it in the beginning and save me all this trouble? The whole affair is absurd. . . . But no; she cannot mean to drown me. She dare not drown me. She cannot drown me. Not after all this work." Afterward the man might have had an impulse to shake his fist at the clouds. "Just you drown me, now, and then hear what I call you!"

The billows that came at this time were more formidable. They seemed always just about to break and roll over the little boat in a turmoil of foam. There was a preparatory and long growl in the speech of them. No mind unused to the sea would have concluded that the dinghy could ascend these sheer heights in time. The shore was still afar. The oiler was a wily surfman. "Boys," he said, swiftly, "she won't live three minutes more, and we're too far out to swim. Shall I take her to sea again, Captain?"

"Yes; go ahead!" said the captain.

This oiler, by a series of quick miracles and fast and steady oarsmanship, turned the boat in the middle of the surf and took her safely to sea again.

There was a considerable silence as the boat bumped over the furrowed sea to deeper water. Then somebody in gloom spoke: "Well, anyhow, they must have seen us from the shore by now."

The gulls went in slanting flight up the wind toward the gray, desolate 75 east. A squall, marked by dingy clouds and clouds brick-red, like smoke from a burning building, appeared from the southeast.

"What do you think of those life-saving people? Ain't they peaches?"

"Funny they haven't seen us."

"Maybe they think we're out here for sport! Maybe they think we're fishin'. Maybe they think we're damned fools."

It was a long afternoon. A changed tide tried to force them southward, but wind and wave said northward. Far ahead, where coast-line, sea, and sky formed their mighty angle, there were little dots which seemed to indicate a city on the shore.

"St. Augustine."

The captain shook his head. "Too near Mosquito Inlet." 80

And the oiler rowed, and then the correspondent rowed; then the oiler moved. It was a weary business. The human back can become the seat of more aches and pains than are registered in books for the composite anatomy of a regiment. It is a limited area, but it can become the theatre of innumerable muscular conflicts, tangles, wrenches, knots, and other comforts.

"Did you ever like to row, Billie?" asked the correspondent.

"No," said the oiler. "Hang it."

When one exchanged the rowing-seat for a place in the bottom of the 85 boat, he suffered a bodily depression that caused him to be careless of everything save an obligation to wiggle one finger. There was cold sea-water swashing to and fro in the boat, and he lay in it. His head, pillowed on a thwart, was within an inch of the swirl of a wave-crest, and sometimes a particularly obstreperous sea came inboard and drenched him once more. But these matters did not annoy him. It is almost certain that if the boat had capsized he would have tumbled comfortably out upon the ocean as if he felt sure that it was a great soft mattress.

"Look! There's a man on the shore!"

"There? See 'im? See 'im?"

"Yes, sure! He's walking along."

"Now he's stopped. Look! He's facing us!"

90   "He's waving at us!"

"So he is! By thunder!"

"Ah, now we're all right! Now we're all right! There'll be a boat out here for us in half an hour."

"He's going on. He's running. He's going up to that house there."

The remote beach seemed lower than the sea, and it required a searching glance to discern the little black figure. The captain saw a floating stick, and they rowed to it. A bath towel was by some weird chance in the boat, and, tying this on the stick, the captain waved it. The oarsman did not dare turn his head, so he was obliged to ask questions.

95   "What's he doing now?"

"He's standing still again. He's looking, I think. . . . There he goes again— toward the house. . . . Now he's stopped again."

"Is he waving at us?"

"No, not now; he was, though."

"Look! There comes another man!"

100   "He's running."

"Look at him go, would you!"

"Why, he's on a bicycle. Now he's met the other man. They're both waving at us. Look!"

"There comes something up the beach."

"What the devil is that thing?"

105   "Why, it looks like a boat."

"Why, certainly, it's a boat."

"No; it's on wheels."

"Yes, so it is. Well, that must be the life-boat. They drag them along shore on a wagon."

"That's the life-boat, sure."

110   "No, by God, it's—it's an omnibus."

"I tell you it's a life-boat."

"It is not! It's an omnibus. I can see it plain. See? One of these big hotel omnibuses."

"By thunder, you're right. It's an omnibus, sure as fate. What do you suppose they are doing with an omnibus? Maybe they are going around collecting the life-crew, hey?"

"That's it, likely. Look! There's a fellow waving a little black flag. He's standing on the steps of the omnibus. There comes those other two fellows. Now they're all talking together. Look at the fellow with the flag. Maybe he ain't waving it!"

"That ain't a flag, is it? That's his coat. Why, certainly, that's his coat." 115

"So it is: it's his coat. He's taken it off and is waving it around his head. But would you look at him swing it!"

"Oh, say, there isn't any life-saving station there. That's just a winter-resort."

"What's that idiot with the coat mean? What's he signaling, anyhow?"

"It looks as if he were trying to tell us to go north. There must be a life-saving station up there."

"No; he thinks we're fishing. Just giving us a merry hand. See? Ah, there, 120 Willie!"

"Well, I wish I could make something out of those signals. What do you suppose he means?"

"He don't mean anything; he's just playing."

"Well, if he'd just signal us to try the surf again, or to go to sea and wait, or go north, or go south, or go to hell, there would be some reason in it. But look at him! He just stands there and keeps his coat revolving like a wheel. The ass!"

"There come more people."

"Now there's quite a mob. Look! Isn't that a boat?" 125

"Where? Oh, I see where you mean. No, that's no boat."

"That fellow is still waving his coat."

"He must think we like to see him to do that. Why don't he quit? It don't mean anything."

"I don't know. I think he is trying to make us go north. It must be that there's a life-saving station there somewhere."

"Say, he ain't tired yet. Look at 'im wave!" 130

"Wonder how long he can keep that up. He's been revolving his coat ever since he caught sight of us. He's an idiot. Why aren't they getting men to bring a boat out? A fishing boat—one of those big yawls—could come out here all right. Why don't he do something?"

"Oh, it's all right now."

"They'll have a boat out here for us in less than no time, now that they've seen us."

A faint yellow tone came into the sky over the low land. The shadows on the sea slowly deepened. The wind bore coldness with it, and the men began to shiver.

"Holy smoke!" said one, allowing his voice to express his impious mood, 135 "if we keep on monkeying out here! If we've got to flounder out here all night!"

"Oh, we'll never have to stay here all night! Don't you worry. They've seen us now, and it won't be long before they'll come chasing out after us."

The shore grew dusky. The man waving a coat blended gradually into this gloom, and it swallowed in the same manner the omnibus and the group of people. The spray, when it dashed uproariously over the side, made the voyagers shrink and swear like men who were being branded.

"I'd like to catch the chump who waved the coat. I feel like socking him one, just for luck."

"Why? What did he do?"

140   "Oh, nothing, but then he seemed so damned cheerful."

In the meantime the oiler rowed, and then the correspondent rowed, and then the oiler rowed. Gray-faced and bowed forward, they mechanically, turn by turn, plied the leaden oars. The form of the lighthouse had vanished from the southern horizon, but finally a pale star appeared, just lifting from the sea. The streaked saffron in the west passed before the all-merging darkness, and the sea to the east was black. The land had vanished, and was expressed only by the low and drear thunder of the surf.

"If I am going to be drowned—if I am going to be drowned—if I am going to be drowned, why, in the name of the seven mad gods who rule the sea, was I allowed to come thus far and contemplate sand and trees? Was I brought here merely to have my nose dragged away as I was about to nibble the sacred cheese of life?"

The patient captain, drooped over the water-jar, was sometimes obliged to speak to the oarsman.

"Keep her head up! Keep her head up!"

145   "Keep her head up, sir." The voices were weary and low.

This was surely a quiet evening. All save the oarsman lay heavily and listlessly in the boat's bottom. As for him, his eyes were just capable of noting the tall black waves that swept forward in a most sinister silence, save for an occasional subdued growl of a crest.

The cook's head was on a thwart, and he looked without interest at the water under his nose. He was deep in other scenes. Finally he spoke. "Billie," he murmured, dreamfully, "what kind of pie do you like best?"

V

"Pie!" said the oiler and the correspondent, agitatedly. "Don't talk about those things, blast you!"

"Well," said the cook, "I was just thinking about ham sandwiches, and——"

150   A night on the sea in an open boat is a long night. As darkness settled finally, the shine of the light, lifting from the sea in the south, changed to full gold. On the northern horizon a new light appeared, a small bluish gleam on the edge of the waters. These two lights were the furniture of the world. Otherwise there was nothing but waves.

Two men huddled in the stern, and distances were so magnificent in the dinghy that the rower was enabled to keep his feet partly warm by thrusting them under his companions. Their legs indeed extended far under the rowing-seat until they touched the feet of the captain forward. Sometimes, despite the efforts of the tired oarsman, a wave came piling into the boat, an icy wave of the night, and the chilling water soaked them anew. They would twist their bodies for a moment and groan, and sleep the dead sleep once more, while the water in the boat gurgled about them as the craft rocked.

The plan of the oiler and the correspondent was for one to row until he lost the ability, and then arouse the other from his sea-water couch in the bottom of the boat.

The oiler plied the oars until his head drooped forward and the over-powering sleep blinded him; and he rowed yet afterward. Then he touched a man in the bottom of the boat, and called his name. "Will you spell me for a little while?" he said meekly.

"Sure, Billie," said the correspondent, awaking and dragging himself to a sitting position. They exchanged places carefully, and the oiler, cuddling down in the sea-water at the cook's side, seemed to go to sleep instantly.

The particular violence of the sea had ceased. The waves came without 155 snarling. The obligation of the man at the oars was to keep the boat headed so that the tilt of the rollers would not capsize her, and to preserve her from filling when the crests rushed past. The black waves were silent and hard to be seen in the darkness. Often one was almost upon the boat before the oarsman was aware.

In a low voice the correspondent addressed the captain. He was not sure that the captain was awake, although this iron man seemed to be always awake. "Captain, shall I keep her making for that light north, sir?"

The same steady voice answered him. "Yes. Keep it about two points off the port bow."

The cook had tied a life-belt around himself in order to get even the warmth which this clumsy cork contrivance could donate, and he seemed almost stove-like when a rower, whose teeth invariably chattered wildly as soon as he ceased his labor, dropped down to sleep.

The correspondent, as he rowed, looked down at the two men sleeping underfoot. The cook's arm was around the oiler's shoulders, and, with their fragmentary clothing and haggard faces, they were the babes of the sea—a grotesque rendering of the old babes in the wood.

Later he must have grown stupid at his work, for suddenly there was a 160 growling of water, and a crest came with a roar and a swash into the boat, and it was a wonder that it did not set the cook afloat in his life-belt. The cook continued to sleep, but the oiler sat up, blinking his eyes and shaking with the new cold.

"Oh, I'm awful sorry, Billie," said the correspondent, contritely.

"That's all right, old boy," said the oiler, and lay down again and was asleep.

Presently it seemed that even the captain dozed, and the correspondent thought that he was the one man afloat on all the ocean. The wind had a voice as it came over the waves, and it was sadder than the end.

There was a long, loud swishing astern of the boat, and a gleaming trail of phosphorescence, like blue flame, was furrowed on the black waters. It might have been made by a monstrous knife.

Then there came a stillness, while the correspondent breathed with open 165 mouth and looked at the sea.

Suddenly there was another swish and another long flash of bluish light, and this time it was alongside the boat, and might almost have been reached with an oar. The correspondent saw an enormous fin speed like a shadow through the water, hurling the crystalline spray and leaving the long glowing trail.

The correspondent looked over his shoulder at the captain. His face was hidden, and he seemed to be asleep. He looked at the babes of the sea. They certainly were asleep. So, being bereft of sympathy, he leaned a little way to one side and swore softly into the sea.

But the thing did not then leave the vicinity of the boat. Ahead or astern, on one side or the other, at intervals long or short, fled the long sparkling streak, and there was to be heard the *whirroo* of the dark fin. The speed and power of the thing was greatly to be admired. It cut the water like a gigantic and keen projectile.

The presence of this biding thing did not affect the man with the same horror that it would if he had been a picnicker. He simply looked at the sea dully and swore in an undertone.

170   Nevertheless, it is true that he did not wish to be alone with the thing. He wished one of his companions to awake by chance and keep him company with it. But the captain hung motionless over the water-jar and the oiler and the cook in the bottom of the boat were plunged in slumber.

VI

"If I am going to be drowned—if I am going to be drowned—if I am going to be drowned, why, in the name of the seven mad gods who rule the sea, was I allowed to come thus far and contemplate sand and trees?"

During this dismal night, it may be remarked that a man would conclude that it was really the intention of the seven mad gods to drown him, despite the abominable injustice of it. For it was certainly an abominable injustice to drown a man who had worked so hard, so hard. The man felt it would be a crime most unnatural. Other people had drowned at sea since galleys swarmed with painted sails, but still—

When it occurs to a man that nature does not regard him as important, and that she feels she would not maim the universe by disposing of him, he at first wishes to throw bricks at the temple, and he hates deeply the fact that there are no bricks and no temples. Any visible expression of nature would surely be pelleted with his jeers.

Then, if there be no tangible thing to hoot, he feels, perhaps, the desire to confront a personification and indulge in pleas, bowed to one knee, and with hands supplicant, saying, "Yes, but I love myself."

175   A high cold star on a winter's night is the word he feels that she says to him. Thereafter he knows the pathos of his situation.

The men in the dinghy had not discussed these matters, but each had, no doubt, reflected upon them in silence and according to his mind. There was seldom any expression upon their faces save the general one of complete weariness. Speech was devoted to the business of the boat.

To chime the notes of his emotions, a verse mysteriously entered the correspondent's head. He had even forgotten that he had forgotten this verse, but it suddenly was in his mind.

> A soldier of the Legion lay dying in Algiers;
> There was lack of woman's nursing, there was dearth of woman's tears;
> But a comrade stood beside him, and he took the comrade's hand,
> And he said, "I never more shall see my own, my native land."[6]

In his childhood the correspondent had been made acquainted with the fact that a soldier of the Legion lay dying in Algiers, but he had never regarded it as important. Myriads of his schoolfellows had informed him of the soldier's plight, but the dinning had naturally ended by making him perfectly indifferent. He had never considered it his affair that a soldier of the Legion lay dying in Algiers, nor had it appeared to him as a matter for sorrow. It was less to him than the breaking of a pencil's point.

Now, however, it quaintly came to him as a human, living thing. It was no longer merely a picture of a few throes in the breast of a poet, meanwhile drinking tea and warming his feet at the grate; it was an actuality—stern, mournful, and fine.

The correspondent plainly saw the soldier. He lay on the sand with his feet out straight and still. While his pale left hand was upon his chest in an attempt to thwart the going of his life, the blood came between his fingers. In the far Algerian distance, a city of low square forms was set against a sky that was faint with the last sunset hues. The correspondent, plying the oars and dreaming of the slow and slower movements of the lips of the soldier, was moved by a profound and perfectly impersonal comprehension. He was sorry for the soldier of the Legion who lay dying in Algiers.

The thing which had followed the boat and waited had evidently grown bored at the delay. There was no longer to be heard the slash of the cutwater, and there was no longer the flame of the long trail. The light in the north still glimmered, but it was apparently no nearer to the boat. Sometimes the boom of the surf rang in the correspondent's ears, and he turned the craft seaward then and rowed harder. Southward, some one had evidently built a watch-fire on the beach. It was too low and too far to be seen, but it made a shimmering, roseate reflection upon the bluff in back of it, and this could be discerned from the boat. The wind came stronger, and sometimes a wave suddenly raged out like a mountain-cat, and there was to be seen the sheen and sparkle of a broken crest.

The captain, in the bow, moved on his water-jar and sat erect. "Pretty long night," he observed to the correspondent. He looked at the shore. "Those life-saving people take their time."

"Did you see that shark playing around?"

"Yes, I saw him. He was a big fellow, all right."

"Wish I had known you were awake."

6. From "Bingen on the Rhine," by Caroline Norton (1808–1877).

185   Later the correspondent spoke into the bottom of the boat. "Billie!" There was a slow and gradual disentanglement. "Billie, will you spell me?" "Sure," said the oiler.

    As soon as the correspondent touched the cold, comfortable seawater in the bottom of the boat and had huddled close to the cook's life-belt he was deep in sleep, despite the fact that his teeth played all the popular airs. This sleep was so good to him that it was but a moment before he heard a voice call his name in a tone that demonstrated the last stages of exhaustion. "Will you spell me?"

    "Sure, Billie."

    The light in the north had mysteriously vanished, but the correspondent took his course from the wide-awake captain.

190   Later in the night they took the boat farther out to sea, and the captain directed the cook to take one oar at the stern and keep the boat facing the seas. He was to call out if he should hear the thunder of the surf. This plan enabled the oiler and the correspondent to get respite together. "We'll give those boys a chance to get into shape again," said the captain. They curled down and, after a few preliminary chatterings and trembles, slept once more the dead sleep. Neither knew they had bequeathed to the cook the company of another shark, or perhaps the same shark.

    As the boat caroused on the waves, spray occasionally bumped over the side and gave them a fresh soaking, but this had no power to break their repose. The ominous slash of the wind and the water affected them as it would have affected mummies.

    "Boys," said the cook, with the notes of every reluctance in his voice, "she's drifted in pretty close. I guess one of you had better take her to sea again." The correspondent, aroused, heard the crash of the toppled crests.

    As he was rowing, the captain gave him some whiskey-and-water, and this steadied the chills out of him. "If I ever get ashore and anybody shows me even a photograph of an oar——"

    At last there was a short conversation.

195   "Billie! . . . Billie, will you spell me?"

    "Sure," said the oiler.

VII

    When the correspondent again opened his eyes, the sea and the sky were each of the gray hue of the dawning. Later, carmine and gold was painted upon the waters. The morning appeared finally, in its splendor, with a sky of pure blue, and the sunlight flamed on the tips of the waves.

    On the distant dunes were set many little black cottages, and a tall white windmill reared above them. No man, nor dog, nor bicycle appeared on the beach. The cottages might have formed a deserted village.

    The voyagers scanned the shore. A conference was held in the boat. "Well," said the captain, "if no help is coming, we might better try a run through the surf right away. If we stay out here much longer we will be too weak to do anything for ourselves at all." The others silently acquiesced in this reasoning. The boat was headed for the beach. The correspondent wondered if none ever ascended the tall wind-tower,[7] and if then they never looked seaward. This tower was a giant, standing with its back to the plight of the ants. It represented in a degree, to the correspondent, the serenity of nature amid the struggles of the individual—nature in the wind, and nature in the vision of men. She did not seem cruel to him then, nor beneficent, nor treacherous, nor wise. But she was indifferent, flatly indifferent. It is, perhaps, plausible that a man in this situation, impressed with the unconcern of the universe, should see the innumerable flaws of his life, and have them taste wickedly in his mind, and wish for another chance. A distinction between right and wrong seems absurdly clear to him, then, in this new ignorance of the grave-edge, and he understands that if he were given another opportunity he would mend his conduct and his words, and be better and brighter during an introduction or at a tea.

"Now, boys," said the captain, "she is going to swamp sure. All we can do is to work her in as far as possible, and then when she swamps, pile out and scramble for the beach. Keep cool now, and don't jump until she swamps sure."

The oiler took the oars. Over his shoulders he scanned the surf. "Captain," he said, "I think I'd better bring her about and keep her head-on to the seas and back her in."

"All right, Billie," said the captain. "Back her in." The oiler swung the boat then, and, seated in the stern, the cook and the correspondent were obliged to look over their shoulders to contemplate the lonely and indifferent shore.

The monstrous inshore rollers heaved the boat high until the men were again enabled to see the white sheets of water scudding up the slanted beach. "We won't get in very close," said the captain. Each time a man could wrest his attention from the rollers, he turned his glance toward the shore, and in the expression of the eyes during this contemplation there was a singular quality. The correspondent, observing the others, knew that they were not afraid, but the full meaning of their glances was shrouded.

As for himself, he was too tired to grapple fundamentally with the fact. He tried to coerce his mind into thinking of it, but the mind was dominated at this time by the muscles, and the muscles said they did not care. It merely occurred to him that if he should drown it would be a shame.

There were no hurried words, no pallor, no plain agitation. The men simply looked at the shore. "Now, remember to get well clear of the boat when you jump," said the captain.

Seaward the crest of a roller suddenly fell with a thunderous crash, and the long white comber came roaring down upon the boat.

"Steady now," said the captain. The men were silent. They turned their eyes from the shore to the comber and waited. The boat slid up the incline, leaped at the furious top, bounced over it, and swung down the long back of the wave. Some water had been shipped, and the cook bailed it out.

But the next crest crashed also. The tumbling, boiling flood of white

7. A watchtower for observing weather.

water caught the boat and whirled it almost perpendicular. Water swarmed in from all sides. The correspondent had his hands on the gunwale at this time, and when the water entered at that place he swiftly withdrew his fingers, as if he objected to wetting them.

The little boat, drunken with this weight of water, reeled and snuggled deeper into the sea.

210 "Bail her out, cook! Bail her out!" said the captain.

"All right, Captain," said the cook.

"Now, boys, the next one will do for us sure," said the oiler. "Mind to jump clear of the boat."

The third wave moved forward, huge, furious, implacable. It fairly swallowed the dinghy, and almost simultaneously the men tumbled into the sea. A piece of life-belt had lain in the bottom of the boat, and as the correspondent went overboard he held this to his chest with his left hand.

The January water was icy, and reflected immediately that it was colder than he had expected to find it off the coast of Florida. This appeared to his dazed mind as a fact important enough to be noted at the time. The coldness of the water was sad; it was tragic. This fact was somehow mixed and confused with his opinion of his own situation, so that it seemed almost a proper reason for tears. The water was cold.

215 When he came to the surface he was conscious of little but the noisy water. Afterward he saw his companions in the sea. The oiler was ahead in the race. He was swimming strongly and rapidly. Off to the correspondent's left, the cook's great white and corked back bulged out of the water, and in the rear the captain was hanging with his one good hand to the keel of the overturned dinghy.

There is a certain immovable quality to a shore, and the correspondent wondered at it amid the confusion of the sea.

It seemed also very attractive; but the correspondent knew that it was a long journey, and he paddled leisurely. The piece of life-preserver lay under him, and sometimes he whirled down the incline of a wave as if he were on a hand-sled.

But finally he arrived at a place in the sea where travel was beset with difficulty. He did not pause swimming to inquire what manner of current had caught him, but there his progress ceased. The shore was set before him like a bit of scenery on a stage, and he looked at it and understood with his eyes each detail of it.

As the cook passed, much farther to the left, the captain was calling to him, "Turn over on your back, cook! Turn over on your back and use the oar."

220 "All right, sir." The cook turned on his back, and, paddling with an oar, went ahead as if he were a canoe.

Presently the boat also passed to the left of the correspondent, with the captain clinging with one hand to the keel. He would have appeared like a man raising himself to look over a board fence if it were not for the extraordinary gymnastics of the boat. The correspondent marvelled that the captain could still hold to it.

They passed on nearer to shore—the oiler, the cook, the captain—and following them went the water-jar, bouncing gaily over the seas.

The correspondent remained in the grip of this strange new enemy, a current. The shore, with its white slope of sand and its green bluff topped with little silent cottages, was spread like a picture before him. It was very near to him then, but he was impressed as one who, in a gallery, looks at a scene from Brittany or Algiers.

He thought: "I am going to drown? Can it be possible? Can it be possible? Can it be possible?" Perhaps an individual must consider his own death to be the final phenomenon of nature.

But later a wave perhaps whirled him out of this small deadly current, for he found suddenly that he could again make progress toward the shore. Later still he was aware that the captain, clinging with one hand to the keel of the dinghy, had his face turned away from the shore and toward him, and was calling his name. "Come to the boat! Come to the boat!"

In his struggle to reach the captain and the boat, he reflected that when one gets properly wearied drowning must really be a comfortable arrangement—a cessation of hostilities accompanied by a large degree of relief; and he was glad of it, for the main thing in his mind for some moments had been horror of the temporary agony; he did not wish to be hurt.

Presently he saw a man running along the shore. He was undressing with most remarkable speed. Coat, trousers, shirt, everything flew magically off him.

"Come to the boat!" called the captain.

"All right, Captain." As the correspondent paddled, he saw the captain let himself down to bottom and leave the boat. Then the correspondent performed his one little marvel of the voyage. A large wave caught him and flung him with ease and supreme speed completely over the boat and far beyond it. It struck him even then as an event in gymnastics and a true miracle of the sea. An overturned boat in the surf is not a plaything to a swimming man.

The correspondent arrived in water that reached only to his waist, but his condition did not enable him to stand for more than a moment. Each wave knocked him into a heap, and the undertow pulled at him.

Then he saw the man who had been running and undressing, and undressing and running, come bounding into the water. He dragged ashore the cook, and then waded toward the captain; but the captain waved him away and sent him to the correspondent. He was naked—naked as a tree in winter; but a halo was about his head, and he shone like a saint. He gave a strong pull, and a long drag, and a bully heave at the correspondent's hand. The correspondent, schooled in the minor formulae, said, "Thanks, old man." But suddenly the man cried, "What's that?" He pointed a swift finger. The correspondent said, "Go."

In the shallows, face downward, lay the oiler. His forehead touched sand that was periodically, between each wave, clear of the sea.

The correspondent did not know all that transpired afterward. When he achieved safe ground he fell, striking the sand with each particular part of his body. It was as if he had dropped from a roof, but the thud was grateful to him.

It seems that instantly the beach was populated with men with blankets, clothes, and flasks, and women with coffee-pots and all the remedies sacred to their minds. The welcome of the land to the men from the sea was warm and generous; but a still and dripping shape was carried slowly up the beach, and the land's welcome for it could only be the different and sinister hospitality of the grave.

235   When it came night, the white waves paced to and fro in the moonlight, and the wind brought the sound of the great sea's voice to the men on the shore, and they felt that they could then be interpreters.

                                                                        1898

QUESTIONS

1. When do you become aware that your view of events in "The Open Boat" is limited to things seen and heard by the four men in the boat? In what specific ways is that important to the story's effect? How much of the story's suspense depends on this limited point of view? How would the effect of the story differ if it were told autobiographically through a first-person narrator?

2. Examine the language of the story's first paragraph. How is the contrast between the sky and the sea significant? What specific colors are mentioned or implied here? How much differentiation in color is discernible to the men? What angles of vision are implied by the color imagery? Which specific words and phrases imply details about body posture and fatigue?

3. How much of the basic plot do you know by the end of the third paragraph? What crucial information is, at this point, still unclear? At what point in the text is each additional plot detail presented?

4. Examine paragraphs 3–6; then differentiate the four men as fully as you can. What distinguishing features help you keep them straight as the narrative proceeds? What facts are provided later about each of the men? How do you account for the general agreeableness of the group toward the individual needs of each other? How does the captain set himself apart from the rest? What details create the sense of hierarchy in the group? How might the plot differ if the makeup of the group were to change?

5. In some ways the story seems almost timeless as the relentless waves threaten the men and the boat. How much time actually passes? How is the passing of time recorded? How are the threats to life different in different parts of the story?

6. At which points in the story does the men's weariness outweigh their sense of danger? How are these points signaled by the language? What functions does the repetitive language perform? Does Crane affect his reader with the monotony experienced by the men in the boat, or does he capture attention by varying the repetitions?

7. Where does the story's perspective "expand" to include larger reflections and generalizations? How are they justified by the narrative point of view? Describe the "voice" in these comments. What is their tone?

8. In which of the men do you become most interested as the story develops? Point to textual indications that the point of view gradually narrows to

increasingly suggest an individual voice rather than the collective one of the four men. Why does such a narrowing occur? What effect does this narrowing point of view have on the story's conclusion?

9. How important is it that the threat to the men involves a natural force? How would the story's theme differ if they faced a human threat? How would the symbolism differ? What do the shifting waves symbolize? How does the language in the story support this symbolism?

SUGGESTIONS FOR WRITING

1. In "The Secret Sharer," when Leggatt is aboard and dressed in the captain's sleeping suit, he is described as looking like the captain's "double." That, plus Leggatt's arriving from the sea naked, looking like a fish, phosphorescent and oblong, together with the title of the story and the narrator's seeing his first command as a test, has led many readers to interpret this story in psychological terms. Write an essay in which you discuss how the narrator-captain and his "double" might represent different aspects of the mind.

2. Can you imagine "The Secret Sharer"—the story of a new captain taking over command of a strange ship, with mates not of his own choosing and not of his own "kind," of the strained relations between the new captain and the other officers, of his emotional state, and of his first daring act of seamanship—without the presence of a Leggatt? Write a 2–3-page synopsis of such a story, and, in the manner of Conrad, an opening or a closing scene. Is there some way in which you might still call your story "The Secret Sharer"? Who has the secret and with whom does he share it?

3. Write a sequel to "The Secret Sharer" recounting what happens to Leggatt after he leaves the ship, using as many of the elements and details of Conrad's story as you can but with a new focus and voice.

4. Voice is a dominant element in "Love Medicine," and it is largely through Lipsha's voice that we infer his character. His language is ungrammatical, and he seems to have a somewhat naive view of reality, or causality. His kindness and good nature show through the errors and naiveté, however, and he is capable of insight and even wisdom. Write an essay that shows how "Love Medicine" 's theme is presented through a character who is not well educated or intellectually profound and how the character's very limitations contribute meaning and force to the theme.

5. Toward the end of "Love Medicine," Lipsha tells Grandma that it was not "love medicine" that brought Grandpa's ghost back to her but love itself, not magic but feeling. Grandma looks at him tenderly and says, " 'Lipsha, . . . you was always my favorite' " (paragraph 159). Write an essay in which you discuss this passage in terms of the plot (but be sure to remember Lulu); in terms of Lipsha's character; in terms of Grandma's; in terms of theme (and you might even want to think of "love medicine" as symbol).

6. Look carefully at paragraphs in "The Open Boat" in which different "elements" (such as plot, character, language, setting, and so on) seem purposely merged or fused. How is such interaction accomplished? Choose a single paragraph that illustrates the close interaction of different elements, and write a

two-page analytical paper showing how the paragraph works to integrate the story's narrative presentation.

7. Amidst all the terrors recounted in "The Open Boat," the narrator pauses to reflect that "there was this comradeship that the correspondent . . . knew even at the time was the best experience of his life" (paragraph 43). Then he adds: "But no one said that it was so. No one mentioned it." Write an essay in which you explain why the correspondent, "who had been taught to be cynical of men," comes to feel this way, and why none of the men talk about it.

8. Write an essay in which you discuss the symbolism of the predicament in "The Open Boat." Consider, for example, the implacable natural force that threatens the men, their defenselessness, the precariousness of the tiny boat, the circling sharks, the maddening nearness to a shore they cannot reach safely. How much does the story's symbolic effect depend upon the traditional "life as voyage" metaphor?

9. In "The Open Boat," Stephen Crane writes: "When it occurs to a man that nature does not regard him as important, and that she feels she would not maim the universe by disposing of him, he at first wishes to throw bricks at the temple, and he hates deeply the fact that there are no bricks and no temples. Any visible expression of nature would surely be pelleted with his jeers" (paragraph 173). Write a short story depicting characters whose lives are imperiled by natural forces beyond their control.

Reading More Fiction

AMBROSE BIERCE

An Occurrence at Owl Creek Bridge

I

A man stood upon a railroad bridge in Northern Alabama, looking down into the swift waters twenty feet below. The man's hands were behind his back, the wrists bound with a cord. A rope loosely encircled his neck. It was attached to a stout cross-timber above his head, and the slack fell to the level of his knees. Some loose boards laid upon the sleepers supporting the metals of the railway supplied a footing for him and his executioners—two private soldiers of the Federal army, directed by a sergeant, who in civil life may have been a deputy sheriff. At a short remove upon the same temporary platform was an officer in the uniform of his rank, armed. He was a captain. A sentinel at each end of the bridge stood with his rifle in the position known as "support," that is to say, vertical in front of the left shoulder, the hammer resting on the forearm thrown straight across the chest—a formal and unnatural position, enforcing an erect carriage of the body. It did not appear to be the duty of these two men to know what was occurring at the centre of the bridge; they merely blockaded the two ends of the foot plank which traversed it.

Beyond one of the sentinels nobody was in sight; the railroad ran straight away into a forest for a hundred yards, then, curving, was lost to view. Doubtless there was an outpost further along. The other bank of the stream was open ground—a gentle acclivity crowned with a stockade of vertical tree trunks, loopholed for rifles, with a single embrasure through which protruded the muzzle of a brass cannon commanding the bridge. Midway of the slope between bridge and fort were the spectators—a single company of infantry in line, at "parade rest," the butts of the rifles on the ground, the barrels inclining slightly backward against the right shoulder, the hands crossed upon the stock. A lieutenant stood at the right of the line, the point of his sword upon the ground, his left hand resting upon his right. Excepting the group of four at the centre of the bridge not a man moved. The company faced the bridge, staring stonily, motionless. The sentinels, facing the banks of the stream, might have been statues to adorn the bridge. The captain stood with folded arms, silent, observing the work of his subordinates but making no sign. Death is a dignitary who, when he comes announced, is to be received with formal manifestations of respect, even by those most familiar with him. In the code of military etiquette silence and fixity are forms of deference.

The man who was engaged in being hanged was apparently about thirty-five years of age. He was a civilian, if one might judge from his dress, which was that of a planter. His features were good—a straight nose, firm mouth, broad forehead, from which his long, dark hair was combed straight back, falling behind his ears to the collar of his well-fitting frock coat. He wore a moustache and pointed beard, but no whiskers; his eyes were large and dark grey and had a kindly expression which one would hardly have expected in one whose neck was in the hemp. Evidently this was no vulgar assassin. The liberal military code makes provision for hanging many kinds of people, and gentlemen are not excluded.

The preparations being complete, the two private soldiers stepped aside and each drew away the plank upon which he had been standing. The sergeant turned to the captain, saluted and placed himself immediately behind that officer, who in turn moved apart one pace. These movements left the condemned man and the sergeant standing on the two ends of the same plank, which spanned three of the cross-ties of the bridge. The end upon which the civilian stood almost, but not quite, reached a fourth. This plank had been held in place by the weight of the captain; it was now held by that of the sergeant. At a signal from the former, the latter would step aside, the plank would tilt and the condemned man go down between two ties. The arrangement commended itself to his judgment as simple and effective. His face had not been covered nor his eyes bandaged. He looked a moment at his "unsteadfast footing," then let his gaze wander to the swirling water of the stream racing madly beneath his feet. A piece of dancing driftwood caught his attention and his eyes followed it down the current. How slowly it appeared to move! What a sluggish stream!

5   He closed his eyes in order to fix his last thoughts upon his wife and children. The water, touched to gold by the early sun, the brooding mists under the banks at some distance down the stream, the fort, the soldiers, the piece of drift—all had distracted him. And now he became conscious of a new disturbance. Striking through the thought of his dear ones was a sound which he could neither ignore nor understand, a sharp, distinct, metallic percussion like the stroke of a blacksmith's hammer upon the anvil; it had the same ringing quality. He wondered what it was, and whether immeasurably distant or near by—it seemed both. Its recurrence was regular, but as slow as the tolling of a death knell. He awaited each stroke with impatience and—he knew not why—apprehension. The intervals of silence grew progressively longer, the delays became maddening. With their greater infrequency the sounds increased in strength and sharpness. They hurt his ear like the thrust of a knife; he feared he would shriek. What he heard was the ticking of his watch.

He unclosed his eyes and saw again the water below him. "If I could free my hands," he thought, "I might throw off the noose and spring into the stream. By diving I could evade the bullets, and, swimming vigorously, reach the bank, take to the woods, and get away home. My home, thank God, is as yet outside their lines; my wife and little ones are still beyond the invader's farthest advance."

As these thoughts, which have here to be set down in words, were flashed into the doomed man's brain rather than evolved from it, the captain nodded to the sergeant. The sergeant stepped aside.

II

Peyton Farquhar was a well-to-do planter, of an old and highly-respected Alabama family. Being a slave owner, and, like other slave owners, a politician, he was naturally an original secessionist and ardently devoted to the Southern cause. Circumstances of an imperious nature which it is unnecessary to relate here, had prevented him from taking service with the gallant army which had fought the disastrous campaigns ending with the fall of Corinth,[1] and he chafed under the inglorious restraint, longing for the release of his energies, the larger life of the soldier, the opportunity for distinction. That opportunity, he felt, would come, as it comes to all in war time. Meanwhile he did what he could. No service was too humble for him to perform in aid of the South, no adventure too perilous for him to undertake if consistent with the character of a civilian who was at heart a soldier, and who in good faith and without too much qualification assented to at least a part of the frankly villainous dictum that all is fair in love and war.

One evening while Farquhar and his wife were sitting on a rustic bench near the entrance to his grounds, a grey-clad soldier rode up to the gate and asked for a drink of water. Mrs. Farquhar was only too happy to serve him with her own white hands. While she was gone to fetch the water, her husband approached the dusty horseman and inquired eagerly for news from the front.

"The Yanks are repairing the railroads," said the man, "and are getting 10
ready for another advance. They have reached the Owl Creek bridge, put it in order, and built a stockade on the other bank. The commandant has issued an order, which is posted everywhere, declaring that any civilian caught interfering with the railroad, its bridges, tunnels, or trains, will be summarily hanged. I saw the order."

"How far is it to the Owl Creek bridge?" Farquhar asked.

"About thirty miles."

"Is there no force on this side the creek?"

"Only a picket post half a mile out, on the railroad, and a single sentinel at this end of the bridge."

"Suppose a man—a civilian and student of hanging—should elude the 15
picket post and perhaps get the better of the sentinel," said Farquhar, smiling, "what could he accomplish?"

The soldier reflected. "I was there a month ago," he replied. "I observed that the flood of last winter had lodged a great quantity of driftwood against the wooden pier at this end of the bridge. It is now dry and would burn like tow."

The lady had now brought the water, which the soldier drank. He

---

1. Corinth, Mississippi, captured by General Ulysses S. Grant in April 1862.

thanked her ceremoniously, bowed to her husband, and rode away. An hour later, after nightfall, he repassed the plantation, going northward in the direction from which he had come. He was a Federal scout.

III

As Peyton Farquhar fell straight downward through the bridge, he lost consciousness and was as one already dead. From this state he was awakened—ages later, it seemed to him—by the pain of a sharp pressure upon his throat, followed by a sense of suffocation. Keen, poignant agonies seemed to shoot from his neck downward through every fibre of his body and limbs. These pains appeared to flash along well-defined lines of ramification, and to beat with an inconceivably rapid periodicity. They seemed like streams of pulsating fire heating him to an intolerable temperature. As to his head, he was conscious of nothing but a feeling of fullness—of congestion. These sensations were unaccompanied by thought. The intellectual part of his nature was already effaced; he had power only to feel, and feeling was torment. He was conscious of motion. Encompassed in a luminous cloud, of which he was now merely the fiery heart, without material substance, he swung through unthinkable arcs of oscillation, like a vast pendulum. Then all at once, with terrible suddenness, the light about him shot upward with the noise of a loud plash; a frightful roaring was in his ears, and all was cold and dark. The power of thought was restored; he knew that the rope had broken and he had fallen into the stream. There was no additional strangulation; the noose about his neck was already suffocating him, and kept the water from his lungs. To die of hanging at the bottom of a river!—the idea seemed to him ludicrous. He opened his eyes in the blackness and saw above him a gleam of light, but how distant, how inaccessible! He was still sinking, for the light became fainter and fainter until it was a mere glimmer. Then it began to grow and brighten, and he knew that he was rising toward the surface—knew it with reluctance, for he was now very comfortable. "To be hanged and drowned," he thought, "that is not so bad; but I do not wish to be shot. No; I will not be shot; that is not fair."

He was not conscious of an effort, but a sharp pain in his wrist apprised him that he was trying to free his hands. He gave the struggle his attention, as an idler might observe the feat of a juggler, without interest in the outcome. What splendid effort!—what magnificent, what superhuman strength! Ah, that was a fine endeavour! Bravo! The cord fell away; his arms parted and floated upward, the hands dimly seen on each side in the growing light. He watched them with a new interest as first one and then the other pounced upon the noose at his neck. They tore it away and thrust it fiercely aside, its undulations resembling those of a water-snake. "Put it back, put it back!" He thought he shouted these words to his hands, for the undoing of the noose had been succeeded by the direst pang which he had yet experienced. His neck ached horribly; his brain was on fire; his heart, which had been fluttering faintly, gave a great leap, trying to force itself out at his mouth. His whole body was racked and wrenched with an insupportable anguish! But his disobedient hands gave no heed to the command. They beat the water vigorously with quick, downward strokes, forcing him to the surface. He felt his head emerge; his eyes were blinded by the sunlight; his chest expanded convulsively, and with a supreme and crowning agony his lungs engulfed a great draught of air, which instantly he expelled in a shriek!

He was now in full possession of his physical senses. They were, indeed, 20 preternaturally keen and alert. Something in the awful disturbance of his organic system had so exalted and refined them that they made record of things never before perceived. He felt the ripples upon his face and heard their separate sounds as they struck. He looked at the forest on the bank of the stream, saw the individual trees, the leaves and the veining of each leaf—the very insects upon them, the locusts, the brilliant-bodied flies, the grey spiders stretching their webs from twig to twig. He noted the prismatic colors in all the dewdrops upon a million blades of grass. The humming of the gnats that danced above the eddies of the stream, the beating of the dragon flies' wings, the strokes of the water spiders' legs, like oars which had lifted their boat—all these made audible music. A fish slid along beneath his eyes and he heard the rush of its body parting the water.

He had come to the surface facing down the stream; in a moment the visible world seemed to wheel slowly round, himself the pivotal point, and he saw the bridge, the fort, the soldiers upon the bridge, the captain, the sergeant, the two privates, his executioners. They were in silhouette against the blue sky. They shouted and gesticulated, pointing at him; the captain had drawn his pistol, but did not fire; the others were unarmed. Their movements were grotesque and horrible, their forms gigantic.

Suddenly he heard a sharp report and something struck the water smartly within a few inches of his head, spattering his face with spray. He heard a second report, and saw one of the sentinels with his rifle at his shoulder, a light cloud of blue smoke rising from the muzzle. The man in the water saw the eye of the man on the bridge gazing into his own through the sights of the rifle. He observed that it was a grey eye, and remembered having read that grey eyes were keenest and that all famous marksmen had them. Nevertheless, this one had missed.

A counter swirl had caught Farquhar and turned him half round; he was again looking into the forest on the bank opposite the fort. The sound of a clear, high voice in a monotonous singsong now rang out behind him and came across the water with a distinctness that pierced and subdued all other sounds, even the beating of the ripples in his ears. Although no soldier, he had frequented camps enough to know the dread significance of that deliberate, drawling, aspirated chant; the lieutenant on shore was taking a part in the morning's work. How coldly and pitilessly—with what an even, calm intonation, presaging and enforcing tranquillity in the men—with what accurately-measured intervals fell those cruel words:

"Attention, company.... Shoulder arms.... Ready.... Aim.... Fire."

Farquhar dived—dived as deeply as he could. The water roared in his 25 ears like the voice of Niagara, yet he heard the dulled thunder of the volley, and rising again toward the surface, met shining bits of metal, singularly flattened, oscillating slowly downward. Some of them touched him on the face and hands, then fell away, continuing their descent. One lodged between his collar and neck; it was uncomfortably warm, and he snatched it out.

As he rose to the surface, gasping for breath, he saw that he had been a long time under water; he was perceptibly farther down stream—nearer to safety. The soldiers had almost finished reloading; the metal ramrods flashed all at once in the sunshine as they were drawn from the barrels, turned in the air, and thrust into their sockets. The two sentinels fired again, independently and ineffectually.

The hunted man saw all this over his shoulder; he was now swimming vigorously with the current. His brain was as energetic as his arms and legs; he thought with the rapidity of lightning.

"The officer," he reasoned, "will not make that martinet's error a second time. It is as easy to dodge a volley as a single shot. He has probably already given the command to fire at will. God help me, I cannot dodge them all!"

An appalling plash within two yards of him, followed by a loud rushing sound, *diminuendo*, which seemed to travel back through the air to the fort and died in an explosion which stirred the very river to its deeps! A rising sheet of water, which curved over him, fell down upon him, blinded him, strangled him! The cannon had taken a hand in the game. As he shook his head free from the commotion of the smitten water, he heard the deflected shot humming through the air ahead, and in an instant it was cracking and smashing the branches in the forest beyond.

30   "They will not do that again," he thought; "the next time they will use a charge of grape. I must keep my eye upon the gun; the smoke will apprise me—the report arrives too late; it lags behind the missile. It is a good gun."

Suddenly he felt himself whirled round and round—spinning like a top. The water, the banks, the forest, the now distant bridge, fort and men—all were commingled and blurred. Objects were represented by their colors only; circular horizontal streaks of color—that was all he saw. He had been caught in a vortex and was being whirled on with a velocity of advance and gyration which made him giddy and sick. In a few moments he was flung upon the gravel at the foot of the left bank of the stream—the southern bank—and behind a projecting point which concealed him from his enemies. The sudden arrest of his motion, the abrasion of one of his hands on the gravel, restored him and he wept with delight. He dug his fingers into the sand, threw it over himself in handfuls and audibly blessed it. It looked like gold, like diamonds, rubies, emeralds; he could think of nothing beautiful which it did not resemble. The trees upon the bank were giant garden plants; he noted a definite order in their arrangement, inhaled the fragrance of their blooms. A strange, roseate light shone through the spaces among their trunks, and the wind made in their branches the music of æolian harps. He had no wish to perfect his escape, was content to remain in that enchanting spot until retaken.

A whizz and rattle of grapeshot among the branches high above his head roused him from his dream. The baffled cannoneer had fired him a random farewell. He sprang to his feet, rushed up the sloping bank, and plunged into the forest.

All that day he travelled, laying his course by the rounding sun. The forest seemed interminable; nowhere did he discover a break in it, not even a woodman's road. He had not known that he lived in so wild a region. There was something uncanny in the revelation.

By nightfall he was fatigued, footsore, famishing. The thought of his wife and children urged him on. At last he found a road which led him in what he knew to be the right direction. It was as wide and straight as a city street, yet it seemed untravelled. No fields bordered it, no dwelling anywhere. Not so much as the barking of a dog suggested human habitation. The black bodies of the great trees formed a straight wall on both sides, terminating on the horizon in a point, like a diagram in a lesson in perspective. Overhead, as he looked up through this rift in the wood, shone great golden stars looking unfamiliar and grouped in strange constellations. He was sure they were arranged in some order which had a secret and malign significance. The wood on either side was full of singular noises, among which—once, twice, and again—he distinctly heard whispers in an unknown tongue.

His neck was in pain, and, lifting his hand to it, he found it horribly 35 swollen. He knew that it had a circle of black where the rope had bruised it. His eyes felt congested; he could no longer close them. His tongue was swollen with thirst; he relieved its fever by thrusting it forward from between his teeth into the cool air. How softly the turf had carpeted the untravelled avenue! He could no longer feel the roadway beneath his feet!

Doubtless, despite his suffering, he fell asleep while walking, for now he sees another scene—perhaps he has merely recovered from a delirium. He stands at the gate of his own home. All is as he left it, and all bright and beautiful in the morning sunshine. He must have travelled the entire night. As he pushes open the gate and passes up the wide white walk, he sees a flutter of female garments; his wife, looking fresh and cool and sweet, steps down from the verandah to meet him. At the bottom of the steps she stands waiting, with a smile of ineffable joy, an attitude of matchless grace and dignity. Ah, how beautiful she is! He springs forward with extended arms. As he is about to clasp her, he feels a stunning blow upon the back of the neck; a blinding white light blazes all about him, with a sound like the shock of a cannon—then all is darkness and silence!

Peyton Farquhar was dead; his body, with a broken neck, swung gently from side to side beneath the timbers of the Owl Creek bridge.

1891

KATE CHOPIN

WEB

The Story of an Hour

Knowing that Mrs. Mallard was afflicted with a heart trouble, great care was taken to break to her as gently as possible the news of her husband's death.

It was her sister Josephine who told her, in broken sentences; veiled hints that revealed in half concealing. Her husband's friend Richards was there, too, near her. It was he who had been in the newspaper office when intelligence of the railroad disaster was received, with Brently Mallard's name leading the list of "killed." He had only taken the time to assure himself of its truth by a second telegram, and had hastened to forestall any less careful, less tender friend in bearing the sad message.

She did not hear the story as many women have heard the same, with a paralyzed inability to accept its significance. She wept at once, with sudden, wild abandonment, in her sister's arms. When the storm of grief had spent itself she went away to her room alone. She would have no one follow her.

There stood, facing the open window, a comfortable, roomy armchair. Into this she sank, pressed down by a physical exhaustion that haunted her body and seemed to reach into her soul.

5 She could see in the open square before her house the tops of trees that were all aquiver with the new spring life. The delicious breath of rain was in the air. In the street below a peddler was crying his wares. The notes of a distant song which some one was singing reached her faintly, and countless sparrows were twittering in the eaves.

There were patches of blue sky showing here and there through the clouds that had met and piled one above the other in the west facing her window.

She sat with her head thrown back upon the cushion of the chair, quite motionless, except when a sob came up into her throat and shook her, as a child who has cried itself to sleep continues to sob in its dreams.

She was young, with a fair, calm face, whose lines bespoke repression and even a certain strength. But now there was a dull stare in her eyes, whose gaze was fixed away off yonder on one of those patches of blue sky. It was not a glance of reflection, but rather indicated a suspension of intelligent thought.

There was something coming to her and she was waiting for it, fearfully. What was it? She did not know; it was too subtle and elusive to name. But she felt it, creeping out of the sky, reaching toward her through the sounds, the scents, the color that filled the air.

10 Now her bosom rose and fell tumultuously. She was beginning to recognize this thing that was approaching to possess her, and she was striving to beat it back with her will—as powerless as her two white slender hands would have been.

When she abandoned herself a little whispered word escaped her slightly parted lips. She said it over and over under her breath: "free, free, free!" The vacant stare and the look of terror that had followed it went from her eyes. They stayed keen and bright. Her pulses beat fast, and the coursing blood warmed and relaxed every inch of her body.

She did not stop to ask if it were or were not a monstrous joy that held her. A clear and exalted perception enabled her to dismiss the suggestion as trivial.

She knew that she would weep again when she saw the kind, tender hands folded in death; the face that had never looked save with love upon her, fixed and gray and dead. But she saw beyond that bitter moment a long procession of years to come that would belong to her absolutely. And she opened and spread her arms out to them in welcome.

There would be no one to live for her during those coming years; she would live for herself. There would be no powerful will bending hers in that blind persistence with which men and women believe they have a right to impose a private will upon a fellow-creature. A kind intention or a cruel intention made the act seem no less a crime as she looked upon it in that brief moment of illumination.

And yet she had loved him—sometimes. Often she had not. What did it 15 matter! What could love, the unsolved mystery, count for in face of this possession of self-assertion which she suddenly recognized as the strongest impulse of her being!

"Free! Body and soul free!" she kept whispering.

Josephine was kneeling before the closed door with her lips to the keyhold, imploring for admission. "Louise, open the door! I beg; open the door—you will make yourself ill. What are you doing, Louise? For heaven's sake open the door."

"Go away. I am not making myself ill." No; she was drinking in a very elixir of life through that open window.

Her fancy was running riot along those days ahead of her. Spring days, and summer days, and all sorts of days that would be her own. She breathed a quick prayer that life might be long. It was only yesterday she had thought with a shudder that life might be long.

She arose at length and opened the door to her sister's importunities. 20 There was a feverish triumph in her eyes, and she carried herself unwittingly like a goddess of Victory. She clasped her sister's waist, and together they descended the stairs. Richards stood waiting for them at the bottom.

Some one was opening the front door with a latchkey. It was Brently Mallard who entered, a little travel-stained, composedly carrying his gripsack and umbrella. He had been far from the scene of accident, and did not even know there had been one. He stood amazed at Josephine's piercing cry; at Richards' quick motion to screen him from the view of his wife.

But Richards was too late.

When the doctors came they said she had died of heart disease—of joy that kills.

1891

CHARLOTTE PERKINS GILMAN

WEB

The Yellow Wallpaper

It is very seldom that mere ordinary people like John and myself secure ancestral halls for the summer.

A colonial mansion, a hereditary estate, I would say a haunted house, and reach the height of romantic felicity—but that would be asking too much of fate!

Still I will proudly declare that there is something queer about it.

Else, why should it be let so cheaply? And why have stood so long untenanted?

5   John laughs at me, of course, but one expects that in marriage.

John is practical in the extreme. He has no patience with faith, an intense horror of superstition, and he scoffs openly at any talk of things not to be felt and seen and put down in figures.

John is a physician, and *perhaps*—(I would not say it to a living soul, of course, but this is dead paper and a great relief to my mind—) *perhaps* that is one reason I do not get well faster.

You see he does not believe I am sick!

And what can one do?

10   If a physician of high standing, and one's own husband, assures friends and relatives that there is really nothing the matter with one but temporary nervous depression—a slight hysterical tendency—what is one to do?

My brother is also a physician, and also of high standing, and he says the same thing.

So I take phosphates or phosphites—whichever it is, and tonics, and journeys, and air, and exercise, and am absolutely forbidden to "work" until I am well again.

Personally, I disagree with their ideas.

Personally, I believe that congenial work, with excitement and change, would do me good.

15   But what is one to do?

I did write for a while in spite of them; but it *does* exhaust me a good deal—having to be so sly about it, or else meet with heavy opposition.

I sometimes fancy that in my condition if I had less opposition and more society and stimulus—but John says the very worst thing I can do is to think about my condition, and I confess it always makes me feel bad.

So I will let it alone and talk about the house.

The most beautiful place! It is quite alone, standing well back from the road, quite three miles from the village. It makes me think of English places that you read about, for there are hedges and walls and gates that lock, and lots of separate little houses for the gardeners and people.

20   There is a *delicious* garden! I never saw such a garden—large and shady, full of box-bordered paths, and lined with long grape-covered arbors with seats under them.

There were greenhouses, too, but they are all broken now.

There was some legal trouble, I believe, something about the heirs and co-heirs; anyhow, the place has been empty for years.

That spoils my ghostliness, I am afraid, but I don't care—there is something strange about the house—I can feel it.

I even said so to John one moonlight evening, but he said what I felt was a *draught,* and shut the window.

I get unreasonably angry with John sometimes. I'm sure I never used to be so sensitive. I think it is due to this nervous condition. 25

But John says if I feel so, I shall neglect proper self-control; so I take pains to control myself—before him, at least, and that makes me very tired.

I don't like our room a bit. I wanted one downstairs that opened on the piazza and had roses all over the window, and such pretty old-fashioned chintz hangings! but John would not hear of it.

He said there was only one window and not room for two beds, and no near room for him if he took another.

He is very careful and loving, and hardly lets me stir without special direction.

I have a schedule prescription for each hour in the day; he takes all care 30 from me, and so I feel basely ungrateful not to value it more.

He said we came here solely on my account, that I was to have perfect rest and all the air I could get. "Your exercise depends on your strength, my dear," said he, "and your food somewhat on your appetite; but air you can absorb all the time." So we took the nursery at the top of the house.

It is a big, airy room, the whole floor nearly, with windows that look all ways, and air and sunshine galore. It was nursery first and then playroom and gymnasium, I should judge; for the windows are barred for little children, and there are rings and things in the walls.

The paint and paper look as if a boys' school had used it. It is stripped off—the paper—in great patches all around the head of my bed, about as far as I can reach, and in a great place on the other side of the room low down. I never saw a worse paper in my life.

One of those sprawling flamboyant patterns committing every artistic sin.

It is dull enough to confuse the eye in following, pronounced enough 35 to constantly irritate and provoke study, and when you follow the lame uncertain curves for a little distance they suddenly commit suicide—plunge off at outrageous angles, destroy themselves in unheard of contradictions.

The color is repellant, almost revolting; a smouldering unclean yellow, strangely faded by the slow-turning sunlight.

It is a dull yet lurid orange in some places, a sickly sulphur tint in others.

No wonder the children hated it! I should hate it myself if I had to live in this room long.

There comes John, and I must put this away,—he hates to have me write a word.

40 We have been here two weeks, and I haven't felt like writing before, since that first day.

I am sitting by the window now, up in this atrocious nursery, and there is nothing to hinder my writing as much as I please, save lack of strength.

John is away all day, and even some nights when his cases are serious.

I am glad my case is not serious!

But these nervous troubles are dreadfully depressing.

45 John does not know how much I really suffer. He knows there is no *reason* to suffer, and that satisfies him.

Of course it is only nervousness. It does weigh on me so not to do my duty in any way!

I mean to be such a help to John, such a real rest and comfort, and here I am a comparative burden already!

Nobody would believe what an effort it is to do what little I am able,—to dress and entertain, and order things.

It is fortunate Mary is so good with the baby. Such a dear baby!

50 And yet I *cannot* be with him, it makes me so nervous.

I suppose John never was nervous in his life. He laughs at me so about this wallpaper!

At first he meant to repaper the room, but afterwards he said that I was letting it get the better of me, and that nothing was worse for a nervous patient than to give way to such fancies.

He said that after the wallpaper was changed it would be the heavy bedstead, and then the barred windows, and then that gate at the head of the stairs, and so on.

"You know the place is doing you good," he said, "and really, dear, I don't care to renovate the house just for a three months' rental."

55 "Then do let us go downstairs," I said, "there are such pretty rooms there."

Then he took me in his arms and called me a blessed little goose, and said he would go down cellar, if I wished, and have it whitewashed into the bargain.

But he is right enough about the beds and windows and things.

It is an airy and comfortable room as any one need wish, and, of course, I would not be so silly as to make him uncomfortable just for a whim.

I'm really getting quite fond of the big room, all but that horrid paper.

60 Out of one window I can see the garden, those mysterious deep-shaded arbors, the riotous old-fashioned flowers, and bushes and gnarly trees.

Out of another I get a lovely view of the bay and a little private wharf belonging to the estate. There is a beautiful shaded lane that runs down there from the house. I always fancy I see people walking in these numerous paths and arbors, but John has cautioned me not to give way to fancy in the least. He says that with my imaginative power and habit of story-making, a nervous weakness like mine is sure to lead to all manner of excited fancies, and that I ought to use my will and good sense to check the tendency. So I try.

I think sometimes that if I were only well enough to write a little it would relieve the press of ideas and rest me.

But I find I get pretty tired when I try.

It is so discouraging not to have any advice and companionship about my work. When I get really well, John says we will ask Cousin Henry and Julia down for a long visit; but he says he would as soon put fireworks in my pillow-case as to let me have those stimulating people about now.

I wish I could get well faster. 65

But I must not think about that. This paper looks to me as if it *knew* what a vicious influence it had!

There is a recurrent spot where the pattern lolls like a broken neck and two bulbous eyes stare at you upside down.

I get positively angry with the impertinence of it and the everlastingness. Up and down and sideways they crawl, and those absurd, unblinking eyes are everywhere. There is one place where two breadths didn't match, and the eyes go all up and down the line, one a little higher than the other.

I never saw so much expression in an inanimate thing before, and we all know how much expression they have! I used to lie awake as a child and get more entertainment and terror out of blank walls and plain furniture than most children could find in a toy-store.

I remember what a kindly wink the knobs of our big, old bureau used 70 to have, and there was one chair that always seemed like a strong friend.

I used to feel that if any of the other things looked too fierce I could always hop into that chair and be safe.

The furniture in this room is no worse than inharmonious, however, for we had to bring it all from downstairs. I suppose when this was used as a playroom they had to take the nursery things out, and no wonder! I never saw such ravages as the children have made here.

The wallpaper, as I said before, is torn off in spots, and it sticketh closer than a brother—they must have had perseverance as well as hatred.

Then the floor is scratched and gouged and splintered, the plaster itself is dug out here and there, and this great heavy bed which is all we found in the room, looks as if it had been through the wars.

But I don't mind it a bit—only the paper. 75

There comes John's sister. Such a dear girl as she is, and so careful of me! I must not let her find me writing.

She is a perfect and enthusiastic housekeeper, and hopes for no better profession. I verily believe she thinks it is the writing which made me sick!

But I can write when she is out, and see her a long way off from these windows.

There is one that commands the road, a lovely shaded winding road, and one that just looks off over the country. A lovely country, too, full of great elms and velvet meadows.

This wallpaper has a kind of sub-pattern in a different shade, a partic- 80 ularly irritating one, for you can only see it in certain lights, and not clearly then.

But in the places where it isn't faded and where the sun is just so—I can see a strange, provoking, formless sort of figure, that seems to skulk about behind that silly and conspicuous front design.

There's sister on the stairs!

Well, the Fourth of July is over! The people are all gone and I am tired out. John thought it might do me good to see a little company, so we just had mother and Nellie and the children down for a week.

Of course I didn't do a thing. Jennie sees to everything now.

85 But it tired me all the same.

John says if I don't pick up faster he shall send me to Weir Mitchell[1] in the fall.

But I don't want to go there at all. I had a friend who was in his hands once, and she says he is just like John and my brother, only more so!

Besides, it is such an undertaking to go so far.

I don't feel as if it was worth while to turn my hand over for anything, and I'm getting dreadfully fretful and querulous.

90 I cry at nothing, and cry most of the time.

Of course I don't when John is here, or anybody else, but when I am alone.

And I am alone a good deal just now. John is kept in town very often by serious cases, and Jennie is good and lets me alone when I want her to.

So I walk a little in the garden or down that lovely lane, sit on the porch under the roses, and lie down up here a good deal.

I'm getting really fond of the room in spite of the wallpaper. Perhaps *because* of the wallpaper.

95 It dwells in my mind so!

I lie here on this great immovable bed—it is nailed down, I believe—and follow that pattern about by the hour. It is as good as gymnastics, I assure you. I start, we'll say, at the bottom, down in the corner over there where it has not been touched, and I determine for the thousandth time that I *will* follow that pointless pattern to some sort of conclusion.

I know a little of the principle of design, and I know this thing was not arranged on any laws of radiation, or alternation, or repetition, or symmetry, or anything else that I ever heard of.

It is repeated, of course, by the breadths, but not otherwise.

Looked at in one way each breadth stands alone, the bloated curves and flourishes—a kind of "debased Romanesque" with *delirium tremens*—go waddling up and down in isolated columns of fatuity.

100 But, on the other hand, they connect diagonally, and the sprawling outlines run off in great slanting waves of optic horror, like a lot of wallowing seaweeds in full chase.

The whole thing goes horizontally, too, at least it seems so, and I exhaust myself in trying to distinguish the order of its going in that direction.

They have used a horizontal breadth for a frieze, and that adds wonderfully to the confusion.

There is one end of the room where it is almost intact, and there, when the crosslights fade and the low sun shines directly upon it, I can almost

---

1. Silas Weir Mitchell (1829–1914), American physician, novelist, and specialist in nerve disorders, popularized the rest cure.

fancy radiation after all,—the interminable grotesque seem to form around a common center and rush off in headless plunges of equal distraction.

It makes me tired to follow it. I will take a nap I guess.

I don't know why I should write this. 105
I don't want to.
I don't feel able.

And I know John would think it absurd. But I *must* say what I feel and think in some way—it is such a relief!

But the effort is getting to be greater than the relief.

Half the time now I am awfully lazy, and lie down ever so much. 110

John says I mustn't lose my strength, and has me take cod liver oil and lots of tonics and things, to say nothing of ale and wine and rare meat.

Dear John! He loves me very dearly, and hates to have me sick. I tried to have a real earnest reasonable talk with him the other day, and tell him how I wish he would let me go and make a visit to Cousin Henry and Julia.

But he said I wasn't able to go, nor able to stand it after I got there; and I did not make out a very good case for myself, for I was crying before I had finished.

It is getting to be a great effort for me to think straight. Just this nervous weakness I suppose.

And dear John gathered me up in his arms, and just carried me upstairs 115 and laid me on the bed, and sat by me and read to me till it tired my head.

He said I was his darling and his comfort and all he had, and that I must take care of myself for his sake, and keep well.

He says no one but myself can help me out of it, that I must use my will and self-control and not let any silly fancies run away with me.

There's one comfort, the baby is well and happy, and does not have to occupy this nursery with the horrid wallpaper.

If we had not used it, that blessed child would have! What a fortunate escape! Why, I wouldn't have a child of mine, an impressionable little thing, live in such a room for worlds.

I never thought of it before, but it is lucky that John kept me here after 120 all, I can stand it so much easier than a baby, you see.

Of course I never mention it to them any more—I am too wise,—but I keep watch of it all the same.

There are things in that paper that nobody knows but me, or ever will.

Behind that outside pattern the dim shapes get clearer every day.

It is always the same shape, only very numerous.

And it is like a woman stooping down and creeping about behind that 125 pattern. I don't like it a bit. I wonder—I begin to think—I wish John would take me away from here!

It is so hard to talk with John about my case, because he is so wise, and because he loves me so.

But I tried it last night.

It was moonlight. The moon shines in all around just as the sun does.

I hate to see it sometimes, it creeps so slowly, and always comes in by one window or another.

130 John was asleep and I hated to waken him, so I kept still and watched the moonlight on that undulating wallpaper till I felt creepy.

The faint figure behind seemed to shake the pattern, just as if she wanted to get out.

I got up softly and went to feel and see if the paper *did* move, and when I came back John was awake.

"What is it, little girl?" he said. "Don't go walking about like that—you'll get cold."

I thought it was a good time to talk, so I told him that I really was not gaining here, and that I wished he would take me away.

135 "Why, darling!" said he, "our lease will be up in three weeks, and I can't see how to leave before.

"The repairs are not done at home, and I cannot possibly leave town just now. Of course if you were in any danger, I could and would, but you really are better, dear, whether you can see it or not. I am a doctor, dear, and I know. You are gaining flesh and color, your appetite is better, I feel really much easier about you."

"I don't weigh a bit more," said I, "nor as much; and my appetite may be better in the evening when you are here, but it is worse in the morning when you are away!"

"Bless her little heart!" said he with a big hug, "she shall be as sick as she pleases! But now let's improve the shining hours by going to sleep, and talk about it in the morning!"

"And you won't go away?" I asked gloomily.

140 "Why, how can I, dear? It is only three weeks more and then we will take a nice little trip of a few days while Jennie is getting the house ready. Really dear you are better!"

"Better in body perhaps—" I began, and stopped short, for he sat up straight and looked at me with such a stern, reproachful look that I could not say another word.

"My darling," said he, "I beg of you, for my sake and for our child's sake, as well as for your own, that you will never for one instant let that idea enter your mind! There is nothing so dangerous, so fascinating, to a temperament like yours. It is a false and foolish fancy. Can you not trust me as a physician when I tell you so?"

So of course I said no more on that score, and we went to sleep before long. He thought I was asleep first, but I wasn't, and lay there for hours trying to decide whether that front pattern and the back pattern really did move together or separately.

On a pattern like this, by daylight, there is a lack of sequence, a defiance of law, that is a constant irritant to a normal mind.

145 The color is hideous enough, and unreliable enough, and infuriating enough, but the pattern is torturing.

You think you have mastered it, but just as you get well underway in following, it turns a back-somersault and there you are. It slaps you in the face, knocks you down, and tramples upon you. It is like a bad dream.

The outside pattern is a florid arabesque, reminding one of a fungus. If you can imagine a toadstool in joints, an interminable string of toadstools, budding and sprouting in endless convolutions—why, that is something like it.

That is, sometimes!

There is one marked peculiarity about this paper, a thing nobody seems to notice but myself, and that is that it changes as the light changes.

When the sun shoots in through the east window—I always watch for   150
that first long, straight ray—it changes so quickly that I never can quite believe it.

That is why I watch it always.

By moonlight—the moon shines in all night when there is a moon—I wouldn't know it was the same paper.

At night in any kind of light, in twilight, candlelight, lamplight, and worst of all by moonlight, it becomes bars! The outside pattern I mean, and the woman behind it is as plain as can be.

I didn't realize for a long time what the thing was that showed behind, that dim sub-pattern, but now I am quite sure it is a woman.

By daylight she is subdued, quiet. I fancy it is the pattern that keeps her   155
so still. It is so puzzling. It keeps me quiet by the hour.

I lie down ever so much now. John says it is good for me, and to sleep all I can.

Indeed he started the habit by making me lie down for an hour after each meal.

It is a very bad habit I am convinced, for you see I don't sleep.

And that cultivates deceit, for I don't tell them I'm awake—O no!

The fact is I am getting a little afraid of John.   160

He seems very queer sometimes, and even Jennie has an inexplicable look.

It strikes me occasionally, just as a scientific hypothesis,—that perhaps it is the paper!

I have watched John when he did not know I was looking, and come into the room suddenly on the most innocent excuses, and I've caught him several times *looking at the paper!* And Jennie too. I caught Jennie with her hand on it once.

She didn't know I was in the room, and when I asked her in a quiet, a very quiet voice, with the most restrained manner possible, what she was doing with the paper—she turned around as if she had been caught stealing, and looked quite angry—asked me why I should frighten her so!

Then she said that the paper stained everything it touched, that she had   165
found yellow smooches on all my clothes and John's, and she wished we would be more careful!

Did not that sound innocent? But I know she was studying that pattern, and I am determined that nobody shall find it out but myself!

Life is very much more exciting now than it used to be. You see I have something more to expect, to look forward to, to watch. I really do eat better, and am more quiet than I was.

John is so pleased to see me improve! He laughed a little the other day, and said I seemed to be flourishing in spite of my wallpaper.

I turned it off with a laugh. I had no intention of telling him it was *because* of the wallpaper—he would make fun of me. He might even want to take me away.

170   I don't want to leave now until I have found it out. There is a week more, and I think that will be enough.

I'm feeling ever so much better! I don't sleep much at night, for it is so interesting to watch developments; but I sleep a good deal in the daytime.

In the daytime it is tiresome and perplexing.

There are always new shoots on the fungus, and new shades of yellow all over it. I cannot keep count of them, though I have tried conscientiously.

It is the strangest yellow, that wallpaper! It makes me think of all the yellow things I ever saw—not beautiful ones like buttercups, but old foul, bad yellow things.

175   But there is something else about that paper—the smell! I noticed it the moment we came into the room, but with so much air and sun it was not bad. Now we have had a week of fog and rain, and whether the windows are open or not, the smell is here.

It creeps all over the house.

I find it hovering in the dining-room, skulking in the parlor, hiding in the hall, lying in wait for me on the stairs.

It gets into my hair.

Even when I go to ride, if I turn my head suddenly and surprise it—there is that smell!

180   Such a peculiar odor, too! I have spent hours in trying to analyze it, to find what it smelled like.

It is not bad—at first, and very gentle, but quite the subtlest, most enduring odor I ever met.

In this damp weather it is awful, I wake up in the night and find it hanging over me.

It used to disturb me at first. I thought seriously of burning the house— to reach the smell.

But now I am used to it. The only thing I can think of that it is like is the *color* of the paper! A yellow smell.

185   There is a very funny mark on this wall, low down, near the mopboard. A streak that runs round the room. It goes behind every piece of furniture, except the bed, a long, straight, even *smooch,* as if it had been rubbed over and over.

I wonder how it was done and who did it, and what they did it for. Round and round and round—round and round and round—it makes me dizzy!

I really have discovered something at last.

Through watching so much at night, when it changes so, I have finally found out.

The front pattern *does* move—and no wonder! The woman behind shakes it!

Sometimes I think there are a great many women behind, and some- 190 times only one, and she crawls around fast, and her crawling shakes it all over.

Then in the very bright spots she keeps still, and in the very shady spots she just takes hold of the bars and shakes them hard.

And she is all the time trying to climb through. But nobody could climb through that pattern—it strangles so; I think that is why it has so many heads.

They get through, and then the pattern strangles them off and turns them upside down, and makes their eyes white!

If those heads were covered or taken off it would not be half so bad.

I think that woman gets out in the daytime! 195

And I'll tell you why—privately—I've seen her!

I can see her out of every one of my windows!

It is the same woman, I know, for she is always creeping, and most women do not creep by daylight.

I see her in that long shaded lane, creeping up and down. I see her in those dark grape arbors, creeping all around the garden.

I see her on that long road under the trees, creeping along, and when a 200 carriage comes she hides under the blackberry vines.

I don't blame her a bit. It must be very humiliating to be caught creeping by daylight!

I always lock the door when I creep by daylight. I can't do it at night, for I know John would suspect something at once.

And John is so queer now, that I don't want to irritate him. I wish he would take another room! Besides, I don't want anybody to get that woman out at night but myself.

I often wonder if I could see her out of all the windows at once.

But, turn as fast as I can, I can only see out of one at one time. 205

And though I always see her, she *may* be able to creep faster than I can turn!

I have watched her sometimes away off in the open country, creeping as fast as a cloud shadow in a high wind.

If only that top pattern could be gotten off from the under one! I mean to try it, little by little.

I have found out another funny thing, but I shan't tell it this time! It does not do to trust people too much.

There are only two more days to get this paper off, and I believe John 210 is beginning to notice. I don't like the look in his eyes.

And I heard him ask Jennie a lot of professional questions about me. She had a very good report to give.

She said I slept a good deal in the daytime.

John knows I don't sleep very well at night, for all I'm so quiet!

He asked me all sorts of questions, too, and pretended to be very loving and kind.

215 As if I couldn't see through him!

Still, I don't wonder he acts so, sleeping under this paper for three months.

It only interests me, but I feel sure John and Jennie are secretly affected by it.

Hurrah! This is the last day, but it is enough. John to stay in town over night, and won't be out until this evening.

Jennie wanted to sleep with me—the sly thing! but I told her I should undoubtedly rest better for a night all alone.

220 That was clever, for really I wasn't alone a bit! As soon as it was moon-light and that poor thing began to crawl and shake the pattern, I got up and ran to help her.

I pulled and she shook, I shook and she pulled, and before morning we had peeled off yards of that paper.

A strip about as high as my head and half around the room.

And then when the sun came and that awful pattern began to laugh at me, I declared I would finish it to-day!

We go away to-morrow, and they are moving all my furniture down again to leave things as they were before.

225 Jennie looked at the wall in amazement, but I told her merrily that I did it out of pure spite at the vicious thing.

She laughed and said she wouldn't mind doing it herself, but I must not get tired.

How she betrayed herself that time!

But I am here, and no person touches this paper but me,—not *alive!*

She tried to get me out of the room—it was too patent! But I said it was so quiet and empty and clean now that I believed I would lie down again and sleep all I could; and not to wake me even for dinner—I would call when I woke.

230 So now she is gone, and the servants are gone, and the things are gone, and there is nothing left but that great bedstead nailed down, with the canvas mattress we found on it.

We shall sleep downstairs to-night, and take the boat home to-morrow.

I quite enjoy the room, now it is bare again.

How those children did tear about here!

This bedstead is fairly gnawed!

235 But I must get to work.

I have locked the door and thrown the key down into the front path.

I don't want to go out, and I don't want to have anybody come in, till John comes.

I want to astonish him.

I've got a rope up here that even Jennie did not find. If that woman does get out, and tries to get away, I can tie her!

But I forgot I could not reach far without anything to stand on! 240
This bed will *not* move!

I tried to lift and push it until I was lame, and then I got so angry I bit off a little piece at one corner—but it hurt my teeth.

Then I peeled off all the paper I could reach standing on the floor. It sticks horribly and the pattern just enjoys it! All those strangled heads and bulbous eyes and waddling fungus growths just shriek with derision!

I am getting angry enough to do something desperate. To jump out of the window would be admirable exercise, but the bars are too strong even to try.

Besides I wouldn't do it. Of course not. I know well enough that a step 245 like that is improper and might be misconstrued.

I don't like to *look* out of the windows even—there are so many of those creeping women, and they creep so fast.

I wonder if they all come out of that wallpaper as I did?

But I am securely fastened now by my well-hidden rope—you don't get *me* out in the road there!

I suppose I shall have to get back behind the pattern when it comes night, and that is hard!

It is so pleasant to be out in this great room and creep around as I 250 please!

I don't want to go outside. I won't, even if Jennie asks me to.

For outside you have to creep on the ground, and everything is green instead of yellow.

But here I can creep smoothly on the floor, and my shoulder just fits in that long smooch around the wall, so I cannot lose my way.

Why there's John at the door!

It is no use, young man, you can't open it! 255

How he does call and pound!

Now he's crying for an axe.

It would be a shame to break down that beautiful door!

"John dear!" said I in the gentlest voice, "the key is down by the front steps, under a plantain leaf!"

That silenced him for a few moments. 260

Then he said—very quietly indeed, "Open the door, my darling!"

"I can't," said I. "The key is down by the front door under a plantain leaf!"

And then I said it again, several times, very gently and slowly, and said it so often that he had to go and see, and he got it of course, and came in. He stopped short by the door.

"What is the matter?" he cried. "For God's sake, what are you doing!"

I kept on creeping just the same, but I looked at him over my shoulder. 265

"I've got out at last," said I, "in spite of you and Jane. And I've pulled off most of the paper, so you can't put me back!"

Now why should that man have fainted? But he did, and right across my path by the wall, so that I had to creep over him every time!

1892

JAMES JOYCE

Araby

North Richmond Street, being blind,[1] was a quiet street except at the hour when the Christian Brothers' School set the boys free. An uninhabited house of two storeys stood at the blind end, detached from its neighbours in a square ground. The other houses of the street, conscious of decent lives within them, gazed at one another with brown imperturbable faces.

The former tenant of our house, a priest, had died in the back drawing-room. Air, musty from having been long enclosed, hung in all the rooms, and the waste room behind the kitchen was littered with old useless papers. Among these I found a few paper-covered books, the pages of which were curled and damp: *The Abbot*, by Walter Scott, *The Devout Communicant* and *The Memoirs of Vidocq*[2] I liked the last best because its leaves were yellow. The wild garden behind the house contained a central apple-tree and a few straggling bushes under one of which I found the late tenant's rusty bicycle-pump. He had been a very charitable priest; in his will he had left all his money to institutions and the furniture of his house to his sister.

When the short days of winter came dusk fell before we had well eaten our dinners. When we met in the street the houses had grown sombre. The space of sky above us was the colour of ever-changing violet and towards it the lamps of the street lifted their feeble lanterns. The cold air stung us and we played till our bodies glowed. Our shouts echoed in the silent street. The career of our play brought us through the dark muddy lanes behind the houses where we ran the gantlet of the rough tribes from the cottages, to the back doors of the dark dripping gardens where odours arose from the ashpits,[3] to the dark odorous stables where a coachman smoothed and combed the horse or shook music from the buckled harness. When we returned to the street light from the kitchen windows had filled the areas. If my uncle was seen turning the corner we hid in the shadow until we had seen him safely housed. Or if Mangan's sister came out on the doorstep to call her brother in to his tea we watched her from our shadow peer up and down the street. We waited to see whether she would remain or go in and, if she remained, we left our shadow and walked up to Mangan's steps resignedly. She was waiting for us, her figure defined by the light from the half-opened door. Her brother always teased her before he obeyed and I stood by the railings looking at her. Her dress swung as she moved her body and the soft rope of her hair tossed from side to side.

1. That is, a dead-end street.
2. The "memoirs" were probably *not* written by François Vidocq (1775–1857), a French criminal who became chief of detectives and who died poor and disgraced for his part in a crime that he solved; the 1820 novel by Sir Walter Scott (1771–1834) is a romance about the Catholic Mary, Queen of Scots (1542–1587), who was beheaded; *The Devout Communicant: or Pious Mediations and Aspirations for the Three Days Before and Three Days After Receiving the Holy Eucharist* (1813) is a Catholic religious tract.   3. Where fireplace ashes and other household refuse were dumped.

Every morning I lay on the floor in the front parlour watching her door. The blind was pulled down to within an inch of the sash so that I could not be seen. When she came out on the doorstep my heart leaped. I ran to the hall, seized my books and followed her. I kept her brown figure always in my eye and, when we came near the point at which our ways diverged, I quickened my pace and passed her. This happened morning after morning. I had never spoken to her, except for a few casual words, and yet her name was like a summons to all my foolish blood.

Her image accompanied me even in places the most hostile to romance. On Saturday evenings when my aunt went marketing I had to go to carry some of the parcels. We walked through the flaring streets, jostled by drunken men and bargaining women, amid the curses of labourers, the shrill litanies of shopboys who stood on guard by the barrels of pigs' cheeks, the nasal chanting of street-singers, who sang a *come-all-you* about O'Donovan Rossa,[4] or a ballad about the troubles in our native land. These noises converged in a single sensation of life for me: I imagined that I bore my chalice safely through a throng of foes. Her name sprang to my lips at moments in strange prayers and praises which I myself did not understand. My eyes were often full of tears (I could not tell why) and at times a flood from my heart seemed to pour itself out into my bosom. I thought little of the future. I did not know whether I would ever speak to her or not or, if I spoke to her, how I could tell her of my confused adoration. But my body was like a harp and her words and gestures were like fingers running upon the wires.

One evening I went into the back drawing-room in which the priest had died. It was a dark rainy evening and there was no sound in the house. Through one of the broken panes I heard the rain impinge upon the earth, the fine incessant needles of water playing in the sodden beds. Some distant lamp or lighted window gleamed below me. I was thankful that I could see so little. All my senses seemed to desire to veil themselves and, feeling that I was about to slip from them, I pressed the palms of my hands together until they trembled, murmuring: *O love! O love!* many times.

At last she spoke to me. When she addressed the first words to me I was so confused that I did not know what to answer. She asked me was I going to *Araby*.[5] I forget whether I answered yes or no. It would be a splendid bazaar, she said; she would love to go.

—And why can't you? I asked.

While she spoke she turned a silver bracelet round and round her wrist. She could not go, she said, because there would be a retreat that week in her convent. Her brother and two other boys were fighting for their caps and I was alone at the railings. She held one of the spikes, bowing her head towards me. The light from the lamp opposite our door caught the white curve of her neck, lit up her hair that rested there and, falling, lit up the

---

4. Jeremiah O'Donovan (1831–1915) was a militant Irish nationalist who fought on despite terms in prison and banishment. *Come-all-you:* a song, of which there were many, that began "Come, all you Irishmen."   5. A bazaar billed as a "Grand Oriental Fete," Dublin, May 1894.

hand upon the railing. It fell over one side of her dress and caught the white border of a petticoat, just visible as she stood at ease.

10   —It's well for you, she said.

—If I go, I said, I will bring you something.

What innumerable follies laid waste my waking and sleeping thoughts after that evening! I wished to annihilate the tedious intervening days. I chafed against the work of school. At night in my bedroom and by day in the classroom her image came between me and the page I strove to read. The syllables of the word *Araby* were called to me through the silence in which my soul luxuriated and cast an Eastern enchantment over me. I asked for leave to go to the bazaar on Saturday night. My aunt was surprised and hoped it was not some Freemason[6] affair. I answered few questions in class. I watched my master's face pass from amiability to sternness; he hoped I was not beginning to idle. I could not call my wandering thoughts together. I had hardly any patience with the serious work of life which, now that it stood between me and my desire, seemed to me child's play, ugly monotonous child's play.

On Saturday morning I reminded my uncle that I wished to go to the bazaar in the evening. He was fussing at the hallstand, looking for the hat-brush, and answered me curtly:

—Yes, boy, I know.

15   As he was in the hall I could not go into the front parlour and lie at the window. I left the house in bad humour and walked slowly towards the school. The air was pitilessly raw and already my heart misgave me.

When I came home to dinner my uncle had not yet been home. Still it was early. I sat staring at the clock for some time and, when its ticking began to irritate me, I left the room. I mounted the staircase and gained the upper part of the house. The high cold empty gloomy rooms liberated me and I went from room to room singing. From the front window I saw my companions playing below in the street. Their cries reached me weakened and indistinct and, leaning my forehead against the cool glass, I looked over at the dark house where she lived. I may have stood there for an hour, seeing nothing but the brown-clad figure cast by my imagination, touched discreetly by the lamplight at the curved neck, at the hand upon the railings and at the border below the dress.

When I came downstairs again I found Mrs. Mercer sitting at the fire. She was an old garrulous woman, a pawnbroker's widow, who collected used stamps for some pious purpose. I had to endure the gossip of the tea-table. The meal was prolonged beyond an hour and still my uncle did not come. Mrs. Mercer stood up to go: she was sorry she couldn't wait any longer, but it was after eight o'clock and she did not like to be out late, as the night air was bad for her. When she had gone I began to walk up and down the room, clenching my fists. My aunt said:

—I'm afraid you may put off your bazaar for this night of Our Lord.

6. Freemasons—members of an influential, secretive, and highly ritualistic fraternal organization—were considered enemies of the Catholics.

At nine o'clock I heard my uncle's latchkey in the halldoor. I heard him talking to himself and heard the hallstand rocking when it had received the weight of his overcoat. I could interpret these signs. When he was midway through his dinner I asked him to give me the money to go to the bazaar. He had forgotten.

—The people are in bed and after their first sleep now, he said.   20

I did not smile. My aunt said to him energetically:

—Can't you give him the money and let him go? You've kept him late enough as it is.

My uncle said he was very sorry he had forgotten. He said he believed in the old saying: *All work and no play makes Jack a dull boy.* He asked me where I was going and, when I had told him a second time he asked me did I know *The Arab's Farewell to his Steed.*[7] When I left the kitchen he was about to recite the opening lines of the piece to my aunt.

I held a florin[8] tightly in my hand as I strode down Buckingham Street towards the station. The sight of the streets thronged with buyers and glaring with gas recalled to me the purpose of my journey. I took my seat in a third-class carriage of a deserted train. After an intolerable delay the train moved out of the station slowly. It crept onward among ruinous houses and over the twinkling river. At Westland Row Station a crowd of people pressed to the carriage doors; but the porters moved them back, saying that it was a special train for the bazaar. I remained alone in the bare carriage. In a few minutes the train drew up beside an improvised wooden platform. I passed out on to the road and saw by the lighted dial of a clock that it was ten minutes to ten. In front of me was a large building which displayed the magical name.

I could not find any sixpenny entrance and, fearing that the bazaar   25
would be closed, I passed in quickly through a turnstile, handing a shilling to a weary-looking man. I found myself in a big hall girdled at half its height by a gallery. Nearly all the stalls were closed and the greater part of the hall was in darkness. I recognised a silence like that which pervades a church after a service. I walked into the centre of the bazaar timidly. A few people were gathered about the stalls which were still open. Before a curtain, over which the words *Café Chantant*[9] were written in coloured lamps, two men were counting money on a salver. I listened to the fall of the coins.

Remembering with difficulty why I had come I went over to one of the stalls and examined porcelain vases and flowered tea-sets. At the door of the stall a young lady was talking and laughing with two young gentlemen. I remarked their English accents and listened vaguely to their conversation.

—O, I never said such a thing!

—O, but you did!

—O, but I didn't!

—Didn't she say that?   30

---

7. Or *The Arab's Farewell to His Horse*, a sentimental nineteenth-century poem by Caroline Norton. The speaker has sold the horse.

8. A two-shilling piece; thus four times the "sixpenny entrance" fee.   9. Café with music.

—Yes. I heard her.

—O, there's a . . . fib!

Observing me the young lady came over and asked me did I wish to buy anything. The tone of her voice was not encouraging; she seemed to have spoken to me out of a sense of duty. I looked humbly at the great jars that stood like eastern guards at either side of the dark entrance to the stall and murmured:

—No, thank you.

35   The young lady changed the position of one of the vases and went back to the two young men. They began to talk of the same subject. Once or twice the young lady glanced at me over her shoulder.

I lingered before her stall, though I knew my stay was useless, to make my interest in her wares seem the more real. Then I turned away slowly and walked down the middle of the bazaar. I allowed the two pennies to fall against the sixpence in my pocket. I heard a voice call from one end of the gallery that the light was out. The upper part of the hall was now completely dark.

Gazing up into the darkness I saw myself as a creature driven and derided by vanity; and my eyes burned with anguish and anger.

1914

D. H. LAWRENCE

Odour of Chrysanthemums

I

The small locomotive engine, Number 4, came clanking, stumbling down from Selston with seven full waggons. It appeared round the corner with loud threats of speed, but the colt that it startled from among the gorse, which still flickered indistinctly in the raw afternoon, outdistanced it at a canter. A woman, walking up the railway line to Underwood, drew back into the hedge, held her basket aside, and watched the footplate of the engine advancing. The trucks thumped heavily past, one by one, with slow inevitable movement, as she stood insignificantly trapped between the jolting black waggons and the hedge; then they curved away towards the coppice where the withered oak leaves dropped noiselessly, while the birds, pulling at the scarlet hips beside the track, made off into the dusk that had already crept into the spinney. In the open, the smoke from the engine sank and cleaved to the rough grass. The fields were dreary and forsaken, and in the marshy strip that led to the whimsey, a reedy pit-pond, the fowls had already abandoned their run among the alders, to roost in the tarred fowl-house. The pit-bank loomed up beyond the pond, flames like red sores licking its ashy sides, in the afternoon's stagnant light. Just beyond rose the tapering chimneys and the clumsy black headstocks of Brinsley Colliery. The two wheels were spinning fast up against the sky, and the winding-engine rapped out its little spasms. The miners were being turned up.

The engine whistled as it came into the wide bay of railway lines beside the colliery, where rows of trucks stood in harbour.

Miners, single, trailing and in groups, passed like shadows diverging home. At the edge of the ribbed level of sidings squat a low cottage, three steps down from the cinder track. A large bony vine clutched at the house, as if to claw down the tiled roof. Round the bricked yard grew a few wintry primroses. Beyond, the long garden sloped down to a bush-covered brook course. There were some twiggy apple trees, winter-crack trees, and ragged cabbages. Beside the path hung dishevelled pink chrysanthemums, like pink cloths hung on bushes. A woman came stooping out of the felt-covered fowl-house, half-way down the garden. She closed and padlocked the door, then drew herself erect, having brushed some bits from her white apron.

She was a tall woman of imperious mien, handsome, with definite black eyebrows. Her smooth black hair was parted exactly. For a few moments she stood steadily watching the miners as they passed along the railway: then she turned towards the brook course. Her face was calm and set, her mouth was closed with disillusionment. After a moment she called:

"John!" There was no answer. She waited, and then said distinctly: 5
"Where are you?"

"Here!" replied a child's sulky voice from among the bushes. The woman looked piercingly through the dusk.

"Are you at that brook?" she asked sternly.

For answer the child showed himself before the raspberry-canes that rose like whips. He was a small, sturdy boy of five. He stood quite still, defiantly.

"Oh!" said the mother, conciliated. "I thought you were down at that 10 wet brook—and you remember what I told you—"

The boy did not move or answer.

"Come, come on in," she said more gently, "it's getting dark. There's your grandfather's engine coming down the line!"

The lad advanced slowly, with resentful, taciturn movement. He was dressed in trousers and waistcoat of cloth that was too thick and hard for the size of the garments. They were evidently cut down from a man's clothes.

As they went slowly towards the house he tore at the ragged wisps of chrysanthemums and dropped the petals in handfuls along the path.

"Don't do that—it does look nasty," said his mother. He refrained, and 15 she, suddenly pitiful, broke off a twig with three or four wan flowers and held them against her face. When mother and son reached the yard her hand hesitated, and instead of laying the flower aside, she pushed it in her apron-band. The mother and son stood at the foot of the three steps looking across the bay of lines at the passing home of the miners. The trundle of the small train was imminent. Suddenly the engine loomed past the house and came to a stop opposite the gate.

The engine-driver, a short man with round grey beard, leaned out of the cab high above the woman.

"Have you got a cup of tea?" he said in a cheery, hearty fashion.

It was her father. She went in, saying she would mash.[1] Directly, she returned.

"I didn't come to see you on Sunday," began the little grey-bearded man.

20   "I didn't expect you," said his daughter.

The engine-driver winced; then, reassuming his cheery, airy manner, he said:

"Oh, have you heard then? Well, and what do you think——?"

"I think it is soon enough," she replied.

At her brief censure the little man made an impatient gesture, and said coaxingly, yet with dangerous coldness:

25   "Well, what's a man to do? It's no sort of life for a man of my years, to sit at my own hearth like a stranger. And if I'm going to marry again it may as well be soon as late—what does it matter to anybody?"

The woman did not reply, but turned and went into the house. The man in the engine-cab stood assertive, till she returned with a cup of tea and a piece of bread and butter on a plate. She went up the steps and stood near the footplate of the hissing engine.

"You needn't 'a' brought me bread an' butter," said her father. "But a cup of tea"—he sipped appreciatively—"it's very nice." He sipped for a moment or two, then: "I hear as Walter's got another bout on," he said.

"When hasn't he?" said the woman bitterly.

"I heered tell of him in the 'Lord Nelson'[2] braggin' as he was going to spend that b——afore he went: half a sovereign[3] that was."

30   "When?" asked the woman.

"A' Sat'day night—I know that's true."

"Very likely," she laughed bitterly. "He gives me twenty-three shillings."

"Aye, it's a nice thing, when a man can do nothing with his money but make a beast of himself!" said the grey-whiskered man. The woman turned her head away. Her father swallowed the last of his tea and handed her the cup.

"Aye," he sighed, wiping his mouth. "It's a settler, it is——"

35   He put his hand on the lever. The little engine strained and groaned, and the train rumbled towards the crossing. The woman again looked across the metals. Darkness was settling over the spaces of the railway and trucks: the miners, in grey sombre groups, were still passing home. The winding-engine pulsed hurriedly, with brief pauses. Elizabeth Bates looked at the dreary flow of men, then she went indoors. Her husband did not come.

The kitchen was small and full of firelight; red coals piled glowing up the chimney mouth. All the life of the room seemed in the white, warm

---

1. Prepare (tea).   2. A public house, pub.

3. A sovereign (a gold coin worth one pound sterling) was about half a week's wage; there are twenty shillings (see below) to the pound.

hearth and the steel fender reflecting the red fire. The cloth was laid for tea; cups glinted in the shadows. At the back, where the lowest stairs protruded into the room, the boy sat struggling with a knife and a piece of white wood. He was almost hidden in the shadow. It was half-past four. They had but to await the father's coming to begin tea. As the mother watched her son's sullen little struggle with the wood, she saw herself in his silence and pertinacity; she saw the father in her child's indifference to all but himself. She seemed to be occupied by her husband. He had probably gone past his home, slunk past his own door, to drink before he came in, while his dinner spoiled and wasted in waiting. She glanced at the clock, then took the potatoes to strain them in the yard. The garden and fields beyond the brook were closed in uncertain darkness. When she rose with the saucepan, leaving the drain steaming into the night behind her, she saw the yellow lamps were lit along the high road that went up the hill away beyond the space of the railway lines and the field.

Then again she watched the men trooping home, fewer now and fewer.

Indoors the fire was sinking and the room was dark red. The woman put her saucepan on the hob, and set a batter pudding near the mouth of the oven. Then she stood unmoving. Directly, gratefully, came quick young steps to the door. Someone hung on the latch a moment, then a little girl entered and began pulling off her outdoor things, dragging a mass of curls, just ripening from gold to brown, over her eyes with her hat.

Her mother chid her for coming late from school, and said she would have to keep her at home the dark winter days.

"Why, mother, it's hardly a bit dark yet. The lamp's not lighted, and my father's not home." 40

"No, he isn't. But it's a quarter to five! Did you see anything of him?"

The child became serious. She looked at her mother with large, wistful blue eyes.

"No, mother, I've never seen him. Why? Has he come up an' gone past, to Old Brinsley? He hasn't, mother, 'cos I never saw him."

"He'd watch that," said the mother bitterly, "he'd take care as you didn't see him. But you may depend upon it, he's seated in the 'Prince o' Wales.' He wouldn't be this late."

The girl looked at her mother piteously. 45

"Let's have our teas, mother, should we?" said she.

The mother called John to table. She opened the door once more and looked out across the darkness of the lines. All was deserted: she could not hear the winding-engines.

"Perhaps," she said to herself, "he's stopped to get some ripping⁴ done."

They sat down to tea. John, at the end of the table near the door, was almost lost in the darkness. Their faces were hidden from each other. The girl crouched against the fender slowly moving a thick piece of bread before the fire. The lad, his face a dusky mark on the shadow, sat watching her who was transfigured in the red glow.

---

4. Coal-mining term for taking down the roof of an underground road in order to make it higher.

50   "I do think it's beautiful to look in the fire," said the child.

"Do you?" said her mother. "Why?"

"It's so red, and full of little caves—and it feels so nice, and you can fair smell it."

"It'll want mending directly," replied her mother, "and then if your father comes he'll carry on and say there never is a fire when a man comes home sweating from the pit.—A public-house is always warm enough."

There was silence till the boy said complainingly: "Make haste, our Annie."

55   "Well, I am doing! I can't make the fire do it no faster, can I?"

"She keeps wafflin'⁵ it about so's to make 'er slow," grumbled the boy.

"Don't have such an evil imagination, child," replied the mother.

Soon the room was busy in the darkness with the crisp sound of crunching. The mother ate very little. She drank her tea determinedly, and sat thinking. When she rose her anger was evident in the stern unbending of her head. She looked at the pudding in the fender, and broke out:

"It is a scandalous thing as a man can't even come home to his dinner! If it's crozzled⁶ up to a cinder I don't see why I should care. Past his very door he goes to get to a public-house, and here I sit with his dinner waiting for him——"

60   She went out. As she dropped piece after piece of coal on the red fire, the shadows fell on the walls, till the room was almost in total darkness.

"I canna see," grumbled the invisible John. In spite of herself, the mother laughed.

"You know the way to your mouth," she said. She set the dustpan outside the door. When she came again like a shadow on the hearth, the lad repeated, complaining sulkily:

"I canna see."

"Good gracious!" cried the mother irritably, "you're as bad as your father if it's a bit dusk!"

65   Nevertheless she took a paper spill from a sheaf on the mantelpiece and proceeded to light the lamp that hung from the ceiling in the middle of the room. As she reached up, her figure displayed itself just rounding with maternity.

"Oh, mother——!" exclaimed the girl.

"What?" said the woman, suspended in the act of putting the lamp-glass over the flame. The copper reflector shone handsomely on her, as she stood with uplifted arm, turning to face her daughter:

"You've got a flower in your apron!" said the child, in a little rapture at this unusual event.

"Goodness me!" exclaimed the woman, relieved. "One would think the house was afire." She replaced the glass and waited a moment before turning up the wick. A pale shadow was seen floating vaguely on the floor.

70   "Let me smell!" said the child, still rapturously, coming forward and putting her face to her mother's waist.

5. Waving.   6. Shriveled.

"Go along, silly!" said the mother, turning up the lamp. The light revealed their suspense so that the woman felt it almost unbearable. Annie was still bending at her waist. Irritably, the mother took the flowers out from her apron-band.

"Oh, mother—don't take them out!" Annie cried, catching her hand and trying to replace the sprig.

"Such nonsense!" said the mother, turning away. The child put the pale chrysanthemums to her lips, murmuring:

"Don't they smell beautiful!"

Her mother gave a short laugh.   75

"No," she said, "not to me. It was chrysanthemums when I married him, and chrysanthemums when you were born, and the first time they ever brought him home drunk, he'd got brown chrysanthemums in his button-hole."

She looked at the children. Their eyes and their parted lips were wondering. The mother sat rocking in silence for some time. Then she looked at the clock.

"Twenty minutes to six!" In a tone of fine bitter carelessness she continued: "Eh, he'll not come now till they bring him. There he'll stick! But he needn't come rolling in here in his pit-dirt, for *I* won't wash him. He can lie on the floor——Eh, what a fool I've been, what a fool! And this is what I came here for, to this dirty hole, rats and all, for him to slink past his very door. Twice last week—he's begun now——"

She silenced herself, and rose to clear the table.

While for an hour or more the children played, subduedly intent, fertile 80
of imagination, united in fear of the mother's wrath, and in dread of their father's home-coming, Mrs. Bates sat in her rocking-chair making a "singlet" of thick cream-coloured flannel, which gave a dull wounded sound as she tore off the grey edge. She worked at her sewing with energy, listening to the children, and her anger wearied itself, lay down to rest, opening its eyes from time to time and steadily watching, its ears raised to listen. Sometimes even her anger quailed and shrank, and the mother suspended her sewing, tracing the footsteps that thudded along the sleepers outside; she would lift her head sharply to bid the children "hush," but she recovered herself in time, and the footsteps went past the gate, and the children were not flung out of their playworld.

But at last Annie sighed, and gave in. She glanced at her waggon of slippers, and loathed the game. She turned plaintively to her mother.

"Mother!"—but she was inarticulate.

John crept out like a frog from under the sofa. His mother glanced up.

"Yes," she said, "just look at those shirtsleeves!"

The boy held them out to survey them, saying nothing. Then somebody 85
called in a hoarse voice away down the line, and suspense bristled in the room, till two people had gone by outside, talking.

"It is time for bed," said the mother.

"My father hasn't come," wailed Annie plaintively. But her mother was primed with courage.

"Never mind. They'll bring him when he does come—like a log." She meant there would be no scene. "And he may sleep on the floor till he wakes himself. I know he'll not go to work tomorrow after this!"

The children had their hands and faces wiped with a flannel.[7] They were very quiet. When they had put on their nightdresses, they said their prayers, the boy mumbling. The mother looked down at them, at the brown silken bush of intertwining curls in the nape of the girl's neck, at the little black head of the lad, and her heart burst with anger at their father who caused all three such distress. The children hid their faces in her skirts for comfort.

90   When Mrs. Bates came down, the room was strangely empty, with a tension of expectancy. She took up her sewing and stitched for some time without raising her head. Meantime her anger was tinged with fear.

II

The clock struck eight and she rose suddenly, dropping her sewing on her chair. She went to the stairfoot door, opened it, listening. Then she went out, locking the door behind her.

Something scuffled in the yard, and she started though she knew it was only the rats with which the place was overrun. The night was very dark. In the great bay of railway lines, bulked with trucks, there was no trace of light, only away back she could see a few yellow lamps at the pit-top, and the red smear of the burning pit-bank on the night. She hurried along the edge of the track, then, crossing the converging lines, came to the stile by the white gates, whence she emerged on the road. Then the fear which had led her shrank. People were walking up to New Brinsley; she saw the lights in the houses; twenty yards further on were the broad windows of the "Prince of Wales," very warm and bright, and the loud voices of men could be heard distinctly. What a fool she had been to imagine that anything had happened to him! He was merely drinking over there at the "Prince of Wales." She faltered. She had never yet been to fetch him, and she never would go. So she continued her walk towards the long straggling line of houses, standing blank on the highway. She entered a passage between the dwellings.

"Mr. Rigley?—Yes! Did you want him? No, he's not in at this minute."

The raw-boned woman leaned forward from her dark scullery and peered at the other, upon whom fell a dim light through the blind of the kitchen window.

95   "Is it Mrs. Bates?" she asked in a tone tinged with respect.

"Yes. I wondered if your Master was at home. Mine hasn't come yet."

" 'Asn't 'e! Oh, Jack's been 'ome an 'ad 'is dinner an' gone out. 'E's just gone for 'alf an hour afore bedtime. Did you call at the 'Prince of Wales'?"

"No——"

"No, you didn't like——! It's not very nice." The other woman was indulgent. There was an awkward pause. "Jack never said nothink about—about your Mester," she said.

7. Washcloth.

"No!—I expect he's stuck in there!"   100

Elizabeth Bates said this bitterly, and with recklessness. She knew that the woman across the yard was standing at her door listening, but she did not care. As she turned:

"Stop a minute! I'll just go an' ask Jack if 'e knows anythink," said Mrs. Rigley.

"Oh, no—I wouldn't like to put—!"

"Yes, I will, if you will just step inside an' see as th' childer doesn't come downstairs and set theirselves afire."

Elizabeth Bates, murmuring a remonstrance, stepped inside. The other   105
woman apologized for the state of the room.

The kitchen needed apology. There were little frocks and trousers and childish undergarments on the squab[8] and on the floor, and a litter of playthings everywhere. On the black American cloth[9] of the table were pieces of bread and cake, crusts, slops, and a teapot with cold tea.

"Eh, ours is just as bad," said Elizabeth Bates, looking at the woman, not at the house. Mrs. Rigley put a shawl over her head and hurried out, saying:

"I shanna be a minute."

The other sat, noting with faint disapproval the general untidiness of the room. Then she fell to counting the shoes of various sizes scattered over the floor. There were twelve. She sighed and said to herself, "No wonder!"—glancing at the litter. There came the scratching of two pairs of feet on the yard, and the Rigleys entered. Elizabeth Bates rose. Rigley was a big man, with very large bones. His head looked particularly bony. Across his temple was a blue scar, caused by a wound got in the pit, a wound in which the coal-dust remained blue like tattooing.

" 'Asna 'e come whoam yit?" asked the man, without any form of greet-   110
ing, but with deference and sympathy. "I couldna say wheer he is—'e's non ower theer!"—he jerked his head to signify the "Prince of Wales."

" 'E's 'appen[1] gone up to th' 'Yew,' " said Mrs. Rigley.

There was another pause. Rigley had evidently something to get off his mind:

"Ah left 'im finishin' a stint," he began. "Loose-all[2] 'ad bin gone about ten minutes when we com'n away, an' I shouted, 'Are ter comin', Walt?' an' 'e said 'Go on, Ah shanna be but a 'ef a minnit,' so we com'n ter th' bottom, me an' Browers, thinkin' as 'e wor just behint, an' 'ud come up i' th' next bantle[3]——"

He stood perplexed, as if answering a charge of deserting his mate. Elizabeth Bates, now again certain of disaster, hastened to reassure him:

"I expect 'e's gone up to th' 'Yew Tree,' as you say. It's not the first time.   115
I've fretted myself into a fever before now. He'll come home when they carry him."

"Ay, isn't it too bad!" deplored the other woman.

---

8. Sofa.   9. Enameled oilcloth.   1. Perhaps.   2. Signal to quit work and come to the surface.
3. An open seat or car of the lift or elevator that takes the miners to the surface.

"I'll just step up to Dick's an' see if 'e *is* theer," offered the man, afraid of appearing alarmed, afraid of taking liberties.

"Oh, I wouldn't think of bothering you that far," said Elizabeth Bates, with emphasis, but he knew she was glad of his offer.

As they stumbled up the entry, Elizabeth Bates heard Rigley's wife run across the yard and open her neighbour's door. At this, suddenly all the blood in her body seemed to switch away from her heart.

120   "Mind!" warned Rigley. "Ah've said many a time as Ah'd fill up them ruts in this entry, sumb'dy 'll be breakin' their legs yit."

She recovered herself and walked quickly along with the miner.

"I don't like leaving the children in bed, and nobody in the house," she said.

"No, you dunna!" he replied courteously. They were soon at the gate of the cottage.

"Well, I shanna be many minnits. Dunna you be frettin' now, 'e'll be all right," said the butty.[4]

125   "Thank you very much, Mr. Rigley," she replied.

"You're welcome!" he stammered, moving away. "I shanna be many minnits."

The house was quiet. Elizabeth Bates took off her hat and shawl, and rolled back the rug. When she had finished, she sat down. It was a few minutes past nine. She was startled by the rapid chuff of the winding-engine at the pit, and the sharp whirr of the brakes on the rope as it descended. Again she felt the painful sweep of her blood, and she put her hand to her side, saying aloud, "Good gracious!—it's only the nine o'clock deputy going down," rebuking herself.

She sat still, listening. Half an hour of this, and she was wearied out.

"What am I working up like this for?" she said pitiably to herself, "I s'll only be doing myself some damage."

130   She took out her sewing again.

At a quarter to ten there were footsteps. One person! She watched for the door to open. It was an elderly woman, in a black bonnet and a black woollen shawl—his mother. She was about sixty years old, pale, with blue eyes, and her face all wrinkled and lamentable. She shut the door and turned to her daughter-in-law peevishly.

"Eh, Lizzie, whatever shall we do, whatever shall we do!" she cried.

Elizabeth drew back a little, sharply.

"What is it, mother?" she said.

135   The elder woman seated herself on the sofa.

"I don't know, child, I can't tell you!"—she shook her head slowly. Elizabeth sat watching her, anxious and vexed.

"I don't know," replied the grandmother, sighing very deeply. "There's no end to my troubles, there isn't. The things I've gone through, I'm sure it's enough——!" She wept without wiping her eyes, the tears running.

"But, mother," interrupted Elizabeth, "what do you mean? What is it?"

---

4. Buddy, fellow worker.

The grandmother slowly wiped her eyes. The fountains of her tears were stopped by Elizabeth's directness. She wiped her eyes slowly. "Poor child! Eh, you poor thing!" she moaned. "I don't know what we're going to do, I don't—and you as you are—it's a thing, it is indeed!" Elizabeth waited.

"Is he dead?" she asked, and at the words her heart swung violently, though she felt a slight flush of shame at the ultimate extravagance of the question. Her words sufficiently frightened the old lady, almost brought her to herself.

"Don't say so, Elizabeth! We'll hope it's not as bad as that; no, may the Lord spare us that, Elizabeth. Jack Rigley came just as I was sittin' down to a glass afore going to bed, an' 'e said, ' 'Appen you'll go down th' line, Mrs. Bates. Walt's had an accident. 'Appen you'll go an' sit wi' 'er till we can get him home.' I hadn't time to ask him a word afore he was gone. An' I put my bonnet on an' come straight down, Lizzie. I thought to myself, 'Eh, that poor blessed child, if anybody should come an' tell her of a sudden, there's no knowin'; what'll 'appen to 'er.' You mustn't let it upset you, Lizzie—or you know what to expect. How long is it, six months—or is it five, Lizzie? Ay!"—the old woman shook her head—"time slips on, it slips on! Ay!"

Elizabeth's thoughts were busy elsewhere. If he was killed—would she be able to manage on the little pension and what she could earn?—she counted up rapidly. If he was hurt—they wouldn't take him to the hospital—how tiresome he would be to nurse!—but perhaps she'd be able to get him away from the drink and his hateful ways. She would—while he was ill. The tears offered to come to her eyes at the picture. But what sentimental luxury was this she was beginning?—She turned to consider the children. At any rate she was absolutely necessary for them. They were her business.

"Ay!" repeated the old woman, "it seems but a week or two since he brought me his first wages. Ay—he was a good lad, Elizabeth, he was, in his way. I don't know why he got to be such a trouble, I don't. He was a happy lad at home, only full of spirits. But there's no mistake he's been a handful of trouble, he has! I hope the Lord'll spare him to mend his ways. I hope so, I hope so. You've had a sight o' trouble with him, Elizabeth, you have indeed. But he was a jolly enough lad wi' me, he was, I can assure you. I don't know how it is...."

The old woman continued to muse aloud, a monotonous irritating sound, while Elizabeth thought concentratedly, startled once, when she heard the winding-engine chuff quickly, and the brakes skirr with a shriek. Then she heard the engine more slowly, and the brakes made no sound. The old woman did not notice. Elizabeth waited in suspense. The mother-in-law talked, with lapses into silence.

"But he wasn't your son, Lizzie, an' it makes a difference. Whatever he was, I remember him when he was little, an' I learned to understand him and to make allowances. You've got to make allowances for them—"

It was half-past ten, and the old woman was saying: "But it's trouble from beginning to end; you're never too old for trouble, never too old for that——" when the gate banged back, and there were heavy feet on the steps.

"I'll go, Lizzie, let me go," cried the old woman, rising. But Elizabeth was at the door. It was a man in pit-clothes.

150 "They're bringin' 'im, Missis," he said. Elizabeth's heart halted a moment. Then it surged on again, almost suffocating her.

"Is he—is it bad?" she asked.

The man turned away, looking at the darkness:

"The doctor says 'e'd been dead hours. 'E saw 'im i' th' lamp-cabin."

The old woman, who stood just behind Elizabeth, dropped into a chair and folded her hands, crying: "Oh, my boy, my boy!"

155 "Hush!" said Elizabeth, with a sharp twitch of a frown. "Be still, mother, don't waken th' children: I wouldn't have them down for anything!"

The old woman moaned softly, rocking herself. The man was drawing away. Elizabeth took a step forward.

"How was it?" she asked.

"Well, I couldn't say for sure," the man replied, very ill at ease. " 'E wor finishin' a stint an' th' butties 'ad gone, an' a lot o' stuff come down atop 'n 'im."

"And crushed him?" cried the widow, with a shudder.

160 "No," said the man, "it fell at th' back of 'im. 'E wor under th' face, an' it niver touched 'im. It shut 'im in. It seems 'e wor smothered."

Elizabeth shrank back. She heard the old woman behind her cry:

"What?—what did 'e say it was?"

The man replied, more loudly: " 'E wor smothered!"

Then the old woman wailed aloud, and this relieved Elizabeth.

165 "Oh, mother," she said, putting her hands on the old woman, "don't waken th' children, don't waken th' children."

She wept a little, unknowing, while the old mother rocked herself and moaned. Elizabeth remembered that they were bringing him home, and she must be ready. "They'll lay him in the parlour," she said to herself, standing a moment pale and perplexed.

Then she lighted a candle and went into the tiny room. The air was cold and damp, but she could not make a fire, there was no fireplace. She set down the candle and looked round. The candlelight glittered on the lustre-glasses,[5] on the two vases that held some of the pink chrysanthemums, and on the dark mahogany. There was a cold, deathly smell of chrysanthemums in the room. Elizabeth stood looking at the flowers. She turned away, and calculated whether there would be room to lay him on the floor, between the couch and the chiffonier. She pushed the chairs aside. There would be room to lay him down and to step round him. Then she fetched the old red tablecloth, and another old cloth, spreading them down to save her bit of carpet. She shivered on leaving the parlour; so, from the dresser-drawer she took a clean shirt and put it at the fire to air. All the time her mother-in-law was rocking herself in the chair and moaning.

5. Glass pendants around the edge of an ornamental vase.

"You'll have to move from there, mother," said Elizabeth. "They'll be bringing him in. Come in the rocker."

The old mother rose mechanically, and seated herself by the fire, continuing to lament. Elizabeth went into the pantry for another candle, and there, in the little penthouse[6] under the naked tiles, she heard them coming. She stood still in the pantry doorway, listening. She heard them pass the end of the house, and come awkwardly down the three steps, a jumble of shuffling footsteps and muttering voices. The old woman was silent. The men were in the yard.

Then Elizabeth heard Matthews, the manager of the pit, say: "You go in first, Jim. Mind!" 170

The door came open, and the two women saw a collier backing into the room, holding one end of a stretcher, on which they could see the nailed pitboots of the dead man. The two carriers halted, the man at the head stooping to the lintel of the door.

"Wheer will you have him?" asked the manager, a short, white-bearded man.

Elizabeth roused herself and came from the pantry carrying the unlighted candle.

"In the parlour," she said.

"In there, Jim!" pointed the manager, and the carriers backed round into 175 the tiny room. The coat with which they had covered the body fell off as they awkwardly turned through the two doorways, and the women saw their man, naked to the waist, lying stripped for work. The old woman began to moan in a low voice of horror.

"Lay th' stretcher at th' side," snapped the manager, "an' put 'im on th' cloths. Mind now, mind! Look you now——!"

One of the men had knocked off a vase of chrysanthemums. He stared awkwardly, then they set down the stretcher. Elizabeth did not look at her husband. As soon as she could get in the room, she went and picked up the broken vase and the flowers.

"Wait a minute!" she said.

The three men waited in silence while she mopped up the water with a duster.

"Eh, what a job, what a job, to be sure!" the manager was saying, rubbing 180 his brow with trouble and perplexity. "Never knew such a thing in my life, never! He'd no business to ha' been left. I never knew such a thing in my life! Fell over him clean as a whistle, an' shut him in. Not four foot of space, there wasn't—yet it scarce bruised him."

He looked down at the dead man, lying prone, half naked, all grimed with coal-dust.

" 'Sphyxiated,' the doctor said. It *is* the most terrible job I've ever known. Seems as if it was done o' purpose. Clean over him, an' shut 'im in, like a mouse-trap"—he made a sharp, descending gesture with his hand.

The colliers standing by jerked aside their heads in hopeless comment.

6. Structure, usually with a sloping roof, attached to a house.

The horror of the thing bristled upon them all.

185   Then they heard the girl's voice upstairs calling shrilly: "Mother, mother—who is it? Mother, who is it?"

Elizabeth hurried to the foot of the stairs and opened the door:

"Go to sleep!" she commanded sharply. "What are you shouting about? Go to sleep at once—there's nothing——"

Then she began to mount the stairs. They could hear her on the boards, and on the plaster floor of the little bedroom. They could hear her distinctly:

"What's the matter now?—what's the matter with you, silly thing?"—her voice was much agitated, with an unreal gentleness.

190   "I thought it was some men come," said the plaintive voice of the child. "Has he come?"

"Yes, they've brought him. There's nothing to make a fuss about. Go to sleep now, like a good child."

They could hear her voice in the bedroom, they waited whilst she covered the children under the bedclothes.

"Is he drunk?" asked the girl, timidly, faintly.

"No! No—he's not! He's—he's asleep."

195   "Is he asleep downstairs?"

"Yes—and don't make a noise."

There was silence for a moment, then the men heard the frightened child again:

"What's that noise?"

"It's nothing, I tell you, what are you bothering for?"

200   The noise was the grandmother moaning. She was oblivious of everything, sitting on her chair rocking and moaning. The manager put his hand on her arm and bade her "Sh-sh!!"

The old woman opened her eyes and looked at him. She was shocked by this interruption, and seemed to wonder.

"What time is it?"—the plaintive thin voice of the child, sinking back unhappily into sleep, asked this last question.

"Ten o'clock," answered the mother more softly. Then she must have bent down and kissed the children.

Matthews beckoned to the men to come away. They put on their caps, and took up the stretcher. Stepping over the body, they tiptoed out of the house. None of them spoke till they were far from the wakeful children.

205   When Elizabeth came down she found her mother alone on the parlour floor, leaning over the dead man, the tears dropping on him.

"We must lay him out," the wife said. She put on the kettle, then returning knelt at the feet, and began to unfasten the knotted leather laces. The room was clammy and dim with only one candle, so that she had to bend her face almost to the floor. At last she got off the heavy boots and put them away.

"You must help me now," she whispered to the old woman. Together they stripped the man.

When they arose, saw him lying in the naïve dignity of death, the women stood arrested in fear and respect. For a few moments they remained still, looking down, the old mother whimpering. Elizabeth felt countermanded. She saw him, how utterly inviolable he lay in himself. She had nothing to do with him. She could not accept it. Stooping, she laid her hand on him, in claim. He was still warm, for the mine was hot where he had died. His mother had his face between her hands, and was murmuring incoherently. The old tears fell in succession as drops from wet leaves; the mother was not weeping, merely her tears flowed. Elizabeth embraced the body of her husband, with cheek and lips. She seemed to be listening, inquiring, trying to get some connection. But she could not. She was driven away. He was impregnable.

She rose, went into the kitchen, where she poured warm water into a bowl, brought soap and flannel and a soft towel.

"I must wash him," she said.

Then the old mother rose stiffly, and watched Elizabeth as she carefully washed his face, carefully brushing the big blonde moustache from his mouth with the flannel. She was afraid with a bottomless fear, so she ministered to him. The old woman, jealous, said:

"Let me wipe him!"—and she kneeled on the other side drying slowly as Elizabeth washed, her big black bonnet sometimes brushing the dark head of her daughter. They worked thus in silence for a long time. They never forgot it was death, and the touch of the man's dead body gave them strange emotions, different in each of the women; a great dread possessed them both, the mother felt the lie was given to her womb, she was denied; the wife felt the utter isolation of the human soul, the child within her was a weight apart from her.

At last it was finished. He was a man of handsome body, and his face showed no traces of drink. He was blonde, full-fleshed, with fine limbs. But he was dead.

"Bless him," whispered his mother, looking always at his face, and speaking out of sheer terror. "Dear lad—bless him!" She spoke in a faint sibilant ecstasy of fear and mother love.

Elizabeth sank down again to the floor, and put her face against his neck, and trembled and shuddered. But she had to draw away again. He was dead, and her living flesh had no place against his. A great dread and weariness held her: she was so unavailing. Her life was gone like this.

"White as milk he is, clear as a twelve-month baby, bless him, the darling!" the old mother murmured to herself. "Not a mark on him, clear and clean and white, beautiful as ever a child was made," she murmured with pride. Elizabeth kept her face hidden.

"He went peaceful, Lizzie—peaceful as sleep. Isn't he beautiful, the lamb? Ay—he must ha' made his peace, Lizzie. 'Appen he made it all right, Lizzie, shut in there. He'd have time. He wouldn't look like this if he hadn't made his peace. The lamb, the dear lamb. Eh, but he had a hearty laugh. I loved to hear it. He had the heartiest laugh, Lizzie, as a lad——"

Elizabeth looked up. The man's mouth was fallen back, slightly open under the cover of the moustache. The eyes, half shut, did not show glazed in the obscurity. Life with its smoky burning gone from him, had left him apart and utterly alien to her. And she knew what a stranger he was to her. In her womb was ice of fear, because of this separate stranger with whom she had been living as one flesh. Was this what it all meant—utter, intact separateness, obscured by heat of living? In dread she turned her face away. The fact was too deadly. There had been nothing between them, and yet they had come together, exchanging their nakedness repeatedly. Each time he had taken her, they had been two isolated beings, far apart as now. He was no more responsible than she. The child was like ice in her womb. For as she looked at the dead man, her mind, cold and detached, said clearly: "Who am I? What have I been doing? I have been fighting a husband who did not exist. *He* existed all the time. What wrong have I done? What was that I have been living with? There lies the reality, this man."—And her soul died in her for fear: she knew she had never seen him, he had never seen her, they had met in the dark and had fought in the dark, not knowing whom they met nor whom they fought. And now she saw, and turned silent in seeing. For she had been wrong. She had said he was something he was not; she had felt familiar with him. Whereas he was apart all the while, living as she never lived, feeling as she never felt.

In fear and shame she looked at his naked body, that she had known falsely. And he was the father of her children. Her soul was torn from her body and stood apart. She looked at his naked body and was ashamed, as if she had denied it. After all, it was itself. It seemed awful to her. She looked at his face, and she turned her own face to the wall. For his look was other than hers, his way was not her way. She had denied him what he was—she saw it now. She had refused him as himself.—And this had been her life, and his life.—She was grateful to death, which restored the truth. And she knew she was not dead.

220   And all the while her heart was bursting with grief and pity for him. What had he suffered? What stretch of horror for this helpless man! She was rigid with agony. She had not been able to help him. He had been cruelly injured, this naked man, this other being, and she could make no reparation. There were the children—but the children belonged to life. This dead man had nothing to do with them. He and she were only channels through which life had flowed to issue in the children. She was a mother—but how awful she knew it now to have been a wife. And he, dead now, how awful he must have felt it to be a husband. She felt that in her next world he would be a stranger to her. If they met there, in the beyond, they would only be ashamed of what had been before. The children had come, for some mysterious reason, out of both of them. But the children did not unite them. Now he was dead, she knew how eternally he was apart from her, how eternally he had nothing more to do with her. She saw this episode of her life closed. They had denied each other in life. Now he had withdrawn. An anguish came over her. It was finished then: it had become hopeless between them long before he died. Yet he had been her husband. But how little!

"Have you got his shirt, 'Lizabeth?"

Elizabeth turned without answering, though she strove to weep and behave as her mother-in-law expected. But she could not, she was silenced. She went into the kitchen and returned with the garment.

"It is aired," she said, grasping the cotton shirt here and there to try. She was almost ashamed to handle him; what right had she or anyone to lay hands on him; but her touch was humble on his body. It was hard work to clothe him. He was so heavy and inert. A terrible dread gripped her all the while: that he could be so heavy and utterly inert, unresponsive, apart. The horror of the distance between them was almost too much for her—it was so infinite a gap she must look across.

At last it was finished. They covered him with a sheet and left him lying, with his face bound. And she fastened the door of the little parlour, lest the children should see what was lying there. Then, with peace sunk heavy on her heart, she went about making tidy the kitchen. She knew she submitted to life, which was her immediate master. But from death, her ultimate master, she winced with fear and shame.

1914

KATHERINE ANNE PORTER

Flowering Judas

Braggioni sits heaped upon the edge of a straight-backed chair much too small for him, and sings to Laura in a furry, mournful voice. Laura has begun to find reasons for avoiding her own house until the latest possible moment, for Braggioni is there almost every night. No matter how late she is, he will be sitting there with a surly, waiting expression, pulling at his kinky yellow hair, thumbing the strings of his guitar, snarling a tune under his breath. Lupe the Indian maid meets Laura at the door, and says with a flicker of a glance towards the upper room, "He waits."

Laura wishes to lie down, she is tired of her hairpins and the feel of her long tight sleeves, but she says to him, "Have you a new song for me this evening?" If he says yes, she asks him to sing it. If he says no, she remembers his favorite one, and asks him to sing it again. Lupe brings her a cup of chocolate and a plate of rice, and Laura eats at the small table under the lamp, first inviting Braggioni, whose answer is always the same: "I have eaten, and besides, chocolate thickens the voice."

Laura says, "Sing, then," and Braggioni heaves himself into song. He scratches the guitar familiarly as though it were a pet animal, and sings passionately off key, taking the high notes in a prolonged painful squeal. Laura, who haunts the markets listening to the ballad singers, and stops every day to hear the blind boy playing his reed-flute in Sixteenth of September Street,[1] listens to Braggioni with pitiless courtesy, because she dares not smile at his miserable performance. Nobody dares to smile at him.

---

1. Street in Morelia, a city in central Mexico.

Braggioni is cruel to everyone, with a kind of specialized insolence, but he is so vain of his talents, and so sensitive to slights, it would require a cruelty and vanity greater than his own to lay a finger on the vast cureless wound of his self-esteem. It would require courage, too, for it is dangerous to offend him, and nobody has this courage.

Braggioni loves himself with such tenderness and amplitude and eternal charity that his followers—for he is a leader of men, a skilled revolutionist, and his skin had been punctured in honorable warfare—warm themselves in the reflected glow, and say to each other: "He has a real nobility, a love of humanity raised above mere personal affections." The excess of this self-love has flowed out, inconveniently for her, over Laura, who, with so many others, owes her comfortable situation and her salary to him. When he is in a very good humor, he tells her, "I am tempted to forgive you for being a *gringa. Gringita!*"[2] and Laura, burning, imagines herself leaning forward suddenly, and with a sound back-handed slap wiping the suety smile from his face. If he notices her eyes at these moments he gives no sign.

5   She knows what Braggioni would offer her, and she must resist tenaciously without appearing to resist, and if she could avoid it she would not admit even to herself the slow drift of his intention. During these long evenings which have spoiled a long month for her, she sits in her deep chair with an open book on her knees, resting her eyes on the consoling rigidity of the printed page when the sight and sound of Braggioni singing threaten to identify themselves with all her remembered afflictions and to add their weight to her uneasy premonitions of the future. The gluttonous bulk of Braggioni has become a symbol of her many disillusions, for a revolutionist should be lean, animated by heroic faith, a vessel of abstract virtues. This is nonsense, she knows it now and is ashamed of it. Revolution must have leaders, and leadership is a career for energetic men. She is, her comrades tell her, full of romantic error, for what she defines as cynicism in them is merely "a developed sense of reality." She is almost too willing to say, "I am wrong, I suppose I don't really understand the principles," and afterward she makes a secret truce with herself, determined not to surrender her will to such expedient logic. But she cannot help feeling that she has been betrayed irreparably by the disunion between her way of living and her feeling of what life should be, and at times she is almost contented to rest in this sense of grievance as a private store of consolation. Sometimes she wishes to run away, but she stays. Now she longs to fly out of this room, down the narrow stairs, and into the street where the houses lean together like conspirators under a single mottled lamp, and leave Braggioni singing to himself.

Instead she looks at Braggioni, frankly and clearly, like a good child who understands the rules of behavior. Her knees cling together under sound blue serge, and her round white collar is not purposely nun-like. She wears the uniform of an idea, and has renounced vanities. She was born Roman Catholic, and in spite of her fear of being seen by someone who might

2. Diminutive of *gringa:* non-Mexican woman, used pejoratively.

make a scandal of it, she slips now and again into some crumbling little church, kneels on the chilly stone, and says a Hail Mary on the gold rosary she bought in Tehuantepec. It is no good and she ends by examining the altar with its tinsel flowers and ragged brocades, and feels tender about the battered doll-shape of some male saint whose white, lace-trimmed drawers hang limply around his ankles below the hieratic dignity of his velvet robe. She has encased herself in a set of principles derived from her early training, leaving no detail of gesture or of personal taste untouched, and for this reason she will not wear lace made on machines. This is her private heresy, for in her special group the machine is sacred, and will be the salvation of the workers. She loves fine lace, and there is a tiny edge of fluted cobweb on this collar, which is one of twenty precisely alike, folded in blue tissue paper in the upper drawer of her clothes chest.

Braggioni catches her glance solidly as if he had been waiting for it, leans forward, balancing his paunch between his spread knees, and sings with tremendous emphasis, weighing his words. He has, the song relates, no father and no mother, nor even a friend to console him; lonely as a wave of the sea he comes and goes, lonely as a wave. His mouth opens round and yearns sideways, his balloon cheeks grow oily with the labor of song. He bulges marvelously in his expensive garments. Over his lavender collar, crushed upon a purple necktie, held by a diamond hoop: over his ammunition belt of tooled leather worked in silver, buckled cruelly around his gasping middle: over the tops of his glossy yellow shoes Braggioni swells with ominous ripeness, his mauve silk hose stretched taut, his ankles bound with the stout leather thongs of his shoes.

When he stretches his eyelids at Laura she notes again that his eyes are the true tawny yellow cat's eyes. He is rich, not in money, he tells her, but in power, and this power brings with it the blameless ownership of things, and the right to indulge his love of small luxuries. "I have a taste for the elegant refinements," he said once, flourishing a yellow silk handkerchief before her nose. "Smell that? It is Jockey Club, imported from New York." Nonetheless he is wounded by life. He will say so presently. "It is true everything turns to dust in the hand, to gall on the tongue." He sighs and his leather belt creaks like a saddle girth. "I am disappointed in everything as it comes. Everything." He shakes his head. "You, poor thing, you will be disappointed too. You are born for it. We are more alike than you realize in some things. Wait and see. Some day you will remember what I have told you, you will know that Braggioni was your friend."

Laura feels a slow chill, a purely physical sense of danger, a warning in her blood that violence, mutilation, a shocking death, wait for her with lessening patience. She has translated this fear into something homely, immediate, and sometimes hesitates before crossing the street. "My personal fate is nothing, except as the testimony of a mental attitude," she reminds herself, quoting from some forgotten philosophic primer, and is sensible enough to add, "Anyhow, I shall not be killed by an automobile if I can help it."

"It may be true I am as corrupt, in another way, as Braggioni," she thinks 10 in spite of herself, "as callous, as incomplete," and if this is so, any kind of death seems preferable. Still she sits quietly, she does not run. Where could she go? Uninvited she has promised herself to this place; she can no longer imagine herself as living in another country, and there is no pleasure in remembering her life before she came here.

Precisely what is the nature of this devotion, its true motives, and what are its obligations? Laura cannot say. She spends part of her days in Xochimilco, near by, teaching Indian children to say in English, "The cat is on the mat." When she appears in the classroom they crowd about her with smiles on their wise, innocent, clay-colored faces, crying "Good morning, my titcher!" in immaculate voices, and they make of her desk a fresh garden of flowers every day.

During her leisure she goes to union meetings and listens to busy important voices quarreling over tactics, methods, internal politics. She visits the prisoners of her own political faith in their cells, where they entertain themselves with counting cockroaches, repenting of their indiscretions, composing their memoirs, writing out manifestoes and plans for their comrades who are still walking about free, hands in pockets, sniffing fresh air. Laura brings them food and cigarettes and a little money, and she brings messages disguised in equivocal phrases from the men outside who dare not set foot in the prison for fear of disappearing into the cells kept empty for them. If the prisoners confuse night and day, and complain, "Dear little Laura, time doesn't pass in this infernal hole, and I won't know when it is time to sleep unless I have a reminder," she brings them their favorite narcotics, and says in a tone that does not wound them with pity, "Tonight will really be night for you," and though her Spanish amuses them, they find her comforting, useful. If they lose patience and all faith, and curse the slowness of their friends in coming to their rescue with money and influence, they trust her not to repeat everything, and if she inquires, "Where do you think we can find money, or influence?" they are certain to answer, "Well, there is Braggioni, why doesn't he do something?"

She smuggles letters from headquarters to men hiding from firing squads in back streets in mildewed houses, where they sit in tumbled beds and talk bitterly as if all Mexico were at their heels, when Laura knows positively they might appear at the band concert in the Alameda on Sunday morning, and no one would notice them. But Braggioni says, "Let them sweat a little. The next time they may be careful. It is very restful to have them out of the way for a while." She is not afraid to knock on any door in any street after midnight, and enter in the darkness, and say to one of these men who is really in danger: "They will be looking for you—seriously—tomorrow morning after six. Here is some money from Vicente. Go to Vera Cruz and wait."

She borrows money from the Roumanian agitator to give to his bitter enemy the Polish agitator. The favor of Braggioni is their disputed territory, and Braggioni holds the balance nicely, for he can use them both. The Polish agitator talks love to her over café tables, hoping to exploit what he believes is her secret sentimental preference for him, and he gives her misinformation which he begs her to repeat as the solemn truth to certain persons. The Roumanian is more adroit. He is generous with his money in all good causes, and lies to her with an air of ingenuous candor, as if he were her good friend and confidant. She never repeats anything they may say. Braggioni never asks questions. He has other ways to discover all that he wishes to know about them.

Nobody touches her, but all praise her gray eyes, and the soft, round 15 under lip which promises gayety, yet is always grave, nearly always firmly closed: and they cannot understand why she is in Mexico. She walks back and forth on her errands, with puzzled eyebrows, carrying her little folder of drawings and music and school papers. No dancer dances more beautifully than Laura walks, and she inspires some amusing, unexpected ardors, which cause little gossip, because nothing comes of them. A young captain who had been a soldier in Zapata's[3] army attempted, during a horseback ride near Cuernavaca, to express his desire for her with the noble simplicity befitting a rude folk-hero: but gently, because he was gentle. This gentleness was his defeat, for when he alighted, and removed her foot from the stirrup, and essayed to draw her down into his arms, her horse, ordinarily a tame one, shied fiercely, reared and plunged away. The young hero's horse careered blindly after his stable-mate, and the hero did not return to the hotel until rather late that evening. At breakfast he came to her table in full charro[4] dress, gray buckskin jacket and trousers with strings of silver buttons down the leg, and he was in a humorous, careless mood. "May I sit with you?" and "You are a wonderful rider. I was terrified that you might be thrown and dragged. I should never have forgiven myself. But I cannot admire you enough for your riding!"

"I learned to ride in Arizona," said Laura.

"If you will ride with me again this morning, I promise you a horse that will not shy with you," he said. But Laura remembered that she must return to Mexico City at noon.

Next morning the children made a celebration and spent their playtime writing on the blackboard, "We lov ar ticher," and with tinted chalks they drew wreaths of flowers around the words. The young hero wrote her a letter: "I am a very foolish, wasteful, impulsive man. I should have first said I love you, and then you would not have run away. But you shall see me again." Laura thought, "I must send him a box of colored crayons," but she was trying to forgive herself for having spurred her horse at the wrong moment.

A brown, shock-haired youth came and stood in her patio one night and sang like a lost soul for two hours, but Laura could think of nothing to do about it. The moonlight spread a wash of gauzy silver over the clear spaces of the garden, and the shadows were cobalt blue. The scarlet blossoms of the Judas tree were dull purple, and the names of the colors repeated themselves automatically in her mind, while she watched not the

---

3. Emiliano Zapata (1879–1919), Mexican peasant-revolutionary general.
4. Costume worn by peasant horsemen of special status.

boy, but his shadow, fallen like a dark garment across the fountain rim, trailing in the water. Lupe came silently and whispered expert counsel in her ear: "If you will throw him one little flower, he will sing another song or two and go away." Laura threw the flower, and he sang a last song and went away with the flower tucked in the band of his hat. Lupe said, "He is one of the organizers of the Typographers Union, and before that he sold corridos[5] in the Merced market, and before that, he came from Guanajuato, where I was born. I would not trust any man, but I trust least those from Guanajuato."

20   She did not tell Laura that he would be back again the next night, and the next, nor that he would follow her at a certain fixed distance around the Merced market, through the Zócolo, up Francisco I. Madero Avenue, and so along the Paseo de la Reforma to that Chapultepec Park, and into the Philosopher's Footpath, still with that flower withering in his hat, and an indivisible attention in his eyes.

Now Laura is accustomed to him, it means nothing except that he is nineteen years old and is observing a convention with all propriety, as though it were founded on a law of nature, which in the end it might well prove to be. He is beginning to write poems which he prints on a wooden press, and he leaves them stuck like handbills in her door. She is pleasantly disturbed by the abstract, unhurried watchfulness of his black eyes which will in time turn easily towards another object. She tells herself that throwing the flower was a mistake, for she is twenty-two years old and knows better; but she refuses to regret it, and persuades herself that her negation of all external events as they occur is a sign that she is gradually perfecting herself in the stoicism she strives to cultivate against that disaster she fears, though she cannot name it.

She is not at home in the world. Every day she teaches children who remain strangers to her, though she loves their tender round hands and their charming opportunist savagery. She knocks at unfamiliar doors not knowing whether a friend or a stranger shall answer, and even if a known face emerges from the sour gloom of that unknown interior, still it is the face of a stranger. No matter what this stranger says to her, nor what her message to him, the very cells of her flesh reject knowledge and kinship in one monotonous word. No. No. No. She draws her strength from this one holy talismanic word which does not suffer her to be led into evil. Denying everything, she may walk anywhere in safety, she looks at everything without amazement.

No, repeats this firm unchanging voice of her blood; and she looks at Braggioni without amazement. He is a great man, he wishes to impress this simple girl who covers her great round breasts with thick dark cloth, and who hides long, invaluably beautiful legs under a heavy skirt. She is almost thin except for the incomprehensible fullness of her breasts, like a nursing mother's, and Braggioni, who considers himself a judge of women, speculates again on the puzzle of her notorious virginity, and takes the

5. Popular ballads.

liberty of speech which she permits without a sign of modesty, indeed, without any sort of sign, which is disconcerting.

"You think you are so cold, *gringita!* Wait and see. You will surprise yourself some day! May I be there to advise you!" He stretches his eyelids at her, and his ill-humored cat's eyes waver in a separate glance for the two points of light marking the opposite ends of a smoothly drawn path between the swollen curve of her breasts. He is not put off by that blue serge, nor by her resolutely fixed gaze. There is all the time in the world. His cheeks are bellying with the wind of song. "O girl with the dark eyes," he sings, and reconsiders. "But yours are not dark. I can change all that. O girl with the green eyes, you have stolen my heart away!" then his mind wanders to the song, and Laura feels the weight of his attention being shifted elsewhere. Singing thus, he seems harmless, he is quite harmless, there is nothing to do but sit patiently and say "No," when the moment comes. She draws a full breath, and her mind wanders also, but not far. She dares not wander too far.

Not for nothing has Braggioni taken pains to be a good revolutionist 25 and a professional lover of humanity. He will never die of it. He has the malice, the cleverness, the wickedness, the sharpness of wit, the hardness of heart, stipulated for loving the world profitably. *He will never die of it.* He will live to see himself kicked out from his feeding trough by other hungry world-saviors. Traditionally he must sing in spite of his life which drives him to bloodshed, he tells Laura, for his father was a Tuscany[6] peasant who drifted to Yucatan and married a Maya woman: a woman of race, an aristocrat. They gave him the love and knowledge of music, thus: and under the rip of his thumbnail, the strings of the instrument complain like exposed nerves.

Once he was called Delgadito by all the girls and married women who ran after him; he was so scrawny all his bones showed under his thin cotton clothing, and he could squeeze his emptiness to the very backbone with his two hands. He was a poet and the revolution was only a dream then; too many women loved him and sapped away his youth, and he could never find enough to eat anywhere, anywhere! Now he is a leader of men, crafty men who whisper in his ear, hungry men who wait for hours outside his office for a word with him, emaciated men with wild faces who waylay him at the street gate with a timid, "Comrade, let me tell you . . ." and they blow the foul breath from their empty stomachs in his face.

He is always sympathetic. He gives them handfuls of small coins from his own pocket, he promises them work, there will be demonstrations, they must join the unions and attend the meetings, above all they must be on the watch for spies. They are closer to him than his own brothers, without them he can do nothing—until tomorrow, comrade!

Until tomorrow. "They are stupid, they are lazy, they are treacherous, they would cut my throat for nothing," he says to Laura. He has good food and abundant drink, he hires an automobile and drives in the Paseo on

6. Region in northern Italy.

Sunday morning, and enjoys plenty of sleep in a soft bed beside a wife who dares not disturb him; and he sits pampering his bones in easy billows of fat, singing to Laura, who knows and thinks these things about him. When he was fifteen, he tried to drown himself because he loved a girl, his first love, and she laughed at him. "A thousand women have paid for that," and his tight little mouth turns down at the corners. Now he perfumes his hair with Jockey Club, and confides to Laura: "One woman is really as good as another for me, in the dark. I prefer them all."

His wife organizes unions among the girls in the cigarette factories, and walks in picket lines, and even speaks at meetings in the evening. But she cannot be brought to acknowledge the benefits of true liberty. "I tell her I must have my freedom, net. She does not understand my point of view." Laura has heard this many times. Braggioni scratches the guitar and meditates. "She is an instinctively virtuous woman, pure gold, no doubt of that. If she were not, I should lock her up, and she knows it."

30   His wife, who works so hard for the good of the factory girls, employs part of her leisure lying on the floor weeping because there are so many women in the world, and only one husband for her, and she never knows where nor when to look for him. He told her: "Unless you can learn to cry when I am not here, I must go away for good." That day he went away and took a room at the Hotel Madrid.

It is this month of separation for the sake of higher principles that has been spoiled not only for Mrs. Braggioni, whose sense of reality is beyond criticism, but for Laura, who feels herself bogged in a nightmare. Tonight Laura envies Mrs. Braggioni, who is alone, and free to weep as much as she pleases about a concrete wrong. Laura has just come from a visit to the prison, and she is waiting for tomorrow with a bitter anxiety as if tomorrow may not come, but time may be caught immovably in this hour, with herself transfixed, Braggioni singing on forever, and Eugenio's body not yet discovered by the guard.

Braggioni says: "Are you going to sleep?" Almost before she can shake her head, he begins telling her about the May-day disturbances coming on in Morelia, for the Catholics hold a festival in honor of the Blessed Virgin, and the Socialists celebrate their martyrs on that day. "There will be two independent processions, starting from either end of town, and they will march until they meet, and the rest depends . . ." He asks her to oil and load his pistols. Standing up, he unbuckles his ammunition belt, and spreads it laden across her knees. Laura sits with the shells slipping through the cleaning cloth dipped in oil, and he says again he cannot understand why she works so hard for the revolutionary idea unless she loves some man who is in it. "Are you not in love with someone?" "No," says Laura. "And no one is in love with you?" "No." "Then it is your own fault. No woman need go begging. Why, what is the matter with you? The legless beggar woman in the Alameda has a perfectly faithful lover. Did you know that?"

Laura peers down the pistol barrel and says nothing, but a long, slow faintness rises and subsides in her; Braggioni curves his swollen fingers around the throat of the guitar and softly smothers the music out of it, and when she hears him again he seems to have forgotten her, and is speaking in the hypnotic voice he uses when talking in small rooms to a listening, close-gathered crowd. Some day this world, now seemingly so composed and eternal, to the edges of every sea shall be merely a tangle of gaping trenches, of crashing walls and broken bodies. Everything must be torn from its accustomed place where it has rotted for centuries, hurled skyward and distributed, cast down again clean as rain, without separate identity. Nothing shall survive that the stiffened hands of poverty have created for the rich and no one shall be left alive except the elect spirits destined to procreate a new world cleansed of cruelty and injustice, ruled by benevolent anarchy: "Pistols are good, I love them, cannon are even better, but in the end I pin my faith to good dynamite," he concludes, and strokes the pistol lying in her hands. "Once I dreamed of destroying this city, in case it offered resistance to General Ortíz, but it fell into his hands like an overripe pear."

He is made restless by his own words, rises and stands waiting. Laura holds up the belt to him: "Put that on, and go kill somebody in Morelia, and you will be happier," she says softly. The presence of death in the room makes her bold. "Today, I found Eugenio going into a stupor. He refused to allow me to call the prison doctor. He had taken all the tablets I brought him yesterday. He said he took them because he was bored."

"He is a fool, and his death is his own business," says Braggioni, fasten- 35
ing his belt carefully.

"I told him if he had waited only a little while longer, you would have got him set free," says Laura. "He said he did not want to wait."

"He is a fool and we are well rid of him," says Braggioni, reaching for his hat.

He goes away. Laura knows his mood has changed, she will not see him any more for a while. He will send word when he needs her to go on errands into strange streets, to speak to the strange faces that will appear, like clay masks with the power of human speech, to mutter their thanks to Braggioni for his help. Now she is free, and she thinks, I must run while there is time. But she does not go.

Braggioni enters his own house where for a month his wife has spent many hours every night weeping and tangling her hair upon her pillow. She is weeping now, and she weeps more at the sight of him, the cause of all her sorrows. He looks about the room. Nothing is changed, the smells are good and familiar, he is well acquainted with the woman who comes toward him with no reproach except grief on her face. He says to her tenderly: "You are so good, please don't cry any more, you dear good creature." She says, "Are you tired, my angel? Sit here and I will wash your feet." She brings a bowl of water, and kneeling, unlaces his shoes, and when from her knees she raises her sad eyes under her blackened lids, he is sorry for everything, and bursts into tears. "Ah, yes, I am hungry, I am tired, let us eat something together," he says, between sobs. His wife leans her head on his arm and says, "Forgive me!" and this time he is refreshed by the solemn, endless rain of her tears.

Laura takes off her serge dress and puts on a white linen nightgown and 40 goes to bed. She turns her head a little to one side, and lying still, reminds herself that it is time to sleep. Numbers tick in her brain like little clocks, soundless doors close of themselves around her. If you would sleep, you must not remember anything, the children will say tomorrow, good morning, my teacher, the poor prisoners who come every day bringing flowers to their jailor. 1-2-3-4-5—it is monstrous to confuse love with revolution, night with day, life with death—ah, Eugenio!

The tolling of the midnight bell is a signal, but what does it mean? Get up, Laura, and follow me: come out of your sleep, out of your bed, out of this strange house. What are you doing in this house? Without a word, without fear she rose and reached for Eugenio's hand, but he eluded her with a sharp, sly smile and drifted away. This is not all, you shall see— Murderer, he said, follow me, I will show you a new country, but it is far away and we must hurry. No, said Laura, not unless you take my hand, no; and she clung first to the stair rail, and then to the topmost branch of the Judas tree that bent down slowly and set her upon the earth, and then to the rocky ledge of a cliff, and then to the jagged wave of a sea that was not water but a desert of crumbling stone. Where are you taking me, she asked in wonder but without fear. To death, and it is a long way off, and we must hurry, said Eugenio. No, said Laura, not unless you take my hand. Then eat these flowers, poor prisoner, said Eugenio in a voice of pity, take and eat: and from the Judas tree he stripped the warm bleeding flowers, and held them to her lips. She saw that his hand was fleshless, a cluster of small white petrified branches, and his eye sockets were without light, but she ate the flowers greedily for they satisfied both hunger and thirst. Murderer! said Eugenio, and Cannibal! This is my body and my blood. Laura cried No! and at the sound of her own voice, she awoke trembling, and was afraid to sleep again.

1929, 1930

WILLIAM FAULKNER

A Rose for Emily

I

When Miss Emily Grierson died, our whole town went to her funeral: the men through a sort of respectful affection for a fallen monument, the women mostly out of curiosity to see the inside of her house, which no one save an old man-servant—a combined gardener and cook—had seen in at least ten years.

It was a big, squarish frame house that had once been white, decorated with cupolas and spires and scrolled balconies in the heavily lightsome style of the seventies,[1] set on what had once been our most select street.

---

1. The 1870s, the decade following the Civil War between the "Union and Confederate soldiers" mentioned at the end of the paragraph.

But garages and cotton gins had encroached and obliterated even the august names of that neighborhood; only Miss Emily's house was left, lifting its stubborn and coquettish decay above the cotton wagons and the gasoline pumps—an eyesore among eyesores. And now Miss Emily had gone to join the representatives of those august names where they lay in the cedar-bemused cemetery among the ranked and anonymous graves of Union and Confederate soldiers who fell at the battle of Jefferson.

Alive, Miss Emily had been a tradition, a duty, and a care; a sort of hereditary obligation upon the town, dating from that day in 1894 when Colonel Sartoris, the mayor—he who fathered the edict that no Negro woman should appear on the streets without an apron—remitted her taxes, the dispensation dating from the death of her father on into perpetuity. Not that Miss Emily would have accepted charity. Colonel Sartoris invented an involved tale to the effect that Miss Emily's father had loaned money to the town, which the town, as a matter of business, preferred this way of repaying. Only a man of Colonel Sartoris' generation and thought could have invented it, and only a woman could have believed it.

When the next generation, with its more modern ideas, became mayors and aldermen, this arrangement created some little dissatisfaction. On the first of the year they mailed her a tax notice. February came, and there was no reply. They wrote her a formal letter, asking her to call at the sheriff's office at her convenience. A week later the mayor wrote her himself, offering to call or to send his car for her, and received in reply a note on paper of an archaic shape, in a thin, flowing calligraphy in faded ink, to the effect that she no longer went out at all. The tax notice was also enclosed, without comment.

They called a special meeting of the Board of Aldermen. A deputation waited upon her, knocked at the door through which no visitor had passed since she ceased giving china-painting lessons eight or ten years earlier. They were admitted by the old Negro into a dim hall from which a stairway mounted into still more shadow. It smelled of dust and disuse—a close, dank smell. The Negro led them into the parlor. It was furnished in heavy, leather-covered furniture. When the Negro opened the blinds of one window, a faint dust rose sluggishly about their thighs, spinning with slow motes in the single sun-ray. On a tarnished gilt easel before the fireplace stood a crayon portrait of Miss Emily's father.

They rose when she entered—a small, fat woman in black, with a thin gold chain descending to her waist and vanishing into her belt, leaning on an ebony cane with a tarnished gold head. Her skeleton was small and spare; perhaps that was why what would have been merely plumpness in another was obesity in her. She looked bloated, like a body long submerged in motionless water, and of that pallid hue. Her eyes, lost in the fatty ridges of her face, looked like two small pieces of coal pressed into a lump of dough as they moved from one face to another while the visitors stated their errand.

She did not ask them to sit. She just stood in the door and listened quietly until the spokesman came to a stumbling halt. Then they could hear the invisible watch ticking at the end of the gold chain.

Her voice was dry and cold. "I have no taxes in Jefferson. Colonel Sartoris explained it to me. Perhaps one of you can gain access to the city records and satisfy yourselves."

"But we have. We are the city authorities, Miss Emily. Didn't you get a notice from the sheriff, signed by him?"

10   "I received a paper, yes," Miss Emily said. "Perhaps he considers himself the sheriff. . . . I have no taxes in Jefferson."

"But there is nothing on the books to show that, you see. We must go by the—"

"See Colonel Sartoris. I have no taxes in Jefferson."

"But, Miss Emily—"

"See Colonel Sartoris." (Colonel Sartoris had been dead almost ten years.) "I have no taxes in Jefferson. Tobe!" The Negro appeared. "Show these gentlemen out."

II

15 So she vanquished them, horse and foot, just as she had vanquished their fathers thirty years before about the smell. That was two years after her father's death and a short time after her sweetheart—the one we believed would marry her—had deserted her. After her father's death she went out very little; after her sweetheart went away, people hardly saw her at all. A few of the ladies had the temerity to call, but were not received, and the only sign of life about the place was the Negro man—a young man then—going in and out with a market basket.

"Just as if a man—any man—could keep a kitchen properly," the ladies said; so they were not surprised when the smell developed. It was another link between the gross, teeming world and the high and mighty Griersons.

A neighbor, a woman, complained to the mayor, Judge Stevens, eighty years old.

"But what will you have me do about it, madam?" he said.

"Why, send her word to stop it," the woman said. "Isn't there a law?"

20   "I'm sure that won't be necessary," Judge Stevens said. "It's probably just a snake or a rat that nigger of hers killed in the yard. I'll speak to him about it."

The next day he received two more complaints, one from a man who came in diffident deprecation. "We really must do something about it, Judge. I'd be the last one in the world to bother Miss Emily, but we've got to do something." That night the Board of Aldermen met—three gray-beards and one younger man, a member of the rising generation.

"It's simple enough," he said. "Send her word to have her place cleaned up. Give her a certain time to do it in, and if she don't . . ."

"Dammit, sir," Judge Stevens said, "will you accuse a lady to her face of smelling bad?"

So the next night, after midnight, four men crossed Miss Emily's lawn and slunk about the house like burglars, sniffing along the base of the brickwork and at the cellar openings while one of them performed a regular sowing motion with his hand out of a sack slung from his shoulder. They broke open the cellar door and sprinkled lime there, and in all the outbuildings. As they recrossed the lawn, a window that had been dark was lighted and Miss Emily sat in it, the light behind her, and her upright torso motionless as that of an idol. They crept quietly across the lawn and into the shadow of the locusts that lined the street. After a week or two the smell went away.

That was when people had begun to feel really sorry for her. People in our town, remembering how old lady Wyatt, her great-aunt, had gone completely crazy at last, believed that the Griersons held themselves a little too high for what they really were. None of the young men were quite good enough for Miss Emily and such. We had long thought of them as a tableau; Miss Emily a slender figure in white in the background, her father a spraddled silhouette in the foreground, his back to her and clutching a horsewhip, the two of them framed by the back-flung front door. So when she got to be thirty and was still single, we were not pleased exactly, but vindicated; even with insanity in the family she wouldn't have turned down all of her chances if they had really materialized.

When her father died, it got about that the house was all that was left to her; and in a way, people were glad. At last they could pity Miss Emily. Being left alone, and a pauper, she had become humanized. Now she too would know the old thrill and the old despair of a penny more or less.

The day after his death all the ladies prepared to call at the house and offer condolence and aid, as is our custom. Miss Emily met them at the door, dressed as usual and with no trace of grief on her face. She told them that her father was not dead. She did that for three days, with the ministers calling on her, and the doctors, trying to persuade her to let them dispose of the body. Just as they were about to resort to law and force, she broke down, and they buried her father quickly.

We did not say she was crazy then. We believed she had to do that. We remembered all the young men her father had driven away, and we knew that with nothing left, she would have to cling to that which had robbed her, as people will.

III

She was sick for a long time. When we saw her again, her hair was cut short, making her look like a girl, with a vague resemblance to those angels in colored church windows—sort of tragic and serene.

The town had just let the contracts for paving the sidewalks, and in the summer after her father's death they began to work. The construction company came with niggers and mules and machinery, and a foreman named Homer Barron, a Yankee—a big, dark, ready man, with a big voice and eyes lighter than his face. The little boys would follow in groups to hear him cuss the niggers, and the niggers singing in time to the rise and fall of picks. Pretty soon he knew everybody in town. Whenever you heard a lot of laughing anywhere about the square, Homer Barron would be in the center of the group. Presently we began to see him and Miss Emily on Sunday afternoons driving in the yellow-wheeled buggy and the matched team of bays from the livery stable.

At first we were glad that Miss Emily would have an interest, because the ladies all said, "Of course a Grierson would not think seriously of a Northerner, a day laborer." But there were still others, older people, who said that even grief could not cause a real lady to forget *noblesse oblige*— without calling it *noblesse oblige*.[2] They just said, "Poor Emily. Her kinsfolk should come to her." She had some kin in Alabama; but years ago her father had fallen out with them over the estate of old lady Wyatt, the crazy woman, and there was no communication between the two families. They had not even been represented at the funeral.

And as soon as the old people said, "Poor Emily," the whispering began. "Do you suppose it's really so?" they said to one another. "Of course it is. What else could . . ." This behind their hands; rustling of craned silk and satin behind jalousies[3] closed upon the sun of Sunday afternoon as the thin, swift clop-clop-clop of the matched team passed: "Poor Emily."

She carried her head high enough—even when we believed that she was fallen. It was as if she demanded more than ever the recognition of her dignity as the last Grierson; as if it had wanted that touch of earthiness to reaffirm her imperviousness. Like when she bought the rat poison, the arsenic. That was over a year after they had begun to say "Poor Emily," and while the two female cousins were visiting her.

"I want some poison," she said to the druggist. She was over thirty then, still a slight woman, though thinner than usual, with cold, haughty black eyes in a face the flesh of which was strained across the temples and about the eyesockets as you imagine a lighthouse-keeper's face ought to look. "I want some poison," she said.

35 "Yes, Miss Emily. What kind? For rats and such? I'd recom—"

"I want the best you have. I don't care what kind."

The druggist named several. "They'll kill anything up to an elephant. But what you want is—"

"Arsenic," Miss Emily said. "Is that a good one?"

"Is . . . arsenic? Yes ma'am. But what you want—"

40 "I want arsenic."

The druggist looked down at her. She looked back at him, erect, her face like a strained flag. "Why, of course," the druggist said. "If that's what you want. But the law requires you to tell what you are going to use it for."

Miss Emily just stared at him, her head tilted back in order to look him eye for eye, until he looked away and went and got the arsenic and wrapped it up. The Negro delivery boy brought her the package; the druggist didn't come back. When she opened the package at home there was written on the box, under the skull and bones: "For rats."

IV

So the next day we all said, "She will kill herself"; and we said it would be the best thing. When she had first begun to be seen with Homer Barron, we had said, "She will marry him." Then we said, "She will persuade him

---

2. The obligation, coming with noble or upper-class birth, to behave with honor and generosity toward those less privileged.   3. Window blinds made of adjustable horizontal slats.

yet," because Homer himself had remarked—he liked men, and it was known that he drank with the younger men in the Elk's Club—that he was not a marrying man. Later we said, "Poor Emily," behind the jalousies as they passed on Sunday afternoon in the glittering buggy, Miss Emily with her head high and Homer Barron with his hat cocked and a cigar in his teeth, reins and whip in a yellow glove.

Then some of the ladies began to say that it was a disgrace to the town and a bad example to the young people. The men did not want to interfere, but at last the ladies forced the Baptist minister—Miss Emily's people were Episcopal—to call upon her. He would never divulge what happened during that interview, but he refused to go back again. The next Sunday they again drove about the streets, and the following day the minister's wife wrote to Miss Emily's relations in Alabama.

So she had blood-kin under her roof again and we sat back to watch 45 developments. At first nothing happened. Then we were sure that they were to be married. We learned that Miss Emily had been to the jeweler's and ordered a man's toilet set in silver, with the letters H. B. on each piece. Two days later we learned that she had bought a complete outfit of men's clothing, including a nightshirt, and we said, "They are married." We were really glad. We were glad because the two female cousins were even more Grierson than Miss Emily had ever been.

So we were not surprised when Homer Barron—the streets had been finished some time since—was gone. We were a little disappointed that there was not a public blowing-off, but we believed that he had gone on to prepare for Miss Emily's coming, or to give her a chance to get rid of the cousins. (By that time it was a cabal, and we were all Miss Emily's allies to help circumvent the cousins.) Sure enough, after another week they departed. And, as we had expected all along, within three days Homer Barron was back in town. A neighbor saw the Negro man admit him at the kitchen door at dusk one evening.

And that was the last we saw of Homer Barron. And of Miss Emily for some time. The Negro man went in and out with the market basket, but the front door remained closed. Now and then we would see her at a window for a moment, as the men did that night when they sprinkled the lime, but for almost six months she did not appear on the streets. Then we knew that this was to be expected too; as if that quality of her father which had thwarted her woman's life so many times had been too virulent and too furious to die.

When we next saw Miss Emily, she had grown fat and her hair was turning gray. During the next few years it grew grayer and grayer until it attained an even pepper-and-salt iron-gray, when it ceased turning. Up to the day of her death at seventy-four it was still that vigorous iron-gray, like the hair of an active man.

From that time on her front door remained closed, save for a period of six or seven years, when she was about forty, during which she gave lessons in china-painting. She fitted up a studio in one of the downstairs rooms, where the daughters and grand-daughters of Colonel Sartoris' contemporaries were sent to her with the same regularity and in the same spirit that they were sent on Sundays with a twenty-five cent piece for the collection plate. Meanwhile her taxes had been remitted.

50   Then the newer generation became the backbone and the spirit of the town, and the painting pupils grew up and fell away and did not send their children to her with boxes of color and tedious brushes and pictures cut from the ladies' magazines. The front door closed upon the last one and remained closed for good. When the town got free postal delivery Miss Emily alone refused to let them fasten the metal numbers above her door and attach a mailbox to it. She would not listen to them.

Daily, monthly, yearly we watched the Negro grow grayer and more stooped, going in and out with the market basket. Each December we sent her a tax notice, which would be returned by the post office a week later, unclaimed. Now and then we would see her in one of the downstairs windows—she had evidently shut up the top floor of the house—like the carven torso of an idol in a niche, looking or not looking at us, we could never tell which. Thus she passed from generation to generation—dear, inescapable, impervious, tranquil, and perverse.

And so she died. Fell ill in the house filled with dust and shadows, with only a doddering Negro man to wait on her. We did not even know she was sick; we had long since given up trying to get any information from the Negro. He talked to no one, probably not even to her, for his voice had grown harsh and rusty, as if from disuse.

She died in one of the downstairs rooms, in a heavy walnut bed with a curtain, her gray head propped on a pillow yellow and moldy with age and lack of sunlight.

V

The Negro met the first of the ladies at the front door and let them in, with their hushed, sibilant voices and their quick, curious glances, and then he disappeared. He walked right through the house and out the back and was not seen again.

55   The two female cousins came at once. They held the funeral on the second day, with the town coming to look at Miss Emily beneath a mass of bought flowers, with the crayon face of her father musing profoundly above the bier and the ladies sibilant and macabre; and the very old men— some in their brushed Confederate uniforms—on the porch and the lawn, talking of Miss Emily as if she had been a contemporary of theirs, believing that they had danced with her and courted her perhaps, confusing time with its mathematical progression, as the old do, to whom all the past is not a diminishing road, but, instead, a huge meadow which no winter ever quite touches, divided from them now by the narrow bottleneck of the most recent decade of years.

Already we knew that there was one room in that region above stairs which no one had seen in forty years, and which would have to be forced. They waited until Miss Emily was decently in the ground before they opened it.

The violence of breaking down the door seemed to fill this room with pervading dust. A thin, acrid pall as of the tomb seemed to lie everywhere upon this room decked and furnished as for a bridal: upon the valance curtains of faded rose color, upon the rose-shaded lights, upon the dressing table, upon the delicate array of crystal and the man's toilet things backed with tarnished silver, silver so tarnished that the monogram was obscured. Among them lay a collar and tie, as if they had just been removed, which, lifted, left upon the surface a pale crescent in the dust. Upon a chair hung the suit, carefully folded; beneath it the two mute shoes and the discarded socks.

The man himself lay in the bed.

For a long while we just stood there, looking down at the profound and fleshless grin. The body had apparently once lain in the attitude of an embrace, but now the long sleep that outlasts love, that conquers even the grimace of love, had cuckolded him. What was left of him, rotted beneath what was left of the nightshirt, had become inextricable from the bed in which he lay; and upon him and upon the pillow beside him lay that even coating of the patient and biding dust.

Then we noticed that in the second pillow was the indentation of a 60 head. One of us lifted something from it, and leaning forward, that faint and invisible dust dry and acrid in the nostrils, we saw a long strand of iron-gray hair.

1931

WILLIAM CARLOS WILLIAMS

The Use of Force

They were new patients to me, all I had was the name, Olson. Please come down as soon as you can, my daughter is very sick. When I arrived I was met by the mother, a big startled looking woman, very clean and apologetic who merely said, Is this the doctor? and let me in. In the back, she added. You must excuse us, doctor, we have her in the kitchen where it is warm. It is very damp here sometimes.

The child was fully dressed and sitting on her father's lap near the kitchen table. He tried to get up, but I motioned for him not to bother, took off my overcoat and started to look things over. I could see that they were all very nervous, eyeing me up and down distrustfully. As often, in such cases, they weren't telling me more than they had to, it was up to me to tell them; that's why they were spending three dollars on me.

The child was fairly eating me up with her cold, steady eyes, and no expression to her face whatever. She did not move and seemed, inwardly, quiet; an unusually attractive little thing, and as strong as a heifer in appearance. But her face was flushed, she was breathing rapidly, and I realized that she had a high fever. She had magnificent blonde hair, in profusion. One of those picture children often reproduced in advertising leaflets and the photogravure[1] sections of the Sunday papers.

She's had a fever for three days, began the father and we don't know what it comes from. My wife has given her things, you know, like people do, but it don't do no good. And there's been a lot of sickness around. So we tho't you'd better look her over and tell us what is the matter.

5   As doctors often do I took a trial shot at it as a point of departure. Has she had a sore throat?

Both parents answered me together, No . . . No, she says her throat don't hurt her.

Does your throat hurt you? added the mother to the child. But the little girl's expression didn't change nor did she move her eyes from my face.

Have you looked?

I tried to, said the mother, but I couldn't see.

10   As it happens we had been having a number of cases of diphtheria in the school to which this child went during that month and we were all, quite apparently, thinking of that, though no one had as yet spoken of the thing.

Well, I said, suppose we take a look at the throat first. I smiled in my best professional manner and asking for the child's first name I said, come on, Mathilda, open your mouth and let's take a look at your throat.

Nothing doing.

Aw, come on, I coaxed, just open your mouth wide and let me take a look. Look, I said opening both hands wide, I haven't anything in my hands. Just open up and let me see.

Such a nice man, put in the mother. Look how kind he is to you. Come on, do what he tells you to. He won't hurt you.

15   At that I ground my teeth in disgust. If only they wouldn't use the word "hurt" I might be able to get somewhere. But I did not allow myself to be hurried or disturbed but speaking quietly and slowly I approached the child again.

As I moved my chair a little nearer suddenly with one catlike movement both her hands clawed instinctively for my eyes and she almost reached them too. In fact she knocked my glasses flying and they fell, though unbroken, several feet away from me on the kitchen floor.

Both the mother and father almost turned themselves inside out in embarrassment and apology. You bad girl, said the mother, taking her and shaking her by one arm. Look what you've done. The nice man . . .

For heaven's sake, I broke in. Don't call me a nice man to her. I'm here to look at her throat on the chance that she might have diphtheria[2] and possibly die of it. But that's nothing to her. Look here, I said to the child, we're going to look at your throat. You're old enough to understand what

---

1. Process for printing photographs.
2. Bacterial disease that killed millions, mostly children, in the era before antibiotic medicines and effective programs of immunization. The most common sign of infection is a thick, bluish-white membrane coating the tonsils and throat.

I'm saying. Will you open it now by yourself or shall we have to open it for you?

Not a move. Even her expression hadn't changed. Her breaths however were coming faster and faster. Then the battle began. I had to do it. I had to have a throat culture for her own protection. But first I told the parents that it was entirely up to them. I explained the danger but said that I would not insist on a throat examination so long as they would take the responsibility.

If you don't do what the doctor says you'll have to go to the hospital, 20 the mother admonished her severely.

Oh yeah? I had to smile to myself. After all, I had already fallen in love with the savage brat, the parents were contemptible to me. In the ensuing struggle they grew more and more abject, crushed, exhausted while she surely rose to magnificent heights of insane fury of effort bred of her terror of me.

The father tried his best, and he was a big man but the fact that she was his daughter, his shame at her behavior and his dread of hurting her made him release her just at the critical times when I had almost achieved success, till I wanted to kill him. But his dread also that she might have diphtheria made him tell me to go on, go on though he himself was almost fainting, while the mother moved back and forth behind us raising and lowering her hands in an agony of apprehension.

Put her in front of you on your lap, I ordered, and hold both her wrists.

But as soon as he did the child let out a scream. Don't, you're hurting me. Let go of my hands. Let them go I tell you. Then she shrieked terrifyingly, hysterically. Stop it! Stop it! You're killing me!

Do you think she can stand it, doctor! said the mother.   25

You get out, said the husband to his wife. Do you want her to die of diphtheria?

Come on now, hold her, I said.

Then I grasped the child's head with my left hand and tried to get the wooden tongue depressor between her teeth. She fought, with clenched teeth, desperately! But now I also had grown furious—at a child. I tried to hold myself down but I couldn't. I know how to expose a throat for inspection. And I did my best. When finally I got the wooden spatula behind the last teeth and just the point of it into the mouth cavity, she opened up for an instant but before I could see anything she came down again and gripping the wooden blade between her molars she reduced it to splinters before I could get it out again.

Aren't you ashamed, the mother yelled at her. Aren't you ashamed to act like that in front of the doctor?

Get me a smooth-handled spoon of some sort, I told the mother. We're 30 going through with this. The child's mouth was already bleeding. Her tongue was cut and she was screaming in wild hysterical shrieks. Perhaps I should have desisted and come back in an hour or more. No doubt it would have been better. But I have seen at least two children lying dead in bed of neglect in such cases, and feeling that I must get a diagnosis now or never I went at it, again. But the worst of it was that I too had got beyond reason. I could have torn the child apart in my own fury and enjoyed it. It was a pleasure to attack her. My face was burning with it.

The damned little brat must be protected against her own idiocy, one says to one's self at such times. Others must be protected against her. It is a social necessity. And all these things are true. But a blind fury, a feeling of adult shame, bred of a longing for muscular release are the operatives. One goes on to the end.

In the final unreasoning assault I overpowered the child's neck and jaws. I forced the heavy silver spoon back of her teeth and down her throat till she gagged. And there it was—both tonsils covered with membrane. She had fought valiantly to keep me from knowing her secret. She had been hiding that sore throat for three days at least and lying to her parents in order to escape just such an outcome as this.

Now truly she was furious. She had been on the defensive before but now she attacked. Tried to get off her father's lap and fly at me while tears of defeat blinded her eyes.

1938

YASUNARI KAWABATA

The Grasshopper and the Bell Cricket[1]

Walking along the tile-roofed wall of the university, I turned aside and approached the upper school. Behind the white board fence of the school playground, from a dusky clump of bushes under the black cherry trees, an insect's voice could be heard. Walking more slowly and listening to that voice, and furthermore reluctant to part with it, I turned right so as not to leave the playground behind. When I turned to the left, the fence gave way to an embankment planted with orange trees. At the corner, I exclaimed with surprise. My eyes gleaming at what they saw up ahead, I hurried forward with short steps.

At the base of the embankment was a bobbing cluster of beautiful varicolored lanterns, such as one might see at a festival in a remote country village. Without going any farther, I knew that it was a group of children on an insect chase among the bushes of the embankment. There were about twenty lanterns. Not only were there crimson, pink, indigo, green, purple, and yellow lanterns, but one lantern glowed with five colors at once. There were even some little red store-bought lanterns. But most of the lanterns were beautiful square ones which the children had made themselves with love and care. The bobbing lanterns, the coming together of children on this lonely slope—surely it was a scene from a fairy tale?

One of the neighborhood children had heard an insect sing on this slope one night. Buying a red lantern, he had come back the next night to find the insect. The night after that, there was another child. This new child

1. Translated by Lane Dunlop.

could not buy a lantern. Cutting out the back and front of a small carton and papering it, he placed a candle on the bottom and fastened a string to the top. The number of children grew to five, and then to seven. They learned how to color the paper that they stretched over the windows of the cutout cartons, and to draw pictures on it. Then these wise child-artists, cutting out round, three-cornered, and lozenge leaf shapes in the cartons, coloring each little window a different color, with circles and diamonds, red and green, made a single and whole decorative pattern. The child with the red lantern discarded it as a tasteless object that could be bought at a store. The child who had made his own lantern threw it away because the design was too simple. The pattern of light that one had had in hand the night before was unsatisfying the morning after. Each day, with cardboard, paper, brush, scissors, penknife, and glue, the children made new lanterns out of their hearts and minds. Look at my lantern! Be the most unusually beautiful! And each night, they had gone out on their insect hunts. These were the twenty children and their beautiful lanterns that I now saw before me.

Wide-eyed, I loitered near them. Not only did the square lanterns have old-fashioned patterns and flower shapes, but the names of the children who had made them were cut out in squared letters of the syllabary. Different from the painted-over red lanterns, others (made of thick cutout cardboard) had their designs drawn onto the paper windows, so that the candle's light seemed to emanate from the form and color of the design itself. The lanterns brought out the shadows of the bushes like dark light. The children crouched eagerly on the slope wherever they heard an insect's voice.

"Does anyone want a grasshopper?" A boy, who had been peering into 5 a bush about thirty feet away from the other children, suddenly straightened up and shouted.

"Yes! Give it to me!" Six or seven children came running up. Crowding behind the boy who had found the grasshopper, they peered into the bush. Brushing away their outstretched hands and spreading out his arms, the boy stood as if guarding the bush where the insect was. Waving the lantern in his right hand, he called again to the other children.

"Does anyone want a grasshopper? A grasshopper!"

"I do! I do!" Four or five more children came running up. It seemed you could not catch a more precious insect than a grasshopper. The boy called out a third time.

"Doesn't anyone want a grasshopper?"

Two or three more children came over. 10

"Yes. I want it."

It was a girl, who just now had come up behind the boy who'd discovered the insect. Lightly turning his body, the boy gracefully bent forward. Shifting the lantern to his left hand, he reached his right hand into the bush.

"It's a grasshopper."

"Yes. I'd like to have it."

The boy quickly stood up. As if to say "Here!" he thrust out his fist that 15 held the insect at the girl. She, slipping her left wrist under the string of her lantern, enclosed the boy's fist with both hands. The boy quietly opened his fist. The insect was transferred to between the girl's thumb and index finger.

"Oh! It's not a grasshopper. It's a bell cricket." The girl's eyes shone as she looked at the small brown insect.

"It's a bell cricket! It's a bell cricket!" The children echoed in an envious chorus.

"It's a bell cricket. It's a bell cricket."

Glancing with her bright intelligent eyes at the boy who had given her the cricket, the girl opened the little insect cage hanging at her side and released the cricket in it.

20   "It's a bell cricket."

"Oh, it's a bell cricket," the boy who'd captured it muttered. Holding up the insect cage close to his eyes, he looked inside it. By the light of his beautiful many colored lantern, also held up at eye level, he glanced at the girl's face.

Oh, I thought. I felt slightly jealous of the boy, and sheepish. How silly of me not to have understood his actions until now! Then I caught my breath in surprise. Look! It was something on the girl's breast which neither the boy who had given her the cricket, nor she who had accepted it, nor the children who were looking at them noticed.

In the faint greenish light that fell on the girl's breast, wasn't the name "Fujio" clearly discernible? The boy's lantern, which he held up alongside the girl's insect cage, inscribed his name, cut out in the green papered aperture, onto her white cotton kimono. The girl's lantern, which dangled loosely from her wrist, did not project its pattern so clearly, but still one could make out, in a trembling patch of red on the boy's waist, the name "Kiyoko." This chance interplay of red and green—if it was chance or play— neither Fujio nor Kiyoko knew about.

Even if they remembered forever that Fujio had given her the cricket and that Kiyoko had accepted it, not even in dreams would Fujio ever know that his name had been written in green on Kiyoko's breast or that Kiyoko's name had been inscribed in red on his waist, nor would Kiyoko ever know that Fujio's name had been inscribed in green on her breast or that her own name had been written in red on Fujio's waist.

25   Fujio! Even when you have become a young man, laugh with pleasure at a girl's delight when, told that it's a grasshopper, she is given a bell cricket; laugh with affection at a girl's chagrin when, told that it's a bell cricket, she is given a grasshopper.

Even if you have the wit to look by yourself in a bush away from the other children, there are not many bell crickets in the world. Probably you will find a girl like a grasshopper whom you think is a bell cricket.

And finally, to your clouded, wounded heart, even a true bell cricket will seem like a grasshopper. Should that day come, when it seems to you that the world is only full of grasshoppers, I will think it a pity that you have no way to remember tonight's play of light, when your name was written in green by your beautiful lantern on a girl's breast.

1988

FLANNERY O'CONNOR

A Good Man Is Hard to Find

The grandmother didn't want to go to Florida. She wanted to visit some of her connections in east Tennessee and she was seizing at every chance to change Bailey's mind. Bailey was the son she lived with, 'her only boy. He was sitting on the edge of his chair at the table, bent over the orange sports section of the *Journal*. "Now look here, Bailey," she said, "see here, read this," and she stood with one hand on her thin hip and the other rattling the newspaper at his bald head. "Here this fellow that calls himself The Misfit is aloose from the Federal Pen and headed toward Florida and you read here what it says he did to these people. Just you read it. I wouldn't take my children in any direction with a criminal like that aloose in it. I couldn't answer to my conscience if I did."

Bailey didn't look up from his reading so she wheeled around then and faced the children's mother, a young woman in slacks, whose face was as broad and innocent as a cabbage and was tied around with a green head-kerchief that had two points on the top like a rabbit's ears. She was sitting on the sofa, feeding the baby his apricots out of a jar. "The children have been to Florida before," the old lady said. "You all ought to take them somewhere else for a change so they would see different parts of the world and be broad. They never have been to east Tennessee."

The children's mother didn't seem to hear her but the eight-year-old boy, John Wesley, a stocky child with glasses, said, "If you don't want to go to Florida, why dontcha stay at home?" He and the little girl, June Star, were reading the funny papers on the floor.

"She wouldn't stay at home to be queen for a day," June Star said without raising her yellow head.

"Yes and what would you do if this fellow, The Misfit, caught you?" the 5 grandmother asked.

"I'd smack his face," John Wesley said.

"She wouldn't stay at home for a million bucks," June Star said. "Afraid she'd miss something. She has to go everywhere we go."

"All right, Miss," the grandmother said. "Just remember that the next time you want me to curl your hair."

June Star said her hair was naturally curly.

The next morning the grandmother was the first one in the car, ready 10 to go. She had her big black valise that looked like the head of a hippopotamus in one corner, and underneath it she was hiding a basket with Pitty Sing,[1] the cat, in it. She didn't intend for the cat to be left alone in the house for three days because he would miss her too much and she was afraid he might brush against one of the gas burners and accidentally

---

1. Named after Pitti-Sing, one of the "three little maids from school" in Gilbert and Sullivan's operetta *The Mikado* (1885).

asphyxiate himself. Her son, Bailey, didn't like to arrive at a motel with a cat.

She sat in the middle of the back seat with John Wesley and June Star on either side of her. Bailey and the children's mother and the baby sat in front and they left Atlanta at eight forty-five with the mileage on the car at 55890. The grandmother wrote this down because she thought it would be interesting to say how many miles they had been when they got back. It took them twenty minutes to reach the outskirts of the city.

The old lady settled herself comfortably, removing her white cotton gloves and putting them up with her purse on the shelf in front of the back window. The children's mother still had on slacks and still had her head tied up in a green kerchief, but the grandmother had on a navy blue straw sailor hat with a bunch of white violets on the brim and a navy blue dress with a small white dot in the print. Her collars and cuffs were white organdy trimmed with lace and at her neckline she had pinned a purple spray of cloth violets containing a sachet. In case of an accident, anyone seeing her dead on the highway would know at once that she was a lady.

She said she thought it was going to be a good day for driving, neither too hot nor too cold, and she cautioned Bailey that the speed limit was fifty-five miles an hour and that the patrolmen hid themselves behind billboards and small clumps of trees and sped out after you before you had a chance to slow down. She pointed out interesting details of the scenery: Stone Mountain; the blue granite that in some places came up to both sides of the highway; the brilliant red clay banks slightly streaked with purple; and the various crops that made rows of green lace-work on the ground. The trees were full of silver-white sunlight and the meanest of them sparkled. The children were reading comic magazines and their mother had gone back to sleep.

"Let's go through Georgia fast so we won't have to look at it much," John Wesley said.

15   "If I were a little boy," said the grandmother, "I wouldn't talk about my native state that way. Tennessee has the mountains and Georgia has the hills."

"Tennessee is just a hillbilly dumping ground," John Wesley said, "and Georgia is a lousy state too."

"You said it," June Star said.

"In my time," said the grandmother, folding her thin veined fingers, "children were more respectful of their native states and their parents and everything else. People did right then. Oh look at the cute little pickaninny!" she said and pointed to a Negro child standing in the door of a shack. "Wouldn't that make a picture, now?" she asked and they all turned and looked at the little Negro out of the back window. He waved.

"He didn't have any britches on," June Star said.

20   "He probably didn't have any," the grandmother explained. "Little niggers in the country don't have things like we do. If I could paint, I'd paint that picture," she said.

The children exchanged comic books.

The grandmother offered to hold the baby and the children's mother passed him over the front seat to her. She set him on her knee and bounced him and told him about the things they were passing. She rolled her eyes and screwed up her mouth and stuck her leathery thin face into his smooth bland one. Occasionally he gave her a faraway smile. They passed a large cotton field with five or six graves fenced in the middle of it, like a small island. "Look at the graveyard!" the grandmother said, pointing it out. "That was the old family burying ground. That belonged to the plantation."

"Where's the plantation?" John Wesley asked.

"Gone with the Wind,"[2] said the grandmother. "Ha. Ha."

When the children finished all the comic books they had brought, they opened the lunch and ate it. The grandmother ate a peanut butter sand- 25 wich and an olive and would not let the children throw the box and the paper napkins out the window. When there was nothing else to do they played a game by choosing a cloud and making the other two guess what shape it suggested. John Wesley took one the shape of a cow and June Star guessed a cow and John Wesley said, no, an automobile, and June Star said he didn't play fair, and they began to slap each other over the grandmother.

The grandmother said she would tell them a story if they would keep quiet. When she told a story, she rolled her eyes and waved her head and was very dramatic. She said once when she was a maiden lady she had been courted by a Mr. Edgar Atkins Teagarden from Jasper, Georgia. She said he was a very good-looking man and a gentleman and that he brought her a watermelon every Saturday afternoon with his initials cut in it, E. A. T. Well, one Saturday, she said, Mr. Teagarden brought the watermelon and there was nobody at home and he left it on the front porch and returned in his buggy to Jasper, but she never got the watermelon, she said, because a nigger boy ate it when he saw the initials, E. A. T.! This story tickled John Wesley's funny bone and he giggled and giggled but June Star didn't think it was any good. She said she wouldn't marry a man that just brought her a watermelon on Saturday. The grandmother said she would have done well to marry Mr. Teagarden because he was a gentleman and had bought Coca-Cola stock when it first came out and that he had died only a few years ago, a very wealthy man.

They stopped at The Tower for barbecued sandwiches. The Tower was a part stucco and part wood filling station and dance hall set in a clearing outside of Timothy. A fat man named Red Sammy Butts ran it and there were signs stuck here and there on the building and for miles up and down the highway saying, TRY RED SAMMY'S FAMOUS BARBECUE. NONE LIKE FAMOUS RED SAMMY'S! RED SAM! THE FAT BOY WITH THE HAPPY LAUGH! A VETERAN! RED SAMMY'S YOUR MAN!

Red Sammy was lying on the bare ground outside The Tower with his head under a truck while a gray monkey about a foot high, chained to a

---

2. The title of an immensely popular novel, published in 1936, by Margaret Mitchell (1900–1949); the novel depicts a large, prosperous Southern plantation, Tara, that is destroyed by Northern troops in the American Civil War.

small chinaberry tree, chattered nearby. The monkey sprang back into the tree and got on the highest limb as soon as he saw the children jump out of the car and run toward him.

Inside, The Tower was a long dark room with a counter at one end and tables at the other and dancing space in the middle. They all sat down at a board table next to the nickelodeon[3] and Red Sam's wife, a tall burnt-brown woman with hair and eyes lighter than her skin, came and took their order. The children's mother put a dime in the machine and played "The Tennessee Waltz," and the grandmother said that tune always made her want to dance. She asked Bailey if he would like to dance but he only glared at her. He didn't have a naturally sunny disposition like she did and trips made him nervous. The grandmother's brown eyes were very bright. She swayed her head from side to side and pretended she was dancing in her chair. June Star said play something she could tap to so the children's mother put in another dime and played a fast number and June Star stepped out onto the dance floor and did her tap routine.

30   "Ain't she cute?" Red Sam's wife said, leaning over the counter. "Would you like to come be my little girl?"

"No I certainly wouldn't," June Star said. "I wouldn't live in a broken-down place like this for a million bucks!" and she ran back to the table.

"Ain't she cute?" the woman repeated, stretching her mouth politely.

"Aren't you ashamed?" hissed the grandmother.

Red Sam came in and told his wife to quit lounging on the counter and hurry up with these people's order. His khaki trousers reached just to his hip bones and his stomach hung over them like a sack of meal swaying under his shirt. He came over and sat down at a table nearby and let out a combination sigh and yodel. "You can't win," he said. "You can't win," and he wiped his sweating red face off with a gray handkerchief. "These days you don't know who to trust," he said. "Ain't that the truth?"

35   "People are certainly not nice like they used to be," said the grandmother.

"Two fellers come in here last week," Red Sammy said, "driving a Chrysler. It was a old beat-up car but it was a good one and these boys looked all right to me. Said they worked at the mill and you know I let them fellers charge the gas they bought? Now why did I do that?"

"Because you're a good man!" the grandmother said at once.

"Yes'm, I suppose so," Red Sam said as if he were struck with this answer.

His wife brought the orders, carrying the five plates all at once without a tray, two in each hand and one balanced on her arm. "It isn't a soul in this green world of God's that you can trust," she said. "And I don't count nobody out of that, not nobody," she repeated, looking at Red Sammy.

40   "Did you read about that criminal, The Misfit, that's escaped?" asked the grandmother.

"I wouldn't be a bit surprised if he didn't attact this place right here,"

---

3. Jukebox.

said the woman. "If he hears about it being here, I wouldn't be none surprised to see him. If he hears it's two cent in the cash register, I wouldn't be a tall surprised if he . . ."

"That'll do," Red Sam said. "Go bring these people their Co'-Colas," and the woman went off to get the rest of the order.

"A good man is hard to find," Red Sammy said. "Everything is getting terrible. I remember the day you could go off and leave your screen door unlatched. Not no more."

He and the grandmother discussed better times. The old lady said that in her opinion Europe was entirely to blame for the way things were now. She said the way Europe acted you would think we were made of money and Red Sam said it was no use talking about it, she was exactly right. The children ran outside into the white sunlight and looked at the monkey in the lacy chinaberry tree. He was busy catching fleas on himself and biting each one carefully between his teeth as if it were a delicacy.

They drove off again into the hot afternoon. The grandmother took cat   45 naps and woke up every few minutes with her own snoring. Outside of Toombsboro she woke up and recalled an old plantation that she had visited in this neighborhood once when she was a young lady. She said the house had six white columns across the front and that there was an avenue of oaks leading up to it and two little wooden trellis arbors on either side in front where you sat down with your suitor after a stroll in the garden. She recalled exactly which road to turn off to get to it. She knew that Bailey would not be willing to lose any time looking at an old house, but the more she talked about it, the more she wanted to see it once again and find out if the little twin arbors were still standing. "There was a secret panel in this house," she said craftily, not telling the truth but wishing that she were, "and the story went that all the family silver was hidden in it when Sherman came through but it was never found . . ."

"Hey!" John Wesley said. "Let's go see it! We'll find it! We'll poke all the woodwork and find it! Who lives there? Where do you turn off at? Hey Pop, can't we turn off there?"

"We never have seen a house with a secret panel!" June Star shrieked. "Let's go to the house with the secret panel! Hey Pop, can't we go see the house with the secret panel!"

"It's not far from here, I know," the grandmother said. "It wouldn't take over twenty minutes."

Bailey was looking straight ahead. His jaw was as rigid as a horseshoe. "No," he said.

The children began to yell and scream that they wanted to see the house   50 with the secret panel. John Wesley kicked the back of the front seat and June Star hung over her mother's shoulder and whined desperately into her ear that they never had any fun even on their vacation, that they could never do what THEY wanted to do. The baby began to scream and John Wesley kicked the back of the seat so hard that his father could feel the blows in his kidney.

"All right!" he shouted and drew the car to a stop at the side of the road. "Will you all shut up? Will you all just shut up for one second? If you don't shut up, we won't go anywhere."

"It would be very educational for them," the grandmother murmured.

"All right," Bailey said, "but get this: this is the only time we're going to stop for anything like this. This is the one and only time."

"The dirt road that you have to turn down is about a mile back," the grandmother directed. "I marked it when we passed."

55   "A dirt road," Bailey groaned.

After they had turned around and were headed toward the dirt road, the grandmother recalled other points about the house, the beautiful glass over the front doorway and the candle-lamp in the hall. John Wesley said that the secret panel was probably in the fireplace.

"You can't go inside this house," Bailey said. "You don't know who lives there."

"While you all talk to the people in front, I'll run around behind and get in a window," John Wesley suggested.

"We'll all stay in the car," his mother said.

60   They turned onto the dirt road and the car raced roughly along in a swirl of pink dust. The grandmother recalled the times when there were no paved roads and thirty miles was a day's journey. The dirt road was hilly and there were sudden washes in it and sharp curves on dangerous embankments. All at once they would be on a hill, looking down over the blue tops of trees for miles around, then the next minute, they would be in a red depression with the dust-coated trees looking down on them.

"This place had better turn up in a minute," Bailey said, "or I'm going to turn around."

The road looked as if no one had traveled on it in months.

"It's not much farther," the grandmother said and just as she said it, a horrible thought came to her. The thought was so embarrassing that she turned red in the face and her eyes dilated and her feet jumped up, upsetting her valise in the corner. The instant the valise moved, the newspaper top she had over the basket under it rose with a snarl and Pitty Sing, the cat, sprang onto Bailey's shoulder.

The children were thrown to the floor and their mother, clutching the baby, out the door onto the ground; the old lady was thrown into the front seat. The car turned over once and landed right-side-up in a gulch off the side of the road. Bailey remained in the driver's seat with the cat—gray-striped with a broad white face and an orange nose—clinging to his neck like a caterpillar.

65   As soon as the children saw they could move their arms and legs, they scrambled out of the car, shouting, "We've had an ACCIDENT!" The grandmother was curled up under the dashboard, hoping she was injured so that Bailey's wrath would not come down on her all at once. The horrible thought she had had before the accident was that the house she had remembered so vividly was not in Georgia but in Tennessee.

Bailey removed the cat from his neck with both hands and flung it out the window against the side of a pine tree. Then he got out of the car and started looking for the children's mother. She was sitting against the side of the red gutted ditch, holding the screaming baby, but she only had a cut down her face and a broken shoulder. "We've had an ACCIDENT!" the children screamed in a frenzy of delight.

"But nobody's killed," June Star said with disappointment as the grandmother limped out of the car, her hat still pinned to her head but the broken front brim standing up at a jaunty angle and the violet spray hanging off the side. They all sat down in the ditch, except the children, to recover from the shock. They were all shaking.

"Maybe a car will come along," said the children's mother hoarsely.

"I believe I have injured an organ," said the grandmother, pressing her side, but no one answered her. Bailey's teeth were clattering. He had on a yellow sport shirt with bright blue parrots designed in it and his face was as yellow as the shirt. The grandmother decided that she would not mention that the house was in Tennessee.

The road was about ten feet above and they could see only the tops of 70 the trees on the other side of it. Behind the ditch they were sitting in there were more woods, tall and dark and deep. In a few minutes they saw a car some distance away on top of a hill, coming slowly as if the occupants were watching them. The grandmother stood up and waved both arms dramatically to attract their attention. The car continued to come on slowly, disappeared around a bend and appeared again, moving even slower, on top of the hill they had gone over. It was a big black battered hearselike automobile. There were three men in it.

It came to a stop just over them and for some minutes, the driver looked down with a steady expressionless gaze to where they were sitting, and didn't speak. Then he turned his head and muttered something to the other two and they got out. One was a fat boy in black trousers and a red sweat shirt with a silver stallion embossed on the front of it. He moved around on the right side of them and stood staring, his mouth partly open in a kind of loose grin. The other had on khaki pants and a blue striped coat and a gray hat pulled down very low, hiding most of his face. He came around slowly on the left side. Neither spoke.

The driver got out of the car and stood by the side of it, looking down at them. He was an older man than the other two. His hair was just beginning to gray and he wore silver-rimmed spectacles that gave him a scholarly look. He had a long creased face and didn't have on any shirt or undershirt. He had on blue jeans that were too tight for him and was holding a black hat and a gun. The two boys also had guns.

"We've had an ACCIDENT!" the children screamed.

The grandmother had the peculiar feeling that the bespectacled man was someone she knew. His face was as familiar to her as if she had known him all her life but she could not recall who he was. He moved away from the car and began to come down the embankment, placing his feet carefully so that he wouldn't slip. He had on tan and white shoes and no socks, and his ankles were red and thin. "Good afternoon," he said. "I see you all had you a little spill."

75   "We turned over twice!" said the grandmother.

"Oncet," he corrected. "We seen it happen. Try their car and see will it run, Hiram," he said quietly to the boy with the gray hat.

"What you got that gun for?" John Wesley asked. "Whatcha gonna do with that gun?"

"Lady," the man said to the children's mother, "would you mind calling them children to sit down by you? Children make me nervous. I want all you all to sit down right together there where you're at."

"What are you telling US what to do for?" June Star asked.

80   Behind them the line of woods gaped like a dark open mouth. "Come here," said their mother.

"Look here now," Bailey began suddenly, "we're in a predicament! We're in . . ."

The grandmother shrieked. She scrambled to her feet and stood staring. "You're The Misfit!" she said. "I recognized you at once!"

"Yes'm," the man said, smiling slightly as if he were pleased in spite of himself to be known, "but it would have been better for all of you, lady, if you hadn't of reckernized me."

Bailey turned his head sharply and said something to his mother that shocked even the children. The old lady began to cry and The Misfit reddened.

85   "Lady," he said, "don't you get upset. Sometimes a man says things he don't mean. I don't reckon he meant to talk to you thataway."

"You wouldn't shoot a lady, would you?" the grandmother said and removed a clean handkerchief from her cuff and began to slap at her eyes with it.

The Misfit pointed the toe of his shoe into the ground and made a little hole and then covered it up again. "I would hate to have to," he said.

"Listen," the grandmother almost screamed, "I know you're a good man. You don't look a bit like you have common blood. I know you must come from nice people!"

"Yes mam," he said, "finest people in the world." When he smiled he showed a row of strong white teeth. "God never made a finer woman than my mother and my daddy's heart was pure gold," he said. The boy with the red sweat shirt had come around behind them and was standing with his gun at his hip. The Misfit squatted down on the ground. "Watch them children, Bobby Lee," he said. "You know they make me nervous." He looked at the six of them huddled together in front of him and he seemed to be embarrassed as if he couldn't think of anything to say. "Ain't a cloud in the sky," he remarked, looking up at it. "Don't see no sun but don't see no cloud neither."

90   "Yes, it's a beautiful day," said the grandmother. "Listen," she said, "you shouldn't call yourself The Misfit because I know you're a good man at heart. I can just look at you and tell."

"Hush!" Bailey yelled. "Hush! Everybody shut up and let me handle this!" He was squatting in the position of a runner about to sprint forward but he didn't move.

"I pre-chate that, lady," The Misfit said and drew a little circle in the ground with the butt of his gun.

"It'll take a half a hour to fix this here car," Hiram called, looking over the raised hood of it.

"Well, first you and Bobby Lee get him and that little boy to step over yonder with you," The Misfit said, pointing to Bailey and John Wesley. "The boys want to ast you something," he said to Bailey. "Would you mind stepping back in them woods there with them?"

"Listen," Bailey began, "we're in a terrible predicament! Nobody realizes   95
what this is," and his voice cracked. His eyes were as blue and intense as the parrots in his shirt and he remained perfectly still.

The grandmother reached up to adjust her hat brim as if she were going to the woods with him but it came off in her hand. She stood staring at it and after a second she let it fall on the ground. Hiram pulled Bailey up by the arm as if he were assisting an old man. John Wesley caught hold of his father's hand and Bobby Lee followed. They went off toward the woods and just as they reached the dark edge, Bailey turned and supporting himself against a gray naked pine trunk, he shouted, "I'll be back in a minute, Mamma, wait on me!"

"Come back this instant!" his mother shrilled but they all disappeared into the woods.

"Bailey Boy!" the grandmother called in a tragic voice but she found she was looking at The Misfit squatting on the ground in front of her. "I just know you're a good man," she said desperately. "You're not a bit common!"

"Nome, I ain't a good man," The Misfit said after a second as if he had considered her statement carefully, "but I ain't the worst in the world neither. My daddy said I was a different breed of dog from my brothers and sisters. 'You know,' Daddy said, 'it's some that can live their whole life out without asking about it and it's others has to know why it is, and this boy is one of the latters. He's going to be into everything!' " He put on his black hat and looked up suddenly and then away deep into the woods as if he were embarrassed again. "I'm sorry I don't have on a shirt before you ladies," he said, hunching his shoulders slightly. "We buried our clothes that we had on when we escaped and we're just making do until we can get better. We borrowed these from some folks we met," he explained.

"That's perfectly all right," the grandmother said. "Maybe Bailey has an   100
extra shirt in his suitcase."

"I'll look and see terrectly," The Misfit said.

"Where are they taking him?" the children's mother screamed.

"Daddy was a card himself," The Misfit said. "You couldn't put anything over on him. He never got in trouble with the Authorities though. Just had the knack of handling them."

"You could be honest too if you'd only try," said the grandmother. "Think how wonderful it would be to settle down and live a comfortable life and not have to think about somebody chasing you all the time."

The Misfit kept scratching in the ground with the butt of his gun as   105 if he were thinking about it. "Yes'm, somebody is always after you," he murmured.

The grandmother noticed how thin his shoulder blades were just behind his hat because she was standing up looking down on him. "Do you ever pray?" she asked.

He shook his head. All she saw was the black hat wiggle between his shoulder blades. "Nome," he said.

There was a pistol shot from the woods, followed closely by another. Then silence. The old lady's head jerked around. She could hear the wind move through the tree tops like a long satisfied insuck of breath. "Bailey Boy!" she called.

"I was a gospel singer for a while," The Misfit said. "I been most everything. Been in the arm service, both land and sea, at home and abroad, been twict married, been an undertaker, been with the railroads, plowed Mother Earth, been in a tornado, seen a man burnt alive oncet," and looked up at the children's mother and the little girl who were sitting close together, their faces white and their eyes glassy; "I even seen a woman flogged," he said.

110   "Pray, pray," the grandmother began, "pray, pray ..."

"I never was a bad boy that I remember of," The Misfit said in an almost dreamy voice, "but somewheres along the line I done something wrong and got sent to the penitentiary. I was buried alive," and he looked up and held her attention to him by a steady stare.

"That's when you should have started to pray," she said. "What did you do to get sent to the penitentiary that first time?"

"Turn to the right, it was a wall," The Misfit said, looking up again at the cloudless sky. "Turn to the left, it was a wall. Look up it was a ceiling, look down it was a floor. I forgot what I done, lady. I set there and set there, trying to remember what it was I done and I ain't recalled it to this day. Oncet in a while, I would think it was coming to me, but it never come."

"Maybe they put you in by mistake," the old lady said vaguely.

115   "Nome," he said. "It wasn't no mistake. They had the papers on me."

"You must have stolen something," she said.

The Misfit sneered slightly. "Nobody had nothing I wanted," he said. "It was a head-doctor at the penitentiary said what I had done was kill my daddy but I known that for a lie. My daddy died in nineteen ought nineteen of the epidemic flu and I never had a thing to do with it. He was buried in the Mount Hopewell Baptist churchyard and you can go there and see for yourself."

"If you would pray," the old lady said, "Jesus would help you."

"That's right," The Misfit said.

120   "Well then, why don't you pray?" she asked trembling with delight suddenly.

"I don't want no hep," he said. "I'm doing all right by myself."

Bobby Lee and Hiram came ambling back from the woods. Bobby Lee was dragging a yellow shirt with bright blue parrots in it.

"Thow me that shirt, Bobby Lee," The Misfit said. The shirt came flying at him and landed on his shoulder and he put it on. The grandmother couldn't name what the shirt reminded her of. "No, lady," The Misfit said while he was buttoning it up, "I found out the crime don't matter. You can do one thing or you can do another, kill a man or take a tire off his car, because sooner or later you're going to forget what it was you done and just be punished for it."

The children's mother had begun to make heaving noises as if she couldn't get her breath. "Lady," he asked, "would you and that little girl like to step off yonder with Bobby Lee and Hiram and join your husband?"

"Yes, thank you," the mother said faintly. Her left arm dangled helplessly 125 and she was holding the baby, who had gone to sleep, in the other. "Hep that lady up, Hiram," The Misfit said as she struggled to climb out of the ditch, "and Bobby Lee, you hold onto that little girl's hand."

"I don't want to hold hands with him," June Star said. "He reminds me of a pig."

The fat boy blushed and laughed and caught her by the arm and pulled her off into the woods after Hiram and her mother.

Alone with The Misfit, the grandmother found that she had lost her voice. There was not a cloud in the sky nor any sun. There was nothing around her but woods. She wanted to tell him that he must pray. She opened and closed her mouth several times before anything came out. Finally she found herself saying, "Jesus, Jesus," meaning, Jesus will help you, but the way she was saying it, it sounded as if she might be cursing.

"Yes'm," The Misfit said as if he agreed. "Jesus thown everything off balance. It was the same case with Him as with me except He hadn't committed any crime and they could prove I had committed one because they had the papers on me. Of course," he said, "they never shown me my papers. That's why I sign myself now. I said long ago, you get you a signature and sign everything you do and keep a copy of it. Then you'll know what you done and you can hold up the crime to the punishment and see do they match and in the end you'll have something to prove you ain't been treated right. I call myself The Misfit," he said, "because I can't make what all I done wrong fit what all I gone through in punishment."

There was a piercing scream from the woods, followed closely by a pistol 130 report. "Does it seem right to you, lady, that one is punished a heap and another ain't punished at all?"

"Jesus!" the old lady cried. "You've got good blood! I know you wouldn't shoot a lady! I know you come from nice people! Pray! Jesus, you ought not to shoot a lady. I'll give you all the money I've got!"

"Lady," The Misfit said, looking beyond her far into the woods, "there never was a body that give the undertaker a tip."

There were two more pistol reports and the grandmother raised her head like a parched old turkey hen crying for water and called, "Bailey Boy, Bailey Boy!" as if her heart would break.

"Jesus was the only One that ever raised the dead." The Misfit continued, "and He shouldn't have done it. He thown everything off balance. If He did what He said, then it's nothing for you to do but thow away everything and follow Him, and if He didn't, then it's nothing for you to do but enjoy the few minutes you got left the best way you can—by killing somebody or burning down his house or doing some other meanness to him. No pleasure but meanness," he said and his voice had become almost a snarl.

135   "Maybe He didn't raise the dead," the old lady mumbled, not knowing what she was saying and feeling so dizzy that she sank down in the ditch with her legs twisted under her.

"I wasn't there so I can't say He didn't," The Misfit said. "I wisht I had of been there," he said, hitting the ground with his fist. "It ain't right I wasn't there because if I had of been there I would of known. Listen lady," he said in a high voice, "if I had of been there I would of known and I wouldn't be like I am now." His voice seemed about to crack and the grandmother's head cleared for an instant. She saw the man's face twisted close to her own as if he were going to cry and she murmured, "Why you're one of my babies. You're one of my own children!" She reached out and touched him on the shoulder. The Misfit sprang back as if a snake had bitten him and shot her three times through the chest. Then he put his gun down on the ground and took off his glasses and began to clean them.

Hiram and Bobby Lee returned from the woods and stood over the ditch, looking down at the grandmother who half sat and half lay in a puddle of blood with her legs crossed under her like a child's and her face smiling up at the cloudless sky.

Without his glasses, The Misfit's eyes were red-rimmed and pale and defenseless-looking. "Take her off and thow her where you thown the others," he said, picking up the cat that was rubbing itself against his leg.

"She was a talker, wasn't she?" Bobby Lee said, sliding down the ditch with a yodel.

140   "She would of been a good woman," The Misfit said, "if it had been somebody there to shoot her every minute of her life."

"Some fun!" Bobby Lee said.

"Shut up, Bobby Lee," The Misfit said. "It's no real pleasure in life."

1955

TONI CADE BAMBARA

Gorilla, My Love

That was the year Hunca Bubba changed his name. Not a change up, but a change back, since Jefferson Winston Vale was the name in the first place. Which was news to me cause he'd been my Hunca Bubba my whole lifetime, since I couldn't manage Uncle to save my life. So far as I was concerned it was a change completely to somethin soundin very geographical weather-like to me, like somethin you'd find in a almanac. Or somethin you'd run across when you sittin in the navigator seat with a wet thumb on the map crinkly in your lap, watchin the roads and signs so when Granddaddy Vale say "Which way, Scout," you got sense enough to say take the next exit or take a left or whatever it is. Not that Scout's my name. Just the name Granddaddy call whoever sittin in the navigator seat. Which is usually me cause I don't feature sittin in the back with the pecans. Now, you figure pecans all right to be sittin with. If you thinks so, that's your business. But they dusty sometime and make you cough. And they got a way of slidin around and dippin down sudden, like maybe a rat in the buckets. So if you scary like me, you sleep with the lights on and blame it on Baby Jason and, so as not to waste good electric, you study the maps. And that's how come I'm in the navigator seat most times and get to be called Scout.

So Hunca Bubba in the back with the pecans and Baby Jason, and he in love. And we got to hear all this stuff about this woman he in love with and all. Which really ain't enough to keep the mind alive, though Baby Jason got no better sense than to give his undivided attention and keep grabbin at the photograph which is just a picture of some skinny woman in a countrified dress with her hand shot up to her face like she shame fore cameras. But there's a movie house in the background which I ax about. Cause I am a movie freak from way back, even though it do get me in trouble sometime.

Like when me and Big Brood and Baby Jason was on our own last Easter and couldn't go to the Dorset cause we'd seen all the Three Stooges they was. And the RKO Hamilton was closed readying up for the Easter Pageant that night. And the West End, the Regun and the Sunset was too far, less we had grownups with us which we didn't. So we walk up Amsterdam Avenue to the Washington and *Gorilla, My Love* playin, they say, which suit me just fine, though the "my love" part kinda drag Big Brood some. As for Baby Jason, shoot, like Granddaddy say, he'd follow me into the fiery furnace if I say come on. So we go in and get three bags of Havmore potato chips which not only are the best potato chips but the best bags for blowin up and bustin real loud so the matron come trottin down the aisle with her chunky self, flashin that flashlight dead in your eye so you can give her some lip, and if she answer back and you already finish seein the show anyway, why then you just turn the place out. Which I love to do, no lie. With Baby Jason kickin at the seat in front, egging me on, and Big Brood mumblin bout what fiercesome things we goin do. Which means me. Like when the big boys come up on us talkin bout Lemme a nickel. It's me that hide the money. Or when the bad boys in the park take Big Brood's Spaudeen[1] way from him. It's me that jump on they back and fight awhile. And it's me that turns out the show if the matron get too salty.

So the movie come on and right away it's this churchy music and clearly not about no gorilla. Bout Jesus. And I am ready to kill, not cause I got anything gainst Jesus. Just that when you fixed to watch a gorilla picture you don't wanna get messed around with Sunday School stuff. So I am

---

1. Probably refers to "Spaldeen," the small pink rubber ball made by the Spalding company and used for stick ball.

mad. Besides, we see this raggedy old brown film *King of Kings*[2] every year
and enough's enough. Grownups figure they can treat you just anyhow.
Which burns me up. There I am, my feet up and my Havmore potato chips
really salty and crispy and two jawbreakers in my lap and the money safe
in my shoe from the big boys, and there comes this Jesus stuff. So we all
go wild. Yellin, booin, stompin and carryin on. Really to wake the man in
the booth up there who musta went to sleep and put on the wrong reels.
But no, cause he holler down to shut up and then he turn the sound up
so we really gotta holler like crazy to even hear ourselves good. And the
matron ropes off the children section and flashes her light all over the
place and we yell some more and some kids slip under the rope and run
up and down the aisle just to show it take more than some dusty ole velvet
rope to tie us down. And I'm flingin the kid in front of me's popcorn. And
Baby Jason kickin seats. And it's really somethin. Then here come the big
and bad matron, the one they let out in case of emergency. And she totin
that flashlight like she gonna use it on somebody. This here the colored
matron Brandy and her friends call Thunderbuns. She do not play. She do
not smile. So we shut up and watch the simple ass picture.

Which is not so simple as it is stupid. Cause I realized that just about
anybody in my family is better than this god they always talkin about. My
daddy wouldn't stand for nobody treatin any of us that way. My mama
specially. And I can just see it now, Big Brood up there on the cross talkin
bout Forgive them Daddy cause they don't know what they doin. And my
Mama say Get on down from there you big fool, whatcha think this is,
playtime? And my Daddy yellin to Granddaddy to get him a ladder cause
Big Brood actin the fool, his mother side of the family showin up. And my
mama and her sister Daisy jumpin on them Romans beatin them with they
pocketbooks. And Hunca Bubba tellin them folks on they knees they better
get out the way and go get some help or they goin to get trampled on. And
Granddaddy Vale sayin Leave the boy alone, if that's what he wants to do
with his life we ain't got nothin to say about it. Then Aunt Daisy givin him
a taste of that pocketbook, fussin bout what a damn fool old man Granddaddy is. Then everybody jumpin in his chest like the time Uncle Clayton
went in the army and come back with only one leg and Granddaddy say
somethin stupid about that's life. And by this time Big Brood off the cross
and in the park playin handball or skully[3] or somethin. And the family in
the kitchen throwin dishes at each other, screamin bout if you hadn't done
this I wouldn't had to do that. And me in the parlor trying to do my
arithmetic yellin Shut it off.

5   Which is what I was yellin all by myself which make me a sittin target
for Thunderbuns. But when I yell We want our money back, that gets
everybody in chorus. And the movie windin up with this heavenly cloud
music and the smartass up there in his hole in the wall turns up the sound

2. Although there is a 1961 version, this probably refers to the silent movie made in the 1920s.
3. A basketball game that tests shooting skill and can be played alone or as a contest between two
people.

again to drown us out. Then there comes Bugs Bunny which we already seen so we know we been had. No gorilla my nuthin. And Big Brood say Awwww sheeet, we goin to see the manager and get our money back. And I know from this we business. So I brush the potato chips out of my hair which is where Baby Jason like to put em, and I march myself up the aisle to deal with the manager who is a crook in the first place for lyin out there sayin *Gorilla, My Love* playin. And I never did like the man cause he oily and pasty at the same time like the bad guy in the serial, the one that got a hideout behind a push-button bookcase and play "Moonlight Sonata"[4] with gloves on. I knock on the door and I am furious. And I am alone, too. Cause Big Brood suddenly got to go so bad even though my mama told us bout goin in them nasty bathrooms. And I hear him sigh like he disgusted when he get to the door and see only a little kid there. And now I'm really furious cause I get so tired grownups messin over kids cause they little and can't take em to court. What is it, he say to me like I lost my mittens or wet myself or am somebody's retarded child. When in reality I am the smartest kid P.S. 186 ever had in its whole lifetime and you can ax anybody. Even them teachers that don't like me cause I won't sing them Southern songs or back off when they tell me my questions are out of order. And cause my Mama come up there in a minute when them teachers start playin the dozens[5] behind colored folks. She stalks in with her hat pulled down bad and that Persian lamb coat draped back over one hip on account of she got her fist planted there so she can talk that talk which gets us all hypnotized, and teacher be comin undone cause she know this could be her job and her behind cause Mama got pull with the Board and bad by her own self anyhow.

So I kick the door open wider and just walk right by him and sit down and tell the man about himself and that I want my money back and that goes for Baby Jason and Big Brood too. And he still trying to shuffle me out the door even though I'm sittin which shows him for the fool he is. Just like them teachers do fore they realize Mama like a stone on that spot and ain't backin up. So he ain't gettin up off the money. So I was forced to leave, takin the matches from under his ashtray, and set a fire under the candy stand, which closed the raggedy ole Washington down for a week. My Daddy had the suspect it was me cause Big Brood got a big mouth. But I explained right quick what the whole thing was about and I figured it was even-steven. Cause if you say Gorilla, My Love, you supposed to mean it. Just like when you say you goin to give me a party on my birthday, you gotta mean it. And if you say me and Baby Jason can go South pecan haulin with Granddaddy Vale, you better not be comin up with no stuff about the weather look uncertain or did you mop the bathroom or any other trickified business. I mean even gangsters in the movies say My word is my bond. So don't nobody get away with nothin far as I'm concerned. So

4. Popular name for Beethoven's *Piano Sonata in C Sharp Minor*, Opus 27, No. 2. The "bad guy" who plays this piece is the Phantom of the Opera.
5. Ritualized game or contest in which two participants exchange artfully stylized insults.

Daddy put his belt back on. Cause that's the way I was raised. Like my Mama say in one of them situations when I won't back down, Okay Badbird, you right. Your point is well-taken. Not that Badbird my name, just what she say when she tired arguin and know I'm right. And Aunt Jo, who is the hardest head in the family and worse even than Aunt Daisy, she say, You absolutely right Miss Muffin, which also ain't my real name but the name she gave me one time when I got some medicine shot in my behind and wouldn't get up off her pillows for nothin. And even Granddaddy Vale—who got no memory to speak of, so sometime you can just plain lie to him, if you want to be like that—he say, Well if that's what I said, then that's it. But this name business was different they said. It wasn't like Hunca Bubba had gone back on his word or anything. Just that he was thinkin bout gettin married and was usin his real name now. Which ain't the way I saw it at all.

So there I am in the navigator seat. And I turned to him and just plain ole ax him. I mean I come right on out with it. No sense goin all around that barn the old folks talk about. And like my mama say, Hazel—which is my real name and what she remembers to call me when she bein serious—when you got somethin on your mind, speak up and let the chips fall where they may. And if anybody don't like it, tell em to come see your mama. And Daddy look up from the paper and say, You hear your Mama good, Hazel. And tell em to come see me first. Like that. That's how I was raised.

So I turn clear round in the navigator seat and say, "Look here, Hunca Bubba or Jefferson Windsong Vale or whatever your name is, you gonna marry this girl?"

"Sure am," he say, all grins.

10 And I say, "Member that time you was baby-sittin me when we lived at four-o-nine and there was this big snow and Mama and Daddy got held up in the country so you had to stay for two days?"

And he say, "Sure do."

"Well. You remember how you told me I was the cutest thing that ever walked the earth?"

"Oh, you were real cute when you were little," he say, which is supposed to be funny. I am not laughin.

"Well. You remember what you said?"

15 And Granddaddy Vale squintin over the wheel and axin Which way, Scout. But Scout is busy and don't care if we all get lost for days.

"Watcha mean, Peaches?"

"My name is Hazel. And what I mean is you said you were going to marry *me* when I grew up. You were going to wait. That's what I mean, my dear Uncle Jefferson." And he don't say nuthin. Just look at me real strange like he never saw me before in life. Like he lost in some weird town in the middle of night and lookin for directions and there's no one to ask. Like it was me that messed up the maps and turned the road posts round. "Well, you said it, didn't you?" And Baby Jason lookin back and forth like we playin ping-pong. Only I ain't playin. I'm hurtin and I can hear that I am screamin. And Granddaddy Vale mumblin how we never gonna get to where we goin if I don't turn around and take my navigator job serious.

"Well, for cryin out loud, Hazel, you just a little girl. And I was just teasin."

" 'And I was just teasin,' " I say back just how he said it so he can hear what a terrible thing it is. Then I don't say nuthin. And he don't say nuthin. And Baby Jason don't say nuthin nohow. Then Granddaddy Vale speak up. "Look here, Precious, it was Hunca Bubba what told you them things. This here, Jefferson Winston Vale." And Hunca Bubba say, "That's right. That was somebody else. I'm a new somebody."

"You a lyin dawg," I say, when I meant to say treacherous dog, but just couldn't get hold of the word. It slipped away from me. And I'm crying and crumplin down in the seat and just don't care. And Granddaddy say to hush and steps on the gas. And I'm losin my bearins and don't even know where to look on the map cause I can't see for cryin. And Baby Jason cryin too. Cause he is my blood brother and understands that we must stick together or be forever lost, what with grown-ups playin change-up and turnin you round every which way so bad. And don't even say they sorry. 20

JAMAICA KINCAID

Girl

Wash the white clothes on Monday and put them on the stone heap; wash the color clothes on Tuesday and put them on the clothesline to dry; don't walk barehead in the hot sun; cook pumpkin fritters in very hot sweet oil; soak your little cloths right after you take them off; when buying cotton to make yourself a nice blouse, be sure that it doesn't have gum on it, because that way it won't hold up well after a wash; soak salt fish overnight before you cook it; is it true that you sing benna[1] in Sunday school?; always eat your food in such a way that it won't turn someone else's stomach; on Sundays try to walk like a lady and not like the slut you are so bent on becoming; don't sing benna in Sunday school; you mustn't speak to wharf-rat boys, not even to give directions; don't eat fruits on the street—flies will follow you; *but I don't sing benna on Sundays at all and never in Sunday school;* this is how to sew on a button; this is how to make a buttonhole for the button you have just sewed on; this is how to hem a dress when you see the hem coming down and so to prevent yourself from looking like the slut I know you are so bent on becoming; this is how you iron your father's khaki shirt so that it doesn't have a crease; this is how you iron your father's khaki pants so that they don't have a crease; this is how you grow okra—far from the house, because okra tree harbors red ants; when you are growing dasheen, make sure it gets plenty of water or else it makes your throat itch when you are eating it; this is how you sweep a corner; this is how you sweep a whole house; this is how you sweep a yard; this is how you smile to someone you don't like too much; this is how you smile to someone

---

1. A Caribbean folk-music style.

you don't like at all; this is how you smile to someone you like completely; this is how you set a table for tea; this is how you set a table for dinner; this is how you set a table for dinner with an important guest; this is how you set a table for lunch; this is how you set a table for breakfast; this is how to behave in the presence of men who don't know you very well, and this way they won't recognize immediately the slut I have warned you against becoming; be sure to wash every day, even if it is with your own spit; don't squat down to play marbles—you are not a boy, you know; don't pick people's flowers—you might catch something; don't throw stones at blackbirds, because it might not be a blackbird at all; this is how to make a bread pudding; this is how to make doukona[2] this is how to make pepper pot; this is how to make a good medicine for a cold; this is how to make a good medicine to throw away a child before it even becomes a child; this is how to catch a fish; this is how to throw back a fish you don't like, and that way something bad won't fall on you; this is how to bully a man; this is how a man bullies you; this is how to love a man, and if this doesn't work there are other ways, and if they don't work don't feel too bad about giving up; this is how to spit up in the air if you feel like it, and this is how to move quick so that it doesn't fall on you; this is how to make ends meet; always squeeze bread to make sure it's fresh; *but what if the baker won't let me feel the bread?*; you mean to say that after all you are really going to be the kind of woman who the baker won't let near the bread?

1983

---

2. A spicy pudding, often made from plantain and wrapped in a plantain or banana leaf.

Biographical Sketches
Fiction Writers

SHERMAN ALEXIE
(b. 1966)

Born on an Indian reservation near Spokane, Washington, Sherman Alexie attended high school in nearby Reardan, where he was the only native American other than the school mascot. Shortly after graduating in American Studies from Washington State University, Alexie received the Washington State Arts Commission Poetry Fellowship in 1991 and the National Endowment for the Arts Poetry Fellowship in 1992. The first of nine collections of poetry, *The Business of Fancydancing* (1991) was named a *New York Times* Notable Book of the Year in 1992. *The Lone Ranger and Tonto Fistfight in Heaven* (1993), a collection of short stories, received a PEN/Hemingway Award for Best First Book of Fiction. Alexie is also the author of two novels, *Reservation Blues* (1995) and *Indian Killer* (1996), as well as screenplays: *Smoke Signals* (1998) and *49?* (2004) were both featured at the Sundance Film Festival. A stand-up comedian and four-time champion of the World Heavyweight Poetry Bout, he lives in Seattle, Washington.

JAMES BALDWIN
(1924–1987)

For much of his life, James Baldwin was a leading literary spokesman for civil rights and racial equality in America. Born in New York City but long a resident of France, he first attracted critical attention with two extraordinary novels, *Go Tell It on the Mountain* (1953), drawing upon his past as a teenage preacher in the Fireside Pentecostal Church, and *Giovanni's Room* (1956), which dealt with the anguish of being black and homosexual in a largely white and heterosexual society; other works include the novels *Another Country* (1962) and *If Beale Street Could Talk* (1974), the play *Blues for Mr. Charlie* (1964), and a story collection, *Going to Meet the Man* (1965). Baldwin is perhaps best remembered as a perceptive and eloquent essayist, the author of *Notes of a Native Son* (1955), *Nobody Knows My Name* (1961), *The Fire Next Time* (1963), *No Name in the Street* (1972), and *The Price of a Ticket* (1985).

TONI CADE BAMBARA (1939–1995)

Born in New York City, Toni Cade Bambara grew up in Harlem and in Bedford-Stuyvesant, two of New York City's poorest neighborhoods. She began writing as a child and took her last name from a signature on a sketchbook she found in a trunk belonging to her great-grandmother. (The Bambara are a people of northwest Africa.) After graduating from Queens College, she wrote fiction in "the predawn in-betweens" while studying for her MA at the City College of New York, and working at a great variety of jobs: dancer, social worker, recreation director, psychiatric counselor, college English teacher, literary critic, and film producer. Bambara began to publish her stories in 1962. Her fiction includes two collections of stories, *Gorilla, My Love*

(1972) and *The Sea Birds Are Still Alive* (1977), as well as two novels, *The Salt Eaters* (1980) and *If Blessing Comes* (1987). Bambara also edited two anthologies, *The Black Woman* (1970) and *Stories for Black Folks* (1971).

AMBROSE BIERCE
(1842–1914?)

The tenth child of a poor Ohio family, Ambrose Bierce served with distinction in the Union Army during the Civil War, rising to the rank of major. After the war he worked as a journalist in California and London, where his boisterous western mannerisms and savage wit made him a celebrity and earned him the name "Bitter Bierce." He is probably best known as the author of *The Cynic's Word Book* (1906; later called *The Devil's Dictionary*), but his finest achievement may be his two volumes of short stories, *Tales of Soldiers and Civilians* (1891; later called *In the Midst of Life*) and *Can Such Things Be?* (1893), and *The Monk and the Hangman's Daughter* (1892), an adaptation of a German story. Disillusioned and depressed after his divorce and the deaths of his two sons, Bierce went to Mexico in 1913, where he reportedly rode with Pancho Villa's revolutionaries. He disappeared and is presumed to have died there.

LINDA BREWER
(b. 1946)

Western writer Linda Brewer grew up in Oregon's Siuslaw and now lives in the Sonora Desert of southern Arizona, where she works in a medical lab and writes features and food articles for a Tucson publication, *The Desert Leaf*. A finalist in the World's Best Short Story Contest, she won the 2002 Raymond Carver Short Story Contest. Her story "20/20" was featured in *Micro Fiction: An Anthology of Really Short Stories* (1996).

ANGELA CARTER
(1940–1992)

Born in Eastbourne, Sussex, England, Angela Carter chose to work as a journalist rather than attend Oxford University, though she later studied medieval literature at the University of Bristol. Her novels include *Shadow Dance* (1966), *The Magic Toyshop* (1967), *Heroes and Villains* (1969), *Several Perceptions* (1968), *The Infernal Desire Machines of Dr. Hoffman* (1973), *The Passion of New Eve* (1977), *Nights at the Circus* (1984), *Black Venus* (1985), *Love* (1988), and *Wise Children* (1991). Her stories are collected in *Burning Your Boats* (1997). Carter's writing gained widespread popularity after the release of the film *The Company of Wolves* (1984), which was based on a story from *The Bloody Chamber* (1979), a collection of macabre and erotic retellings of fairy tales. Her chief nonfiction work is *The Sadeian Woman: An Exercise in Cultural History* (1979). When she died in 1992, novelist Salman Rushdie wrote that "English literature has lost its high sorceress, its benevolent witch queen."

RAYMOND CARVER
(1938–1988)

Born in the logging town of Clatskanie, Oregon, to a working-class family, Raymond Carver married at nineteen and had two children by the time he was twenty-one. Despite these early responsibilities and a struggle with alcoholism that was to continue for the rest of his life, Carver published his first story in 1961 and graduated from Humboldt State College in 1963. He published his first book, *Near Klamath,* a collection of poems, in 1968, and thereafter supported himself with visiting lectureships at the University of California at Berkeley, Syracuse University, and the Iowa Writer's Workshop, among other institutions. His short-story collections include *What We Talk About When We Talk About Love* (1981), *Will You Please Be Quiet, Please?* (1976), *Cathedral* (1983), *My Father's*

Life (1986), and *Where I'm Calling From* (1989). His poetry is collected in *All of Us* (2000).

JOHN CHEEVER
(1912–1982)

John Cheever was born in Quincy, Massachusetts. His formal education ended when he was expelled from Thayer Academy at seventeen; he moved to New York City and devoted himself to fiction writing, except for brief interludes of writing scripts for television and of teaching at Barnard College and the University of Iowa. Cheever published his first story when he was sixteen, and even after his first novel, *The Wapshot Chronicle*, won the National Book Award in 1958, he was known primarily as a prolific writer of superb short stories. Collections include *The Way Some People Live* (1943), *The Enormous Radio* (1953), and *The Stories of John Cheever* (1978), which won the Pulitzer Prize. Known as "the Chekhov of the suburbs," Cheever was awarded the National Medal for Literature by the American Academy of Arts and Letters in 1982, shortly before he died.

ANTON CHEKHOV
(1860–1904)

The grandson of an emancipated serf, Anton Chekhov was born in the Russian town of Taganrog. In 1875, his father, a grocer facing bankruptcy and imprisonment, fled to Moscow and soon the rest of the family lost their house to a former friend and lodger, a situation that Chekhov would revisit in his play *The Cherry Orchard*. In 1884, Chekhov received his M.D. from the University of Moscow. He purchased an estate near Moscow in the early 1890s and became both an industrious landowner and doctor to the local peasants. After contributing stories to magazines and journals throughout the 1880s, he began writing for the stage in 1887. His plays, now regarded as classics, were generally ill-received in his lifetime.

The Wood Demon (later rewritten as *Uncle Vanya*) was performed only a few times in 1889 before closing, while the 1896 premiere of *The Seagull* turned into a riot when an audience expecting comedy was confronted with an experimental tragedy.

KATE CHOPIN
(1850–1904)

Katherine O'Flaherty was born in St. Louis, Missouri, to a Creole-Irish family that enjoyed a high place in society. Her father died when she was four, and Kate was raised by her mother, grandmother, and great-grandmother. Very well read at a young age, she received her formal education at the St. Louis Academy of the Sacred Heart. In 1870, she married Oscar Chopin, a Louisiana businessman, and lived with him in Natchitoches parish and New Orleans, where she became a close observer of Creole and Cajun life. Following her husband's sudden death in 1884, she returned to St. Louis, where she raised her six children and began her literary career. In slightly more than a decade she produced a substantial body of work, including the story collections *Bayou Folk* (1894) and *A Night in Acadie* (1897) and the classic novel *The Awakening* (1899), which was greeted with a storm of criticism for its frank treatment of female sexuality.

JOSEPH CONRAD
(1857–1924)

Jozeph Teodor Konrad Nalecz Korzeniowski was born in Berdyczew, Polish Ukraine. Orphaned at eleven, he eventually made his way to Marseilles and by the age of seventeen had made several trips to the West Indies as an apprentice seaman. After some troubles in France involving gambling debts, he sailed on a British ship, landed in England in 1878, and spent the next sixteen years in the British merchant service, rising to master in 1886, the year he became a British subject. In 1890, he worked on a boat that sailed up the

Congo, a trip that would inspire his best-known work, the novella *Heart of Darkness* (1899). Although he began writing in 1889, he did not publish his first novel, *Almayer's Folly*, until 1896, and enjoyed little popular success until the publication of *Chance* in 1913. Among his major novels are *Lord Jim* (1900), *Nostromo* (1904), *The Secret Agent* (1907), *Under Western Eyes* (1910), *Chance* (1913), and *Victory* (1915).

STEPHEN CRANE
(1871–1900)

One of fourteen children, Stephen Crane and his family moved frequently before settling, after his father's death in 1880, in Asbury Park, New Jersey. Crane sporadically attended various preparatory schools and colleges without excelling at much besides baseball. Determined to be a journalist, he left school for the last time in 1891 and began contributing pieces to New York newspapers. His city experiences led him to write *Maggie: A Girl of the Streets,* a realist social-reform novel published in 1893 at his own expense. His next novel, *The Red Badge of Courage* (1895), presented a stark picture of the Civil War and brought him widespread fame; many of his stories were published in the collections *The Open Boat and Other Tales of Adventure* (1898) and *The Monster and Other Stories* (1899). Crane served as a foreign correspondent, reporting on conflicts in Cuba and Greece, and lived his last years abroad, dying of tuberculosis at the age of 28.

LOUISE ERDRICH
(b. 1954)

Born in Minnesota of German-American and French-Chippewa descent, Louise Erdrich grew up in Wahpeton, North Dakota, as a member of the Turtle Mountain Band of Chippewa. She attended Dartmouth College and received an MFA in creative writing from Johns Hopkins University. Her first novel, *Love Medicine* (1984), a collection of linked stories, won the National

Book Critics Circle Award. In her subsequent publications—*The Beet Queen* (1986), *Tracks* (1988), *The Bingo Palace* (1993), and *Tales of Burning Love* (1996)—she pursued her focus on the lives of Native Americans in contemporary North Dakota. In 1991, she jointly authored the best-selling novel *The Crown of Columbus* with her husband, Michael Dorris. Her recent works include the novels *The Antelope Wife* (1998), *The Last Report on the Miracles at Little No Horse* (2001), *The Master Butchers Singing Club* (2003), *Four Souls* (2004), and a novel for young readers, *The Birchbark House* (2002).

WILLIAM FAULKNER
(1897–1962)

A native of Oxford, Mississippi, William Faulkner left high school without graduating, joined the Royal Canadian Air Force in 1918, and in the mid-1920s lived briefly in New Orleans, where he was encouraged as a writer by Sherwood Anderson. He then spent a few miserable months as a clerk in a New York bookstore, published a collection of poems, *The Marble Faun*, in 1924, and took a long walking tour of Europe in 1925 before returning to Mississippi. With the publication of *Sartoris* in 1929, Faulkner began a cycle of works, featuring recurrent characters and families in fictional Yoknapatawpha County, including *The Sound and the Fury* (1929), *As I Lay Dying* (1930), *Light in August* (1932), *Absalom, Absalom!* (1936), *The Hamlet* (1940), and *Go Down, Moses* (1942). He spent time in Hollywood, writing screenplays for *The Big Sleep* and other films, and lived his last years in Charlottesville, Virginia. Faulkner received the Nobel Prize for Literature in 1950.

CHARLOTTE PERKINS GILMAN
(1860–1935)

Charlotte Anna Perkins was born in Hartford, Connecticut. After a painful, lonely childhood and several

years of supporting herself as a governess, art teacher, and designer of greeting cards, Perkins married the artist Charles Stetson. Following Gilman's suffering several extended periods of depression, her husband put her in the care of a doctor who "sent me home with the solemn advice to 'live as domestic a life as . . . possible,' to 'have but two hours' intellectual life a day,' and 'never to touch pen, brush, or pencil again' as long as I lived." Three months of this regimen brought her "near the borderline of utter mortal ruin" and inspired her masterpiece, "The Yellow Wallpaper." In 1900, she married George Houghton Gilman, having divorced Stetson in 1892. Her nonfiction works, springing from the early women's movement, include *Women and Economics* (1898) and *Man-Made World* (1911). She also wrote several utopian novels, including *Moving the Mountain* (1911) and *Herland* (1915).

NATHANIEL HAWTHORNE (1804–1864)

Nathaniel Hawthorne was born in Salem, Massachusetts, a descendant of Puritan immigrants. Educated at Bowdoin College, he was agonizingly slow in winning recognition for his work, and supported himself from time to time in government service—working in the customhouses of Boston and Salem and serving as the United States consul in Liverpool. His early collections of stories, *Twice-Told Tales* (1837) and *Mosses from an Old Manse* (1846), did not sell well, and it was not until the publication of his most famous novel, *The Scarlet Letter* (1850), that his fame spread beyond a discerning few. His other novels include *The House of the Seven Gables* (1851) and *The Blithedale Romance* (1852). Burdened by a deep sense of guilt for his family's role in the notorious Salem witchcraft trials over a century before he was born (one ancestor had been a judge), Hawthorne used fiction as a means of exploring the moral dimensions of sin and the human soul.

ERNEST HEMINGWAY (1899–1961)

Born in Oak Park, Illinois, Ernest Hemingway became a reporter after graduating from high school. During World War I, he served as an ambulance-service volunteer in France and an infantryman in Italy, where he was wounded and decorated for valor. After the war, he lived for a time in Paris, part of the "Lost Generation" of American expatriates such as Gertrude Stein and F. Scott Fitzgerald. Two volumes of stories, *In Our Time* (1925) and *Death in the Afternoon* (1932), and two major novels, *The Sun Also Rises* (1926) and *A Farewell to Arms* (1929), established his international reputation. Hemingway supported the Loyalists in the Spanish Civil War—the subject of *For Whom the Bell Tolls* (1940)—served as a war correspondent during World War II, and from 1950 until his death lived in Cuba. His novel *The Old Man and the Sea* (1952) won a Pulitzer Prize, and Hemingway was awarded the Nobel Prize for Literature in 1954.

JAMES JOYCE (1882–1941)

In 1902, after graduating from University College, Dublin, James Joyce left Ireland for Paris, returning a year later to teach school. In October 1904, he eloped with Nora Barnacle and settled in Trieste, where he taught English for the Berlitz school. Though he lived as an expatriate for the rest of his life, all of his fiction is set in his native Dublin. Joyce had more than his share of difficulties with publication and censorship. His volume of short stories, *Dubliners*, completed in 1905, was not published until 1914. His novel *Portrait of the Artist as a Young Man*, dated "Dublin 1904, Trieste 1914," appeared first in America, in 1916. His great novel, *Ulysses* (1921), was banned for a dozen years in the United States and as long or longer elsewhere. In addition, Joyce published a play, *Exiles* (1918); two collections of poetry, *Chamber*

Music (1907) and *Pomes Penyeach* (1927); and the monumental, experimental, and puzzling novel *Finnegans Wake* (1939).

FRANZ KAFKA
(1883–1924)

Born into a middle-class Jewish family in Prague, Franz Kafka earned a doctorate in law from the German University in that city and held an inconspicuous position in the civil service for many years. Emotionally and physically ill for the last seven or eight years of his short life, he died of tuberculosis in Vienna, never having married (though he was twice engaged to the same woman and lived with an actress in Berlin for some time before he died) and not having published his three major novels, *The Trial* (1925), *The Castle* (1926), and *Amerika* (1927). Indeed, he ordered his friend Max Brod to destroy them and other works he had left in manuscript. Fortunately, Brod did not; and not long after Kafka's death, his sometimes-dreamlike, sometimes-nightmarish work was known and admired all over the world. His stories in English translation are collected in *The Great Wall of China* (1933), *The Penal Colony* (1948), and *The Complete Stories* (1976).

YASUNARI KAWA-
BATA (1899–1972)

Born in Osaka, Japan, to a prosperous family, Yasunari Kawabata graduated from Tokyo Imperial University in 1924 and had his first literary success with the semiautobiographical novella *The Izu Dancer* (1926). He cofounded the journal *Contemporary Literature* in support of the Neosensualist movement, which had much in common with the European literary movements of Dadaism, Expressionism, and Cubism. His best-known works include *Snow Country* (1937), *Thousand Cranes* (1952), *The Sound of the Mountain* (1954), *The Lake* (1955), *The Sleeping Beauty* (1960), *The Old Capital* (1962), and the collection *Palm-of-the-Hand Stories* (translated in 1988). Kawabata was

awarded the Nobel Prize for Literature in 1968. After long suffering from poor health, he committed suicide in 1972.

JAMAICA KINCAID
(b. 1949)

Born in St. John's, Antigua, Elaine Potter Richardson left her native island and her family at seventeen. Changing her name to Jamaica Kincaid, she worked in New York City as an au pair and a receptionist before studying photography at the New School for Social Research, then briefly continuing her studies at Franconia College in New Hampshire. After returning to New York, she became a regular contributor to *The New Yorker,* for which she wrote from 1976 until 1995. Her publications include a collection of short stories, *At the Bottom of the River* (1983); a book-length essay about Antigua, *A Small Place* (1988); a book for children, *Annie, Gwen, Lilly, Pam, and Tulip* (1986); the novels *Annie John* (1985), *Lucy* (1990), and *The Autobiography of My Mother* (1996); the memoir *My Brother* (1997); and a collection of her *New Yorker* pieces, *Talk Stories* (2001). Her most recent novel, *Mr. Potter* (2002), takes place on the island of Antigua.

D. H. LAWRENCE
(1885–1930)

The son of a coal miner and a schoolteacher, David Herbert Lawrence was able to attend high school only briefly. He worked for a surgical-appliance manufacturer, attended Nottingham University College, and taught school in Croydon, near London. After publishing his first novel, *The White Peacock* (1911), he devoted his time exclusively to writing; *Sons and Lovers* (1913) established him as a major literary figure. In 1912, he eloped with Frieda von Richthofen, and in 1914, after her divorce, they were married. During World War I, both his novels and his wife's German nationality gave him trouble: *The Rainbow* was published in September 1915 and suppressed in November. In 1919, the Lawrences left England and began years of wandering: first Italy, then Ceylon, Australia, Mexico, and New Mexico, then back to England and Italy. Lawrence published *Women in Love* in 1920 and *Lady Chatterley's Lover*, his most sexually explicit novel, in 1928. Through it all he suffered from tuberculosis and eventually died from the disease.

HERMAN MELVILLE
(1819–1891)

When his father died in debt, twelve-year-old Herman Melville's life of privilege became one of struggle. At eighteen, he left his native New York to teach in a backwoods Massachusetts school, then trained as a surveyor; finding no work, he became a sailor in 1839. After five years in the South Seas, he wrote *Typee* (1846) and *Omoo* (1847), sensationalized accounts of his voyages that were wildly popular. They proved the pinnacle of Melville's career in his lifetime, however; *Mardi* (1849) was judged too abstruse, the travel narratives *Redburn* (1849) and *White-Jacket* (1850), too listless. Melville's magnum opus, *Moby-Dick* (1851), was alternately shunned and condemned. His later novels—*Pierre* (1852), *Israel Potter* (1853), and *The Confidence-Man* (1856)—as well as his poetry collection *Battle-Pieces* (1866) were all but ignored. Melville's reputation as one of the giants of American literature was established only after his death; the novel *Billy Budd, Sailor* (not published until 1924), like *Moby-Dick*, was judged a masterpiece.

BHARATI MUKHERJEE
(b. 1940)

Born to wealthy parents in Calcutta, Bharati Mukherjee attended private schools in India, London, and Switzerland before studying at the University of Iowa, where she earned both an MFA in creative writing and a Ph.D. in English and Comparative Literature. At Iowa she met and married Canadian novelist Clark Blaise, with whom she has lived in Canada and the United States, and with whom she wrote *Days and Nights in Calcutta* (1977), an acclaimed account of their visit to her native India in 1972. In addition to her novels *The Tiger's Daughter* (1971), *Wife* (1975), *Jasmine* (1989), *The Holder of the World* (1993), *Leave It to Me* (1997), *Desirable Daughters* (2002), and *The Tree Bride* (2004), Mukherjee has published the short-story collections *Darkness* (1985) and *The Middleman* (1988). She teaches at the University of California at Berkeley.

FLANNERY O'CONNOR
(1925–1964)

Mary Flannery O'Connor was born in Savannah, Georgia, studied at the Georgia State College for Women, and won a fellowship to the Writer's Workshop of the University of Iowa, from which she received her MFA. In 1950, she was first diagnosed with lupus, a painful autoimmune disorder that had killed her father and would trouble her for the rest of her brief life. Her first novel, *Wise Blood*, was published in 1952, and her first collection of stories, *A Good Man Is Hard to Find*, in 1955. She was able to complete only one more novel, *The Violent Bear It Away* (1960), and a second collection of stories, *Everything That Rises Must Converge* (1965), before dying of lupus, in Milledgeville, Georgia. Her posthumously published *Complete Stories* won the National Book Award in 1972. A collection of letters, edited by Sally Fitzgerald under the title *The Habit of Being*, appeared in 1979.

GRACE PALEY
(b. 1922)

Born to Russian immigrants in the Bronx, New York, Grace Paley attended Hunter College and New York University but never finished college because she was too busy reading and writing poetry before she turned to fiction. Her short stories, first published in *The Little Disturbances of Man: Stories of Men and Women at Love* (1959), *Enormous Changes at the Last Minute* (1974), and *Later the Same Day* (1985), are assembled in *The Collected Stories* (1994); her poetry, in *Begin Again: Collected Poems* (2000); and her essays, reviews, and lectures, in *Just as I Thought* (1998). In 1987, she was awarded a Senior Fellowship by the National Endowment for the Arts, in recognition of her lifetime contribution to literature. In 1988, she was named the first New York State Author. Always politically engaged, she was an outspoken critic of the Vietnam War and has been a lifelong anti-nuclear activist and an outspoken feminist.

EDGAR ALLAN POE
(1809–1849)

Orphaned before he was three, Edgar Poe was adopted by John Allan, a wealthy Richmond businessman. Poe received his early schooling in Richmond and in England before a brief, unsuccessful stint at the University of Virginia. After serving for two years in the army, he was appointed to West Point in 1830 but was expelled within the year for cutting classes. Living in Baltimore with his grandmother, aunt, and cousin Virginia (whom he married in 1835, when she was thirteen), Poe eked out a precarious living as an editor; his keen-edged reviews earned him numerous literary enemies. His two-volume *Tales of the Grotesque and Arabesque* received little critical attention when published in 1839, but his poem "The Raven" (1845) made him a literary celebrity. After his wife's death of tuberculosis in 1847, Poe, already an alcoholic, became increasingly erratic and two years later he died mysteriously in Baltimore. His poems and stories have been collected in many editions.

KATHERINE ANNE
PORTER (1890–
1980)

A native of Indian Creek, Texas, and a descendant of Daniel Boone, Katherine Anne Porter was raised by her grandmother and educated in convent schools. Forced by tuberculosis to abandon an acting career, she worked as a journalist in Denver, Chicago, and Mexico. She published her first short story in 1922; her first collection *Flowering Judas* (1930), won critical acclaim. Porter's only full-length novel, *Ship of Fools* (1962), established her as a major American writer and made her rich. She won numerous awards for her work, including both a Pulitzer Prize and a National Book Award for her *Collected Short Stories* (1965) and a Gold Medal from the National Institute of Arts and Letters. Among her works are the story collections *Pale Horse, Pale Rider* (1939) and *The Leaning Tower and Other Stories* (1944); a volume of essays, *The Days Before* (1952); and an account of the controversial Sacco and Vanzetti murder trial, *The Never-Ending Wrong* (1977).

AMY TAN (b. 1952)

Amy Tan was born in Oakland, California, just two and a half years after her parents immigrated from China. She received her M.A. in linguistics from San Jose State University and has worked on programs for disabled children and as a freelance writer. In 1987, she visited China for the first time—"As soon as my feet touched China, I became Chinese"—and returned to write her first book, *The Joy Luck Club* (1989). Tan has since published three more novels—*The Kitchen God's Wife* (1991), *The Hundred Secret Senses* (1995), and *The Bonesetter's Daughter* (2000)—and has co-authored two children's books. Her first book of nonfiction, *The Opposite of Fate: A Book of Musings* (2003), explores lucky accidents, choice, and memory. Tan is also the lead singer for the Rock Bottom Remainders, a rock band made up of fellow writers, including Stephen King and Dave Barry; they make appearances at benefits that support literacy programs for children.

EUDORA WELTY
(1909–2001)

Known as the "First Lady of Southern Literature," Eudora Welty was born and raised in Jackson, Mississippi, attended Mississippi State College for Women, and earned a B.A. from the University of Wisconsin. Among the countless awards she received were two Guggenheim Fellowships, six O. Henry Awards, a Pulitzer Prize, the French Legion of Honor, the National Medal for Literature, and the Presidential Medal of Freedom. Although she wrote five novels, including *The Robber Bridegroom* (1942), *Ponder Heart* (1954), and *The Optimist's Daughter* (1972), she is best known for her short stories, many of which have been published in *The Collected Stories of Eudora Welty* (1980). Among her nonfiction works are *One Writer's Beginnings* (1984), *A Writer's Eye: Collected Book Reviews* (1994), and five collections of her photographs, including *One Place, One Time* (1978) and *Photographs* (1989). In 1998 the Library of America published a two-volume edition of her selected works, making her the first living author they had published.

WILLIAM CARLOS WILLIAMS (1883–1963)

Born in Rutherford, New Jersey, William Carlos Williams attended school in Switzerland and New York and studied medicine at the University of Pennsylvania and the University of Leipzig in Germany. He spent most of his life in Rutherford, practicing medicine and gradually establishing himself as one of the great figures in American poetry. Early in his writing career he left the European-inspired Imagist movement in favor of a more uniquely American poetic style comprised of vital, local language and "no ideas but in things." His shorter poems have been published in numerous collected editions and other volumes, including the Pulitzer Prize–winning *Brueghel, and Other Poems* (1963); his five-volume philosophical poem, *Paterson*, was published in 1963. Among his other works are plays such as *A Dream of Love* (1948) and *Many Loves* (1950); a trilogy of novels: *White Mules* (1937), *In the Money* (1940), and *The Build-Up* (1952); his *Autobiography* (1951); his *Selected Essays* (1954); and his *Selected Letters* (1957).

POETRY

Poetry

Poetry: Reading, Responding, Writing

If you're a reader of poetry, you already know: poetry reading is not just an intellectual and bookish activity; it is about feeling. Reading poetry well means responding to it: if you respond on a feeling level, you are likely to read more accurately, with deeper understanding, and with greater pleasure. And, conversely, if you read poetry accurately, and with attention to detail, you will almost certainly respond to it—or learn how to respond—on an emotional level. Reading poetry involves conscious articulation through language, and reading and responding come to be, for experienced readers of poetry, very nearly one. But those who teach poetry—and there are a lot of us, almost all enthusiasts about both poetry as a subject and reading as a craft—have discovered something else: writing about poetry helps both the reading and the responding processes. Responding involves remembering and reflecting as well. As you recall your own past and make associations between things in the text and things you already know and feel, you will not only respond more fully to a particular poem, but improve your reading skills more generally. Your knowledge and life experience inform your reading of what is before you and allow you to connect elements within the text—events, images, words, sounds—so that meanings and feelings develop and accumulate. Prior learning creates expectations: of pattern, repetition, association, or causality. Reflecting on the text—and on expectations produced by themes and ideas in the text—re-creates old feelings but directs them in new, often unusual ways. Poems, even when they are about things we have no experience of, connect to things we do know and order our memories, thoughts, and feelings in new and newly challenging ways.

> *Poetry is a way of taking life by the throat.*
> —ROBERT FROST

A course in reading poetry can ultimately enrich your life by helping you become more articulate and more sensitive to both ideas and feelings: that's the larger goal. But the more immediate goal—and the route to the larger one—is to make you a better reader of texts and a more precise and careful writer yourself. Close attention to one text makes you appreciate, and understand, textuality and its possibilities more generally. Texts may be complex and even unstable in some ways; they do not affect all readers the same way, and they work through language that has its own volatilities and complexities. But paying attention to how you read—developing specific questions to ask and working on your reading skills systematically—can take a lot of the guess-work out of reading texts and give you a sense of greater satisfaction in your interpretations.

READING

Poems, perhaps even more than other texts, can sharpen your reading skills because they tend to be so compact, so fully dependent on concise expressions of feeling. In poems, ideas and feelings are packed tightly into just a few lines. The experiences of life are very concentrated here, and meanings emerge quickly, word by word. Poems often show us the very process of putting feelings into a language that can be shared with others—to *say* feelings in a communicable way. Poetry can be intellectual too, explaining and exploring ideas, but its focus is more often on how people feel than how they think. Poems work out a shareable language for feeling, and one of poetry's most insistent virtues arises from its attempt to express the inexpressible. How can anyone, for example, put into words what it means to be in love or how it feels to lose someone one cares about? Poetry tries, and it often captures a shade of emotion that feels just right to a reader. No single poem can be said to represent all the things that love or death feels like or means, but one of the joys of experiencing poetry occurs when we read a poem and want to say, "Yes, that is just what it is like; I know exactly what that line means but I've never been able to express it so well." Poetry can be the voice of our feelings even when our minds are speechless with grief or joy. Reading is no substitute for living, but it can make living more abundant and more available.

Here are two poems that talk about the sincerity and depth of love between two people. Each is written as if it were spoken by one person to his or her lover, and each is definite and powerful about the intensity and quality of love; but the poems work in quite different ways—the first one asserting the strength and depth of love, the second implying intense feeling by reminiscing about earlier events in the relationship between the two people.

ELIZABETH BARRETT BROWNING

How Do I Love Thee?

How do I love thee? Let me count the ways.
I love thee to the depth and breadth and height
My soul can reach, when feeling out of sight
For the ends of Being and ideal Grace.
5 I love thee to the level of every day's
Most quiet need, by sun and candlelight.
I love thee freely, as men strive for Right;
I love thee purely, as they turn from Praise;
I love thee with the passion put to use
10 In my old griefs, and with my childhood's faith.
I love thee with a love I seemed to lose

With my lost saints—I love thee with the breath,
Smiles, tears of all my life!—and, if God choose,
I shall but love thee better after death.

1850

JAROLD RAMSEY

The Tally Stick

Here from the start, from our first of days, look:
I have carved our lives in secret on this stick
of mountain mahogany the length of your arms
outstretched, the wood clear red, so hard and rare.
5 It is time to touch and handle what we know we share.

Near the butt, this intricate notch where the grains
converge and join: it is our wedding.
I can read it through with a thumb and tell you now
who danced, who made up the songs, who meant us joy.
10 These little arrowheads along the grain,
they are the births of our children. See,
they make a kind of design with these heavy crosses,
the deaths of our parents, the loss of friends.

Over it all as it goes, of course, I
15 have chiseled Events, History—random
hashmarks cut against the swirling grain.
See, here is the Year the World Went Wrong,
we thought, and here the days the Great Men fell.
The lengthening runes of our lives run through it all.

20 See, our tally stick is whittled nearly end to end;
delicate as scrimshaw, it would not bear you up.
Regrets have polished it, hand over hand.
Yet let us take it up, and as our fingers
like children leading on a trail cry back
25 our unforgotten wonders, sign after sign,
we will talk softly as of ordinary matters,
and in one another's blameless eyes go blind.

1977

"How Do I Love Thee?" is direct but fairly abstract. It lists several ways in which the poet feels love and connects them to some noble ideas of higher obligations—to justice (line 7), for example, and to spiritual aspiration (lines 2–4). It suggests a wide range of things that love can mean and notices a variety of emotions. It is an ardent statement of feeling and asserts a permanence that will extend even beyond death. It contains admirable thoughts and memorable phrases that many lovers would like to hear said to themselves. What it does not do is say very much about what the relationship between the two lovers is like on an everyday basis, what experiences they have had together, what distinguishes their relationship from that of other devoted or ideal lovers. Its appeal is to our general sense of what love is like and of how intense feelings can be; it does not offer details.

"The Tally Stick" is much more concrete. The whole poem concentrates on a single object that, like "How Do I Love Thee?," "counts" or "tallies" the ways in which this couple love one another. This stick stands for their love and becomes a kind of physical totem for it: its natural features (lines 6, 10, and 12) and the marks carved on it (lines 15–16, 20–21) indicate events in the story of the relationship. We could say that the stick *symbolizes* their love—later on, we will look at terms like this that make it easier to talk about poems—but for now it is enough to notice that the stick serves the lovers as a marker and a reminder of some specific details of their love. It is a special kind of reminder because its language is "secret" (line 2), something they can share privately (except that we as readers of the poem are looking over their shoulders, not intruding but sharing their secret). The poet interprets the particular features of the stick as standing for particular events—their wedding and the births of their children, for example—and carves marks into it as reminders of other events (lines 15 ff.). The stick itself becomes a very personal object, and in the last stanza of the poem it is as if we watch the lovers touching the stick together and reminiscing over it, gradually dissolving into their emotions and each other as they recall the "unforgotten wonders" (line 25) of their lives together.

Both poems are powerful statements of feelings, each in its own way. Various readers will respond differently to each poem; the effect these poems have on their readers will lead some to prefer one and some the other. Personal preference does not mean that objective standards for poetry cannot be found—some poems *are* better than others, and later we will look in detail at features that help us to evaluate poems—but we need no preconceived standards as to what poetry must be or how it must work. Some good poems are quite abstract, others quite specific. Any poem that helps us to articulate and clarify human feelings and ideas has a legitimate claim on us as readers.

Both "How Do I Love Thee?" and "The Tally Stick" are written as if they were addressed to the partner in the love relationship, and both talk directly about the intensity of the love. The next poem talks only indirectly about the quality and intensity of love. It is written as if it were a letter from a woman to her husband, who has gone on a long journey on business. It directly expresses how much she misses him and indirectly suggests how much she cares about him.

EZRA POUND

The River-Merchant's Wife: A Letter

(after Rihaku)[1]

While my hair was still cut straight across my forehead
I played about the front gate, pulling flowers.
You came by on bamboo stilts, playing horse,
You walked about my seat, playing with blue plums.
5 And we went on living in the village of Chokan:
Two small people, without dislike or suspicion.

At fourteen I married My Lord you.
I never laughed, being bashful.
Lowering my head, I looked at the wall.
10 Called to, a thousand times, I never looked back.

At fifteen I stopped scowling,
I desired my dust to be mingled with yours
For ever and for ever and for ever.
Why should I climb the look out?

15 At sixteen you departed,
You went into far Ku-to-yen, by the river of swirling eddies,
And you have been gone five months.
The monkeys make sorrowful noise overhead.

You dragged your feet when you went out.
20 By the gate now, the moss is grown, the different mosses,
Too deep to clear them away!
The leaves fall early this autumn, in wind.
The paired butterflies are already yellow with August
Over the grass in the West garden;
25 They hurt me. I grow older.
If you are coming down through the narrows of the river Kiang,
Please let me know beforehand,
And I will come out to meet you
As far as Cho-fu-Sa.

1915

    The "letter" tells us only a few facts about the nameless merchant's wife: that she is about sixteen and a half years old, that she married at fourteen and fell in love with her husband a year later, that she is now very lonely. About their relationship we know only that they were childhood playmates

---

1. The Japanese name for Li Po, an eighth-century Chinese poet. Pound's poem is a loose paraphrase of one by Li Po.

in a small Chinese village, that their marriage originally was not a matter of personal choice, and that the husband unwillingly went away on a long journey five months ago. But the words tell us a great deal about how the young wife feels, and the simplicity of her language suggests her sincere and deep longing. The daily noises she hears seem "sorrowful" (line 18), and she worries about the dangers of the faraway place where her husband is, thinking of it in terms of its perilous "river of swirling eddies" (line 16). She thinks of how moss has grown up over the unused gate, and more time seems to her to have passed than actually has (lines 22–25). Nostalgically she remembers their innocent childhood, when they played together without deeper love or commitment (lines 1–6), and contrasts that with her later satisfaction in their love (lines 11–14) and with her present anxiety, loneliness, and desire. We do not need to know the geography of the river Kiang or how far Cho-fu-Sa is to sense that her wish to see him is very strong, that her desire is powerful enough to make her venture beyond the ordinary geographical bounds of her existence so that their reunion will happen sooner. The closest she comes to a direct statement about her love is "I desired my dust to be mingled with yours / For ever and for ever and for ever" (lines 12–13). But her single-minded vision of the world, her perception of even the beauty of nature as only a record of her husband's absence and the passage of time, and her plain, apparently uncalculated language about her rejection of other suitors and her shutting out of the rest of the world all show her to be committed, desirous, nearly desperate for his presence. In a different sense, she too has counted the ways that she loves her man.

RESPONDING

The poems we have looked at so far all describe, though in different ways, feelings associated with loving or being attached to someone and the expression—either physical or verbal—of those feelings. Watching how poems discover a language for feeling can help us to discover a language for our own feelings, but the process is also reciprocal: being conscious of feelings we already have can lead us into poems more surely and with more satisfaction.

> *If I feel physically as if the top of my head were taken off, I know that is poetry.*
> —EMILY DICKINSON

Poems can be about all kinds of experiences, and not all the things we find in them will replicate (or even relate to) experiences we may have had individually. But sharing through language will often enable us to uncover feelings—of love or anger, fear or confidence—we did not know we had. The next few poems involve another, far less pleasant set of feelings than those usually generated by love, but even here, where our experience may be limited, we are able to respond, to feel the tug of emotions within us that we may not be fully aware of. In the following poem, a father struggles to understand and control his grief over the death of a seven-year-old son. We don't have to be a father or to have lost a loved one to be aware of—and even share—the speaker's pain, because our own experiences will have given us some idea of what such a loss would feel like. And the words and strategies of the poem may arouse expectations created by our previous experiences.

BEN JONSON

On My First Son

Farewell, thou child of my right hand,[1] and joy;
My sin was too much hope of thee, loved boy:
Seven years thou wert lent to me, and I thee pay,
Exacted by thy fate, on the just[2] day.
5 O could I lose all father now! for why
Will man lament the state he should envý,
To have so soon 'scaped world's and flesh's rage,
And, if no other misery, yet age?
Rest in soft peace, and asked, say, "Here doth lie
10 Ben Jonson his[3] best piece of poetry."
For whose sake henceforth all his vows be such
As what he loves may never like too much.

1616

This poem's attempts to rationalize the boy's death are quite conventional. Although the father tries to be comforted by pious thoughts, his feelings keep showing through. The poem's beginning—with its formal "farewell" and the rather distant-sounding address to the dead boy ("child of my right hand")—cannot be sustained for long: both of the first two lines end with bursts of emotion. It is as if the father is trying to explain the death to himself and to keep his emotions under control, but cannot quite manage it. Even the punctuation suggests the way his feelings compete with conventional attempts to put the death into some sort of perspective that will soften the grief, and the comma near the end of each of the first two lines marks a pause that cannot quite hold back the overflowing emotion. But finally the only "idea" that the poem supports is that the father wishes he did not feel so intensely; in the fifth line he fairly blurts that he wishes he could lose his fatherly emotions, and in the final lines he resolves never again to "like" so much that he can be this deeply hurt. Philosophy and religion offer their useful counsels in this poem, but they prove far less powerful than feeling. Rather than drawing some kind of moral about what death means, the poem presents the actuality of feeling as inevitable and nearly all-consuming.

The poem that follows also tries to suppress the rawness of feelings about

1. A literal translation of the son's name, Benjamin.
2. Exact; the son died on his seventh birthday, in 1603.
3. That is, Ben Jonson's (this was a common Renaissance form of the possessive).

the death of a loved one, but here the survivor is haunted by memories of his wife when he sees a physical object—a vacuum cleaner—that he associates with her.

HOWARD NEMEROV

The Vacuum

The house is so quiet now
The vacuum cleaner sulks in the corner closet,
Its bag limp as a stopped lung, its mouth
Grinning into the floor, maybe at my
5 Slovenly life, my dog-dead youth.

I've lived this way long enough,
But when my old woman died her soul
Went into that vacuum cleaner, and I can't bear
To see the bag swell like a belly, eating the dust
10 And the woolen mice, and begin to howl

Because there is old filth everywhere
She used to crawl, in the corner and under the stair.
I know now how life is cheap as dirt,
And still the hungry, angry heart
15 Hangs on and howls, biting at air.

1955

The poem is about a vacuum in the husband's life, but the title refers most obviously to the vacuum cleaner that, like the tally stick we looked at earlier, seems to stand for many of the things that were once important in the life he had together with his wife. The cleaner is a reminder of the dead wife ("my old woman," line 7) because of her devotion to cleanliness. But to the surviving husband buried in the filth of his life it seems as if the machine has become almost human, a kind of ghost of her: it "sulks" (line 2), it has lungs and a mouth (line 3), and it seems to grin, making fun of what has become of him. He "can't bear" (line 8) to see it in action because it then seems too much alive, too much a reminder of her life. The poem records his paralysis, his inability to do more than discover that life is "cheap as dirt" without her ordering and cleansing presence for him. At the end it is *his* angry heart that acts like the haunting machine, howling and biting at air as if he has merged with her spirit and the physical object that memorializes her. This poem puts a strong emphasis on the stillness of death and the way it makes things seem to stop; it captures in words the hurt, the anger, the inability to understand, the vacuum that remains when a loved one dies and leaves a vacant space. But here we do not see the body or hear a direct good-bye to the dead person; rather we encounter the feeling that lingers and won't go away, recalled through memory by an especially significant object, a mere thing but one that has been personalized to the point of becoming nearly human in itself. (The event described here is, by the way, fictional; the poet's wife did not actually die. Like a dramatist or writer of fiction, the poet may simply *imagine* an event in order to analyze and articulate how such an event might feel in certain circumstances. A work of literature can be *true* without being *actual*.)

Here is another poem about a death:

SEAMUS HEANEY

Mid-Term Break

I sat all morning in the college sick bay
Counting bells knelling classes to a close.
At two o'clock our neighbors drove me home.

In the porch I met my father crying—
5　He had always taken funerals in his stride—
And Big Jim Evans saying it was a hard blow.

The baby cooed and laughed and rocked the pram
When I came in, and I was embarrassed
By old men standing up to shake my hand

10　And tell me they were "sorry for my trouble,"
Whispers informed strangers I was the eldest,
Away at school, as my mother held my hand

In hers and coughed out angry tearless sighs.
At ten o'clock the ambulance arrived
15　With the corpse, stanched and bandaged by the nurses.

Next morning I went up into the room. Snowdrops
And candles soothed the bedside; I saw him
For the first time in six weeks. Paler now,

Wearing a poppy bruise on his left temple,
20　He lay in the four foot box as in his cot.
No gaudy scars, the bumper knocked him clear.

A four foot box, a foot for every year.

1966

If, in "The Vacuum," the grief is displaced onto an object left behind, here grief seems almost wordless. The speaker of the poem, the older brother of the dead four-year-old, cannot really articulate his grief and instead provides a lot of meticulous detail, as if giving us information can substitute for an expression of feeling. He is "embarrassed" (line 8) by the attempts of others to say how they feel and to empathize with him. He records the feelings of other family members in detail, but never fully expresses his own feelings, as if he has taken on a kind of deadness of his own that eludes, and substitutes for, articulation. Only when he confronts the bruised body itself can he begin to come to terms with the loss, and even there he resorts to a kind of mathematical formula to displace the feeling so that he doesn't have to talk about it. Though the feelings in the poem are extremely powerful, the power is expressed (as in the Jonson poem above) by suppression. It is not restraint that holds back the young man's grief, but a silence that cannot be put into any words except those of enumerated facts.

Sometimes poems are a way of confronting feelings. Sometimes they explore feelings in detail and try to intellectualize or rationalize them. At other times, poems generate responses by recalling experiences many years in the past. In the following poem, for example, a childhood memory takes an adult almost physically back into childhood. As you read the poem, keep track of (or perhaps even jot down) your responses. How much of your feeling is due to your own past experiences? In which specific places? Which feelings expressed in the poem are similar to your own? Where do your feelings differ most strongly? How would you articulate your responses to such memories differently? In what ways does an awareness of your similar—and different—experiences and feelings make you a better reader of the poem?

ANNE SEXTON

WEB *The Fury of Overshoes*

They sit in a row
outside the kindergarten,
black, red, brown, all
with those brass buckles.
5 Remember when you couldn't
buckle your own
overshoe
or tie your own
shoe
10 or cut your own meat
and the tears
running down like mud
because you fell off your
tricycle?
15 Remember, big fish,
when you couldn't swim
and simply slipped under
like a stone frog?
The world wasn't
20 yours.

It belonged to
the big people.
Under your bed
sat the wolf
25   and he made a shadow
when cars passed by
at night.
They made you give up
your nightlight
30   and your teddy
and your thumb.
Oh overshoes,
don't you
remember me,
35   pushing you up and down
in the winter snow?
Oh thumb,
I want a drink,
it is dark,
40   where are the big people,
when will I get there,
taking giant steps
all day,
each day
45   and thinking
nothing of it?

                    1974

There is much more going on in the poems we have glanced far at than
we have taken time to consider, but even the quickest look at these poems
suggests the range of feelings that poems offer—the depth of feeling, the
clarity, the experience that may be articulately and precisely shared. Not all
poems are as accessible as those we've looked at so far, and even the accessible ones yield themselves to us more readily and more fully if we approach
them systematically by developing specific reading habits and skills—just as
someone learning to play tennis or to make pottery systematically learns the
rules, the techniques, the things to watch out for that are distinctive to the
pleasures and hazards of that skill or craft. It helps if you develop a sense
of what to expect, and the chapters that follow will show you the things that
poets can do—and thus what poems can do for you.

But knowing what to expect isn't everything. As a reader of poetry, you
should always be open—to new experiences, new feelings, new ideas. Every
poem is a potential new experience, and no matter how sophisticated you
become, you can still be surprised (and delighted) by new poems—and by
rereading old ones. Good poems bear many, many rereadings, and often one
discovers something new with every new reading: there is no such thing as
"mastering" a poem, and good poems are not exhausted by repeated read-

ings. Let poems surprise you when you come to them, let them come on their own terms, let them be themselves. If you are open to poetry, you are also open to much more that the world can offer you.

No one can give you a method that will offer you total experience of all poems. But because individual poems often share characteristics with other poems, the following guidelines can prompt you to ask the right questions:

1. *Read the syntax literally.* What the words say literally in normal sentences is only a starting point, but it is the place to start. Not all poems use normal prose syntax, but most of them do, and you can save yourself embarrassment by paraphrasing accurately (that is, rephrasing what the poem literally says, in plain prose) and not simply free-associating from an isolated word or phrase.

2. *Articulate for yourself what the title, subject, and situation make you expect.* Poets often use false leads and try to surprise you by doing shocking things, but defining expectation lets you become conscious of where you are when you begin.

3. *Identify the poem's situation.* What is said is often conditioned by where it is said and by whom. Identifying the speaker and his or her place in the situation puts what he or she says in perspective.

4. *Find out what is implied by the traditions behind the poem.* Verse forms, poetic kinds, and metrical patterns all have a frame of reference, traditions of the way they are usually used and for what. For example, the **anapest** (two unstressed syllables followed by a stressed one, as in the word *Tennessee*) is usually used for comic poems, and when poets use it "straight" they are probably making a point with this "departure" from tradition.

5. *Use your dictionary, other reference books, and reliable Web sites.* Look up anything you don't understand: an unfamiliar word (or an ordinary word used in an unfamiliar way), a place, a person, a myth, an idea—anything the poem uses. When you can't find what you need or don't know where to look, ask the reference librarian for help.

6. *Remember that poems exist in time, and times change.* Not only the meanings of words, but whole ways of looking at the universe vary in different ages. Consciousness of time works two ways: your knowledge of history provides a context for reading the poem, and the poem's use of a word or idea may modify your notion of a particular age.

7. *Take a poem on its own terms.* Adjust to the poem; don't make the poem adjust to you. Be prepared to hear things you do not want to hear. Not all poems are about your ideas, nor will they always present emotions you want to feel. But be tolerant and listen to the poem's ideas, not only to your wish to revise them for yourself.

8. *Be willing to be surprised.* Things often happen in poems that turn them around. A poem may seem to suggest one thing at first, then persuade you of its opposite, or at least of a significant qualification or variation.

9. *Assume there is a reason for everything.* Poets do make mistakes, but when a poem shows some degree of verbal control it is usually safest to assume that the poet chose each word carefully; if the choice seems peculiar, you

may be missing something. Try to account for everything in a poem, see what kind of sense you can make of it, and figure out a coherent **pattern** that explains the text as it stands.

10. *Argue.* Discussion usually results in clarification and keeps you from being too dependent on personal biases and preoccupations that sometimes mislead even the best readers. Talking a poem over with someone else (especially someone who thinks very differently) can expand your perspective.

WRITING ABOUT POEMS

If you have been keeping notes on your personal responses to the poems you've read, you have already taken an important step toward writing about them. There are many different ways to write about poems, just as there are many different things to say. (The section of the anthology called "Writing about Literature" suggests some ways to come up with a good topic.) But all writing begins with a clear sense of the poem itself and your responses to it, so the first steps (long before formally sitting down to write) are to read the poem several times and keep notes on the things that strike you and the questions that remain.

Formulating a clear series of questions will usually suggest an appropriate approach to the poem and a good topic. Learning to ask the right questions can save you a lot of time. Some questions—the kinds of questions implied in the ten guidelines for reading listed above—are basic and apply, more or less, to all poems. But each poem makes demands of its own, too, because of its distinctive way of going about its business, so you will usually want to list what seem to you the crucial questions for that poem. Here, just to give you an example, are some questions that could lead you to a paper topic about the Aphra Behn poem on p. 412.

1. How does the **title** affect your reading of and response to the poem?
2. What is the poem about?
3. What makes the poem interesting?
4. Who is the **speaker**? What role does the speaker have?
5. What effect does the poem have on you? Do you think the poet intended such an effect?
6. What is distinctive about the poet's use of language? Which words especially contribute to the poem's effect?

What *is* poetry? Let your definition be cumulative as you read more and more poems. No dictionary definition will cover all that you find, and it is better to discover for yourself poetry's many ingredients, its many effects, its many ways of acting. What can it do for you? Wait and see. Add up its effects after you have read carefully—after you have reread and studied—a hundred or so poems; then continue to read new poems or reread old ones.

PRACTICING READING: SOME POEMS ON LOVE

W. H. AUDEN

[*Stop all the clocks, cut off the telephone*]

Stop all the clocks, cut off the telephone,
Prevent the dog from barking with a juicy bone,
Silence the pianos and with muffled drum
Bring out the coffin, let the mourners come.

5 Let aeroplanes circle moaning overhead
Scribbling on the sky the message He Is Dead,
Put crêpe bows round the white necks of the public doves,
Let the traffic policemen wear black cotton gloves.

He was my North, my South, my East and West,
10 My working week and my Sunday rest,
My noon, my midnight, my talk, my song;
I thought that love would last for ever: I was wrong.

The stars are not wanted now: put out every one;
Pack up the moon and dismantle the sun;
15 Pour away the ocean and sweep up the wood;
For nothing now can ever come to any good.

ca. 1936

- Whom does the speaker of this poem seem to be addressing?
  Why might the poet have proclaimed his grief with such a
  public declaration as this poem?

ANNE BRADSTREET

WEB ## To My Dear and Loving Husband

If ever two were one, then surely we.
If ever man were loved by wife, then thee;
If ever wife was happy in a man,
Compare with me ye women if you can.
5 I prize thy love more than whole mines of gold,
Or all the riches that the East doth hold.
My love is such that rivers cannot quench,
Nor aught but love from thee give recompense.
Thy love is such I can no way repay;

10 The heavens reward thee manifold, I pray.
Then while we live, in love let's so persever,
That when we live no more we may live ever.

1678

- How does Bradstreet's strategy of characterizing her love through a series of comparisons compare with Barrett Browning's strategy in "How Do I Love Thee?"

WILLIAM SHAKESPEARE

[*Let me not to the marriage of true minds*]

Let me not to the marriage of true minds
Admit impediments.[1] Love is not love
Which alters when it alteration finds,
Or bends with the remover to remove:
5 Oh, no! it is an ever-fixéd mark,
That looks on tempests and is never shaken;
It is the star to every wandering bark,
Whose worth's unknown, although his height be taken.[2]
Love's not Time's fool, though rosy lips and cheeks
10 Within his bending sickle's compass come;
Love alters not with his brief hours and weeks,
But bears it out even to the edge of doom.
If this be error and upon me proved,
I never writ, nor no man ever loved.

1609

- What might the speaker mean when he says that love doesn't "ben[d] with the remover to remove"?

APHRA BEHN

On Her Loving Two Equally

I

How strongly does my passion flow,
Divided equally twixt[3] two?
Damon had ne'er subdued my heart

---

1. The Marriage Service contains this address to the witnesses: "If any of you know cause or just impediments why these persons should not be joined together. . . ."
2. That is, measuring the altitude of stars (for purposes of navigation) is not a way to measure value. 3. Between.

Had not Alexis took his part;
5 Nor could Alexis powerful prove,
Without my Damon's aid, to gain my love.

II

When my Alexis present is,
Then I for Damon sigh and mourn;
But when Alexis I do miss,
10 Damon gains nothing but my scorn.
But if it chance they both are by,
For both alike I languish, sigh, and die.

III

Cure then, thou mighty wingéd god,[4]
This restless fever in my blood;
15 One golden-pointed dart take back:
But which, O Cupid, wilt thou take?
If Damon's, all my hopes are crossed;
Or that of my Alexis, I am lost.

1684

• What is this poem saying about the nature of love if the speaker's passions are stronger when "divided"?

MARY, LADY CHUDLEIGH

To the Ladies

Wife and servant are the same,
But only differ in the name:
For when that fatal knot is tied,
Which nothing, nothing can divide,
5 When she the word *Obey* has said,
And man by law supreme has made,
Then all that's kind is laid aside,
And nothing left but state[5] and pride.
Fierce as an eastern prince he grows,
10 And all his innate rigor shows:
Then but to look, to laugh, or speak,
Will the nuptial contract break.
Like mutes, she signs alone must make,
And never any freedom take,
15 But still be governed by a nod,

4. Cupid, who, according to myth, shot darts of lead and of gold at the hearts of lovers, corresponding to false love and true love, respectively. 5. Social position.

And fear her husband as her god:
Him still must serve, him still obey,
And nothing act, and nothing say,
But what her haughty lord thinks fit,
20 Who, with the power, has all the wit.
Then shun, oh! shun that wretched state,
And all the fawning flatterers hate.
Value yourselves, and men despise:
You must be proud, if you'll be wise.

                                                    1703

- Who do you think is the intended audience for this poem? If
  the speaker overstates her case to some degree, why might she
  do so?

W. B. YEATS

A Last Confession

What lively lad most pleasured me
Of all that with me lay?
I answer that I gave my soul
And loved in misery,
5 But had great pleasure with a lad
That I loved bodily.

Flinging from his arms I laughed
To think his passion such
He fancied that I gave a soul
10 Did but our bodies touch,
And laughed upon his breast to think
Beast gave beast as much.

I gave what other women gave
That stepped out of their clothes,
15 But when this soul, its body off,
Naked to naked goes,
He it has found shall find therein
What none other knows,

And give his own and take his own
20 And rule in his own right;
And though it loved in misery
Close and cling so tight,
There's not a bird of day that dare
Extinguish that delight.

                                                    1933

- What distinction is the speaker making between physical and spiritual love? Why would this poem be someone's "last confession"?

SUGGESTIONS FOR WRITING

1. Of all the love poems in this chapter, which one would you most like to have addressed to you? which least? Write an essay in which you answer the author of either poem you have chosen, explaining what seemed to you most (or least) complimentary in what the poem said about you.

2. Paraphrase—that is, put into different words line by line and stanza by stanza— Behn's "On Her Loving Two Equally" or Yeats's "A Last Confession." Summarize the poem's basic statement in one sentence. How accurately do your paraphrase and summary represent the feelings recorded in the poem? Write an essay in which you discuss the differences between poetry and paraphrases of poetry.

3. Consider your responses to the marriage poems in this chapter. Which one most accurately expresses your ideal of a good marriage? Why do you think so? What does your choice say about you? Write an essay in which you reflect upon how these poems reinforce, refine, or perhaps even challenge your views of marriage.

Understanding the Text

8   TONE

Poetry is full of surprises. Poems express anger or outrage just as effectively as love or sadness, and good poems can be written about going to a rock concert or having lunch or mowing the lawn, as well as about making love or smelling flowers or listening to Beethoven. Even poems on "predictable" subjects can surprise us with unpredicted attitudes, unusual events, or sudden twists. Knowing that a poem is about some particular subject—love, for example, or death—may give us a general idea of what to expect, but it never tells us altogether what we will find in a particular poem. Responding to a poem fully means being open to the poem and its surprises, letting the poem guide us to its own stances, feelings, and ideas—to an illumination of a topic that may be very different from what we expect or what we have thought before. Letting a poem speak to us means listening to *how* the poem says what it says—hearing the tone of voice implied in the way the words are spoken. *What* a poem says involves its **theme,** a statement about its subject. *How* a poem makes that statement involves its **tone,** the poem's attitude or feelings toward the theme.

The following two poems—one about death and one about love—express attitudes and feelings quite different from those in the poems we have read so far.

MARGE PIERCY
WEB   *Barbie Doll*

This girlchild was born as usual
and presented dolls that did pee-pee
and miniature GE stoves and irons
and wee lipsticks the color of cherry candy.
5 Then in the magic of puberty, a classmate said:
You have a great big nose and fat legs.

She was healthy, tested intelligent,
possessed strong arms and back,
abundant sexual drive and manual dexterity.
10 She went to and fro apologizing.
Everyone saw a fat nose on thick legs.

She was advised to play coy,
exhorted to come on hearty,
exercise, diet, smile and wheedle.
15 Her good nature wore out
like a fan belt.
So she cut off her nose and her legs
and offered them up.

In the casket displayed on satin she lay
20 with the undertaker's cosmetics painted on,
a turned-up putty nose,
dressed in a pink and white nightie.
Doesn't she look pretty? everyone said.
Consummation at last.
25 To every woman a happy ending.

1973

W. D. SNODGRASS

Leaving the Motel

Outside, the last kids holler
Near the pool: they'll stay the night.
Pick up the towels; fold your collar
Out of sight.

5 Check: is the second bed
Unrumpled, as agreed?
Landlords have to think ahead
In case of need,

Too. Keep things straight: don't take
10 The matches, the wrong keyrings—
We've nowhere we could keep a keepsake—
Ashtrays, combs, things

That sooner or later others
Would accidentally find.
15 Check: take nothing of one another's
And leave behind

Your license number only,
Which they won't care to trace;
We've paid. Still, should such things get lonely,
20 Leave in their vase

An aspirin to preserve
Our lilacs, the wayside flowers

We've gathered and must leave to serve
A few more hours;

25 That's all. We can't tell when
We'll come back, can't press claims,
We would no doubt have other rooms then,
Or other names.

1968

The first poem, "Barbie Doll," has the strong note of sadness that characterizes many death poems, but it emphasizes not the girl's death but the disappointments in her life. The only "scene" in the poem (lines 19–23) portrays the unnamed girl at rest in her casket, but the still body in the casket contrasts not with vitality but with frustration and anxiety: her life since puberty (lines 5–6) had been full of apologies and attempts to change her physical appearance and emotional makeup. The "consummation" she achieves in death is not, however, a triumph, despite what people say (line 23). Although the poem's last two words are "happy ending," this girl without a name has died in embarrassment and without fulfillment, and the final lines are ironic, questioning the whole idea of what "happy" means. The cheerful comments at the end lack force and truth because of what we already know; we understand them as ironic because they underline how unhappy the girl was and how false her cosmeticized corpse is to the sad truth of her life.

The poem suggests the falsity and destructiveness of those standards of female beauty that have led to the tragedy of the girl's life. In an important sense, the poem is not really *about* death at all in spite of the fact that the girl's death and her repaired corpse are central to it. As the title suggests, the poem dramatizes how standardized, commercialized notions of femininity and prettiness can be painful and destructive to those whose bodies do not precisely fit the conformist models, and the poem vigorously attacks those conventional standards and the widespread, unthinking acceptance of them.

"Leaving the Motel" similarly goes in quite a different direction from many poems on the subject of love. Instead of expressing assurance about how love lasts and endures, or about the sincerity and depth of affection, this poem describes a parting of lovers after a brief, surreptitious sexual encounter. But it does not emphasize sexuality or eroticism in the meeting of the nameless lovers (we see them only as they prepare to leave), nor does it suggest why or how they have found each other, or what either of them is like as a person. It focuses on how careful they must be not to get caught, how exact and calculating they must be in their planning, how finite and limited their encounter must be, how sealed off this encounter is from the rest of their lives. The poem relates the tiny details the lovers must think of, the agreements they must observe, and the ritual checklist of their duties ("Check . . . Keep things straight . . . Check . . . ," lines 5, 9, 15). Affection and sentiment have their small place in the poem (notice the care for the flowers, lines 19–24, and the thought of "press[ing] claims," line 26), but the emphasis is on temporariness, uncertainty, and limits. Although it is about an illicit, perhaps adulterous, sexual encounter, there is no sex in the poem, only a kind of archaeological record of lust.

Labeling a poem a "love poem" or a "death poem" is primarily a matter of convenience; such categories indicate the **subject** of a poem, or the event or **topic** it chooses to engage. But as the poems we have been looking at suggest, poems that may be loosely called "love poems" or "death poems" may differ widely from one another, express totally different attitudes or ideas, and concentrate on very different aspects of the subject. The main advantages of grouping poems in this way is that a reader can become conscious of individual differences; a reading of two poems side by side may suggest how each is distinctive in what it has to say and how it says it.

The theme of a poem may be expressed in several different ways, and poems often have more than one theme. We could say, for example, that the theme of "Leaving the Motel" is that illicit love is secretive, careful, transitory, and short on emotion and sentiment, or that secret sexual encounters tend to be brief, calculated, and characterized by restrained or hesitant feelings. "Barbie Doll" suggests that commercialized standards destroy humane values; that rigid and idealized notions of normality cripple those who are different; that people are easily and tragically led to accept evaluations thrust upon them by others; that American consumers tend to be conformists, easily influenced in their outlook by advertising and by commercial products; that children who do not conform to middle-class standards and notions don't have a chance. The poem implies each of these ideas, and all are quite central to it. But none of these assertions individually nor all of them together can fully express or explain the poem itself. To state the themes in such a brief and abstract way—though it may help to clarify what the poem does and does not say—cannot do justice to the experience of the poem, the way it works on us as readers, the way we respond. Poems affect us in all sorts of ways—emotional and psychological as well as rational—and often a poem's dramatization of a story, an event, or a moment bypasses our rational responses and affects us far more deeply than a clear and logical argument would.

Here is a poem even more directly about desire and its implications. It too is cautious, even critical, but it represents the appeal of both drugs and sex as powerfully as it depicts the fear of their consequences. The "Plague" is here the AIDS epidemic in America, especially among gay men, in the early 1990s.

THOM GUNN

In Time of Plague

My thoughts are crowded with death
and it draws so oddly on the sexual
that I am confused
confused to be attracted
5   by, in effect, my own annihilation.
Who are these two, these fiercely attractive men

who want me to stick their needle in my arm?
They tell me they are called Brad and John,
one from here, one from Denver, sitting the same
10   on the bench as they talk to me,
their legs spread apart, their eyes attentive.
I love their daring, their looks, their jargon,
and what they have in mind.

Their mind is the mind of death.
15   They know it, and do not know it,
and they are like me in that
(I know it, and do not know it)
and like the flow of people through this bar.
Brad and John thirst heroically together
20   for euphoria—for a state of ardent life
in which we could all stretch ourselves
and lose our differences. I seek
to enter their minds: am I a fool,
and they direct and right, properly
25   testing themselves against risk,
as a human must, and does,
or are they the fools, their alert faces
mere death's heads lighted glamorously?

I weigh possibilities
30   till I am afraid of the strength
of my own health
and of their evident health.

They get restless at last with my indecisiveness
and so, first one, and then the other,
35   move off into the moving concourse of people
who are boisterous and bright
carrying in their faces and throughout their bodies
the news of life and death.

1992

Delicate subject, sensitive poem. The situation and narrative here are quite clear, and the speaker is plainly attracted by the two men and "what they have in mind" (line 13), but the poem is about a mental state rather than physical action. The tone is carefully poised between excitement and fear—so much so that the two emotions don't just coexist but are nearly one, and a lust for life and attraction to death are very close. The speaker realizes that he is "attracted by . . . my own annihilation" (lines 4–5), and his vacillation about action involves an internal debate ("I weigh possibilities," line 29) between desire and self-protection. The tone of voice here is both excited and cautionary—at the same time.

Poems, then, can differ widely from one another even when they share a common subject. And the subjects of poetry can also vary widely. It isn't true that certain subjects are "poetic" and that others aren't appropriate to poetry. Any human activity, thought, or feeling can be the subject of poetry. Poetry often deals with beauty and the softer, more attractive human emotions, but it can deal with ugliness and unattractive human conduct as well, for poetry seeks to represent human beings and human events, showing us ourselves not only as we would like to be but as we are. Good poetry gets written about all kinds of topics, in all kinds of forms, with all kinds of attitudes. Here, for example, is a poem about a prison inmate—and about the conflict between individual and societal values.

ETHERIDGE KNIGHT

Hard Rock Returns to Prison from the Hospital for the Criminal Insane

Hard Rock was "known not to take no shit
From nobody," and he had the scars to prove it:
Split purple lips, lumped ears, welts above
His yellow eyes, and one long scar that cut
5 Across his temple and plowed through a thick
Canopy of kinky hair.

The WORD was that Hard Rock wasn't a mean nigger
Anymore, that the doctors had bored a hole in his head,
Cut out part of his brain, and shot electricity
10 Through the rest. When they brought Hard Rock back,
Handcuffed and chained, he was turned loose,
Like a freshly gelded stallion, to try his new status.
And we all waited and watched, like indians at a corral,
To see if the WORD was true.

15 As we waited we wrapped ourselves in the cloak
Of his exploits: "Man, the last time, it took eight
Screws to put him in the Hole."[1] "Yeah, remember when he
Smacked the captain with his dinner tray?" "He set
The record for time in the Hole—67 straight days!"
20 "Ol Hard Rock! man, that's one crazy nigger."
And then the jewel of a myth that Hard Rock had once bit
A screw on the thumb and poisoned him with syphilitic spit.

The testing came, to see if Hard Rock was really tame.
A hillbilly called him a black son of a bitch
25 And didn't lose his teeth, a screw who knew Hard Rock
From before shook him down and barked in his face.

---

1. Solitary confinement. *Screws*: guards.

And Hard Rock did *nothing*. Just grinned and looked silly,
His eyes empty like knot holes in a fence.

And even after we discovered that it took Hard Rock
30 Exactly 3 minutes to tell you his first name,
We told ourselves that he had just wised up,
Was being cool; but we could not fool ourselves for long,
And we turned away, our eyes on the ground. Crushed.
He had been our Destroyer, the doer of things
35 We dreamed of doing but could not bring ourselves to do,
The fears of years, like a biting whip,
Had cut grooves too deeply across our backs.

1968

The picture of Hard Rock as a kind of hero to other prison inmates is
established early in the poem through a retelling of the legends circulated
about him; the straightforward chronology of the poem sets up the mystery
of how he will react after his "treatment" in the hospital. The poem identifies
with those who wait; they are hopeful that Hard Rock's spirit has not been
broken by surgery or shock treatments, and the lines crawl almost to a stop
with disappointment in stanza 4. The *"nothing"* (line 27) of Hard Rock's
response to taunting and the emptiness of his eyes ("like knot holes in a
fence," line 28) reduce the narrator's hopes to despair. The final stanza
recounts the observers' attempts to reinterpret, to hang onto hope that their
symbol of heroism can stand up against the best efforts to tame him, but
the spirit has gone out of the hero-worshipers, too, and the poem records
them as beaten, tamed, deprived of their spirit as Hard Rock has been of his.
The poem records the despair of the hopeless, and it protests against the
cruel exercise of power that can quash even as defiant a figure as Hard Rock.

The following poem is equally full of anger and disappointment, but it
expresses its attitudes in a very different way.

WILLIAM BLAKE

 London

I wander through each chartered street,
Near where the chartered Thames does flow,
And mark in every face I meet
Marks of weakness, marks of woe.

5 In every cry of every man,
In every Infant's cry of fear,
In every voice, in every ban,
The mind-forged manacles I hear.

How the Chimney-sweeper's cry
10 Every black'ning Church appalls;

And the hapless Soldier's sigh
Runs in blood down Palace walls.

But most through midnight streets I hear
How the youthful Harlot's curse
15 Blasts the new-born Infant's tear,
And blights with plagues the Marriage hearse.

1794

The poem gives a strong sense of how London feels to this particular observer; it is cluttered, constricting, oppressive. The wordplay here articulates and connects the strong emotions he associates with London experiences. The repeated words—"every," for example, and "cry"—intensify the sense of total despair in the city and create connections between things not necessarily related, such as the cries of street vendors with the cries for help. The twice-used word "chartered" implies strong feelings, too. The streets, instead of seeming alive with people or bustling with movement, are rigidly, coldly determined, controlled, cramped. Likewise the river seems as if it were planned, programmed, laid out by an oppressor. In actual fact, the course of the Thames through the city had been altered (slightly) by the government before Blake's time, but most important is the word's emotional force, the sense it projects of constriction and artificiality: the speaker experiences London as if human artifice had totally usurped nature. Moreover, according to the poem, people are victimized, "marked" by their confrontations with the city and its faceless institutions: the "Soldier's sigh" that "runs in blood down Palace walls" vividly suggests, through metaphor, both the powerlessness of the individual and the callousness of power. The description of the city has clearly become, by now, a subjective, highly emotional, and vivid expression of how the speaker feels about London and what it represents to him.

> *Poetry makes nothing happen.*
> —W. H. AUDEN

Another thing about "London": at first it looks like an account of a personal experience, as if the speaker is describing and interpreting as he goes along: "I wander through each chartered street." But soon it is clear that he is describing many wanderings, putting together impressions from many walks, re-creating a typical walk—which shows him "every" person in the streets, allows him to generalize about the churches being "appalled" (literally, made white) by the cry of the representative Chimney-sweeper, and leads to his conclusions about soldiers, prostitutes, and infants. We receive not a personal record of an event, but a representation of it in retrospect—not a story, not a narrative or chronological account of events, but a dramatization of self that compresses many experiences and impressions into one.

> *When power leads man toward arrogance, poetry reminds him of his limitations. When power narrows the areas of man's concern, poetry reminds him of the richness and diversity of his existence. When power corrupts, poetry cleanses.*
> —JOHN F. KENNEDY

"London" is somber in spite of the poet's playfulness with words. Word-play may be witty and funny if it calls attention to its own cleverness, but here it prompts the discovery of unsuspected (but meaningful) connections between things. The tone of the poem is sad, despairing, and angry; reading it aloud, one would try to show in the tone of one's voice the strong feelings that the poem expresses, just as one would try to reproduce tenderness and caring and passion in reading aloud "The Tally Stick" or "How Do I Love Thee?"

The following two poems are "about" animals, although both of them place their final emphasis on human beings: the animal in each case is only the means to the end of exploring human nature. The poems share a common assumption that animal behavior may appear to reflect human habits and conduct and may reveal much about ourselves, and in each case the character central to the poem is revealed to be surpris-ingly unlike the way she thinks of herself. But the poems are very different. Read each poem aloud, and try to imagine what each main character is like. What tones of voice do you use to help express the character of the "killer" (line 24) in the first poem? What demands on your voice does the second poem make?

MAXINE KUMIN

Woodchucks

Gassing the woodchucks didn't turn out right.
The knockout bomb from the Feed and Grain Exchange
was featured as merciful, quick at the bone
and the case we had against them was airtight,
5   both exits shoehorned shut with puddingstone,[2]
but they had a sub-sub-basement out of range.

Next morning they turned up again, no worse
for the cyanide than we for our cigarettes
and state-store Scotch, all of us up to scratch.
10 They brought down the marigolds as a matter of course
and then took over the vegetable patch
nipping the broccoli shoots, beheading the carrots.

The food from our mouths, I said, righteously thrilling
to the feel of the .22, the bullets' neat noses.
15 I, a lapsed pacifist fallen from grace
puffed with Darwinian pieties for killing,
now drew a bead on the littlest woodchuck's face.
He died down in the everbearing roses.

---

2. A mixture of cement, pebbles, and gravel.

Ten minutes later I dropped the mother. She
20 flipflopped in the air and fell, her needle teeth
still hooked in a leaf of early Swiss chard.
Another baby next. O one-two-three
the murderer inside me rose up hard,
the hawkeye killer came on stage forthwith.

25 There's one chuck left. Old wily fellow, he keeps
me cocked and ready day after day after day.
All night I hunt his humped-up form. I dream
I sight along the barrel in my sleep.
If only they'd all consented to die unseen
30 gassed underground the quiet Nazi way.

1972

ADRIENNE RICH

Aunt Jennifer's Tigers

Aunt Jennifer's tigers prance across a screen,
Bright topaz denizens of a world of green.
They do not fear the men beneath the tree;
They pace in sleek chivalric certainty.

5 Aunt Jennifer's fingers fluttering through her wool
Find even the ivory needle hard to pull.
The massive weight of Uncle's wedding band
Sits heavily upon Aunt Jennifer's hand.

When Aunt is dead, her terrified hands will lie
10 Still ringed with ordeals she was mastered by.
The tigers in the panel that she made
Will go on prancing, proud and unafraid.

1951

If you read "Woodchucks" aloud, how would your tone of voice change
from beginning to end? What tone would you use to read the ending? How
does the hunter feel about her increasing attraction to violence? Why does
the poem begin by calling the gassing of the woodchucks "merciful" and
end by describing it as "the quiet Nazi way"? What names does the hunter
call herself? How does the name-calling affect your feelings about her?
Exactly when does the hunter begin to *enjoy* the feel of the gun and the idea
of killing? How does the poet make that clear?

In the second poem, why are tigers a particularly appropriate contrast to
the quiet and subdued manner of Aunt Jennifer? What words describing the
tigers seem particularly significant? How is the tiger an opposite of Aunt
Jennifer? In what ways does it externalize her secrets? Why are Aunt Jennifer's

hands described as "terrified"? What clues does the poem give about why Aunt Jennifer is so afraid? How does the poem make you feel about Aunt Jennifer? about her tigers? about her life? How would you describe the tone of the poem? How does the poet feel about Aunt Jennifer?

Subject, theme, and tone: each of these categories gives us a way to begin considering poems and how one poem differs from another. Comparing poems with the same subject or a similar theme or tone can lead to a clearer understanding of each individual poem and can refine our responses to their subtle differences. The title of a poem ("Leaving the Motel," for example) or the way a poem first introduces its subject can often give us a sense of what to expect, but we must be open to surprise, too. No two poems affect us in exactly the same way; the variety of possible poems multiplies when you think of all the possible themes and tones that can be explored within any single subject. Varieties of feeling often coincide with varieties of thinking, and readers open to the pleasures of the unexpected may find themselves learning, growing, becoming more sensitive to ideas and human issues—as well as more articulate about feelings and thoughts they already have.

MANY TONES: POEMS ABOUT FAMILY RELATIONSHIPS

GALWAY KINNELL

After Making Love We Hear Footsteps

For I can snore like a bullhorn
or play loud music
or sit up talking with any reasonably sober Irishman
and Fergus will only sink deeper
5 into his dreamless sleep, which goes by all in one flash,
but let there be that heavy breathing
or a stifled come-cry anywhere in the house
and he will wrench himself awake
and make for it on the run—as now, we lie together,
10 after making love, quiet, touching along the length of our bodies,
familiar touch of the long-married,
and he appears—in his baseball pajamas, it happens,
the neck opening so small
he has to screw them on, which one day may make him wonder
15 about the mental capacity of baseball players—
and says, "Are you loving and snuggling? May I join?"
He flops down between us and hugs us and snuggles himself to sleep,
his face gleaming with satisfaction at being this very child.

In the half darkness we look at each other
20 and smile
and touch arms across his little, startlingly muscled body—
this one whom habit of memory propels to the ground of his
    making,
sleeper only the mortal sounds can sing awake,
this blessing love gives again into our arms.

1980

• How does the language in lines 1–5 establish the poem's tone? Do the last
  lines (starting with line 22) alter the tone in any way?

ROBERT HAYDEN

Those Winter Sundays

Sundays too my father got up early
and put his clothes on in the blueblack cold,
then with cracked hands that ached
from labor in the weekday weather made
5 banked fires blaze. No one ever thanked him.

I'd wake and hear the cold splintering, breaking.
When the rooms were warm, he'd call,
and slowly I would rise and dress,
fearing the chronic angers of that house,

10 Speaking indifferently to him,
who had driven out the cold
and polished my good shoes as well.
What did I know, what did I know
of love's austere and lonely offices?

1966

• Why does the poem begin with the words "Sundays too"
  (rather than, say, "On Sundays")? What are the "austere and
  lonely offices" of love in the poem's final line?

DANIEL TOBIN

The Clock

Bored with plastic armies,
he climbs onto the parlor loveseat
and watches the wide expression of the clock.
He doesn't know what time is,

5　doesn't know how in no time
　　those numbers will fill his days
　　the way water fills a bath
　　into which an exhausted man
　　lowers himself, not wanting to rise.
10　Sun and moon gaze back at him
　　from the glaze of the silver frame,
　　each with a human face,
　　his own face mirrored there.
　　Look closer, his mother says,
15　and you can see the small hand move.
　　And he leans closer now, steadied
　　in her arms, the hand a winded runner
　　lapped on the track. That's hours,
　　she says, the big hand's minutes, the quick,
20　seconds. And the boy fingers the pivot
　　anchoring them, his touch
　　stirs with the machine.
　　I'm older now, and now, and now. The gears
　　start to tick through every room of that house.

1999

- How do the language and tone shift when the boy touches the clock? What exactly has changed?

AGHA SHAHID ALI

Postcard from Kashmir

(for Pavan Sahgal)

Kashmir shrinks into my mailbox,
my home a neat four by six inches.

I always loved neatness. Now I hold
the half-inch Himalayas in my hand.
5　This is home. And this the closest
I'll ever be to home. When I return,
the colors won't be so brilliant,
the Jhelum's waters[1] so clean,
so ultramarine. My love
10　so overexposed.

---

1. The river Jhelum runs through Kashmir and Pakistan.

And my memory will be a little
out of focus, in it
a giant negative, black
and white, still undeveloped.

1987

- What words characterize the speaker's dreams of home in this
  poem? What words reveal a more realistic attitude?

KELLY CHERRY

Alzheimer's

He stands at the door, a crazy old man
Back from the hospital, his mind rattling
Like the suitcase, swinging from his hand,
That contains shaving cream, a piggy bank,
5 A book he sometimes pretends to read,
His clothes. On the brick wall beside him
Roses and columbine slug it out for space, claw the mortar.
The sun is shining, as it does late in the afternoon
In England, after rain.
10 Sun hardens the house, reifies it,
Strikes the iron grillwork like a smithy
And sparks fly off, burning in the bushes—
The rosebushes—
While the white wood trim defines solidity in space.
15 This is his house. He remembers it as his,
Remembers the walkway he built between the front room
And the garage, the rhododendron he planted in back,
The car he used to drive. He remembers himself,
A younger man, in a tweed hat, a man who loved
20 Music. There is no time for that now. No time for music,
The peculiar screeching of strings, the luxurious
Fiddling with emotion.
Other things have become more urgent.
Other matters are now of greater import, have more
25 Consequence, must be attended to. The first
Thing he must do, now that he is home, is decide who
This woman is, this old, white-haired woman
Standing here in the doorway,
Welcoming him in.

1997

- How do phrases like "a crazy old man" and "a book he sometimes pretends to read" indicate the speaker's feelings toward
  her father? Does her attitude shift at some point? Where?

SUGGESTIONS FOR WRITING

1. "The Clock," by Daniel Tobin, use shifts of tone to elevate the poems subject
   matter from the narrow concerns of children to the more universal issues that
   face adults. Where, in this poem, does the shift of tone occur? How is the shift
   revealed through language? Write an essay in which you describe this broad-
   ening of perspective.
2. What words in Robert Hayden's "Those Winter Sundays" suggest the son's
   feelings toward his father and his home? What words indicate that the poet's
   attitudes have changed since the time depicted in the poem? Write an essay
   in which you compare the speaker's feelings, as a youth and then later as a
   man, about his father and his home.
3. Write an essay in which you consider the use of language to create tone in any
   grouping of two or more poems in this chapter.

9 SPEAKER: WHOSE VOICE DO WE HEAR?

Poems are personal. The thoughts and feelings they express belong to a specific person, and however general or universal their sentiments seem to be, poems come to us as the expression of an individual human voice. That voice is often the voice of the poet. But not always. Poets sometimes create "characters" just as writers of fiction or drama do—people who speak for them only indirectly. A character may, in fact, be very different from the poet, just as a character in a play or story is not necessarily the author, and that person, the **speaker** of the poem, may express ideas or feelings very different from the poet's own. In the following poem, rather than speaking directly to us himself, the poet has created two speakers, both female, each of whom has a distinctive voice, personality, and character.

THOMAS HARDY

The Ruined Maid

"O 'Melia,[1] my dear, this does everything crown!
Who could have supposed I should meet you in Town?
And whence such fair garments, such prosperi-ty?"—
"O didn't you know I'd been ruined?" said she.

5 —"You left us in tatters, without shoes or socks,
Tired of digging potatoes, and spudding up docks;[2]
And now you've gay bracelets and bright feathers three!"—
"Yes: that's how we dress when we're ruined," said she.

  —"At home in the barton[3] you said 'thee' and 'thou,'
10 And 'thik oon,' and 'theäs oon,' and 't'other'; but now
Your talking quite fits 'ee for high compa-ny!"—
"Some polish is gained with one's ruin," said she.

  —"Your hands were like paws then, your face blue and bleak
But now I'm bewitched by your delicate cheek,
15 And your little gloves fit as on any la-dy!"—
"We never do work when we're ruined," said she.

1. Short for Amelia.   2. Spading up weeds.   3. Farmyard.

—"You used to call home-life a hag-ridden dream,
And you'd sigh, and you'd sock;[4] but at present you seem
To know not of megrims[5] or melancho-ly!"—
20 "True. One's pretty lively when ruined," said she.

—"I wish I had feathers, a fine sweeping gown,
And a delicate face, and could strut about Town!"—
"My dear—a raw country girl, such as you be,
Cannot quite expect that. You ain't ruined," said she.

1866

The first voice, that of a young woman who has remained back on the farm, is designated typographically (that is, by the way the poem is printed): there are dashes at the beginning and end of all but the first of her speeches. She speaks the first part of each **stanza** (a stanza is a section of a poem designated by spacing), usually the first three lines. The second young woman, a companion and coworker on the farm in years gone by, regularly gets the last line in each stanza (and in the last stanza, two lines), so it is clear who is talking at every point. Also, the two speakers are just as clearly distinguished by what they say, how they say it, and what sort of person each proves to be. The nameless stay-at-home shows little knowledge of the world, and everything surprises her: seeing her former companion at all, but especially seeing her well clothed, cheerful, and polished; and as the poem develops she shows increasing envy of her more worldly friend. She is the "raw country girl" (line 23) that the other speaker says she is, and she still speaks the country dialect ("fits 'ee," line 11, for example) that she notices her friend has lost (lines 9–11). The "ruined" young woman ('Melia), on the other hand, says little except the refrain about having been ruined, but even the slight variations she plays on that theme suggest her sophistication and amusement at her rural friend, although she still uses a country "ain't" at the end. We are not told the full story of their lives (was the "ruined" young woman thrown out? did she run away from home or work?), but we know enough (that they've been separated for some time, that the stay-at-home did not know where the other had gone) to allow the dialogue to articulate the contrast between them: one is still rural, inexperienced, and innocent; the other is sophisticated, citified—and "ruined." Each speaker's style of speech then does the rest.

Sometimes poets "borrow" a character from history and ask readers to factor in historical facts and contexts. In the following poem, for example, the Canadian poet Margaret Atwood draws heavily upon facts and traditions about a nineteenth-century émigré from Scotland to Canada:

---

4. Deliver angry blows.   5. Migraine headaches.

MARGARET ATWOOD

Death of a Young Son by Drowning

He, who navigated with success
the dangerous river of his own birth
once more set forth

on a voyage of discovery
5 into the land I floated on
but could not touch to claim.

His feet slid on the bank,
the currents took him;
he swirled with ice and trees in the swollen water

10 and plunged into distant regions,
his head a bathysphere;
through his eyes' thin glass bubbles

he looked out, reckless adventurer
on a landscape stranger than Uranus
15 we have all been to and some remember.

There was an accident; the air locked,
he was hung in the river like a heart.
They retrieved the swamped body,

cairn of my plans and future charts,
20 with poles and hooks
from among the nudging logs.

It was spring, the sun kept shining, the new grass
leapt to solidity;
my hands glistened with details.

25 After the long trip I was tired of waves.
My foot hit rock. The dreamed sails
collapsed, ragged.

I planted him in this country
like a flag.

1970

The poem comes from a volume called *The Journals of Susanna Moodie: Poems by Margaret Atwood* (1970). A frontier pioneer, Moodie herself had written two books about Canada, *Roughing It in the Bush* and *Life in the Clearings*, and Atwood found their observations rather stark and disorganized. She wrote her Susanna Moodie poems to refocus the "character" and to reconstruct Moodie's actual geographical exploration and self-discovery. To truly understand these thoughts and meditations, then, we need to know something of the history behind them. Read in context, they present very powerful psychological and cultural analyses.

Some speakers in poems are not, however, nearly so heroic or attractive, and some poems create a speaker we are made to dislike, as the following poem does. Here the speaker, as the title implies, is a monk, but he shows himself to be most unspiritual: mean, petty, self-righteous, and despicable.

ROBERT BROWNING

WEB   *Soliloquy of the Spanish Cloister*

> Gr-r-r—there go, my heart's abhorrence!
>   Water your damned flower-pots, do!
> If hate killed men, Brother Lawrence,
>   God's blood, would not mine kill you!
> 5 What? your myrtle-bush wants trimming?
>   Oh, that rose has prior claims—
> Needs its leaden vase filled brimming?
>   Hell dry you up with its flames!
>
> At the meal we sit together:
> 10   *Salve tibi!*[6] I must hear
> Wish talk of the kind of weather,
>   Sort of season, time of year:
> *Not a plenteous cork-crop: scarcely*
>   *Dare we hope oak-galls,*[7] *I doubt:*
> 15 *What's the Latin name for "parsley"?*
>   What's the Greek name for Swine's Snout?
>
> Whew! We'll have our platter burnished,
>   Laid with care on our own shelf!
> With a fire-new spoon we're furnished,
> 20   And a goblet for ourself,
> Rinsed like something sacrificial
>   Ere 'tis fit to touch our chaps[8]—
> Marked with L. for our initial!
>   (He-he! There his lily snaps!)
>
> 25 *Saint,* forsooth! While brown Dolores
>   —Squats outside the Convent bank
> With Sanchicha, telling stories,
>   Steeping tresses in the tank,
> Blue-black, lustrous, thick like horsehairs,
> 30   —Can't I see his dead eye glow,

6. Hail to thee (Latin). Italics usually indicate the words of Brother Lawrence.
7. Abnormal growth on oak trees, used for tanning.   8. Jaws.

Bright as 'twere a Barbary corsair's?[9]
(That is, if he'd let it show!)

When he finishes refection,
    Knife and fork he never lays
35 Cross-wise, to my recollection,
    As do I, in Jesu's praise.
I the Trinity illustrate,
    Drinking watered orange-pulp—
In three sips the Arian[1] frustrate;
40 —While he drains his at one gulp.

Oh, those melons? If he's able
    We're to have a feast! so nice!
One goes to the Abbot's table,
    All of us get each a slice.
45 How go on your flowers? None double?
    Not one fruit-sort can you spy?
Strange!—And I, too, at such trouble,
    —Keep them close-nipped on the sly!

There's a great text in Galatians,
50 Once you trip on it, entails
Twenty-nine distinct damnations,[2]
    One sure, if another fails:
If I trip him just a-dying,
    Sure of heaven as sure can be,
55 Spin him round and send him flying
    Off to hell, a Manichee?[3]

Or, my scrofulous French novel
    On gray paper with blunt type!
Simply glance at it, you grovel
60 Hand and foot in Belial's gripe:[4]
If I double down its pages
    At the woeful sixteenth print,
When he gathers his greengages,
    Ope a sieve and slip it in't?

65 Or, there's Satan!—one might venture
    Pledge one's soul to him, yet leave
Such a flaw in the indenture
    —As he'd miss till, past retrieve,

9. African pirate's.   1. A heretical sect that denied the Trinity.
2. Galatians 5.15–23 provides a long list of possible offenses, though they do not add up to twenty-nine.
3. A heretic. According to the Manichean heresy, the world was divided into the forces of good and evil, equally powerful.   4. In the clutches of Satan.

Blasted lay that rose-acacia
70 We're so proud of! *Hy, Zy, Hine* . . .[5]
'St, there's Vespers! *Plena gratiâ*
Ave, Virgo.[6] Gr-r-r—you swine!

1842

Not many poems begin with a growl, and this harsh sound turns out to be fair warning that we are about to meet a real beast, even though he is in the clothing of a religious man. In line 1 he shows himself to hold a most uncharitable attitude toward his fellow monk, Brother Lawrence, and by line 4 he has uttered two profanities and admitted his intense feelings of hatred and vengefulness. His ranting and roaring is full of exclamation points, and he reveals his own personality and character when he imagines curses and unflattering nicknames for Brother Lawrence or plots malicious jokes on him. By the end, we have accumulated no knowledge of Brother Lawrence that makes him seem a fit target for such rage (except that he is pious, dutiful, and pleasant—perhaps enough to make this sort of speaker despise him), but we have discovered the speaker to be lecherous (stanza 4), full of false piety (stanza 5), malicious in trivial matters (stanza 6), ready to use his theological learning to sponsor damnation rather than salvation (stanza 7), a closet reader and viewer of pornography within the monastery (stanza 8)— even willing to risk his own soul in order to torment Brother Lawrence (last stanza).

The speaker characterizes himself; the details accumulate into a fairly full portrait, and here we do not have even an opening and closing "objective" description or another speaker to give us perspective. Except for the moments when the speaker mimics or parodies Brother Lawrence (usually in italic type), we have only the speaker's own words and thoughts. But that is enough; the poet has controlled them so carefully that we know what he thinks of the speaker—that he is a mean-spirited, vengeful hypocrite, a thoroughly disreputable and unlikable character. The whole poem has been about him and his attitudes; the point has been to characterize the speaker and develop in us a dislike of him and what he stands for—hypocrisy.

In reading a poem like this aloud, we would want our voice to suggest all the unlikable features of a hypocrite. We would also need to suggest, through tone of voice, the author's contemptuous mocking of the rage and hypocrisy, and we would want, like an actor, to create strong disapproval in the hearer. The poem's words (the ones the author has given to the speaker) clearly imply those attitudes, and we would want our voice to express them. Usually there is much more to a poem than the characterization of the speaker, but in many cases it is necessary first to identify the speaker and determine his or her character before we can appreciate what else goes on in the poem. And sometimes, as here, in looking for the speaker of the poem, we approach the center of the poem itself.

---

5. Possibly the beginning of an incantation or curse.
6. The opening words of the *Ave Maria*, here reversed: "Full of grace, Hail, Virgin" (Latin).

Sometimes the effect of a poem depends on our recognizing the **emporal setting** as well as the speaker's identity. The following poem, for example, quickly makes plain that a childhood experience is at the center of the action and that the speaker is female:

TESS GALLAGHER

Sudden Journey

Maybe I'm seven in the open field—
the straw-grass so high
only the top of my head makes a curve
of brown in the yellow. Rain then.
5 First a little. A few drops on my
wrist, the right wrist. More rain.
My shoulders, my chin. Until I'm looking up
to let my eyes take the bliss.
I open my face. Let the teeth show. I
10 pull my shirt down past the collar-bones.
I'm still a boy under my breast spots.
I can drink anywhere. The rain. My
skin shattering. Up suddenly, needing
to gulp, turning with my tongue, my arms out
15 running, running in the hard, cold plenitude
of all those who reach earth by falling.

1984

The sense of adventure and wonder here has a lot to do with the childlike syntax and choice of words at the beginning of the poem. Sentences are short, observations direct and simple. The rain becomes exciting and blissful and totally absorbing as the child's actions and reactions take over the poem in lines 2-13. But not all of the poem takes place in a child's mind in spite of the precise and impressive re-creation of childish responses and feelings. The opening line makes clear that we are sliding into a supposition of the past; "maybe I'm seven" makes clear that we, as conspiring adults, are pretending ourselves into earlier time. And at the end the word "plenitude"— crucial to interpreting the poem's full effect and meaning—makes clear that we are now encountering an adult perspective on the incident. Elsewhere, too, the adult world gives the incident meaning. In line 12, for example, the joke about being able to drink anywhere depends on an adult sense of what being a boy might mean. The "journey" of the poem's title is not only the little girl's running in the rain, but also the adult's return to a past re-created and newly understood.

The speaker in the following poem positions herself very differently, but we do not get a full sense of her until we are well into the poem. As you read, try to imagine the tone of voice you think this person would use. Exactly when do you begin to know what she sounds like?

DOROTHY PARKER

A Certain Lady

Oh, I can smile for you, and tilt my head,
   And drink your rushing words with eager lips,
And paint my mouth for you a fragrant red,
   And trace your brows with tutored finger-tips.
5 When you rehearse your list of loves to me,
   Oh, I can laugh and marvel, rapturous-eyed.
And you laugh back, nor can you ever see
   The thousand little deaths my heart has died.
And you believe, so well I know my part,
10   That I am gay as morning, light as snow,
And all the straining things within my heart
   You'll never know.

Oh, I can laugh and listen, when we meet,
   And you bring tales of fresh adventurings—
15 Of ladies delicately indiscreet,
   Of lingering hands, and gently whispered things.
And you are pleased with me, and strive anew
   To sing me sagas of your late delights.
Thus do you want me—marveling, gay, and true—
20   Nor do you see my staring eyes of nights.
And when, in search of novelty, you stray,
   Oh, I can kiss you blithely as you go . . .
And what goes on, my love, while you're away,
   You'll never know.

                                                        1937

To whom does the speaker seem to be talking? What sort of person is he? How do you feel about him? Which habits and attitudes of his do you like least? How soon can you tell that the speaker is not altogether happy about his conversation and conduct? In what tone of voice would you read the first twenty-two lines aloud? What attitude would you try to express toward the person spoken to? What tone would you use for the last two lines? How would you describe the speaker's personality? What aspects of her behavior are most crucial to the poem's effect?

It is easy to assume that the speaker in a poem is an extension of the poet, especially when the voice is as distinctively self-assured as in "A Certain Lady." So, is the speaker in this poem Dorothy Parker? Maybe. A lot of Parker's poems present a similar world-weary posture and a wry cynicism about romantic love. But the poem is hardly a case of self-revelation, a giving away of personal secrets. If it were, it would be silly, not to say risky, to address her lover in a way that gives damaging facts about a pose she has been so careful to set up.

In poems such as "The Ruined Maid" and "Soliloquy of the Spanish Cloister," we are in no danger of mistaking the speaker for the poet, once we have recognized that poets may create speakers who participate in specific situations, much as in fiction or drama. When there is a pointed discrepancy between the speaker and what we know of the poet—when the speaker is a woman, for example, and the poet is a man—we know we have a created speaker to contend with and that the point (or at least *one* point) in the poem is to observe the characterization carefully. In "A Certain Lady" we may be less sure, and in other poems the discrepancy between speaker and poet may be even more uncertain.

Even when poets present themselves as if they were speaking directly to us in their own voices, their poems present only a partial portrait, something considerably less than the full personality and character of the poet. Even when there is not an obviously created character—someone with distinct characteristics that are different from those of the poet—strategies of characterization are used to present the person speaking in one way and not another. Even in a poem like the following one, which contains identifiable autobiographical details, it is still a good idea to think of the speaker instead of the poet, although here the poet is probably writing about a personal, actual experience, and he is certainly making a character of himself—that is, characterizing himself in a certain way, emphasizing some parts of himself and not others.

WILLIAM WORDSWORTH

She Dwelt among the Untrodden Ways

> She dwelt among the untrodden ways
>   Beside the springs of Dove,[7]
> A Maid whom there were none to praise
>   And very few to love:
>
> 5 A violet by a mossy stone
>   Half hidden from the eye!
> —Fair as a star, when only one
>   Is shining in the sky.
>
> She lived unknown, and few could know
> 10   When Lucy ceased to be;
> But she is in her grave, and, oh,
>   The difference to me!

1800

---

7. A small stream in the Lake District in northern England, near where Wordsworth lived in Dove Cottage at Grasmere.

Is this poem more about Lucy or about the speaker's feelings concerning her death? Her simple life, far removed from fame and known only to a few, is said to have been beautiful, but we know little about her beyond her name and where she lived, in a beautiful but then-isolated section of northern England. We don't know if she was young or old, only that the speaker thinks of her as "fair" and compares her to a "violet by a mossy stone." We do know that the speaker is deeply pained by her death, so deeply that he is almost inarticulate with grief, lapsing into simple exclamation ("oh," line 11) and hardly able to articulate the "difference" that her death makes.

Did Lucy actually live? Was she a friend of the poet? We don't know; the poem doesn't tell us, and even biographers of Wordsworth are unsure. What we do know is that Wordsworth was able to represent grief very powerfully. Whether the speaker is the historical Wordsworth or not, that speaker is a major focus of the poem, and it is his feelings that the poem isolates and expresses. We need to recognize some characteristics of the speaker and be sensitive to his feelings for the poem to work.

The poems we have looked at in this chapter—and the group that follows—all suggest the value of beginning the reading of any poem with simple questions: Who is speaking? What do we know about him or her? What kind of person is she or he? Putting together the evidence that the poem presents in answer to such questions can often take us a long way into the poem. For some poems, such questions won't help a great deal because the speaking voice is too indistinct or the character behind the poem too scantily presented. But starting with such questions will often lead you toward the central experience the poem offers. At the very least, the question of speaker helps clarify the tone of voice, and it often provides guidance to the larger situation the poem explores.

• • •

SIR THOMAS WYATT

They Flee from Me

They flee from me, that sometime did me seek,
With naked foot stalking in my chamber.
I have seen them, gentle, tame, and meek,
That now are wild, and do not remember
5 That sometime they put themselves in danger
To take bread at my hand; and now they range,
Busily seeking with a continual change.

Thankéd be Fortune it hath been otherwise,
Twenty times better; but once in special,
10 In thin array, after a pleasant guise,
When her loose gown from her shoulders did fall,

And she me caught in her arms long and small.[8]
And therewith all sweetly did me kiss
And softly said, "Dear heart, how like you this?"

15 It was no dream, I lay broad waking.
But all is turned, thorough[9] my gentleness,
Into a strange fashion of forsaking;
And I have leave to go, of her goodness,
And she also to use newfangleness.[1]
20 But since that I so kindely[2] am servéd,
I fain[3] would know what she hath deservéd.

1557

- Who are "they" who now "flee" the speaker? What is his explanation for their fleeing?

ROBERT BURNS

To a Louse

On Seeing One on a Lady's Bonnet at Church

Ha! whare ya gaun, ye crowlan ferlie![4]
Your impudence protects you sairly:[5]
I canna say but ye strunt[6] rarely,
    Owre gauze and lace;
5 Tho' faith, I fear ye dine but sparely,
    On sic a place.

Ye ugly, creepan, blastit wonner,[7]
Detested, shunn'd, by saunt an' sinner,
How daur ye set your fit[8] upon her,
10   Sae fine a Lady!
Gae somewhere else and seek your dinner,
    On some poor body.

Swith, in some beggar's haffet squattle;[9]
There ye may creep, and sprawl, and sprattle,[1]
15 Wi'ither kindred, jumping cattle,
    In shoals and, nations;
Whare horn nor bane[2] ne'er daur unsettle,
    Your thick plantations.

---

8. Slender.   9. Through.   1. Fondness for novelty.   2. That is, in kind.   3. Eagerly.
4. Crawling miracle!   5. Sorely.   6. Strut.   7. Wonder.   8. Foot.
9. Swift, in some beggar's hair sprawl.   1. Struggle.   2. Bone.

Now haud you there ye're out o'sight,
20   Below the fatt'rels,³ snug and tight,
Na faith ye yet!⁴ ye'll no be right,
      Till ye've got on it,
The vera tapmost, towrin height
      O' Miss's bonnet.

25   My sooth! right bauld ye set your nose out,
As plump an' gray as onie grozet:⁵
O for some rank, mercurial rozet,⁶
      Or fell, red smeddum,⁷
I'd gie you sic a hearty dose o't,
30   Wad dress your droddum!⁸

I wad na been surpriz'd to spy
You on an auld wife's flainen toy,⁹
Or aiblins some bit duddie boy,¹
      On 's wylecoat;²
35   But Miss's fine Lunardi,³ fye!
      How daur ye do't?

O Jenny dinna toss your head,
An' set your beauties a' abroad!⁴
Ye little ken what cursed speed
40   The blastie's⁵ makin!
Thae⁶ winks and finger-ends, I dread,
      Are notice takin!

O wad some Pow'r the giftie gie us
To see oursels as others see us!
45   It wad frae monie a blunder free us
      An foolish notion:
What airs in dress an' gait wad lea'e us,
      And ev'n Devotion!⁷

                   1785

- What is the speaker's attitude toward the louse? toward Jenny?
  What lines best summarize the speaker's main point?

---

3. Ribbon ends.   4. No matter!   5. Gooseberry.   6. Rosin.   7. Or sharp, red powder.
8. Buttocks.   9. Flannel cap.   1. Or perhaps some small ragged boy.   2. Undershirt.
3. Bonnet.   4. Abroad.   5. Creature's.   6. Those.   7. Piety.

EDNA ST. VINCENT MILLAY

[*Women have loved before as I love now*]

Women have loved before as I love now;
At least, in lively chronicles of the past—
Of Irish waters by a Cornish prow
Or Trojan waters by a Spartan mast
5 Much to their cost invaded—here and there,
Hunting the amorous line, skimming the rest,
I find some woman bearing as I bear
Love like a burning city in the breast.
I think however that of all alive
10 I only in such utter, ancient way
Do suffer love; in me alone survive
The unregenerate passions of a day
When treacherous queens, with death upon the tread,
Heedless and wilful, took their knights to bed.

                                                    1931

`WEB` # [*I, being born a woman and distressed*]

I, being born a woman and distressed
By all the needs and notions of my kind,
Am urged by your propinquity to find
Your person fair, and feel a certain zest
5 To bear your body's weight upon my breast:
So subtly is the fume of life designed,
To clarify the pulse and cloud the mind,
And leave me once again undone, possessed.
Think not for this, however, the poor treason
10 Of my stout blood against my staggering brain,
I shall remember you with love, or season
My scorn with pity,—let me make it plain:
I find this frenzy insufficient reason
For conversation when we meet again.

                                                    1923

- Do both of these poems by Edna St. Vincent Millay seem to
  have the same speaker? Why or why not?

GWENDOLYN BROOKS

WEB **We Real Cool**

THE POOL PLAYERS,
SEVEN AT THE GOLDEN SHOVEL.

We real cool. We
Left school. We

Lurk late. We
Strike straight. We

5 Sing sin. We
Thin gin. We

Jazz June. We
Die soon.

1950

• Who are "we" in this poem? Do you think that the speaker and the poet share the same idea of what is "cool"?

WALT WHITMAN

WEB **[I celebrate myself, and sing myself]**

I celebrate myself, and sing myself,
And what I assume you shall assume,
For every atom belonging to me as good belongs to you.
I loafe and invite my soul,
5 I lean and loafe at my ease observing a spear of summer grass.

My tongue, every atom of my blood, form'd from this soil, this air,
Born here of parents born here from parents the same, and their
    parents the same,
I, now thirty-seven years old in perfect health begin,
Hoping to cease not till death.
10 Creeds and schools in abeyance,
Retiring back a while sufficed at what they are, but never forgotten,
I harbor for good or bad, I permit to speak at every hazard,
Nature without check with original energy.

1855, 1881

• What is characteristically American about the speaker of this poem?

SUGGESTIONS FOR WRITING

1. Some of the poems in this chapter create characters and imply situations, as in drama. Write an essay in which you describe and analyze the speaker of either "The Ruined Maid" by Thomas Hardy, "Soliloquy of the Spanish Cloister" by Robert Browning, or "A Certain Lady" by Dorothy Parker.
2. Choose any of the poems in this or the previous chapter and write an essay about the way a poet can create irony and humor through the use of a speaker who is clearly distinct from the poet him- or herself.

10 SITUATION AND SETTING: WHAT HAPPENS? WHERE? WHEN?

Questions about the speaker ("Who" questions) in a poem almost always lead to questions of "Where?" "When?" and "Why?" Identifying the speaker is, in fact, usually part of a larger process of defining the entire imagined **situation** in a poem: What is happening? Where is it happening? Who is the speaker speaking to? Who else is present? Why is this event occurring? In order to understand the dialogue in Hardy's "The Ruined Maid," for example, we need to recognize that the friends are meeting after an extended

> *It is difficult / to get the news*
> *from poems / yet men die*
> *miserably every day / for lack*
> */ of what is found there.*
> —WILLIAM CARLOS WILLIAMS

period of separation, and that they meet in a town setting rather than the rural area in which they grew up together. We infer (from the opening lines) that the meeting is accidental, and that no other friends are present for the conversation. The poem's whole "story" depends on their situation: after leading separate lives for a

while they have some catching up to do. We don't know what specific town, year, season, or time of day is involved because those details are not important to the poem's effect. But crucial to the poem are the where and when questions that define the situation and relationship of the two speakers, and the answer to the why question—that the meeting is by chance—is important, too. In another poem we looked at in the previous chapter, Parker's "A Certain Lady," the specific moment and place are not important, but we do need to notice that the "lady" is talking to (or having an imaginary conversation with) her lover and that they are talking about a relationship of some duration.

Sometimes a *specific* time and place (**setting**) may be important. In Browning's "Soliloquy of the Spanish Cloister," the setting (a monastery) adds to the irony because of the gross inappropriateness of such sentiments and attitudes in a supposedly holy place, just as the setting of Betjeman's "In Westminster Abbey" (below, page 461) similarly helps us to judge the speaker's ideas, attitudes, and self-conception.

The title of the following poem suggests that place may be important, and it is, although you may be surprised to discover exactly what exists at this address and what uses the speaker makes of it.

JAMES DICKEY

Cherrylog Road

Off Highway 106
At Cherrylog Road I entered
The '34 Ford without wheels,
Smothered in kudzu,
5 With a seat pulled out to run
Corn whiskey down from the hills,

And then from the other side
Crept into an Essex
With a rumble seat of red leather
10 And then out again, aboard
A blue Chevrolet, releasing
The rust from its other color,

Reared up on three building blocks.
None had the same body heat;
15 I changed with them inward, toward
The weedy heart of the junkyard,
For I knew that Doris Holbrook
Would escape from her father at noon

And would come from the farm
20 To seek parts owned by the sun
Among the abandoned chassis,
Sitting in each in turn
As I did, leaning forward
As in a wild stock-car race

25 In the parking lot of the dead.
Time after time, I climbed in
And out the other side, like
An envoy or movie star
Met at the station by crickets.
30 A radiator cap raised its head,

Become a real toad or a kingsnake
As I neared the hub of the yard,
Passing through many states,
Many lives, to reach
35 Some grandmother's long Pierce-Arrow
Sending platters of blindness forth

From its nickel hubcaps
And spilling its tender upholstery
On sleepy roaches,

40   The glass panel in between
     Lady and colored driver
     Not all the way broken out,

     The back-seat phone
     Still on its hook.
45   I got in as though to exclaim,
     "Let us go to the orphan asylum,
     John; I have some old toys
     For children who say their prayers."

     I popped with sweat as I thought
50   I heard Doris Holbrook scrape
     Like a mouse in the southern-state sun
     That was eating the paint in blisters
     From a hundred car tops and hoods.
     She was tapping like code,

55   Loosening the screws,
     Carrying off headlights,
     Sparkplugs, bumpers,
     Cracked mirrors and gear-knobs,
     Getting ready, already,
60   To go back with something to show

     Other than her lips' new trembling
     I would hold to me soon, soon,
     Where I sat in the ripped back seat
     Talking over the interphone,
65   Praying for Doris Holbrook
     To come from her father's farm

     And to get back there
     With no trace of me on her face
     To be seen by her red-haired father
70   Who would change, in the squalling barn,
     Her back's pale skin with a strop,
     Then lay for me

     In a bootlegger's roasting car
     With a string-triggered 12-gauge shotgun
75   To blast the breath from the air.
     Not cut by the jagged windshields,
     Through the acres of wrecks she came
     With a wrench in her hand,

     Through dust where the blacksnake dies
80   Of boredom, and the beetle knows
     The compost has no more life.
     Someone outside would have seen

The oldest car's door inexplicably
Close from within:

85 I held her and held her and held her,
Convoyed at terrific speed
By the stalled, dreaming traffic around us,
So the blacksnake, stiff
With inaction, curved back
90 Into life, and hunted the mouse

With deadly overexcitement,
The beetles reclaimed their field
As we clung, glued together,
With the hooks of the seat springs
95 Working through to catch us red-handed
Amidst the gray breathless batting

That burst from the seat at our backs.
We left by separate doors
Into the changed, other bodies
100 Of cars, she down Cherrylog Road
And I to my motorcycle
Parked like the soul of the junkyard

Restored, a bicycle fleshed
With power, and tore off
105 Up Highway 106, continually
Drunk on the wind in my mouth,
Wringing the handlebar for speed,
Wild to be wreckage forever.

1964

The *exact* location of the junkyard is not important (there is no Highway 106 near the real Cherrylog Road in North Georgia), but we do need to know that the setting is rural, that the time is summer and the summer is hot, and that moonshine whiskey is native to the area. Following the story is no problem once we have sorted out these few facts, and we are prepared to meet the cast of characters: Doris Holbrook, her red-haired father, and the speaker. About each we learn just enough to appreciate the sense of vitality, adventure, power, and disengagement that constitute the major effects of the poem.

The situation of lovemaking in a setting other than the junkyard would not produce the same effects, and the exotic sense of a forbidden meeting in this unlikely place helps to re-create the speaker's sense of the episode. For him, it is memorable (notice all the tiny details he recalls), powerful (notice his reaction when he gets back on his motorcycle), dreamlike (notice the sense of time standing still, especially in lines 85–89), and important (notice how the speaker perceives his environment as changed by their love-making, lines 88–91 and 98–100). The wealth of details about setting also helps us to raise other, related questions. Why does the speaker fantasize about being shot by the father (lines 72–75)? Why, in a poem so full of details, do we find out so little about what Doris Holbrook looks like and thinks about? What gives us the sense that this incident is a composite of episodes, an event that was repeated many times? What gives us the impression that the events occurred long ago? What makes the speaker feel so powerful at the end? What does he mean when he talks of himself as being "wild to be wreckage forever"? All of the poem's attention to the speaker's reactions, reflections, and memories is intricately tied up with the particulars of setting. Making love in a junkyard is crucial to the speaker's sense of both power and wreckage, and to him Doris is merely a matter of excitement, adventure, and pale skin, appreciated because she makes the world seem different and because she is willing to take risks and to suffer for meeting him like this. The more we probe the poem with questions about situation, the more likely we are to get a sense of the speaker and to catch the poem's full effect.

The **plot** of "Cherrylog Road" is fairly easy to sort out, but its effect is more complex than the simple story suggests. The next poem we will look at is initially much more difficult to follow. Part of the difficulty is that the poem comes from an earlier age and its language and sentence structure are a bit unfamiliar, and part is that the action in the poem is so closely connected to what is being said. But its opening lines—addressed to someone who is resisting the speaker's suggestions—disclose the situation, and gradually we figure out the scene: a man, trying to convince a woman that they should make love, uses a nearby flea for an unlikely example; it becomes part of his argument. And once we recognize the situation, we can readily follow (and be amused by) the speaker's witty, intricate, and specious argument.

JOHN DONNE

The Flea

> Mark but this flea, and mark in this[1]
> How little that which thou deny'st me is;
> It sucked me first, and now sucks thee,
> And in this flea our two bloods mingled be;
> 5 Thou know'st that this cannot be said
> A sin, nor shame, nor loss of maidenhead.
>   Yet this enjoys before it woo,
>   And pampered[2] swells with one blood made of two,
>   And this, alas, is more than we would do.[3]

1. Medieval preachers and rhetoricians asked their hearers to "mark" (look at) an object that illustrated a moral or philosophical lesson they wished to emphasize.   2. Fed luxuriously.
3. According to the medical theory of Donne's era, conception involved the literal mingling of the lovers' blood.

10 Oh stay,[4] three lives in one flea spare,
Where we almost, yea more than, married are.
This flea is you and I, and this
Our marriage bed, and marriage temple is;
Though parents grudge, and you, we're met
15 And cloistered in these living walls of jet.
　　Though use[5] make you apt to kill me,
　　Let not to that, self-murder added be,
　　And sacrilege, three sins in killing three.

　　Cruel and sudden, hast thou since
20 Purpled thy nail in blood of innocence?
Wherein could this flea guilty be,
Except in that drop which it sucked from thee?
Yet thou triumph'st, and say'st that thou
Find'st not thyself, nor me, the weaker now;
25 　'Tis true; then learn how false, fears be;
　　Just so much honor, when thou yield'st to me,
　　Will waste, as this flea's death took life from thee.

1633

The scene in "The Flea" develops, action occurs, even as the poem unfolds. Between stanzas 1 and 2, the woman makes a move to kill the flea (as stanza 2 opens, the speaker is trying to stop her), and between stanzas 2 and 3 she has squashed the flea with her fingernail. Once we make sense of what the speaker says, the action is just as clear from the words as if we had stage directions in the margin. All of the speaker's verbal cleverness and all of his silly arguments follow from the situation, and in this poem (as in Browning's "Soliloquy of the Spanish Cloister") we watch as if we were observing a scene in a play. The speaker is, in effect, giving a dramatic monologue for our benefit.

Neither time nor place is important to "The Flea," except that we assume the speaker and his friend are in the same place and have the leisure for some playfulness. The situation could occur anywhere a man, a woman, and a flea could be together: indoors, outdoors, morning, evening, city, country, in a cottage or a castle, on a boat or in a bedroom. We know, from the date of publication, that Donne was writing about people of almost four centuries ago, but the conduct he describes might occur in any age. Only the habits of language (and perhaps the outmoded medical ideas) date the poem.

Some poems, however, depend heavily on historical specifics. In the preceding chapter, for example, we saw how Margaret Atwood based "Death of a Young Son by Drowning" on an actual person's journal entries. While the following poem refers to a particular event, it also draws on the parallels between that event and circumstances surrounding the poet and his immediate readers:

4. Desist.　5. Habit.

JOHN MILTON

On the Late Massacre in Piedmont

Avenge, O Lord, thy slaughtered saints, whose bones
    Lie scattered on the Alpine mountains cold;
    Even them who kept thy truth so pure of old
    When all our fathers worshiped stocks and stones,[6]
5 Forget not: in thy book record their groans
    Who were thy sheep and in their ancient fold
    Slain by the bloody Piemontese that rolled
    Mother with infant down the rocks. Their moans
The vales redoubled to the hills, and they
10   To heaven. Their martyred blood and ashes sow
    O'er all th' Italian fields, where still doth sway
    The triple tyrant:[7] that from these may grow
    A hundredfold, who having learnt thy way
    Early may fly the Babylonian woe.[8]

1655

The "slaughtered saints" were members of the Waldensians—a heretical sect that had long been settled in southern France and northern Italy (the Piedmont). Though a minority, the Waldensians were allowed freedom of worship until 1655, when their protection under the law was taken away and locals attacked them, killing large numbers. This poem, then, is not a private meditation, but rather a public statement about a well-known "news" event. To fully understand the poem and respond to it meaningfully, the reader must therefore be acquainted with its historical context, including the massacre itself and the significance it had for Milton and his English audience.

Milton wrote the poem shortly after the massacre became known in England, and implicit in its "meaning" is a parallel Milton's readers would have perceived between events in the Piedmont and current English politics. Milton signals the analogy early on by calling the dead Piedmontese "saints," the term then regularly used by English Protestants of the Puritan stamp to describe themselves and to thereby assert their belief that every individual Christian—not just those few "special" religious heroes singled out in the Catholic tradition—lived a heroic life. By identifying the Waldensians with the English Puritans—their beliefs were in some ways quite similar, and both were minorities in a larger political and cultural context—Milton was warning his fellow Puritans that, if the Stuart monarchy were reestablished, what had just happened to the Waldensians could happen to them as well. Indeed,

6. Idols of wood and stone.   7. The pope's tiara featured three crowns.
8. In Milton's day, Protestants often likened the Roman Church to Babylonian decadence, calling the church "the whore of Babylon," and they read Revelation 17 and 18 as an allegory of its coming destruction.

following the Restoration in 1660, tight restrictions were placed on the Puritan "sects" under the new British monarchy. In lines 12 and 14, the poem alludes to dangers of religious rule by dominant groups by invoking standard images of Catholic power and persecution; the heir to the English throne (who succeeded to the throne as Charles II in 1660) was spending his exile in Catholic Europe and was, because of his sympathetic treatment of Catholic associates and friends, suspected of being a Catholic. Chauvinistic Englishmen, who promoted rivalries with Catholic powers like France, considered him a traitor.

Many poems, like this one, make use of historical occurrences and situations to create a widely evocative set of angers, sympathies, and conclusions. Sometimes a poet's intention in recording a particular moment or event is to commemorate it or comment upon it. A poem written about a specific occasion is usually called an **occasional poem,** and such a poem is **referential;** that is, it *refers* to a certain historical time or event. Sometimes, it is hard to place ourselves fully enough in another time or place to imagine sympathetically what a particular historical moment would have been like, and even the best poetic efforts do not necessarily transport us there. For such poems we need, at the least, specific historical information—plus a willingness on our part as readers to be transported by a name, a date, or a dramatic situation.

Time or place may, of course, be used much less specifically and still be important to a poem; frequently a poem's setting draws upon common notions of a particular time or place. Setting a poem in a garden, for example, or writing about apples almost inevitably reminds many readers of the Garden of Eden because it is part of the Western heritage of belief or knowledge. Even people who don't read at all or who lack Judeo-Christian religious commitments are likely to know about Eden, and a poet writing in our culture can count on that. An **allusion** is a reference to something outside the poem that carries a history of meaning and strong emotional associations. (For a longer account of allusion, see chapter 11.) For example, gardens may carry suggestions of innocence and order, or temptation and the Fall, or both, depending on how the poem handles the allusion. Well-known places from history or myth may be popularly associated with particular ideas or values or ways of life.

The place involved in a poem is its **spatial setting,** and the time is its **temporal setting.** The temporal setting may be a specific date or an era, a season of the year or a time of day. We tend, for example, to think of spring as a time of discovery and growth, and poems set in spring are likely to make use of that association; morning usually suggests discovery as well—beginnings, vitality, the world fresh and new—even to those of us who in reality take our waking slow. Temporal or spatial setting often influences our expectation of theme and tone, although a poet may surprise us by making something very different of what we had thought was familiar. Setting is often an important factor in creating the mood in poems just as in stories, plays, or films. Often the details of setting have a lot to do with the way we ultimately respond to the poem's subject or theme, as in this poem:

MATTHEW ARNOLD

WEB *Dover Beach*[9]

The sea is calm tonight.
The tide is full, the moon lies fair
Upon the straits; on the French coast the light
Gleams and is gone; the cliffs of England stand,
5 Glimmering and vast, out in the tranquil bay.
Come to the window, sweet is the night-air!
Only, from the long line of spray
Where the sea meets the moon-blanched land,
Listen! you hear the grating roar
10 Of pebbles which the waves draw back, and fling,
At their return, up the high strand,
Begin, and cease, and then again begin,
With tremulous cadence slow, and bring
The eternal note of sadness in.

15 Sophocles long ago
Heard it on the Aegean, and it brought
Into his mind the turbid ebb and flow
Of human misery;[1] we
Find also in the sound a thought,
20 Hearing it by this distant northern sea.

The Sea of Faith
Was once, too, at the full, and round earth's shore
Lay like the folds of a bright girdle furled.
But now I only hear
25 Its melancholy, long, withdrawing roar,
Retreating, to the breath
Of the night-wind, down the vast edges drear
And naked shingles[2] of the world.

Ah, love, let us be true
30 To one another! for the world, which seems
To lie before us like a land of dreams,
So various, so beautiful, so new,
Hath really neither joy, nor love, nor light,
Nor certitude, nor peace, nor help for pain;

---

9. At the narrowest point on the English Channel. The light on the French coast (lines 3–4) would be about twenty miles away.
1. In Sophocles' *Antigone,* lines 637–46, the chorus compares the fate of the house of Oedipus to the waves of the sea.   2. Pebble-strewn beaches.

35 And we are here as on a darkling plain
   Swept with confused alarms of struggle and flight,
   Where ignorant armies clash by night.

ca. 1851

Exactly what is the dramatic situation in "Dover Beach"? How soon are you aware that someone is being spoken to? How much do you learn about the person spoken to? How would you describe the speaker's mood? What does the speaker's mood have to do with time and place? Do any details of present time and place help to account for his tendency to talk repeatedly of the past and the future? How important is it to the poem's total effect that the beach here involves an international border? What particulars of Dover Beach seem especially important to the poem's themes? to its emotional effects?

Not all poems have an identifiable situation or setting, just as not all poems have a speaker who is entirely distinct from the author. Poems that simply present a series of thoughts and feelings directly, in a contemplative, meditative, or reflective way, may not set up any kind of action, plot, or situation at all, preferring to speak directly without the intermediary of a dramatic device. But most poems depend crucially upon a sense of place, a sense of time, and an understanding of human interaction in scenes that resemble the strategies of drama or film. And questions about these matters will often lead you to define not only the "facts" but also the feelings central to the design a poem has upon its readers.

SITUATIONS

EMILY BRONTË

The Night-Wind

In summer's mellow midnight,
A cloudless moon shone through
Our open parlor window
And rosetrees wet with dew.

5 I sat in silent musing,
The soft wind waved my hair:
It told me Heaven was glorious,
And sleeping Earth was fair.

I needed not its breathing
10 To bring such thoughts to me,
But still it whispered lowly,
"How dark the woods will be!

"The thick leaves in my murmur
Are rustling like a dream,
15 And all their myriad voices
Instinct[1] with spirit seem."

I said, "Go, gentle singer,
Thy wooing voice is kind,
But do not think its music
20 Has power to reach my mind.

"Play with the scented flower,
The young tree's supple bough,
And leave my human feelings
In their own course to flow."

25 The wanderer would not leave me;
Its kiss grew warmer still—
"O come," it sighed so sweetly,
"I'll win thee 'gainst thy will.

"Have we not been from childhood friends?
30 Have I not loved thee long?
As long as thou hast loved the night
Whose silence wakes my song.

"And when thy heart is laid at rest
Beneath the church-yard stone
35 I shall have time enough to mourn
And thou to be alone."

September 11, 1840

- **What might it mean that the speaker feels tempted by the wind to go wandering in the darkness? What might she find there?**

ANDREW MARVELL

To His Coy Mistress

Had we but world enough, and time,
This coyness,[2] lady, were no crime.
We would sit down, and think which way
To walk, and pass our long love's day.
5 Thou by the Indian Ganges' side
Shouldst rubies[3] find: I by the tide

---

1. Infused.   2. Hesitancy, modesty (not necessarily suggesting calculation).
3. Talismans that are supposed to preserve virginity.

Of Humber would complain.⁴ I would
Love you ten years before the Flood,
And you should if you please refuse
10 Till the conversion of the Jews.⁵
My vegetable love⁶ should grow
Vaster than empires, and more slow;
An hundred years should go to praise
Thine eyes, and on thy forehead gaze;
15 Two hundred to adore each breast,
But thirty thousand to the rest.
An age at least to every part,
And the last age should show your heart.
For, lady, you deserve this state;⁷
20 Nor would I love at lower rate.
   But at my back I always hear
Time's wingéd chariot hurrying near;
And yonder all before us lie
Deserts of vast eternity.
25 Thy beauty shall no more be found,
Nor, in thy marble vault, shall sound
My echoing song; then worms shall try
That long preserved virginity,
And your quaint honor turn to dust,
30 And into ashes all my lust:
The grave's a fine and private place,
But none, I think, do there embrace.
   Now therefore, while the youthful hue
Sits on thy skin like morning dew,⁸
35 And while thy willing soul transpires⁹
At every pore with instant fires,
Now let us sport us while we may,
And now, like am'rous birds of prey,
Rather at once our time devour
40 Than languish in his slow-chapped¹ pow'r.
Let us roll all our strength and all
Our sweetness up into one ball,
And tear our pleasures with rough strife

---

4. Write love complaints, conventional songs lamenting the cruelty of love. *Humber:* a river and estuary in Marvell's hometown of Hull.
5. Which, according to popular Christian belief, will occur just before the end of the world.
6. Which is capable only of passive growth, not of consciousness. The "vegetable soul" is lower than the other two divisions of the soul, "animal" and "rational."   7. Dignity.
8. The text reads "glew." "Lew" (warmth) has also been suggested as an emendation.
9. Breathes forth.
1. Slow-jawed. Chronos (Time), ruler of the world in early Greek myth, devoured all of his children except Zeus, who was hidden. Later, Zeus seized power (see line 46 and note).

Thorough[2] the iron gates of life.
45 Thus, though we cannot make our sun
Stand still,[3] yet we will make him run.[4]

1681

- Whom is the speaker trying to persuade in this poem? Is his argument persuasive?

HOWARD NEMEROV

A Way of Life

It's been going on a long time.
For instance, these two guys, not saying much, who slog
Through sun and sand, fleeing the scene of their crime,
Till one turns, without a word, and smacks
5 His buddy flat with the flat of an axe,
Which cuts down on the dialogue
Some, but is viewed rather as normal than sad
By me, as I wait for the next ad.

It seems to me it's been quite a while
10 Since the last vision of blonde loveliness
Vanished, her shampoo and shower and general style
Replaced by this lean young lunk-
head parading along with a gun in his back to confess
How yestereve, being drunk
15 And in a state of existential despair,
He beat up his grandma and pawned her invalid chair.

But here at last is a pale beauty
Smoking a filter beside a mountain stream,
Brief interlude, before the conflict of love and duty
20 Gets moving again, as sheriff and posse expound,
Between jail and saloon, the American Dream
Where Justice, after considerable horsing around,
Turns out to be Mercy; when the villain is knocked off,
A kindly uncle offers syrup for my cough.

25 And now these clean-cut athletic types
In global hats are having a nervous debate
As they stand between their individual rocket ships
Which have landed, appropriately, on some rocks
Somewhere in Space, in an atmosphere of hate

2. Through.   3. To lengthen his night of love with Alcmene, Zeus made the sun stand still.
4. Each sex act was believed to shorten life by one day.

30 Where one tells the other to pull up his socks
And get going, he doesn't say where; they fade,
And an angel food cake flutters in the void.

I used to leave now and again;
No more. A lot of violence in American life
35 These days, mobsters and cops all over the scene.
But there's a lot of love, too, mixed with the strife,
And kitchen-kindness, like a bedtime story
With rich food and a more kissable depilatory.
Still, I keep my weapons handy, sitting here
40 Smoking and shaving and drinking the dry beer.

1967

- What does the succession of images represent to the speaker
  of this poem? Would the situation be different today?

TIMES

WILLIAM SHAKESPEARE

[*Full many a glorious morning have I seen*]

Full many a glorious morning have I seen
Flatter the mountain-tops with sovereign eye,
Kissing with golden face the meadows green,
Gilding pale streams with heavenly alchymy;
5 Anon permit the basest clouds to ride
With ugly rack[1] on his celestial face,
And from the forlorn world his visage hide,
Stealing unseen to west with this disgrace:
Even so my sun one early morn did shine,
10 With all-triumphant splendor on my brow;
But, out! alack! he was but one hour mine,
The region cloud hath mask'd him from me now.
  Yet him for this my love no whit disdaineth;
  Suns of the world may stain when heaven's sun staineth.

1609

- What words and phrases mark the shifts of the clouds back
  and forth across the face of the sun in "Full many a glorious
  morning"? What distinction is Shakespeare making between
  "suns of the world" and "heaven's sun"?

---

1. Moss.

JOHN DONNE

The Good-Morrow

I wonder, by my troth, what thou and I
  Did, till we loved? were we not weaned till then?
But sucked on country pleasures, childishly?
  Or snorted we in the Seven Sleepers' den?[2]
5   'Twas so; but[3] this, all pleasures fancies be.
  If ever any beauty I did see,
Which I desired, and got,[4] twas but a dream of thee.

And now good-morrow to our waking souls,
  Which watch not one another out of fear;
10   For love, all love of other sights controls,
  And makes one little room an everywhere.
Let sea-discoverers to new worlds have gone,
Let maps to other,[5] worlds on worlds have shown,
Let us possess one world, each hath one, and is one.

15   My face in thine eye, thine in mine appears,[6]
  And true plain hearts do in the faces rest;
Where can we find two better hemispheres,
  Without sharp north, without declining west?
Whatever dies was not mixed equally,[7]
20   If our two loves be one, or, thou and I
Love so alike that none do slacken, none can die.

                                                    1633

- Like so many of Donne's poems, this one attempts to persuade. What is the situation of this poem? What does the speaker wish to demonstrate?

SYLVIA PLATH

WEB ### Morning Song

Love set you going like a fat gold watch.
The midwife slapped your footsoles, and your bald cry
Took its place among the elements.

---

2. According to legend, seven Christian youths escaped Roman persecution by sleeping in a cave for 187 years. *Snorted:* snored.   3. Except for.   4. Sexually possessed.   5. Other people.
6. That is, each is reflected in the other's eyes.
7. Perfectly mixed elements, according to scholastic philosophy, were stable and immortal.

Our voices echo, magnifying your arrival. New statue.
5 In a drafty museum, your nakedness
Shadows our safety. We stand round blankly as walls.

I'm no more your mother
Than the cloud that distils a mirror to reflect its own slow
Effacement at the wind's hand.

10 All night your moth-breath
Flickers among the flat pink roses. I wake to listen:
A far sea moves in my ear.

One cry, and I stumble from bed, cow-heavy and floral
In my Victorian nightgown.
15 Your mouth opens clean as a cat's. The window square

Whitens and swallows its dull stars. And now you try
Your handful of notes;
The clear vowels rise like balloons.

1961

- How does this poem's language emphasize the distinctions
  between the speaker and her baby? How does the poem's setting in time—morning—affect its meaning?

PLACES

JOHN BETJEMAN

In Westminster Abbey[1]

Let me take this other glove off
   As the *vox humana*[2] swells,
And the beauteous fields of Eden
   Bask beneath the Abbey bells.
5 Here, where England's statesmen lie,
Listen to a lady's cry.

Gracious Lord, oh bomb the Germans.
   Spare their women for Thy Sake,
And if that is not too easy
10   We will pardon Thy Mistake.
But, gracious Lord, whate'er shall be,
Don't let anyone bomb me.

---

1. Gothic church in London in which English monarchs are crowned and many famous Englishmen
are buried (see lines 5, 39–40).   2. Organ tones that resemble the human voice.

Keep our Empire undismembered
   Guide our Forces by Thy Hand,
15 Gallant blacks from far Jamaica,
   Honduras and Togoland;
Protect them Lord in all their fights,
   And, even more, protect the whites.

Think of what our Nation stands for,
20   Books from Boots³ and country lanes,
Free speech, free passes, class distinction,
   Democracy and proper drains.
Lord, put beneath Thy special care
One-eighty-nine Cadogan Square.⁴

25 Although dear Lord I am a sinner,
   I have done no major crime;
Now I'll come to Evening Service
   Whensoever I have the time.
So, Lord, reserve for me a crown,⁵
30 And do not let my shares go down.

I will labor for Thy Kingdom,
   Help our lads to win the war,
Send white feathers to the cowards⁶
   Join the Women's Army Corps,⁷
35 Then wash the Steps around Thy Throne
   In the Eternal Safety Zone.

Now I feel a little better,
   What a treat to hear Thy Word
Where the bones of leading statesmen,
40   Have so often been interred.
And now, dear Lord, I cannot wait
Because I have a luncheon date.

1940

- How do the poem's setting in place—a historic church in London—and time—1940, during the German bombardment of Britain—affect the tone?

---

3. A chain of British pharmacies.
4. Presumably where the speaker lives, in a fashionable section of central London.
5. Coin worth five shillings (but also an afterlife reward).
6. White feathers were sometimes given or sent to men not in uniform to suggest that they were cowards and should join the armed forces.
7. The speaker uses the old World War I name (Women's Army Auxiliary Corps) of the Auxiliary Territorial Service, an organization that performed domestic (and some foreign) defense duties.

DEREK WALCOTT

Midsummer

Certain things here[8] are quietly American—
that chain-link fence dividing the absent roars
of the beach from the empty ball park, its holes
muttering the word umpire instead of empire;
5 the gray, metal light where an early pelican
coasts, with its engine off, over the pink fire
of a sea whose surface is as cold as Maine's.
The light warms up the sides of white, eager Cessnas[9]
parked at the airstrip under the freckling hills
10 of St. Thomas. The sheds, the brown, functional hangar,
are like those of the Occupation in the last war.
The night left a rank smell under the casuarinas,
the villas have fenced-off beaches where the natives walk,
illegal immigrants from unlucky islands
15 who envy the smallest polyp its right to work.
Here the wetback crab and the mollusc are citizens,
and the leaves have green cards. Bulldozers jerk
and gouge out a hill, but we all know that the dust
is industrial and must be suffered. Soon—
20 the sea's corrugations are sheets of zinc
soldered by the sun's steady acetylene. This
drizzle that falls now is American rain,
stitching stars in the sand. My own corpuscles
are changing as fast. I fear what the migrant envies:
25 the starry pattern they make—the flag on the post office—
the quality of the dirt, the fealty changing under my foot.

                                                    1984

- What is "American" (line 22) about the images described in
  this poem? Why does the speaker say he fears "the starry pattern" made by the raindrops in the sand (line 25)?

THOM GUNN

A Map of the City

I stand upon a hill and see
A luminous country under me,
Through which at two the drunk must weave;
The transient's pause, the sailor's leave.

---

8. Trinidad.   9. Small airplanes.

5   I notice, looking down the hill,
    Arms braced upon a window sill;
    And on the web of fire escapes
    Move the potential, the grey shapes.

    I hold the city here, complete:
10 And every shape defined by light
    Is mine, or corresponds to mine,
    Some flickering or some steady shine.

    This map is ground of my delight.
    Between the limits, night by night,
15 I watch a malady's advance,
    I recognize my love of chance.

    By the recurrent lights I see
    Endless potentiality,
    The crowded, broken, and unfinished!
20 I would not have the risk diminished.

                                    1954

- In what way does the speaker's view of a city at night constitute a "map"? How is this map "complete" (line 9)?

_____

SUGGESTIONS FOR WRITING

1. Matthew Arnold's "Dover Beach" is a meditation on history and human destiny derived from the poet's close observation of the ebb and flow of the sea.
   Write an essay in which you examine the poem's descriptive language and the
   way this creates a suitable setting for Arnold's philosophical musings.

2. Certain seventeenth-century poets, such as John Donne and Andrew Marvell,
   have been called "metaphysical poets" for their ingenuity in using apparently
   far-fetched analogies to create apt and insightful comparisons, usually
   intended to persuade. What is the line of reasoning in Donne's "The Flea" or
   Marvell's "To His Coy Mistress?" Who is the intended audience for each poem?
   Write an essay in which you discuss the way that either or both of these poems
   uses situation as the basis for comparison and persuasion.

3. Choose any of the poems in this or the previous chapters and write an essay
   about the way a poet can use situation and setting to evoke a rich intermingling of language, subject, and feeling.

11 LANGUAGE

Fiction and drama depend upon language just as poetry does, but in a poem almost everything comes down to the particular meanings and implications of individual words. When we read stories and plays, we generally focus our attention on character and plot, and although words determine how we imagine those characters and how we respond to what happens to them, we are not as likely to pause over any one word as we may need to when reading a poem. Because poems are often short, a lot depends on every word in them. Sometimes, as though they were distilled prose, poems contain only the essential words. They say just barely enough to communicate in the most basic way, using elemental signs—with each chosen for exactly the right shade of meaning or feeling or both. But elemental does not necessarily mean simple, and these signs may be very rich in their meanings and complex in their effects. The poet's word choice—the **diction** of a poem—determines not only meaning but just about every effect the poem produces.

PRECISION AND AMBIGUITY

Let's look first at poems that create some of their effects by examining—or playing with—a single word. Often multiple meanings or shiftiness and uncertainty of a word are at issue. The following short poem, for example, depends almost entirely on the way we use the word *play*.

SARAH CLEGHORN

[The golf links lie so near the mill]

The golf links lie so near the mill
That almost every day
The laboring children can look out
And see the men at play.

1915

While traveling in the American South, Cleghorn had seen, right next to a golf course, a textile mill that employed quite young children. Her poem doesn't *say* that we expect men to work and children to play; it just assumes our expectation and builds an effect of **dramatic irony**—an incongruity between what we expect and what actually occurs—out of the observation.

The poem saves almost all of its devastating effect for the final word, after the situation has been carefully described and the irony set up.

Here is a far more personal and emotional poem, which uses a single word, "terminal," to explore the changing relationship between two people—a father (who speaks the poem) and daughter.

YVOR WINTERS

At the San Francisco Airport

to my daughter, 1954

This is the terminal: the light
Gives perfect vision, false and hard;
The metal glitters, deep and bright.
Great planes are waiting in the yard—
5   They are already in the night.

And you are here beside me, small,
Contained and fragile, and intent
On things that I but half recall—
Yet going whither you are bent.
10 I am the past, and that is all.

But you and I in part are one:
The frightened brain, the nervous will,
The knowledge of what must be done,
The passion to acquire the skill
15 To face that which you dare not shun.

The rain of matter upon sense
Destroys me momently. The score:
There comes what will come. The expense
Is what one thought, and something more—
20 One's being and intelligence.

This is the terminal, the break.
Beyond this point, on lines of air,
You take the way that you must take;
And I remain in light and stare—
25 In light, and nothing else, awake.

1954

In this case, the poem soberly and thoughtfully probes the several possible meanings of its key word. The importance of the word involves its **ambiguity** (its having more than one possible meaning) rather than its **precision** (its exactness).

What does it *mean* to be in a place called a "terminal"? As the parting of father and daughter is explored carefully, the place of parting and the means of transportation take on meanings larger than their simple referential ones. The poem presents contrasts—young and old, light and dark, past and present, security and adventure. The father ("I am the past," line 10) remains in the light, among known objects and experiences familiar to his many years; the daughter is about to depart into the night, the unknown, the uncertain future. But they both share a sense of the necessity of the parting, of the need for the daughter to mature, gain knowledge, acquire experience. Is she going off to school? to college? to her first job? We don't know, but her plane ride clearly means a new departure and a clean break with childhood, dependency, the past.

So much depends upon the word "terminal." It refers to the airport building, of course, but it also implies a boundary, an extremity, a terminus, something that is limited, a junction, a place where a connection may be broken. Important as well is the unambiguous or "dictionary" meaning of certain other words—that is, what these words **denote**. The final stanza is articulated flatly, as if the speaker has recovered from the momentary confusion of stanza 4, when "being and intelligence" are lost in the emotion of the parting itself. The words "break," "point," "way," and "remain" are almost unemotional and colorless; they do not make value judgments or offer personal views, but rather define and describe. The sharp articulation of the last stanza stresses the **denotations** of the words employed, as though the speaker is trying to disengage himself from the emotion of the situation and just give the facts.

Words, however, are more than hard blocks of meaning on whose sense everyone agrees. They also have a more personal side, and they carry emotional force and shades of suggestion. The words we use indicate not only what we mean but how we feel about it, and we choose words that we hope will engage others emotionally and persuasively, in conversation and daily usage as well as in poems. A person who holds office is, quite literally (and unemotionally), an *officeholder*—the word denotes what he or she does. But if we want to convey that a particular officeholder is wise, trustworthy, and deserving of political support we may call that person a *civil servant*, a *political leader*, or an *elected official*, whereas if we want to promote distrust or contempt of that same officeholder we might say *politician* or *bureaucrat* or *political hack*. These latter terms have clear **connotations**— suggestions of emotional coloration that imply our attitude and invite a similar one from our hearers. What words **connote** can be just as important to a poem as what they denote; some poems work primarily through denotation and some more through connotation.

> *A poet is, before anything else, a person who is passionately in love with language.*
>
> —W. H. AUDEN

"At the San Francisco Airport," certainly, depends primarily on denotation. The speaker tries to *specify* the meanings and implications of the parting with his daughter, and his tendency to split categories neatly for the two of them at first contributes to the sense of clarity and certainty he wants to project. He is the past (line 10) and what remains (line 24); he has age and experience, his life is the known quantity, he stands in the light. She, on the other hand, is committed to the adventure of going into the night; she seems small, fragile, and her identity blurs into the uncertain future. Yet the connotations of some words carry strong emotional force as well as clear definition: that the daughter seems "small" and "fragile" to the speaker suggests his fear for her, something quite different from her own sense of adventure. The neat, clean categories keep breaking down, and the speaker's feelings keep showing through. In stanza 1, the light in the terminal gives "perfect vision," but the speaker also notices, indirectly, its artificial quality: it is "false" and "hard," suggesting the limits of the rationalism he tries to maintain. That artificial light shines over most of the poem and honors the speaker's effort, but the whole poem represents his struggle, and in stanza 4 the signals of disturbance are very strong as, despite an insistence on a vocabulary of calculation, his rational facade collapses completely. If we have observed his verbal strategies carefully, we should not be surprised to find him at the end just *staring* in the artificial light, merely awake, although the poem has shown him to be unconsciously awake to much more than he will candidly admit.

"At the San Francisco Airport" is an unusually intricate and complicated poem, and it offers us, if we are willing to examine precisely its carefully crafted fabric, rich insight into how complex it is to be human and to have human feelings and foibles when we think we must be rational machines.

But connotations can work more simply. The following epitaph, for example, even though it describes the mixed feelings one person has about another, depends heavily on the connotations of fairly common words.

WALTER DE LA MARE
Slim Cunning Hands

Slim cunning hands at rest, and cozening eyes—
Under this stone one loved too wildly lies;
How false she was, no granite could declare;
    Nor all earth's flowers, how fair.

1950

What the speaker in "Slim Cunning Hands" remembers about the dead woman—her hands, her eyes—tells part of the story; her physical presence was clearly important to him. The poem's other nouns—stone, granite, flowers—all remind us of her death and its finality. All these words denote objects having to do with the rituals that memorialize a departed life. Granite and stone connote finality as well, and flowers connote fragility and suggest the shortness of life (which is why they have become the symbolic language of funerals). The way the speaker talks about the woman expresses, in just a few words, the complexity of his love for her. She was loved, he says, too "wildly"—by him perhaps, and apparently by others. The excitement she offered is suggested by the word, and also the lack of control. The words "cunning" and "cozening" help us interpret both her wildness and her falsity; they suggest her calculation, cleverness, and untrustworthiness as well as her skill, persuasiveness, and ability to please. Moreover, coming at the end of the second line the word "lies" has more than one meaning. The body "lies" under the stone, but the woman's falsity has by now become too prominent to ignore as a second meaning. And the word "fair," a simple yet very inclusive word, suggests how totally attractive the speaker finds her: her beauty can no more be expressed by flowers than her fickleness can be expressed by something as permanent as words in stone. But the word "fair," in the emphatic position as the final word, also implies two other meanings that seem to resonate, ironically, with what we have already learned about her from the speaker: "impartial" and "just." "Impartial" she may be in her preferences (as the word "false" suggests), but to the speaker she is hardly "just," and the final defining word speaks both to her appearance and (ironically) to her character. Simple words here tell us perhaps all we need to know of a long story—or at least the speaker's version of it.

Words like "fair" and "cozening" are clearly loaded. They imply more emotionally than they mean literally. They have strong, clear connotations; they tell us what to think, what evaluation to make; and they suggest the basis for the evaluation. Sometimes word choice in poems is less dramatic and less obviously "significant" but equally important. Often, in fact, simple appropriateness makes the words in a poem work, and words that do not call special attention to themselves can be the most effective. Precision of denotation may be just as impressive and productive of specific effects as the resonance or ambiguous suggestiveness of connotation. Often poems achieve their power by a combination of verbal effects, setting off elaborate figures of speech (which we will discuss shortly) or other complicated strategies with simple words chosen to mark exact actions, moments, or states of mind. Notice, for example, how carefully the following poem produces its complex description of emotional patterns by delineating and then elaborating precise stages of feeling.

EMILY DICKINSON

[*After great pain, a formal feeling comes—*]

After great pain, a formal feeling comes—
The Nerves sit ceremonious, like Tombs—
The stiff Heart questions was it He, that bore,
And Yesterday, or Centuries before?

5   The Feet, mechanical, go round—
     Of Ground, or Air, or Ought—
     A Wooden way
     Regardless grown,
     A Quartz contentment, like a stone—

10 This is the Hour of Lead—
   Remembered, if outlived,
   As Freezing Persons recollect the Snow—
   First—Chill—then Stupor—then the letting go—

ca. 1862

As you read the following poem, notice how the title calls upon us to wonder, from the beginning, how playful and how patterned the boy's bedtime romp with his father is. Try to be conscious of the emotional effects created by what seem to be the key words. Which words establish the bond between the two males?

THEODORE ROETHKE

My Papa's Waltz

The whiskey on your breath
Could make a small boy dizzy;
But I hung on like death:
Such waltzing was not easy.

5 We romped until the pans
Slid from the kitchen shelf;
My mother's countenance
Could not unfrown itself.

The hand that held my wrist
10 Was battered on one knuckle;
At every step you missed
My right ear scraped a buckle.

You beat time on my head
With a palm caked hard by dirt,
15 Then waltzed me off to bed
Still clinging to your shirt.

1948

Exactly what is the situation in "My Papa's Waltz"? What are the family's economic circumstances? How can you tell? What indications are there of the family's social class, or of the father's line of work? How would you characterize the speaker? How does the poem indicate his pleasure in the bedtime ritual? Which words suggest the boy's excitement? Which suggest his anxiety? How can you tell the speaker's feelings about his father? What clues are there about what the mother is like? What clues are there in the word choice that an adult is remembering a childhood experience? How scared was the boy at the time? How does the grown adult now evaluate his emotions when he was a boy? In what sense is the poem a tribute to memories of the father? How would you describe the poem's tone?

The subtlety and force of word choice is sometimes very much affected by **word order,** the way the sentences are put together. Some poems employ unusual word order because of the demands of rhyme and meter, but ordinarily poets use word order very much as prose writers do, to create a particular emphasis. When you find an unusual word order, you can be pretty sure that something there merits special attention. Notice the odd constructions in the second and third stanzas of "My Papa's Waltz"—the way the speaker talks about the abrasion of buckle on ear in line 12, for example. He does not say that the buckle scraped his ear, but rather puts it the other way round—a big difference in the kind of effect created, for it avoids placing blame and refuses to specify any unpleasant effect. Had he said that the buckle scraped his ear—the normal way of putting it—we would have to worry about the fragile ear. The **syntax** (sentence structure) of the poem channels our feeling and helps to control what we think of the "waltz."

In the most curious part of the poem, the second stanza, the silent mother appears, and the syntax is peculiar in two places. In lines 5-6, the connection between the romping and the pans falling is stated oddly: "We romped *until* the pans / Slid from the kitchen shelf" (emphasis added). The speaker does not say that they knocked down the pans or imply awkwardness, but he does suggest energetic activity and duration. He implies intensity, almost intention—as though the romping would not be complete until the pans fell. And the sentence about the mother—odd but effective—makes her position clear. A silent bystander in this male ritual, she doesn't seem frightened or angry. She seems to be holding a frown, or to have it molded on her face, as though it were part of her own ritual, and perhaps a facet of her stern character as well. The syntax implies that she *has to* maintain the frown, and the falling of the pans almost seems to be for her benefit. She disapproves, but she remains their audience.

Words, the basic materials of poetry, come in many kinds and can be used in many different ways and in different—sometimes surprising—combinations. They are seldom simple or transparent, even when we know their meanings and recognize their syntactical combinations as ordinary and conventional. Carefully examining them, individually and collectively, is a crucial part of reading poems, and being able to ask good questions about the words that poems use is one of the most basic—and rewarding—skills a reader of poetry can develop.

• • •

EMILY DICKINSON

[*I dwell in Possibility—*]

I dwell in Possibility—
A fairer House than Prose—
More numerous of Windows—
Superior—for Doors—

5 Of Chambers as the Cedars—
Impregnable of Eye—
And for an Everlasting Roof
The Gambrels[1] of the Sky—

Of Visitors—the fairest—
10 For Occupation—This—
The spreading wide my narrow Hands
To gather Paradise—

ca. 1862

- What does Dickinson seem to mean by "Possibility"? How does the poem's ending broaden this meaning?

WILLIAM CARLOS WILLIAMS

The Red Wheelbarrow

so much depends
upon

a red wheel
barrow

5 glazed with rain
water

beside the white
chickens.

1923

- Why do you think the poet has included the details of the "rain / water" and "the white / chickens"?

[WEB] *This Is Just to Say*

I have eaten
the plums
that were in
the icebox

5 and which
you were probably
saving
for breakfast

1. Roofs with double slopes.

Forgive me
10 they were delicious
so sweet
and so cold

1934

- What is meant by "This" in the poem's title? What is the apparent occasion for this poem?

GERARD MANLEY HOPKINS

Pied Beauty[2]

Glory be to God for dappled things—
    For skies of couple-color as a brinded[3] cow;
      For rose-moles all in stipple[4] upon trout that swim;
Fresh-firecoal chestnut-falls;[5] finches' wings;
5   Landscape plotted and pieced—fold, fallow, and plow;
    And all trades, their gear and tackle and trim.
All things counter, original, spare, strange;
    Whatever is fickle, freckled (who knows how?)
      With swift, slow; sweet, sour; adazzle, dim;
10 He fathers-forth whose beauty is past change;
      Praise him.

1887

- How many ways of expressing mixed color can you find in this poem? How does Hopkins expand the meaning of "pied beauty"?

E. E. CUMMINGS

[in Just-][6]

in Just-
spring   when the world is mud-
luscious the little
lame balloonman

5 whistles   far   and wee

and eddieandbill come
running from marbles and

2. Particolored beauty: having patches or sections of more than one color.
3. Streaked or spotted. 4. Rose-colored dots or flecks.
5. Fallen chestnuts as red as burning coals. 6. The first poem in the series *Chansons innocentes*.

piracies and it's
spring

10   when the world is puddle-wonderful

the queer
old balloonman whistles
far   and   wee
and bettyandisbel come dancing

15   from hop-scotch and jump-rope and
it's
spring
and
      the
20   goat-footed

balloonMan   whistles
far
and
wee[7]

                                    1923

- What are some connotations of "mud-luscious" and "puddle-wonderful"? What are some of the ways in which this poem challenges a reader's expectations of diction and syntax?

BEN JONSON

Still to Be Neat[8]

Still[9] to be neat, still to be dressed,
As you were going to a feast;
Still to be powdered, still perfumed;
Lady, it is to be presumed,
5   Though art's hid causes are not found,
All is not sweet, all is not sound.

Give me a look, give me a face
That makes simplicity a grace;
Robes loosely flowing, hair as free;
10   Such sweet neglect more taketh me
Than all th' adulteries of art.
They strike mine eyes, but not my heart.

                                    1609

---

7. Pan, whose Greek name means "everything," is traditionally represented with a syrinx (or the pipes of Pan). The upper half of his body is human, the lower half goat, and as the father of Silenus he is associated with the spring rites of Dionysus.
8. A song from Jonson's play *The Silent Woman* (1609–10).   9. Continually.

- What are at least two possible meanings of the poem's assertion that "all is not sound"? What are some connotations of "th' adulteries of art"?

ROBERT HERRICK

Delight in Disorder

A sweet disorder in the dress
Kindles in clothes a wantonness.
A lawn[1] about the shoulders thrown
Into a fine distractiön;
5 An erring lace, which here and there
Enthralls the crimson stomacher,[2]
A cuff neglectful, and thereby
Ribbands[3] to flow confusedly;
A winning wave, deserving note,
10 In the tempestuous petticoat;
A careless shoestring, in whose tie
I see a wild civility;
Do more bewitch me than when art
Is too precise[4] in every part.

1648

- What are some of the words that this poem uses to indicate "disorder"? Why do you think the speaker finds disorder "sweet"?

PICTURING: THE LANGUAGES OF DESCRIPTION

The language of poetry is most often visual and pictorial. Rather than depending primarily on abstract ideas and elaborate reasoning, poems depend mainly on concrete and specific words that create images in our minds. Poems thus help us to see things afresh and anew or to feel them suggestively through our other physical senses, such as hearing or touch. But mostly, poetry uses the sense of sight to help us form, in our minds, visual impressions, images that communicate more directly than concepts. We "see" yellow leaves on a branch, a father and son waltzing precariously, or two lovers sitting together on the bank of a stream, so that our response begins from a vivid impression of exactly what is happening. Some people think that those media and arts that challenge the imagination of a hearer or reader—radio drama, for example, or poetry—allow us to respond more

1. Scarf of fine linen. 2. Ornamental covering for the breasts. 3. Ribbons.
4. In the sixteenth and seventeenth centuries, Puritans were often called Precisians because of their fastidiousness.

fully than those (such as television or theater) that actually show things more fully to our physical senses. Certainly they leave more to our imagination, to our mind's eye.

Visual applications of language stem from the nature and direction of the poetic process itself, and some of them have to do with how poems are conceived and then, gradually, fleshed out in words. Poems are sometimes quite abstract—they can even be *about* abstractions. But usually, they are quite concrete in what they ask us to see. One reason is that they often begin in a poet's mind with a picture or an image: of a person, a place, an event, or an object of observation. That image may be based on something the poet has seen—that is, it may be a picture of something remembered by the poet—but it may also be totally imaginary and only based on the "real world" in the sense that it draws on the poet's physical sense of what the world is like, including the people and things in it. Sometimes a poet represents an imagined scene or object in a highly stylized or feeling-centered way, as do, for example, impressionist or surrealist painters. But that process often begins from a quite specific image in the poet's mind that he or she then tries to **represent,** in words, in such a way that readers can "see" it, too, through the poet's vivid verbal representation of what he or she has already "seen" (imagined) in the mind.

Think of it this way: a painter or sculptor uses strategies of form, color, texture, viewpoint, and relationship to create a visual idea, and so the viewer begins with an *actual* image, something that can be seen physically (though the viewer's understanding and interpretation may be many steps away). Even when a poet begins with an idea that draws on visual experience, however, the reader still has to *imagine* (through the poem's words) an image, some person or thing or action that the poem describes. The poet must help the reader to flesh out that mental image on the basis of the words he or she uses. In a sense, then, the reader becomes a visual artist, but the poet directs how the visualization is to be done by evoking specific responses through words. *How* that happens can involve quite complicated verbal strategies—or even *visual* ones that draw on the possibilities of print.

The languages of description are quite varied. The visual qualities of poetry result partly from the two aspects of poetic language described in the previous section: on the one hand, the precision of individual words, and, on the other hand, precision's opposite—the reach, richness, and ambiguity of suggestion that words sometimes accrue. Visualization can also derive from sophisticated rhetorical and literary devices (figures of speech and symbols, for example, as we will see later in this chapter). But often description begins simply with naming—providing the word (noun, verb, adjective, or adverb) that will trigger images familiar from a reader's own experience. A reader can readily imagine a *dog* or *cat* or *house* or *flower* when each word is named, but not all readers will have the same kind of dog or flower come to mind (because of our individual experiences) until the word is qualified in some way. So the poet may specify that the dog is a greyhound or poodle, or that the flower is a daffodil or a lilac or Queen Anne's lace; or the poet may provide colors, sizes, specific movements, or particular identifying features. Such description can involve either narrowing by category or expansion through detail, and often comparisons are either explicitly or implicitly involved. In Richard Wilbur's "The Beautiful Changes," for example, the similarity between wading through flowers in a meadow and wading among waves in the sea helps to suggest how the first experience feels as well as to etch it visually in our minds. More than just a matter of naming, using precise words, and providing basic information, description involves qualification and comparison; sometimes the poet needs to tell us what a picture is not, dissociating what the poem describes from other possible images we may have in mind. Different features in the language of description add up to something that describes a whole—a picture or scene—as well as a series of individualized objects.

Seeing in the mind's eye—the re-creation of visual experience—requires different skills from poets and readers. Poets use all the language strategies they can think of to re-create for us something they have already "seen." Poets depend on our having had a rich variety of visual experiences and try to draw on those experiences by using common, evocative words and then refining the process through more elaborate verbal devices. We as readers inhabit the process the other way around, trying to draw on our previous knowledge so that we can "see" by following verbal clues. In the poems that follow, notice the ways that description leads to specific images, and pay attention to how shape, color, relationship, and perspective become clear, not only through individual words but also through combinations of words and phrases that suggest appearance and motion.

• • •

OSCAR WILDE

Symphony in Yellow

An omnibus across the bridge
  Crawls like a yellow butterfly,
  And, here and there, a passer-by
Shows like a little restless midge.[1]

5 Big barges full of yellow hay
  Are moored against the shadowy wharf,
  And, like a yellow silken scarf,
The thick fog hangs along the quay.

The yellow leaves begin to fade
10 And flutter from the Temple[2] elms,
  And at my feet the pale green Thames
Lies like a rod of rippled jade.

                 1909

---

1. Tiny mosquito-like insect.   2. The law-courts area of London.

- What can you infer about London and its climate and the season from each of the yellow images in this poem?

RICHARD WILBUR

The Beautiful Changes

One wading a Fall meadow finds on all sides
The Queen Anne's Lace[3] lying like lilies
On water; it glides
So from the walker, it turns
5 Dry grass to a lake, as the slightest shade of you
Valleys my mind in fabulous blue Lucernes.[4]

The beautiful changes as a forest is changed
By a chameleon's tuning his skin to it;
As a mantis, arranged
10 On a green leaf, grows
Into it, makes the leaf leafier, and proves
Any greenness is deeper than anyone knows.

Your hands hold roses always in a way that says
They are not only yours; the beautiful changes
15 In such kind ways,
Wishing ever to sunder
Things and things' selves for a second finding, to lose
For a moment all that it touches back to wonder.
                                                    1947

- What part of speech is "Beautiful" in the poem's title and lines 7 and 14? What part of speech is "Changes"? What is meant by "the beautiful changes / In such kind ways" (lines 14–15)?

TED HUGHES

To Paint a Water Lily

A green level of lily leaves
Roofs the pond's chamber and paves

The flies' furious arena: study
These, the two minds of this lady.

---

3. A plant sometimes called "wild carrot," with delicate, finger-like leaves and flat clusters of small white flowers.
4. Alfalfa, a plant resembling clover, with small purple flowers. Lake Lucerne is famed for its deep blue color and picturesque Swiss setting amid limestone mountains.

5 First observe the air's dragonfly
 That eats meat, that bullets by

 Or stands in space to take aim;
 Others as dangerous comb the hum

 Under the trees. There are battle-shouts
10 And death-cries everywhere hereabouts

 But inaudible, so the eyes praise
 To see the colors of these flies

 Rainbow their arcs, spark, or settle
 Cooling like beads of molten metal

15 Through the spectrum. Think what worse
 Is the pond-bed's matter of course;

 Prehistoric bedragonned times
 Crawl that darkness with Latin names,

 Have evolved no improvements there,
20 Jaws for heads, the set stare,

 Ignorant of age as of hour—
 Now paint the long-necked lily-flower

 Which, deep in both worlds, can be still
 As a painting, trembling hardly at all

25 Though the dragonfly alight,
 Whatever horror nudge her root.

 1960

- What are "the two minds of this lady" (line 4)? Whom do you
  think the speaker is addressing when he commands, "Now
  paint the long-necked lily flower" (line 22)?

ANDREW MARVELL

On a Drop of Dew

See how the orient[5] dew
Shed from the bosom of the morn
 Into the blowing roses,
Yet careless of its mansion new
5 For[6] the clear region where 'twas born
 Round in itself incloses,
 And in its little globe's extent

5. Shining.   6. By reason of.

Frames as it can its native element;
  How it the purple flow'r does slight,
10   Scarce touching where it lies,
  But gazing back upon the skies,
    Shines with a mournful light
      Like its own tear,
  Because so long divided from the sphere.[7]
15   Restless it rolls and unsecure,
    Trembling lest it grow impure,

    Till the warm sun pity its pain,
  And to the skies exhale it back again.
    So the soul, that drop, that ray
20 Of the clear fountain of eternal day,
  Could it within the human flower be seen,
    Rememb'ring still its former height,
    Shuns the sweet leaves and blossoms green;
    And, recollecting its own light,
25 Does, in its pure and circling thoughts, express
  The greater Heaven in an Heaven less.
    In how coy[8] a figure wound,
    Every way it turns away;
    So the world excluding round,
30   Yet receiving in the day:
    Dark beneath, but bright above,
    Here disdaining, there in love.

    How loose and easy hence to go,
    How girt and ready to ascend;
35   Moving but on a point below,
    It all about does upwards bend.
  Such did the manna's sacred dew distill,
  White and entire, though congealed and chill;[9]
  Congealed on earth, but does, dissolving, run
40 Into the glories of th' almighty sun.

                                        1681

- How does the sun "exhale" (line 17) the drop of dew? "Back
  again" to where? Explain the comparison between the dew-
  drop and the human soul.

---

7. Of heaven.   8. Reserved, withdrawn, modest.
9. In the wilderness, the Israelites fed upon manna from heaven (distilled from the dew; see Exodus
16.10–21); manna became a traditional symbol for divine grace.

METAPHOR AND SIMILE

Being visual does not just mean describing, telling us facts, indicating shapes, colors, and specific details, and giving us precise discriminations through exacting verbs, nouns, adverbs, and adjectives. Often the vividness of the picture in our minds depends upon comparisons through **figures of speech**. What we are trying to imagine is pictured in terms of something else familiar to us, and we are asked to think of one thing as if it were something else. Many such comparisons, in which something is pictured or figured forth in terms of something already familiar to us, are taken for granted in daily life. Things we can't see or that aren't familiar to us are imaged as things we already know; for example, God is said to be like a father; Italy is said to be shaped like a boot; life is compared to a forest, a journey, or a sea. When the comparison is explicit—that is, when one thing is directly compared to something else—the figure is called a **simile**. When the comparison is implicit, with something described as if it were something else, it is called a **metaphor**.

Poems use **figurative language** much of the time. A poem may insist that death is like a sunset or sex like an earthquake or that the way to imagine how it feels to be spiritually secure is to think of the way a sheep is taken care of by a shepherd. The pictorialness of our imagination may *clarify* things for us—scenes, states of mind, ideas—but at the same time it stimulates us to think of how those pictures make us *feel*. Pictures, even when they are mental pictures or imagined visions, may be both denotative and connotative, just as individual words are: they may clarify and make precise, and they may evoke a range of feelings. In the poem that follows, the poet helps us visualize the old age and approaching death of the speaker by making comparisons with familiar things—the coming of winter, the approach of sunset, and the dying embers of a fire.

WILLIAM SHAKESPEARE

[*That time of year thou mayst in me behold*]

That time of year thou mayst in me behold
When yellow leaves, or none, or few, do hang
Upon those boughs which shake against the cold,
Bare ruined choirs, where late the sweet birds sang.
5 In me thou see'st the twilight of such day
As after sunset fadeth in the west;
Which by and by[1] black night doth take away,

1. Shortly.

Death's second self,[2] that seals up all in rest.
In me thou see'st the glowing of such fire,
10 That on the ashes of his youth doth lie,
As the deathbed whereon it must expire,
Consumed with that which it was nourished by.
This thou perceiv'st, which makes thy love more strong,
To love that well which thou must leave ere long.

                                              1609

The first four lines of "That time of year" evoke images of the late autumn;
but notice that the poet does not have the speaker say directly that his physical condition and age make him resemble autumn. He draws the
comparison without stating it as a comparison: you can see my own state,
he says, in the coming of winter, when almost all the leaves have fallen from
the trees. The speaker portrays himself *indirectly* by talking about the passing
of the year. The poem uses metaphor; that is, one thing is pictured *as if* it
were something else. "That time of year" goes on to another metaphor in
lines 5–8 and still another in lines 9–12, and each metaphor contributes to
our understanding of the speaker's sense of his old age and approaching
death. More important, however, is the way the metaphors give us feelings,
an emotional sense of the speaker's age and of his own attitude toward aging.
Through the metaphors we come to understand, appreciate, and to some
extent share the increasing sense of urgency that the poem expresses. Our
emotional sense of the poem depends largely on the way each metaphor is
developed and by the way each metaphor leads, with its own kind of internal
logic, to another.

    The images of late autumn in the first four lines all suggest loneliness,
loss, and nostalgia for earlier times. As in the rest of the poem, the speaker
presents our eyes as the main vehicle for noticing his age and condition; in
the phrase "thou mayst in me behold" (line 1) he introduces what he is
asking us to see, and in both lines 5 and 9 he tells us similarly "In me thou
see'st. . . ." The picture of the trees shedding their leaves suggests that
autumn is nearly over, and we can imagine trees either with yellow leaves,
or without leaves, or with just a trace of foliage remaining—the latter perhaps
most feelingly suggesting the bleakness and loneliness that characterize the
change of seasons, the ending of the life cycle. But other senses are invoked,
too. The boughs shaking against the cold represent an appeal to our tactile
sense, and the next line appeals to our sense of hearing, although only by
the silence of birds no longer singing. (Notice how exact the visual representation is of the bare, or nearly bare, limbs, even as the speaker notes the
cold and the lack of birds; birds lined up like a choir on risers would have
made a striking visual image on the barren limbs one above the other, but
now there is only the *reminder* of what used to be. The present is quiet, bleak,
and lonely; it is the absence of color, song, and life that underscores the
visual impression, a reminder of what formerly was.)

2. Sleep.

The next four lines have a slightly different tone, and the color changes. From a black-and-white landscape with a few yellow leaves, we come upon a rich and almost warm reminder of a faded sunset. But a somber note enters the poem in these lines through another figure of speech, **personification,** which involves treating an abstraction, such as death or justice or beauty, as if it were a person. As the poem talks about the coming of night and of sleep, Sleep is personified as the "second self" of Death (that is, as a kind of "double" for death). The main emphasis is on how night and sleep close in on the twilight, and only secondarily does a reminder of death enter the poem. But it does enter.

The third metaphor—that of the dying embers of a fire—begins in line 9 and continues to color and warm the bleak cold that the poem began with, but it also sharpens the reminder of death. The three main metaphors in the poem work to make our sense of old age and approaching death more familiar but also more immediate: moving from barren trees, to fading twilight, to dying embers suggests a sensuous increase of color and warmth but also an increasing urgency. The first metaphor involves a whole season, or at least a segment of one, a matter of days or possibly weeks; the second involves the passing of a single day, reducing the time scale to a matter of minutes, and the third draws our attention to that split second when a glowing ember dies into a gray ash. The final part of the fire metaphor introduces the most explicit sense of death so far, as the metaphor of embers shifts into a direct reminder of death. Embers, which had been a metaphor of the speaker's aging body, now themselves become, metaphorically, a deathbed; the vitality that nourishes youth is used up just as a log in a fire is. The urgency of the reminder of coming death has now peaked. It is friendlier but now seems immediate and inevitable, a natural part of the life process, and the final two lines then offer an explicit plea to make good and intense use of the remaining moments of human relationship.

"That time of year" represents an unusually intricate use of images to organize a poem and focus its emotional impact. Not all poems are so skillfully made, and not all depend on such a full and varied use of metaphor. But most poems use metaphors for at least part of their effect, and often a poem fully develops a single metaphor as its statement as in the following poem.

LINDA PASTAN

Marks

My husband gives me an A
for last night's supper,
an incomplete for my ironing,
a B plus in bed.
5 My son says I am average,
an average mother, but if

I put my mind to it
I could improve.
My daughter believes
10 in Pass/Fail and tells me
I pass. Wait 'til they learn
I'm dropping out.

1978

The speaker in "Marks" is obviously less than pleased with the idea of continually being judged, and the metaphor of marks (or grades) as a way of talking about her performance of family duties suggests her irritation. The list of the roles implies the many things expected of her, and the three different systems of marking (letter grades, categories to be checked off on a chart, and pass/fail) detail the difficulties of multiple standards. The poem retains the language of schooldays all the way to the end ("learn," line 11; "dropping out," line 12), and the major effect of the poem depends on the irony of the speaker's surrendering to the metaphor the family has thrust upon her; if she is to be judged as if she were a student, she retains the right to leave the system. Ironically, she joins the system (adopts the metaphor for herself) in order to defeat it.

Sometimes, in poetry as in prose, comparisons are made explicitly, as in the following poem:

ROBERT BURNS

A Red, Red Rose

O, my luve's like a red, red rose
That's newly sprung in June.
O, my luve is like the melodie
That's sweetly played in tune.

5 As fair art thou, my bonnie lass,
So deep in luve am I;
And I will luve thee still, my dear,
Till a' the seas gang³ dry.

Till a' the seas gang dry, my dear,
10 And the rocks melt wi' the sun;
And I will luve thee still, my dear,
While the sands o' life shall run.

And fare thee weel, my only luve,
And fare thee weel a while!
15 And I will come again, my luve,
Though it were ten thousand mile.

1796

3. Go.

The first four lines make two explicit comparisons: the speaker says that his love is "like a . . . rose" and "like [a] melodie." As we noted earlier, such *explicit* comparisons are called similes, and usually (as here) the comparison involves the word *like* or the word *as*. Similes work much as do metaphors, except that usually they are used more passingly, more incidentally; they make a quick comparison and usually do not elaborate, whereas metaphors often extend over a long section of a poem (in which case they are called **extended metaphors**) or even over the whole poem, as in "Marks" (in which case they are called **controlling metaphors**).

The two similes in "A Red, Red Rose" assume that we already have a favorable opinion of roses and of melodies. Here the poet does not develop the comparison or even remind us of attractive details about roses or tunes. He pays the quick compliment and moves on. Similes sometimes develop more elaborate comparisons than this and occasionally, as in Marvell's "On a Drop of Dew," even govern long sections of a poem (in which case they are called **analogies**). Usually, though, a simile is briefer and relies more fully on something we already know. The speaker in "My Papa's Waltz" says that he hung on "like death"; he doesn't have to explain or elaborate the comparison: we know the anxiety he refers to.

Like metaphors, similes may imply both meaning and feeling; they may both explain something and invoke feelings about it. All figurative language involves an attempt to clarify something *and* to prompt readers to feel a certain way about it. Saying that one's love is like a rose implies a delicate and fragile beauty and invites our senses into play so that we can share sensuously a response to appealing fragrance and soft touch, just as the shivering boughs and dying embers in "That time of year" suggest separation and loss at the same time that they invite us to share both the cold sense of loneliness and the warmth of old friendship.

Once you start looking for them, you will find figures of speech in poem after poem; they are among the most common devices through which poets share their visions with us.

· · ·

WILLIAM SHAKESPEARE

[*Shall I compare thee to a summer's day?*]

Shall I compare thee to a summer's day?
Thou art more lovely and more temperate.
Rough winds do shake the darling buds of May,
And summer's lease hath all too short a date.
5 Sometime too hot the eye of heaven shines,
And often is his gold complexion dimmed;
And every fair from fair sometime declines,
By chance or nature's changing course untrimmed.
But thy eternal summer shall not fade,

10 Nor lose possession of that fair thou ow'st,
    Nor shall Death brag thou wand'rest in his shade,
    When in eternal lines to time thou grow'st.
        So long as men can breathe or eyes can see,
        So long lives this,[4] and this gives life to thee.

                                                    1609

- What sort of promise does the speaker make with this poem?
  Why can he boast that "thy eternal summer shall not fade"?

ANONYMOUS[5]

The Twenty-third Psalm

The Lord is my shepherd; I shall not want.
He maketh me to lie down in green pastures: he leadeth me beside
    the still waters.
He restoreth my soul: he leadeth me in the paths of righteousness
    for his name's sake.
Yea, though I walk through the valley of the shadow of death,
    I will fear no evil: for thou art with me;
    thy rod and thy staff they comfort me.
5 Thou preparest a table before me in the presence of mine enemies:
    thou anointest my head with oil; my cup runneth over.
Surely goodness and mercy shall follow me all the days of my life:
    and I will dwell in the house of the Lord for ever.

- What is the controlling metaphor in this poem? At what point in the psalm
  does the controlling metaphor shift?

JOHN DONNE

[Batter my heart, three-personed God][6]

Batter my heart, three-personed God; for You
As yet but knock, breathe, shine, and seek to mend;
That I may rise and stand, o'erthrow me, and bend
Your force, to break, blow, burn, and make me new.
5 I, like an usurped town, to another due,
Labor to admit You, but Oh, to no end!

---

4. This poem.
5. Traditionally attributed to King David. This English translation is from the King James Version
of the Bible.   6. *Holy Sonnets,* 14.

Reason, Your viceroy[7] in me, me should defend,
But is captived, and proves weak or untrue.
Yet dearly I love You, and would be loved fain,[8]
10 But am betrothed unto Your enemy:
Divorce me, untie or break that knot again,
Take me to You, imprison me, for I,
Except You enthrall me, never shall be free,
Nor ever chaste, except You ravish me.

1633

- In the poem's controlling metaphor, who is the speaker? Who, or what, is God? To whom is the speaker "betrothed"?

The Computation

For the first twenty years, since yesterday,
I scarce believed thou couldst be gone away;
For forty more, I fed on favors past,
And forty on hopes—that thou wouldst, they might, last.
5 Tears drowned one hundred, and sighs blew out two;
A thousand, I did neither think, nor do,
Or not divide, all being one thought of you;
Or in a thousand more forgot that too.
Yet call not this long life, but think that I
10 Am, by being dead, immortal. Can ghosts die?

1633

- Who, or what, might be "thou" in the second line? What seems to be the cause of the speaker's "death"?

The Canonization

For God's sake hold your tongue and let me love!
   Or[9] chide my palsy or my gout,
My five gray hairs or ruined fortune flout;
With wealth your state, your mind with arts improve,
5   Take you a course, get you a place,
   Observe his Honor or his Grace,
Or the king's real or his stampéd face[1]
   Contemplate; what you will, approve,
      So you will let me love.

10 Alas, alas, who's injured by my love?
   What merchant's ships have my sighs drowned?
Who says my tears have overflowed his ground?

---

7. One who rules as the representative of a higher power.   8. Gladly.   9. Either.   1. On coins.

When did my colds a forward spring remove?
  When did the heats which my veins fill
15   Add one man to the plaguy bill?[2]
When did the heats which my veins fill
Soldiers find wars, and lawyers find out still
  Litigious men which quarrels move,
    Though she and I do love.

Call us what you will, we are made such by love.
20   Call her one, me another fly,
We're tapers too, and at our own cost die;[3]
And we in us find th' eagle and the dove.[4]
  The phoenix riddle hath more wit[5]
    By us; we two, being one, are it.
25 So to one neutral thing both sexes fit,
  We die and rise the same, and prove
    Mysterious by this love.

We can die by it, if not live by love;
  And if unfit for tombs and hearse
30 Our legend be, it will be fit for verse;[6]
  And if no piece of chronicle we prove,
We'll build in sonnets pretty rooms[7]
(As well a well-wrought urn becomes[8]
The greatest ashes, as half-acre tombs),
35 And by these hymns all shall approve
    Us canonized for love.

And thus invoke us: "You whom reverent love
  Made one another's hermitage,
You to whom love was peace, that now is rage,
40 Who did the whole world's soul extract, and drove[9]
  Into the glasses of your eyes
(So made such mirrors and such spies
That they did all to you epitomize)
  Countries, towns, courts; beg from above
45   A pattern of your love!"

                               1633

---

2. List of plague victims.
3. Tapers—candles—consume themselves. To "die" is Renaissance slang for consummating the sexual act, which was popularly believed to shorten life by one day. *Fly:* a traditional symbol of transitory life.   4. Traditional symbols of strength and purity.
5. Meaning. According to tradition, only one phoenix existed at a time, dying in a funeral pyre of its own making and being reborn from its own ashes. The bird's existence was thus a riddle akin to a religious mystery (line 27), and a symbol sometimes fused with Christian representations of immortality.   6. That is, if we don't turn out to be an authenticated piece of historical narrative.
7. In Italian, *stanza* means room.   8. Befits.   9. Compressed.

- Whom does the speaker address in the first line, "hold your tongue"? Why does the speaker concede that he and his lover may not "prove" a "piece of chronicle" (line 31)?

DAVID FERRY

At the Hospital

She was the sentence the cancer spoke at last,
Its blurred grammar finally clarified.

1983

- What, exactly, has "clarified" the cancer's "blurred grammar"?

RANDALL JARRELL

The Death of the Ball Turret Gunner[1]

From my mother's sleep I fell into the State,
And I hunched in its belly till my wet fur froze.
Six miles from earth, loosed from its dream of life,
I woke to black flak and the nightmare fighters.
5 When I died they washed me out of the turret with a hose.

1945

- What is meant by "I fell into the State"? What do the words "sleep," "dream," and "nightmare" suggest about the poem's basic situation?

FRANCIS WILLIAM BOURDILLON

The Night Has a Thousand Eyes

The night has a thousand eyes,
    And the day but one;
Yet the light of the bright world dies
    With the dying sun.

---

1. A ball turret was a plexiglass sphere set into the belly of a B-17 or B-24 and inhabited by two .50 caliber machine-guns and one man, a short, small man. When this gunner tracked with his machine-guns a fighter attacking his bomber from below, he revolved with the turret; hunched upside-down in his little sphere, he looked like the foetus in the womb. The fighters which attacked him were armed with cannon firing explosive shells. The hose was a steam hose. [Jarrell's note]

5 The mind has a thousand eyes,
  And the heart but one;
Yet the light of a whole life dies
  When the love is gone.

1889

- What are the "thousand eyes" of the night? the single eye of the day? What, exactly, are the comparisons to the mind and the heart?

EMILY DICKINSON

[*Wild Nights—Wild Nights!*]

Wild Nights—Wild Nights!
Were I with thee
Wild Nights should be
Our luxury!

5 Futile—the Winds—
To a Heart in port—
Done with the Compass—
Done with the Chart!

Rowing in Eden—
10 Ah, the Sea!
Might I but moor—Tonight—
In Thee!

ca. 1861

- To what, exactly, does the speaker compare her love? What are some possible, even opposite, interpretations of the line "Done with the Chart"?

SYMBOL

The word *symbol* is often used sloppily and sometimes pretentiously, but properly used the term suggests one of the most basic things about poems— their ability to get beyond what words signify and to make larger claims about meanings in the verbal world. All words go beyond themselves. They are not simply a collection of sounds: they signify something beyond their sounds, often things or actions or ideas. Words describe not only a verbal universe but also a world in which actions occur, acts have implications, and events have meaning. Sometimes words signify something beyond themselves, say *rock* or *tree* or *cloud*, and symbolize something as well, such as solidity or life or dreams. Words can—when their implications are agreed on by tradition, convention, or habit—stand for things beyond their most immediate meanings or significations and become symbols, and even simple words that have accumulated no special power from previous use may be given special significance in special circumstances—in poetry as in life itself.

A **symbol** is, put simply, something that stands for something else. The everyday world is full of common examples; a flag, a logo, a trademark, or a skull and crossbones all suggest things beyond themselves, and everyone likely understands what their display indicates, whether or not each viewer shares a commitment to what is thus represented. In common usage a prison symbolizes confinement, constriction, and loss of freedom, and in specialized traditional usage a cross may symbolize oppression, cruelty, suffering, death, resurrection, triumph, or an intersection of some kind (as in *crossroads* and *crosscurrents*). The specific symbolic significance depends on the context; for example, a reader might determine significance by looking at contiguous details in a poem and by examining the poem's attitude toward a particular tradition or body of beliefs. A star means one thing to a Jewish poet and something else to a Christian poet, still something else to a sailor or an actor. In a very literal sense, words themselves are all symbols (they stand for objects, actions, or qualities, not just for letters or sounds), but symbols in poetry are said to be those words and phrases that have a range of reference beyond their literal signification or denotation.

Poems sometimes create a symbol out of a thing, action, or event that has no previously agreed-upon symbolic significance. The following poem, for example, gives a seemingly random gesture symbolic significance:

SHARON OLDS

Leningrad Cemetery, Winter of 1941[1]

That winter, the dead could not be buried.
The ground was frozen, the gravediggers weak from hunger,
the coffin wood used for fuel. So they were covered with something
and taken on a child's sled to the cemetery
5   in the sub-zero air. They lay on the soil,
some of them wrapped in dark cloth
bound with rope like the tree's ball of roots
when it waits to be planted; others wound in sheets,
their pale, gauze, tapered shapes
10 stiff as cocoons that will split down the center
when the new life inside is prepared;

1. The 900-day siege of Leningrad (now Saint Petersburg) during World War II began in September 1941.

but most lay like corpses, their coverings
coming undone, naked calves
hard as corded wood spilling
15 from under a cloak, a hand reaching out
with no sign of peace, wanting to come back
even to the bread made of glue and sawdust,
even to the icy winter, and the siege.

1979

All of these corpses—frozen, neglected, uncovered—vividly stamp upon our minds a picture of the horrors of war, one likely to stay in our minds long after we have finished reading the poem. Several details are striking, and the poem's language heightens our sense of them. The corpses wound in sheets, for example, are described in "their pale, gauze, tapered shapes" (line 9), and they are compared to cocoons that one day will split and emit new life; and the limbs that dangle loose when the coverings come undone are "hard as corded wood spilling" (line 14). But clearly the most memorable sight is the hand dangling from one corpse that is coming unwrapped, for the poet invests that hand with special significance, giving its gesture *meaning*. The hand is "reaching out . . . wanting to come back" (lines 15–16); it is as if the dead can still gesture even if they cannot speak, and the gesture seems to signify the desire of the dead to return at any price. They would be glad to live, even under the grim conditions that attend life in Leningrad during the war. Suddenly the grimness that we—the living—have been witnessing pales by comparison with what the dead have lost simply by being dead. The hand has been made to *symbolize* the desire of the dead to return, to live, to be still among us, anywhere. The hand reaches out in the poem as a gesture that means something; the poet has made it a symbol of desire.

The whole array of dead bodies in the poem might be called symbolic as well. As a group, they stand for the war's human waste, and their dramatic presence provides the poem with a dramatic visualization of how war leaves no time for decency, not even the decency of burial. The bodies are a symbol: they stand for what the poem as a whole asserts.

Some objects and acts have a built-in significance because of past usage in literature, or tradition, or the stories a culture develops to explain itself and its beliefs. Over the years some things have acquired an agreed-upon significance, an accepted value in our minds. They already stand for something before the poet cites them; they are **traditional symbols.** Their uses in poetry have to do with the fact that poets can count on a recognition of their traditional suggestions and meanings outside the poem, and the poem does not have to propose or argue a particular symbolic value. Birds, for example, traditionally symbolize flight, freedom from confinement, detachment from earthbound limits, the ability to soar beyond rationality and transcend mortal limits. Traditionally, birds have also been linked with imagination, especially poetic imagination, and poets often identify with them as pure and ideal singers of songs, as in Keats's "Ode to a Nightingale" (see p. 595). One of the most traditional symbols, the rose, may be a simple and fairly plentiful flower in its season, but it has so long stood for particular qualities that merely to name it raises predictable expectations. Its beauty, delicacy, fragrance, shortness of life, and depth of color have made it a symbol of the transitoriness of beauty, and countless poets have counted on its accepted symbolism—sometimes to compliment a friend (as Burns does in "A Red, Red Rose") or sometimes to make a point about the nature of symbolism. The following poem draws, in quite a traditional way, on the traditional meanings.

EDMUND WALLER

Song

 Go, lovely rose!
Tell her that wastes her time and me
 That now she knows,
When I resemble² her to thee,
5 How sweet and fair she seems to be.

 Tell her that's young,
And shuns to have her graces spied,
 That hadst thou sprung
In deserts, where no men abide,
10 Thou must have uncommended died.

 Small is the worth
Of beauty from the light retired;
 Bid her come forth,
Suffer herself to be desired,
15 And not blush so to be admired.

 Then die! that she
The common fate of all things rare
 May read in thee;
How small a part of time they share
20 That are so wondrous sweet and fair!

1645

  The speaker in "Song" sends the rose to his love in order to have it speak its traditional meanings of not only beauty but also transitoriness. He counts on accepted symbolism to make his point and hurry her into accepting his advances. Likewise, the poet does not elaborate or argue these things because he does not need to; he counts on the familiarity of the tradition (though, of course, readers unfamiliar with the tradition will not respond in the same

---

2. Compare.

way—that is one reason it is difficult to fully appreciate texts from another linguistic or cultural tradition).

Poets may use traditional symbols to invoke predictable responses—in effect using shortcuts to meaning by repeating acts of signification sanctioned by time and cultural habit. But often poets examine the tradition even as they employ it, and sometimes they revise or reverse meanings built into the tradition. Symbols do not necessarily stay the same over time, and poets often turn even the most traditional symbols to their own original uses. Knowing the traditions of poetry—reading a lot of poems and observing how they tend to use certain words, metaphors, and symbols—can be very useful in reading new poems, but traditions evolve and individual poems do highly individual things. Knowing the past never means being able to interpret new texts with confidence. Symbolism makes things happen, but individual poets and texts determine what will happen and how. The following two poems work important variations on the traditional associations of roses:

D. H. LAWRENCE

I Am Like a Rose

I am myself at last; now I achieve
My very self. I, with the wonder mellow,
Full of fine warmth, I issue forth in clear
And single me, perfected from my fellow.

5 Here I am all myself. No rose-bush heaving
Its limpid sap to culmination has brought
Itself more sheer and naked out of the green
In stark-clear roses, than I to myself am brought.

1917

DOROTHY PARKER

One Perfect Rose

A single flow'r he sent me, since we met.
All tenderly his messenger he chose;
Deep-hearted, pure, with scented dew still wet—
One perfect rose.

5 I knew the language of the floweret;
"My fragile leaves," it said, "his heart enclose."
Love long has taken for his amulet
One perfect rose.

Why is it no one ever sent me yet
10   One perfect limousine, do you suppose?
Ah no, it's always just my luck to get
One perfect rose.

1937

Sometimes symbols—traditional or not—become so insistent in the world of a poem that the larger referential world is left almost totally behind. In such cases the symbol is everything, and the poem does not just *use* symbols but becomes a **symbolic poem,** usually a highly individualized one dependent on an internal system introduced by the individual poet.

Here is an example of such a poem:

WILLIAM BLAKE

The Sick Rose[3]

O rose, thou art sick.
The invisible worm
That flies in the night
In the howling storm

5 Has found out thy bed
Of crimson joy,
And his dark secret love
Does thy life destroy.

1794

The poem does not seem to be about a rose, but about what the rose represents—not in this case something altogether understandable through the traditional meanings of *rose.*

We usually associate the rose with beauty and love, often with sex; and here several key terms have sexual connotations: "worm," "bed," and "crimson joy." The violation of the rose by the worm is the poem's main concern; the violation seems to have involved secrecy, deceit, and "dark" motives, and the result is sickness rather than the joy of love. The poem is sad; it involves a sense of hurt and tragedy, nearly of despair. The poem cries out against the misuse of the rose, against its desecration, implying that instead of a healthy joy in sensuality and sexuality, there has been in this case destruction and hurt, perhaps because of misunderstanding and repression and lack of sensitivity.

But to say so much about this poem we have to extrapolate from other poems by Blake, and we have to introduce information from outside the

---

3. In Renaissance emblem books, the scarab beetle, worm, and rose are closely associated: the beetle feeds on dung, and the smell of the rose is fatal to it.

poem. Fully symbolic poems often require that, and thus they ask us to go beyond the formal procedures of reading that we have discussed so far. As presented in this poem, the rose is not part of the normal world that we ordinarily see, and it is symbolic in a special sense. The poet does not simply take an object from our everyday world and give it special significance, making it a symbol in the same sense that the leap or the corpse's hand is a symbol. Here the rose seems to belong to its own world, a world made entirely inside the poem or the poet's head. The rose is not referential, or not primarily so. The whole poem is symbolic; it is not paraphrasable; it lives in its own world. But what is the rose here a symbol of? In general terms, we can say from what the poem tells us; but we may not be as confident as we can be in the more nearly recognizable world of "Leningrad Cemetery, Winter of 1941." In "The Sick Rose," it seems inappropriate to ask the standard questions: What rose? Where? Which worm? What are the particulars here? In the world of this poem worms can fly and may be invisible. We are altogether in a world of meanings that have been formulated according to a special system of knowledge and code of belief. We will feel comfortable and confident in that world only if we read many poems written by the poet (in this case William Blake) within the same symbolic system.

Negotiation of meanings in symbolic poems can be very difficult indeed. Reading symbolic poems is an advanced skill that depends on special knowledge of authors and of the special traditions they work from. But usually the symbols you will find in poems *are* referential of meanings we all share and you can readily discover these meanings by carefully studying the poems themselves.

. . .

ROBERT FROST
Fireflies in the Garden

Here come real stars to fill the upper skies,
And here on earth come emulating flies,
That though they never equal stars in size,
(And they were never really stars at heart)
5   Achieve at times a very star-like start.
Only, of course, they can't sustain the part.

1928

- What is the tone of this poem? What does the poem say about the limits of symbolism?

ADRIENNE RICH

WEB

Diving into the Wreck

First having read the book of myths,
and loaded the camera,
and checked the edge of the knife-blade,
I put on
5　the body-armor of black rubber
the absurd flippers
the grave and awkward mask.
I am having to do this
not like Cousteau[4] with his
10　assiduous team
aboard the sun-flooded schooner
but here alone.

There is a ladder.
The ladder is always there
15　hanging innocently
close to the side of the schooner.
We know what it is for,
we who have used it.
Otherwise
20　it's a piece of maritime floss
some sundry equipment.

I go down.
Rung after rung and still
the oxygen immerses me
25　the blue light
the clear atoms
of our human air.
I go down.
My flippers cripple me,
30　I crawl like an insect down the ladder
and there is no one
to tell me when the ocean
will begin.

First the air is blue and then
35　it is bluer and then green and then
black I am blacking out and yet
my mask is powerful
it pumps my blood with power

4. Jacques-Yves Cousteau (1910–1997), French underwater explorer and writer.

the sea is another story
40 the sea is not a question of power
I have to learn alone
to turn my body without force
in the deep element.

And now: it is easy to forget
45 what I came for
among so many who have always
lived here
swaying their crenellated fans
between the reefs
50 and besides
you breathe differently down here.

I came to explore the wreck.
The words are purposes.
The words are maps.
55 I came to see the damage that was done
and the treasures that prevail.
I stroke the beam of my lamp
slowly along the flank
of something more permanent
60 than fish or weed

the thing I came for:
the wreck and not the story of the wreck
the thing itself and not the myth
the drowned face always staring
65 toward the sun
the evidence of damage
worn by salt and sway into this threadbare beauty
the ribs of the disaster
curving their assertion
70 among the tentative haunters.

This is the place.
And I am here, the mermaid whose dark hair
streams black, the merman in his armored body
We circle silently
75 about the wreck
we dive into the hold.
I am she: I am he

whose drowned face sleeps with open eyes
whose breasts still bear the stress
80 whose silver, copper, vermeil cargo lies
obscurely inside barrels
half-wedged and left to rot

we are the half-destroyed instruments
that once held to a course
85 the water-eaten log
the fouled compass

We are, I am, you are
by cowardice or courage
the one who find our way
90 back to this scene
carrying a knife, a camera
a book of myths
in which
our names do not appear.

1972   1973

- What word or phrase first signals the reader that "Diving into
  the Wreck" is to be understood symbolically, not literally?
  What are some possible symbolic interpretations of the wreck
  and the dive?

ROO BORSON

After a Death

Seeing that there's no other way,
I turn his absence into a chair.
I can sit in it,
gaze out through the window.
5 I can do what I do best
and then go out into the world.
And I can return then with my useless love,
to rest,
because the chair is there.

1989

- Why do you think the speaker chooses to symbolize her absent
  loved one with a chair?

SUGGESTIONS FOR WRITING

1. Choose one poem in this book in which a single word seems crucial to the poem's total effect. Write an essay in which you work out carefully how the poem's meaning and tone depend on that one word.
2. Compare Dickinson's "I dwell in Possibility—" and "Wild Nights—Wild Nights!" (both in this chapter). What patterns of word use do you see in the two poems? What kinds of vocabulary do they have in common? Syntax? Strategies of organization? Find other poems by Dickinson (there are a number in this book) and look for similar patterns of thought and language. What might her poems be like if they were written "normally"? Write an essay in which you explore Dickinson's unique poetic style.
3. Consider the poems about roses found in this chapter and write a paragraph about each poem showing how it establishes specific symbolism for the rose. What generalizations can you draw about the rose's traditional meanings in poetry? If you can, find other poems about roses outside of this book to determine if your generalizations still apply.

12 THE SOUNDS OF POETRY

A lot of what happens in a poem happens in your mind's eye, but some of it happens in your "mind's ear" and in your voice. Poems are full of meaningful sounds and silences as well as words and sentences. Besides choosing words for their meanings, poets sometimes choose words because they have certain sounds, and poems use sound effects to create a mood or establish a tone, just as films do. Sometimes the sounds of words are crucial to what is happening in the text of the poem.

Here is a poem that explores the sounds of a particular word, tries them on, and analyzes them in relation to the word itself.

HELEN CHASIN

The Word Plum

> The word *plum* is delicious
>
> pout and push, luxury of
> self-love, and savoring murmur
>
> full in the mouth and falling
> 5 like fruit
>
> taut skin
> pierced, bitten, provoked into
> juice, and tart flesh
>
> question
> 10 and reply, lip and tongue
> of pleasure.
>
> 1968

The poem savors the sounds of the word as well as the taste and feel of the fruit itself. It is almost as if the poem is tasting the sounds and rolling them slowly on the tongue. The second and third lines even replicate the *p, l, uh,* and *m* sounds of the word while at the same time imitating the squishy sounds of eating the fruit. Words like "delicious" and "luxury" sound juicy, and other words imitate sounds of satisfaction and pleasure—"murmur," for example. Even the process of eating is in part re-created aurally. The tight, clipped sounds of "taut skin/pierced" suggest the way teeth sharply break the skin and slice quickly into the soft flesh of a plum, and as they describe the tartness, the words ("provoked," "question") force the lips to pucker and the tongue and palate to meet and hold, as if the mouth were savoring a tart fruit. The poet is having fun here re-creating the sensual appeal of a plum, teasing the sounds and meanings out of available words. The words must mean something appropriate and describe something accurately first of all, of course, but when they can also imitate the sounds and feel of the process, they can do double duty. Not many poems manipulate sound as intensely or as fully as "The Word *Plum*," but many poems at least contain passages in which the sounds of life are reproduced by the human voice reading the poem. To get the full effect of this poem—and of many others—*you must read aloud*; that way, you can attend to the vocal rhythms and articulate the sounds as the poem calls for them to be reproduced by the human voice.

You will almost always enhance a poem's effect by reading aloud, using your voice to pronounce the words so that the poem becomes a spoken communication. Historically, poetry began as an oral phenomenon, and often poems that seem very difficult when looked at silently come alive when turned into sound. Early bards in many cultures chanted or recited their verses, and the music of poetry—its cadences and rhythms—developed from this kind of performance. The presentation of primitive poetry (and some later work as well) was often accompanied by some kind of musical instrument. The rhythms of any poem become clearer when you say or hear them.

Poetry is almost always a vocal art, dependent on the human voice to become its full self. In a sense, it only begins to exist as a real phenomenon when a reader reads and actualizes it. Poems don't really achieve their full meaning when they exist merely on a page; a poem on a page is more a score or set of stage directions for a poem than a poem itself. Sometimes, in fact, it is hard to experience the poem at all unless you hear it; the actual experience of saying the words aloud or hearing them spoken is very good practice for learning to hear in your mind's ear when you read silently. A good poetry reading might easily convince you of the importance of a good voice sensitive to the poem's requirements, but you can also persuade yourself by reading poems aloud in the privacy of your own room. An audience is even better, however—an occasion to share the pleasure in the sounds themselves and what they imply. At its oral best, much poetry is communal.

KENNETH FEARING

Dirge

1-2-3 was the number he played but today the number came 3-2-1;
Bought his Carbide at 30, and it went to 29; had the favorite at
Bowie[1] but the track was slow—

---

1. A racetrack in Maryland. *Carbide:* stock in the Union Carbide Corporation.

O executive type, would you like to drive a floating-power, knee-
action, silk-upholstered six? Wed a Hollywood star? Shoot the
course in 58? Draw to the ace, king, jack?
O fellow with a will who won't take no, watch out for three
cigarettes on the same, single match; O democratic voter born
in August under Mars, beware of liquidated rails—

5 Denouement to denouement, he took a personal pride in the
certain, certain way he lived his own, private life,
But nevertheless, they shut off his gas; nevertheless, the bank
foreclosed; nevertheless, the landlord called; nevertheless, the
radio broke,

And twelve o'clock arrived just once too often,
Just the same he wore one gray tweed suit, bought one straw hat,
drank one straight Scotch, walked one short step, took one
long look, drew one deep breath,
Just one too many,

10 And wow he died as wow he lived,
Going whop to the office and blooie home to sleep and biff got
married and bam had children and oof got fired,
Zowie did he live and zowie did he die,

With who the hell are you at the corner of his casket, and where
the hell're we going on the right-hand silver knob, and who
the hell cares walking second from the end with an American
Beauty² wreath from why the hell not,

Very much missed by the circulation staff of the New York
Evening Post; deeply, deeply mourned by the B.M.T.³

Wham, Mr. Roosevelt; pow, Sears Roebuck; awk, big dipper; bop,
15 summer rain;
Bong, Mr., bong, Mr., bong, Mr., bong.

1935

As the title implies, "Dirge" is a kind of musical lament, in this case for
a certain sort of businessman who took many chances and saw his investments and life go down the drain in the depression of the early 1930s. Reading this poem aloud helps a lot, in part because of the expressive cartoon
words here that echo the action, words like "oof" and "blooie" (which primarily carry their meaning in their sounds, for they have practically no literal
or referential meaning). Reading aloud also helps us notice that the poem
employs rhythms much as a song would and that it frequently shifts its pace
and mood. Notice how carefully the first two lines are balanced, and then
how quickly the rhythm shifts as the "executive type" is addressed directly
in line 3. (Line 2 is long and dribbles over in the narrow pages of a book like

2. A variety of rose.   3. A New York City subway line.

There are only three things ... that a poem must reach: the eye, the ear, and what we may call the heart or the mind. It is the most important of all to reach the heart of the reader. And the surest way to reach the heart is through the ear.

—ROBERT FROST

this; the especially long lines and irregular line lengths here create some of the poem's special sound effects.) In the direct address, the poem first picks up the lingo of advertising, which it recites in rapid-fire order rather like advertising phrases. In stanza 3 here, the rhythm shifts again, but the poem gives us helpful clues about how to read. Line 5 sounds like prose and is long, drawn out, and rather dull (rather like its subject), but line 6 sets up a regular (and monotonous) rhythm with its repeated "never-theless," which punctuates the rhythm like a drumbeat: "But nevertheless, *tuh-tuh-tuh-tuh-tuh;* nevertheless, *tuh-tuh-tuh-tuh;* nevertheless, *tuh-tuh-tuh-tuh;* nevertheless, *tuh-tuh-tuh-tuh-tuh.*" In the next stanza, the repetitive phrasing comes again, this time guided by the word "one" in cooperation with other words of one syllable: "wore *one* gray tweed suit, bought *one* straw hat, *tuh* one *tuh-tuh, tuh* one *tuh-tuh, tuh* one *tuh-tuh, tuh* one *tuh-tuh.*" And then a new rhythm and a new technique begin in stanza 5, which imitates the language of comic books to describe in violent, exaggerated terms the routine of the businessman's life. You have to say words like "whop" and "zowie" aloud and in the rhythm of the whole sentence to get the full effect of how boring his life is, no matter how he tries to jazz it up with exciting words. And so it goes—repeated words, shifting rhythms, emphasis on routine and aver-ageness—until the final bell ("Bong.... bong ... bong ... bong") tolls rhyth-mically for the dead man in the final clanging line.

Sometimes the sounds in poems just provide special effects, rather like a musical score behind a film, setting mood and getting us into an appropriate frame of mind. But often sound and meaning go hand in hand, and the poet finds words that in their sounds echo the action. A word that captures or approximates the sound of what it describes, such as "splash" or "squish" or "murmur," is an **onomatopoeic** word, and the device itself is **onomato-poeia.** And poets can do similar things with pacing and rhythm, sounds and pauses. The punctuation, the length of vowels, and the combination of con-sonant sounds help to control the way we read so that we use our voice to imitate what is being described.

Here is a classic passage in which a skillful poet talks about the virtues of making the sound echo the sense—and shows at the same time how to do it:

ALEXANDER POPE

Sound and Sense[4]

337   But most by numbers[5] judge a poet's song,
And smooth or rough, with them, is right or wrong;
In the bright muse though thousand charms conspire,[6]
340 Her voice is all these tuneful fools admire,
Who haunt Parnassus[7] but to please their ear,
Not mend their minds; as some to church repair,
Not for the doctrine, but the music there.
These, equal syllables[8] alone require,
345 Though oft the ear the open vowels tire,
While expletives[9] their feeble aid do join,
And ten low words oft creep in one dull line,
While they ring round the same unvaried chimes,
With sure returns of still expected rhymes.
350 Where'er you find "the cooling western breeze,"
In the next line, it "whispers through the trees";
If crystal streams "with pleasing murmurs creep,"
The reader's threatened (not in vain) with "sleep."
Then, at the last and only couplet fraught
355 With some unmeaning thing they call a thought,
A needless Alexandrine[1] ends the song,
That, like a wounded snake, drags its slow length along.
Leave such to tune their own dull rhymes, and know
What's roundly smooth, or languishingly slow;
360 And praise the easy vigor of a line,
Where Denham's strength and Waller's[2] sweetness join.
True ease in writing comes from art, not chance,
As those move easiest who have learned to dance.
'Tis not enough no harshness gives offense,
365 The sound must seem an echo to the sense:
Soft is the strain when Zephyr[3] gently blows,
And the smooth stream in smoother numbers flows;
But when loud surges lash the sounding shore,

---

4. From *An Essay on Criticism*, Pope's poem on the art of poetry and the problems of literary criticism. The passage excerpted here follows a discussion of several common weaknesses of critics—failure to regard an author's intention, for example, or overemphasis on clever metaphors and ornate style.
5. Meter, rhythm, sound.   6. Unite.
7. A mountain in Greece, traditionally associated with the Muses and considered the seat of poetry and music.   8. Regular accents.   9. Filler words, such as "do."
1. A line of six metrical feet, sometimes used in pentameter poems to vary the pace mechanically. Line 357 is an alexandrine.
2. Sir John Denham and Edmund Waller, seventeenth-century poets credited with perfecting the heroic couplet.   3. The west wind.

The hoarse, rough verse should like the torrent roar.
370 When Ajax[4] strives, some rock's vast weight to throw,
The line too labors, and the words move slow;
Not so, when swift Camilla[5] scours the plain,
Flies o'er th' unbending corn, and skims along the main.
Hear how Timotheus'[6] varied lays surprise,
375 And bid alternate passions fall and rise!
While, at each change, the son of Libyan Jove[7]
Now burns with glory, and then melts with love;
Now his fierce eyes with sparkling fury glow,
Now sighs steal out, and tears begin to flow:
380 Persians and Greeks like turns of nature[8] found,
And the world's victor stood subdued by sound!
The pow'r of music all our hearts allow,
And what Timotheus was, is DRYDEN now.

                                                    1711

A lot of things are going on here simultaneously. The poem uses a number of echoic or onomatopoeic words, and in some lines pleasant and unpleasant consonant sounds underline a particular point or add some mood music. When the poet talks about a particular weakness in poetry, he illustrates it at the same time—by using open vowels (line 345), expletives (line 346), monosyllabic words (line 347), predictable rhymes (lines 350–53), or long, slow lines (line 357). And the good qualities of poetry he talks about and illustrates as well (line 360, for example). But the main effects of the passage come from an interaction of several strategies at once. The effects are fairly simple and easy to spot, but their causes involve a lot of poetic ingenuity. In line 340, for example, Pope achieves a careful cacophonous effect by repeating the o̅o̅ vowel sound and repeating the *l* consonant sound together with (twice) interrupting the rough *f* sound in the middle; no one wants to be caught admiring that music, but the careful harmony of the preceding sounds has set us up beautifully. And the pace of lines 347, 357, and 359 is carefully controlled by clashing consonant sounds as well as by the use of long vowels. Line 347 moves incredibly slowly and seems much longer than it is because almost all the one-syllable words end in a consonant that refuses to blend with the beginning of the next word, making the words hard to say without distinct, awkward pauses between them. In lines 357 and 359, long vowels such as those in "wounded," "snake," "slow," "along," "roundly," and "smooth" help to slow down the pace, and awkward, hard-to-pronounce consonants are again juxtaposed. The commas also provide nearly a full stop

---

4. A Greek hero of the Trojan War, noted for his strength.   5. A woman warrior in Virgil's *Aeneid*.
6. The court musician of Alexander the Great, celebrated in a famous poem by John Dryden (see line 383) for the power of his music over Alexander's emotions.
7. In Greek tradition, the chief god of any people was often given the name Zeus (Jove), and the chief god of Libya (the Greek name for all of Africa) was called Zeus Ammon. Alexander visited his oracle and was proclaimed son of the god.   8. Similar alternations of emotion.

in the midst of these lines to slow us down still more. Similarly, the harsh lashing of the shore in lines 368–69 is accomplished partly by onomatopoeia, partly by a shift in the pattern of stress, which creates irregular waves in line 368, and partly by the dominance of rough consonants in line 369. (In Pope's time, the English *r* was still trilled gruffly so that it could be made to sound extremely rrrough and harrrsh.) Almost every line in this passage demonstrates how to make sound echo sense.

As "Sound and Sense" and "Dirge" suggest, poets most effectively manipulate sound by carefully controlling the rhythm of the voice so that not only are the proper sounds heard, but they are heard at precisely the right moment. Pace and rhythm are as important to a good poem as they are to a good piece of music. The human voice naturally develops certain rhythms in speech; some syllables and some words receive more stress than others. Just as multisyllabic words put more stress on some syllables than others (dictionaries always indicate which syllables are stressed), words in the context of a sentence receive more or less stress, depending on meaning. One-syllable words are thus sometimes stressed and sometimes not. A careful poet controls the flow of stresses so that, in many poems, a certain basic pattern of rhythm (or **meter**) develops almost like a quiet percussion instrument in the background. Not all poems have meter, and not all metered poems follow a single dominant rhythm, but many poems employ one pervasive pattern, and it is useful to look for patterns of stress.

In the Western world, we can thank the ancient Greeks for systematizing an understanding of meter and giving us a vocabulary (including the words *rhythm* and *meter*) that enables us to discuss the art of poetry. *Meter* comes from a Greek word meaning "measure": what we measure in the English language are the patterns of stressed (or "accented") syllables that occur naturally when we speak, and, just as when we measure length, the unit we use in measuring poetry is the **foot.** Most traditional poetry in English uses the accentual-syllabic form of meter—meaning that its rhythmic pattern is based on both a set number of syllables per line and a regular pattern of accents in each line. The most common metrical pattern is **iambic,** in which each foot contains an unstressed syllable followed by a stressed one. Consider, for example, the first two lines of Alexander Pope's "Sound and Sense," here marked to show the stressed syllables:

> But móst | by núm- | bers júdge | a pó- | et's sóng,
> And smóoth | or róugh, | with thém, | is ríght | or wróng.

These lines, like so many in English literature, provide an example of **iambic pentameter**—that is, the lines are written in a meter consisting of five iambic feet. Notice that there is nothing forced or artificial in the sound of these lines; the words flow easily. In fact, linguists contend that English is naturally iambic, and even the most ordinary, "unpoetic" utterances often fall into this pattern: "Please tell me if you've heard this one before." "They said she had a certain way with words." "The baseball game was televised at nine."

Besides the iamb, other metrical feet include the following:

trochee—an accented syllable followed by an unstressed one ("méter," "Hómer")

anapest—two unaccented syllables followed by a stressed one ("comprehénd," "after yóu")

dactyl—an accented syllable followed by two unstressed ones ("róundabout," "dínnertime")

Line lengths are sometimes described in terms of the number of syllables: a *decasyllabic* line, for example, is ten syllables long; an *octosyllabic* is eight, etc. Much more commonly though, lines are described in terms of the number of feet. It is possible to write regular lines using any of the feet shown above:

iambic pentameter—"In sé- | quent tóil | all fór- | wards dó | con- | ténd . . ." (William Shakespeare)

trochaic octameter—"Ónce u- | pón a | mídnight | dréary, | whíle I | póndered, | wéak and | wéary . . ." (Edgar Allan Poe)

anapestic tetrameter—"There are mán- | y who sáy | that a dóg | has his dáy . . ." (Dylan Thomas)

dactylic hexameter—"Thís is the | fórest pri- | méval. The | múrmuring | pínes and the | hémlocks . . ." (Henry Wadsworth Longfellow)

Notice that this final example is perfectly regular until the final foot, a trochee. Few poems, in fact, are written entirely in regular lines, and substitution of one metrical foot for another—to accommodate idioms and conversational habits or to create a special effect or emphasis—is quite common, especially in the first foot of a line. Shakespeare often begins an iambic line with a trochee:

Líke as | the wáves | make towárds | the péb- | bled shóre . . .

The poet may introduce a **spondee,** for example—a pair of accented syllables. Consider this line from John Milton's *Paradise Lost,* a poem written mainly in iambic pentameter:

Rócks, cáves, | lákes, féns, | bógs, déns, | and Shádes | of Déath . . .

Here Milton substitutes three spondees for the first three iambs in a pentameter line. John Dryden's "To the Memory of Mr. Oldham" begins with two spondees:

Fárewéll, tóo líttle, and tóo látely knówn

A **caesura,** a short pause often (though not always) signaled by a mark of punctuation such as a comma, may interrupt a line, as in the example from Poe's "The Raven," above, or in most lines of more than five or six syllables. (Sometimes, other even more elaborate accentual variations are used—*amphybrachs,* for example, involve an unstressed syllable, a stressed one, and then another unstressed one—but such hybrids are seldom used in English verse.)

In traditional metrical poetry, the poet's art, just like the musician's, consists of establishing metrical patterns and then varying the patterns without breaking them. With just the few rhythmic building blocks shown above, poets can create an almost infinite variety of rhythms. Here is a poem that names and illustrates many of the meters. If someone read it aloud and you charted the stressed (–) and unstressed (˘) syllables, you would have a chart similar to that done by the poet himself in the text.

SAMUEL TAYLOR COLERIDGE

Metrical Feet

Lesson for a Boy

Trōchĕe trīps frŏm lōng tŏ shōrt;[9]
From long to long in solemn sort
Slōw Spōndēe stālks; strōng fōot! yet ill able
Ēvĕr tŏ cōme ŭp wĭth Dāctȳl trĭsȳllăblĕ.
5 Ĭāmbĭcs mārch frŏm shōrt tŏ lōng—
Wĭth ă lēap ănd ă bōund thĕ swĭft Ānăpĕsts thrōng;
One syllable long, with one short at each side,
Ămphībrăchȳs hāstes wĭth ă stātelȳ stride—
Fīrst ănd lāst bēing lōng, mīddlĕ shōrt, Ămphĭmācer
10 Strīkes hĭs thūndērĭng hōofs līke ă prōud hīgh-brĕd Rācer.
If Derwent[1] be innocent, steady, and wise,
And delight in the things of earth, water, and skies;

Tender warmth at his heart, with these meters to show it,
With sound sense in his brains, may make Derwent a poet—
15 May crown him with fame, and must win him the love
Of his father on earth and his Father above.
     My dear, dear child!
Could you stand upon Skiddaw,[2] you would not from its
     whole ridge
See a man who so loves you as your fond S. T. COLERIDGE.

1806

The following poem exemplifies **dactylic** rhythm (– ˘ ˘ or stressed syllable followed by two unstressed ones).

---

9. The long and short marks over syllables are Coleridge's.
1. Written originally for Coleridge's son Hartley, the poem was later adapted for his younger son, Derwent.
2. A mountain in the lake country of northern England (where Coleridge lived in his early years), near the town of Derwent.

WENDY COPE

Emily Dickinson

Higgledy-piggledy
Emily Dickinson
Liked to use dashes
Instead of full stops.

5   Nowadays, faced with such
Idiosyncrasy,
Critics and editors
Send for the cops.

1986

Limericks rely on **anapestic** meter ($\smile \smile -$, or two unstressed syllables followed by a stressed one), although usually the first two syllables are in iambic meter (see below).

ANONYMOUS

There was a young girl from St. Paul,
Wore a newspaper-dress to a ball.
The dress caught on fire
And burned her entire
Front page, sporting section and all.

The following poem is composed in the more common **trochaic** meter ($- \smile$, a stressed syllable followed by an unstressed one).

SIR JOHN SUCKLING

Song

Why so pale and wan, fond Lover?
Prithee why so pale?
Will, when looking well can't move her,
Looking ill prevail?
5   Prithee why so pale?

Why so dull and mute, young Sinner?
Prithee why so mute?
Will, when speaking well can't win her,
Saying nothing do 't?
10   Prithee why so mute?

> Quit, quit, for shame, this will not move,
>   This cannot take her;
> If of her self she will not love,
>   Nothing can make her,
> 15 The Devil take her.

1646

Like Pope's "Sound and Sense," the following poem uses the English language's most common poetic meter, **iambic** (ˇ ‒, an unstressed syllable followed by a stressed one, which some would argue is the most "natural" rhythm for English).

JOHN DRYDEN

To the Memory of Mr. Oldham[3]

> Farewell, too little, and too lately known,
> Whom I began to think and call my own;
> For sure our souls were near allied, and thine
> Cast in the same poetic mold with mine.
> 5 One common note on either lyre did strike,
> And knaves and fools we both abhorred alike.
> To the same goal did both our studies drive;
> The last set out the soonest did arrive.
> Thus Nisus fell upon the slippery place,
> 10 While his young friend performed and won the race.[4]
> O early ripe! to thy abundant store
> What could advancing age have added more?
> It might (what nature never gives the young)
> Have taught the numbers[5] of thy native tongue.
> 15 But satire needs not those, and wit will shine
> Through the harsh cadence of a rugged line.[6]
> A noble error, and but seldom made,
> When poets are by too much force betrayed.
> Thy generous fruits, though gathered ere their prime,
> 20 Still showed a quickness; and maturing time
> But mellows what we write to the dull sweets of rhyme.
> Once more, hail and farewell; farewell, thou young,
> But ah too short, Marcellus[7] of our tongue;

3. John Oldham (1653–1683), who like Dryden (see lines 3–6) wrote satiric poetry.
4. In Virgil's *Aeneid* (Book 5), Nisus (who is leading the race) falls and then trips the second runner so that his friend Euryalus can win.   5. Rhythms.
6. In Dryden's time, the English *r* was pronounced with a harsh, trilling sound.
7. Nephew of the Roman emperor Augustus who died at twenty, celebrated by Virgil in the *Aeneid*, Book 6.

Thy brows with ivy, and with laurels bound;
25 But fate and gloomy night encompass thee around.

1684

Scanning a poem line by line—that is, sorting out its metrical pattern—can be hard work, and few people enjoy the process (which is called **scansion**). Doing it right involves listening carefully to your voice as you read aloud, marking the stressed and unstressed syllables, counting the syllables and feet, and checking the rhyme patterns. Though there is no easy substitute for this work, there is often a major payoff in seeing the subtleties of a poet's craft as well as in hearing the poetry itself more fully and resonantly. If, for example, you chart "To the Memory of Mr. Oldham," you will notice some extraordinary variations in the basic iambic pattern, variations that signal special emphasis on certain key terms and that indicate structural changes and directions. Even the first line is highly irregular—even though no pattern has yet been established in our ears. (Often, in fact, you will need to scan several lines before you can be sure of the "controlling" metrical pattern of a poem.) Possibly as many as seven syllables in this first line are stressed, rather than the expected five in a regular iambic pentameter line, and the effect is both to strongly emphasize Oldham's relatively unknown status (*too lit-*tle *and too late-*ly *known*) and to draw out, lengthily, in conjunction with the use of a series of long vowels, the reading of the line.

Hearing a poem properly involves practice—listening to others read poetry and especially to yourself as you read poems aloud, so that you get used to hearing your voice, so that you become confident about where the stresses fall, and so that the rhythms begin to play themselves out "naturally." Your dictionary will show you the stresses for every word of more than one syllable, and the governing stress of individual words will largely control the patterns in a line: if you read a line for its basic sense (almost, for a moment, as if it were prose), you will usually see the line's basic pattern. But single-syllable words can be a challenge because they may or may not get a stress depending on their syntactic function and the full meaning of the sentence. Normally, important functional words, such as nouns and verbs of one syllable, get stressed (as in normal conversation or in prose); but conjunctions (such as *and* or *but*), prepositions (such as *on* or *with*), and articles (such as *an* or *the*) do not. But you often need to make decisions as you say words aloud, decisions based on what the words actually convey and what the sentence means. Listen to yourself as you read aloud and be prepared for uncertainties. Sometimes you will even find your "normal" pronunciation being influenced or modified by the pattern your voice develops as you hear basic rhythms. The way you actually read a line, once you have "heard" the basic rhythm, is influenced by two factors: normal pronunciations and prose sense (on the one hand) and the predominant pattern of the poem (on the other). Since these two forces are constantly in tension and are sometimes contradictory, you can almost never fully predict the actual reading of a line, and good reading aloud (like every other art) depends less on formula than on subtlety and flexibility.

Because scanning lines is an imprecise craft, sometimes very good readers plausibly disagree about whether or not to stress certain syllables. Then, too, some stresses are stronger than others: the convention of calling syllables "stressed" or "unstressed" fails to measure degrees of stress—and meaning often dictates that some syllables be stressed *much* more heavily than others.

In addition, not every poem relies on a formal pattern of stresses. As we saw in "Sound and Sense" and "To the Memory of Mr. Oldham," a poem dominated by iambic meter might incorporate trochaic, anapestic, spondaic, or dactylic feet in one place or another to create a stylistic effect. Beyond that, a poet tired of or resistant to traditional vocal patterns might follow or create other patterns—or employ patternlessness—to form the sound of a poem. Counting only the number of syllables (and *not* stresses) in a line is one common variation, which early-twentieth-century poets such as Marianne Moore were especially fond of. Even more widespread is **free verse,** which does without any governing pattern of stresses or line lengths.

• • •

EDGAR ALLAN POE

[WEB]

The Raven

Once upon a midnight dreary, while I pondered, weak and weary,
Over many a quaint and curious volume of forgotten lore,
While I nodded, nearly napping, suddenly there came a tapping,
As of some one gently rapping, rapping at my chamber door.
5 " 'Tis some visitor," I muttered, "tapping at my chamber door—
                Only this, and nothing more."

Ah, distinctly I remember it was in the bleak December,
And each separate dying ember wrought its ghost upon the floor.
Eagerly I wished the morrow;—vainly I had sought to borrow
10 From my books surcease of sorrow—sorrow for the lost Lenore—
For the rare and radiant maiden whom the angels name Lenore—
                Nameless here for evermore.

And the silken sad uncertain rustling of each purple curtain
Thrilled me—filled me with fantastic terrors never felt before;
15 So that now, to still the beating of my heart, I stood repeating
" 'Tis some visitor entreating entrance at my chamber door;—
Some late visitor entreating entrance at my chamber door;
                This it is, and nothing more."

Presently my soul grew stronger; hesitating then no longer,
20 "Sir," said I, "or Madam, truly your forgiveness I implore;
But the fact is I was napping, and so gently you came rapping,
And so faintly you came tapping, tapping at my chamber door,
That I scarce was sure I heard you"—here I opened wide the door;—
                Darkness there, and nothing more.

25 Deep into that darkness peering, long I stood there wondering, fearing,
    Doubting, dreaming dreams no mortal ever dared to dream before;
    But the silence was unbroken, and the darkness gave no token,
    And the only word there spoken was the whispered word, "Lenore!"
    This I whispered, and an echo murmured back the word, "Lenore!"—
30   Merely this, and nothing more.

    Back into the chamber turning, all my soul within me burning,
    Soon I heard again a tapping somewhat louder than before.
    "Surely," said I, "surely that is something at my window lattice;
    Let me see, then, what thereat is, and this mystery explore—
35 Let my heart be still a moment and this mystery explore;—
             'Tis the wind and nothing more!"

    Open here I flung the shutter, when, with many a flirt and flutter,
    In there stepped a stately raven of the saintly days of yore;
    Not the least obeisance made he; not an instant stopped or stayed he;
40 But, with mien of lord or lady, perched above my chamber door—
    Perched upon a bust of Pallas[8] just above my chamber door—
           Perched, and sat, and nothing more.

    Then this ebony bird beguiling my sad fancy into smiling,
    By the grave and stern decorum of the countenance it wore,
45 "Though thy crest be shorn and shaven, thou," I said, "art sure no craven,
    Ghastly grim and ancient raven wandering from the Nightly shore—
    Tell me what thy lordly name is on the Night's Plutonian[9] shore!"
          Quoth the raven, "Nevermore."

    Much I marvelled this ungainly fowl to hear discourse so plainly,
50 Though its answer little meaning—little relevancy bore,
    For we cannot help agreeing that no living human being
    Ever yet was blessed with seeing bird above his chamber door—
    Bird or beast upon the sculptured bust above his chamber door,
          With such name as "Nevermore."

55 But the raven, sitting lonely on the placid bust, spoke only
    That one word, as if his soul in that one word he did outpour.
    Nothing farther then he uttered—not a feather then he fluttered—
    Till I scarcely more than muttered "Other friends have flown before—
    On the morrow *he* will leave me, as my hopes have flown before."
60   Then the bird said "Nevermore."

    Startled at the stillness broken by reply so aptly spoken,
    "Doubtless," said I, "what it utters is its only stock and store
    Caught from some unhappy master whom unmerciful Disaster

---

8. Athena, the Greek goddess of wisdom.   9. Dark; Pluto was god of the underworld.

Followed fast and followed faster till his songs one burden bore—
65 Till the dirges of his Hope that melancholy burden bore
                    Of 'Never—nevermore.' "

But the raven still beguiling all my sad soul into smiling,
Straight I wheeled a cushioned seat in front of bird and bust and
    door;
Then, upon the velvet sinking, I betook myself to linking
70 Fancy unto fancy, thinking what this ominous bird of yore—
What this grim, ungainly, ghastly, gaunt, and ominous bird of yore
                    Meant in croaking "Nevermore."

This I sat engaged in guessing, but no syllable expressing
To the fowl whose fiery eyes now burned into my bosom's core;
75 This and more I sat divining, with my head at ease reclining
On the cushion's velvet lining that the lamplight gloated o'er,
But whose velvet violet lining with the lamplight gloating o'er,
                  She shall press, ah, nevermore!

Then, methought, the air grew denser, perfumed from an unseen
    censer
80 Swung by angels whose faint foot-falls tinkled on the tufted floor.
"Wretch," I cried, "thy God hath lent thee—by these angels he hath
    sent thee
Respite—respite and nepenthe[1] from thy memories of Lenore!
Quaff, oh quaff this kind nepenthe and forget this lost Lenore!"
                  Quoth the raven, "Nevermore."

85 "Prophet!" said I, "thing of evil!—prophet still, if bird or devil!—
Whether Tempter sent, or whether tempest tossed thee here ashore,
Desolate, yet all undaunted, on this desert land enchanted—
On this home by Horror haunted—tell me truly, I implore—
Is there—*is* there balm in Gilead?[2]—tell me—tell me, I implore!"
90   Quoth the raven, "Nevermore."

"Prophet!" said I, "thing of evil—prophet still, if bird or devil!
By that Heaven that bends above us—by that God we both adore—
Tell this soul with sorrow laden if, within the distant Aidenn,[3]
It shall clasp a sainted maiden whom the angels name Lenore—
95 Clasp a rare and radiant maiden whom the angels name Lenore."
                  Quoth the raven, "Nevermore."

"Be that word our sign of parting, bird or fiend!" I shrieked
    upstarting—
"Get thee back into the tempest and the Night's Plutonian shore!
Leave no black plume as a token of that lie thy soul hath spoken!

---

1. A drug reputed by the Greeks to cause forgetfulness or sorrow (pronounced "ne-PEN-thee").
2. See Jeremiah 8.22.   3. Eden.

100   Leave my loneliness unbroken!—quit the bust above my door!
      Take thy beak from out my heart, and take thy form from off my
         door!"
                           Quoth the raven, "Nevermore."

      And the raven, never flitting, still is sitting, still is sitting
      On the pallid bust of Pallas just above my chamber door;
105   And his eyes have all the seeming of a demon's that is dreaming,
      And the lamp-light o'er him streaming throws his shadow on the
         floor;
      And my soul from out that shadow that lies floating on the floor
                           Shall be lifted—nevermore!

                                                              1844

- Describing the composition of "The Raven," Poe wrote of the need to use
  sounds "in the fullest possible keeping with that melancholy which I had
  predetermined as the tone of the poem." List at least five of the sound
  effects (e.g., rhyme, alliteration, etc.) that Poe uses in "The Raven." How
  does each of these contribute to the poem's tone of "melancholy"?

WILLIAM SHAKESPEARE

[*Like as the waves make towards the pebbled shore*]

      Like as the waves make towards the pebbled shore,
      So do our minutes hasten to their end,
      Each changing place with that which goes before,
      In sequent toil all forwards do contend.[4]
5   Nativity, once in the main[5] of light,
      Crawls to maturity, wherewith being crowned,
      Crooked[6] eclipses 'gainst his glory fight,
      And Time that gave doth now his gift confound.[7]
      Time doth transfix[8] the flourish set on youth
10   And delves the parallels[9] in beauty's brow,
      Feeds on the rarities of nature's truth,
      And nothing stands but for his scythe to mow.
      And yet to times in hope[1] my verse shall stand,
      Praising thy worth, despite his cruel hand.

                                                              1609

- Which lines in this poem vary the basic iambic metric scheme?
  What is the effect of these variations?

4. Struggle. *Sequent:* successive.   5. High seas. *Nativity:* newborn life.   6. Perverse.
7. Bring to nothing.   8. Pierce.   9. Lines, wrinkles.   1. In the future.

GERARD MANLEY HOPKINS

Spring and Fall:

to a young child

Márgarét áre you gríeving[2]
Over Goldengrove unleaving?
Leáves, like the things of man, you
With your fresh thoughts care for, can you?
5 Áh! ás the heart grows older
It will come to such sights colder
By and by, nor spare a sigh
Though worlds of wanwood leafmeal[3] lie;
And yet you wíll weep and know why.
10 Now no matter, child, the name:
Sórrow's spríngs áre the same.
Nor mouth had, no nor mind, expressed
What heart heard of, ghost[4] guessed:
It ís the blight man was born for,
15 It is Margaret you mourn for.

1880

- How does this poem's heavy use of alliteration serve its themes of youth and age, life and death?

EMILY DICKINSON

[*A narrow Fellow in the Grass*]

A narrow Fellow in the Grass
Occasionally rides—
You may have met Him—did you not
His notice sudden is—

5 The Grass divides as with a Comb—
A spotted shaft is seen—
And then it closes at your feet
And opens further on—

He likes a Boggy Acre
10 A Floor too cool for Corn—
Yet when a Boy, and Barefoot—
I more than once at Noon

---

2. Hopkins's own accent markings.
3. Broken up, leaf by leaf (analogous to "piecemeal"). *Wanwood:* pale, gloomy woods.   4. Soul.

Have passed, I thought, a Whip lash
Unbraiding in the Sun
15 When stooping to secure it
It wrinkled, and was gone—

Several of Nature's People
I know, and they know me—
I feel for them a transport
20 Of cordiality—

But never met this Fellow
Attended, or alone
Without a tighter breathing
And Zero at the Bone—

1866

- How does Dickinson use sound devices such as alliteration to underscore the images and themes of the poem?

THOMAS CAMPION

When to Her Lute Corinna Sings

When to her lute Corinna sings,
Her voice revives the leaden[5] strings,
And doth in highest notes appear
As any challenged[6] echo clear;
5 But when she doth of mourning speak,
Ev'n with her sighs the strings do break.

And as her lute doth live or die,
Led by her passion, so must I:
For when of pleasure she doth sing,
10 My thoughts enjoy a sudden spring;
But if she doth of sorrow speak,
Ev'n from my heart the strings do break.

1601

- How does Campion mimic an "echo" in this poem? What is the effect of this echoing?

---

5. Heavy.   6. Aroused.

ROBERT HAYDEN

Homage to the Empress of the Blues[7]

Because there was a man somewhere in a candystripe silk shirt,
gracile and dangerous as a jaguar and because a woman moaned
for him in sixty-watt gloom and mourned him Faithless Love
Twotiming Love Oh Love Oh Careless Aggravating Love,

5   She came out on the stage in yards of pearls, emerging like
a favorite scenic view, flashed her golden smile and sang.

Because grey laths began somewhere to show from underneath
torn hurdygurdy[8] lithographs of dollfaced heaven;
and because there were those who feared alarming fists of snow
10 on the door and those who feared the riot-squad of statistics,

She came out on the stage in ostrich feathers, beaded satin,
and shone that smile on us and sang.

1962

- How do the two short stanzas beginning with "She came out"
  complete the thoughts of the longer stanzas that start with
  "Because"?

SUGGESTIONS FOR WRITING

1. Read Poe's "The Raven" aloud, paying particular attention to pacing. Do you
   find yourself speeding up as you continue through the poem? Does a quick-
   ening pace suit the speaker's growing exasperation and madness? Write an
   essay in which you examine the way that Poe underlines the poem's story and
   emotional flow with a range of poetic devices: line length, punctuation, rhyme,
   meter, and the sounds of words.
2. Pope's "Sound and Sense" contains this advice for poets: "But when loud
   surges lash the sounding shore, / The hoarse, rough verse should like the torrent roar" (lines 368–69). In other words, he counsels that the sound of the
   poet's description should match the sense of what the poem is describing.
   Write an essay in which you examine the sound and sense in Shakespeare's
   "[Like as the waves make towards the pebbled shore]"—how does the poem
   achieve a harmony of meaning and sound?
3. Write an essay in which you discuss any of the poems you have read in this
   book in which sound seems a more important element than anything else,
   even the meaning of words. What is the point of writing and reading this kind
   of poetry? Can it achieve its effects through silent reading, or must it be
   experienced aloud?

7. Bessie Smith (1894 [or 1898?]-1937); legendary blues singer whose theatrical style grew out of
the black American vaudeville tradition.   8. A disreputable kind of dance hall.

13 INTERNAL STRUCTURE

"Proper words in proper places": that is how one great writer of English prose, Jonathan Swift, described good writing. A good poet finds appropriate words, and already we have looked at some implications for readers of the verbal choices a poet makes. But the poet must also decide where to put those words—how to arrange them for maximum effect—because individual words, metaphors, and symbols exist not only within phrases and sentences and rhythmic patterns but also within the larger whole of the poem. How should the words be arranged and the poem organized? What comes first and what last? Will the poem have a "plot"? What principle or idea of organization will inform it? How can words, sentences, images, ideas, and feelings be combined into a structure that holds together, seems complete, and affects readers?

Considering these questions from the poet's point of view (What is my plan? Where shall I begin?) can help us notice the effects of structural choices. Every poem works in its own unique way, and therefore every poet must make independent decisions about how to organize an individual poem. But poems do fall into patterns of organization, sometimes because of subject matter, sometimes because of effects intended, sometimes for other reasons. A poet may consciously decide on a particular strategy, may reach instinctively for one, or may happen into one that suits the needs of the moment—a framework onto which words and sentences will hang, one by one and group by group.

When a poem tells a story, the organization may be fairly straightforward. The following poem, for example, tells a simple story largely in chronological order:

EDWIN ARLINGTON ROBINSON

Mr. Flood's Party

Old Eben Flood, climbing alone one night
Over the hill between the town below
And the forsaken upland hermitage
That held as much as he should ever know
5   On earth again of home, paused warily.
The road was his and not a native near;
And Eben, having leisure, said aloud,
For no man else in Tilbury Town to hear:

"Well, Mr. Flood, we have the harvest moon
10 Again, and we may not have many more;
The bird is on the wing, the poet says,[1]
And you and I have said it here before.
Drink to the bird." He raised up to the light
The jug that he had gone so far to fill,
15 And answered huskily: "Well, Mr. Flood,
Since you propose it, I believe I will."

Alone, as if enduring to the end
A valiant armor of scarred hopes outworn
He stood there in the middle of the road
20 Like Roland's ghost winding a silent horn.[2]
Below him, in the town among the trees,
Where friends of other days had honored him,
A phantom salutation of the dead
Rang thinly till old Eben's eyes were dim.

25 Then, as a mother lays her sleeping child
Down tenderly, fearing it may awake
He set the jug down slowly at his feet
With trembling care, knowing that most things break;
And only when assured that on firm earth
30 It stood, as the uncertain lives of men
Assuredly did not, he paced away,
And with his hand extended paused again:

"Well, Mr. Flood, we have not met like this
In a long time; and many a change has come
35 To both of us, I fear, since last it was
We had a drop together. Welcome home!"
Convivially returning with himself,
Again he raised the jug up to the light;
And with an acquiescent quaver said:
40 "Well, Mr. Flood, if you insist, I might.

"Only a very little, Mr. Flood—
For auld lang syne. No more, sir; that will do."
So, for the time, apparently it did,
And Eben evidently thought so too;
45 For soon amid the silver loneliness
Of night he lifted up his voice and sang,
Secure, with only two moons listening,
Until the whole harmonious landscape rang—

1. Edward FitzGerald, in "The Rubáiyát of Omar Khayyám" (more or less a translation of an Arab original), so describes the "Bird of Time."
2. According to French legend, the hero Roland used his powerful ivory horn to warn his allies of impending attack.

"For auld lang syne." The weary throat gave out,
50 The last word wavered, and the song was done.
He raised again the jug regretfully
And shook his head, and was again alone.
There was not much that was ahead of him,
And there was nothing in the town below—
55 Where strangers would have shut the many doors
That many friends had opened long ago.

1921

The fairly simple **narrative structure** here is based on the gradual unfolding of the story. After old Eben is introduced and situated in relation to the town and his home, the "plot" unfolds: he sits down in the road, reviews his life, reflects on the present, and has a drink—several drinks, in fact, as he thinks about passing time and growing old; then he sings and considers going "home." Not much happens, really; we get a vignette of Mr. Flood between two places and two times. But there *is* action, and the poem's movement—its organization and structure—depends on it: Mr. Flood in motion, in stasis, and then, again, contemplating motion. This counts as event, and a certain, limited chronological movement. The poem's organization—its structural principle—involves the passing of time, action moving forward, a larger story being revealed by the few moments depicted here.

"Mr. Flood's Party" presents about as much story as a short poem ever does, but like most poems it doesn't really emphasize the developing action—which all seems fairly predictable once we "get" who Eben is, how old he is, and what place he occupies in the communal memory of Tilbury Town and vice versa. Rather, the movement forward in time dictates the shape of the poem, determines the way it presents its images, ideas, themes. Nearly everything occurs within an easy-to-follow chronology.

But even here, in this most simple narrative structure, we note complications. One complication is in the use of time itself, for "old" time and "present" time seem posed against each other as a structural principle, too, one in tension with the chronological movement: Eben's past, as contrasted with his present and limited future, focuses the poem's attention, and in some ways the contrast between what was and what is seems even more important than the brief movement through present time that gets the most obvious attention in the poem. Then, too, "character"—Eben's character and that of the townspeople of later generations—gets a lot of attention, even as the chronology moves forward. More than one structural principle is at work here. We may identify the main movement of the poem as chronological and its principal structure as narrative, but to be fair and full in our discussion we have to note several other competing organizational forces at work—principles of comparison and contrast, for example, and of descriptive elaboration.

Most poems work with this kind of complexity, and identifying a single structure behind any poem involves a sense of the organizational principle that makes it work, while at the same time recognizing that other principles repeatedly, perhaps continually, compete for our attention. A poem's structure involves its conceptual framework—what principle best explains its organization and movement—and it is often useful to identify one dominating kind of structure, such as narrative structure, that gives the poem its shape. But we need to recognize from the start that most poems follow structural models loosely. Finding an appropriate label to describe the structure of a particular poem can help in analyzing the poem's other aspects, but the label itself has no magic.

Purely narrative poems are often very long and often include many features that are not, strictly speaking, closely connected to the narrative or linked to a strict chronology. Very often a poem moves from a narrative of an event to some sort of commentary or reflection on it, as in Philip Larkin's "Church Going" (below, in this chapter). Reflection can be included along the way or may be implicit in the way the story is narrated, as in Maxine Kumin's "Woodchucks" (chapter 8), where we focus more on the narrator and her responses than on the events in the story.

> *Back of the idea of organic form is the concept that there is a form in all things (and in our experience) which the poet can discover and reveal.*
> —DENISE LEVERTOV

Just as poems sometimes take on a structure like that of a story, they sometimes borrow the structures of plays. The following poem has a **dramatic structure;** it consists of a series of scenes, each of which is presented vividly and in detail, as if on stage.

HOWARD NEMEROV

The Goose Fish

On the long shore, lit by the moon
To show them properly alone,
Two lovers suddenly embraced
So that their shadows were as one.
5 The ordinary night was graced
For them by the swift tide of blood
That silently they took at flood.
And for a little time they prized
   Themselves emparadised.

10 Then, as if shaken by stage-fright
Beneath the hard moon's bony light,
They stood together on the sand
Embarrassed in each other's sight
But still conspiring hand in hand,
15 Until they saw, there underfoot,
As though the world had found them out,
The goose fish turning up, though dead,
   His hugely grinning head.

There in the china light he lay,
20   Most ancient and corrupt and gray.
They hesitated at his smile,
Wondering what it seemed to say
To lovers who a little while
Before had thought to understand,
25   By violence upon the sand,
The only way that could be known
    To make a world their own.

It was a wide and moony grin
Together peaceful and obscene;
30   They knew not what he would express,
So finished a comedian
He might mean failure or success,
But took it for an emblem of
Their sudden, new and guilty love
35   To be observed by, when they kissed,
    That rigid optimist.

So he became their patriarch,
Dreadfully mild in the half-dark.
His throat that the sand seemed to choke,
40   His picket teeth, these left their mark
But never did explain the joke
That so amused him, lying there
While the moon went down to disappear
Along the still and tilted track
45   That bears the zodiac.

1955

The first stanza sets the scene—a sandy shore in moonlight—and presents, in fact, the major action of the poem. The rest of the poem dramatizes the lovers' reactions: their initial embarrassment and feelings of guilt (stanza 2), their attempt to interpret the goose fish's smile (stanza 3), their decision to make him, whatever his meaning, the "emblem" of their love (stanza 4), and their acceptance of the fish's ambiguity and of their own relationship (stanza 5). The five stanzas do not exactly present five different scenes or angles on the action, but they do present separate dramatic moments, even if little time has elapsed between them. Almost like a play of five very short acts, the poem traces the drama of the lovers' discovery of themselves and their coming to terms with the meaning of their action. As in many plays, the central event (their lovemaking) is not the central focus of the drama, although the drama is based upon that event and could not take place without it. The poem depicts that event swiftly but very vividly through figurative language: "they took at flood" the "swift tide of blood." The lovers then briefly feel "emparadised," but the poem concentrates on their later reactions.

Their sudden discovery of the fish, a rude shock, injects a grotesque, almost macabre, note into the poem. From a vision of paradise, the poem seems for a moment to turn toward gothic horror when the lovers discover that they have, after all, been seen—and by such a ghoulish spectator. The last three stanzas gradually re-create the intruder in their minds, as they admit that their act of love exists not in isolation, but rather as part of a continuum, as part of their relationship to the larger world, even (at the end) within the context of the earth itself, and the moon, and the stars. In retrospect, we can see that even at the moment of passion the lovers were in touch with larger processes controlled by the presiding moon ("the swift *tide* of blood"), but neither they nor we had understood their act as such then, and the poem is about this gradual recognition of their "place" in time and space.

Stages of feeling and knowing rather than specific visual scenes determine the poem's progress, and its dramatic structure depends upon internal perceptions and internal states of mind rather than dialogue and events. Visualization and images help to organize the poem, too. Notice in particular how the two most striking visual features—the fish and the moon—are presented stanza by stanza. In stanza 1, the fish does not appear, and the moon exists plain; it is only mentioned, not described, and its light provides a stage spotlight to assure not center-stage attention, but rather total privacy: the moon serves as a lookout for the lovers. The stage imagery, barely suggested by the light in stanza 1, is articulated in stanza 2, and there the moon is "hard" and its light "bony"; its characteristics seem more appropriate to the fish, which has now become visible. In stanza 3, the moon's light comes to seem fragile ("china") as it exposes the fish directly; the moon's role as lookout and protector seems abandoned, or at least endangered. No moon appears in stanza 4, but the fish's grin is "wide and moony," almost as if the two onlookers, one earthly and dead, the other heavenly and eternal, have merged, as they nearly were by the imagery in stanza 2. And in stanza 5, the fish becomes a friend, a comedian, an optimist, an emblem, and a patriarch of their love—and his new position in collaboration with the lovers is presided over by the moon going about its eternal business. The moon—providing the stage light for the poem and the means by which not only the fish but the meaning of the lovers' act is discovered—has also helped to organize the poem, partly as a dramatic accessory, partly as imagery.

The following dramatic poem represents a composite of several similar experiences rather than a single event—a fairly common pattern in dramatic poems:

PHILIP LARKIN

Church Going

Once I am sure there's nothing going on
I step inside, letting the door thud shut.
Another church: matting, seats, and stone,

And little books; sprawlings of flowers, cut
5 For Sunday, brownish now; some brass and stuff
Up at the holy end; the small neat organ;
And a tense, musty, unignorable silence,
Brewed God knows how long. Hatless, I take off
My cycle-clips in awkward reverence,

10 Move forward, run my hand around the font.
From where I stand, the roof looks almost new—
Cleaned, or restored? Someone would know: I don't.
Mounting the lectern, I peruse a few
Hectoring large-scale verses, and pronounce
15 "Here endeth" much more loudly than I'd meant.
The echoes snigger briefly. Back at the door
I sign the book, donate an Irish sixpence,
Reflect the place was not worth stopping for.

Yet stop I did: in fact I often do,
20 And always end much at a loss like this,
Wondering what to look for; wondering, too,
When churches fall completely out of use
What we shall turn them into, if we shall keep
A few cathedrals chronically on show,
25 Their parchment, plate and pyx in locked cases,
And let the rest rent-free to rain and sheep.
Shall we avoid them as unlucky places?

Or, after dark, will dubious women come
To make their children touch a particular stone;
30 Pick simples[3] for a cancer; or on some
Advised night see walking a dead one?
Power of some sort or other will go on
In games, in riddles, seemingly at random;
But superstition, like belief, must die,
35 And what remains when disbelief has gone?
Grass, weedy pavement, brambles, buttress, sky,

A shape less recognizable each week,
A purpose more obscure. I wonder who
Will be the last, the very last, to seek
40 This place for what it was; one of the crew
That tap and jot and know what rood-lofts[4] were?
Some ruin-bibber,[5] randy for antique,
Or Christmas-addict, counting on a whiff

---

3. Medicinal herbs.
4. Galleries atop the screens (on which crosses are mounted) that divide the naves or main bodies
of churches from the choirs or chancels.
5. Literally, ruin-drinker: someone extremely attracted to antiquarian objects.

Of gown-and-bands and organ-pipes and myrrh?
45 Or will he be my representative,

Bored, uninformed, knowing the ghostly silt
Dispersed, yet tending to this cross of ground
Through suburb scrub because it held unspilt
So long and equably what since is found
50 Only in separation—marriage, and birth,
And death, and thoughts of these—for whom was built
This special shell? For, though I've no idea
What this accoutered frowsty barn is worth,
It pleases me to stand in silence here;

55 A serious house on serious earth it is,
In whose blent[6] air all our compulsions meet,
Are recognized, and robed as destinies.
And that much never can be obsolete,
Since someone will forever be surprising
60 A hunger in himself to be more serious,
And gravitating with it to this ground,
Which, he once heard, was proper to grow wise in,
If only that so many dead lie round.

1955

Ultimately, Larkin's poem focuses on what it means to visit churches, what it might be that church buildings represent, and what we should make of the fact that "church going" (in the usual sense of the word) has declined so much. The poem uses a *different* sort of church going (visitation by tourists) to consider larger questions about the relationship of religion to culture and history. The poem is, finally, a rather philosophical one about the directions of English culture, and through an enumeration of religious objects and rituals it reviews part of the history of that culture. It tells a kind of story first, through one lengthy dramatized scene, in order to comment later on what the place and the experience may mean, and the larger conclusion derives from the particulars of what the speaker does and touches. By the end of stanza 2 the action is over, but that action, we are told, stands for many such visits to similar churches; after that, the next five stanzas present reflection and discussion.

"Church Going" is a curious poem in many ways. It goes to a lot of trouble to characterize its speaker, who seems a rather odd choice as a commentator on the state of religion. His informal attire (he takes off his cycle-clips at the end of stanza 1) and his less than worshipful behavior do not at first make him seem like a serious philosopher. He is not disrespectful or sacrilegious, and before the end of stanza 1 he has tried to describe the "awkward reverence" he feels; but his overly emphatic imitation of part of the service stamps him as playful, a little satirical. He is a tourist here, not someone who reg-

6. Blended.

ularly drops in for prayer or meditation in the usual sense. And yet those early details give him credentials, in a way; he knows the names of religious objects and has some history of churches in his grasp. Clearly he does this sort of church going habitually ("Yet stop I did: in fact I often do," line 19) because he wonders seriously what it all means—now—in comparison to what it meant to religious worshipers in times past. Ultimately, he takes the church, its cultural meaning, and its function seriously (lines 55 ff.), and he understands the importance of the church in the history of his culture. Thus the relatively brief drama provides a context for the rambling reflections that grow out of the speaker's dramatic experience.

Sometimes poems are organized by contrasts, and they conveniently set one thing up against another that is quite different. Notice, for example, how the following poem carefully contrasts two worlds:

PAT MORA

Sonrisas

I live in a doorway
between two rooms, I hear
quiet clicks, cups of black
coffee, *click, click* like facts
5   budgets, tenure, curriculum,
from careful women in crisp beige
suits, quick beige smiles
that seldom sneak into their eyes.

I peek
10 in the other room señoras
in faded dresses stir sweet
milk coffee, laughter whirls
with steam from fresh *tamales*
   sh, sh, mucho ruido,[7]
15 they scold one another,
press their lips, trap smiles
in their dark, Mexican eyes.

               1986

Here different words, habits, and values characterize the worlds of the two sets of characters, and the poem is organized largely by the contrasts between them. The meaning of the poem (the difference between the two worlds) is very nearly the same as the structure.

Poems often have **discursive structures**, too; that is, they may be organized like a treatise, an argument, or an essay. "First," they say, "and second . . . and third . . ." This sort of 1-2-3 structure takes a variety of forms

---

7. A lot of noise.

depending on what is being enumerated or argued. Discursive structures help organize poems such as Shelley's "Ode to the West Wind" (later in this chapter), where the wind drives a leaf in Part I, a cloud in Part II, a wave in Part III, and then, after a summary and statement of the speaker's ambitious hope in Part IV, is asked to make the speaker a lyre in Part V.

Poems may borrow their organizational strategies from many places, imitating chronological, visual, or discursive shapes in reality or in other works of art. Sometimes poems strive to be almost purely descriptive of someone or something (using **descriptive structures**), in which case poets have to make organizational decisions much as painters or photographers would, deciding first how a whole scene should look, then putting the parts into proper place for the whole. Of course, poems must present their details sequentially, not all at once as actual pictures more or less can, so poets must decide where to start a description (at the left? center? top?) and what sort of movement to use (linear across the scene? clockwise?). But if using words instead of paint or film has some drawbacks, it also has particular advantages: figurative language can be a part of description, or an adjunct to it. Poets can insert comparisons at any point without necessarily disturbing the unity of their descriptions.

Some poems use **imitative structures,** mirroring as exactly as possible the structure of something that already exists as an object and can be seen—another poem perhaps. Other poems use **reflective (or meditative) structures,** pondering a subject, theme, or event, and letting the mind play with it, skipping (logically or not) from one sound to another, or to related thoughts or objects as the mind encounters them.

Although the following poem employs several organizational principles, it ultimately takes its structure from an important shift in the speaker's attitude as she reviews, ponders, and rethinks events of long ago.

SHARON OLDS

The Victims

When Mother divorced you, we were glad. She took it and
took it, in silence, all those years and then
kicked you out, suddenly, and her
kids loved it. Then you were fired, and we
5 grinned inside, the way people grinned when
Nixon's helicopter lifted off the South
Lawn for the last time.[8] We were tickled
to think of your office taken away,
your secretaries taken away,
10 your lunches with three double bourbons,

---

8. When Richard Nixon resigned the U.S. presidency on August 8, 1974, his exit from the White House (by helicopter from the lawn) was televised live.

> your pencils, your reams of paper. Would they take your
> suits back, too, those dark
> carcasses hung in your closet, and the black
> noses of your shoes with their large pores?
> 15 She had taught us to take it, to hate you and take it
> until we pricked with her for your
> annihilation, Father. Now I
> pass the bums in doorways, the white
> slugs of their bodies gleaming through slits in their
> 20 suits of compressed silt, the stained
> flippers of their hands, the underwater
> fire of their eyes, ships gone down with the
> lanterns lit, and I wonder who took it and
> took it from them in silence until they had
> 25 given it all away and had nothing
> left but this.

1984

"The Victims" divides basically into two parts. In the first two-thirds of the poem (from line 1 to the middle of line 17), the speaker evokes her father (the "you" of lines 1, 3, and so forth), who had been guilty of terrible habits and behavior when the speaker was young and was kicked out suddenly and divorced by the speaker's mother (lines 1–3). He was then fired from his job (line 4) and lost his whole way of life (lines 8–12), and the speaker (taught by the mother, lines 15–17) recalls celebrating every defeat and every loss ("we pricked with her for your annihilation," lines 16–17). The mother is regarded as a victim ("She took it and took it, in silence, all those years" [lines 1–2]), and the speaker forms an indivisible unit with her and the other children ("her kids," lines 3–4). They are the "we" of the first part of the poem. They were "glad" (line 1) at the divorce; they "loved it" (line 4) when the mother kicked out the father; they "grinned" (line 5) when the father was fired; they were "tickled" (line 7) when he lost his job, his secretaries, and his daily life. Only at the end of the first section does the speaker (now older but remembering what it was like to be a child) recognize that the mother was responsible for the easy, childish vision of the father's guilt ("She had taught us to take it, to hate you and take it" [line 15]); nevertheless, all sympathy in this part of the poem is with the mother and her children, while all of the imagery is entirely unfavorable to the father. The family reacted to the father's misfortunes the way observers responded to the retreat in disgrace of Richard Nixon from the U.S. presidency. The father seems to have led a luxurious and insensitive life, with lots of support in his office (lines 8–11), fancy clothes (lines 12–14), and decadent lunches (line 10); his artificial identity seemed haunting and frightening (lines 11–14) to the speaker as child.

But in line 17, the poem shifts its focus and tone. The "you" in the poem is now, suddenly, "Father." A bit of sympathy begins to surface for "bums in doorways" (line 18), who begin to seem like victims, too; their bodies are "slugs" (line 19), their suits are made of residual waste (lines 19–20), and their hands are reduced to nearly useless "flippers" (line 21). Their eyes contain fire (line 22), but it is as if they retain only a spark of life in their submerged and dying state. The speaker has not forgotten the cruelty and insensitivity remembered in the first part of the poem, but the blame seems to have shifted somewhat and the father is not the only villain, nor are the mother and children the only victims. Look carefully at how the existence of street people recalls earlier details about the father, how sympathy for his plight is elicited from us, and how the definition of *victim* shifts.

Imagery, words, attitudes, and narrative are different in the two parts of the poem, and the second half carefully qualifies the first, as if to illustrate the more mature and considered attitudes of the speaker in her older years—a qualification of the easy imitation of the earlier years, when the mother's views dominated and set the tone. Change has governed the poem's structure here; differences in age and attitude are supported by an entirely different point of view and frame of reference.

The paradigms (or models) for organizing poems are, finally, not all that different from those of prose. It may be easier to organize something short rather than something long, but the question of intensity becomes comparatively more important in shorter works. Basically, the problem of how to organize one's material is, for the writer, first of all a matter of deciding what kind of thing one wants to create, of having its purposes and effects clearly in mind. That means that every poem will differ somewhat from every other, but it also means that purposeful patterns—narrative, dramatic, descriptive, imitative, or reflective—may help writers organize and develop their ideas. A consciousness of purpose and effect can help the reader see *how* a poem proceeds toward its goal. And seeing how a poem is organized is, in turn, often a good way of seeing where it is going and what its real concerns and purposes may be. Often a poem's organization helps to clarify the particular effects that the poet wishes to generate. In a good poem, means and ends are closely related, and a reader who is a good observer of one will be rewarded with the other.

• • •

ANONYMOUS

Sir Patrick Spens

The king sits in Dumferling toune,[9]
  Drinking the blude-reid[1] wine:
"O whar will I get guid sailor,
  To sail this ship of mine?"

---

9. Town. 1. Blood-red.

5 Up and spake an eldern knicht,
    Sat at the king's richt knee:
"Sir Patrick Spens is the best sailor
    That sails upon the sea."

    The king has written a braid[2] letter
10   And signed it wi' his hand,
And sent it to Sir Patrick Spens,
    Was walking on the sand.

    The first line that Sir Patrick read,
    A loud lauch[3] lauched he;
15 The next line that Sir Patrick read,
    The tear blinded his ee.[4]

"O wha is this has done this deed,
    This il deed done to me,
To send me out this time o' the year,
20   To sail upon the sea?

"Make haste, make haste, my merry men all,
    Our guid ship sails the morn."
"O say na sae,[5] my master dear,
    For I fear a deadly storm.

25 "Late, late yestre'en I saw the new moon
    Wi' the auld moon in her arm,
And I fear, I fear, my dear mastér,
    That we will come to harm."

O our Scots nobles were richt laith[6]
30   To weet their cork-heeled shoon,[7]
But lang owre a'[8] the play were played
    Their hats they swam aboon.[9]

O lang, lang, may their ladies sit,
    Wi' their fans into their hand,
35 Or ere they see Sir Patrick Spens
    Come sailing to the land.

O lang, lang, may the ladies stand
    Wi' their gold kems[1] in their hair,
Waiting for their ain[2] dear lords,
40   For they'll see them na mair.

Half o'er, half o'er to Aberdour
    It's fifty fadom deep,

---

2. Broad: explicit.   3. Laugh.   4. Eye.   5. Not so.   6. Right loath: very reluctant.
7. To wet their cork-heeled shoes. Cork was expensive, and, therefore, such shoes were a mark of wealth and status.   8. Before all.   9. Their hats swam above them.   1. Combs.   2. Own.

And there lies guid Sir Patrick Spens
  Wi' the Scots lords at his feet.

probably 13th century

- What event is hinted at in line 32 ("Their hats they swam
  aboon") and in the poem's final stanza? What is the effect of
  depicting the poem's principal action indirectly?

WILLIAM CARLOS WILLIAMS

The Dance

In Brueghel's great picture, The Kermess,[3]
the dancers go round, they go round and
around, the squeal and the blare and the
tweedle of bagpipes, a bugle and fiddles
5 tipping their bellies (round as the thick-
sided glasses whose wash they impound)
their hips and their bellies off balance
to turn them. Kicking and rolling about
the Fair Grounds, swinging their butts, those
10 shanks must be sound to bear up under such
rollicking measures, prance as they dance
in Brueghel's great picture, The Kermess.

1944

- Why is it appropriate to the subject, a painting, to begin and
  end the poem with the same line? In what ways is the poem
  like the dance it depicts?

EMILY DICKINSON

[The Wind begun to knead the Grass—]

The Wind begun to knead the Grass—
As Women do a Dough—
He flung a Hand full at the Plain—
A Hand full at the Sky—
5 The Leaves unhooked themselves from Trees—
And started all abroad—
The Dust did scoop itself like Hands—
And throw away the Road—

---

3. A painting by Pieter Brueghel the Elder (1525?–1569).

The Wagons quickened on the Street—
10 The Thunders gossiped low—
The Lightning showed a Yellow Head—
And then a livid Toe—
The Birds put up the Bars to Nests—
The Cattle flung to Barns—
15 Then came one drop of Giant Rain—
And then, as if the Hands
That held the Dams—had parted hold—
The Waters Wrecked the Sky—
But overlooked my Father's House—
20 Just Quartering a Tree—

1864

- What happens in this poem's final line? How is this the work of "the Hands"?

WILLIAM SHAKESPEARE

[Th'expense of spirit in a waste of shame]

Th'expense of spirit in a waste[4] of shame
Is lust in action; and, till action, lust
Is perjured, murderous, bloody, full of blame,
Savage, extreme, rude, cruel, not to trust;
5 Enjoyed no sooner but despisèd straight:
Past reason hunted; and no sooner had,
Past reason hated, as a swallowed bait,
On purpose laid to make the taker mad:
Mad in pursuit, and in possession so;
10 Had, having, and in quest to have, extreme;
A bliss in proof;[5] and proved, a very woe;
Before, a joy proposed; behind, a dream.
All this the world well knows; yet none knows well
To shun the heaven that leads men to this hell.

1609

- Paraphrase this poem. What emotional stages accompany the carrying out of a violent or lustful act? Is Shakespeare an insightful psychologist? What is his major insight about how lust works?

4. Using up; also, desert. *Expense*: expending   5. In the act.

PERCY BYSSHE SHELLEY

Ode to the West Wind

I

O wild West Wind, thou breath of Autumn's being,
Thou, from whose unseen presence the leaves dead
Are driven, like ghosts from an enchanter fleeing,

Yellow, and black, and pale, and hectic red,
5 Pestilence-stricken multitudes: O thou,
Who chariotest to their dark wintry bed

The wingéd seeds, where they lie cold and low,
Each like a corpse within its grave, until
Thine azure sister of the Spring shall blow

10 Her clarion[6] o'er the dreaming earth, and fill
(Driving sweet buds like flocks to feed in air)
With living hues and odors plain and hill:

Wild Spirit, which art moving everywhere;
Destroyer and preserver; hear, oh, hear!

II

15 Thou on whose stream, mid the steep sky's commotion,
Loose clouds like earth's decaying leaves are shed,
Shook from the tangled boughs of Heaven and Ocean,

Angels[7] of rain and lightning: there are spread
On the blue surface of thine aëry surge,
20 Like the bright hair uplifted from the head

Of some fierce Maenad,[8] even from the dim verge
Of the horizon to the zenith's height,
The locks of the approaching storm. Thou dirge

Of the dying year, to which this closing night
25 Will be the dome of a vast sepulcher,
Vaulted with all thy congregated might

Of vapors, from whose solid atmosphere
Black rain, and fire, and hail will burst: oh, hear!

---

6. Trumpet call.   7. Messengers.
8. A frenzied female votary of Dionysus, the Greek god of vegetation and fertility who was supposed
to die in the fall and rise again each spring.

III

Thou who didst waken from his summer dreams
30 The blue Mediterranean, where he lay,
Lulled by the coil of his crystálline streams,

Beside a pumice isle in Baiae's bay,[9]
And saw in sleep old palaces and towers
Quivering within the wave's intenser day,

35 All overgrown with azure moss and flowers
So sweet, the sense faints picturing them! Thou
For whose path the Atlantic's level powers

Cleave themselves into chasms, while far below
The sea-blooms and the oozy woods which wear
40 The sapless foliage of the ocean, know

Thy voice, and suddenly grow gray with fear,
And tremble and despoil themselves:[1] oh, hear!

IV

If I were a dead leaf thou mightest bear;
If I were a swift cloud to fly with thee;
45 A wave to pant beneath thy power, and share

The impulse of thy strength, only less free
Than thou, O uncontrollable! If even
I were as in my boyhood, and could be

The comrade of thy wanderings over Heaven,
50 As then, when to outstrip thy skyey speed
Scarce seemed a vision; I would ne'er have striven

As thus with thee in prayer in my sore need.
Oh, lift me as a wave, a leaf, a cloud!
I fall upon the thorns of life! I bleed!

55 A heavy weight of hours has chained and bowed
One too like thee: tameless, and swift, and proud.

V

Make me thy lyre, even as the forest is:
What if my leaves are falling like its own!
The tumult of thy mighty harmonies

---

9. Where Roman emperors had erected villas, west of Naples.
1. The vegetation at the bottom of the sea . . . sympathizes with that of the land in the change of seasons [Shelley's note].

60 Will take from both a deep, autumnal tone,
Sweet though in sadness. Be thou, Spirit fierce,
My spirit! Be thou me, impetuous one!

Drive my dead thoughts over the universe
Like withered leaves to quicken a new birth!
65 And, by the incantation of this verse,

Scatter, as from an unextinguished hearth
Ashes and sparks, my words among mankind!
Be through my lips to unawakened earth

The trumpet of a prophecy! O Wind,
70 If Winter comes, can Spring be far behind?

1820

- What attributes of the West Wind does the speaker want his
  poetry to embody? In what ways is this poem like the wind it
  describes?

W. H. AUDEN

In Memory of W. B. Yeats

(d. January, 1939)

I

He disappeared in the dead of winter:
The brooks were frozen, the airports almost deserted,
And snow disfigured the public statues;
The mercury sank in the mouth of the dying day.
5 What instruments we have agree
The day of his death was a dark cold day.

Far from his illness
The wolves ran on through the evergreen forests,
The peasant river was untempted by the fashionable quays;
10 By mourning tongues
The death of the poet was kept from his poems.

But for him it was his last afternoon as himself,
An afternoon of nurses and rumors;
The provinces of his body revolted,
15 The squares of his mind were empty,
Silence invaded the suburbs,
The current of his feeling failed; he became his admirers.

Now he is scattered among a hundred cities
And wholly given over to unfamiliar affections,
20 To find his happiness in another kind of wood

And be punished under a foreign code of conscience.
The words of a dead man
Are modified in the guts of the living.

But in the importance and noise of tomorrow
25   When the brokers are roaring like beasts on the floor of the
        Bourse,[2]
And the poor have the sufferings to which they are fairly
        accustomed,
And each in the cell of himself is almost convinced of his
        freedom,
A few thousand will think of this day
As one thinks of a day when one did something slightly unusual.
30   What instruments we have agree
The day of his death was a dark cold day.

        II

You were silly like us; your gift survived it all:
The parish of rich women, physical decay,
Yourself. Mad Ireland hurt you into poetry.
35   Now Ireland has her madness and her weather still,
For poetry makes nothing happen: it survives
In the valley of its making where executives
Would never want to tamper, flows on south
From ranches of isolation and the busy griefs,
40   Raw towns that we believe and die in; it survives,
A way of happening, a mouth.

        III

Earth, receive an honored guest:
William Yeats is laid to rest.
Let the Irish vessel lie
45   Emptied of its poetry.

In the nightmare of the dark
All the dogs of Europe bark,
And the living nations wait,
Each sequestered in its hate;

50   Intellectual disgrace
Stares from every human face,
And the seas of pity lie
Locked and frozen in each eye.

Follow, poet, follow right
55   To the bottom of the night,

---

2. The Paris stock exchange.

With your unconstraining voice
Still persuade us to rejoice;

With the farming of a verse
Make a vineyard of the curse,
60 Sing of human unsuccess
In a rapture of distress;

In the deserts of the heart
Let the healing fountain start,
In the prison of his days
65 Teach the free man how to praise.

1939

- What is meant by "he became his admirers" (line 17)? What meaning is added to line 36 ("For poetry makes nothing happen . . .") by the poem's final three stanzas?

SUGGESTIONS FOR WRITING

1. What words and patterns are repeated in the different stanzas of Shelley's "Ode to the West Wind"? What differences are there from stanza to stanza? What "progress" does the poem make? Write an essay in which you discuss the ways that meaning and structure are intertwined in Shelley's poem.

2. Write an essay in which you explore the structure of Auden's "In Memory of W. B. Yeats." What is the logic of the poem? Why does each of the three parts have its own distinct subject, tone, and poetic approach? What subjects does the poem encompass besides the death of Yeats?

3. Pick out any poem you have read in this book that seems particularly effective in the way it is put together. Write an essay in which you consider how the poem is organized—that is, what structural principles it employs. What do the choices of speaker, situation, and setting have to do with the poem's structure? What other artistic decisions contribute to its structure?

14 EXTERNAL FORM

Most poems of more than a few lines are divided into **stanzas**—groups of lines divided from other groups by white space on the page. Putting some space between groupings of lines has the effect of sectioning a poem, giving its physical appearance a series of divisions that often mark turns of thought, changes of scene or image, or other shifts in structure or direction. In Donne's "The Flea" (chapter 10), for example, the stanza divisions mark distinct stages in the action: between the first and second stanzas, the speaker stops his companion from killing the flea; between the second and third stanzas, the companion follows through on her intention and kills the flea. In Nemerov's "The Goose Fish" (chapter 13), the stanzas mark stages in the self-perception of the lovers: each stanza is a more or less distinct scene, and the scenes unfold almost like a series of slides. Not all stanzas are quite so neatly patterned as these, but any formal division of a poem into stanzas is important to consider; what appear to be gaps or silences may be structural markers.

Historically, stanzas have most often been organized by patterns of rhyme, and thus stanza divisions have been a visual indicator of patterns in sound. In most traditional stanza forms, the pattern of rhyme is repeated in stanza after stanza throughout the poem, until voice and ear become familiar with the pattern and come to expect and, in a sense, depend on it. The accumulation of pattern allows us to "hear" deviations from the pattern as well, just as we do in music. The rhyme thus becomes an organizational device in the poem—a formal, external determiner of organization, as distinguished from the internal, structural determiners we considered in chapter 13—and ordinarily the metrical patterns stay constant from stanza to stanza. (That is, a formal rhyme scheme is *external* to the unique inner logic of a poem's narrative, descriptive, or discursive design.) In Shelley's "Ode to the West Wind," for example, the first and third lines in each stanza rhyme, and the middle line then rhymes with the first and third lines of the next stanza. (In indicating rhyme, we conventionally use a different letter of the alphabet to represent each rhyme sound; in the following example, if we begin with "being" as *a* and "dead" as *b*, then "fleeing" is also *a*, and "red" and "bed" are *b*.)

O wild West Wind, thou breath of Autumn's being,	*a*
Thou, from whose unseen presence the leaves dead	*b*
Are driven, like ghosts from an enchanter fleeing,	*a*
Yellow, and black, and pale, and hectic red,	*b*
Pestilence-stricken multitudes: O thou,	*c*
Who chariotest to their dark wintry bed	*b*

The wingéd seeds, where they lie cold and low,   *c*
Each like a corpse within its grave, until   *d*
Thine azure sister of the Spring shall blow   *c*

In this stanza form, known as **terza rima**, the stanzas are linked to each other by a common sound: one rhyme sound from each stanza is picked up in the next stanza, and so on to the end of the poem (though sometimes poems in this form have sections that use varied rhyme schemes). This stanza form was used by Dante in *The Divine Comedy*, written in Italian in the early 1300s. Terza rima is not all that common in English because it is a rhyme-rich stanza form—that is, it requires many rhymes, and thus many different rhyme words—and English is, relatively speaking, a rhyme-poor language (not as rich in rhyme possibilities as Italian or French). One reason for this is that English is derived from so many different language families that it has fewer similar word endings than languages that have remained "pure"—that is, more dependent for vocabulary on the roots and patterns found in a single language family.

Many contemporary poets use rhyme sparingly, finding it neither necessary nor appealing, but until the twentieth century the music of rhyme was central to both the sound and the formal conception of most poems. Because poetry was originally an oral art (and its texts not always written down), various kinds of **memory devices** (sometimes called **mnemonic devices**) were built into poems to help reciters remember them. Rhyme was one such device, and most people still find it easier to memorize poetry that rhymes. The simple pleasure of hearing familiar sounds repeated at regular intervals may also help to account for the traditional popularity of rhyme, and perhaps plain habit (for both poets and hearers) had a lot to do with why rhyme flourished for so many centuries in so many languages as an expected feature of poetry. Rhyme also helps to give poetry a special aural quality that distinguishes it from prose, a significant advantage in ages that worry about decorum and propriety and are anxious to preserve a strong sense of poetic tradition. Some ages have been very concerned that poetry should not in any way be mistaken for prose or made to serve prosaic functions, and the literary critics and theorists in those ages made extraordinary efforts to emphasize the distinctions between poetry, which was thought to be artistically superior, and prose, which was thought to be primarily utilitarian. An elitist pride and a fear that an expanded reading public could ultimately dilute the possibilities of traditional art forms have been powerful cultural forces in Western civilization, and if such forces were not themselves responsible for creating rhyme in poetry, they at least helped to preserve a sense of its necessity. But rhyme and other patterns of repeated sounds are also important, for countless historical and cultural reasons, to non-Western languages and poetic traditions as well.

There are at least two other reasons for rhyme. One is complex and hard to state justly without long explanations. It involves traditional ideas about the symmetrical relationship of different aspects of the world and the function of poetry to reflect the universe as human learning has understood it.

Many cultures (especially in earlier centuries) have assumed that rhyme was proper to verse, perhaps even essential. Poets in these ages and cultures would have felt themselves eccentric or even foolish to compose poems any other way. Some English poets (especially in the Renaissance) did experiment—often very successfully—with **blank verse** (that is, verse that did not rhyme but that nevertheless had strict metrical requirements), but the cultural pressure for rhyme was almost constant. Why? As noted above, custom or habit may account in part for the assumption that rhyme was necessary, but there was probably more to it than that. Rather, the poets' sense that poetry was an imitation of larger relationships in the universe made it seem natural to use rhyme to represent or re-create a sense of pattern, harmony, correspondence, symmetry, and order. The sounds of poetry were thus, they reasoned, reminders of the harmonious cosmos, of the music of the spheres that animated the planets, the processes of nature, the interrelationship of all created things and beings. Probably no poet ever thought, "I shall now tunefully emulate the harmony of God's carefully ordered universe," but the tendency to use rhyme and other repetitions or re-echoings of sound (such as **alliteration** or **assonance**) nevertheless stemmed ultimately from basic assumptions about how the universe worked. In a modern world increasingly perceived as fragmented and chaotic, there is less of a tendency to assert a sense of harmony and symmetry. It would be far too easy and too mechanical, of course, to think that rhyme in a poem specifically means that the poet has a firm sense of cosmic order, and that an unrhymed poem testifies to chaos, but cultural assumptions do affect the expectations of both poets and readers, and cultural tendencies create a kind of pressure on the individual creator. If you take a survey course (or a series of related "period" courses) in English or American literature, you will readily notice the diminishing sense that rhyme is an indispensable aspect of poetry. And similarly, other linguistic and national traditions vary usages in different times, depending on their own evolving philosophical and cultural assumptions.

Concentration is the very essence of poetry.
—AMY LOWELL

One other reason for using rhyme is that it provides a kind of discipline for the poet, a way of harnessing poetic talents and keeping a rein on the imagination, so that the results are ordered, controlled, put into some kind of meaningful and recognizable form. Robert Frost said that writing poems without rhyme or regular meter was pointless, like playing tennis without a net. Writing good poetry does require a lot of discipline, and Frost speaks for many (perhaps most) traditional poets in suggesting that rhyme or rhythm can be a major source of that discipline. But neither one is the only possible source, and more recent poets have usually felt they would rather play by new rules or invent their own as they go along; they have, therefore, sought their sources of discipline elsewhere, preferring the sparer tones that unrhymed poetry provides. It is not that contemporary poets cannot think of rhyme words or that they do not care about the sounds of their poetry; rather, many recent poets have consciously decided not to work with rhyme and to use instead other aural and metrical devices and other strategies for organizing stanzas, just as they have chosen to work with experimental and variable rhythms instead of writing necessarily in the traditional English meters. Nevertheless, many modern poets have continued to write rhymed verse successfully in a more or less traditional way, finding that, in fact, rhyme can be a useful spur to the imagination—the search for a rhyme word can often lead to unexpected discoveries. It might well be, for example, that the need to find a rhyme for "dirt" led Theodore Roethke to the wonderful final line of "My Papa's Waltz" (chapter 11): "Still clinging to your shirt." A free-verse poet might have judged the poem complete after the previous line: "Then waltzed me off to bed."

The amount and density of rhyme vary widely in stanza and verse forms, from elaborate and intricate patterns of rhyme to more casual or spare sound repetitions. The **Spenserian stanza,** for example, is even more rhyme-rich than terza rima, using only three rhyme sounds in nine rhymed lines, as in Keats's *The Eve of St. Agnes:*

Her falt'ring hand upon the balustrade,	*a*
Old Angela was feeling for the stair,	*b*
When Madeline, St. Agnes' charméd maid,	*a*
Rose, like a missioned spirit, unaware:	*b*
With silver taper's light, and pious care,	*b*
She turned, and down the agéd gossip led	*c*
To a safe level matting. Now prepare,	*b*
Young Porphyro, for gazing on that bed;	*c*
She comes, she comes again, like ring dove frayed and fled	*c*

On the other hand, the **ballad stanza** (as in "Sir Patrick Spens") has only one set of rhymes in four lines; lines 1 and 3 in each stanza do not rhyme at all:

The king sits in Dumferling toune,	*a*
Drinking the blude-reid wine:	*b*
"O whar will I get guid sailor,	*c*
To sail this ship of mine?"	*b*

Most stanza forms use a metrical pattern as well as a rhyme scheme. Terza rima, for example, involves **iambic meter** (unstressed and stressed syllables alternating regularly), and each line has five beats (**pentameter**). Most of the Spenserian stanza (the first eight lines) is also in iambic pentameter, but the ninth line in each stanza has one extra foot (thus, the last line is in iambic hexameter). The ballad stanza, also iambic, as are most English stanza and verse forms, alternates three-beat and four-beat lines; lines 1 and 3 are unrhymed iambic tetrameter (four beats), and lines 2 and 4 are rhymed iambic trimeter (three beats).

THE SONNET

The **sonnet,** one of the most persistent verse forms, originated in the Middle Ages as a prominent form in Italian and French poetry. It dominated English poetry in the late sixteenth and early seventeenth centuries and then was revived several times from the early–nineteenth century onward. Except for some early experiments with length, the sonnet has always been fourteen lines long, and it usually is written in iambic pentameter. It is most often printed as if it were a *single* stanza, although it actually has several formal divisions that represent its rhyme schemes and formal breaks. As a popular and traditional verse form in English for more than four centuries, the sonnet has been surprisingly resilient even in ages that largely reject rhyme. It continues to attract a variety of poets, including (curiously) radical and even revolutionary poets, who find its formal demands, discipline, and fixed outcome very appealing. Its uses, although quite varied, can be illustrated fairly precisely. As a verse form, the sonnet is contained, compact, demanding; whatever it does, it must do concisely and quickly. To be effective, it must take advantage of the possibilities inherent in its shortness and its relative rigidity. It is best suited to intensity of feeling and concentration of expression. Not too surprisingly, one subject it frequently discusses is confinement itself.

WILLIAM WORDSWORTH

Nuns Fret Not

Nuns fret not at their convent's narrow room;
And hermits are contented with their cells;
And students with their pensive citadels;
Maids at the wheel, the weaver at his loom,
5 Sit blithe and happy; bees that soar for bloom,
High as the highest Peak of Furness-fells,[1]
Will murmur by the hour in foxglove bells:
In truth the prison, unto which we doom
Ourselves, no prison is: and hence for me,
10 In sundry moods,'twas pastime to be bound
Within the sonnet's scanty plot of ground;
Pleased if some souls (for such there needs must be)
Who have felt the weight of too much liberty,
Should find brief solace there, as I have found.

1807

    Most sonnets are structured according to one of two principles of division. On one principle, the sonnet divides into three units of four lines each and a final unit of two lines, and sometimes the line spacing reflects this division. On the other, the fundamental break is between the first eight lines (called an octave) and the last six (called a sestet). The 4-4-4-2 sonnet is usually called the **English** or **Shakespearean sonnet,** and ordinarily

---

1. Mountains in England's Lake District, where Wordsworth lived.

its rhyme scheme reflects the structure: the scheme of *abab cdcd efef gg* is the classic one, but many variations from that pattern still reflect the basic 4-4-4-2 division. The 8-6 sonnet is usually called the **Italian** or **Petrarchan sonnet** (the Italian poet Petrarch was an early master of this structure), and its "typical" rhyme scheme is *abbaabba cdecde*, although it too produces many variations that still reflect the basic division into two parts, an **octave** and a **sestet**.

The two kinds of sonnet structures are useful for two different sorts of argument. The 4-4-4-2 structure works very well for constructing a poem that wants to make a three-step argument (with a quick summary at the end), or for setting up brief, cumulative images. "That time of year thou mayst in me behold" (chapter 11), for example, uses the 4-4-4-2 structure to mark the progressive steps toward death and the parting of friends by using three distinct images, then summarizing. "Let me not to the marriage of true minds" (page 412) works very similarly, following the kind of organization that in chapter 13 was referred to as the 1-2-3 structure—and doing it compactly and economically.

Here, on the other hand, is a poem that uses the 8-6 pattern:

HENRY CONSTABLE

[*My lady's presence makes the roses red*]

My lady's presence makes the roses red,
Because to see her lips they blush for shame.
The lily's leaves, for envy, pale became,
And her white hands in them this envy bred.
5 The marigold the leaves abroad doth spread,
Because the sun's and her power is the same.
The violet of purple colour came,
Dyed in the blood she made my heart to shed.
In brief: all flowers from her their virtue take;
10 From her sweet breath their sweet smells do proceed;
The living heat which her eyebeams doth make
Warmeth the ground and quickeneth the seed.
The rain, wherewith she watereth the flowers,
Falls from mine eyes, which she dissolves in showers.

1594

The first eight lines argue that the lady's presence is responsible for the color of all of nature's flowers, and the final six lines summarize and extend that argument to smells and heat—and finally to the rain that the lady draws from the speaker's eyes. That kind of two-part structure, in which the octave states a proposition or generalization and the sestet provides a particularization or application of it, has a variety of uses. The final lines may, for example, reverse the first eight and achieve a paradox or irony in the poem, or the poem may nearly balance two comparable arguments. Basically, the 8-6 structure lends itself to poems with two points to make, or to those that wish to make one point and then illustrate it.

Sometimes the neat and precise structure is altered—either slightly, as in Wordsworth's "Nuns Fret Not," above (where the 8-6 structure is more of an 8½-5½ or 7-7 structure), or more radically as particular needs or effects may demand. And the two basic structures certainly do not define all the structural possibilities within a fourteen-line poem, even if they do suggest the most traditional ways of taking advantage of the sonnet's compact and well-kept container.

During the Renaissance, poets regularly employed the sonnet for love poems, and many modern sonnets continue to be about love or private life. And many continue to use a personal, apparently open and sincere tone. But poets often find the sonnet's compact form and rigid demands equally useful for many varieties of subject, theme, and tone. Besides love, sonnets often treat other subjects: politics, philosophy, discovery. And tones vary widely too, from the anger and remorse of "Th' expense of spirit in a waste of shame" (chapter 13) and righteous outrage of "On the Late Massacre in Piedmont" (chapter 10) to the tender awe of "How Do I Love Thee?" (page 399). Many poets seem to take the kind of comfort Wordsworth describes in the careful limits of the form, finding in its two basic variations (the English sonnet, such as "That time of year," and the Italian sonnet, such as "On First Looking into Chapman's Homer" [p. 594]) a sufficiency of ways to organize their materials into coherent structures.

· · ·

DANTE GABRIEL ROSSETTI

A Sonnet Is a Moment's Monument

A Sonnet is a moment's monument—
    Memorial from the Soul's eternity
    To one dead deathless hour. Look that it be,
    Whether for lustral[2] rite or dire portent,
5 Of its own arduous fullness reverent.
        Carve it in ivory or in ebony,
        As Day or Night may rule; and let Time see
    Its flowering crest impearled and orient.[3]

    A Sonnet is a coin: its face reveals
10   The soul—its converse, to what Power 'tis due—
        Whether for tribute to the august appeals
        Of Life or dower in Love's high retinue,

2. Purificatory.   3. Sparkling.

It serve; or 'mid the dark wharf's cavernous breath,
In Charon's palm it pay the toll to Death.[4]

1881

- In Rossetti's metaphor comparing the sonnet to a coin (lines 9–14), what are the two "sides" of a sonnet?

JOHN KEATS

On the Sonnet

If by dull rhymes our English must be chained,
And like Andromeda,[5] the sonnet sweet
Fettered, in spite of painéd loveliness,
Let us find, if we must be constrained,
5 Sandals more interwoven and complete
To fit the naked foot of Poesy:[6]
Let us inspect the lyre, and weigh the stress
Of every chord,[7] and see what may be gained
By ear industrious, and attention meet;
10 Misers of sound and syllable, no less
Than Midas[8] of his coinage, let us be
Jealous of dead leaves in the bay-wreath crown;[9]
So, if we may not let the Muse be free,
She will be bound with garlands of her own.

1819

- What is the rhyme scheme of this poem? How well does this unusual structure meet the challenge implied by the poem?

---

4. In classical myth, Charon was the boatman who rowed the souls of the dead across the river Styx. Ancient Greeks put a small coin in the hand of the dead to pay his fee.

5. According to Greek myth, Andromeda was chained to a rock so that she would be devoured by a sea monster. She was rescued by Perseus, who married her. When she died she was placed among the stars.

6. In a letter that contained this sonnet, Keats expressed impatience with the traditional Petrarchan and Shakespearean sonnet forms: "I have been endeavoring to discover a better sonnet stanza than we have."   7. Lyre string; *Meet:* proper.

8. The legendary king of Phrygia who asked, and got, the power to turn all he touched to gold.

9. The bay tree was sacred to Apollo, god of poetry, and bay wreaths came to symbolize true poetic achievement. The withering of the bay tree is sometimes considered an omen of death. *Jealous:* suspiciously watchful.

GWENDOLYN BROOKS

First Fight. Then Fiddle.

First fight. Then fiddle. Ply the slipping string
With feathery sorcery; muzzle the note
With hurting love; the music that they wrote
Bewitch, bewilder. Qualify to sing
5 Threadwise. Devise no salt, no hempen thing
For the dear instrument to bear. Devote
The bow to silks and honey. Be remote
A while from malice and from murdering.
But first to arms, to armor. Carry hate
10 In front of you and harmony behind.
Be deaf to music and to beauty blind.
Win war. Rise bloody, maybe not too late
For having first to civilize a space
Wherein to play your violin with grace.   1949

- After advising "First Fight. Then fiddle," the speaker discusses
  first music, then conflict. Why do you think the poet has
  arranged her argument this way?

EMMA LAZARUS

The New Colossus[1]

Not like the brazen giant of Greek fame,[2]
With conquering limbs astride from land to land;
Here at our sea-washed, sunset gates shall stand
A mighty woman with a torch, whose flame
5 Is the imprisoned lightning, and her name
Mother of Exiles. From her beacon-hand
Glows world-wide welcome; her mild eyes command
The air-bridged harbor that twin cities[3] frame.
"Keep ancient lands, your storied pomp!" cries she
10 With silent lips. "Give me your tired, your poor,
Your huddled masses yearning to breathe free,
The wretched refuse of your teeming shore.
Send these, the homeless, tempest-tost to me,
I lift my lamp beside the golden door!"

November 1883

- What comparison is the speaker making between old and new
  worlds?

1. The poem was written to commemorate the opening of the Statue of Liberty, in New York harbor.
2. The Colossus of Rhodes, one of the seven wonders of the ancient world, a 100-foot statue of
Helios, the sun god.   3. Manhattan and Brooklyn.

ROBERT FROST

Range-Finding

The battle rent a cobweb diamond-strung
And cut a flower beside a groundbird's nest
Before it stained a single human breast.
The stricken flower bent double and so hung.
5 And still the bird revisited her young.
A butterfly its fall had dispossessed,
A moment sought in air his flower of rest,
Then slightly stooped to it and fluttering clung.
On the bare upland pasture there had spread
10 O'ernight 'twixt mullein stalks a wheel of thread
And straining cables wet with silver dew.
A sudden passing bullet shook it dry.
The indwelling spider ran to greet the fly,
But finding nothing, sullenly withdrew.

1916

- What is the "battle" of line 1? What is the poem's actual subject?

WILLIAM WORDSWORTH

London, 1802

Milton! thou should'st be living at this hour:
England hath need of thee: she is a fen
Of stagnant waters: altar, sword, and pen,
Fireside, the heroic wealth of hall and bower,
5 Have forfeited their ancient English dower
Of inward happiness. We are selfish men;
Oh! raise us up, return to us again;
And give us manners, virtue, freedom, power.
Thy soul was like a star, and dwelt apart:
10 Thou hadst a voice whose sound was like the sea:
Pure as the naked heavens, majestic, free,
So didst thou travel on life's common way,
In cheerful godliness; and yet thy heart
The lowliest duties on herself did lay.

1802

- What is Wordsworth asserting about the power of poetry in
  this sonnet? Why do you think he chose the sonnet form for
  this poem?

JOHN MILTON

[*When I consider how my light is spent*]

When I consider how my light is spent,
   Ere half my days, in this dark world and wide,
   And that one talent which is death to hide[4]
   Lodged with me useless, though my soul more bent
5 To serve therewith my Maker, and present
   My true account, lest he returning chide;
   "Doth God exact day-labor, light denied?"
   I fondly ask; but Patience to prevent[5]
That murmur, soon replies, "God doth not need
10   Either man's work or his own gifts; who best
   Bear his mild yoke, they serve him best. His state
Is kingly. Thousands at his bidding speed
   And post o'er land and ocean without rest:
   They also serve who only stand and wait."

1652?

- Paraphrase the speaker's question and Patience's reply. Does knowing that Milton was blind alter your interpretation of this poem?

ELIZABETH BARRETT BROWNING

[WEB]

[*When our two souls stand up*]

When our two souls stand up erect and strong,
Face to face, silent, drawing nigh and nigher,
Until the lengthening wings break into fire
At either curvéd point,—what bitter wrong
5 Can the earth do to us, that we should not long
Be here contented? Think. In mounting higher,
The angels would press on us and aspire
To drop some golden orb of perfect song
Into our deep, dear silence. Let us stay
10   Rather on earth, Belovéd,—where the unfit
Contrarious moods of men recoil away

---

4. In the parable of the talents (Matthew 25), the servants who earned interest on their master's money (his talents) while he was away were called "good and faithful"; the one who simply hid the money and then returned it was condemned and sent away.   5. Forestall. *Fondly*: foolishly.

And isolate pure spirits, and permit
A place to stand and love in for a day,
With darkness and the death-hour rounding it.

1897

- Explain the metaphor of this poem's first four lines. What will
cause "the lengthening wings" to "break into fire"?

CHRISTINA ROSSETTI

In an Artist's Studio

One face looks out from all his canvases,
  One selfsame figure sits or walks or leans;
    We found her hidden just behind those screens,
That mirror gave back all her loveliness.
5 A queen in opal or in ruby dress,
  A nameless girl in freshest summer-greens,
    A saint, an angel—every canvass means
The same one meaning, neither more nor less.
He feeds upon her face by day and night,
10 And she with true kind eyes looks back on him
Fair as the moon and joyful as the light:
  Not wan with waiting, not with sorrow dim;
  Not as she is, but was when hope shone bright;
  Not as she is, but as she fills his dream.

1856

- What do you think is "The same one meaning" the speaker
sees in every portrait in the studio?

EDNA ST. VINCENT MILLAY

[*What lips my lips have kissed, and where, and why*]

What lips my lips have kissed, and where, and why,
I have forgotten, and what arms have lain
Under my head till morning; but the rain
Is full of ghosts tonight, that tap and sigh
5 Upon the glass and listen for reply,
  And in my heart there stirs a quiet pain
For unremembered lads that not again
Will turn to me at midnight with a cry.
Thus in the winter stands the lonely tree,

10 Nor knows what birds have vanished one by one,
    Yet knows its boughs more silent than before:
    I cannot say what loves have come and gone;
    I only know that summer sang in me
    A little while, that in me sings no more.

                                            1923

- **What are the poem's principal parts? Why does the Petrarchan model suit this sonnet?**

GWEN HARWOOD

In the Park

She sits in the park. Her clothes are out of date.
Two children whine and bicker, tug her skirt.
A third draws aimless patterns in the dirt.
Someone she loved once passes by—too late

5 to feign indifference to that casual nod.
   "How nice," et cetera. "Time holds great surprises."
   From his neat head unquestionably rises
   a small balloon . . . "but for the grace of God . . ."

They stand a while in flickering light, rehearsing
10 the children's names and birthdays. "It's so sweet
   to hear their chatter, watch them grow and thrive,"
   she says to his departing smile. Then, nursing
   the youngest child, sits staring at her feet.
   To the wind she says, "They have eaten me alive."

                                            1963

- **What is the implication of the "small balloon" that rises from the head of the man who passes by?**

WILLIAM SHAKESPEARE

[My mistress' eyes are nothing like the sun]

My mistress' eyes are nothing like the sun;
Coral is far more red than her lips' red;
If snow be white, why then her breasts are dun;[6]
If hairs be wires, black wires grow on her head.

6. Mouse-colored.

5 I have seen roses damasked[7] red and white,
But no such roses see I in her cheeks;
And in some perfumes is there more delight
Than in the breath that from my mistress reeks.
I love to hear her speak, yet well I know
10 That music hath a far more pleasing sound;
I grant I never saw a goddess go;[8]
My mistress, when she walks, treads on the ground.
And yet, by heaven, I think my love as rare
As any she belied with false compare.

1609

- In addition to the speaker's mistress, what might be another subject of this poem?

BILLY COLLINS

Sonnet

All we need is fourteen lines, well, thirteen now,
and after this one just a dozen
to launch a little ship on love's storm-tossed seas,
then only ten more left like rows of beans.
5 How easily it goes unless you get Elizabethan
and insist the iambic bongos must be played
and rhymes positioned at the ends of lines,
one for every station of the cross.
But hang on here while we make the turn
10 into the final six where all will be resolved,
where longing and heartache will find an end,
where Laura will tell Petrarch to put down his pen,
take off those crazy medieval tights,
blow out the lights, and come at last to bed.

1999

- In what respects is Collins's poem a traditional sonnet? In what respects is it not?

STANZA FORMS

Many stanza forms are represented in this book. Some have names, because they have been used over and over by different poets. Others (such as Poe's stanza form for "The Raven" [chapter 12]) were invented for a particular use

7. Variegated.   8. Walk.

in a particular poem and may never be repeated again. Most traditional stanzas are based on rhyme schemes, but some use other kinds of predictable sound patterns; early English poetry, for example, used alliteration to construct a balance between the first and second half of each line. Sometimes, especially when poets interact with each other within a strong community, highly elaborate *verse forms* have been developed that set up stanzas as part of a scheme for the whole poem. The poets of medieval Provence were especially inventive, subtle, and elaborate in their construction of complex verse forms, some of which have been copied by poets ever since. The **sestina,** for example, depends on the measured repetition of words (rather than just sounds) in particular places; see, for example, Bishop's "Sestina" (later in this chapter) and try to decipher the pattern. (There are also double and even triple sestinas, tough tests of a poet's ingenuity.) And the **villanelle,** another Provençal form, depends on the patterned repetition of whole lines (see Dylan Thomas's "Do Not Go Gentle into That Good Night" [next page]). Different cultures and different languages develop their own patterns and measures—not all poetries are parallel to English poetry—and they vary from age to age as well as nation to nation.

You can probably deduce the principles involved in each of the following stanza or verse forms by looking carefully at a poem that uses it; if you have trouble, look at the definitions in the glossary.

heroic couplet	"Sound and Sense"	chapter 12
tetrameter couplet	"To His Coy Mistress"	chapter 10
limerick	"There was a young girl from St. Paul"	chapter 12
free verse	"Dirge"	chapter 12

What are stanza forms good for? What use is it to recognize them? Why do poets bother? Matters discussed in this chapter so far have suggested two reasons: (1) Breaks between stanzas provide convenient pauses for reader and writer, something roughly equivalent to paragraphs in prose. The eye thus picks up the places where some kind of pause or break or change of focus occurs. (2) Poets sometimes use stanza forms, as they do rhyme itself, as a discipline: writing in a certain kind of stanza form imposes a shape on the act of imagination. But visual spaces and unexpected print divisions also mean that poems sometimes *look* unusual and require special visual attention, attention that does not always follow the logic of sound patterns or syntax. After the following poems illustrating some common stanza forms, you will find a section on poems that employ special configurations and shapes, using spaces and print in other ways, to establish their meanings and effects.

• • •

DYLAN THOMAS

Do Not Go Gentle into That Good Night[1]

Do not go gentle into that good night,
Old age should burn and rave at close of day;
Rage, rage against the dying of the light.

Though wise men at their end know dark is right,
5 Because their words had forked no lightning they
Do not go gentle into that good night.

Good men, the last wave by, crying how bright
Their frail deeds might have danced in a green bay,
Rage, rage against the dying of the light.

10 Wild men who caught and sang the sun in flight,
And learn, too late, they grieved it on its way,
Do not go gentle into that good night.

Grave men, near death, who see with blinding sight
Blind eyes could blaze like meteors and be gay,
15 Rage, rage against the dying of the light.

And you, my father, there on the sad height,
Curse, bless, me now with your fierce tears, I pray.
Do not go gentle into that good night.
Rage, rage against the dying of the light.

1952

- What do the wise, good, wild, and grave men have in common with the speaker's father? Why do you think Thomas chose such a strict form, the villanelle, for such an emotionally charged subject?

MARIANNE MOORE

Poetry

I, too, dislike it: there are things that are important beyond
   all this fiddle.
  Reading it, however, with a perfect contempt for it, one
   discovers in
   it after all, a place for the genuine.
    Hands that can grasp, eyes

---

1. Written during the final illness of the poet's father.

5   that can dilate, hair that can rise
          if it must, these things are important not because a

high-sounding interpretation can be put upon them but
     because they are
useful. When they become so derivative as to become
     unintelligible,
    the same thing may be said for all of us, that we
10   do not admire what
     we cannot understand: the bat
       holding on upside down or in quest of something to

eat, elephants pushing, a wild horse taking a roll, a tireless
     wolf under
a tree, the immovable critic twitching his skin like a horse
     that feels a
    flea, the base-
15 ball fan, the statistician—
     nor is it valid
       to discriminate against "business documents and

school-books"[2]; all these phenomena are important. One
     must make a distinction
however: when dragged into prominence by half poets, the
     result is not poetry,
20 nor till the poets among us can be
     "literalists of
    the imagination"[3]—above
      insolence and triviality and can present

for inspection, "imaginary gardens with real toads in them,"
     shall we have
25 it. In the meantime, if you demand on the one hand,
    the raw material of poetry in
     all its rawness and
     that which is on the other hand
      genuine, you are interested in poetry.

                              1921

---

2. *Diary of Tolstoy* (Dutton), p. 84. "Where the boundary between prose and poetry lies, I shall never be able to understand. The question is raised in manuals of style, yet the answer to it lies beyond me. Poetry is verse: Prose is not verse. Or else poetry is everything with the exception of business documents and school books" [Moore's note].

3. Yeats, *Ideas of Good and Evil* (A. H. Bullen, 1903), p. 182. "The limitation of [William Blake's] view was from the very intensity of his vision; he was a too literal realist of imagination, as others are of nature; and because he believed that the figures seen by the mind's eye, when exalted by inspiration, were 'eternal existences,' symbols of divine essences, he hated every grace of style that might obscure their lineaments" [Moore's note].

- Is this poem more about the reading or the writing of poetry? What does the poem suggest is the relationship between poetry and "the genuine" (line 3)?

ELIZABETH BISHOP

Sestina

September rain falls on the house.
In the failing light, the old grandmother
sits in the kitchen with the child
beside the Little Marvel Stove,
5 reading the jokes from the almanac,
laughing and talking to hide her tears.

She thinks that her equinoctial tears
and the rain that beats on the roof of the house
were both foretold by the almanac,
10 but only known to a grandmother.
The iron kettle sings on the stove.
She cuts some bread and says to the child,

It's time for tea now; but the child
is watching the teakettle's small hard tears
15 dance like mad on the hot black stove,
the way the rain must dance on the house.
Tidying up, the old grandmother
hangs up the clever almanac

on its string. Birdlike, the almanac
20 hovers half open above the child,
hovers above the old grandmother
and her teacup full of dark brown tears.
She shivers and says she thinks the house
feels chilly, and puts more wood in the stove.

25 *It was to be,* says the Marvel Stove.
I know what I know, says the almanac.
With crayons the child draws a rigid house
and a winding pathway. Then the child
puts in a man with buttons like tears
30 and shows it proudly to the grandmother.

But secretly, while the grandmother
busies herself about the stove,
the little moons fall down like tears
from between the pages of the almanac
35 into the flower bed the child
has carefully placed in the front of the house.

Time to plant tears, says the almanac.
The grandmother sings to the marvellous stove
and the child draws another inscrutable house.

1965

- Try to derive from "Sestina" the "rules" that govern the sestina
  form. Why do you think Bishop chose this form for her poem?

ARCHIBALD MacLEISH

Ars Poetica[4]

A poem should be palpable and mute
As a globed fruit,

Dumb
As old medallions to the thumb,

5 Silent as the sleeve-worn stone
Of casement ledges where the moss has grown—

A poem should be wordless
As the flight of birds.

A poem should be motionless in time
10 As the moon climbs.

Leaving, as the moon releases
Twig by twig the night-entangled trees,

Leaving, as the moon behind the winter leaves,
Memory by memory the mind—

15 A poem should be motionless in time
As the moon climbs.

A poem should be equal to:
Not true.

For all the history of grief
20 An empty doorway and a maple leaf.

For love
The leaning grasses and two lights above the sea—

A poem should not mean
But be.

1926

---

4. "The Art of Poetry," title of a poetical treatise by the Roman poet Horace (65–8 B.C.E.).

- Can you summarize this poem's ideas about what poetry should be? How does the poem itself illustrate these principles?

SUGGESTIONS FOR WRITING

1. Chart the rhyme scheme of Keats's "On the Sonnet," and then, after reading the poem aloud, mark the major structural divisions of the poem. At what points do these structural divisions and the breaks in rhyme coincide? At what points do they conflict? Write an essay in which you discuss how these patterns and variations relate to the poem's meaning.
2. Some of the sonnets in this book, such as those by Shakespeare, adhere closely to the classic English model; others, such as Milton's "When I consider how my light is spent," follow the Italian model; and some, bear only slight resemblance to either of the traditional sonnet models. Take any four sonnets found in this book as the basis for an essay in which you compare and contrast the various ways poets have used the sonnet form to achieve their unique artistic purposes.
3. Trace the variations on imagery of light and darkness in Thomas's "Do Not Go Gentle into That Good Night." How do we know that light represents life and darkness death (rather than, say, sight and blindness)? How does the poet use the strict formal requirements of the villanelle to emphasize this interplay of light and darkness? Write an essay in which you discuss the interaction of form and content in "Do Not Go Gentle into That Good Night."

15 THE WHOLE TEXT

In the previous seven chapters, we have been thinking about one thing at a
time—setting, word choice, symbolism, meter, stanza form, and so on—and
we have discussed each poem primarily in terms of a single issue. Learning
to deal with one problem at a time is good educational practice and in the
long run will make you a more careful and more effective reader of poems.
Still, the elements of poems do not work individually but in combination,
and in considering even the simplest elements (speaker, for example, or setting) we have noticed how categories overlap—how, for example, the question of setting in Dickey's "Cherrylog Road" quickly merges into questions
about the speaker, his state of mind, his personality, his distance from the
central events in the poem. Thinking about a single issue never does complete justice to an individual poem; no poem depends for all its effects on
just one device or one element of the poet's craft. Poems are complex wholes
that demand various kinds of attention, and, ultimately, to read any poem
fully and well you need to ask every question about craft, form, and tradition
that we've asked so far, and many more questions you may learn to ask after
more experience in reading poems. Not all questions are equally relevant to
all poems, of course, but moving systematically through your whole reper-
toire of questions will enable you to get beyond the fragmentation of particular issues in order to approach the whole poem and its multiple effects.
In this chapter we will consider how the various elements in poems work
together.

Below is a short poem in which several issues we have considered come
up almost simultaneously.

ELIZABETH JENNINGS

Delay

The radiance of that star that leans on me
Was shining years ago. The light that now
Glitters up there my eye may never see
And so the time lag teases me with how

5 Love that loves now may not reach me until
Its first desire is spent. The star's impulse
Must wait for eyes to claim it beautiful
And love arrived may find us somewhere else.

1953

In most poems, several issues arise more or less at once, and the analytic practice of separating issues is a convenience rather than an assertion of priorities. In "Delay," a lot of the basic questions (about speaker, situation, and setting, for example) seem to be put on hold in the beginning, but if we proceed systematically the poem opens itself to us. The first line identifies the "I" (or rather, in this case, "me") of the poem as an observer of the bright star that is the main object in the poem and the principal source of its imagery, its "plot," and its analogical argument. But we learn little about the speaker. She surfaces again in lines 4 and 5 and with someone else ("us") in line 8, but she is always "me" in the objective case—acted on rather than acting. All we know for certain about her is that she can speak about the time it takes a star's light to reach her and that she contemplates deeply about the meaning and effect of such time lags. We know even less about the setting and situation; somewhere the speaker watches a bright star and meditates on the fact that she is seeing it long, long after its light was actually sent forth. Her location is not specified, and the time, though probably night, could be any night (in the age of modern astronomy, that is, because the speaker knows about the speed of light and the distance of the stars from Earth); the only other explicit clues we have about the situation involve the "us" of the final line and the fact that the speaker's concern with time seems oddly personal, something that matters to her emotional life—not merely a matter of scientific knowledge.

The poem's language helps us understand much more about the speaker and her situation, as do the poem's structure and stanza form. The most crucial word in the first stanza is probably the verb "leans" (line 1); certainly it is the poem's most unusual and surprising word. Because a star cannot literally *lean* on its observer, the word seems to suggest the speaker's perception of her relationship to the star. Perhaps she feels that the star impinges on her, that she is somehow *subject* to its influence, though not in the popular, astrological sense. Here the star influences the speaker because she understands something about the way the universe works and can apply her knowledge of light and the vastness of space in an analogical way to her own life: it "leans" because it tells her something about how observers are affected by what they observe. And it is worth noticing how fully the speaker thinks of herself as object rather than actor or agent. Here, as throughout the poem, she is acted upon; things happen *to* her—the star leans on her, the time lag teases her (line 4), love may not reach her (line 5), and she (along with someone else) is the object sought in the final line.

Other crucial words also help clarify the speaker and her situation. The words "radiance" (line 1) and "[g]litters" (line 3) are fairly standard ones to describe stars, but here their standard meanings are carefully qualified by their position in time. The actual radiance of the starlight occurred many eons before and seems to be unavailable to the speaker, who now sees only glitter, something far less warm and resonant. And the word "impulse" in line 6 invokes technical knowledge about light. Rather than being impulsive or quickly spent, a star must "wait" for its reception in the eye of the beholder, where it becomes "beautiful"; in physics, an impulse combines force and duration. Hence, the receiver of light—the beholder, the acted-upon—becomes important, and we begin to see why the speaker always appears as the object: she is the receiver and interpreter, and the light is not complete—its duration not established—until she receives and interprets it. The star does, after all, "lean" on (depend on) her in some objective sense as well as the subjective one in which she first seems to report it.

The stanza form suggests that the poem may have stages and that its meaning may emerge in two parts, a suggestion confirmed by the poem's form and structure. The first stanza is entirely about stars and stargazing, but the second stanza establishes the analogy with love that becomes the poem's central metaphor. Now, too, more becomes clear about the speaker and her situation. Her concern is about delay, "time lag" (line 4), and the fact that "[l]ove that loves now may not reach me until / Its first desire is spent" (lines 5–6), a strong indication that her initial observation of the star is driven by feeling and her emotional context. Her attempt to put the remoteness of feeling into a perspective that will enable understanding and patience becomes the "plot" of the poem, and her final calm recognition about "us"—that "love arrived may find us somewhere else"—is, if not comforting, nevertheless a recognition that patience is important and that some things do last. Even the sounds of the poem—in this case the way rhyme is used—help support the meaning of the poem and the tone it achieves. The rhymes in the first part of the poem reflect perfectly the stable sense of ancient stars, while in the second stanza we find near-rhymes: there is harmony here, but in human life and emotion nothing is quite perfect.

Here is another short poem whose several elements deserve some detailed attention:

ANONYMOUS

Western Wind

Western wind, when wilt thou blow,
    The small rain down can rain?
Christ, if my love were in my arms
    And I in my bed again!

    15th century

Perhaps the most obvious thing here is the poem's structure: its first two lines seem to have little to do with the last two. How can we account for these two distinct and apparently unrelated directions, the calm concern with natural processes in the first part and the emotional outburst about loneliness and lovelessness in the second? The best route to the whole poem is still to begin with the most simple of questions—who? when? where? what is happening?—and proceed to more difficult and complex ones.

As in Jennings's "Delay," the speaker here offers little explicit autobiography. The first two lines provide no personal information, but ask a question that could be delivered quite impersonally: they could be part of a philosophical meditation. The abbreviated syntax at the end of line 1 (the question of causality is not fully stated, and we have to supply the "so that" implied at the end of the line) may suggest strong feeling and emotional upset, but it tells us nothing intimate, only that the time is spring (which is when the western wind blows). No place is indicated, no year, no particulars of situation. But lines 3–4, while remaining inexplicit about exact details, make the speaker's situation clear enough: his love is no longer in his arms, and he wishes she were. (We don't really know genders here, but we can make a guess based on what we know of typical practices in fifteenth-century England.)

The poem's language, a study in contrast, guides us to see the two-part structure clearly. The question asked of the wind in lines 1–2 involves straightforward, steady language, but line 3 bursts with agony and personal despair. The power of the first word of line 3—especially in an age of belief—suggests a speaker ready to bewail his loss in the strongest possible terms, and the parallel statements of loss in lines 3 and 4 suggest not only the speaker's physical relationship to his love but also his displacement from home: he is deprived of both place and love, human contact and contact with his past. His longing for a world ordered according to his past experience is structured to parallel his longing for the spring wind that brings the world back to life. The two parts of the poem both express a desire for return—to life, to order, to causal relationships within the world. Setting has in fact become a central theme in the poem, and what the poem expresses tonally involves a powerful desire for stability and belonging—an effect that grows out of our sense of the speaker's situation and character. Speaker, setting, language, and structure here intertwine to create the intense focus of the poem.

In the following short poem, several elements likewise interrelate:

ROBERT HERRICK

Upon Julia's Clothes

Whenas in silks my Julia goes
Then, then, methinks, how sweetly flows
That liquefaction of her clothes.

Next, when I cast mine eyes, and see
5 That brave[1] vibration, each way free,
O, how that glittering taketh me!

1648

---

1. Handsome, showy.

The poem is unabashed in its admiration of the way Julia looks, and nearly everything in its six short lines contributes to its celebratory tone. Perhaps the most striking thing about the poem is its unusual, highly suggestive use of words. "[G]oes" at the end of line 1 may be the first word to call special attention to itself, though we will return in a minute to the very first word of the poem. "Walks" or "moves" would seem to be more obvious choices; "goes" is more neutral and less specific and in most circumstances would seem an inferior choice, but here the point seems to be to describe Julia in a kind of seamless and unspecified motion and from a specific angle, because the poem wants to record the effect of Julia's movement on the speaker (already a second element becomes crucial) rather than the specifics of Julia herself. Another word that seems especially important is "liquefaction" (line 3), also an unusual and suggestive word about motion. Again it implies no specific kind of motion, just smoothness and seamlessness, and it applies not to Julia but to her clothes. Other words that might repay a close look include "vibration" in line 5 (the speaker is finally a little more direct); "brave" and "free," also in line 5; and "glittering" and "taketh" in line 6.

Had we begun conventionally by thinking about speaker, situation, and setting, we would have quickly noticed the precise way that the speaker clothes Julia: "in silks," which move almost as one with her body. And we would have noticed that the speaker positions himself almost as voyeur (standing for us as observers, of course, but also for himself as the central figure in the poem). Not much detail about situation or setting is given (and the speaker is characterized only as a viewer and appreciator), but one thing about the scene is crucial, and this takes us back to the first word of the poem, "whenas." The slightly quaint quality of the word may at first obscure, to a modern reader, just what it tells us about the situation, that it is a *generic* scene rather than a single event. "Whenas" is very close to "whenever"; the speaker's claim seems to be that he responds this way *whenever* Julia dons her silks—apparently fairly often, at least in his memory or imagination.

Most of the speaker's language is sensual and rather provocative (he is anxious to share his responses with others so that *everyone* will know just how "taking" Julia is), but one rather elaborate (though somewhat disguised) metaphor suggests his awareness of his own calculation and its consequences. In the beginning of the second stanza he describes how he "cast" his eyes: it is a metaphor from fishing, a frequent one in love poetry about luring, chasing, and catching. Julia, of course, is the object. The metaphor continues two lines later, but the angler has caught himself: he is taken by the "glittering" lure. This turning of the tables, drawing as it does on a traditional, common image that is then modified to help characterize the speaker, gives a little depth to the show: whatever the slither and glitter, there is not just showing off and sensuality but a catch in this angling.

Many other elements deserve comment, especially because they quickly relate to each other. Consider the way the poet uses sounds, first of all in picking words like "liquefaction" that are almost onomatopoeic, but then also using rhyme very cleverly. There are only two rhyme sounds in the poem, one in the first stanza, the other in the second. The long *ee* of the second becomes almost exclamatory, and the three words of the first seem to become linked in a kind of separate grammar of their own, as if "goes," "flows," and "clothes" were all part of a single action—pretty much what the poem claims on a thematic level. A lot happens in this short and simple poem, and although a reader can get at it step by step by thinking about element after element, the interlocking of the elements is finally the most impressive effect of all. Although the plot reenacts familiar stances of woman as object and man as gazer, our analysis and reading need to be flexible enough to consider not only all the analytical categories, but also the ways in which they work together.

Here are several more poems to analyze. As you read them, think about the elements discussed in the previous seven chapters—but rather than thinking about a single element at a time, try to consider relationships, how the different elements combine to make you respond not to a single device but to a complex set of strategies and effects.

· · ·

W. H. AUDEN

[WEB] *Musée des Beaux Arts*[2]

About suffering they were never wrong,
The Old Masters: how well they understood
Its human position; how it takes place
While someone else is eating or opening a window or just walking
    dully along;
5 How, when the aged are reverently, passionately waiting
For the miraculous birth, there always must be
Children who did not specially want it to happen, skating
On a pond at the edge of the wood:
They never forgot
10 That even the dreadful martyrdom must run its course
Anyhow in a corner, some untidy spot
Where the dogs go on with their doggy life and the torturer's horse
Scratches its innocent behind on a tree.

In Brueghel's *Icarus*,[3] for instance: how everything turns away
15 Quite leisurely from the disaster; the plowman may

2. The Museum of the Fine Arts, in Brussels.
3. *Landscape with the Fall of Icarus*, by Pieter Brueghel the Elder (1525?–1569), located in the Brussels museum. According to Greek myth, Daedalus and his son, Icarus, escaped from imprisonment by using homemade wings of feathers and wax; but Icarus flew too near the sun, the wax melted, and he fell into the sea and drowned. In the Brueghel painting the central figure is a peasant plowing, and several other figures are more immediately noticeable than Icarus, who, disappearing into the sea, is easy to miss in the lower right-hand corner.

Have heard the splash, the forsaken cry,
But for him it was not an important failure; the sun shone
As it had to on the white legs disappearing into the green
Water; and the expensive delicate ship that must have seen
20 Something amazing, a boy falling out of the sky,
Had somewhere to get to and sailed calmly on.

1938

- Find a reproduction of the painting—*Landscape with the Fall of Icarus*, by Pieter Brueghel the Elder—that is the subject of this poem. How is your interpretation affected by examining the painting?

GEORGE HERBERT

The Collar

I struck the board[4] and cried, "No more;
        I will abroad!
What? shall I ever sigh and pine?
My lines[5] and life are free, free as the road,
5   Loose as the wind, as large as store.[6]
        Shall I be still in suit?[7]
Have I no harvest but a thorn
To let me blood, and not restore
What I have lost with cordial[8] fruit?
10   Sure there was wine
Before my sighs did dry it; there was corn
    Before my tears did drown it.
Is the year only lost to me?
    Have I no bays[9] to crown it,
15 No flowers, no garlands gay? All blasted?
        All wasted?
Not so, my heart; but there is fruit,
        And thou hast hands.
Recover all thy sigh-blown age
20 On double pleasures: leave thy cold dispute
Of what is fit, and not. Forsake thy cage,[1]
        Thy rope of sands,
Which petty thoughts have made, and made to thee
    Good cable, to enforce and draw,
25   And be thy law,
While thou didst wink[2] and wouldst not see.

4. Table. 5. Lot. 6. A storehouse; that is, abundance. 7. In service to another.
8. Reviving, restorative. 9. Laurel wreaths of triumph. 1. Moral restrictions.
2. That is, close your eyes to the weaknesses of such restrictions.

Away! take heed;
I will abroad.
Call in thy death's-head³ there; tie up thy fears.
30   He that forbears
To suit and serve his need,
Deserves his load."
But as I raved and grew more fierce and wild
At every word,
35 Methought I heard one calling, *Child!*
And I replied, *My Lord.*

1633

- How does knowledge of Herbert's profession—clergyman—
  help you to interpret the title and the rest of the poem? What
  do the many metaphors in the poem suggest about the
  speaker's state of mind?

ROBERT FROST

WEB *Design*

I found a dimpled spider, fat and white,
On a white heal-all,⁴ holding up a moth
Like a white piece of rigid satin cloth—
Assorted characters of death and blight
5 Mixed ready to begin the morning right,
Like the ingredients of a witches' broth—
A snow-drop spider, a flower like a froth,
And dead wings carried like a paper kite.

What had that flower to do with being white,
10 The wayside blue and innocent heal-all?
What brought the kindred spider to that height,
Then steered the white moth thither in the night?
What but design of darkness to appall?—
If design govern in a thing so small.

1936

- How does this poem confound our usual preconceptions
  about "light" and "darkness"? How does its elaborate form
  complement its theme?

3. *Memento mori*, a skull intended to remind people of their mortality.
4. A plant, also called the "all-heal" and "self-heal," with tightly clustered violet-blue flowers.

EDEN PHILLPOTTS

The Learned

The grey beards wag, the bald heads nod,
And gather thick as bees,
To talk electrons, gases, God,
Old nebulae, new fleas.
5 Each specialist, each dry-as-dust
And professional oaf,
Holds up his little crumb of crust
And cries, "Behold the loaf!"

1942

- What light does the simile "thick as bees" cast on this poem
  as a whole? How does the poem's scheme of rhyme and meter
  contribute to its tone?

EMILY DICKINSON

[My Life had stood—a Loaded Gun—]

My Life had stood—a Loaded Gun—
In Corners—till a Day
The Owner passed—identified—
And carried Me away—

5 And now We roam in Sovereign Woods—
And now We hunt the Doe—
And every time I speak for Him—
The Mountains straight reply—

And do I smile, such cordial light
10 Upon the Valley glow—
It is as a Vesuvian face
Had let its pleasure through—

And when at Night—Our good Day done—
I guard My Master's Head—
15 'Tis better than the Eider-Duck's
Deep Pillow—to have shared—

To foe of His—I'm deadly foe—
None stir the second time—
On whom I lay a Yellow Eye—
20 Or an emphatic Thumb—

Though I than He—may longer live
He longer must—than I—
For I have but the power to kill,
Without—the power to die—

ca. 1863

- How does Dickinson set up and then defy the reader's expectations through the poem's central metaphor—the speaker's life as a loaded gun? How do the poem's quirks (e.g., the jerky rhythm, the strange syntax, the slant rhymes) contribute to its overall effect?

BEN JONSON

Epitaph on Elizabeth, L. H.

Wouldst thou hear what man can say
In a little? Reader, stay.
Underneath this stone doth lie
As much beauty as could die;
5 Which in life did harbor give
To more virtue than doth live.
If at all she had a fault,
Leave it buried in this vault.
One name was Elizabeth;
10 Th' other, let it sleep with death:
Fitter, where it died, to tell,
Than that it lived at all. Farewell.

1616

- How are lines 4 and 6 expressing more than just common courtliness? In what ways is poetry as much this poem's subject as the beauty and virtue of Elizabeth?

SUGGESTIONS FOR WRITING

1. Consider the setting of Auden's "Musée des Beaux Arts" in the sense of both the painting and its location in the museum. In what different ways do the two settings become important? How do they function to frame the story of Icarus, or the theme of suffering? Write an essay in which you discuss the way the poem's setting and structure contribute to the overall effect of the poem.

2. Consider both speaker and situation as you analyze Herbert's "The Collar." How does one of these elements illuminate the other? Write an essay in which you examine the way the poem's whole effect arises from an understanding of the speaker and situation.

3. Discussing Dickinson's "My Life had stood—a Loaded Gun," the poet Adrienne Rich has written, "I think it is a poem about possession by the daemon [of artistic creativity], about the dangers and risks of such possession if you are a woman, about the knowledge that power in a woman can seem destructive, and that you cannot live without the daemon once it has possessed you." Write an essay in which you respond to Rich's interpretation of Dickinson's poem.

Reading More Poetry

MAYA ANGELOU

Africa

Thus she had lain
sugar cane sweet
deserts her hair
golden her feet
5 mountains her breasts
two Niles her tears
Thus she has lain
Black through the years.

Over the white seas
10 rime white and cold
brigands ungentled
icicle bold
took her young daughters
sold her strong sons
15 churched her with Jesus
bled her with guns.
Thus she has lain.

Now she is rising
remember her pain
20 remember the losses
her screams loud and vain
remember her riches
her history slain
now she is striding
25 although she had lain.

1975

ELIZABETH BISHOP

Exchanging Hats

Unfunny uncles who insist
in trying on a lady's hat,
—oh, even if the joke falls flat,
we share your slight transvestite twist

5 in spite of our embarrassment.
Costume and custom are complex.
The headgear of the other sex
inspires us to experiment.

Anandrous[1] aunts, who, at the beach
10 with paper plates upon your laps,
keep putting on the yachtsmen's caps
with exhibitionistic screech,

the visors hanging o'er the ear
so that the golden anchors drag,
15 —the tides of fashion never lag.
Such caps may not be worn next year.

Or you who don the paper plate
itself, and put some grapes upon it,
or sport the Indian's feather bonnet,
20 —perversities may aggravate

the natural madness of the hatter.
And if the opera hats collapse
and crowns grow drafty, then, perhaps,
he thinks what might a miter matter?

25 Unfunny uncle, you who wore a
hat too big, or one too many,
tell us, can't you, are there any
stars inside your black fedora?

Aunt exemplary and slim,
30 with avernal[2] eyes, we wonder
what slow changes they see under
their vast, shady, turned-down brim.

1956

---

1. Literally, "husbandless." 2. Infernal.

WILLIAM BLAKE

The Lamb

    Little Lamb, who made thee?
    Dost thou know who made thee?
    Gave thee life, and bid thee feed
    By the stream and o'er the mead;
5   Gave thee clothing of delight,
    Softest clothing woolly bright;
    Gave thee such a tender voice,
    Making all the vales rejoice?
    Little Lamb, who made thee?
10 Dost thou know who made thee?

    Little Lamb, I'll tell thee!
    Little Lamb, I'll tell thee:
    He is callèd by thy name,
    For he calls himself a Lamb,
15 He is meek and he is mild;
    He became a little child.
    I a child and thou a lamb,
    We are callèd by his name.
    Little Lamb, God bless thee!
20 Little Lamb, God bless thee!

1789

The Tyger

    Tyger! Tyger! burning bright
    In the forests of the night,
    What immortal hand or eye
    Could frame thy fearful symmetry?

5 In what distant deeps or skies
    Burnt the fire of thine eyes?
    On what wings dare he aspire?
    What the hand dare seize the fire?

    And what shoulder, & what art,
10 Could twist the sinews of thy heart?
    And when thy heart began to beat,
    What dread hand? & what dread feet?

    What the hammer? what the chain?
    In what furnace was thy brain?
15 What the anvil? what dread grasp
    Dare its deadly terrors clasp?

When the stars threw down their spears
And water'd heaven with their tears,
Did he smile his work to see?
20 Did he who made the Lamb make thee?

Tyger! Tyger! burning bright
In the forests of the night,
What immortal hand or eye
Dare frame thy fearful symmetry?

1790

ROBERT BROWNING

My Last Duchess

Ferrara[3]

That's my last Duchess painted on the wall,
Looking as if she were alive. I call
That piece a wonder, now: Frà Pandolf's hands[4]
Worked busily a day, and there she stands.
5 Will't please you sit and look at her? I said
"Frà Pandolf" by design, for never read
Strangers like you that pictured countenance,
The depth and passion of its earnest glance,
But to myself they turned (since none puts by
10 The curtain I have drawn for you, but I)
And seemed as they would ask me, if they durst,
How such a glance came there; so, not the first
Are you to turn and ask thus. Sir,'twas not
Her husband's presence only, called that spot
15 Of joy into the Duchess' cheek: perhaps
Frà Pandolf chanced to say "Her mantle laps
Over my lady's wrist too much," or "Paint
Must never hope to reproduce the faint
Half-flush that dies along her throat": such stuff
20 Was courtesy, she thought, and cause enough
For calling up that spot of joy. She had
A heart—how shall I say?—too soon made glad,
Too easily impressed; she liked whate'er
She looked on, and her looks went everywhere.

3. Alfonso II, duke of Ferrara in Italy in the mid-sixteenth century, is the presumed speaker of the
poem, which is loosely based on historical events. The duke's first wife—whom he had married when
she was fourteen—died under suspicious circumstances at seventeen, and he then negotiated through
an agent (to whom the poem is spoken) for the hand of the niece of the count of Tyrol in Austria.
4. Frà Pandolf is, like Claus (line 56), fictitious.

25 Sir,'twas all one! My favor at her breast,
The dropping of the daylight in the West,
The bough of cherries some officious fool
Broke in the orchard for her, the white mule
She rode with round the terrace—all and each
30 Would draw from her alike the approving speech,
Or blush, at least. She thanked men,—good! but thanked
Somehow—I know not how—as if she ranked
My gift of a nine-hundred-years-old name
With anybody's gift. Who'd stoop to blame
35 This sort of trifling? Even had you skill
In speech—which I have not—to make your will
Quite clear to such an one, and say, "Just this
Or that in you disgusts me; here you miss,
Or there exceed the mark"—and if she let
40 Herself be lessoned so, nor plainly set
Her wits to yours, forsooth, and made excuse,
—E'en then would be some stooping; and I choose
Never to stoop. Oh sir, she smiled, no doubt,
Whene'er I passed her; but who passed without
45 Much the same smile? This grew; I gave commands;
Then all smiles stopped together. There she stands
As if alive. Will't please you rise? We'll meet
The company below, then. I repeat,
The Count your master's known munificence
50 Is ample warrant that no just pretense
Of mine for dowry will be disallowed;
Though his fair daughter's self, as I avowed
At starting, is my object. Nay, we'll go
Together down, sir. Notice Neptune, though,
55 Taming a sea-horse, thought a rarity,
Which Claus of Innsbruck cast in bronze for me!

1842

SAMUEL TAYLOR COLERIDGE

Kubla Khan

Or, a Vision in a Dream[5]

In Xanadu did Kubla Khan
A stately pleasure-dome decree:
Where Alph, the sacred river, ran

---

5. Coleridge said he wrote this fragment immediately after waking from an opium dream and that after he was interrupted by a caller he was unable to finish the poem.

Through caverns measureless to man
5   Down to a sunless sea.
So twice five miles of fertile ground
With walls and towers were girdled round:
And here were gardens bright with sinuous rills
Where blossomed many an incense-bearing tree;
10   And here were forests ancient as the hills,
Enfolding sunny spots of greenery.

But oh! that deep romantic chasm which slanted
Down the green hill athwart a cedarn cover![6]
A savage place! as holy and enchanted
15   As e'er beneath a waning moon was haunted
By woman wailing for her demon-lover![7]
And from this chasm, with ceaseless turmoil seething,
As if this earth in fast thick pants were breathing,
A mighty fountain momently[8] was forced,
20   Amid whose swift half-intermitted burst
Huge fragments vaulted like rebounding hail,
Or chaffy grain beneath the thresher's flail:
And 'mid these dancing rocks at once and ever
It flung up momently the sacred river.
25   Five miles meandering with a mazy motion
Through wood and dale the sacred river ran,
Then reached the caverns measureless to man,
And sank in tumult to a lifeless ocean:
And 'mid this tumult Kubla heard from far
30   Ancestral voices prophesying war!

The shadow of the dome of pleasure
Floated midway on the waves;
Where was heard the mingled measure
From the fountain and the caves.
35   It was a miracle of rare device,
A sunny pleasure-dome with caves of ice!

A damsel with a dulcimer
In a vision once I saw:
It was an Abyssinian maid,
40   And on her dulcimer she played,
Singing of Mount Abora.
Could I revive within me
Her symphony and song,
To such a deep delight 'twould win me,

6. From side to side beneath a cover of cedar trees.
7. In a famous and often-imitated German ballad, the lady Lenore is carried off on horseback by
the specter of her lover and married to him at his grave.   8. Suddenly.

45 That with music loud and long,
I would build that dome in air,
That sunny dome! those caves of ice!
And all who heard should see them there,
And all should cry, Beware! Beware!
50 His flashing eyes, his floating hair!
Weave a circle round him thrice,
And close your eyes with holy dread,
For he on honey-dew hath fed,
And drunk the milk of Paradise.

1798

COUNTEE CULLEN

WEB *Yet Do I Marvel*

I doubt not God is good, well-meaning, kind,
And did He stoop to quibble could tell why
The little buried mole continues blind,
Why flesh that mirrors Him must some day die,
5 Make plain the reason tortured Tantalus[9]
Is baited by the fickle fruit, declare
If merely brute caprice dooms Sisyphus[1]
To struggle up a never-ending stair.
Inscrutable His ways are, and immune
10 To catechism by a mind too strewn
With petty cares to slightly understand
What awful brain compels His awful hand.
Yet do I marvel at this curious thing:
To make a poet black, and bid him sing!

1925

EMILY DICKINSON

WEB *[Because I could not stop for Death—]*

Because I could not stop for Death—
He kindly stopped for me—
The Carriage held but just Ourselves—
And Immortality.

---

9. In Greek myth he was condemned, for ambiguous reasons, to stand up to his neck in water he couldn't drink and to be within sight of fruit he couldn't reach to eat.
1. The king of Corinth who, in Greek myth, was condemned eternally to roll a huge stone uphill.

5 We slowly drove—He knew no haste
And I had put away
My labor and my leisure too,
For His Civility—

We passed the School, where Children strove
10 At Recess—in the Ring—
We passed the Fields of Gazing Grain—
We passed the Setting Sun—

Or rather—He passed Us—
The Dews drew quivering and chill—
15 For only Gossamer,[2] my Gown—
My Tippet—only Tulle[3]—

We paused before a House that seemed
A Swelling of the Ground—
The Roof was scarcely visible—
20 The Cornice—in the Ground—

Since then—'tis Centuries—and yet
Feels shorter than the Day
I first surmised the Horses' Heads
Were toward Eternity—

ca. 1863

[*I stepped from Plank to Plank*]

I stepped from Plank to Plank
A slow and cautious way
The Stars about my Head I felt
About my Feet the Sea.

5 I knew not but the next
Would be my final inch—
This gave me that precarious Gait
Some call Experience.

ca. 1864

[*We do not play on Graves—*]

We do not play on Graves—
Because there isn't Room—
Besides—it isn't even—it slants
And People come—

---

2. A soft, sheer fabric.   3. A fine net fabric. *Tippet:* scarf.

5 And put a Flower on it—
  And hang their faces so—
  We're fearing that their Hearts will drop—
  And crush our pretty play—

   And so we move as far
10 As Enemies—away—
   Just looking round to see how far
   It is—Occasionally—

ca. 1862

[The Brain—is wider than the Sky—]

   The Brain—is wider than the Sky—
   For—put them side by side—
   The one the other will contain
   With ease—and You—beside—

5 The Brain is deeper than the sea—
   For—hold them—Blue to Blue—
   The one the other will absorb—
   As Sponges—Buckets—do—

   The Brain is just the weight of God—
10 For—Heft them—Pound for Pound—
   And they will differ—if they do—
   As Syllable from Sound—

ca. 1862

[She dealt her pretty words like Blades—]

   She dealt her pretty words like Blades—
   How glittering they shone—
   And every One unbared a Nerve
   Or wantoned with a Bone—

5 She never deemed—she hurt—
   That—is not Steel's Affair—
   A vulgar grimace in the Flesh—
   How ill the Creatures bear—

   To Ache is human—not polite—
10 The Film upon the eye
   Mortality's old Custom—
   Just locking up—to Die.

1862

JOHN DONNE

[*Death, be not proud*]

Death be not proud, though some have calléd thee
Mighty and dreadful, for thou art not so;
For those whom thou think'st thou dost overthrow
Die not, poor Death, nor yet canst thou kill me.
5   From rest and sleep, which but thy pictures[4] be,
Much pleasure; then from thee much more must flow,
And soonest[5] our best men with thee do go,
Rest of their bones, and soul's delivery.[6]
Thou art slave to Fate, Chance, kings, and desperate men,
10   And dost with Poison, War, and Sickness dwell;
And poppy or charms can make us sleep as well,
And better than thy stroke; why swell'st[7] thou then?
One short sleep past, we wake eternally
And death shall be no more; Death, thou shalt die.

1633

WEB *A Valediction: Forbidding Mourning*

As virtuous men pass mildly away,
And whisper to their souls to go,
Whilst some of their sad friends do say,
"The breath goes now," and some say,
"No,"

5   So let us melt, and make no noise,
No tear-floods, nor sigh-tempests move;
'Twere profanation of our joys
To tell the laity our love.

Moving of the earth[8] brings harms and fears,
810   Men reckon what it did and meant;
But trepidation of the spheres,[9]
Though greater far, is innocent.

Dull sublunary[1] lovers' love
(Whose soul is sense) cannot admit

---

4. Likenesses.   5. Most willingly.   6. Deliverance.   7. Puff with pride.   8. Earthquakes.
9. The Renaissance hypothesis that the celestial spheres trembled and thus caused unexpected variations in their orbits. Such movements are "innocent" because earthlings do not observe or fret about them.
1. Below the moon—that is, changeable. According to the traditional cosmology that Donne invokes here, the moon was considered the dividing line between the immutable celestial world and the earthly mortal one.

15 Absence, because it doth remove
   Those things which elemented[2] it.

But we, by a love so much refined
   That our selves know not what it is,
Inter-assured of the mind,
20   Care less, eyes, lips, and hands to miss.

Our two souls therefore, which are one,
   Though I must go, endure not yet
A breach, but an expansion,
   Like gold to airy thinness beat.

25 If they be two, they are two so
   As stiff twin compasses are two:
Thy soul, the fixed foot, makes no show
   To move, but doth, if the other do;

And though it in the center sit,
30   Yet when the other far doth roam,
It leans, and hearkens after it,
   And grows erect, as that comes home.

Such wilt thou be to me, who must,
   Like the other foot, obliquely run;
35 Thy firmness makes my circle[3] just,
   And makes me end where I begun.

1611?

PAUL LAURENCE DUNBAR

Sympathy

I know what the caged bird feels, alas!
   When the sun is bright on the upland slopes;
When the wind stirs soft through the springing grass,
   And the river flows like a stream of glass;
5   When the first bird sings and the first bud opens,
And the faint perfume from its chalice steals—
I know what the caged bird feels!

I know why the caged bird beats his wing
   Till its blood is red on the cruel bars;
10 For he must fly back to his perch and cling
When he fain[4] would be on the bough a-swing;
   And a pain still throbs in the old, old scars

---

2. Comprised.   3. A traditional symbol of perfection.   4. Gladly.

And they pulse again with a keener sting—
I know why he beats his wing!

15 I know why the caged bird sings, ah me,
    When his wing is bruised and his bosom sore,—
When he beats his bars and he would be free;
It is not a carol of joy or glee,
    But a prayer that he sends from his heart's deep core,
20 But a plea, that upward to Heaven he flings—
I know why the caged bird sings!

1893

We Wear the Mask

We wear the mask that grins and lies,
It hides our cheeks and shades our eyes,—
This debt we pay to human guile;
With torn and bleeding hearts we smile,
5 And mouth with myriad subtleties.

Why should the world be over-wise,
In counting all our tears and sighs?
Nay, let them only see us, while
    We wear the mask.

10 We smile, but, O great Christ, our cries
To thee from tortured souls arise.
We sing, but oh the clay is vile
Beneath our feet, and long the mile;
But let the world dream otherwise,
15   We wear the mask!

1895

T. S. ELIOT

Journey of the Magi[5]

"A cold coming we had of it,
Just the worst time of the year
For a journey, and such a long journey:
The ways deep and the weather sharp,
5 The very dead of winter."[6]
And the camels galled, sore-footed, refractory,
Lying down in the melting snow.
There were times we regretted

5. The wise men who followed the star of Bethleham. See Matthew 2.1–12.
6. An adaptation of a passage from a 1622 sermon by Lancelot Andrews.

The summer palaces on slopes, the terraces,
10 And the silken girls bringing sherbet.
Then the camel men cursing and grumbling
And running away, and wanting their liquor and women,
And the night-fires going out, and the lack of shelters,
And the cities hostile and the towns unfriendly
15 And the villages dirty and charging high prices:
A hard time we had of it.
At the end we preferred to travel all night,
Sleeping in snatches,
With the voices singing in our ears, saying
20 That this was all folly.

Then at dawn we came down to a temperate valley,
Wet, below the snow line, smelling of vegetation;
With a running stream and a water-mill beating the darkness,
And three trees on the low sky,[7]
25 And an old white horse galloped away in the meadow.
Then we came to a tavern with vine-leaves over the lintel,
Six hands at an open door dicing for pieces of silver,
And feet kicking the empty wine-skins.
But there was no information, and so we continued
30 And arrived at evening, not a moment too soon
Finding the place; it was (you may say) satisfactory.

All this was a long time ago, I remember,
And I would do it again, but set down
This set down
35 This: were we led all that way for
Birth or Death? There was a Birth, certainly,
We had evidence and no doubt. I had seen birth and death,
But had thought they were different; this Birth was
Hard and bitter agony for us, like Death, our death.
40 We returned to our places, these Kingdoms,[8]
But no longer at ease here, in the old dispensation,
With an alien people clutching their gods.
I should be glad of another death.

1927

7. Suggesting the three crosses of the Crucifixion (Luke 23.32–33). The Magi see several objects that suggest later events in Christ's life: pieces of silver (see Matthew 26.14–16), the dicing (see Matthew 27.35), the white horse (see Revelation 6.2 and 19.11–16), and the empty wine skins (see Matthew 9.17, possibly relevant also to lines 41–42).
8. The Bible identifies the wise men only as "from the east," and subsequent tradition has made them kings. In Persia, magi were members of an ancient priestly caste.

ROBERT FROST

The Road Not Taken

Two roads diverged in a yellow wood,
And sorry I could not travel both
And be one traveler, long I stood
And looked down one as far as I could
5 To where it bent in the undergrowth;

Then took the other, as just as fair,
And having perhaps the better claim,
Because it was grassy and wanted wear;
Though as for that the passing there
10 Had worn them really about the same,

And both that morning equally lay
In leaves no step had trodden black.
Oh, I kept the first for another day!
Yet knowing how way leads on to way,
15 I doubted if I should ever come back.

I shall be telling this with a sigh
Somewhere ages and ages hence:
Two roads diverged in a wood, and I—
I took the one less traveled by,
20 And that has made all the difference.

1916

Stopping by Woods on a Snowy Evening

Whose woods these are I think I know.
His house is in the village, though;
He will not see me stopping here
To watch his woods fill up with snow.

5 My little horse must think it queer
To stop without a farmhouse near
Between the woods and frozen lake
The darkest evening of the year.

He gives his harness bells a shake
10 To ask if there is some mistake.
The only other sound's the sweep
Of easy wind and downy flake.

The woods are lovely, dark, and deep,
But I have promises to keep,

15 And miles to go before I sleep,
And miles to go before I sleep.

1923

THOMAS GRAY

Elegy Written in a Country Churchyard

The curfew tolls the knell of parting day,
   The lowing herd wind slowly o'er the lea,
The plowman homeward plods his weary way,
   And leaves the world to darkness and to me.

5 Now fades the glimmering landscape on the sight,
   And all the air a solemn stillness holds,
Save where the beetle wheels his droning flight,
   And drowsy tinklings lull the distant folds;

Save that from yonder ivy-mantled tower
10   The moping owl does to the moon complain
Of such, as wandering near her secret bower,
   Molest her ancient solitary reign.

Beneath those rugged elms, that yew tree's shade,
   Where heaves the turf in many a moldering heap,
15 Each in his narrow cell forever laid,
   The rude⁹ forefathers of the hamlet sleep.

The breezy call of incense-breathing Morn,
   The swallow twittering from the straw-built shed,
The cock's shrill clarion, or the echoing horn.¹
20   No more shall rouse them from their lowly bed.

For them no more the blazing hearth shall burn,
   Or busy housewife ply her evening care;
No children run to lisp their sire's return,
   Or climb his knees the envied kiss to share.

25 Oft did the harvest to their sickle yield,
   Their furrow oft the stubborn glebe² has broke;
How jocund did they drive their team afield!
   How bowed the woods beneath their sturdy stroke!

Let not Ambition mock their useful toil,
30   Their homely joys, and destiny obscure;
Nor Grandeur hear with a disdainful smile
   The short and simple annals of the poor.

---

9. Unlearned.   1. The hunter's horn.   2. Soil.

The boast of heraldry,[3] the pomp of power,
    And all that beauty, all that wealth e'er gave,
35 Awaits alike the inevitable hour.
    The paths of glory lead but to the grave.

Nor you, ye proud, impute to these the fault,
    If Memory o'er their tomb no trophies[4] raise,
Where through the long-drawn aisle and fretted[5] vault
40   The pealing anthem swells the note of praise

Can storied urn or animated[6] bust
    Back to its mansion call the fleeting breath?
Can Honor's voice provoke the silent dust,
    Or Flattery soothe the dull cold ear of Death?

45 Perhaps in this neglected spot is laid
    Some heart once pregnant with celestial fire;
Hands that the rod of empire might have swayed,
    Or waked to ecstasy the living lyre.

But Knowledge to their eyes her ample page
50   Rich with the spoils of time did ne'er unroll;
Chill Penury repressed their noble rage,
    And froze the genial current of the soul.

Full many a gem of purest ray serene,
    The dark unfathomed caves of ocean bear:
55 Full many a flower is born to blush unseen,
    And waste its sweetness on the desert air.

Some village Hampden,[7] that with dauntless breast
    The little tyrant of his fields withstood;
Some mute inglorious Milton[8] here may rest,
60   Some Cromwell[9] guiltless of his country's blood.

The applause of listening senates to command,
    The threats of pain and ruin to despise,
To scatter plenty o'er a smiling land,
    And read their history in a nation's eyes,

65 Their lot forbade: nor circumscribed alone
    Their growing virtues, but their crimes confined;

---

3. Noble birth.
4. An ornamental or symbolic group of figures depicting the achievements of the deceased.
5. Decorated with intersecting lines in relief.
6. Lifelike. *Storied urn:* a funeral urn with an epitaph or pictured story inscribed on it.
7. John Hampden (1594–1643), who, both as a private citizen and as a member of Parliament, zealously defended the rights of the people against the autocratic policies of Charles I.
8. John Milton (1608–1674), great English poet.
9. Oliver Cromwell (1599–1658), lord protector of England during the Interregnum, noted for military genius but also cruelty and intolerance.

Forbade to wade through slaughter to a throne,
And shut the gates of mercy on mankind,

The struggling pangs of conscious truth to hide,
70   To quench the blushes of ingenuous shame,
Or heap the shrine of Luxury and Pride
With incense kindled at the Muse's flame.

Far from the madding crowd's ignoble strife,
Their sober wishes never learned to stray;
75 Along the cool sequestered vale of life
They kept the noiseless tenor of their way.

Yet even these bones from insult to protect
Some frail memorial still erected nigh,
With uncouth rhymes and shapeless sculpture decked,[1]
80   Implores the passing tribute of a sigh.

Their name, their years, spelt by the unlettered Muse,
The place of fame and elegy supply:
And many a holy text around she strews,
That teach the rustic moralist to die.

85 For who to dumb Forgetfulness a prey,
This pleasing anxious being e'er resigned,
Left the warm precincts of the cheerful day,
Nor cast one longing lingering look behind?

On some fond breast the parting soul relies,
90   Some pious drops the closing eye requires;
Even from the tomb the voice of Nature cries,
Even in our ashes live their wonted fires.

For thee, who mindful of the unhonored dead
Dost in these lines their artless tale relate;
95 If chance, by lonely contemplation led,
Some kindred spirit shall inquire thy fate,

Haply some hoary-headed swain may say,
"Oft have we seen him at the peep of dawn
Brushing with hasty steps the dews away
100   To meet the sun upon the upland lawn.

"There at the foot of yonder nodding beech
That wreathes its old fantastic roots so high,
His listless length at noontide would he stretch,
And pore upon the brook that babbles by.

105 "Hard by yon wood, now smiling as in scorn,
Muttering his wayward fancies he would rove,

---

1. Cf. the "storied urn or animated bust" (line 41) dedicated inside the church to the "proud" (line 37).

Now drooping, woeful wan, like one forlorn,
Or crazed with care, or crossed in hopeless love.

"One morn I missed him on the customed hill,
110   Along the heath and near his favorite tree;
Another came; nor yet beside the rill,
Nor up the lawn, nor at the wood was he;

"The next with dirges due in sad array
Slow through the churchway path we saw him borne.
115 Approach and read (for thou canst read) the lay,
Graved on the stone beneath yon aged thorn."

The Epitaph

Here rests his head upon the lap of Earth
A youth to Fortune and to Fame unknown.
Fair Science[2] *frowned not on his humble birth,*
120   *And Melancholy marked him for her own.*

Large was his bounty, and his soul sincere,
Heaven did a recompense as largely send:
He gave to Misery all he had, a tear,
He gained from Heaven ('twas all he wished) a friend.

125 *No farther seek his merits to disclose,*
Or draw his frailties from their dread abode
(There they alike in trembling hope repose),
The bosom of his Father and his God.

                                                            1751

ANGELINA GRIMKE

Tenebris[3]

There is a tree, by day,
That, at night,
Has a shadow,
A hand huge and black,
5 With fingers long and black.
     All through the dark,
Against the white man's house,
     In the little wind,
The black hand plucks and plucks
10   At the bricks.
The bricks are the color of blood and very small.
     Is it a black hand,
     Or is it a shadow?

                                                            1927

2. Learning.   3. In darkness (Latin).

THOMAS HARDY

Channel Firing

That night your great guns, unawares,
Shook all our coffins as we lay,
And broke the chancel window squares,⁴
We thought it was the Judgment-day

5 And sat upright. While drearisome
Arose the howl of wakened hounds:
The mouse let fall the altar-crumb,⁵
The worms drew back into the mounds,

The glebe cow⁶ drooled. Till God called, "No;
10 It's gunnery practice out at sea
Just as before you went below;
The world is as it used to be:

"All nations striving strong to make
Red war yet redder. Mad as hatters
15 They do no more for Christés sake
Than you who are helpless in such matters.

"That this is not the judgment-hour
For some of them's a blessed thing,
For if it were they'd have to scour
20 Hell's floor for so much threatening . . .

"Ha, ha. It will be warmer when
I blow the trumpet (if indeed
I ever do; for you are men,
And rest eternal sorely need)."

25 So down we lay again. "I wonder,
Will the world ever saner be,"
Said one, "than when He sent us under
In our indifferent century!"

And many a skeleton shook his head.
30 "Instead of preaching forty year,"
My neighbor Parson Thirdly said,
"I wish I had stuck to pipes and beer."

Again the guns disturbed the hour,
Roaring their readiness to avenge.

---

4. The windows near the altar in a church.   5. Breadcrumbs from the sacrament of Communion.
6. Parish cow pastured on the meadow next to the churchyard.

35 As far inland as Stourton Tower,
And Camelot, and starlit Stonehenge.[7]

April 1914

SEAMUS HEANEY

Digging

Between my finger and my thumb
The squat pen rests; snug as a gun.

Under my window, a clean rasping sound
When the spade sinks into gravelly ground:
5 My father, digging. I look down

Till his straining rump among the flowerbeds
Bends low, comes up twenty years away
Stooping in rhythm through potato drills[8]
Where he was digging.

10 The coarse boot nestled on the lug, the shaft
Against the inside knee was levered firmly.
He rooted out tall tops, buried the bright edge deep
To scatter new potatoes that we picked
Loving their cool hardness in our hands.

15 By God, the old man could handle a spade.
Just like his old man.

My grandfather cut more turf[9] in a day
Than any other man on Toner's bog.
Once I carried him milk in a bottle
20 Corked sloppily with paper. He straightened up
To drink it, then fell to right away
Nicking and slicing neatly, heaving sods
Over his shoulder, going down and down
For the good turf. Digging.

25 The cold smell of potato mould, the squelch and slap
Of soggy peat, the curt cuts of an edge

---

7. A circular formation of upright stones dating from about 1600 B.C.E. on Salisbury Plain, Wiltshire; it is thought to have been a ceremonial site for political and religious occasions or perhaps an early astronomical observatory. *Stourton Tower:* a monument in Stourhead Park, Wiltshire, built in the eighteenth century to commemorate King Alfred's ninth-century victory over the Danes. *Camelot:* the legendary site of King Arthur's court, said to have been in Cornwall or Somerset.
8. Small furrows in which seeds are sown.
9. Peat cut into slabs and dried to be used as fuel in stoves and furnaces.

Through living roots awaken in my head.
But I've no spade to follow men like them.

Between my finger and my thumb
30   The squat pen rests.
I'll dig with it.

1966

GERARD MANLEY HOPKINS

God's Grandeur

The world is charged with the grandeur of God.
    It will flame out, like shining from shook foil;[1]
    It gathers to a greatness, like the ooze of oil
Crushed. Why do men then now not reck his rod?[2]
5 Generations have trod, have trod, have trod;
    And all is seared with trade; bleared, smeared with toil;
    And wears man's smudge and shares man's smell: the soil
Is bare now, nor can foot feel, being shod.

And for all this, nature is never spent;
10   There lives the dearest freshness deep down things;
And though the last lights off the black West went
    Oh, morning, at the brown brink eastward, springs—
Because the Holy Ghost over the bent
    World broods with warm breast and with ah! bright wings.

1918

The Windhover[3]

To Christ our Lord

I caught this morning morning's minion,[4] king-
    dom of daylight's dauphin,[5] dapple-dawn-drawn Falcon, in
    his riding
Of the rolling level underneath him steady air, and striding
High there, how he rung upon the rein of a wimpling[6] wing
5 In his ecstasy! then off, off forth on swing,

---

1. "I mean foil in its sense of leaf or tinsel.... Shaken goldfoil gives off broad glares like sheet
lightning and also, and this is true of nothing else, owing to its zig-zag dints and creasings and
network of small many cornered facets, a sort of fork lightning too" (*Letters of Gerard Manley Hopkins
to Robert Bridges*, ed. C. C. Abbott [1955], p. 169).

2. Heed his authority.

3. A small hawk, the kestrel, which habitually hovers in the air, headed into the wind.

4. Favorite, beloved. 5. Heir to regal splendor. 6. Rippling.

As a skate's heel sweeps smooth on a bow-bend: the hurl and
   gliding
Rebuffed the big wind. My heart in hiding
Stirred for a bird,—the achieve of, the mastery of the thing!

Brute beauty and valor and act, oh, air, pride, plume, here
10   Buckle![7] AND the fire that breaks from thee then, a billion
Times told lovelier, more dangerous, O my chevalier![8]

No wonder of it: shéer plód makes plow down sillion[9]
Shine, and blue-bleak embers, ah my dear,
   Fall, gall themselves, and gash gold-vermilion.

1877

LANGSTON HUGHES

Harlem

What happens to a dream deferred?

   Does it dry up
   like a raisin in the sun?
   Or fester like a sore—
5   And then run?
   Does it stink like rotten meat?
   Or crust and sugar over—
   like a syrupy sweet?

   Maybe it just sags
10   like a heavy load.

   Or does it explode?

1951

The Negro Speaks of Rivers

I've known rivers:
I've known rivers ancient as the world and older than the flow of
   human blood in human veins.

My soul has grown deep like the rivers.

7. Several meanings may apply: to join closely, to prepare for battle, to grapple with, to collapse.
8. Horseman, knight.
9. The narrow strip of land between furrows in an open field divided for separate cultivation.

I bathed in the Euphrates when dawns were young.
5 I built my hut near the Congo and it lulled me to sleep.
I looked upon the Nile and raised the pyramids above it.
I heard the singing of the Mississippi when Abe Lincoln went down
    to New Orleans, and I've seen its muddy bosom turn all golden
    in the sunset.

I've known rivers:
Ancient, dusky rivers.

10 My soul has grown deep like the rivers.

                         1926

BEN JONSON

[*Come, my Celia, let us prove*][1]

Come, my Celia, let us prove,[2]
While we can, the sports of love;
Time will not be ours forever:
He at length our good will sever.
5 Spend not, then, his gifts in vain;
Suns that set may rise again,
But if once we lose this light,
'Tis with us perpetual night.
Why should we defer our joys?
10 Fame and rumor are but toys.
Cannot we delude the eyes
Of a few poor household spies?
Or his easier ears beguile,
Thus removéd by our wile?
15 'Tis no sin love's fruits to steal,
But the sweet thefts to reveal;
To be taken, to be seen,
These have crimes accounted been.

1606

---

1. A song from *Volpone*, sung by the play's villain and would-be seducer. Part of the poem paraphrases
Catullus, poem 5.　2. Experience.

JOHN KEATS

On First Looking into Chapman's Homer[3]

Much have I traveled in the realms of gold,
And many goodly states and kingdoms seen;
Round many western islands have I been
Which bards in fealty to Apollo[4] hold.
5   Oft of one wide expanse had I been told
That deep-browed Homer ruled as his demesne;
Yet did I never breathe its pure serene[5]
Till I heard Chapman speak out loud and bold:
Then felt I like some watcher of the skies
10 When a new planet swims into his ken;[6]
Or like stout Cortez[7] when with eagle eyes
He stared at the Pacific—and all his men
Looked at each other with a wild surmise—
Silent, upon a peak in Darien.

1816

On Seeing the Elgin Marbles[8]

My spirit is too weak—mortality
Weighs heavily on me like unwilling sleep,
And each imagined pinnacle and steep
Of godlike hardship tells me I must die
5   Like a sick eagle looking at the sky.
Yet 'tis a gentle luxury to weep
That I have not the cloudy winds to keep
Fresh for the opening of the morning's eye.
Such dim-conceivéd glories of the brain
10 Bring round the heart an indescribable feud;
So do these wonders a most dizzy pain,
That mingles Grecian grandeur with the rude

3. George Chapman's were among the most famous Renaissance translations; he completed his *Iliad* in 1611, his *Odyssey* in 1616. Keats wrote the sonnet after being led to Chapman by a former teacher and reading the *Iliad* all night long.
4. Greek god of poetry and music. *Fealty:* literally, the loyalty owed by a vassal to his feudal lord.
5. Atmosphere.   6. Range of vision.
7. Actually, Balboa; he first viewed the Pacific from Darien, in Panama.
8. Figures and friezes from the Athenian Parthenon, they were taken from the site by Lord Elgin, brought to England in 1806, and then sold to the British Museum, where Keats saw them.

Wasting of old Time—with a billowy main—
A sun—a shadow of a magnitude.

1817

Ode to a Nightingale

I

My heart aches, and a drowsy numbness pains
  My sense, as though of hemlock I had drunk,
Or emptied some dull opiate to the drains
  One minute past, and Lethe-wards[9] had sunk:
5 'Tis not through envy of thy happy lot,
    But being too happy in thine happiness,
      That thou, light-wingéd Dryad[1] of the trees,
        In some melodious plot
    Of beechen green, and shadows numberless,
10   Singest of summer in full-throated ease.

II

O, for a draught of vintage! that hath been
  Cooled a long age in the deep-delvéd earth,
Tasting of Flora[2] and the country green,
  Dance, and Provençal song,[3] and sunburnt mirth!
15 O for a beaker full of the warm South,
    Full of the true, the blushful Hippocrene,[4]
      With beaded bubbles winking at the brim,
        And purple-stainéd mouth;
    That I might drink, and leave the world unseen,
20   And with thee fade away into the forest dim:

III

Fade far away, dissolve, and quite forget
  What thou among the leaves hast never known,
The weariness, the fever, and the fret
  Here, where men sit and hear each other groan;
25 Where palsy shakes a few, sad, last gray hairs,
    Where youth grows pale, and specter-thin, and dies;

---

9. Toward the river of forgetfulness (Lethe) in Hades.   1. Wood nymph.
2. Roman goddess of flowers.
3. The medieval troubadours of Provence were famous for their love songs.
4. The fountain of the Muses on Mt. Helicon, whose waters bring poetic inspiration.

Where but to think is to be full of sorrow
And leaden-eyed despairs,
Where Beauty cannot keep her lustrous eyes,
30   Or new Love pine at them beyond tomorrow.

IV

Away! away! for I will fly to thee,
Not charioted by Bacchus and his pards,[5]
But on the viewless[6] wings of Poesy,
Though the dull brain perplexes and retards:
35 Already with thee! tender is the night,
And haply the Queen-Moon is on her throne,
Clustered around by all her starry Fays;[7]
But here there is no light,
Save what from heaven is with the breezes blown
40   Through verdurous glooms and winding mossy ways.

V

I cannot see what flowers are at my feet,
Nor what soft incense hangs upon the boughs,
But, in embalméd[8] darkness, guess each sweet
Wherewith the seasonable month endows
45 The grass, the thicket, and the fruit-tree wild;
White hawthorn, and the pastoral eglantine;[9]
Fast fading violets covered up in leaves;
And mid-May's eldest child,
The coming musk-rose, full of dewy wine,
50   The murmurous haunt of flies on summer eves.

VI

Darkling[1] I listen; and, for many a time
I have been half in love with easeful Death,
Called him soft names in many a muséd rhyme,
To take into the air my quiet breath;
55 Now more than ever seems it rich to die,
To cease upon the midnight with no pain,
While thou art pouring forth thy soul abroad
In such an ecstasy!
Still wouldst thou sing, and I have ears in vain—
60   To thy high requiem become a sod.

---

5. The Roman god of wine was sometimes portrayed in a chariot drawn by leopards.   6. Invisible.
7. Fairies.   8. Fragrant, aromatic.   9. Sweetbriar or honeysuckle.   1. In the dark.

VII

Thou wast not born for death, immortal Bird!
No hungry generations tread thee down;
The voice I hear this passing night was heard
In ancient days by emperor and clown:
65 Perhaps the selfsame song that found a path
Through the sad heart of Ruth,[2] when, sick for home,
　　She stood in tears amid the alien corn;
　　　The same that ofttimes hath
Charmed magic casements, opening on the foam
70 　Of perilous seas, in faery lands forlorn.

VIII

Forlorn! the very word is like a bell
To toll me back from thee to my sole self!
Adieu! the fancy cannot cheat so well
As she is famed to do, deceiving elf.
75 Adieu! adieu! thy plaintive anthem fades
Past the near meadows, over the still stream,
　　Up the hillside; and now 'tis buried deep
　　　In the next valley-glades:
Was it a vision, or a waking dream?
80 　Fled is that music:—Do I wake or sleep?

May 1819

Ode on a Grecian Urn

I

Thou still unravished bride of quietness,
　Thou foster-child of silence and slow time,
Sylvan historian, who canst thus express
　A flowery tale more sweetly than our rhyme:
5 What leaf-fringed legend haunts about thy shape
　Of deities or mortals, or of both,
　　In Tempe or the dales of Arcady?[3]
What men or gods are these? What maidens loath?
What mad pursuit? What struggle to escape?
10 　What pipes and timbrels? What wild ecstasy?

---

2. A virtuous Moabite widow who, according to the Old Testament Book of Ruth, left her own country to accompany her mother-in-law, Naomi, back to Naomi's native land. She supported herself as a gleaner.

3. Arcadia. Tempe is a beautiful valley near Mt. Olympus in Greece, and the valleys ("dales") of Arcadia a picturesque section of the Peloponnesus; both came to be associated with the pastoral ideal.

II

Heard melodies are sweet, but those unheard
  Are sweeter; therefore, ye soft pipes, play on;
Not to the sensual[4] ear, but, more endeared,
  Pipe to the spirit ditties of no tone:
15 Fair youth, beneath the trees, thou canst not leave
  Thy song, nor ever can those trees be bare;
    Bold Lover, never, never canst thou kiss,
Though winning near the goal—yet, do not grieve;
  She cannot fade, though thou hast not thy bliss,
20   For ever wilt thou love, and she be fair!

III

Ah, happy, happy boughs! that cannot shed
  Your leaves, nor ever bid the Spring adieu;
And, happy melodist, unweariéd,
  For ever piping songs for ever new;
25 More happy love! more happy, happy love!
  For ever warm and still to be enjoyed,
    For ever panting, and for ever young;
All breathing human passion far above,
  That leaves a heart high-sorrowful and cloyed,
30   A burning forehead, and a parching tongue.

IV

Who are these coming to the sacrifice?
  To what green altar, O mysterious priest,
Lead'st thou that heifer lowing at the skies,
  And all her silken flanks with garlands dressed?
35 What little town by river or sea shore,
  Or mountain-built with peaceful citadel,
    Is emptied of this folk, this pious morn?
And, little town, thy streets for evermore
  Will silent be; and not a soul to tell
40   Why thou art desolate, can e'er return.

V

O Attic shape! Fair attitude! with brede[5]
  Of marble men and maidens overwrought,[6]
With forest branches and the trodden weed;
  Thou, silent form, dost tease us out of thought

---

4. Of the senses, as distinguished from the "ear" of the spirit or imagination.
5. Woven pattern. *Attic:* Attica was the district of ancient Greece surrounding Athens.
6. Ornamented all over.

45 As doth eternity: Cold Pastoral!
   When old age shall this generation waste,
     Thou shalt remain, in midst of other woe
   Than ours, a friend to man, to whom thou say'st,
   Beauty is truth, truth beauty[7]—that is all
50   Ye know on earth, and all ye need to know.

May 1819

GALWAY KINNELL

Blackberry Eating

I love to go out in late September
among the fat, overripe, icy, black blackberries
to eat blackberries for breakfast,
the stalks very prickly, a penalty
5 they earn for knowing the black art
of blackberry-making; and as I stand among them
lifting the stalks to my mouth, the ripest berries
fall almost unbidden to my tongue,
as words sometimes do, certain peculiar words
10 like *strengths* or *squinched*,
many-lettered, one-syllabled lumps,
which I squeeze, squinch open, and splurge well
in the silent, startled, icy, black language
of blackberry-eating in late September.

                          1980

ROBERT LOWELL

Skunk Hour

for Elizabeth Bishop

Nautilus Island's hermit
heiress still lives through winter in her Spartan cottage;
her sheep still graze above the sea.
Her son's a bishop. Her farmer
5 is first selectman[8] in our village,
she's in her dotage.

---

7. In some texts of the poem "Beauty is truth, truth beauty" is in quotation marks and in some texts it is not, leading to critical disagreements about whether the last line and a half are also inscribed on the urn or spoken by the poet.   8. An elected New England town official.

Thirsting for
the hierarchic privacy
of Queen Victoria's century,
10   she buys up all
the eyesores facing her shore,
and lets them fall.

The season's ill—
we've lost our summer millionaire,
15   who seemed to leap from an L. L. Bean[9]
catalogue. His nine-knot yawl
was auctioned off to lobstermen.
A red fox stain covers Blue Hill.

And now our fairy
20   decorator brightens his shop for fall,
his fishnet's filled with orange cork,
orange, his cobbler's bench and awl,
there is no money in his work,
he'd rather marry.

25   One dark night,
my Tudor Ford climbed the hill's skull,
I watched for love-cars. Lights turned down,
they lay together, hull to hull,
where the graveyard shelves on the town....
30   My mind's not right.

A car radio bleats,
"Love, O careless Love...."[1] I hear
my ill-spirit sob in each blood cell,
as if my hand were at its throat....
35   I myself am hell;
nobody's here—

only skunks, that search
in the moonlight for a bite to eat.
They march on their soles up Main Street:
40   white stripes, moonstruck eyes' red fire
under the chalk-dry and spar spire
of the Trinitarian Church.

I stand on top
of our back steps and breathe the rich air—
45   a mother skunk with her column of kittens swills the garbage pail.
She jabs her wedge head in a cup
of sour cream, drops her ostrich tail,
and will not scare.

1959

9. Famous old Maine sporting goods firm.
1. A popular folk song recorded many times, as by Frankie Laine (1959).

CHRISTOPHER MARLOWE

The Passionate Shepherd to His Love

Come live with me and be my love,
And we will all the pleasures prove[2]
That valleys, groves, hills, and fields,
Woods, or steepy mountain yields.

5　And we will sit upon the rocks,
Seeing the shepherds feed their flocks,
By shallow rivers to whose falls
Melodious birds sing madrigals.

And I will make thee beds of roses
10　And a thousand fragrant posies,
A cap of flowers, and a kirtle[3]
Embroidered all with leaves of myrtle;

A gown made of the finest wool
Which from our pretty lambs we pull;
15　Fair linéd slippers for the cold,
With buckles of the purest gold;

A belt of straw and ivy buds,
With coral clasps and amber studs:
And if these pleasures may thee move,
20　Come live with me, and be my love.

The shepherd swains[4] shall dance and sing
For thy delight each May morning:
If these delights thy mind may move,
Then live with me and be my love.

　　　　　　　　　　　　　　　　1600

ANDREW MARVELL

The Garden

　How vainly men themselves amaze[5]
To win the palm, the oak, or bays,[6]
And their incessant labors see
Crowned from some single herb, or tree,
5　Whose short and narrow-vergéd[7] shade
7Does prudently their toils upbraid;

---

2. Experience.　3. Gown.　4. Youths.　5. Become frenzied.
6. Awards for athletic, civic, and literary achievements.　7. Narrowly cropped.

While all flowers and all trees do close[8]
To weave the garlands of repose!

Fair Quiet, have I found thee here,
10 And Innocence, thy sister dear?
Mistaken long, I sought you then
In busy companies of men.
Your sacred plants,[9] if here below,
Only among the plants will grow;
15 Society is all but rude[1]
To[2] this delicious solitude.

No white nor red was ever seen
So am'rous as this lovely green.
Fond lovers, cruel as their flame,
20 Cut in these trees their mistress' name:
Little, alas, they know, or heed
How far these beauties hers exceed!
Fair trees, wheresoe'er your barks I wound,
No name shall but your own be found.

25 When we have run our passion's heat,
Love hither makes his best retreat.
The gods, that mortal beauty chase,
Still in a tree did end their race:
Apollo hunted Daphne so,
30 Only that she might laurel grow;
And Pan did after Syrinx speed,
Not as a nymph, but for a reed.[3]

What wondrous life is this I lead!
Ripe apples drop about my head;
35 The luscious clusters of the vine
Upon my mouth do crush their wine;
The nectarine and curious[4] peach
Into my hands themselves do reach;
Stumbling on melons, as I npass,
40 Insnared with flowers, I fall on grass.

Meanwhile the mind, from pleasure less,
Withdraws into its happiness;[5]
The mind, that ocean where each kind
Does straight its own resemblance find;[6]

---

8. Unite.   9. Cuttings.   1. Barbarous.   2. Compared to.

3. In Ovid's *Metamorphoses*, Daphne, pursued by Apollo, is turned into a laurel, and Syrinx, pursued by Pan, into a reed that Pan makes into a flute.   4. Exquisite.

5. That is, the mind withdraws from lesser-sense pleasure into contemplation.

6. All land creatures supposedly had corresponding sea creatures.

45 Yet it creates, transcending these,
   Far other worlds and other seas,
   Annihilating[7] all that's made
   To a green thought in a green shade.

   Here at the fountain's sliding foot,
50 Or at some fruit tree's mossy root,
   Casting the body's vest[8] aside,
   My soul into the boughs does glide:
   There, like a bird, it sits and sings,
   Then whets[9] and combs its silver wings,
55 And, till prepared for longer flight,
   Waves in its plumes the various[1] light.

   Such was that happy garden-state,
   While man there walked without a mate:
   After a place so pure, and sweet,
60 What other help could yet be meet![2]
   But 'twas beyond a mortal's share
   To wander solitary there:
   Two paradises 'twere in one
   To live in paradise alone.

65   How well the skillful gardener drew
   Of flowers and herbs this dial[3] new,
   Where, from above, the milder sun
   Does through a fragrant zodiac run;
   And as it works, th' industrious bee
70 Computes its time as well as we!
   How could such sweet and wholesome hours
   Be reckoned but with herbs and flowers?

                                        1681

CLAUDE McKAY

The Harlem Dancer

Applauding youths laughed with young prostitutes
And watched her perfect, half-clothed body sway;
Her voice was like the sound of blended flutes
Blown by black players upon a picnic day.
5 She sang and danced on gracefully and calm,

---

7. Reducing to nothing by comparison.
8. Vestment, clothing; the flesh is being considered as simply clothing for the soul.   9. Preens.
1. Many-colored.   2. Appropriate.
3. A garden planted in the shape of a sundial, complete with zodiac.

The light gauze hanging loose about her form;
To me she seemed a proudly-swaying palm
Grown lovelier for passing through a storm.
Upon her swarthy neck black shiny curls
10 Luxuriant fell; and tossing coins in praise,
The wine-flushed, bold-eyed boys, and even the girls,
Devoured her shape with eager, passionate gaze;
But looking at her falsely-smiling face,
I knew her self was not in that strange place.

1922

The White House

Your door is shut against my tightened face,
And I am sharp as steel with discontent;
But I possess the courage and the grace
To bear my anger proudly and unbent.
5   The pavement slabs burn loose beneath my feet,
And passion rends my vitals as I pass,
A chafing savage, down the decent street,
Where boldly shines your shuttered door of glass.
Oh, I must search for wisdom every hour,
10 Deep in my wrathful bosom sore and raw,
And find in it the superhuman power
To hold me to the letter of your law!
Oh, I must keep my heart inviolate
Against the poison of your deadly hate.

1937

WILFRED OWEN

[WEB] *Dulce et Decorum Est*[4]

Bent double, like old beggars under sacks,
Knock-kneed, coughing like hags, we cursed through sludge,
Till on the haunting flares we turned our backs
And towards our distant rest began to trudge.
5   Men marched asleep. Many had lost their boots
But limped on, blood-shod. All went lame; all blind;
Drunk with fatigue; deaf even to the hoots
Of disappointed shells that dropped behind.

Gas! Gas! Quick, boys!—An ecstasy of fumbling,
10 Fitting the clumsy helmets just in time;

---

4. Part of a phrase from Horace (Roman poet and satirist, 65–8 B.C.E.), quoted in full in the last lines: "It is sweet and proper to die for one's country."

But someone still was yelling out and stumbling
And floundering like a man in fire or lime.—
Dim, through the misty panes and thick green light
As under a green sea, I saw him drowning.

15 In all my dreams, before my helpless sight,
He plunges at me, guttering, choking, drowning.

If in some smothering dreams you too could pace
Behind the wagon that we flung him in,
And watch the white eyes writhing in his face,
20 His hanging face, like a devil's sick of sin;
If you could hear, at every jolt, the blood
Come gargling from the froth-corrupted lungs,
Obscene as cancer, bitter as the cud
Of vile, incurable sores on innocent tongues,—
25 My friend, you would not tell with such high zest
To children ardent for some desperate glory,
The old Lie: Dulce et decorum est
Pro patria mori.

1917

SYLVIA PLATH

Daddy[5]

You do not do, you do not do
Any more, black shoe
In which I have lived like a foot
For thirty years, poor and white,
5 Barely daring to breathe or Achoo.

Daddy, I have had to kill you.
You died before I had time—
Marble-heavy, a bag full of God,
Ghastly statue with one gray toe[6]
10 Big as a Frisco seal

And a head in the freakish Atlantic
Where it pours bean green over blue
In the waters off beautiful Nauset.[7]
I used to pray to recover you.
15 Ach, du.[8]

---

5. First published in *Ariel,* a volume of poems that appeared two years after Plath's suicide.
6. Otto Plath, Sylvia's father, lost a toe to gangrene that resulted from diabetes.
7. An inlet on Cape Cod.
8. Oh, you (German). Plath often portrays herself as Jewish and her oppressors as German.

In the German tongue, in the Polish town[9]
Scraped flat by the roller
Of wars, wars, wars.
But the name of the town is common.
20 My Polack friend

Says there are a dozen or two.
So I never could tell where you
Put your foot, your root,
I never could talk to you.
25 The tongue stuck in my jaw.

It stuck in a barb wire snare.
Ich,[1] ich, ich, ich,
I could hardly speak.
I thought every German was you.
30 And the language obscene

An engine, an engine
Chuffing me off like a Jew.
A Jew to Dachau, Auschwitz, Belsen.[2]
I began to talk like a Jew.
35 I think I may well be a Jew.

The snows of the Tyrol, the clear beer of Vienna[3]
Are not very pure or true.
With my gypsy-ancestress and my weird luck
And my Taroc[4] pack and my Taroc pack
40 I may be a bit of a Jew.

I have always been scared of *you,*
With your Luftwaffe,[5] your gobbledygoo.
And your neat moustache
And your Aryan[6] eye, bright blue.
45 Panzer[7]-man, panzer-man, O You—

Not God but a swastika
So black no sky could squeak through.
Every woman adores a Fascist,
The boot in the face, the brute
50 Brute heart of a brute like you.

---

9. Otto Plath, an ethnic German, was born in Grabow, Poland.   1. German for "I."
2. Sites of World War II Nazi death camps.
3. The snow in the Tyrol (an Alpine region in Austria and northern Italy) is, legendarily, as pure as the beer is clear in Vienna.   4. Tarot, playing cards used mainly for fortune-telling.
5. The German air force.   6. People of Germanic lineage, often blond-haired and blue-eyed.
7. Literally "panther," the Nazi tank corps' term for an armored vehicle.

You stand at the blackboard, daddy,
In the picture I have of you,
A cleft in your chin instead of your foot
But no less a devil for that, no not
55 Any less the black man who

Bit my pretty red heart in two.
I was ten when they buried you.
At twenty I tried to die
And get back, back, back to you.
60 I thought even the bones would do

But they pulled me out of the sack,
And they stuck me together with glue.[8]
And then I knew what to do.
I made a model of you,
65 A man in black with a Meinkampf[9] look

And a love of the rack and the screw.
And I said I do, I do.
So daddy, I'm finally through.
The black telephone's off at the root,
70 The voices just can't worm through.

If I've killed one man, I've killed two—
The vampire who said he was you
And drank my blood for a year,
Seven years, if you want to know.
75 Daddy, you can lie back now.

There's a stake in your fat black heart
And the villagers never liked you.
They are dancing and stamping on you.
They always *knew* it was you.
80 Daddy, daddy, you bastard, I'm through.

1966

Lady Lazarus

I have done it again.
One year in every ten
I manage it—

A sort of walking miracle, my skin
5 Bright as a Nazi lampshade,
My right foot

---

8. An allusion to Plath's recovery from her first suicide attempt.
9. The title of Adolf Hitler's autobiography and manifesto (1925–27); German for "my struggle."

A paperweight,
My face a featureless, fine
Jew linen.[1]

10 Peel off the napkin
O my enemy.
Do I terrify?—

The nose, the eye pits, the full set of teeth?
The sour breath
15 Will vanish in a day.

Soon, soon the flesh
The grave cave ate will be
At home on me

And I a smiling woman.
20 I am only thirty.
And like the cat I have nine times to die.

This is Number Three.
What a trash
To annihilate each decade.

25 What a million filaments.
The peanut-crunching crowd
Shoves in to see

Them unwrap me hand and foot—
The big strip tease.
30 Gentlemen, ladies

These are my hands
My knees.
I may be skin and bone,

Nevertheless, I am the same, identical woman.
35 The first time it happened I was ten.
It was an accident.

The second time I meant
To last it out and not come back at all.
I rocked shut

40 As a seashell.
They had to call and call
And pick the worms off me like sticky pearls.

Dying
Is an art, like everything else.
45 I do it exceptionally well.

---

1. During World War II, in some Nazi camps, prisoners were gassed to death and their body parts then turned into objects such as lampshades and paperweights.

I do it so it feels like hell.
I do it so it feels real.
I guess you could say I've a call.

It's easy enough to do it in a cell.
50 It's easy enough to do it and stay put.
It's the theatrical

Comeback in broad day
To the same place, the same face, the same brute
Amused shout:

55 "A miracle!"
That knocks me out.
There is a charge

For the eyeing of my scars, there is a charge
For the hearing of my heart—
60 It really goes.

And there is a charge, a very large charge
For a word or a touch
Or a bit of blood

Or a piece of my hair or my clothes.
65 So, so Herr Doktor.
So, Herr Enemy.

I am your opus,
I am your valuable,
The pure gold baby

70 That melts to a shriek.
I turn and burn.
Do not think I underestimate your great concern

Ash, ash—
You poke and stir.
75 Flesh, bone, there is nothing there—

A cake of soap,
A wedding ring,
A gold filling.

Herr God, Herr Lucifer
80 Beware
Beware.

Out of the ash
I rise with my red hair
And I eat men like air.

1965

EZRA POUND

In a Station of the Metro[2]

The apparition of these faces in the crowd;
Petals on a wet, black bough.

1913

SIR WALTER RALEGH

The Nymph's Reply to the Shepherd

If all the world and love were young,
And truth in every shepherd's tongue,
These pretty pleasures might me move
To live with thee and be thy love.

5   Time drives the flocks from field to fold,
When rivers rage, and rocks grow cold,
And Philomel[3] becometh dumb;
The rest complain of cares to come.

The flowers do fade, and wanton fields
10 To wayward winter reckoning yields:
A honey tongue, a heart of gall,
Is fancy's spring, but sorrow's fall.

Thy gowns, thy shoes, thy beds of roses,
Thy cap, thy kirtle, and thy posies
15 Soon break, soon wither, soon forgotten;
In folly ripe, in reason rotten.

Thy belt of straw and ivy buds,
Thy coral clasps and amber studs,
All these in me no means can move
20 To come to thee and be thy love.

But could youth last, and love still breed,
Had joys no date,[4] nor age no need,
Then these delights my mind might move
To live with thee and be thy love.

1600

2. The Paris subway.   3. The nightingale.   4. End.

JOHN CROWE RANSOM

Bells for John Whiteside's Daughter

There was such speed in her little body,
And such lightness in her footfall,
It is no wonder her brown study[5]
Astonishes us all.

5   Her wars were bruited in our high window.
We looked among orchard trees and beyond
Where she took arms against her shadow,
Or harried unto the pond

The lazy geese, like a snow cloud
10 Dripping their snow on the green grass,
Tricking and stopping, sleepy and proud,
Who cried in goose, Alas,

For the tireless heart within the little
Lady with rod that made them rise
15 From their noon apple-dreams and scuttle
Goose-fashion under the skies!

But now go the bells, and we are ready,
In one house we are sternly stopped
To say we are vexed at her brown study,
20 Lying so primly propped.

                                        1924

ADRIENNE RICH

Storm Warnings

The glass has been falling all the afternoon,
And knowing better than the instrument
What winds are walking overhead, what zone
Of gray unrest is moving across the land,
5   I leave the book upon a pillowed chair
And walk from window to closed window, watching
Boughs strain against the sky

And think again, as often when the air
Moves inward toward a silent core of waiting,
10 How with a single purpose time has traveled
By secret currents of the undiscerned

---

5. Stillness, as if in meditation or deep thought.

Into this polar realm. Weather abroad
And weather in the heart alike come on
Regardless of prediction.

15 Between foreseeing and averting change
Lies all the mastery of elements
Which clocks and weatherglasses cannot alter.
Time in the hand is not control of time,
Nor shattered fragments of an instrument
20 A proof against the wind; the wind will rise,
We can only close the shutters.

I draw the curtains as the sky goes black
And set a match to candles sheathed in glass
Against the keyhole draught, the insistent whine
25 Of weather through the unsealed aperture.
This is our sole defense against the season;
These are the things that we have learned to do
Who live in troubled regions.

                                            1951

History[6]

Should I simplify my life for you?
Don't ask how I began to love men.
Don't ask how I began to love women.
Remember the forties songs, the slowdance numbers
5 the small sex-filled gas-rationed Chevrolet?
Remember walking in the snow and who was gay?
Cigarette smoke of the movies, silver-and-gray
profiles, dreaming the dreams of he-and-she
breathing the dissolution of the wisping silver plume?
10 Dreaming that dream we leaned applying lipstick
by the gravestone's mirror when we found ourselves
playing in the cemetery. In Current Events she said
the war in Europe is over, the Allies
and she wore no lipstick have won the war
15 and we raced screaming out of Sixth Period.

Dreaming that dream
we had to maze our ways through a wood
where lips were knives breasts razors and I hid
in the cage of my mind scribbling
20 *this map stops where it all begins*
into a red-and-black notebook.

6. This is poem 4 in Rich's series "Inscriptions."

Remember after the war when peace came down
as plenty for some and they said we were saved
in an eternal present and we knew the world could end?
25 —remember after the war when peace rained down
on the winds from Hiroshima Nagasaki Utah Nevada?[7]
and the socialist queer Christian teacher jumps from the hotel
     window?[8]
and L.G. saying *I want to sleep with you but not for sex*
and the red-and-black enamelled coffee-pot dripped slow
     through the dark grounds
30 —appetite terror power tenderness
the long kiss in the stairwell the switch thrown
on two Jewish Communists[9] married to each other
the definitive crunch of glass at the end of the wedding?
(When shall we learn, what should be clear as day,
35 *We cannot choose what we are free to love?)*

                                                              1995

WILLIAM SHAKESPEARE

[*Not marble, nor the gilded monuments*]

Not marble, nor the gilded monuments
Of princes, shall outlive this powerful rhyme;
But you shall shine more bright in these conténts
Than unswept stone, besmeared with sluttish time.
5 When wasteful war shall statues overturn,
And broils[1] root out the work of masonry,
Nor[2] Mars his sword nor war's quick fire shall burn
The living record of your memory.
'Gainst death and all-oblivious enmity
10 Shall you pace forth; your praise shall still find room
Even in the eyes of all posterity
That wear this world out to the ending doom.[3]
So, till the judgment that yourself arise,
You live in this, and dwell in lovers' eyes.

                                                              1609

---

7. Sites of atom bomb explosions, the first two in Japan near the end of World War II, the last two at test sites in the American desert.
8. This line alludes to the critic Francis Otto Matthiessen (1902–1950), who taught at Harvard while Rich was an undergraduate there.
9. Julius and Ethel Rosenberg, executed as spies by the United States in 1953.   1. Riots.
2. Neither. *Mars his:* Mars's.   3. Judgment Day.

WALLACE STEVENS

The Emperor of Ice-Cream

Call the roller of big cigars,
The muscular one, and bid him whip
In kitchen cups concupiscent curds.[4]
Let the wenches dawdle in such dress
5   As they are used to wear, and let the boys
Bring flowers in last month's newspapers.
Let be be finale of seem.[5]
The only emperor is the emperor of ice-cream.

Take from the dresser of deal,
10 Lacking the three glass knobs, that sheet
On which she embroidered fantails[6] once
And spread it so as to cover her face.
If her horny feet protrude, they come
To show how cold she is, and dumb.
15 Let the lamp affix its beam.
The only emperor is the emperor of ice-cream.

1923

Anecdote of the Jar

I placed a jar in Tennessee,
And round it was, upon a hill.
It made the slovenly wilderness
Surround that hill.

5   The wilderness rose up to it,
And sprawled around, no longer wild.
The jar was round upon the ground
And tall and of a port in air.

It took dominion everywhere.
10 The jar was gray and bare.
It did not give of bird or bush,
Like nothing else in Tennessee.

1923

---

4. "The words 'concupiscent curds' have no genealogy; they are merely expressive: at least, I hope they are expressive. They express the concupiscence of life, but, by contrast with the things in relation in the poem, they express or accentuate life's destitution, and it is this that gives them something more than a cheap lustre" (*Letters*, p. 500).

5. "[T]he true sense of Let be be the finale of seem is let being become the conclusion of denouement of appearing to be: in short, ice cream is an absolute good. The poem is obviously not about ice cream, but about being as distinguished from seeming to be" (*Letters*, p. 341).   6. Fantail pigeons.

Sunday Morning

I

Complacencies of the peignoir, and late
Coffee and oranges in a sunny chair,
And the green freedom of a cockatoo
Upon a rug mingle to dissipate
5 The holy hush of ancient sacrifice.
She dreams a little, and she feels the dark
Encroachment of that old catastrophe,[7]
As a calm darkens among water-lights.
The pungent oranges and bright, green wings
10 Seem things in some procession of the dead,
Winding across wide water, without sound,
The day is like wide water, without sound,
Stilled for the passing of her dreaming feet
Over the seas, to silent Palestine,
15 Dominion of the blood and sepulchre.

II

Why should she give her bounty to the dead?
What is divinity if it can come
Only in silent shadows and in dreams?
Shall she not find in comforts of the sun,
20 In pungent fruit and bright, green wings, or else
In any balm or beauty of the earth,
Things to be cherished like the thought of heaven?
Divinity must live within herself
Passions of rain, or moods in falling snow;
25 Grievings in loneliness, or unsubdued
Elations when the forest blooms; gusty
Emotions on wet roads on autumn nights;
All pleasures and all pains, remembering
The bough of summer and the winter branch.
30 These are the measures destined for her soul.

III

Jove in the clouds has his inhuman birth.
No mother suckled him, no sweet land gave
Large-mannered motions to his mythy mind
He moved among us, as a muttering king,
35 Magnificent, would move among his hinds,[8]

---

7. The Crucifixion.   8. Lowliest rural subjects.

Until our blood, commingling, virginal,
With heaven, brought such requital to desire
The very hinds discerned it, in a star.[9]
Shall our blood fail? Or shall it come to be
40 The blood of paradise? And shall the earth
Seem all of paradise that we shall know?
The sky will be much friendlier then than now,
A part of labor and a part of pain,
And next in glory to enduring love,
45 Not this dividing and indifferent blue.

IV

She says, "I am content when wakened birds,
Before they fly, test the reality
Of misty fields, by their sweet questionings;
But when the birds are gone, and their warm fields
50 Return no more, where, then, is paradise?"
There is not any haunt of prophecy,
Nor any old chimera of the grave,
Neither the golden underground, nor isle
Melodious, where spirits gat[1] them home,
55 Nor visionary south, nor cloudy palm
Remote on heaven's hill, that has endured
As April's green endures, or will endure
Like her remembrance of awakened birds,
Or her desire for June and evening, tipped
60 By the consummation of the swallow's wings.

V

She says, "But in contentment I still feel
The need of some imperishable bliss."
Death is the mother of beauty; hence from her,
Alone, shall come fulfillment to our dreams
65 And our desires. Although she strews the leaves
Of sure obliteration on our paths,
The path sick sorrow took, the many paths
Where triumph rang its brassy phrase, or love
Whispered a little out of tenderness,
70 She makes the willow shiver in the sun
For maidens who were wont to sit and gaze
Upon the grass, relinquished to their feet.
She causes boys to pile new plums and pears

---

9. The star of Bethlehem.   1. Got.

On disregarded plate.[2] The maidens taste
75 And stray impassioned in the littering leaves.

VI

Is there no change of death in paradise?
Does ripe fruit never fall? Or do the boughs
Hang always heavy in that perfect sky,
Unchanging, yet so like our perishing earth,
80 With rivers like our own that seek for seas
They never find, the same receding shores
That never touch with inarticulate pang?
Why set the pear upon those river-banks
Or spice the shores with odors of the plum?
85 Alas, that they should wear our colors there,
The silken weavings of our afternoons,
And pick the strings of our insipid lutes!
Death is the mother of beauty, mystical,
Within whose burning bosom we devise
90 Our earthly mothers awaiting, sleeplessly.

VII

Supple and turbulent, a ring of men
Shall chant in orgy[3] on a summer morn
Their boisterous devotion to the sun,
Not as a god, but as a god might be,
95 Naked among them, like a savage source.
Their chant shall be a chant of paradise,
Out of their blood, returning to the sky;
And in their chant shall enter, voice by voice,
The windy lake wherein their lord delights,
100 The trees, like serafin,[4] and echoing hills,
That choir among themselves long afterward.
They shall know well the heavenly fellowship
Of men that perish and of summer morn.
And whence they came and whither they shall go
105 The dew upon their feet shall manifest.

VIII

She hears, upon that water without sound,
A voice that cries, "The tomb in Palestine
Is not the porch of spirits lingering.

---

2. "Plate is used in the sense of so-called family plate. Disregarded refers to the disuse into which things fall that have been possessed for a long time. I mean, therefore, that death releases and renews. What the old have come to disregard, the young inherit and make use of" (*Letters*, pp. 183–84).
3. Ceremonial revelry.   4. Seraphim, the highest of the nine orders of angels.

It is the grave of Jesus, where he lay."
110 We live in an old chaos of the sun,
Or old dependency of day and night,
Or island solitude, unsponsored, free,
Of that wide water, inescapable.
Deer walk upon our mountains, and the quail
115 Whistle about us their spontaneous cries;
Sweet berries ripen in the wilderness;
And, in the isolation of the sky,
At evening, casual flocks of pigeons make
Ambiguous undulations as they sink,
120 Downward to darkness, on extended wings.

1915

ALFRED, LORD TENNYSON

Tears, Idle Tears[5]

Tears, idle tears, I know not what they mean,
Tears from the depth of some divine despair
Rise in the heart, and gather to the eyes,
In looking on the happy autumn-fields,
5 And thinking of the days that are no more.

Fresh as the first beam glittering on a sail,
That brings our friends up from the underworld,
Sad as the last which reddens over one
That sinks with all we love below the verge;
10 So sad, so fresh, the days that are no more.

Ah, sad and strange as in dark summer dawns
The earliest pipe of half-awakened birds
To dying ears, when unto dying eyes
The casement slowly grows a glimmering square;
15 So sad, so strange, the days that are no more.

Dear as remembered kisses after death,
And sweet as those by hopeless fancy feigned
On lips that are for others; deep as love,
Deep as first love, and wild with all regret;
20 O Death in Life, the days that are no more!

1847

---

5. A song from *The Princess*.

Tithonus[6]

The woods decay, the woods decay and fall,
The vapors weep their burthen[7] to the ground,
Man comes and tills the field and lies beneath,
And after many a summer dies the swan.
5 Me only cruel immortality
Consumes; I wither slowly in thine arms,
Here at the quiet limit of the world,
A white-haired shadow roaming like a dream
The ever-silent spaces of the East,
10 Far-folded mists, and gleaming halls of morn.
    Alas! for this gray shadow, once a man—
So glorious in his beauty and thy choice,
Who madest him thy chosen, that he seemed
To his great heart none other than a God!
15 I asked thee, "Give me immortality."
Then didst thou grant mine asking with a smile,
Like wealthy men who care not how they give.
But thy strong Hours indignant worked their wills,
And beat me down and marred and wasted me,
20 And though they could not end me, left me maimed
To dwell in presence of immortal youth,
Immortal age beside immortal youth,
And all I was in ashes. Can thy love,
Thy beauty, make amends, though even now,
25 Close over us, the silver star, thy guide,
Shines in those tremulous eyes that fill with tears
To hear me? Let me go; take back thy gift.
Why should a man desire in any way
To vary from the kindly race of men,
30 Or pass beyond the goal of ordinance
Where all should pause, as is most meet[8] for all?
    A soft air fans the cloud apart; there comes
A glimpse of that dark world where I was born.
Once more the old mysterious glimmer steals
35 From thy pure brows, and from thy shoulders pure
And bosom beating with a heart renewed.
Thy cheek begins to redden through the gloom,
Thy sweet eyes brighten slowly close to mine,
Ere yet they blind the stars, and the wild team
40 Which love thee, yearning for thy yoke, arise,

---

6. Prince of Troy, loved by Aurora, goddess of the dawn, to whom he speaks the poem. Aurora obtained for him the gift of eternal life but forgot to ask for eternal youth.
7. Burden.   8. Proper.

And shake the darkness from their loosened manes,
And beat the twilight into flakes of fire.
    Lo! ever thus thou growest beautiful
In silence, then before thine answer given
45 Departest, and thy tears are on my cheek.
    Why wilt thou ever scare me with thy tears,
And make me tremble lest a saying learnt,
In days far-off, on that dark earth, be true?
"The Gods themselves cannot recall their gifts."
50   Ay me! ay me! with what another heart
In days far-off, and with what other eyes
I used to watch—if I be he that watched—
The lucid outline forming round thee; saw
The dim curls kindle into sunny rings;
55 Changed with thy mystic change, and felt my blood
Glow with the glow that slowly crimsoned all
Thy presence and thy portals, while I lay,
Mouth, forehead, eyelids, growing dewy-warm
With kisses balmier than half-opening buds
60 Of April, and could hear the lips that kissed
Whispering I knew not what of wild and sweet,
Like that strange song I heard Apollo sing,
While Ilion like a mist rose into towers.[9]
    Yet hold me not forever in thine East;
65 How can my nature longer mix with thine?
Coldly thy rosy shadows bathe me, cold
Are all thy lights, and cold my wrinkled feet
Upon thy glimmering thresholds, when the steam
Floats up from those dim fields about the homes
70 Of happy men that have the power to die,
And grassy barrows of the happier dead.
Release me, and restore me to the ground.
Thou seest all things, thou wilt see my grave;
Thou wilt renew thy beauty morn by morn,
75 I earth in earth forget these empty courts,
And thee returning on thy silver wheels.

                                   1860

---

9. According to Ovid's *Heroides*, music by the god of poetic inspiration accompanied the creation
of walls and towers around Troy (Ilion).

WEB *Ulysses*[1]

It little profits that an idle king,
By this still hearth, among these barren crags,
Matched with an agéd wife,[2] I mete and dole
Unequal laws unto a savage race,
5 That hoard, and sleep, and feed, and know not me.

I cannot rest from travel; I will drink
Life to the lees.[3] All times I have enjoyed
Greatly, have suffered greatly, both with those
That loved me, and alone; on shore, and when
10 Through scudding drifts the rainy Hyades[4]
Vexed the dim sea. I am become a name;
For always roaming with a hungry heart
Much have I seen and known—cities of men
And manners, climates, councils, governments,
15 Myself not least, but honored of them all—
And drunk delight of battle with my peers,
Far on the ringing plains of windy Troy.
I am a part of all that I have met;
Yet all experience is an arch wherethrough
20 Gleams that untraveled world, whose margin fades
For ever and for ever when I move.
How dull it is to pause, to make an end,
To rust unburnished, not to shine in use!
As though to breathe were life. Life piled on life
25 Were all too little, and of one to me
Little remains; but every hour is saved
From that eternal silence, something more,
A bringer of new things; and vile it were
For some three suns to store and hoard myself,
30 And this gray spirit yearning in desire
To follow knowledge like a sinking star,
Beyond the utmost bound of human thought.

This is my son, mine own Telemachus,
To whom I leave the scepter and the isle—
35 Well-loved of me, discerning to fulfill
This labor by slow prudence to make mild
A rugged people, and through soft degrees

---

1. After the end of the Trojan War, Ulysses (or Odysseus), king of Ithaca and one of the Greek heroes of the war, returned to his island home (line 34). Homer's account of the situation is in the *Odyssey* 11, but Dante's account of Ulysses in the *Inferno* 26 is the more immediate background of the poem.   2. Penelope.   3. All the way down to the bottom of the cup.
4. A group of stars that were supposed to predict the rain when they rose at the same time as the sun.

Subdue them to the useful and the good.
Most blameless is he, centered in the sphere
40 Of common duties, decent not to fail
In offices of tenderness, and pay
Meet adoration to my household gods,
When I am gone. He works his work, I mine.

There lies the port; the vessel puffs her sail:
45 There gloom the dark, broad seas. My mariners,
Souls that have toiled, and wrought, and thought with me—
That ever with a frolic welcome took
The thunder and the sunshine, and opposed
Free hearts, free foreheads—you and I are old;
50 Old age hath yet his honor and his toil.
Death closes all; but something ere the end,
Some work of noble note, may yet be done,
Not unbecoming men that strove with Gods.
The lights begin to twinkle from the rocks;
55 The long day wanes; the slow moon climbs; the deep
Moans round with many voices. Come, my friends.
'Tis not too late to seek a newer world.
Push off, and sitting well in order smite
The sounding furrows; for my purpose holds
60 To sail beyond the sunset, and the baths
Of all the western stars, until I die.
It may be that the gulfs will wash us down;[5]
It may be we shall touch the Happy Isles,[6]
And see the great Achilles, whom we knew.
65 Though much is taken, much abides; and though
We are not now that strength which in old days
Moved earth and heaven, that which we are, we are:
One equal temper of heroic hearts,
Made weak by time and fate, but strong in will
70 To strive, to seek, to find, and not to yield.

1833

DYLAN THOMAS

Fern Hill

Now as I was young and easy under the apple boughs
About the lilting house and happy as the grass was green,
   The night above the dingle starry,

---

5. Beyond the Gulf of Gibraltar was supposed to be a chasm that led to Hades.
6. Elysium, the Islands of the Blessed, where heroes like Achilles (line 64) go after death.

Time let me hail and climb
5 Golden in the heydays of his eyes,
And honored among wagons I was prince of the apple towns
And once below a time I lordly had the trees and leaves
   Trail with daisies and barley
   Down the rivers of the windfall light.

10 And as I was green and carefree, famous among the barns
About the happy yard and singing as the farm was home,
   In the sun that is young once only,
      Time let me play and be
   Golden in the mercy of his means,
15 And green and golden I was huntsman and herdsman, the calves
Sang to my horn, the foxes on the hills barked clear and cold,
   And the sabbath rang slowly
   In the pebbles of the holy streams.

All the sun long it was running, it was lovely, the hay
20 Fields high as the house, the tunes from the chimneys, it was air
   And playing, lovely and watery
      And fire green as grass.
   And nightly under the simple stars
As I rode to sleep the owls were bearing the farm away,
25 All the moon long I heard, blessed among stables, the nightjars[7]
   Flying with the ricks,[8] and the horses
      Flashing into the dark.

And then to awake, and the farm, like a wanderer white
With the dew, come back, the cock on his shoulder: it was all
30   Shining, it was Adam and maiden,
      The sky gathered again
   And the sun grew round that very day.
So it must have been after the birth of the simple light
In the first, spinning place, the spellbound horses walking warm
35   Out of the whinnying green stable
      On to the fields of praise.

And honored among foxes and pheasants by the gay house
Under the new made clouds and happy as the heart was long,
   In the sun born over and over,
40   I ran my heedless ways,
   My wishes raced through the house-high hay
And nothing I cared, at my sky-blue trades, that time allows
In all his tuneful turning so few and such morning songs
   Before the children green and golden
45   Follow him out of grace,

7. Birds also known as goatsuckers.   8. Haystacks.

Nothing I cared, in the lamb white days, that time would take me
Up to the swallow-thronged loft by the shadow of my hand,
   In the moon that is always rising,
     Nor that riding to sleep
50   I should hear him fly with the high fields
And wake to the farm forever fled from the childless land.
Oh as I was young and easy in the mercy of his means,
    Time held me green and dying
   Though I sang in my chains like the sea.

1946

DEREK WALCOTT

WEB   *A Far Cry from Africa*

A wind is ruffling the tawny pelt
Of Africa. Kikuyu,[9] quick as flies,
Batten upon the bloodstreams of the veldt.[1]
Corpses are scattered through a paradise.
5 Only the worm, colonel of carrion, cries:
"Waste no compassion on these separate dead!"
Statistics justify and scholars seize
The salients of colonial policy.
What is that to the white child hacked in bed?
10 To savages, expendable as Jews?

Threshed out by beaters,[2] the long rushes break
In a white dust of ibises whose cries
Have wheeled since civilization's dawn
From the parched river or beast-teeming plain.
15 The violence of beast on beast is read
As natural law, but upright man
Seeks his divinity by inflicting pain.
Delirious as these worried beasts, his wars
Dance to the tightened carcass of a drum,
20 While he calls courage still that native dread
Of the white peace contracted by the dead.

Again brutish necessity wipes its hands
Upon the napkin of a dirty cause, again

9. An East African tribe whose members, as Mau Mau fighters, conducted an eight-year insurrection against British colonial settlers in Kenya.
1. Open plains, neither cultivated nor thickly forested (Afrikaans).
2. In big-game hunting, natives are hired to beat the brush, driving birds—such as ibises—and animals into the open.

A waste of our compassion, as with Spain,[3]
25 The gorilla wrestles with the superman.
I who am poisoned with the blood of both,
Where shall I turn, divided to the vein?
I who have cursed
The drunken officer of British rule, how choose
30 Between this Africa and the English tongue I love?
Betray them both, or give back what they give?
How can I face such slaughter and be cool?
How can I turn from Africa and live?

1962

PHILLIS WHEATLEY

WEB

On Being Brought from Africa to America

'Twas mercy brought me from my Pagan land,
Taught my benighted soul to understand
That there's a God, that there's a Saviour too:
Once I redemption neither sought nor knew.
5 Some view our sable race with scornful eye,
"Their colour is a diabolic die."
Remember, Christians, Negroes, black as Cain,[4]
May be refin'd, and join th' angelic train.

1773

WALT WHITMAN

Facing West from California's Shores

Facing west, from California's shores,
Inquiring, tireless, seeking what is yet unfound,
I, a child, very old, over waves, towards the house of maternity,[5] the
    land of migrations, look afar,
Look off the shores of my Western sea, the circle almost circled:
5 For starting westward from Hindustan, from the vales of
    Kashmere,
From Asia, from the north, from the God, the sage, and the hero,
From the south, from the flowery peninsulas and the spice islands,
Long having wandered since, round the earth having wandered,

---

3. The Spanish Civil War (1936–39), in which the Republican loyalists were supported politically by
liberals in the West and militarily by Soviet Communists, and the Nationalist rebels by Nazi Germany
and Fascist Italy.
4. One of Adam's sons, he killed his brother Abel. See Genesis 4.
5. Asia, as the supposed birthplace of the human race.

Now I face home again, very pleased and joyous;
10 (But where is what I started for, so long ago?
And why is it yet unfound?)

1860

I Hear America Singing

I hear America singing, the varied carols I hear,
Those of mechanics, each one singing his as it should be blithe
and strong,
The carpenter singing his as he measures his plank or beam,
The mason singing his as he makes ready for work, or leaves off
work,
5 The boatman singing what belongs to him in his boat, the
deckhand singing on the steamboat deck,
The shoemaker singing as he sits on his bench, the hatter singing
as he stands,
The wood-cutter's song, the ploughboy's on his way in the
morning, or at noon intermission or at sundown,
The delicious singing of the mother, or of the young wife at
work, or of the girl sewing or washing,
Each singing what belongs to him or her and to none else,
10 The day what belongs to the day—at night the party of young
fellows, robust, friendly,
Singing with open mouths their strong melodious songs.

1860

A Noiseless Patient Spider

A noiseless patient spider,
I marked where on a little promontory it stood isolated,
Marked how to explore the vacant vast surrounding,
It launched forth filament, filament, filament, out of itself,
5 Ever unreeling them, ever tirelessly speeding them.

And you O my soul where you stand,
Surrounded, detached, in measureless oceans of space,
Ceaselessly musing, venturing, throwing, seeking the spheres to
connect them,
Till the bridge you will need be formed, till the ductile anchor
hold,
10 Till the gossamer thread you fling catch somewhere, O my soul.

1881

RICHARD WILBUR

Love Calls Us to the Things of This World

The eyes open to a cry of pulleys,
And spirited from sleep, the astounded soul
Hangs for a moment bodiless and simple
As false dawn.
5   Outside the open window
The morning air is all awash with angels.

Some are in bed-sheets, some are in blouses,
Some are in smocks: but truly there they are.
Now they are rising together in calm swells
10 Of halcyon[6] feeling, filling whatever they wear
With the deep joy of their impersonal breathing;
    Now they are flying in place,[7] conveying
The terrible speed of their omnipresence, moving
And staying like white water; and now of a sudden
15 They swoon down into so rapt a quiet
That nobody seems to be there.
                    The soul shrinks

From all that it is about to remember,
From the punctual rape of every blessed day,
20 And cries,
        "Oh, let there be nothing on earth but laundry,
Nothing but rosy hands in the rising steam
And clear dances done in the sight of heaven."

Yet, as the sun acknowledges
25 With a warm look the world's hunks and colors,
The soul descends once more in bitter love
To accept the waking body, saying now
In a changed voice as the man yawns and rises,

"Bring them down from their ruddy gallows;
30 Let there be clean linen for the backs of thieves;
Let lovers go fresh and sweet to be undone,
And the heaviest nuns walk in a pure floating
Of dark habits,
            keeping their difficult balance."

                                    1956

---

6. Serene.   7. Like planes in a formation.

WILLIAM WORDSWORTH

Lines Written a Few Miles above Tintern Abbey, On Revisiting the Banks of the Wye during a Tour, July 13, 1798[8]

Five years have passed; five summers, with the length
Of five long winters! and again I hear
These waters, rolling from their mountain-springs
With a soft inland murmur. Once again
5 Do I behold these steep and lofty cliffs,
That on a wild secluded scene impress
Thoughts of more deep seclusion; and connect
The landscape with the quiet of the sky.
The day is come when I again repose
10 Here, under this dark sycamore, and view
These plots of cottage-ground, these orchard tufts,
Which at this season, with their unripe fruits,
Are clad in one green hue, and lose themselves
'Mid groves and copses.[9] Once again I see
15 These hedge-rows, hardly hedge-rows, little lines
Of sportive wood run wild: these pastoral farms,
Green to the very door; and wreaths of smoke
Sent up, in silence, from among the trees!
With some uncertain notice, as might seem
20 Of vagrant dwellers in the houseless woods,
Or of some hermit's cave, where by his fire
The hermit sits alone.

                    These beauteous forms,
Through a long absence, have not been to me
As is a landscape to a blind man's eye;
25 But oft, in lonely rooms, and 'mid the din
Of towns and cities, I have owed to them,
In hours of weariness, sensations sweet,
Felt in the blood, and felt along the heart;
And passing even into my purer mind,
30 With tranquil restoration—feelings too
Of unremembered pleasure: such, perhaps,
As have no slight or trivial influence
On that best portion of a good man's life,

---

8. Wordsworth had first visited the Wye valley and the ruins of the medieval abbey there in 1793, while on a solitary walking tour. He was twenty-three then, twenty-eight when he wrote this poem.
9. Thickets.

His little, nameless, unremembered acts
35 Of kindness and of love. Nor less, I trust,
To them I may have owed another gift,
Of aspect more sublime; that blessèd mood,
In which the burthen[1] of the mystery,
In which the heavy and the weary weight
40 Of all this unintelligible world,
Is lightened—that serene and blessèd mood,
In which the affections gently lead us on—
Until, the breath of this corporeal frame
And even the motion of our human blood
45 Almost suspended, we are laid asleep
In body, and become a living soul;
While with an eye made quiet by the power
Of harmony, and the deep power of joy,
We see into the life of things.
                                        If this
50 Be but a vain belief, yet, oh! how oft—
In darkness and amid the many shapes
Of joyless daylight; when the fretful stir
Unprofitable, and the fever of the world,
Have hung upon the beatings of my heart—
55 How oft, in spirit, have I turned to thee,
O sylvan Wye! thou wanderer through the woods,
How often has my spirit turned to thee!

    And now, with gleams of half-extinguished thought,
With many recognitions dim and faint,
60 And somewhat of a sad perplexity,
The picture of the mind revives again;
While here I stand, not only with the sense
Of present pleasure, but with pleasing thoughts
That in this moment there is life and food
65 For future years. And so I dare to hope,
Though changed, no doubt, from what I was when first
I came among these hills; when like a roe
I bounded o'er the mountains, by the sides
Of the deep rivers, and the lonely streams,
70 Wherever nature led: more like a man
Flying from something that he dreads than one
Who sought the thing he loved. For nature then
(The coarser[2] pleasures of my boyish days,
And their glad animal movements all gone by)
75 To me was all in all—I cannot paint
What then I was. The sounding cataract

1. Burden.   2. Physical.

Haunted me like a passion; the tall rock,
The mountain, and the deep and gloomy wood,
Their colors and their forms, were then to me
80 An appetite; a feeling and a love,
That had no need of a remoter charm,
By thought supplied, nor any interest
Unborrowed from the eye. That time is past,
And all its aching joys are now no more,
85 And all its dizzy raptures. Not for this
Faint I,[3] nor mourn nor murmur; other gifts
Have followed; for such loss, I would believe,
Abundant recompense. For I have learned
To look on nature, not as in the hour
90 Of thoughtless youth; but hearing oftentimes
The still, sad music of humanity,
Nor[4] harsh nor grating, though of ample power
To chasten and subdue. And I have felt
A presence that disturbs me with the joy
95 Of elevated thoughts, a sense sublime
Of something far more deeply interfused,
Whose dwelling is the light of setting suns,
And the round ocean and the living air,
And the blue sky, and in the mind of man:
100 A motion and a spirit, that impels
All thinking things, all objects of all thought,
And rolls through all things. Therefore am I still
A lover of the meadows and the woods
And mountains; and of all that we behold
105 From this green earth; of all the mighty world
Of eye, and ear—both what they half create,
And what perceive; well pleased to recognize
In nature and the language of the sense
The anchor of my purest thoughts, the nurse,
110 The guide, the guardian of my heart, and soul
Of all my moral being.

                        Nor perchance,
If I were not thus taught, should I the more
Suffer my genial spirits[5] to decay:
For thou art with me here upon the banks
115 Of this fair river; thou my dearest Friend,[6]
My dear, dear Friend; and in thy voice I catch
The language of my former heart, and read
My former pleasures in the shooting lights

---

3. Am I discouraged.   4. Neither.
5. Natural disposition; that is, the spirits are part of his individual genius.   6. His sister Dorothy.

Of thy wild eyes. Oh! yet a little while
120 May I behold in thee what I was once,
My dear, dear Sister! and this prayer I make,
Knowing that Nature never did betray
The heart that loved her; 'tis her privilege,
Through all the years of this our life, to lead
125 From joy to joy: for she can so inform
The mind that is within us, so impress
With quietness and beauty, and so feed
With lofty thoughts, that neither evil tongues,
Rash judgments, nor the sneers of selfish men,
130 Nor greetings where no kindness is, nor all
The dreary intercourse of daily life,
Shall e'er prevail against us, or disturb
Our cheerful faith that all which we behold
Is full of blessings. Therefore let the moon
135 Shine on thee in thy solitary walk;
And let the misty mountain-winds be free
To blow against thee: and, in after years,
When these wild ecstasies shall be matured
Into a sober pleasure; when thy mind
140 Shall be a mansion for all lovely forms,
Thy memory be as a dwelling-place
For all sweet sounds and harmonies; oh! then,
If solitude, or fear, or pain, or grief,
Should be thy portion, with what healing thoughts
145 Of tender joy wilt thou remember me,
And these my exhortations! No, perchance—
If I should be where I no more can hear
Thy voice, nor catch from thy wild eyes these gleams
Of past existence—wilt thou then forget
150 That on the banks of this delightful stream
We stood together; and that I, so long
A worshiper of Nature, hither came
Unwearied in that service; rather say
With warmer love—oh! with far deeper zeal
155 Of holier love. Nor wilt thou then forget,
That after many wanderings, many years
Of absence, these steep woods and lofty cliffs,
And this green pastoral landscape, were to me
More dear, both for themselves and for thy sake!

1798

W. B. YEATS

The Lake Isle of Innisfree[7]

I will arise and go now, and go to Innisfree,
And a small cabin build there, of clay and wattles made,
Nine bean-rows will I have there, a hive for the honey-bee,
And live alone in the bee-loud glade.

5 And I shall have some peace there, for peace comes dropping slow,
Dropping from the veils of the morning to where the cricket sings;
There midnight's all a glimmer, and noon a purple glow,
And evening full of the linnet's wings.

I will arise and go now, for always night and day
10 I hear lake water lapping with low sounds by the shore;
While I stand on the roadway, or on the pavements grey,
I hear it in the deep heart's core.

1890

The Second Coming[8]

Turning and turning in the widening gyre[9]
The falcon cannot hear the falconer;
Things fall apart; the center cannot hold;
Mere anarchy is loosed upon the world,
5 The blood-dimmed tide is loosed, and everywhere
The ceremony of innocence is drowned;
The best lack all conviction, while the worst
Are full of passionate intensity.
Surely some revelation is at hand;
10 Surely the Second Coming is at hand.
The Second Coming! Hardly are those words out
When a vast image out of *Spiritus Mundi*[1]

7. Island in Lough Gill, County Sligo, Ireland.
8. The Second Coming of Christ, according to Matthew 24.29–44, will be after a time of "tribulation." Disillusioned by Ireland's continued civil strife, Yeats saw his time as the end of another historical cycle. In *A Vision* (1937), Yeats describes his view of history as dependent on cycles of about two thousand years: the birth of Christ had ended the cycle of Greco-Roman civilization, and now the Christian cycle seemed near an end, to be followed by an antithetical cycle, ominous in its portents.
9. Literally, the widening spiral of a falcon's flight. "Gyre" is Yeats's term for a cycle of history, which he diagrammed as a series of interpenetrating cones.
1. Or *Anima Mundi*, the spirit or soul of the world. Yeats considered this universal consciousness or memory a fund from which poets drew their images and symbols.

Troubles my sight: somewhere in sands of the desert
A shape with lion body and the head of a man,
15 A gaze blank and pitiless as the sun,
Is moving its slow thighs, while all about it
Reel shadows of the indignant desert birds.²
The darkness drops again; but now I know
That twenty centuries of stony sleep
20 Were vexed to nightmare by a rocking cradle,
And what rough beast, its hour come round at last,
Slouches towards Bethlehem to be born?

January 1919

Leda and the Swan³

A sudden blow: the great wings beating still
Above the staggering girl, her thighs caressed
By the dark webs, her nape caught in his bill,
He holds her helpless breast upon his breast.

5 How can those terrified vague fingers push
The feathered glory from her loosening thighs?
And how can body, laid in that white rush,
But feel the strange heart beating where it lies?

A shudder in the loins engenders there
10 The broken wall, the burning roof and tower
And Agamemnon dead.
      Being so caught up,
So mastered by the brute blood of the air,
Did she put on his knowledge with his power
Before the indifferent beak could let her drop?

1923

---

2. Yeats later wrote of the "brazen winged beast . . . described in my poem *The Second Coming*" as "associated with laughing, ecstatic destruction."
3. According to Greek myth, Zeus took the form of a swan to rape Leda, who became the mother of Helen of Troy; of Castor; and also of Clytemnestra, Agamemnon's wife and murderer. Helen's abduction from her husband, Menelaus, brother of Agamemnon, began the Trojan War (line 10). Yeats described the visit of Zeus to Leda as an annunciation like that to Mary (see Luke 1.26–38); "I imagine the annunciation that founded Greece as made to Leda" (*A Vision*).

Sailing to Byzantium[4]

I

That[5] is no country for old men. The young
In one another's arms, birds in the trees
—Those dying generations—at their song,
The salmon-falls, the mackerel-crowded seas,
5 Fish, flesh, or fowl, commend all summer long
Whatever is begotten, born, and dies.
Caught in that sensual music all neglect
Monuments of unaging intellect.

II

An aged man is but a paltry thing,
10 A tattered coat upon a stick, unless
Soul clap its hands and sing, and louder sing
For every tatter in its mortal dress,
Nor is there singing school but studying
Monuments of its own magnificence;
15 And therefore I have sailed the seas and come
To the holy city of Byzantium.

III

O sages standing in God's holy fire
As in the gold mosaic of a wall,
Come from the holy fire, perne in a gyre,[6]
20 And be the singing-masters of my soul.
Consume my heart away; sick with desire
And fastened to a dying animal
It knows not what it is; and gather me
Into the artifice of eternity.

IV

25 Once out of nature I shall never take
My bodily form from any natural thing,
But such a form as Grecian goldsmiths make

---

4. The ancient name of Istanbul, the capital and holy city of Eastern Christendom from the late fourth century until 1453. It was famous for its stylized and formal mosaics; its symbolic, nonnaturalistic art; and its highly developed intellectual life. Yeats repeatedly uses it to symbolize a world of artifice and timelessness, free from the decay and death of the natural and sensual world.

5. Ireland, as an instance of the natural, temporal world.

6. That is, whirl in a coiling motion, so that his soul may merge with its motion as the timeless world invades the cycles of history and nature. "Perne" is Yeats's coinage (from the noun *pim*): to spin around in the kind of spiral pattern that thread makes as it comes off a bobbin or spool.

Of hammered gold and gold enameling
To keep a drowsy Emperor awake;[7]
30 Or set upon a golden bough[8] to sing
To lords and ladies of Byzantium
Of what is past, or passing, or to come.

1927

---

7. "I have read somewhere that in the Emperor's palace at Byzantium was a tree made of gold and silver, and artificial birds that sang" [Yeats's note].
8. In Book 6 of the *Aeneid,* the sibyl tells Aeneas that he must pluck a golden bough from a nearby tree in order to descend to Hades. Each time Aeneas plucks the one such branch there, an identical one takes its place.

Biographical Sketches
Poets

Sketches are included for poets represented by two or more poems.

W. H. AUDEN
(1907–1973)

Wystan Hugh Auden was born in York, England, to a medical officer and a nurse. Intending at first to become a scientist, Auden studied at Oxford, where he became the center of the "Oxford Group" of poets and leftist intellectuals. His travels during the 1930s led him to Germany, Iceland, China, Spain (where he was an ambulance driver in the civil war), and the United States (where he taught at various universities and, in 1946, became a naturalized citizen). A prolific writer of poems, plays, essays, and criticism, Auden won the Pulitzer Prize in 1948 for his collection of poems *The Age of Anxiety,* set in a New York City bar. Late in life he returned to Christ Church College, Oxford, where he was writer in residence. He is regarded as a masterly poet of political and intellectual conscience as well as one of the twentieth century's greatest lyric craftsmen.

ELIZABETH BISHOP
(1911–1979)

Born in Worcester, Massachusetts, Elizabeth Bishop endured the death of her father before she was a year old and the institutionalization of her mother when she was five. Bishop was raised by her maternal grandmother in Nova Scotia, then by her paternal grandparents back in Worcester. At Vassar College she met the poet Marianne Moore, who encouraged her to give up plans for medical school and pursue a career in poetry. Bishop traveled through Canada, Europe, and South America, finally settling in Rio de Janeiro, where she lived for nearly twenty years. Her four volumes of poetry are *North and South* (1946); *A Cold Spring* (1955), which won the Pulitzer Prize; *Questions of Travel* (1965); and *Geography III* (1976), which won the National Book Critics' Circle Award. *Complete Poems 1929–1979* and *Collected Prose* gather most of her published work.

WILLIAM BLAKE
(1757–1828)

The son of a London haberdasher and his wife, William Blake studied drawing at ten and at fourteen was apprenticed to an engraver for seven years. After a first book of poems, *Poetical Sketches* (1783), he began experimenting with what he called "illuminated printing"—the words and pictures of each page were engraved in relief on copper, which was used to print sheets that were then partly colored by hand—a laborious and time-consuming process that resulted in books of singular beauty, no two of which were exactly alike. His great *Songs of Innocence* (1789) and *Songs of Experience* (1794) were produced in this manner, as were his increasingly mythic and prophetic books, including *The Marriage of Heaven and Hell* (1793), *The Four Zoas* (1803), *Milton* (1804), and *Jerusalem* (1809). Blake devoted his later life to pictorial art, illustrating *The Canterbury Tales,* the Book of Job, and *The Divine Comedy,* on which he was hard at work when he died.

GWENDOLYN BROOKS
(1917–2000)

Gwendolyn Brooks was born in Topeka, Kansas, and raised in Chicago, where she began writing poetry at the age of seven, and where she graduated from Wilson Junior College in 1936. Shortly after beginning her formal study of modern poetry at Chicago's Southside Community Art Center, Brooks produced her first book of poems, *A Street in Bronzeville* (1945). With her second volume, *Annie Allen* (1949), she became the first African American to win the Pulitzer Prize. Though her early work focused on what Langston Hughes called the "ordinary aspects of black life," during the mid-1960s she devoted her poetry to raising African American consciousness and to social activism. In 1968, she was named the Poet Laureate of Illinois; from 1985 to 1986, she served as poetry consultant to the Library of Congress. Her *Selected Poems* appeared in 1999.

ELIZABETH BARRETT BROWNING
(1806–1861)

Elizabeth Barrett was born into a wealthy family in Durham, England, and raised in Herefordshire. She received no formal schooling, but was very well educated at home in the classics and in English literature, and published her first volume of poetry at the age of thirteen. Despite her status as a prominent woman of letters, deteriorating health forced Barrett to live in semi-seclusion. Her collection *Poems* (1844) inspired the poet Robert Browning to write to her in May 1845, and thus began a courtship that resulted in their eloping to Italy in 1846. Following the publication of *Sonnets from the Portuguese* (1850), Barrett Browning received serious consideration to succeed Wordsworth as Poet Laureate (although the laureateship went instead to Tennyson); one critic hailed her as "the greatest female poet that England has produced." Her most admired work is *Aurora Leigh* (1857), a nine-book verse novel.

ROBERT BROWNING
(1812–1889)

Born in London, Robert Browning attended London University but was largely self-educated, learning Latin, Greek, French, and Italian by the time he was fourteen. He was an accomplished but little-known poet and playwright when he began courting the already famous poet Elizabeth Barrett. After they eloped to Italy in 1846, the Brownings enjoyed a period of happiness during which they produced most of their best-known work. Following Elizabeth's death in 1861, Robert returned to England with their son and for the rest of his life enjoyed great literary and social success. His major collections are *Men and Women* (1855), dedicated to his wife, and *Dramatis Personae* (1864), which contains some of his finest dramatic monologues. Lionized as one of England's greatest poets by the time of his death, Browning is buried in the Poets' Corner at Westminster Abbey.

ROBERT BURNS
(1759–1796)

Robert Burns was born and raised in Ayrshire, Scotland. The son of impoverished tenant farmers, he attended school sporadically but was largely self-taught. He collected subscriptions to publish his first collection, *Poems, Chiefly in the Scottish Dialect* (1786), which made his reputation in both Edinburgh and London. These poems were new in their rebellious individualism and in their pre-Romantic sensitivity to nature, yet they seemed to speak in an authentic "auld Scots" voice. A perennial failure as a farmer, Burns became a tax inspector and settled in the country town of Dumfries. Despite financial difficulties and failing health, he continued to write poems and songs (including "Auld Lang

Syne") and devoted his last years to collecting Scottish folk songs for a cultural-preservation project. His work, frequently bawdy, politically zealous, and critical of organized religion, remains deeply loved throughout the world.

SAMUEL TAYLOR COLERIDGE
(1772–1834)

Born in the small town of Ottery St. Mary in rural Devonshire, England, Samuel Taylor Coleridge is among the greatest and most original of the nineteenth-century Romantic poets. He wrote three of the most haunting and powerful poems in English—*The Rime of the Ancient Mariner* (1798), *Christabel* (1816), and "Kubla Khan" (1816)—as well as immensely influential literary criticism and a treatise on biology. In 1795, in the midst of a failed experiment to establish a "Pantisocracy" (his form of ideal community), he met William Wordsworth, and in 1798 they jointly published their enormously influential *Lyrical Ballads*. Coleridge's physical ailments, addiction to opium, and profound sense of despair made his life difficult and tumultuous and certainly affected his work. Still, he remains a central figure in English literature.

EMILY DICKINSON
(1830–1886)

From childhood on, Emily Dickinson led a sequestered and obscure life. Yet her verse has traveled far beyond the cultured yet relatively circumscribed environment in which she lived: her room, her father's house, her family, a few close friends, and the small town of Amherst, Massachusetts. Indeed, along with Walt Whitman, her far more public contemporary, she all but invented American poetry. Born in Amherst, the daughter of a respected lawyer whom she revered ("His heart was pure and terrible," she once wrote), Dickinson studied for less than a year at the Mount Holyoke Female Seminary, returning permanently to her family home. She became more and more reclusive, dressing only in white, seeing no visitors, yet working ceaselessly at her poems—nearly eighteen hundred in all, only a few of which were published during her lifetime. After her death, her sister Lavinia discovered the rest in a trunk, neatly bound into packets with blue ribbons—among the most important bodies of work in all of American literature.

JOHN DONNE
(1572–1631)

The first and greatest of the English writers who came to be known as the Metaphysical poets, John Donne wrote in a revolutionary style that combined highly intellectual conceits with complex, compressed phrasing. Born into an old Roman Catholic family at a time when Catholics were subject to constant harassment, Donne quietly abandoned his religion and had a promising legal career until a politically disastrous marriage ruined his worldly hopes. He struggled for years to support a large family; impoverished and despairing, he even wrote a treatise (*Biathanatos*) on the lawfulness of suicide. King James (who had ambitions for him as a preacher) eventually pressured Donne to take Anglican orders in 1615, and Donne became one of the great sermonizers of his day, rising to the position of dean of St. Paul's Cathedral in 1621. Donne's private devotions ("Meditations") were published in 1624, and he continued to write poetry until a few years before his death.

PAUL LAURENCE DUNBAR
(1872–1906)

The son of former slaves, Paul Laurence Dunbar was born in Dayton, Ohio. He attended a white high school, where he showed an early talent for writing and was elected class president. Unable to afford further education, he then worked as an elevator operator, writing poems and newspaper articles in his spare time. Dunbar took out a loan to subsidize the printing of his first book, *Oak and Ivy* (1893), but with the publication of *Majors and Minors* (1895) and *Lyrics of Lowly Life* (1896), his growing reputation enabled him to support himself by writing and lecturing. Though acclaimed during his lifetime for his lyrical use of rural black dialect in volumes such as *Candle-Lightin' Time* (1902), Dunbar was later criticized for adopting "white" literary conventions and accused of pandering to racist images of slaves and ex-slaves. He wrote novels and short stories in addition to poetry, and dealt frankly with racial injustice in works such as *The Sport of the Gods* (1903) and *The Fourth of July and Race Outrages* (1903).

T. S. ELIOT
(1888–1965)

Thomas Stearns Eliot—from his formally experimental and oblique writings to his brilliant arguments in defense of "orthodoxy" and "tradition"—dominated the world of English poetry between the world wars. Born in St. Louis, Missouri, into a family that hailed from New England, Eliot studied literature and philosophy at Harvard and later in France and Germany. He went to England in 1914, read Greek philosophy at Oxford, and published his first major poem, "The Love Song of J. Alfred Prufrock," the next year. In 1922, with the help of Ezra Pound, Eliot published *The Waste Land*, which profoundly influenced a generation of poets and became a cornerstone of literary modernism. In his later work, particularly the *Four Quartets* (completed in 1945), Eliot explored religious questions in a quieter, more controlled idiom. By the middle of the twentieth century, Eliot was regarded as a towering figure in modern literature, renowned as a poet, critic, essayist, editor, and dramatist.

He was awarded the Nobel Prize for Literature in 1948.

ROBERT FROST
(1874–1963)

Though his poetry identifies Frost with rural New England, he was born and lived to the age of eleven in San Francisco. Moving to New England after his father's death, Frost studied classics in high school, entered and dropped out of both Dartmouth and Harvard, and spent difficult years as an unrecognized poet before his first book, *A Boy's Will* (1913), was accepted and published in England. Frost's character was full of contradiction—he held "that we get forward as much by hating as by loving"— yet by the end of his long life he was one of the most honored poets of his time, and the most widely read. In 1961, two years before his death, he was invited to read a poem at John F. Kennedy's presidential inauguration ceremony. Frost's poems— masterfully crafted, sometimes deceptively simple—are collected in *The Poetry of Robert Frost* (1969).

THOM GUNN
(1929–2004)

With the irony that characterizes much of his poetry, Thom Gunn once claimed, "I am a completely anonymous person—my life contains no events, and I lack any visible personality." Nevertheless, Gunn impressed himself on American poetry, producing more than thirty volumes and winning the Lenore Marshall Prize for *The Man with Night Sweats* (1992). Although he was born and educated in England, earning by 1958 both a B.A. and an M.A. from Trinity College, Cambridge, he lived and worked in California for many years. His poetry combines an appreciation of formal tradition with frank treatments of such subjects as homosexuality and hallucinogens. Much of his best work can be found in his *Selected Poems 1950–1975* (1979) and *Collected Poems* (1994). His last collection is

Boss Cupid (2000). In 2003, Gunn received the David Cohen British Literature Award for lifetime achievement.

ROBERT HAYDEN (1913–1980)

Robert Hayden was born Asa Bundy Sheffey, in Detroit, Michigan, and raised by foster parents. He studied at Detroit City College (later Wayne State University), but left in 1936 to work for the Federal Writers' Project, where he researched black history and folk culture. He received an M.A. from the University of Michigan, taught at Fisk University from 1949 until 1969, and then taught at Michigan until his retirement. Although he published ten volumes of poetry, he did not receive acclaim until late in life. His collections include *Heart-Shape in the Dust* (1940), *The Lion and the Archer*, *Figures of Time* (1955), *A Ballad of Remembrance* (1962), *Selected Poems* (1966), *Words in the Mourning Time* (1970), *Night-Blooming Cereus* (1972), *Angle of Ascent* (1975), *American Journal* (1978 and 1982), and *Collected Poems* (1985).

SEAMUS HEANEY
(b. 1939)

Seamus Heaney, whose poems explore themes of rural life, memory, and history, was born on a farm in Mossbawn, County Derry (Castledawson, Londonderry), Northern Ireland. Educated at Queen's University in Belfast, he has taught at the University of California at Berkeley, Carysfort College in Dublin, and Oxford University; he currently teaches at Harvard. Once called by Robert Lowell "the most important Irish poet since Yeats," Heaney received the 1995 Nobel Prize for Literature. His poetry collections include *Eleven Poems* (1965), *Death of a Naturalist* (1966), *Wintering Out* (1972), *The Haw Lantern* (1987), *Seeing Things* (1991), *The Spirit Level* (1996), and *Electric Light* (2001). Heaney's translation of *Beowulf* (2000) from Anglo-Saxon into modern English gave new life to the oldest of English poems; it not only won Britain's prestigious Whitbread Award but also become a best-seller.

ROBERT HERRICK
(1591–1674)

The son of a London goldsmith and his wife, Robert Herrick would have liked nothing better than a life of leisured study, spent discussing literature and drinking sack with his hero, Ben Jonson. Instead, he answered the call of religion, taking holy orders and reluctantly accepting a remote parish in Devonshire. Herrick eventually made himself at home there, inventing dozens of imaginary mistresses with exotic names and practicing, half-seriously, his own peculiar form of paganism. When the Puritans came to power, Herrick was driven from his post to London, where in 1648 he published a volume of over fourteen hundred poems with two titles: *Hesperides* for the secular poems and *Noble Numbers* for those with sacred subjects. The poems did not fit the harsh atmosphere of Puritanism, but after the restoration of the Stuart monarchy in 1660, Herrick was eventually returned to his Devonshire parish, where he lived out his last years quietly.

GERARD MANLEY HOPKINS
(1844–1889)

Born the eldest of eight children of a marine-insurance adjuster and his wife, Gerard Manley Hopkins attended Oxford, where his ambition was to become a painter—until, at the age of 22, he converted to Roman Catholicism and burned all his early poetry as too worldly. Not until after his seminary training and ordination as a Jesuit priest, in 1877, did he resume writing poetry, though he made few attempts to publish his verse, which many of his contemporaries found nearly incomprehensible. Near the end of his life, Hopkins was appointed professor of Greek at University College, Dublin, where—out of place, deeply depressed, and all but unknown—he died of typhoid. His poetry, collected and published by his friends, has been championed by modern poets, who admire its controlled tension, strong rhythm, and sheer exuberance.

LANGSTON HUGHES
(1902–1967)

Born in Joplin, Missouri, Langston Hughes was raised mainly by his maternal grandmother, though he lived intermittently with each of his parents. He studied at Columbia University, but left to travel and work at a variety of jobs. Having already published poems in periodicals, anthologies, and his own first collection, *The Weary Blues* (1926), he graduated from Lincoln University; published a successful novel, *Not without Laughter* (1930); and became a major writer in the intellectual and literary movement called the Harlem Renaissance. During the 1930s, he became involved in radical politics and traveled the world as a correspondent and columnist; during the 1950s, though, the FBI classified him as a security risk and limited his ability to travel. In addition to poems and novels, he wrote essays, plays, screenplays, and an autobiography; he also edited anthologies of literature and folklore. His *Collected Poems* appeared in 1994.

BEN JONSON
(1572?–1637)

Poet, playwright, actor, scholar, critic, and translator, Ben Jonson was the posthumous son of a clergyman and the stepson of a master bricklayer of Westminster. Jonson had an eventful early life, going to war against the Spanish, working as an actor, killing an associate in a duel, and converting to Roman Catholicism. Meanwhile, Jonson wrote a number of plays that have remained popular to this day, including *Every Man in His Humour* (in which Shakespeare acted a leading role; 1598), *Volpone* (1606), and *The Alchemist* (1610). He was named Poet Laureate in 1616 and spent the latter part of his life at the center of a large circle of friends and admirers known as the "Tribe of Ben." Often considered the

first English author to deem writing his primary career, he published *The Works of Benjamin Jonson* in 1616.

JOHN KEATS
(1795–1821)

John Keats was the son of a London livery stable owner and his wife; reviewers would later disparage him as a working-class "Cockney poet." At fifteen he was apprenticed to a surgeon, and at twenty-one he became a licensed pharmacist—in the same year that his first two published poems, including the sonnet "On First Looking into Chapman's Homer," appeared in *The Examiner*, a journal edited by the critic and poet Leigh Hunt. Hunt introduced Keats to such literary figures as the poet Percy Bysshe Shelley and helped him publish *Poems by John Keats* (1817). When his second book, the long poem *Endymion* (1818), was fiercely attacked by critics, Keats, suffering from a steadily worsening case of tuberculosis, knew that he would not live to realize his poetic promise. In July 1820, he published *Lamia, Isabella, The Eve of St. Agnes, and Other Poems,* which contained the poignant "To Autumn" and three great odes: "Ode on a Grecian Urn," "Ode on Melancholy," and "Ode to a Nightingale"; early the next year, he died in Rome. In the years after Keats's death, his letters became almost as famous as his poetry.

GALWAY KINNELL
(b. 1927)

Born in Providence, Rhode Island, Galway Kinnell earned a B.A. from Princeton and an M.A. from the University of Rochester. He served in the navy and has been a journalist, a civil-rights field-worker, and a teacher at numerous colleges and universities. His early poetry, collected in *What a Kingdom It Was* (1960) and *First Poems 1946–1954* (1970), is highly formal; his subsequent work employs a more colloquial style. "Poetry," he has said, "is the attempt to find a language that can speak the unspeakable." He received both a Pulitzer Prize and the American Book Award for *Selected Poems* (1982), and in 2000 he culled *A New Selected Poems* from eight collections spanning twenty-four years. He lives in New York and Vermont.

ANDREW MARVELL
(1621–1678)

The son of a clergyman and his wife, Andrew Marvell was born in Yorkshire, England, and educated at Trinity College, Cambridge. There is no evidence that he fought in the English Civil War, which broke out in 1642, but his poem "An Horatian Ode upon Cromwell's Return from Ireland" appeared in 1650, shortly after the beheading of King Charles I in 1649, and may represent straightforward praise of England's new Puritan leader. Some regard it as strong satire, however—Marvell was known in his day for his satirical prose and verse. Today he is better known for lyric poems, such as the carpe diem manifesto "To His Coy Mistress," which he probably wrote while serving as tutor to a Yorkshire noble's daughter. In 1657, on the recommendation of John Milton, Marvell accepted a position in Cromwell's government that he held until his election to Parliament in 1659. After helping restore the monarchy in 1660, he continued to write and to serve as a member of Parliament until the end of his life.

CLAUDE McKAY
(1889–1948)

Festus Claudis McKay was born and raised in Sunny Ville, Clarendon Parish, Jamaica, the youngest of eleven children. He worked as a wheelwright and cabinetmaker, then briefly as a police constable, before writing and publishing two books of poetry in Jamaican dialect. In 1912, he emigrated to the United States, where he attended Booker T. Washington's Tuskegee Institute in Alabama, studied agricultural science at Kansas State College, and then moved to New York City. McKay sup-

ported himself through various jobs while becoming a prominent literary and political figure. The oldest Harlem Renaissance writer, McKay was also the first to publish, with the poetry collection *Harlem Shadows* (1922); his other works include the novels *Home to Harlem* (1928) and *Banana Bottom* (1933) and his autobiography, *A Long Way from Home* (1937).

EDNA ST. VINCENT MILLAY
(1892–1950)

Born in Rockland, Maine, Edna St. Vincent Millay published her first poem at twenty, her first poetry collection at twenty-five. After graduating from Vassar College, she moved to New York City's Greenwich Village, where, as she gained a reputation as a brilliant poet, she also became notorious for her bohemian life and her association with prominent artists, writers, and radicals. In 1923, she won the Pulitzer Prize for her collection *The Ballad of the Harp-Weaver;* in 1925, growing weary of fame, she and her husband moved to Austerlitz, New York, where she lived for the rest of her life. Although her work fell out of favor with mid-twentieth century modernists, who rejected her formalism as old-fashioned, her poetry—witty, acerbic, and superbly crafted—has found many new admirers today.

JOHN MILTON
(1608–1674)

Born in London, the elder son of a self-made businessman and his wife, John Milton exhibited unusual literary and scholarly gifts at an early age; even before entering Cambridge University, he was adept at Latin and Greek and was well on his way to mastering Hebrew and a number of European languages. After graduation, he spent six more years of intense study and composed, among other works, his great pastoral elegy, "Lycidas" (1637). After a year of travel in Europe, Milton return to England and found his country embroiled in religious strife and civil war. Milton took up the Puritan cause and, in 1641, began writing pamphlets defending everything from free speech to Cromwell's execution of Charles I; Milton also served as Cromwell's Latin secretary until, in 1651, he lost his sight. After the monarchy was restored in 1660, Milton was briefly imprisoned and his property was confiscated. Blind, impoverished, and isolated, he devoted himself to the great spiritual epics of his later years: *Paradise Lost* (1667), *Paradise Regained* (1671), and *Samson Agonistes* (1671).

PAT MORA (b. 1942)

Born to Mexican American parents in El Paso, Texas, Pat Mora earned a B.A. and an M.A. from the University of Texas at El Paso. She has been a consultant on U.S.-Mexico youth exchanges; a museum director and administrator at her alma mater; and a teacher of English at all levels. Her poetry—collected in *Chants* (1985), *Borders* (1986), *Communion* (1991), *Agua Santa* (1995), and *Aunt Carmen's Book of Practical Saints* (1997)—reflects and addresses her Chicana and southwestern background. Mora's other publications include *Nepantla: Essays from the Land in the Middle* (1993); a family memoir, *House of Houses* (1997); and many works for children.

HOWARD NEMEROV
(1920–1991)

Born and raised in New York City, Howard Nemerov graduated from Harvard University, served in the U.S. Army Air Corps during World War II, and returned to New York to complete his first book, *The Image and the Law* (1948). He taught at a number of colleges and universities and published books of poetry, plays, short stories, novels, and essays. His *Collected Poems* won the Pulitzer Prize and the National Book Award in 1978. He served as Consultant in Poetry to the Library of Congress from 1963 to 1964, and Poet Laureate of the United States from 1988 to 1990. *Trying Conclusions: New and Selected Poems 1961–1991* was published in 1991.

SHARON OLDS
(b. 1942)

Born in San Francisco, Sharon Olds earned a B.A. from Stanford University and a Ph.D. from Columbia University. She was founding chair of the Writing Program at Goldwater Hospital (a public facility for the severely physically disabled), and she currently chairs New York University's Creative Writing Program. She has received a National Endowment for the Arts Grant and a Guggenheim Fellowship and was named New York State Poet in 1998. Her books include *Satan Says* (1980); the National Book Critics Circle Award–winning *The Dead and the Living* (1983); *The Gold Cell* (1987); *The Father* (1992); *The Wellspring* (1997); *Blood, Tin, Straw* (1999); and *The Unswept Room*, a National Book Award nominee in 2002.

DOROTHY PARKER
(1893–1967)

Born in West End, New Jersey, Dorothy Rothschild worked for both *Vogue* and *Vanity Fair* magazines before becoming a freelance writer. In 1917, she married Edwin Pond Parker II, whom she divorced in 1928. Her first book of verse, *Enough Rope* (1926), was a best-seller and was followed by *Sunset Gun* (1928), *Death and Taxes* (1931), and *Collected Poems: Not So Deep as a Well* (1936). In 1927, Parker became a book reviewer for *The New Yorker,* to which she contributed for most of her career. In 1933, Parker and her second husband, Alan Campbell, moved to Hollywood, where they collaborated as film writers. In addition, Parker wrote criticism, two plays, short stories, and news reports from the Spanish Civil War. She is probably best remembered, though, as the reigning wit at the "Round Table" at Manhattan's Algonquin Hotel, where, in the 1920s and '30s, she traded barbs with other prominent writers and humorists.

SYLVIA PLATH
(1932–1963)

Sylvia Plath was born in Boston; her father, a Polish immigrant, died when she was eight. After graduating from Smith College, Plath attended Cambridge University on a Fulbright scholarship, and there she met and married the poet Ted Hughes, with whom she had two children. As she documented in her novel *The Bell Jar* (1963), in 1953—between her junior and senior years of college—Plath became seriously depressed, attempted suicide, and was hospitalized. In 1963, the break-up of her marriage led to another suicide attempt, this time successful. Plath has attained cult status as much for her poems as for her "martyrdom" to art and life. In addition to her first volume of poetry, *The Colossus* (1960), Plath's work has been collected in *Ariel* (1966), *Crossing the Water* (1971), and *Winter Trees* (1972). Her selected letters were published in 1975; her expurgated journals, in 1983; and her unabridged journals, in 2000.

EZRA POUND
(1885–1972)

Born in Hailey, Idaho, Ezra Pound studied at the University of Pennsylvania and Hamilton College before traveling to Europe in 1908. He remained there, living in Ireland, England, France, and Italy, for much of his life. Pound's tremendous ambition—to succeed in his own work and to influence the development of poetry and Western culture in general—led him to found the Imagist school of poetry, to advise and assist many great writers (Eliot, Joyce, Williams, Frost, and Hemingway, to name a few), and to write a number of highly influential critical works. His increasingly fiery and erratic behavior led to a charge of treason (he served as a propagandist for Mussolini during World War II), a diagnosis of insanity, and twelve years at St. Elizabeth's, an institution for the criminally insane. His verse is collected in *Personae: The Collected Poems* (1949) and *The Cantos* (1976).

ADRIENNE RICH
(b. 1929)

Adrienne Rich was born in Baltimore. Since the selection of her first volume by W. H. Auden for the Yale Series of Younger Poets (1951), her work has continually evolved, from the tightly controlled early poems to the politically and personally charged verse for which she is known today. Rich's books of poetry include *Collected Early Poems 1950–1970* (1993), *The Dream of a Common Language* (1978), *Your Native Land, Your Life* (1986), *Time's Power* (1988), *An Atlas of the Difficult World* (1991), *Dark Fields of the Republic* (1995), *Midnight Salvage* (1999), *Fox* (2001), and *The School among the Ruins* (2004). Her prose works include *Of Woman Born: Motherhood as Experience and Institution* (1976), *On Lies, Secrets, and Silence* (1979), and *Blood, Bread, and Poetry* (1986), all influential feminist texts; *What Is Found There: Notebooks on Poetry and Politics* (1993); and *Arts of the Possible: Essays and Conversations* (2001). Her many awards include a MacArthur Fellowship and a Lanning Foundation Lifetime Achievement Award.

WILLIAM SHAKESPEARE
(1554–1616)

Considering the great fame of his work, surprisingly little is known of William Shakespeare's life. Between 1585 and 1592, he left his birthplace of Stratford-upon-Avon for London to begin a career as playwright and actor. No dates of his professional career are recorded, however, nor can the order in which he composed his plays and poetry be determined with any certainty. By 1594, he had established himself as a poet with two long works—*Venus and Adonis* and *The Rape of Lucrece*—and his more than 150 sonnets are supreme expressions of the form. His reputation, though, rests on the works he wrote for the theater. Shakespeare produced perhaps thirty-five plays in twenty-five years, proving himself a master of every dramatic genre: tragedy (in works such as *Macbeth, Hamlet, King Lear,* and *Othello*); historical drama (for example, *Richard III* and *Henry IV*); comedy (*Twelfth Night, As You Like It,* and many more); and romance (in plays such as *The Tempest* and *Cymbaline*). Without question, Shakespeare is the most quoted, discussed, and beloved writer in English literature.

WALLACE STEVENS
(1879–1955)

Born and raised in Reading, Pennsylvania, Wallace Stevens attended Harvard University and New York Law School. In New York City, he worked for a number of law firms, published poems in magazines, and befriended such literary figures as William Carlos Williams and Marianne Moore. In 1916, Stevens moved to Connecticut and began working for the Hartford Accident and Indemnity Company, where he became a vice-president in 1934 and where he worked for the rest of his life, writing poetry at night and during vacations. He published his first collection, *Harmonium,* in 1923, and followed it with a series of volumes from 1935 until 1950, establishing himself as one of the twentieth century's most important poets. His lectures were collected in *The Necessary Angel: Essays on Reality and Imagination* (1951); his *Collected Poems* appeared in 1954.

ALFRED, LORD TENNYSON
(1809–1892)

Perhaps the most important and certainly the most popular of the Victorian poets, Alfred, Lord Tennyson demonstrated his talents at an early age; he published his first volume in 1827. Encouraged to devote his life to poetry by a group of undergraduates at Cambridge University known as the "Apostles," Tennyson was particularly close to Arthur Hallam, whose sudden death in 1833 inspired the long elegy *In Memoriam* (1850). With that poem he achieved lasting fame and recognition; he was appointed Poet Laureate the year of its publication, succeeding Wordsworth. Despite the great popularity of his "journalistic" poems—"The Charge of the Light Brigade" (1854) is perhaps the best known—Tennyson's great theme was the past, both personal (*In the Valley of Cauteretz,* 1864) and national (*Idylls of the King,* 1869). Tennyson was made a baron in 1884; when he died, eight years later, he was buried in Poets' Corner in Westminster Abbey.

DYLAN THOMAS
(1914–1953)

Born in Swansea, Wales, into what he called "the smug darkness of a provincial town," Dylan Thomas published his first book, *Eighteen Poems* (1934), at twenty, in the same year that he moved to London. Thereafter he had a successful, though turbulent, career publishing poetry, short stories, and plays, including the highly successful *Under Milk Wood* (1954). In his last years he supported himself with lecture tours and poetry readings in the United States, but his excessive drinking caught up with him and he died in New York City of chronic alcoholism. His *Collected Poems, 1934–1952* (1952) was the last book he published during his short lifetime; his comic novel, *Adventures in the Skin Trade,* was never completed.

DEREK WALCOTT
(b. 1930)

Born of mixed heritage on the West Indian island of St. Lucia, Derek Walcott grew up speaking French and patois but was educated in English. In 1953, he earned his B.A. in English, French, and Latin from the University College of the West Indies in Jamaica. In 1950, with his twin brother, Roderick, he founded the St. Lucia Arts Guild, a dramatic society; nine years later, he founded the Little Carib Theatre Workshop in Trinidad, which he ran until 1976, writing many plays for production there. Walcott has published many volumes of poetry, including *In a Green Night* (1962), *The Castaway* (1965), *Another Life* (1973), *Sea Grapes* (1976), *The Fortunate Traveller* (1981), *Omeros* (1990), *The Bounty* (1997), *Tiepolo's Hound* (2000), and *The Prodigal* (2004). His work draws on diverse influences, from West Indian folk tales to Homer to Yeats. The first Caribbean poet to win the Nobel Prize (in 1992), Walcott now lives and teaches in the United States.

WALT WHITMAN
(1819–1892)

Walt Whitman was born on a farm in West Hills, Long Island, to a British father and a Dutch mother. After working as a journalist throughout New York for many years, he taught for a while and founded his own newspaper, *The Long Islander*, in 1838; he then left journalism to work on *Leaves of Grass*, originally intended as a poetic treatise on American democratic idealism. Published privately in multiple editions from 1855 to 1874, the book at first failed to reach a mass audience. In 1881, Boston's Osgood and Company published another edition of *Leaves of Grass*, which sold well until the district attorney called it "obscene literature" and stipulated that Whitman remove certain poems and phrases. He refused, and it was many years before his works were again published, this time in Philadelphia. By the time Whitman died, his work was revered, as it still is today, for its greatness of spirit and its exuberant American voice.

RICHARD WILBUR
(b. 1921)

Born in New York City and raised in New Jersey, Richard Wilbur received his B.A. from Amherst College and his M.A. from Harvard. He started to write while serving as an army cryptographer during World War II, and his collections *The Beautiful Changes* (1947) and *Ceremony* (1950) established his reputation as a serious poet. In addition to subsequent volumes such as the Pulitzer Prize-winning *Things of This World* (1956), *Walking to Sleep* (1969), *The Mind Reader* (1976), the Pulitzer Prize-winning *New and Collected Poems* (1988), and *Mayflies: New Poems and Translations* (2000), he has published children's books, critical essays, and numerous translations of classic French works by Racine and Molière. He has taught at various colleges and universities, including Harvard, Wellesley, Wesleyan, and Smith. In 1987, he was named Poet Laureate of the United States.

WILLIAM CARLOS WILLIAMS (1883–1963)

Born in Rutherford, New Jersey, William Carlos Williams attended school in Switzerland and New York and studied medicine at the University of Pennsylvania and the University of Leipzig in Germany. He spent most of his life in Rutherford, practicing medicine and gradually establishing himself as one of the great figures in American poetry. Early in his writing career he left the European-inspired Imagist movement in favor of a more uniquely American poetic style comprised of vital, local language and "no ideas but in things." His shorter poems have been published in numerous collected editions and other volumes, including the Pulitzer Prize-winning *Brueghel*, *and Other Poems* (1963); his five-volume philosophical poem, *Paterson,* was published in 1963. Among his other works are plays such as *A Dream of Love* (1948) and *Many Loves* (1950); a trilogy of novels: *White Mules* (1937), *In the Money* (1940), and *The Build-Up* (1952); his *Autobiography* (1951); his *Selected Essays* (1954); and his *Selected Letters* (1957).

WILLIAM WORDSWORTH (1770–1850)

Regarded by many as the greatest of the Romantic poets, William Wordsworth was born in Cockermouth in the English Lake District, a beautiful, mountainous region that figured as a deep inspiration for his poetry. He studied at Cambridge and then spent a year in France, hoping to witness the French Revolution firsthand; as the Revolution's "glorious renovation" dissolved into anarchy and then tyranny, Wordsworth was forced to return to England. Remarkably, he managed to establish "a saving intercourse with my true self" and to write some of his finest poetry, including the early version of his masterpiece, *The Prelude,* which first appeared in 1805 and then again, much altered, in 1850. In 1798, Wordsworth and his friend Samuel Taylor Coleridge published *Lyrical Ballads,* which contained many of their greatest poems and can be considered the founding document of English Romanticism. Wordsworth was revered by the reading public and in 1843 was named Poet Laureate.

WILLIAM BUTLER YEATS (1865–1939)

William Butler Yeats was born in Dublin and, though he spent most of his youth in London, became the pre-eminent Irish poet of the twentieth century. Immersed in Irish history, folklore, and politics, as well as spiritualism and the occult, he attended art school for a time, but left to devote himself to poetry that was, early in his career, self-consciously dreamy and ethereal. Yeats's poems became tighter and more passionate with his reading of philosophers such as Nietzsche, his involvement (mainly through theater) with the Irish nationalist cause, and his desperate love for the actress and nationalist Maud Gonne. He was briefly a senator in the newly independent Irish government before withdrawing from active public life to Thoor Ballylee, a crumbling Norman tower that Yeats and his wife fashioned into a home. There he developed an elaborate mythology (published as *A Vision* in 1925) and wrote poems that explored fundamental questions of history and identity. He was awarded the Nobel Prize for Literature in 1923. His works, in many genres, have been selected and collected in various editions.

DRAMA

Drama

Drama: Reading, Responding, Writing

As we noted in our introduction, many cultures have had oral literatures: histories, romances, poems to be recited or sung. Our own era has its share of oral art forms, of course, but "literary" fiction and poetry are now most often read privately, silently, from the printed page. Most contemporary fiction writers and poets write with an understanding that this is how their work will be experienced and enjoyed.

In contrast, **drama** is written primarily to be performed—by actors, on a stage, for an audience. Playwrights work with an understanding that the words on the page are just the first step—a map of sorts—toward the ultimate goal: a collaborative, publicly performed work of art. They create plays fully aware of the possibilities that go beyond printed words and extend to physical actions, stage devices, and other theatrical techniques for creating special effects and modifying our responses. Although the script of a play may be the most essential piece in the puzzle that makes up the final work of art, the play text is not the final, complete work.

> *On the stage it is always now; the personages are standing on that razor-edge, between the past and the future, which is the essential character of conscious being; the words are rising to their lips in immediate spontaneity.*
>
> —THORNTON WILDER

To attend a play—to be part of an audience—represents a very different kind of experience from the usually solitary act of reading. On the stage, real human beings, standing for imaginary characters, deliver lines and perform actions for you to see and hear. In turn, the actors adapt in subtle ways to the reactions of the people who attend the performance, and whose responses are no longer wholly private but have become, in part, communal.

When you attend the performance of a play, then, you become a collaborator in the creation of a unique work of art: not the play *text,* but instead a specific *interpretation* of that text. The play has been *mediated* by all the people involved in a particular production—the director, producers, actors, and designers of lighting, set, sound, costume, makeup—who help to interpret the author's text. These mediators have made decisions about how to convey the meaning and spirit of the play, and they perform for viewers part of the act of imagination that readers of a story or a poem must perform for themselves. Consciously or not, every director interprets every scene by the way he or she stages the action; casting, set design, the "blocking" or physical interaction of the actors, and the timing, phrasing, and tone of every speech affect how the play comes across. Every syllable uttered by every actor in some sense reshapes the play; the delivery of lines and even the slightest gestures correspond, for an actor, to the choices of words and sentence rhythms for a writer. With so many fine details affecting the outcome, it's inevitable that no two performances of a play can ever be identical.

Similarly, no two interpretations of a play can be exactly the same. We speak of "Olivier's Hamlet" (meaning the performance of the title role by Sir Laurence Olivier), of "Dame Maggie Smith's" or "Glenda Jackson's Hedda Gabler," or of "Baz Luhrmann's *Romeo and Juliet*" (meaning the film directed by Luhrmann), because in each case the actor or director creates a distinctive interpretation of the play. In the written text Hamlet may seem indecisive, melancholy, conniving, mad, vindictive, ambitious, or some combination of these qualities; individual performances emphasize one attribute or another, inevitably by downplaying other characteristics and interpretations. No play can be all things in any one performance or run (all the performances of a particular production).

The power of the best plays to be interpreted in so many ways, and the complementary limitation of the performed play (its necessary exclusion of many possible interpretations) once led the nineteenth-century writer Charles Lamb to come home from the theater vowing never to see another play of Shakespeare's on the stage. He found that no matter how good the performance, the enacted play restricted his imagination and robbed the play of some of the richness he found in reading it—and imagining it—for himself. Without having to renounce the theater as Lamb did or deprive ourselves of the thrilling experience of a brilliantly directed and performed interpretation of a play, we agree with Lamb that reading a play, rather than being a poor substitute for attending a performance, gives us an opportunity to be creative and collaborative in ways that are different from the ways we read a story or a poem.

In some respects, of course, reading drama is similar to reading fiction. In both cases we anticipate what will happen next; we imagine the characters, settings, and actions; we respond to the symbolic suggestiveness of images; and we notice thematic patterns that are likely to matter in the end. The chief difference between narrative fiction and drama on the page is the absence, in drama, of a mediator or narrator, someone standing between the reader and the events to help us relate to the characters, actions, and meanings. Description in drama is usually limited to a few **stage directions**— the italicized descriptions of the set, characters, and actions—while **exposition**—the explanation of the past and current situation—emerges only here and there in the dialogue.

For this reason, reading drama may place a greater demand on the imagination than reading fiction does: the reader must be his or her own narrator and interpreter. Such an exercise for the imagination can prove rewarding, however, for it has much in common with the imaginative work that a director, actors, and other artists involved in a staged production bring to their performance of a play. Recreating a play as we read it, we are essentially imagining the play as if it were being performed by live actors in real time.

The dream is the theater where the dreamer is at once scene, actor, prompter, stage manager, author, audience, and critic.

—C. G. JUNG

We "cast" the characters, we design the set with its furniture and props, and we choreograph or "block" the physical action, according to the cues in the text.

Those cues, of course, can be few and far between. Stage directions, which were rare in plays before the later nineteenth century, seldom spell out many details of the lighting, costume design, or other effects that live audiences see. Susan Glaspell assumes directors or readers will easily re-create a standard realistic set for her play, *Trifles*: the kitchen of a farmhouse in the early twentieth century, one that is partially heated by a coal stove and not yet wired for a party-line telephone. Obviously, both of these one-act plays allow directors, actors, and readers considerable discretion in fleshing out the skeleton of the script. Making the most of this freedom is one of the unique pleasures of reading drama.

In reading drama even more than in reading fiction, we construct our ideas of character and personality from what a character says. In some plays, especially those with a modernist or experimental bent, certain lines of dialogue can be mystifying; other characters and the audience or readers can be left wondering what a speech meant. On the one hand, such puzzling lines can become clearer in performance, in which actors physically express the intentions and interactions of the characters. On the other hand, plays that call for several characters to speak at once or to talk at cross purposes can be much easier to understand from the printed script than in performance. In interpreting dialogue, you will naturally draw on your own experiences of comparable situations or similar personalities, as well as your familiarity with other plays or stories.

As you read scene by scene, you should not only make mental or written notes about your expectations, but you should raise some of the questions an actor might ask in preparing a role, or a director might ask before choosing a cast: How should this line be spoken? What kind of person is this character and what are his or her motives in each scene? What does the play imply or state about what made the character this way—family, environment, experience? Which characters are present or absent (onstage or off) in which scenes, and how do the characters onstage or off influence each other? What are characters aware of and what is the audience aware of? When and how does the audience know something that the characters don't? With these sorts of questions in mind, you may want to read the following short play now. In the discussion that follows the play text, we will trace stages of a first reading, but we necessarily reveal something of the ending. You will want to enjoy on your own the experience of a first reading when you don't yet know what will happen.

SUSAN GLASPELL

Trifles

CHARACTERS

SHERIFF	MRS. PETERS, *Sheriff's wife*
COUNTY ATTORNEY	MRS. HALE
HALE	

SCENE: *The kitchen in the now abandoned farmhouse of* JOHN WRIGHT, *a gloomy kitchen, and left without having been put in order—unwashed pans under the sink, a loaf of bread outside the bread-box, a dish-towel on the table—other signs of incompleted work. At the rear the outer door opens and the* SHERIFF *comes in followed by the* COUNTY ATTORNEY *and* HALE. *The* SHERIFF *and* HALE *are men in middle life, the* COUNTY ATTORNEY *is a young man; all are much bundled up and go at once to the stove. They are followed by the two women—the* SHERIFF'S *wife first; she is a slight wiry woman, a thin nervous face.* MRS. HALE *is larger and would ordinarily be called more comfortable looking, but she is disturbed now and looks fearfully about as she enters. The women have come in slowly, and stand close together near the door.*

COUNTY ATTORNEY: [*Rubbing his hands.*] This feels good. Come up to the fire, ladies.

MRS. PETERS: [*After taking a step forward.*] I'm not—cold.

SHERIFF: [*Unbuttoning his overcoat and stepping away from the stove as if to mark the beginning of official business.*] Now, Mr. Hale, before we move things about, you explain to Mr. Henderson just what you saw when you came here yesterday morning.

COUNTY ATTORNEY: By the way, has anything been moved? Are things just as you left them yesterday?

SHERIFF: [*Looking about.*] It's just the same. When it dropped below zero last night I thought I'd better send Frank out this morning to make a fire for us—no use getting pneumonia with a big case on, but I told him not to touch anything except the stove—and you know Frank.

COUNTY ATTORNEY: Somebody should have been left here yesterday.

SHERIFF: Oh—yesterday. When I had to send Frank to Morris Center for that man who went crazy—I want you to know I had my hands full yesterday. I knew you could get back from Omaha by today and as long as I went over everything here myself—

COUNTY ATTORNEY: Well, Mr. Hale, tell just what happened when you came here yesterday morning.

HALE: Harry and I had started to town with a load of potatoes. We came along the road from my place and as I got here I said, "I'm going to see if I can't get John Wright to go in with me on a party telephone." I spoke to Wright about it once before and he put me off, saying folks talked too much anyway, and all he asked was peace and quiet—I guess you know about how much he talked himself; but I thought maybe if I went to the house and talked about it before his wife, though I said to Harry that I didn't know as what his wife wanted made much difference to John—

COUNTY ATTORNEY: Let's talk about that later, Mr. Hale. I do want to talk about that, but tell now just what happened when you got to the house.

HALE: I didn't hear or see anything; I knocked at the door, and still it was all quiet inside. I knew they must be up, it was past eight o'clock. So I knocked again, and I thought I heard somebody say, "Come in." I wasn't sure, I'm not sure yet, but I opened the door—this door [*Indicating the door by which the two women are still standing.*] and there in that rocker— [*Pointing to it.*] sat Mrs. Wright.

[*They all look at the rocker.*]

COUNTY ATTORNEY: What—was she doing?

HALE: She was rockin' back and forth. She had her apron in her hand and was kind of—pleating it.

COUNTY ATTORNEY: And how did she—look?

HALE: Well, she looked queer.

COUNTY ATTORNEY: How do you mean—queer?

HALE: Well, as if she didn't know what she was going to do next. And kind of done up.

COUNTY ATTORNEY: How did she seem to feel about your coming?

HALE: Why, I don't think she minded—one way or other. She didn't pay much attention. I said, "How do, Mrs. Wright, it's cold, ain't it?" And she said, "Is it?"—and went on kind of pleating at her apron. Well, I was surprised; she didn't ask me to come up to the stove, or to set down, but just sat there, not even looking at me, so I said, "I want to see John." And then she—laughed. I guess you would call it a laugh. I thought of Harry and the team outside, so I said a little sharp: "Can't I see John?" "No," she says, kind o' dull like. "Ain't he home?" says I. "Yes," says she, "he's home." "Then why can't I see him?" I asked her, out of patience. " 'Cause he's dead," says she. "*Dead?*" says I. She just nodded her head, not getting a bit excited, but rockin' back and forth. "Why—where is he?" says I, not knowing what to say. She just pointed upstairs—like that. [*Himself pointing to the room above.*] I got up, with the idea of going up there. I walked from there to here—then I says, "Why, what did he die of?" "He died of a rope round his neck," says she, and just went on pleatin' at her apron. Well, I went out and called Harry. I thought I might—need help. We went upstairs and there he was lyin'—

COUNTY ATTORNEY: I think I'd rather have you go into that upstairs, where you can point it all out. Just go on now with the rest of the story.

HALE: Well, my first thought was to get that rope off. It looked . . . [*Stops, his face twitches.*] . . . but Harry, he went up to him, and he said, "No, he's dead all right, and we'd better not touch anything." So we went back down stairs. She was still sitting that same way. "Has anybody been notified?" I asked. "No," says she unconcerned. "Who did this, Mrs. Wright?" said Harry. He said it business-like—and she stopped pleatin' of her apron. "I don't know," she says. "You don't *know?*" says Harry.

"No," says she. "Weren't you sleepin' in the bed with him?" says Harry. "Yes," says she, "but I was on the inside." "Somebody slipped a rope round his neck and strangled him and you didn't wake up?" says Harry. "I didn't wake up," she said after him. We must 'a looked as if we didn't see how that could be, for after a minute she said, "I sleep sound." Harry was going to ask her more questions but I said maybe we ought to let her tell her story first to the coroner, or the sheriff, so Harry went fast as he could to Rivers' place, where there's a telephone.

COUNTY ATTORNEY: And what did Mrs. Wright do when she knew that you had gone for the coroner?

HALE: She moved from that chair to this one over here [*Pointing to a small chair in the corner.*] and just sat there with her hands held together and looking down. I got a feeling that I ought to make some conversation, so I said I had come in to see if John wanted to put in a telephone, and at that she started to laugh, and then she stopped and looked at me—scared. [*The* COUNTY ATTORNEY, *who has had his notebook out, makes a note.*] I dunno, maybe it wasn't scared. I wouldn't like to say it was. Soon Harry got back, and then Dr. Lloyd came, and you, Mr. Peters, and so I guess that's all I know that you don't.

COUNTY ATTORNEY: [*Looking around.*] I guess we'll go upstairs first—and then out to the barn and around there. [*To the* SHERIFF.] You're convinced that there was nothing important here—nothing that would point to any motive?

SHERIFF: Nothing here but kitchen things.

[*The* COUNTY ATTORNEY, *after again looking around the kitchen, opens the door of a cupboard closet. He gets up on a chair and looks on a shelf. Pulls his hand away, sticky.*]

COUNTY ATTORNEY: Here's a nice mess.

[*The women draw nearer.*]

MRS. PETERS: [*To the other woman.*] Oh, her fruit; it did freeze. [*To the* LAWYER.] She worried about that when it turned so cold. She said the fire'd go out and her jars would break.

SHERIFF: Well, can you beat the women! Held for murder and worryin' about her preserves.

COUNTY ATTORNEY: I guess before we're through she may have something more serious than preserves to worry about.

HALE: Well, women are used to worrying over trifles.

[*The two women move a little closer together.*]

COUNTY ATTORNEY: [*With the gallantry of a young politician.*] And yet, for all their worries, what would we do without the ladies? [*The women do not unbend. He goes to the sink, takes a dipperful of water from the pail and pouring it into a basin, washes his hands. Starts to wipe them on the roller towel, turns it for a cleaner place.*] Dirty towels! [*Kicks his foot against the pans under the sink.*] Not much of a housekeeper, would you say, ladies?

MRS. HALE: [*Stiffly.*] There's a great deal of work to be done on a farm.

COUNTY ATTORNEY: To be sure. And yet [*With a little bow to her.*] I know there are some Dickson county farmhouses which do not have such roller towels. [*He gives it a pull to expose its length again.*]

MRS. HALE: Those towels get dirty awful quick. Men's hands aren't always as clean as they might be.

COUNTY ATTORNEY: Ah, loyal to your sex, I see. But you and Mrs. Wright were neighbors. I suppose you were friends, too.

MRS. HALE: [*Shaking her head.*] I've not seen much of her of late years. I've not been in this house—it's more than a year.

COUNTY ATTORNEY: And why was that? You didn't like her?

MRS. HALE: I liked her all well enough. Farmers' wives have their hands full, Mr. Henderson. And then—

COUNTY ATTORNEY: Yes—?

MRS. HALE: [*Looking about.*] It never seemed a very cheerful place.

COUNTY ATTORNEY: No—it's not cheerful. I shouldn't say she had the homemaking instinct.

MRS. HALE: Well, I don't know as Wright had, either.

COUNTY ATTORNEY: You mean that they didn't get on very well?

MRS. HALE: No, I don't mean anything. But I don't think a place'd be any cheerfuller for John Wright's being in it.

COUNTY ATTORNEY: I'd like to talk more of that a little later. I want to get the lay of things upstairs now. [*He goes to the left, where three steps lead to a stair door.*]

SHERIFF: I suppose anything Mrs. Peters does'll be all right. She was to take in some clothes for her, you know, and a few little things. We left in such a hurry yesterday.

COUNTY ATTORNEY: Yes, but I would like to see what you take, Mrs. Peters, and keep an eye out for anything that might be of use to us.

MRS. PETERS: Yes, Mr. Henderson. [*The women listen to the men's steps on the stairs, then look about the kitchen.*]

MRS. HALE: I'd hate to have men coming into my kitchen, snooping around and criticizing. [*She arranges the pans under sink which the LAWYER had shoved out of place.*]

MRS. PETERS: Of course it's no more than their duty.

MRS. HALE: Duty's all right, but I guess that deputy sheriff that came out to make the fire might have got a little of this on. [*Gives the roller towel a pull.*] Wish I'd thought of that sooner. Seems mean to talk about her for not having things slicked up when she had to come away in such a hurry.

MRS. PETERS: [*Who has gone to a small table in the left rear corner of the room, and lifted one end of a towel that covers a pan.*] She had bread set. [*Stands still.*]

MRS. HALE: [*Eyes fixed on a loaf of bread beside the bread box, which is on a low shelf at the other side of the room. Moves slowly toward it.*] She was going to put this in there. [*Picks up loaf, then abruptly drops it. In a manner of returning to familiar things.*] It's a shame about her fruit. I wonder if it's all gone. [*Gets up on the chair and looks.*] I think there's some here that's all right,

Mrs. Peters. Yes—here; [*Holding it toward the window.*] this is cherries, too. [*Looking again.*] I declare I believe that's the only one. [*Gets down, bottle in her hand. Goes to the sink and wipes it off on the outside.*] She'll feel awful bad after all her hard work in the hot weather. I remember the afternoon I put up my cherries last summer. [*She puts the bottle on the big kitchen table, center of the room. With a sigh, is about to sit down in the rocking-chair. Before she is seated realizes what chair it is; with a slow look at it, steps back. The chair, which she has touched, rocks back and forth.*]

MRS. PETERS: Well, I must get those things from the front room closet. [*She goes to the door at the right, but after looking into the other room, steps back.*] You coming with me, Mrs. Hale? You could help me carry them. [*They go in the other room; reappear,* MRS. PETERS *carrying a dress and skirt,* MRS. HALE *following with a pair of shoes.*] My, it's cold in there. [*She puts the clothes on the big table, and hurries to the stove.*]

MRS. HALE: [*Examining the skirt.*] Wright was close. I think maybe that's why she kept so much to herself. She didn't even belong to the Ladies Aid. I suppose she felt she couldn't do her part, and then you don't enjoy things when you feel shabby. She used to wear pretty clothes and be lively, when she was Minnie Foster, one of the town girls singing in the choir. But that—oh, that was thirty years ago. This all you was to take in?

MRS. PETERS: She said she wanted an apron. Funny thing to want, for there isn't much to get you dirty in jail, goodness knows. But I suppose just to make her feel more natural. She said they was in the top drawer in this cupboard. Yes, here. And then her little shawl that always hung behind the door. [*Opens stair door and looks.*] Yes, here it is. [*Quickly shuts door leading upstairs.*]

MRS. HALE: [*Abruptly moving toward her.*] Mrs. Peters?

MRS. PETERS: Yes, Mrs. Hale?

MRS. HALE: Do you think she did it?

MRS. PETERS: [*In a frightened voice.*] Oh, I don't know.

MRS. HALE: Well, I don't think she did. Asking for an apron and her little shawl. Worrying about her fruit.

MRS. PETERS: [*Starts to speak, glances up, where footsteps are heard in the room above. In a low voice.*] Mr. Peters says it looks bad for her. Mr. Henderson is awful sarcastic in a speech and he'll make fun of her sayin' she didn't wake up.

MRS. HALE: Well, I guess John Wright didn't wake when they was slipping that rope under his neck.

MRS. PETERS: No, it's strange. It must have been done awful crafty and still. They say it was such a—funny way to kill a man, rigging it all up like that.

MRS. HALE: That's just what Mr. Hale said. There was a gun in the house. He says that's what he can't understand.

MRS. PETERS: Mr. Henderson said coming out that what was needed for the case was a motive; something to show anger, or—sudden feeling.

MRS. HALE: [*Who is standing by the table.*] Well, I don't see any signs of anger around here. [*She puts her hand on the dish towel which lies on the table, stands looking down at table, one half of which is clean, the other half messy.*] It's wiped to here. [*Makes a move as if to finish work, then turns and looks at loaf of bread outside the bread box. Drops towel. In that voice of coming back to familiar things.*] Wonder how they are finding things upstairs. I hope she had it a little more red-up[1] up there. You know, it seems kind of *sneaking*. Locking her up in town and then coming out here and trying to get her own house to turn against her!

MRS. PETERS: But Mrs. Hale, the law is the law.

MRS. HALE: I s'pose 'tis. [*Unbuttoning her coat.*] Better loosen up your things, Mrs. Peters. You won't feel them when you go out.

[MRS. PETERS *takes off her fur tippet, goes to hang it on hook at back of room, stands looking at the under part of the small corner table.*]

MRS. PETERS: She was piecing a quilt. [*She brings the large sewing basket and they look at the bright pieces.*]

MRS. HALE: It's log cabin pattern. Pretty, isn't it? I wonder if she was goin' to quilt it or just knot it?

[*Footsteps have been heard coming down the stairs. The* SHERIFF *enters followed by* HALE *and the* COUNTY ATTORNEY.]

SHERIFF: They wonder if she was going to quilt it or just knot it!

[*The men laugh, the women look abashed.*]

COUNTY ATTORNEY: [*Rubbing his hands over the stove.*] Frank's fire didn't do much up there, did it? Well, let's go out to the barn and get that cleared up.

[*The men go outside.*]

MRS. HALE: [*Resentfully.*] I don't know as there's anything so strange, our takin' up our time with little things while we're waiting for them to get the evidence. [*She sits down at the big table smoothing out a block with decision.*] I don't see as it's anything to laugh about.

MRS. PETERS: [*Apologetically.*] Of course they've got awful important things on their minds. [*Pulls up a chair and joins* MRS. HALE *at the table.*]

MRS. HALE: [*Examining another block.*] Mrs. Peters, look at this one. Here, this is the one she was working on, and look at the sewing! All the rest of it has been so nice and even. And look at this! It's all over the place! Why, it looks as if she didn't know what she was about! [*After she has said this they look at each other, then start to glance back at the door. After an instant* MRS. HALE *has pulled at a knot and ripped the sewing.*]

MRS. PETERS: Oh, what are you doing, Mrs. Hale?

MRS. HALE: [*Mildly.*] Just pulling out a stitch or two that's not sewed very good. [*Threading the needle.*] Bad sewing always made me fidgety.

MRS. PETERS: [*Nervously.*] I don't think we ought to touch things.

---

1. Tidied up.

MRS. HALE: I'll just finish up this end. [*Suddenly stopping and leaning forward.*] Mrs. Peters?

MRS. PETERS: Yes, Mrs. Hale?

MRS. HALE: What do you suppose she was so nervous about?

MRS. PETERS: Oh—I don't know. I don't know as she was nervous. I sometimes sew awful queer when I'm just tired. [MRS. HALE *starts to say something, looks at* MRS. PETERS, *then goes on sewing.*] Well I must get these things wrapped up. They may be through sooner than we think. [*Putting apron and other things together.*] I wonder where I can find a piece of paper, and string.

MRS. HALE: In that cupboard, maybe.

MRS. PETERS: [*Looking in cupboard.*] Why, here's a bird-cage. [*Holds it up.*] Did she have a bird, Mrs. Hale?

MRS. HALE: Why, I don't know whether she did or not—I've not been here for so long. There was a man around last year selling canaries cheap, but I don't know as she took one; maybe she did. She used to sing real pretty herself.

MRS. PETERS: [*Glancing around.*] Seems funny to think of a bird here. But she must have had one, or why would she have a cage? I wonder what happened to it.

MRS. HALE: I s'pose maybe the cat got it.

MRS. PETERS: No, she didn't have a cat. She's got that feeling some people have about cats—being afraid of them. My cat got in her room and she was real upset and asked me to take it out.

MRS. HALE: My sister Bessie was like that. Queer, ain't it?

MRS. PETERS: [*Examining the cage.*] Why, look at this door. It's broke. One hinge is pulled apart.

MRS. HALE: [*Looking too.*] Looks as if someone must have been rough with it.

MRS. PETERS: Why, yes. [*She brings the cage forward and puts it on the table.*]

MRS. HALE: I wish if they're going to find any evidence they'd be about it. I don't like this place.

MRS. PETERS: But I'm awful glad you came with me, Mrs. Hale. It would be lonesome for me sitting here alone.

MRS. HALE: It would, wouldn't it? [*Dropping her sewing.*] But I tell you what I do wish, Mrs. Peters. I wish I had come over sometimes when *she* was here. I—[*Looking around the room.*]—wish I had.

MRS. PETERS: But of course you were awful busy, Mrs. Hale—your house and your children.

MRS. HALE: I could've come. I stayed away because it weren't cheerful—and that's why I ought to have come. I—I've never liked this place. Maybe because it's down in a hollow and you don't see the road. I dunno what it is, but it's a lonesome place and always was. I wish I had come over to see Minnie Foster sometimes. I can see now—[*Shakes her head.*]

MRS. PETERS: Well, you mustn't reproach yourself, Mrs. Hale. Somehow we just don't see how it is with other folks until—something comes up.

MRS. HALE: Not having children makes less work—but it makes a quiet house, and Wright out to work all day, and no company when he did come in. Did you know John Wright, Mrs. Peters?

MRS. PETERS: Not to know him; I've seen him in town. They say he was a good man.

MRS. HALE: Yes—good; he didn't drink, and kept his word as well as most, I guess, and paid his debts. But he was a hard man, Mrs. Peters. Just to pass the time of day with him—[*Shivers.*] Like a raw wind that gets to the bone. [*Pauses, her eye falling on the cage.*] I should think she would 'a wanted a bird. But what do you suppose went with it?

MRS. PETERS: I don't know, unless it got sick and died. [*She reaches over and swings the broken door, swings it again, both women watch it.*]

MRS. HALE: You weren't raised round here, were you? [MRS. PETERS *shakes her head.*] You didn't know—her?

MRS. PETERS: Not till they brought her yesterday.

MRS. HALE: She—come to think of it, she was kind of like a bird herself—real sweet and pretty, but kind of timid and—fluttery. How—she—did—change. [*Silence; then as if struck by a happy thought and relieved to get back to everyday things.*] Tell you what, Mrs. Peters, why don't you take the quilt in with you? It might take up her mind.

MRS. PETERS: Why, I think that's a real nice idea, Mrs. Hale. There couldn't possibly be any objection to it, could there? Now, just what would I take? I wonder if her patches are in here—and her things. [*They look in the sewing basket.*]

MRS. HALE: Here's some red. I expect this has got sewing things in it. [*Brings out a fancy box.*] What a pretty box. Looks like something somebody would give you. Maybe her scissors are in here. [*Opens box. Suddenly puts her hand to her nose.*] Why—[MRS. PETERS *bends nearer, then turns her face away.*] There's something wrapped up in this piece of silk.

MRS. PETERS: Why, this isn't her scissors.

MRS. HALE: [*Lifting the silk.*] Oh, Mrs. Peters—it's—

[MRS. PETERS *bends closer.*]

MRS. PETERS: It's the bird.

MRS. HALE: [*Jumping up.*] But, Mrs. Peters—look at it! Its neck! Look at its neck! It's all—other side *to.*

MRS. PETERS: Somebody—wrung—its—neck.

[*Their eyes meet. A look of growing comprehension, of horror. Steps are heard outside.* MRS. HALE *slips box under quilt pieces, and sinks into her chair. Enter* SHERIFF *and* COUNTY ATTORNEY. MRS. PETERS *rises.*]

COUNTY ATTORNEY: [*As one turning from serious things to little pleasantries.*] Well ladies, have you decided whether she was going to quilt it or knot it?

MRS. PETERS: We think she was going to—knot it.

COUNTY ATTORNEY: Well, that's interesting, I'm sure. [*Seeing the bird-cage.*] Has the bird flown?

MRS. HALE: [*Putting more quilt pieces over the box.*] We think the—cat got it.

COUNTY ATTORNEY: [*Preoccupied.*] Is there a cat?

[MRS. HALE *glances in a quick covert way at* MRS. PETERS.]

MRS. PETERS: Well, not *now.* They're superstitious, you know. They leave.

COUNTY ATTORNEY: [*To* SHERIFF PETERS, *continuing an interrupted conversation.*] No sign at all of anyone having come from the outside. Their own rope. Now let's go up again and go over it piece by piece. [*They start upstairs.*] It would have to have been someone who knew just the—

[MRS. PETERS *sits down. The two women sit there not looking at one another, but as if peering into something and at the same time holding back. When they talk now it is in the manner of feeling their way over strange ground, as if afraid of what they are saying, but as if they cannot help saying it.*]

MRS. HALE: She liked the bird. She was going to bury it in that pretty box.

MRS. PETERS: [*In a whisper.*] When I was a girl—my kitten—there was a boy took a hatchet, and before my eyes—and before I could get there—[*Covers her face an instant.*] If they hadn't held me back I would have—[*Catches herself, looks upstairs where steps are heard, falters weakly.*]—hurt him.

MRS. HALE: [*With a slow look around her.*] I wonder how it would seem never to have had any children around. [*Pause.*] No, Wright wouldn't like the bird—a thing that sang. She used to sing. He killed that, too.

MRS. PETERS: [*Moving uneasily.*] We don't know who killed the bird.

MRS. HALE: I knew John Wright.

MRS. PETERS: It was an awful thing was done in this house that night, Mrs. Hale. Killing a man while he slept, slipping a rope around his neck that choked the life out of him.

MRS. HALE: His neck. Choked the life out of him. [*Her hand goes out and rests on the bird-cage.*]

MRS. PETERS: [*With rising voice.*] We don't know who killed him. We don't *know.*

MRS. HALE: [*Her own feeling not interrupted.*] If there's been years and years of nothing, then a bird to sing to you, it would be awful—still, after the bird was still.

MRS. PETERS: [*Something within her speaking.*] I know what stillness is. When we homesteaded in Dakota, and my first baby died—after he was two years old, and me with no other then—

MRS. HALE: [*Moving.*] How soon do you suppose they'll be through, looking for the evidence?

MRS. PETERS: I know what stillness is. [*Pulling herself back.*] The law has got to punish crime, Mrs. Hale.

MRS. HALE: [*Not as if answering that.*] I wish you'd seen Minnie Foster when she wore a white dress with blue ribbons and stood up there in the choir and sang. [*A look around the room.*] Oh, I *wish* I'd come over here once in a while! That was a crime! That was a crime! Who's going to punish that?

MRS. PETERS: [*Looking upstairs.*] We mustn't—take on.

MRS. HALE: I might have known she needed help! I know how things can be—for women. I tell you, it's queer, Mrs. Peters. We live close together and we live far apart. We all go through the same things—it's all just a different kind of the same thing. [*Brushes her eyes, noticing the bottle of fruit, reaches out for it.*] If I was you, I wouldn't tell her her fruit was gone. Tell her it *ain't*. Tell her it's all right. Take this in to prove it to her. She—she may never know whether it was broke or not.

MRS. PETERS: [*Takes the bottle, looks about for something to wrap it in; takes petticoat from the clothes brought from the other room, very nervously begins winding this around the bottle. In a false voice.*] My, it's a good thing the men couldn't hear us. Wouldn't they just laugh! Getting all stirred up over a little thing like a—dead canary. As if that could have anything to do with—with—wouldn't they *laugh!*

[*The men are heard coming down stairs.*]

MRS. HALE: [*Under her breath.*] Maybe they would—maybe they wouldn't.

COUNTY ATTORNEY: No, Peters, it's all perfectly clear except a reason for doing it. But you know juries when it comes to women. If there was some definite thing. Something to show—something to make a story about—a thing that would connect up with this strange way of doing it—

[*The women's eyes meet for an instant. Enter* HALE *from outer door.*]

HALE: Well, I've got the team around. Pretty cold out there.

COUNTY ATTORNEY: I'm going to stay here a while by myself. [*To the* SHERIFF.] You can send Frank out for me, can't you? I want to go over everything. I'm not satisfied that we can't do better.

SHERIFF: Do you want to see what Mrs. Peters is going to take in?

[*The* LAWYER *goes to the table, picks up the apron, laughs.*]

COUNTY ATTORNEY: Oh, I guess they're not very dangerous things the ladies have picked out. [*Moves a few things about, disturbing the quilt pieces which cover the box. Steps back.*] No, Mrs. Peters doesn't need supervising. For that matter, a sheriff's wife is married to the law. Ever think of it that way, Mrs. Peters?

MRS. PETERS: Not—just that way.

SHERIFF: [*Chuckling.*] Married to the law. [*Moves toward the other room.*] I just want you to come in here a minute, George. We ought to take a look at these windows.

COUNTY ATTORNEY: [*Scoffingly.*] Oh, windows!

SHERIFF: We'll be right out, Mr. Hale.

[HALE *goes outside. The* SHERIFF *follows the* COUNTY ATTORNEY *into the other room. Then* MRS. HALE *rises, hands tight together, looking intensely at* MRS. PETERS, *whose eyes make a slow turn, finally meeting* MRS. HALE's. *A moment* MRS. HALE *holds her, then her own eyes point the way to where the box is concealed. Suddenly* MRS. PETERS *throws back quilt pieces and tries to put the box in the bag she is wearing. It is too big. She opens box, starts to take bird out, cannot touch it, goes to pieces, stands there helpless. Sound of a knob turning in the other room.* MRS. HALE *snatches the box and puts it in the pocket of her big coat. Enter* COUNTY ATTORNEY *and* SHERIFF.]

COUNTY ATTORNEY: [*Facetiously.*] Well, Henry, at least we found out that she was not going to quilt it. She was going to—what is it you call it, ladies?

MRS. HALE: [*Her hand against her pocket.*] We call it—knot it, Mr. Henderson.

CURTAIN

1916

A title is always a key to an interpretation. Does the title "*Trifles*" lead you to expect a light comedy, something "trifling"? The list of characters that follows Glaspell's title, however, includes a sheriff and a county attorney along with some common Anglo American names, suggesting a serious situation involving the law (compare these ordinary names with Stoppard's inventions of an inspector named Hound, or a housekeeper named Drudge, which is another word for a servant). A few lines into Glaspell's play, the county attorney asks Mr. Hale if "things are just as you left them," and then asks him to "tell just what happened." Probably most readers expect at this point that the house is the scene of a crime. What does a reader expect Hale to say in the next lines as he describes his visit the day before? Are your expectations confirmed or altered when you find out more?

As the talkative Hale describes his visit to the home of people who seldom talk and don't answer the door, you probably feel curious. You don't yet know more than Hale did at the time, so you probably expect nothing too alarming. Why do the stage directions instruct all the actors to look at the rocking chair, if Mrs. Wright is obviously not there? It is a cue to imagine her and the rather strange behavior that Hale describes. When Hale reports that Mrs. Wright said her husband "died of a rope round his neck," curiosity changes to suspicion. Could she actually have slept so soundly that she didn't know someone had put a rope around his neck and pulled him upright, killing him? Though we anticipate the discovery of the murderer—or perhaps Mrs. Wright's confession—our attention is really more focused on the behavior of the people on stage. Why does Hale remark that "women are used to worrying over trifles"? Why do the men scoff at the women's discussion of Mrs. Wright's intentions for finishing the quilt, whether to quilt-stitch or knot it? Depending on how alert we are, we may have noticed that the county attorney dismisses information about Mr. Wright's treatment of Mrs. Wright, and that the sheriff remarks that there is "nothing here but kitchen things." With the help of the title, we begin to see the flaw in the habitual way male characters devalue what women care about: they will miss the clues to a motive for the murder.

> *What is drama but life with the dull bits cut out?*
> —ALFRED HITCHCOCK

The situation now raises a number of questions. How offensive are these sexist remarks? Do you prefer the "gallantry" of the county attorney, who consistently flatters the women? Maybe the women's concerns are too trivial and practical. Obviously, losing all but one of the bottles of preserves, or leaving a quilt unfinished, is less important than the death of a husband. The women's sympathies and concerns evolve during the scene, whereas the men learn little from the visit to the house except that the rope belonged to the Wrights. Can you find the moments that Mrs. Peters shifts her allegiance from her husband and the law to Mrs. Hale? To what extent do the men's assumptions justify the women's suppression of their evidence (which the men might not have thought "real" evidence anyway)? Where do your own sympathies lie? Should Mrs. Wright get away with it? Does the play strongly suggest an answer to these questions? Does the answer make you like or dislike the play? How important is your acceptance or rejection of the social theme to your emotional response to the play?

There is nothing particularly difficult or unfamiliar about *Trifles* as a "story." (Glaspell did, indeed, turn the play into a story—"A Jury of Her Peers.") Like some detective stories, it asks not "who done it?" but why the murder was committed. Its **mode** of representation is a familiar type—domestic realism—in which the places, people, and even events are more or less ordinary (unfortunately, domestic violence is too common to be extraordinary). Its staging is also conventional in the modern theater: it shows three walls of a room, with the front of the stage—the **proscenium arch**—where the imaginary fourth wall would be. It also has—though somewhat in miniature—the traditional five-part structure: the **exposition**—the situation at the beginning of a play (here, Mr. Hale's description of what happened); the **rising action**—the complicating of the plot (the men leaving the women alone with the evidence that reveals the motive); the **climax**—the turning point (here, perhaps, the discovery of the dead bird); the **falling action**—the unwinding of the plot toward the conclusion (the women covering up the "trifling" evidence); and the **conclusion.** This does not suggest that the play is *too* conventional, but only that its type, subject matter, manner of presentation, and form are familiar—which might also be said, for example, of *Oedipus* or *Hamlet.*

Working with the conventions of her time, Glaspell made ingenious decisions about how to dramatize her story. To dramatize the story of what happened, Glaspell could have designed several scene changes over a longer period of time, showing the deteriorating marriage, the crisis over the bird, the murder itself, the sleepless night for Mrs. Wright, and the arrival of Mr. Hale the day before the scene we witness. Instead, the story unfolds in a single scene after the fact: in one room, on the second morning after the murder, between the entrance and exit of Mrs. Hale and Mrs. Peters. Mrs. Wright never appears. Instead, her old neighbors, Mr. and Mrs. Hale, describe her both as she is now and as she was when young. (When directors choose the plays they will put on, they have to think about the availability of actors and, if it is a professional production, the cost of paying them; plays with smaller casts are easier as well as cheaper to stage.) What is the effect of such a deliberate omission? Rather than watching Mrs. Wright to judge her guilt, the audience or readers focus on the process of detection and the motivation of the two visiting women. The other crucial omission from the play is the victim himself. The men go offstage to look at the corpse that everyone knows (or imagines) is lying upstairs. (Again, no actor is needed.) This separation of the women from the men brings out the theme of the different outlooks and values of the sexes. The growing allegiance of the two women with the absent housewife elicits the audience's sympathy as the secrets of Mrs. Wright's motivation are discovered. This evidence remains invisible to the men when they return to the kitchen, Mrs. Wright's environment. The audience now knows that space quite intimately.

• • •

How do you write about a play? If you are not a reviewer assigned to evaluate the acting, the staging, or the script, why should you analyze the elements of the play or present an interpretation of what it means? As with fiction and poetry, writing an essay about drama can sharpen your responses and focus your reading, while it can demonstrate effects in the work that other readers may have missed. When you write about drama, in a very real sense you perform the role that directors and actors take on in a stage performance: you offer your "reading" of the text, interpreting it in order to guide other readers' responses. But as when you write about a story or a poem, you also shape and refine your own response by attempting to express it clearly. Normally, you consider the whole play before you actually write about it, but jotting down your initial impressions as you read can be a constructive first step in writing an essay. Recording your thoughts before you've finished a play may help you clarify your expectations. Try stopping your reading at some reasonable point—the end of a scene or an act, or when you are puzzled, or where the action seems to pause briefly—and writing out your current expectations for the play. Very likely you will choose what the playwright expected the audience to expect at this point. Why would the clues have been designed this way? When you find out that your expectations are met—or not met—ask what difference it makes for a playwright to have prepared a surprise for the audience, or to have led them to confirm their own predictions.

With such notes, however informal, you can now return to the text to locate the specific lines that have contributed to your expectations or your discoveries. Are these lines at the beginning, the middle, or the end of the play? Who gives most of the hints or misleading information? If there is one character who is especially unseeing, especially devious, or especially insightful, you might decide to write an essay describing the function of that character in the play. A good way to undertake such a study of a character in drama (as in fiction) is to imagine the work without that character. Mrs. Hale in *Trifles* is certainly the cleverest "detective"; why do we need Mrs. Peters as well? One answer is that plays need dialogue, and we would find it artificial if Mrs. Hale talked mainly to herself. But a more interesting answer is that the audience learns by witnessing different temperaments responding to a situation. Mrs. Peters speaks for our misgivings about protecting a murderer.

In addition to character studies, essays on drama can focus on the kinds of observations we made above: expectations and structure of plot, from its rising action to its turning point and resolution; the presence and absence of characters or actions onstage; the different degrees of awareness of characters and audience at various points in the action; titles, stage directions, and other stylistic details including metaphors or other imagery; and, of course, themes such as the importance of feminine "trifles". As you write, you will probably discover that you can imagine directing or acting in a performance of the play, and you'll realize that interpreting a play is a crucial step in bringing it to life.

SUGGESTIONS FOR WRITING

1. How do your sympathies for Mrs. Peters change over the course of *Trifles*? What might Mrs. Peters be said to represent in the clash of attitudes at the heart of the play? Write an essay in which you examine both Mrs. Peters's evolving character as it is revealed in *Trifles* and her dramatic function in relation to the other characters and to the plot.

2. How would you characterize Susan Glaspell's feminism as revealed in *Trifles*— does it seem radical or moderate? How does it compare to feminist political and social ideas of our own time? (Consult three or more educational or library Web sites for biographical background on Glaspell; there are several sites offering teaching materials on *Trifles* as well. If time allows, you might also pursue sources that provide an overview of women's movements in the United States in the twentieth century.) Write an essay in which you explore the political leanings apparent in *Trifles*, both in the context of Glaspell's play (published in 1920) and in the broader historical context of the struggle for women's rights over the past century.

3. Write an essay in which you propose a production of *Trifles*, complete with details of how you would handle the casting, costumes, set design, lighting, and direction of the actors. What would be your overall controlling vision for the production? Would you attempt to reproduce faithfully the look and feel of the play as it might have been in 1916, or would you introduce innovations? How would you justify your choices in terms of dramatic effectiveness?

Understanding the Text

16 ELEMENTS OF DRAMA

Most of us read more fiction than drama and are likely to encounter drama by watching videotaped or filmed versions of it. Nonetheless, the skills you have developed in reading stories and poems come in handy when reading plays. Just as with fiction and poetry, you will understand and appreciate drama more fully by becoming familiar with the various elements of the genre.

Character

Character is possibly the most familiar and accessible of the elements; both fiction and drama feature one or more imaginary persons who take part in the action. The word "character" refers not only to a person represented in an imagined plot, whether narrated or acted out, but also to the unique qualities that make up a personality. From one point of view, "character" as a part in a plot and "character" as a kind of personality are both predictions: this sort of person is likely to see things from a certain angle and behave in certain ways. Notice that the idea of character includes both the individual differences among people and the classification of similar people into types. To have character is positive, but to have too much of it can be objectionable. A person has "a lot of character" if he or she has integrity and stands up to pressure; but to *be* "a character" is to provoke laughter, annoyance, or reproach. Whereas much realistic fiction emphasizes unique individuals rather than general character types, drama usually compresses and simplifies personalities—a play has only about two hours in which to show situations, appearances, and behaviors, without description or background other than exposition spoken by the actors. The advantage of portraying character in broader strokes is that it heightens the contrasts between character types, adding to the drama: differences provoke stronger reactions. Whether a play favors exceptional or typical characters, authors, actors, and readers collaborate in creating these roles, drawing on their experience of varieties of personality in life and in literature.

Plays are especially concerned with characters because of the concrete manner in which they portray people on the stage. With a few exceptions (such as experiments in multimedia performance), the only words in the performance of a play are spoken by actors, and usually these actors are *in character*—that is, speaking as though they really were the people they play in the drama. (Sometimes plays have a narrator who observes and comments on the action from the sidelines, and in some plays a character may address the audience directly, but even when apparently stepping outside of the imaginary frame the actors are still part of the play.) In fiction, the narrator's description and commentary can guide a reader's judgment about characters. Reading a play, you will have no such guide; apart from some clues about characters in the stage directions, you will need to imagine the appearance, manners, and movement of someone speaking the lines assigned to any one character. You can do this even as you read through a play for the first time, discovering the characters' attitudes and motivations as the scenes unfold. This ability to predict character and then to revise expectations as situations change is based not only on our experiences of people in real life, but also on our familiarity with types of characters or roles that occur in many dramatic forms.

Consider the patterns of characters in many stories that are narrated or acted out, whether in novels, children's books, comic books, cartoons, television series, Hollywood feature films, animated films by Disney or Pixar, and even some kinds of video games. In many of these forms, there is a leading role, a main character: the **protagonist**. The titles of plays such as *Hamlet, Oedipus the King,* or, a little less obviously, *Death of a Salesman* imply that the play will be about a central character, the chief object of the playwright's and the reader's or audience's concern. Understanding the character of the protagonist—sometimes in contrast with an **antagonist,** the counterpart or opponent of the main character—becomes the consuming interest of such a play. Especially in more traditional or popular genres, the protagonist may be called a **hero** or **heroine,** and the antagonist may be called the **villain.** We have been trained since infancy to identify with the good guys and to oppose the bully, the stepmother, the madman out to destroy the planet, or other agents of hostility and evil. This lifelong training helps us quickly immerse ourselves in the conflict between characters in a play, even if the style and form are far removed from more typical examples of their genres.

Most characterization in professional theater avoids depicting pure good and pure evil in a fight to the death. Not only are most roles qualified with flaws or redeeming qualities, but most plays portray more than two imagined people, so the conflicts are necessarily more complex than a simple good-guy-vs.-bad-guy comic-book plot. As in other genres that represent people in action, in drama too there are minor characters or supporting roles. At least since ancient Rome, romantic comedies have been structured around a leading man, a leading woman, and a comparable pair whose problems may be less serious, whose characters may be less complex, or who in other ways support rather than lead the action. Sometimes a supporting role can be said to be a **foil,** a character designed to bring out qualities in another character by contrast. Curiously, actors who are usually cast in the minor parts are sometimes called *character actors.* We might exclaim "what a character!" about a supporting role. But usually the less important parts could be said to have less character, or to require less characterization; they reveal a few traits in brief, sharp contrast rather than complex development. The main point to remember is that all the characters in a drama are interdependent and help to characterize each other. In dialogue and in behavior, each brings out what is characteristic in the others.

Like movies and other "shows," plays must respect certain limitations: the time an audience can be expected to sit and watch; the attention and sympathy an audience is likely to give to various characters; the amount of exposition that can be shown rather than spoken aloud. Because of these constraints, playwrights, screenwriters, casting directors, and actors must rely on shortcuts to convey character. Everyone involved, including the audience, consciously or unconsciously relies on **stereotypes** of various social roles to flesh out the dramatic action that is concentrated into two hours, more or less. Even a play that seeks to undermine stereotypes must still invoke them. In the United States today, casting—or typecasting—usually relies on an actor's social identity, from gender and race to occupation, region, age, and values. It might be difficult to cast someone to play the part of a middle-aged Korean American truck driver from Georgia, and even more difficult if the part specifies that this truck driver is a woman who spends her days off learning to tap dance. Such a unique role might be very desirable to an actress who has found that there are few parts for Asian American women or older women. The fact that the role defies stereotypes makes it more interesting to perform and more interesting to watch. If an actor is cast too far "against type," however, it begins to be funny, which can be an intentional effect in a play that is making fun of stereotypes. Or the role can be so exceptional and unfamiliar that audiences will fail to recognize any connection to people they might meet, and their response will fall flat. At times, however, plays or other dramatic forms can rely too much on stereotypes, positive or negative, and the familiarity leaves everyone disappointed (or offended).

All dramatic roles, then, must have some connection to types of personality, and good roles modify such types just enough to make the character deeper and more interesting. Playwrights often overturn or modify expectations of character in order to surprise an audience. Some theatrical roles have become famous because of

> *Art always aims at the* **individual.** *. . . Nothing could be more unique than the character of Hamlet. Though he may resemble other men in some respects, it is clearly not on that account that he interests us most.*
>
> **—HENRI BERGSON**

their larger-than-life complexity within certain types, and because they have been performed to great acclaim. In *A Streetcar Named Desire,* Blanche DuBois does to some extent fit the type of the southern aristocrat who has lost wealth, status, and her "mansion" in the Civil War and is too frail for the rapid changes of the new postwar, industrial society. In fact, she likes to imagine herself in this tragic role in spite of the generations and World Wars that have made her pre-Civil-War dream obsolete. It is the way that she simultaneously conforms to this stereotype, artificially impersonates it, and contradicts it that makes this role so rich and compelling. It is one of the great women's roles of the twentieth century, and in 1951 it earned Vivien Leigh an Oscar for Best Actress. A similarly complex leading role, likewise from a play that became a hit film, is Henry Higgins in *Pygmalion.* Rex Harrison immortalized the part in both the stage and film versions of the musical *My Fair Lady*, which closely follows Shaw's play. Higgins is an irascible middle-aged bachelor "rather like a very impetuous baby," a brilliant linguist who is ignorant about people, an idealistic reformer who hates any threats to his own privileges; he treats everyone alike—as a true gentleman should—but treats everyone badly, and his manners and vocabulary are crude. Should an actor in this role try to match Harrison's performance—including even his rough style of talking through his songs? Should he reveal that he is actually a soft romantic under his gruff exterior? Or would it be more authentic and interesting to give the impression that he enjoys other people's suffering and has no heart for his protégée, Eliza?

Every production of a play is an interpretation. Not just "adaptations"—Greek or Elizabethan plays set in modern times and performed in modern dress, for example—but even productions that seek the "essence" of a play are interpretations of what is vital or essential in it. John Malkovich, in the 1983–84 production of *Death of a Salesman*, did not project Biff Loman as an outgoing, successful, hail-fellow-well-met jock, though that is what Arthur Miller intended and how he wanted the part played. Malkovich saw Biff as only pretending to be a jock. Big-time athletes, he insisted, don't glad-hand people; they wait for people to come to them. The actor did not change the author's words, but by intonation, body language, and "stage business" (wordless gestures and actions) he suggested his own view of the character's nature. In other words, he broke with the expectations associated with the character's type. As you read and develop your own interpretation or imaginary performance of a play, try adding unexpected qualities to one or more of the characters, to reveal different possible meanings in the drama.

Plot and Structure

An important part of any storyteller's task, whether in narrative or dramatic forms, is the invention, selection, and arrangement of the action. Even carefully structured action cannot properly be called a full-scale **plot** without some unifying sense of purpose that joins character, story line, and theme. That is, what happens should seem to happen for meaningful reasons. This does not mean, of course, that characters or audience need be satisfied in their hopes or expectations, or that effective plays need to wrap up all loose ends of cause and effect. It does mean that a reader or theatergoer should feel that the playwright has completed *this* play—that nothing essential is missing—though the play's outcome or overall effect may be difficult to sum up.

The plot is the first principle and, as it were, the soul of tragedy; character comes second.

—ARISTOTLE

Conflict is the engine that drives plot, and the presentation of conflict shapes the dramatic structure of a play. A conflict whose outcome is never in doubt may have other kinds of interest, but it is not truly dramatic. In a dramatic conflict each of the opposing forces must at some point seem likely to triumph or worthy of such triumph—whether it is one character versus another, one group of characters versus another group, the values of an individual versus those of a group or society or nature, or one idea or ideology versus another one. In *Hamlet*, for example, our interest in the struggle between Hamlet and Claudius depends on their being evenly matched, though few viewers would ever wish the new king to defeat the young hero. Claudius has possession of the throne and the queen, but Hamlet's role as the heir to the late king and his popularity with the people offset his opponent's strength. As we have seen in the previous chapter, the typical structure of a dramatic plot involves five stages in the progression of the conflict: exposition, rising action, climax, falling action, and conclusion. Even a short play such as *Trifles* contains all five stages.

In addition to plot, there are other devices that can give a play coherent structure and effect. Thematic concerns are a primary means of holding together varieties of characters and expansive plots. In *The Piano Lesson*, for example, the desire to define family, ancestry, and identity brings together the various conflicts—between races, classes, generations, genders, individuals, and ways of life.

The intricate developments of conflict between characters—and hence the plot—may be supported not only by events and themes but also by such elements as symbols or controlling metaphors. In *The Piano Lesson*, the constant presence of the piano onstage reminds us of the family's past and its relationship to slavery, and the ways that people have treated human beings as material property.

Another structural device that often supports and propels plot is **dramatic irony**, the fulfillment of a plan, action, or expectation in a surprising way, often the opposite of what the characters intend. One example occurs in *Trifles*, when the women notice all the everyday things in the house while the official investigators—the men—keep looking for large and unusual things. Of course, the women's "trifles" reveal the truth about the murder while the men's search for evidence has missed it.

In addition to the above kinds of elements that provide structural unity in a play, most plays also have formal divisions such as acts and scenes that emphasize the five phases of the plot. In the Greek theater, scenes were separated by choral odes (see *Oedipus the King*). In many French plays, a new scene begins with any significant entrance or exit of a character. Many "classic" plays, like *Hamlet*, have five acts, but modern plays tend to have two or three acts. It has become customary to have at least one intermission in the performance of a play that is longer than one act, in part for the practical reasons of the audience's need for restrooms or refreshments. Breaks may be signaled by turning down stage lighting and turning up the house lights, lowering the curtain (if there is one), or other means. Playwrights since the early twentieth century have sometimes deliberately challenged audience expectations concerning the beginning, middle, and end—the rising action, climax, and resolution. (Every now and then, audiences find themselves wondering whether the play is over or whether there is still more to come. When the actors all come out and take their bows, it is a safe bet the play is over!) Experimental playwrights of the later twentieth century sometimes crossed the boundaries of the stage and introduced actors into the audience or induced audiences to participate in the action. The plays in this collection follow the traditions of theater that maintain a realistic illusion and a separation (sometimes called "the fourth wall") between actors and audience. Some recent plays, however, show a contemporary flexibility in their treatment of time, with brief scenes out of chronological order, and of structure, with the protagonist developing an understanding of her life story as she now and then addresses the audience directly.

Stages, Sets, and Setting

Most of us have been to a theater at one time or another, if only for a school play, and we know what a conventional modern stage (the proscenium stage) looks like: a room with the wall missing between us and it. So when we read a modern play—that is, one written during the past two or three hundred years—and imagine it taking place before us, we think of its happening on such a stage. There are other types of modern stages—the **thrust stage**, where the audience sits around three sides of the major acting area, and the **arena stage**, where the audience sits all the way around the acting area and players make their entrances and their exits through the auditorium—but most plays are set on a proscenium stage. Most of the plays in this textbook can be readily imagined to be taking place on such a stage.

The Shakespeare play and the Greek play in this anthology were staged quite differently, and although they may be played today on a proscenium stage, we might be confused as we read if we are unaware of the original layout of the staging. In the Greek theater, the audience sat on a raised semicircle of seats (**amphitheater**) halfway around a circular area (**orchestra**) used primarily for dancing by the chorus. At the back of the orchestra was the **skene**, or stage house, representing the palace or temple before which the action took place. Shakespeare's stage, in contrast, basically involved a rectangular area built inside one end of a large enclosure like a circular walled-in yard; the audience stood on the ground or sat in stacked balconies around three sides of the principal acting area (rather like a thrust stage). There were additional acting areas on either side of this stage, as well as a recessed area at the back of the stage (which could represent Gertrude's chamber in *Hamlet,* for example) and an upper acting area (which could serve as Juliet's balcony). There was a trap door in the stage floor used for occasional effects; the ghost of Hamlet's father probably came and went this way. Until three centuries ago—and certainly in Shakespeare's time—plays for large paying audiences were performed outdoors in daylight, due to the difficulty and expense of lighting. If you are curious about Shakespeare's stage, you can visit a reconstruction of his Globe Theatre (according to what scholars have been able to determine) in Southwark, London, England, in person or online at <www.shakespearesglobe.org>. Every summer, plays by Shakespeare are performed there for large international audiences willing to sit on hard benches around the arena or to stand with the "groundlings" (of whom a lucky few can lean on the stage near the feet of the actors). The walls in the background of the stage are beautifully carved and painted, but there is no painted scenery, minimal furniture, few costume changes, no lighting, and no curtain around the stage (a cloth hanging usually covers the recessed area at the back of the stage). Three or four musicians may play period instruments on the balcony.

As the design of the Globe suggests, the conventions of dramatic writing and stage production have changed considerably since the advent of theater. Certainly this is true of the way playwrights convey a sense of location. Usually the audience is asked to imagine that the featured section of the auditorium is actually a particular place or **setting** somewhere else. The audience of course knows it is a stage, more or less bare or disguised, but they accept it as a public square, a wooded park, an open road, or a room in a castle or a hut. *Oedipus the King* takes place entirely before the palace at Thebes. Following the general convention of Greek drama, the play never changes place. When the action demands the presence of Teiresias, for example, the scene does not shift to him, but instead escorts bring him to the front of the palace. Similarly, important events that take place elsewhere are described by witnesses who arrive on the scene.

In Shakespeare's theater the conventions of place are quite different: the acting arena does not represent a specific place, but assumes a temporary identity according to the characters who inhabit it, the costumes, and their speeches. At the opening of *Hamlet* we know we are at a sentry station because a man dressed as a soldier challenges two others. By line 15, we know that we are in Denmark because the actors profess to be "liegemen to the Dane." At the end of the scene the actors leave the stage and in a sense take the sentry station with them. Shortly a group of people dressed in court costumes and a man and a woman wearing crowns appear. As a theater audience, we must surmise from costumes and dialogue that the acting area has now become a royal court; when we read the play, the stage directions give us a cue that the place has changed.

In a modern play, there are likely to be several changes of scene. The scene changes in modern plays involve lowering a curtain or darkening the stage while different sets and props are arranged. **Sets** (the design, decoration, and scenery) and **props** (articles or objects used on stage) vary greatly in modern productions of plays written in any period. Sometimes space is merely suggested—a circle of sand at one end of the stage, a blank wall behind—to emphasize abstraction and universal themes, or to exercise the audience's imagination. More typically, a set uses realistic aids to the imagination. The set of *Trifles*, for example, must include at least a sink, a cupboard, a stove, a small table, a large kitchen table, and a rocking chair, as well as certain props: a bird cage, quilting pieces, and an ornamental box.

In addition to representing place and the changing of place, dramatic conventions represent time and the changing of times, and these conventions, too, have altered across the centuries. Three or four centuries ago, European dramatists and critics admired the conventions of classical Greek drama which, they believed, dictated that the action of a play should represent a very short time—sometimes as short as the actual performance time (two or three hours), and certainly no longer than a single day. This **unity of time,** one of the so-called **classical unities,** impels a dramatist to select the moment when a stable situation should change and to fill in the necessary prior details by exposition. (These same critics maintained that a play should be unified in place and action as well; the kind of leaping from Denmark to England, or from court to forest, that happens in Shakespeare's plays was off limits according to such standards.) Thus, as we noted in *Trifles,* all the action before the investigators' visit to the farmhouse is summarized by characters during their brief visit, and the kitchen is the only part of the house that is seen by the audience.

Sometimes plays will use a more elaborate device to reveal characters' memories, as when Willy Loman's dreams or memories are acted out in *Death of a Salesman.* Gaps in time are often indicated between scenes, with the help of scenery, sound effects, stage directions, or notes in the program. Actors must assist in conveying the idea of time if their character appears at different ages. Various conventions of classical or Elizabethan drama have also worked effectively to communicate to the audience the idea of the passage of time, from the choral odes in *Oedipus the King* to the breaks between scenes in Shakespeare plays. There is a short time, for example, between Hamlet's departure to see his mother at the end of act 3, scene 2, and the entrance of the king with Rosencrantz and Guildenstern at the beginning of the next scene; in other parts of the play the elapsed time might be as long as that between scenes 4 and 5 of act 4, during which the news of Polonius's death reaches Paris and Laertes returns to Denmark and there rallies his friends. Action from the beginning to the end of a play thus can reach across a wide range of locations and represent many years rather than remaining in one place for the twenty-four hours demanded by critics who believed in the classical unities.

Tone, Style, and Imagery

In plays as in other literary genres, the **tone**—the style or manner of expression—is difficult to specify or explain. Perhaps tone is more important in drama than in other genres because it is, in performance, a spoken form, and vocal tone always affects the meaning of spoken words to some extent, in any culture or language. The actor—and any reader who wishes to imagine a play as spoken aloud—must infer from the written language just how to read a line, what tone of voice to use. The choice of tone must be a negotiation between the words of the playwright and the interpretation and skill of the actor. At times the stage directions will specify the tone of a line of dialogue, though even that must be only a hint, since there are many ways of speaking "intensely" or "angrily." Try it yourself; find a line in one of the plays printed here that has a stage direction telling the actor how to deliver it, and with one or two other people take turns saying it that way. If nothing else, such an experiment may help all of us appreciate the talent of good actors who can put on a certain tone of voice and make it seem natural and convincing. But it will also show you the many options for interpreting tone.

Never hesitate to apply the skills you have developed in interpreting poetry to drama; after all, most early plays were written in some form of verse. Aspects of poetry emerge in modern plays; for example, **monologues** or extended speeches by one character, while they rarely rhyme or have regular meter, may allow greater eloquence than is usual in everyday speech, expressing character and theme in well-chosen images or metaphors.

Not only can names, monologues, or recurrent memories stand in for webs of meaning in a play, but so can simple actions or objects. Effective plays often use props almost metaphorically. For instance, Boy Willie and Lymon, in *The Piano Lesson,* bring a load of watermelons rather than squash or other produce, because watermelons have become part of a nasty caricature of rural African Americans, who supposedly lived a happy life consuming the cheap, sweet fruit. The carved family heirloom is a piano for several good reasons: it can be seen on stage as something difficult to move and impossible to divide without destruction; characters can play it and the child of the next generation can be taught to play it; and it can symbolize both the great art of African American music and the way African Americans might take on European forms of culture and art and make them their own. As you read any play, pay close attention to metaphors or images, whether in language, concepts, or concrete forms.

Theme

Theme—usually defined as a statement or assertion about the subject of a work—is by its very nature the most comprehensive of the elements, embracing the impact of the entire work. Theme indeed is not part of the work, but abstracted from it by the reader or audience. Since we, as interpreters, infer the theme and put it in our own words, we understandably often disagree about nuances of emphasis or phrasing or even entire conceptions. To arrive at your own statement of a theme it is necessary to consider all the elements of a play together: character, structure, setting (including time and place), tone, and other aspects of the style or the potential staging that create the entire effect. Above all, try to understand a play on its own terms. You may dislike symbolic or unrealistic drama until you get more used to it; if a play is not supposed to represent what real people would do in everyday life in that place and time, then it should not be criticized for failing to do so. Or you may find realistic plays about ordinary adults in middle America in the mid-twentieth century to be devoid of excitement or appeal. Yet if you read carefully, you may discover vigorous, moving portrayals of people trapped in situations all too familiar to them, if alien to you. Tastes may vary as widely as tones of speech, but equipped with familiarity with the elements of drama and the ways they have changed over time you can become a good judge of theatrical literature, and notice more and more of the fine effects it can achieve. Nothing replaces the exhilaration of the one-time immediacy of a live theater performance, but reading and rereading plays can yield a rich and rewarding appreciation of the dramatic art.

SOPHOCLES

Oedipus the King[1]

CHARACTERS

OEDIPUS, *King of Thebes*	FIRST MESSENGER
JOCASTA, *His Wife*	SECOND MESSENGER
CREON, *His Brother-in-Law*	A HERDSMAN
TEIRESIAS, *an Old Blind Prophet*	A CHORUS *of Old Men of Thebes*
A PRIEST	

SCENE: *In front of the palace of* OEDIPUS *at Thebes. To the right of the stage near the altar stands the* PRIEST *with a crowd of children.* OEDIPUS *emerges from the central door.*

OEDIPUS: Children, young sons and daughters of old Cadmus,[2]
why do you sit here with your suppliant crowns?
The town is heavy with a mingled burden
of sounds and smells, of groans and hymns and incense;
5   I did not think it fit that I should hear
of this from messengers but came myself,—
I Oedipus whom all men call the Great.

[*He turns to the* PRIEST.]

You're old and they are young; come, speak for them.
What do you fear or want, that you sit here
10   suppliant? Indeed I'm willing to give all
that you may need; I would be very hard
should I not pity suppliants like these.
PRIEST: O ruler of my country, Oedipus,
you see our company around the altar;
15   you see our ages; some of us, like these,
who cannot yet fly far, and some of us
heavy with age; these children are the chosen
among the young, and I the priest of Zeus.
Within the market place sit others crowned
20   with suppliant garlands, at the double shrine
of Pallas[3] and the temple where Ismenus
gives oracles by fire. King, you yourself
have seen our city reeling like a wreck
already; it can scarcely lift its prow
25   out of the depths, out of the bloody surf.
A blight is on the fruitful plants of the earth,
a blight is on the cattle in the fields,
a blight is on our women that no children

---

1. Translated by David Grene.   2. The founder of Thebes.   3. Athena, the goddess of wisdom.

are born to them; a God that carries fire,
a deadly pestilence, is on our town,   30
strikes us and spares not, and the house of Cadmus
is emptied of its people while black Death
grows rich in groaning and in lamentation.
We have not come as suppliants to this altar
because we thought of you as of a God,   35
but rather judging you the first of men
in all the chances of this life and when
we mortals have to do with more than man.
You came and by your coming saved our city,
freed us from tribute which we paid of old   40
to the Sphinx, cruel singer. This you did
in virtue of no knowledge we could give you,
in virtue of no teaching; it was God
that aided you, men say, and you are held
with God's assistance to have saved our lives.   45
Now Oedipus, Greatest in all men's eyes,
here falling at your feet we all entreat you,
find us some strength for rescue.
Perhaps you'll hear a wise word from some God,
perhaps you will learn something from a man   50
(for I have seen that for the skilled of practice
the outcome of their counsels live the most).
Noblest of men, go, and raise up our city,
go,—and give heed. For now this land of ours
calls you its savior since you saved it once.   55
So, let us never speak about your reign
as of a time when first our feet were set
secure on high, but later fell to ruin.
Raise up our city, save it and raise it up.
Once you have brought us luck with happy omen;   60
be no less now in fortune.
If you will rule this land, as now you rule it,
better to rule it full of men than empty.
For neither tower nor ship is anything
when empty, and none live in it together.   65
OEDIPUS: I pity you, children. You have come full of longing,
but I have known the story before you told it
only too well. I know you are all sick,
yet there is not one of you, sick though you are,
that is as sick as I myself.   70
Your several sorrows each have single scope
and touch but one of you. My spirit groans
for city and myself and you at once.
You have not roused me like a man from sleep;
know that I have given many tears to this,   75

gone many ways wandering in thought,
but as I thought I found only one remedy
and that I took. I sent Menoeceus' son
Creon, Jocasta's brother, to Apollo,
80   to his Pythian temple,
that he might learn there by what act or word
I could save this city. As I count the days,
it vexes me what ails him; he is gone
far longer than he needed for the journey.
85   But when he comes, then, may I prove a villain,
if I shall not do all the God commands.
PRIEST: Thanks for your gracious words. Your servants here
signal that Creon is this moment coming.
OEDIPUS: His face is bright. O holy Lord Apollo,
90   grant that his news too may be bright for us
and bring us safety.
PRIEST: It is happy news,
I think, for else his head would not be crowned
with sprigs of fruitful laurel.
OEDIPUS: We will know soon,
95   he's within hail. Lord Creon, my good brother,
what is the word you bring us from the God?

[CREON *enters.*]

CREON: A good word,—for things hard to bear themselves
if in the final issue all is well
I count complete good fortune.
OEDIPUS: What do you mean?
100   What you have said so far
leaves me uncertain whether to trust or fear.
CREON: If you will hear my news before these others
I am ready to speak, or else to go within.
OEDIPUS: Speak it to all;
105   the grief I bear, I bear it more for these
than for my own heart.
CREON: I will tell you, then,
what I heard from the God.
King Phoebus[4] in plain words commanded us
to drive out a pollution from our land,
110   pollution grown ingrained within the land;
drive it out, said the God, not cherish it,
till it's past cure.
OEDIPUS: What is the rite
of purification? How shall it be done?
CREON: By banishing a man, or expiation

4. Apollo, the god of truth.

of blood by blood, since it is murder guilt   115
    which holds our city in this destroying storm.
OEDIPUS: Who is this man whose fate the God pronounces?
CREON: My Lord, before you piloted the state
    we had a king called Laius.
OEDIPUS: I know of him by hearsay. I have not seen him.   120
CREON: The God commanded clearly: let some one
    punish with force this dead man's murderers.
OEDIPUS: Where are they in the world? Where would a trace
    of this old crime be found? It would be hard
    to guess where.
CREON: The clue is in this land;   125
    that which is sought is found;
    the unheeded thing escapes:
    so said the God.
OEDIPUS: Was it at home,
    or in the country that death came upon him,
    or in another country travelling?   130
CREON: He went, he said himself, upon an embassy,
    but never returned when he set out from home.
OEDIPUS: Was there no messenger, no fellow traveller
    who knew what happened? Such a one might tell
    something of use.   135
CREON: They were all killed save one. He fled in terror
    and he could tell us nothing in clear terms
    of what he knew, nothing, but one thing only.
OEDIPUS: What was it?
    If we could even find a slim beginning   140
    in which to hope, we might discover much.
CREON: This man said that the robbers they encountered
    were many and the hands that did the murder
    were many; it was no man's single power.
OEDIPUS: How could a robber dare a deed like this   145
    were he not helped with money from the city,
    money and treachery?
CREON: That indeed was thought.
    But Laius was dead and in our trouble
    there was none to help.
OEDIPUS: What trouble was so great to hinder you   150
    inquiring out the murder of your king?
CREON: The riddling Sphinx induced us to neglect
    mysterious crimes and rather seek solution
    of troubles at our feet.
OEDIPUS: I will bring this to light again. King Phoebus⁵   155
    fittingly took this care about the dead,

---

5. Apollo, god of light.

and you too fittingly.
And justly you will see in me an ally,
a champion of my country and the God.
160 For when I drive pollution from the land
I will not serve a distant friend's advantage,
but act in my own interest. Whoever
he was that killed the king may readily
wish to dispatch me with his murderous hand;
165 so helping the dead king I help myself.

Come, children, take your suppliant boughs and go;
up from the altars now. Call the assembly
and let it meet upon the understanding
that I'll do everything. God will decide
170 whether we prosper or remain in sorrow.
PRIEST: Rise, children—it was this we came to seek,
which of himself the king now offers us.
May Phoebus who gave us the oracle
come to our rescue and stay the plague.

[*Exeunt*[6] *all but the* CHORUS.]

175 CHORUS: [*Strophe.*] What is the sweet spoken word of God from the
shrine of Pythorich in gold
that has come to glorious Thebes?
I am stretched on the rack of doubt, and terror and trembling hold
my heart, O Delian Healer, and I worship full of fears
for what doom you will bring to pass, new or renewed in the revolving
years.
180 Speak to me, immortal voice,
child of golden Hope.

[*Antistrophe.*]

First I call on you, Athene,[7] deathless daughter of Zeus,
and Artemis, Earth Upholder,
who sits in the midst of the market place in the throne which men
call Fame,
185 and Phoebus, the Far Shooter, three averters of Fate,
come to us now, if ever before, when ruin rushed upon the state,
you drove destruction's flame away
out of our land.

[*Strophe.*]

---

6. Exit the stage (Latin for "they go out"). *Strophe* (line 175): in Greek stagecraft, a choral song and the corresponding dance of the chorus to one side. *Antistrophe* (stage direction following line 181): after the strophe, the chorus's answering song and returning dance.
7. Goddess of both war and peace as well as wisdom. Artemis (line 183): goddess of the earth and the hunt, twin sister of Apollo.

Our sorrows defy number;
all the ship's timbers are rotten;
taking of thought is no spear for the driving away of the plague. 190
There are no growing children in this famous land;
there are no women bearing the pangs of childbirth.
You may see them one with another, like birds swift on the wing,
quicker than fire unmastered, 195
speeding away to the coast of the Western God.

[*Antistrophe.*]

In the unnumbered deaths
of its people the city dies;
those children that are born lie dead on the naked earth
unpitied, spreading contagion of death; and grey haired mothers and 200
wives
everywhere stand at the altar's edge, suppliant, moaning;
the hymn to the healing God rings out but with it the wailing voices
are blended.
From these our sufferings grant us, O golden Daughter of Zeus,
glad-faced deliverance.

[*Strophe.*]

There is no clash of brazen shields but our fight is with the War God, 205
a War God ringed with the cries of men, a savage God who burns us;
grant that he turn in racing course backwards out of our country's
bounds
to the great palace of Amphitrite[8] or where the waves of the Thracian
sea
deny the stranger safe anchorage.
Whatsoever escapes the night 210
at last the light of day revisits;
so smite the War God, Father Zeus,
beneath your thunderbolt,
for you are the Lord of the lightning, the lightning that carries fire.

[*Antistrophe.*]

And your unconquered arrow shafts, winged by the golden corded 215
bow,
Lycean King, I beg to be at our side for help;
and the gleaming torches of Artemis with which she scours the Lycean
hills,
and I call on the God with the turban of gold, who gave his name to
this country of ours,
the Bacchic God with the wind flushed face,
Evian One, who travel 220

---

8. Queen of the sea and wife of Poseidon, sometimes said to dwell in the Atlantic Ocean.

with the Maenad[9] company,
combat the God that burns us
with your torch of pine;
for the God that is our enemy is a God unhonoured among the Gods.

[OEDIPUS *returns.*]

225   OEDIPUS: For what you ask me—if you will hear my words,
and hearing welcome them and fight the plague,
you will find strength and lightening of your load
Hark to me; what I say to you, I say
as one that is a stranger to the story
230   as stranger to the deed. For I would not
be far upon the track if I alone
were tracing it without a clue. But now,
since after all was finished, I became
a citizen among you, citizens—
235   now I proclaim to all the men of Thebes:
who so among you knows the murderer
by whose hand Laius, son of Labdacus,
died—I command him to tell everything
to me,—yes, though he fears himself to take the blame
240   on his own head; for bitter punishment
he shall have none, but leave this land unharmed.
Or if he knows the murderer, another,
a foreigner, still let him speak the truth.
For I will pay him and be grateful, too.
245   But if you shall keep silence, if perhaps
some one of you, to shield a guilty friend,
or for his own sake shall reject my words—
hear what I shall do then:
I forbid that man, whoever he be, my land,
250   my land where I hold sovereignty and throne;
and I forbid any to welcome him
or cry him greeting or make him a sharer
in sacrifice or offering to the gods,
or give him water for his hands to wash.
255   I command all to drive him from their homes,
since he is our pollution, as the oracle
of Pytho's god proclaimed him now to me.
So I stand forth a champion of the god
and of the man who died.
260   Upon the murderer I invoke this curse—
whether he is one man and all unknown,
or one of many—may he wear out his life

9. Female worshipers of Bacchus (see line 219): Dionysus (Bacchus to the Romans), god of fertility and wine. *Evian one* (line 220): Dionysus (also known as Evius).

in misery to miserable doom!
If with my knowledge he lives at my hearth
I pray that I myself may feel my curse.   265
On you I lay my charge to fulfill all this
for me, for the god, and for this land of ours
destroyed and blighted, by the god forsaken.

Even were this no matter of God's ordinance
it would not fit you so to leave it lie,   270
unpurified, since a good man is dead
and one that was a king. Search it out.
Since I am now the holder of his office,
and have his bed and wife that once was his,
and had his line not been unfortunate   275
we would have common children—(fortune leaped
upon his head)—because of all these things,
I fight in his defence as for my father,
and I shall try all means to take the murderer
of Laius the son of Labdacus   280
the son of Polydorus and before him
of Cadmus and before him of Agenor.
Those who do not obey me, may the Gods
grant no crops springing from the ground they plough
nor children to their women! May a fate   285
like this, or one still worse than this consume them!
For you whom these words please, the other Thebans,
may Justice as your ally and all the Gods
live with you, blessing you now and for ever!
CHORUS: As you have held me to my oath, I speak: 290
I neither killed the king nor can declare
the killer; but since Phoebus set the quest
it is his part to tell who the man is.
OEDIPUS: Right; but to put compulsion on the Gods
against their will—no man can do that.   295
CHORUS: May I then say what I think second best?
OEDIPUS: If there's a third best, too, spare not to tell it.
CHORUS: I know that what the Lord Teiresias
sees, is most often what the Lord Apollo
sees. If you should inquire of this from him   300
you might find out most clearly.
OEDIPUS: Even in this my actions have not been sluggard.
On Creon's word I have sent two messengers
and why the prophet is not here already
I have been wondering.
CHORUS: His skill apart   305
there is besides only an old faint story.
OEDIPUS: What is it?

I look at every story.

CHORUS: It was said
that he was killed by certain wayfarers.

310 OEDIPUS: I heard that, too, but no one saw the killer.

CHORUS: Yet if he has a share of fear at all,
his courage will not stand firm, hearing your curse.

OEDIPUS: The man who in the doing did not shrink
will fear no word.

CHORUS: Here comes his prosecutor:

315 led by your men the godly prophet comes
in whom alone of mankind truth is native.

[*Enter* TEIRESIAS, *led by a* LITTLE BOY.]

OEDIPUS: Teiresias, you are versed in everything,
things teachable and things not to be spoken,
things of the heaven and earth-creeping things.

320 You have no eyes but in your mind you know
with what a plague our city is afflicted.
My lord, in you alone we find a champion,
in you alone one that can rescue us.
Perhaps you have not heard the messengers,

325 but Phoebus sent in answer to our sending
an oracle declaring that our freedom
from this disease would only come when we
should learn the names of those who killed King Laius,
and kill them or expel from our country.

330 Do not begrudge us oracles from birds,
or any other way of prophecy
within your skill; save yourself and the city,
save me; redeem the debt of our pollution
that lies on us because of this dead man.

335 We are in your hands; pains are most nobly taken
to help another when you have means and power.

TEIRESIAS: Alas, how terrible is wisdom when
it brings no profit to the man that's wise!
This I knew well, but had forgotten it,
else I would not have come here.

340 OEDIPUS: What is this?
How sad you are now you have come!

TEIRESIAS: Let me
go home. It will be easiest for us both
to bear our several destinies to the end
if you will follow my advice.

OEDIPUS: You'd rob us

345 of this your gift of prophecy? You talk
as one who had no care for law nor love
for Thebes who reared you.

TEIRESIAS: Yes, but I see that even your own words
    miss the mark; therefore I must fear for mine.

OEDIPUS: For God's sake if you know of anything,   350
    do not turn from us; all of us kneel to you,
    all of us here, your suppliants.

TEIRESIAS: All of you here know nothing. I will not
    bring to the light of day my troubles, mine—
    rather than call them yours.

OEDIPUS: What do you mean?   355
    You know of something but refuse to speak.
    Would you betray us and destroy the city?

TEIRESIAS: I will not bring this pain upon us both,
    neither on you nor on myself. Why is it
    you question me and waste your labour? I   360
    will tell you nothing.

OEDIPUS: You would provoke a stone! Tell us, you villain,
    tell us, and do not stand there quietly
    unmoved and balking at the issue.

TEIRESIAS: You blame my temper but you do not see   365
    your own that lives within you; it is me
    you chide.

OEDIPUS: Who would not feel his temper rise
    at words like these with which you shame our city?

TEIRESIAS: Of themselves things will come, although I hide them   370
    and breathe no word of them.

OEDIPUS: Since they will come
    tell them to me.

TEIRESIAS: I will say nothing further.
    Against this answer let your temper rage
    as wildly as you will.

OEDIPUS: Indeed I am
    so angry I shall not hold back a jot   375
    of what I think. For I would have you know
    I think you were complotter of the deed
    and doer of the deed save in so far
    as for the actual killing. Had you had eyes
    I would have said alone you murdered him.   380

TEIRESIAS: Yes? Then I warn you faithfully to keep
    the letter of your proclamation and
    from this day forth to speak no word of greeting
    to these nor me; you are the land's pollution.

OEDIPUS: How shamelessly you started up this taunt!   385
    How do you think you will escape?

TEIRESIAS: I have.
    I have escaped; the truth is what I cherish
    and that's my strength.

OEDIPUS: And who has taught you truth?

Not your profession surely!

TEIRESIAS: You have taught me,
390   for you have made me speak against my will.

OEDIPUS: Speak what? Tell me again that I may learn it better.

TEIRESIAS: Did you not understand before or would you
        provoke me into speaking?

OEDIPUS: I did not grasp it,
        not so to call it known. Say it again.

395   TEIRESIAS: I say you are the murderer of the king
        whose murderer you seek.

OEDIPUS: Not twice you shall
        say calumnies like this and stay unpunished.

TEIRESIAS: Shall I say more to tempt your anger more?

OEDIPUS: As much as you desire; it will be said
        in vain.

400   TEIRESIAS: I say that with those you love best
        you live in foulest shame unconsciously
        and do not see where you are in calamity.

OEDIPUS: Do you imagine you can always talk
        like this, and live to laugh at it hereafter?

405   TEIRESIAS: Yes, if the truth has anything of strength.

OEDIPUS: It has, but not for you; it has no strength
        for you because you are blind in mind and ears
        as well as in your eyes.

TEIRESIAS: You are a poor wretch
        to taunt me with the very insults which
410   every one soon will heap upon yourself.

OEDIPUS: Your life is one long night so that you cannot
        hurt me or any other who sees the light.

TEIRESIAS: It is not fate that I should be your ruin,
        Apollo is enough; it is his care
        to work this out.

415   OEDIPUS: Was this your own design
        or Creon's?

TEIRESIAS: Creon is no hurt to you,
        but you are to yourself.

OEDIPUS: Wealth, sovereignty and skill outmatching skill
        for the contrivance of an envied life!
420   Great store of jealousy fill your treasury chests,
        if my friend Creon, friend from the first and loyal,
        thus secretly attacks me, secretly
        desires to drive me out and secretly
        suborns this juggling, trick devising quack,
425   this wily beggar who has only eyes
        for his own gains, but blindness in his skill.
        For, tell me, where have you seen clear, Teiresias,
        with your prophetic eyes? When the dark singer,

the sphinx, was in your country, did you speak
word of deliverance to its citizens? 430
And yet the riddle's answer was not the province
of a chance comer. It was a prophet's task
and plainly you had no such gift of prophecy
from birds nor otherwise from any God
to glean a word of knowledge. But I came, 435
Oedipus, who knew nothing, and I stopped her.
I solved the riddle by my wit alone.
Mine was no knowledge got from birds.[1] And now
you would expel me,
because you think that you will find a place 440
by Creon's throne. I think you will be sorry,
both you and your accomplice, for your plot
to drive me out. And did I not regard you
as an old man, some suffering would have taught you
that what was in your heart was treason. 445
CHORUS: We look at this man's words and yours, my king,
and we find both have spoken them in anger.
We need no angry words but only thought
how we may best hit the God's meaning for us.
TEIRESIAS: If you are king, at least I have the right 450
no less to speak in my defence against you.
Of that much I am master. I am no slave
of yours, but Loxias',[2] and so I shall not
enroll myself with Creon for my patron.
Since you have taunted me with being blind, 455
here is my word for you.
You have your eyes but see not where you are
in sin, nor where you live, nor whom you live with.
Do you know who your parents are? Unknowing
you are an enemy to kith and kin 460
in death, beneath the earth, and in this life.
A deadly footed, double striking curse,
from father and mother both, shall drive you forth
out of this land, with darkness on your eyes,
that now have such straight vision. Shall there be 465
a place will not be harbour to your cries,
a corner of Cithaeron[3] will not ring
in echo to your cries, soon, soon,—
when you shall learn the secret of your marriage,
which steered you to a haven in this house,— 470
haven no haven, after lucky voyage?

---

1. Prophetic knowledge derived from observing the flight of birds, or sometimes from inspecting
bird entrails.   2. Yet another name for Apollo.

3. The mountain where Oedipus was abandoned as a child.

And of the multitude of other evils
establishing a grim equality
between you and your children, you know nothing.
475   So, muddy with contempt my words and Creon's!
Misery shall grind no man as it will you.
OEDIPUS: Is it endurable that I should hear
such words from him? Go and a curse go with you
Quick, home with you! Out of my house at once!
480 TEIRESIAS: I would not have come either had you not called me.
OEDIPUS: I did not know then you would talk like a fool—
or it would have been long before I called you.
TEIRESIAS: I am a fool then, as it seems to you—
but to the parents who have bred you, wise.
485 OEDIPUS: What parents? Stop! Who are they of all the world?
TEIRESIAS: This day will show your birth and will destroy you.
OEDIPUS: How needlessly your riddles darken everything.
TEIRESIAS: But it's in riddle answering you are strongest.
OEDIPUS: Yes. Taunt me where you will find me great.
490 TEIRESIAS: It is this very luck that has destroyed you.
OEDIPUS: I do not care, if it has saved this city.
TEIRESIAS: Well, I will go. Come, boy, lead away.
OEDIPUS: Yes, lead him off. So long as you are here,
you'll be a stumbling block and a vexation;
once gone, you will not trouble me again.
495 TEIRESIAS: I have said
what I came here to say not fearing your
countenance: there is no way you can hurt me.
I tell you, king, this man, this murderer
(whom you have long declared you are in search of,
500   indicting him in threatening proclamation
as murderer of Laius)—he is here.
In name he is a stranger among citizens
but soon he will be shown to be a citizen
true native Theban, and he'll have no joy
505   of the discovery: blindness for sight
and beggary for riches his exchange,
he shall go journeying to a foreign country
tapping his way before him with a stick.
He shall be proved father and brother both
510   to his own children in his house; to her
that gave him birth, a son and husband both;
a fellow sower in his father's bed
with that same father that he murdered.
Go within, reckon that out, and if you find me
515   mistaken, say I have no skill in prophecy.

[*Exeunt separately* TEIRESIAS *and* OEDIPUS.]

CHORUS: [*Strophe*.] Who is the man proclaimed
    by Delphi's prophetic rock
    as the bloody handed murderer,
    the doer of deeds that none dare name?
    Now is the time for him to run   520
    with a stronger foot
    than Pegasus[4]
    for the child of Zeus leaps in arms upon him
    with fire and the lightning bolt,
    and terribly close on his heels   525
    are the Fates[5] that never miss.

      [*Antistrophe*.]

    Lately from snowy Parnassus[6]
    clearly the voice flashed forth,
    bidding each Theban track him down,
    the unknown murderer.   530
    In the savage forests he lurks and in
    the caverns like
    the mountain bull.
    He is sad and lonely, and lonely his feet
    that carry him far from the navel of earth;   535
    but its prophecies, ever living,
    flutter around his head.

      [*Strophe*.]

    The augur has spread confusion,
    terrible confusion;
    I do not approve what was said   540
    nor can I deny it.
    I do not know what to say;
    I am in a flutter of foreboding;
    I never heard in the present
    nor past of a quarrel between   545
    the sons of Labdacus and Polybus,[7]
    that I might bring as proof
    in attacking the popular fame
    of Oedipus, seeking
    to take vengeance for undiscovered   550
    death in the line of Labdacus.

      [*Antistrophe*.]

    Truly Zeus and Apollo are wise
    and in human things all knowing;

---

4. Winged horse.   5. Goddesses who decide the course of human life.
6. Mountain sacred to Apollo.   7. King who adopted Oedipus.

but amongst men there is no
555 distinct judgment, between the prophet
and me—which of us is right.
One man may pass another in wisdom
but I would never agree
with those that find fault with the king
560 till I should see the word
proved right beyond doubt. For once
in visible form the Sphinx
came on him and all of us
saw his wisdom and in that test
565 he saved the city. So he will not be condemned by my mind.

[*Enter* CREON.]

CREON: Citizens, I have come because I heard
deadly words spread about me, that the king
accuses me. I cannot take that from him.
If he believes that in these present troubles
570 he has been wronged by me in word or deed
I do not want to live on with the burden
of such a scandal on me. The report
injures me doubly and most vitally—
for I'll be called a traitor to my city
575 and traitor also to my friends and you.
CHORUS: Perhaps it was a sudden gust of anger
that forced that insult from him, and no judgment.
CREON: But did he say that it was in compliance
with schemes of mine that the seer told him lies?
580 CHORUS: Yes, he said that, but why, I do not know.
CREON: Were his eyes straight in his head? Was his mind right
when he accused me in this fashion?
CHORUS: I do not know; I have no eyes to see
what princes do. Here comes the king himself.

[*Enter* OEDIPUS.]

585 OEDIPUS: You, sir, how is it you come here? Have you so much
brazen-faced daring that you venture in
my house although you are proved manifestly
the murderer of that man, and though you tried,
openly, highway robbery of my crown?
590 For God's sake, tell me what you saw in me,
what cowardice or what stupidity,
that made you lay a plot like this against me?
Did you imagine I should not observe
the crafty scheme that stole upon me or
595 seeing it, take no means to counter it?
Was it not stupid of you to make the attempt,

to try to hunt down royal power without
the people at your back or friends? For only
with the people at your back or money can
the hunt end in the capture of a crown.   600
CREON: Do you know what you're doing? Will you listen
    to words to answer yours, and then pass judgment?
OEDIPUS: You're quick to speak, but I am slow to grasp you,
    for I have found you dangerous,—and my foe.
CREON: First of all hear what I shall say to that.   605
OEDIPUS: At least don't tell me that you are not guilty.
CREON: If you think obstinacy without wisdom
    a valuable possession, you are wrong.
OEDIPUS: And you are wrong if you believe that one,
    a criminal, will not be punished only   610
    because he is my kinsman.
CREON: This is but just—
    but tell me, then, of what offense I'm guilty?
OEDIPUS: Did you or did you not urge me to send
    to this prophetic mumbler?
CREON: I did indeed,
    and I shall stand by what I told you.   615
OEDIPUS: How long ago is it since Laius . . .
CREON: What about Laius? I don't understand.
OEDIPUS: Vanished—died—was murdered?
CREON: It is long,
    a long, long time to reckon.
OEDIPUS: Was this prophet
    in the profession then?
CREON: He was, and honoured   620
    as highly as he is today.
OEDIPUS: At that time did he say a word about me?
CREON: Never, at least when I was near him.
OEDIPUS: You never made a search for the dead man?
CREON: We searched, indeed, but never learned of anything.   625
OEDIPUS: Why did our wise old friend not say this then?
CREON: I don't know; and when I know nothing, I
    usually hold my tongue.
OEDIPUS: You know this much,
    and can declare this much if you are loyal.
CREON: What is it? If I know, I'll not deny it.   630
OEDIPUS: That he would not have said that I killed Laius
    had he not met you first.
CREON: You know yourself
    whether he said this, but I demand that I
    should hear as much from you as you from me.
OEDIPUS: Then hear,—I'll not be proved a murderer.   635
CREON: Well, then. You're married to my sister.

OEDIPUS: Yes,
   that I am not disposed to deny.
CREON: You rule
   this country giving her an equal share
   in the government?
OEDIPUS: Yes, everything she wants
   she has from me.
640 CREON: And I, as thirdsman to you,
   am rated as the equal of you two?
OEDIPUS: Yes, and it's there you've proved yourself false friend.
CREON: Not if you will reflect on it as I do.
   Consider, first, if you think any one
645 would choose to rule and fear rather than rule
   and sleep untroubled by a fear if power
   were equal in both cases. I, at least,
   I was not born with such a frantic yearning
   to be a king—but to do what kings do.
650 And so it is with every one who has learned
   wisdom and self-control. As it stands now,
   the prizes are all mine—and without fear.
   But if I were the king myself, I must
   do much that went against the grain.
655 How should despotic rule seem sweeter to me
   than painless power and an assured authority?
   I am not so besotted yet that I
   want other honours than those that come with profit.
   Now every man's my pleasure; every man greets me;
660 now those who are your suitors fawn on me,—
   success for them depends upon my favour.
   Why should I let all this go to win that?
   My mind would not be traitor if it's wise;
   I am no treason lover, of my nature,
665 nor would I ever dare to join a plot.
   Prove what I say. Go to the oracle
   at Pytho and inquire about the answers,
   if they are as I told you. For the rest,
   if you discover I laid any plot
670 together with the seer, kill me, I say,
   not only by your vote but by my own.
   But do not charge me on obscure opinion
   without some proof to back it. It's not just
   lightly to count your knaves as honest men,
675 nor honest men as knaves. To throw away
   an honest friend is, as it were, to throw
   your life away, which a man loves the best.
   In time you will know all with certainty;
   time is the only test of honest men,

one day is space enough to know a rogue.   680

CHORUS: His words are wise, king, if one fears to fall.
Those who are quick of temper are not safe.

OEDIPUS: When he that plots against me secretly
moves quickly, I must quickly counterplot.
If I wait taking no decisive measure   685
his business will be done, and mine be spoiled.

CREON: What do you want to do then? Banish me?

OEDIPUS: No, certainly; kill you, not banish you.[8]

CREON: I do not think that you've your wits about you.

OEDIPUS: For my own interests, yes.

CREON: But for mine, too,   690
you should think equally.

OEDIPUS: You are a rogue.

CREON: Suppose you do not understand?

OEDIPUS: But yet
I must be ruler.

CREON: Not if you rule badly.

OEDIPUS: O, city, city!

CREON: I too have some share
in the city; it is not yours alone.   695

CHORUS: Stop, my lords! Here—and in the nick of time
I see Jocasta coming from the house;
with her help lay the quarrel that now stirs you.

   [*Enter* JOCASTA.]

JOCASTA: For shame! Why have you raised this foolish squabbling
brawl? Are you not ashamed to air your private   700
griefs when the country's sick? Go in, you, Oedipus,
and you, too, Creon, into the house. Don't magnify
your nothing troubles.

CREON: Sister, Oedipus,
your husband, thinks he has the right to do
terrible wrongs—he has but to choose between   705
two terrors: banishing or killing me.

OEDIPUS: He's right, Jocasta; for I find him plotting
with knavish tricks against my person.

CREON: That God may never bless me! May I die
accursed, if I have been guilty of   710
one tittle of the charge you bring against me!

JOCASTA: I beg you, Oedipus, trust him in this,
spare him for the sake of this his oath to God,

8. *Translator's note:* Two lines omitted here owing to the confusion in the dialogue consequent on the loss of a third line. The lines as they stand in Jebb's edition (1902) are: OED.: That you may show what manner of thing is envy. / CREON: You speak as one that will not yield or trust. / [OED. *lost line.*]

for my sake, and the sake of those who stand here.
715 CHORUS: Be gracious, be merciful,
we beg of you.
OEDIPUS: In what would you have me yield?
CHORUS: He has been no silly child in the past.
He is strong in his oath now.
720 Spare him.
OEDIPUS: Do you know what you ask?
CHORUS: Yes.
OEDIPUS: Tell me then.
CHORUS: He has been your friend before all men's eyes; do not cast him
725 away dishonoured on an obscure conjecture.
OEDIPUS: I would have you know that this request of yours
really requests my death or banishment.
CHORUS: May the Sun God,[9] king of Gods, forbid! May I die without
God's blessing, without friends' help, if I had any such thought. But
730 my spirit is broken by my unhappiness for my wasting country; and
this would but add troubles amongst ourselves to the other troubles.
OEDIPUS: Well, let him go then—if I must die ten times for it,
or be sent out dishonoured into exile.
It is your lips that prayed for him I pitied,
735 not his; wherever he is, I shall hate him.
CREON: I see you sulk in yielding and you're dangerous
when you are out of temper; natures like yours
are justly heaviest for themselves to bear.
OEDIPUS: Leave me alone! Take yourself off, I tell you.
740 CREON: I'll go, you have not known me, but they have,
and they have known my innocence.

[*Exit.*]

CHORUS: Won't you take him inside, lady?
JOCASTA: Yes, when I've found out what was the matter.
CHORUS: There was some misconceived suspicion of a story, and on the
745 other side the sting of injustice.
JOCASTA: So, on both sides?
CHORUS: Yes.
JOCASTA: What was the story?
CHORUS: I think it best, in the interests of the country, to leave it where
it ended.
750 OEDIPUS: You see where you have ended, straight of judgment
although you are, by softening my anger.
CHORUS: Sir, I have said before and I say again—be sure that I would have
been proved a madman, bankrupt in sane council, if I should put you

9. Helios, closely associated with Apollo, the god of light.

away, you who steered the country I love safely when she was crazed
with troubles. God grant that now, too, you may prove a fortunate guide   755
for us.
JOCASTA: Tell me, my lord, I beg of you, what was it
　　that roused your anger so?
OEDIPUS:　　　　　　　　　　Yes, I will tell you.
　　I honour you more than I honour them.
　　It was Creon and the plots he laid against me.
JOCASTA: Tell me—if you can clearly tell the quarrel—
OEDIPUS:　　　　　　　　　　Creon says   760
　　that I'm the murderer of Laius.
JOCASTA: Of his own knowledge or on information?
OEDIPUS: He sent this rascal prophet to me, since
　　he keeps his own mouth clean of any guilt.
JOCASTA: Do not concern yourself about this matter;   765
　　listen to me and learn that human beings
　　have no part in the craft of prophecy.
　　Of that I'll show you a short proof.
　　There was an oracle once that came to Laius,—
　　I will not say that it was Phoebus' own,   770
　　but it was from his servants—and it told him
　　that it was fate that he should die a victim
　　at the hands of his own son, a son to be born
　　of Laius and me. But, see now, he,
　　the king, was killed by foreign highway robbers   775
　　at a place where three roads meet—so goes the story;
　　and for the son—before three days were out
　　after his birth King Laius pierced his ankles
　　and by the hands of others cast him forth
　　upon a pathless hillside. So Apollo   780
　　failed to fulfill his oracle to the son,
　　that he should kill his father, and to Laius
　　also proved false in that the thing he feared,
　　death at his son's hands, never came to pass.
　　So clear in this case were the oracles,   785
　　so clear and false. Give them no heed, I say;
　　what God discovers need of, easily
　　he shows to us himself.
OEDIPUS:　　　　　　　　　O dear Jocasta,
　　as I hear this from you, there comes upon me
　　a wandering of the soul—I could run mad.   790
JOCASTA: What trouble is it, that you turn again
　　and speak like this?
OEDIPUS:　　　　　　　　I thought I heard you say
　　that Laius was killed at a crossroads.
JOCASTA: Yes, that was how the story went and still
　　that word goes round.

795 OEDIPUS: Where is this place, Jocasta,
    where he was murdered?

JOCASTA: Phocis is the country
    and the road splits there, one of two roads from Delphi,
    another comes from Daulia.

OEDIPUS: How long ago is this?

JOCASTA: The news came to the city just before
800   you became king and all men's eyes looked to you.
    What is it, Oedipus, that's in your mind?

OEDIPUS: What have you designed, O Zeus, to do with me?

JOCASTA: What is the thought that troubles your heart?

OEDIPUS: Don't ask me yet—tell me of Laius—
805   How did he look? How old or young was he?

JOCASTA: He was a tall man and his hair was grizzled
    already—nearly white—and in his form
    not unlike you.

OEDIPUS: O God, I think I have
    called curses on myself in ignorance.

810 JOCASTA: What do you mean? I am terrified
    when I look at you.

OEDIPUS: I have a deadly fear
    that the old seer had eyes. You'll show me more
    if you can tell me one more thing.

JOCASTA: I will.
    I'm frightened,—but if I can understand,
    I'll tell you all you ask.

815 OEDIPUS: How was his company?
    Had he few with him when he went this journey,
    or many servants, as would suit a prince?

JOCASTA: In all there were but five, and among them
    a herald; and one carriage for the king.

820 OEDIPUS: It's plain—it's plain—who was it told you this?

JOCASTA: The only servant that escaped safe home.

OEDIPUS: Is he at home now?

JOCASTA: No, when he came home again
    and saw you king and Laius was dead,
    he came to me and touched my hand and begged
825   that I should send him to the fields to be
    my shepherd and so he might see the city
    as far off as he might. So I
    sent him away. He was an honest man,
    as slaves go, and was worthy of far more
830   than what he asked of me.

OEDIPUS: O, how I wish that he could come back quickly!

JOCASTA: He can. Why is your heart so set on this?

OEDIPUS: O dear Jocasta, I am full of fears
    that I have spoken far too much; and therefore

I wish to see this shepherd.

JOCASTA: He will come;   835
but, Oedipus, I think I'm worthy too
to know what it is that disquiets you.

OEDIPUS: It shall not be kept from you, since my mind
has gone so far with its forebodings. Whom
should I confide in rather than you, who is there   840
of more importance to me who have passed
through such a fortune?
Polybus was my father, king of Corinth,
and Merope, the Dorian, my mother.
I was held greatest of the citizens   845
in Corinth till a curious chance befell me
as I shall tell you—curious, indeed,
but hardly worth the store I set upon it.
There was a dinner and at it a man,
a drunken man, accused me in his drink   850
of being bastard. I was furious
but held my temper under for that day.
Next day I went and taxed my parents with it;
they took the insult very ill from him,
the drunken fellow who had uttered it.   855
So I was comforted for their part, but
still this thing rankled always, for the story
crept about widely. And I went at last
to Pytho, though my parents did not know.
But Phoebus sent me home again unhonoured   860
in what I came to learn, but he foretold
other and desperate horrors to befall me,
that I was fated to lie with my mother,
and show to daylight an accursed breed
which men would not endure, and I was doomed   865
to be murderer of the father that begot me.
When I heard this I fled, and in the days
that followed I would measure from the stars
the whereabouts of Corinth—yes, I fled
to somewhere where I should not see fulfilled   870
the infamies told in that dreadful oracle.
And as I journeyed I came to the place
where, as you say, this king met with his death.
Jocasta, I will tell you the whole truth.
When I was near the branching of the crossroads,   875
going on foot, I was encountered by
a herald and a carriage with a man in it,
just as you tell me. He that led the way
and the old man himself wanted to thrust me
out of the road by force. I became angry   880

and struck the coachman who was pushing me.
When the old man saw this he watched his moment,
and as I passed he struck me from his carriage,
full on the head with his two pointed goad.
885   But he was paid in full and presently
my stick had struck him backwards from the car
and he rolled out of it. And then I killed them
all. If it happened there was any tie
of kinship twixt this man and Laius,
890   who is then now more miserable than I,
what man on earth so hated by the Gods,
since neither citizen nor foreigner
may welcome me at home or even greet me,
but drive me out of doors? And it is I,
895   I and no other have so cursed myself.
And I pollute the bed of him I killed
by the hands that killed him. Was I not born evil?
Am I not utterly unclean? I had to fly
and in my banishment not even see
900   my kindred nor set foot in my own country,
or otherwise my fate was to be yoked
in marriage with my mother and kill my father,
Polybus who begot me and had reared me.
Would not one rightly judge and say that on me
905   these things were sent by some malignant God?
O no, no, no—O holy majesty
of God on high, may I not see that day!
May I be gone out of men's sight before
I see the deadly taint of this disaster
910   come upon me.
CHORUS: Sir, we too fear these things. But until you see this man face to
       face and hear his story, hope.
OEDIPUS: Yes, I have just this much of hope—to wait until the herdsman
       comes.
JOCASTA: And when he comes, what do you want with him?
915   OEDIPUS: I'll tell you; if I find that his story is the same as yours, I at least
       will be clear of this guilt.
JOCASTA: Why what so particularly did you learn from my story?
OEDIPUS: You said that he spoke of highway *robbers* who killed Laius. Now
       if he uses the same number, it was not I who killed him. One man cannot
920   be the same as many. But if he speaks of a man travelling alone, then
       clearly the burden of the guilt inclines towards me.
JOCASTA: Be sure, at least, that this was how he told the story. He cannot
       unsay it now, for every one in the city heard it—not I alone. But, Oedipus,
       even if he diverges from what he said then, he shall never prove that the
925   murder of Laius squares rightly with the prophecy—for Loxias declared
       that the king should be killed by his own son. And that poor creature

did not kill him surely,—for he died himself first. So as far as prophecy
goes, henceforward I shall not look to the right hand or the left.

OEDIPUS: Right. But yet, send some one for the peasant to bring him here;
do not neglect it.　　　　　　　　　　　　　　　　　　　　　　　930

JOCASTA: I will send quickly. Now let me go indoors. I will do nothing
except what pleases you.

　　[*Exeunt.*]

CHORUS: [*Strophe.*] May destiny ever find me
pious in word and deed
prescribed by the laws that live on high:　　　　　　　　　　　　935
laws begotten in the clear air of heaven,
whose only father is Olympus;
no mortal nature brought them to birth,
no forgetfulness shall lull them to sleep;
for God is great in them and grows not old.　　　　　　　　　　　940

　　[*Antistrophe.*]

Insolence breeds the tyrant, insolence
if it is glutted with a surfeit, unseasonable, unprofitable,
climbs to the roof-top and plunges
sheer down to the ruin that must be,
and there its feet are no service.　　　　　　　　　　　　　　　945
But I pray that the God may never
abolish the eager ambition that profits the state.
For I shall never cease to hold the God as our protector.

　　[*Strophe.*]

If a man walks with haughtiness
of hand or word and gives no heed　　　　　　　　　　　　　　950
to Justice and the shrines of Gods
despises—may an evil doom
smite him for his ill-starred pride of heart!—
if he reaps gains without justice
and will not hold from impiety　　　　　　　　　　　　　　　955
and his fingers itch for untouchable things.
When such things are done, what man shall contrive
to shield his soul from the shafts of the God?
When such deeds are held in honour,
why should I honour the Gods in the dance?　　　　　　　　　　960

　　[*Antistrophe.*]

No longer to the holy place,
to the navel of earth I'll go
to worship, nor to Abae
nor to Olympia,
unless the oracles are proved to fit,　　　　　　　　　　　　　965

for all men's hands to point at.
O Zeus, if you are rightly called
the sovereign lord, all-mastering,
let this not escape you nor your ever-living power!
970 The oracles concerning Laius
are old and dim and men regard them not.
Apollo is nowhere clear in honour; God's service perishes.

[*Enter* JOCASTA, *carrying garlands.*]

JOCASTA: Princes of the land, I have had the thought to go
to the Gods' temples, bringing in my hand
975 garlands and gifts of incense, as you see.
For Oedipus excites himself too much
at every sort of trouble, not conjecturing,
like a man of sense, what will be from what was,
but he is always at the speaker's mercy,
980 when he speaks terrors. I can do no good
by my advice, and so I came as suppliant
to you, Lycaean Apollo, who are nearest.
These are the symbols of my prayer and this
my prayer: grant us escape free of the curse.
985 Now when we look to him we are all afraid;
he's pilot of our ship and he is frightened.

[*Enter* MESSENGER.]

MESSENGER: Might I learn from you, sirs, where is the house of Oedipus?
Or best of all, if you know, where is the king himself?
CHORUS: This is his house and he is within doors. This lady is his wife and
990 mother of his children.
MESSENGER: God bless you, lady, and God bless your household! God bless
Oedipus' noble wife!
JOCASTA: God bless you, sir, for your kind greeting! What do you want of
us that you have come here? What have you to tell us?
995 MESSENGER: Good news, lady. Good for your house and for your husband.
JOCASTA: What is your news? Who sent you to us?
MESSENGER: I come from Corinth and the news I bring will give you plea-
sure. Perhaps a little pain too.
JOCASTA: What is this news of double meaning?
1000 MESSENGER: The people of the Isthmus will choose Oedipus to be their
king. That is the rumour there.
JOCASTA: But isn't their king still old Polybus?
MESSENGER: No. He is in his grave. Death has got him.
JOCASTA: Is that the truth? Is Oedipus' father dead?
1005 MESSENGER: May I die myself if it be otherwise!
JOCASTA: [*To a* SERVANT.] Be quick and run to the King with the news! O
oracles of the Gods, where are you now? It was from this man Oedipus

fled, lest he should be his murderer! And now he is dead, in the course of nature, and not killed by Oedipus.

[*Enter* OEDIPUS.]

OEDIPUS: Dearest Jocasta, why have you sent for me?　　　　　　1010

JOCASTA: Listen to this man and when you hear reflect what is the outcome of the holy oracles of the Gods.

OEDIPUS: Who is he? What is his message for me?

JOCASTA: He is from Corinth and he tells us that your father Polybus is dead and gone.　　　　　　　　　　　　　　　　　1015

OEDIPUS: What's this you say, sir? Tell me yourself.

MESSENGER: Since this is the first matter you want clearly told: Polybus has gone down to death. You may be sure of it.

OEDIPUS: By treachery or sickness?

MESSENGER: A small thing will put old bodies asleep.　　　　　　1020

OEDIPUS: So he died of sickness, it seems,—poor old man!

MESSENGER: Yes, and of age—the long years he had measured.

OEDIPUS: Ha! Ha! O dear Jocasta, why should one
　　look to the Pythian hearth?[1] Why should one look
　　to the birds screaming overhead? They prophesied　　　　1025
　　that I should kill my father! But he's dead,
　　and hidden deep in earth, and I stand here
　　who never laid a hand on spear against him,—
　　unless perhaps he died of longing for me,
　　and thus I am his murderer. But they,　　　　　　　1030
　　the oracles, as they stand—he's taken them
　　away with him, they're dead as he himself is,
　　and worthless.

JOCASTA:　　　　　　　　That I told you before now.

OEDIPUS: You did, but I was misled by my fear.

JOCASTA: Then lay no more of them to heart, not one.　　　　　1035

OEDIPUS: But surely I must fear my mother's bed?

JOCASTA: Why should man fear since chance is all in all
　　for him, and he can clearly foreknow nothing?
　　Best to live lightly, as one can, unthinkingly.
　　As to your mother's marriage bed,—don't fear it.　　　　1040
　　Before this, in dreams too, as well as oracles,
　　many a man has lain with his own mother.
　　But he to whom such things are nothing bears
　　his life most easily.

OEDIPUS: All that you say would be said perfectly　　　　　　1045
　　if she were dead; but since she lives I must
　　still fear, although you talk so well, Jocasta.

JOCASTA: Still in your father's death there's light of comfort?

OEDIPUS: Great light of comfort; but I fear the living.

---

1. Delphi.

1050   MESSENGER: Who is the woman that makes you afraid?
OEDIPUS: Merope, old man, Polybus' wife.
MESSENGER: What about her frightens the queen and you?
OEDIPUS: A terrible oracle, stranger, from the Gods.
MESSENGER: Can it be told? Or does the sacred law
1055   forbid another to have knowledge of it?
OEDIPUS: O no! Once on a time Loxias said
that I should lie with my own mother and
take on my hands the blood of my own father.
And so for these long years I've lived away
1060   from Corinth; it has been to my great happiness;
but yet it's sweet to see the face of parents.
MESSENGER: This was the fear which drove you out of Corinth?
OEDIPUS: Old man, I did not wish to kill my father.
MESSENGER: Why should I not free you from this fear, sir,
1065   since I have come to you in all goodwill?
OEDIPUS: You would not find me thankless if you did.
MESSENGER: Why, it was just for this I brought the news,—
to earn your thanks when you had come safe home.
OEDIPUS: No, I will never come near my parents.
MESSENGER: Son,
1070   it's very plain you don't know what you're doing.
OEDIPUS: What do you mean, old man? For God's sake, tell me.
MESSENGER: If your homecoming is checked by fears like these.
OEDIPUS: Yes, I'm afraid that Phoebus may prove right.
MESSENGER: The murder and the incest?
OEDIPUS: Yes, old man;
that is my constant terror.
1075   MESSENGER: Do you know
that all your fears are empty?
OEDIPUS: How is that,
if they are father and mother and I their son?
MESSENGER: Because Polybus was no kin to you in blood.
OEDIPUS: What, was not Polybus my father?
MESSENGER: No more than I but just so much.
1080   OEDIPUS: How can
my father be my father as much as one
that's nothing to me?
MESSENGER: Neither he nor I
begat you.
OEDIPUS: Why then did he call me son?
MESSENGER: A gift he took you from these hands of mine.
1085   OEDIPUS: Did he love so much what he took from another's hand?
MESSENGER: His childlessness before persuaded him.
OEDIPUS: Was I a child you bought or found when I
was given to him?
MESSENGER: On Cithaeron's slopes

in the twisting thickets you were found.
OEDIPUS: And why
were you a traveller in those parts?
MESSENGER: I was   1090
in charge of mountain flocks.
OEDIPUS: You were a shepherd?
A hireling vagrant?
MESSENGER: Yes, but at least at that time
the man that saved your life, son.
OEDIPUS: What ailed me when you took me in your arms?
MESSENGER: In that your ankles should be witnesses.   1095
OEDIPUS: Why do you speak of that old pain?
MESSENGER: I loosed you;
the tendons of your feet were pierced and fettered,—
OEDIPUS: My swaddling clothes brought me a rare disgrace.
MESSENGER: So that from this you're called your present name.[2]
OEDIPUS: Was this my father's doing or my mother's?   1100
For God's sake, tell me.
MESSENGER: I don't know, but he
who gave you to me has more knowledge than I.
OEDIPUS: You yourself did not find me then? You took me
from someone else?
MESSENGER: Yes, from another shepherd.
OEDIPUS: Who was he? Do you know him well enough   1105
to tell?
MESSENGER: He was called Laius' man.
OEDIPUS: You mean the king who reigned here in the old days?
MESSENGER: Yes, he was that man's shepherd.
OEDIPUS: Is he alive
still, so that I could see him?
MESSENGER: You who live here
would know that best.
OEDIPUS: Do any of you here   1110
know of this shepherd whom he speaks about
in town or in the fields? Tell me. It's time
that this was found out once for all.
CHORUS: I think he is none other than the peasant
whom you have sought to see already; but   1115
Jocasta here can tell us best of that.
OEDIPUS: Jocasta, do you know about this man
whom we have sent for? Is he the man he mentions?
JOCASTA: Why ask of whom he spoke? Don't give it heed;
nor try to keep in mind what has been said.   1120
It will be wasted labour.
OEDIPUS: With such clues

2. *Oedipus* means, literally, "swollen foot."

I could not fail to bring my birth to light.
JOCASTA: I beg you—do not hunt this out—I beg you,
    if you have any care for your own life.
    What I am suffering is enough.
1125 OEDIPUS: Keep up
    your heart, Jocasta. Though I'm proved a slave,
    thrice slave, and though my mother is thrice slave,
    you'll not be shown to be of lowly lineage.
JOCASTA: O be persuaded by me, I entreat you;
1130   do not do this.
OEDIPUS: I will not be persuaded to let be
    the chance of finding out the whole thing clearly.
JOCASTA: It is because I wish you well that I
    give you this counsel—and it's the best counsel.
1135 OEDIPUS: Then the best counsel vexes me, and has
    for some while since.
JOCASTA: O Oedipus, God help you!
    God keep you from the knowledge of who you are!
OEDIPUS: Here, someone, go and fetch the shepherd for me;
    and let her find her joy in her rich family!
1140 JOCASTA: O Oedipus, unhappy Oedipus!
    that is all I can call you, and the last thing
    that I shall ever call you.

    [*Exit.*]

CHORUS: Why has the queen gone, Oedipus, in wild
    grief rushing from us? I am afraid that trouble
1145   will break out of this silence.
OEDIPUS: Break out what will! I at least shall be
    willing to see my ancestry, though humble.
    Perhaps she is ashamed of my low birth,
    for she has all a woman's high-flown pride.
1150   But I account myself a child of Fortune,
    beneficent Fortune, and I shall not be
    dishonoured. She's the mother from whom I spring;
    the months, my brothers, marked me, now as small,
    and now again as mighty. Such is my breeding,
1155   and I shall never prove so false to it,
    as not to find the secret of my birth.
CHORUS: [*Strophe.*] If I am a prophet and wise of heart
    you shall not fail, Cithaeron,
    by the limitless sky, you shall not!—
1160   to know at tomorrow's full moon
    that Oedipus honours you,
    as native to him and mother and nurse at once;
    and that you are honoured in dancing by us, as finding favour in
        sight of our king.
    Apollo, to whom we cry, find these things pleasing!

[*Antistrophe.*]

Who was it bore you, child? One of   1165
the long-lived nymphs who lay with Pan[3]—
the father who treads the hills?
Or was she a bride of Loxias, your mother? The grassy slopes
are all of them dear to him. Or perhaps Cyllene's[4] king
or the Bacchants' God[5] that lives on the tops   1170
of the hills received you a gift from some
one of the Helicon Nymphs,[6] with whom he mostly plays?

[*Enter an* OLD MAN, *led by* OEDIPUS' *servants.*]

OEDIPUS: If someone like myself who never met him
  may make a guess,—I think this is the herdsman,
  whom we were seeking. His old age is consonant   1175
  with the other. And besides, the men who bring him
  I recognize as my own servants. You
  perhaps may better me in knowledge since
  you've seen the man before.
CHORUS: You can be sure
  I recognize him. For if Laius   1180
  had ever an honest shepherd, this was he.
OEDIPUS: You, sir, from Corinth, I must ask you first,
  is this the man you spoke of?
MESSENGER: This is he
  before your eyes.
OEDIPUS: Old man, look here at me
  and tell me what I ask you. Were you ever   1185
  a servant of King Laius?
HERDSMAN: I was,—
  no slave he bought but reared in his own house.
OEDIPUS: What did you do as work? How did you live?
HERDSMAN: Most of my life was spent among the flocks.
OEDIPUS: In what part of the country did you live?   1190
HERDSMAN: Cithaeron and the places near to it.
OEDIPUS: And somewhere there perhaps you knew this man?
HERDSMAN: What was his occupation? Who?
OEDIPUS: This man here
  have you had any dealings with him?
HERDSMAN: No—
  not such that I can quickly call to mind.   1195
MESSENGER: That is no wonder, master. But I'll make him remember what
  he does not know. For I know, that he well knows the country of Cithae-

---

3. God of nature; half man, half goat.
4. Mountain reputed to be the birthplace of Hermes, the messenger god.
5. Dionysus.
6. The Muses; nine sister goddesses who presided over poetry, music, and the arts.

ron, how he with two flocks, I with one kept company for three years—
each year half a year—from spring till autumn time and then when
1200   winter came I drove my flocks to our fold home again and he to Laius'
steadings. Well—am I right or not in what I said we did?

HERDSMAN: You're right—although it's a long time ago.

MESSENGER: Do you remember giving me a child
to bring up as my foster child?

HERDSMAN: What's this?
Why do you ask this question?

1205 MESSENGER: Look old man,
here he is—here's the man who was that child!

HERDSMAN: Death take you! Won't you hold your tongue?

OEDIPUS: No, no,
do not find fault with him, old man. Your words
are more at fault than his.

HERDSMAN: O best of masters,
how do I give offense?

1210 OEDIPUS: When you refuse
to speak about the child of whom he asks you.

HERDSMAN: He speaks out of his ignorance, without meaning.

OEDIPUS: If you'll not talk to gratify me, you
will talk with pain to urge you.

HERDSMAN: O please, sir,
don't hurt an old man, sir.

1215 OEDIPUS: [To the SERVANTS.] Here, one of you,
twist his hands behind him.

HERDSMAN: Why, God help me, why?
What do you want to know?

OEDIPUS: You gave a child
to him,—the child he asked you of?

HERDSMAN: I did.
I wish I'd died the day I did.

OEDIPUS: You will
unless you tell me truly.

1220 HERDSMAN: And I'll die
far worse if I should tell you.

OEDIPUS: This fellow
is bent on more delays, as it would seem.

HERDSMAN: O no, no! I have told you that I gave it.

OEDIPUS: Where did you get this child from? Was it your own or did you
get it from another?

1225 HERDSMAN: Not
my own at all; I had it from someone.

OEDIPUS: One of these citizens? or from what house?

HERDSMAN: O master, please—I beg you, master, please don't ask me
more.

OEDIPUS: You're a dead man if I
ask you again.

HERDSMAN: It was one of the children   1230
  of Laius.
OEDIPUS: A slave? Or born in wedlock?
HERDSMAN: O God, I am on the brink of frightful speech.
OEDIPUS: And I of frightful hearing. But I must hear.
HERDSMAN: The child was called his child; but she within,
  your wife would tell you best how all this was.   1235
OEDIPUS: *She* gave it to you?
HERDSMAN: Yes, she did, my lord.
OEDIPUS: To do what with it?
HERDSMAN: Make away with it.
OEDIPUS: She was so hard—its mother?
HERDSMAN: Aye, through fear
  of evil oracles.
OEDIPUS: Which?
HERDSMAN: They said that he
  should kill his parents.
OEDIPUS: How was it that you   1240
  gave it away to this old man?
HERDSMAN: O master,
  I pitied it, and thought that I could send it
  off to another country and this man
  was from another country. But he saved it
  for the most terrible troubles. If you are   1245
  the man he says you are, you're bred to misery.
OEDIPUS: O, O, O, they will all come,
  all come out clearly! Light of the sun, let me
  look upon you no more after today!
  I who first saw the light bred of a match   1250
  accursed, and accursed in my living
  with them I lived with, cursed in my killing.

  [*Exeunt all but the* CHORUS.]

CHORUS: [*Strophe.*] O generations of men, how I
  count you as equal with those who live
  not at all!   1255
  What man, what man on earth wins more
  of happiness than a seeming
  and after that turning away?
  Oedipus, you are my pattern of this,
  Oedipus, you and your fate!   1260
  Luckless Oedipus, whom of all men
  I envy not at all.

  [*Antistrophe.*]

  In as much as he shot his bolt
  beyond the others and won the prize
  of happiness complete—   1265

O Zeus—and killed and reduced to nought
the hooked taloned maid of the riddling speech,[7]
standing a tower against death for my land:
hence he was called my king and hence
1270 was honoured the highest of all
honours; and hence he ruled
in the great city of Thebes.

  [*Strophe.*]

But now whose tale is more miserable?
Who is there lives with a savager fate?
1275 Whose troubles so reverse his life as his?

O Oedipus, the famous prince
for whom a great haven
the same both as father and son
sufficed for generation,
1280 how, O how, have the furrows ploughed
by your father endured to bear you, poor wretch,
and hold their peace so long?

  [*Antistrophe.*]

Time who sees all has found you out
against your will; judges your marriage accursed,
1285 begetter and begot at one in it.

O child of Laius,
would I had never seen you.
I weep for you and cry
a dirge of lamentation.

1290 To speak directly, I drew my breath
from you at the first and so now I lull
my mouth to sleep with your name.

  [*Enter a* SECOND MESSENGER.]

SECOND MESSENGER: O Princes always honoured by our country,
what deeds you'll hear of and what horrors see,
1295 what grief you'll feel, if you as true born Thebans
care for the house of Labdacus' sons.[8]
Phasis nor Ister cannot purge this house,
I think, with all their streams, such things
it hides, such evils shortly will bring forth

---

7. The sphinx, who killed herself when Oedipus was the first to give a correct answer to her riddle:
"What walks on four feet in the morning, on two at noon, and on three in the evening?"
8. Labdacus, king of Thebes, was father of Laïus and grandfather of Oedipus. *Phasis . . . Ister* (line
1297): rivers near Thebes.

into the light, whether they will or not; 1300
and troubles hurt the most
when they prove self-inflicted.
CHORUS: What we had known before did not fall short
of bitter groaning's worth; what's more to tell?
SECOND MESSENGER: Shortest to hear and tell—our glorious queen 1305
Jocasta's dead.
CHORUS: Unhappy woman! How?
SECOND MESSENGER: By her own hand. The worst of what was done
you cannot know. You did not see the sight.
Yet in so far as I remember it
you'll hear the end of our unlucky queen. 1310
When she came raging into the house she went
straight to her marriage bed, tearing her hair
with both her hands, and crying upon Laius
long dead—Do you remember, Laius,
that night long past which bred a child for us 1315
to send you to your death and leave
a mother making children with her son?
And then she groaned and cursed the bed in which
she brought forth husband by her husband, children
by her own child, an infamous double bond. 1320
How after that she died I do not know,—
for Oedipus distracted us from seeing.
He burst upon us shouting and we looked
to him as he paced frantically around,
begging us always: Give me a sword, I say, 1325
to find this wife no wife, this mother's womb,
this field of double sowing whence I sprang
and where I sowed my children! As he raved
some god showed him the way—none of us there.
Bellowing terribly and led by some 1330
invisible guide he rushed on the two doors,—
wrenching the hollow bolts out of their sockets,
he charged inside. There, there, we saw his wife
hanging, the twisted rope around her neck.
When he saw her, he cried out fearfully 1335
and cut the dangling noose. Then, as she lay,
poor woman, on the ground, what happened after,
was terrible to see. He tore the brooches—
the gold chased[9] brooches fastening her robe—
away from her and lifting them up high 1340
dashed them on his own eyeballs, shrieking out
such things as: they will never see the crime
I have committed or had done upon me!

9. Decorated with ornamental grooves.

Dark eyes, now in the days to come look on
1345   forbidden faces, do not recognize
those whom you long for—with such imprecations
he struck his eyes again and yet again
with the brooches. And the bleeding eyeballs gushed
and stained his beard—no sluggish oozing drops
1350   but a black rain and bloody hail poured down.

So it has broken—and not on one head
but troubles mixed for husband and for wife.
The fortune of the days gone by was true
good fortune—but today groans and destruction
1355   and death and shame—of all ills can be named
not one is missing.
CHORUS: Is he now in any ease from pain?
SECOND MESSENGER: He shouts
for someone to unbar the doors and show him
to all the men of Thebes, his father's killer,
1360   his mother's—no I cannot say the word,
it is unholy—for he'll cast himself,
out of the land, he says, and not remain
to bring a curse upon his house, the curse
he called upon it in his proclamation. But
1365   he wants for strength, aye, and some one to guide him;
his sickness is too great to bear. You, too,
will be shown that. The bolts are opening.
Soon you will see a sight to waken pity
even in the horror of it.

[*Enter the blinded* OEDIPUS.]

1370 CHORUS: This is a terrible sight for men to see!
I never found a worse!
Poor wretch, what madness came upon you!
What evil spirit leaped upon your life
to your ill-luck—a leap beyond man's strength!
1375   Indeed I pity you, but I cannot
look at you, though there's much I want to ask
and much to learn and much to see.
I shudder at the sight of you.
OEDIPUS: O, O,
1380   where am I going? Where is my voice
borne on the wind to and fro?
Spirit, how far have you sprung?
CHORUS: To a terrible place whereof men's ears
may not hear, nor their eyes behold it.
1385 OEDIPUS: Darkness!
Horror of darkness enfolding, resistless, unspeakable visitant sped by
an ill wind in haste!

madness and stabbing pain and memory
of evil deeds I have done!
CHORUS: In such misfortunes it's no wonder
if double weighs the burden of your grief.   1390
OEDIPUS: My friend,
you are the only one steadfast, the only one that attends on me;
you still stay nursing the blind man.
Your care is not unnoticed. I can know
your voice, although this darkness is my world.   1395
CHORUS: Doer of dreadful deeds, how did you dare
so far to do despite to your own eyes?
what spirit urged you to it?
OEDIPUS: It was Apollo, friends, Apollo,
that brought this bitter bitterness, my sorrows to completion.   1400
But the hand that struck me
was none but my own.
Why should I see
whose vision showed me nothing sweet to see?
CHORUS: These things are as you say.   1405
OEDIPUS: What can I see to love?
What greeting can touch my ears with joy?
Take me away, and haste—to a place out of the way!
Take me away, my friends, the greatly miserable,
the most accursed, whom God too hates   1410
above all men on earth!
CHORUS: Unhappy in your mind and your misfortune,
would I had never known you!
OEDIPUS: Curse on the man who took
the cruel bonds from off my legs, as I lay in the field.   1415
He stole me from death and saved me,
no kindly service.
Had I died then
I would not be so burdensome to friends.
CHORUS: I, too, could have wished it had been so.   1420
OEDIPUS: Then I would not have come
to kill my father and marry my mother infamously.
Now I am godless and child of impurity,
begetter in the same seed that created my wretched self.
If there is any ill worse than ill,   1425
that is the lot of Oedipus.
CHORUS: I cannot say your remedy was good;
you would be better dead than blind and living.
OEDIPUS: What I have done here was best done—don't tell me
otherwise, do not give me further counsel.   1430
I do not know with what eyes I could look
upon my father when I die and go
under the earth, nor yet my wretched mother—
those two to whom I have done things deserving

1435   worse punishment than hanging. Would the sight
of children, bred as mine are, gladden me?
No, not these eyes, never. And my city,
its towers and sacred places of the Gods,
of these I robbed my miserable self
1440   when I commanded all to drive *him* out,
the criminal since proved by God impure
and of the race of Laius.
To this guilt I bore witness against myself—
with what eyes shall I look upon my people?
1445   No. If there were a means to choke the fountain
of hearing I would not have stayed my hand
from locking up my miserable carcase,
seeing and hearing nothing; it is sweet
to keep our thoughts out of the range of hurt.

1450   Cithaeron, why did you receive me? why
having received me did you not kill me straight?
And so I had not shown to men my birth.

O Polybus and Corinth and the house,
the old house that I used to call my father's—
1455   what fairness you were nurse to, and what foulness
festered beneath! Now I am found to be
a sinner and a son of sinners. Crossroads,
and hidden glade, oak and the narrow way
at the crossroads, that drank my father's blood
1460   offered you by my hands, do you remember
still what I did as you looked on, and what
I did when I came here? O marriage, marriage!
you bred me and again when you had bred
bred children of your child and showed to men
1465   brides, wives and mothers and the foulest deeds
that can be in this world of ours.

    Come—it's unfit to say what is unfit
to do.—I beg of you in God's name hide me
somewhere outside your country, yes, or kill me,
1470   or throw me into the sea, to be forever
out of your sight. Approach and deign to touch me
for all my wretchedness, and do not fear.
No man but I can bear my evil doom.
    CHORUS: Here Creon comes in fit time to perform
1475   or give advice in what you ask of us.
Creon is left sole ruler in your stead.
    OEDIPUS: Creon! Creon! What shall I say to him?
How can I justly hope that he will trust me?
In what is past I have been proved towards him
an utter liar.

[*Enter* CREON.]

CREON: Oedipus, I've come   1480
not so that I might laugh at you nor taunt you
with evil of the past. But if you still
are without shame before the face of men
reverence at least the flame that gives all life,
our Lord the Sun, and do not show unveiled   1485
to him pollution such that neither land
nor holy rain nor light of day can welcome.

    [*To a* SERVANT.]

Be quick and take him in. It is most decent
that only kin should see and hear the troubles
of kin.

OEDIPUS: I beg you, since you've torn me from   1490
my dreadful expectations and have come
in a most noble spirit to a man
that has used you vilely—do a thing for me.
I shall speak for your own good, not for my own.

CREON: What do you need that you would ask of me?   1495

OEDIPUS: Drive me from here with all the speed you can
to where I may not hear a human voice.

CREON: Be sure, I would have done this had not I
wished first of all to learn from the God the course
of action I should follow.

OEDIPUS: But his word   1500
has been quite clear to let the parricide,
the sinner, die.

CREON: Yes, that indeed was said.
But in the present need we had best discover
what we should do.

OEDIPUS: And will you ask about
a man so wretched?

CREON: Now even you will trust   1505
the God.

OEDIPUS: So. I command you—and will beseech you—
to her that lies inside that house give burial
as you would have it; she is yours and rightly
you will perform the rites for her. For me—
never let this my father's city have me   1510
living a dweller in it. Leave me live
in the mountains where Cithaeron is, that's called
my mountain, which my mother and my father
while they were living would have made my tomb.
So I may die by their decree who sought   1515
indeed to kill me. Yet I know this much:
no sickness and no other thing will kill me.

I would not have been saved from death if not
for some strange evil fate. Well, let my fate
go where it will.

1520   Creon, you need not care
about my sons; they're men and so wherever
they are, they will not lack a livelihood.
But my two girls—so sad and pitiful—
whose table never stood apart from mine,
1525 and everything I touched they always shared—
O Creon, have a thought for them! And most
I wish that you might suffer me to touch them
and sorrow with them.

> [*Enter* ANTIGONE *and* ISMENE, OEDIPUS' *two daughters.*]

O my lord! O true noble Creon! Can I
1530 really be touching them, as when I saw?
What shall I say?
Yes, I can hear them sobbing—my two darlings!
and Creon has had pity and has sent me
what I loved most?
1535 Am I right?
CREON: You're right: it was I gave you this
because I knew from old days how you loved them
as I see now.
OEDIPUS: God bless you for it, Creon,
and may God guard you better on your road
than he did me!
1540   O children,
where are you? Come here, come to my hands,
a brother's hands which turned your father's eyes,
those bright eyes you knew once, to what you see,
a father seeing nothing, knowing nothing,
1545 begetting you from his own source of life.
I weep for you—I cannot see your faces—
I weep when I think of the bitterness
there will be in your lives, how you must live
before the world. At what assemblages
1550 of citizens will you make one? to what
gay company will you go and not come home
in tears instead of sharing in the holiday?
And when you're ripe for marriage, who will he be,
the man who'll risk to take such infamy
1555 as shall cling to my children, to bring hurt
on them and those that marry with them? What
curse is not there? "Your father killed his father
and sowed the seed where he had sprung himself
and begot you out of the womb that held him."

These insults you will hear. Then who will marry you? 1560
No one, my children; clearly you are doomed
to waste away in barrenness unmarried.
Son of Menoeceus,[1] since you are all the father
left these two girls, and we, their parents, both
are dead to them—do not allow them wander 1565
like beggars, poor and husbandless.
They are of your own blood.
And do not make them equal with myself
in wretchedness; for you can see them now
so young, so utterly alone, save for you only. 1570
Touch my hand, noble Creon, and say yes.
If you were older, children, and were wiser,
there's much advice I'd give you. But as it is,
let this be what you pray: give me a life
wherever there is opportunity 1575
to live, and better life than was my father's.
CREON: Your tears have had enough of scope; now go within the house.
OEDIPUS: I must obey, though bitter of heart.
CREON: In season, all is good.
OEDIPUS: Do you know on what conditions I obey?
CREON: You tell me them, 1580
  and I shall know them when I hear.
OEDIPUS: That you shall send me out
  to live away from Thebes.
CREON: That gift you must ask of the Gods.
OEDIPUS: But I'm now hated by the Gods.
CREON: So quickly you'll obtain your prayer.
OEDIPUS: You consent then?
CREON: What I do not mean, I do not use to say.
OEDIPUS: Now lead me away from here.
CREON: Let go the children, then, and come. 1585
OEDIPUS: Do not take them from me.
CREON: Do not seek to be master in everything,
  for the things you mastered did not follow you throughout your life.

[*As* CREON *and* OEDIPUS *go out.*]

CHORUS: You that live in my ancestral Thebes, behold this Oedipus,—
  him who knew the famous riddles and was a man most masterful;
  not a citizen who did not look with envy on his lot— 1590
  see him now and see the breakers of misfortune swallow him!
  Look upon that last day always. Count no mortal happy till
  he has passed the final limit of his life secure from pain.

ca. 429 B.C.E.

1. Father of Creon and Jocasta.

AUGUST WILSON

The Piano Lesson

Gin my cotton
Sell my seed
Buy my baby
Everything she need
      —Skip James

CHARACTERS

DOAKER	MARETHA
BOY WILLIE	AVERY
LYMON	WINING BOY
BERNIECE	GRACE

THE SETTING: *The action of the play takes place in the kitchen and parlor of the house where* DOAKER CHARLES *lives with his niece,* BERNIECE, *and her eleven-year-old daughter,* MARETHA. *The house is sparsely furnished, and although there is evidence of a woman's touch, there is a lack of warmth and vigor.* BERNIECE *and* MARETHA *occupy the upstairs rooms.* DOAKER'*s room is prominent and opens onto the kitchen. Dominating the parlor is an old upright piano. On the legs of the piano, carved in the manner of African sculpture, are mask-like figures resembling totems. The carvings are rendered with a grace and power of invention that lifts them out of the realm of craftsmanship and into the realm of art. At left is a staircase leading to the upstairs.*

ACT I
Scene 1

[*The lights come up on the Charles household. It is five o'clock in the morning. The dawn is beginning to announce itself, but there is something in the air that belongs to the night. A stillness that is a portent, a gathering, a coming together of something akin to a storm. There is a loud knock at the door.*]

BOY WILLIE: [*Off stage, calling.*] Hey, Doaker . . . Doaker! [*He knocks again and calls.*] Hey, Doaker! Hey, Berniece! Berniece!

[DOAKER *enters from his room. He is a tall, thin man of forty-seven, with severe features, who has for all intents and purposes retired from the world though he works full-time as a railroad cook.*]

DOAKER: Who is it?

BOY WILLIE: Open the door, nigger! It's me . . . Boy Willie!

DOAKER: Who?

BOY WILLIE: Boy Willie! Open the door!

[DOAKER *opens the door and* BOY WILLIE *and* LYMON *enter.* BOY WILLIE *is thirty years old. He has an infectious grin and a boyishness that is apt for his name. He is brash and impulsive, talkative and somewhat crude in speech and manner.* LYMON *is twenty-nine.* BOY WILLIE's *partner, he talks little, and then with a straightforwardness that is often disarming.*]

DOAKER: What you doing up here?

BOY WILLIE: I told you, Lymon. Lymon talking about you might be sleep. This is Lymon. You remember Lymon Jackson from down home? This my Uncle Doaker.

DOAKER: What you doing up here? I couldn't figure out who that was. I thought you was still down in Mississippi.

BOY WILLIE: Me and Lymon selling watermelons. We got a truck out there. Got a whole truckload of watermelons. We brought them up here to sell. Where's Berniece? [*Calls.*] Hey, Berniece!

DOAKER: Berniece up there sleep.

BOY WILLIE: Well, let her get up. [*Calls.*] Hey, Berniece!

DOAKER: She got to go to work in the morning.

BOY WILLIE: Well she can get up and say hi. It's been three years since I seen her. [*Calls.*] Hey, Berniece! It's me . . . Boy Willie.

DOAKER: Berniece don't like all that hollering now. She got to work in the morning.

BOY WILLIE: She can go on back to bed. Me and Lymon been riding two days in that truck . . . the least she can do is get up and say hi.

DOAKER: [*Looking out the window.*] Where you all get that truck from?

BOY WILLIE: It's Lymon's. I told him let's get a load of watermelons and bring them up here.

LYMON: Boy Willie say he going back, but I'm gonna stay. See what it's like up here.

BOY WILLIE: You gonna carry me down there first.

LYMON: I told you I ain't going back down there and take a chance on that truck breaking down again. You can take the train. Hey, tell him Doaker, he can take the train back. After we sell them watermelons he have enough money he can buy him a whole railroad car.

DOAKER: You got all them watermelons stacked up there no wonder the truck broke down. I'm surprised you made it this far with a load like that. Where you break down at?

BOY WILLIE: We broke down three times! It took us two and a half days to get here. It's a good thing we picked them watermelons fresh.

LYMON: We broke down twice in West Virginia. The first time was just as soon as we got out of Sunflower. About forty miles out she broke down. We got it going and got all the way to West Virginia before she broke down again.

BOY WILLIE: We had to walk about five miles for some water.

LYMON: It got a hole in the radiator but it runs pretty good. You have to pump the brakes sometime before they catch. Boy Willie have his door open and be ready to jump when that happens.

BOY WILLIE: Lymon think that's funny. I told the nigger I give him ten dollars to get the brakes fixed. But he thinks that funny.

LYMON: They don't need fixing. All you got to do is pump them till they catch.

[BERNIECE *enters on the stairs. Thirty-five years old, with an eleven-year-old daughter, she is still in mourning for her husband after three years.*]

BERNIECE: What you doing all that hollering for?

BOY WILLIE: Hey, Berniece. Doaker said you was sleep. I said at least you could get up and say hi.

BERNIECE: It's five o'clock in the morning and you come in here with all this noise. You can't come like normal folks. You got to bring all that noise with you.

BOY WILLIE: Hell, I ain't done nothing but come in and say hi. I ain't got in the house good.

BERNIECE: That's what I'm talking about. You start all that hollering and carry on as soon as you hit the door.

BOY WILLIE: Aw hell, woman, I was glad to see Doaker. You ain't had to come down if you didn't want to. I come eighteen hundred miles to see my sister I figure she might want to get up and say hi. Other than that you can go back upstairs. What you got, Doaker? Where your bottle? Me and Lymon want a drink. [*To* BERNIECE.] This is Lymon. You remember Lymon Jackson from down home.

LYMON: How you doing, Berniece. You look just like I thought you looked.

BERNIECE: Why you all got to come in hollering and carrying on? Waking the neighbors with all that noise.

BOY WILLIE: They can come over and join the party. We fixing to have a party. Doaker, where your bottle? Me and Lymon celebrating. The Ghosts of the Yellow Dog got Sutter.

BERNIECE: Say what?

BOY WILLIE: Ask Lymon, they found him the next morning. Say he drowned in his well.

DOAKER: When this happen, Boy Willie?

BOY WILLIE: About three weeks ago. Me and Lymon was over in Stoner County when we heard about it. We laughed. We thought it was funny. A great big old three-hundred-and-forty-pound man gonna fall down his well.

LYMON: It remind me of Humpty Dumpty.

BOY WILLIE: Everybody say the Ghosts of the Yellow Dog pushed him.

BERNIECE: I don't want to hear that nonsense. Somebody down there pushing them people in their wells.

DOAKER: What was you and Lymon doing over in Stoner County?

BOY WILLIE: We was down there working. Lymon got some people down there.

LYMON: My cousin got some land down there. We was helping him.

BOY WILLIE: Got near about a hundred acres. He got it set up real nice. Me and Lymon was down there chopping down trees. We was using Lymon's truck to haul the wood. Me and Lymon used to haul wood all around them parts. [*To* BERNIECE.] Me and Lymon got a truckload of watermelons out there.

[BERNIECE *crosses to the window to the parlor.*]

Doaker, where your bottle? I know you got a bottle stuck up in your room. Come on, me and Lymon want a drink.

[DOAKER *exits into his room.*]

BERNIECE: Where you all get that truck from?

BOY WILLIE: I told you it's Lymon's.

BERNIECE: Where you get the truck from, Lymon?

LYMON: I bought it.

BERNIECE: Where he get that truck from, Boy Willie?

BOY WILLIE: He told you he bought it. Bought it for a hundred and twenty dollars. I can't say where he got that hundred and twenty dollars from ... but he bought that old piece of truck from Henry Porter. [*To* LYMON.] Where you get that hundred and twenty dollars from, nigger?

LYMON: I got it like you get yours. I know how to take care of money.

[DOAKER *brings a bottle and sets it on the table.*]

BOY WILLIE: Aw hell, Doaker got some of that good whiskey. Don't give Lymon none of that. He ain't used to good whiskey. He liable to get sick.

LYMON: I done had good whiskey before.

BOY WILLIE: Lymon bought that truck so he have him a place to sleep. He down there wasn't doing no work or nothing. Sheriff looking for him. He bought that truck to keep away from the sheriff. Got Stovall looking for him too. He down there sleeping in that truck ducking and dodging both of them. I told him come on let's go up and see my sister.

BERNIECE: What the sheriff looking for you for, Lymon?

BOY WILLIE: The man don't want you to know all his business. He's my company. He ain't asking you no questions.

LYMON: It wasn't nothing. It was just a misunderstanding.

BERNIECE: He in my house. You say the sheriff looking for him, I wanna know what he looking for him for. Otherwise you all can go back out there and be where nobody don't have to ask you nothing.

LYMON: It was just a misunderstanding. Sometimes me and the sheriff we don't think alike. So we just got crossed on each other.

BERNIECE: Might be looking for him about that truck. He might have stole that truck.

BOY WILLIE: We ain't stole no truck, woman. I told you Lymon bought it.

DOAKER: Boy Willie and Lymon got more sense than to ride all the way up here in a stolen truck with a load of watermelons. Now they might have stole them watermelons, but I don't believe they stole that truck.

BOY WILLIE: You don't even know the man good and you calling him a thief. And we ain't stole them watermelons either. Them old man Pitterford's watermelons. He give me and Lymon all we could load for ten dollars.

DOAKER: No wonder you got them stacked up out there. You must have five hundred watermelons stacked up out there.

BERNIECE: Boy Willie, when you and Lymon planning on going back?

BOY WILLIE: Lymon say he staying. As soon as we sell them watermelons I'm going on back.

BERNIECE: [*Starts to exit up the stairs.*] That's what you need to do. And you need to do it quick. Come in here disrupting the house. I don't want all that loud carrying on around here. I'm surprised you ain't woke Maretha up.

BOY WILLIE: I was fixing to get her now. [*Calls.*] Hey, Maretha!

DOAKER: Berniece don't like all that hollering now.

BERNIECE: Don't you wake that child up!

BOY WILLIE: You going up there . . . wake her up and tell her her uncle's here. I ain't seen her in three years. Wake her up and send her down here. She can go back to bed.

BERNIECE: I ain't waking that child up . . . and don't you be making all that noise. You and Lymon need to sell them watermelons and go on back.

[BERNIECE *exits up the stairs.*]

BOY WILLIE: I see Berniece still try to be stuck up.

DOAKER: Berniece alright. She don't want you making all that noise. Maretha up there sleep. Let her sleep until she get up. She can see you then.

BOY WILLIE: I ain't thinking about Berniece. You hear from Wining Boy? You know Cleotha died?

DOAKER: Yeah, I heard that. He come by here about a year ago. Had a whole sack of money. He stayed here about two weeks. Ain't offered nothing. Berniece asked him for three dollars to buy some food and he got mad and left.

LYMON: Who's Wining Boy?

BOY WILLIE: That's my uncle. That's Doaker's brother. You heard me talk about Wining Boy. He play piano. He done made some records and everything. He still doing that, Doaker?

DOAKER: He made one or two records a long time ago. That's the only ones I ever known him to make. If you let him tell it he a big recording star.

BOY WILLIE: He stopped down home about two years ago. That's what I hear. I don't know. Me and Lymon was up on Parchman Farm doing them three years.

DOAKER: He don't never stay in one place. Now, he been here about eight months ago. Back in the winter. Now, you subject not to see him for another two years. It's liable to be that long before he stop by.

BOY WILLIE: If he had a whole sack of money you liable never to see him. You ain't gonna see him until he get broke. Just as soon as that sack of money is gone you look up and he be on your doorstep.

LYMON: [*Noticing the piano.*] Is that the piano?

BOY WILLIE: Yeah . . . look here, Lymon. See how it's carved up real nice and polished and everything? You never find you another piano like that.

LYMON: Yeah, that look real nice.

BOY WILLIE: I told you. See how it's polished? My mama used to polish it every day. See all them pictures carved on it? That's what I was talking about. You can get a nice price for that piano.

LYMON: That's all Boy Willie talked about the whole trip up here. I got tired of hearing him talk about the piano.

BOY WILLIE: All you want to talk about is women. You ought to hear this nigger, Doaker. Talking about all the women he gonna get when he get up here. He ain't had none down there but he gonna get a hundred when he get up here.

DOAKER: How your people doing down there, Lymon?

LYMON: They alright. They still there. I come up here to see what it's like up here. Boy Willie trying to get me to go back and farm with him.

BOY WILLIE: Sutter's brother selling the land. He say he gonna sell it to me. That's why I come up here. I got one part of it. Sell them watermelons and get me another part. Get Berniece to sell that piano and I'll have the third part.

DOAKER: Berniece ain't gonna sell that piano.

BOY WILLIE: I'm gonna talk to her. When she see I got a chance to get Sutter's land she'll come around.

DOAKER: You can put that thought out your mind. Berniece ain't gonna sell that piano.

BOY WILLIE: I'm gonna talk to her. She been playing on it?

DOAKER: You know she won't touch that piano. I ain't never known her to touch it since Mama Ola died. That's over seven years now. She say it got blood on it. She got Maretha playing on it though. Say Maretha can go on and do everything she can't do. Got her in an extra school down at the Irene Kaufman Settlement House. She want Maretha to grow up and be a schoolteacher. Say she good enough she can teach on the piano.

BOY WILLIE: Maretha don't need to be playing on no piano. She can play on the guitar.

DOAKER: How much land Sutter got left?

BOY WILLIE: Got a hundred acres. Good land. He done sold it piece by piece, he kept the good part for himself. Now he got to give that up. His brother come down from Chicago for the funeral . . . he up there in Chicago got some kind of business with soda fountain equipment. He anxious to sell the land, Doaker. He don't want to be bothered with it. He called me to him and said cause of how long our families done known each other and how we been good friends and all, say he wanted to sell the land to me. Say he'd rather see me with it than Jim Stovall. Told me he'd let me have it for two thousand dollars cash money. He don't know I found out the most Stovall would give him for it was fifteen hundred dollars. He trying to get that extra five hundred out of me telling me he doing me a favor. I thanked him just as nice. Told him what a good man Sutter was and how he had my sympathy and all. Told him to give me two weeks. He said he'd wait on me. That's why I come up here. Sell them watermelons. Get Berniece to sell that piano. Put them two parts with the part I done saved. Walk in there. Tip my hat. Lay my money down on the table. Get my deed and walk on out. This time I get to keep all the cotton. Hire me some men to work it for me. Gin my cotton. Get my seed. And I'll see you again next year. Might even plant some tobacco or some oats.

DOAKER: You gonna have a hard time trying to get Berniece to sell that piano. You know Avery Brown from down there don't you? He up here now. He followed Berniece up here trying to get her to marry him after Crawley got killed. He been up here about two years. He call himself a preacher now.

BOY WILLIE: I know Avery. I know him from when he used to work on the Willshaw place. Lymon know him too.

DOAKER: He after Berniece to marry him. She keep telling him no but he won't give up. He keep pressing her on it.

BOY WILLIE: Avery think all white men is bigshots. He don't know there some white men ain't got as much as he got.

DOAKER: He supposed to come past here this morning. Berniece going down to the bank with him to see if he can get a loan to start his church. That's why I know Berniece ain't gonna sell that piano. He tried to get her to sell it to help him start his church. Sent the man around and everything.

BOY WILLIE: What man?

DOAKER: Some white fellow was going around to all the colored people's houses looking to buy up musical instruments. He'd buy anything. Drums. Guitars. Harmonicas. Pianos. Avery sent him past here. He looked at the piano and got excited. Offered her a nice price. She turned him down and got on Avery for sending him past. The man kept on her about two weeks. He seen where she wasn't gonna sell it, he gave her his number and told her if she ever wanted to sell it to call him first. Say he'd go one better than what anybody else would give her for it.

BOY WILLIE: How much he offer her for it?

DOAKER: Now you know me. She didn't say and I didn't ask. I just know it was a nice price.

LYMON: All you got to do is find out who he is and tell him somebody else wanna buy it from you. Tell him you can't make up your mind who to sell it to, and if he like Doaker say, he'll give you anything you want for it.

BOY WILLIE: That's what I'm gonna do. I'm gonna find out who he is from Avery.

DOAKER: It ain't gonna do you no good. Berniece ain't gonna sell that piano.

BOY WILLIE: She ain't got to sell it. I'm gonna sell it. I own just as much of it as she does.

BERNIECE: [Offstage, hollers.] Doaker! Go on get away. Doaker!

DOAKER: [Calling.] Berniece?

[DOAKER and BOY WILLIE rush to the stairs, BOY WILLIE runs up the stairs, passing BERNIECE as she enters, running.]

DOAKER: Berniece, what's the matter? You alright? What's the matter?

[BERNIECE tries to catch her breath. She is unable to speak.]

DOAKER: That's alright. Take your time. You alright. What's the matter? [He calls.] Hey, Boy Willie?

BOY WILLIE: [*Offstage.*] Ain't nobody up here.

BERNIECE: Sutter . . . Sutter's standing at the top of the steps.

DOAKER: [*Calls.*] Boy Willie!

[LYMON *crosses to the stairs and looks up.* BOY WILLIE *enters from the stairs.*]

BOY WILLIE: Hey Doaker, what's wrong with her? Berniece, what's wrong? Who was you talking to?

DOAKER: She say she seen Sutter's ghost standing at the top of the stairs.

BOY WILLIE: Seen what? Sutter? She ain't seen no Sutter.

BERNIECE: He was standing right up there.

BOY WILLIE: [*Entering on the stairs.*] That's all in Berniece's head. Ain't nobody up there. Go on up there, Doaker.

DOAKER: I'll take your word for it. Berniece talking about what she seen. She say Sutter's ghost standing at the top of the steps. She ain't just make all that up.

BOY WILLIE: She up there dreaming. She ain't seen no ghost.

LYMON: You want a glass of water, Berniece? Get her a glass of water, Boy Willie.

BOY WILLIE: She don't need no water. She ain't seen nothing. Go on up there and look. Ain't nobody up there but Maretha.

DOAKER: Let Berniece tell it.

BOY WILLIE: I ain't stopping her from telling it.

DOAKER: What happened, Berniece?

BERNIECE: I come out my room to come back down here and Sutter was standing there in the hall.

BOY WILLIE: What he look like?

BERNIECE: He look like Sutter. He look like he always look.

BOY WILLIE: Sutter couldn't find his way from Big Sandy to Little Sandy. How he gonna find his way all the way up here to Pittsburgh? Sutter ain't never even heard of Pittsburgh.

DOAKER: Go on, Berniece.

BERNIECE: Just standing there with the blue suit on.

BOY WILLIE: The man ain't never left Marlin County when he was living . . . and he's gonna come all the way up here now that he's dead?

DOAKER: Let her finish. I want to hear what she got to say.

BOY WILLIE: I'll tell you this. If Berniece had seen him like she think she seen him she'd still be running.

DOAKER: Go on, Berniece. Don't pay Boy Willie no mind.

BERNIECE: He was standing there . . . had his hand on top of his head. Look like he might have thought if he took his hand down his head might have fallen off.

LYMON: Did he have on a hat?

BERNIECE: Just had on that blue suit . . . I told him to go away and he just stood there looking at me . . . calling Boy Willie's name.

BOY WILLIE: What he calling my name for?

BERNIECE: I believe you pushed him in the well.

BOY WILLIE: Now what kind of sense that make? You telling me I'm gonna go out there and hide in the weeds with all them dogs and things he got around there ... I'm gonna hide and wait till I catch him looking down his well just right ... then I'm gonna run over and push him in. A great big old three-hundred-and-forty-pound man.

BERNIECE: Well, what he calling your name for?

BOY WILLIE: He bending over looking down his well, woman ... how he know who pushed him? It could have been anybody. Where was you when Sutter fell in his well? Where was Doaker? Me and Lymon was over in Stoner County. Tell her, Lymon. The Ghosts of the Yellow Dog got Sutter. That's what happened to him.

BERNIECE: You can talk all that Ghosts of the Yellow Dog stuff if you want. I know better.

LYMON: The Ghosts of the Yellow Dog pushed him. That's what the people say. They found him in his well and all the people say it must be the Ghosts of the Yellow Dog. Just like all them other men.

BOY WILLIE: Come talking about he looking for me. What he come all the way up here for? If he looking for me all he got to do is wait. He could have saved himself a trip if he looking for me. That ain't nothing but in Berniece's head. Ain't no telling what she liable to come up with next.

BERNIECE: Boy Willie, I want you and Lymon to go ahead and leave my house. Just go on somewhere. You don't do nothing but bring trouble with you everywhere you go. If it wasn't for you Crawley would still be alive.

BOY WILLIE: Crawley what? I ain't had nothing to do with Crawley getting killed. Crawley three time seven.[1] He had his own mind.

BERNIECE: Just go on and leave. Let Sutter go somewhere else looking for you.

BOY WILLIE: I'm leaving. Soon as we sell them watermelons. Other than that I ain't going nowhere. Hell, I just got here. Talking about Sutter looking for me. Sutter was looking for that piano. That's what he was looking for. He had to die to find out where that piano was at ... If I was you I'd get rid of it. That's the way to get rid of Sutter's ghost. Get rid of that piano.

BERNIECE: I want you and Lymon to go on and take all this confusion out of my house!

BOY WILLIE: Hey, tell her, Doaker. What kind of sense that make? I told you, Lymon, as soon as Berniece see me she was gonna start something. Didn't I tell you that? Now she done made up that story about Sutter just so she could tell me to leave her house. Well, hell, I ain't going nowhere till I sell them watermelons.

BERNIECE: Well why don't you go out there and sell them! Sell them and go on back!

BOY WILLIE: We waiting till the people get up.

LYMON: Boy Willie say if you get out there too early and wake the people up they get mad at you and won't buy nothing from you.

---

1. That is, Crawley was 21 years old—an adult.

DOAKER: You won't be waiting long. You done let the sun catch up with you. This the time everybody be getting up around here.

BERNIECE: Come on, Doaker, walk up here with me. Let me get Maretha up and get her started. I got to get ready myself. Boy Willie, just go on out there and sell them watermelons and you and Lymon leave my house.

[BERNIECE *and* DOAKER *exit up the stairs.*]

BOY WILLIE: [*Calling after them.*] If you see Sutter up there . . . tell him I'm down here waiting on him.

LYMON: What if she see him again?

BOY WILLIE: That's all in her head. There ain't no ghost up there. [*Calls.*] Hey, Doaker . . . I told you ain't nothing up there.

LYMON: I'm glad he didn't say he was looking for me.

BOY WILLIE: I wish I would see Sutter's ghost. Give me a chance to put a whupping on him.

LYMON: You ought to stay up here with me. You be down there working his land . . . he might come looking for you all the time.

BOY WILLIE: I ain't thinking about Sutter. And I ain't thinking about staying up here. You stay up here. I'm going back and get Sutter's land. You think you ain't got to work up here. You think this the land of milk and honey. But I ain't scared of work. I'm going back and farm every acre of that land.

[DOAKER *enters from the stairs.*]

I told you there ain't nothing up there, Doaker. Berniece dreaming all that.

DOAKER: I believe Berniece seen something. Berniece levelheaded. She ain't just made all that up. She say Sutter had on a suit. I don't believe she ever seen Sutter in a suit. I believe that's what he was buried in, and that's what Berniece saw.

BOY WILLIE: Well, let her keep on seeing him then. As long as he don't mess with me.

[DOAKER *starts to cook his breakfast.*]

I heard about you, Doaker. They say you got all the women looking out for you down home. They be looking to see you coming. Say you got a different one every two weeks. Say they be fighting one another for you to stay with them. [*To* LYMON.] Look at him, Lymon. He know it's true.

DOAKER: I ain't thinking about no women. They never get me tied up with them. After Coreen I ain't got no use for them. I stay up on Jack Slattery's place when I be down there. All them women want is somebody with a steady payday.

BOY WILLIE: That ain't what I hear. I hear every two weeks the women all put on their dresses and line up at the railroad station.

DOAKER: I don't get down there but once a month. I used to go down there every two weeks but they keep switching me around. They keep switching all the fellows around.

BOY WILLIE: Doaker can't turn that railroad loose. He was working the railroad when I was walking around crying for sugartit. My mama used to brag on him.

DOAKER: I'm cooking now, but I used to line track. I pieced together the Yellow Dog stitch by stitch. Rail by rail. Line track all up around there. I lined track all up around Sunflower and Clarksdale. Wining Boy worked with me. He helped put in some of that track. He'd work it for six months and quit. Go back to playing piano and gambling.

BOY WILLIE: How long you been with the railroad now?

DOAKER: Twenty-seven years. Now, I'll tell you something about the railroad. What I done learned after twenty-seven years. See, you got North. You got West. You look over here you got South. Over there you got East. Now, you can start from anywhere. Don't care where you at. You got to go one of them four ways. And whichever way you decide to go they got a railroad that will take you there. Now, that's something simple. You think anybody would be able to understand that. But you'd be surprised how many people trying to go North get on a train going West. They think the train's supposed to go where they going rather than where it's going.

Now, why people going? Their sister's sick. They leaving before they kill somebody ... and they sitting across from somebody who's leaving to keep from getting killed. They leaving cause they can't get satisfied. They going to meet someone. I wish I had a dollar for every time that someone wasn't at the station to meet them. I done seen that a lot. In between the time they sent the telegram and the time the person get there ... they done forgot all about them.

They got so many trains out there they have a hard time keeping them from running into each other. Got trains going every whichaway. Got people on all of them. Somebody going where somebody just left. If everybody stay in one place I believe this would be a better world. Now what I done learned after twenty-seven years of railroading is this ... if the train stays on the track ... it's going to get where it's going. It might not be where you going. If it ain't, then all you got to do is sit and wait cause the train's coming back to get you. The train don't never stop. It'll come back every time. Now I'll tell you another thing ...

BOY WILLIE: What you cooking over there, Doaker? Me and Lymon's hungry.

DOAKER: Go on down there to Wylie and Kirkpatrick to Eddie's restaurant. Coffee cost a nickel and you can get two eggs, sausage, and grits for fifteen cents. He even give you a biscuit with it.

BOY WILLIE: That look good what you got. Give me a little piece of that grilled bread.

DOAKER: Here ... go on take the whole piece.

BOY WILLIE: Here you go, Lymon ... you want a piece?

[*He gives* LYMON *a piece of toast.* MARETHA *enters from the stairs.*]

BOY WILLIE: Hey, sugar. Come here and give me a hug. Come on give Uncle Boy Willie a hug. Don't be shy. Look at her, Doaker. She done got bigger. Ain't she got big?

DOAKER: Yeah, she getting up there.

BOY WILLIE: How you doing, sugar?

MARETHA: Fine.

BOY WILLIE: You was just a little old thing last time I seen you. You remember me, don't you? This your Uncle Boy Willie from down South. That there's Lymon. He my friend. We come up here to sell watermelons. You like watermelons?

[MARETHA *nods.*]

We got a whole truckload out front. You can have as many as you want. What you been doing?

MARETHA: Nothing.

BOY WILLIE: Don't be shy now. Look at you getting all big. How old is you?

MARETHA: Eleven. I'm gonna be twelve soon.

BOY WILLIE: You like it up here? You like the North?

MARETHA: It's alright.

BOY WILLIE: That there's Lymon. Did you say hi to Lymon?

MARETHA: Hi.

LYMON: How you doing? You look just like your mama. I remember you when you was wearing diapers.

BOY WILLIE: You gonna come down South and see me? Uncle Boy Willie gonna get him a farm. Gonna get a great big old farm. Come down there and I'll teach you how to ride a mule. Teach you how to kill a chicken, too.

MARETHA: I seen my mama do that.

BOY WILLIE: Ain't nothing to it. You just grab him by his neck and twist it. Get you a real good grip and then you just wring his neck and throw him in the pot. Cook him up. Then you got some good eating. What you like to eat? What kind of food you like?

MARETHA: I like everything . . . except I don't like no black-eyed peas.

BOY WILLIE: Uncle Doaker tell me your mama got you playing that piano. Come on play something for me.

[BOY WILLIE *crosses over to the piano followed by* MARETHA.]

Show me what you can do. Come on now. Here . . . Uncle Boy Willie give you a dime . . . show me what you can do. Don't be bashful now. That dime say you can't be bashful.

[MARETHA *plays. It is something any beginner first learns.*]

Here, let me show you something.

[BOY WILLIE *sits and plays a simple boogie-woogie.*]

See that? See what I'm doing? That's what you call the boogie-woogie. See now . . . you can get up and dance to that. That's how good it sound. It sound like you wanna dance. You can dance to that. It'll hold you up.

Whatever kind of dance you wanna do you can dance to that right there. See that? See how it go? Ain't nothing to it. Go on you do it.

MARETHA: I got to read it on the paper.

BOY WILLIE: You don't need no paper. Go on. Do just like that there.

BERNIECE: Maretha! You get up here and get ready to go so you be on time. Ain't no need you trying to take advantage of company.

MARETHA: I got to go.

BOY WILLIE: Uncle Boy Willie gonna get you a guitar. Let Uncle Doaker teach you how to play that. You don't need to read no paper to play the guitar. Your mama told you about that piano? You know how them pictures got on there?

MARETHA: She say it just always been like that since she got it.

BOY WILLIE: You hear that, Doaker? And you sitting up here in the house with Berniece.

DOAKER: I ain't got nothing to do with that. I don't get in the way of Berniece's raising her.

BOY WILLIE: You tell your mama to tell you about that piano. You ask her how them pictures got on there. If she don't tell you I'll tell you.

BERNIECE: Maretha!

MARETHA: I got to get ready to go.

BOY WILLIE: She getting big, Doaker. You remember her, Lymon?

LYMON: She used to be real little.

[*There is a knock on the door.* DOAKER *goes to answer it.* AVERY *enters. Thirty-eight years old, honest and ambitious, he has taken to the city like a fish to water, finding in it opportunities for growth and advancement that did not exist for him in the rural South. He is dressed in a suit and tie with a gold cross around his neck. He carries a small Bible.*]

DOAKER: Hey, Avery, come on in. Berniece upstairs.

BOY WILLIE: Look at him . . . look at him . . . he don't know what to say. He wasn't expecting to see me.

AVERY: Hey, Boy Willie. What you doing up here?

BOY WILLIE: Look at him, Lymon.

AVERY: Is that Lymon? Lymon Jackson?

BOY WILLIE: Yeah, you know Lymon.

DOAKER: Berniece be ready in a minute, Avery.

BOY WILLIE: Doaker say you a preacher now. What . . . we supposed to call you Reverend? You used to be plain old Avery. When you get to be a preacher, nigger?

LYMON: Avery say he gonna be a preacher so he don't have to work.

BOY WILLIE: I remember when you was down there on the Willshaw place planting cotton. You wasn't thinking about no Reverend then.

AVERY: That must be your truck out there. I saw that truck with them watermelons, I was trying to figure out what it was doing in front of the house.

BOY WILLIE: Yeah, me and Lymon selling watermelons. That's Lymon's truck.

DOAKER: Berniece say you all going down to the bank.

AVERY: Yeah, they give me a half day off work. I got an appointment to talk to the bank about getting a loan to start my church.

BOY WILLIE: Lymon say preachers don't have to work. Where you working at, nigger?

DOAKER: Avery got him one of them good jobs. He working at one of them skyscrapers downtown.

AVERY: I'm working down there at the Gulf Building running an elevator. Got a pension and everything. They even give you a turkey on Thanksgiving.

LYMON: How you know the rope ain't gonna break? Ain't you scared the rope's gonna break?

AVERY: That's steel. They got steel cables hold it up. It take a whole lot of breaking to break that steel. Naw, I ain't worried about nothing like that. It ain't nothing but a little old elevator. Now, I wouldn't get in none of them airplanes. You couldn't pay me to do nothing like that.

LYMON: That be fun. I'd rather do that than ride in one of them elevators.

BOY WILLIE: How many of them watermelons you wanna buy?

AVERY: I thought you was gonna give me one seeing as how you got a whole truck full.

BOY WILLIE: You can get one, get two. I'll give you two for a dollar.

AVERY: I can't eat but one. How much are they?

BOY WILLIE: Aw, nigger, you know I'll give you a watermelon. Go on, take as many as you want. Just leave some for me and Lymon to sell.

AVERY: I don't want but one.

BOY WILLIE: How you get to be a preacher, Avery? I might want to be a preacher one day. Have everybody call me Reverend Boy Willie.

AVERY: It come to me in a dream. God called me and told me he wanted me to be a shepherd for his flock. That's what I'm gonna call my church . . . The Good Shepherd Church of God in Christ.

DOAKER: Tell him what you told me. Tell him about the three hobos.

AVERY: Boy Willie don't want to hear all that.

LYMON: I do. Lots a people say your dreams can come true.

AVERY: Naw. You don't want to hear all that.

DOAKER: Go on. I told him you was a preacher. He didn't want to believe me. Tell him about the three hobos.

AVERY: Well, it come to me in a dream. See . . . I was sitting out in this railroad yard watching the trains go by. The train stopped and these three hobos got off. They told me they had come from Nazareth and was on their way to Jerusalem. They had three candles. They gave me one and told me to light it . . . but to be careful that it didn't go out. Next thing I knew I was standing in front of this house. Something told me to go knock on the door. This old woman opened the door and said they had been waiting on me. Then she led me into this room. It was a big room and it was full of all kinds of different people. They looked like anybody else except they all had sheep heads and was making noise like sheep make. I heard somebody call my name. I looked around and there was these same three hobos. They told me to take off my clothes and they give me a blue robe with gold thread. They washed my feet and combed my hair. Then they showed me these three doors and told me to pick one.

I went through one of them doors and that flame leapt off that candle and it seemed like my whole head caught fire. I looked around and there was four or five other men standing there with these same blue robes on. Then we heard a voice tell us to look out across this valley. We looked out and saw the valley was full of wolves. The voice told us that these sheep people that I had seen in the other room had to go over to the other side of this valley and somebody had to take them. Then I heard another voice say, "Who shall I send?" Next thing I knew I said, "Here I am. Send me." That's when I met Jesus. He say, "If you go, I'll go with you." Something told me to say, "Come on. Let's go." That's when I woke up. My head still felt like it was on fire . . . but I had a peace about myself that was hard to explain. I knew right then that I had been filled with the Holy Ghost and called to be a servant of the Lord. It took me a while before I could accept that. But then a lot of little ways God showed me that it was true. So I became a preacher.

LYMON: I see why you gonna call it the Good Shepherd Church. You dreaming about them sheep people. I can see that easy.

BOY WILLIE: Doaker say you sent some white man past the house to look at that piano. Say he was going around to all the colored people's houses looking to buy up musical instruments.

AVERY: Yeah, but Berniece didn't want to sell that piano. After she told me about it . . . I could see why she didn't want to sell it.

BOY WILLIE: What's this man's name?

AVERY: Oh, that's a while back now. I done forgot his name. He give Berniece a card with his name and telephone number on it, but I believe she throwed it away.

[BERNIECE *and* MARETHA *enter from the stairs.*]

BERNIECE: Maretha, run back upstairs and get my pocketbook. And wipe that hair grease off your forehead. Go ahead, hurry up.

[MARETHA *exits up the stairs.*]

How you doing, Avery? You done got all dressed up. You look nice. Boy Willie, I thought you and Lymon was going to sell them watermelons.

BOY WILLIE: Lymon done got sleepy. We liable to get some sleep first.

LYMON: I ain't sleepy.

DOAKER: As many watermelons as you got stacked up on that truck out there, you ought to have been gone.

BOY WILLIE: We gonna go in a minute. We going.

BERNIECE: Doaker. I'm gonna stop down there on Logan Street. You want anything?

DOAKER: You can pick up some ham hocks if you going down there. See if you can get the smoked ones. If they ain't got that get the fresh ones.

Don't get the ones that got all that fat under the skin. Look for the long ones. They nice and lean. [*He gives her a dollar.*] Don't get the short ones lessen they smoked. If you got to get the fresh ones make sure that they the long ones. If they ain't got them smoked then go ahead and get the short ones. [*Pause.*] You may as well get some turnip greens while you down there. I got some buttermilk ... if you pick up some cornmeal I'll make me some cornbread and cook up them turnip greens.

[MARETHA *enters from the stairs.*]

MARETHA: We gonna take the streetcar?

BERNIECE: Me and Avery gonna drop you off at the settlement house. You mind them people down there. Don't be going down there showing your color. Boy Willie, I done told you what to do. I'll see you later, Doaker.

AVERY: I'll be seeing you again, Boy Willie.

BOY WILLIE: Hey, Berniece ... what's the name of that man Avery sent past say he want to buy the piano?

BERNIECE: I knew it. I knew it when I first seen you. I knew you was up to something.

BOY WILLIE: Sutter's brother say he selling the land to me. He waiting on me now. Told me he'd give me two weeks. I got one part. Sell them watermelons get me another part. Then we can sell that piano and I'll have the third part.

BERNIECE: I ain't selling that piano, Boy Willie. If that's why you come up here you can just forget about it. [*To* DOAKER.] Doaker, I'll see you later. Boy Willie ain't nothing but a whole lot of mouth. I ain't paying him no mind. If he come up here thinking he gonna sell that piano then he done come up here for nothing.

[BERNIECE, AVERY, *and* MARETHA *exit the front door.*]

BOY WILLIE: Hey, Lymon! You ready to go sell these watermelons.

[BOY WILLIE *and* LYMON *start to exit. At the door* BOY WILLIE *turns to* DOAKER.]

Hey, Doaker ... if Berniece don't want to sell that piano ... I'm gonna cut it in half and go on and sell my half.

[BOY WILLIE *and* LYMON *exit.*]

[*The lights go down on the scene.*]

Scene 2

[*The lights come up on the kitchen. It is three days later.* WINING BOY *sits at the kitchen table. There is a half-empty pint bottle on the table.* DOAKER *busies himself washing pots.* WINING BOY *is fifty-six years old.* DOAKER's *older brother, he tries to present the image of a successful musician and gambler, but his music, his clothes, and even his manner of presentation are old.*

He is a man who looking back over his life continues to live it with an odd mixture of zest and sorrow.]

WINING BOY: So the Ghosts of the Yellow Dog got Sutter. That just go to show you I believe I always lived right. They say every dog gonna have his day and time it go around it sure come back to you. I done seen that a thousand times. I know the truth of that. But I'll tell you outright . . . if I see Sutter's ghost I'll be on the first thing I find that got wheels on it.

[DOAKER *enters from his room.*]

DOAKER: Wining Boy!

WINING BOY: And I'll tell you another thing . . . Berniece ain't gonna sell that piano.

DOAKER: That's what she told him. He say he gonna cut it in half and go on and sell his half. They been around here three days trying to sell them watermelons. They trying to get out to where the white folks live but the truck keep breaking down. They go a block or two and it break down again. They trying to get out to Squirrel Hill and can't get around the corner. He say soon as he can get that truck empty to where he can set the piano up in there he gonna take it out of here and go sell it.

WINING BOY: What about them boys Sutter got? How come they ain't farming that land?

DOAKER: One of them going to school. He left down there and come North to school. The other one ain't got as much sense as that frying pan over yonder. That is the dumbest white man I ever seen. He'd stand in the river and watch it rise till it drown him.

WINING BOY: Other than seeing Sutter's ghost how's Berniece doing?

DOAKER: She doing alright. She still got Crawley on her mind. He been dead three years but she still holding on to him. She need to go out here and let one of these fellows grab a whole handful of whatever she got. She act like it done got precious.

WINING BOY: They always told me any fish will bite if you got good bait.

DOAKER: She stuck up on it. She think it's better than she is. I believe she messing around with Avery. They got something going. He a preacher now. If you let him tell it the Holy Ghost sat on his head and heaven opened up with thunder and lightning and God was calling his name. Told him to go out and preach and tend to his flock. That's what he gonna call his church. The Good Shepherd Church.

WINING BOY: They had that joker down in Spear walking around talking about he Jesus Christ. He gonna live the life of Christ. Went through the Last Supper and everything. Rented him a mule on Palm Sunday and rode through the town. Did everything . . . talking about he Christ. He did everything until they got up to that crucifixion part. Got up to that part and told everybody to go home and quit pretending. He got up to the crucifixion part and changed his mind. Had a whole bunch of folks come down there to see him get nailed to the cross. I don't know who's the worse fool. Him or them. Had all them folks come down there . . . even carried the cross up this little hill. People standing around waiting to see him get nailed to the cross and he stop everything and preach a little sermon and told everybody to go home. Had enough nerve to tell them to come to church on Easter Sunday to celebrate his resurrection.

DOAKER: I'm surprised Avery ain't thought about that. He trying every little thing to get him a congregation together. They meeting over at his house till he get him a church.

WINING BOY: Ain't nothing wrong with being a preacher. You got the preacher on one hand and the gambler on the other. Sometimes there ain't too much difference in them.

DOAKER: How long you been in Kansas City?

WINING BOY: Since I left here. I got tied up with some old gal down there. [*Pause.*] You know Cleotha died.

DOAKER: Yeah, I heard that last time I was down there. I was sorry to hear that.

WINING BOY: One of her friends wrote and told me. I got the letter right here. [*He takes the letter out of his pocket.*] I was down in Kansas City and she wrote and told me Cleotha had died. Name of Willa Bryant. She say she know cousin Rupert. [*He opens the letter and reads.*] Dear Wining Boy: I am writing this letter to let you know Miss Cleotha Holman passed on Saturday the first of May she departed this world in the loving arms of her sister Miss Alberta Samuels. I know you would want to know this and am writing as a friend of Cleotha. There have been many hardships since last you seen her but she survived them all and to the end was a good woman whom I hope have God's grace and is in His Paradise. Your cousin Rupert Bates is my friend also and he give me your address and I pray this reaches you about Cleotha. Miss Willa Bryant. A friend. [*He folds the letter and returns it to his pocket.*] They was nailing her coffin shut by the time I heard about it. I never knew she was sick. I believe it was that yellow jaundice. That's what killed her mama.

DOAKER: Cleotha wasn't but forty-some.

WINING BOY: She was forty-six. I got ten years on her. I met her when she was sixteen. You remember I used to run around there. Couldn't nothing keep me still. Much as I loved Cleotha I loved to ramble. Couldn't nothing keep me still. We got married and we used to fight about it all the time. Then one day she asked me to leave. Told me she loved me before I left. Told me, Wining Boy, you got a home as long as I got mine. And I believe in my heart I always felt that and that kept me safe.

DOAKER: Cleotha always did have a nice way about her.

WINING BOY: Man that woman was something. I used to thank the Lord. Many a night I sat up and looked out over my life. Said, well, I had Cleotha. When it didn't look like there was nothing else for me, I said, thank God, at least I had that. If ever I go anywhere in this life I done known a good woman. And that used to hold me till the next morning. [*Pause.*] What you got? Give me a little nip. I know you got something stuck up in your room.

DOAKER: I ain't seen you walk in here and put nothing on the table. You done sat there and drank up your whiskey. Now you talking about what you got.

WINING BOY: I got plenty money. Give me a little nip.

[DOAKER *carries a glass into his room and returns with it half-filled. He sets it on the table in front of* WINING BOY.]

WINING BOY: You hear from Coreen?

DOAKER: She up in New York. I let her go from my mind.

WINING BOY: She was something back then. She wasn't too pretty but she had a way of looking at you made you know there was a whole lot of woman there. You got married and snatched her out from under us and we all got mad at you.

DOAKER: She up in New York City. That's what I hear.

[*The door opens and* BOY WILLIE *and* LYMON *enter.*]

BOY WILLIE: Aw hell . . . look here! We was just talking about you. Doaker say you left out of here with a whole sack of money. I told him we wasn't going see you till you got broke.

WINING BOY: What you mean broke? I got a whole pocketful of money.

DOAKER: Did you all get that truck fixed?

BOY WILLIE: We got it running and got halfway out there on Centre and it broke down again. Lymon went out there and messed it up some more. Fellow told us we got to wait till tomorrow to get it fixed. Say he have it running like new. Lymon going back down there and sleep in the truck so the people don't take the watermelons.

LYMON: Lymon nothing. You go down there and sleep in it.

BOY WILLIE: You was sleeping in it down home, nigger! I don't know nothing about sleeping in no truck.

LYMON: I ain't sleeping in no truck.

BOY WILLIE: They can take all the watermelons. I don't care. Wining Boy, where you coming from? Where you been?

WINING BOY: I been down in Kansas City.

BOY WILLIE: You remember Lymon? Lymon Jackson.

WINING BOY: Yeah, I used to know his daddy.

BOY WILLIE: Doaker say you don't never leave no address with nobody. Say he got to depend on your whim. See when it strike you to pay a visit.

WINING BOY: I got four or five addresses.

BOY WILLIE: Doaker say Berniece asked you for three dollars and you got mad and left.

WINING BOY: Berniece try and rule over you too much for me. That's why I left. It wasn't about no three dollars.

BOY WILLIE: Where you getting all these sacks of money from? I need to be with you. Doaker say you had a whole sack of money . . . turn some of it loose.

WINING BOY: I was just fixing to ask you for five dollars.

BOY WILLIE: I ain't got no money. I'm trying to get some. Doaker tell you about Sutter? The Ghosts of the Yellow Dog got him about three weeks ago. Berniece done seen his ghost and everything. He right upstairs. [*Calls.*] Hey Sutter! Wining Boy's here. Come on, get a drink!

WINING BOY: How many that make the Ghosts of the Yellow Dog done got?

BOY WILLIE: Must be about nine or ten, eleven or twelve. I don't know.

DOAKER: You got Ed Saunders. Howard Peterson. Charlie Webb.

WINING BOY: Robert Smith. That fellow that shot Becky's boy . . . say he was stealing peaches . . .

DOAKER: You talking about Bob Mallory.

BOY WILLIE: Berniece say she don't believe all that about the Ghosts of the Yellow Dog.

WINING BOY: She ain't got to believe. You go ask them white folks in Sunflower County if they believe. You go ask Sutter if he believe. I don't care if Berniece believe or not. I done been to where the Southern cross the Yellow Dog and called out their names. They talk back to you, too.

LYMON: What they sound like? The wind or something?

BOY WILLIE: You done been there for real, Wining Boy?

WINING BOY: Nineteen thirty. July of nineteen thirty I stood right there on that spot. It didn't look like nothing was going right in my life. I said everything can't go wrong all the time . . . let me go down there and call on the Ghosts of the Yellow Dog, see if they can help me. I went down there and right there where them two railroads cross each other . . . I stood right there on that spot and called out their names. They talk back to you, too.

LYMON: People say you can ask them questions. They talk to you like that?

WINING BOY: A lot of things you got to find out on your own. I can't say how they talked to nobody else. But to me it just filled me up in a strange sort of way to be standing there on that spot. I didn't want to leave. It felt like the longer I stood there the bigger I got. I seen the train coming and it seem like I was bigger than the train. I started not to move. But something told me to go ahead and get on out the way. The train passed and I started to go back up there and stand some more. But something told me not to do it. I walked away from there feeling like a king. Went on and had a stroke of luck that run on for three years. So I don't care if Berniece believe or not. Berniece ain't got to believe. I know cause I been there. Now Doaker'll tell you about the Ghosts of the Yellow Dog.

DOAKER: I don't try and talk that stuff with Berniece. Avery got her all tied up in that church. She just think it's a whole lot of nonsense.

BOY WILLIE: Berniece don't believe in nothing. She just think she believe. She believe in anything if it's convenient for her to believe. But when that convenience run out then she ain't got nothing to stand on.

WINING BOY: Let's not get on Berniece now. Doaker tell me you talking about selling that piano.

BOY WILLIE: Yeah . . . hey, Doaker, I got the name of that man Avery was talking about. The man what's fixing the truck gave me his name. Everybody know him. Say he buy up anything you can make music with. I got his name and his telephone number. Hey, Wining Boy, Sutter's brother say he selling the land to me. I got one part. Sell them water-melons get me the second part. Then . . . soon as I get them watermelons out that truck I'm gonna take and sell that piano and get the third part.

DOAKER: That land ain't worth nothing no more. The smart white man's up here in these cities. He cut the land loose and step back and watch you and the dumb white man argue over it.

WINING BOY: How you know Sutter's brother ain't sold it already? You talking about selling the piano and the man's liable to sold the land two or three times.

BOY WILLIE: He say he waiting on me. He say he give me two weeks. That's two weeks from Friday. Say if I ain't back by then he might gonna sell it to somebody else. He say he wanna see me with it.

WINING BOY: You know as well as I know the man gonna sell the land to the first one walk up and hand him the money.

BOY WILLIE: That's just who I'm gonna be. Look, you ain't gotta know he waiting on me. I know. Okay. I know what the man told me. Stovall already done tried to buy the land from him and he told him no. The man say he waiting on me . . . he waiting on me. Hey, Doaker . . . give me a drink. I see Wining Boy got his glass.

[DOAKER *exits into his room.*]

Wining Boy, what you doing in Kansas City? What they got down there?

LYMON: I hear they got some nice-looking women in Kansas City. I sure like to go down there and find out.

WINING BOY: Man, the women down there is something else.

[DOAKER *enters with a bottle of whiskey. He sets it on the table with some glasses.*]

DOAKER: You wanna sit up here and drink up my whiskey, leave a dollar on the table when you get up.

BOY WILLIE: You ain't doing nothing but showing your hospitality. I know we ain't got to pay for your hospitality.

WINING BOY: Doaker say they had you and Lymon down on the Parchman Farm. Had you on my old stomping grounds.

BOY WILLIE: Me and Lymon was down there hauling wood for Jim Miller and keeping us a little bit to sell. Some white fellows tried to run us off of it. That's when Crawley got killed. They put me and Lymon in the penitentiary.

LYMON: They ambushed us right there where that road dip down and around that bend in the creek. Crawley tried to fight them. Me and Boy Willie got away but the sheriff got us. Say we was stealing wood. They shot me in my stomach.

BOY WILLIE: They looking for Lymon down there now. They rounded him up and put him in jail for not working.

LYMON: Fined me a hundred dollars. Mr. Stovall come and paid my hundred dollars and the judge say I got to work for him to pay him back his hundred dollars. I told them I'd rather take my thirty days but they wouldn't let me do that.

BOY WILLIE: As soon as Stovall turned his back, Lymon was gone. He down there living in that truck dodging the sheriff and Stovall. He got both of them looking for him. So I brought him up here.

LYMON: I told Boy Willie I'm gonna stay up here. I ain't going back with him.

BOY WILLIE: Ain't nobody twisting your arm to make you go back. You can do what you want to do.

WINING BOY: I'll go back with you. I'm on my way down there. You gonna take the train? I'm gonna take the train.

LYMON: They treat you better up here.

BOY WILLIE: I ain't worried about nobody mistreating me. They treat you like you let them treat you. They mistreat me I mistreat them right back. Ain't no difference in me and the white man.

WINING BOY: Ain't no difference as far as how somebody supposed to treat you. I agree with that. But I'll tell you the difference between the colored man and the white man. Alright. Now you take and eat some berries. They taste real good to you. So you say I'm gonna go out and get me a whole pot of these berries and cook them up to make a pie or whatever. But you ain't looked to see them berries is sitting in the white fellow's yard. Ain't got no fence around them. You figure anybody want something they'd fence it in. Alright. Now the white man come along and say that's my land. Therefore everything that grow on it belong to me. He tell the sheriff, "I want you to put this nigger in jail as a warning to all the other niggers. Otherwise first thing you know these niggers have everything that belong to us."

BOY WILLIE: I'd come back at night and haul off his whole patch while he was sleep.

WINING BOY: Alright. Now Mr. So and So, he sell the land to you. And he come to you and say, "John, you own the land. It's all yours now. But them is my berries. And come time to pick them I'm gonna send my boys over. You got the land . . . but them berries, I'm gonna keep them. They mine." And he go and fix it with the law that them is his berries. Now that's the difference between the colored man and the white man. The colored man can't fix nothing with the law.

BOY WILLIE: I don't go by what the law say. The law's liable to say anything. I go by if it's right or not. It don't matter to me what the law say. I take and look at it for myself.

LYMON: That's why you gonna end up back down there on the Parchman Farm.

BOY WILLIE: I ain't thinking about no Parchman Farm. You liable to go back before me.

LYMON: They work you too hard down there. All that weeding and hoeing and chopping down trees. I didn't like all that.

WINING BOY: You ain't got to like your job on Parchman. Hey, tell him, Doaker, the only one got to like his job is the waterboy.

DOAKER: If he don't like his job he need to set that bucket down.

BOY WILLIE: That's what they told Lymon. They had Lymon on water and everybody got mad at him cause he was lazy.

LYMON: That water was heavy.

BOY WILLIE: They had Lymon down there singing:

[*Sings.*]

O Lord Berta Berta O Lord gal oh-ah
O Lord Berta Berta O Lord gal well

[LYMON *and* WINING BOY *join in.*]

Go 'head marry don't you wait on me oh-ah
Go 'head marry don't you wait on me well
Might not want you when I go free oh-ah
Might not want you when I go free well

BOY WILLIE: Come on, Doaker. Doaker know this one.

[*As* DOAKER *joins in the men stamp and clap to keep time. They sing in harmony with great fervor and style.*]

O Lord Berta Berta O Lord gal oh-ah
O Lord Berta Berta O Lord gal well

Raise them up higher, let them drop on down oh-ah
Raise them up higher, let them drop on down well
Don't know the difference when the sun go down oh-ah
Don't know the difference when the sun go down well

Berta in Meridan and she living at ease oh-ah
Berta in Meridan and she living at ease well
I'm on old Parchman, got to work or leave oh-ah
I'm on old Parchman, got to work or leave well

O Alberta, Berta, O Lord gal oh-ah
O Alberta, Berta, O Lord gal well

When you marry, don't marry no farming man oh-ah
When you marry, don't marry no farming man well
Everyday Monday, hoe handle in your hand oh-ah
Everyday Monday, hoe handle in your hand well

When you marry, marry a railroad man, oh-ah
When you marry, marry a railroad man, well
Everyday Sunday, dollar in your hand oh-ah
Everyday Sunday, dollar in your hand well

O Alberta, Berta, O Lord gal oh-ah
O Alberta, Berta, O Lord gal well

BOY WILLIE: Doaker like that part. He like that railroad part.

LYMON: Doaker sound like Tangleye.[2] He can't sing a lick.

BOY WILLIE: Hey, Doaker, they still talk about you down on Parchman.

---

2. Or Tangle Eye, one of the prisoners field-recorded at Parchman Farm by Alan Lomax in the 1930s and 1940s.

They ask me, "You Doaker Boy's nephew?" I say, "Yeah, me and him is family." They treated me alright soon as I told them that. Say, "Yeah, he my uncle."

DOAKER: I don't never want to see none of them niggers no more.

BOY WILLIE: I don't want to see them either. Hey, Wining Boy, come on play some piano. You a piano player, play some piano. Lymon wanna hear you.

WINING BOY: I give that piano up. That was the best thing that ever happened to me, getting rid of that piano. That piano got so big and I'm carrying it around on my back. I don't wish that on nobody. See, you think it's all fun being a recording star. Got to carrying that piano around and man did I get slow. Got just like molasses. The world just slipping by me and I'm walking around with that piano. Alright. Now, there ain't but so many places you can go. Only so many road wide enough for you and that piano. And that piano get heavier and heavier. Go to a place and they find out you play piano, the first thing they want to do is give you a drink, find you a piano, and sit you right down. And that's where you gonna be for the next eight hours. They ain't gonna let you get up! Now, the first three or four years of that is fun. You can't get enough whiskey and you can't get enough women and you don't never get tired of playing that piano. But that only last so long. You look up one day and you hate the whiskey, and you hate the women, and you hate the piano. But that's all you got. You can't do nothing else. All you know how to do is play that piano. Now, who am I? Am I me? Or am I the piano player? Sometime it seem like the only thing to do is shoot the piano player cause he the cause of all the trouble I'm having.

DOAKER: What you gonna do when your troubles get like mine?

LYMON: If I knew how to play it, I'd play it. That's a nice piano.

BOY WILLIE: Whoever playing better play quick. Sutter's brother say he waiting on me. I sell them watermelons. Get Berniece to sell that piano. Put them two parts with the part I done saved . . .

WINING BOY: Berniece ain't gonna sell that piano. I don't see why you don't know that.

BOY WILLIE: What she gonna do with it? She ain't doing nothing but letting it sit up there and rot. That piano ain't doing nobody no good.

LYMON: That's a nice piano. If I had it I'd sell it. Unless I knew how to play like Wining Boy. You can get a nice price for that piano.

DOAKER: Now I'm gonna tell you something, Lymon don't know this . . . but I'm gonna tell you why me and Wining Boy say Berniece ain't gonna sell that piano.

BOY WILLIE: She ain't got to sell it! I'm gonna sell it! Berniece ain't got no more rights to that piano than I do.

DOAKER: I'm talking to the man . . . let me talk to the man. See, now . . . to understand why we say that . . . to understand about that piano . . . you got to go back to slavery time. See, our family was owned by a fellow named Robert Sutter. That was Sutter's grandfather. Alright. The piano was owned by a fellow named Joel Nolander. He was one of the Nolander brothers from down in Georgia. It was coming up on Sutter's wedding anniversary and he was looking to buy his wife . . . Miss Ophelia was her name . . . he was looking to buy her an anniversary present. Only thing with him . . . he ain't had no money. But he had some niggers. So he asked Mr. Nolander to see if maybe he could trade off some of his niggers for that piano. Told him he would give him one and a half niggers for it. That's the way he told him. Say he could have one full grown and one half grown. Mr. Nolander agreed only he say he had to pick them. He didn't want Sutter to give him just any old nigger. He say he wanted to have the pick of the litter. So Sutter lined up his niggers and Mr. Nolander looked them over and out of the whole bunch he picked my grandmother . . . her name was Berniece . . . same like Berniece . . . and he picked my daddy when he wasn't nothing but a little boy nine years old. They made the trade off and Miss Ophelia was so happy with that piano that it got to be just about all she would do was play on that piano.

WINING BOY: Just get up in the morning, get all dressed up and sit down and play on that piano.

DOAKER: Alright. Time go along. Time go along. Miss Ophelia got to missing my grandmother . . . the way she would cook and clean the house and talk to her and what not. And she missed having my daddy around the house to fetch things for her. So she asked to see if maybe she could trade back that piano and get her niggers back. Mr. Nolander said no. Said a deal was a deal. Him and Sutter had a big falling out about it and Miss Ophelia took sick to the bed. Wouldn't get out of the bed in the morning. She just lay there. The doctor said she was wasting away.

WINING BOY: That's when Sutter called our granddaddy up to the house.

DOAKER: Now, our granddaddy's name was Boy Willie. That's who Boy Willie's named after . . . only they called him Willie Boy. Now, he was a worker of wood. He could make you anything you wanted out of wood. He'd make you a desk. A table. A lamp. Anything you wanted. Them white fellows around there used to come up to Mr. Sutter and get him to make all kinds of things for them. Then they'd pay Mr. Sutter a nice price. See, everything my granddaddy made Mr. Sutter owned cause he owned him. That's why when Mr. Nolander offered to buy him to keep the family together Mr. Sutter wouldn't sell him. Told Mr. Nolander he didn't have enough money to buy him. Now . . . am I telling it right, Wining Boy?

WINING BOY: You telling it.

DOAKER: Sutter called him up to the house and told him to carve my grandmother and my daddy's picture on the piano for Miss Ophelia. And he took and carved this . . .

[DOAKER *crosses over to the piano.*]

See that right there? That's my grandmother, Berniece. She looked just like that. And he put a picture of my daddy when he wasn't nothing but a little boy the way he remembered him. He made them up out of his memory. Only thing... he didn't stop there. He carved all this. He got a picture of his mama... Mama Esther... and his daddy, Boy Charles.

WINING BOY: That was the first Boy Charles.

DOAKER: Then he put on the side here all kinds of things. See that? That's when him and Mama Berniece got married. They called it jumping the broom. That's how you got married in them days. Then he got here when my daddy was born... and here he got Mama Esther's funeral... and down here he got Mr. Nolander taking Mama Berniece and my daddy away down to his place in Georgia. He got all kinds of things what happened with our family. When Mr. Sutter seen the piano with all them carvings on it he got mad. He didn't ask for all that. But see... there wasn't nothing he could do about it. When Miss Ophelia seen it... she got excited. Now she had her piano and her niggers too. She took back to playing it and played on it right up till the day she died. Alright... now see, our brother Boy Charles... that's Berniece and Boy Willie's daddy... he was the oldest of us three boys. He's dead now. But he would have been fifty-seven if he had lived. He died in 1911 when he was thirty-one years old. Boy Charles used to talk about that piano all the time. He never could get it off his mind. Two or three months go by and he be talking about it again. He be talking about taking it out of Sutter's house. Say it was the story of our whole family and as long as Sutter had it... he had us. Say we was still in slavery. Me and Wining Boy tried to talk him out of it but it wouldn't do any good. Soon as he quiet down about it he'd start up again. We seen where he wasn't gonna get it off his mind... so, on the Fourth of July, 1911... when Sutter was at the picnic what the county give every year... me and Wining Boy went on down there with him and took that piano out of Sutter's house. We put it on a wagon and me and Wining Boy carried it over into the next county with Mama Ola's people. Boy Charles decided to stay around there and wait until Sutter got home to make it look like business as usual.

Now, I don't know what happened when Sutter came home and found that piano gone. But somebody went up to Boy Charles's house and set it on fire. But he wasn't in there. He must have seen them coming cause he went down and caught the 3:57 Yellow Dog. He didn't know they was gonna come down and stop the train. Stopped the train and found Boy Charles in the boxcar with four of them hobos. Must have got mad when they couldn't find the piano cause they set the boxcar afire and killed everybody. Now, nobody know who done that. Some people say it was Sutter cause it was his piano. Some people say it was Sheriff Carter. Some people say it was Robert Smith and Ed Saunders. But don't nobody know for sure. It was about two months after that that Ed Saunders fell down his well. Just upped and fell down his well for no reason. People say it was the ghost of them men who burned up in the boxcar that pushed him in his well. They started calling them the Ghosts of the Yellow Dog. Now, that's how all that got started and that why we say Berniece ain't gonna sell that piano. Cause her daddy died over it.

BOY WILLIE: All that's in the past. If my daddy had seen where he could have traded that piano in for some land of his own, it wouldn't be sitting up here now. He spent his whole life farming on somebody else's land. I ain't gonna do that. See, he couldn't do no better. When he come along he ain't had nothing he could build on. His daddy ain't had nothing to give him. The only thing my daddy had to give me was that piano. And he died over giving me that. I ain't gonna let it sit up there and rot without trying to do something with it. If Berniece can't see that, then I'm gonna go ahead and sell my half. And you and Wining Boy know I'm right.

DOAKER: Ain't nobody said nothing about who's right and who's wrong. I was just telling the man about the piano. I was telling him why we say Berniece ain't gonna sell it.

LYMON: Yeah, I can see why you say that now. I told Boy Willie he ought to stay up here with me.

BOY WILLIE: You stay! I'm going back! That's what I'm gonna do with my life! Why I got to come up here and learn to do something I don't know how to do when I already know how to farm? You stay up here and make your own way if that's what you want to do. I'm going back and live my life the way I want to live it.

[WINING BOY *gets up and crosses to the piano.*]

WINING BOY: Let's see what we got here. I ain't played on this thing for a while.

DOAKER: You can stop telling that. You was playing on it the last time you was through here. We couldn't get you off of it. Go on and play something.

[WINING BOY *sits down at the piano and plays and sings. The song is one which has put many dimes and quarters in his pocket, long ago, in dimly remembered towns and way stations. He plays badly, without hesitation, and sings in a forceful voice.*]

WINING BOY: [*Singing.*]

I am a rambling gambling man
I gambled in many towns
I rambled this wide world over
I rambled this world around
I had my ups and downs in life
And bitter times I saw
But I never knew what misery was
Till I lit on old Arkansas.

I started out one morning
To meet that early train
He said, "You better work for me
I have some land to drain.

I'll give you fifty cents a day,
Your washing, board and all
And you shall be a different man
In the state of Arkansas."

I worked six months for the rascal
Joe Herrin was his name
He fed me old corn dodgers
They was hard as any rock
My tooth is all got loosened
And my knees begin to knock
That was the kind of hash I got
In the state of Arkansas.

Traveling man
I've traveled all around this world
Traveling man
I've traveled from land to land
Traveling man
I've traveled all around this world
Well it ain't no use
Writing no news
I'm a traveling man.

[*The door opens and* BERNIECE *enters with* MARETHA.]

BERNIECE: Is that . . . Lord, I know that ain't Wining Boy sitting there.

WINING BOY: Hey, Berniece.

BERNIECE: You all had this planned. You and Boy Willie had this planned.

WINING BOY: I didn't know he was gonna be here. I'm on my way down home. I stopped by to see you and Doaker first.

DOAKER: I told the nigger he left out of here with that sack of money, we thought we might never see him again. Boy Willie say he wasn't gonna see him till he got broke. I looked up and seen him sitting on the doorstep asking for two dollars. Look at him laughing. He know it's the truth.

BERNIECE: Boy Willie, I didn't see that truck out there. I thought you was out selling watermelons.

BOY WILLIE: We done sold them all. Sold the truck too.

BERNIECE: I don't want to go through none of your stuff. I done told you to go back where you belong.

BOY WILLIE: I was just teasing you, woman. You can't take no teasing?

BERNIECE: Wining Boy, when you get here?

WINING BOY: A little while ago. I took the train from Kansas City.

BERNIECE: Let me go upstairs and change and then I'll cook you something to eat.

BOY WILLIE: You ain't cooked me nothing when I come.

BERNIECE: Boy Willie, go on and leave me alone. Come on, Maretha, get up here and change your clothes before you get them dirty.

[BERNIECE *exits up the stairs, followed by* MARETHA.]

WINING BOY: Maretha sure getting big, ain't she, Doaker. And just as pretty as she want to be. I didn't know Crawley had it in him.

[BOY WILLIE *crosses to the piano.*]

BOY WILLIE: Hey, Lymon . . . get up on the other side of this piano and let me see something.

WINING BOY: Boy Willie, what is you doing?

BOY WILLIE: I'm seeing how heavy this piano is. Get up over there, Lymon.

WINING BOY: Go on and leave that piano alone. You ain't taking that piano out of here and selling it.

BOY WILLIE: Just as soon as I get them watermelons out that truck.

WINING BOY: Well, I got something to say about that.

BOY WILLIE: This my daddy's piano.

WINING BOY: He ain't took it by himself. Me and Doaker helped him.

BOY WILLIE: He died by himself. Where was you and Doaker at then? Don't come telling me nothing about this piano. This is me and Berniece's piano. Am I right, Doaker?

DOAKER: Yeah, you right.

BOY WILLIE: Let's see if we can lift it up, Lymon. Get a good grip on it and pick it up on your end. Ready? Lift!

[*As they start to move the piano, the sound of* SUTTER'S GHOST *is heard.* DOAKER *is the only one to hear it. With difficulty they move the piano a little bit so it is out of place.*]

BOY WILLIE: What you think?

LYMON: It's heavy . . . but you can move it. Only it ain't gonna be easy.

BOY WILLIE: It wasn't that heavy to me. Okay, let's put it back.

[*The sound of* SUTTER'S GHOST *is heard again. They all hear it as* BERNIECE *enters on the stairs.*]

BERNIECE: Boy Willie . . . you gonna play around with me one too many times. And then God's gonna bless you and West is gonna dress you. Now set that piano back over there. I done told you a hundred times I ain't selling that piano.

BOY WILLIE: I'm trying to get me some land, woman. I needthat piano to get me some money so I can buy Sutter's land.

BERNIECE: Money can't buy what that piano cost. You can't sell your soul for money. It won't go with the buyer. It'll shrivel and shrink to know that you ain't taken on to it. But it won't go with the buyer.

BOY WILLIE: I ain't talking about all that, woman. I ain't talking about selling my soul. I'm talking about trading that piece of wood for some land. Get something under your feet. Land the only thing God ain't making no more of. You can always get you another piano. I'm talking about some land. What you get something out the ground from. That's what I'm talking about. You can't do nothing with that piano but sit up there and look at it.

BERNIECE: That's just what I'm gonna do. Wining Boy, you want me to fry you some pork chops?

BOY WILLIE: Now, I'm gonna tell you the way I see it. The only thing that make that piano worth something is them carvings Papa Willie Boy put on there. That's what make it worth something. That was my great-grandaddy. Papa Boy Charles brought that piano into the house. Now, I'm supposed to build on what they left me. You can't do nothing with that piano sitting up here in the house. That's just like if I let them watermelons sit out there and rot. I'd be a fool. Alright now, if you say to me, Boy Willie, I'm using that piano. I give out lessons on it and that help me make my rent or whatever. Then that be something else. I'd have to go on and say, well, Berniece using that piano. She building on it. Let her go on and use it. I got to find another way to get Sutter's land. But Doaker say you ain't touched that piano the whole time it's been up here. So why you wanna stand in my way? See, you just looking at the sentimental value. See, that's good. That's alright. I take my hat off whenever somebody say my daddy's name. But I ain't gonna be no fool about no sentimental value. You can sit up here and look at the piano for the next hundred years and it's just gonna be a piano. You can't make more than that. Now I want to get Sutter's land with that piano. I get Sutter's land and I can go down and cash in the crop and get my seed. As long as I got the land and the seed then I'm alright. I can always get me a little something else. Cause that land give back to you. I can make me another crop and cash that in. I still got the land and the seed. But that piano don't put out nothing else. You ain't got nothing working for you. Now, the kind of man my daddy was he would have understood that. I'm sorry you can't see it that way. But that's why I'm gonna take that piano out of here and sell it.

BERNIECE: You ain't taking that piano out of my house. [*She crosses to the piano.*] Look at this piano. Look at it. Mama Ola polished this piano with her tears for seventeen years. For seventeen years she rubbed on it till her hands bled. Then she rubbed the blood in . . . mixed it up with the rest of the blood on it. Every day that God breathed life into her body she rubbed and cleaned and polished and prayed over it. "Play something for me, Berniece. Play something for me, Berniece." Every day. "I cleaned it up for you, play something for me, Berniece." You always talking about your daddy but you ain't never stopped to look at what his foolishness cost your mama. Seventeen years' worth of cold nights and an empty bed. For what? For a piano? For a piece of wood? To get even with somebody? I look at you and you're all the same. You, Papa Boy Charles, Wining Boy, Doaker, Crawley . . . you're all alike. All this thieving and killing and thieving and killing. And what it ever lead to? More killing and more thieving. I ain't never seen it come to nothing. People getting burned up. People getting shot. People falling down their wells. It don't never stop.

DOAKER: Come on now, Berniece, ain't no need in getting upset.

BOY WILLIE: I done a little bit of stealing here and there, but I ain't never killed nobody. I can't be speaking for nobody else. You all got to speak for yourself, but I ain't never killed nobody.

BERNIECE: You killed Crawley just as sure as if you pulled the trigger.

BOY WILLIE: See, that's ignorant. That's downright foolish for you to say something like that. You ain't doing nothing but showing your ignorance. If the nigger was here I'd whup his ass for getting me and Lymon shot at.

BERNIECE: Crawley ain't knew about the wood.

BOY WILLIE: We told the man about the wood. Ask Lymon. He knew all about the wood. He seen we was sneaking it. Why else we gonna be out there at night? Don't come telling me Crawley ain't knew about the wood. Them fellows come up on us and Crawley tried to bully them. Me and Lymon seen the sheriff with them and give in. Wasn't no sense in getting killed over fifty dollars' worth of wood.

BERNIECE: Crawley ain't knew you stole that wood.

BOY WILLIE: We ain't stole no wood. Me and Lymon was hauling wood for Jim Miller and keeping us a little bit on the side. We dumped our little bit down there by the creek till we had enough to make a load. Some fellows seen us and we figured we better get it before they did. We come up there and got Crawley to help us load it. Figured we'd cut him in. Crawley trying to keep the wolf from his door . . . we was trying to help him.

LYMON: Me and Boy Willie told him about the wood. We told him some fellows might be trying to beat us to it. He say let me go back and get my thirty-eight. That's what caused all the trouble.

BOY WILLIE: If Crawley ain't had the gun he'd be alive today.

LYMON: We had it about half loaded when they come up on us. We seen the sheriff with them and we tried to get away. We ducked around near the bend in the creek . . . but they was down there too. Boy Willie say let's give in. But Crawley pulled out his gun and started shooting. That's when they started shooting back.

BERNIECE: All I know is Crawley would be alive if you hadn't come up there and got him.

BOY WILLIE: I ain't had nothing to do with Crawley getting killed. That was his own fault.

BERNIECE: Crawley's dead and in the ground and you still walking around here eating. That's all I know. He went off to load some wood with you and ain't never come back.

BOY WILLIE: I told you, woman . . . I ain't had nothing to do with . . .

BERNIECE: He ain't here, is he? He ain't here!

[BERNIECE *hits* BOY WILLIE.]

I said he ain't here. Is he?

[BERNIECE *continues to hit* BOY WILLIE, *who doesn't move to defend himself, other than back up and turning his head so that most of the blows fall on his chest and arms.*]

DOAKER: [*Grabbing* BERNIECE.] Come on, Berniece . . . let it go, it ain't his fault.

BERNIECE: He ain't here, is he? Is he?

BOY WILLIE: I told you I ain't responsible for Crawley.

BERNIECE: He ain't here.

BOY WILLIE: Come on now, Berniece . . . don't do this now. Doaker get her. I ain't had nothing to do with Crawley . . .

BERNIECE: You come up there and got him!

BOY WILLIE: I done told you now. Doaker, get her. I ain't playing.

DOAKER: Come on. Berniece.

[MARETHA *is heard screaming upstairs. It is a scream of stark terror.*]

MARETHA: Mama! . . . Mama!

[*The lights go down to black. End of Act One.*]

ACT II

Scene 1

[*The lights come up on the kitchen. It is the following morning.* DOAKER *is ironing the pants to his uniform. He has a pot cooking on the stove at the same time. He is singing a song. The song provides him with the rhythm for his work and he moves about the kitchen with the ease born of many years as a railroad cook*]

DOAKER:

Gonna leave Jackson Mississippi
And go to Memphis
And double back to Jackson
Come on down to Hattiesburg
Change cars on the Y.D.
Coming through the territory to
Meridian
And Meridian to Greenville
And Greenville to Memphis
I'm on my way and I know where

Change cars on the Katy
Leaving Jackson
And going through Clarksdale
Hello Winona!
Courtland!
Bateville!
Como!
Senitobia!
Lewisberg!
Sunflower!
Glendora!
Sharkey!
And double back to Jackson
Hello Greenwood

I'm on my way Memphis
Clarksdale
Moorhead
Indianola
Can a highball pass through?
Highball on through sir
Grand Carson!
Thirty First Street Depot
Fourth Street Depot
Memphis!

[WINING BOY *enters carrying a suit of clothes.*]

DOAKER: I thought you took that suit to the pawnshop?

WINING BOY: I went down there and the man tell me the suit is too old. Look at this suit. This is one hundred percent silk! How a silk suit gonna get too old? I know what it was he just didn't want to give me five dollars for it. Best he wanna give me is three dollars. I figure a silk suit is worth five dollars all over the world. I wasn't gonna part with it for no three dollars so I brought it back.

DOAKER: They got another pawnshop up on Wylie.

WINING BOY: I carried it up there. He say he don't take no clothes. Only thing he take is guns and radios. Maybe a guitar or two. Where's Berniece?

DOAKER: Berniece still at work. Boy Willie went down there to meet Lymon this morning. I guess they got that truck fixed, they had been out there all day and ain't come back yet. Maretha scared to sleep up there now. Berniece don't know, but I seen Sutter before she did.

WINING BOY: Say what?

DOAKER: About three weeks ago. I had just come back from down there. Sutter couldn't have been dead more than three days. He was sitting over there at the piano. I come out to go to work . . . and he was sitting right there. Had his hand on top of his head just like Berniece said. I believe he broke his neck when he fell in the well. I kept quiet about it. I didn't see no reason to upset Berniece.

WINING BOY: Did he say anything? Did he say he was looking for Boy Willie?

DOAKER: He was just sitting there. He ain't said nothing. I went on out the door and left him sitting there. I figure as long as he was on the other side of the room everything be alright. I don't know what I would have done if he had started walking toward me.

WINING BOY: Berniece say he was calling Boy Willie's name.

DOAKER: I ain't heard him say nothing. He was just sitting there when I seen him. But I don't believe Boy Willie pushed him in the well. Sutter here cause of that piano. I heard him playing on it one time. I thought it was Berniece but then she don't play that kind of music. I come out here and ain't seen nobody, but them piano keys was moving a mile a minute. Berniece need to go on and get rid of it. It ain't done nothing but cause trouble.

WINING BOY: I agree with Berniece. Boy Charles ain't took it to give it back. He took it cause he figure he had more right to it than Sutter did. If Sutter can't understand that ... then that's just the way that go. Sutter dead and in the ground ... don't care where his ghost is. He can hover around and play on the piano all he want. I want to see him carry it out the house. That's what I want to see. What time Berniece get home? I don't see how I let her get away from me this morning.

DOAKER: You up there sleep. Berniece leave out of here early in the morning. She out there in Squirrel Hill cleaning house for some bigshot down there at the steel mill. They don't like you to come late. You come late they won't give you your carfare. What kind of business you got with Berniece?

WINING BOY: My business. I ain't asked you what kind of business you got.

DOAKER: Berniece ain't got no money. If that's why you was trying to catch her. She having a hard enough time trying to get by as it is. If she go ahead and marry Avery ... he working every day ... she go ahead and marry him they could do alright for themselves. But as it stands she ain't got no money.

WINING BOY: Well, let me have five dollars.

DOAKER: I just give you a dollar before you left out of here. You ain't gonna take my five dollars out there and gamble and drink it up.

WINING BOY: Aw, nigger, give me five dollars. I'll give it back to you.

DOAKER: You wasn't looking to give me five dollars when you had that sack of money. You wasn't looking to throw nothing my way. Now you wanna come in here and borrow five dollars. If you going back with Boy Willie you need to be trying to figure out how you gonna get train fare.

WINING BOY: That's why I need the five dollars. If I had five dollars I could get me some money.

[DOAKER *goes into his pocket.*]

Make it seven.

DOAKER: You take this five dollars ... and you bring my money back here too.

[BOY WILLIE *and* LYMON *enter. They are happy and excited. They have money in all of their pockets and are anxious to count it.*]

DOAKER: How'd you do out there?

BOY WILLIE: They was lining up for them.

LYMON: Me and Boy Willie couldn't sell them fast enough. Time we got one sold we'd sell another.

BOY WILLIE: I seen what was happening and told Lymon to up the price on them.

LYMON: Boy Willie say charge them a quarter more. They didn't care. A couple of people give me a dollar and told me to keep the change.

BOY WILLIE: One fellow bought five. I say now what he gonna do with five watermelons? He can't eat them all. I sold him the five and asked him did he want to buy five more.

LYMON: I ain't never seen nobody snatch a dollar fast as Boy Willie.

BOY WILLIE: One lady asked me say, "Is they sweet?" I told her say, "Lady, where we grow these watermelons we put sugar in the ground." You know, she believed me. Talking about she had never heard of that before. Lymon was laughing his head off. I told her, "Oh, yeah, we put the sugar right in the ground with the seed." She say, "Well, give me another one." Them white folks is something else . . . ain't they, Lymon?

LYMON: Soon as you holler watermelons they come right out their door. Then they go and get their neighbors. Look like they having a contest to see who can buy the most.

WINING BOY: I got something for Lymon.

[WINING BOY *goes to get his suit.* BOY WILLIE *and* LYMON *continue to count their money.*]

BOY WILLIE: I know you got more than that. You ain't sold all them watermelons for that little bit of money.

LYMON: I'm still looking. That ain't all you got either. Where's all them quarters?

BOY WILLIE: You let me worry about the quarters. Just put the money on the table.

WINING BOY: [*Entering with his suit.*] Look here, Lymon . . . see this? Look at his eyes getting big. He ain't never seen a suit like this. This is one hundred percent silk. Go ahead . . . put it on. See if it fit you.

[LYMON *tries the suit coat on.*]

Look at that. Feel it. That's one hundred percent genuine silk. I got that in Chicago. You can't get clothes like that nowhere but New York and Chicago. You can't get clothes like that in Pittsburgh. These folks in Pittsburgh ain't never seen clothes like that.

LYMON: This is nice, feel real nice and smooth.

WINING BOY: That's a fifty-five-dollar suit. That's the kind of suit the big-shots wear. You need a pistol and a pocketful of money to wear that suit. I'll let you have it for three dollars. The women will fall out their windows they see you in a suit like that. Give me three dollars and go on and wear it down the street and get you a woman.

BOY WILLIE: That looks nice, Lymon. Put the pants on. Let me see it with the pants.

[LYMON *begins to try on the pants.*]

WINING BOY: Look at that . . . see how it fits you? Give me three dollars and go on and take it. Look at that, Doaker . . . don't he look nice?

DOAKER: Yeah . . . that's a nice suit.

WINING BOY: Got a shirt to go with it. Cost you an extra dollar. Four dollars you got the whole deal.

LYMON: How this look, Boy Willie?

BOY WILLIE: That look nice . . . if you like that kind of thing. I don't like them dress-up kind of clothes. If you like it, look real nice.

WINING BOY: That's the kind of suit you need for up here in the North.

LYMON: Four dollars for everything? The suit and the shirt?

WINING BOY: That's cheap. I should be charging you twenty dollars. I give you a break cause you a homeboy. That's the only way I let you have it for four dollars.

LYMON: [*Going into his pocket.*] Okay . . . here go the four dollars.

WINING BOY: You got some shoes? What size you wear?

LYMON: Size nine.

WINING BOY: That's what size I got! Size nine. I let you have them for three dollars.

LYMON: Where they at? Let me see them.

WINING BOY: They real nice shoes, too. Got a nice tip to them. Got pointy toe just like you want.

[WINING BOY *goes to get his shoes.*]

LYMON: Come on, Boy Willie, let's go out tonight. I wanna see what it looks like up here. Maybe we go to a picture show. Hey, Doaker, they got picture shows up here?

DOAKER: The Rhumba Theater. Right down there on Fullerton Street. Can't miss it. Got the speakers outside on the sidewalk. You can hear it a block away. Boy Willie know where it's at.

[DOAKER *exits into his room.*]

LYMON: Let's go to the picture show, Boy Willie. Let's go find some women.

BOY WILLIE: Hey, Lymon, how many of them watermelons would you say we got left? We got just under a half a load . . . right?

LYMON: About that much. Maybe a little more.

BOY WILLIE: You think that piano will fit up in there?

LYMON: If we stack them watermelons you can sit it up in the front there.

BOY WILLIE: I'm gonna call that man tomorrow.

WINING BOY: [*Returns with his shoes.*] Here you go . . . size nine. Put them on. Cost you three dollars. That's a Florsheim shoe. That's the kind Staggerlee[3] wore.

LYMON: [*Trying on the shoes.*] You sure these size nine?

WINING BOY: You can look at my feet and see we wear the same size. Man, you put on that suit and them shoes and you got something there. You ready for whatever's out there. But is they ready for you? With them shoes on you be the King of the Walk. Have everybody stop to look at your shoes. Wishing they had a pair. I'll give you a break. Go on and take them for two dollars.

[LYMON *pays* WINING BOY *two dollars.*]

---

3. In African American folklore, a flashy figure (also called Stagger Lee, Stagolee, Stagalee, Stackolee, Stack O'Lee, Stack-o-lee, and so on) who murdered the man who stole his Stetson hat. The story is frequently retold (and reinterpreted) in song.

LYMON: Come on, Boy Willie . . . let's go find some women. I'm gonna go upstairs and get ready. I'll be ready to go in a minute. Ain't you gonna get dressed?

BOY WILLIE: I'm gonna wear what I got on. I ain't dressing up for these city niggers.

[LYMON *exits up the stairs.*]

That's all Lymon think about is women.

WINING BOY: His daddy was the same way. I used to run around with him. I know his mama too. Two strokes back and I would have been his daddy! His daddy's dead now . . . but I got the nigger out of jail one time. They was fixing to name him Daniel and walk him through the Lion's Den.[4] He got in a tussle with one of them white fellows and the sheriff lit on him like white on rice. That's how the whole thing come about between me and Lymon's mama. She knew me and his daddy used to run together and he got in jail and she went down there and took the sheriff a hundred dollars. Don't get me to lying about where she got it from. I don't know. The sheriff *looked at that hundred dollars and turned his nose up.* Told her, say, "That ain't gonna do him no good. You got to put another hundred on top of that." She come up *there and got me where I was playing at this saloon* . . . said she had all but fifty dollars and asked me if I could help. Now the way I figured it . . . without that fifty dollars the sheriff was gonna turn him over to Parchman. The sheriff turn him over to Parchman it be three years before anybody see him again. Now I'm gonna say it right . . . I will give anybody fifty dollars to keep them out of jail for three years. I give her the fifty dollars and she told me to come over to the house. I ain't asked her. I figure if she was nice enough to invite me I ought to go. I ain't had to say a word. She invited me over just as nice. Say, "Why don't you come over to the house?" She ain't had to say nothing else. Them words rolled off her tongue just as nice. I went on down there and sat about three hours. Started to leave and changed my mind. She grabbed hold to me and say, "Baby, it's all night long." That was one of the shortest nights I have ever spent on this earth! I could have used another eight hours. Lymon's daddy didn't even say nothing to me when he got out. He just looked at me funny. He had a good notion something had happened between me an' her. L. D. Jackson. That was one bad-luck nigger. Got killed at some dance. Fellow walked in and shot him thinking he was somebody else.

[DOAKER *enters from his room.*]

Hey, Doaker, you remember L. D. Jackson?

DOAKER: That's Lymon's daddy. That was one bad-luck nigger.

---

4. See Daniel 6.23: "My God has sent his angel and closed the lions' mouths so that they have not hurt me."

BOY WILLIE: Look like you ready to railroad some.

DOAKER: Yeah, I got to make that run.

[LYMON *enters from the stairs. He is dressed in his new suit and shoes, to which he has added a cheap straw hat.*]

LYMON: How I look?

WINING BOY: You look like a million dollars. Don't he look good, Doaker? Come on, let's play some cards. You wanna play some cards?

BOY WILLIE: We ain't gonna play no cards with you. Me and Lymon gonna find some women. Hey, Lymon, don't play no cards with Wining Boy. He'll take all your money.

WINING BOY: [*To* LYMON.] You got a magic suit there. You can get you a woman easy with that suit . . . but you got to know the magic words. You know the magic words to get you a woman?

LYMON: I just talk to them to see if I like them and they like me.

WINING BOY: You just walk right up to them and say, "If you got the harbor I got the ship." If that don't work ask them if you can put them in your pocket. The first thing they gonna say is, "It's too small." That's when you look them dead in the eye and say, "Baby, ain't nothing small about me." If that don't work then you move on to another one. Am I telling him right, Doaker?

DOAKER: That man don't need you to tell him nothing about no women. These women these days ain't gonna fall for that kind of stuff. You got to buy them a present. That's what they looking for these days.

BOY WILLIE: Come on, I'm ready. You ready, Lymon? Come on, let's go find some women.

WINING BOY: Here, let me walk out with you. I wanna see the women fall out their window when they see Lymon.

[*They all exit and the lights go down on the scene.*]

Scene 2

[*The lights come up on the kitchen. It is late evening of the same day.* BER-NIECE *has set a tub for her bath in the kitchen. She is heating up water on the stove. There is a knock at the door.*]

BERNIECE: Who is it?

AVERY: It's me, Avery.

[BERNIECE *opens the door and lets him in.*]

BERNIECE: Avery, come on in. I was just fixing to take my bath.

AVERY: Where Boy Willie? I see that truck out there almost empty. They done sold almost all them watermelons.

BERNIECE: They was gone when I come home. I don't know where they went off to. Boy Willie around here about to drive me crazy.

AVERY: They sell them watermelons . . . he'll be gone soon.

BERNIECE: What Mr. Cohen say about letting you have the place?

AVERY: He say he'll let me have it for thirty dollars a month. I talked him out of thirty-five and he say he'll let me have it for thirty.

BERNIECE: That's a nice spot next to Benny Diamond's store.

AVERY: Berniece . . . I be at home and I get to thinking you up here an' I'm down there. I get to thinking how that look to have a preacher that ain't married. It makes for a better congregation if the preacher was settled down and married.

BERNIECE: Avery . . . not now. I was fixing to take my bath.

AVERY: You know how I feel about you, Berniece. Now . . . I done got the place from Mr. Cohen. I get the money from the bank and I can fix it up real nice. They give me a ten cents a hour raise down there on the job . . . now Berniece, I ain't got much in the way of comforts. I got a hole in my pockets near about as far as money is concerned. I ain't never found no way through life to a woman I care about like I care about you. I need that. I need somebody on my bond side. I need a woman that fits in my hand.

BERNIECE: Avery, I ain't ready to get married now.

AVERY: You too young a woman to close up, Berniece.

BERNIECE: I ain't said nothing about closing up. I got a lot of woman left in me.

AVERY: Where's it at? When's the last time you looked at it?

BERNIECE: [Stunned by his remark.] That's a nasty thing to say. And you call yourself a preacher.

AVERY: Anytime I get anywhere near you . . . you push me away.

BERNIECE: I got enough on my hands with Maretha. I got enough people to love and take care of.

AVERY: Who you got to love you? Can't nobody get close enough to you. Doaker can't half say nothing to you. You jump all over Boy Willie. Who you got to love you, Berniece?

BERNIECE: You trying to tell me a woman can't be nothing without a man. But you alright, huh? You can just walk out of here without me—without a woman—and still be a man. That's alright. Ain't nobody gonna ask you, "Avery, who you got to love you?" That's alright for you. But everybody gonna be worried about Berniece. "How Berniece gonna take care of herself? How she gonna raise that child without a man? Wonder what she do with herself. How she gonna live like that?" Everybody got all kinds of questions for Berniece. Everybody telling me I can't be a woman unless I got a man. Well, you tell me, Avery—you know—how much woman am I?

AVERY: It wasn't me, Berniece. You can't blame me for nobody else. I'll own up to my own shortcomings. But you can't blame me for Crawley or nobody else.

BERNIECE: I ain't blaming nobody for nothing. I'm just stating the facts.

AVERY: How long you gonna carry Crawley with you, Berniece? It's been over three years. At some point you got to let go and go on. Life's got all kinds of twists and turns. That don't mean you stop living. That don't mean you cut yourself off from life. You can't go through life carrying Crawley's ghost with you. Crawley's been dead three years. Three years, Berniece.

BERNIECE: I know how long Crawley's been dead. You ain't got to tell me that. I just ain't ready to get married right now.

AVERY: What is you ready for, Berniece? You just gonna drift along from day to day. Life is more than making it from one day to another. You gonna look up one day and it's all gonna be past you. Life's gonna be gone out of your hands—there won't be enough to make nothing with. I'm standing here now, Berniece—but I don't know how much longer I'm gonna be standing here waiting on you.

BERNIECE: Avery, I told you . . . when you get your church we'll sit down and talk about this. I got too many other things to deal with right now. Boy Willie and the piano . . . and Sutter's ghost. I thought I might have been seeing things, but Maretha done seen Sutter's ghost, too.

AVERY: When this happen, Berniece?

BERNIECE: Right after I came home yesterday. Me and Boy Willie was arguing about the piano and Sutter's ghost was standing at the top of the stairs. Maretha scared to sleep up there now. Maybe if you bless the house he'll go away.

AVERY: I don't know, Berniece. I don't know if I should fool around with something like that.

BERNIECE: I can't have Maretha scared to go to sleep up there. Seem like if you bless the house he would go away.

AVERY: You might have to be a special kind of preacher to do something like that.

BERNIECE: I keep telling myself when Boy Willie leave he'll go on and leave with him. I believe Boy Willie pushed him in the well.

AVERY: That's been going on down there a long time. The Ghosts of the Yellow Dog been pushing people in their wells long before Boy Willie got grown.

BERNIECE: Somebody down there pushing them people in their wells. They ain't just upped and fell. Ain't no wind pushed nobody in their well.

AVERY: Oh, I don't know. God works in mysterious ways.

BERNIECE: He ain't pushed nobody in their wells.

AVERY: He caused it to happen. God is the Great Causer. He can do anything. He parted the Red Sea.[5] He say I will smite my enemies. Reverend Thompson used to preach on the Ghosts of the Yellow Dog as the hand of God.

BERNIECE: I don't care who preached what. Somebody down there pushing them people in their wells. Somebody like Boy Willie. I can see him doing something like that. You ain't gonna tell me that Sutter just upped and fell in his well. I believe Boy Willie pushed him so he could get his land.

AVERY: What Doaker say about Boy Willie selling the piano?

BERNIECE: Doaker don't want no part of that piano. He ain't never wanted

---

5. See Exodus 14.21: "Then Moses stretched out his hand over the sea, and the Lord swept the sea with a strong east wind throughout the night and so turned it into dry land."

no part of it. He blames himself for not staying behind with Papa Boy Charles. He washed his hands of that piano a long time ago. He didn't want me to bring it up here—but I wasn't gonna leave it down there.

AVERY: Well, it seems to me somebody ought to be able to talk to Boy Willie.

BERNIECE: You can't talk to Boy Willie. He been that way all his life. Mama Ola had her hands full trying to talk to him. He don't listen to nobody. He just like my daddy. He get his mind fixed on something and can't nobody turn him from it.

AVERY: You ought to start a choir at the church. Maybe if he seen you was doing something with it—if you told him you was gonna put it in my church—maybe he'd see it different. You ought to put it down in the church and start a choir. The Bible say "Make a joyful noise unto the Lord." Maybe if Boy Willie see you was doing something with it he'd see it different.

BERNIECE: I done told you I don't play on that piano. Ain't no need in you to keep talking this choir stuff. When my mama died I shut the top on that piano and I ain't never opened it since. I was only playing it for her. When my daddy died seem like all her life went into that piano. She used to have me playing on it . . . had Miss Eula come in and teach me . . . say when I played it she could hear my daddy talking to her. I used to think them pictures came alive and walked through the house. Sometime late at night I could hear my mama talking to them. I said that wasn't gonna happen to me. I don't play that piano cause I don't want to wake them spirits. They never be walking around in this house.

AVERY: You got to put all that behind you, Berniece.

BERNIECE: I got Maretha playing on it. She don't know nothing about it. Let her go on and be a schoolteacher or something. She don't have to carry all of that with her. She got a chance I didn't have. I ain't gonna burden her with that piano.

AVERY: You got to put all of that behind you. Berniece. That's the same thing like Crawley. Everybody got stones in their passway. You got to step over them or walk around them. You picking them up and carrying them with you. All you got to do is set them down by the side of the road. You ain't got to carry them with you. You can walk over there right now and play that piano. You can walk over there right now and God will walk over there with you. Right now you can set that sack of stones down by the side of the road and walk away from it. You don't have to carry it with you. You can do it right now.

[AVERY *crosses over to the piano and raises the lid.*]

Come on, Berniece . . . set it down and walk away from it. Come on, play "Old Ship of Zion." Walk over here and claim it as an instrument of the Lord. You can walk over here right now and make it into a celebration.

[BERNIECE *moves toward the piano.*]

BERNIECE: Avery . . . I done told you I don't want to play that piano. Now or no other time.

AVERY: The Bible say, "The Lord is my refuge . . . and my strength!" With the strength of God you can put the past behind you, Berniece. With the strength of God you can do anything! God got a bright tomorrow. God don't ask what you done . . . God ask what you gonna do. The strength of God can move mountains! God's got a bright tomorrow for you . . . all you got to do is walk over here and claim it.

BERNIECE: Avery, just go on and let me finish my bath. I'll see you tomorrow.

AVERY: Okay, Berniece. I'm gonna go home. I'm gonna go home and read up on my Bible. And tomorrow . . . if the good Lord give me strength tomorrow . . . I'm gonna come by and bless the house . . . and show you the power of the Lord.

[AVERY *crosses to the door.*]

It's gonna be alright, Berniece. God say he will soothe the troubled waters. I'll come by tomorrow and bless the house.

[*The lights go down to black.*]

Scene 3

[*Several hours later. The house is dark.* BERNIECE *has retired for the night.* BOY WILLIE *enters the darkened house with* GRACE.]

BOY WILLIE: Come on in. This is my sister's house. My sister live here. Come on, I ain't gonna bite you.

GRACE: Put some light on. I can't see.

BOY WILLIE: You don't need to see nothing, baby. This here is all you need to see. All you need to do is see me. If you can't see me you can feel me in the dark. How's that, sugar? [*He attempts to kiss her.*]

GRACE: Go on now . . . wait!

BOY WILLIE: Just give me one little old kiss.

GRACE: [*Pushing him away.*] Come on, now. Where I'm gonna sleep at?

BOY WILLIE: We got to sleep out here on the couch. Come on, my sister don't mind. Lymon come back he just got to sleep on the floor. He run off with Dolly somewhere he better stay there. Come on, sugar.

GRACE: Wait now . . . you ain't told me nothing about no couch. I thought you had a bed. Both of us can't sleep on that little old couch.

BOY WILLIE: It don't make no difference. We can sleep on the floor. Let Lymon sleep on the couch.

GRACE: You ain't told me nothing about no couch.

BOY WILLIE: What difference it make? You just wanna be with me.

GRACE: I don't want to be with you on no couch. Ain't you got no bed?

BOY WILLIE: You don't need no bed, woman. My granddaddy used to take women on the backs of horses. What you need a bed for? You just want to be with me.

GRACE: You sure is country. I didn't know you was this country.

BOY WILLIE: There's a lot of things you don't know about me. Come on, let me show you what this country boy can do.

GRACE: Let's go to my place. I got a room with a bed if Leroy don't come back there.

BOY WILLIE: Who's Leroy? You ain't said nothing about no Leroy.

GRACE: He used to be my man. He ain't coming back. He gone off with some other gal.

BOY WILLIE: You let him have your key?

GRACE: He ain't coming back.

BOY WILLIE: Did you let him have your key?

GRACE: He got a key but he ain't coming back. He took off with some other gal.

BOY WILLIE: I don't wanna go nowhere he might come. Let's stay here. Come on, sugar. [*He pulls her over to the couch.*] Let me heist your hood and check your oil. See if your battery needs charged. [*He pulls her to him. They kiss and tug at each other's clothing. In their anxiety they knock over a lamp.*]

BERNIECE: Who's that . . . Wining Boy?

BOY WILLIE: It's me . . . Boy Willie. Go on back to sleep. Everything's alright. [*To* GRACE.] That's my sister. Everything's alright, Berniece. Go on back to sleep.

BERNIECE: What you doing down there? What you done knocked over?

BOY WILLIE: It wasn't nothing. Everything's alright. Go on back to sleep. [*To* GRACE.] That's my sister. We alright. She gone back to sleep.

[*They begin to kiss.* BERNIECE *enters from the stairs dressed in a nightgown. She cuts on the light.*]

BERNIECE: Boy Willie, what you doing down here?

BOY WILLIE: It was just that there lamp. It ain't broke. It's okay. Everything's alright. Go on back to bed.

BERNIECE: Boy Willie, I don't allow that in my house. You gonna have to take your company someplace else.

BOY WILLIE: It's alright. We ain't doing nothing. We just sitting here talking. This here is Grace. That's my sister Berniece.

BERNIECE: You know I don't allow that kind of stuff in my house.

BOY WILLIE: Allow what? We just sitting here talking.

BERNIECE: Well, your company gonna have to leave. Come back and talk in the morning.

BOY WILLIE: Go on back upstairs now.

BERNIECE: I got an eleven-year-old girl upstairs. I can't allow that around here.

BOY WILLIE: Ain't nobody said nothing about that. I told you we just talking.

GRACE: Come on . . . let's go to my place. Ain't nobody got to tell me to leave but once.

BOY WILLIE: You ain't got to be like that, Berniece.

BERNIECE: I'm sorry, Miss. But he know I don't allow that in here.

GRACE: You ain't got to tell me but once. I don't stay nowhere I ain't wanted.

BOY WILLIE: I don't know why you want to embarrass me in front of my company.

GRACE: Come on, take me home.

BERNIECE: Go on, Boy Willie. Just go on with your company.

[BOY WILLIE *and* GRACE *exit.* BERNIECE *puts the light on in the kitchen and puts on the teakettle. Presently there is a knock at the door.* BERNIECE *goes to answer it.* BERNIECE *opens the door.* LYMON *enters.*]

LYMON: How you doing, Berniece? I thought you'd be asleep. Boy Willie been back here?

BERNIECE: He just left out of here a minute ago.

LYMON: I went out to see a picture show and never got there. We always end up doing something else. I was with this woman she just wanted to drink up all my money. So I left her there and came back looking for Boy Willie.

BERNIECE: You just missed him. He just left out of here.

LYMON: They got some nice-looking women in this city. I'm gonna like it up here real good. I like seeing them with their dresses on. Got them high heels. I like that. Make them look like they real precious. Boy Willie met a real nice one today. I wish I had met her before he did.

BERNIECE: He come by here with some woman a little while ago. I told him to go on and take all that out of my house.

LYMON: What she look like, the woman he was with? Was she a brown-skinned woman about this high? Nice and healthy? Got nice hips on her?

BERNIECE: She had on a red dress.

LYMON: That's her! That's Grace. She real nice. Laugh a lot. Lot of fun to be with. She don't be trying to put on. Some of these woman act like they the Queen of Sheba. I don't like them kind. Grace ain't like that. She real nice with herself.

BERNIECE: I don't know what she was like. He come in here all drunk knocking over the lamp, and making all kind of noise. I told them to take that somewhere else. I can't really say what she was like.

LYMON: She real nice. I seen her before he did. I was trying not to act like I seen her. I wanted to look at her a while before I said something. She seen me when I come into the saloon. I tried to act like I didn't see her. Time I looked around Boy Willie was talking to her. She was talking to him kept looking at me. That's when her friend Dolly came. I asked her if she wanted to go to the picture show. She told me to buy her a drink while she thought about it. Next thing I knew she done had three drinks talking about she too tired to go. I bought her another drink, then I left. Boy Willie was gone and I thought he might have come back here. Doaker gone, huh? He say he had to make a trip.

BERNIECE: Yeah, he gone on his trip. This is when I can usually get me some peace and quiet, Maretha asleep.

LYMON: She look just like you. Got them big eyes. I remember her when she was in diapers.

BERNIECE: Time just keep on. It go on with or without you. She going on twelve.

LYMON: She sure is pretty. I like kids.

BERNIECE: Boy Willie say you staying . . . what you gonna do up here in this big city? You thought about that?

LYMON: They never get me back down there. The sheriff looking for me. All because they gonna try and make me work for somebody when I don't want to. They gonna try and make me work for Stovall when he don't pay nothing. It ain't like that up here. Up here you more or less do what you want to. I figure I find me a job and try to get set up and then see what the year brings. I tried to do that two or three times down there . . . but it never would work out. I was always in the wrong place.

BERNIECE: This ain't a bad city once you get to know your way around.

LYMON: Up here is different. I'm gonna get me a job unloading boxcars or something. One fellow told me say he know a place. I'm gonna go over there with him next week. Me and Boy Willie finish selling them watermelons I'll have enough money to hold me for a while. But I'm gonna go over there and see what kind of jobs they have.

BERNIECE: You shouldn't have too much trouble finding a job. It's all in how you present yourself. See now, Boy Willie couldn't get no job up here. Somebody hire him they got a pack of trouble on their hands. Soon as they find that out they fire him. He don't want to do nothing unless he do it his way.

LYMON: I know. I told him let's go to the picture show first and see if there was any women down there. They might get tired of sitting at home and walk down to the picture show. He say he wanna look around first. We never did get down there. We tried a couple of places and then we went to this saloon where he met Grace. I tried to meet her before he did but he beat me to her. We left Wining Boy sitting down there running his mouth. He told me if I wear this suit I'd find me a woman. He was almost right.

BERNIECE: You don't need to be out there in them saloons. Ain't no telling what you liable to run into out there. This one liable to cut you as quick as that one shoot you. You don't need to be out there. You start out that fast life you can't keep it up. It makes you old quick. I don't know what them women out there be thinking about.

LYMON: Mostly they be lonely and looking for somebody to spend the night with them. Sometimes it matters who it is and sometimes it don't. I used to be the same way. Now it got to matter. That's why I'm here now. Dolly liable not to even recognize me if she sees me again. I don't like women like that. I like my women to be with me in a nice and easy way. That way we can both enjoy ourselves. The way I see it we the only two people like us in the world. We got to see how we fit together. A woman that don't want to take the time to do that I don't bother with. Used to. Used to bother with all of them. Then I woke up one time with this woman and I didn't know who she was. She was the prettiest woman I had ever seen in my life. I spent the whole night with her and didn't even know it. I had never taken the time to look at her. I guess she kinda knew I ain't never really looked at her. She must have known that cause she ain't wanted to see me no more. If she had wanted to see me I believe we might have got married. How come you ain't married? It seem like to me you would be married. I remember Avery from down home. I used to call him plain old Avery. Now he Reverend Avery. That's kinda funny about him becoming a preacher. I like when he told about how that come to him in a dream about them sheep people and them hobos. Nothing ever come to me in a dream like that. I just dream about women. Can't never seem to find the right one.

BERNIECE: She out there somewhere. You just got to get yourself ready to meet her. That's what I'm trying to do. Avery's alright. I ain't really got nobody in mind.

LYMON: I get me a job and a little place and get set up to where I can make a woman comfortable I might get married. Avery's nice. You ought to go ahead and get married. You be a preacher's wife you won't have to work. I hate living by myself. I didn't want to be no strain on my mama so I left home when I was about sixteen. Everything I tried seem like it just didn't work out. Now I'm trying this.

BERNIECE: You keep trying it'll work out for you.

LYMON: You ever go down there to the picture show?

BERNIECE: I don't go in for all that.

LYMON: Ain't nothing wrong with it. It ain't like gambling and sinning. I went to one down in Jackson once. It was fun.

BERNIECE: I just stay home most of the time. Take care of Maretha.

LYMON: It's getting kind of late. I don't know where Boy Willie went off to. He's liable not to come back. I'm gonna take off these shoes. My feet hurt. Was you in bed? I don't mean to be keeping you up.

BERNIECE: You ain't keeping me up. I couldn't sleep after that Boy Willie woke me up.

LYMON: You got on that nightgown. I likes women when they wear them fancy nightclothes and all. It makes their skin look real pretty.

BERNIECE: I got this at the five-and-ten-cents store. It ain't so fancy.

LYMON: I don't too often get to see a woman dressed like that. [*There is a long pause.* LYMON *takes off his suit coat.*] Well, I'm gonna sleep here on the couch. I'm supposed to sleep on the floor but I don't reckon Boy Willie's coming back tonight. Wining Boy sold me this suit. Told me it was a magic suit. I'm gonna put it on again tomorrow. Maybe it bring me a woman like he say. [*He goes into his coat pocket and takes out a small bottle of perfume.*] I almost forgot I had this. Some man sold me this for a dollar. Say it come from Paris. This is the same kind of perfume the Queen of France wear. That's what he told me. I don't know if it's true or not. I smelled it. It smelled good to me. Here . . . smell it see if you like it. I was gonna give it to Dolly. But I didn't like her too much.

BERNIECE: [*Takes the bottle.*] It smells nice.

LYMON: I was gonna give it to Dolly if she had went to the picture with me. Go on, you take it.

BERNIECE: I can't take it. Here . . . go on you keep it. You'll find somebody to give it to.

LYMON: I wanna give it to you. Make you smell nice. [*He takes the bottle and puts perfume behind* BERNIECE'*s ear.*] They tell me you supposed to put it right here behind your ear. Say if you put it there you smell nice all day.

[BERNIECE *stiffens at his touch.* LYMON *bends down to smell her.*]

There . . . you smell real good now. [*He kisses her neck.*] You smell real good for Lymon.

[*He kisses her again.* BERNIECE *returns the kiss, then breaks the embrace and crosses to the stairs. She turns and they look silently at each other.* LYMON *hands her the bottle of perfume.* BERNIECE *exits up the stairs.* LYMON *picks up his suit coat and strokes it lovingly with the full knowledge that it is indeed a magic suit. The lights go down on the scene.*]

Scene 4

[*It is late the next morning. The lights come up on the parlor.* LYMON *is asleep on the sofa.* BOY WILLIE *enters the front door.*]

BOY WILLIE: Hey, Lymon! Lymon, come on get up.

LYMON: Leave me alone.

BOY WILLIE: Come on, get up, nigger! Wake up, Lymon.

LYMON: What you want?

BOY WILLIE: Come on, let's go. I done called the man about the piano.

LYMON: What piano?

BOY WILLIE: [*Dumps* LYMON *on the floor.*] Come on, get up!

LYMON: Why you leave, I looked around and you was gone.

BOY WILLIE: I come back here with Grace, then I went looking for you. I figured you'd be with Dolly.

LYMON: She just want to drink and spend up your money. I come on back here looking for you to see if you wanted to go to the picture show.

BOY WILLIE: I been up at Grace's house. Some nigger named Leroy come by but I had a chair up against the door. He got mad when he couldn't get in. He went off somewhere and I got out of there before he could come back. Berniece got mad when we came here.

LYMON: She say you was knocking over the lamp busting up the place.

BOY WILLIE: That was Grace doing all that.

LYMON: Wining Boy seen Sutter's ghost last night.

BOY WILLIE: Wining Boy's liable to see anything. I'm surprised he found the right house. Come on, I done called the man about the piano.

LYMON: What he say?

BOY WILLIE: He say to bring it on out. I told him I was calling for my sister, Miss Berniece Charles. I told him some man wanted to buy it for eleven hundred dollars and asked him if he would go any better. He said yeah, he would give me eleven hundred and fifty dollars for it if it was the same piano. I described it to him again and he told me to bring it out.

LYMON: Why didn't you tell him to come and pick it up?

BOY WILLIE: I didn't want to have no problem with Berniece. This way we just take it on out there and it be out the way. He want to charge twenty-five dollars to pick it up.

LYMON: You should have told him the man was gonna give you twelve hundred for it.

BOY WILLIE: I figure I was taking a chance with that eleven hundred. If I had told him twelve hundred he might have run off. Now I wish I had told him twelve-fifty. It's hard to figure out white folks sometimes.

LYMON: You might have been able to tell him anything. White folks got a lot of money.

BOY WILLIE: Come on, let's get it loaded before Berniece come back. Get that end over there. All you got to do is pick it up on that side. Don't worry about this side. You wanna stretch you' back for a minute?

LYMON: I'm ready.

BOY WILLIE: Get a real good grip on it now.

[*The sound of* SUTTER's GHOST *is heard. They do not hear it.*]

LYMON: I got this end. You get that end.

BOY WILLIE: Wait till I say ready now. Alright. You got it good? You got a grip on it?

LYMON: Yeah, I got it. You lift up on that end.

BOY WILLIE: Ready? Lift!

[*The piano will not budge.*]

LYMON: Man, this piano is heavy! It's gonna take more than me and you to move this piano.

BOY WILLIE: We can do it. Come on—we did it before.

LYMON: Nigger—you crazy! That piano weighs five hundred pounds!

BOY WILLIE: I got three hundred pounds of it! I know you can carry two hundred pounds! You be lifting them cotton sacks! Come on lift this piano!

[*They try to move the piano again without success.*]

LYMON: It's stuck. Something holding it.

BOY WILLIE: How the piano gonna be stuck? We just moved it. Slide you' end out.

LYMON: Naw—we gonna need two or three more people. How this big old piano get in the house?

BOY WILLIE: I don't know how it got in the house. I know how it's going out though! You get on this end. I'll carry three hundred and fifty pounds of it. All you got to do is slide your end out. Ready?

[*They switch sides and try again without success.* DOAKER *enters from his room as they try to push and shove it.*]

LYMON: Hey, Doaker . . . how this piano get in the house?

DOAKER: Boy Willie, what you doing?

BOY WILLIE: I'm carrying this piano out the house. What it look like I'm doing? Come on, Lymon, let's try again.

DOAKER: Go on let the piano sit there till Berniece come home.

BOY WILLIE: You ain't got nothing to do with this, Doaker. This my business.

DOAKER: This is my house, nigger! I ain't gonna let you or nobody else carry nothing out of it. You ain't gonna carry nothing out of here without my permission!

BOY WILLIE: This is my piano. I don't need your permission to carry my belongings out of your house. This is mine. This ain't got nothing to do with you.

DOAKER: I say leave it over there till Berniece come home. She got part of it too. Leave it set there till you see what she say.

BOY WILLIE: I don't care what Berniece say. Come on, Lymon. I got this side.

DOAKER: Go on and cut it half in two if you want to. Just leave Berniece's half sitting over there. I can't tell you what to do with your piano. But I can't let you take her half out of here.

BOY WILLIE: Go on, Doaker. You ain't got nothing to do with this. I don't want you starting nothing now. Just go on and leave me alone. Come on, Lymon. I got this end.

[DOAKER *goes into his room.* BOY WILLIE *and* LYMON *prepare to move the piano.*]

LYMON: How we gonna get it in the truck?

BOY WILLIE: Don't worry about how we gonna get it on the truck. You got to get it out the house first.

LYMON: It's gonna take more than me and you to move this piano.

BOY WILLIE: Just lift up on that end, nigger!

[DOAKER *comes to the doorway of his room and stands.*]

DOAKER: [*Quietly with authority.*] Leave that piano set over there till Berniece come back. I don't care what you do with it then. But you gonna leave it sit over there right now.

BOY WILLIE: Alright.... I'm gonna tell you this, Doaker. I'm going out of here ... I'm gonna get me some rope ... find me a plank and some wheels ... and I'm coming back. Then I'm gonna carry that piano out of here ... sell it and give Berniece half the money. See ... now that's what I'm gonna do. And you ... or nobody else is gonna stop me. Come on, Lymon ... let's go get some rope and stuff. I'll be back, Doaker.

[BOY WILLIE *and* LYMON *exit. The lights go down on the scene.*]

Scene 5

[*The lights come up.* BOY WILLIE *sits on the sofa, screwing casters on a wooden plank.* MARETHA *is sitting on the piano stool.* DOAKER *sits at the table playing solitaire.*]

BOY WILLIE: [*To* MARETHA.] Then after that them white folks down around there started falling down their wells. You ever seen a well? A well got a wall around it. It's hard to fall down a well. You got to be leaning way over. Couldn't nobody figure out too much what was making these fellows fall down their well . . . so everybody says the Ghosts of the Yellow Dog must have pushed them. That's what everybody called them four men what got burned up in the boxcar.

MARETHA: Why they call them that?

BOY WILLIE: Cause the Yazoo Delta railroad got yellow boxcars. Sometime the way the whistle blow sound like an old dog howling so the people call it the Yellow Dog.

MARETHA: Anybody ever see the Ghosts?

BOY WILLIE: I told you they like the wind. Can you see the wind?

MARETHA: No.

BOY WILLIE: They like the wind you can't see them. But sometimes you be in trouble they might be around to help you. They say if you go where the Southern cross the Yellow Dog . . . you go to where them two railroads cross each other . . . and call out their names . . . they say they talk back to you. I don't know, I ain't never done that. But Uncle Wining Boy he say he been down there and talked to them. You have to ask him about that part.

[BERNIECE *has entered from the front door.*]

BERNIECE: Maretha, you go on and get ready for me to do your hair.

[MARETHA *crosses to the steps.*]

Boy Willie, I done told you to leave my house. [*To* MARETHA.] Go on, Maretha.

[MARETHA *is hesitant about going up the stairs.*]

BOY WILLIE: Don't be scared. Here, I'll go up there with you. If we see Sutter's ghost I'll put a whupping on him. Come on, Uncle Boy Willie going with you.

[BOY WILLIE *and* MARETHA *exit up the stairs.*]

BERNIECE: Doaker—what is going on here?

DOAKER: I come home and him and Lymon was moving the piano. I told them to leave it over there till you got home. He went out and got that board and them wheels. He say he gonna take that piano out of here and ain't nobody gonna stop him.

BERNIECE: I ain't playing with Boy Willie. I got Crawley's gun upstairs. He don't know but I'm through with it. Where Lymon go?

DOAKER: Boy Willie sent him for some rope just before you come in.

BERNIECE: I ain't studying Boy Willie or Lymon—or the rope. Boy Willie ain't taking that piano out this house. That's all there is to it.

[BOY WILLIE *and* MARETHA *enter on the stairs.* MARETHA *carries a hot comb and a can of hair grease.* BOY WILLIE *crosses over and continues to screw the wheels on the board.*]

MARETHA: Mama, all the hair grease is gone. There ain't but this little bit left.

BERNIECE: [*Gives her a dollar.*] Here . . . run across the street and get another can. You come straight back, too. Don't you be playing around out there. And watch the cars. Be careful when you cross the street.

[MARETHA *exits out the front door.*]

Boy Willie, I done told you to leave my house.

BOY WILLIE: I ain't in you' house. I'm in Doaker's house. If he ask me to leave then I'll go on and leave. But consider me done left your part.

BERNIECE: Doaker, tell him to leave. Tell him to go on.

DOAKER: Boy Willie ain't done nothing for me to put him out of the house. I told you if you can't get along just go on and don't have nothing to do with each other.

BOY WILLIE: I ain't thinking about Berniece. [*He gets up and draws a line across the floor with his foot.*] There! Now I'm out of your part of the house. Consider me done left your part. Soon as Lymon come back with that rope. I'm gonna take that piano out of here and sell it.

BERNIECE: You ain't gonna touch that piano.

BOY WILLIE: Carry it out of here just as big and bold. Do like my daddy would have done come time to get Sutter's land.

BERNIECE: I got something to make you leave it over there.

BOY WILLIE: It's got to come better than this thirty-two-twenty.[6]

DOAKER: Why don't you stop all that! Boy Willie, go on and leave her alone. You know how Berniece get. Why you wanna sit there and pick with her?

BOY WILLIE: I ain't picking with her. I told her the truth. She the one talking about what she got. I just told her what she better have.

BERNIECE: That's alright, Doaker. Leave him alone.

BOY WILLIE: She trying to scare me. Hell, I ain't scared of dying. I look around and see people dying every day. You got to die to make room for somebody else. I had a dog that died. Wasn't nothing but a puppy. I picked it up and put it in a bag and carried it up there to Reverend C. L. Thompson's church. I carried it up there and prayed and asked Jesus to make it live like he did the man in the Bible.[7] I prayed real hard. Knelt down and everything. Say ask in Jesus' name. Well, I must have called Jesus' name two hundred times. I called his name till my mouth got sore. I got up and looked in the bag and the dog still dead. It ain't moved a muscle! I say, "Well, ain't nothing precious." And then I went out and killed me a cat. That's when I discovered the power of death. See, a nigger that ain't afraid to die is the worse kind of nigger for the white man. He can't hold that power over you. That's what I learned when I killed that cat. I got the power of death too. I can command him. I can call him up. The white man don't like to see that. He don't

---

6. That is, this thirty-two-twenty-caliber gun I'm (figuratively) holding.

7. Lazarus, who was raised from the dead by Jesus; see John 11.1–44.

like for you to stand up and look him square in the eye and say, "I got it too." Then he got to deal with you square up.

BERNIECE: That's why I don't talk to him, Doaker. You try and talk to him and that's the only kind of stuff that comes out his mouth.

DOAKER: You say Avery went home to get his Bible?

BOY WILLIE: What Avery gonna do? Avery can't do nothing with me. I wish Avery would say something to me about this piano.

DOAKER: Berniece ain't said about that. Avery went home to get his Bible. He coming by to bless the house see if he can get rid of Sutter's ghost.

BOY WILLIE: Ain't nothing but a house full of ghosts down there at the church. What Avery look like chasing away somebody's ghost?

[MARETHA *enters the front door.*]

BERNIECE: Light that stove and set that comb over there to get hot. Get something to put around your shoulders.

BOY WILLIE: The Bible say an eye for an eye, a tooth for a tooth, and a life for a life. Tit for tat. But you and Avery don't want to believe that. You gonna pass up that part and pretend it ain't in there. Everything else you gonna agree with. But if you gonna agree with part of it you got to agree with all of it. You can't do nothing halfway. You gonna go at the Bible halfway. You gonna act like that part ain't in there. But you pull out the Bible and open it and see what it say. Ask Avery. He a preacher. He'll tell you it's in there. He the Good Shepherd. Unless he gonna shepherd you to heaven with half the Bible.

BERNIECE Maretha, bring me that comb. Make sure it's hot.

[MARETHA *brings the comb.* BERNIECE *begins to do her hair.*]

BOY WILLIE: I will say this for Avery. He done figured out a path to go through life. I don't agree with it. But he done fixed it so he can go right through it real smooth. Hell, he liable to end up with a million dollars that he done got from selling bread and wine.

MARETHA: OWWWWWW!

BERNIECE: Be still, Maretha. If you was a boy I wouldn't be going through this.

BOY WILLIE: Don't you tell that girl that. Why you wanna tell her that?

BERNIECE: You ain't got nothing to do with this child.

BOY WILLIE: Telling her you wished she was a boy. How's that gonna make her feel?

BERNIECE: Boy Willie, go on and leave me alone.

DOAKER: Why don't you leave her alone? What you got to pick with her for? Why don't you go on out and see what's out there in the streets? Have something to tell the fellows down home.

BOY WILLIE: I'm waiting on Lymon to get back with that truck. Why don't you go on out and see what's out there in the streets? You ain't got to work tomorrow. Talking about me . . . why don't you go out there? It's Friday night.

DOAKER: I got to stay around here and keep you all from killing one another.

BOY WILLIE: You ain't got to worry about me. I'm gonna be here just as long as it takes Lymon to get back here with that truck. You ought to be talking to Berniece. Sitting up there telling Maretha she wished she was a boy. What kind of thing is that to tell a child? If you want to tell her something tell her about that piano. You ain't even told her about that piano. Like that's something to be ashamed of. Like she supposed to go off and hide somewhere about that piano. You ought to mark down on the calendar the day that Papa Boy Charles brought that piano into the house. You ought to mark that day down and draw a circle around it . . . and every year when it come up throw a party. Have a celebration. If you did that she wouldn't have no problem in life. She could walk around here with her head held high. I'm talking about a big party!

Invite everybody! Mark that day down with a special meaning. That way she know where she at in the world. You got her going out here thinking she wrong in the world. Like there ain't no part of it belong to her.

BERNIECE: Let me take care of my child. When you get one of your own then you can teach it what you want to teach it.

[DOAKER exits into his room.]

BOY WILLIE: What I want to bring a child into this world for? Why I wanna bring somebody else into all this for? I'll tell you this . . . If I was Rockefeller[8] I'd have forty or fifty. I'd make one every day. Cause they gonna start out in life with all the advantages. I ain't got no advantages to offer nobody. Many is the time I looked at my daddy and seen him staring off at his hands. I got a little older I know what he was thinking. He sitting there saying, "I got these big old hands but what I'm gonna do with them? Best I can do is make a fifty-acre crop for Mr. Stovall. Got these big old hands capable of doing anything. I can take and build something with these hands. But where's the tools? All I got is these hands. Unless I go out here and kill me somebody and take what they got . . . it's a long row to hoe for me to get something of my own. So what I'm gonna do with these big old hands? What would you do?"

See now . . . if he had his own land he wouldn't have felt that way. If he had something under his feet that belonged to him he could stand up taller. That's what I'm talking about. Hell, the land is there for everybody. All you got to do is figure out how to get you a piece. Ain't no mystery to life. You just got to go out and meet it square on. If you got a piece of land you'll find everything else fall right into place. You can stand right up next to the white man and talk about the price of cotton . . . the weather, and anything else you want to talk about. If you teach

---

8. John D. Rockefeller (1839–1937), American oil magnate and philanthropist; the Rockefeller family is known for its wealth.

that girl that she living at the bottom of life, she's gonna grow up and hate you.

BERNIECE: I'm gonna teach her the truth. That's just where she living. Only she ain't got to stay there. [*To* MARETHA.] Turn you' head over to the other side.

BOY WILLIE: This might be your bottom but it ain't mine. I'm living at the top of life. I ain't gonna just take my life and throw it away at the bottom. I'm in the world like everybody else. The way I see it everybody else got to come up a little taste to be where I am.

BERNIECE: You right at the bottom with the rest of us.

BOY WILLIE: I'll tell you this . . . and ain't a living soul can put a come back on it. If you believe that's where you at then you gonna act that way. If you act that way then that's where you gonna be. It's as simple as that. Ain't no mystery to life. I don't know how you come to believe that stuff. Crawley didn't think like that. He wasn't living at the bottom of life. Papa Boy Charles and Mama Ola wasn't living at the bottom of life. You ain't never heard them say nothing like that. They would have taken a strap to you if they heard you say something like that.

[DOAKER *enters from his room.*]

Hey, Doaker . . . Berniece say the colored folks is living at the bottom of life. I tried to tell her if she think that . . . that's where she gonna be. You think you living at the bottom of life? Is that how you see yourself?

DOAKER: I'm just living the best way I know how. I ain't thinking about no top or no bottom.

BOY WILLIE: That's what I tried to tell Berniece. I don't know where she got that from. That sound like something Avery would say. Avery think cause the white man give him a turkey for Thanksgiving that makes him better than everybody else. That's gonna raise him out of the bottom of life. I don't need nobody to give me a turkey. I can get my own turkey. All you have to do is get out my way. I'll get me two or three turkeys.

BERNIECE: You can't even get a chicken let alone two or three turkeys. Talking about get out your way. Ain't nobody in your way. [*To* MARETHA.] Straighten your head, Maretha! Don't be bending down like that. Hold your head up! [*To* BOY WILLIE.] All you got going for you is talk. You' whole life that's all you ever had going for you.

BOY WILLIE: See now . . . I'll tell you something about me. I done strung along and strung along. Going this way and that. Whatever way would lead me to a moment of peace. That's all I want. To be as easy with everything. But I wasn't born to that. I was born to a time of fire.

The world ain't wanted no part of me. I could see that since I was about seven. The world say it's better off without me. See, Berniece accept that. She trying to come up to where she can prove something to the world. Hell, the world a better place cause of me. I don't see it like Berniece. I got a heart that beats here and it beats just as loud as the next fellow's. Don't care if he black or white. Sometime it beats louder. When it beats louder, then everybody can hear it. Some people get scared of that. Like Berniece. Some people get scared to hear a nigger's heart beating. They think you ought to lay low with that heart. Make it beat quiet and go along with everything the way it is. But my mama ain't birthed me for nothing. So what I got to do? I got to mark my passing on the road. Just like you write on a tree, "Boy Willie was here."

That's all I'm trying to do with that piano. Trying to put my mark on the road. Like my daddy done. My heart say for me to sell that piano and get me some land so I can make a life for myself to live in my own way. Other than that I ain't thinking about nothing Berniece got to say.

[*There is a knock at the door.* BOY WILLIE *crosses to it and yanks it open thinking it is* LYMON. AVERY *enters. He carries a Bible.*]

BOY WILLIE: Where you been, nigger? Aw . . . I thought you was Lymon. Hey, Berniece, look who's here.

BERNIECE: Come on in, Avery. Don't you pay Boy Willie no mind.

BOY WILLIE: Hey . . . Hey, Avery . . . tell me this . . . can you get to heaven with half the Bible?

BERNIECE: Boy Willie . . . I done told you to leave me alone.

BOY WILLIE: I just ask the man a question. He can answer. He don't need you to speak for him. Avery . . . if you only believe on half the Bible and don't want to accept the other half . . . you think God let you in heaven? Or do you got to have the whole Bible? Tell Berniece . . . if you only believe in part of it . . . when you see God he gonna ask you why you ain't believed in the other part . . . then he gonna send you straight to Hell.

AVERY: You got to be born again. Jesus say unless a man be born again he cannot come unto the Father and who so ever heareth my words and believeth them not shall be cast into a fiery pit.

BOY WILLIE: That's what I was trying to tell Berniece. You got to believe in it all. You can't go at nothing halfway. She think she going to heaven with half the Bible. [*To* BERNIECE.] You hear that . . . Jesus say you got to believe in it all.

BERNIECE: You keep messing with me.

BOY WILLIE: I ain't thinking about you.

DOAKER: Come on in, Avery, and have a seat. Don't pay neither one of them no mind. They been arguing all day.

BERNIECE: Come on in, Avery.

AVERY: How's everybody in here?

BERNIECE: Here, set this comb back over there on that stove. [*To* AVERY.] Don't pay Boy Willie no mind. He been around here bothering me since I come home from work.

BOY WILLIE: Boy Willie ain't bothering you. Boy Willie ain't bothering nobody. I'm just waiting on Lymon to get back. I ain't thinking about you. You heard the man say I was right and you still don't want to believe it. You just wanna go and make up anythin'. Well there's Avery . . . there's the preacher . . . go on and ask him.

AVERY: Berniece believe in the Bible. She been baptized.

BOY WILLIE: What about that part that say an eye for an eye a tooth for a tooth and a life for a life? Ain't that in there?

DOAKER: What they say down there at the bank, Avery?

AVERY: Oh, they talked to me real nice. I told Berniece . . . they say maybe they let me borrow the money. They done talked to my boss down at work and everything.

DOAKER: That's what I told Berniece. You working every day you ought to be able to borrow some money.

AVERY: I'm getting more people in my congregation every day. Berniece says she gonna be the Deaconess. I get me my church I can get married and settled down. That's what I told Berniece.

DOAKER: That be nice. You all ought to go ahead and get married. Berniece don't need to be by herself. I tell her that all the time.

BERNIECE: I ain't said nothing about getting married. I said I was thinking about it.

DOAKER: Avery get him his church you all can make it nice. [*To* AVERY.] Berniece said you was coming by to bless the house.

AVERY: Yeah, I done read up on my Bible. She asked me to come by and see if I can get rid of Sutter's ghost.

BOY WILLIE: Ain't no ghost in this house. That's all in Berniece's head. Go on up there and see if you see him. I'll give you a hundred dollars if you see him. That's all in her imagination.

DOAKER: Well, let her find that out then. If Avery blessing the house is gonna make her feel better . . . what you got to do with it?

AVERY: Berniece say Maretha seen him too. I don't know, but I found a part in the Bible to bless the house. If he is here then that ought to make him go.

BOY WILLIE: You worse than Berniece believing all that stuff. Talking about . . . if he here. Go on up there and find out. I been up there I ain't seen him. If you reading from that Bible gonna make him leave out of Berniece imagination, well, you might be right. But if you talking about . . .

DOAKER: Boy Willie, why don't you just be quiet? Getting all up in the man's business. This ain't got nothing to do with you. Let him go ahead and do what he gonna do.

BOY WILLIE: I ain't stopping him. Avery ain't got no power to do nothing.

AVERY: Oh, I ain't got no power. God got the power! God got power over everything in His creation. God can do anything. God say, "As I commandeth so it shall be." God said, "Let there be light," and there was light.[9] He made the world in six days and rested on the seventh. God's got a wonderful power. He got power over life and death. Jesus raised Lazareth from the dead. They was getting ready to bury him and Jesus told him say, "Rise up and walk." He got up and walked and the people made great rejoicing at the power of God. I ain't worried about him chasing away a little old ghost!

---

9. See Genesis 1.3. *Lazareth:* Lazarus.

[*There is a knock at the door.* BOY WILLIE *goes to answer it.* LYMON *enters carrying a coil of rope.*]

BOY WILLIE: Where you been? I been waiting on you and you run off somewhere.

LYMON: I ran into Grace. I stopped and bought her drink. She say she gonna go to the picture show with me.

BOY WILLIE: I ain't thinking about no Grace nothing.

LYMON: Hi, Berniece.

BOY WILLIE: Give me that rope and get up on this side of the piano.

DOAKER: Boy Willie, don't start nothing now. Leave the piano alone.

BOY WILLIE: Get that board there, Lymon. Stay out of this, Doaker.

[BERNIECE *exits up the stairs.*]

DOAKER: You just can't take the piano. How you gonna take the piano? Berniece ain't said nothing about selling that piano.

BOY WILLIE: She ain't got to say nothing. Come on, Lymon. We got to lift one end at a time up on the board. You got to watch so that the board don't slide up under there.

LYMON: What we gonna do with the rope?

BOY WILLIE: Let me worry about the rope. You just get up on this side over here with me.

[BERNIECE *enters from the stairs. She has her hand in her pocket where she has Crawley's gun.*]

AVERY: Boy Willie ... Berniece ... why don't you all sit down and talk this out now?

BERNIECE: Ain't nothing to talk out.

BOY WILLIE: I'm through talking to Berniece. You can talk to Berniece till you get blue in the face, and it don't make no difference. Get up on that side, Lymon. Throw that rope around there and tie it to the leg.

LYMON: Wait a minute ... wait a minute, Boy Willie. Berniece got to say. Hey, Berniece ... did you tell Boy Willie he could take this piano?

BERNIECE: Boy Willie ain't taking nothing out of my house but himself. Now you let him go ahead and try.

BOY WILLIE: Come on, Lymon, get up on this side with me.

[LYMON *stands undecided.*]

Come on, nigger! What you standing there for?

LYMON: Maybe Berniece is right, Boy Willie. Maybe you shouldn't sell it.

AVERY: You all ought to sit down and talk it out. See if you can come to an agreement.

DOAKER: That's what I been trying to tell them. Seem like one of them ought to respect the other one's wishes.

BERNIECE: I wish Boy Willie would go on and leave my house. That's what I wish. Now, he can respect that. Cause he's leaving here one way or another.

BOY WILLIE: What you mean one way or another? What's that supposed to mean? I ain't scared of no gun.

DOAKER: Come on, Berniece, leave him alone with that.

BOY WILLIE: I don't care what Berniece say. I'm selling my half. I can't help it if her half got to go along with it. It ain't like I'm trying to cheat her out of her half. Come on, Lymon.

LYMON: Berniece . . . I got to do this . . . Boy Willie say he gonna give you half of the money . . . say he want to get Sutter's land.

BERNIECE: Go on, Lymon. Just go on . . . I done told Boy Willie what to do.

BOY WILLIE: Here, Lymon . . . put that rope up over there.

LYMON: Boy Willie, you sure you want to do this? The way I figure it . . . I might be wrong . . . but I figure she gonna shoot you first.

BOY WILLIE: She just gonna have to shoot me.

BERNIECE: Maretha, get on out the way. Get her out the way, Doaker.

DOAKER: Go on, do what your mama told you.

BERNIECE: Put her in your room.

[MARETHA *exits to Doaker's room.* BOY WILLIE *and* LYMON *try to lift the piano. The door opens and* WINING BOY *enters. He has been drinking.*]

WINING BOY: Man, these niggers around here! I stopped down there at Seefus. . . . These folks standing around talking about Patchneck Red's coming. They jumping back and getting off the sidewalk talking about Patchneck Red this and Patchneck Red that. Come to find out . . . you know who they was talking about? Old John D. from up around Tyler! Used to run around with Otis Smith. He got everybody scared of him. Calling him Patchneck Red. They don't know I whupped the nigger's head in one time.

BOY WILLIE: Just make sure that board don't slide, Lymon.

LYMON: I got this side. You watch that side.

WINING BOY: Hey, Boy Willie, what you got? I know you got a pint stuck up in your coat.

BOY WILLIE: Wining Boy, get out the way!

WINING BOY: Hey, Doaker. What you got? Gimme a drink. I want a drink.

DOAKER: It look like you had enough of whatever it was. Come talking about "What you got?" You ought to be trying to find somewhere to lay down.

WINING BOY: I ain't worried about no place to lay down. I can always find me a place to lay down in Berniece's house. Ain't that right, Berniece?

BERNIECE: Wining Boy, sit down somewhere. You been out there drinking all day. Come in here smelling like an old polecat. Sit on down there, you don't need nothing to drink.

DOAKER: You know Berniece don't like all that drinking.

WINING BOY: I ain't disrespecting Berniece. Berniece, am I disrespecting you? I'm just trying to be nice. I been with strangers all day and they treated me like family. I come in here to family and you treat me like a stranger. I don't need your whiskey. I can buy my own. I wanted your company, not your whiskey.

DOAKER: Nigger, why don't you go upstairs and lay down? You don't need
nothing to drink.

WINING BOY: I ain't thinking about no laying down. Me and Boy Willie
fixing to party. Ain't that right, Boy Willie? Tell him. I'm fixing to play
me some piano. Watch this.

[WINING BOY *sits down at the piano.*]

BOY WILLIE: Come on, Wining Boy! Me and Lymon fixing to move the
piano.

WINING BOY: Wait a minute . . . wait a minute. This a song I wrote for
Cleotha. I wrote this song in memory of Cleotha. [*He begins to play and
sing.*]

> Hey little woman what's the matter with you now
> Had a storm last night and blowed the line all down
>
> Tell me how long
> Is I got to wait
> Can I get it now
> Or must I hesitate
>
> It takes a hesitating stocking in her hesitating shoe
> It takes a hesitating woman wanna sing the blues
>
> Tell me how long
> Is I got to wait
> Can I kiss you now
> Or must I hesitate.

BOY WILLIE: Come on, Wining Boy, get up! Get up, Wining Boy! Me and
Lymon's fixing to move the piano.

WINING BOY: Naw . . . Naw . . . you ain't gonna move this piano!

BOY WILLIE: Get out the way, Wining Boy.

[WINING BOY, *his back to the piano, spreads his arms out over the piano.*]

WINING BOY: You ain't taking this piano out the house. You got to take
me with it!

BOY WILLIE: Get on out the way, Wining Boy! Doaker get him!

[*There is a knock on the door.*]

BERNIECE: I got him, Doaker. Come on, Wining Boy. I done told Boy Willie
he ain't taking the piano.

[BERNIECE *tries to take* WINING BOY *away from the piano.*]

WINING BOY: He got to take me with it!

[DOAKER *goes to answer the door.* GRACE *enters.*]

GRACE: Is Lymon here?

DOAKER: Lymon.

WINING BOY: He ain't taking that piano.

BERNIECE: I ain't gonna let him take it.

GRACE: I thought you was coming back. I ain't gonna sit in that truck all day.

LYMON: I told you I was coming back.

GRACE: [*Sees* BOY WILLIE.] Oh, hi, Boy Willie. Lymon told me you was gone back down South.

LYMON: I said he was going back. I didn't say he had left already.

GRACE: That's what you told me.

BERNIECE: Lymon, you got to take your company someplace else.

LYMON: Berniece, this is Grace. That there is Berniece. That's Boy Willie's sister.

GRACE: Nice to meet you. [*To* LYMON.] I ain't gonna sit out in that truck all day. You told me you was gonna take me to the movie.

LYMON: I told you I had something to do first. You supposed to wait on me.

BERNIECE: Lymon, just go on and leave. Take Grace or whoever with you. Just go on get out my house.

BOY WILLIE: You gonna help me move this piano first, nigger!

LYMON: [*To* GRACE.] I got to help Boy Willie move the piano first.

[*Everybody but* GRACE *suddenly senses* SUTTER'*s presence.*]

GRACE: I ain't waiting on you. Told me you was coming right back. Now you got to move a piano. You just like all the other men. [GRACE *now senses something.*] Something ain't right here. I knew I shouldn't have come back up in this house. [GRACE *exits.*]

LYMON: Hey, Grace! I'll be right back, Boy Willie.

BOY WILLIE: Where you going, nigger?

LYMON: I'll be back. I got to take Grace home.

BOY WILLIE: Come on, let's move the piano first!

LYMON: I got to take Grace home. I told you I'll be back.

[LYMON *exits.* BOY WILLIE *exits and calls after him.*]

BOY WILLIE: Come on, Lymon! Hey . . . Lymon! Lymon . . . come on!

[*Again, the presence of* SUTTER *is felt.*]

WINING BOY: Hey, Doaker, did you feel that? Hey, Berniece . . . did you get cold? Hey, Doaker . . .

DOAKER: What you calling me for?

WINING BOY: I believe that's Sutter.

DOAKER: Well, let him stay up there. As long as he don't mess with me.

BERNIECE: Avery, go on and bless the house.

DOAKER: You need to bless that piano. That's what you need to bless. It ain't done nothing but cause trouble. If you gonna bless anything go on and bless that.

WINING BOY: Hey, Doaker, if he gonna bless something let him bless everything. The kitchen . . . the upstairs. Go on and bless it all.

BOY WILLIE: Ain't no ghost in this house. He need to bless Berniece's head. That's what he need to bless.

AVERY: Seem like that piano's causing all the trouble. I can bless that. Berniece, put me some water in that bottle.

[AVERY *takes a small bottle from his pocket and hands it to* BERNIECE, *who goes into the kitchen to get water.* AVERY *takes a candle from his pocket and lights it. He gives it to* BERNIECE *as she gives him the water.*]

Hold this candle. Whatever you do make sure it don't go out.

O Holy Father we gather here this evening in the Holy Name to cast out the spirit of one James Sutter. May this vial of water be empowered with thy spirit. May each drop of it be a weapon and a shield against the presence of all evil and may it be a cleansing and blessing of this humble abode. ·

Just as Our Father taught us how to pray so He say, "I will prepare a table for you in the midst of mine enemies," and in His hands we place ourselves to come unto his presence. Where there is Good so shall it cause Evil to scatter to the Four Winds. [*He throws water at the piano at each commandment.*] Get thee behind me, Satan! Get thee behind the face of Righteousness as we Glorify His Holy Name! Get thee behind the Hammer of Truth that breaketh down the Wall of Falsehood! Father. Father. Praise. Praise. We ask in Jesus' name and call forth the power of the Holy Spirit as it is written. . . . [*He opens the Bible and reads from it.*] I will sprinkle clean water upon thee and ye shall be clean.

BOY WILLIE: All this old preaching stuff. Hell, just tell him to leave.

[AVERY *continues reading throughout* BOY WILLIE*'s outburst.*]

AVERY: I will sprinkle clean water upon you and you shall be clean: from all your uncleanliness, and from all your idols, will I cleanse you. A new heart also will I give you, and a new spirit will I put within you: and I will take out of your flesh the heart of stone, and I will give you a heart of flesh. And I will put my spirit within you, and cause you to walk in my statutes, and ye shall keep my judgments, and do them.

[BOY WILLIE *grabs a pot of water from the stove and begins to fling it around the room.*]

BOY WILLIE: Hey Sutter! Sutter! Get your ass out this house! Sutter! Come on and get some of this water! You done drowned in the well, come on and get some more of this water!

[BOY WILLIE *is working himself into a frenzy as he runs around the room throwing water and calling* SUTTER*'s name.* AVERY *continues reading.*]

BOY WILLIE: Come on, Sutter! [*He starts up the stairs.*] Come on, get some water! Come on, Sutter!

[*The sound of* SUTTER*'S GHOST is heard. As* BOY WILLIE *approaches the steps he is suddenly thrown back by the unseen force, which is choking him. As he struggles he frees himself, then dashes up the stairs.*]

BOY WILLIE: Come on, Sutter!

AVERY: [*Continuing.*] A new heart also will I give you and a new spirit will I put within you: and I will take out of your flesh the heart of stone, and I will give you a heart of flesh. And I will put my spirit within you, and cause you to walk in my statutes, and ye shall keep my judgments, and do them.

[*There are loud sounds heard from upstairs as* BOY WILLIE *begins to wrestle with* SUTTER's GHOST. *It is a life-and-death struggle fraught with perils and faultless terror.* BOY WILLIE *is thrown down the stairs.* AVERY *is stunned into silence.* BOY WILLIE *picks himself up and dashes back upstairs.*]

AVERY: Berniece, I can't do it.

[*There are more sounds heard from upstairs.* DOAKER *and* WINING BOY *stare at one another in stunned disbelief. It is in this moment, from somewhere old, that* BERNIECE *realizes what she must do. She crosses to the piano. She begins to play. The song is found piece by piece. It is an old urge to song that is both a commandment and a plea. With each repetition it gains in strength. It is intended as an exorcism and a dressing for battle. A rustle of wind blowing across two continents.*]

BERNIECE: [*Singing.*]

I want you to help me
I want you to help me
I want you to help me
I want you to help me
I want you to help me
I want you to help me
Mama Berniece
I want you to help me
Mama Esther
I want you to help me
Papa Boy Charles
I want you to help me
Mama Ola
I want you to help me
I want you to help me
I want you to help me
I want you to help me
I want you to help me
I want you to help me
I want you to help me
I want you to help me

[*The sound of a train approaching is heard. The noise upstairs subsides.*]

BOY WILLIE: Come on, Sutter! Come back, Sutter!

[BERNIECE *begins to chant:*]
BERNIECE:

Thank you.
Thank you.
Thank you.

[*A calm comes over the house.* MARETHA *enters from* DOAKER*'s room.* BOY WILLIE *enters on the stairs. He pauses a moment to watch* BERNIECE *at the piano.*]

BERNIECE:

Thank you.
Thank you.
Thank you.

BOY WILLIE: Wining Boy, you ready to go back down home? Hey, Doaker, what time the train leave?

DOAKER: You still got time to make it.

[MARETHA *crosses and embraces* BOY WILLIE.]

BOY WILLIE: Hey Berniece . . . if you and Maretha don't keep playing on that piano . . . ain't no telling . . . me and Sutter both liable to be back. [*He exits.*]

BERNIECE: Thank you.

[*The lights go down to black.*]

1987

SUGGESTIONS FOR WRITING

1. *Oedipus the King* poses intriguing questions about the mysteries of sight and blindness, light and darkness. Why, for example, is it significant that Apollo, the sun god, is also a god of prophecy? Why is Teiresias, a prophet inspired by Apollo, blind? How does his blindness compare to that of Oedipus? What distinction does Sophocles draw between sight and insight? Citing specific actions, images, and passages, write an essay in which you examine what *seeing* means in *Oedipus the King*. With what kinds of enlightenment and darkness is the play concerned?

2. What is "tragic," and what is "heroic," about a tragic hero? To the modern sensibility, Oedipus's poor judgment and stubborn unwillingness to face facts are what bring down on him, and on his family and the people of Thebes, the fate shown in the play. But to the ancients, Oedipus was the model of nobility in his innate sense of justice, selfless concern for the well-being of his people, and ultimate embrace of his destiny. What, then, is the nature of Oedipus's responsibility for his fate and the fate of Thebes? Write an essay in which you discuss the role of the "tragic hero" in *Oedipus the King*. What is the play's intended "lesson"?

3. What is the role of music in *The Piano Lesson?* How does the music function to reveal character and to provide a counterpoint to the action of the plot? What is the thematic importance of the music? Write an essay in which you explore the many uses of music in Wilson's play.

4. What is the legacy of slavery in the lives of the African American characters in *The Piano Lesson?* How fully does each character acknowledge slavery's influence on the late-twentieth-century lives depicted in the play? How does each character try to break free of this influence? Write an essay in which you explore slavery's lingering power to shape the attitudes and behavior of the characters in *The Piano Lesson.*

5. Were you surprised by the play's ending? A longstanding "rule" for playwrights is that if a gun appears onstage, it must be fired by the end of the play. *The Piano Lesson,* though, seems to build steadily toward a violent climax that is averted at the last moment. Write an essay in which you examine the way August Wilson both uses and subverts the audience's conventional expectations that drama is resolved by violence.

17 THE WHOLE TEXT

Now that you have read more plays and have encountered the various elements of drama, you are ready to view two plays in their entirety, both in comparison to other plays and in the context of theater history. This larger scope can be approached with some of the specific skills you already have.

As you read each play, consider its title, the cast of characters and stage directions, and the representation of time and place (in terms of both the historical period and geographical setting as well as the timing and location of the scenes shown on stage). Imagine the appearance, costumes, vocal styles, movements of each of the characters, and "run" each scene before your mental vision: who is on stage, who is claiming the attention or yielding to whom, who walks, who sits, who busies himself or herself with a book, game, or chore? Would there be any sound or lighting effects needed? Any props to be picked up, brought on stage or carried off? Once you have a good idea of what happens step by step in a performance of a play, you are in a better position to raise questions about what it all means. Especially if you know you will write about this play, you should make notes on a first reading. Mark passages directly on the page as you read, or use post-it flags that can be removed. Then write down your observations and questions. Which differences between the characters seem most important? What causes the decisive conflict that must be resolved or at least softened by the play's end? For the sake of analysis, pinpoint which portion of the play corresponds with each of the five stages of plot: exposition, rising action, climax, falling action, and conclusion. Are there surprises, delays, or disappointments in how the conflict is set up, how it is brought out in the open, how it is resolved? What does each character know at the end that he or she did not know earlier? Has the power shifted from one character to another at the end? Once you understand the characters and the plot or structure, look again more closely at specific scenes and lines. Why is any scene or exchange of dialogue necessary to the understanding of the whole play? (To understand the effect of any aspect or element of a literary work, it always helps to imagine what would be lost if it were missing.) Do you notice intriguing or puzzling language in any of the dialogue? Are there interesting patterns of imagery, or is there a symbol or concept that unites the whole play? How would you state the theme of the play?

If you follow the sequence of questions that we suggest above, you can accumulate specific observations about the parts of a play, and from these you can shape an overview—a sense of the play's spirit, coherence, or fundamental aim. Of course, a literary work, being more than the sum of its parts, may trace more than one thematic pattern.

Inevitably, your critical assessment of the whole play will entail one matter that is often the beginning and the end of discussion: do you like it? We have had little to say about this factor in your response because it does indeed tend to stop discussion. You either like the play or you don't. But very interesting and productive questions can follow when you ask what it is in the play or in this kind of play that pleases or alienates you. You might be encouraged to articulate what you think a better play would be like, or how this play might be improved. Or you might learn to classify different plays, recognizing that the one you don't like belongs with a class of plays that you tend not to like, though others might value plays of this kind. Your judgment will always be your own, but others will respect it if it is based on fair standards of comparison and on accurate observation of each work.

Tastes and preferences in drama as in other genres can be placed in historical perspective. Each reader, student, or critic is part of a time, place, and culture—a context that will influence any interpretation of a play. If theater reviewers from Moscow in 1904 or New York in 1947 were somehow to attend the opening night of a contemporary play in New York, they might feel almost as alienated and dumbfounded as if they had suddenly been dropped into an ancient Athenian arena to watch a play by Sophocles. You may find it easier to appreciate a recent play with a contemporary style and current themes. Or like many subscribers to repertory theaters, you

> *All theories of what a good play is, or how a good play should be written, are futile. A good play is a play which when acted upon the boards makes an audience interested and pleased. A play that fails in this is a bad play.*
>
> —MAURICE BARING

may prefer classics of forty or a hundred years ago—or even four centuries ago, if it's Shakespeare you want. Or you may enjoy plays of many different contexts, reaching beyond your first reactions to engage with each work as much as possible on its own terms.

Samuel Johnson, the most respected arbiter of taste in England in the late eighteenth century, said that "nothing can please many and please long but just representations of general nature." Johnson was trying to explain why Shakespeare had continued to charm readers and playgoers for a century and a half, and his comments form both a commonsense argument about actual responses to texts (based on consensus and durability) and a proposition about the relation between literature and reality. Good literature, says Johnson, accurately reflects patterns that exist across culture and time; to last, literature must have something appropriate and valid ("just") to say about what is true regardless of time or place ("general nature").

Not everyone in Johnson's time agreed that such a universal standard could be found, and in the early twenty-first century's enlarged and varied world, fewer still believe that there are any universals that are shared by all human beings. Yet even if we no longer expect plots and characters that assure us that we are all essentially alike, and even if we try not to measure a play from Iran or Sri Lanka by the same yardstick as one from London or New York, we still seek some shared ground in order to understand any play. We must find a way to translate it, to some extent, into our language and our sense of what is human.

Our response to a play depends a great deal on how it is interpreted in performance, which in turn is influenced by the artistic standards of the playwright's time as well as our own. When you read a play from an earlier century you should bear in mind that the style of acting then would probably strike us as artificial, if we could see it now. And there may come another revolution in acting styles during the twenty-first century.

Different dramatic styles have developed to express different themes or different conceptions of character and experience. Realistic theater allows us to pretend that we are observing real people who would behave this way even if we were not watching; often such plays will imply that sincere self-expression, listening, and forgiveness can resolve conflict. Experimental staging may do little to hide its fictionality and may have the effect of "breaking down the fourth wall," so that we become aware of ourselves in the seats watching a performance on a set that represents only three sides of a room or other location. Such plays tend to distance the audience from characters, and may suggest the impossibility of honest communication and reconciliation between people. Yet in comparing the structure and staging of plays from different stylistic periods, we should remember to consider each play as a whole, on its own terms. A well-designed play will create an effect (in reading or performance) that coordinates well with all its elements and that can be expressed in a coherent theme. Comparing plays in different styles that deal with similar themes can help you to understand how each play produces its unique effects.

Through a careful reading of details, connecting parts to the whole, discovering themes, and noticing the tone, whether tragic or comic, as well as considering other works, we can approach a sound interpretation of a literary work. In the process, it helps to place each work historically and to approach the spirit in which it was first created. If we ask a Disney cartoon to be a classical ballet, or imagine a Shakespeare play performed in the manner of *Star Trek*—or vice versa—the works lose their integrity, and we will be disappointed all around. Some sense of historical context is indispensable to an evaluation that goes beyond current fashions or personal likes and dislikes.

What we bring to a text, from our own lives and experience, will likely influence our judgment at every point. But the fact that our judgments are both highly subjective and influenced by our ideologies and cultural identities does not mean that our responses are predetermined and beyond discussion or change. The better we can articulate our values and adduce evidence from the text, the more we will be able to learn, to grow, and to teach. You may never convince someone else that a particular play is as good or bad as you think it is. And you may never be convinced by someone else's arguments. But the grounds of judgment are ultimately more important than the judgment of any single play, and argument helps clarify your grounds of judgment. Knowing the reasons behind your interpretation of the whole play will certainly make it more interesting and meaningful to you, and probably help you to enjoy it more.

Your challenge now is to read these plays, imagining how you would see and hear them on a stage. Reading, you can pay extra attention to the words, which might fly past you in a theatrical performance. Pay attention as well to your changing responses and, as you respond, begin the open-ended process of understanding the whole play. Don't be alarmed if at times you come to a moment of speechless admiration. It is all right to hold your breath with excitement, to laugh aloud, or to let tears come to your eyes—no one is watching you read, and the house lights in the theater are turned down! Remember that plays are supposed to be physical experiences. Applause was invented to let audiences discharge all that pent-up feeling. Writing about a play is just a more sustained and shared way than these physical reactions to express the kind of response that drama can provoke in performance or even in reading.

ANTON CHEKHOV

The Cherry Orchard[1]

CHARACTERS IN THE PLAY

MADAME RANEVSKY (LYUBOV
  ANDREYEVNA), *the owner of the Cherry*
  Orchard
ANYA, *her daughter, aged 17*
VARYA, *her adopted daughter, aged 24*
SEMYONOV-PISHTCHIK, *a landowner*
CHARLOTTA IVANOVNA, *a governess*
EPIHODOV (SEMYON
  PANTALEYEVITCH), *a clerk*
DUNYASHA, *a maid*
FIRS, *an old valet, aged 87*

GAEV (LEONID ANDREYEVITCH),
  brother of Madame Ranevsky
LOPAHIN (YERMOLAY ALEXEYEVITCH), *a*
  merchant
TROFIMOV (PYOTR SERGEYEVITCH), *a*
  student
YASHA, *a young valet*
A WAYFARER
THE STATION MASTER
A POST-OFFICE CLERK
VISITORS, SERVANTS

The action takes place on the estate of MADAME RANEVSKY.

ACT I

A room, which has always been called the nursery. One of the doors leads into ANYA'S *room. Dawn, sun rises during the scene. May, the cherry trees in flower, but it is cold in the garden with the frost of early morning. Windows closed.*
  Enter DUNYASHA *with a candle and* LOPAHIN *with a book in his hand.*

LOPAHIN: The train's in, thank God. What time is it?
DUNYASHA: Nearly two o'clock. [*Puts out the candle.*] It's daylight already.
LOPAHIN: The train's late! Two hours, at least. [*Yawns and stretches.*] I'm a
  pretty one; what a fool I've been. Came here on purpose to meet them
  at the station and dropped asleep. . . . Dozed off as I sat in the chair. It's
  annoying. . . . You might have waked me.

---

1. Translated by Constance Garnett.

DUNYASHA: I thought you had gone. [*Listens.*] There, I do believe they're coming!

LOPAHIN: [*Listens.*] No, what with the luggage and one thing and another. [*A pause.*] Lyubov Andreyevna has been abroad five years; I don't know what she is like now.... She's a splendid woman. A good-natured, kind-hearted woman. I remember when I was a lad of fifteen, my poor father—he used to keep a little shop here in the village in those days—gave me a punch in the face with his fist and made my nose bleed. We were in the yard here, I forget what we'd come about—he had had a drop. Lyubov Andreyevna—I can see her now—she was a slim young girl then—took me to wash my face, and then brought me into this very room, into the nursery. "Don't cry, little peasant," says she, "it will be well in time for your wedding day." ... [*A pause.*] Little peasant.... My father was a peasant, it's true, but here am I in a white waistcoat and brown shoes, like a pig in a bun shop. Yes, I'm a rich man, but for all my money, come to think, a peasant I was, and a peasant I am. [*Turns over the pages of the book.*] I've been reading this book and I can't make head or tail of it. I fell asleep over it. [*A pause.*]

DUNYASHA: The dogs have been awake all night, they feel that the mistress is coming.

LOPAHIN: Why, what's the matter with you, Dunyasha?

DUNYASHA: My hands are all of a tremble. I feel as though I should faint.

LOPAHIN: You're a spoilt soft creature, Dunyasha. And dressed like a lady too, and your hair done up. That's not the thing. One must know one's place.

[*Enter* EPIHODOV *with a nosegay;*[2] he wears a pea-jacket and highly polished creaking topboots; he drops the nosegay as he comes in.]

EPIHODOV: [*Picking up the nosegay.*] Here! the gardener's sent this, says you're to put it in the dining-room. [*Gives* DUNYASHA *the nosegay.*]

LOPAHIN: And bring me some kvass.[3]

DUNYASHA: I will. [*Goes out.*]

EPIHODOV: It's chilly this morning, three degrees of frost,[4] though the cherries are all in flower. I can't say much for our climate. [*Sighs.*] I can't. Our climate is not often propitious to the occasion. Yermolay Alexeyevitch, permit me to call your attention to the fact that I purchased myself a pair of boots the day before yesterday, and they creak, I venture to assure you, so that there's no tolerating them. What ought I to grease them with?

LOPAHIN: Oh, shut up! Don't bother me.

EPIHODOV: Every day some misfortune befalls me. I don't complain, I'm used to it, and I wear a smiling face.

[DUNYASHA *comes in, hands* LOPAHIN *the kvass.*]

---

2. Bouquet.   3. Weak homemade beer.   4. That is, 29°F (−2°C).

EPIHODOV: I am going. [*Stumbles against a chair, which falls over.*] There! [*As though triumphant.*] There you see now, excuse the expression, an accident like that among others. . . . It's positively remarkable. [*Goes out.*]

DUNYASHA: Do you know, Yermolay Alexeyevitch, I must confess, Epihodov has made me a proposal.

LOPAHIN: Ah!

DUNYASHA: I'm sure I don't know. . . . He's a harmless fellow, but sometimes when he begins talking, there's no making anything of it. It's all very fine and expressive, only there's no understanding it. I've a sort of liking for him too. He loves me to distraction. He's an unfortunate man; every day there's something. They tease him about it—two and twenty misfortunes they call him.

LOPAHIN: [*Listening.*] There! I do believe they're coming.

DUNYASHA: They are coming! What's the matter with me? . . . I'm cold all over.

LOPAHIN: They really are coming. Let's go and meet them. Will she know me? It's five years since I saw her.

DUNYASHA: [*In a flutter.*] I shall drop this very minute. . . . Ah, I shall drop.

[*There is a sound of two carriages driving up to the house.* LOPAHIN *and* DUNYASHA *go out quickly. The stage is left empty. A noise is heard in the adjoining rooms.* FIRS, *who has driven to meet* MADAME RANEVSKY, *crosses the stage hurriedly leaning on a stick. He is wearing old-fashioned livery and a high hat. He says something to himself, but not a word can be distinguished. The noise behind the scenes goes on increasing. A voice: "Come, let's go in here." Enter* LYUBOV ANDREYEVNA, ANYA, *and* CHARLOTTA IVANOVNA *with a pet dog on a chain, all in traveling dresses.* VARYA *in an out-door coat with a kerchief over her head,* GAEV, SEMYONOV-PISHTCHIK, LOPAHIN, DUNYASHA *with bag and parasol, servants with other articles. All walk across the room.*]

ANYA: Let's come in here. Do you remember what room this is, mamma?

LYUBOV: [*Joyfully, through her tears.*] The nursery!

VARYA: How cold it is, my hands are numb. [*To* LYUBOV ANDREYEVNA.] Your rooms, the white room and the lavender one, are just the same as ever, mamma.

LYUBOV: My nursery, dear delightful room. . . . I used to sleep here when I was little. . . . [*Cries.*] And here I am, like a little child. . . . [*Kisses her brother and* VARYA, *and then her brother again.*] Varya's just the same as ever, like a nun. And I knew Dunyasha. [*Kisses* DUNYASHA.]

GAEV: The train was two hours late. What do you think of that? Is that the way to do things?

CHARLOTTA: [*To* PISHTCHIK.] My dog eats nuts, too.

PISHTCHIK: [*Wonderingly.*] Fancy that!

[*They all go out except* ANYA *and* DUNYASHA.]

DUNYASHA: We've been expecting you so long. [*Takes* ANYA's *hat and coat.*]

ANYA: I haven't slept for four nights on the journey. I feel dreadfully cold.

DUNYASHA: You set out in Lent, there was snow and frost, and now? My darling! [*Laughs and kisses her.*] I *have* missed you, my precious, my joy. I must tell you . . . I can't put it off a minute. . . .

ANYA: [*Wearily.*] What now?

DUNYASHA: Epihodov, the clerk, made me a proposal just after Easter.

ANYA: It's always the same thing with you. . . . [*Straightening her hair.*] I've lost all my hairpins. . . . [*She is staggering from exhaustion.*]

DUNYASHA: I don't know what to think, really. He does love me, he does love me so!

ANYA: [*Looking towards her door, tenderly.*] My own room, my windows just as though I had never gone away. I'm home! To-morrow morning I shall get up and run into the garden. . . . Oh, if I could get to sleep! I haven't slept all the journey, I was so anxious and worried.

DUNYASHA: Pyotr Sergeyevitch came the day before yesterday.

ANYA: [*Joyfully.*] Petya!

DUNYASHA: He's asleep in the bath house, he has settled in there. I'm afraid of being in their way, says he. [*Glancing at her watch.*] I was to have waked him, but Varvara Mihalovna told me not to. Don't you wake him, says she.

[*Enter* VARYA *with a bunch of keys at her waist.*]

VARYA: Dunyasha, coffee and make haste. . . . Mamma's asking for coffee.

DUNYASHA: This very minute. [*Goes out.*]

VARYA: Well, thank God, you've come. You're home again. [*Petting her.*] My little darling has come back! My precious beauty has come back again!

ANYA: I have had a time of it!

VARYA: I can fancy.

ANYA: We set off in Holy Week—it was so cold then, and all the way Charlotta would talk and show off her tricks. What did you want to burden me with Charlotta for?

VARYA: You couldn't have traveled all alone, darling. At seventeen!

ANYA: We got to Paris at last, it was cold there—snow. I speak French shockingly. Mamma lives on the fifth floor, I went up to her and there were a lot of French people, ladies, an old priest with a book. The place smelt of tobacco and so comfortless. I felt sorry, oh! so sorry for mamma all at once, I put my arms round her neck, and hugged her and wouldn't let her go. Mamma was as kind as she could be, and she cried. . . .

VARYA: [*Through her tears.*] Don't speak of it, don't speak of it!

ANYA: She had sold her villa at Mentone, she had nothing left, nothing. I hadn't a farthing left either, we only just had enough to get here. And mamma doesn't understand! When we had dinner at the stations, she always ordered the most expensive things and gave the waiters a whole rouble. Charlotta's just the same. Yasha too must have the same as we do; it's simply awful. You know Yasha is mamma's valet now, we brought him here with us.

VARYA: Yes, I've seen the young rascal.

ANYA: Well, tell me—have you paid the arrears on the mortgage?

VARYA: How could we get the money?

ANYA: Oh, dear! Oh, dear!

VARYA: In August the place will be sold.

ANYA: My goodness!

LOPAHIN: [*Peeps in at the door and moos like a cow.*] Moo! [*Disappears.*]

VARYA: [*Weeping.*] There, that's what I could do to him. [*Shakes her fist.*]

ANYA: [*Embracing* VARYA, *softly.*] Varya, has he made you an offer? [VARYA *shakes her head.*] Why, but he loves you. Why is it you don't come to an understanding? What are you waiting for?

VARYA: I believe that there never will be anything between us. He has a lot to do, he has no time for me ... and takes no notice of me. Bless the man, it makes me miserable to see him.... Everyone's talking of our being married, everyone's congratulating me, and all the while there's really nothing in it; it's all like a dream. [*In another tone.*] You have a new brooch like a bee.

ANYA: [*Mournfully.*] Mamma bought it. [*Goes into her own room and in a lighthearted childish tone.*] And you know, in Paris I went up in a balloon!

VARYA: My darling's home again! My pretty is home again!

[DUNYASHA *returns with the coffee-pot and is making the coffee.*]

VARYA: [*Standing at the door.*] All day long, darling, as I go about looking after the house, I keep dreaming all the time. If only we could marry you to a rich man, then I should feel more at rest. Then I would go off by myself on a pilgrimage to Kiev, to Moscow ... and so I would spend my life going from one holy place to another.... I would go on and on. ... What bliss!

ANYA: The birds are singing in the garden. What time is it?

VARYA: It must be nearly three. It's time you were asleep, darling. [*Going into* ANYA'*s room.*] What bliss!

[YASHA *enters with a rug and a traveling bag.*]

YASHA: [*Crosses the stage, mincingly.*] May one come in here, pray?

DUNYASHA: I shouldn't have known you, Yasha. How you have changed abroad.

YASHA: H'm! ... And who are you?

DUNYASHA: When you went away, I was that high. [*Shows distance from floor.*] Dunyasha, Fyodor's daughter.... You don't remember me!

YASHA: H'm! ... You're a peach! [*Looks round and embraces her: she shrieks and drops a saucer.* YASHA *goes out hastily.*]

VARYA: [*In the doorway, in a tone of vexation.*] What now?

DUNYASHA: [*Through her tears.*] I have broken a saucer.

VARYA: Well, that brings good luck.

ANYA: [*Coming out of her room.*] We ought to prepare mamma: Petya is here.

VARYA: I told them not to wake him.

ANYA: [*Dreamily.*] It's six years since father died. Then only a month later little brother Grisha was drowned in the river, such a pretty boy he was, only seven. It was more than mamma could bear, so she went away, went away without looking back. [*Shuddering.*] . . . How well I understand her, if only she knew! [*A pause.*] And Petya Trofimov was Grisha's tutor, he may remind her.

[*Enter* FIRS: *he is wearing a pea-jacket and a white waistcoat.*]

FIRS: [*Goes up to the coffee-pot, anxiously.*] The mistress will be served here. [*Puts on white gloves.*] Is the coffee ready? [*Sternly to* DUNYASHA.] Girl! Where's the cream?

DUNYASHA: Ah, mercy on us! [*Goes out quickly.*]

FIRS: [*Fussing round the coffee-pot.*] Ech! you good-for-nothing! [*Muttering to himself.*] Come back from Paris. And the old master used to go to Paris too . . . horses all the way. [*Laughs.*]

VARYA: What is it, Firs?

FIRS: What is your pleasure? [*Gleefully.*] My lady has come home! I have lived to see her again! Now I can die. [*Weeps with joy.*]

[*Enter* LYUBOV ANDREYEVNA, GAEV *and* SEMYONOV-PISHTCHIK; *the latter is in a short-waisted full coat of fine cloth, and full trousers.* GAEV, *as he comes in, makes a gesture with his arms and his whole body, as though he were playing billiards.*]

LYUBOV: How does it go? Let me remember. Cannon off the red!

GAEV: That's it—in off the white! Why, once, sister, we used to sleep together in this very room, and now I'm fifty-one, strange as it seems.

LOPAHIN: Yes, time flies.

GAEV: What do you say?

LOPAHIN: Time, I say, flies.

GAEV: What a smell of patchouli!

ANYA: I'm going to bed. Good-night, mamma. [*Kisses her mother.*]

LYUBOV: My precious darling. [*Kisses her hands.*] Are you glad to be home? I can't believe it.

ANYA: Good-night, uncle.

GAEV: [*Kissing her face and hands.*] God bless you! How like you are to your mother! [*To his sister.*] At her age you were just the same, Lyuba.

[ANYA *shakes hands with* LOPAHIN *and* PISHTCHIK, *then goes out, shutting the door after her.*]

LYUBOV: She's quite worn out.

PISHTCHIK: Aye, it's a long journey, to be sure.

VARYA: [*To* LOPAHIN *and* PISHTCHIK.] Well, gentlemen? It's three o'clock and time to say good-bye.

LYUBOV: [*Laughs.*] You're just the same as ever, Varya. [*Draws her to her and kisses her.*] I'll just drink my coffee and then we will all go and rest. [FIRS *puts a cushion under her feet.*] Thanks, friend. I am so fond of coffee, I drink it day and night. Thanks, dear old man. [*Kisses* FIRS.]

VARYA: I'll just see whether all the things have been brought in. [*Goes out.*]

LYUBOV: Can it really be me sitting here? [*Laughs.*] I want to dance about and clap my hands. [*Covers her face with her hands.*] And I could drop asleep in a moment! God knows I love my country, I love it tenderly; I couldn't look out of the window in the train, I kept crying so. [*Through her tears.*] But I must drink my coffee, though. Thank you, Firs, thanks, dear old man. I'm so glad to find you still alive.

FIRS: The day before yesterday.

GAEV: He's rather deaf.

LOPAHIN: I have to set off for Harkov directly, at five o'clock. . . . It is annoying! I wanted to have a look at you, and a little talk. . . . You are just as splendid as ever.

PISHTCHIK: [*Breathing heavily.*] Handsomer, indeed. . . . Dressed in Parisian style . . . completely bowled me over.

LOPAHIN: Your brother, Leonid Andreyevitch here, is always saying that I'm a low-born knave, that I'm a money-grubber, but I don't care one straw for that. Let him talk. Only I do want you to believe in me as you used to. I do want your wonderful tender eyes to look at me as they used to in the old days. Merciful God! My father was a serf of your father and of your grandfather, but you—you—did so much for me once, that I've forgotten all that; I love you as though you were my kin . . . more than my kin.

LYUBOV: I can't sit still, I simply can't. . . . [*Jumps up and walks about in violent agitation.*] This happiness is too much for me. . . . You may laugh at me, I know I'm silly. . . . My own bookcase. [*Kisses the bookcase.*] My little table.

GAEV: Nurse died while you were away.

LYUBOV: [*Sits down and drinks coffee.*] Yes, the Kingdom of Heaven be hers! You wrote me of her death.

GAEV: And Anastasy is dead. Squinting Petruchka has left me and is in service now with the police captain in the town. [*Takes a box of caramels out of his pocket and sucks one.*]

PISHTCHIK: My daughter, Dashenka, wishes to be remembered to you.

LOPAHIN: I want to tell you something very pleasant and cheering. [*Glancing at his watch.*] I'm going directly . . . there's no time to say much . . . well, I can say it in a couple of words. I needn't tell you your cherry orchard is to be sold to pay your debts; the 22nd of August is the date fixed for the sale; but don't you worry, dearest lady, you may sleep in peace, there is a way of saving it. . . . This is what I propose. I beg your attention! Your estate is not twenty miles from the town, the railway runs close by it, and if the cherry orchard and the land along the river bank were cut up into building plots and then let on lease for summer villas, you would make an income of at least 25,000 roubles a year out of it.[5]

GAEV: That's all rot, if you'll excuse me.

LYUBOV: I don't quite understand you, Yermolay Alexeyevitch.

LOPAHIN: You will get a rent of at least 25 roubles a year for a three-acre plot from summer visitors, and if you say the word now, I'll bet you what you like there won't be one square foot of ground vacant by the

---

5. Over $400,000 per year in today's U.S. currency; a rental fee of 25 roubles is the equivalent of about $400.

autumn, all the plots will be taken up. I congratulate you; in fact, you are saved. It's a perfect situation with that deep river. Only, of course, it must be cleared—all the old buildings, for example, must be removed, this house too, which is really good for nothing and the old cherry orchard must be cut down.

LYUBOV: Cut down? My dear fellow, forgive me, but you don't know what you are talking about. If there is one thing interesting—remarkable indeed—in the whole province, it's just our cherry orchard.

LOPAHIN: The only thing remarkable about the orchard is that it's a very large one. There's a crop of cherries every alternate year, and then there's nothing to be done with them, no one buys them.

GAEV: This orchard is mentioned in the *Encyclopædia*.[6]

LOPAHIN: [*Glancing at his watch.*] If we don't decide on something and don't take some steps, on the 22nd of August the cherry orchard and the whole estate too will be sold by auction. Make up your minds! There is no other way of saving it, I'll take my oath on that. No, no!

FIRS: In old days, forty or fifty years ago, they used to dry the cherries, soak them, pickle them, make jam too, and they used—

GAEV: Be quiet, Firs.

FIRS: And they used to send the preserved cherries to Moscow and to Harkov by the wagon-load. That brought the money in! And the preserved cherries in those days were soft and juicy, sweet and fragrant. . . . They knew the way to do them then. . . .

LYUBOV: And where is the recipe now?

FIRS: It's forgotten. Nobody remembers it.

PISHTCHIK: [*To* LYUBOV ANDREYEVNA.] What's it like in Paris? Did you eat frogs there?

LYUBOV: Oh, I ate crocodiles.

PISHTCHIK: Fancy that now!

LOPAHIN: There used to be only the gentlefolks and the peasants in the country, but now there are these summer visitors. All the towns, even the small ones, are surrounded nowadays by these summer villas. And one may say for sure, that in another twenty years there'll be many more of these people and that they'll be everywhere. At present the summer visitor only drinks tea in his verandah, but maybe he'll take to working his bit of land too, and then your cherry orchard would become happy, rich and prosperous. . . .

GAEV: [*Indignant.*] What rot!

[*Enter* VARYA *and* YASHA.]

VARYA: There are two telegrams for you, mamma. [*Takes out keys and opens an old-fashioned bookcase with a loud crack.*] Here they are.

LYUBOV: From Paris. [*Tears the telegrams, without reading them.*] I have done with Paris.

---

6. Perhaps the *Great Russian Encyclopedic Dictionary,* an authoritative 86-volume reference work edited by Brockhaus and Efron.

GAEV: Do you know, Lyuba, how old that bookcase is? Last week I pulled out the bottom drawer and there I found the date branded on it. The bookcase was made just a hundred years ago. What do you say to that? We might have celebrated its jubilee. Though it's an inanimate object, still it is a *book* case.

PISHTCHIK: [*Amazed.*] A hundred years! Fancy that now.

GAEV: Yes. . . . It is a thing. . . . [*Feeling the bookcase.*] Dear, honored, bookcase! Hail to thee who for more than a hundred years hast served the pure ideals of good and justice; thy silent call to fruitful labor has never flagged in those hundred years, maintaining [*In tears.*] in the generations of man, courage and faith in a brighter future and fostering in us ideals of good and social consciousness. [*A pause.*]

LOPAHIN: Yes. . . .

LYUBOV: You are just the same as ever, Leonid.

GAEV: [*A little embarrassed.*] Cannon off the right into the pocket!

LOPAHIN: [*Looking at his watch.*] Well, it's time I was off.

YASHA: [*Handing* LYUBOV ANDREYEVNA *medicine.*] Perhaps you will take your pills now.

PISHTCHIK: You shouldn't take medicines, my dear madam . . . they do no harm and no good. Give them here . . . honored lady. [*Takes the pill-box, pours the pills into the hollow of his hand, blows on them, puts them in his mouth and drinks off some kvass.*] There!

LYUBOV: [*In alarm.*] Why, you must be out of your mind!

PISHTCHIK: I have taken all the pills.

LOPAHIN: What a glutton! [*All laugh.*]

FIRS: His honor stayed with us in Easter week, ate a gallon and a half of cucumbers. . . . [*Mutters.*]

LYUBOV: What is he saying?

VARYA: He has taken to muttering like that for the last three years. We are used to it.

YASHA: His declining years!

[CHARLOTTA IVANOVNA, *a very thin, lanky figure in a white dress with a lorgnette in her belt, walks across the stage.*]

LOPAHIN: I beg your pardon, Charlotta Ivanovna, I have not had time to greet you. [*Tries to kiss her hand.*]

CHARLOTTA: [*Pulling away her hand.*] If I let you kiss my hand, you'll be wanting to kiss my elbow, and then my shoulder.

LOPAHIN: I've no luck to-day! [*All laugh.*] Charlotta Ivanovna, show us some tricks!

LYUBOV: Charlotta, do show us some tricks!

CHARLOTTA: I don't want to. I'm sleepy. [*Goes out.*]

LOPAHIN: In three weeks' time we shall meet again. [*Kisses* LYUBOV ANDREY-EVNA's *hand.*] Good-bye till then—I must go. [*To* GAEV.] Good-bye. [*Kisses* PISHTCHIK.] Good-bye. [*Gives his hand to* VARYA, *then to* FIRS *and* YASHA.] I don't want to go. [*To* LYUBOV ANDREYEVNA.] If you think over my plan for the villas and make up your mind, then let me know; I will lend you 50,000 roubles.[7] Think of it seriously.

VARYA: [*Angrily.*] Well, do go, for goodness sake.

LOPAHIN: I'm going, I'm going. [*Goes out.*]

GAEV: Low-born knave! I beg pardon, though . . . Varya is going to marry him, he's Varya's fiancé.

VARYA: Don't talk nonsense, uncle.

LYUBOV: Well, Varya, I shall be delighted. He's a good man.

PISHTCHIK: He is, one must acknowledge, a most worthy man. And my Dashenka . . . says too that . . . she says . . . various things. [*Snores, but at once wakes up.*] But all the same, honored lady, could you oblige me . . . with a loan of 240 roubles . . . to pay the interest on my mortgage to-morrow?

VARYA: [*Dismayed.*] No, no.

LYUBOV: I really haven't any money.

PISHTCHIK: It will turn up. [*Laughs.*] I never lose hope. I thought everything was over, I was a ruined man, and lo and behold—the railway passed through my land and . . . they paid me for it. And something else will turn up again, if not to-day, then to-morrow . . . Dashenka'll win two hundred thousand . . . she's got a lottery ticket.

LYUBOV: Well, we've finished our coffee, we can go to bed.

FIRS: [*Brushes GAEV, reprovingly.*] You have got on the wrong trousers again! What am I to do with you?

VARYA: [*Softly.*] Anya's asleep. [*Softly opens the window.*] Now the sun's risen, it's not a bit cold. Look, mamma, what exquisite trees! My goodness! And the air! The starlings are singing!

GAEV: [*Opens another window.*] The orchard is all white. You've not forgotten it, Lyuba? That long avenue that runs straight, straight as an arrow, how it shines on a moonlight night. You remember? You've not forgotten?

LYUBOV: [*Looking out of the window into the garden.*] Oh, my childhood, my innocence! It was in this nursery I used to sleep, from here I looked out into the orchard, happiness waked with me every morning and in those days the orchard was just the same, nothing has changed. [*Laughs with delight.*] All, all white! Oh, my orchard! After the dark gloomy autumn, and the cold winter; you are young again, and full of happiness, the heavenly angels have never left you. . . . If I could cast off the burden that weighs on my heart, if I could forget the past!

GAEV: H'm! and the orchard will be sold to pay our debts; it seems strange. . . .

LYUBOV: See, our mother walking . . . all in white, down the avenue! [*Laughs with delight.*] It is she!

GAEV: Where?

VARYA: Oh, don't, mamma!

---

7. The equivalent of over $800,000 in today's U.S. currency. *A loan of 240 roubles:* a loan of nearly $4000 in today's U.S. currency.

LYUBOV: There is no one. It was my fancy. On the right there, by the path to the arbor, there is a white tree bending like a woman.…

[*Enter* TROFIMOV *wearing a shabby student's uniform and spectacles.*]

LYUBOV: What a ravishing orchard! White masses of blossom, blue sky.…

TROFIMOV: Lyubov Andreyevna! [*She looks round at him.*] I will just pay my respects to you and then leave you at once. [*Kisses her hand warmly.*] I was told to wait until morning, but I hadn't the patience to wait any longer.…

[LYUBOV ANDREYEVNA *looks at him in perplexity.*]

VARYA: [*Through her tears.*] This is Petya Trofimov.

TROFIMOV: Petya Trofimov, who was your Grisha's tutor.… Can I have changed so much?

[LYUBOV ANDREYEVNA *embraces him and weeps quietly.*]

GAEV: [*In confusion.*] There, there, Lyuba.

VARYA: [*Crying.*] I told you, Petya, to wait till to-morrow.

LYUBOV: My Grisha … my boy … Grisha … my son!

VARYA: We can't help it, mamma, it is God's will.

TROFIMOV: [*Softly through his tears.*] There … there.

LYUBOV: [*Weeping quietly.*] My boy was lost … drowned. Why? Oh, why, dear Petya? [*More quietly.*] Anya is asleep in there, and I'm talking loudly … making this noise.… But, Petya? Why have you grown so ugly? Why do you look so old?

TROFIMOV: A peasant-woman in the train called me a mangy-looking gentleman.

LYUBOV: You were quite a boy then, a pretty little student, and now your hair's thin—and spectacles. Are you really a student still? [*Goes towards the door.*]

TROFIMOV: I seem likely to be a perpetual student.

LYUBOV: [*Kisses her brother, then* VARYA.] Well, go to bed.… You are older too, Leonid.

PISHTCHIK: [*Follows her.*] I suppose it's time we were asleep.… Ugh! my gout. I'm staying the night! Lyubov Andreyevna, my dear soul, if you could … to-morrow morning … 240 roubles.

GAEV: That's always his story.

PISHTCHIK: 240 roubles … to pay the interest on my mortgage.

LYUBOV: My dear man, I have no money.

PISHTCHIK: I'll pay it back, my dear … a trifling sum.

LYUBOV: Oh, well, Leonid will give it you.… You give him the money, Leonid.

GAEV: Me give it him! Let him wait till he gets it!

LYUBOV: It can't be helped, give it him. He needs it. He'll pay it back.

[LYUBOV ANDREYEVNA, TROFIMOV, PISHTCHIK *and* FIRS *go out.* GAEV, VARYA *and* YASHA *remain.*]

GAEV: Sister hasn't got out of the habit of flinging away her money. [*To* YASHA.] Get away, my good fellow, you smell of the hen-house.

YASHA: [*With a grin.*] And you, Leonid Andreyevitch, are just the same as ever.

GAEV: What's that? [*To* VARYA.] What did he say?

VARYA: [*To* YASHA.] Your mother has come from the village; she has been sitting in the servants' room since yesterday, waiting to see you.

YASHA: Oh, bother her!

VARYA: For shame!

YASHA: What's the hurry? She might just as well have come to-morrow. [*Goes out.*]

VARYA: Mamma's just the same as ever, she hasn't changed a bit. If she had her own way, she'd give away everything.

GAEV: Yes. [*A pause.*] If a great many remedies are suggested for some disease, it means that the disease is incurable. I keep thinking and racking my brains; I have many schemes, a great many, and that really means none. If we could only come in for a legacy from somebody, or marry our Anya to a very rich man, or we might go to Yaroslavl[8] and try our luck with our old aunt, the Countess. She's very, very rich, you know.

VARYA: [*Weeps.*] If God would help us.

GAEV: Don't blubber. Aunt's very rich, but she doesn't like us. First, sister married a lawyer instead of a nobleman. . . .

[ANYA *appears in the doorway.*]

GAEV: And then her conduct, one can't call it virtuous. She is good, and kind, and nice, and I love her, but, however one allows for extenuating circumstances, there's no denying that she's an immoral woman. One feels it in her slightest gesture.

VARYA: [*In a whisper.*] Anya's in the doorway.

GAEV: What do you say? [*A pause.*] It's queer, there seems to be something wrong with my right eye. I don't see as well as I did. And on Thursday when I was in the district Court . . .

[*Enter* ANYA.]

VARYA: Why aren't you asleep, Anya?

ANYA: I can't get to sleep.

GAEV: My pet. [*Kisses* ANYA'S *face and hands.*] My child. [*Weeps.*] You are not my niece, you are my angel, you are everything to me. Believe me, believe. . . .

ANYA: I believe you, uncle. Everyone loves you and respects you . . . but, uncle dear, you must be silent . . . simply be silent. What were you saying just now about my mother, about your own sister? What made you say that?

GAEV: Yes, yes. . . . [*Puts his hand over his face.*] Really, that was awful! My God,

---

8. Major industrial city located on the Volga River, 170 miles northeast of Moscow.

save me! And to-day I made a speech to the bookcase . . . so stupid! And only when I had finished, I saw how stupid it was.

VARYA: It's true, uncle, you ought to keep quiet. Don't talk, that's all.

ANYA: If you could keep from talking, it would make things easier for you, too.

GAEV: I won't speak. [*Kisses* ANYA's *and* VARYA's *hands.*] I'll be silent. Only this is about business. On Thursday I was in the district Court; well, there was a large party of us there and we began talking of one thing and another, and this and that, and do you know, I believe that it will be possible to raise a loan on an I.O.U. to pay the arrears on the mortgage.

VARYA: If the Lord would help us!

GAEV: I'm going on Tuesday; I'll talk of it again. [*To* VARYA.] Don't blubber. [*To* ANYA.] Your mamma will talk to Lopahin; of course, he won't refuse her. And as soon as you're rested you shall go to Yaroslavl to the Countess, your great-aunt. So we shall all set to work in three directions at once, and the business is done. We shall pay off arrears, I'm convinced of it. [*Puts a caramel in his mouth.*] I swear on my honor, I swear by anything you like, the estate shan't be sold. [*Excitedly.*] By my own happiness, I swear it! Here's my hand on it, call me the basest, vilest of men, if I let it come to an auction! Upon my soul I swear it!

ANYA: [*Her equanimity has returned, she is quite happy.*] How good you are, uncle, and how clever! [*Embraces her uncle.*] I'm at peace now! Quite at peace! I'm happy!

[*Enter* FIRS.]

FIRS: [*Reproachfully.*] Leonid Andreyevitch, have you no fear of God? When are you going to bed?

GAEV: Directly, directly. You can go, Firs. I'll . . . yes, I will undress myself. Come, children, bye-bye. We'll go into details to-morrow, but now go to bed. [*Kisses* ANYA *and* VARYA.] I'm a man of the eighties.[9] They run down that period, but still I can say I have had to suffer not a little for my convictions in my life, it's not for nothing that the peasant loves me. One must know the peasant! One must know how. . . .

ANYA: At it again, uncle!

VARYA: Uncle dear, you'd better be quiet!

FIRS: [*Angrily.*] Leonid Andreyevitch!

GAEV: I'm coming. I'm coming. Go to bed. Potted the shot—there's a shot for you![1] A beauty! [*Goes out,* FIRS *hobbling after him.*]

ANYA: My mind's at rest now. I don't want to go to Yaroslavl, I don't like my great-aunt, but still my mind's at rest. Thanks to uncle. [*Sits down.*]

VARYA: We must go to bed. I'm going. Something unpleasant happened while you were away. In the old servants' quarters there are only the old

---

9. That is, the 1880s, a period of reactionary conservatism in Russia under Tsar Alexander III.

1. Gaev is preoccupied with billiards; the terminology is fanciful because Chekhov admittedly knew nothing about the game.

servants, as you know—Efimyushka, Polya and Yevstigney—and Karp too. They began letting stray people in to spend the night—I said nothing. But all at once I heard they had been spreading a report that I gave them nothing but pease pudding to eat. Out of stinginess, you know. ... And it was all Yevstigney's doing.... Very well, I said to myself.... If that's how it is, I thought, wait a bit. I sent for Yevstigney.... [*Yawns.*] He comes.... "How's this, Yevstigney," I said, "you could be such a fool as to?..." [*Looking at* ANYA.] Anitchka! [*A pause.*] She's asleep. [*Puts her arm around* ANYA.] Come to bed ... come along! [*Leads her.*] My darling has fallen asleep! Come.... [*They go.*]

[*Far away beyond the orchard a shepherd plays on a pipe.* TROFIMOV *crosses the stage and, seeing* VARYA *and* ANYA, *stands still.*]

VARYA: 'Sh! asleep, asleep. Come, my own.

ANYA: [*Softly, half asleep.*] I'm so tired. Still those bells. Uncle ... dear ... mamma and uncle....

VARYA: Come, my own, come along.

[*They go into* ANYA's *room.*]

TROFIMOV: [*Tenderly.*] My sunshine! My spring.

CURTAIN

ACT II

The open country. An old shrine,[2] *long abandoned and fallen out of the perpendicular; near it a well, large stones that have apparently once been tombstones, and an old garden seat. The road to* GAEV's *house is seen. On one side rise dark poplars; and there the cherry orchard begins. In the distance a row of telegraph poles and far, far away on the horizon there is faintly outlined a great town, only visible in very fine clear weather. It is near sunset.* CHARLOTTA, YASHA *and* DUNYASHA *are sitting on the seat.* EPIHODOV *is standing near, playing something mournful on a guitar. All sit plunged in thought.* CHARLOTTA *wears an old forage cap; she has taken a gun from her shoulder and is tightening the buckle on the strap.*

CHARLOTTA: [*Musingly.*] I haven't a real passport[3] of my own, and I don't know how old I am, and I always feel that I'm a young thing. When I was a little girl, my father and mother used to travel about to fairs and give performances—very good ones. And I used to dance *salto-mortale*[4] and all sorts of things. And when papa and mamma died, a German lady took me and had me educated. And so I grew up and become a governess. But where I came from, and who I am, I don't know.... Who my parents were, very likely they weren't married.... I don't know. [*Takes a cucumber out of her pocket and eats.*] I know nothing at all. [*A pause.*] One wants to talk and has no one to talk to.... I have nobody.

---

2. That is, a chapel.   3. A document required for travel within Russia.
4. *Salto mortal*, literally "deadly leap," is Spanish for "somersault."

EPIHODOV: [*Plays on the guitar and sings.*] "What care I for the noisy world! What care I for friends or foes!"[5] How agreeable it is to play on the mandoline!

DUNYASHA: That's a guitar, not a mandoline. [*Looks in a hand-mirror and powders herself.*]

EPIHODOV: To a man mad with love, it's a mandoline. [*Sings.*] "Were her heart but aglow with love's mutual flame." [YASHA *joins in.*]

CHARLOTTA: How shockingly these people sing! Foo! Like jackals!

DUNYASHA: [*To* YASHA.] What happiness, though, to visit foreign lands.

YASHA: Ah, yes! I rather agree with you there. [*Yawns, then lights a cigar.*]

EPIHODOV: That's comprehensible. In foreign lands everything has long since reached full complexion.

YASHA: That's so, of course.

EPIHODOV: I'm a cultivated man, I read remarkable books of all sorts, but I can never make out the tendency I am myself precisely inclined for, whether to live or to shoot myself, speaking precisely, but nevertheless I always carry a revolver. Here it is.... [*Shows revolver.*]

CHARLOTTA: I've had enough, and now I'm going. [*Puts on the gun.*] Epihodov, you're a very clever fellow, and a very terrible one too, all the women must be wild about you. Br-r-r! [*Goes.*] These clever fellows are all so stupid; there's not a creature for me to speak to.... Always alone, alone, nobody belonging to me ... and who I am, and why I'm on earth, I don't know. [*Walks away slowly.*]

EPIHODOV: Speaking precisely, not touching upon other subjects, I'm bound to admit about myself, that destiny behaves mercilessly to me, as a storm to a little boat. If, let us suppose, I am mistaken, then why did I wake up this morning, to quote an example, and look round, and there on my chest was a spider of fearful magnitude ... like this. [*Shows with both hands.*] And then I take up a jug of kvass, to quench my thirst, and in it there is something in the highest degree unseemly of the nature of a cockroach. [*A pause.*] Have you read Buckle?[6] [*A pause.*] I am desirous of troubling you, Dunyasha, with a couple of words.

DUNYASHA: Well, speak.

EPIHODOV: I should be desirous to speak with you alone. [*Sighs.*]

DUNYASHA: [*Embarrassed.*] Well—only bring me my mantle first. It's by the cupboard. It's rather damp here.

EPIHODOV: Certainly. I will fetch it. Now I know what I must do with my revolver. [*Takes guitar and goes off playing on it.*]

YASHA: Two and twenty misfortunes! Between ourselves, he's a fool. [*Yawns.*]

DUNYASHA: God grant he doesn't shoot himself! [*A pause.*] I am so nervous,

---

5. Words of a popular ballad.

6. Henry Thomas Buckle (1821–1861), a learned but eccentric historian known as a freethinker whose *History of Civilization in England* (1857) was the talk of Moscow a generation earlier. His work, initially respected for its empirical methods, quickly fell into disrepute in sophisticated intellectual circles.

I'm always in a flutter. I was a little girl when I was taken into our lady's house, and now I have quite grown out of peasant ways, and my hands are white, as white as a lady's. I'm such a delicate, sensitive creature, I'm afraid of everything. I'm so frightened. And if you deceive me, Yasha, I don't know what will become of my nerves.

YASHA: [*Kisses her.*] You're a peach! Of course a girl must never forget herself; what I dislike more than anything is a girl being flighty in her behavior.

DUNYASHA: I'm passionately in love with you, Yasha; you are a man of culture—you can give your opinion about anything. [*A pause.*]

YASHA: [*Yawns.*] Yes, that's so. My opinion is this: if a girl loves anyone, that means that she has no principles. [*A pause.*] It's pleasant smoking a cigar in the open air. [*Listens.*] Someone's coming this way . . . it's the gentlefolk. [DUNYASHA *embraces him impulsively.*] Go home, as though you had been to the river to bathe; go by that path, or else they'll meet you and suppose I have made an appointment with you here. That I can't endure.

DUNYASHA: [*Coughing softly.*] The cigar has made my head ache. . . . [*Goes off.*]

[YASHA *remains sitting near the shrine. Enter* LYUBOV ANDREYEVNA, GAEV *and* LOPAHIN.]

LOPAHIN: You must make up your mind once for all—there's no time to lose. It's quite a simple question, you know. Will you consent to letting the land for building or not? One word in answer: Yes or no? Only one word!

LYUBOV: Who is smoking such horrible cigars here? [*Sits down.*]

GAEV: Now the railway line has been brought near, it's made things very convenient. [*Sits down.*] Here we have been over and lunched in town. Cannon off the white! I should like to go home and have a game.

LYUBOV: You have plenty of time.

LOPAHIN: Only one word! [*Beseechingly.*] Give me an answer!

GAEV: [*Yawning.*] What do you say?

LYUBOV: [*Looks in her purse.*] I had quite a lot of money here yesterday, and there's scarcely any left to-day. My poor Varya feeds us all on milk soup for the sake of economy; the old folks in the kitchen get nothing but pease pudding, while I waste my money in a senseless way. [*Drops purse, scattering gold pieces.*] There, they have all fallen out! [*Annoyed.*]

YASHA: Allow me, I'll soon pick them up. [*Collects the coins.*]

LYUBOV: Pray do, Yasha. And what did I go off to the town to lunch for? Your restaurant's a wretched place with its music and the tablecloth smelling of soap. . . . Why drink so much, Leonid? And eat so much? And talk so much? To-day you talked a great deal again in the restaurant, and all so inappropriately. About the era of the seventies,[7] about the decadents. And to whom? Talking to waiters about decadents!

LOPAHIN: Yes.

7. The 1870s, a relatively liberal period in Russia that ended abruptly with the assassination of Alexander II in 1881. *The decadents:* probably a reference to the group of flamboyant French poets of the 1880s who called themselves *les décadents*.

GAEV: [*Waving his hand.*] I'm incorrigible; that's evident. [*Irritably to* YASHA.] Why is it you keep fidgeting about in front of us!

YASHA: [*Laughs.*] I can't help laughing when I hear your voice.

GAEV: [*To his sister.*] Either I or he. . . .

LYUBOV: Get along! Go away, Yasha.

YASHA: [*Gives* LYUBOV ANDREYEVNA *her purse.*] Directly. [*Hardly able to suppress his laughter.*] This minute. . . . [*Goes off.*]

LOPAHIN: Deriganov, the millionaire, means to buy your estate. They say he is coming to the sale himself.

LYUBOV: Where did you hear that?

LOPAHIN: That's what they say in town.

GAEV: Our aunt in Yaroslavl has promised to send help; but when, and how much she will send, we don't know.

LOPAHIN: How much will she send? A hundred thousand? Two hundred?

LYUBOV: Oh, well! . . . Ten or fifteen thousand, and we must be thankful to get that.

LOPAHIN: Forgive me, but such reckless people as you are—such queer, unbusiness-like people—I never met in my life. One tells you in plain Russian your estate is going to be sold, and you seem not to understand it.

LYUBOV: What are we to do? Tell us what to do.

LOPAHIN: I do tell you every day. Every day I say the same thing. You absolutely must let the cherry orchard and the land on building leases; and do it at once, as quick as may be—the auction's close upon us! Do understand! Once make up your mind to build villas, and you can raise as much money as you like, and then you are saved.

LYUBOV: Villas and summer visitors—forgive me saying so—it's so vulgar.

GAEV: There I perfectly agree with you.

LOPAHIN: I shall sob, or scream, or fall into a fit. I can't stand it! You drive me mad! [*To* GAEV.] You're an old woman!

GAEV: What do you say?

LOPAHIN: An old woman! [*Gets up to go.*]

LYUBOV: [*In dismay.*] No, don't go! Do stay, my dear friend! Perhaps we shall think of something.

LOPAHIN: What is there to think of?

LYUBOV: Don't go, I entreat you! With you here it's more cheerful, anyway. [*A pause.*] I keep expecting something, as though the house were going to fall about our ears.

GAEV: [*In profound dejection.*] Potted the white! It fails—a kiss.

LYUBOV: We have been great sinners. . . .

LOPAHIN: You have no sins to repent of.

GAEV: [*Puts a caramel in his mouth.*] They say I've eaten up my property in caramels. [*Laughs.*]

LYUBOV: Oh, my sins! I've always thrown my money away recklessly like a lunatic. I married a man who made nothing but debts. My husband died of champagne—he drank dreadfully. To my misery I loved another man, and immediately—it was my first punishment—the blow fell upon me, here, in the river ... my boy was drowned and I went abroad—went away for ever, never to return, not to see that river again ... I shut my eyes, and fled, distracted, and *he* after me ... pitilessly, brutally. I bought a villa at Mentone, for *he* fell ill there, and for three years I had no rest day or night. His illness wore me out, my soul was dried up. And last year, when my villa was sold to pay my debts, I went to Paris and there he robbed me of everything and abandoned me for another woman; and I tried to poison myself.... So stupid, so shameful! ... And suddenly I felt a yearning for Russia, for my country, for my little girl.... [*Dries her tears.*] Lord, Lord, be merciful! Forgive my sins! Do not chastise me more! [*Takes a telegram out of her pocket.*] I got this to-day from Paris. He implores forgiveness, entreats me to return. [*Tears up the telegram.*] I fancy there is music somewhere. [*Listens.*]

GAEV: That's our famous Jewish orchestra. You remember, four violins, a flute and a double bass.

LYUBOV: That still in existence? We ought to send for them one evening, and give a dance.

LOPAHIN: [*Listens.*] I can't hear.... [*Hums softly.*] "For money the Germans will turn a Russian into a Frenchman." [*Laughs.*] I did see such a piece at the theater yesterday! It was funny!

LYUBOV: And most likely there was nothing funny in it. You shouldn't look at plays, you should look at yourselves a little oftener. How gray your lives are! How much nonsense you talk.

LOPAHIN: That's true. One may say honestly, we live a fool's life. [*Pause.*] My father was a peasant, an idiot; he knew nothing and taught me nothing, only beat me when he was drunk, and always with his stick. In reality I am just such another blockhead and idiot. I've learnt nothing properly. I write a wretched hand. I write so that I feel ashamed before folks, like a pig.

LYUBOV: You ought to get married, my dear fellow.

LOPAHIN: Yes ... that's true.

LYUBOV: You should marry our Varya, she's a good girl.

LOPAHIN: Yes.

LYUBOV: She's a good-natured girl, she's busy all day long, and what's more, she loves you. And you have liked her for ever so long.

LOPAHIN: Well? I'm not against it.... She's a good girl. [*Pause.*]

GAEV: I've been offered a place in the bank: 6,000 roubles a year.[8] Did you know?

LYUBOV: You would never do for that! You must stay as you are.

    [*Enter* FIRS *with overcoat.*]

FIRS: Put it on, sir, it's damp.

GAEV: [*Putting it on.*] You bother me, old fellow.

FIRS: You can't go on like this. You went away in the morning without leaving word. [*Looks him over.*]

---

8. Nearly $100,000 per year in today's U.S. currency.

LYUBOV: You look older, Firs!

FIRS: What is your pleasure?

LOPAHIN: You look older, she said.

FIRS: I've had a long life. They were arranging my wedding before your papa was born.... [*Laughs.*] I was the head footman before the emancipation came.[9] I wouldn't consent to be set free then; I stayed on with the old master.... [*A pause.*] I remember what rejoicings they made and didn't know themselves what they were rejoicing over.

LOPAHIN: Those were fine old times. There was flogging anyway.

FIRS: [*Not hearing.*] To be sure! The peasants knew their place, and the masters knew theirs; but now they're all at sixes and sevens,[1] there's no making it out.

GAEV: Hold your tongue, Firs. I must go to town to-morrow. I have been promised an introduction to a general, who might let us have a loan.

LOPAHIN: You won't bring that off. And you won't pay your arrears, you may rest assured of that.

LYUBOV: That's all his nonsense. There is no such general.

[*Enter* TROFIMOV, ANYA *and* VARYA.]

GAEV: Here come our girls.

ANYA: There's mamma on the seat.

LYUBOV: [*Tenderly.*] Come here, come along. My darlings! [*Embraces* ANYA *and* VARYA.] If you only knew how I love you both. Sit beside me, there, like that. [*All sit down.*]

LOPAHIN: Our perpetual student is always with the young ladies.

TROFIMOV: That's not your business.

LOPAHIN: He'll soon be fifty, and he's still a student.

TROFIMOV: Drop your idiotic jokes.

LOPAHIN: Why are you so cross, you queer fish?

TROFIMOV: Oh, don't persist!

LOPAHIN: [*Laughs.*] Allow me to ask you what's your idea of me?

TROFIMOV: I'll tell you my idea of you, Yermolay Alexeyevitch: you are a rich man, you'll soon be a millionaire. Well, just as in the economy of nature a wild beast is of use, who devours everything that comes in his way, so you too have your use.

[*All laugh.*]

VARYA: Better tell us something about the planets, Petya.

LYUBOV: No, let us go on with the conversation we had yesterday.

TROFIMOV: What was it about?

GAEV: About pride.

TROFIMOV: We had a long conversation yesterday, but we came to no conclusion. In pride, in your sense of it, there is something mystical. Perhaps

---

9. In 1861 Tsar Alexander II issued the Edict of Emancipation, which freed the serfs (agricultural workers held in feudal bondage, who represented about one-third of Russia's population).

1. That is, they are confused, unsettled.

you are right from your point of view; but if one looks at it simply, without subtlety, what sort of pride can there be, what sense is there in it, if man in his physiological formation is very imperfect, if in the immense majority of cases he is coarse, dull-witted, profoundly unhappy? One must give up glorification of self. One should work, and nothing else.

GAEV: One must die in any case.

TROFIMOV: Who knows? And what does it mean—dying? Perhaps man has a hundred senses, and only the five we know are lost at death, while the other ninety-five remain alive.

LYUBOV: How clever you are, Petya!

LOPAHIN: [*Ironically.*] Fearfully clever!

TROFIMOV: Humanity progresses, perfecting its powers. Everything that is beyond its ken now will one day become familiar and comprehensible; only we must work, we must with all our powers aid the seeker after truth. Here among us in Russia the workers are few in number as yet. The vast majority of the intellectual people I know, seek nothing, do nothing, are not fit as yet for work of any kind. They call themselves intellectual, but they treat their servants as inferiors, behave to the peasants as though they were animals, learn little, read nothing seriously, do practically nothing, only talk about science and know very little about art. They are all serious people, they all have severe faces, they all talk of weighty matters and air their theories, and yet the vast majority of us—ninety-nine per cent—live like savages, at the least thing fly to blows and abuse, eat piggishly, sleep in filth and stuffiness, bugs everywhere, stench and damp and moral impurity. And it's clear all our fine talk is only to divert our attention and other people's. Show me where to find the *crèches* there's so much talk about, and the reading-rooms?[2] They only exist in novels: in real life there are none of them. There is nothing but filth and vulgarity and Asiatic apathy. I fear and dislike very serious faces. I'm afraid of serious conversations. We should do better to be silent.

LOPAHIN: You know, I get up at five o'clock in the morning, and I work from morning to night; and I've money, my own and other people's, always passing through my hands, and I see what people are made of all round me. One has only to begin to do anything to see how few honest, decent people there are. Sometimes when I lie awake at night, I think: "Oh! Lord, thou hast given us immense forests, boundless plains, the widest horizons, and living here we ourselves ought really to be giants."

LYUBOV: You ask for giants! They are no good except in story-books; in real life they frighten us.

[EPIHODOV *advances in the background, playing on the guitar.*]

2. Nursery schools and centers offering free reading material—that is, the social services and civilizing influences that have been imagined but never created.

LYUBOV: [*Dreamily.*] There goes Epihodov.

ANYA: [*Dreamily.*] There goes Epihodov.

GAEV: The sun has set, my friends.

TROFIMOV: Yes.

GAEV: [*Not loudly, but, as it were, declaiming.*] O nature, divine nature, thou art bright with eternal luster, beautiful and indifferent! Thou, whom we call mother, thou dost unite within thee life and death! Thou dost give life and dost destroy!

VARYA: [*In a tone of supplication.*] Uncle!

ANYA: Uncle, you are at it again!

TROFIMOV: You'd much better be cannoning off the red!

GAEV: I'll hold my tongue, I will.

[*All sit plunged in thought. Perfect stillness. The only thing audible is the muttering of* FIRS. *Suddenly there is a sound in the distance, as it were from the sky—the sound of a breaking harp-string, mournfully dying away.*]

LYUBOV: What is that?

LOPAHIN: I don't know. Somewhere far away a bucket fallen and broken in the pits. But somewhere very far away.

GAEV: It might be a bird of some sort—such as a heron.

TROFIMOV: Or an owl.

LYUBOV: [*Shudders.*] I don't know why, but it's horrid. [*A pause.*]

FIRS: It was the same before the calamity—the owl hooted and the samovar hissed all the time.

GAEV: Before what calamity?

FIRS: Before the emancipation. [*A pause.*]

LYUBOV: Come, my friends, let us be going; evening is falling. [*To* ANYA.] There are tears in your eyes. What is it, darling? [*Embraces her.*]

ANYA: Nothing, mamma; it's nothing.

TROFIMOV: There is somebody coming.

[*The* WAYFARER *appears in a shabby white forage cap and an overcoat; he is slightly drunk.*]

WAYFARER: Allow me to inquire, can I get to the station this way?

GAEV: Yes. Go along that road.

WAYFARER: I thank you most feelingly. [*Coughing.*] The weather is superb. [*Declaims.*] My brother, my suffering brother![3] . . . Come out to the Volga! Whose groan do you hear? . . . [*To* VARYA.] Mademoiselle, vouchsafe a hungry Russian thirty kopecks.[4]

[VARYA *utters a shriek of alarm.*]

---

3. A line from a poem by Semen Nadson (1862–1887), persecuted in Russia because of his Jewish origins.

4. *Come out to the Volga!:* from a poem by Nikolai Nekrasov (1821–1878), a poet known as a champion of the lower classes. (The Volga is Europe's longest river and Russia's principal waterway.) Thirty kopecks is the equivalent of about $5 in today's U.S. currency.

LOPAHIN: [*Angrily.*] There's a right and a wrong way of doing everything!

LYUBOV: [*Hurriedly.*] Here, take this. [*Looks in her purse.*] I've no silver. No matter—here's gold for you.

WAYFARER: I thank you most feelingly! [*Goes off.*]

[*Laughter.*]

VARYA: [*Frightened.*] I'm going home—I'm going. . . . Oh, mamma, the servants have nothing to eat, and you gave him gold!

LYUBOV: There's no doing anything with me. I'm so silly! When we get home, I'll give you all I possess. Yermolay Alexeyevitch, you will lend me some more! . . .

LOPAHIN: I will.

LYUBOV: Come, friends, it's time to be going. And Varya, we have made a match of it for you. I congratulate you.

VARYA: [*Through her tears.*] Mamma, that's not a joking matter.

LOPAHIN: "Ophelia, get thee to a nunnery!"[5]

GAEV: My hands are trembling; it's a long while since I had a game of billiards.

LOPAHIN: "Ophelia! Nymph, in thy orisons be all my sins remember'd."

LYUBOV: Come, it will soon be supper-time.

VARYA: How he frightened me! My heart's simply throbbing.

LOPAHIN: Let me remind you, ladies and gentlemen: on the 22nd of August the cherry orchard will be sold. Think about that! Think about it!

[*All go off, except* TROFIMOV *and* ANYA.]

ANYA: [*Laughing.*] I'm grateful to the wayfarer! He frightened Varya and we are left alone.

TROFIMOV: Varya's afraid we shall fall in love with each other, and for days together she won't leave us. With her narrow brain she can't grasp that we are above love. To eliminate the petty and transitory which hinder us from being free and happy—that is the aim and meaning of our life. Forward! We go forward irresistibly towards the bright star that shines yonder in the distance. Forward! Do not lag behind, friends.

ANYA: [*Claps her hands.*] How well you speak! [*A pause.*] It is divine here today.

TROFIMOV: Yes, it's glorious weather.

ANYA: Somehow, Petya, you've made me so that I don't love the cherry orchard as I used to. I used to love it so dearly. I used to think that there was no spot on earth like our garden.

TROFIMOV: All Russia is our garden. The earth is great and beautiful—there are many beautiful places in it. [*A pause.*] Think only, Anya, your grandfather, and great-grandfather, and all your ancestors were slave-owners—the owners of living souls—and from every cherry in the orchard, from every leaf, from every trunk there are human creatures looking at you. Cannot you hear their voices? Oh, it is awful! Your orchard is a fearful

---

5. For this quotation and the one below, see *Hamlet* 3.1.

thing, and when in the evening or at night one walks about the orchard, the old bark on the trees glimmers dimly in the dusk, and the old cherry trees seem to be dreaming of centuries gone by and tortured by fearful visions.[6] Yes! We are at least two hundred years behind, we have really gained nothing yet, we have no definite attitude to the past, we do nothing but theorize or complain of depression or drink vodka. It is clear that to begin to live in the present we must first expiate our past, we must break with it; and we can expiate it only by suffering, by extraordinary unceasing labor. Understand that, Anya.

ANYA: The house we live in has long ceased to be our own, and I shall leave it, I give you my word.

TROFIMOV: If you have the house keys, fling them into the well and go away. Be free as the wind.

ANYA: [*In ecstasy.*] How beautifully you said that!

TROFIMOV: Believe me, Anya, believe me! I am not thirty yet, I am young, I am still a student, but I have gone through so much already! As soon as winter comes I am hungry, sick, careworn, poor as a beggar, and what ups and downs of fortune have I not known! And my soul was always, every minute, day and night, full of inexplicable forebodings. I have a foreboding of happiness, Anya. I see glimpses of it already.

ANYA: [*Pensively.*] The moon is rising.

[EPIHODOV *is heard playing still the same mournful song on the guitar. The moon rises. Somewhere near the poplars* VARYA *is looking for* ANYA *and calling* "Anya! where are you?"]

TROFIMOV: Yes, the moon is rising. [*A pause.*] Here is happiness—here it comes! It is coming nearer and nearer; already I can hear its footsteps. And if we never see it—if we may never know it—what does it matter? Others will see it after us.

VARYA'S VOICE: Anya! Where are you?

TROFIMOV: That Varya again! [*Angrily.*] It's revolting!

ANYA: Well, let's go down to the river. It's lovely there.

TROFIMOV: Yes, let's go. [*They go.*]

VARYA'S VOICE: Anya! Anya!

CURTAIN

ACT III

A drawing-room divided by an arch from a larger drawing-room.[7] A chandelier burning. The Jewish orchestra, the same that was mentioned in Act II, is heard playing in the ante-room. It is evening. In the larger drawing-room they are dancing

---

6. *Oh, it is awful!... fearful visions.* Chekhov wrote this passage to replace one that official censors found objectionable: "To own human beings has affected every one of you—those who lived before and those who live now. Your mother, your uncle, and you don't notice that you are living off the labors of others—in fact, the very people you won't even let in the front door." This passage was restored following the 1917 revolution.   7. That is, ballroom.

the grand chain. The voice of SEMYONOV-PISHTCHIK: "Promenade à une paire!"[8]
Then enter the drawing-room in couples first PISHTCHIK *and* CHARLOTTA IVA-
NOVA, *then* TROFIMOV *and* LYUBOV ANDREYEVNA, *thirdly* ANYA *with the* POST-
OFFICE CLERK, *fourthly* VARYA *with the* STATION MASTER, *and other guests.*
VARYA *is quietly weeping and wiping away her tears as she dances. In the last couple
is* DUNYASHA. *They move across the drawing-room.* PISHTCHIK *shouts:* "Grand
rond, balancez!" *and* "Les Cavaliers à genou et remerciez vos dames."

FIRS *in a swallow-tail coat brings in seltzer water on a tray.* PISHTCHIK *and*
TROFIMOV *enter the drawing-room.*

PISHTCHIK: I am a full-blooded man; I have already had two strokes. Dancing's hard work for me, but as they say, if you're in the pack, you must
bark with the rest. I'm as strong, I may say, as a horse. My parent, who
would have his joke—may the Kingdom of Heaven be his!—used to say
about our origin that the ancient stock of the Semyonov-Pishtchiks was
derived from the very horse that Caligula made a member of the senate.[9]
[*Sits down.*] But I've no money, that's where the mischief is. A hungry
dog believes in nothing but meat. [*Snores, but at once wakes up.*] That's
like me . . . I can think of nothing but money.
TROFIMOV: There really is something horsy about your appearance.
PISHTCHIK: Well . . . a horse is a fine beast . . . a horse can be sold.

[*There is the sound of billiards being played in an adjoining room.* VARYA
appears in the arch leading to the larger drawing-room.]

TROFIMOV: [*Teasing.*] Madame Lopahin! Madame Lopahin!
VARYA: [*Angrily.*] Mangy-looking gentleman!
TROFIMOV: Yes, I am a mangy-looking gentleman, and I'm proud of it!
VARYA: [*Pondering bitterly.*] Here we have hired musicians and nothing to
pay them! [*Goes out.*]
TROFIMOV: [*To* PISHTCHIK.] If the energy you have wasted during your life-
time in trying to find the money to pay your interest had gone to some-
thing else, you might in the end have turned the world upside down.
PISHTCHIK: Nietzsche, the philosopher, a very great and celebrated man[1]
. . . of enormous intellect . . . says in his works, that one can make forged
bank-notes.
TROFIMOV: Why, have you read Nietzsche?
PISHTCHIK: What next . . . Dashenka told me. . . . And now I am in such a
position, I might just as well forge banknotes. The day after to-morrow

---

8. In this French phrase and those quoted below, Semyonov-Pishtchik is calling out the moves in
the "grand chain" dance: promenade (walk) to a couple; grand circle, step to the side (that is, *balancez*
as in ballet); and gentlemen (knights), kneel and thank your ladies. (French was widely spoken as a
second language among the upper classes in pre-Soviet Russia.)
9. Caligula (12–41 C.E.), Roman emperor known for tyrannical cruelty, is said to have gone insane
and to have appointed his horse as a consul.
1. Friedrich Wilhelm Nietzsche (1844–1900), German philosopher who rejected what he termed the
"slave morality" of Western bourgeois civilization.

I must pay 310 roubles²—130 I have procured. [*Feels in his pockets, in alarm.*] The money's gone! I have lost my money! [*Through his tears.*] Where's the money? [*Gleefully.*] Why, here it is behind the lining. . . . It has made me hot all over.

[*Enter* LYUBOV ANDREYEVNA *and* CHARLOTTA IVANOVNA.]

LYUBOV: [*Hums the Lezginka.*] Why is Leonid so long? What can he be doing in town? [*To* DUNYASHA.] Offer the musicians some tea.

TROFIMOV: The sale hasn't taken place, most likely.

LYUBOV: It's the wrong time to have the orchestra, and the wrong time to give a dance. Well, never mind. [*Sits down and hums softly.*]

CHARLOTTA: [*Gives* PISHTCHIK *a pack of cards.*] Here's a pack of cards. Think of any card you like.

PISHTCHIK: I've thought of one.

CHARLOTTA: Shuffle the pack now. That's right. Give it here, my dear Mr. Pishtchik. *Ein, zwei, drei*³—now look, it's in your breast pocket.

PISHTCHIK: [*Taking a card out of his breast pocket.*] The eight of spades! Perfectly right! [*Wonderingly.*] Fancy that now!

CHARLOTTA: [*Holding pack of cards in her hands, to* TROFIMOV.] Tell me quickly which is the top card.

TROFIMOV: Well, the queen of spades.

CHARLOTTA: It is! [*To* PISHTCHIK.] Well, which card is uppermost?

PISHTCHIK: The ace of hearts.

CHARLOTTA: It is! [*Claps her hands, pack of cards disappears.*] Ah! what lovely weather it is to-day!

[*A mysterious feminine voice which seems coming out of the floor answers her.* "Oh, yes, it's magnificent weather, madam."]

CHARLOTTA: You are my perfect ideal.

VOICE: And I greatly admire you too, madam.

STATION MASTER: [*Applauding.*] The lady ventriloquist—bravo!

PISHTCHIK: [*Wonderingly.*] Fancy that now! Most enchanting Charlotta Ivanovna. I'm simply in love with you.

CHARLOTTA: In love? [*Shrugging shoulders.*] What do you know of love, *guter Mensch, aber schlechter Musikant.*⁴

TROFIMOV: [*Pats* PISHTCHIK *on the shoulder.*] You dear old horse. . . .

CHARLOTTA: Attention, please! Another trick! [*Takes a traveling rug from a chair.*] Here's a very good rug; I want to sell it. [*Shaking it out.*] Doesn't anyone want to buy it?

PISHTCHIK: [*Wonderingly.*] Fancy that!

CHARLOTTA: *Ein, zwei, drei!* [*Quickly picks up rug she has dropped; behind the rug stands* ANYA; *she makes a curtsey, runs to her mother, embraces her and runs back into the larger drawing-room amidst general enthusiasm.*]

---

2. The equivalent of over $5000 in today's U.S. currency.
3. One, two, three (German). Charlotta speaks the language she associates with her childhood of performing at carnivals.   4. A good man, but a poor musician (German).

LYUBOV: [*Applauds.*] Bravo! Bravo!

CHARLOTTA: Now again! *Ein, zwei, drei!* [*Lifts up the rug; behind the rug stands* VARYA, *bowing.*]

PISHTCHIK: [*Wonderingly.*] Fancy that now!

CHARLOTTA: That's the end. [*Throws the rug at* PISHTCHIK, *makes a curtsey, runs into the larger drawing-room.*]

PISHTCHIK: [*Hurries after her.*] Mischievous creature! Fancy! [*Goes out.*]

LYUBOV: And still Leonid doesn't come. I can't understand what he's doing in the town so long! Why, everything must be over by now. The estate is sold, or the sale has not taken place. Why keep us so long in suspense?

VARYA: [*Trying to console her.*] Uncle's bought it. I feel sure of that.

TROFIMOV: [*Ironically.*] Oh, yes!

VARYA: Great-aunt sent him an authorization to buy it in her name, and transfer the debt. She's doing it for Anya's sake, and I'm sure God will be merciful. Uncle will buy it.

LYUBOV: My aunt in Yaroslavl sent fifteen thousand to buy the estate in her name, she doesn't trust us—but that's not enough even to pay the arrears. [*Hides her face in her hands.*] My fate is being sealed to-day, my fate. . . .

TROFIMOV: [*Teasing* VARYA.] Madame Lopahin.

VARYA: [*Angrily.*] Perpetual student! Twice already you've been sent down[5] from the University.

LYUBOV: Why are you angry, Varya? He's teasing you about Lopahin. Well, what of that? Marry Lopahin if you like, he's a good man, and interesting; if you don't want to, don't! Nobody compels you, darling.

VARYA: I must tell you plainly, mamma, I look at the matter seriously; he's a good man, I like him.

LYUBOV: Well, marry him. I can't see what you're waiting for.

VARYA: Mamma. I can't make him an offer myself. For the last two years, everyone's been talking to me about him. Everyone talks; but he says nothing or else makes a joke. I see what it means. He's growing rich, he's absorbed in business, he has no thoughts for me. If I had money, were it ever so little, if I had only a hundred roubles, I'd throw everything up and go far away. I would go into a nunnery.

TROFIMOV: What bliss!

VARYA: [*To* TROFIMOV.] A student ought to have sense! [*In a soft tone with tears.*] How ugly you've grown, Petya! How old you look! [*To* LYUBOV ANDREYEVNA, *no longer crying.*] But I can't do without work, mamma; I must have something to do every minute.

[*Enter* YASHA.]

YASHA: [*Hardly restraining his laughter.*] Epihodov has broken a billiard cue! [*Goes out.*]

VARYA: What is Epihodov doing here? Who gave him leave to play billiards? I can't make these people out. [*Goes out.*]

5. Expelled.

LYUBOV: Don't tease her, Petya. You see she has grief enough without that.

TROFIMOV: She is so very officious, meddling in what's not her business. All the summer she's given Anya and me no peace. She's afraid of a love affair between us. What's it to do with her? Besides, I have given no grounds for it. Such triviality is not in my line. We are above love!

LYUBOV: And I suppose I am beneath love. [*Very uneasily.*] Why is it Leonid's not here? If only I could know whether the estate is sold or not! It seems such an incredible calamity that I really don't know what to think. I am distracted... I shall scream in a minute... I shall do something stupid. Save me, Petya, tell me something, talk to me!

TROFIMOV: What does it matter whether the estate is sold to-day or not? That's all done with long ago. There's no turning back, the path is overgrown. Don't worry yourself, dear Lyubov Andreyevna. You mustn't deceive yourself; for once in your life you must face the truth!

LYUBOV: What truth? You see where the truth lies, but I seem to have lost my sight, I see nothing. You settle every great problem so boldly, but tell me, my dear boy, isn't it because you're young—because you haven't yet understood one of your problems through suffering? You look forward boldly, and isn't it that you don't see and don't expect anything dreadful because life is still hidden from your young eyes? You're bolder, more honest, deeper than we are, but think, be just a little magnanimous, have pity on me. I was born here, you know, my father and mother lived here, my grandfather lived here, I love this house. I can't conceive of life without the cherry orchard, and if it really must be sold, then sell me with the orchard. [*Embraces* TROFIMOV, *kisses him on the forehead.*] My boy was drowned here. [*Weeps.*] Pity me, my dear kind fellow.

TROFIMOV: You know I feel for you with all my heart.

LYUBOV: But that should have been said differently, so differently. [*Takes out her handkerchief, telegram falls on the floor.*] My heart is so heavy to-day. It's so noisy here, my soul is quivering at every sound, I'm shuddering all over, but I can't go away; I'm afraid to be quiet and alone. Don't be hard on me, Petya... I love you as though you were one of ourselves. I would gladly let you marry Anya—I swear I would—only, my dear boy, you must take your degree, you do nothing—you're simply tossed by fate from place to place. That's so strange. It is, isn't it? And you must do something with your beard to make it grow somehow. [*Laughs.*] You look so funny!

TROFIMOV: [*Picks up the telegram.*] I've no wish to be a beauty.

LYUBOV: That's a telegram from Paris. I get one every day. One yesterday and one to-day. That savage creature is ill again, he's in trouble again. He begs forgiveness, beseeches me to go, and really I ought to go to Paris to see him. You look shocked, Petya. What am I to do, my dear boy, what am I to do? He is ill, he is alone and unhappy, and who'll look after him, who'll keep him from doing the wrong thing, who'll give him his medicine at the right time? And why hide it or be silent? I love him, that's clear. I love him! I love him! He's a millstone about my neck, I'm going to the bottom with him, but I love that stone and can't live without it. [*Presses* TROFIMOV's *hand.*] Don't think ill of me, Petya, don't tell me anything, don't tell me....

TROFIMOV: [*Through his tears*] For God's sake forgive my frankness: why, he robbed you!

LYUBOV: No! No! No! You mustn't speak like that. [*Covers her ears.*]

TROFIMOV: He is a wretch! You're the only person that doesn't know it! He's a worthless creature! A despicable wretch!

LYUBOV: [*Getting angry, but speaking with restraint.*] You're twenty-six or twenty-seven years old, but you're still a schoolboy.

TROFIMOV: Possibly.

LYUBOV: You should be a man at your age! You should understand what love means! And you ought to be in love yourself. You ought to fall in love! [*Angrily.*] Yes, yes, and it's not purity in you, you're simply a prude, a comic fool, a freak.

TROFIMOV: [*In horror.*] The things she's saying!

LYUBOV: I am above love! You're not above love, but simply as our Firs here says, "You are a good-for-nothing." At your age not to have a mistress!

TROFIMOV: [*In horror.*] This is awful! The things she is saying! [*Goes rapidly into the larger drawing-room clutching his head.*] This is awful! I can't stand it! I'm going. [*Goes off, but at once returns.*] All is over between us! [*Goes off into the ante-room.*]

LYUBOV: [*Shouts after him.*] Petya! Wait a minute! You funny creature! I was joking! Petya! [*There is a sound of somebody running quickly downstairs and suddenly falling with a crash.* ANYA *and* VARYA *scream, but there is a sound of laughter at once.*]

LYUBOV: What has happened?

[ANYA *runs in.*]

ANYA: [*Laughing.*] Petya's fallen downstairs! [*Runs out.*]

LYUBOV: What a queer fellow that Petya is!

[*The* STATION MASTER *stands in the middle of the larger room and reads* The Magdalene, *by Alexey Tolstoy.*[6] *They listen to him, but before he has recited many lines strains of a waltz are heard from the ante-room and the reading is broken off. All dance.* TROFIMOV, ANYA, VARYA *and* LYUBOV ANDREYEVNA *come in from the ante-room.*]

LYUBOV: Come, Petya—come, pure heart! I beg your pardon. Let's have a dance! [*Dances with* PETYA.]

[ANYA *and* VARYA *dance.* FIRS *comes in, puts his stick down near the side door.* YASHA *also comes into the drawing-room and looks on at the dancing.*]

YASHA: What is it, old man?

FIRS: I don't feel well. In old days we used to have generals, barons and admirals dancing at our balls, and now we send for the post-office clerk

---

6. A poem sometimes translated as "The Sinful Woman," by Alexsey Tolstoy (1817–1875), a distant cousin of novelist Leo Tolstoy.

and the station master and even they're not overanxious to come. I am getting feeble. The old master, the grandfather, used to give sealing-wax for all complaints. I have been taking sealing-wax for twenty years or more. Perhaps that's what's kept me alive.

YASHA: You bore me, old man! [*Yawns.*] It's time you were done with.

FIRS: *Ach*, you're a good-for-nothing! [*Mutters.*]

[TROFIMOV *and* LYUBOV ANDREYEVNA *dance in larger room and then on to the stage.*]

LYUBOV: *Merci.* I'll sit down a little. [*Sits down.*] I'm tired.

[*Enter* ANYA.]

ANYA: [*Excitedly.*] There's a man in the kitchen has been saying that the cherry orchard's been sold to-day.

LYUBOV: Sold to whom?

ANYA: He didn't say to whom. He's gone away.

[*She dances with* TROFIMOV, *and they go off into the larger room.*]

YASHA: There was an old man gossiping there, a stranger.

FIRS: Leonid Andreyevitch isn't here yet, he hasn't come back. He has his light overcoat on, *demi-saison*, he'll catch cold for sure. *Ach!* Foolish young things!

LYUBOV: I feel as though I should die. Go, Yasha, find out to whom it has been sold.

YASHA: But he went away long ago, the old chap. [*Laughs.*]

LYUBOV: [*With slight vexation.*] What are you laughing at? What are you pleased at?

YASHA: Epihodov is so funny. He's a silly fellow, two and twenty misfortunes.

LYUBOV: Firs, if the estate is sold, where will you go?

FIRS: Where you bid me, there I'll go.

LYUBOV: Why do you look like that? Are you ill? You ought to be in bed.

FIRS: Yes. [*Ironically.*] Me go to bed and who's to wait here? Who's to see to things without me? I'm the only one in all the house.

YASHA: [*To* LYUBOV ANDREYEVNA.] Lyubov Andreyevna, permit me to make a request of you; if you go back to Paris again, be so kind as to take me with you. It's positively impossible for me to stay here. [*Looking about him; in an undertone.*] There's no need to say it, you see for yourself—an uncivilized country, the people have no morals, and then the dullness! The food in the kitchen's abominable, and then Firs runs after one muttering all sorts of unsuitable words. Take me with you, please do!

[*Enter* PISHTCHIK.]

PISHTCHIK: Allow me to ask you for a waltz, my dear lady. [LYUBOV ANDREYEVNA *goes with him.*] Enchanting lady, I really must borrow of you just 180 roubles, [*Dances.*] only 180 roubles. [*They pass into the larger room.*]

[*In the larger drawing-room, a figure in a gray top hat and in check trousers is gesticulating and jumping about. Shouts of* "Bravo, Charlotta Ivanovna."]

DUNYASHA: [*She has stopped to powder herself.*] My young lady tells me to dance. There are plenty of gentlemen, and too few ladies, but dancing makes me giddy and makes my heart beat. Firs, the post-office clerk said something to me just now that quite took my breath away.

[*Music becomes more subdued.*]

FIRS: What did he say to you?
DUNYASHA: He said I was like a flower.
YASHA: [*Yawns.*] What ignorance! [*Goes out.*]
DUNYASHA: Like a flower. I am a girl of such delicate feelings, I am awfully fond of soft speeches.
FIRS: Your head's being turned.

[*Enter* EPIHODOV.]

EPIHODOV: You have no desire to see me, Dunyasha. I might be an insect. [*Sighs.*] Ah! life!
DUNYASHA: What is it you want?
EPIHODOV: Undoubtedly you may be right. [*Sighs.*] But, of course, if one looks at it from that point of view, if I may so express myself, you have, excuse my plain speaking, reduced me to a complete state of mind. I know my destiny. Every day some misfortune befalls me and I have long ago grown accustomed to it, so that I look upon my fate with a smile. You gave me your word, and though I——
DUNYASHA: Let us have a talk later, I entreat you, but now leave me in peace, for I am lost in reverie. [*Plays with her fan.*]
EPIHODOV: I have a misfortune every day, and if I may venture to express myself, I merely smile at it, I even laugh.

[VARYA *enters from the larger drawing-room.*]

VARYA: You still have not gone, Epihodov. What a disrespectful creature you are, really! [*To* DUNYASHA.] Go along, Dunyasha! [*To* EPIHODOV.] First you play billiards and break the cue, then you go wandering about the drawing-room like a visitor!
EPIHODOV: You really cannot, if I may so express myself, call me to account like this.
VARYA: I'm not calling you to account, I'm speaking to you. You do nothing but wander from place to place and don't do your work. We keep you as a counting-house clerk, but what use you are I can't say.
EPIHODOV: [*Offended.*] Whether I work or whether I walk, whether I eat or whether I play billiards, is a matter to be judged by persons of understanding and my elders.
VARYA: You dare to tell me that! [*Firing up.*] You dare! You mean to say I've no understanding. Begone from here! This minute!
EPIHODOV: [*Intimidated.*] I beg you to express yourself with delicacy.

VARYA: [*Beside herself with anger.*] This moment! get out! away! [*He goes towards the door, she following him.*] Two and twenty misfortunes! Take yourself off! Don't let me set eyes on you! [EPIHODOV *has gone out, behind the door his voice,* "I shall lodge a complaint against you."] What! You're coming back? [*Snatches up the stick* FIRS *has put down near the door.*] Come! Come! Come! I'll show you! What! you're coming? Then take that! [*She swings the stick, at the very moment that* LOPAHIN *comes in.*]

LOPAHIN: Very much obliged to you!

VARYA: [*Angrily and ironically.*] I beg your pardon!

LOPAHIN: Not at all! I humbly thank you for your kind reception!

VARYA: No need of thanks for it. [*Moves away, then looks round and asks softly.*] I haven't hurt you?

LOPAHIN: Oh, no! Not at all! There's an immense bump coming up, though!

VOICES FROM LARGER ROOM: Lopahin has come! Yermolay Alexeyevitch!

PISHTCHIK: What do I see and hear? [*Kisses* LOPAHIN.] There's a whiff of cognac about you, my dear soul, and we're making merry here too!

[*Enter* LYUBOV ANDREYEVNA.]

LYUBOV: Is it you, Yermolay Alexeyevitch? Why have you been so long? Where's Leonid?

LOPAHIN: Leonid Andreyevitch arrived with me. He is coming.

LYUBOV: [*In agitation.*] Well! Well! Was there a sale? Speak!

LOPAHIN: [*Embarrassed, afraid of betraying his joy.*] The sale was over at four o'clock. We missed our train—had to wait till half-past nine. [*Sighing heavily.*] Ugh! I feel a little giddy.

[*Enter* GAEV. *In his right hand he has purchases, with his left hand he is wiping away his tears.*]

LYUBOV: Well, Leonid? What news? [*Impatiently, with tears.*] Make haste, for God's sake!

GAEV: [*Makes her no answer, simply waves his hand. To* FIRS, *weeping.*] Here, take them; there's anchovies, Kertch herrings. I have eaten nothing all day. What I have been through! [*Door into the billiard room is open. There is heard a knocking of balls and the voice of* YASHA *saying* "Eighty-seven." GAEV's *expression changes, he leaves off weeping.*] I am fearfully tired. Firs, come and help me change my things. [*Goes to his own room across the larger drawing-room.*]

PISHTCHIK: How about the sale? Tell us, do!

LYUBOV: Is the cherry orchard sold?

LOPAHIN: It is sold.

LYUBOV: Who has bought it?

LOPAHIN: I have bought it. [*A pause.* LYUBOV *is crushed; she would fall down if she were not standing near a chair and table.*]

[VARYA *takes keys from her waistband, flings them on the floor in middle of drawing-room and goes out.*]

LOPAHIN: I have bought it! Wait a bit, ladies and gentlemen, pray. My head's a bit muddled, I can't speak. [*Laughs.*] We came to the auction. Deriganov was there already. Leonid Andreyevitch only had 15,000 and Deriganov bid 30,000, besides the arrears, straight off. I saw how the land lay. I bid against him. I bid 40,000, he bid 45,000, I said 55, and so he went on, adding 5 thousands and I adding 10. Well . . . So it ended. I bid 90, and it was knocked down to me.[7] Now the cherry orchard's mine! Mine! [*Chuckles.*] My God, the cherry orchard's mine! Tell me that I'm drunk, that I'm out of my mind, that it's all a dream. [*Stamps with his feet.*] Don't laugh at me! If my father and my grandfather could rise from their graves and see all that has happened! How their Yermolay, ignorant, beaten Yermolay, who used to run about barefoot in winter, how that very Yermolay has bought the finest estate in the world! I have bought the estate where my father and grandfather were slaves, where they weren't even admitted into the kitchen. I am asleep, I am dreaming! It is all fancy, it is the work of your imagination plunged in the darkness of ignorance. [*Picks up keys, smiling fondly.*] She threw away the keys; she means to show she's not the housewife now. [*Jingles the keys.*] Well, no matter. [*The orchestra is heard tuning up.*] Hey, musicians! Play! I want to hear you. Come, all of you, and look how Yermolay Lopahin will take the ax to the cherry orchard, how the trees will fall to the ground! We will build houses on it and our grandsons and great-grandsons will see a new life springing up there. Music! Play up!

[*Music begins to play.* LYUBOV ANDREYEVNA *has sunk into a chair and is weeping bitterly.*]

LOPAHIN: [*Reproachfully.*] Why, why didn't you listen to me? My poor friend! Dear lady, there's no turning back now. [*With tears.*] Oh, if all this could be over, oh, if our miserable disjointed life could somehow soon be changed!

PISHTCHIK: [*Takes him by the arm, in an undertone.*] She's weeping, let us go and leave her alone. Come. [*Takes him by the arm and leads him into the larger drawing-room.*]

LOPAHIN: What's that? Musicians, play up! All must be as I wish it. [*With irony.*] Here comes the new master, the owner of the cherry orchard! [*Accidentally tips over a little table, almost upsetting the candelabra.*] I can pay for everything! [*Goes out with* PISHTCHIK. *No one remains on the stage or in the larger drawing-room except* LYUBOV, *who sits huddled up, weeping bitterly. The music plays softly.* ANYA *and* TROFIMOV *come in quickly.* ANYA *goes up to her mother and falls on her knees before her.* TROFIMOV *stands at the entrance to the larger drawing-room.*]

ANYA: Mamma! Mamma, you're crying, dear, kind, good mamma! My precious! I love you! I bless you! The cherry orchard is sold, it is gone, that's

---

7. Lopahin's winning bid for the estate was 90,000 roubles, the equivalent of nearly $1.5 million in today's U.S. currency—about twice what Lopahin had offered to lend Lyubov and her family to save the estate (act 1).

true, that's true! But don't weep, mamma! Life is still before you, you have still your good, pure heart! Let us go, let us go, darling, away from here! We will make a new garden, more splendid than this one; you will see it, you will understand. And joy, quiet, deep joy, will sink into your soul like the sun at evening! And you will smile, mamma! Come, darling, let us go!

CURTAIN

ACT IV

SCENE: *Same as in First Act. There are neither curtains on the windows nor pictures on the walls: only a little furniture remains piled up in a corner as if for sale. There is a sense of desolation; near the outer door and in the background of the scene are packed trunks, traveling bags, etc. On the left the door is open, and from here the voices of* VARYA *and* ANYA *are audible.* LOPAHIN *is standing waiting.* YASHA *is holding a tray with glasses full of champagne. In front of the stage* EPI-HODOV *is tying up a box. In the background behind the scene a hum of talk from the peasants who have come to say good-bye. The voice of* GAEV: "Thanks, brothers, thanks!"*

YASHA: The peasants have come to say good-bye. In my opinion, Yermolay Alexeyevitch, the peasants are good-natured, but they don't know much about things.

[*The hum of talk dies away. Enter across front of stage* LYUBOV ANDREYEVNA *and* GAEV. *She is not weeping, but is pale; her face is quivering—she cannot speak.*]

GAEV: You gave them your purse, Lyuba. That won't do—that won't do!
LYUBOV: I couldn't help it! I couldn't help it!

[*Both go out.*]

LOPAHIN: [*In the doorway, calls after them.*] You will take a glass at parting? Please do. I didn't think to bring any from the town, and at the station I could only get one bottle. Please take a glass. [*A pause.*] What? You don't care for any? [*Comes away from the door.*] If I'd known, I wouldn't have bought it. Well, and I'm not going to drink it. [YASHA *carefully sets the tray down on a chair.*] You have a glass, Yasha, anyway.

YASHA: Good luck to the travelers, and luck to those that stay behind! [*Drinks.*] This champagne isn't the real thing, I can assure you.
LOPAHIN: It cost eight roubles the bottle. [*A pause.*] It's devilish cold here.
YASHA: They haven't heated the stove today—it's all the same since we're going. [*Laughs.*]
LOPAHIN: What are you laughing for?
YASHA: For pleasure.
LOPAHIN: Though it's October, it's as still and sunny as though it were summer. It's just right for building! [*Looks at his watch; says in doorway.*] Take note, ladies and gentlemen, the train goes in forty-seven minutes;

so you ought to start for the station in twenty minutes. You must hurry up!

[TROFIMOV *comes in from out of doors wearing a great-coat.*]

TROFIMOV: I think it must be time to start, the horses are ready. The devil only knows what's become of my goloshes; they're lost. [*In the doorway.*] Anya! My goloshes aren't here. I can't find them.

LOPAHIN: And I'm getting off to Harkov. I am going in the same train with you. I'm spending all the winter at Harkov. I've been wasting all my time gossiping with you and fretting with no work to do. I can't get on without work. I don't know what to do with my hands, they flap about so queerly, as if they didn't belong to me.

TROFIMOV: Well, we're just going away, and you will take up your profitable labors again.

LOPAHIN: Do take a glass.

TROFIMOV: No, thanks.

LOPAHIN: Then you're going to Moscow now?

TROFIMOV: Yes. I shall see them as far as the town, and to-morrow I shall go on to Moscow.

LOPAHIN: Yes, I daresay, the professors aren't giving any lectures, they're waiting for your arrival.

TROFIMOV: That's not your business.

LOPAHIN: How many years have you been at the University?

TROFIMOV: Do think of something newer than that—that's stale and flat. [*Hunts for goloshes.*] You know we shall most likely never see each other again, so let me give you one piece of advice at parting: don't wave your arms about—get out of the habit. And another thing, building villas, reckoning up that the summer visitors will in time become independent farmers—reckoning like that, that's not the thing to do either. After all, I am fond of you: you have fine delicate fingers like an artist, you've a fine delicate soul.

LOPAHIN: [*Embraces him.*] Good-bye, my dear fellow. Thanks for everything. Let me give you money for the journey, if you need it.

TROFIMOV: What for? I don't need it.

LOPAHIN: Why, you haven't got a half-penny.

TROFIMOV: Yes, I have, thank you. I got some money for a translation. Here it is in my pocket, [*Anxiously.*] but where can my goloshes be!

VARYA: [*From the next room.*] Take the nasty things! [*Flings a pair of goloshes on to the stage.*]

TROFIMOV: Why are you so cross, Varya? h'm!...but those aren't my goloshes.

LOPAHIN: I sowed three thousand acres with poppies in the spring, and now I have cleared forty thousand profit.[8] And when my poppies were in flower, wasn't it a picture! So here, as a I say, I made forty thousand,

8. That is, a profit equivalent to about $650,000 in today's U.S. currency.

and I'm offering you a loan because I can afford to. Why turn up your nose? I am a peasant—I speak bluntly.

TROFIMOV: Your father was a peasant, mine was a chemist[9]—and that proves absolutely nothing whatever. [LOPAHIN *takes out his pocket-book.*] Stop that—stop that. If you were to offer me two hundred thousand I wouldn't take it. I am an independent man, and everything that all of you, rich and poor alike, prize so highly and hold so dear, hasn't the slightest power over me—it's like so much fluff fluttering in the air. I can get on without you. I can pass by you. I am strong and proud. Humanity is advancing towards the highest truth, the highest happiness, which is possible on earth, and I am in the front ranks.

LOPAHIN: Will you get there?

TROFIMOV: I shall get there. [*A pause.*] I shall get there, or I shall show others the way to get there.

[*In the distance is heard the stroke of an ax on a tree.*]

LOPAHIN: Good-bye, my dear fellow; it's time to be off. We turn up our noses at one another, but life is passing all the while. When I am working hard without resting, then my mind is more at ease, and it seems to me as though I too know what I exist for; but how many people there are in Russia, my dear boy, who exist, one doesn't know what for. Well, it doesn't matter. That's not what keeps things spinning. They tell me Leonid Andreyevitch has taken a situation. He is going to be a clerk at the bank—6,000 roubles a year.[1] Only, of course, he won't stick to it—he's too lazy.

ANYA: [*In the doorway.*] Mamma begs you not to let them chop down the orchard until she's gone.

TROFIMOV: Yes, really, you might have the tact. [*Walks out across the front of the stage.*]

LOPAHIN: I'll see to it! I'll see to it! Stupid fellows! [*Goes out after him.*]

ANYA: Has Firs been taken to the hospital?

YASHA: I told them this morning. No doubt they have taken him.

ANYA: [*To* EPIHODOV, *who passes across the drawing-room.*] Semyon Pantaleyevitch, inquire, please, if Firs has been taken to the hospital.

YASHA: [*In a tone of offence.*] I told Yegor this morning—why ask a dozen times?

EPIHODOV: Firs is advanced in years. It's my conclusive opinion no treatment would do him good; it's time he was gathered to his fathers. And I can only envy him. [*Puts a trunk down on a cardboard hat-box and crushes it.*] There, now, of course—I knew it would be so.

YASHA: [*Jeeringly.*] Two and twenty misfortunes!

VARYA: [*Through the door.*] Has Firs been taken to the hospital?

ANYA: Yes.

VARYA: Why wasn't the note for the doctor taken too?

ANYA: Oh, then, we must send it after them. [*Goes out.*]

---

9. Pharmacist.   1. A salary equivalent to nearly $100,000 in today's U.S. currency.

VARYA: [*From the adjoining room.*] Where's Yasha? Tell him his mother's come to say good-bye to him.

YASHA: [*Waves his hand.*] They put me out of all patience! [DUNYASHA *has all this time been busy about the luggage. Now, when* YASHA *is left alone, she goes up to him.*]

DUNYASHA: You might just give me one look, Yasha. You're going away. You're leaving me. [*Weeps and throws herself on his neck.*]

YASHA: What are you crying for? [*Drinks the champagne.*] In six days I shall be in Paris again. To-morrow we shall get into the express train and roll away in a flash. I can scarcely believe it! *Vive la France!* It doesn't suit me here—it's not the life for me; there's no doing anything. I have seen enough of the ignorance here. I have had enough of it. [*Drinks champagne.*] What are you crying for? Behave yourself properly, and then you won't cry.

DUNYASHA: [*Powders her face, looking in a pocket-mirror.*] Do send me a letter from Paris. You know how I loved you, Yasha—how I loved you! I am a tender creature, Yasha.

YASHA: Here they are coming!

[*Busies himself about the trunks, humming softly. Enter* LYUBOV ANDREY-EVNA, GAEV, ANYA *and* CHARLOTTA IVANOVNA.]

GAEV: We ought to be off. There's not much time now. [*Looking at* YASHA.] What a smell of herrings!

LYUBOV: In ten minutes we must get into the carriage. [*Casts a look about the room.*] Farewell, dear house, dear old home of our fathers! Winter will pass and spring will come, and then you will be no more; they will tear you down! How much those walls have seen! [*Kisses her daughter passionately.*] My treasure, how bright you look! Your eyes are sparkling like diamonds! Are you glad? Very glad?

ANYA: Very glad! A new life is beginning, mamma.

GAEV: Yes, really, everything is all right now. Before the cherry orchard was sold, we were all worried and wretched, but afterwards, when once the question was settled conclusively, irrevocably, we all felt calm and even cheerful. I am a bank clerk now—I am a financier—cannon off the red. And you, Lyuba, after all, you are looking better; there's no question of that.

LYUBOV: Yes. My nerves are better, that's true. [*Her hat and coat are handed to her.*] I'm sleeping well. Carry out my things, Yasha. It's time. [*To* ANYA.] My darling, we shall soon see each other again. I am going to Paris. I can live there on the money your Yaroslavl auntie sent us to buy the estate with—hurrah for auntie—but that money won't last long.

ANYA: You'll come back soon, mamma, won't you? I'll be working up for my examination in the high school, and when I have passed that, I shall set to work and be a help to you. We will read all sorts of things together, mamma, won't we? [*Kisses her mother's hands.*] We will read in the autumn evenings. We'll read lots of books, and a new wonderful world will open out before us. [*Dreamily.*] Mamma, come soon.

LYUBOV: I shall come, my precious treasure. [*Embraces her.*]

[*Enter* LOPAHIN. CHARLOTTA *softly hums a song.*]

GAEV: Charlotta's happy; she's singing!

CHARLOTTA: [*Picks up a bundle like a swaddled baby.*] Bye, bye, my baby. [*A baby is heard crying: "Ooah! ooah!"*] Hush, hush, my pretty boy! [*Ooah! ooah!*] Poor little thing! [*Throws the bundle back.*] You must please find me a situation. I can't go on like this.

LOPAHIN: We'll find you one, Charlotta Ivanovna. Don't you worry yourself.

GAEV: Everyone's leaving us. Varya's going away. We have become of no use all at once.

CHARLOTTA: There's nowhere for me to be in the town. I must go away. [*Hums.*] What care I . . .

[*Enter* PISHTCHIK.]

LOPAHIN: The freak of nature!

PISHTCHIK: [*Gasping.*] Oh! . . . let me get my breath. . . . I'm worn out . . . my most honored . . . Give me some water.

GAEV: Want some money, I suppose? Your humble servant! I'll go out of the way of temptation. [*Goes out.*]

PISHTCHIK: It's a long while since I have been to see you . . . dearest lady. [*To* LOPAHIN.] You are here . . . glad to see you . . . a man of immense intellect . . . take . . . here. [*Gives* LOPAHIN.] 400 roubles.[2] That leaves me owing 840.

LOPAHIN: [*Shrugging his shoulders in amazement.*] It's like a dream. Where did you get it?

PISHTCHIK: Wait a bit . . . I'm hot . . . a most extraordinary occurrence! Some Englishmen came along and found in my land some sort of white clay. [*To* LYUBOV ANDREYEVNA.] And 400 for you . . . most lovely . . . wonderful. [*Gives money.*] The rest later. [*Sips water.*] A young man in the train was telling me just now that a great philosopher advises jumping off a house-top. "Jump!" says he; "the whole gist of the problem lies in that." [*Wonderingly.*] Fancy that, now! Water, please!

LOPAHIN: What Englishmen?

PISHTCHIK: I have made over to them the rights to dig the clay for twenty-four years . . . and now, excuse me . . . I can't stay . . . I must be trotting on. I'm going to Znoikovo . . . to Kardamanovo. . . . I'm in debt all round. [*Sips.*] . . . To your very good health! . . . I'll come in on Thursday.

LYUBOV: We are just off to the town, and to-morrow I start for abroad.

PISHTCHIK: What! [*In agitation.*] Why to the town? Oh, I see the furniture . . . the boxes. No matter . . . [*Through his tears.*] . . . no matter . . . men of enormous intellect . . . these Englishmen. . . . Never mind . . . be happy. God will succor you . . . no matter . . . everything in this world must have an end. [*Kisses* LYUBOV ANDREYEVNA's *hand.*] If the rumor reaches you that my end has come, think of this . . . old horse, and say: "There once was such a man in the world . . . Semyonov-Pishtchik . . . the Kingdom of Heaven be his!" . . . most extraordinary weather . . . yes. [*Goes out in*

---

2. About $6500 in today's U.S. currency.

violent agitation, but at once returns and says in the doorway.] Dashenka wishes to be remembered to you. [*Goes out.*]

LYUBOV: Now we can start. I leave with two cares in my heart. The first is leaving Firs ill. [*Looking at her watch.*] We have still five minutes.

ANYA: Mamma, Firs has been taken to the hospital. Yasha sent him off this morning.

LYUBOV: My other anxiety is Varya. She is used to getting up early and working; and now, without work, she's like a fish out of water. She is thin and pale, and she's crying, poor dear! [*A pause.*] You are well aware, Yermolay Alexeyevitch, I dreamed of marrying her to you, and everything seemed to show that you would get married. [*Whispers to* ANYA *and motions to* CHARLOTTA *and both go out.*] She loves you—she suits you. And I don't know—I don't know why it is you seem, as it were, to avoid each other. I can't understand it!

LOPAHIN: I don't understand it myself, I confess. It's queer somehow, altogether. If there's still time, I'm ready now at once. Let's settle it straight off, and go ahead; but without you, I feel I shan't make her an offer.

LYUBOV: That's excellent. Why, a single moment's all that's necessary. I'll call her at once.

LOPAHIN: And there's champagne all ready too. [*Looking into the glasses.*] Empty! Someone's emptied them already. [YASHA *coughs.*] I call that greedy.

LYUBOV: [*Eagerly.*] Capital! We will go out. Yasha, *allez!*[3] I'll call her in. [*At the door.*] Varya, leave all that; come here. Come along! [*Goes out with* YASHA.]

LOPAHIN: [*Looking at his watch.*] Yes.

[*A pause. Behind the door, smothered laughter and whispering, and, at last, enter* VARYA.]

VARYA: [*Looking a long while over the things.*] It is strange, I can't find it anywhere.

LOPAHIN: What are you looking for?

VARYA: I packed it myself, and I can't remember. [*A pause.*]

LOPAHIN: Where are you going now, Varvara Mihailova?

VARYA: I? To the Ragulins. I have arranged to go to them to look after the house—as a housekeeper.

LOPAHIN: That's in Yashnovo? It'll be seventy miles away. [*A pause.*] So this is the end of life in this house!

VARYA: [*Looking among the things.*] Where is it? Perhaps I put it in the trunk. Yes, life in this house is over—there will be no more of it.

LOPAHIN: And I'm just off to Harkov—by this next train. I've a lot of business there. I'm leaving Epihodov here, and I've taken him on.

VARYA: Really!

LOPAHIN: This time last year we had snow already, if you remember; but

---

3. Go! (French).

now it's so fine and sunny. Though it's cold, to be sure—three degrees of frost.

VARYA: I haven't looked. [*A pause.*] And besides, our thermometer's broken. [*A pause.*]

[*Voice at the door from the yard:* "Yermolay Alexeyevitch!"]

LOPAHIN: [*As though he had long been expecting this summons.*] This minute!

[LOPAHIN *goes out quickly.* VARYA *sitting on the floor and laying her head on a bag full of clothes, sobs quietly. The door opens.* LYUBOV ANDREYEVNA *comes in cautiously.*]

LYUBOV: Well? [*A pause.*] We must be going.

VARYA: [*Has wiped her eyes and is no longer crying.*] Yes, mamma, it's time to start. I shall have time to get to the Ragulins to-day, if only you're not late for the train.

LYUBOV: [*In the doorway.*] Anya, put your things on.

[*Enter* ANYA, *then* GAEV *and* CHARLOTTA IVANOVNA. GAEV *has on a warm coat with a hood. Servants and cabmen come in.* EPIHODOV *bustles about the luggage.*]

LYUBOV: Now we can start on our travels.

ANYA: [*Joyfully.*] On our travels!

GAEV: My friends—my dear, my precious friends! Leaving this house for ever, can I be silent? Can I refrain from giving utterance at leave-taking to those emotions which now flood all my being?

ANYA: [*Supplicatingly.*] Uncle!

VARYA: Uncle, you mustn't!

GAEV: [*Dejectedly.*] Cannon and into the pocket . . . I'll be quiet. . . .

[*Enter* TROFIMOV *and afterwards* LOPAHIN.]

TROFIMOV: Well, ladies and gentlemen, we must start.

LOPAHIN: Epihodov, my coat!

LYUBOV: I'll stay just one minute. It seems as though I have never seen before what the walls, what the ceilings in this house were like, and now I look at them with greediness, with such tender love.

GAEV: I remember when I was six years old sitting in that window on Trinity Day watching my father going to church.

LYUBOV: Have all the things been taken?

LOPAHIN: I think all. [*Putting on overcoat, to* EPIHODOV.] You, Epihodov, mind you see everything is right.

EPIHODOV: [*In a husky voice.*] Don't you trouble, Yermolay Alexeyevitch.

LOPAHIN: Why, what's wrong with your voice?

EPIHODOV: I've just had a drink of water, and I choked over something.

YASHA: [*Contemptuously.*] The ignorance!

LYUBOV: We are going—and not a soul will be left here.

LOPAHIN: Not till the spring.

VARYA: [*Pulls a parasol out of a bundle, as though about to hit someone with it.*

LOPAHIN *makes a gesture as though alarmed.*] What is it? I didn't mean anything.

TROFIMOV: Ladies and gentlemen, let us get into the carriage. It's time. The train will be in directly.

VARYA: Petya, here they are, your goloshes, by that box. [*With tears.*] And what dirty old things they are!

TROFIMOV: [*Putting on his goloshes.*] Let us go, friends!

GAEV: [*Greatly agitated, afraid of weeping.*] The train—the station! Double baulk, ah!

LYUBOV: Let us go!

LOPAHIN: Are we all here? [*Locks the side-door on left.*] The things are all here. We must lock up. Let us go!

ANYA: Good-bye, home! Good-bye to the old life!

TROFIMOV: Welcome to the new life!

[TROFIMOV *goes out with* ANYA. VARYA *looks round the room and goes out slowly.* YASHA *and* CHARLOTTA IVANOVNA, *with her dog, go out.*]

LOPAHIN: Till the spring, then! Come, friends, till we meet! [*Goes out.*]

[LYUBOV ANDREYEVNA *and* GAEV *remain alone. As though they had been waiting for this, they throw themselves on each other's necks, and break into subdued smothered sobbing, afraid of being overheard.*]

GAEV: [*In despair.*] Sister, my sister!

LYUBOV: Oh, my orchard!—my sweet, beautiful orchard! My life, my youth, my happiness, good-bye! good-bye!

VOICE OF ANYA: [*Calling gaily.*] Mamma!

VOICE OF TROFIMOV: [*Gaily, excitedly.*] Aa—oo!

LYUBOV: One last look at the walls, at the windows. My dear mother loved to walk about this room.

GAEV: Sister, sister!

VOICE OF ANYA: Mamma!

VOICE OF TROFIMOV: Aa—oo!

LYUBOV: We are coming. [*They go out.*]

[*The stage is empty. There is the sound of the doors being locked up, then of the carriages driving away. There is silence. In the stillness there is the dull stroke of an ax in a tree, clanging with a mournful lonely sound. Footsteps are heard.* FIRS *appears in the doorway on the right. He is dressed as always— in a pea-jacket and white waistcoat, with slippers on his feet. He is ill.*]

FIRS: [*Goes up to the doors, and tries the handles.*] Locked! They have gone . . . [*Sits down on sofa.*] They have forgotten me. . . . Never mind . . . I'll sit here a bit. . . . I'll be bound Leonid Andreyevitch hasn't put his fur coat on and has gone off in his thin overcoat. [*Sighs anxiously.*] I didn't see after him. . . . These young people . . . [*Mutters something that can't be distinguished.*] Life has slipped by as though I hadn't lived. [*Lies down.*] I'll lie down a bit. . . . There's no strength in you, nothing left you—all gone! Ech! I'm good for nothing. [*Lies motionless.*]

[*A sound is heard that seems to come from the sky, like a breaking harpstring, dying away mournfully. All is still again, and there is heard nothing but the strokes of the ax far away in the orchard.*]

CURTAIN

1903–04

Hamlet

CHARACTERS

CLAUDIUS, *King of Denmark*
HAMLET, *son of the former and nephew to the present King*
POLONIUS, *Lord Chamberlain*
HORATIO, *friend of Hamlet*
LAERTES, *son of Polonius*
VOLTEMAND
CORNELIUS
ROSENCRANTZ } *courtiers*
GUILDENSTERN
OSRIC
A GENTLEMAN
A PRIEST

MARCELLUS } *officers*
BERNARDO
FRANCISCO, *a soldier*
REYNALDO, *servant to Polonius*
PLAYERS
TWO CLOWNS, *gravediggers*
FORTINBRAS, *Prince of Norway*
A NORWEGIAN CAPTAIN
ENGLISH AMBASSADORS
GERTRUDE, *Queen of Denmark, and mother of Hamlet*
OPHELIA, *daughter of Polonius*
GHOST OF HAMLET'S FATHER

LORDS, LADIES, OFFICERS, SOLDIERS, SAILORS, MESSENGERS, AND ATTENDANTS

SCENE: *The action takes place in or near the royal castle of Denmark at Elsinore.*

ACT I

Scene 1

A guard station atop the castle. Enter BERNARDO *and* FRANCISCO, *two sentinels.*

BERNARDO: Who's there?
FRANCISCO: Nay, answer me. Stand and unfold yourself.
BERNARDO: Long live the king!
FRANCISCO: Bernardo?
BERNARDO: He.   5
FRANCISCO: You come most carefully upon your hour.
BERNARDO: 'Tis now struck twelve. Get thee to bed, Francisco.
FRANCISCO: For this relief much thanks. 'Tis bitter cold,
    And I am sick at heart.
BERNARDO: Have you had quiet guard?
FRANCISCO: Not a mouse stirring.   10
BERNARDO: Well, good night.
    If you do meet Horatio and Marcellus,
    The rivals[1] of my watch, bid them make haste.

1. Companions.

[*Enter* HORATIO *and* MARCELLUS.]

FRANCISCO: I think I hear them. Stand, ho! Who is there?

HORATIO: Friends to this ground.

15 MARCELLUS: And liegemen to the Dane.[2]

FRANCISCO: Give you good night.

MARCELLUS: O, farewell, honest soldier!
    Who hath relieved you?

FRANCISCO: Bernardo hath my place.
    Give you good night.   [*Exit* FRANCISCO.]

MARCELLUS: Holla, Bernardo!

BERNARDO: Say—
    What, is Horatio there?

HORATIO: A piece of him.

20 BERNARDO: Welcome, Horatio. Welcome, good Marcellus.

HORATIO: What, has this thing appeared again tonight?

BERNARDO: I have seen nothing.

MARCELLUS: Horatio says 'tis but our fantasy,
    And will not let belief take hold of him

25 Touching this dreaded sight twice seen of us.
    Therefore I have entreated him along
    With us to watch the minutes of this night,
    That if again this apparition come,
    He may approve[3] our eyes and speak to it.

HORATIO: Tush, tush, 'twill not appear.

30 BERNARDO: Sit down awhile,
    And let us once again assail your ears,
    That are so fortified against our story,
    What we have two nights seen.

HORATIO: Well, sit we down.
    And let us hear Bernardo speak of this.

35 BERNARDO: Last night of all,
    When yond same star that's westward from the pole[4]
    Had made his course t' illume that part of heaven
    Where now it burns, Marcellus and myself,
    The bell then beating one—

        [*Enter* GHOST.]

40 MARCELLUS: Peace, break thee off. Look where it comes again.

BERNARDO: In the same figure like the king that's dead.

MARCELLUS: Thou art a scholar; speak to it, Horatio.

BERNARDO: Looks 'a[5] not like the king? Mark it, Horatio.

HORATIO: Most like. It harrows me with fear and wonder.

---

2. The "Dane" is the king of Denmark, who is also called "Denmark," as in line 48 of this scene. In line 61 the same figure is used for the king of Norway.   3. Confirm the testimony of.   4. Polestar.
5. He.

BERNARDO: It would be spoke to.
MARCELLUS: Speak to it, Horatio.   45
HORATIO: What art thou that usurp'st this time of night
  Together with that fair and warlike form
  In which the majesty of buried Denmark
  Did sometimes march? By heaven I charge thee, speak.
MARCELLUS: It is offended.
BERNARDO: See, it stalks away.   50
HORATIO: Stay. Speak, speak. I charge thee, speak.   [*Exit* GHOST.]
MARCELLUS: 'Tis gone and will not answer.
BERNARDO: How now, Horatio! You tremble and look pale.
  Is not this something more than fantasy?
  What think you on't?   55
HORATIO: Before my God, I might not this believe
  Without the sensible[6] and true avouch
  Of mine own eyes.
MARCELLUS: It is not like the king?
HORATIO: As thou art to thyself.
  Such was the very armor he had on   60
  When he the ambitious Norway combated.
  So frowned he once when, in an angry parle,[7]
  He smote the sledded Polacks on the ice.
  'Tis strange.
MARCELLUS: Thus twice before, and jump[8] at this dead hour,   65
  With martial stalk hath he gone by our watch.
HORATIO: In what particular thought to work I know not,
  But in the gross and scope of mine opinion,
  This bodes some strange eruption to our state.
MARCELLUS: Good now, sit down, and tell me he that knows,   70
  Why this same strict and most observant watch
  So nightly toils the subject[9] of the land,
  And why such daily cast of brazen cannon
  And foreign mart for implements of war;
  Why such impress of shipwrights, whose sore task   75
  Does not divide the Sunday from the week.
  What might be toward that this sweaty haste
  Doth make the night joint-laborer with the day?
  Who is't that can inform me?
HORATIO: That can I.
  At last, the whisper goes so. Our last king,   80
  Whose image even but now appeared to us,
  Was as you know by Fortinbras of Norway,
  Thereto pricked on by a most emulate pride,
  Dared to the combat; in which our valiant Hamlet
  (For so this side of our known world esteemed him)   85

6. Perceptible.   7. Parley.   8. Precisely.   9. People.

Did slay this Fortinbras; who by a sealed compact
Well ratified by law and heraldry,
Did forfeit, with his life, all those his lands
Which he stood seized of,[1] to the conqueror;
90   Against the which a moiety competent[2]
Was gagéd[3] by our king; which had returned
To the inheritance of Fortinbras,
Had he been vanquisher; as, by the same covenant
And carriage of the article designed,
95   His fell to Hamlet. Now, sir, young Fortinbras,
Of unimprovéd mettle hot and full,
Hath in the skirts of Norway here and there
Sharked up a list of lawless resolutes
For food and diet to some enterprise
100   That hath a stomach in't; which is no other,
As it doth well appear unto our state,
But to recover of us by strong hand
And terms compulsatory, those foresaid lands
So by his father lost; and this, I take it,
105   Is the main motive of our preparations,
The source of this our watch, and the chief head
Of this post-haste and romage[4] in the land.
BERNARDO: I think it be no other but e'en so.
Well may it sort[5] that this portentous figure
110   Comes arméd through our watch so like the king
That was and is the question of these wars.
HORATIO: A mote[6] it is to trouble the mind's eye.
In the most high and palmy state of Rome,
A little ere the mightiest Julius fell,
115   The graves stood tenantless, and the sheeted dead
Did squeak and gibber in the Roman streets;
As stars with trains of fire, and dews of blood,
Disasters in the sun; and the moist star,
Upon whose influence Neptune's empire stands,[7]
120   Was sick almost to doomsday with eclipse.
And even the like precurse[8] of feared events,
As harbingers preceding still the fates
And prologue to the omen coming on,
Have heaven and earth together demonstrated
125   Unto our climatures[9] and countrymen.

[*Enter* GHOST.]

---

1. Possessed.   2. Portion of similar value.   3. Pledged.   4. Stir.   5. Chance.
6. Speck of dust.   7. Neptune was the Roman sea god; the "moist star" is the moon.
8. Precursor.   9. Regions.

But soft, behold, lo where it comes again!
I'll cross it[1] though it blast me.—Stay, illusion.

[*It spreads (its) arms.*]

If thou hast any sound or use of voice,
Speak to me.
If there be any good thing to be done,   130
That may to thee do ease, and grace to me,
Speak to me.
If thou art privy to thy country's fate,
Which happily foreknowing may avoid,
O, speak!   135
Or if thou hast uphoarded in thy life
Extorted treasure in the womb of earth,
For which, they say, you spirits oft walk in death,

[*The cock crows.*]

Speak of it. Stay, and speak. Stop it, Marcellus.
MARCELLUS: Shall I strike at it with my partisan?[2]   140
HORATIO: Do, if it will not stand.
BERNARDO: 'Tis here.
HORATIO: 'Tis here.
MARCELLUS: 'Tis gone.   [*Exit* GHOST.]
We do it wrong, being so majestical,
To offer it the show of violence;
For it is as the air, invulnerable,   145
And our vain blows malicious mockery.
BERNARDO: It was about to speak when the cock crew.
HORATIO: And then it started like a guilty thing
Upon a fearful summons. I have heard
The cock, that is the trumpet to the morn,   150
Doth with his lofty and shrill-sounding throat
Awake the god of day, and at his warning,
Whether in sea or fire, in earth or air,
Th' extravagant and erring[3] spirit hies
To his confine; and of the truth herein   155
This present object made probation.[4]
MARCELLUS: It faded on the crowing of the cock.
Some say that ever 'gainst that season comes
Wherein our Savior's birth is celebrated,
This bird of dawning singeth all night long,   160
And then, they say, no spirit dare stir abroad,

---

1. Horatio means either that he will move across the ghost's path in order to stop him or that he will make the sign of the cross to gain power over him. The stage direction that follows is somewhat ambiguous. "It" seems to refer to the ghost, but the movement would be appropriate to Horatio.
2. Halberd.   3. Wandering out of bounds.   4. Proof.

The nights are wholesome, then no planets strike,
No fairy takes,[5] nor witch hath power to charm,
So hallowed and so gracious is that time.
165 HORATIO: So have I heard and do in part believe it.
But look, the morn in russet mantle clad
Walks o'er the dew of yon high eastward hill.
Break we our watch up, and by my advice
Let us impart what we have seen tonight
170 Unto young Hamlet, for upon my life
This spirit, dumb to us, will speak to him.
Do you consent we shall acquaint him with it,
As needful in our loves, fitting our duty?
MARCELLUS: Let's do't, I pray, and I this morning know
175 Where we shall find him most conveniently.   [*Exeunt.*]

Scene 2

A chamber of state. Enter KING CLAUDIUS, QUEEN GERTRUDE, HAMLET,
POLONIUS, LAERTES, VOLTEMAND, CORNELIUS *and other members of the court.*

KING: Though yet of Hamlet our dear brother's death
The memory be green, and that it us befitted
To bear our hearts in grief, and our whole kingdom
To be contracted in one brow of woe,
5 Yet so far hath discretion fought with nature
That we with wisest sorrow think on him,
Together with remembrance of ourselves.
Therefore our sometime sister, now our queen,
Th' imperial jointress[6] to this warlike state,
10 Have we, as 'twere with a defeated joy,
With an auspicious and a dropping eye,
With mirth in funeral, and with dirge in marriage,
In equal scale weighing delight and dole,
Taken to wife; nor have we herein barred
15 Your better wisdoms, which have freely gone
With this affair along. For all, our thanks.
Now follows that you know young Fortinbras,
Holding a weak supposal of our worth,
Or thinking by our late dear brother's death
20 Our state to be disjoint and out of frame,
Colleaguéd with this dream of his advantage,
He hath not failed to pester us with message
Importing the surrender of those lands
Lost by his father, with all bonds of law,
25 To our most valiant brother. So much for him.

5. Enchants.
6. A "jointress" is a widow who holds a *jointure* or life interest in the estate of her deceased husband.

Now for ourself, and for this time of meeting,
Thus much the business is: we have here writ
To Norway, uncle of young Fortinbras—
Who, impotent and bedrid, scarcely hears
Of this his nephew's purpose—to suppress   30
His further gait[7] herein, in that the levies,
The lists, and full proportions are all made
Out of his subject; and we here dispatch
You, good Cornelius, and you, Voltemand,
For bearers of this greeting to old Norway,   35
Giving to you no further personal power
To business with the king, more than the scope
Of these dilated[8] articles allow.
Farewell, and let your haste commend your duty.

CORNELIUS: ⎫
VOLTEMAND: ⎬ In that, and all things will we show our duty.   40

KING: We doubt it nothing, heartily farewell.

               [*Exeunt* VOLTEMAND *and* CORNELIUS.]

And now, Laertes, what's the news with you?
You told us of some suit. What is't, Laertes?
You cannot speak of reason to the Dane
And lose your voice. What wouldst thou beg, Laertes,   45
That shall not be my offer, not thy asking?
The head is not more native to the heart,
The hand more instrumental[9] to the mouth,
Than is the throne of Denmark to thy father.
What wouldst thou have, Laertes?

LAERTES: My dread lord,   50
Your leave and favor to return to France,
From whence, though willingly, I came to Denmark
To show my duty in your coronation,
Yet now I must confess, that duty done,
My thoughts and wishes bend again toward France,   55
And bow them to your gracious leave and pardon.

KING: Have you your father's leave? What says Polonius?

POLONIUS: He hath, my lord, wrung from me my slow leave
By laborsome petition, and at last
Upon his will I sealed my hard consent.   60
I do beseech you give him leave to go.

KING: Take thy fair hour, Laertes. Time be thine,
And thy best graces spend it at thy will.
But now, my cousin[1] Hamlet, and my son—

HAMLET: [*Aside.*] A little more than kin, and less than kind.   65

KING: How is it that the clouds still hang on you?

---

7. Progress. 8. Fully expressed. 9. Serviceable.
1. "Cousin" is used here as a general term of kinship.

HAMLET: Not so, my lord. I am too much in the sun.

QUEEN: Good Hamlet, cast thy nighted color off,
　　　And let thine eye look like a friend on Denmark.
70　　Do not for ever with thy vailéd lids[2]
　　　Seek for thy noble father in the dust.
　　　Thou know'st 'tis common—all that lives must die,
　　　Passing through nature to eternity.

HAMLET: Ay, madam, it is common.

QUEEN:　　　　　　　　　　　　　　If it be,
75　　Why seems it so particular with thee?

HAMLET: Seems, madam? Nay, it is. I know not "seems."
　　　'Tis not alone my inky cloak, good mother,
　　　Nor customary suits of solemn black,
　　　Nor windy suspiration of forced breath,
80　　No, nor the fruitful river in the eye,
　　　Nor the dejected havior[3] of the visage,
　　　Together with all forms, moods, shapes of grief,
　　　That can denote me truly. These indeed seem,
　　　For they are actions that a man might play,
85　　But I have that within which passes show—
　　　These but the trappings and the suits of woe.

KING: 'Tis sweet and commendable in your nature, Hamlet,
　　　To give these mourning duties to your father,
　　　But you must know your father lost a father,
90　　That father lost, lost his, and the survivor bound
　　　In filial obligation for some term
　　　To do obsequious[4] sorrow. But to persever
　　　In obstinate condolement is a course
　　　Of impious stubbornness. 'Tis unmanly grief.
95　　It shows a will most incorrect to[5] heaven,
　　　A heart unfortified, a mind impatient,
　　　An understanding simple and unschooled.
　　　For what we know must be, and is as common
　　　As any the most vulgar thing to sense,
100　　Why should we in our peevish opposition
　　　Take it to heart? Fie, 'tis a fault to heaven,
　　　A fault against the dead, a fault to nature,
　　　To reason most absurd, whose common theme
　　　Is death of fathers, and who still hath cried,
105　　From the first corse[6] till he that died today,
　　　"This must be so." We pray you throw to earth
　　　This unprevailing woe, and think of us
　　　As of a father, for let the world take note
　　　You are the most immediate[7] to our throne,

---

2. Lowered eyes.　3. Appearance.　4. Suited for funeral obsequies.
5. Uncorrected toward.　6. Corpse.　7. Next in line.

And with no less nobility of love   110
Than that which dearest father bears his son
Do I impart toward you. For your intent
In going back to school in Wittenberg,
It is most retrograde[8] to our desire,
And we beseech you, bend you to remain   115
Here in the cheer and comfort of our eye,
Our chiefest courtier, cousin, and our son.
QUEEN: Let not thy mother lose her prayers, Hamlet.
I pray thee stay with us, go not to Wittenberg.
HAMLET: I shall in all my best obey you, madam.   120
KING: Why, 'tis a loving and a fair reply.
Be as ourself in Denmark. Madam, come.
This gentle and unforced accord of Hamlet
Sits smiling to my heart, in grace whereof,
No jocund health that Denmark drinks today   125
But the great cannon to the clouds shall tell,
And the king's rouse the heaven shall bruit[9] again,
Respeaking earthly thunder. Come away.
                          [*Flourish. Exeunt all but* HAMLET.]
HAMLET: O, that this too too solid flesh would melt,
Thaw, and resolve itself into a dew,   130
Or that the Everlasting had not fixed
His canon[1] 'gainst self-slaughter. O God, God,
How weary, stale, flat, and unprofitable
Seem to me all the uses of this world!
Fie on't, ah, fie, 'tis an unweeded garden   135
That grows to seed. Things rank and gross in nature
Possess it merely.[2] That it should come to this,
But two months dead, nay, not so much, not two.
So excellent a king, that was to this
Hyperion to a satyr,[3] so loving to my mother,   140
That he might not beteem[4] the winds of heaven
Visit her face too roughly. Heaven and earth,
Must I remember? Why, she would hang on him
As if increase of appetite had grown
By what it fed on, and yet, within a month—   145
Let me not think on't. Frailty, thy name is woman—
A little month, or ere those shoes were old
With which she followed my poor father's body
Like Niobe,[5] all tears, why she, even she—

8. Contrary.   9. Echo. *Rouse:* carousal.   1. Law.   2. Entirely.
3. Hyperion, a Greek god, stands here for beauty in contrast to the monstrous satyr, a lecherous
creature, half man and half goat.   4. Permit.
5. In Greek mythology, Niobe was turned to stone after a tremendous fit of weeping over the death
of her fourteen children, a misfortune brought about by her boasting over her fertility.

150   O God, a beast that wants discourse of reason
       Would have mourned longer—married with my uncle,
       My father's brother, but no more like my father
       Than I to Hercules.[6] Within a month,
       Ere yet the salt of most unrighteous tears
155   Had left the flushing in her gallèd eyes,
       She married. O, most wicked speed, to post
       With such dexterity to incestuous sheets!
       It is not, nor it cannot come to good.
       But break my heart, for I must hold my tongue.

       [*Enter* HORATIO, MARCELLUS, *and* BERNARDO.]

       HORATIO: Hail to your lordship!
160   HAMLET: I am glad to see you well.
          Horatio—or I do forget myself.
       HORATIO: The same, my lord, and your poor servant ever.
       HAMLET: Sir, my good friend, I'll change[7] that name with you.
          And what make you from Wittenberg, Horatio?
165   Marcellus?
       MARCELLUS: My good lord!
       HAMLET: I am very glad to see you. [*To* BERNARDO.] Good even, sir.—
          But what, in faith, make you from Wittenberg?
       HORATIO: A truant disposition, good my lord.
170   HAMLET: I would not hear your enemy say so,
          Nor shall you do my ear that violence
          To make it truster of your own report
          Against yourself. I know you are no truant.
          But what is your affair in Elsinore?
175   We'll teach you to drink deep ere you depart.
       HORATIO: My lord, I came to see your father's funeral.
       HAMLET: I prithee do not mock me, fellow-student,
          I think it was to see my mother's wedding.
       HORATIO: Indeed, my lord, it followed hard upon.
180   HAMLET: Thrift, thrift, Horatio. The funeral-baked meats
          Did coldly furnish forth the marriage tables.
          Would I had met my dearest[8] foe in heaven
          Or ever I had seen that day, Horatio!
          My father—methinks I see my father.
       HORATIO: Where, my lord?
185   HAMLET: In my mind's eye, Horatio.
       HORATIO: I saw him once, 'a was a goodly king.
       HAMLET: 'A was a man, take him for all in all,
          I shall not look upon his like again.
       HORATIO: My lord, I think I saw him yesternight.

       ---

6. The demigod Hercules was noted for his strength and the series of spectacular labors that it allowed him to accomplish.   7. Exchange.   8. Bitterest.

HAMLET: Saw who?   190
HORATIO: My lord, the king your father.
HAMLET: The king my father?
HORATIO: Season your admiration⁹ for a while
    With an attent ear till I may deliver¹
    Upon the witness of these gentlemen
    This marvel to you.
HAMLET: For God's love, let me hear!   195
HORATIO: Two nights together had these gentlemen,
    Marcellus and Bernardo, on their watch
    In the dead waste and middle of the night
    Been thus encountered. A figure like your father,
    Arméd at point exactly, cap-a-pe,²   200
    Appears before them, and with solemn march
    Goes slow and stately by them. Thrice he walked
    By their oppressed and fear-surpriséd eyes
    Within his truncheon's³ length, whilst they, distilled
    Almost to jelly with the act of fear,   205
    Stand dumb and speak not to him. This to me
    In dreadful secrecy impart they did,
    And I with them the third night kept the watch,
    Where, as they had delivered, both in time,
    Form of the thing, each word made true and good,   210
    The apparition comes. I knew your father.
    These hands are not more like.
HAMLET: But where was this?
MARCELLUS: My lord, upon the platform where we watch.
HAMLET: Did you not speak to it?
HORATIO: My lord, I did,
    But answer made it none. Yet once methought   215
    It lifted up it head and did address
    Itself to motion, like as it would speak;
    But even then the morning cock crew loud,
    And at the sound it shrunk in haste away
    And vanished from our sight.
HAMLET: 'Tis very strange.   220
HORATIO: As I do live, my honored lord, 'tis true,
    And we did think it writ down in our duty
    To let you know of it.
HAMLET: Indeed, sirs, but
    This troubles me. Hold you the watch tonight?
ALL: We do, my lord.
HAMLET: Armed, say you?
ALL: Armed, my lord.   225

---

9. Moderate your wonder.   1. Relate. *Attent:* attentive.   2. From head to toe. *Exactly:* completely.
3. Baton of office.

HAMLET: From top to toe?

ALL: My lord, from head to foot.

HAMLET: Then saw you not his face.

HORATIO: O yes, my lord, he wore his beaver[4] up.

HAMLET: What, looked he frowningly?

230 HORATIO: A countenance more in sorrow than in anger.

HAMLET: Pale or red?

HORATIO: Nay, very pale.

HAMLET: And fixed his eyes upon you?

HORATIO: Most constantly.

HAMLET: I would I had been there.

HORATIO: It would have much amazed you.

HAMLET: Very like.

235 Stayed it long?

HORATIO: While one with moderate haste might tell a hundred.

BOTH: Longer, longer.

HORATIO: Not when I saw't.

HAMLET: His beard was grizzled, no?

HORATIO: It was as I have seen it in his life,
A sable silvered.

240 HAMLET: I will watch tonight.
Perchance 'twill walk again.

HORATIO: I warr'nt it will.

HAMLET: If it assume my noble father's person,
I'll speak to it though hell itself should gape[5]
And bid me hold my peace. I pray you all,

245 If you have hitherto concealed this sight,
Let it be tenable[6] in your silence still,
And whatsomever else shall hap tonight,
Give it an understanding but no tongue.
I will requite your loves. So fare you well.

250 Upon the platform 'twixt eleven and twelve
I'll visit you.

ALL: Our duty to your honor.

HAMLET: Your loves, as mine to you. Farewell.   [*Exeunt all but* HAMLET.]
My father's spirit in arms? All is not well.
I doubt[7] some foul play. Would the night were come!

255 Till then sit still, my soul. Foul deeds will rise,
Though all the earth o'erwhelm them, to men's eyes.   [*Exit.*]

Scene 3

The dwelling of POLONIUS. *Enter* LAERTES *and* OPHELIA.

LAERTES: My necessaries are embarked. Farewell.
And, sister, as the winds give benefit

---

4. Movable face protector.   5. Open (its mouth) wide.   6. Held.   7. Suspect.

And convoy is assistant,[8] do not sleep,
But let me hear from you.

OPHELIA: Do you doubt that?

LAERTES: For Hamlet, and the trifling of his favor,   5
Hold it a fashion and a toy in blood,
A violet in the youth of primy[9] nature,
Forward, not permanent, sweet, not lasting,
The perfume and suppliance of a minute,
No more.

OPHELIA: No more but so?

LAERTES: Think it no more.   10
For nature crescent[1] does not grow alone
In thews and bulk, but as this temple[2] waxes
The inward service of the mind and soul
Grows wide withal. Perhaps he loves you now,
And now no soil nor cautel[3] doth besmirch   15
The virtue of his will, but you must fear,
His greatness weighted,[4] his will is not his own,
For he himself is subject to his birth.
He may not, as unvalued persons do,
Carve for himself, for on his choice depends   20
The safety and health of this whole state,
And therefore must his choice be circumscribed
Unto the voice[5] and yielding of that body
Whereof he is the head. Then if he says he loves you,
It fits your wisdom so far to believe it   25
As he in his particular act and place
May give his saying deed, which is no further
Than the main voice of Denmark goes withal.
Then weigh what loss your honor may sustain
If with too credent ear you list[6] his songs,   30
Or lose your heart, or your chaste treasure open
To his unmastered importunity.
Fear it, Ophelia, fear it, my dear sister,
And keep you in the rear of your affection,
Out of the shot and danger of desire.   35
The chariest[7] maid is prodigal enough
If she unmask her beauty to the moon.
Virtue itself scapes not calumnious strokes.
The canker[8] galls the infants of the spring
Too oft before their buttons[9] be disclosed,   40
And in the morn and liquid dew of youth

8. Means of transport is available.   9. Of the spring.   1. Growing.   2. Body.
3. Deceit.   4. Rank considered.   5. Assent.   6. Too credulous an ear you listen to.
7. Most circumspect.   8. Rose caterpillar.   9. Buds.

Contagious blastments[1] are most imminent.
Be wary then; best safety lies in fear.
Youth to itself rebels, though none else near.

45 OPHELIA: I shall the effect of this good lesson keep
As watchman to my heart. But, good my brother,
Do not as some ungracious pastors do,
Show me the steep and thorny way to heaven,
Whiles like a puffed and reckless libertine

50 Himself the primrose path of dalliance treads
And recks not his own rede.[2]

LAERTES: O, fear me not.

[Enter POLONIUS.]

I stay too long. But here my father comes.
A double blessing is a double grace;
Occasion smiles upon a second leave.

55 POLONIUS: Yet here, Laertes? Aboard, aboard, for shame!
The wind sits in the shoulder of your sail,
And you are stayed for. There—my blessing with thee,
And these few precepts in thy memory
Look thou character.[3] Give thy thoughts no tongue,

60 Nor any unproportioned thought his act.
Be thou familiar, but by no means vulgar.
Those friends thou hast, and their adoption tried,
Grapple them unto thy soul with hoops of steel;
But do not dull[4] thy palm with entertainment

65 Of each new-hatched, unfledged comrade. Beware
Of entrance to a quarrel, but being in,
Bear't that th' opposéd[5] may beware of thee.
Give every man thy ear, but few thy voice;[6]
Take each man's censure, but reserve thy judgment.

70 Costly thy habit as thy purse can buy,
But not expressed in fancy; rich not gaudy,
For the apparel oft proclaims the man,
And they in France of the best rank and station
Are of a most select and generous chief[7] in that.

75 Neither a borrower nor a lender be,
For loan oft loses both itself and friend,
And borrowing dulls th' edge of husbandry.
This above all, to thine own self be true,
And it must follow as the night the day

80 Thou canst not then be false to any man.
Farewell. My blessing season this in thee!

LAERTES: Most humbly do I take my leave, my lord.

---

1. Blights.   2. Heeds not his own advice.   3. Write.   4. Make callous.
5. Conduct it so that the opponent.   6. Approval.   7. Eminence.

POLONIUS: The time invests you. Go, your servants tend.[8]
LAERTES: Farewell, Ophelia, and remember well
    What I have said to you.
OPHELIA: 'Tis in my memory locked,   85
    And you yourself shall keep the key of it.
LAERTES: Farewell.   *[Exit.]*
POLONIUS: What is't, Ophelia, he hath said to you?
OPHELIA: So please you, something touching the Lord Hamlet.
POLONIUS: Marry, well bethought.   90
    'Tis told me he hath very oft of late
    Given private time to you, and you yourself
    Have of your audience been most free and bounteous.
    If it be so—as so 'tis put on me,
    And that in way of caution—I must tell you,   95
    You do not understand yourself so clearly
    As it behooves my daughter and your honor.
    What is between you? Give me up the truth.
OPHELIA: He hath, my lord, of late made many tenders
    Of his affection to me.   100
POLONIUS: Affection? Pooh! You speak like a green girl,
    Unsifted in such perilous circumstance.
    Do you believe his tenders, as you call them?
OPHELIA: I do not know, my lord, what I should think.
POLONIUS: Marry, I will teach you. Think yourself a baby   105
    That you have ta'en these tenders for true pay
    Which are not sterling. Tender yourself more dearly,
    Or (not to crack the wind of the poor phrase,
    Running it thus) you'll tender me a fool.
OPHELIA: My lord, he hath importuned me with love   110
    In honorable fashion.
POLONIUS: Ay, fashion you may call it. Go to, go to.
OPHELIA: And hath given countenance[9] to his speech, my lord,
    With almost all the holy vows of heaven.
POLONIUS: Ay, springes[1] to catch woodcocks. I do know,   115
    When the blood burns, how prodigal the soul
    Lends the tongue vows. These blazes, daughter,
    Giving more light than heat, extinct in both
    Even in their promise, as it is a-making,
    You must not take for fire. From this time   120
    Be something scanter of your maiden presence.
    Set your entreatments[2] at a higher rate
    Than a command to parle. For Lord Hamlet,
    Believe so much in him that he is young,
    And with a larger tether may he walk   125
    Than may be given you. In few, Ophelia,

8. Await.   9. Confirmation.   1. Snares.   2. Negotiations before a surrender.

Do not believe his vows, for they are brokers,[3]
Not of that dye which their investments[4] show,
But mere implorators[5] of unholy suits,
130   Breathing like sanctified and pious bawds,
The better to beguile. This is for all:
I would not, in plain terms, from this time forth
Have you so slander any moment leisure
As to give words or talk with the Lord Hamlet.
135   Look to't, I charge you. Come your ways.
OPHELIA: I shall obey, my lord.   [*Exeunt.*]

Scene 4

The guard station. Enter HAMLET, HORATIO *and* MARCELLUS.

HAMLET: The air bites shrewdly;[6] it is very cold.
HORATIO: It is a nipping and an eager[7] air.
HAMLET: What hour now?
HORATIO: I think it lacks of twelve.
MARCELLUS: No, it is struck.
HORATIO: Indeed? I heard it not.
5   It then draws near the season
Wherein the spirit held his wont to walk.

[*A flourish of trumpets, and two pieces go off.*]

What does this mean, my lord?
HAMLET: The king doth wake tonight and takes his rouse,
Keeps wassail, and the swagg'ring up-spring[8] reels,
10   And as he drains his draughts of Rhenish down,
The kettledrum and trumpet thus bray out
The triumph of his pledge.
HORATIO: Is it a custom?
HAMLET: Ay, marry, is't,
But to my mind, though I am native here
15   And to the manner born, it is a custom
More honored in the breach than the observance.
This heavy-headed revel east and west
Makes us traduced and taxed of other nations.
They clepe[9] us drunkards, and with swinish phrase
20   Soil our addition,[1] and indeed it takes
From our achievements, though performed at height,
The pith and marrow of our attribute.[2]
So oft it chances in particular men,
That for some vicious mole of nature in them,
25   As in their birth, wherein they are not guilty
(Since nature cannot choose his origin),

3. Panderers.   4. Garments.   5. Solicitors.   6. Sharply.   7. Keen.   8. A German dance.
9. Call.   1. Reputation.   2. Honor.

By their o'ergrowth of some complexion,
Oft breaking down the pales[3] and forts of reason,
Or by some habit that too much o'er-leavens
The form of plausive[4] manners—that these men,   30
Carrying, I say, the stamp of one defect,
Being nature's livery or fortune's star,
His virtues else, be they as pure as grace,
As infinite as man may undergo,
Shall in the general censure take corruption   35
From that particular fault. The dram of evil
Doth all the noble substance often doubt[5]
To his own scandal.

      [*Enter* GHOST.]

HORATIO: Look, my lord, it comes.
HAMLET: Angels and ministers of grace defend us!
  Be thou a spirit of health or goblin damned,
  Bring with thee airs from heaven or blasts from hell,   40
  Be thy intents wicked or charitable,
  Thou com'st in such a questionable[6] shape
  That I will speak to thee. I'll call thee Hamlet,
  King, father, royal Dane. O, answer me!   45
  Let me not burst in ignorance, but tell
  Why thy canonized[7] bones, hearsèd in death,
  Have burst their cerements;[8] why the sepulchre
  Wherein we saw thee quietly inurned
  Hath oped his ponderous and marble jaws   50
  To cast thee up again. What may this mean
  That thou, dead corse, again in complete steel[9]
  Revisits thus the glimpses of the moon,
  Making night hideous, and we fools of nature
  So horridly to shake our disposition   55
  With thoughts beyond the reaches of our souls?
  Say, why is this? wherefore? What should we do?

      [GHOST *beckons.*]

HORATIO: It beckons you to go away with it,
  As if it some impartment[1] did desire
  To you alone.
MARCELLUS: Look with what courteous action   60
  It waves you to a more removèd[2] ground.
  But do not go with it.
HORATIO: No, by no means.

---

3. Barriers.   4. Pleasing.   5. Put out.   6. Prompting question.
7. Buried in accordance with church canons.   8. Graveclothes.   9. Armor.
1. Communication.   2. Beckons you to a more distant.

HAMLET: It will not speak; then I will follow it.
HORATIO: Do not, my lord.
HAMLET: Why, what should be the fear?
65   I do not set my life at a pin's fee,[3]
      And for my soul, what can it do to that,
      Being a thing immortal as itself?
      It waves me forth again. I'll follow it
HORATIO: What if it tempt you toward the flood, my lord,
70   Or to the dreadful summit of the cliff
      That beetles[4] o'er his base into the sea,
      And there assume some other horrible form,
      Which might deprive your sovereignty of reason[5]
      And draw you into madness? Think of it.
75   The very place puts toys of desperation,[6]
      Without more motive, into every brain
      That looks so many fathoms to the sea
      And hears it roar beneath.
HAMLET: It wafts me still.
      Go on. I'll follow thee.
MARCELLUS: You shall not go, my lord.
80 HAMLET: Hold off your hands.
HORATIO: Be ruled. You shall not go.
HAMLET: My fate cries out
      And makes each petty artere in this body
      As hardy as the Nemean lion's nerve.[7]
      Still am I called. Unhand me, gentlemen.
85   By heaven, I'll make a ghost of him that lets[8] me.
      I say, away! Go on. I'll follow thee.   [*Exeunt* GHOST *and* HAMLET.]
HORATIO: He waxes desperate with imagination.
MARCELLUS: Let's follow. 'Tis not fit thus to obey him.
HORATIO: Have after. To what issue will this come?
90 MARCELLUS: Something is rotten in the state of Denmark.
HORATIO: Heaven will direct it.
MARCELLUS: Nay, let's follow him.   [*Exeunt.*]

Scene 5

Near the guard station. Enter GHOST *and* HAMLET.

HAMLET: Whither wilt thou lead me? Speak. I'll go no further.
GHOST: Mark me.
HAMLET: I will.
GHOST: My hour is almost come,
      When I to sulph'rous and tormenting flames
      Must render up myself.

---

3. Price.   4. Juts out.   5. Rational power. *Deprive:* take away.   6. Desperate fancies.
7. The Nemean lion was a mythological monster slain by Hercules as one of his twelve labors.
8. Hinders.

HAMLET: Alas, poor ghost!
GHOST: Pity me not, but lend thy serious hearing   5
  To what I shall unfold.
HAMLET: Speak. I am bound to hear.
GHOST: So art thou to revenge, when thou shalt hear.
HAMLET: What?
GHOST: I am thy father's spirit,
  Doomed for a certain term to walk the night,   10
  And for the day confined to fast in fires,
  Till the foul crimes done in my days of nature[9]
  Are burnt and purged away. But that I am forbid
  To tell the secrets of my prison house,
  I could a tale unfold whose lightest word   15
  Would harrow up thy soul, freeze thy young blood,
  Make thy two eyes like stars start from their spheres,
  Thy knotted and combinéd[1] locks to part,
  And each particular hair to stand an end,
  Like quills upon the fretful porpentine.[2]   20
  But this eternal blazon[3] must not be
  To ears of flesh and blood. List, list, O, list!
  If thou didst every thy dear father love—
HAMLET: O God!
GHOST: Revenge his foul and most unnatural murder.   25
HAMLET: Murder!
GHOST: Murder most foul, as in the best it is,
  But this most foul, strange, and unnatural.
HAMLET: Haste me to know't, that I, with wings as swift
  As meditation or the thoughts of love,   30
  May sweep to my revenge.
GHOST: I find thee apt.
  And duller shouldst thou be than the fat weed
  That rots itself in ease on Lethe[4] wharf,—
  Wouldst thou not stir in this. Now, Hamlet, hear.
  'Tis given out that, sleeping in my orchard,   35
  A serpent stung me. So the whole ear of Denmark
  Is by a forgéd process[5] of my death
  Rankly abused. But know, thou noble youth,
  The serpent that did sting thy father's life
  Now wears his crown.
HAMLET: O my prophetic soul!   40
  My uncle!
GHOST: Ay, that incestuous, that adulterate beast,
  With witchcraft of his wits, with traitorous gifts—

---

9. That is, while I was alive.   1. Tangled.   2. Porcupine.   3. Description of eternity.
4. The waters of the Lethe, one of the rivers of the classical underworld, when drunk, induced
forgetfulness. The "fat weed" is the asphodel that grew there; some texts have "roots" for "rots."
5. False report.

O wicked wit and gifts that have the power
45   So to seduce!—won to his shameful lust
The will of my most seeming virtuous queen.
O Hamlet, what a falling off was there,
From me, whose love was of that dignity
That it went hand in hand even with the vow
50   I made to her in marriage, and to decline[6]
Upon a wretch whose natural gifts were poor
To those of mine!
But virtue, as it never will be moved,
Though lewdness court it in a shape of heaven,
55   So lust, though to a radiant angel linked,
Will sate itself in a celestial bed
And prey on garbage.
But soft, methinks I scent the morning air.
Brief let me be. Sleeping within my orchard,
60   My custom always of the afternoon,
Upon my secure hour thy uncle stole,
With juice of cursed hebona[7] in a vial,
And in the porches of my ears did pour
The leperous distilment, whose effect
65   Holds such an enmity with blood of man
That swift as quicksilver it courses through
The natural gates and alleys of the body,
And with a sudden vigor it doth posset[8]
And curd, like eager[9] droppings into milk,
70   The thin and wholesome blood. So did it mine,
And a most instant tetter barked about[1]
Most lazar-like[2] with vile and loathsome crust
All my smooth body.
Thus was I sleeping by a brother's hand
75   Of life, of crown, of queen at once dispatched,
Cut off even in the blossoms of my sin,
Unhouseled, disappointed, unaneled,[3]
No reck'ning made, but sent to my account
With all my imperfections on my head.
80   O, horrible! O, horrible! most horrible!
If thou hast nature in thee, bear it not.
Let not the royal bed of Denmark be
A couch of luxury[4] and damnéd incest.
But howsomever thou pursues this act,
85   Taint not thy mind, nor let thy soul contrive
Against thy mother aught. Leave her to heaven,

---

6. Sink.   7. A poison.   8. Coagulate.   9. Acid. *Curd:* curdle.
1. Covered like bark. *Tetter:* a skin disease.   2. Leperlike.
3. The ghost means that he died without the customary rites of the church, that is, without receiving the Sacrament, without confession, and without Extreme Unction.   4. Lust.

And to those thorns that in her bosom lodge
To prick and sting her. Fare thee well at once.
The glowworm shows the matin[5] to be near,
And gins to pale his uneffectual fire.   90
Adieu, adieu, adieu. Remember me.   [*Exit.*]
HAMLET: O all you host of heaven! O earth! What else?
And shall I couple hell? O, fie! Hold, hold, my heart,
And you, my sinews, grow not instant old,
But bear me stiffly up. Remember thee?   95
Ay, thou poor ghost, whiles memory holds a seat
In this distracted globe.[6] Remember thee?
Yea, from the table[7] of my memory
I'll wipe away all trivial fond[8] records,
All saws of books, all forms, all pressures past   100
That youth and observation copied there,
And thy commandment all alone shall live
Within the book and volume of my brain,
Unmixed with baser matter. Yes, by heaven!
O most pernicious woman!   105
O villain, villain, smiling, damnéd villain!
My tables—meet it is I set it down
That one may smile, and smile, and be a villain.
At least I am sure it may be so in Denmark.
So, uncle, there you are. Now to my word:[9]   110
It is "Adieu, adieu. Remember me."
I have sworn't.

   [*Enter* HORATIO *and* MARCELLUS.]

HORATIO: My lord, my lord!
MARCELLUS: Lord Hamlet!
HORATIO: Heavens secure him!
HAMLET: So be it!
MARCELLUS: Illo, ho, ho, my lord!   115
HAMLET: Hillo, ho, ho, boy![1] Come, bird, come.
MARCELLUS: How is't, my noble lord?
HORATIO: What news, my lord?
HAMLET: O, wonderful!
HORATIO: Good my lord, tell it.
HAMLET: No, you will reveal it.
HORATIO: Not I, my lord, by heaven.
MARCELLUS: Nor I, my lord.   120
HAMLET: How say you then, would heart of man once think it?
   But you'll be secret?
BOTH: Ay, by heaven, my lord.
HAMLET: There's never a villain dwelling in all Denmark

---

5. Morning. 6. Skull. 7. Writing tablet. 8. Foolish. 9. For my motto.
1. A falconer's cry.

But he's an arrant knave.

125 HORATIO: There needs no ghost, my lord, come from the grave
To tell us this.

HAMLET: Why, right, you are in the right,
And so without more circumstance at all
I hold it fit that we shake hands and part,
You, as your business and desire shall point you,
130 For every man hath business and desire
Such as it is, and for my own poor part,
Look you, I'll go pray.

HORATIO: These are but wild and whirling words, my lord.

HAMLET: I am sorry they offend you, heartily;
Yes, faith, heartily.

135 HORATIO: There's no offence, my lord.

HAMLET: Yes, by Saint Patrick, but there is, Horatio,
And much offence too. Touching this vision here,
It is an honest ghost, that let me tell you.
For your desire to know what is between us,
140 O'ermaster't as you may. And now, good friends,
As you are friends, scholars, and soldiers,
Give me one poor request.

HORATIO: What is't, my lord? We will.

HAMLET: Never make known what you have seen tonight.

BOTH: My lord, we will not.

HAMLET: Nay, but swear't.

145 HORATIO: In faith,
My lord, not I.

MARCELLUS: Nor I, my lord, in faith.

HAMLET: Upon my sword.

MARCELLUS: We have sworn, my lord, already.

HAMLET: Indeed, upon my sword, indeed.
[GHOST *cries under the stage.*]

GHOST: Swear.

HAMLET: Ha, ha, boy, say'st thou so? Art thou there, truepenny?[2]
150 Come on. You hear this fellow in the cellarage.[3]
Consent to swear.

HORATIO: Propose the oath, my lord.

HAMLET: Never to speak of this that you have seen,
Swear by my sword.

GHOST: [*Beneath.*] Swear.

155 HAMLET: Hic et ubique?[4] Then we'll shift our ground.
Come hither, gentlemen,
And lay your hands again upon my sword.
Swear by my sword
Never to speak of this that you have heard.

160 GHOST: [*Beneath.*] Swear by his sword.

2. Old fellow.   3. Below.   4. Here and everywhere?

HAMLET: Well said, old mole! Canst work i' th' earth so fast?
  A worthy pioneer![5] Once more remove, good friends.
HORATIO: O day and night, but this is wondrous strange!
HAMLET: And therefore as a stranger give it welcome.
  There are more things in heaven and earth, Horatio,   165
  Than are dreamt of in your philosophy.
  But come.
  Here as before, never, so help you mercy,
  How strange or odd some'er I bear myself
  (As I perchance hereafter shall think meet   170
  To put an antic[6] disposition on),
  That you, at such times, seeing me, never shall,
  With arms encumbered[7] thus, or this head-shake,
  Or by pronouncing of some doubtful phrase,
  As "Well, we know," or "We could, and if we would"   175
  Or "If we list to speak," or "There be, and if they might"
  Or such ambiguous giving out, to note
  That you know aught of me—this do swear,
  So grace and mercy at your most need help you.
GHOST: [*Beneath.*] Swear.   [*They swear.*] 180
HAMLET: Rest, rest, perturbéd spirit! So, gentlemen,
  With all my love I do commend me to you,
  And what so poor a man as Hamlet is
  May do t'express his love and friending[8] to you,
  God willing, shall not lack. Let us go in together,   185
  And still your fingers on your lips, I pray.
  The time is out of joint. O curséd spite
  That ever I was born to set it right!
  Nay, come, let's go together.   [*Exeunt.*]

ACT II
Scene 1

The dwelling of POLONIUS. *Enter* POLONIUS *and* REYNALDO.

POLONIUS: Give him this money and these notes, Reynaldo.
REYNALDO: I will, my lord.
POLONIUS: You shall do marvellous wisely, good Reynaldo,
  Before you visit him, to make inquire[9]
  Of his behavior.
REYNALDO: My lord, I did intend it.   5
POLONIUS: Marry, well said, very well said. Look you, sir.
  Enquire me first what Danskers[1] are in Paris,
  And how, and who, what means, and where they keep,[2]
  What company, at what expense; and finding
  By this encompassment[3] and drift of question   10

5. Soldier who digs trenches.   6. Mad.   7. Folded.   8. Friendship.
9. Inquiry.   1. Danes.   2. Live.   3. Indirect means.

That they do know my son, come you more nearer
Than your particular demands[4] will touch it.
Take you as 'twere some distant knowledge of him,
As thus, "I know his father and his friends,
15   And in part him." Do you mark this, Reynaldo?
REYNALDO: Ay, very well, my lord.
POLONIUS: "And in part him, but," you may say, "not well,
But if't be he I mean, he's very wild,
Addicted so and so." And there put on him
20   What forgeries you please; marry, none so rank[5]
As may dishonor him. Take heed of that.
But, sir, such wanton, wild, and usual slips
As are companions noted and most known
To youth and liberty.
REYNALDO: As gaming, my lord.
25 POLONIUS: Ay, or drinking, fencing, swearing,
Quarrelling, drabbing[6]—you may go so far.
REYNALDO: My lord, that would dishonor him.
POLONIUS: Faith, no, as you may season it in the charge.[7]
You must not put another scandal on him,
30   That he is open to incontinency.[8]
That's not my meaning. But breathe his faults so quaintly[9]
That they may seem the taints of liberty,[1]
The flash and outbreak of a fiery mind,
A savageness in unreclaiméd[2] blood,
Of general assault.[3]
35 REYNALDO: But, my good lord—
POLONIUS: Wherefore should you do this?
REYNALDO: Ay, my lord,
I would know that.
POLONIUS: Marry, sir, here's my drift,
And I believe it is a fetch of warrant.[4]
You laying these slight sullies on my son,
40   As 'twere a thing a little soiled wi' th' working,
Mark you,
Your party in converse,[5] him you would sound,
Having ever seen in the prenominate[6] crimes
The youth you breathe[7] of guilty, be assured
45   He closes with you in this consequence,
"Good sir," or so, or "friend," or "gentleman,"
According to the phrase or the addition
Of man and country.
REYNALDO: Very good, my lord.

---

4. Direct questions.   5. Foul. *Forgeries:* lies.   6. Whoring.   7. Soften the accusation.
8. Sexual excess.   9. With delicacy.   1. Faults of freedom.   2. Untamed.
3. Touching everyone.   4. Permissible trick.   5. Conversation.   6. Already named.   7. Speak.

POLONIUS: And then, sir, does 'a this—'a does—What was I about to say?
By the mass, I was about to say something.   50
Where did I leave?
REYNALDO: At "closes in the consequence."
POLONIUS: At "closes in the consequence"—ay, marry,
He closes thus: "I know the gentleman.
I saw him yesterday, or th' other day,   55
Or then, or then, with such, or such, and as you say,
There was 'a gaming, there o'ertook in's rouse,
There falling out at tennis," or perchance
"I saw him enter such a house of sale,"
Videlicet,[8] a brothel, or so forth.   60
See you, now—
Your bait of falsehood takes this carp of truth,
And thus do we of wisdom and of reach,[9]
With windlasses and with assays of bias,[1]
By indirections find directions out;   65
So by my former lecture and advice
Shall you my son. You have me, have you not?
REYNALDO: My lord, I have.
POLONIUS: God b'wi' ye; fare ye well.
REYNALDO: Good my lord.
POLONIUS: Observe his inclination in yourself.   70
REYNALDO: I shall, my lord.
POLONIUS: And let him ply[2] his music.
REYNALDO: Well, my lord.
POLONIUS: Farewell.   [*Exit* REYNALDO.]

[*Enter* OPHELIA.]

                    How now, Ophelia, what's the matter?
OPHELIA: O my lord, my lord, I have been so affrighted!
POLONIUS: With what, i' th' name of God?   75
OPHELIA: My lord, as I was sewing in my closet,[3]
Lord Hamlet with his doublet all unbraced,[4]
No hat upon his head, his stockings fouled,
Ungartered and down-gyvéd[5] to his ankle,
Pale as his shirt, his knees knocking each other,   80
And with a look so piteous in purport
As if he had been looséd out of hell
To speak of horrors—he comes before me.
POLONIUS: Mad for thy love?
OPHELIA: My lord, I do not know,
But truly I do fear it.
POLONIUS: What said he?   85

8. Namely.   9. Ability.   1. Indirect tests.   2. Practice.   3. Chamber.
4. Unlaced. *Doublet:* jacket.   5. Fallen down like fetters.

OPHELIA: He took me by the wrist, and held me hard,
Then goes he to the length of all his arm,
And with his other hand thus o'er his brow,
He falls to such perusal of my face
90   As 'a would draw it. Long stayed he so.
At last, a little shaking of mine arm,
And thrice his head thus waving up and down,
He raised a sigh so piteous and profound
As it did seem to shatter all his bulk,[6]
95   And end his being. That done, he lets me go,
And with his head over his shoulder turned
He seemed to find his way without his eyes,
For out adoors he went without their helps,
And to the last bended[7] their light on me.
100 POLONIUS: Come, go with me. I will go seek the king.
This is the very ecstasy of love,
Whose violent property fordoes[8] itself,
And leads the will to desperate undertakings
As oft as any passion under heaven
105   That does afflict our natures. I am sorry.
What, have you given him any hard words of late?
OPHELIA: No, my good lord, but as you did command
I did repel[9] his letters, and denied
His access to me.
POLONIUS: That hath made him mad.
110 I am sorry that with better heed and judgment
I had not quoted[1] him. I feared he did but trifle,
And meant to wrack[2] thee; but beshrew my jealousy.
By heaven, it is as proper to our age
To cast beyond ourselves in our opinions
115   As it is common for the younger sort
To lack discretion. Come, go we to the king.
This must be known, which being kept close, might move
More grief to hide than hate to utter love.
Come.   [*Exeunt.*]

Scene 2

A public room. Enter KING, QUEEN, ROSENCRANTZ *and* GUILDENSTERN.

KING: Welcome, dear Rosencrantz and Guildenstern.
Moreover that[3] we much did long to see you,
The need we have to use you did provoke
Our hasty sending. Something have you heard
5   Of Hamlet's transformation—so call it,
Sith[4] nor th' exterior nor the inward man
Resembles that it was. What it should be,

6. Body.   7. Directed.   8. Destroys. *Property:* character.   9. Refuse.   1. Observed.
2. Harm.   3. In addition to the fact that.   4. Since.

More than his father's death, that thus hath put him
So much from th' understanding of himself,
I cannot deem of. I entreat you both   10
That, being of so young days[5] brought up with him,
And sith so neighbored[6] to his youth and havior,
That you vouchsafe your rest here in our court
Some little time, so by your companies
To draw him on to pleasures, and to gather   15
So much as from occasion you may glean,
Whether aught to us unknown afflicts him thus,
That opened lies within our remedy.

QUEEN: Good gentlemen, he hath much talked of you,
And sure I am two men there are not living   20
To whom he more adheres. If it will please you
To show us so much gentry[7] and good will
As to expend your time with us awhile
For the supply and profit of our hope,
Your visitation shall receive such thanks   25
As fits a king's remembrance.

ROSENCRANTZ: Both your majesties
Might, by the sovereign power you have of us,
Put your dread pleasures more into command
Than to entreaty.

GUILDENSTERN: But we both obey,
And here give up ourselves in the full bent[8]   30
To lay our service freely at your feet,
To be commanded.

KING: Thanks, Rosencrantz and gentle Guildenstern.

QUEEN: Thanks, Guildenstern and gentle Rosencrantz.
And I beseech you instantly to visit   35
My too much changed son. Go, some of you,
And bring these gentlemen where Hamlet is.

GUILDENSTERN: Heavens make our presence and our practices
Pleasant and helpful to him!

QUEEN: Ay, amen!
                    [*Exeunt* ROSENCRANTZ *and* GUILDENSTERN.]

        [*Enter* POLONIUS.]

POLONIUS: Th' ambassadors from Norway, my good lord,   40
Are joyfully returned.

KING: Thou still[9] hast been the father of good news.

POLONIUS: Have I, my lord? I assure you, my good liege,
I hold my duty as I hold my soul,
Both to my God and to my gracious king;   45
And I do think—or else this brain of mine

---

5. From childhood.   6. Closely allied.   7. Courtesy.   8. Completely.   9. Ever.

Hunts not the trail of policy[1] so sure
As it hath used to do—that I have found
The very cause of Hamlet's lunacy.
50   KING: O, speak of that, that do I long to hear.
POLONIUS: Give first admittance to th' ambassadors.
My news shall be the fruit[2] to that great feast.
KING: Thyself do grace to them, and bring them in.   [*Exit* POLONIUS.]
He tells me, my dear Gertrude, he hath found
55   The head and source of all your son's distemper.
QUEEN: I doubt it is no other but the main,
His father's death and our o'erhasty marriage.
KING: Well, we shall sift[3] him.

[*Enter Ambassadors (*VOLTEMAND *and* CORNELIUS*) with* POLONIUS.]

                              Welcome, my good friends,
Say, Voltemand, what from our brother Norway?
60   VOLTEMAND: Most fair return of greetings and desires.
Upon our first,[4] he sent out to suppress
His nephew's levies, which to him appeared
To be a preparation 'gainst the Polack,
But better looked into, he truly found
65   It was against your highness, whereat grieved,
That so his sickness, age, and impotence
Was falsely borne in hand, sends out arrests[5]
On Fortinbras, which he in brief obeys,
Receives rebuke from Norway, and in fine,
70   Makes vow before his uncle never more
To give th' assay[6] of arms against your majesty.
Whereon old Norway, overcome with joy,
Gives him three thousand crowns in annual fee,
And his commission to employ those soldiers,
75   So levied as before, against the Polack,
With an entreaty, herein further shown,   [*Gives* CLAUDIUS *a paper.*]
That it might please you to give quiet pass[7]
Through your dominions for this enterprise,
On such regards of safety and allowance
As therein are set down.
80   KING: It likes[8] us well,
And at our more considered time[9] we'll read,
Answer, and think upon this business.
Meantime we thank you for your well-took[1] labor.
Go to your rest; at night we'll feast together.
Most welcome home!   [*Exeunt* AMBASSADORS.]

---

1. Statecraft.   2. Dessert.   3. Examine.   4. That is, first appearance.
5. Orders to stop. *Falsely borne in hand:* deceived.   6. Trial.   7. Safe conduct.   8. Pleases.
9. Time for more consideration.   1. Successful.

POLONIUS: This business is well ended.   85
My liege and madam, to expostulate[2]
What majesty should be, what duty is,
Why day is day, night night, and time is time,
Were nothing but to waste night, day, and time.
Therefore, since brevity is the soul of wit,   90
And tediousness the limbs and outward flourishes,[3]
I will be brief. Your noble son is mad.
Mad call I it, for to define true madness,
What is't but to be nothing else but mad?
But let that go.
QUEEN: More matter with less art.   95
POLONIUS: Madam, I swear I use no art at all.
That he is mad, 'tis true: 'tis true 'tis pity,
And pity 'tis 'tis true. A foolish figure,
But farewell it, for I will use no art.
Mad let us grant him, then, and now remains   100
That we find out the cause of this effect,
Or rather say the cause of this defect,
For this effect defective comes by cause.
Thus it remains, and the remainder thus.
Perpend.[4]   105
I have a daughter—have while she is mine—
Who in her duty and obedience, mark,
Hath given me this. Now gather, and surmise.
    "To the celestial, and my soul's idol, the most beautified Ophelia."—
That's an ill phrase, a vile phrase, "beautified" is a vile phrase. But you 110
shall hear. Thus:
    "In her excellent white bosom, these, etc."
QUEEN: Came this from Hamlet to her?
POLONIUS: Good madam, stay awhile. I will be faithful.

    "Doubt thou the stars are fire,   115
        Doubt that the sun doth move;
    Doubt truth to be a liar;
        But never doubt I love.

    O dear Ophelia, I am ill at these numbers.[5] I have not art to reckon
my groans, but that I love thee best, O most best, believe it. Adieu.   120
        Thine evermore, most dear lady, whilst this machine[6] is to him,
    Hamlet."
This in obedience hath my daughter shown me,
And more above, hath his solicitings,
As they fell out by time, by means, and place,   125
All given to mine ear.
KING: But how hath she

2. Discuss.   3. Adornments.   4. Consider.   5. Verses.   6. Body.

Received his love?

POLONIUS: What do you think of me?

KING: As of a man faithful and honorable.

POLONIUS: I would fain prove so. But what might you think,
130   When I had seen this hot love on the wing.
       (As I perceived it, I must tell you that,
       Before my daughter told me), what might you,
       Or my dear majesty your queen here, think,
       If I had played the desk or table-book,
135   Or given my heart a winking, mute and dumb,
       Or looked upon this love with idle sight,[7]
       What might you think? No, I went round[8] to work,
       And my young mistress thus I did bespeak:
       "Lord Hamlet is a prince out of thy star.[9]
140   This must not be." And then I prescripts[1] gave her,
       That she should lock herself from his resort,
       Admit no messengers, receive no tokens.
       Which done, she took[2] the fruits of my advice;
       And he repelled, a short tale to make,
145   Fell into a sadness, then into a fast,
       Thence to a watch, thence into a weakness,
       Thence to a lightness, and by this declension,
       Into the madness wherein now he raves,
       And all we mourn for.

KING: Do you think 'tis this?

150 QUEEN: It may be, very like.

POLONIUS: Hath there been such a time—I would fain know that—
       That I have positively said " 'Tis so,"
       When it proved otherwise?

KING: Not that I know.

POLONIUS: [Pointing to his head and shoulder.] Take this from this, if this be
       otherwise.
155   If circumstances lead me, I will find
       Where truth is hid, though it were hid indeed
       Within the centre.[3]

KING: How may we try it further?

POLONIUS: You know sometimes he walks four hours together
       Here in the lobby.

QUEEN: So he does, indeed.

160 POLONIUS: At such a time I'll loose[4] my daughter to him.
       Be you and I behind an arras[5] then.

---

7. Polonius means that he would have been at fault if, having seen Hamlet's attention to Ophelia,
he had winked at it or not paid attention, an "idle sight," and if he had remained silent and kept
the information to himself, as if it were written in a "desk" or "table-book."   8. Directly.
9. Beyond your sphere.   1. Orders.   2. Followed.   3. Of the earth.   4. Let loose.
5. Tapestry.

Mark the encounter. If he love her not,
And be not from his reason fall'n thereon,
Let me be no assistant for a state,
But keep a farm and carters.

KING: We will try it.   165

[*Enter* HAMLET *reading a book.*]

QUEEN: But look where sadly the poor wretch comes reading.
POLONIUS: Away, I do beseech you both away,
    I'll board[6] him presently.   [*Exeunt* KING *and* QUEEN.]
                              O, give me leave.
    How does my good Lord Hamlet?
HAMLET: Well, God-a-mercy.   170
POLONIUS: Do you know me, my lord?
HAMLET: Excellent well, you are a fishmonger.
POLONIUS: Not I, my lord.
HAMLET: Then I would you were so honest a man.
POLONIUS: Honest, my lord?   175
HAMLET: Ay, sir, to be honest as this world goes, is to be one man picked
    out of ten thousand.
POLONIUS: That's very true, my lord.
HAMLET: For if the sun breed maggots in a dead dog, being a god kissing
    carrion[7]—Have you a daughter?   180
POLONIUS: I have, my lord.
HAMLET: Let her not walk i' th' sun. Conception is a blessing, but as your
    daughter may conceive—friend, look to't.
POLONIUS: How say you by that? [*Aside.*] Still harping on my daughter. Yet
    he knew me not at first. 'A said I was a fishmonger. 'A is far gone. And 185
    truly in my youth I suffered much extremity for love. Very near this. I'll
    speak to him again.—What do you read, my lord?
HAMLET: Words, words, words.
POLONIUS: What is the matter, my lord?
HAMLET: Between who?   190
POLONIUS: I mean the matter that you read, my lord.
HAMLET: Slanders, sir; for the satirical rogue says here that old men have
    grey beards, that their faces are wrinkled, their eyes purging thick amber
    and plum-tree gum, and that they have a plentiful lack of wit, together
    with most weakhams[8]—all which, sir, though I most powerfully and 195
    potently believe, yet I hold it not honesty to have it thus set down, for
    yourself, sir, shall grow old as I am, if like a crab you could go backward.
POLONIUS: [*Aside.*] Though this be madness, yet there is method in't.—Will
    you walk out of the air, my lord?
HAMLET: Into my grave?   200

---

6. Accost.
7. A reference to the belief of the period that maggots were produced spontaneously by the action
of sunshine on carrion.   8. Limbs.

POLONIUS: [*Aside.*] Indeed, that's out of the air. How pregnant sometime his replies are! a happiness that often madness hits on, which reason and sanity could not so prosperously be delivered of. I will leave him, and suddenly contrive the means of meeting between him and my
205   daughter.—My honorablelord. I will most humbly take my leave of you.
HAMLET: You cannot take from me anything that I will more willingly part withal—except my life, except my life, except my life.

[*Enter* GUILDENSTERN *and* ROSENCRANTZ.]

POLONIUS: Fare you well, my lord.
HAMLET: These tedious old fools!
210   POLONIUS: You go to seek the Lord Hamlet. There he is.
ROSENCRANTZ: [*To* POLONIUS.] God save you, sir!   [*Exit* POLONIUS.]
GUILDENSTERN: My honored lord!
ROSENCRANTZ: My most dear lord!
HAMLET: My excellent good friends! How dost thou, Guildenstern?
215   Ah, Rosencrantz! Good lads, how do you both?
ROSENCRANTZ: As the indifferent[9] children of the earth.
GUILDENSTERN: Happy in that we are not over-happy;
    On Fortune's cap we are not the very button.[1]
HAMLET: Nor the soles of her shoe?
220   ROSENCRANTZ: Neither, my lord.
HAMLET: Then you live about her waist, or in the middle of her favors?
GUILDENSTERN: Faith, her privates we.
HAMLET: In the secret parts of Fortune? O, most true, she is a strumpet.[2] What news?
225   ROSENCRANTZ: None, my lord, but that the world's grown honest.
HAMLET: Then is doomsday near. But your news is not true. Let me question more in particular. What have you, my good friends, deserved at the hands of Fortune, that she sends you to prison hither?
GUILDENSTERN: Prison, my lord?
230   HAMLET: Denmark's a prison.
ROSENCRANTZ: Then is the world one.
HAMLET: A goodly one, in which there are many confines, wards[3] and dungeons. Denmark being one o' th' worst.
ROSENCRANTZ: We think not so, my lord.
235   HAMLET: Why then 'tis none to you; for there is nothing either good or bad, but thinking makes it so. To me it is a prison.
ROSENCRANTZ: Why then your ambition makes it one. 'Tis too narrow for your mind.
HAMLET: O God, I could be bounded in a nutshell and count myself a king
240   of infinite space, were it not that I have bad dreams.

---

9. Ordinary.   1. That is, on top.
2. Prostitute. Hamlet is indulging in characteristic ribaldry. Guildenstern means that they are "privates" = ordinary citizens, but Hamlet takes him to mean "privates" = sexual organs and "middle of her favors" = waist = sexual organs.   3. Cells.

GUILDENSTERN: Which dreams indeed are ambition; for the very substance of the ambitious is merely the shadow of a dream.

HAMLET: A dream itself is but a shadow.

ROSENCRANTZ: Truly, and I hold ambition of so airy and light a quality that it is but a shadow's shadow. 245

HAMLET: Then are our beggars bodies, and our monarchs and outstretched heroes the beggars' shadows. Shall we to th' court? for, by my fay,[4] I cannot reason.

BOTH: We'll wait upon you.

HAMLET: No such matter. I will not sort[5] you with the rest of my servants; 250 for to speak to you like an honest man, I am most dreadfully attended. But in the beaten way of friendship, what make you at Elsinore?

ROSENCRANTZ: To visit you, my lord; no other occasion.

HAMLET: Beggar that I am, I am even poor in thanks, but I thank you; and sure dear friends, my thanks are too dear a halfpenny.[6] Were you not 255 sent for? Is it your own inclining? Is it a free visitation? Come, come, deal justly with me. Come, come, nay speak.

GUILDENSTERN: What should we say, my lord?

HAMLET: Anything but to th' purpose. You were sent for, and there is a kind of confession in your looks, which your modesties have not craft 260 enough to color. I know the good king and queen have sent for you.

ROSENCRANTZ: To what end, my lord?

HAMLET: That you must teach me. But let me conjure you by the rights of our fellowship, by the consonancy of our youth, by the obligation of our ever-preserved love, and by what more dear a better proposer can 265 charge you withal, be even and direct[7] with me whether you were sent for or no.

ROSENCRANTZ: [*Aside to* GUILDENSTERN.] What say you?

HAMLET: [*Aside.*] Nay, then, I have an eye of you.—If you love me, hold not off. 270

GUILDENSTERN: My lord, we were sent for.

HAMLET: I will tell you why; so shall my anticipation prevent your discovery,[8] and your secrecy to the king and queen moult no feather. I have of late—but wherefore I know not—lost all my mirth, forgone all custom of exercises; and indeed it goes so heavily with my disposition, that this 275 goodly frame the earth seems to me a sterile promontory, this most excellent canopy the air, look you, this brave o'er-hanging firmament, this majestical roof fretted[9] with golden fire, why it appeareth nothing to me but a foul and pestilent congregation of vapors. What a piece of work is a man, how noble in reason, how infinite in faculties, in form 280 and moving, how express[1] and admirable in action, how like an angel in apprehension, how like a god: the beauty of the world, the paragon of animals. And yet to me, what is this quintessence of dust? Man

---

4. Faith.   5. Include.   6. Not worth a halfpenny.   7. Straightforward.   8. Disclosure.
9. Ornamented with fretwork.   1. Well built.

delights not me, nor woman neither, though by your smiling you seem
285   to say so.

ROSENCRANTZ: My lord, there was no such stuff in my thoughts.

HAMLET: Why did ye laugh, then, when I said "Man delights not me"?

ROSENCRANTZ: To think, my lord, if you delight not in man, what lenten
entertainment the players shall receive from you. We coted[2] them on the
290   way, and hither are they coming to offer you service.

HAMLET: He that plays the king shall be welcome—his majesty shall have
tribute of me; the adventurous knight shall use his foil and target; the
lover shall not sigh gratis; the humorous[3] man shall end his part in
peace; the clown shall make those laugh whose lungs are tickle o' th'
295   sere;[4] and the lady shall say her mind freely, or the blank verse shall halt
for't. What players are they?

ROSENCRANTZ: Even those you were wont to take such delight in, the
tragedians of the city.

HAMLET: How chances it they travel? Their residence, both in reputation
300   and profit, was better both ways.

ROSENCRANTZ: I think their inhibition comes by the means of the late
innovation.

HAMLET: Do they hold the same estimation they did when I was in the city?
Are they so followed?

305   ROSENCRANTZ: No, indeed, are they not.

HAMLET: How comes it? Do they grow rusty?

ROSENCRANTZ: Nay, their endeavor keeps in the wonted pace; but there is,
sir, an eyrie of children, little eyases,[5] that cry out on the top of question,[6]
and are most tyrannically clapped for't. These are now the fashion, and
310   so berattle the common stages (so they call them) that many wearing
rapiers are afraid of goose quills[7] and dare scarce come thither.[8]

HAMLET: What, are they children? Who maintains 'em? How are they
escoted?[9] Will they pursue the quality no longer than they can sing? Will
they not say afterwards, if they should grow themselves to common
315   players (as it is most like, if their means are no better), their writers do
them wrong to make them exclaim against their own succession?[1]

ROSENCRANTZ: Faith, there has been much todo on both sides; and the
nation holds it no sin to tarre[2] them to controversy. There was for a
while no money bid for argument,[3] unless the poet and the player went
320   to cuffs[4] in the question.

HAMLET: Is't possible?

GUILDENSTERN: O, there has been much throwing about of brains.

HAMLET: Do the boys carry it away?

---

2. Passed. *Lenten:* scanty.   3. Eccentric. *Foil and target:* sword and shield.   4. Easily set off.
5. Little hawks.   6. With a loud, high delivery.   7. Pens of satirical writers.
8. The passage refers to the emergence at the time of the play of theatrical companies made up of
children from London choir schools. Their performances became fashionable and hurt the business
of the established companies. Hamlet says that if they continue to act, "pursue the quality," when
they are grown, they will find that they have been damaging their own future careers.
9. Supported.   1. Future careers.   2. Urge.   3. Paid for a play plot.   4. Blows.

ROSENCRANTZ: Ay, that they do, my lord. Hercules and his load too.[5]

HAMLET: It is not very strange, for my uncle is King of Denmark, and those 325
that would make mouths[6] at him while my father lived give twenty, forty,
fifty, a hundred ducats apiece for his picture in little.[7] 'Sblood, there is
something in this more than natural, if philosophy could find it out.

[*A flourish.*]

GUILDENSTERN: There are the players.

HAMLET: Gentlemen, you are welcome to Elsinore. Your hands. Come then, 330
th' appurtenance of welcome is fashion and ceremony. Let me comply
with you in this garb, lest my extent[8] to the players, which I tell you
must show fairly outwards should more appear like entertainment[9] than
yours. You are welcome. But my uncle-father and aunt-mother are
deceived. 335

GUILDENSTERN: In what, my dear lord?

HAMLET: I am but mad north-north-west; when the wind is southerly I
know a hawk from a handsaw.[1]

[*Enter* POLONIUS.]

POLONIUS: Well be with you, gentlemen.

HAMLET: Hark you, Guildenstern—and you too—at each ear a hearer. That 340
great baby you see there is not yet out of his swaddling clouts.[2]

ROSENCRANTZ: Happily he is the second time come to them, for they say
an old man is twice a child.

HAMLET: I will prophesy he comes to tell me of the players. Mark it.—You
say right, sir, a Monday morning, 'twas then indeed. 345

POLONIUS: My lord, I have news to tell you.

HAMLET: My lord, I have news to tell you. When Roscius was an actor in
Rome—[3]

POLONIUS: The actors are come hither, my lord.

HAMLET: Buzz, buzz. 350

POLONIUS: Upon my honor—

HAMLET: Then came each actor on his ass—

POLONIUS: The best actors in the world, either for tragedy, comedy, history, pastoral, pastoral-comical, historical-pastoral, tragical-historical,
tragical-comical-historical-pastoral, scene individable, or poem unlim- 355
ited. Seneca cannot be too heavy nor Plautus too light. For the law of
writ and the liberty, these are the only men.[4]

---

5. During one of his labors Hercules assumed for a time the burden of the Titan Atlas, who supported the heavens on his shoulders. Also a reference to the effect on business at Shakespeare's
theater, the Globe. 6. Sneer. 7. Miniature. 8. Fashion. *Comply with:* welcome.
9. Cordiality.
1. A "hawk" is a plasterer's tool; Hamlet may also be using "handsaw" = hernshaw = heron.
2. Wrappings for an infant. 3. Roscius was the most famous actor of classical Rome.
4. Seneca and Plautus were Roman writers of tragedy and comedy, respectively. The "law of writ"
refers to plays written according to such rules as the three unities; the "liberty" to those written
otherwise.

HAMLET: O Jephtha, judge of Israel, what a treasure hadst thou![5]
POLONIUS: What a treasure had he, my lord?
360 HAMLET: Why—

> "One fair daughter, and no more,
> The which he loved passing well."

POLONIUS: [*Aside.*] Still on my daughter.
HAMLET: Am I not i' th' right, old Jephtha?
365 POLONIUS: If you call me Jephtha, my lord, I have a daughter that I love
passing well.
HAMLET: Nay, that follows not.
POLONIUS: What follows then, my lord?
HAMLET: Why—

370 > "As by lot, God wot"

and then, you know,

> "It came to pass, as most like it was."

The first row of the pious chanson[6] will show you more, for look where
my abridgement[7] comes.

[*Enter the* PLAYERS.]

375 You are welcome, masters; welcome, all.—I am glad to see thee well.—
Welcome, good friends.—O, old friend! Why thy face is valanced[8] since
I saw thee last. Com'st thou to beard me in Denmark?—What, my young
lady and mistress? By'r lady, your ladyship is nearer to heaven than when
I saw you last by the altitude of a chopine.[9] Pray God your voice, like a
380 piece of uncurrent gold, be not cracked within the ring.—Masters, you
are all welcome. We'll e'en to 't like French falconers, fly at anything we
see. We'll have a speech straight. Come give us a taste of your quality,[1]
come a passionate speech.
FIRST PLAYER: What speech, my good lord?
385 HAMLET: I heard thee speak me a speech once, but it was never acted, or if
it was, not above once, for the play, I remember, pleased not the million;
'twas caviary to the general.[2] But it was—as I received it, and others
whose judgments in such matters cried in the top of[3] mine—an excellent
play, well digested[4] in the scenes, set down with as much modesty as

---

5. To insure victory, Jephtha promised to sacrifice the first creature to meet him on his return.
Unfortunately, his only daughter outstripped his dog and was the victim of his vow. The biblical
story is told in Judges 11.   6. Song. *Row:* stanza.   7. That which cuts short by interrupting.
8. Fringed (with a beard).
9. A reference to the contemporary theatrical practice of using boys to play women's parts. The
company's "lady" has grown in height by the size of a woman's thick-soled shoe, "chopine," since
Hamlet saw him last. The next sentence refers to the possibility, suggested by his growth, that the
young actor's voice may soon begin to change.   1. Trade.   2. Masses. *Caviary:* caviar.
3. Were weightier than.   4. Arranged.

cunning. I remember one said there were no sallets[5] in the lines to make 390
the matter savory, nor no matter in the phrase that might indict the
author of affectation, but called it an honest method, as wholesome as
sweet, and by very much more handsome than fine. One speech in't I
chiefly loved. 'Twas Æneas' tale to Dido, and thereabout of it especially
where he speaks of Priam's slaughter.[6] If it live in your memory, 395
begin at this line—let me see, let me see:

"The rugged Pyrrhus, like th' Hyrcanian beast"[7]—

'tis not so; it begins with Pyrrhus—

"The rugged Pyrrhus, he whose sable arms,
Black as his purpose, did the night resemble 400
When he lay couchéd in th' ominous horse,[8]
Hath now this dread and black complexion smeared
With heraldry more dismal; head to foot
Now is he total gules, horridly tricked[9]
With blood of fathers, mothers, daughters, sons, 405
Baked and impasted with the parching[1] streets,
That lend a tyrannous and a damnéd light
To their lord's murder. Roasted in wrath and fire,
And thus o'er-sizéd with coagulate[2] gore,
With eyes like carbuncles, the hellish Pyrrhus 410
Old grandsire Priam seeks."

So proceed you.
POLONIUS: Fore God, my lord, well spoken, with good accent and good
discretion.
FIRST PLAYER: "Anon he finds him[3] 415
Striking too short at Greeks. His antique[4] sword,
Rebellious[5] to his arm, lies where it falls,
Repugnant to command. Unequal matched,
Pyrrhus at Priam drives, in rage strikes wide.
But with the whiff and wind of his fell sword 420
Th' unnervéd father falls. Then senseless[6] Ilium,
Seeming to feel this blow, with flaming top
Stoops[7] to his base, and with a hideous crash
Takes prisoner Pyrrhus' ear. For, lo! his sword,
Which was declining[8] on the milky head 425

---

5. Spicy passages.
6. Aeneas, fleeing with his band from fallen Troy (Ilium), arrives in Carthage, where he tells Dido,
the queen of Carthage, of the fall of Troy. Here he is describing the death of Priam, the aged king
of Troy, at the hands of Pyrrhus, the son of the slain Achilles.   7. Tiger.
8. That is, the Trojan horse.   9. Adorned. *Total gules:* completely red.
1. Burning. *Impasted:* crusted.   2. Clotted. *O'er-sizéd:* glued over.   3. That is, Pyrrhus finds Priam.
4. Which he used when young.   5. Refractory.   6. Without feeling.   7. Falls.
8. About to fall.

Of reverend Priam, seemed i' th' air to stick.
So as a painted tyrant Pyrrhus stood,
And like a neutral to his will and matter,⁹
Did nothing.
430 But as we often see, against some storm,
A silence in the heavens, the rack¹ stand still,
The bold winds speechless, and the orb below
As hush as death, anon the dreadful thunder
Doth rend the region; so, after Pyrrhus' pause,
435 A rouséd vengeance sets him new awork,²
And never did the Cyclops' hammers fall
On Mars's armor, forged for proof eterne,³
With less remorse than Pyrrhus' bleeding sword
Now falls on Priam.
440 Out, out, thou strumpet, Fortune! All you gods,
In general synod take away her power,
Break all the spokes and fellies⁴ from her wheel,
And bowl the round nave⁵ down the hill of heaven
As low as to the fiends."
445 POLONIUS: This is too long.
HAMLET: It shall to the barber's with your beard.—Prithee say on. He's for
a jig,⁶ or a tale of bawdry, or he sleeps. Say on; come to Hecuba.⁷
FIRST PLAYER: "But who, ah woe! had seen the mobléd⁸ queen—"
HAMLET: "The mobléd queen"?
450 POLONIUS: That's good. "Mobléd queen" is good.
FIRST PLAYER: "Run barefoot up and down, threat'ning the flames
With bisson rheum, a clout⁹ upon that head
Where late the diadem stood, and for a robe,
About her lank and all o'er-teeméd loins,
455 A blanket, in the alarm of fear caught up—
Who this had seen, with tongue in venom steeped,
'Gainst Fortune's state¹ would treason have pronounced.
But if the gods themselves did see her then,
When she saw Pyrrhus make malicious sport
460 In mincing² with his sword her husband's limbs,
The instant burst of clamor that she made,
Unless things mortal move them not at all,

---

9. Between his will and the fulfillment of it.   1. Clouds.   2. To work.
3. Mars, as befits a Roman war god, had armor made for him by the blacksmith god Vulcan and
his assistants, the Cyclopes. It was suitably impenetrable, of "proof eterne."   4. Parts of the rim.
5. Hub. *Bowl:* roll.   6. A comic act.
7. Hecuba was the wife of Priam and queen of Troy. Her "loins" are described below as "o'erteemed"
because of her unusual fertility. The number of her children varies in different accounts, but twenty
is a safe minimum.   8. Muffled (in a hood).
9. Cloth. *Bisson rheum:* blinding tears.   1. Government.   2. Cutting up.

Would have made milch[3] the burning eyes of heaven,
And passion in the gods."
POLONIUS: Look whe'r[4] he has not turned his color, and has tears in's eyes. 465
   Prithee no more.
HAMLET: 'Tis well. I'll have thee speak out the rest of this soon.—Good my
   lord, will you see the players well bestowed?[5] Do you hear, let them be
   well used, for they are the abstract[6] and brief chronicles of the time; after
   your death you were better have a bad epitaph than their ill report while 470
   you live.
POLONIUS: My lord, I will use them according to their desert.
HAMLET: God's bodkin, man, much better. Use every man after his desert,
   and who shall 'scape whipping? Use them after your own honor and
   dignity. The less they deserve, the more merit is in your bounty. Take 475
   them in.
POLONIUS: Come, sirs.
HAMLET: Follow him, friends. We'll hear a play tomorrow.
                                        [*Aside to* FIRST PLAYER.]
   Dost thou hear me, old friend, can you play "The Murder of Gonzago"?
FIRST PLAYER: Ay, my lord.   480
HAMLET: We'll ha't tomorrow night. You could for a need study a speech
   of some dozen or sixteen lines which I would set down and insert in't,
   could you not?
FIRST PLAYER: Ay, my lord.
HAMLET: Very well. Follow that lord, and look you mock him not.   485
                        [*Exeunt* POLONIUS *and* PLAYERS.]
   My good friends, I'll leave you till night. You are welcome to Elsinore.
ROSENCRANTZ: Good my lord.
                        [*Exeunt* ROSENCRANTZ *and* GUILDENSTERN.]
HAMLET: Ay, so God b'wi'ye. Now I am alone.
   O, what a rogue and peasant slave am I!
   Is it not monstrous that this player here,
   But in a fiction, in a dream of passion,   490
   Could force his soul so to his own conceit[7]
   That from her working all his visage wanned;[8]
   Tears in his eyes, distraction in his aspect[9]
   A broken voice, and his whole function suiting   495
   With forms to his conceit? And all for nothing,
   For Hecuba!
   What's Hecuba to him or he to Hecuba,
   That he should weep for her? What would he do
   Had he the motive and the cue for passion
   That I have? He would drown the stage with tears,   500
   And cleave the general ear with horrid speech,
   Make mad the guilty, and appal the free,

3. Tearful (literally, milk-giving).   4. Whether.   5. Provided for.   6. Summary.
7. Imagination.   8. Grew pale.   9. Face.

Confound the ignorant, and amaze indeed
505   The very faculties of eyes and ears.
Yet I,
A dull and muddy-mettled rascal, peak[1]
Like John-a-dreams, unpregnant[2] of my cause,
And can say nothing; no, not for a king
510   Upon whose property and most dear life
A damned defeat was made. Am I a coward?
Who calls me villain, breaks my pate across,
Plucks off my beard and blows it in my face,
Tweaks me by the nose, gives me the lie i' th' throat
515   As deep as to the lungs? Who does me this?
Ha, 'swounds, I should take it; for it cannot be
But I am pigeon-livered and lack gall[3]
To make oppression bitter, or ere this
I should 'a fatted all the region kites[4]
520   With this slave's offal. Bloody, bawdy villain!
Remorseless, treacherous, lecherous, kindless[5] villain!
O, vengeance!
Why, what an ass am I! This is most brave,
That I, the son of a dear father murdered,
525   Prompted to my revenge by heaven and hell,
Must like a whore unpack[6] my heart with words,
And fall a-cursing like a very drab,
A scullion![7] Fie upon't! foh!
About, my brains. Hum—I have heard
530   That guilty creatures sitting at a play,
Have by the very cunning of the scene
Been struck so to the soul that presently
They have proclaimed[8] their malefactions;
For murder, though it have no tongue, will speak
535   With most miraculous organ. I'll have these players
Play something like the murder of my father
Before mine uncle. I'll observe his looks.
I'll tent him to the quick. If 'a do blench,[9]
I know my course. The spirit that I have seen
540   May be a devil, and the devil hath power
T' assume a pleasing shape, yea, and perhaps
Out of my weakness and my melancholy,
As he is very potent with such spirits,
Abuses me to damn me. I'll have grounds

---

1. Mope. *Muddy-mettled:* dull-spirited.   2. Not quickened by. *John-a-dreams:* a man dreaming.
3. Bitterness.   4. Birds of prey of the area.   5. Unnatural.   6. Relieve.
7. In some versions of the play, the word "stallion," a slang term for a prostitute, appears in place
of "scullion."   8. Admitted.   9. Turn pale. *Tent:* try.

More relative[1] than this. The play's the thing   545
Wherein I'll catch the conscience of the king.   [*Exit.*]

ACT III
Scene 1

A room in the castle. Enter KING, QUEEN, POLONIUS, OPHELIA, ROSEN-
CRANTZ *and* GUILDENSTERN.

KING: And can you by no drift of conference[2]
  Get from him why he puts on this confusion,
  Grating so harshly all his days of quiet
  With turbulent[3] and dangerous lunacy?
ROSENCRANTZ: He does confess he feels himself distracted,   5
  But from what cause 'a will by no means speak.
GUILDENSTERN: Nor do we find him forward to be sounded,[4]
  But with a crafty madness keeps aloof
  When we would bring him on to some confession
  Of his true state.
QUEEN: Did he receive you well?   10
ROSENCRANTZ: Most like a gentleman.
GUILDENSTERN: But with much forcing of his disposition.[5]
ROSENCRANTZ: Niggard of question, but of our demands[6]
  Most free in his reply.
QUEEN: Did you assay[7] him
  To any pastime?   15
ROSENCRANTZ: Madam, it so fell out that certain players
  We o'er-raught[8] on the way. Of these we told him,
  And there did seem in him a kind of joy
  To hear of it. They are here about the court,
  And as I think, they have already order   20
  This night to play before him.
POLONIUS: 'Tis most true,
  And he beseeched me to entreat your majesties
  To hear and see the matter.[9]
KING: With all my heart, and it doth much content me
  To hear him so inclined.   25
  Good gentlemen, give him a further edge,
  And drive his purpose[1] into these delights.
ROSENCRANTZ: We shall, my lord.
          [*Exeunt* ROSENCRANTZ *and* GUILDENSTERN.]
KING: Sweet Gertrude, leave us too,
  For we have closely sent for Hamlet hither,
  That he, as 'twere by accident, may here   30

---

1. Conclusive.   2. Line of conversation.   3. Disturbing.   4. Questioned. *Forward:* eager.
5. Conversation.   6. To our questions.   7. Tempt.   8. Passed.   9. Performance.
1. Sharpen his intention.

Affront[2] Ophelia.
Her father and myself (lawful espials[3])
Will so bestow ourselves that, seeing unseen,
We may of their encounter frankly judge,
35 And gather by him, as he is behaved,
If 't be th' affliction of his love or no
That thus he suffers for.
QUEEN: I shall obey you.—
And for your part, Ophelia, I do wish
That your good beauties be the happy cause
40 Of Hamlet's wildness. So shall I hope your virtues
Will bring him to his wonted[4] way again,
To both your honors.
OPHELIA: Madam, I wish it may.   [*Exit* QUEEN.]
POLONIUS: Ophelia, walk you here.—Gracious,[5] so please you,
We will bestow ourselves.—[*To* OPHELIA.] Read on this book,
45 That show of such an exercise may color[6]
Your loneliness.—We are oft to blame in this,
'Tis too much proved, that with devotion's visage
And pious action we do sugar o'er
The devil himself.
KING: [*Aside.*]   O, 'tis too true.
50 How smart a lash that speech doth give my conscience!
The harlot's cheek, beautied with plast'ring[7] art,
Is not more ugly to the thing that helps it
Than is my deed to my most painted word.
O heavy burden!
55 POLONIUS: I hear him coming. Let's withdraw, my lord.
                         [*Exeunt* KING *and* POLONIUS.]

[*Enter* HAMLET.]

HAMLET: To be, or not to be, that is the question:
Whether 'tis nobler in the mind to suffer
The slings and arrows of outrageous fortune,
Or to take arms against a sea of troubles,
60 And by opposing end them. To die, to sleep—
No more; and by a sleep to say we end
The heartache, and the thousand natural shocks
That flesh is heir to. 'Tis a consummation
Devoutly to be wished—to die, to sleep—
65 To sleep, perchance to dream, ay there's the rub;
For in that sleep of death what dreams may come
When we have shuffled off this mortal coil[8]
Must give us pause—there's the respect[9]

---

2. Confront.   3. Justified spies.   4. Usual.   5. Majesty.   6. Explain. *Exercise:* act of devotion.
7. Thickly painted.   8. Turmoil.   9. Consideration.

That makes calamity of so long life.
For who would bear the whips and scorns of time,   70
Th' oppressor's wrong, the proud man's contumely,[1]
The pangs of despised love, the law's delay,
The insolence of office, and the spurns[2]
That patient merit of th' unworthy takes,
When he himself might his quietus[3] make   75
With a bare bodkin? Who would fardels[4] bear,
To grunt and sweat under a weary life,
But that the dread of something after death,
The undiscovered country, from whose bourn[5]
No traveller returns, puzzles the will,   80
And makes us rather bear those ills we have
Than fly to others that we know not of?
Thus conscience does make cowards of us all;
And thus the native[6] hue of resolution
Is sicklied o'er with the pale cast of thought,   85
And enterprises of great pitch and moment[7]
With this regard their currents turn awry
And lose the name of action.—Soft you now,
The fair Ophelia.—Nymph, in thy orisons[8]
Be all my sins remembered.

OPHELIA: Good my lord,   90
How does your honor for this many a day?
HAMLET: I humbly thank you, well, well, well.
OPHELIA: My lord, I have remembrances of yours
That I have longéd long to re-deliver.
I pray you now receive them.
HAMLET: No, not I,   95
I never gave you aught.
OPHELIA: My honored lord, you know right well you did,
And with them words of so sweet breath composed
As made the things more rich. Their perfume lost,
Take these again, for to the noble mind   100
Rich gifts wax[9] poor when givers prove unkind.
There, my lord.
HAMLET: Ha, ha! are you honest?[1]
OPHELIA: My lord?
HAMLET: Are you fair?   105
OPHELIA: What means your lordship?
HAMLET: That if you be honest and fair, your honesty should admit no
     discourse to your beauty.

---

1. Insulting behavior.   2. Rejections.   3. Settlement.   4. Burdens. *Bodkin:* dagger.
5. Boundary.   6. Natural.   7. Importance. *Pitch:* height.   8. Prayers.   9. Become.
1. Chaste.

OPHELIA: Could beauty, my lord, have better commerce[2] than with honesty?
110 HAMLET: Ay, truly, for the power of beauty will sooner transform honesty
from what it is to a bawd than the force of honesty can translate beauty
into his likeness. This was sometimes a paradox, but now the time gives
it proof. I did love you once.
OPHELIA: Indeed, my lord, you made me believe so.
115 HAMLET: You should not have believed me, for virtue cannot so inoculate[3]
our old stock but we shall relish of it. I loved you not.
OPHELIA: I was the more deceived.
HAMLET: Get thee to a nunnery.[4] Why wouldst thou be a breeder of sinners?
I am myself indifferent[5] honest, but yet I could accuse me of such things
120 that it were better my mother had not borne me: I am very proud,
revengeful, ambitious, with more offences at my beck[6] than I have
thoughts to put them in, imagination to give them shape, or time to
act them in. What should such fellows as I do crawling between earth
and heaven? We are arrant[7] knaves all; believe none of us. Go thy ways
125 to a nunnery. Where's your father?
OPHELIA: At home, my lord.
HAMLET: Let the doors be shut upon him, that he may play the fool
nowhere but in's own house. Farewell.
OPHELIA: O, help him, you sweet heavens!
130 HAMLET: If thou dost marry, I'll give thee this plague for thy dowry: be
thou as chaste as ice, as pure as snow, thou shalt not escape calumny.
Get thee to a nunnery, farewell. Or if thou wilt needs marry, marry a
fool, for wise men know well enough what monsters[8] you make of them.
To a nunnery, go, and quickly too. Farewell.
135 OPHELIA: Heavenly powers, restore him!
HAMLET: I have heard of your paintings, too, well enough. God hath given
you one face, and you make yourselves another. You jig, you amble, and
you lisp;[9] you nickname God's creatures, and make your wantonness
your ignorance.[1] Go to, I'll no more on't, it hath made me mad. I say
140 we will have no more marriage. Those that are married already, all but
one, shall live. The rest shall keep as they are. To a nunnery, go. [*Exit.*]
OPHELIA: O, what a noble mind is here o'erthrown!
The courtier's, soldier's, scholar's, eye, tongue, sword,
Th' expectancy and rose[2] of the fair state,
145 The glass of fashion and the mould[3] of form,
Th' observed of all observers, quite quite down!
And I of ladies most deject and wretched,
That sucked the honey of his music[4] vows,

---

2. Intercourse.   3. Change by grafting.
4. With typical ribaldry Hamlet uses "nunnery" in two senses, the second as a slang term for brothel.
5. Moderately.   6. Command.   7. Thorough.   8. Horned because cuckolded.
9. Walk and talk affectedly.
1. Hamlet means that women call things by pet names and then blame the affectation on ignorance.
2. Ornament. *Expectancy:* hope.   3. Model. *Glass:* mirror.   4. Musical.

Now see that noble and most sovereign reason
Like sweet bells jangled, out of time and harsh; 150
That unmatched form and feature of blown[5] youth
Blasted with ecstasy. O, woe is me
T' have seen what I have seen, see what I see!

[*Enter* KING *and* POLONIUS.]

KING: Love! His affections do not that way tend,
Nor what he spake, though it lacked form a little, 155
Was not like madness. There's something in his soul
O'er which his melancholy sits on brood,[6]
And I do doubt the hatch and the disclose[7]
Will be some danger; which to prevent,
I have in quick determination 160
Thus set it down: he shall with speed to England
For the demand of our neglected tribute.
Haply the seas and countries different,
With variable objects, shall expel
This something-settled matter in his heart 165
Whereon his brains still beating puts him thus
From fashion of himself. What think you on't?
POLONIUS: It shall do well. But yet do I believe
The origin and commencement of his grief
Sprung from neglected love.—How now, Ophelia? 170
You need not tell us what Lord Hamlet said,
We heard it all.—My lord, do as you please,
But if you hold it fit, after the play
Let his queen-mother all alone entreat him
To show his grief. Let her be round[8] with him, 175
And I'll be placed, so please you, in the ear[9]
Of all their conference. If she find him not,[1]
To England send him; or confine him where
Your wisdom best shall think.
KING: It shall be so.
Madness in great ones must not unwatched go.   [*Exeunt.*] 180

Scene 2

A public room in the castle. Enter HAMLET *and three of the* PLAYERS.

HAMLET: Speak the speech, I pray you, as I pronounced it to you, trippingly
on the tongue; but if you mouth it as many of our players do, I had as
lief the town-crier spoke my lines. Nor do not saw the air too much
with your hand thus, but use all gently, for in the very torrent, tempest,
and as I may say, whirlwind of your passion, you must acquire and beget 5

---

5. Full-blown.   6. That is, like a hen.   7. Result. *Doubt:* fear.   8. Direct.   9. Hearing.
1. Does not discover his problem.

a temperance that may give it smoothness. O, it offends me to the soul to hear a robustious periwig-pated[2] fellow tear a passion to tatters, to very rags, to split the ears of the groundlings, who for the most part are capable of[3] nothing but inexplicable dumb shows and noise. I would

10 have such a fellow whipped for o'erdoing Termagant. It out-herods Herod.[4] Pray you avoid it.

FIRST PLAYER: I warrant your honor.

HAMLET: Be not too tame neither, but let your own discretion be your tutor.

Suit the action to the word, the word to the action, with this special

15 observance, that you o'erstep not the modesty of nature; for anything so o'erdone is from[5] the purpose of playing, whose end both at the first, and now, was and is, to hold as 'twere the mirror up to nature, to show virtue her own feature, scorn her own image, and the very age and body of the time his form and pressure.[6] Now this overdone, or come tardy

20 off, though it makes the unskilful[7] laugh, cannot but make the judicious grieve, the censure[8] of the which one must in your allowance o'erweigh a whole theatre of others. O, there be players that I have seen play—and heard others praise, and that highly—not to speak it profanely, that neither having th' accent of Christians, nor the gait of Christian, pagan,

25 nor man, have so strutted and bellowed that I have thought some of nature's journeymen[9] had made men, and not made them well, they imitated humanity so abominably.

FIRST PLAYER: I hope we have reformed that indifferently[1] with us, sir.

HAMLET: O, reform it altogether. And let those that play your clowns speak

30 no more than is set down for them, for there be of them that will themselves laugh, to set on some quantity of barren[2] spectators to laugh too, though in the meantime some necessary question of the play be then to be considered. That's villainous, and shows a most pitiful ambition in the fool that uses it. Go, make you ready.   [*Exeunt* PLAYERS.]

[*Enter* POLONIUS, GUILDENSTERN, *and* ROSENCRANTZ.]

35 How now, my lord? Will the king hear this piece of work?

POLONIUS: And the queen too, and that presently.

HAMLET: Bid the players make haste.   [*Exit* POLONIUS.]

Will you two help to hasten them?

ROSENCRANTZ: Ay, my lord.   [*Exeunt they two.*]

40 HAMLET: What, ho, Horatio!

[*Enter* HORATIO.]

HORATIO: Here, sweet lord, at your service.

HAMLET: Horatio, thou art e'en as just a man

---

2. Bewigged. *Robustious:* noisy.
3. That is, capable of understanding. *Groundlings:* the spectators who paid least.
4. Termagant, a "Saracen" deity, and the biblical Herod were stock characters in popular drama noted for the excesses of sound and fury used by their interpreters.   5. Contrary to.   6. Shape.
7. Ignorant.   8. Judgment.   9. Inferior craftsmen.   1. Somewhat.   2. Dull-witted.

As e'er my conversation coped³ withal.
HORATIO: O my dear lord!
HAMLET: Nay, do not think I flatter,
For what advancement may I hope from thee,   45
That no revenue hast but thy good spirits
To feed and clothe thee? Why should the poor be flattered?
No, let the candied tongue lick absurd pomp,
And crook the pregnant⁴ hinges of the knee
Where thrift⁵ may follow fawning. Dost thou hear?   50
Since my dear soul was mistress of her choice
And could of men distinguish her election,
S'hath sealed thee for herself, for thou hast been
As one in suff'ring all that suffers nothing,
A man that Fortune's buffets and rewards   55
Hast ta'en with equal thanks; and blest are those
Whose blood and judgment are so well commingled
That they are not a pipe⁶ for Fortune's finger
To sound what stop⁷ she please. Give me that man
That is not passion's slave, and I will wear him   60
In my heart's core, ay, in my heart of heart,
As I do thee. Something too much of this.
There is a play tonight before the king.
One scene of it comes near the circumstance
Which I have told thee of my father's death.   65
I prithee, when thou seest that act afoot,
Even with the very comment⁸ of thy soul
Observe my uncle. If his occulted⁹ guilt
Do not itself unkennel¹ in one speech,
It is a damnéd ghost that we have seen,   70
And my imaginations are as foul
As Vulcan's stithy. Give him heedful note,²
For I mine eyes will rivet to his face,
And after we will both our judgments join
In censure of his seeming.³
HORATIO: Well, my lord.   75
If 'a steal aught the whilst this play in playing,
And 'scape detecting, I will pay⁴ the theft.

[*Enter Trumpets and Kettledrums,* KING, QUEEN, POLONIUS, OPHELIA,
ROSENCRANTZ, GUILDENSTERN, *and other* LORDS *attendant.*]

HAMLET: They are coming to the play. I must be idle.
Get you a place.
KING: How fares our cousin Hamlet?

---

3. Encountered.   4. Quick to bend.   5. Profit.   6. Musical instrument.   7. Note. *Sound:* play.
8. Keenest observation.   9. Hidden.   1. Break loose.   2. Careful attention. *Stithy:* smithy.
3. Manner.   4. Repay.

80 HAMLET: Excellent, i' faith, of the chameleon's dish.[5] I eat the air, promise-crammed. You cannot feed capons so.

KING: I have nothing with this answer, Hamlet. These words are not mine.

HAMLET: No, nor mine now. [*To* POLONIUS.] My lord, you played once i' th' university, you say?

85 POLONIUS: That did I, my lord, and was accounted a good actor.

HAMLET: What did you enact?

POLONIUS: I did enact Julius Cæsar. I was killed i' th' Capitol; Brutus killed me.[6]

HAMLET: It was a brute part of him to kill so capital a calf there. Be the
90   players ready?

ROSENCRANTZ: Ay, my lord, they stay upon your patience.[7]

QUEEN: Come hither, my dear Hamlet, sit by me.

HAMLET: No, good mother, here's metal more attractive.

POLONIUS: [*To the* KING.] O, ho! do you mark that?

95 HAMLET: Lady, shall I lie in your lap?

[*Lying down at* OPHELIA's *feet.*]

OPHELIA: No, my lord.

HAMLET: I mean, my head upon your lap?

OPHELIA: Ay, my lord.

HAMLET: Do you think I meant country matters?[8]

100 OPHELIA: I think nothing, my lord.

HAMLET: That's a fair thought to lie between maids' legs.

OPHELIA: What is, my lord?

HAMLET: Nothing.

OPHELIA: You are merry, my lord.

105 HAMLET: Who, I?

OPHELIA: Ay, my lord.

HAMLET: O God, your only jig-maker![9] What should a man do but be merry? For look you how cheerfully my mother looks, and my father died within's two hours.

110 OPHELIA: Nay, 'tis twice two months, my lord.

HAMLET: So long? Nay then, let the devil wear black, for I'll have a suit of sables. O heavens! die two months ago, and not forgotten yet? Then there's hope a great man's memory may outlive his life half a year, but by'r lady 'a must build churches then, or else shall 'a suffer not thinking
115   on, with the hobby-horse, whose epitaph is "For O, for O, the hobby-horse is forgot!"[1]

---

5. A reference to a popular belief that the chameleon subsisted on a diet of air. Hamlet has deliberately misunderstood the king's question.

6. The assassination of Julius Caesar by Brutus and others is the subject of another play by Shakespeare.   7. Leisure. *Stay:* wait.

8. Presumably, rustic misbehavior, but here and elsewhere in this exchange Hamlet treats Ophelia to some ribald double meanings.   9. Writer of comic scenes.

1. In traditional games and dances one of the characters was a man represented as riding a horse. The horse was made of something like cardboard and was worn about the "rider's" waist.

The trumpets sound. Dumb Show follows. Enter a KING *and a* QUEEN *very lovingly; the* QUEEN *embracing him and he her. She kneels, and makes show of protestation unto him. He takes her up, and declines[2] his head upon her neck. He lies him down upon a bank of flowers; she, seeing him asleep, leaves him. Anon come in another man, takes off his crown, kisses it, pours poison in the sleeper's ears, and leaves him. The* QUEEN *returns, finds the* KING *dead, makes passionate action. The* POISONER *with some three or four come in again, seem to condole with her. The dead body is carried away. The* POISONER *woos the* QUEEN *with gifts; she seems harsh awhile, but in the end accepts love.*   *[Exeunt.]*

OPHELIA: What means this, my lord?

HAMLET: Marry, this is miching mallecho;[3] it means mischief.

OPHELIA: Belike this show imports the argument[4] of the play.

[Enter PROLOGUE.*]*

HAMLET: We shall know by this fellow. The players cannot keep counsel;   120
     they'll tell all.

OPHELIA: Will 'a tell us what this show meant?

HAMLET: Ay, or any show that you will show him. Be not you ashamed to
     show, he'll not shame to tell you what it means.

OPHELIA: You are naught, you are naught. I'll mark[5] the play.   125

PROLOGUE: *For us, and for our tragedy,*
     Here stooping to your clemency,
     We beg your hearing patiently.   *[Exit.]*

HAMLET: Is this a prologue, or the posy[6] of a ring?

OPHELIA: 'Tis brief, my lord.   130

HAMLET: As woman's love.

[Enter the PLAYER KING *and* QUEEN.*]*

PLAYER KING: *Full thirty times hath Phœbus' cart gone round*
     Neptune's salt wash and Tellus' orbéd ground,
     And thirty dozen moons with borrowed sheen[7]
     About the world have times twelve thirties been,   135
     Since love our hearts and Hymen did our hands
     Unite comutual in most sacred bands.[8]

PLAYER QUEEN: *So many journeys may the sun and moon*
     Make us again count o'er ere love be done!
     But woe is me, you are so sick of late,   140
     So far from cheer and from your former state,
     That I distrust[9] you. Yet though I distrust,

2. Lays.   3. Sneaking crime.   4. Plot. *Imports:* explains.   5. Attend to. *Naught:* obscene.
6. Motto engraved inside.   7. Light.
8. The speech contains several references to Greek mythology. Phoebus was the sun god, and his chariot or "cart" is the sun. The "salt wash" of Neptune is the ocean; Tellus was an earth goddess, and her "orbed ground" is the Earth, or globe. Hymen was the god of marriage. *Comutual:* mutually.
9. Fear for.

Discomfort you, my lord, it nothing must.
For women's fear and love hold quantity,[1]
145   *In neither aught, or in extremity.*[2]
Now what my love is proof hath made you know,
And as my love is sized,[3] *my fear is so.*
Where love is great, the littlest doubts are fear;
Where little fears grow great, great love grows there.
150 PLAYER KING: *Faith, I must leave thee, love, and shortly too;*
My operant powers their functions leave[4] *to do.*
And thou shalt live in this fair world behind,
Honored, beloved, and haply one as kind
For husband shalt thou—
PLAYER QUEEN: *O, confound the rest!*
155   *Such love must needs be treason in my breast.*
In second husband let me be accurst!
None wed the second but who killed the first.[5]
HAMLET: That's wormwood.
PLAYER QUEEN: *The instances*[6] *that second marriage move*
160   *Are base respects*[7] *of thrift, but none of love.*
A second time I kill my husband dead,
When second husband kisses me in bed.
PLAYER KING: *I do believe you think what now you speak,*
But what we do determine oft we break.
165   *Purpose is but the slave to memory,*
Of violent birth, but poor validity;
Which now, like fruit unripe, sticks on the tree,
But fall unshaken when they mellow be.
Most necessary 'tis that we forget
170   *To pay ourselves what to ourselves is debt.*
What to ourselves in passion we propose,
The passion ending, doth the purpose lose.
The violence of either grief or joy
Their own enactures[8] *with themselves destroy.*
175   *Where joy most revels, grief doth most lament;*
Grief joys, joy grieves, on slender accident.
This world is not for aye,[9] *nor 'tis not strange*
That even our loves should with our fortunes change;
For 'tis a question left us yet to prove,
180   *Whether love lead fortune, or else fortune love.*
The great man down, you mark his favorite flies;
The poor advanced makes friends of enemies;

---

1. Agree in weight.   2. Without regard to too much or too little.   3. In size.
4. Cease. *Operant powers:* active forces.
5. Though there is some ambiguity, she seems to mean that the only kind of woman who would
remarry is one who has killed or would kill her first husband.   6. Causes.   7. Concerns.
8. Actions.   9. Eternal.

And hitherto doth love on fortune tend,
For who not needs shall never lack a friend,
And who in want a hollow¹ friend doth try, 185
Directly seasons him² his enemy.
But orderly to end where I begun,
Our wills and fates do so contrary run
That our devices³ still are overthrown;
Our thoughts are ours, their ends none of our own. 190
So think thou wilt no second husband wed,
But die thy thoughts when thy first lord is dead.
PLAYER QUEEN: Nor earth to me give food, nor heaven light,
Sport and repose lock from me day and night,
To desperation turn my trust and hope, 195
An anchor's cheer⁴ in prison be my scope,
Each opposite that blanks⁵ the face of joy
Meet what I would have well, and it destroy,
Both here and hence⁶ pursue me lasting strife,
If once a widow, ever I be wife! 200
HAMLET: If she should break it now!
PLAYER KING: 'Tis deeply sworn. Sweet, leave me here awhile.
My spirits grow dull, and fain I would beguile
The tedious day with sleep.   [Sleeps.]
PLAYER QUEEN: Sleep rock thy brain,
And never come mischance between us twain!   [Exit.] 205
HAMLET: Madam, how like you this play?
QUEEN: The lady doth protest too much, methinks.
HAMLET: O, but she'll keep her word.
KING: Have you heard the argument? Is there no offence in't?
HAMLET: No, no, they do but jest, poison in jest; no offence i' th' world. 210
KING: What do you call the play?
HAMLET: "The Mouse-trap." Marry, how? Tropically.⁷ This play is the image
of a murder done in Vienna. Gonzago is the duke's name; his wife,
Baptista. You shall see anon. 'Tis a knavish piece of work, but what of
that? Your majesty, and we that have free souls, it touches us not. Let 215
the galled jade wince, our withers are unwrung.⁸

[Enter LUCIANUS.]

This is one Lucianus, nephew to the king.
OPHELIA: You are as good as a chorus, my lord.
HAMLET: I could interpret between you and your love, if I could see the
puppets dallying. 220
OPHELIA: You are keen, my lord, you are keen.

---

1. False.   2. Ripens him into.   3. Plans.   4. Anchorite's food.   5. Blanches.
6. In the next world.   7. Figuratively.
8. A "galled jade" is a horse, particularly one of poor quality, with a sore back. The "withers" are
the ridge between a horse's shoulders; "unwrung withers" are not chafed by the harness.

HAMLET: It would cost you a groaning to take off mine edge.

OPHELIA: Still better, and worse.

HAMLET: So you mistake your husbands.—Begin, murderer. Leave thy dam-
225   nable faces and begin. Come, the croaking raven doth bellow for revenge.

LUCIANUS: *Thoughts black, hands apt, drugs fit, and time agreeing,*
Confederate season,[9] *else no creature seeing,*
Thou mixture rank, of midnight weeds collected,
With Hecate's ban thrice blasted, thrice infected,[1]
230   *Thy natural magic*[2] *and dire property*
On wholesome life usurp immediately.   [*Pours the poison in his ears.*]

HAMLET: 'A poisons him i' th' garden for his estate. His name's Gonzago.
The story is extant, and written in very choice Italian. You shall see anon
how the murderer gets the love of Gonzago's wife.

235 OPHELIA: The king rises.

HAMLET: What, frighted with false fire?

QUEEN: How fares my lord?

POLONIUS: Give o'er the play.

KING: Give me some light. Away!

240 POLONIUS: Lights, lights, lights!   [*Exeunt all but* HAMLET *and* HORATIO.]

HAMLET:

Why, let the strucken deer go weep,
    The hart ungallèd[3] play.
For some must watch while some must sleep;
    Thus runs the world away.

245   Would not this, sir, and a forest of feathers[4]—if the rest of my fortunes
turn Turk with me—with two Provincial roses on my razed shoes, get
me a fellowship in a cry of players?[5]

HORATIO: Half a share.

HAMLET: A whole one, I.

250   For thou dost know, O Damon dear,[6]
    This realm dismantled was
Of Jove himself, and now reigns here
    A very, very—peacock.

HORATIO: You might have rhymed.

255 HAMLET: O good Horatio, I'll take the ghost's word for a thousand pound.
Didst perceive?

---

9. A helpful time for the crime.   1. Hecate was a classical goddess of witchcraft.
2. Native power.   3. Uninjured.   4. Plumes.
5. Hamlet asks Horatio if "this" recitation, accompanied with a player's costume, including plumes
and rosettes on shoes that have been slashed for decorative effect, might not entitle him to become
a shareholder in a theatrical company in the event that Fortune goes against him, "turn Turk." *Cry:*
company.
6. Damon was a common name for a young man or a shepherd in lyric, especially pastoral poetry.
Jove was the chief god of the Romans. Readers may supply for themselves the rhyme referred to by
Horatio.

HORATIO: Very well, my lord.

HAMLET: Upon the talk of the poisoning.

HORATIO: I did very well note[7] him.

HAMLET: Ah, ha! Come, some music. Come, the recorders.[8]   260

For if the king like not the comedy.
Why then, belike he likes it not, perdy.[9]

Come, some music.

[*Enter* ROSENCRANTZ *and* GUILDENSTERN.]

GUILDENSTERN: Good my lord, vouchsafe me a word with you.

HAMLET: Sir, a whole history.   265

GUILDENSTERN: The king, sir—

HAMLET: Ay, sir, what of him?

GUILDENSTERN: Is in his retirement marvellous distempered.[1]

HAMLET: With drink, sir?

GUILDENSTERN: No, my lord, with choler.[2]   270

HAMLET: Your wisdom should show itself more richer to signify this to the
doctor, for for me to put him to his purgation[3] would perhaps plunge
him into more choler.

GUILDENSTERN: Good my lord, put your discourse into some frame,[4] and
start not so wildly from my affair.   275

HAMLET: I am tame, sir. Pronounce.

GUILDENSTERN: The queen your mother, in most great affliction of spirit,
hath sent me to you.

HAMLET: You are welcome.

GUILDENSTERN: Nay, good my lord, this courtesy is not of the right breed.   280
If it shall please you to make me a wholesome[5] answer, I will do your
mother's commandment. If not, your pardon and my return[6] shall be
the end of my business.

HAMLET: Sir, I cannot.

ROSENCRANTZ: What, my lord?   285

HAMLET: Make you a wholesome answer; my wit's diseased. But, sir, such
answer as I can make, you shall command, or rather, as you say, my
mother. Therefore no more, but to the matter. My mother, you say—

ROSENCRANTZ: Then thus she says: your behavior hath struck her into
amazement and admiration.[7]   290

HAMLET: O wonderful son, that can so stonish a mother! But is there no
sequel at the heels of his mother's admiration? Impart.[8]

ROSENCRANTZ: She desires to speak with you in her closet[9] ere you go to
bed.

---

7. Observe.   8. Wooden, end-blown flutes.   9. *Par Dieu* (by God).
1. Vexed. *Retirement:* place to which he has retired.   2. Bile.   3. Treatment with a laxative.
4. Order. *Discourse:* speech.   5. Reasonable.   6. That is, to the queen.   7. Wonder.   8. Tell me.
9. Bedroom.

295 HAMLET: We shall obey, were she ten times our mother. Have you any
further trade[1] with us?

ROSENCRANTZ: My lord, you once did love me.

HAMLET: And do still, by these pickers and stealers.[2]

ROSENCRANTZ: Good my lord, what is your cause of distemper? You do
300   surely bar the door upon your own liberty, if you deny your griefs to
your friend.

HAMLET: Sir, I lack advancement.

ROSENCRANTZ: How can that be, when you have the voice of the king
himself for your succession in Denmark?

305 HAMLET: Ay, sir, but "while the grass grows"—the proverb[3] is something
musty.

[*Enter the* PLAYERS *with recorders.*]

O, the recorders! Let me see one. To withdraw with you[4]—why do you
go about to recover the wind of me, as if you would drive me into a
toil?[5]

310 GUILDENSTERN: O my lord, if my duty be too bold, my love is too unman-
nerly.

HAMLET: I do not well understand that. Will you play upon this pipe?[6]

GUILDENSTERN: My lord, I cannot.

HAMLET: I pray you.

GUILDENSTERN: Believe me, I cannot.

315 HAMLET: I do beseech you.

GUILDENSTERN: I know no touch of it,[7] my lord.

HAMLET: It is as easy as lying. Govern these ventages[8] with your fingers and
thumb, give it breath with your mouth, and it will discourse most eloquent music. Look you, these are the stops.[9]

320 GUILDENSTERN: But these cannot I command to any utt'rance of harmony.
I have not the skill.

HAMLET: Why, look you now, how unworthy a thing you make of me! You
would play upon me, you would seem to know my stops, you would
pluck out the heart of my mystery, you would sound[1] me from my lowest
325   note to the top of my compass;[2] and there is much music, excellent
voice, in this little organ, yet cannot you make it speak. 'Sblood, do you
think I am easier to be played on than a pipe? Call me what instrument
you will, though you can fret[3] me, you cannot play upon me.

[*Enter* POLONIUS.]

---

1. Business.   2. Hands.   3. The proverb ends "the horse starves."   4. Let me step aside.
5. The figure is from hunting. Hamlet asks why Guildenstern is attempting to get windward of him,
as if he would drive him into a net.   6. Recorder.   7. Have no ability.
8. Holes. *Govern:* cover and uncover.   9. Wind-holes.   1. Play.   2. Range.
3. "Fret" is used in a double sense, to annoy and to play a guitar or similar instrument using the
"frets" or small bars on the neck.

God bless you, sir!

POLONIUS: My lord, the queen would speak with you, and presently.[4]   330

HAMLET: Do you see yonder cloud that's almost in shape of a camel?

POLONIUS: By th' mass, and 'tis like a camel indeed.

HAMLET: Methinks it is like a weasel.

POLONIUS: It is backed like a weasel.

HAMLET: Or like a whale.   335

POLONIUS: Very like a whale.

HAMLET: Then I will come to my mother by and by. [*Aside.*] They fool me
to the top of my bent.[5]—I will come by and by.

POLONIUS: I will say so.   [*Exit.*]

HAMLET: "By and by" is easily said. Leave me, friends.   340

[*Exeunt all but* HAMLET.]

'Tis now the very witching time of night,
When churchyards yawn, and hell itself breathes out
Contagion to this world. Now could I drink hot blood,
And do such bitter business as the day
Would quake to look on. Soft, now to my mother.   345
O heart, lose not thy nature; let not ever
The soul of Nero[6] enter this firm bosom.
Let me be cruel, not unnatural;
I will speak daggers to her, but use none.
My tongue and soul in this be hypocrites—   350
How in my words somever she be shent,[7]
To give them seals[8] never, my soul, consent!   [*Exit.*]

Scene 3

A room in the castle. Enter KING, ROSENCRANTZ *and* GUILDENSTERN.

KING: I like him not,[9] nor stands it safe with us
To let his madness range.[1] Therefore prepare you.
I your commission will forthwith dispatch,
And he to England shall along with you.
The terms of our estate[2] may not endure   5
Hazard so near's as doth hourly grow
Out of his brows.

GUILDENSTERN: We will ourselves provide,[3]
Most holy and religious fear it is
To keep those many many bodies safe
That live and feed upon your majesty.   10

ROSENCRANTZ: The single and peculiar[4] life is bound
With all the strength and armor of the mind

---

4. At once.   5. Treat me as an utter fool.
6. The Roman emperor Nero, known for his excesses, was believed to have been responsible for the
death of his mother.   7. Shamed.   8. Fulfillment in action.   9. Distrust him.   1. Roam freely.
2. Condition of the state.   3. Equip (for the journey).   4. Individual.

To keep itself from noyance,[5] but much more
That spirit upon whose weal[6] depends and rests
15   The lives of many. The cess[7] of majesty
Dies not alone, but like a gulf[8] doth draw
What's near it with it. It is a massy[9] wheel
Fixed on the summit of the highest mount,
To whose huge spokes ten thousand lesser things
20   Are mortised and adjoined,[1] which when it falls,
Each small annexment, petty consequence,
Attends[2] the boist'rous ruin. Never alone
Did the king sigh, but with a general groan.
KING: Arm you, I pray you, to this speedy voyage,
25   For we will fetters put about this fear,
Which now goes too free-footed.
ROSENCRANTZ: We will haste us.
                          [*Exeunt* ROSENCRANTZ *and* GUILDENSTERN.]

       [*Enter* POLONIUS.]

POLONIUS: My lord, he's going to his mother's closet.
Behind the arras I'll convey[3] myself
To hear the process. I'll warrant she'll tax him home,[4]
30   And as you said, and wisely was it said,
'Tis meet that some more audience than a mother,
Since nature makes them partial, should o'erhear
The speech, of vantage.[5] Fare you well, my liege.
I'll call upon you ere you go to bed,
And tell you what I know.
35   KING: Thanks, dear my lord.   [*Exit* POLONIUS.]
O, my offence is rank, it smells to heaven;
It hath the primal eldest curse[6] upon't,
A brother's murder. Pray can I not,
Though inclination be as sharp as will.
40   My stronger guilt defeats my strong intent,
And like a man to double business[7] bound,
I stand in pause where I shall first begin,
And both neglect. What if this cursèd hand
Were thicker than itself with brother's blood,
45   Is there not rain enough in the sweet heavens
To wash it white as snow? Whereto serves mercy
But to confront the visage of offence?
And what's in prayer but this twofold force,
To be forestallèd[8] ere we come to fall,

---

5. Harm.   6. Welfare.   7. Cessation.   8. Whirlpool.   9. Massive.   1. Attached.
2. Joins in.   3. Station.   4. Sharply. *Process:* proceedings.   5. From a position of vantage.
6. That is, of Cain.   7. Two mutually opposed interests.   8. Prevented (from sin).

Or pardoned being down?[9] Then I'll look up.   50
My fault is past. But, O, what form of prayer
Can serve my turn? "Forgive me my foul murder"?
That cannot be, since I am still possessed
Of those effects[1] for which I did the murder—
My crown, mine own ambition, and my queen.   55
May one be pardoned and retain th' offence?[2]
In the corrupted currents of this world
Offence's gilded[3] hand may shove by justice,
And oft 'tis seen the wicked prize itself
Buys out the law. But 'tis not so above.   60
There is no shuffling; there the action[4] lies
In his true nature, and we ourselves compelled,
Even to the teeth and forehead of[5] our faults,
To give in evidence. What then? What rests?[6]
Try what repentance can. What can it not?   65
Yet what can it when one cannot repent?
O wretched state! O bosom black as death!
O liméd[7] soul, that struggling to be free
Art more engaged! Help, angels! Make assay.
Bow, stubborn knees, and heart with strings of steel,   70
Be soft as sinews of the new-born babe.
All may be well.   [*He kneels.*]

   [*Enter* HAMLET.]

HAMLET: Now might I do it pat,[8] now 'a is a-praying,
  And now I'll do't—and so 'a goes to heaven,
  And so am I revenged. That would be scanned.[9]   75
  A villain kills my father, and for that,
  I, his sole son, do this same villain send
  To heaven.
  Why, this is hire and salary, not revenge.
  'A took my father grossly, full of bread,[1]   80
  With all his crimes broad blown, as flush[2] as May;
  And how his audit stands who knows save heaven?
  But in our circumstance and course of thought
  'Tis heavy with him; and am I then revenged
  To take him in the purging of his soul,   85
  When he is fit and seasoned[3] for his passage?
  No.
  Up, sword, and know thou a more horrid hent.[4]
  When he is drunk, asleep, or in his rage,

---

9. Having sinned.   1. Gains.   2. That is, benefits of the offense.   3. Bearing gold as a bribe.
4. Case at law.   5. Face-to-face with.   6. Remains.   7. Caught as with birdlime.   8. Easily.
9. Deserves consideration.   1. In a state of sin and without fasting.
2. Vigorous. *Broad blown:* full-blown.   3. Ready.   4. Opportunity.

90 Or in th' incestuous pleasure of his bed,
  At game a-swearing, or about some act
  That has no relish[5] of salvation in't—
  Then trip him, that his heels may kick at heaven,
  And that his soul may be as damned and black
95 As hell, whereto it goes. My mother stays.
  This physic[6] but prolongs thy sickly days.   [*Exit.*]
 KING: [*Rising.*] My words fly up, my thoughts remain below.
  Words without thoughts never to heaven go. [*Exit.*]

Scene 4

The Queen's chamber. Enter QUEEN *and* POLONIUS.

 POLONIUS: 'A will come straight. Look you lay home to[7] him.
  Tell him his pranks have been too broad[8] to bear with,
  And that your grace hath screen'd[9] and stood between
  Much heat and him. I'll silence me even here.
5 Pray you be round with him.
 HAMLET: [*Within.*] Mother, mother, mother!
 QUEEN: I'll warrant you. Fear[1] me not.
  Withdraw, I hear him coming.

   [POLONIUS *goes behind the arras. Enter* HAMLET.]

 HAMLET: Now, mother, what's the matter?
10 QUEEN: Hamlet, thou hast thy father much offended.
 HAMLET: Mother, you have my father much offended.
 QUEEN: Come, come, you answer with an idle tongue.
 HAMLET: Go, go, you question with a wicked tongue.
 QUEEN: Why, how now, Hamlet?
 HAMLET: What's the matter now?
 QUEEN: Have you forgot me?
15 HAMLET: No, by the rood,[2] not so.
  You are the queen, your husband's brother's wife,
  And would it were not so, you are my mother.
 QUEEN: Nay, then I'll set those to you that can speak.
 HAMLET: Come, come, and sit you down. You shall not budge.
20 You go not till I set you up a glass[3]
  Where you may see the inmost part of you.
 QUEEN: What wilt thou do? Thou wilt not murder me?
  Help, ho!
 POLONIUS: [*Behind.*] What, ho! help!
25 HAMLET: [*Draws.*] How now, a rat?
  Dead for a ducat, dead!

   [*Kills* POLONIUS *with a pass through the arras.*]

---

5. Flavor. 6. Medicine. 7. Be sharp with. 8. Outrageous. 9. Acted as a fire screen.
1. Doubt. 2. Cross. 3. Mirror.

POLONIUS: [*Behind.*] O, I am slain!
QUEEN: O me, what hast thou done?
HAMLET: Nay, I know not.
  Is it the king?
QUEEN: O, what a rash and bloody deed is this!   30
HAMLET: A bloody deed!—almost as bad, good mother,
  As kill a king and marry with his brother.
QUEEN: As kill a king?
HAMLET: Ay, lady, it was my word.   [*Parting the arras.*]
  Thou wretched, rash, intruding fool, farewell!
  I took thee for thy better. Take thy fortune.   35
  Thou find'st to be too busy⁴ is some danger.—
  Leave wringing of your hands. Peace, sit you down
  And let me wring your heart, for so I shall
  If it be made of penetrable stuff,
  If damnéd custom have not brazed it⁵ so   40
  That it be proof and bulwark against sense.⁶
QUEEN: What have I done that thou dar'st wag thy tongue
  In noise so rude against me?
HAMLET: Such an act
  That blurs the grace and blush of modesty,
  Calls virtue hypocrite, takes off the rose   45
  From the fair forehead of an innocent love.
  And sets a blister⁷ there, makes marriage-vows
  As false as dicers' oaths. O, such a deed
  As from the body of contraction⁸ plucks
  The very soul, and sweet religion makes   50
  A rhapsody of words. Heaven's face does glow
  O'er this solidity and compound mass⁹
  With heated visage, as against the doom¹—
  Is thought-sick at the act.
QUEEN: Ay me, what act
  That roars so loud and thunders in the index?²   55
HAMLET: Look here upon this picture³ and on this,
  The counterfeit presentment of two brothers.
  See what a grace was seated on this brow:
  Hyperion's curls, the front⁴ of Jove himself,
  An eye like Mars, to threaten and command,   60
  A station like the herald Mercury⁵
  New lighted⁶ on a heaven-kissing hill—
  A combination and a form indeed

4. Officious.   5. Plated it with brass.   6. Feeling. *Proof:* armor.   7. Brand.
8. The marriage contract.   9. Meaningless mass (Earth).   1. Judgment Day.
2. Table of contents.   3. Portrait.   4. Forehead.
5. In Roman mythology, Mercury served as the messenger of the gods. *Station:* bearing.
6. Newly alighted.

Where every god did seem to set his seal,[7]
65   To give the world assurance of a man.
This was your husband. Look you now what follows.
Here is your husband, like a mildewed ear
Blasting his wholesome brother. Have you eyes?
Could you on this fair mountain leave to feed,
70   And batten[8] on this moor? Ha! have you eyes?
You cannot call it love, for at your age
The heyday in the blood is tame, it's humble,
And waits upon the judgment, and what judgment
Would step from this to this? Sense sure you have
75   Else could you not have motion, but sure that sense
Is apoplexed[9] for madness would not err,
Nor sense to ecstasy was ne'er so thralled
But it reserved some quantity[1] of choice
To serve in such a difference. What devil was't
80   That thus hath cozened you at hoodman-blind?[2]
Eyes without feeling, feeling without sight,
Ears without hands or eyes, smelling sans[3] all,
Or but a sickly part of one true sense
Could not so mope.[4] O shame! where is thy blush?
85   Rebellious hell,
If thou canst mutine[5] in a matron's bones,
To flaming youth let virtue be as wax
And melt in her own fire. Proclaim no shame
When the compulsive ardor gives the charge,[6]
90   Since frost itself as actively doth burn,
And reason panders[7] will.
QUEEN: O Hamlet, speak no more!
Thou turn'st my eyes into my very soul;
And there I see such black and grainéd[8] spots
As will not leave their tinct.[9]
HAMLET: Nay, but to live
95   In the rank sweat of an enseaméd[1] bed,
Stewed in curruption, honeying and making love
Over the nasty sty—
QUEEN: O, speak to me no more!
These words like daggers enter in my ears;
No more, sweet Hamlet.
HAMLET: A murderer and a villain,
100   A slave that is not twentieth part the tithe[2]
Of your precedent lord, a vice of kings,[3]

---

7. Mark of approval.   8. Feed greedily.   9. Paralyzed.   1. Power.
2. Blindman's buff. *Cozened:* cheated.   3. Without.   4. Be stupid.   5. Commit mutiny.
6. Attacks.   7. Pimps for.   8. Ingrained.   9. Lose their color.   1. Greasy.   2. One-tenth.
3. The "Vice," a common figure in the popular drama, was a clown or buffoon. *Precedent lord:* first
husband.

A cutpurse[4] of the empire and the rule,
That from a shelf the precious diadem stole
And put it in his pocket—
QUEEN: No more.   105

[*Enter* GHOST.]

HAMLET: A king of shreds and patches—
   Save me and hover o'er me with your wings,
   You heavenly guards! What would your gracious figure?
QUEEN: Alas, he's mad.
HAMLET: Do you not come your tardy[5] son to chide,   110
   That lapsed in time and passion lets go by
   Th' important acting of your dread command?
   O, say!
GHOST: Do not forget. This visitation
   Is but to whet thy almost blunted purpose.   115
   But look, amazement on thy mother sits.
   O, step between her and her fighting soul!
   Conceit[6] in weakest bodies strongest works.
   Speak to her, Hamlet.
HAMLET: How is it with you, lady?
QUEEN: Alas, how is't with you,   120
   That you do bend[7] your eye on vacancy,
   And with th' incorporal air do hold discourse?
   Forth at your eyes your spirits wildly peep,
   And as the sleeping soldiers in th' alarm,
   Your bedded hairs like life in excrements[8]   125
   Start up and stand an end. O gentle son,
   Upon the heat and flame of thy distemper
   Sprinkle cool patience. Whereon do you look?
HAMLET: On him, on him! Look you how pale he glares.
   His form and cause conjoined,[9] preaching to stones,   130
   Would make them capable.[1]—Do not look upon me,
   Lest with this piteous action you convert
   My stern effects.[2] Then what I have to do
   Will want true color—tears perchance for blood.
QUEEN: To whom do you speak this?   135
HAMLET: Do you see nothing there?
QUEEN: Nothing at all, yet all that is I see.
HAMLET: Nor did you nothing hear?
QUEEN: No, nothing but ourselves.
HAMLET: Why, look you there. Look how it steals away.   140
   My father, in his habit[3] as he lived!
   Look where he goes even now out at the portal.   [*Exit* GHOST.]

---

4. Pickpocket.   5. Slow to act.   6. Imagination.   7. Turn.   8. Nails and hair.
9. Working together.   1. Of responding.   2. Deeds.   3. Costume.

QUEEN: This is the very coinage[4] of your brain.
Ths bodiless creation ecstasy[5]
Is very cunning[6] in.
145 HAMLET: Ecstasy?
My pulse as yours doth temperately keep time,
And makes as healthful music. It is not madness
That I have uttered. Bring me to the test,
And I the matter will re-word, which madness
150 Would gambol[7] from. Mother, for love of grace,
Lay not that flattering unction[8] to your soul,
That not your trespass but my madness speaks.
It will but skin and film the ulcerous place
Whiles rank corruption, mining[9] all within,
155 Infects unseen. Confess yourself to heaven,
Repent what's past, avoid what is to come.
And do not spread the compost on the weeds,
To make them ranker. Forgive me this my virtue,
For in the fatness of these pursy[1] times
160 Virtue itself of vice must pardon beg,
Yea, curb[2] and woo for leave to do him good.
QUEEN: O Hamlet, thou hast cleft my heart in twain.
HAMLET: O, throw away the worser part of it,
And live the purer with the other half.
165 Good night—but go not to my uncle's bed.
Assume a virtue, if you have it not.
That monster custom[3] who all sense doth eat
Of habits devil, is angel yet in this,
That to the use of actions fair and good
170 He likewise gives a frock or livery
That aptly[4] is put on. Refrain tonight,
And that shall lend a kind of easiness
To the next abstinence; the next more easy;
For use almost can change the stamp of nature,
175 And either curb the devil, or throw him out
With wondrous potency. Once more, good night,
And when you are desirous to be blest,
I'll blessing beg of you. For this same lord
I do repent; but heaven hath pleased it so,
180 To punish me with this, and this with me,
That I must be their scourge and minister.
I will bestow[5] him and will answer well
The death I gave him. So, again, good night.
I must be cruel only to be kind.
185 Thus bad begins and worse remains behind.

---

4. Invention.   5. Madness.   6. Skilled.   7. Shy away.   8. Ointment.   9. Undermining.
1. Bloated.   2. Bow.   3. Habit.   4. Easily.   5. Dispose of.

One word more, good lady.
QUEEN: What shall I do?
HAMLET: Not this, by no means, that I bid you do:
Let the bloat[6] king tempt you again to bed,
Pinch wanton[7] on your cheek, call you his mouse,
And let him, for a pair of reechy[8] kisses,   190
Or paddling in your neck with his damned fingers,
Make you to ravel[9] all this matter out,
That I essentially am not in madness,
But mad in craft. 'Twere good you let him know,
For who that's but a queen, fair, sober, wise,   195
Would from a paddock, from a bat, a gib,[1]
Such dear concernings hide? Who would so do?
No, in despite of sense and secrecy,
Unpeg the basket on the house's top,
Let the birds fly, and like the famous ape,   200
To try conclusions, in the basket creep
And break your own neck down.[2]
QUEEN: Be thou assured, if words be made of breath
And breath of life, I have no life to breathe
What thou hast said to me.   205
HAMLET: I must to England; you know that?
QUEEN: Alack,
I had forgot. 'Tis so concluded on.
HAMLET: There's letters sealed, and my two school-fellows,
Whom I will trust as I will adders fanged,
They bear the mandate; they must sweep[3] my way   210
And marshal me to knavery. Let it work,
For 'tis the sport to have the enginer
Hoist with his own petard;[4] and't shall go hard
But I will delve[5] one yard below their mines
And blow them at the moon. O, 'tis most sweet   215
When in one line two crafts directly meet.
This man shall set me packing.
I'll lug the guts into the neighbor room.
Mother, good night. Indeed, this counsellor
Is now most still, most secret, and most grave,   220
Who was in life a foolish prating knave.

---

6. Bloated.   7. Lewdly.   8. Foul.   9. Reveal.   1. Tomcat. *Paddock:* toad.
2. Apparently a reference to a now-lost fable in which an ape, finding a basket containing a cage of
birds on a housetop, opens the cage. The birds fly away. The ape, thinking that if he were in the
basket he too could fly, enters, jumps out, and breaks his neck.   3. Prepare. *Mandate:* command.
4. The "enginer," or engineer, is a military man who is here described as being blown up by a bomb
of his own construction, "hoist with his own petard." The military figure continues in the succeeding
lines where Hamlet describes himself as digging a countermine or tunnel beneath the one Claudius
is digging to defeat Hamlet. In line 216 the two tunnels unexpectedly meet.   5. Dig.

Come sir, to draw toward an end with you.
Good night, mother.

> [*Exit the* QUEEN. *Then exit* HAMLET *tugging* POLONIUS.]

ACT IV
Scene 1

A room in the castle. Enter KING, QUEEN, ROSENCRANTZ *and* GUILDEN-STERN.

KING: There's matter in these sighs, these profound heaves,
  You must translate;[6] 'tis fit we understand them.
  Where is your son?
QUEEN: Bestow this place on us a little while.

> [*Exeunt* ROSENCRANTZ *and* GUILDENSTERN.]

5   Ah, mine own lord, what have I seen tonight!
KING: What, Gertrude? How does Hamlet?
QUEEN: Mad as the sea and wind when both contend
  Which is the mightier. In his lawless fit,
  Behind the arras hearing something stir,
10 Whips out his rapier, cries "A rat, a rat!"
  And in this brainish apprehension[7] kills
  The unseen good old man.
KING: O heavy deed!
  It had been so with us had we been there.
  His liberty is full of threats to all—
15 To you yourself, to us, to every one.
  Alas, how shall this bloody deed be answered?
  It will be laid to us, whose providence[8]
  Should have kept short, restrained, and out of haunt,[9]
  This mad young man. But so much was our love,
20 We would not understand what was most fit;
  But, like the owner of a foul disease,
  To keep it from divulging, let it feed
  Even on the pith of life. Where is he gone?
QUEEN: To draw apart the body he hath killed,
25 O'er whom his very madness, like some ore
  Among a mineral of metals base,
  Shows itself pure: 'a weeps for what is done.
KING: O Gertrude, come away!
  The sun no sooner shall the mountains touch
30 But we will ship him hence, and this vile deed
  We must with all our majesty and skill
  Both countenance and excuse. Ho, Guildenstern!

> [*Enter* ROSENCRANTZ *and* GUILDENSTERN.]

---

6. Explain.   7. Insane notion.   8. Prudence.   9. Away from court.

Friends both, go join you with some further aid.
Hamlet in madness hath Polonius slain,
And from his mother's closet hath he dragged him.   35
Go seek him out; speak fair, and bring the body
Into the chapel. I pray you haste in this.
                                    [*Exeunt* ROSENCRANTZ *and* GUILDENSTERN.]
Come, Gertrude, we'll call up our wisest friends
And let them know both what we mean to do
And what's untimely done;   40
Whose whisper o'er the world's diameter,
As level as the cannon to his blank,[1]
Transports his poisoned shot—may miss our name,
And hit the woundless air. O, come away!
My soul is full of discord and dismay.   [*Exeunt.*] 45

Scene 2

A passageway. Enter HAMLET.

HAMLET: Safely stowed.
ROSENCRANTZ *and* GUILDENSTERN: [*Within.*] Hamlet! Lord Hamlet!
HAMLET: But soft, what noise? Who calls on Hamlet?
    O, here they come.

[*Enter* ROSENCRANTZ, GUILDENSTERN, *and* OTHERS.]

ROSENCRANTZ: What have you done, my lord, with the dead body?   5
HAMLET: Compounded it with dust, whereto 'tis kin.
ROSENCRANTZ: Tell us where 'tis, that we may take it thence
    And bear it to the chapel.
HAMLET: Do not believe it.
ROSENCRANTZ: Believe what?   10
HAMLET: That I can keep your counsel and not mine own. Besides, to be
    demanded of a sponge—what replication[2] should be made by the son of
    a king?
ROSENCRANTZ: Take you me for a sponge, my lord?
HAMLET: Ay, sir, that soaks up the king's countenance,[3] his rewards, his   15
    authorities. But such officers do the king best service in the end. He
    keeps them like an apple in the corner of his jaw, first mouthed to be
    last swallowed. When he needs what you have gleaned, it is but squeezing
    you and, sponge, you you shall be dry again.
ROSENCRANTZ: I understand you not, my lord.   20
HAMLET: I am glad of it. A knavish speech sleeps in a foolish ear.
ROSENCRANTZ: My lord, you must tell us where the body is, and go with
    us to the king.
HAMLET: The body is with the king, but the king is not with the body.
    The king is a thing—   25

---

1. Mark. *Level:* direct.   2. Answer. *Demanded of:* questioned by.   3. Favor.

GUILDENSTERN: A thing, my lord!

HAMLET: Of nothing. Bring me to him. Hide fox, and all after.[4]   [*Exeunt.*]

Scene 3

A room in the castle. Enter KING.

KING: I have sent to seek him, and to find the body.
  How dangerous is it that this man goes loose!
  Yet must not we put the strong law on him.
  He's loved of the distracted[5] multitude,
5   Who like not in their judgment but their eyes,
  And where 'tis so, th' offender's scourge[6] is weighed,
  But never the offence. To bear all smooth and even,
  This sudden sending him away must seem
  Deliberate pause.[7] Diseases desperate grown
10   By desperate appliance are relieved,
  Or not at all.

  [*Enter* ROSENCRANTZ, GUILDENSTERN, *and all the rest.*]

           How now! what hath befall'n?

ROSENCRANTZ: Where the dead body is bestowed, my lord,
  We cannot get from him.

KING: But where is he?

ROSENCRANTZ: Without, my lord; guarded, to know[8] your pleasure.

KING: Bring him before us.

15 ROSENCRANTZ: Ho! bring in the lord.

  [*They enter with* HAMLET.]

KING: Now, Hamlet, where's Polonius?

HAMLET: At supper.

KING: At supper? Where?

HAMLET: Not where he eats, but where 'a is eaten. A certain convocation of
20   politic[9] worms are e'en at him. Your worm is your only emperor for diet.
  We fat all creatures else to fat us, and we fat ourselves for maggots. Your
  fat king and your lean beggar is but variable service—two dishes, but to
  one table. That's the end.

KING: Alas, alas!

25 HAMLET: A man may fish with the worm that hath eat of a king, and eat
  of the fish that hath fed of that worm.

KING: What dost thou mean by this?

HAMLET: Nothing but to show you how a king may go a progress through
  the guts of a beggar.

30 KING: Where is Polonius?

HAMLET: In heaven. Send thither to see. If your messenger find him not

---

4. Apparently a reference to a children's game like hide-and-seek.   5. Confused.   6. Punishment.
7. That is, not an impulse.   8. Await.   9. Statesmanlike. *Convocation:* gathering.

there, seek him i' th' other place yourself. But if, indeed, you find him
not within this month, you shall nose[1] him as you go up the stairs into
the lobby.

KING: [*To* ATTENDANTS.] Go seek him there.   35

HAMLET: 'A will stay till you come.   [*Exeunt* ATTENDANTS.]

KING: Hamlet, this deed, for thine especial safety—
   Which we do tender, as we dearly[2] grieve
   For that which thou hast done—must send thee hence
   With fiery quickness. Therefore prepare thyself.   40
   The bark is ready, and the wind at help,
   Th' associates tend, and everything is bent
   For England.

HAMLET: For England?

KING: Ay, Hamlet.

HAMLET: Good.

KING: So it is, if thou knew'st our purposes.

HAMLET: I see a cherub that sees them. But come, for England!   45
   Farewell, dear mother.

KING: Thy loving father, Hamlet.

HAMLET: My mother. Father and mother is man and wife, man and wife is
   one flesh. So, my mother. Come, for England.   [*Exit.*]

KING: Follow him at foot;[3] tempt him with speed aboard.   50
   Delay it not; I'll have him hence tonight.
   Away! for everything is sealed and done
   That else leans on th' affair. Pray you make haste.
                                              [*Exeunt all but the* KING.]
   And, England, if my love thou hold'st at aught—
   As my great power thereof may give thee sense,[4]   55
   Since yet thy cicatrice[5] looks raw and red
   After the Danish sword, and thy free awe
   Pays homage to us—thou mayst not coldly set[6]
   Our sovereign process,[7] which imports at full
   By letters congruing[8] to that effect   60
   The present death of Hamlet. Do it, England,
   For like the hectic[9] in my blood he rages,
   And thou must cure me. Till I know 'tis done,
   Howe'er my haps, my joys were ne'er begun.   [*Exit.*]

Scene 4

Near Elsinore. Enter FORTINBRAS *with his army.*

FORTINBRAS: Go, captain, from me greet the Danish king.
   Tell him that by his license Fortinbras

---

1. Smell.   2. Deeply. *Tender:* consider.   3. Closely.   4. Of its value.   5. Wound scar.
6. Set aside.   7. Mandate.   8. Agreeing.   9. Chronic fever.

Craves the conveyance[1] of a promised march
Over his kingdom. You know the rendezvous.
5   If that his majesty would aught with us,
We shall express our duty in his eye,[2]
And let him know so.
CAPTAIN: I will do't, my lord.
FORTINBRAS: Go softly on.   [*Exeunt all but the* CAPTAIN.]

[*Enter* HAMLET, ROSENCRANTZ, GUILDENSTERN, *and* OTHERS.]

HAMLET: Good sir, whose powers are these?
10 CAPTAIN: They are of Norway, sir.
HAMLET: How purposed, sir, I pray you?
CAPTAIN: Against some part of Poland.
HAMLET: Who commands them, sir?
CAPTAIN: The nephew to old Norway, Fortinbras.
15 HAMLET: Goes it against the main[3] of Poland, sir,
Or for some frontier?
CAPTAIN: Truly to speak, and with no addition,[4]
We go to gain a little patch of ground
That hath in it no profit but the name.
20   To pay five ducats,[5] five, I would not farm it;
Nor will it yield to Norway or the Pole
A ranker rate should it be sold in fee.[6]
HAMLET: Why, then the Polack never will defend it.
CAPTAIN: Yes, it is already garrisoned.
25 HAMLET: Two thousand souls and twenty thousand ducats
Will not debate the question of this straw.
This is th' imposthume[7] of much wealth and peace,
That inward breaks, and shows no cause without
Why the man dies. I humbly thank you, sir.
CAPTAIN: God b'wi'ye, sir.   [*Exit.*]
30 ROSENCRANTZ: Will't please you go, my lord?
HAMLET: I'll be with you straight. Go a little before.
[*Exeunt all but* HAMLET.]
How all occasions do inform against me,
And spur my dull revenge! What is a man,
If his chief good and market[8] of his time
35   Be but to sleep and feed? A beast, no more.
Sure he that made us with such large discourse,[9]
Looking before and after, gave us not
That capability and godlike reason
To fust[1] in us unused. Now, whether it be
40   Bestial oblivion, or some craven scruple

---

1. Escort.   2. Presence.   3. Central part.   4. Exaggeration.   5. That is, in rent.
6. Outright. *Ranker:* higher.   7. Abscess.   8. Occupation.   9. Ample reasoning power.
1. Grow musty.

Of thinking too precisely on th' event[2]—
A thought which, quartered, hath but one part wisdom
And ever three parts coward—I do not know
Why yet I live to say "This thing's to do,"
Sith[3] I have cause, and will, and strength, and means,   45
To do't. Examples gross as earth exhort me.
Witness this army of such mass and charge,[4]
Led by a delicate and tender prince,
Whose spirit, with divine ambition puffed,
Makes mouths at[5] the invisible event,   50
Exposing what is mortal and unsure
To all that fortune, death, and danger dare,
Even for an eggshell. Rightly to be great
Is not to stir without great argument,
But greatly to find quarrel in a straw   55
When honor's at the stake. How stand I then,
That have a father killed, a mother stained,
Excitements of my reason and my blood,
And let all sleep, while to my shame I see
The imminent death of twenty thousand men   60
That for a fantasy and trick of fame
Go to their graves like beds, fight for a plot
Whereon the numbers cannot try the cause,
Which is not tomb enough and continent
To hide the slain?[6] O, from this time forth,   65
My thoughts be bloody, or be nothing worth!   [*Exit.*]

Scene 5

A room in the castle. Enter QUEEN, HORATIO *and a* GENTLEMAN.

QUEEN: I will not speak with her.
GENTLEMAN: She is importunate, indeed distract.
    Her mood will needs to be pitied.
QUEEN: What would she have?
GENTLEMAN: She speaks much of her father, says she hears
    There's tricks i' th' world, and hems, and beats her heart,   5
    Spurns enviously at straws,[7] speaks things in doubt
    That carry but half sense. Her speech is nothing,
    Yet the unshapéd use of it doth move
    The hearers to collection;[8] they yawn at it,
    And botch the words up fit to their own thoughts,   10
    Which, as her winks and nods and gestures yield them,

2. Outcome.   3. Since.   4. Expense.   5. Scorns.
6. The plot of ground involved is so small that it cannot contain the number of men involved in
fighting or furnish burial space for the number of those who will die.   7. Takes offense at trifles.
8. An attempt to order.

Indeed would make one think there might be thought,
Though nothing sure, yet much unhappily.
HORATIO: 'Twere good she were spoken with, for she may strew
15   Dangerous conjectures in ill-breeding minds.
QUEEN: Let her come in.   [*Exit* GENTLEMAN.]
        [*Aside.*] To my sick soul, as sin's true nature is,
        Each toy seems prologue to some great amiss.[9]
        So full of artless jealousy is guilt,
20   It spills itself in fearing to be spilt.

                    [*Enter* OPHELIA *distracted.*]

OPHELIA: Where is the beauteous majesty of Denmark?
QUEEN: How now, Ophelia!
OPHELIA:

            [*Sings.*]

        How should I your true love know
            From another one?
25   By his cockle hat and staff,[1]
            And his sandal shoon.[2]

QUEEN: Alas, sweet lady, what imports this song?
OPHELIA: Say you? Nay, pray you mark.

            [*Sings.*]

        He is dead and gone, lady,
30   He is dead and gone;
        At his head a grass-green turf,
            At his heels a stone.

    O, ho!
QUEEN: Nay, but Ophelia—
OPHELIA: Pray you mark.

            [*Sings.*]

        White his shroud as the mountain snow—

            [*Enter* KING.]

35 QUEEN: Alas, look here, my lord.
OPHELIA:

            [*Sings.*]

---

9. Catastrophe. *Toy:* trifle.
1. A cockle hat, one decorated with a shell, indicated that the wearer had made a pilgrimage to the shrine of St. James at Compostela in Spain. The staff also marked the carrier as a pilgrim.
2. Shoes.

Larded all with sweet flowers;
Which bewept to the grave did not go
    With true-love showers.

KING: How do you, pretty lady?

OPHELIA: Well, God dild³ you! They say the owl was a baker's daughter. 40
Lord, we know what we are, but know not what we may be. God be at
your table!

KING: Conceit⁴ upon her father.

OPHELIA: Pray let's have no words of this, but when they ask you what it
means, say you this: 45

[*Sings.*]

Tomorrow is Saint Valentine's day,
    All in the morning betime,
And I a maid at your window,
    To be your Valentine.

Then up he rose, and donn'd his clo'es, 50
    And dupped⁵ the chamber-door,
Let in the maid, that out a maid
    Never departed more.

KING: Pretty Ophelia!

OPHELIA: Indeed, without an oath, I'll make an end on't. 55

[*Sings.*]

By Gis⁶ and by Saint Charity,
    Alack, and fie for shame!
Young men will do't, if they come to't;
    By Cock,⁷ they are to blame.
Quoth she "before you tumbled me, 60
    You promised me to wed."

He answers:

"So would I'a done, by yonder sun,
An thou hadst not come to my bed."

KING: How long hath she been thus? 65

OPHELIA: I hope all will be well. We must be patient, but I cannot choose
but weep to think they would lay him i' th' cold ground. My brother
shall know of it, and so I thank you for your good counsel. Come, my
coach! Good night, ladies, good night. Sweet ladies, good night, good
night. [*Exit.*] 70

KING: Follow her close; give her good watch, I pray you.
                [*Exeunt* HORATIO *and* GENTLEMAN.]
O, this is the poison of deep grief; it springs

---

3. Yield. 4. Thought. 5. Opened. 6. Jesus. 7. God.

All from her father's death, and now behold!
O Gertrude, Gertrude!
75   When sorrows come, they come not single spies,
But in battalions: first, her father slain;
Next, your son gone, and he most violent author
Of his own just remove; the people muddied,[8]
Thick and unwholesome in their thoughts and whispers
80   For good Polonius' death; and we have done but greenly[9]
In hugger-mugger[1] to inter him; poor Ophelia
Divided from herself and her fair judgment,
Without the which we are pictures, or mere beasts;
Last, and as much containing as all these,
85   Her brother is in secret come from France,
Feeds on his wonder, keeps himself in clouds,
And wants not buzzers to infect his ear
With pestilent speeches of his father's death,
Wherein necessity, of matter beggared,[2]
90   Will nothing stick our person to arraign[3]
In ear and ear.[4] O my dear Gertrude, this,
Like to a murd'ring piece,[5] in many places
Gives me superfluous death.   [A noise within.]
QUEEN: Alack, what noise is this?
95 KING: Attend!
Where are my Switzers?[6] Let them guard the door.
What is the matter?
MESSENGER: Save yourself, my lord.
The ocean, overpeering of his list,[7]
Eats not the flats with more impiteous[8] haste
100   Than young Laertes, in a riotous head,[9]
O'erbears your officers. The rabble call him lord,
And as the world were now but to begin,
Antiquity forgot, custom not known,
The ratifiers and props of every word,
105   They cry "Choose we, Laertes shall be king."
Caps, hands, and tongues, applaud it to the clouds,
"Laertes shall be king, Laertes king."
QUEEN: How cheerfully on the false trail they cry![1]

[A noise within.]

O, this is counter,[2] you false Danish dogs!
110 KING: The doors are broke.

---

8. Disturbed.   9. Without judgment.   1. Haste.   2. Short on facts.   3. Accuse. *Stick:* hesitate.
4. From both sides.   5. A weapon designed to scatter its shot.   6. Swiss guards.
7. Towering above its limits.   8. Pitiless.   9. With an armed band.   1. As if following the scent.
2. Backward.

[*Enter* LAERTES, *with* OTHERS.]

LAERTES: Where is this king?—Sirs, stand you all without.

ALL: No, let's come in.

LAERTES: I pray you give me leave.

ALL: We will, we will.

LAERTES: I thank you. Keep[3] the door.   [*Exeunt his followers.*]
              O thou vile king,
    Give me my father!

QUEEN: Calmly, good Laertes.   115

LAERTES: That drop of blood that's calm proclaims me bastard,
    Cries cuckold to my father, brands the harlot
    Even here between the chaste unsmirchéd brow
    Of my true mother.

KING: What is the cause, Laertes,
    That thy rebellion looks so giant-like?   120
    Let him go, Gertrude. Do not fear[4] our person.
    There's such divinity doth hedge a king
    That treason can but peep to[5] what it would,
    Acts little of his will. Tell me, Laertes,
    Why thou art thus incensed. Let him go, Gertrude.   125
    Speak, man.

LAERTES: Where is my father?

KING: Dead.

QUEEN: But not by him.

KING: Let him demand[6] his fill.

LAERTES: How came he dead? I'll not be juggled with.
    To hell allegiance, vows to the blackest devil,
    Conscience and grace to the profoundest pit!   130
    I dare damnation. To this point I stand,
    That both the worlds I give to negligence,[7]
    Let come what comes, only I'll be revenged
    Most throughly for my father.

KING: Who shall stay you?

LAERTES: My will, not all the world's.   135
    And for my means, I'll husband[8] them so well
    They shall go far with little.

KING: Good Laertes,
    If you desire to know the certainty
    Of your dear father, is't writ in your revenge
    That, swoopstake,[9] you will draw both friend and foe,   140
    Winner and loser?

LAERTES: None but his enemies.

KING: Will you know them, then?

---

3. Guard.   4. Fear for.   5. Look at over or through a barrier.   6. Question.
7. Disregard. *Both the worlds:* that is, this and the next.   8. Manage.   9. Sweeping the board.

LAERTES: To his good friends thus wide I'll ope my arms,
    And like the kind life-rend'ring pelican,[1]
    Repast them with my blood.
145 KING: Why, now you speak
    Like a good child and a true gentleman.
    That I am guiltless of your father's death,
    And am most sensibly in grief for it,
    It shall as level[2] to your judgment 'pear
150 As day does to your eye.

        [A noise within: "Let her come in."]

LAERTES: How now? What noise is that?

        [Enter OPHELIA.]

    O, heat dry up my brains! tears seven times salt
    Burn out the sense and virtue[3] of mine eye!
    By heaven, thy madness shall be paid with weight
155 Till our scale turn the beam. O rose of May,
    Dear maid, kind sister, sweet Ophelia!
    O heavens! is't possible a young maid's wits
    Should be as mortal as an old man's life?
    Nature is fine[4] in love, and where 'tis fine
160 It sends some precious instances of itself
    After the thing it loves.[5]
OPHELIA:

        [Sings.]

    They bore him barefac'd on the bier;
      Hey non nonny, nonny, hey nonny;
    And in his grave rain'd many a tear—

165 Fare you well, my dove!
LAERTES: Hadst thou thy wits, and didst persuade revenge,
    It could not move thus.
OPHELIA: You must sing "A-down, a-down, and you call him a-down-a." O,
    how the wheel becomes it! It is the false steward, that stole his master's
170 daughter.[6]
LAERTES: This nothing's more than matter.

---

1. The pelican was believed to feed her young with her own blood.   2. Plain.
3. Function. *Sense:* feeling.   4. Refined.
5. Laertes means that Ophelia, because of her love for her father, gave up her sanity as a token of
grief at his death.
6. The "wheel" refers to the "burden" or refrain of a song, in this case "A-down, a-down, and you
call him a-down-a." The ballad to which she refers was about a false steward. Others have suggested
that the "wheel" is the Wheel of Fortune, a spinning wheel to whose rhythm such a song might
have been sung or a kind of dance movement performed by Ophelia as she sings.

OPHELIA: There's a rosemary, that's for remembrance. Pray you, love, remember And there is pansies, that's for thoughts.

LAERTES: A document[7] in madness, thoughts and remembrance fitted.

OPHELIA: There's fennel for you, and columbines. There's rue for you, and 175 here's some for me. We may call it herb of grace a Sundays. O, you must wear your rue with a difference. There's a daisy. I would give you some violets, but they withered all when my father died. They say 'a made a good end.

[*Sings.*]

For bonny sweet Robin is all my joy. 180

LAERTES: Thought and affliction, passion, hell itself,
She turns to favor[8] and to prettiness.

OPHELIA:

[*Sings.*]

And will 'a not come again?
And will 'a not come again?
No, no, he is dead, 185
Go to thy death-bed,
He never will come again.

His beard was as white as snow,
All flaxen was his poll;[9]
He is gone, he is gone, 190
And we cast away moan:
God-a-mercy on his soul!

And of all Christian souls, I pray God. God b'wi'you. [*Exit.*]

LAERTES: Do you see this, O God?

KING: Laertes, I must commune with your grief, 195
Or you deny me right. Go but apart,
Make choice of whom your wisest friends you will,
And they shall hear and judge 'twixt you and me.
If by direct or by collateral[1] hand
They find us touched,[2] we will our kingdom give, 200
Our crown, our life, and all that we call ours,
To you in satisfaction; but if not,
Be you content to lend your patience to us,
And we shall jointly labor with your soul
To give it due content.

LAERTES: Let this be so. 205
His means of death, his obscure funeral—
No trophy, sword, nor hatchment,[3] o'er his bones,
No noble rite nor formal ostentation[4]—

---

7. Lesson.   8. Beauty.   9. Head.   1. Indirect.   2. By guilt.   3. Coat of arms.   4. Pomp.

Cry to be heard, as 'twere from heaven to earth,
That I must call't in question.

210   KING: So you shall;
And where th' offence is, let the great axe fall.
I pray you go with me.   [*Exeunt.*]

Scene 6

Another room in the castle. Enter HORATIO *and a* GENTLEMAN.

HORATIO: What are they that would speak with me?
GENTLEMAN: Sea-faring men, sir. They say they have letters for you.
HORATIO: Let them come in.   [*Exit* GENTLEMAN.]
I do not know from what part of the world
5   I should be greeted, if not from Lord Hamlet.

[*Enter* SAILORS.]

SAILOR: God bless you, sir.
HORATIO: Let him bless thee too.
SAILOR: 'A shall, sir, an't please him. There's a letter for you, sir—it came
from th' ambassador that was bound for England—if your name be
10   Horatio, as I am let to know[5] it is.
HORATIO: [*Reads.*] "Horatio, when thou shalt have overlooked[6] this, give
these fellows some means[7] to the king. They have letters for him. Ere
we were two days old at sea, a pirate of very warlike appointment[8] gave
us chase. Finding ourselves too slow of sail, we put on a compelled valor,
15   and in the grapple I boarded them. On the instant they got clear of our
ship, so I alone became their prisoner. They have dealt with me like
thieves of mercy, but they knew what they did; I am to do a good turn
for them. Let the king have the letters I have sent, and repair thou to
me with as much speed as thou wouldest fly death. I have words to
20   speak in thine ear will make thee dumb; yet are they much too light for
the bore of the matter.[9] These good fellows will bring thee where I am.
Rosencrantz and Guildenstern hold their course for England. Of them
I have much to tell thee. Farewell.

He that thou knowest thine, Hamlet."
Come, I will give you way[1] for these your letters,
25   And do't the speedier that you may direct me
To him from whom you brought them.   [*Exeunt.*]

Scene 7

Another room in the castle. Enter KING *and* LAERTES.

KING: Now must your conscience my acquittance seal,[2]
And you must put me in your heart for friend,

---

5. Informed.   6. Read through.   7. Access.   8. Equipment.
9. A figure from gunnery, referring to shot that is too small for the size of the weapons to be fired.
1. Means of delivery.   2. Grant me innocent.

Sith you have heard, and with a knowing ear,
That he which hath your noble father slain
Pursued my life.
LAERTES: It well appears. But tell me   5
Why you proceeded not against these feats,
So criminal and so capital in nature,
As by your safety, greatness, wisdom, all things else,
You mainly were stirred up.
KING: O, for two special reasons,
Which may to you, perhaps, seem much unsinewed,[3]   10
But yet to me th' are strong. The queen his mother
Lives almost by his looks, and for myself—
My virtue or my plague, be it either which—
She is so conjunctive[4] to my life and soul
That, as the star moves not but in his sphere,[5]   15
I could not but by her. The other motive,
Why to a public count[6] I might not go,
Is the great love the general gender[7] bear him,
Who, dipping all his faults in their affection,
Work like the spring that turneth wood to stone,[8]   20
Convert his gyves[9] to graces; so that my arrows,
Too slightly timbered[1] for so loud a wind,
Would have reverted to my bow again,
But not where I had aimed them.
LAERTES: And so have I a noble father lost,   25
A sister driven into desp'rate terms,
Whose worth, if praises may go back again,
Stood challenger on mount of all the age
For her perfections. But my revenge will come.
KING: Break not your sleeps for that. You must not think   30
That we are made of stuff so flat and dull
That we can let our beard be shook with danger,
And think it pastime. You shortly shall hear more.
I loved you father, and we love our self,
And that, I hope, will teach you to imagine—   35

[*Enter a* MESSENGER *with letters.*]

How now? What news?
MESSENGER: Letters, my lord, from Hamlet.
These to your majesty; this to the queen.
KING: From Hamlet! Who brought them?

---

3. Weak.   4. Closely joined.
5. A reference to the Ptolemaic cosmology, in which planets and stars were believed to revolve in crystalline spheres concentrically about the Earth.   6. Reckoning.   7. Common people.
8. Certain English springs contain so much lime that a lime covering will be deposited on a log placed in one of them for a length of time.   9. Fetters.   1. Shafted.

MESSENGER: Sailors, my lord, they say. I saw them not.
40   They were given me by Claudio; he received them
      Of him that brought them.
      KING: Laertes, you shall hear them.—
      Leave us.   [*Exit* MESSENGER.]
          [*Reads.*] "High and mighty, you shall know I am set naked on your
      kingdom. Tomorrow shall I beg leave to see your kingly eyes; when I
      shall, first asking your pardon thereunto, recount the occasion of my
45   sudden and more strange return.
                                              Hamlet."
      What should this mean? Are all the rest come back?
      Or is it some abuse,[2] and no such thing?
      LAERTES: Know you the hand?
50   KING: 'Tis Hamlet's character.[3] "Naked"!
      And in a postscript here, he says "alone."
      Can you devise[4] me?
      LAERTES: I am lost in it, my lord. But let him come.
      It warms the very sickness in my heart
55   That I shall live and tell him to his teeth
      "Thus didest thou."
      KING: If it be so, Laertes—
      As how should it be so, how otherwise?—
      Will you be ruled by me?
      LAERTES: Ay, my lord,
      So you will not o'errule me to a peace.
60   KING: To thine own peace. If he be now returned,
      As checking at[5] his voyage, and that he means
      No more to undertake it, I will work him
      To an exploit now ripe in my device,
      Under the which he shall not choose but fall;
65   And for his death no wind of blame shall breathe
      But even his mother shall uncharge[6] the practice
      And call it accident.
      LAERTES: My lord, I will be ruled;
      The rather if you could devise it so
      That I might be the organ.[7]
      KING: It falls right.
70   You have been talked of since your travel much,
      And that in Hamlet's hearing, for a quality
      Wherein they say you shine. Your sum of parts
      Did not together pluck such envy from him
      As did that one, and that, in my regard,
      Of the unworthiest siege.[8]
75 LAERTES: What part is that, my lord?

---

2. Trick.   3. Handwriting.   4. Explain it to.   5. Turning aside from.   6. Not accuse.
7. Instrument.   8. Rank.

KING: A very riband in the cap of youth,
    Yet needful too, for youth no less becomes
    The light and careless livery that it wears
    Than settled age his sables and his weeds,[9]
    Importing health and graveness. Two months since   80
    Here was a gentleman of Normandy.
    I have seen myself, and served against, the French,
    And they can[1] well on horseback, but this gallant
    Had witchcraft in't. He grew unto his seat,
    And to such wondrous doing brought his horse,   85
    As had he been incorpsed and demi-natured
    With the brave beast. So far he topped my thought
    That I, in forgery[2] of shapes and tricks,
    Come short of what he did.[3]
LAERTES: A Norman was't?
KING: A Norman.   90
LAERTES: Upon my life, Lamord.
KING: The very same.
LAERTES: I know him well. He is the brooch indeed
    And gem of all the nation.
KING: He made confession[4] of you,
    And gave you such a masterly report   95
    For art and exercise in your defence,[5]
    And for your rapier most especial,
    That he cried out 'twould be a sight indeed
    If one could match you. The scrimers[6] of their nation
    He swore had neither motion, guard, nor eye,   100
    If you opposed them. Sir, this report of his
    Did Hamlet so envenom with his envy
    That he could nothing do but wish and beg
    Your sudden coming o'er, to play with you.
    Now out of this—
LAERTES: What out of this, my lord?   105
KING: Laertes, was your father dear to you?
    Or are you like the painting of a sorrow,
    A face without a heart?
LAERTES: Why ask you this?
KING: Not that I think you did not love your father,
    But that I know love is begun by time,   110
    And that I see in passages of proof,[7]

---

9. Dignified clothing.   1. Perform.   2. Imagination.
3. The gentleman referred to was so skilled in horsemanship that he seemed to share one body with the horse, "incorpsed." The king further extends the compliment by saying that he appeared like the mythical centaur, a creature who was man from the waist up and horse from the waist down, therefore "demi-natured."   4. Gave a report.   5. Skill in fencing.   6. Fencers.
7. Tests of experience.

Time qualifies the spark and fire of it.
There lives within the very flame of love
A kind of wick or snuff that will abate it,
115   And nothing is at a like goodness still,
For goodness, growing to a plurisy,[8]
Dies in his own too much.[9] That we would do,
We should do when we would; for this "would" changes,
And hath abatements and delays as many
120   As there are tongues, are hands, are accidents,
And then this "should" is like a spendthrift's sigh
That hurts by easing. But to the quick of th' ulcer—
Hamlet comes back; what would you undertake
To show yourself in deed your father's son
More than in words?
125 LAERTES: To cut his throat i' th' church.
KING: No place indeed should murder sanctuarize;[1]
Revenge should have no bounds. But, good Laertes,
Will you do this? Keep close within your chamber.
Hamlet returned shall know you are come home.
130   We'll put on those shall praise your excellence,
And set a double varnish[2] on the fame
The Frenchman gave you, bring you in fine[3] together,
And wager on your heads. He, being remiss,[4]
Most generous, and free from all contriving,
135   Will not peruse[5] the foils, so that with ease,
Or with a little shuffling, you may choose
A sword unbated,[6] and in a pass of practice
Requite him for your father.
LAERTES: I will do't,
And for that purpose I'll anoint my sword.
140   I bought an unction of a mountebank
So mortal that but dip a knife in it,
Where it draws blood no cataplasm[7] so rare,
Collected from all simples[8] that have virtue
Under the moon, can save the thing from death
145   That is but scratched withal. I'll touch my point
With this contagion, that if I gall[9] him slightly,
It may be death.
KING: Let's further think of this,
Weigh what convenience both of time and means
May fit us to our shape. If this should fail,
150   And that our drift look[1] through our bad performance,
'Twere better not assayed. Therefore this project

---

8. Fullness.   9. Excess.   1. Provide sanctuary for murder.   2. Gloss.   3. In short.
4. Careless.   5. Examine.   6. Not blunted.   7. Poultice.   8. Herbs.   9. Scratch.
1. Intent become obvious.

Should have a back or second that might hold
If this did blast in proof.[2] Soft, let me see.
We'll make a solemn wager on your cunnings—
I ha't.   155
When in your motion you are hot and dry—
As make your bouts more violent to that end—
And that he calls for drink, I'll have prepared him
A chalice for the nonce, whereon but sipping,
If he by chance escape your venomed stuck,[3]   160
Our purpose may hold there.—But stay, what noise?

    [*Enter* QUEEN.]

QUEEN: One woe doth tread upon another's heel,
  So fast they follow. Your sister's drowned, Laertes.
LAERTES: Drowned? O, where?
QUEEN: There is a willow grows aslant the brook   165
  That shows his hoar leaves in the glassy stream.
  Therewith fantastic garlands did she make
  Of crowflowers, nettles, daisies, and long purples
  That liberal shepherds give a grosser[4] name,
  But our cold[5] maids do dead men's fingers call them.   170
  There on the pendent boughs her coronet weeds
  Clamb'ring to hang, an envious[6] sliver broke,
  When down her weedy trophies and herself
  Fell in the weeping brook. Her clothes spread wide,
  And mermaid-like awhile they bore her up,   175
  Which time she chanted snatches of old tunes,
  As one incapable[7] of her own distress,
  Or like a creature native and indued[8]
  Unto that element. But long it could not be
  Till that her garments, heavy with their drink,   180
  Pulled the poor wretch from her melodious lay
  To muddy death.
LAERTES: Alas, then she is drowned?
QUEEN: Drowned, drowned.
LAERTES: Too much of water hast thou, poor Ophelia,
  And therefore I forbid my tears; but yet   185
  It is our trick; nature her custom holds,
  Let shame say what it will. When these are gone,
  The woman will be out. Adieu, my lord.
  I have a speech o' fire that fain would blaze
  But that this folly drowns it.   [*Exit.*]
KING: Let's follow, Gertrude.   190
  How much I had to do to calm his rage!

---

2. Fail when tried.   3. Thrust.   4. Coarser. *Liberal:* vulgar.   5. Chaste.   6. Malicious.
7. Unaware.   8. Habituated.

Now fear I this will give it start again;
Therefore let's follow.   [*Exeunt.*]

ACT V
Scene 1

A churchyard. Enter two CLOWNS.[9]

CLOWN: Is she to be buried in Christian burial when she wilfully seeks her
     own salvation?
OTHER: I tell thee she is. Therefore make her grave straight. The crowner
     hath sat on her,[1] and finds it Christian burial.
5 CLOWN: How can that be, unless she drowned herself in her own defence?
OTHER: Why, 'tis found so.
CLOWN: It must be "se offendendo";[2] it cannot be else. For here lies the
     point: if I drown myself wittingly, it argues an act, and an act hath three
     branches—it is to act, to do, to perform; argal,[3] she drowned herself
10   wittingly.
OTHER: Nay, but hear you, Goodman Delver.
CLOWN: Give me leave. Here lies the water; good. Here stands the man;
     good. If the man go to this water and drown himself, it is, will he, nill
     he, he goes—mark you that. But if the water come to him and drown
15   him, he drowns not himself. Argal, he that is not guilty of his own death
     shortens not his own life.
OTHER: But is this law?
CLOWN: Ay, marry, is't; crowner's quest[4] law.
OTHER: Will you ha' the truth on't? If this had not been a gentlewoman,
20   she should have been buried out o' Christian burial.
CLOWN: Why, there thou say'st. And the more pity that great folk should
     have count'nance[5] in this world to drown or hang themselves more
     than their even-Christen.[6] Come, my spade. There is no ancient gentle-
     men but gard'ners, ditchers, and grave-makers. They hold up Adam's
     profession.
25 OTHER: Was he a gentleman?
CLOWN: 'A was the first that ever bore arms.
OTHER: Why, he had none.
CLOWN: What, art a heathen? How dost thou understand the Scripture?
     The Scripture says Adam digged. Could he dig without arms? I'll put
30   another question to thee. If thou answerest me not to the purpose,
     confess thyself—
OTHER: Go to.
CLOWN: What is he that builds stronger than either the mason, the ship-
     wright, or the carpenter?
35 OTHER: The gallows-maker, for that frame outlives a thousand tenants.

---

9. Rustics.   1. Held an inquest. *Crowner:* coroner.   2. An error for *se defendendo,* in self-defense.
3. Therefore.   4. Inquest.   5. Approval.   6. Fellow Christians.

CLOWN: I like thy wit well, in good faith. The gallows does well. But how does it well? It does well to those that do ill. Now thou dost ill to say the gallows is built stronger than the church. Argal, the gallows may do well to thee. To't again,[7] come.

OTHER: Who builds stronger than a mason, a shipwright, or a carpenter? 40

CLOWN: Ay tell me that, and unyoke.[8]

OTHER: Marry, now I can tell.

CLOWN: To't.

OTHER: Mass, I cannot tell.

CLOWN: Cudgel thy brains no more about it, for your dull ass will not 45
mend his pace with beating. And when you are asked this question next,
say "a grave maker." The houses he makes lasts till doomsday. Go, get
thee in, and fetch me a stoup[9] of liquor.   [*Exit* OTHER CLOWN.]

    [*Enter* HAMLET *and* HORATIO *as* CLOWN *digs and sings.*]

   In youth, when I did love, did love,
     Methought it was very sweet,   50
   To contract the time for-a my behove,[1]
     O, methought there-a was nothing-a meet.[2]

HAMLET: Has this fellow no feeling of his business, that 'a sings in grave-
making?

HORATIO: Custom hath made it in him a property of easiness.   55

HAMLET: 'Tis e'en so. The hand of little employment hath the daintier sense.

CLOWN:

    [*Sings.*]

   But age, with his stealing steps,
     Hath clawed me in his clutch,
   And hath shipped me into the land,
     As if I had never been such.   60

    [*Throws up a skull.*]

HAMLET: That skull had a tongue in it, and could sing once. How the knave
jowls[3] it to the ground, as if 'twere Cain's jawbone, that did the first
murder! This might be the pate of a politician, which this ass now
o'erreaches;[4] one that would circumvent God, might it not?

HORATIO: It might, my lord.   65

HAMLET: Or of a courtier, which could say, "Good morrow, sweet lord!
How does thou, sweet lord?" This might be my Lord Such-a-one, that
praised my Lord Such-a-one's horse, when 'a meant to beg it, might it
not?

HORATIO: Ay, my lord.   70

---

7. Guess again.   8. Finish the matter.   9. Mug.   1. Advantage. *Contract:* shorten.
2. The gravedigger's song is a free version of "The aged lover renounceth love" by Thomas, Lord
Vaux, published in *Tottel's Miscellany,* 1557.   3. Hurls.   4. Gets the better of.

HAMLET: Why, e'en so, and now my Lady Worm's, chapless,[5] and knock'd
about the mazzard[6] with a sexton's spade. Here's fine revolution,[7] an we
had the trick to see't. Did these bones cost no more the breeding but
to play at loggets with them?[8] Mine ache to think on't.

CLOWN:

[*Sings.*]

75   A pick-axe and a spade, a spade,
           For and a shrouding sheet:
       O, a pit of clay for to be made
           For such a guest is meet.

[*Throws up another skull.*]

HAMLET: There's another. Why may not that be the skull of a lawyer? Where
80   be his quiddities now, his quillets, his cases, his tenures, and his tricks?
     Why does he suffer this mad knave now to knock him about the sconce[9]
     with a dirty shovel, and will not tell him of his action of battery? Hum!
     This fellow might be in's time a great buyer of land, with his statutes,
     his recognizances, his fines, his double vouchers, his recoveries. Is this
85   the fine[1] his fines, and the recovery of his recoveries, to have his fine
     pate full of fine dirt? Will his vouchers vouch him no more of his pur-
     chases, and double ones too, than the length and breadth of a pair of
     indentures?[2] The very conveyances of his lands will scarcely lie in this
     box, and must th' inheritor himself have no more, ha?[3]
90   HORATIO: Not a jot more, my lord.
     HAMLET: Is not parchment made of sheepskins?
     HORATIO: Ay, my lord, and of calves' skins too.
     HAMLET: They are sheep and calves which seek out assurance in that. I will
     speak to this fellow. Whose grave's this, sirrah?
95   CLOWN: Mine, sir.

[*Sings.*]

       O, a pit of clay for to be made
           For such a guest is meet.

HAMLET: I think it be thine indeed, for thou liest in't.
CLOWN: You lie out on't, sir, and therefore 'tis not yours. For my part, I do
100 not lie in't, yet it is mine.
     HAMLET: Thou dost lie in't, to be in't and say it is thine. 'Tis for the dead,
     not for the quick;[4] therefore thou liest.
     CLOWN: 'Tis a quick lie, sir; 'twill away again from me to you.
     HAMLET: What man dost thou dig it for?

---

5. Lacking a lower jaw.   6. Head.   7. Skill.
8. "Loggets" were small pieces of wood thrown as part of a game.   9. Head.   1. End.
2. Contracts.
3. In this speech Hamlet reels off a list of legal terms relating to property transactions.   4. Living.

CLOWN: For no man, sir.   105
HAMLET: What woman, then?
CLOWN: For none neither.
HAMLET: Who is to be buried in't?
CLOWN: One that was a woman, sir; but, rest her soul, she's dead.
HAMLET: How absolute the knave is! We must speak by the card,[5] or equiv- 110
   ocation will undo us. By the Lord, Horatio, this three years I have took
   note of it, the age is grown so picked[6] that the toe of the peasant comes
   so near the heel of the courtier, he galls his kibe.[7] How long hast thou
   been a grave-maker?
CLOWN: Of all the days i' th' year, I came to't that day that our last King 115
   Hamlet overcame Fortinbras.
HAMLET: How long is that since?
CLOWN: Cannot you tell that? Every fool can tell that. It was that very day
   that young Hamlet was born—he that is mad, and sent into England.
HAMLET: Ay, marry, why was he sent into England?   120
CLOWN: Why, because 'a was mad. 'A shall recover his wits there; or, if 'a
   do not, 'tis no great matter there.
HAMLET: Why?
CLOWN: 'Twill not be seen in him there. There the men are as mad as he.
HAMLET: How came he mad?   125
CLOWN: Very strangely, they say.
HAMLET: How strangely?
CLOWN: Faith, e'en with losing his wits.
HAMLET: Upon what ground?
CLOWN: Why, here in Denmark. I have been sexton here, man and boy, 130
   thirty years.
HAMLET: How long will a man lie i' th' earth ere he rot?
CLOWN: Faith, if 'a be not rotten before 'a die—as we have many pocky[8]
   corses now-a-days that will scarce hold the laying in—'a will last you
   some eight year or nine year. A tanner will last you nine year.   135
HAMLET: Why he more than another?
CLOWN: Why, sir, his hide is so tanned with his trade that 'a will keep out
   water a great while; and your water is a sore decayer of your whoreson
   dead body. Here's a skull now hath lien[9] you i' th' earth three and twenty
   years.   140
HAMLET: Whose was it?
CLOWN: A whoreson mad fellow's it was. Whose do you think it was?
HAMLET: Nay, I know not.
CLOWN: A pestilence on him for a mad rogue! 'A poured a flagon of Rhenish
   on my head once. This same skull, sir, was, sir, Yorick's skull, the king's 145
   jester.
HAMLET: [*Takes the skull.*] This?
CLOWN: E'en that.

5. Exactly. *Absolute:* precise.   6. Refined.   7. Rubs a blister on his heel.
8. Corrupted by syphilis.   9. Lain. *Whoreson:* bastard (not literally).

HAMLET: Alas, poor Yorick! I knew him, Horatio—a fellow of infinite jest,
150   of most excellent fancy. He hath bore me on his back a thousand times,
and now how abhorred in my imagination it is! My gorge[1] rises at it.
Here hung those lips that I have kissed I know not how oft. Where be
your gibes now, your gambols, your songs, your flashes of merriment
that were wont to set the table on a roar? Not one now to mock your
155   own grinning? Quite chap-fall'n?[2] Now get you to my lady's chamber,
and tell her, let her paint an inch thick, to this favor[3] she must come.
Make her laugh at that. Prithee, Horatio, tell me one thing.
HORATIO: What's that, my lord?
HAMLET: Dost thou think Alexander looked o' this fashion i' th' earth?
160 HORATIO: E'en so.
HAMLET: And smelt so? Pah!   [*Throws down the skull.*]
HORATIO: E'en so, my lord.
HAMLET: To what base uses we may return, Horatio! Why may not imagi-
nation trace the noble dust of Alexander till 'a find it stopping a bung-
165   hole?
HORATIO: 'Twere to consider too curiously[4] to consider so.
HAMLET: No, faith, not a jot, but to follow him thither with modesty[5]
enough, and likelihood to lead it. Alexander died, Alexander was buried,
Alexander returneth to dust; the dust is earth; of earth we make loam;
170   and why of that loam whereto he was converted might they not stop a
beerbarrel?

> Imperious Cæsar, dead and turned to clay,
> Might stop a hole to keep the wind away.
> O, that that earth which kept the world in awe
175   > Should patch a wall t'expel the winter's flaw![6]

But soft, but soft awhile! Here comes the king,
The queen, the courtiers.

[*Enter* KING, QUEEN, LAERTES, *and the Corse with a* PRIEST *and* LORDS
attendant.]

                              Who is this they follow?
And with such maiméd[7] rites? This doth betoken
The corse they follow did with desperate hand
180   Fordo its own life. 'Twas of some estate.[8]
Couch[9] we awhile and mark.   [*Retires with* HORATIO.]
LAERTES: What ceremony else?[1]
HAMLET: That is Laertes, a very noble youth. Mark.
LAERTES: What ceremony else?
185 PRIEST: Here obsequies have been as far enlarged[2]
As we have warranty. Her death was doubtful,

---

1. Throat.   2. Lacking a lower jaw.   3. Appearance.   4. Precisely.   5. Moderation.
6. Gusty wind.   7. Cut short.   8. Rank. *Fordo:* destroy.   9. Conceal ourselves.   1. More.
2. Extended.

And but that great command o'ersways the order,[3]
She should in ground unsanctified been lodged
Till the last trumpet. For charitable prayers,
Shards, flints, and pebbles, should be thrown on her.   190
Yet here she is allowed her virgin crants,[4]
Her maiden strewments,[5] and the bringing home
Of bell and burial.

LAERTES: Must there no more be done?

PRIEST: No more be done.
We should profane the service of the dead   195
To sing a requiem and such rest to her
As to peace-parted souls.

LAERTES: Lay her i' th' earth,
And from her fair and unpolluted flesh
May violets spring! I tell thee, churlish priest,
A minist'ring angel shall my sister be   200
When thou liest howling.[6]

HAMLET: What, the fair Ophelia!

QUEEN: Sweets to the sweet. Farewell!   *[Scatters flowers.]*
I hoped thou shouldst have been my Hamlet's wife.
I thought thy bride-bed to have decked, sweet maid,
And not t' have strewed thy grave.

LAERTES: O, treble woe   205
Fall ten times treble on that cursèd head
Whose wicked deed thy most ingenious sense[7]
Deprived thee of! Hold off the earth awhile,
Till I have caught her once more in mine arms.   *[Leaps into the grave.]*
Now pile your dust upon the quick and dead,   210
Till of this flat a mountain you have made
T' o'er-top old Pelion or the skyish head
Of blue Olympus.[8]

HAMLET: *[Coming forward.]* What is he whose grief
Bears such an emphasis, whose phrase of sorrow
Conjures[9] the wand'ring stars, and makes them stand   215
Like wonder-wounded hearers? This is I,
Hamlet the Dane.

[HAMLET *leaps into the grave and they grapple.*]

LAERTES: The devil take thy soul!

HAMLET: Thou pray'st not well.

---

3. Usual rules.   4. Wreaths.   5. Flowers strewn on the grave.   6. In Hell.   7. Lively mind.
8. The rivalry between Laertes and Hamlet in this scene extends even to their rhetoric. Pelion and
Olympus, mentioned here by Laertes, and Ossa, mentioned below by Hamlet, are Greek mountains
noted in mythology for their height. Olympus was the reputed home of the gods, and the other two
were piled one on top of the other by the Giants in an attempt to reach the top of Olympus and
overthrow the gods.   9. Casts a spell on.

I prithee take thy fingers from my throat,
220 For though I am not splenitive[1] and rash,
Yet have I in me something dangerous,
Which let thy wisdom fear. Hold off thy hand.
KING: Pluck them asunder.
QUEEN: Hamlet! Hamlet!
225 ALL: Gentlemen!
HORATIO: Good my lord, be quiet.

[*The* ATTENDANTS *part them, and they come out of the grave.*]

HAMLET: Why, I will fight with him upon this theme
Until my eyelids will no longer wag.[2]
QUEEN: O my son, what theme?
230 HAMLET: I loved Ophelia. Forty thousand brothers
Could not with all their quantity of love
Make up my sum. What wilt thou do for her?
KING: O, he is mad, Laertes.
QUEEN: For love of God, forbear[3] him.
235 HAMLET: 'Swounds, show me what th'owt do.
Woo't[4] weep, woo't fight, woo't fast, woo't tear thyself,
Woo't drink up eisel,[5] eat a crocodile?
I'll do't. Dost come here to whine?
To outface[6] me with leaping in her grave?
240 Be buried quick with her, and so will I.
And if thou prate of mountains, let them throw
Millions of acres on us, till our ground,
Singeing his pate against the burning zone,[7]
Make Ossa like a wart! Nay, an thou'lt mouth,
I'll rant as well as thou.
245 QUEEN: This is mere madness
And thus awhile the fit will work on him.
Anon, as patient as the female dove
When that her golden couplets[8] are disclosed,
His silence will sit drooping.
HAMLET: Hear you, sir.
250 What is the reason that you use me thus?
I loved you ever. But it is no matter.
Let Hercules himself do what he may,
The cat will mew, and dog will have his day.   [*Exit.*]
KING: I pray thee, good Horatio, wait upon[9] him.

[*Exit* HORATIO.]

255 [*To* LAERTES.] Strengthen your patience in our last night's speech.
We'll put the matter to the present push.[1]—

---

1. Hot-tempered.   2. Move.   3. Bear with.   4. Will you.   5. Vinegar.   6. Get the best of.
7. Sky in the torrid zone.   8. Pair of eggs.   9. Attend.   1. Immediate trial.

Good Gertrude, set some watch over your son.—
This grave shall have a living monument.
An hour of quiet shortly shall we see;
Till then in patience our proceeding be.   [*Exeunt.*] 260

Scene 2

A hall or public room. Enter HAMLET *and* HORATIO.

HAMLET: So much for this, sir; now shall you see the other.
     You do remember all the circumstance?
HORATIO: Remember it, my lord!
HAMLET: Sir, in my heart there was a kind of fighting
     That would not let me sleep. Methought I lay   5
     Worse than the mutines in the bilboes.² Rashly,
     And praised be rashness for it—let us know,
     Our indiscretion sometime serves us well,
     When our deep plots do pall; and that should learn³ us
     There's a divinity that shapes our ends,   10
     Rough-hew them how we will—
HORATIO: That is most certain.
HAMLET: Up from my cabin,
     My sea-gown scarfed⁴ about me, in the dark
     Groped I to find out them, had my desire,
     Fingered their packet, and in fine⁵ withdrew   15
     To mine own room again, making so bold,
     My fears forgetting manners, to unseal
     Their grand commission; where I found, Horatio—
     Ah, royal knavery!—an exact⁶ command,
     Larded⁷ with many several sorts of reasons,   20
     Importing Denmark's health, and England's too,
     With, ho! such bugs and goblins in my life,⁸
     That on the supervise,⁹ no leisure bated,
     No, not to stay the grinding of the axe,
     My head should be struck off.
HORATIO: Is't possible?   25
HAMLET: Here's the commission; read it at more leisure.
     But wilt thou hear now how I did proceed?
HORATIO: I beseech you.
HAMLET: Being thus benetted¹ round with villainies,
     Ere I could make a prologue to my brains,   30
     They had begun the play. I sat me down,
     Devised a new commission, wrote it fair.²

---

2. Stocks. *Mutines:* mutineers.   3. Teach.   4. Wrapped.   5. Quickly. *Fingered:* stole.
6. Precisely stated.   7. Garnished.   8. Such dangers if I remained alive.
9. As soon as the commission was read.   1. Caught in a net.   2. Legibly. *Devised:* made.

I once did hold it, as our statists[3] do,
A baseness to write fair, and labored much
35   How to forget that learning; but sir, now
It did me yeoman's service. Wilt thou know
Th' effect[4] of what I wrote?

HORATIO: Ay, good my lord.

HAMLET: An earnest conjuration from the king,
As England was his faithful tributary,[5]
40   As love between them like the palm might flourish,
As peace should still her wheaten garland wear
And stand a comma 'tween their amities[6]
And many such like as's of great charge,[7]
That on the view and knowing of these contents,
45   Without debatement[8] further more or less,
He should those bearers put to sudden death,
Not shriving-time allowed.[9]

HORATIO: How was this sealed?

HAMLET: Why, even in that was heaven ordinant,[1]
I had my father's signet in my purse,
50   Which was the model of that Danish seal,
Folded the writ up in the form of th' other,
Subscribed it, gave't th' impression,[2] placed it safely,
The changeling[3] never known. Now, the next day
Was our sea-fight, and what to this was sequent[4]
55   Thou knowest already.

HORATIO: So Guildenstern and Rosencrantz go to't.

HAMLET: Why, man, they did make love to this employment.
They are not near my conscience; their defeat[5]
Does by their own insinuation grow.
60   'Tis dangerous when the baser nature comes
Between the pass and fell[6] incensèd points
Of mighty opposites.

HORATIO: Why, what a king is this!

HAMLET: Does it not, think thee, stand me now upon—
He that hath killed my king and whored my mother,
65   Popped in between th' election and my hopes,
Thrown out his angle[7] for my proper life,
And with such coz'nage[8]—is't not perfect conscience
To quit[9] him with this arm? And is't not to be damned
To let this canker of our nature come
70   In further evil?

HORATIO: It must be shortly known to him from England

---

3. Politicians.   4. Contents.   5. Vassal.   6. Link friendships.   7. Import.
8. Consideration.   9. Without time for confession.   1. Operative.   2. Of the seal.
3. Alteration.   4. Followed.   5. Death. *Are not near:* do not touch.   6. Cruel. *Pass:* thrust.
7. Fishhook.   8. Trickery.   9. Repay.

What is the issue[1] of the business there.

HAMLET: It will be short;[2] the interim is mine.
And a man's life's no more than to say "one."
But I am very sorry, good Horatio,   75
That to Laertes I forgot myself;
For by the image of my cause I see
The portraiture of his. I'll court his favors.
But sure the bravery[3] of his grief did put me
Into a tow'ring passion.

HORATIO: Peace; who comes here?   80

[*Enter* OSRIC.]

OSRIC: Your lordship is right welcome back to Denmark.

HAMLET: I humbly thank you, sir. [*Aside to* HORATIO.] Dost know this water-
fly?

HORATIO: [*Aside to* HAMLET.] No, my good lord.

HAMLET: [*Aside to* HORATIO.] Thy state is the more gracious, for 'tis a vice   85
to know him. He hath much land, and fertile. Let a beast be lord of
beasts, and his crib shall stand at the king's mess. 'Tis a chough,[4] but
as I say, spacious in the possession of dirt.

OSRIC: Sweet lord, if your lordship were at leisure, I should impart a thing
to you from his majesty.   90

HAMLET: I will receive it, sir, with all diligence of spirit. Put your bonnet to
his right use. 'Tis for the head.

OSRIC: I thank your lordship, it is very hot.

HAMLET: No, believe me, 'tis very cold; the wind is northerly.

OSRIC: It is indifferent[5] cold, my lord, indeed.   95

HAMLET: But yet methinks it is very sultry and hot for my complexion.[6]

OSRIC: Exceedingly, my lord; it is very sultry, as 'twere—I cannot tell how.
My lord, his majesty bade me signify to you that 'a has laid a great wager
on your head. Sir, this is the matter—

HAMLET: I beseech you, remember.   [*Moves him to put on his hat.*]   100

OSRIC: Nay, good my lord; for my ease, in good faith. Sir, here is newly
come to court Laertes; believe me, an absolute[7] gentleman, full of most
excellent differences,[8] of very soft society and great showing.[9] Indeed, to
speak feelingly of him, he is the card or calendar of gentry, for you shall
find in him the continent[1] of what part a gentleman would see.   105

HAMLET: Sir, his definement[2] suffers no perdition in you, though I know
to divide him inventorially would dozy[3] th' arithmetic of memory, and
yet but yaw[4] neither in respect of his quick sail. But in the verity of
extolment, I take him to be a soul of great article,[5] and his infusion[6] of

---

1. Outcome. 2. Soon. 3. Exaggerated display. 4. Jackdaw. 5. Moderately.
6. Temperament. 7. Perfect. 8. Qualities. 9. Good manners.
1. Sum total. *Calendar:* measure. 2. Description.
3. Daze. *Divide him inventorially:* examine bit by bit. 4. Steer wildly. 5. Scope. 6. Nature.

110   such dearth and rareness as, to make true diction of him, his semblage[7] is his mirror, and who else would trace him, his umbrage,[8] nothing more.

OSRIC: Your lordship speaks most infallibly of him.

HAMLET: The concernancy,[9] sir? Why do we wrap the gentleman in our more rawer breath?[1]

115   OSRIC: Sir?

HORATIO: Is't not possible to understand in another tongue? You will to't, sir, really.

HAMLET: What imports the nomination[2] of this gentleman?

OSRIC: Of Laertes?

120   HORATIO: [Aside.] His purse is empty already. All's golden words are spent.

HAMLET: Of him, sir.

OSRIC: I know you are not ignorant—

HAMLET: I would you did, sir; yet, in faith, if you did, it would not much approve me. Well, sir.

125   OSRIC: You are not ignorant of what excellence Laertes is—

HAMLET: I dare not confess that, lest I should compare[3] with him in excellence; but to know a man well were to know himself.

OSRIC: I mean, sir, for his weapon; but in the imputation[4] laid on him by them, in his meed he's unfellowed.[5]

130   HAMLET: What's his weapon?

OSRIC: Rapier and dagger.

HAMLET: That's two of his weapons—but well.

OSRIC: The king, sir, hath wagered with him six Barbary horses, against the which he has impawned,[6] as I take it, six French rapiers and poniards,

135   with their assigns,[7] as girdle, hangers, and so. Three of the carriages, in faith, are very dear to fancy,[8] very responsive to the hilts, most delicate carriages, and of very liberal conceit.[9]

HAMLET: What call you the carriages?

HORATIO: [Aside to HAMLET.] I knew you must be edified by the margent[1]

140   ere you had done.

OSRIC: The carriages, sir, are the hangers.

HAMLET: The phrase would be more germane to the matter if we could carry a cannon by our sides. I would it might be hangers till then. But on! Six Barbary horses against six French swords, their assigns, and three

145   liberal conceited carriages; that's the French bet against the Danish. Why is this all impawned, as you call it?

OSRIC: The king, sir, hath laid, sir, that in a dozen passes between yourself and him he shall not exceed you three hits; he hath laid on twelve for nine, and it would come to immediate trial if your lordship would

150   vouchsafe the answer.

HAMLET: How if I answer no?

---

7. Rival. *Diction:* telling.   8. Shadow. *Trace:* keep pace with.   9. Meaning.   1. Cruder words.
2. Naming.   3. That is, compare myself.   4. Reputation.   5. Unequaled in his excellence.
6. Staked.   7. Appurtenances.   8. Finely designed.   9. Elegant design. *Delicate:* well adjusted.
1. Marginal gloss.

OSRIC: I mean, my lord, the opposition of your person in trial.

HAMLET: Sir, I will walk here in the hall. If it please his majesty, it is the breathing time[2] of day with me. Let the foils be brought, the gentleman willing, and the king hold his purpose; I will win for him an I can. If not, I will gain nothing but my shame and the odd hits.

OSRIC: Shall I deliver you so?

HAMLET: To this effect, sir, after what flourish your nature will.

OSRIC: I commend my duty to your lordship.

HAMLET: Yours, yours. [*Exit* OSRIC.] He does well to commend it himself; there are no tongues else for's turn.

HORATIO: This lapwing runs away with the shell on his head.[3]

HAMLET: 'A did comply, sir, with his dug[4] before 'a sucked it. Thus has he, and many more of the same bevy that I know the drossy age dotes on, only got the tune of the time; and out of an habit of encounter, a king of yesty[5] collection which carries them through and through the most fanned and winnowed opinions; and do but blow them to their trial, the bubbles are out.

[*Enter a* LORD.]

LORD: My lord, his majesty commended him to you by young Osric, who brings back to him that you attend[6] him in the hall. He sends to know if your pleasure hold to play with Laertes, or that you will take longer time.

HAMLET: I am constant to my purposes; they follow the king's pleasure. If his fitness speaks, mine is ready; now or whensoever, provided I be so able as now.

LORD: The king and queen and all are coming down.

HAMLET: In happy time.

LORD: The queen desires you to use some gentle entertainment[7] to Laertes before you fall to play.

HAMLET: She well instructs me. [*Exit* LORD.]

HORATIO: You will lose this wager, my lord.

HAMLET: I do not think so. Since he went into France I have been in continual practice. I shall win at the odds. But thou wouldst not think how ill[8] all's here about my heart. But it's no matter.

HORATIO: Nay, good my lord—

HAMLET: It is but foolery, but it is such a kind of gaingiving[9] as would perhaps trouble a woman.

HORATIO: If your mind dislike anything, obey it. I will forestall their repair[1] hither, and say you are not fit.

HAMLET: Not a whit, we defy augury. There is special providence in the fall of a sparrow. If it be now, 'tis not to come; if it be not to come, it will

---

2. Time for exercise.
3. The lapwing was thought to be so precocious that it could run immediately after being hatched, even, as here, with bits of the shell still on its head.   4. Mother's breast. *Comply:* deal formally.
5. Yeasty.   6. Await.   7. Cordiality.   8. Uneasy.   9. Misgiving.   1. Coming.

be now; if it be not now, yet it will come. The readiness is all. Since no
man of aught he leaves knows, what is't to leave betimes? Let be.

[*A table prepared. Enter* TRUMPETS, DRUMS, *and* OFFICERS *with cushions;*
KING, QUEEN, OSRIC *and* ATTENDANTS *with foils, daggers, and* LAERTES.]

KING: Come, Hamlet, come and take this hand from me.

[*The* KING *puts* LAERTES' *hand into* HAMLET'*s.*]

195   HAMLET: Give me your pardon, sir. I have done you wrong,
But pardon 't as you are a gentleman.
This presence[2] knows, and you must needs have heard,
How I am punished with a sore distraction.
What I have done
200   That might your nature, honor, and exception,[3]
Roughly awake, I here proclaim was madness.
Was 't Hamlet wronged Laertes? Never Hamlet.
If Hamlet from himself be ta'en away,
And when he's not himself does wrong Laertes,
205   Then Hamlet does it not, Hamlet denies it.
Who does it then? His madness. If 't be so,
Hamlet is of the faction that is wronged;
His madness is poor Hamlet's enemy.
Sir, in this audience,
210   Let my disclaiming from[4] a purposed evil
Free[5] me so far in your most generous thoughts
That I have shot my arrow o'er the house
And hurt my brother.

LAERTES: I am satisfied in nature,
Whose motive in this case should stir me most
215   To my revenge. But in my terms of honor
I stand aloof, and will no reconcilement
Till by some elder masters of known honor
I have a voice[6] and precedent of peace
To keep my name ungored.[7] But till that time
220   I do receive your offered love like love,
And will not wrong it.

HAMLET: I embrace it freely,
And will this brother's wager frankly[8] play.
Give us the foils. Come on.

LAERTES: Come, one for me.

HAMLET: I'll be your foil, Laertes. In mine ignorance
225   Your skill shall, like a star i' th' darkest night,
Stick fiery off[9] indeed.

LAERTES: You mock me, sir.

---

2. Company.   3. Resentment.   4. Denying of.   5. Absolve.   6. Authority.   7. Unshamed.
8. Without rancor.   9. Shine brightly.

HAMLET: No, by this hand.
KING: Give them the foils, young Osric. Cousin Hamlet,
　You know the wager?
HAMLET:　　　　　　　Very well, my lord;
　Your Grace has laid the odds o' th' weaker side.　　　　　230
KING: I do not fear it, I have seen you both;
　But since he is bettered[1] we have therefore odds.
LAERTES: This is too heavy; let me see another.
HAMLET: This likes me well. These foils have all a[2] length?

　[*They prepare to play.*]

OSRIC: Ay, my good lord.　　　　　　　　　　　　　　　　235
KING: Set me the stoups of wine upon that table.
　If Hamlet give the first or second hit,
　Or quit in answer of[3] the third exchange,
　Let all the battlements their ordnance fire.
　The king shall drink to Hamlet's better breath,　　　　240
　And in the cup an union[4] shall he throw,
　Richer than that which four successive kings
　In Denmark's crown have worn. Give me the cups,
　And let the kettle[5] to the trumpet speak,
　The trumpet to the cannoneer without,　　　　　　　　245
　The cannons to the heavens, the heaven to earth,
　"Now the king drinks to Hamlet." Come, begin—

　[*Trumpets the while.*]

　And you, the judges, bear a wary eye.
HAMLET: Come on, sir.
LAERTES:　　　　　　　Come, my lord.

　[*They play.*]

HAMLET:　　　　　　　　　　　One.
LAERTES:　　　　　　　　　　　No.
HAMLET:　　　　　　　　　　　　　　　Judgment?
OSRIC: A hit, a very palpable hit.　　　　　　　　　　　　250

　[*Drums, trumpets, and shot. Flourish; a piece goes off.*]

LAERTES: Well, again.
KING: Stay, give me drink. Hamlet, this pearl is thine.
　Here's to thy health. Give him the cup.
HAMLET: I'll play this bout first; set it by awhile.
　Come.　　　　　　　　　　　　　　　　　　　　　　255

　[*They play.*]

---

1. Reported better.　2. The same. *Likes:* suits.　3. Repay.　4. Pearl.　5. Kettledrum.

Another hit; what say you?
LAERTES: A touch, a touch, I do confess't.
KING: Our son shall win.
QUEEN: He's fat,[6] and scant of breath.
Here, Hamlet, take my napkin, rub thy brows.
260   The queen carouses to thy fortune, Hamlet.
HAMLET: Good madam!
KING: Gertrude, do not drink.
QUEEN: I will, my lord; I pray you pardon me.
KING: [Aside.] It is the poisoned cup; it is too late.
265 HAMLET: I dare not drink yet, madam; by and by.
QUEEN: Come, let me wipe thy face.
LAERTES: My lord, I'll hit him now.
KING: I do not think't.
LAERTES: [Aside.] And yet it is almost against my conscience.
HAMLET: Come, for the third, Laertes. You do but dally.
270   I pray you pass[7] with your best violence;
I am afeard you make a wanton of me.[8]
LAERTES: Say you so? Come on.

[They play.]

OSRIC: Nothing, neither way.
LAERTES: Have at you now!

[LAERTES wounds HAMLET: then, in scuffling, they change rapiers, and HAM-
LET wounds LAERTES.]

275 KING: Part them. They are incensed.
HAMLET: Nay, come again.

[The QUEEN falls.]

OSRIC: Look to the queen there, ho!
HORATIO: They bleed on both sides. How is it, my lord?
OSRIC: How is't, Laertes?
280 LAERTES: Why, as a woodcock to mine own springe,[9] Osric.
I am justly killed with mine own treachery.
HAMLET: How does the queen?
KING: She swoons to see them bleed.
QUEEN: No, no, the drink, the drink! O my dear Hamlet!
The drink, the drink! I am poisoned.   [Dies.]
285 HAMLET: O, villainy! Ho! let the door be locked.
Treachery! seek it out.
LAERTES: It is here, Hamlet. Hamlet, thou art slain;
No med'cine in the world can do thee good.
In thee there is not half an hour's life.
290   The treacherous instrument is in thy hand,

6. Out of shape.   7. Attack.   8. Trifle with me.   9. Snare.

Unbated[1] and envenomed. The foul practice
Hath turned itself on me. Lo, here I lie,
Never to rise again. Thy mother's poisoned.
I can no more. The king, the king's to blame.
HAMLET: The point envenomed too?   295
Then, venom, to thy work.   [*Hurts the* KING.]
ALL: Treason! treason!
KING: O, yet defend me, friends. I am but hurt.[2]
HAMLET: Here, thou incestuous, murd'rous, damnéd Dane,
Drink off this potion. Is thy union here?   300
Follow my mother.

   [*The* KING *dies.*]

LAERTES: He is justly served.
It is a poison tempered[3] by himself.
Exchange forgiveness with me, noble Hamlet.
Mine and my father's death come not upon thee,
Nor thine on me!   [*Dies.*] 305
HAMLET: Heaven make thee free of[4] it! I follow thee.
I am dead, Horatio. Wretched queen, adieu!
You that look pale and tremble at this chance,[5]
That are but mutes or audience to this act,
Had I but time, as this fell sergeant Death   310
Is strict in his arrest,[6] O, I could tell you—
But let it be. Horatio, I am dead:
Thou livest; report me and my cause aright
To the unsatisfied.[7]
HORATIO: Never believe it.
I am more an antique Roman than a Dane.   315
Here's yet some liquor left.
HAMLET: As th'art a man,
Give me the cup. Let go. By heaven, I'll ha't.
O God, Horatio, what a wounded name,
Things standing thus unknown, shall live behind me!
If thou didst ever hold me in thy heart,   320
Absent thee from felicity awhile,
And in this harsh world draw thy breath in pain,
To tell my story.

   [*A march afar off.*]

                  What warlike noise is this?
OSRIC: Young Fortinbras, with conquest come from Poland,
To th' ambassadors of England gives   325

---

1. Unblunted.   2. Wounded.   3. Mixed.   4. Forgive.   5. Circumstance.
6. Summons to court.   7. Uninformed.

This warlike volley.[8]

HAMLET: O, I die, Horatio!
The potent poison quite o'er-crows[9] my spirit.
I cannot live to hear the news from England,
But I do prophesy th' election lights
On Fortinbras. He has my dying voice.[1]
So tell him, with th' occurrents,[2] more and less,
Which have solicited[3]—the rest is silence.   [*Dies.*]

HORATIO: Now cracks a noble heart. Good night, sweet prince,
And flights of angels sing thee to thy rest!

[*March within.*]

Why does the drum come hither?

[*Enter* FORTINBRAS, *with the* AMBASSADORS *and with drum, colors, and*
ATTENDANTS.]

FORTINBRAS: Where is this sight?

HORATIO: What is it you would see?
If aught of woe or wonder, cease your search.

FORTINBRAS: This quarry cries on havoc.[4] O proud death,
What feast is toward[5] in thine eternal cell
That thou so many princes at a shot
So bloodily hast struck?

AMBASSADORS: The sight is dismal;
And our affairs from England come too late.
The ears are senseless[6] that should give us hearing
To tell him his commandment is fulfilled,
That Rosencrantz and Guildenstern are dead.
Where should we have our thanks?

HORATIO: Not from his mouth,
Had it th' ability of life to thank you.
He never gave commandment for their death.
But since, so jump[7] upon this bloody question,
You from the Polack wars, and you from England,
Are here arrived, give orders that these bodies
High on a stage be placed to the view,
And let me speak to th' yet unknowing world
How these things came about. So shall you hear
Of carnal, bloody, and unnatural acts;
Of accidental judgments, casual[8] slaughters;

---

8. The staging presents some difficulties here. Unless Osric is clairvoyant, he must have left the
stage at some point and returned. One possibility is that he might have left to carry out Hamlet's
order to lock the door (line 280) and returned when the sound of the distant march is heard.
9. Overcomes.   1. Support.   2. Circumstances.   3. Brought about this scene.
4. The game killed in the hunt proclaims a slaughter.   5. In preparation.
6. Without sense of hearing.   7. Exactly.   8. Brought about by apparent accident.

Of deaths put on by cunning and forced cause;
And, in this upshot,[9] purposes mistook
Fall'n on th' inventors' heads. All this can I
Truly deliver.
FORTINBRAS: Let us haste to hear it,   360
And call the noblest to the audience.[1]
For me, with sorrow I embrace my fortune.
I have some rights of memory[2] in this kingdom,
Which now to claim my vantage[3] doth invite me.
HORATIO: Of that I shall have also cause to speak,   365
And from his mouth whose voice will draw on more.
But let this same be presently performed,
Even while men's minds are wild, lest more mischance
On plots and errors happen.
FORTINBRAS: Let four captains
Bear Hamlet like a soldier to the stage,   370
For he was likely, had he been put on,[4]
To have proved most royal; and for his passage
The soldier's music and the rite of war
Speak loudly for him.
Take up the bodies. Such a sight as this   375
Becomes the field, but here shows much amiss.
Go, bid the soldiers shoot. [*Exeunt marching. A peal of ordnance shot off.*]

ca. 1600

SUGGESTIONS FOR WRITING

1. At times, Chekhov's method of providing exposition—background information—may seem stiff and artificial, with characters saying things that the other
characters know already. For example, to explain why Madame Ranevsky has
been in Paris, Chekhov has Anya say, "It's six years since father died. Then
only a month later little brother Grisha was drowned in the river, such a pretty
boy he was, only seven years. It was more than mamma could bear, so she
went away without looking back." There are numerous such expository set-
pieces throughout the play. Do the play's key moments occur onstage, or are
they contained in these set-pieces? Is such summary of the past believable? Is
there a thematic significance in "looking back" or restating the past in this
way? Write an essay in which you discuss Chekhov's methods of conveying
the "pre-history" of his characters, or mixing exposition with present action.
2. Throughout *The Cherry Orchard* Madame Ranevsky (Lyubov) keeps doing what
she tells herself she should not do. For example, she gives money to a beggar
although she has no money of her own to give; she hosts a dance on the eve
of the estate's sale although she tells herself this is inappropriate. Write an
essay in which you examine Lyubov's often self-contradictory behavior. What

9. Result.   1. Hearing.   2. Succession.   3. Position.   4. Elected king.

"should" Madame Ranevsky (Lyubov) do, given her circumstances? What options does she really have?

3. When Trofimov makes his grand declaration about how he will further the advancement of humanity, Chekhov answers him with the stage direction "[*In the distance is heard the stroke of an axe on a tree.*]" Focusing on this and other stage directions, write an essay in which you discuss various aspects of Chekhov's stagecraft besides the dialogue.

4. What are the politics of *The Cherry Orchard*, a play written during a period of great social upheaval in Russia, barely a decade before the revolution that brought the Communists to power? Is the play "conservative"? Is it "revolutionary"? Idealistic? Cynical? Citing specific passages from the play, write an essay in which you argue either for or against the interpretation that *The Cherry Orchard* is an indictment of an old social order that has grown corrupt and will soon be swept away.

5. What does the cherry orchard itself symbolize to the various characters in the play? What does it come to symbolize to the audience? Write an essay examining *The Cherry Orchard*'s central symbol. Is there, finally, any one "correct" interpretation? How does the ambiguity of this symbol serve Chekhov's overall artistic purposes in the play?

6. In ancient Greek tragedy, misfortune is often the result of *hubris*—the excessive pride that leads a hero to overstep the bounds of his destiny and thus to offend the gods. More recent writing about tragedy develops the concept of *hamartia*—the notion that the protagonist's fate is brought about by a tragic flaw or failing of character. What propels *Hamlet*—the prince's proud wish to avenge his father's death and assert his rights? a tragic flaw in Hamlet's otherwise noble character? or something else altogether? Write an essay examining the circumstances and motivations that lead to Hamlet's death and the fall of Denmark.

7. Some critics have focused on the psychological underpinnings of *Hamlet*; others have seen the play as political commentary. In 1600 (the approximate date of *Hamlet*'s first performance), Queen Elizabeth I was sixty-seven and had no direct heirs, a situation that promised no end to the wars and rebellions over succession to the throne that had plagued England for the preceding two centuries. Drawing on the play and, if need be, your own research into the politics of Shakespeare's era, write an essay showing how England's historical circumstances may be reflected in *Hamlet*.

8. In *Hamlet*, characters perform a play. What are the functions and effects of this device? What might the play within the play suggest about the value of drama—including the value of plays like Shakespeare's own? Write an essay exploring the function and significance of the play within the play. What attitudes toward drama does Shakespeare encourage seem to us to adopt?

9. For centuries Shakespeare's plays have been celebrated for their originality and variety. Samuel Johnson, the great eighteenth-century literary critic, once wrote of Shakespeare that "Each change of many-colour'd life he drew." T. S. Eliot claimed that, of all writers, "Shakespeare gives the greatest width of human passion." Still, for all their variety, most of Shakespeare's plays follow fairly rigid formulas. Write an essay in which you discuss how *Hamlet* and at least one other Shakespeare play (for example, *Romeo and Juliet*, *Julius Caesar*, or *Macbeth*) embody Shakespearean tragedy.

Reading More Drama

ARTHUR MILLER

Death of a Salesman

Certain Private Conversations in Two Acts and a Requiem

CHARACTERS

WILLY LOMAN	THE WOMAN	STANLEY
LINDA	CHARLEY	MISS FORSYTHE
BIFF	UNCLE BEN	LETTA
HAPPY	HOWARD WAGNER	
BERNARD	JENNY	

The action takes place in WILLY LOMAN'*s house and yard and in various places he visits in the New York and Boston of today.*

ACT I

A melody is heard, playing upon a flute. It is small and fine, telling of grass and trees and the horizon. The curtain rises.

Before us is the Salesman's house. We are aware of towering, angular shapes behind it, surrounding it on all sides. Only the blue light of the sky falls upon the house and forestage; the surrounding area shows an angry flow of orange. As more light appears, we see a solid vault of apartment houses around the small, fragile-seeming home. An air of the dream clings to the place, a dream rising out of reality. The kitchen at center seems actual enough, for there is a kitchen table with three chairs, and a refrigerator. But no other fixtures are seen. At the back of the kitchen there is a draped entrance, which leads to the living-room. To the right of the kitchen, on a level raised two feet, is a bedroom furnished only with a brass bedstead and a straight chair. On a shelf over the bed a silver athletic trophy stands. A window opens onto the apartment house at the side.

Behind the kitchen, on a level raised six and a half feet, is the boys' bedroom, at present barely visible. Two beds are dimly seen, and at the back of the room a dormer window. (This bedroom is above the unseen living-room.) At the left a stairway curves up to it from the kitchen.

The entire setting is wholly or, in some places, partially transparent. The roof-line of the house is one-dimensional; under and over it we see the apartment buildings. Before the house lies an apron, curving beyond the forestage into the orchestra. This forward area serves as the back yard as well as the locale of all WILLY'*s imaginings and of his city scenes. Whenever the action is in the present the actors observe the imaginary wall-lines, entering the house only through its door at the left. But in the scenes of the past these boundaries are broken, and characters enter or leave a room by stepping "through" a wall onto the forestage.*

From the right, WILLY LOMAN, *the Salesman, enters, carrying two large sample cases. The flute plays on. He hears but is not aware of it. He is past sixty years of age, dressed quietly. Even as he crosses the stage to the doorway of the house, his exhaustion is apparent. He unlocks the door, comes into the kitchen, and thankfully lets his burden down, feeling the soreness of his palms. A word-sigh escapes his lips—it might be "Oh, boy, oh, boy." He closes the door, then carries his cases out into the living-room, through the draped kitchen doorway.*

LINDA, *his wife, has stirred in her bed at the right. She gets out and puts on a robe, listening. Most often jovial, she has developed an iron repression of her exceptions to* WILLY's *behavior—she more than loves him, she admires him, as though his mercurial nature, his temper, his massive dreams and little cruelties, served her only as sharp reminders of the turbulent longings within him, longings which she shares but lacks the temperament to utter and follow to their end.*

LINDA: [*Hearing* WILLY *outside the bedroom, calls with some trepidation.*] Willy!

WILLY: It's all right. I came back.

LINDA: Why? What happened? [*Slight pause.*] Did something happen, Willy?

WILLY: No, nothing happened.

LINDA: You didn't smash the car, did you?

WILLY: [*With casual irritation.*] I said nothing happened. Didn't you hear me?

LINDA: Don't you feel well?

WILLY: I'm tired to the death. [*The flute has faded away. He sits on the bed beside her, a little numb.*] I couldn't make it. I just couldn't make it, Linda.

LINDA: [*Very carefully, delicately.*] Where were you all day? You look terrible.

WILLY: I got as far as a little above Yonkers. I stopped for a cup of coffee. Maybe it was the coffee.

LINDA: What?

WILLY: [*After a pause.*] I suddenly couldn't drive any more. The car kept going off onto the shoulder, y'know?

LINDA: [*Helpfully.*] Oh. Maybe it was the steering again. I don't think Angelo knows the Studebaker.

WILLY: No, it's me, it's me. Suddenly I realize I'm goin' sixty miles an hour and I don't remember the last five minutes. I'm—I can't seem to—keep my mind to it.

LINDA: Maybe it's your glasses. You never went for your new glasses.

WILLY: No, I see everything. I came back ten miles an hour. It took me nearly four hours from Yonkers.

LINDA: [*Resigned.*] Well, you'll just have to take a rest, Willy, you can't continue this way.

WILLY: I just got back from Florida.

LINDA: But you didn't rest your mind. Your mind is overactive, and the mind is what counts, dear.

WILLY: I'll start out in the morning. Maybe I'll feel better in the morning. [*She is taking off his shoes.*] These goddam arch supports are killing me.

LINDA: Take an aspirin. Should I get you an aspirin? It'll soothe you.

WILLY: [*With wonder.*] I was driving along, you understand? And I was fine. I was even observing the scenery. You can imagine, me looking at scenery, on the road every week of my life. But it's so beautiful up there, Linda, the trees are so thick, and the sun is warm. I opened the windshield and just let the warm air bathe over me. And then all of a sudden I'm goin' off the road! I'm tellin' ya, I absolutely forgot I was driving. If I'd've gone the other way over the white line I might've killed somebody. So I went on again—and five minutes later I'm dreamin' again, and I nearly—[*He presses two fingers against his eyes.*] I have such thoughts, I have such strange thoughts.

LINDA: Willy, dear. Talk to them again. There's no reason why you can't work in New York.

WILLY: They don't need me in New York. I'm the New England man. I'm vital in New England.

LINDA: But you're sixty years old. They can't expect you to keep traveling every week.

WILLY: I'll have to send a wire[1] to Portland. I'm supposed to see Brown and Morrison tomorrow morning at ten o'clock to show the line. Goddammit, I could sell them! [*He starts putting on his jacket.*]

LINDA: [*Taking the jacket from him.*] Why don't you go down to the place tomorrow and tell Howard you've simply got to work in New York? You're too accommodating, dear.

WILLY: If old man Wagner was alive I'da been in charge of New York now! That man was a prince, he was a masterful man. But that boy of his, that Howard, he don't appreciate. When I went north the first time, the Wagner Company didn't know where New England was!

LINDA: Why don't you tell those things to Howard, dear?

WILLY: [*Encouraged.*] I will, I definitely will. Is there any cheese?

LINDA: I'll make you a sandwich.

WILLY: No, go to sleep. I'll take some milk. I'll be up right away. The boys in?

LINDA: They're sleeping. Happy took Biff on a date tonight.

WILLY: [*Interested.*] That so?

LINDA: It was so nice to see them shaving together, one behind the other, in the bathroom. And going out together. You notice? The whole house smells of shaving lotion.

WILLY: Figure it out. Work a lifetime to pay off a house. You finally own it, and there's nobody to live in it.

LINDA: Well, dear, life is a casting off. It's always that way.

WILLY: No, no, some people—some people accomplish something. Did Biff say anything after I went this morning?

LINDA: You shouldn't have criticized him, Willy, especially after he just got off the train. You mustn't lose your temper with him.

WILLY: When the hell did I lose my temper? I simply asked him if he was making any money. Is that a criticism?

1. Telegram.

LINDA: But, dear, how could he make any money?

WILLY: [*Worried and angered.*] There's such an undercurrent in him. He became a moody man. Did he apologize when I left this morning?

LINDA: He was crestfallen, Willy. You know how he admires you. I think if he finds himself, then you'll both be happier and not fight any more.

WILLY: How can he find himself on a farm? Is that a life? A farmhand? In the beginning, when he was young, I thought, well, a young man, it's good for him to tramp around, take a lot of different jobs. But it's more than ten years now and he has yet to make thirty-five dollars a week!

LINDA: He's finding himself, Willy.

WILLY: Not finding yourself at the age of thirty-four is a disgrace!

LINDA: Shh!

WILLY: The trouble is he's lazy, goddammit!

LINDA: Willy, please!

WILLY: Biff is a lazy bum!

LINDA: They're sleeping. Get something to eat. Go on down.

WILLY: Why did he come home? I would like to know what brought him home.

LINDA: I don't know. I think he's still lost, Willy. I think he's very lost.

WILLY: Biff Loman is lost. In the greatest country in the world a young man with such—personal attractiveness, gets lost. And such a hard worker. There's one thing about Biff—he's not lazy.

LINDA: Never.

WILLY: [*With pity and resolve.*] I'll see him in the morning; I'll have a nice talk with him. I'll get him a job selling. He could be big in no time. My God! Remember how they used to follow him around in high school? When he smiled at one of them their faces lit up. When he walked down the street . . . [*He loses himself in reminiscences.*]

LINDA: [*Trying to bring him out of it.*] Willy, dear, I got a new kind of American-type cheese today. It's whipped.

WILLY: Why do you get American when I like Swiss?

LINDA: I just thought you'd like a change—

WILLY: I don't want a change! I want Swiss cheese. Why am I always being contradicted?

LINDA: [*With a covering laugh.*] I thought it would be a surprise.

WILLY: Why don't you open a window in here, for God's sake?

LINDA: [*With infinite patience.*] They're all open, dear.

WILLY: The way they boxed us in here. Bricks and windows, windows and bricks.

LINDA: We should've bought the land next door.

WILLY: The street is lined with cars. There's not a breath of fresh air in the neighborhood. The grass don't grow any more, you can't raise a carrot in the back yard. They should've had a law against apartment houses. Remember those two beautiful elm trees out there? When I and Biff hung the swing between them?

LINDA: Yeah, like being a million miles from the city.

WILLY: They should've arrested the builder for cutting those down. They massacred the neighborhood. [*Lost.*] More and more I think of those days, Linda. This time of year it was lilac and wisteria. And then the peonies would come out, and the daffodils. What fragrance in this room!

LINDA: Well, after all, people had to move somewhere.

WILLY: No, there's more people now.

LINDA: I don't think there's more people. I think—

WILLY: There's more people! That's what ruining this country! Population is getting out of control. The competition is maddening! Smell the stink from that apartment house! And another one on the other side . . . How can they whip cheese?

[*On* WILLY's *last line,* BIFF *and* HAPPY *raise themselves up in their beds, listening.*]

LINDA: Go down, try it. And be quiet.

WILLY: [*Turning to* LINDA, *guiltily.*] You're not worried about me, are you, sweetheart?

BIFF: What's the matter?

HAPPY: Listen!

LINDA: You've got too much on the ball to worry about.

WILLY: You're my foundation and my support, Linda.

LINDA: Just try to relax, dear. You make mountains out of mole-hills.

WILLY: I won't fight with him anymore. If he wants to go back to Texas, let him go.

LINDA: He'll find his way.

WILLY: Sure. Certain men just don't get started till later in life. Like Thomas Edison, I think. Or B. F. Goodrich. One of them was deaf. [*He starts for the bedroom doorway.*] I'll put my money on Biff.

LINDA: And Willy—if it's warm Sunday we'll drive in the country. And we'll open the windshield, and take lunch.

WILLY: No, the windshields don't open on the new cars.

LINDA: But you opened it today.

WILLY: Me? I didn't. [*He stops.*] Now isn't that peculiar! Isn't that a remarkable—[*He breaks off in amazement and fright as the flute is heard distantly.*]

LINDA: What, darling?

WILLY: That is the most remarkable thing.

LINDA: What, dear?

WILLY: I was thinking of the Chevvy. [*Slight pause.*] Nineteen twenty-eight . . . when I had that red Chevvy—[*Breaks off.*] That funny? I coulda sworn I was driving that Chevvy today.

LINDA: Well, that's nothing. Something must've reminded you.

WILLY: Remarkable. *Ts.*[2] Remember those days? The way Biff used to simonize that car? The dealer refused to believe there was eighty thousand miles on it. [*He shakes his head.*] Heh! [*To* LINDA.] Close your eyes, I'll be right up. [*He walks out of the bedroom.*]

---

2. Ford Model Ts, extraordinarily popular cars manufactured from 1908 to 1928. *Simonize:* polish with car wax.

HAPPY: [*To* BIFF.] Jesus, maybe he smashed up the car again!

LINDA: [*Calling after* WILLY.] Be careful on the stairs, dear! The cheese is on the middle shelf! [*She turns, goes over to the bed, takes his jacket, and goes out of the bedroom.*]

[*Light has risen on the boys' room. Unseen,* WILLY *is heard talking to himself,* "*Eighty thousand miles,*" *and a little laugh.* BIFF *gets out of bed, comes downstage a bit, and stands attentively.* BIFF *is two years older than his brother,* HAPPY, *well built, but in these days bears a worn air and seems less self-assured. He has succeeded less, and his dreams are stronger and less acceptable than* HAPPY'*s.* HAPPY *is tall, powerfully made. Sexuality is like a visible color on him, or a scent that many women have discovered. He, like his brother, is lost, but in a different way, for he has never allowed himself to turn his face toward defeat and is thus more confused and hard-skinned, although seemingly more content.*]

HAPPY: [*Getting out of bed.*] He's going to get his license taken away if he keeps that up. I'm getting nervous about him, y'know, Biff?

BIFF: His eyes are going.

HAPPY: No, I've driven with him. He sees all right. He just doesn't keep his mind on it. I drove into the city with him last week. He stops at a green light and then it turns red and he goes. [*He laughs.*]

BIFF: Maybe he's color-blind.

HAPPY: Pop? Why he's got the finest eye for color in the business. You know that.

BIFF: [*Sitting down on his bed.*] I'm going to sleep.

HAPPY: You're not still sour on Dad, are you Biff?

BIFF: He's all right, I guess.

WILLY: [*Underneath them, in the living-room.*] Yes, sir, eighty thousand miles—eighty-two thousand!

BIFF: You smoking?

HAPPY: [*Holding out a pack of cigarettes.*] Want one?

BIFF: [*Taking a cigarette.*] I can never sleep when I smell it.

WILLY: What a simonizing job, heh!

HAPPY: [*With deep sentiment.*] Funny, Biff, y'know? Us sleeping in here again? The old beds. [*He pats his bed affectionately.*] All the talk that went across those two beds, huh? Our whole lives.

BIFF: Yeah. Lotta dreams and plans.

HAPPY: [*With a deep and masculine laugh.*] About five hundred women would like to know what was said in this room.

[*They share a soft laugh.*]

BIFF: Remember that big Betsy something—what the hell was her name—over on Bushwick Avenue?

HAPPY: [*Combing his hair.*] With the collie dog!

BIFF: That's the one. I got you in there, remember?

HAPPY: Yeah, that was my first time—I think. Boy, there was a pig! [*They laugh, almost crudely.*] You taught me everything I know about women. Don't forget that.

BIFF: I bet you forgot how bashful you used to be. Especially with girls.

HAPPY: Oh, I still am, Biff.

BIFF: Oh, go on.

HAPPY: I just control it, that's all. I think I got less bashful and you got more so. What happened, Biff? Where's the old humor, the old confidence? [*He shakes* BIFF's *knee.* BIFF *gets up and moves restlessly about the room.*] What's the matter?

BIFF: Why does Dad mock me all the time?

HAPPY: He's not mocking you, he—

BIFF: Everything I say there's a twist of mockery on his face. I can't get near him.

HAPPY: He just wants you to make good, that's all. I wanted to talk to you about Dad for a long time, Biff. Something's—happening to him. He—talks to himself.

BIFF: I noticed that this morning. But he always mumbled.

HAPPY: But not so noticeable. It got so embarrassing I sent him to Florida. And you know something? Most of the time he's talking to you.

BIFF: What's he say about me?

HAPPY: I can't make it out.

BIFF: What's he say about me?

HAPPY: I think the fact that you're not settled, that you're still kind of up in the air . . .

BIFF: There's one or two things depressing him, Happy.

HAPPY: What do you mean?

BIFF: Never mind. Just don't lay it all to me.

HAPPY: But I think if you just got started—I mean—is there any future for you out there?

BIFF: I tell ya, Hap, I don't know what the future is. I don't know—what I'm supposed to want.

HAPPY: What do you mean?

BIFF: Well, I spent six or seven years after high school trying to work myself up. Shipping clerk, salesman, business of one kind or another. And it's a measly manner of existence. To get on that subway on the hot mornings in summer. To devote your whole life to keeping stock, or making phone calls, or selling or buying. To suffer fifty weeks of the year for the sake of a two-week vacation, when all you really desire is to be outdoors, with your shirt off. And always to have to get ahead of the next fella. And still—that's how you build a future.

HAPPY: Well, you really enjoy it on a farm? Are you content out there?

BIFF: [*With rising agitation.*] Hap, I've had twenty or thirty different kinds of jobs since I left home before the war, and it always turns out the same. I just realized it lately. In Nebraska when I herded cattle, and the Dakotas, and Arizona, and now in Texas. It's why I came home now, I guess, because I realized it. This farm I work on, it's spring there now, see? And they've got about fifteen new colts. There's nothing more inspiring or—beautiful than the sight of a mare and a new colt. And it's cool there now, see? Texas is cool now, and it's spring. And whenever spring comes to where I am, I suddenly get the feeling, my God, I'm not gettin' anywhere! What the hell am I doing, playing around with horses, twenty-eight dollars a week! I'm thirty-four years old. I oughta be makin' my future. That's when I come running home. And now, I get there, and I don't know what to do with myself. [*After a pause.*] I've always made a point of not wasting my life, and everytime I come back here I know that all I've done is to waste my life.

HAPPY: You're a poet, you know that, Biff? You're a—you're an idealist!

BIFF: No, I'm mixed up very bad. Maybe I oughta get married. Maybe I oughta get stuck into something. Maybe that's my trouble. I'm like a boy. I'm not married. I'm not in business, I just—I'm like a boy. Are you content, Hap? You're a success, aren't you? Are you content?

HAPPY: Hell, no!

BIFF: Why? You're making money, aren't you?

HAPPY: [*Moving about with energy, expressiveness.*] All I can do now is wait for the merchandise manager to die. And suppose I get to be merchandise manager? He's a good friend of mine, and he just built a terrific estate on Long Island. And he lived there about two months and sold it, and now he's building another one. He can't enjoy it once it's finished. And I know that's just what I would do. I don't know what the hell I'm workin' for. Sometimes I sit in my apartment—all alone. And I think of the rent I'm paying. And it's crazy. But then, it's what I always wanted. My own apartment, a car, and plenty of women. And still, goddammit, I'm lonely.

BIFF: [*With enthusiasm.*] Listen, why don't you come out West with me?

HAPPY: You and I, heh?

BIFF: Sure, maybe we could buy a ranch. Raise cattle, use our muscles. Men built like we are should be working out in the open.

HAPPY: [*Avidly.*] The Loman Brothers, heh?

BIFF: [*With vast affection.*] Sure, we'd be known all over the counties!

HAPPY: [*Enthralled.*] That's what I dream about, Biff. Sometimes I want to just rip my clothes off in the middle of the store and outbox that goddam merchandise manager. I mean I can outbox, outrun, and outlift anybody in that store, and I have to take orders from those common, petty sons-of-bitches till I can't stand it any more.

BIFF: I'm tellin' you, kid, if you were with me I'd be happy out there.

HAPPY: [*Enthused.*] See, Biff, everybody around me is so false that I'm constantly lowering my ideals . . .

BIFF: Baby, together we'd stand up for one another, we'd have someone to trust.

HAPPY: If I were around you—

BIFF: Hap, the trouble is we weren't brought up to grub for money. I don't know how to do it.

HAPPY: Neither can I!

BIFF: Then let's go!

HAPPY: The only thing is—what can you make out there?

BIFF: But look at your friend. Builds an estate and then hasn't the peace of mind to live in it.

HAPPY: Yeah, but when he walks into the store the waves part in front of him. That's fifty-two thousand dollars a year coming through the revolving door, and I got more in my pinky finger than he's got in his head.

BIFF: Yeah, but you just said—

HAPPY: I gotta show some of those pompous, self-important executives over there that Hap Loman can make the grade. I want to walk into the store the way he walks in. Then I'll go with you, Biff. We'll be together yet, I swear. But take those two we had tonight. Now weren't they gorgeous creatures?

BIFF: Yeah, yeah, most gorgeous I've had in years.

HAPPY: I get that any time I want, Biff. Whenever I feel disgusted. The only trouble is, it gets like bowling or something. I just keep knockin' them over and it doesn't mean anything. You still run around a lot?

BIFF: Naa. I'd like to find a girl—steady, somebody with substance.

HAPPY: That's what I long for.

BIFF: Go on! You'd never come home.

HAPPY: I would! Somebody with character, with resistance! Like Mom, y'know? You're gonna call me a bastard when I tell you this. That girl Charlotte I was with tonight is engaged to be married in five weeks. [*He tries on his new hat.*]

BIFF: No kiddin'!

HAPPY: Sure, the guy's in line for the vice-presidency of the store. I don't know what gets into me, maybe I just have an overdeveloped sense of competition or something, but I went and ruined her, and furthermore I can't get rid of her. And he's the third executive I've done that to. Isn't that a crummy characteristic? And to top it all, I go to their weddings! [*Indignantly, but laughing.*] Like I'm not supposed to take bribes. Manufacturers offer me a hundred-dollar bill now and then to throw an order their way. You know how honest I am, but it's like this girl, see. I hate myself for it. Because I don't want the girl, and, still, I take it and—I love it!

BIFF: Let's go to sleep.

HAPPY: I guess we didn't settle anything, heh?

BIFF: I just got one idea that I'm going to try.

HAPPY: What's that?

BIFF: Remember Bill Oliver?

HAPPY: Sure, Oliver is very big now. You want to work for him again?

BIFF: No, but when I quit he said something to me. He put his arm on my shoulder, and he said, "Biff, if you ever need anything, come to me."

HAPPY: I remember that. That sounds good.

BIFF: I think I'll go to see him. If I could get ten thousand or even seven or eight thousand dollars I could buy a beautiful ranch.

HAPPY: I bet he'd back you. 'Cause he thought highly of you, Biff. I mean, they all do. You're well liked, Biff. That's why I say to come back here, and we both have the apartment. And I'm tellin' you, Biff, any babe you want . . .

BIFF: No, with a ranch I could do the work I like and still be something. I just wonder though. I wonder if Oliver still thinks I stole that carton of basketballs.

HAPPY: Oh, he probably forgot that long ago. It's almost ten years. You're too sensitive. Anyway, he didn't really fire you.

BIFF: Well, I think he was going to. I think that's why I quit. I was never sure whether he knew or not. I know he thought the world of me, though. I was the only one he'd let lock up the place.

WILLY: [Below.] You gonna wash the engine, Biff?

HAPPY: Shh! [BIFF looks at HAPPY, who is gazing down, listening. WILLY is mumbling in the parlor.] You hear that?

[They listen. WILLY laughs warmly.]

BIFF: [Growing angry.] Doesn't he know Mom can hear that?

WILLY: Don't get your sweater dirty, Biff!

[A look of pain crosses BIFF's face.]

HAPPY: Isn't that terrible? Don't leave again, will you? You'll find a job here. You gotta stick around. I don't know what to do about him, it's getting embarrassing.

WILLY: What a simonizing job!

BIFF: Mom's hearing that!

WILLY: No kiddin', Biff, you got a date? Wonderful!

HAPPY: Go on to sleep. But talk to him in the morning, will you?

BIFF: [Reluctantly getting into bed.] With her in the house. Brother!

HAPPY: [Getting into bed.] I wish you'd have a good talk with him.

[The light on their room begins to fade.]

BIFF: [To himself in bed.] That selfish, stupid . . .

HAPPY: Sh . . . Sleep, Biff.

[Their light is out. Well before they have finished speaking, WILLY's form is dimly seen below in the darkened kitchen. He opens the refrigerator, searches in there, and takes out a bottle of milk. The apartment houses are fading out, and the entire house and surroundings become covered with leaves. Music insinuates itself as the leaves appear.]

WILLY: Just wanna be careful with those girls, Biff, that's all. Don't make any promises. No promises of any kind. Because a girl, y'know, they always believe what you tell 'em, and you're very young, Biff, you're too young to be talking seriously to girls. [Light rises on the kitchen. WILLY, talking, shuts the refrigerator door and comes downstage to the kitchen table. He pours milk into a glass. He is totally immersed in himself, smiling faintly.] Too young entirely, Biff. You want to watch your schooling first. Then when you're all set, there'll be plenty of girls for a boy like you. [He smiles broadly at a kitchen chair.] That so? The girls pay for you? [He laughs.] Boy, you must really be makin' a hit. [WILLY is gradually addressing—physically—a point offstage, speaking through the wall of the kitchen, and his voice has been rising in volume to that of a normal conversation.] I been wondering why you polish the car so careful. Ha! Don't leave the hubcaps, boys. Get the chamois to the hubcaps. Happy, use newspaper on the windows, it's the easiest thing. Show him how to do it, Biff! You see, Happy? Pad it up, use it like a pad. That's it, that's it, good work. You're doin' all right, Hap. [*He pauses, then nods in approbation for a few seconds, then looks upward.*] Biff, first thing we gotta do when we get time is clip that big branch over the house. Afraid it's gonna fall in a storm and hit the roof. Tell you what. We get a rope and sling her around, and then we climb up there with a couple of saws and take her down. Soon as you finish the car, boys, I wanna see ya. I got a surprise for you, boys.

BIFF: [*Offstage.*] Whatta ya got, Dad?

WILLY: No, you finish first. Never leave a job till you're finished—remember that. [*Looking toward the "big trees."*] Biff, up in Albany I saw a beautiful hammock. I think I'll buy it next trip, and we'll hang it right between those two elms. Wouldn't that be something? Just swingin' there under those branches. Boy, that would be . . .

[YOUNG BIFF *and* YOUNG HAPPY *appear from the direction* WILLY *was addressing.* HAPPY *carries rags and a pail of water.* BIFF, *wearing a sweater with a block "S," carries a football.*]

BIFF: [*Pointing in the direction of the car offstage.*] How's that, Pop, professional?

WILLY: Terrific. Terrific job, boys. Good work, Biff.

HAPPY: Where's the surprise, Pop?

WILLY: In the back seat of the car.

HAPPY: Boy! [*He runs off.*]

BIFF: What is it, Dad? Tell me, what'd you buy?

WILLY: [*Laughing, cuffs him.*] Never mind, something I want you to have.

BIFF: [*Turns and starts off.*] What is it, Hap?

HAPPY: [*Offstage.*] It's a punching bag!

BIFF: Oh, Pop!

WILLY: It's got Gene Tunney's[3] signature on it!

[HAPPY *runs onstage with a punching bag.*]

BIFF: Gee, how'd you know we wanted a punching bag?

WILLY: Well, it's the finest thing for the timing.

HAPPY: [*Lies down on his back and pedals with his feet.*] I'm losing weight, you notice, Pop?

WILLY: [*To* HAPPY.] Jumping rope is good too.

BIFF: Did you see the new football I got?

WILLY: [*Examining the ball.*] Where'd you get a new ball?

BIFF: The coach told me to practice my passing.

WILLY: That so? And he gave you the ball, heh?

BIFF: Well, I borrowed it from the locker room. [*He laughs confidentially.*]

WILLY: [*Laughing with him at the theft.*] I want you to return that.

3. Tunney (1897–1978) was world heavyweight boxing champion from 1926 to 1928 and retired undefeated.

HAPPY: I told you he wouldn't like it!

BIFF: [*Angrily.*] Well, I'm bringing it back!

WILLY: [*Stopping the incipient argument, to* HAPPY.] Sure, he's gotta practice with a regulation ball, doesn't he? [*To* BIFF.] Coach'll probably congratulate you on your initiative!

BIFF: Oh, he keeps congratulating my initiative all the time, Pop.

WILLY: That's because he likes you. If somebody else took that ball there'd be an uproar. So what's the report, boys, what's the report?

BIFF: Where'd you go this time, Dad? Gee we were lonesome for you.

WILLY: [*Pleased, puts an arm around each boy and they come down to the apron.*] Lonesome, heh?

BIFF: Missed you every minute.

WILLY: Don't say? Tell you a secret, boys. Don't breathe it to a soul. Someday I'll have my own business, and I'll never have to leave home anymore.

HAPPY: Like Uncle Charley, heh?

WILLY: Bigger than Uncle Charley! Because Charley is not—liked. He's liked, but he's not—well liked.

BIFF: Where'd you go this time, Dad?

WILLY: Well, I got on the road, and I went north to Providence. Met the mayor.

BIFF: The mayor of Providence!

WILLY: He was sitting in the hotel lobby.

BIFF: What'd he say?

WILLY: He said, "Morning!" And I said, "You got a fine city here, Mayor." And then he had coffee with me. And then I went to Waterbury. Waterbury is a fine city. Big clock city, the famous Waterbury clock. Sold a nice bill there. And then Boston—Boston is the cradle of the Revolution. A fine city. And a couple of other towns in Mass., and on to Portland and Bangor and straight home!

BIFF: Gee, I'd love to go with you sometime, Dad.

WILLY: Soon as summer comes.

HAPPY: Promise?

WILLY: You and Hap and I, and I'll show you all the towns. America is full of beautiful towns and fine, upstanding people. And they know me, boys, they know me up and down New England. The finest people. And when I bring you fellas up, there'll be open sesame for all of us, 'cause one thing, boys: I have friends. I can park my car in any street in New England, and the cops protect it like their own. This summer, heh?

BIFF and HAPPY: [*Together.*] Yeah! You bet!

WILLY: We'll take our bathing suits.

HAPPY: We'll carry your bags, Pop!

WILLY: Oh, won't that be something! Me comin' into the Boston stores with you boys carryin' my bags. What a sensation! [BIFF *is prancing around, practicing passing the ball.*] You nervous, Biff, about the game?

BIFF: Not if you're gonna be there.

WILLY: What do they say about you in school, now that they made you captain?

HAPPY: There's a crowd of girls behind him everytime the classes change.

BIFF: [*Taking* WILLY's *hand.*] This Saturday, Pop, this Saturday—just for you, I'm going to break through for a touchdown.

HAPPY: You're supposed to pass.

BIFF: I'm takin' one play for Pop. You watch me, Pop, and when I take off my helmet, that means I'm breakin' out. Then you watch me crash through that line!

WILLY: [*Kisses* BIFF.] Oh, wait'll I tell this in Boston!

[BERNARD *enters in knickers. He is younger than* BIFF, *earnest and loyal, a worried boy.*]

BERNARD: Biff, where are you? You're supposed to study with me today.

WILLY: Hey, looka Bernard. What're you lookin' so anemic about, Bernard?

BERNARD: He's gotta study, Uncle Willy. He's got Regents[4] next week.

HAPPY: [*Tauntingly, spinning* BERNARD *around.*] Let's box, Bernard!

BERNARD: Biff! [*He gets away from* HAPPY.] Listen, Biff, I heard Mr. Birnbaum say that if you don't start studyin' math he's gonna flunk you, and you won't graduate. I heard him!

WILLY: You better study with him, Biff. Go ahead now.

BERNARD: I heard him!

BIFF: Oh, Pop, you didn't see my sneakers! [*He holds up a foot for* WILLY *to look at.*]

WILLY: Hey, that's a beautiful job of printing!

BERNARD: [*Wiping his glasses.*] Just because he printed University of Virginia on his sneakers doesn't mean they've got to graduate him, Uncle Willy!

WILLY: [*Angrily.*] What're you talking about? With scholarships to three universities they're gonna flunk him?

BERNARD: But I heard Mr. Birnbaum say—

WILLY: Don't be a pest, Bernard! [*To his boys.*] What an anemic!

BERNARD: Okay, I'm waiting for you in my house, Biff.

[BERNARD *goes off. The* LOMANS *laugh.*]

WILLY: Bernard is not well liked, is he?

BIFF: He's liked, but he's not well liked.

HAPPY: That's right, Pop.

WILLY: That's just what I mean. Bernard can get the best marks in school, y'understand, but when he gets out in the business world, y'understand, you are going to be five times ahead of him. That's why I thank Almighty God you're both built like Adonises. Because the man who makes an appearance in the business world, the man who creates personal interest, is the man who gets ahead. Be liked and you will never want. You take me, for instance. I never have to wait in line to see a buyer. "Willy Loman is here!" That's all they have to know, and I go right through.

BIFF: Did you knock them dead, Pop?

---

4. Examinations administered to New York State high-school students.

WILLY: Knocked 'em cold in Providence, slaughtered 'em in Boston.

HAPPY: [*On his back, pedaling again.*] I'm losing weight, you notice, Pop?

[LINDA *enters, as of old, a ribbon in her hair, carrying a basket of washing.*]

LINDA: [*With youthful energy.*] Hello, dear!

WILLY: Sweetheart!

LINDA: How'd the Chevvy run?

WILLY: Chevrolet, Linda, is the greatest car ever built. [*To the boys.*] Since when do you let your mother carry wash up the stairs?

BIFF: Grab hold there, boy!

HAPPY: Where to, Mom?

LINDA: Hang them up on the line. And you better go down to your friends, Biff. The cellar is full of boys. They don't know what to do with themselves.

BIFF: Ah, when Pop comes home they can wait!

WILLY: [*Laughs appreciatively.*] You better go down and tell them what to do, Biff.

BIFF: I think I'll have them sweep out the furnace room.

WILLY: Good work, Biff.

BIFF: [*Goes through wall-line of kitchen to doorway at back and calls down.*] Fellas! Everybody sweep out the furnace room! I'll be right down!

VOICES: All right! Okay, Biff.

BIFF: George and Sam and Frank, come out back! We're hangin' up the wash! Come on, Hap, on the double!

[*He and* HAPPY *carry out the basket.*]

LINDA: The way they obey him!

WILLY: Well, that training, the training. I'm tellin' you, I was sellin' thousands and thousands, but I had to come home.

LINDA: Oh, the whole block'll be at that game. Did you sell anything?

WILLY: I did five hundred gross in Providence and seven hundred gross in Boston.

LINDA: No! Wait a minute, I've got a pencil. [*She pulls pencil and paper out of her apron pocket.*] That makes your commission . . . Two hundred—my God! Two hundred and twelve dollars!

WILLY: Well, I didn't figure it yet, but . . .

LINDA: How much did you do?

WILLY: Well, I—I did—about a hundred and eighty gross in Providence. Well, no—it came to—roughly two hundred gross on the whole trip.

LINDA: [*Without hesitation.*] Two hundred gross. That's . . . [*She figures.*]

WILLY: The trouble was that three of the stores were half closed for inventory in Boston. Otherwise I woulda broke records.

LINDA: Well, it makes seventy dollars and some pennies. That's very good.

WILLY: What do we owe?

LINDA: Well, on the first there's sixteen dollars on the refrigerator—

WILLY: Why sixteen?

LINDA: Well, the fan belt broke, so it was a dollar eighty.

WILLY: But it's brand new.

LINDA: Well, the man said that's the way it is. Till they work themselves in, y'know.

[*They move through the wall-line into the kitchen.*]

WILLY: I hope we didn't get stuck on that machine.

LINDA: They got the biggest ads of any of them!

WILLY: I know, it's a fine machine. What else?

LINDA: Well, there's nine-sixty for the washing machine. And for the vacuum cleaner there's three and a half due on the fifteenth. Then the roof, you got twenty-one dollars remaining.

WILLY: It don't leak, does it?

LINDA: No, they did a wonderful job. Then you owe Frank for the carburetor.

WILLY: I'm not going to pay that man! That goddam Chevrolet, they ought to prohibit the manufacture of that car!

LINDA: Well, you owe him three and a half. And odds and ends, comes to around a hundred and twenty dollars by the fifteenth.

WILLY: A hundred and twenty dollars! My God, if business don't pick up I don't know what I'm gonna do!

LINDA: Well, next week you'll do better.

WILLY: Oh, I'll knock 'em dead next week. I'll go to Hartford. I'm very well liked in Hartford. You know, the trouble is, Linda, people don't seem to take to me.

[*They move onto the forestage.*]

LINDA: Oh, don't be foolish.

WILLY: I know it when I walk in. They seem to laugh at me.

LINDA: Why? Why would they laugh at you? Don't talk that way, Willy.

[WILLY *moves to the edge of the stage.* LINDA *goes into the kitchen and starts to darn stockings.*]

WILLY: I don't know the reason for it, but they just pass me by. I'm not noticed.

LINDA: But you're doing wonderful, dear. You're making seventy to a hundred dollars a week.

WILLY: But I gotta be at it ten, twelve hours a day. Other men—I don't know—they do it easier. I don't know why—I can't stop myself—I talk too much. A man oughta come in with a few words. One thing about Charley. He's a man of few words, and they respect him.

LINDA: You don't talk too much, you're just lively.

WILLY: [*Smiling.*] Well, I figure, what the hell, life is short, a couple of jokes. [*To himself.*] I joke too much! [*The smile goes.*]

LINDA: Why? You're—

WILLY: I'm fat. I'm very—foolish to look at, Linda. I didn't tell you, but Christmas time I happened to be calling on F. H. Stewarts, and a salesman I know, as I was going in to see the buyer I heard him say something about—walrus. And I—I cracked him right across the face. I won't take that. I simply will not take that. But they do laugh at me. I know that.

LINDA: Darling . . .

WILLY: I gotta overcome it. I know I gotta overcome it. I'm not dressing to advantage, maybe.

LINDA: Willy, darling, you're the handsomest man in the world—

WILLY: Oh, no, Linda.

LINDA: To me you are. [*Slight pause.*] The handsomest. [*From the darkness is heard the laughter of a woman.* WILLY *doesn't turn to it, but it continues through* LINDA's *lines.*] And the boys, Willy. Few men are idolized by their children the way you are.

[*Music is heard as behind a scrim, to the left of the house,* THE WOMAN, *dimly seen, is dressing.*]

WILLY: [*With great feeling.*] You're the best there is, Linda, you're a pal, you know that? On the road—on the road I want to grab you sometimes and just kiss the life outa you. [*The laughter is loud now, and he moves into a brightening area at the left, where* THE WOMAN *has come from behind the scrim and is standing, putting on her hat, looking into a "mirror" and laughing.*] 'Cause I get so lonely—especially when business is bad and there's nobody to talk to. I get the feeling that I'll never sell anything again, that I won't make a living for you, or a business, a business for the boys. [*He talks through* THE WOMAN's *subsiding laughter.* THE WOMAN *primps at the "mirror."*] There's so much I want to make for—

THE WOMAN: Me? You didn't make me, Willy. I picked you.

WILLY: [*Pleased.*] You picked me?

THE WOMAN: [*Who is quite proper-looking,* WILLY's *age.*] I did. I've been sitting at that desk watching all the salesmen go by, day in, day out. But you've got such a sense of humor, and we do have such a good time together, don't we?

WILLY: Sure, sure. [*He takes her in his arms.*] Why do you have to go now?

THE WOMAN: It's two o'clock . . .

WILLY: No, come on in! [*He pulls her.*]

THE WOMAN: . . . my sisters'll be scandalized. When'll you be back?

WILLY: Oh, two weeks about. Will you come up again?

THE WOMAN: Sure thing. You do make me laugh. It's good for me. [*She squeezes his arm, kisses him.*] And I think you're a wonderful man.

WILLY: You picked me, heh?

THE WOMAN: Sure. Because you're so sweet. And such a kidder.

WILLY: Well, I'll see you next time I'm in Boston.

THE WOMAN: I'll put you right through to the buyers.

WILLY: [*Slapping her bottom.*] Right. Well, bottoms up!

THE WOMAN: [*Slaps him gently and laughs.*] You just kill me, Willy. [*He suddenly grabs her and kisses her roughly.*] You kill me. And thanks for the stockings. I love a lot of stockings. Well, good night.

WILLY: Good night. And keep your pores open!

THE WOMAN: Oh, Willy!

[THE WOMAN *bursts out laughing, and* LINDA's *laughter blends in.* THE WOMAN *disappears into the dark. Now the area at the kitchen table brightens.* LINDA *is sitting where she was at the kitchen table, but now is mending a pair of her silk stockings.*]

LINDA: You are, Willy. The handsomest man. You've got no reason to feel that—

WILLY: [*Coming out of* THE WOMAN's *dimming area and going over to* LINDA.] I'll make it all up to you, Linda. I'll—

LINDA: There's nothing to make up, dear. You're doing fine, better than—

WILLY: [*Noticing her mending.*] What's that?

LINDA: Just mending my stockings. They're so expensive—

WILLY: [*Angrily, taking them from her.*] I won't have you mending stockings in this house! Now throw them out!

[LINDA *puts the stockings in her pocket.*]

BERNARD: [*Entering on the run.*] Where is he? If he doesn't study!

WILLY: [*Moving to the forestage, with great agitation.*] You'll give him the answers!

BERNARD: I do, but I can't on a Regents! That's a state exam! They're liable to arrest me!

WILLY: Where is he? I'll whip him, I'll whip him!

LINDA: And he'd better give back that football, Willy, it's not nice.

WILLY: Biff! Where is he? Why is he taking everything?

LINDA: He's too rough with the girls, Willy. All the mothers are afraid of him!

WILLY: I'll whip him!

BERNARD: He's driving the car without a license!

[THE WOMAN's *laugh is heard.*]

WILLY: Shut up!

LINDA: All the mothers—

WILLY: Shut up!

BERNARD: [*Backing quietly away and out.*] Mr. Birnbaum says he's stuck up.

WILLY: Get outa here!

BERNARD: If he doesn't buckle down he'll flunk math! [*He goes off.*]

LINDA: He's right, Willy, you've gotta—

WILLY: [*Exploding at her.*] There's nothing the matter with him! You want him to be a worm like Bernard? He's got spirit, personality... [*As he speaks,* LINDA, *almost in tears, exits into the living room.* WILLY *is alone in the kitchen, wilting and staring. The leaves are gone. It is night again, and the apartment houses look down from behind.*] Loaded with it. Loaded! What is he stealing? He's giving it back, isn't he? Why is he stealing? What did I tell him? I never in my life told him anything but decent things.

[HAPPY *in pajamas has come down the stairs;* WILLY *suddenly becomes aware of* HAPPY's *presence.*]

HAPPY: Let's go now, come on.

WILLY: [*Sitting down at the kitchen table.*] Huh! Why did she have to wax the floors herself? Everytime she waxes the floors she keels over. She knows that!

HAPPY: Shh! Take it easy. What brought you back tonight?

WILLY: I got an awful scare. Nearly hit a kid in Yonkers. God! Why didn't I go to Alaska with my brother Ben that time! Ben! That man was a genius, that man was success incarnate! What a mistake! He begged me to go.

HAPPY: Well, there's no use in—

WILLY: You guys! There was a man started with the clothes on his back and ended up with diamond mines!

HAPPY: Boy, someday I'd like to know how he did it.

WILLY: What's the mystery? The man knew what he wanted and went out and got it! Walked into a jungle, and comes out, the age of twenty-one, and he's rich! The world is an oyster, but you don't crack it open on a mattress!

HAPPY: Pop, I told you I'm gonna retire you for life.

WILLY: You'll retire me for life on seventy goddam dollars a week? And your women and your car and your apartment, and you'll retire me for life! Christ's sake, I couldn't get past Yonkers today! Where are you guys, where are you? The woods are burning! I can't drive a car!

[CHARLEY *has appeared in the doorway. He is a large man, slow of speech, laconic, immovable. In all he says, despite what he says, there is pity, and now, trepidation. He has a robe over pajamas, slippers on his feet. He enters the kitchen.*]

CHARLEY: Everything all right?

HAPPY: Yeah, Charley, everything's . . .

WILLY: What's the matter?

CHARLEY: I heard some noise. I thought something happened. Can't we do something about the walls? You sneeze in here, and in my house hats blow off.

HAPPY: Let's go to bed, Dad. Come on.

[CHARLEY *signals to* HAPPY *to go.*]

WILLY: You go ahead, I'm not tired at the moment.

HAPPY: [*To* WILLY.] Take it easy, huh? [*He exits.*]

WILLY: What're you doin' up?

CHARLEY: [*Sitting down at the kitchen table opposite* WILLY.] Couldn't sleep good. I had a heartburn.

WILLY: Well, you don't know how to eat.

CHARLEY: I eat with my mouth.

WILLY: No, you're ignorant. You gotta know about vitamins and things like that.

CHARLEY: Come on, let's shoot. Tire you out a little.

WILLY: [*Hesitantly.*] All right. You got cards?

CHARLEY: [*Taking a deck from his pocket.*] Yeah, I got them. Someplace. What is it with those vitamins?

WILLY: [*Dealing.*] They build up your bones. Chemistry.

CHARLEY: Yeah, but there's no bones in a heartburn.

WILLY: What are you talkin' about? Do you know the first thing about it?

CHARLEY: Don't get insulted.

WILLY: Don't talk about something you don't know anything about.

[*They are playing. Pause.*]

CHARLEY: What're you doin' home?

WILLY: A little trouble with the car.

CHARLEY: Oh. [*Pause.*] I'd like to take a trip to California.

WILLY: Don't say.

CHARLEY: You want a job?

WILLY: I got a job, I told you that. [*After a slight pause.*] What the hell are you offering me a job for?

CHARLEY: Don't get insulted.

WILLY: Don't insult me.

CHARLEY: I don't see no sense in it. You don't have to go on this way.

WILLY: I got a good job. [*Slight pause.*] What do you keep comin' in here for?

CHARLEY: You want me to go?

WILLY: [*After a pause, withering.*] I can't understand it. He's going back to Texas again. What the hell is that?

CHARLEY: Let him go.

WILLY: I got nothin' to give him, Charley, I'm clean, I'm clean.

CHARLEY: He won't starve. None a them starve. Forget about him.

WILLY: Then what have I got to remember?

CHARLEY: You take it too hard. To hell with it. When a deposit bottle is broken you don't get your nickel back.

WILLY: That's easy enough for you to say.

CHARLEY: That ain't easy for me to say.

WILLY: Did you see the ceiling I put up in the living-room?

CHARLEY: Yeah, that's a piece of work. To put up a ceiling is a mystery to me. How do you do it?

WILLY: What's the difference?

CHARLEY: Well, talk about it.

WILLY: You gonna put up a ceiling?

CHARLEY: How could I put up a ceiling?

WILLY: Then what the hell are you bothering me for?

CHARLEY: You're insulted again.

WILLY: A man who can't handle tools is not a man. You're disgusting.

CHARLEY: Don't call me disgusting, Willy.

[UNCLE BEN, *carrying a valise and an umbrella, enters the forestage from around the right corner of the house. He is a stolid man, in his sixties, with a mustache and an authoritative air. He is utterly certain of his destiny, and there is an aura of far places about him. He enters exactly as* WILLY *speaks.*]

WILLY: I'm getting awfully tired, Ben.

[BEN's *music is heard.* BEN *looks around at everything.*]

CHARLEY: Good, keep playing; you'll sleep better. Did you call me Ben?

[BEN *looks at his watch.*]

WILLY: That's funny. For a second there you reminded me of my brother Ben.

BEN: I only have a few minutes. [*He strolls, inspecting the place.* WILLY *and* CHARLEY *continue playing.*]

CHARLEY: You never heard from him again, heh? Since that time?

WILLY: Didn't Linda tell you? Couple of weeks ago we got a letter from his wife in Africa. He died.

CHARLEY: That so.

BEN: [*Chuckling.*] So this is Brooklyn, eh?

CHARLEY: Maybe you're in for some of his money.

WILLY: Naa, he had seven sons. There's just one opportunity I had with that man . . .

BEN: I must make a train, William. There are several properties I'm looking at in Alaska.

WILLY: Sure, sure! If I'd gone with him to Alaska that time, everything would've been totally different.

CHARLEY: Go on, you'da froze to death up there.

WILLY: What're you talking about?

BEN: Opportunity is tremendous in Alaska, William. Surprised you're not up there.

WILLY: Sure, tremendous.

CHARLEY: Heh?

WILLY: There was the only man I ever met who knew the answers.

CHARLEY: Who?

BEN: How are you all?

WILLY: [*Taking a pot, smiling.*] Fine, fine.

CHARLEY: Pretty sharp tonight.

BEN: Is Mother living with you?

WILLY: No, she died a long time ago.

CHARLEY: Who?

BEN: That's too bad. Fine specimen of a lady, Mother.

WILLY: [*To* CHARLEY.] Heh?

BEN: I'd hoped to see the old girl.

CHARLEY: Who died?

BEN: Heard anything from Father, have you?

WILLY: [*Unnerved.*] What do you mean, who died?

CHARLEY: [*Taking a pot.*] What're you talkin' about?

BEN: [*Looking at his watch.*] William, it's half-past eight!

WILLY: [*As though to dispel his confusion he angrily stops* CHARLEY's *hand.*] That's my build!

CHARLEY: I put the ace—

WILLY: If you don't know how to play the game I'm not gonna throw my money away on you!

CHARLEY: [*Rising.*] It was my ace, for God's sake!

WILLY: I'm through, I'm through!

BEN: When did Mother die?

WILLY: Long ago. Since the beginning you never knew how to play cards.

CHARLEY: [*Picks up the cards and goes to the door.*] All right! Next time I'll bring a deck with five aces.

WILLY: I don't play that kind of game!

CHARLEY: [*Turning to him.*] You ought to be ashamed of yourself!

WILLY: Yeah?

CHARLEY: Yeah! [*He goes out.*]

WILLY: [*Slamming the door after him.*] Ignoramus!

BEN: [*As* WILLY *comes toward him through the wall-line of the kitchen.*] So you're William.

WILLY: [*Shaking* BEN's *hand.*] Ben! I've been waiting for you so long! What's the answer? How did you do it?

BEN: Oh, there's a story in that.

[LINDA *enters the forestage, as of old, carrying the wash basket.*]

LINDA: Is this Ben?

BEN: [*Gallantly.*] How do you do, my dear.

LINDA: Where've you been all these years? Willy's always wondered why you—

WILLY: [*Pulling* BEN *away from her impatiently.*] Where is Dad? Didn't you follow him? How did you get started?

BEN: Well, I don't know how much you remember.

WILLY: Well, I was just a baby, of course, only three or four years old—

BEN: Three years and eleven months.

WILLY: What a memory, Ben!

BEN: I have many enterprises, William, and I have never kept books.

WILLY: I remember I was sitting under the wagon in—was it Nebraska?

BEN: It was South Dakota, and I gave you a bunch of wild flowers.

WILLY: I remember you walking away down some open road.

BEN: [*Laughing.*] I was going to find Father in Alaska.

WILLY: Where is he?

BEN: At that age I had a very faulty view of geography, William. I discovered after a few days that I was heading due south, so instead of Alaska, I ended up in Africa.

LINDA: Africa!

WILLY: The Gold Coast!

BEN: Principally diamond mines.

LINDA: Diamond mines!

BEN: Yes, my dear. But I've only a few minutes—

WILLY: No! Boys! Boys! [*Young* BIFF *and* HAPPY *appear.*] Listen to this. This is your Uncle Ben, a great man! Tell my boys, Ben!

BEN: Why, boys, when I was seventeen I walked into the jungle, and when I was twenty-one I walked out. [*He laughs.*] And by God I was rich.

WILLY: [*To the boys.*] You see what I been talking about? The greatest things can happen!

BEN: [*Glancing at his watch.*] I have an appointment in Ketchikan Tuesday week.

WILLY: No, Ben! Please tell about Dad. I want my boys to hear. I want them to know the kind of stock they spring from. All I remember is a man with a big beard, and I was in Mamma's lap, sitting around a fire, and some kind of high music.

BEN: His flute. He played the flute.

WILLY: Sure, the flute, that's right!

[*New music is heard, a high, rollicking tune.*]

BEN: Father was a very great and a very wild-hearted man. We would start in Boston, and he'd toss the whole family into the wagon, and then he'd drive the team right across the country; through Ohio, and Indiana, Michigan, Illinois, and all the Western states. And we'd stop in the towns and sell the flutes that he'd made on the way. Great inventor, Father. With one gadget he made more in a week than a man like you could make in a lifetime.

WILLY: That's just the way I'm bringing them up, Ben—rugged, well liked, all-around.

BEN: Yeah? [*To* BIFF.] Hit that, boy—hard as you can. [*He pounds his stomach.*]

BIFF: Oh, no, sir!

BEN: [*Taking boxing stance.*] Come on, get to me! [*He laughs.*]

WILLY: Go to it, Biff! Go ahead, show him!

BIFF: Okay! [*He cocks his fist and starts in.*]

LINDA: [*To* WILLY.] Why must he fight, dear?

BEN: [*Sparring with* BIFF.] Good boy! Good boy!

WILLY: How's that, Ben, heh?

HAPPY: Give him the left, Biff!

LINDA: Why are you fighting?

BEN: Good boy! [*Suddenly comes in, trips* BIFF, *and stands over him, the point of his umbrella poised over* BIFF's *eye.*]

LINDA: Look out, Biff!

BIFF: Gee!

BEN: [*Patting* BIFF's *knee.*] Never fight fair with a stranger, boy. You'll never get out of the jungle that way. [*Taking* LINDA's *hand and bowing.*] It was an honor and a pleasure to meet you, Linda.

LINDA: [*Withdrawing her hand coldly, frightened.*] Have a nice—trip.

BEN: [*To* WILLY.] And good luck with your—what do you do?

WILLY: Selling.

BEN: Yes. Well . . . [*He raises his hand in farewell to all.*]

WILLY: No, Ben, I don't want you to think . . . [*He takes* BEN's *arm to show him.*] It's Brooklyn, I know, but we hunt too.

BEN: Really, now.

WILLY: Oh, sure, there's snakes and rabbits and—that's why I moved out here. Why, Biff can fell any one of these trees in no time! Boys! Go right over to where they're building the apartment house and get some sand. We're gonna rebuild the entire front stoop right now! Watch this, Ben!

BIFF: Yes, sir! On the double, Hap!

HAPPY: [*As he and* BIFF *run off.*] I lost weight, Pop, you notice?

[CHARLEY *enters in knickers, even before the boys are gone.*]

CHARLEY: Listen, if they steal any more from that building the watchman'll put the cops on them!

LINDA: [*To* WILLY.] Don't let Biff...

[BEN *laughs lustily.*]

WILLY: You shoulda seen the lumber they brought home last week. At least a dozen six-by-tens worth all kinds a money.

CHARLEY: Listen, if that watchman—

WILLY: I gave them hell, understand. But I got a couple of fearless characters there.

CHARLEY: Willy, the jails are full of fearless characters.

BEN: [*Clapping* WILLY *on the back, with a laugh at* CHARLEY.] And the stock exchange, friend!

WILLY: [*Joining in* BEN's *laughter.*] Where are the rest of your pants?

CHARLEY: My wife bought them.

WILLY: Now all you need is a golf club and you can go upstairs and go to sleep. [*To* BEN.] Great athlete! Between him and his son Bernard they can't hammer a nail!

BERNARD: [*Rushing in.*] The watchman's chasing Biff!

WILLY: [*Angrily.*] Shut up! He's not stealing anything!

LINDA: [*Alarmed, hurrying off left.*] Where is he? Biff, dear! [*She exits.*]

WILLY: [*Moving toward the left, away from* BEN.] There's nothing wrong. What's the matter with you?

BEN: Nervy boy. Good!

WILLY: [*Laughing.*] Oh, nerves of iron, that Biff!

CHARLEY: Don't know what it is. My New England man comes back and he's bleedin', they murdered him up there.

WILLY: It's contacts, Charley, I got important contacts!

CHARLEY: [*Sarcastically.*] Glad to hear it, Willy. Come in later, we'll shoot a little casino. I'll take some of your Portland money. [*He laughs at* WILLY *and exits.*]

WILLY: [*Turning to* BEN.] Business is bad, it's murderous. But not for me, of course.

BEN: I'll stop by on my way back to Africa.

WILLY: [*Longingly.*] Can't you stay a few days? You're just what I need, Ben, because I—I have a fine position here, but I—well, Dad left when I was such a baby and I never had a chance to talk to him and I still feel— kind of temporary about myself.

BEN: I'll be late for my train.

[*They are at opposite ends of the stage.*]

WILLY: Ben, my boys—can't we talk? They'd go into the jaws of hell for me, see, but I—

BEN: William, you're being first-rate with your boys. Outstanding, manly chaps!

WILLY: [*Hanging on to his words.*] Oh, Ben, that's good to hear! Because sometimes I'm afraid that I'm not teaching them the right kind of—Ben, how should I teach them?

BEN: [*Giving great weight to each word, and with a certain vicious audacity.*] William, when I walked into the jungle, I was seventeen. When I walked out I was twenty-one. And, by God, I was rich! [*He goes off into darkness around the right corner of the house.*]

WILLY: . . . was rich! That's just the spirit I want to imbue them with! To walk into a jungle! I was right! I was right! I was right!

> [BEN *is gone, but* WILLY *is still speaking to him as* LINDA, *in nightgown and robe, enters the kitchen, glances around for* WILLY, *then goes to the door of the house, looks out and sees him. Comes down to his left. He looks at her.*]

LINDA: Willy, dear? Willy?

WILLY: I was right!

LINDA: Did you have some cheese? [*He can't answer.*] It's very late, darling. Come to bed, heh?

WILLY: [*Looking straight up.*] Gotta break your neck to see a star in this yard.

LINDA: You coming in?

WILLY: Whatever happened to that diamond watch fob? Remember? When Ben came from Africa that time? Didn't he give me a watch fob with a diamond in it?

LINDA: You pawned it, dear. Twelve, thirteen years ago. For Biff's radio correspondence course.

WILLY: Gee, that was a beautiful thing. I'll take a walk.

LINDA: But you're in your slippers.

WILLY: [*Starting to go around the house at the left.*] I was right! I was! [*Half to* LINDA, *as he goes, shaking his head.*] What a man! There was a man worth talking to. I was right!

LINDA: [*Calling after* WILLY.] But in your slippers, Willy!

> [WILLY *is almost gone when* BIFF, *in his pajamas, comes down the stairs and enters the kitchen.*]

BIFF: What is he doing out there?

LINDA: Sh!

BIFF: God Almighty, Mom, how long has he been doing this?

LINDA: Don't, he'll hear you.

BIFF: What the hell is the matter with him?

LINDA: It'll pass by morning.

BIFF: Shouldn't we do anything?

LINDA: Oh, my dear, you should do a lot of things, but there's nothing to do, so go to sleep.

> [HAPPY *comes down the stairs and sits on the steps.*]

HAPPY: I never heard him so loud, Mom.

LINDA: Well, come around more often; you'll hear him. [*She sits down at the table and mends the lining of* WILLY's *jacket.*]

BIFF: Why didn't you ever write me about this, Mom?

LINDA: How would I write to you? For over three months you had no address.

BIFF: I was on the move. But you know I thought of you all the time. You know that, don't you, pal?

LINDA: I know, dear, I know. But he likes to have a letter. Just to know that there's still a possibility for better things.

BIFF: He's not like this all the time, is he?

LINDA: It's when you come home he's always the worst.

BIFF: When I come home?

LINDA: When you write you're coming, he's all smiles, and talks about the future, and—he's just wonderful. And then the closer you seem to come, the more shaky he gets, and then, by the time you get here, he's arguing, and he seems angry at you. I think it's just that maybe he can't bring himself to—to open up to you. Why are you so hateful to each other? Why is that?

BIFF: [*Evasively.*] I'm not hateful, Mom.

LINDA: But you no sooner come in the door than you're fighting!

BIFF: I don't know why. I mean to change. I'm tryin', Mom, you understand?

LINDA: Are you home to stay now?

BIFF: I don't know. I want to look around, see what's doin'.

LINDA: Biff, you can't look around all your life, can you?

BIFF: I just can't take hold, Mom. I can't take hold of some kind of a life.

LINDA: Biff, a man is not a bird, to come and go with the springtime.

BIFF: Your hair . . . [*He touches her hair.*] Your hair got so gray.

LINDA: Oh, it's been gray since you were in high school. I just stopped dyeing it, that's all.

BIFF: Dye it again, will ya? I don't want my pal looking old. [*He smiles.*]

LINDA: You're such a boy! You think you can go away for a year and . . . You've got to get it into your head now that one day you'll knock on this door and there'll be strange people here—

BIFF: What are you talking about? You're not even sixty, Mom.

LINDA: But what about your father?

BIFF: [*Lamely.*] Well, I meant him too.

HAPPY: He admires Pop.

LINDA: Biff, dear, if you don't have any feeling for him, then you can't have any feeling for me.

BIFF: Sure I can, Mom.

LINDA: No. You can't just come to see me, because I love him. [*With a threat, but only a threat, of tears.*] He's the dearest man in the world to me, and I won't have anyone making him feel unwanted and low and blue. You've got to make up your mind now, darling, there's no leeway anymore. Either he's your father and you pay him that respect, or else you're not to come here. I know he's not easy to get along with—nobody knows that better than me—but . . .

WILLY: [*From the left, with a laugh.*] Hey, hey, Biffo!

BIFF: [*Starting to go out after* WILLY.] What the hell is the matter with him? [HAPPY *stops him.*]

LINDA: Don't—don't go near him!

BIFF: Stop making excuses for him! He always, always wiped the floor with you. Never had an ounce of respect for you.

HAPPY: He's always had respect for—

BIFF: What the hell do you know about it?

HAPPY: [*Surlily.*] Just don't call him crazy!

BIFF: He's got no character—Charley wouldn't do this. Not in his own house—spewing out that vomit from his mind.

HAPPY: Charley never had to cope with what he's got to.

BIFF: People are worse off than Willy Loman. Believe me, I've seen them!

LINDA: Then make Charley your father, Biff. You can't do that, can you? I don't say he's a great man. Willy Loman never made a lot of money. His name was never in the paper. He's not the finest character that ever lived. But he's a human being, and a terrible thing is happening to him. So attention must be paid. He's not to be allowed to fall into his grave like an old dog. Attention, attention must be finally paid to such a person. You called him crazy—

BIFF: I didn't mean—

LINDA: No, a lot of people think he's lost his—balance. But you don't have to be very smart to know what his trouble is. The man is exhausted.

HAPPY: Sure!

LINDA: A small man can be just as exhausted as a great man. He works for a company thirty-six years this March, opens up unheard-of territories to their trademark, and now in his old age they take his salary away.

HAPPY: [*Indignantly.*] I didn't know that, Mom.

LINDA: You never asked, my dear! Now that you get your spending money someplace else you don't trouble your mind with him.

HAPPY: But I gave you money last—

LINDA: Christmas time, fifty dollars! To fix the hot water it cost ninety-seven fifty! For five weeks he's been on straight commission, like a beginner, an unknown!

BIFF: Those ungrateful bastards!

LINDA: Are they any worse than his sons? When he brought them business, when he was young, they were glad to see him. But now his old friends, the old buyers that loved him so and always found some order to hand him in a pinch—they're all dead, retired. He used to be able to make six, seven calls a day in Boston. Now he takes his valises out of the car and puts them back and takes them out again and he's exhausted. Instead of walking he talks now. He drives seven hundred miles, and when he gets there no one knows him anymore, no one welcomes him. And what goes through a man's mind, driving seven hundred miles home without having earned a cent? Why shouldn't he talk to himself? Why? When he has to go to Charley and borrow fifty dollars a week and pretend to me that it's his pay? How long can that go on? How long? You see what I'm sitting here and waiting for? And you tell me he has no character? The man who never worked a day but for your benefit? When does he get the medal for that? Is this his reward—to turn around at the age of sixty-three and find his sons, who he loved better than his life, one a philandering bum—

HAPPY: Mom!

LINDA: That's all you are, my baby! [*To* BIFF.] And you! What happened to the love you had for him? You were such pals! How you used to talk to him on the phone every night! How lonely he was till he could come home to you!

BIFF: All right, Mom. I'll live here in my room, and I'll get a job. I'll keep away from him, that's all.

LINDA: No, Biff. You can't stay here and fight all the time.

BIFF: He threw me out of this house, remember that.

LINDA: Why did he do that? I never knew why.

BIFF: Because I know he's a fake and he doesn't like anybody around who knows!

LINDA: Why a fake? In what way? What do you mean?

BIFF: Just don't lay it all at my feet. It's between me and him—that's all I have to say. I'll chip in from now on. He'll settle for half my paycheck. He'll be all right. I'm going to bed. [*He starts for the stairs.*]

LINDA: He won't be all right.

BIFF: [*Turning on the stairs, furiously.*] I hate this city and I'll stay here. Now what do you want?

LINDA: He's dying, BIFF.

[HAPPY *turns quickly to her, shocked.*]

BIFF: [*After a pause.*] Why is he dying?

LINDA: He's been trying to kill himself.

BIFF: [*With great horror.*] How?

LINDA: I live from day to day.

BIFF: What're you talking about?

LINDA: Remember I wrote you that he smashed up the car again? In February?

BIFF: Well?

LINDA: The insurance inspector came. He said that they have evidence. That all these accidents in the last year—weren't—weren't—accidents.

HAPPY: How can they tell that? That's a lie.

LINDA: It seems there's a woman . . . [*She takes a breath as. . . .*]

{ BIFF: [*Sharply but contained.*] What woman?

{ LINDA: [*Simultaneously.*] . . . and this woman . . .

LINDA: What?

BIFF: Nothing. Go ahead.

LINDA: What did you say?

BIFF: Nothing. I just said what woman?

HAPPY: What about her?

LINDA: Well, it seems she was walking down the road and saw his car. She says that he wasn't driving fast at all, and that he didn't skid. She says he came to that little bridge, and then deliberately smashed into the railing, and it was only the shallowness of the water that saved him.

BIFF: Oh, no, he probably just fell asleep again.

LINDA: I don't think he fell asleep.

BIFF: Why not?

LINDA: Last month... [*With great difficulty.*] Oh, boys, it's so hard to say a thing like this! He's just a big stupid man to you, but I tell you there's more good in him than in many other people. [*She chokes, wipes her eyes.*] I was looking for a fuse. The lights blew out, and I went down the cellar. And behind the fuse box—it happened to fall out—was a length of rubber pipe—just short.

HAPPY: No kidding?

LINDA: There's a little attachment on the end of it. I knew right away. And sure enough, on the bottom of the water heater there's a new little nipple on the gas pipe.

HAPPY: [*Angrily.*] That—jerk.

BIFF: Did you have it taken off?

LINDA: I'm—I'm ashamed to. How can I mention it to him? Every day I go down and take away that little rubber pipe. But, when he comes home, I put it back where it was. How can I insult him that way? I don't know what to do. I live from day to day, boys. I tell you, I know every thought in his mind. It sounds so old-fashioned and silly, but I tell you he put his whole life into you and you've turned your backs on him. [*She is bent over in the chair, weeping, her face in her hands.*] Biff, I swear to God! Biff, his life is in your hands!

HAPPY: [*To* BIFF.] How do you like that damned fool!

BIFF: [*Kissing her.*] All right, pal, all right. It's all settled now. I've been remiss. I know that, Mom. But now I'll stay, and I swear to you, I'll apply myself. [*Kneeling in front of her, in a fever of self-reproach.*] It's just—you see, Mom, I don't fit in business. Not that I won't try. I'll try, and I'll make good.

HAPPY: Sure you will. The trouble with you in business was you never tried to please people.

BIFF: I know, I—

HAPPY: Like when you worked for Harrison's. Bob Harrison said you were tops, and then you go and do some damn fool thing like whistling whole songs in the elevator like a comedian.

BIFF: [*Against* HAPPY.] So what? I like to whistle sometimes.

HAPPY: You don't raise a guy to a responsible job who whistles in the elevator!

LINDA: Well, don't argue about it now.

HAPPY: Like when you'd go off and swim in the middle of the day instead of taking the line around.

BIFF: [*His resentment rising.*] Well, don't you run off? You take off sometimes, don't you? On a nice summer day?

HAPPY: Yeah, but I cover myself!

LINDA: Boys!

HAPPY: If I'm going to take a fade the boss can call any number where I'm supposed to be and they'll swear to him that I just left. I'll tell you something that I hate to say, Biff, but in the business world some of them think you're crazy.

BIFF: [*Angered.*] Screw the business world!

HAPPY: All right, screw it! Great, but cover yourself!

LINDA: Hap, Hap!

BIFF: I don't care what they think! They've laughed at Dad for years, and you know why? Because we don't belong in this nuthouse of a city! We should be mixing cement on some open plain, or—or carpenters. A carpenter is allowed to whistle!

[WILLY *walks in from the entrance of the house, at left.*]

WILLY: Even your grandfather was better than a carpenter. [*Pause. They watch him.*] You never grew up. Bernard does not whistle in the elevator, I assure you.

BIFF: [*As though to laugh* WILLY *out of it.*] Yeah, but you do, Pop.

WILLY: I never in my life whistled in an elevator! And who in the business world thinks I'm crazy?

BIFF: I didn't mean it like that, Pop. Now don't make a whole thing out of it, will ya?

WILLY: Go back to the West! Be a carpenter, a cowboy, enjoy yourself!

LINDA: Willy, he was just saying—

WILLY: I heard what he said!

HAPPY: [*Trying to quiet* WILLY.] Hey, Pop, come on now . . .

WILLY: [*Continuing over* HAPPY's *line.*] They laugh at me, heh? Go to Filene's, go to the Hub, go to Slattery's Boston. Call out the name Willy Loman and see what happens! Big shot!

BIFF: All right, Pop.

WILLY: Big!

BIFF: All right!

WILLY: Why do you always insult me?

BIFF: I didn't say a word. [*To* LINDA.] Did I say a word?

LINDA: He didn't say anything, Willy.

WILLY: [*Going to the doorway of the living-room.*] All right, good night, good night.

LINDA: Willy, dear, he just decided . . .

WILLY: [*To* BIFF.] If you get tired hanging around tomorrow, paint the ceiling I put up in the living-room.

BIFF: I'm leaving early tomorrow.

HAPPY: He's going to see Bill Oliver, Pop.

WILLY: [*Interestedly.*] Oliver? For what?

BIFF: [*With reserve, but trying, trying.*] He always said he'd stake me. I'd like to go into business, so maybe I can take him up on it.

LINDA: Isn't that wonderful?

WILLY: Don't interrupt. What's wonderful about it? There's fifty men in the City of New York who'd stake him. [*To* BIFF.] Sporting goods?

BIFF: I guess so. I know something about it and—

WILLY: He knows something about it! You know sporting goods better than Spalding,[5] for God's sake! How much is he giving you?

BIFF: I don't know, I didn't even see him yet, but—

WILLY: Then what're you talkin' about?

BIFF: [*Getting angry.*] Well, all I said was I'm gonna see him, that's all!

WILLY: [*Turning away.*] Ah, you're counting your chickens again.

BIFF: [*Starting left for the stairs.*] Oh, Jesus, I'm going to sleep!

WILLY: [*Calling after him.*] Don't curse in this house!

BIFF: [*Turning.*] Since when did you get so clean?

HAPPY: [*Trying to stop them.*] Wait a ...

WILLY: Don't use that language to me! I won't have it!

HAPPY: [*Grabbing* BIFF, *shouts.*] Wait a minute! I got an idea. I got a feasible idea. Come here, Biff, let's talk this over now, let's talk some sense here. When I was down in Florida last time, I thought of a great idea to sell sporting goods. It just came back to me. You and I, Biff—we have a line, the Loman Line. We train a couple of weeks, and put on a couple of exhibitions, see?

WILLY: That's an idea!

HAPPY: Wait! We form two basketball teams, see? Two water-polo teams. We play each other. It's a million dollars' worth of publicity. Two brothers, see? The Loman Brothers. Displays in the Royal Palms—all the hotels. And banners over the ring and the basketball court: "Loman Brothers." Baby, we could sell sporting goods!

WILLY: That is a one-million-dollar idea!

LINDA: Marvelous!

BIFF: I'm in great shape as far as that's concerned.

HAPPY: And the beauty of it is, Biff, it wouldn't be like a business. We'd be out playin' ball again ...

BIFF: [*Enthused.*] Yeah, that's ...

WILLY: Million-dollar ...

HAPPY: And you wouldn't get fed up with it, Biff. It'd be the family again. There'd be the old honor, and comradeship, and if you wanted to go off for a swim or somethin'—well, you'd do it! Without some smart cooky gettin' up ahead of you!

WILLY: Lick the world! You guys together could absolutely lick the civilized world.

BIFF: I'll see Oliver tomorrow. Hap, if we could work that out ...

LINDA: Maybe things are beginning to—

WILLY: [*Wildly enthused, to* LINDA.] Stop interrupting! [*To* BIFF.] But don't wear sport jacket and slacks when you see Oliver.

BIFF: No, I'll—

WILLY: A business suit, and talk as little as possible, and don't crack any jokes.

BIFF: He did like me. Always liked me.

---

5. Albert G. Spalding (1850–1915), American baseball player and sporting-goods manufacturer.

LINDA: He loved you!

WILLY: [*To* LINDA.] Will you stop! [*To* BIFF.] Walk in very serious. You are not applying for a boy's job. Money is to pass. Be quiet, fine, and serious. Everybody likes a kidder, but nobody lends him money.

HAPPY: I'll try to get some myself, Biff. I'm sure I can.

WILLY: I see great things for you kids, I think your troubles are over. But remember, start big and you'll end big. Ask for fifteen. How much you gonna ask for?

BIFF: Gee, I don't know—

WILLY: And don't say "Gee." "Gee" is a boy's word. A man walking in for fifteen thousand dollars does not say "Gee!"

BIFF: Ten, I think, would be top though.

WILLY: Don't be so modest. You always started too low. Walk in with a big laugh. Don't look worried. Start off with a couple of your good stories to lighten things up. It's not what you say, it's how you say it—because personality always wins the day.

LINDA: Oliver always thought the highest of him—

WILLY: Will you let me talk?

BIFF: Don't yell at her, Pop, will ya?

WILLY: [*Angrily.*] I was talking, wasn't I?

BIFF: I don't like you yelling at her all the time, and I'm tellin' you, that's all.

WILLY: What're you, takin' over this house?

LINDA: Willy—

WILLY: [*Turning on her.*] Don't take his side all the time, goddammit!

BIFF: [*Furiously.*] Stop yelling at her!

WILLY: [*Suddenly pulling on his cheek, beaten down, guilt ridden.*] Give my best to Bill Oliver—he may remember me. [*He exits through the living-room doorway.*]

LINDA: [*Her voice subdued.*] What'd you have to start that for? [BIFF *turns away.*] You see how sweet he was as soon as you talked hopefully? [*She goes over to* BIFF.] Come up and say good night to him. Don't let him go to bed that way.

HAPPY: Come on, Biff, let's buck him up.

LINDA: Please, dear. Just say good night. It takes so little to make him happy. Come. [*She goes through the living-room doorway, calling upstairs from within the living-room.*] Your pajamas are hanging in the bathroom, Willy!

HAPPY: [*Looking toward where* LINDA *went out.*] What a woman! They broke the mold when they made her. You know that, Biff?

BIFF: He's off salary. My God, working on commission!

HAPPY: Well, let's face it: he's no hot-shot selling man. Except that sometimes, you have to admit, he's a sweet personality.

BIFF: [*Deciding.*] Lend me ten bucks, will ya? I want to buy some new ties.

HAPPY: I'll take you to a place I know. Beautiful stuff. Wear one of my striped shirts tomorrow.

BIFF: She got gray. Mom got awful old. Gee, I'm gonna go in to Oliver tomorrow and knock him for a—

HAPPY: Come on up. Tell that to Dad. Let's give him a whirl. Come on.

BIFF: [*Steamed up.*] You know, with ten thousand bucks, boy!

HAPPY: [*As they go into the living-room.*] That's the talk, Biff, that's the first time I've heard the old confidence out of you! [*From within the living-room, fading off.*] You're gonna live with me, kid, and any babe you want just say the word . . .

[*The last lines are hardly heard. They are mounting the stairs to their parents' bedroom.*]

LINDA: [*Entering her bedroom and addressing* WILLY, *who is in the bathroom. She is straightening the bed for him.*] Can you do anything about the shower? It drips.

WILLY: [*From the bathroom.*] All of a sudden everything falls to pieces! Goddam plumbing, oughta be sued, those people. I hardly finished putting it in and the thing . . . [*His words rumble off.*]

LINDA: I'm just wondering if Oliver will remember him. You think he might?

WILLY: [*Coming out of the bathroom in his pajamas.*] Remember him? What's the matter with you, you crazy? If he'd've stayed with Oliver he'd be on top by now! Wait'll Oliver gets a look at him. You don't know the average caliber anymore. The average young man today—[*He is getting into bed.*]—is got a caliber of zero. Greatest thing in the world for him was to bum around. [BIFF *and* HAPPY *enter the bedroom. Slight pause.* WILLY *stops short, looking at* BIFF.] Glad to hear it, boy.

HAPPY: He wanted to say good night to you, sport.

WILLY: [*To* BIFF.] Yeah. Knock him dead, boy. What'd you want to tell me?

BIFF: Just take it easy, Pop. Good night. [*He turns to go.*]

WILLY: [*Unable to resist.*] And if anything falls off the desk while you're talking to him—like a package or something—don't you pick it up. They have office boys for that.

LINDA: I'll make a big breakfast—

WILLY: Will you let me finish? [*To* BIFF.] Tell him you were in the business in the West. Not farm work.

BIFF: All right, Dad.

LINDA: I think everything—

WILLY: [*Going right through her speech.*] And don't undersell yourself. No less than fifteen thousand dollars.

BIFF: [*Unable to bear him.*] Okay. Good night, Mom. [*He starts moving.*]

WILLY: Because you got a greatness in you, Biff, remember that. You got all kinds of greatness . . . [*He lies back, exhausted.* BIFF *walks out.*]

LINDA: [*Calling after* BIFF.] Sleep well, darling!

HAPPY: I'm gonna get married, Mom. I wanted to tell you.

LINDA: Go to sleep, dear.

HAPPY: [*Going.*] I just wanted to tell you.

WILLY: Keep up the good work. [HAPPY *exits.*] God . . . remember that Ebbets Field[6] game? The championship of the city?

---

6. Stadium where the Dodgers, Brooklyn's major-league baseball team, played from 1913 to 1957.

LINDA: Just rest. Should I sing to you?

WILLY: Yeah. Sing to me. [LINDA *hums a soft lullaby.*] When that team came out—he was the tallest, remember?

LINDA: Oh, yes. And in gold.

[BIFF *enters the darkened kitchen, takes a cigarette, and leaves the house. He comes downstage into a golden pool of light. He smokes, staring at the night.*]

WILLY: Like a young god. Hercules—something like that. And the sun, the sun all around him. Remember how he waved to me? Right up from the field, with the representatives of three colleges standing by? And the buyers I brought, and the cheers when he came out—Loman, Loman, Loman! God Almighty, he'll be great yet. A star like that, magnificent, can never really fade away!

[*The light on* WILLY *is fading. The gas heater begins to glow through the kitchen wall, near the stairs, a blue flame beneath red coils.*]

LINDA: [*Timidly.*] Willy dear, what has he got against you?

WILLY: I'm so tired. Don't talk anymore.

[BIFF *slowly returns to the kitchen. He stops, stares toward the heater.*]

LINDA: Will you ask Howard to let you work in New York?

WILLY: First thing in the morning. Everything'll be all right.

[BIFF *reaches behind the heater and draws out a length of rubber tubing. He is horrified and turns his head toward* WILLY's *room, still dimly lit, from which the strains of* LINDA's *desperate but monotonous humming rise.*]

WILLY: [*Staring through the window into the moonlight.*] Gee, look at the moon moving between the buildings!

[BIFF *wraps the tubing around his hand and quickly goes up the stairs.*]

CURTAIN

ACT II

Music is heard, gay and bright. The curtain rises as the music fades away. WILLY, *in shirt sleeves, is sitting at the kitchen table, sipping coffee, his hat in his lap.* LINDA *is filling his cup when she can.*

WILLY: Wonderful coffee. Meal in itself.

LINDA: Can I make you some eggs?

WILLY: No. Take a breath.

LINDA: You look so rested, dear.

WILLY: I slept like a dead one. First time in months. Imagine, sleeping till ten on a Tuesday morning. Boys left nice and early, heh?

LINDA: They were out of here by eight o'clock.

WILLY: Good work!

LINDA: It was so thrilling to see them leaving together. I can't get over the shaving lotion in this house!

WILLY: [*Smiling.*] Mmm—

LINDA: Biff was very changed this morning. His whole attitude seemed to be hopeful. He couldn't wait to get downtown to see Oliver.

WILLY: He's heading for a change. There's no question, there simply are certain men that take longer to get—solidified. How did he dress?

LINDA: His blue suit. He's so handsome in that suit. He could be a—anything in that suit!

[WILLY *gets up from the table.* LINDA *holds his jacket for him.*]

WILLY: There's no question, no question at all. Gee, on the way home tonight I'd like to buy some seeds.

LINDA: [*Laughing.*] That'd be wonderful. But not enough sun gets back there. Nothing'll grow any more.

WILLY: You wait, kid, before it's all over we're gonna get a little place out in the country, and I'll raise some vegetables, a couple of chickens ...

LINDA: You'll do it yet, dear.

[WILLY *walks out of his jacket.* LINDA *follows him.*]

WILLY: And they'll get married, and come for a weekend. I'd build a little guest house. 'Cause I got so many fine tools, all I'd need would be a little lumber and some peace of mind.

LINDA: [*Joyfully.*] I sewed the lining ...

WILLY: I could build two guest houses, so they'd both come. Did he decide how much he's going to ask Oliver for?

LINDA: [*Getting him into the jacket.*] He didn't mention it, but I imagine ten or fifteen thousand. You going to talk to Howard today?

WILLY: Yeah. I'll put it to him straight and simple. He'll just have to take me off the road.

LINDA: And Willy, don't forget to ask for a little advance, because we've got the insurance premium. It's the grace period now.

WILLY: That's a hundred ... ?

LINDA: A hundred and eight, sixty-eight. Because we're a little short again.

WILLY: Why are we short?

LINDA: Well, you had the motor job on the car ...

WILLY: That goddam Studebaker!

LINDA: And you got one more payment on the refrigerator ...

WILLY: But it just broke again!

LINDA: Well, it's old, dear.

WILLY: I told you we should've bought a well-advertised machine. Charley bought a General Electric and it's twenty years old and it's still good, that son-of-a-bitch.

LINDA: But, Willy—

WILLY: Whoever heard of a Hastings refrigerator? Once in my life I would like to own something outright before it's broken! I'm always in a race with the junkyard! I just finished paying for the car and it's on its last legs. The refrigerator consumes belts like a goddam maniac. They time those things. They time them so when you finally paid for them, they're used up.

LINDA: [*Buttoning up his jacket as he unbuttons it.*] All told, about two hundred dollars would carry us, dear. But that includes the last payment on the mortgage. After this payment, Willy, the house belongs to us.

WILLY: It's twenty-five years!

LINDA: Biff was nine years old when we bought it.

WILLY: Well, that's a great thing. To weather a twenty-five year mortgage is—

LINDA: It's an accomplishment.

WILLY: All the cement, the lumber, the reconstruction I put in this house! There ain't a crack to be found in it anymore.

LINDA: Well, it served its purpose.

WILLY: What purpose? Some stranger'll come along, move in, and that's that. If only Biff would take this house, and raise a family . . . [*He starts to go.*] Good-bye, I'm late.

LINDA: [*Suddenly remembering.*] Oh, I forgot! You're supposed to meet them for dinner.

WILLY: Me?

LINDA: At Frank's Chop House on Forty-eighth near Sixth Avenue.

WILLY: Is that so! How about you?

LINDA: No, just the three of you. They're gonna blow you to a big meal!

WILLY: Don't say! Who thought of that?

LINDA: Biff came to me this morning, Willy, and he said, "Tell Dad, we want to blow him to a big meal." Be there six o'clock. You and your two boys are going to have dinner.

WILLY: Gee whiz! That's really somethin'. I'm gonna knock Howard for a loop, kid. I'll get an advance, and I'll come home with a New York job. Goddammit, now I'm gonna do it!

LINDA: Oh, that's the spirit, Willy!

WILLY: I will never get behind a wheel the rest of my life!

LINDA: It's changing, Willy, I can feel it changing!

WILLY: Beyond a question. G'bye, I'm late. [*He starts to go again.*]

LINDA: [*Calling after him as she runs to the kitchen table for a handkerchief.*] You got your glasses?

WILLY: [*Feels for them, then comes back in.*] Yeah, yeah, got my glasses.

LINDA: [*Giving him the handkerchief.*] And a handkerchief.

WILLY: Yeah, handkerchief.

LINDA: And your saccharine?[7]

WILLY: Yeah, my saccharine.

LINDA: Be careful on the subway stairs.

[*She kisses him, and a silk stocking is seen hanging from her hand.* WILLY *notices it.*]

WILLY: Will you stop mending stockings? At least while I'm in the house. It gets me nervous. I can't tell you. Please.

---

7. Artificial sweetener once recommended as a healthy alternative to sugar.

[LINDA *hides the stocking in her hand as she follows* WILLY *across the forestage in front of the house.*]

LINDA: Remember, Frank's Chop House.

WILLY: [*Passing the apron.*] Maybe beets would grow out there.

LINDA: [*Laughing.*] But you tried so many times.

WILLY: Yeah. Well, don't work hard today. [*He disappears around the right corner of the house.*]

LINDA: Be careful! [*As* WILLY *vanishes,* LINDA *waves to him. Suddenly the phone rings. She runs across the stage and into the kitchen and lifts it.*] Hello? Oh, Biff! I'm so glad you called, I just . . . Yes, sure, I just told him. Yes, he'll be there for dinner at six o'clock, I didn't forget. Listen, I was just dying to tell you. You know that little rubber pipe I told you about? That he connected to the gas heater? I finally decided to go down the cellar this morning and take it away and destroy it. But it's gone! Imagine? He took it away himself, it isn't there! [*She listens.*] When? Oh, then you took it. Oh—nothing, it's just that I'd hoped he'd taken it away himself. Oh, I'm not worried, darling, because this morning he left in such high spirits, it was like the old days! I'm not afraid anymore. Did Mr. Oliver see you? . . . Well, you wait there then. And make a nice impression on him, darling. Just don't perspire too much before you see him. And have a nice time with Dad. He may have big news too! . . . That's right, a New York job. And be sweet to him tonight, dear. Be loving to him. Because he's only a little boat looking for a harbor. [*She is trembling with sorrow and joy.*] Oh, that's wonderful, Biff, you'll save his life. Thanks, darling. Just put your arm around him when he comes into the restaurant. Give him a smile. That's the boy . . . Good-bye, dear . . . You got your comb? . . . That's fine. Good-bye, Biff dear.

[*In the middle of her speech,* HOWARD WAGNER, *thirty-six, wheels on a small typewriter table on which is a wire-recording machine and proceeds to plug it in. This is on the left forestage. Light slowly fades on* LINDA *as it rises on* HOWARD. HOWARD *is intent on threading the machine and only glances over his shoulder as* WILLY *appears.*]

WILLY: Pst! Pst!

HOWARD: Hello, Willy, come in.

WILLY: Like to have a little talk with you, Howard.

HOWARD: Sorry to keep you waiting. I'll be with you in a minute.

WILLY: What's that, Howard?

HOWARD: Didn't you ever see one of these? Wire recorder.

WILLY: Oh. Can we talk a minute?

HOWARD: Records things. Just got delivery yesterday. Been driving me crazy, the most terrific machine I ever saw in my life. I was up all night with it.

WILLY: What do you do with it?

HOWARD: I bought it for dictation, but you can do anything with it. Listen to this. I had it home last night. Listen to what I picked up. The first one is my daughter. Get this. [*He flicks the switch and "Roll out the Barrel" is heard being whistled.*] Listen to that kid whistle.

WILLY: That is lifelike, isn't it?

HOWARD: Seven years old. Get that tone.

WILLY: Ts, ts. Like to ask a little favor if you . . .

[*The whistling breaks off, and the voice of* HOWARD*'s daughter is heard.*]

HIS DAUGHTER: "Now you, Daddy."

HOWARD: She's crazy for me! [*Again the same song is whistled.*] That's me! Ha! [*He winks.*]

WILLY: You're very good!

[*The whistling breaks off again. The machine runs silent for a moment.*]

HOWARD: Sh! Get this now, this is my son.

HIS SON: "The capital of Alabama is Montgomery; the capital of Arizona is Phoenix; the capital of Arkansas is Little Rock; the capital of California is Sacramento . . ." [*And on, and on.*]

HOWARD: [*Holding up five fingers.*] Five years old, Willy!

WILLY: He'll make an announcer some day!

HIS SON: [*Continuing.*] "The capital . . ."

HOWARD: Get that—alphabetical order! [*The machine breaks off suddenly.*] Wait a minute. The maid kicked the plug out.

WILLY: It certainly is a—

HOWARD: Sh, for God's sake!

HIS SON: "It's nine o'clock, Bulova watch time.[8] So I have to go to sleep."

WILLY: That really is—

HOWARD: Wait a minute! The next is my wife.

[*They wait.*]

HOWARD'S VOICE: "Go on, say something." [*Pause.*] "Well, you gonna talk?"

HIS WIFE: "I can't think of anything."

HOWARD'S VOICE: "Well, talk—it's turning."

HIS WIFE: [*Shyly, beaten.*] "Hello." [*Silence.*] "Oh, Howard, I can't talk into this . . ."

HOWARD: [*Snapping the machine off.*] That was my wife.

WILLY: That is a wonderful machine. Can we—

HOWARD: I tell you, Willy, I'm gonna take my camera, and my bandsaw, and all my hobbies, and out they go. This is the most fascinating relaxation I ever found.

WILLY: I think I'll get one myself.

HOWARD: Sure, they're only a hundred and a half. You can't do without it. Supposing you wanna hear Jack Benny,[9] see? But you can't be at home

8. Phrase commonly heard on radio programs sponsored by the Bulova Watch Company.
9. A vaudeville, radio, television, and movie star (1894–1974); he hosted America's most popular radio show from 1932 to 1955.

at that hour. So you tell the maid to turn the radio on when Jack Benny comes on, and this automatically goes on with the radio...

WILLY: And when you come home you...

HOWARD: You can come home twelve o'clock, one o'clock, any time you like, and you get yourself a Coke and sit yourself down, throw the switch, and there's Jack Benny's program in the middle of the night!

WILLY: I'm definitely going to get one. Because lots of time I'm on the road, and I think to myself, what I must be missing on the radio!

HOWARD: Don't you have a radio in the car?

WILLY: Well, yeah, but who ever thinks of turning it on?

HOWARD: Say, aren't you supposed to be in Boston?

WILLY: That's what I want to talk to you about, Howard. You got a minute? [He draws a chair in from the wing.]

HOWARD: What happened? What're you doing here?

WILLY: Well...

HOWARD: You didn't crack up again, did you?

WILLY: Oh, no. No...

HOWARD: Geez, you had me worried there for a minute. What's the trouble?

WILLY: Well, tell you the truth, Howard. I've come to the decision that I'd rather not travel anymore.

HOWARD: Not travel! Well, what'll you do?

WILLY: Remember, Christmas time, when you had the party here? You said you'd try to think of some spot for me here in town.

HOWARD: With us?

WILLY: Well, sure.

HOWARD: Oh, yeah, yeah. I remember. Well, I couldn't think of anything for you, Willy.

WILLY: I tell ya, Howard. The kids are all grown up, y'know. I don't need much anymore. If I could take home—well, sixty-five dollars a week, I could swing it.

HOWARD: Yeah, but Willy, see I—

WILLY: I tell ya why, Howard. Speaking frankly and between the two of us, y'know—I'm just a little tired.

HOWARD: Oh, I could understand that, Willy. But you're a road man, Willy, and we do a road business. We've only got a half-dozen salesmen on the floor here.

WILLY: God knows, Howard, I never asked a favor of any man. But I was with the firm when your father used to carry you in here in his arms.

HOWARD: I know that, Willy, but—

WILLY: Your father came to me the day you were born and asked me what I thought of the name of Howard, may he rest in peace.

HOWARD: I appreciate that, Willy, but there just is no spot here for you. If I had a spot I'd slam you right in, but I just don't have a single solitary spot.

[He looks for his lighter. WILLY has picked it up and gives it to him. Pause.]

WILLY: [With increasing anger.] Howard, all I need to set my table is fifty dollars a week.

HOWARD: But where am I going to put you, kid?

WILLY: Look, it isn't a question of whether I can sell merchandise, is it?

HOWARD: No, but it's a business, kid, and everybody's gotta pull his own weight.

WILLY: [*Desperately.*] Just let me tell you a story, Howard—

HOWARD: 'Cause you gotta admit, business is business.

WILLY: [*Angrily.*] Business is definitely business, but just listen for a minute. You don't understand this. When I was a boy—eighteen, nineteen—I was already on the road. And there was a question in my mind as to whether selling had a future for me. Because in those days I had a yearning to go to Alaska. See, there were three gold strikes in one month in Alaska, and I felt like going out. Just for the ride, you might say.

HOWARD: [*Barely interested.*] Don't say.

WILLY: Oh, yeah, my father lived many years in Alaska. He was an adventurous man. We've got quite a little streak of self-reliance in our family. I thought I'd go out with my older brother and try to locate him, and maybe settle in the North with the old man. And I was almost decided to go, when I met a salesman in the Parker House. His name was Dave Singleman. And he was eighty-four years old, and he'd drummed merchandise in thirty-one states. And old Dave, he'd go up to his room, y'understand, put on his green velvet slippers—I'll never forget—and pick up his phone and call the buyers, and without ever leaving his room, at the age of eighty-four, he made a living. And when I saw that, I realized that selling was the greatest career a man could want. 'Cause what could be more satisfying than to be able to go, at the age of eighty-four, into twenty or thirty different cities, and pick up his phone and be remembered and loved and helped by so many different people? Do you know? when he died—and by the way he died the death of a salesman, in his green velvet slippers in the smoker of the New York, New Haven and Hartford, going into Boston—when he died, hundreds of salesmen and buyers were at his funeral. Things were sad on a lotta trains for months after that. [*He stands up.* HOWARD *has not looked at him.*] In those days there was personality in it, Howard. There was respect, and comradeship, and gratitude in it. Today, it's all cut and dried, and there's no chance for bringing friendship to bear—or personality. You see what I mean? They don't know me anymore.

HOWARD: [*Moving away, toward the right.*] That's just the thing, Willy.

WILLY: If I had forty dollars a week—that's all I'd need. Forty dollars, Howard.

HOWARD: Kid, I can't take blood from a stone, I—

WILLY: [*Desperation is on him now.*] Howard, the year Al Smith[1] was nominated, your father came to me and—

HOWARD: [*Starting to go off.*] I've got to see some people, kid.

WILLY: [*Stopping him.*] I'm talking about your father! There were promises made across this desk! You mustn't tell me you've got people to see—I

---

1. Alfred E. Smith (1873–1944), Democratic presidential nominee who lost to Herbert Hoover in 1928.

put thirty-four years into this firm, Howard, and now I can't pay my insurance! You can't eat the orange and throw the peel away—a man is not a piece of fruit! [*After a pause.*] Now pay attention. Your father—in 1928 I had a big year. I averaged a hundred and seventy dollars a week in commissions.

HOWARD: [*Impatiently.*] Now, Willy, you never averaged—

WILLY: [*Banging his hand on the desk.*] I averaged a hundred and seventy dollars a week in the year of 1928! And your father came to me—or rather, I was in the office here—it was right over this desk—and he put his hand on my shoulder—

HOWARD: [*Getting up.*] You'll have to excuse me, Willy, I gotta see some people. Pull yourself together. [*Going out.*] I'll be back in a little while.

[*On* HOWARD's *exit, the light on his chair grows very bright and strange.*]

WILLY: Pull myself together! What the hell did I say to him? My God, I was yelling at him! How could I! [WILLY *breaks off, staring at the light, which occupies the chair, animating it. He approaches this chair, standing across the desk from it.*] Frank, Frank, don't you remember what you told me that time? How you put your hand on my shoulder, and Frank . . . [*He leans on the desk and as he speaks the dead man's name he accidentally switches on the recorder, and instantly.*]

HOWARD'S SON: ". . . of New York is Albany. The capital of Ohio is Cincinnati, the capital of Rhode Island is . . ." [*The recitation continues.*]

WILLY: [*Leaping away with fright, shouting.*] Ha! Howard! Howard! Howard!

HOWARD: [*Rushing in.*] What happened?

WILLY: [*Pointing at the machine, which continues nasally, childishly, with the capital cities.*] Shut it off! Shut it off!

HOWARD: [*Pulling the plug out.*] Look, Willy . . .

WILLY: [*Pressing his hands to his eyes.*] I gotta get myself some coffee. I'll get some coffee . . .

[WILLY *starts to walk out.* HOWARD *stops him.*]

HOWARD: [*Rolling up the cord.*] Willy, look . . .

WILLY: I'll go to Boston.

HOWARD: Willy, you can't go to Boston for us.

WILLY: Why can't I go?

HOWARD: I don't want you to represent us. I've been meaning to tell you for a long time now.

WILLY: Howard, are you firing me?

HOWARD: I think you need a good long rest, Willy.

WILLY: Howard—

HOWARD: And when you feel better, come back, and we'll see if we can work something out.

WILLY: But I gotta earn money, Howard. I'm in no position to—

HOWARD: Where are your sons? Why don't your sons give you a hand?

WILLY: They're working on a very big deal.

HOWARD: This is no time for false pride, Willy. You go to your sons and you tell them that you're tired. You've got two great boys, haven't you?

WILLY: Oh, no question, no question, but in the meantime...

HOWARD: Then that's that, heh?

WILLY: All right, I'll go to Boston tomorrow.

HOWARD: No, no.

WILLY: I can't throw myself on my sons. I'm not a cripple!

HOWARD: Look, kid, I'm busy, I'm busy this morning.

WILLY: [*Grasping* HOWARD's *arm.*] Howard, you've got to let me go to Boston!

HOWARD: [*Hard, keeping himself under control.*] I've got a line of people to see this morning. Sit down, take five minutes, and pull yourself together, and then go home, will ya? I need the office, Willy. [*He starts to go, turns, remembering the recorder, starts to push off the table holding the recorder.*] Oh, yeah. Whenever you can this week, stop by and drop off the samples. You'll feel better, Willy, and then come back and we'll talk. Pull yourself together, kid, there's people outside.

[HOWARD *exits, pushing the table off left.* WILLY *stares into space, exhausted. Now the music is heard*—BEN's *music—first distantly, then closer, closer. As* WILLY *speaks*, BEN *enters from the right. He carries valise and umbrella.*]

WILLY: Oh, Ben, how did you do it? What is the answer? Did you wind up the Alaska deal already?

BEN: Doesn't take much time if you know what you're doing. Just a short business trip. Boarding ship in an hour. Wanted to say good-by.

WILLY: Ben, I've got to talk to you.

BEN: [*Glancing at his watch.*] Haven't the time, William.

WILLY: [*Crossing the apron to* BEN.] Ben, nothing's working out. I don't know what to do.

BEN: Now, look here, William. I've bought timberland in Alaska and I need a man to look after things for me.

WILLY: God, timberland! Me and my boys in those grand outdoors!

BEN: You've a new continent at your doorstep, William. Get out of these cities, they're full of talk and time payments and courts of law. Screw on your fists and you can fight for a fortune up there.

WILLY: Yes, yes! Linda, Linda!

[LINDA *enters as of old, with the wash.*]

LINDA: Oh, you're back?

BEN: I haven't much time.

WILLY: No, wait! Linda, he's got a proposition for me in Alaska.

LINDA: But you've got—[*To* BEN.] He's got a beautiful job here.

WILLY: But in Alaska, kid, I could—

LINDA: You're doing well enough, Willy!

BEN: [*To* LINDA.] Enough for what, my dear?

LINDA: [*Frightened of* BEN *and angry at him.*] Don't say those things to him! Enough to be happy right here, right now. [*To* WILLY, *while* BEN *laughs.*]

Why must everybody conquer the world? You're well liked, and the boys love you, and someday—[*To* BEN.]—why, old man Wagner told him just the other day that if he keeps it up he'll be a member of the firm, didn't he, Willy?

WILLY: Sure, sure. I am building something with this firm, Ben, and if a man is building something he must be on the right track, mustn't he?

BEN: What are you building? Lay your hand on it. Where is it?

WILLY: [*Hesitantly.*] That's true, Linda, there's nothing.

LINDA: Why? [*To* BEN.] There's a man eighty-four years old—

WILLY: That's right, Ben, that's right. When I look at that man I say, what is there to worry about?

BEN: Bah!

WILLY: It's true, Ben. All he has to do is go into any city, pick up the phone, and he's making his living and you know why?

BEN: [*Picking up his valise.*] I've got to go.

WILLY: [*Holding* BEN *back.*] Look at this boy! [BIFF, *in his high school sweater, enters carrying suitcase.* HAPPY *carries* BIFF's *shoulder guards, gold helmet, and football pants.*] Without a penny to his name, three great universities are begging for him, and from there the sky's the limit, because it's not what you do, Ben. It's who you know and the smile on your face! It's contacts, Ben, contacts! The whole wealth of Alaska passes over the lunch table at the Commodore Hotel, and that's the wonder, the wonder of this country, that a man can end with diamonds here on the basis of being liked! [*He turns to* BIFF.] And that's why when you get out on that field today it's important. Because thousands of people will be rooting for you and loving you. [*To* BEN, *who has again begun to leave.*] And Ben! when he walks into a business office his name will sound out like a bell and all the doors will open to him! I've seen it, Ben, I've seen it a thousand times! You can't feel it with your hand like timber, but it's there!

BEN: Good-by, William.

WILLY: Ben, am I right? Don't you think I'm right? I value your advice.

BEN: There's a new continent at your doorstep, William. You could walk out rich. Rich! [*He is gone.*]

WILLY: We'll do it here, Ben! You hear me? We're gonna do it here!

[*Young* BERNARD *rushes in. The gay music of the Boys is heard.*]

BERNARD: Oh, gee, I was afraid you left already!

WILLY: Why? What time is it?

BERNARD: It's half-past one!

WILLY: Well, come on, everybody! Ebbets Field next stop! Where's the pennants? [*He rushes through the wall-line of the kitchen and out into the living room.*]

LINDA: [*To* BIFF.] Did you pack fresh underwear?

BIFF: [*Who has been limbering up.*] I want to go!

BERNARD: Biff, I'm carrying your helmet, ain't I?

HAPPY: No, I'm carrying the helmet.

BERNARD: Oh, Biff, you promised me.

HAPPY: I'm carrying the helmet.

BERNARD: How am I going to get in the locker room?

LINDA: Let him carry the shoulder guards. [*She puts her coat and hat on in the kitchen.*]

BERNARD: Can I, Biff? 'Cause I told everybody I'm going to be in the locker room.

HAPPY: In Ebbets Field it's the clubhouse.

BERNARD: I meant the clubhouse, Biff!

HAPPY: Biff!

BIFF: [*Grandly, after a slight pause.*] Let him carry the shoulder guards.

HAPPY: [*As he gives* BERNARD *the shoulder guards.*] Stay close to us now.

[WILLY *rushes in with the pennants.*]

WILLY: [*Handing them out.*] Everybody wave when Biff comes out on the field. [HAPPY *and* BERNARD *run off.*] You set now, boy?

[*The music has died away.*]

BIFF: Ready to go, Pop. Every muscle is ready.

WILLY: [*At the edge of the apron.*] You realize what this means?

BIFF: That's right, Pop.

WILLY: [*Feeling* BIFF's *muscles.*] You're comin' home this afternoon captain of the All-Scholastic Championship Team of the City of New York.

BIFF: I got it, Pop. And remember, pal, when I take off my helmet, that touchdown is for you.

WILLY: Let's go! [*He is starting out, with his arm around* BIFF, *when* CHARLEY *enters, as of old, in knickers.*] I got no room for you, Charley.

CHARLEY: Room? For what?

WILLY: In the car.

CHARLEY: You goin' for a ride? I wanted to shoot some casino.

WILLY: [*Furiously.*] Casino! [*Incredulously.*] Don't you realize what today is?

LINDA: Oh, he knows, Willy. He's just kidding you.

WILLY: That's nothing to kid about!

CHARLEY: No, Linda, what's goin' on?

LINDA: He's playing in Ebbets Field.

CHARLEY: Baseball in this weather?

WILLY: Don't talk to him. Come on, come on! [*He is pushing them out.*]

CHARLEY: Wait a minute, didn't you hear the news?

WILLY: What?

CHARLEY: Don't you listen to the radio? Ebbets Field just blew up.

WILLY: You go to hell! [CHARLEY *laughs. Pushing them out.*] Come on, come on! We're late.

CHARLEY: [*As they go.*] Knock a homer, Biff, knock a homer!

WILLY: [*The last to leave, turning to* CHARLEY.] I don't think that was funny, Charley. This is the greatest day of my life.

CHARLEY: Willy, when are you going to grow up?

WILLY: Yeah, heh? When this game is over, Charley, you'll be laughing out of the other side of your face. They'll be calling him another Red Grange.[2] Twenty-five thousand a year.

CHARLEY: [*Kidding.*] Is that so?

WILLY: Yeah, that's so.

CHARLEY: Well, then, I'm sorry, Willy. But tell me something.

WILLY: What?

CHARLEY: Who is Red Grange?

WILLY: Put up your hands. Goddam you, put up your hands! [CHARLEY, *chuckling, shakes his head and walks away, around the left corner of the stage.* WILLY *follows him. The music rises to a mocking frenzy.*] Who the hell do you think you are, better than everybody else? You don't know everything, you big, ignorant, stupid . . . Put up your hands!

[*Light rises, on the right side of the forestage, on a small table in the reception room of* CHARLEY's *office. Traffic sounds are heard.* BERNARD, *now mature, sits whistling to himself. A pair of tennis rackets and an overnight bag are on the floor beside him.*]

WILLY: [*Offstage.*] What are you walking away for? Don't walk away! If you're going to say something say it to my face! I know you laugh at me behind my back. You'll laugh out of the other side of your goddam face after this game. Touchdown! Touchdown! Eighty thousand people! Touchdown! Right between the goal posts.

[BERNARD *is a quiet, earnest, but self-assured young man.* WILLY's *voice is coming from right upstage now.* BERNARD *lowers his feet off the table and listens.* JENNY, *his father's secretary, enters.*]

JENNY: [*Distressed.*] Say, Bernard, will you go out in the hall?

BERNARD: What is that noise? Who is it?

JENNY: Mr. Loman. He just got off the elevator.

BERNARD: [*Getting up.*] Who's he arguing with?

JENNY: Nobody. There's nobody with him. I can't deal with him anymore, and your father gets all upset everytime he comes. I've got a lot of typing to do, and your father's waiting to sign it. Will you see him?

WILLY: [*Entering.*] Touchdown! Touch—[*He sees* JENNY.] Jenny, Jenny, good to see you. How're ya? Workin'? Or still honest?

JENNY: Fine. How've you been feeling?

WILLY: Not much anymore, Jenny. Ha, ha! [*He is surprised to see the rackets.*]

BERNARD: Hello, Uncle Willy.

WILLY: [*Almost shocked.*] Bernard! Well, look who's here! [*He comes quickly, guiltily to* BERNARD *and warmly shakes his hand.*]

BERNARD: How are you? Good to see you.

WILLY: What are you doing here?

BERNARD: Oh, just stopped by to see Pop. Get off my feet till my train leaves. I'm going to Washington in a few minutes.

---

2. Harold Edward Grange (1903–1991), All-American halfback at the University of Illinois from 1923 to 1925; he played professionally for the Chicago Bears.

WILLY: Is he in?

BERNARD: Yes, he's in his office with the accountant. Sit down.

WILLY: [*Sitting down.*] What're you going to do in Washington?

BERNARD: Oh, just a case I've got there, Willy.

WILLY: That so? [*Indicating the rackets.*] You going to play tennis there?

BERNARD: I'm staying with a friend who's got a court.

WILLY: Don't say. His own tennis court. Must be fine people, I bet.

BERNARD: They are, very nice. Dad tells me Biff's in town.

WILLY: [*With a big smile.*] Yeah, Biff's in. Working on a very big deal, Bernard.

BERNARD: What's Biff doing?

WILLY: Well, he's been doing very big things in the West. But he decided to establish himself here. Very big. We're having dinner. Did I hear your wife had a boy?

BERNARD: That's right. Our second.

WILLY: Two boys! What do you know!

BERNARD: What kind of a deal has Biff got?

WILLY: Well, Bill Oliver—very big sporting-goods man—he wants Biff very badly. Called him in from the West. Long distance, carte blanche, special deliveries. Your friends have their own private tennis court?

BERNARD: You still with the old firm, Willy?

WILLY: [*After a pause.*] I'm—I'm overjoyed to see how you made the grade, Bernard, overjoyed. It's an encouraging thing to see a young man really—really—Looks very good for Biff—very—[*He breaks off, then.*] Bernard—[*He is so full of emotion, he breaks off again.*]

BERNARD: What is it, Willy?

WILLY: [*Small and alone.*] What—what's the secret?

BERNARD: What secret?

WILLY: How—how did you? Why didn't he ever catch on?

BERNARD: I wouldn't know that, Willy.

WILLY: [*Confidentially, desperately.*] You were his friend, his boyhood friend. There's something I don't understand about it. His life ended after that Ebbets Field game. From the age of seventeen nothing good ever happened to him.

BERNARD: He never trained himself for anything.

WILLY: But he did, he did. After high school he took so many correspondence courses. Radio mechanics; television; God knows what, and never made the slightest mark.

BERNARD: [*Taking off his glasses.*] Willy, do you want to talk candidly?

WILLY: [*Rising, faces* BERNARD.] I regard you as a very brilliant man, Bernard. I value your advice.

BERNARD: Oh, the hell with the advice, Willy. I couldn't advise you. There's just one thing I've always wanted to ask you. When he was supposed to graduate, and the math teacher flunked him—

WILLY: Oh, that son-of-a-bitch ruined his life.

BERNARD: Yeah, but, Willy, all he had to do was go to summer school and make up that subject.

WILLY: That's right, that's right.

BERNARD: Did you tell him not to go to summer school?

WILLY: Me? I begged him to go. I ordered him to go!

BERNARD: Then why wouldn't he go?

WILLY: Why? Why! Bernard, that question has been trailing me like a ghost for the last fifteen years. He flunked the subject, and laid down and died like a hammer hit him!

BERNARD: Take it easy, kid.

WILLY: Let me talk to you—I got nobody to talk to. Bernard, Bernard, was it my fault? Y'see? It keeps going around in my mind, maybe I did something to him. I got nothing to give him.

BERNARD: Don't take it so hard.

WILLY: Why did he lay down? What is the story there? You were his friend!

BERNARD: Willy, I remember, it was June, and our grades came out. And he'd flunked math.

WILLY: That son-of-a-bitch!

BERNARD: No, it wasn't right then. Biff just got very angry, I remember, and he was ready to enroll in summer school.

WILLY: [Surprised.] He was?

BERNARD: He wasn't beaten by it at all. But then, Willy, he disappeared from the block for almost a month. And I got the idea that he'd gone up to New England to see you. Did he have a talk with you then? [WILLY stares in silence.] Willy?

WILLY: [With a strong edge of resentment in his voice.] Yeah, he came to Boston. What about it?

BERNARD: Well, just that when he came back—I'll never forget this, it always mystifies me. Because I'd thought so well of Biff, even though he'd always taken advantage of me. I loved him, Willy, y'know? And he came back after that month and took his sneakers—remember those sneakers with "University of Virginia" printed on them? He was so proud of those, wore them every day. And he took them down in the cellar, and burned them up in the furnace. We had a fist fight. It lasted at least half an hour. Just the two of us, punching each other down the cellar, and crying right through it. I've often thought of how strange it was that I knew he'd given up his life. What happened in Boston, Willy? [WILLY looks at him as at an intruder.] I just bring it up because you asked me.

WILLY: [Angrily.] Nothing. What do you mean, "What happened?" What's that got to do with anything?

BERNARD: Well, don't get sore.

WILLY: What are you trying to do, blame it on me? If a boy lays down is that my fault?

BERNARD: Now, Willy, don't get—

WILLY: Well, don't—don't talk to me that way! What does that mean, "What happened?"

[CHARLEY enters. He is in his vest, and he carries a bottle of bourbon.]

CHARLEY: Hey, you're going to miss that train. [He waves the bottle.]

BERNARD: Yeah, I'm going. [He takes the bottle.] Thanks, Pop. [He picks up his *rackets and bag.*] Good-bye, Willy, and don't worry about it. You know, "If at first you don't succeed..."

WILLY: Yes, I believe in that.

BERNARD: But sometimes, Willy, it's better for a man just to walk away.

WILLY: Walk away?

BERNARD: That's right.

WILLY: But if you can't walk away?

BERNARD: [*After a slight pause.*] I guess that's when it's tough. [*Extending his hand.*] Good-bye, Willy.

WILLY: [*Shaking* BERNARD's *hand.*] Good-bye, boy.

CHARLEY: [*An arm on* BERNARD's *shoulder.*] How do you like this kid? Gonna argue a case in front of the Supreme Court.

BERNARD: [*Protesting.*] Pop!

WILLY: [*Genuinely shocked, pained, and happy.*] No! The Supreme Court!

BERNARD: I gotta run. 'Bye, Dad!

CHARLEY: Knock 'em dead, Bernard!

[BERNARD *goes off.*]

WILLY: [*As* CHARLEY *takes out his wallet.*] The Supreme Court! And he didn't even mention it!

CHARLEY: [*Counting out money on the desk.*] He don't have to—he's gonna do it.

WILLY: And you never told him what to do, did you? You never took any interest in him.

CHARLEY: My salvation is that I never took any interest in anything. There's some money—fifty dollars. I got an accountant inside.

WILLY: Charley, look... [*With difficulty.*] I got my insurance to pay. If you can manage it—I need a hundred and ten dollars. [CHARLEY *doesn't reply for a moment; merely stops moving.*] I'd draw it from my bank but Linda would know, and I...

CHARLEY: Sit down, Willy.

WILLY: [*Moving toward the chair.*] I'm keeping an account of everything, remember. I'll pay every penny back. [*He sits.*]

CHARLEY: Now listen to me, Willy.

WILLY: I want you to know I appreciate...

CHARLEY: [*Sitting down on the table.*] Willy, what're you doin'? What the hell is goin' on in your head?

WILLY: Why? I'm simply...

CHARLEY: I offered you a job. You can make fifty dollars a week. And I won't send you on the road.

WILLY: I've got a job.

CHARLEY: Without pay? What kind of job is a job without pay? [*He rises.*] Now, look kid, enough is enough. I'm no genius but I know when I'm being insulted.

WILLY: Insulted!

CHARLEY: Why don't you want to work for me?

WILLY: What's the matter with you? I've got a job.

CHARLEY: Then what're you walkin' in here every week for?

WILLY: [*Getting up.*] Well, if you don't want me to walk in here—

CHARLEY: I am offering you a job!

WILLY: I don't want your goddam job!

CHARLEY: When the hell are you going to grow up?

WILLY: [*Furiously.*] You big ignoramus, if you say that to me again I'll rap you one! I don't care how big you are! [*He's ready to fight. Pause.*]

CHARLEY: [*Kindly, going to him.*] How much do you need, Willy?

WILLY: Charley, I'm strapped, I'm strapped. I don't know what to do. I was just fired.

CHARLEY: Howard fired you?

WILLY: That snotnose. Imagine that? I named him. I named him Howard.

CHARLEY: Willy, when're you gonna realize that them things don't mean anything? You named him Howard, but you can't sell that. The only thing you got in this world is what you can sell. And the funny thing is that you're a salesman, and you don't know that.

WILLY: I've always tried to think otherwise, I guess. I always felt that if a man was impressive, and well liked, that nothing—

CHARLEY: Why must everybody like you? Who liked J. P. Morgan?[3] Was he impressive? In a Turkish bath he'd look like a butcher. But with his pockets on he was very well liked. Now listen, Willy, I know you don't like me, and nobody can say I'm in love with you, but I'll give you a job because—just for the hell of it, put it that way. Now what do you say?

WILLY: I—I just can't work for you, Charley.

CHARLEY: What're you, jealous of me?

WILLY: I can't work for you, that's all, don't ask me why.

CHARLEY: [*Angered, takes out more bills.*] You been jealous of me all your life, you damned fool! Here, pay your insurance. [*He puts the money in* WILLY's *hand.*]

WILLY: I'm keeping strict accounts.

CHARLEY: I've got some work to do. Take care of yourself. And pay your insurance.

WILLY: [*Moving to the right.*] Funny, y'know? After all the highways and the trains, and the appointments, and the years, you end up worth more dead than alive.

CHARLEY: Willy, nobody's worth nothin' dead. [*After a slight pause.*] Did you hear what I said? [WILLY *stands still, dreaming.*] Willy!

WILLY: Apologize to Bernard for me when you see him. I didn't mean to argue with him. He's a fine boy. They're all fine boys, and they'll end up big—all of them. Someday they'll all play tennis together. Wish me luck, Charley. He saw Bill Oliver today.

CHARLEY: Good luck.

---

3. American financier (1837–1890), widely criticized for his business dealings with the U.S. government.

WILLY: [*On the verge of tears.*] Charley, you're the only friend I got. Isn't that a remarkable thing? [*He goes out.*]

CHARLEY: Jesus!

[CHARLEY *stares after him a moment and follows. All light blacks out. Suddenly raucous music is heard, and a red glow rises behind the screen at right.* STANLEY, *a young waiter, appears, carrying a table, followed by* HAPPY, *who is carrying two chairs.*]

STANLEY: [*Putting the table down.*] That's all right, Mr. Loman, I can handle it myself. [*He turns and takes the chairs from* HAPPY *and places them at the table.*]

HAPPY: [*Glancing around.*] Oh, this is better.

STANLEY: Sure, in the front there you're in the middle of all kinds a noise. Whenever you got a party. Mr. Loman, you just tell me and I'll put you back here. Y'know, there's a lotta people they don't like it private, because when they go out they like to see a lotta action around them because they're sick and tired to stay in the house by theirself. But I know you, you ain't from Hackensack. You know what I mean?

HAPPY: [*Sitting down.*] So how's it coming, Stanley?

STANLEY: Ah, it's a dog life. I only wish during the war they'd a took me in the Army. I couda been dead by now.

HAPPY: My brother's back, Stanley.

STANLEY: Oh, he come back, heh? From the Far West.

HAPPY: Yeah, big cattle man, my brother, so treat him right. And my father's coming too.

STANLEY: Oh, your father too!

HAPPY: You got a couple of nice lobsters?

STANLEY: Hundred per cent, big.

HAPPY: I want them with the claws.

STANLEY: Don't worry, I don't give you no mice. [HAPPY *laughs.*] How about some wine? It'll put a head on the meal.

HAPPY: No. You remember, Stanley, that recipe I brought you from overseas? With the champagne in it?

STANLEY: Oh, yeah, sure. I still got it tacked up yet in the kitchen. But that'll have to cost a buck apiece anyways.

HAPPY: That's all right.

STANLEY: What'd you, hit a number or somethin'?

HAPPY: No, it's a little celebration. My brother is—I think he pulled off a big deal today. I think we're going into business together.

STANLEY: Great! That's the best for you. Because a family business, you know what I mean?—that's the best.

HAPPY: That's what I think.

STANLEY: 'Cause what's the difference? Somebody steals? It's in the family. Know what I mean? [*Sotto voce.*] Like this bartender here. The boss is goin' crazy what kinda leak he's got in the cash register. You put it in but it don't come out.

HAPPY: [*Raising his head.*] Sh!

STANLEY: What?

HAPPY: You notice I wasn't lookin' right or left, was I?

STANLEY: No.

HAPPY: And my eyes are closed.

STANLEY: So what's the—?

HAPPY: Strudel's comin'.

STANLEY: [*Catching on, looks around.*] Ah, no, there's no—[*He breaks off as a furred, lavishly dressed* GIRL *enters and sits at the next table. Both follow her with their eyes.*] Geez, how'd ya know?

HAPPY: I got radar or something. [*Staring directly at her profile.*] Oooooooo . . . Stanley.

STANLEY: I think, that's for you, Mr. Loman.

HAPPY: Look at that mouth. Oh, God. And the binoculars.

STANLEY: Geez, you got a life, Mr. Loman.

HAPPY: Wait on her.

STANLEY: [*Going to the* GIRL'*s table.*] Would you like a menu, ma'am?

GIRL: I'm expecting someone, but I'd like a—

HAPPY: Why don't you bring her—excuse me, miss, do you mind? I sell champagne, and I'd like you to try my brand. Bring her a champagne, Stanley.

GIRL: That's awfully nice of you.

HAPPY: Don't mention it. It's all company money. [*He laughs.*]

GIRL: That's a charming product to be selling, isn't it?

HAPPY: Oh, gets to be like everything else. Selling is selling, y'know.

GIRL: I suppose.

HAPPY: You don't happen to sell, do you?

GIRL: No, I don't sell.

HAPPY: Would you object to a compliment from a stranger? You ought to be on a magazine cover.

GIRL: [*Looking at him a little archly.*] I have been.

[STANLEY *comes in with a glass of champagne.*]

HAPPY: What'd I say before, Stanley? You see? She's a cover girl.

STANLEY: Oh, I could see, I could see.

HAPPY: [*To the* GIRL.] What magazine?

GIRL: Oh, a lot of them. [*She takes the drink.*] Thank you.

HAPPY: You know what they say in France, don't you? "Champagne is the drink of the complexion"—Hya, Biff!

[BIFF *has entered and sits with* HAPPY.]

BIFF: Hello, kid. Sorry I'm late.

HAPPY: I just got here. Uh, Miss—?

GIRL: Forsythe.

HAPPY: Miss Forsythe, this is my brother.

BIFF: Is Dad here?

HAPPY: His name is Biff. You might've heard of him. Great football player.

GIRL: Really? What team?

HAPPY: Are you familiar with football?

GIRL: No, I'm afraid I'm not.

HAPPY: Biff is quarterback with the New York Giants.

GIRL: Well, that's nice, isn't it? [*She drinks.*]

HAPPY: Good health.

GIRL: I'm happy to meet you.

HAPPY: That's my name, Hap. It's really Harold, but at West Point they called me Happy.

GIRL: [*Now really impressed.*] Oh, I see. How do you do? [*She turns her profile.*]

BIFF: Isn't Dad coming?

HAPPY: You want her?

BIFF: Oh, I could never make that.

HAPPY: I remember the time that idea would never come into your head. Where's the old confidence, Biff?

BIFF: I just saw Oliver—

HAPPY: Wait a minute. I've got to see that old confidence again. Do you want her? She's on call.

BIFF: Oh, no. [*He turns to look at the* GIRL.]

HAPPY: I'm telling you. Watch this. [*Turning to see the* GIRL.] Honey? [*She turns to him.*] Are you busy?

GIRL: Well, I am . . . but I could make a phone call.

HAPPY: Do that, will you, honey? And see if you can get a friend. We'll be here for a while. Biff is one of the greatest football players in the country.

GIRL: [*Standing up.*] Well, I'm certainly happy to meet you.

HAPPY: Come back soon.

GIRL: I'll try.

HAPPY: Don't try, honey, try hard. [*The* GIRL *exits.* STANLEY *follows, shaking his head in bewildered admiration.*] Isn't that a shame now? A beautiful girl like that? That's why I can't get married. There's not a good woman in a thousand. New York is loaded with them, kid!

BIFF: Hap, look—

HAPPY: I told you she was on call!

BIFF: [*Strangely unnerved.*] Cut it out, will ya? I want to say something to you.

HAPPY: Did you see Oliver?

BIFF: I saw him all right. Now look, I want to tell Dad a couple of things and I want you to help me.

HAPPY: What? Is he going to back you?

BIFF: Are you crazy? You're out of your goddam head, you know that?

HAPPY: Why? What happened?

BIFF: [*Breathlessly.*] I did a terrible thing today, Hap. It's been the strangest day I ever went through. I'm all numb, I swear.

HAPPY: You mean he wouldn't see you?

BIFF: Well, I waited six hours for him, see? All day. Kept sending my name in. Even tried to date his secretary so she'd get me to him, but no soap.

HAPPY: Because you're not showin' the old confidence, Biff. He remembered you, didn't he?

BIFF: [*Stopping* HAPPY *with a gesture.*] Finally, about five o'clock, he comes out. Didn't remember who I was or anything. I felt like such an idiot, Hap.

HAPPY: Did you tell him my Florida idea?

BIFF: He walked away. I saw him for one minute. I got so mad I could've torn the walls down! How the hell did I ever get the idea I was a salesman there? I even believed myself that I'd been a salesman for him! And then he gave me one look and—I realized what a ridiculous lie my whole life has been! We've been talking in a dream for fifteen years. I was a shipping clerk.

HAPPY: What'd you do?

BIFF: [*With great tension and wonder.*] Well, he left, see. And the secretary went out. I was all alone in the waiting-room. I don't know what came over me, Hap. The next thing I know I'm in his office—paneled walls, everything. I can't explain it. I—Hap, I took his fountain pen.

HAPPY: Geez, did he catch you?

BIFF: I ran out. I ran down all eleven flights. I ran and ran and ran.

HAPPY: That was an awful dumb—what'd you do that for?

BIFF: [*Agonized.*] I don't know, I just—wanted to take something, I don't know. You gotta help me, Hap, I'm gonna tell Pop.

HAPPY: You crazy? What for?

BIFF: Hap, he's got to understand that I'm not the man somebody lends that kind of money to. He thinks I've been spiting him all these years and it's eating him up.

HAPPY: That's just it. You tell him something nice.

BIFF: I can't.

HAPPY: Say you got a lunch date with Oliver tomorrow.

BIFF: So what do I do tomorrow?

HAPPY: You leave the house tomorrow and come back at night and say Oliver is thinking it over. And he thinks it over for a couple of weeks, and gradually it fades away and nobody's the worse.

BIFF: But it'll go on forever!

HAPPY: Dad is never so happy as when he's looking forward to something! [WILLY *enters.*] Hello, scout!

WILLY: Gee, I haven't been here in years!

[STANLEY *has followed* WILLY *in and sets a chair for him.* STANLEY *starts off but* HAPPY *stops him.*]

HAPPY: Stanley!

[STANLEY *stands by, waiting for an order.*]

BIFF: [*Going to* WILLY *with guilt, as to an invalid.*] Sit down, Pop. You want a drink?

WILLY: Sure, I don't mind.

BIFF: Let's get a load on.

WILLY: You look worried.

BIFF: N-no. [*To* STANLEY.] Scotch all around. Make it doubles.

STANLEY: Doubles, right. [*He goes.*]

WILLY: You had a couple already, didn't you?

BIFF: Just a couple, yeah.

WILLY: Well, what happened, boy? [*Nodding affirmatively, with a smile.*] Every-thing go all right?

BIFF: [*Takes a breath, then reaches out and grasps* WILLY's *hand.*] Pal . . . [*He is smiling bravely, and* WILLY *is smiling too.*] I had an experience today.

HAPPY: Terrific, Pop.

WILLY: That so? What happened?

BIFF: [*High, slightly alcoholic, above the earth.*] I'm going to tell you everything from first to last. It's been a strange day. [*Silence. He looks around, composes himself as best he can, but his breath keeps breaking the rhythm of his voice.*] I had to wait quite a while for him, and—

WILLY: Oliver?

BIFF: Yeah, Oliver. All day, as a matter of cold fact. And a lot of—instances—facts, Pop, facts about my life came back to me. Who was it, Pop? Who ever said I was a salesman with Oliver?

WILLY: Well, you were.

BIFF: No, Dad, I was shipping clerk.

WILLY: But you were practically—

BIFF: [*With determination.*] Dad, I don't know who said it first, but I was never a salesman for Bill Oliver.

WILLY: What're you talking about?

BIFF: Let's hold on to the facts tonight, Pop. We're not going to get any-where bullin' around. I was a shipping clerk.

WILLY: [*Angrily.*] All right, now listen to me—

BIFF: Why don't you let me finish?

WILLY: I'm not interested in stories about the past or any crap of that kind because the woods are burning, boys, you understand? There's a big blaze going on all around. I was fired today.

BIFF: [*Shocked.*] How could you be?

WILLY: I was fired, and I'm looking for a little good news to tell your mother, because the woman has waited and the woman has suffered. The gist of it is that I haven't got a story left in my head, Biff. So don't give me a lecture about facts and aspects. I am not interested. Now what've you got to say to me? [STANLEY *enters with three drinks. They wait until he leaves.*] Did you see Oliver?

BIFF: Jesus, Dad!

WILLY: You mean you didn't go up there?

HAPPY: Sure he went up there.

BIFF: I did. I—saw him. How could they fire you?

WILLY: [*On the edge of his chair.*] What kind of a welcome did he give you?

BIFF: He won't even let you work on commission?

WILLY: I'm out. [*Driving.*] So tell me, he gave you a warm welcome?

HAPPY: Sure, Pop, sure!

BIFF: [*Driven.*] Well, it was kind of—

WILLY: I was wondering if he'd remember you. [*To* HAPPY.] Imagine, man doesn't see him for ten, twelve years and gives him that kind of a welcome!

HAPPY: Damn right!

BIFF: [*Trying to return to the offensive.*] Pop, look—

WILLY: You know why he remembered you, don't you? Because you impressed him in those days.

BIFF: Let's talk quietly and get this down to the facts, huh?

WILLY: [*As though* BIFF *had been interrupting.*] Well, what happened? It's great news, Biff. Did he take you into his office or'd you talk in the waiting-room?

BIFF: Well, he came in, see and—

WILLY: [*With a big smile.*] What'd he say? Betcha he threw his arm around you.

BIFF: Well, he kinda—

WILLY: He's a fine man. [*To* HAPPY.] Very hard man to see, y'know.

HAPPY: [*Agreeing.*] Oh, I know.

WILLY: [*To* BIFF.] Is that where you had the drinks?

BIFF: Yeah, he gave me a couple of—no, no!

HAPPY: [*Cutting in.*] He told him my Florida idea.

WILLY: Don't interrupt. [*To* BIFF.] How'd he react to the Florida idea?

BIFF: Dad, will you give me a minute to explain?

WILLY: I've been waiting for you to explain since I sat down here! What happened? He took you into his office and what?

BIFF: Well—I talked. And—he listened, see.

WILLY: Famous for the way he listens, y'know. What was his answer?

BIFF: His answer was—[*He breaks off, suddenly angry.*] Dad, you're not letting me tell you what I want to tell you!

WILLY: [*Accusing, angered.*] You didn't see him, did you?

BIFF: I did see him!

WILLY: What'd you insult him or something? You insulted him, didn't you?

BIFF: Listen, will you let me out of it, will you just let me out of it!

HAPPY: What the hell!

WILLY: Tell me what happened!

BIFF: [*To* HAPPY.] I can't talk to him!

[*A single trumpet note jars the ear. The light of green leaves stains the house, which holds the air of night and a dream.* YOUNG BERNARD *enters and knocks on the door of the house.*]

YOUNG BERNARD: [*Frantically.*] Mrs. Loman, Mrs. Loman!

HAPPY: Tell him what happened!

BIFF: [*To* HAPPY.] Shut up and leave me alone!

WILLY: No, no. You had to go and flunk math!

BIFF: What math? What're you talking about?

YOUNG BERNARD: Mrs. Loman, Mrs. Loman!

[LINDA *appears in the house, as of old.*]

WILLY: [*Wildly.*] Math, math, math!

BIFF: Take it easy, Pop!

YOUNG BERNARD: Mrs. Loman!

WILLY: [*Furiously.*] If you hadn't flunked you'd've been set by now!

BIFF: Now, look, I'm gonna tell you what happened, and you're going to listen to me.

YOUNG BERNARD: Mrs. Loman!

BIFF: I waited six hours—

HAPPY: What the hell are you saying?

BIFF: I kept sending in my name but he wouldn't see me. So finally he . . . [*He continues unheard as light fades low on the restaurant.*]

YOUNG BERNARD: Biff flunked math!

LINDA: No!

YOUNG BERNARD: Birnbaum flunked him! They won't graduate him!

LINDA: But they have to. He's gotta go to the university. Where is he? Biff! Biff!

YOUNG BERNARD: No, he left. He went to Grand Central.

LINDA: Grand—You mean he went to Boston!

YOUNG BERNARD: Is Uncle Willy in Boston?

LINDA: Oh, maybe Willy can talk to the teacher. Oh, the poor, poor boy!

[*Light on house area snaps out.*]

BIFF: [*At the table, now audible, holding up a gold fountain pen.*] . . . so I'm washed up with Oliver, you understand? Are you listening to me?

WILLY: [*At a loss.*] Yeah, sure. If you hadn't flunked—

BIFF: Flunked what? What're you talking about?

WILLY: Don't blame everything on me! I didn't flunk math—you did! What pen?

HAPPY: That was awful dumb, Biff, a pen like that is worth—

WILLY: [*Seeing the pen for the first time.*] You took Oliver's pen?

BIFF: [*Weakening.*] Dad, I just explained it to you.

WILLY: You stole Bill Oliver's fountain pen!

BIFF: I didn't exactly steal it! That's just what I've been explaining to you!

HAPPY: He had it in his hand and just then Oliver walked in, so he got nervous and stuck it in his pocket!

WILLY: My God, Biff!

BIFF: I never intended to do it, Dad!

OPERATOR'S VOICE: Standish Arms, good evening!

WILLY: [*Shouting.*] I'm not in my room!

BIFF: [*Frightened.*] Dad, what's the matter? [*He and* HAPPY *stand up.*]

OPERATOR: Ringing Mr. Loman for you!

BIFF: [*Horrified, gets down on one knee before* WILLY.] Dad, I'll make good, I'll make good. [WILLY *tries to get to his feet.* BIFF *holds him down.*] Sit down now.

WILLY: No, you're no good, you're no good for anything.

BIFF: I am, Dad, I'll find something else, you understand? Now don't worry about anything. [*He holds up* WILLY's *face.*] Talk to me, Dad.

OPERATOR: Mr. Loman does not answer. Shall I page him?

WILLY: [*Attempting to stand, as though to rush and silence the* OPERATOR.] No, no, no!

HAPPY: He'll strike something, Pop.

WILLY: No, no . . .

BIFF: [*Desperately, standing over* WILLY.] Pop, listen! Listen to me! I'm telling you something good. Oliver talked to his partner about the Florida idea. You listening? He—he talked to his partner, and he came to me . . . I'm going to be all right, you hear? Dad, listen to me, he said it was just a question of the amount!

WILLY: Then you . . . got it?

HAPPY: He's gonna be terrific, Pop!

WILLY: [*Trying to stand.*] Then you got it, haven't you? You got it! You got it!

BIFF: [*Agonized, holds* WILLY *down.*] No, no. Look, Pop. I'm supposed to have lunch with them tomorrow. I'm just telling you this so you'll know that I can still make an impression, Pop. And I'll make good somewhere, but I can't go tomorrow, see?

WILLY: Why not? You simply—

BIFF: But the pen, Pop!

WILLY: You give it to him and tell him it was an oversight!

HAPPY: Sure, have lunch tomorrow!

BIFF: I can't say that—

WILLY: You were doing a crossword puzzle and accidentally used his pen!

BIFF: Listen, kid, I took those balls years ago, now I walk in with his fountain pen? That clinches it, don't you see? I can't face him like that! I'll try elsewhere.

PAGE'S VOICE: Paging Mr. Loman!

WILLY: Don't you want to be anything?

BIFF: Pop, how can I go back?

WILLY: You don't want to be anything, is that what's behind it?

BIFF: [*Now angry at* WILLY *for not crediting his sympathy.*] Don't take it that way! You think it was easy walking into that office after what I'd done to him? A team of horses couldn't have dragged me back to Bill Oliver!

WILLY: Then why'd you go?

BIFF: Why did I go? Why did I go! Look at you! Look at what's become of you!

[*Off left,* THE WOMAN *laughs.*]

WILLY: Biff, you're going to go to that lunch tomorrow, or—

BIFF: I can't go. I've got an appointment!

HAPPY: Biff, for . . . !

WILLY: Are you spiting me?

BIFF: Don't take it that way! Goddammit!

WILLY: [*Strikes* BIFF *and falters away from the table.*] You rotten little louse! Are you spiting me?

THE WOMAN: Someone's at the door, Willy!

BIFF: I'm no good, can't you see what I am?

HAPPY: [*Separating them.*] Hey, you're in a restaurant! Now cut it out, both of you! [*The* GIRLS *enter.*] Hello, girls, sit down.

[THE WOMAN *laughs, off left.*]

MISS FORSYTHE: I guess we might as well. This is Letta.

THE WOMAN: Willy, are you going to wake up?

BIFF: [*Ignoring* WILLY.] How're ya, miss, sit down. What do you drink?

MISS FORSYTHE: Letta might not be able to stay long.

LETTA: I gotta get up early tomorrow. I got jury duty. I'm so excited! Were you fellows ever on a jury?

BIFF: No, but I been in front of them! [*The* GIRLS *laugh.*] This is my father.

LETTA: Isn't he cute? Sit down with us, Pop.

HAPPY: Sit him down, Biff!

BIFF: [*Going to him.*] Come on, slugger, drink us under the table. To hell with it! Come on, sit down, pal.

[*On* BIFF*'s last insistence,* WILLY *is about to sit.*]

THE WOMAN: [*Now urgently.*] Willy, are you going to answer the door!

[THE WOMAN'S *call pulls* WILLY *back. He starts right, befuddled.*]

BIFF: Hey, where are you going?

WILLY: Open the door.

BIFF: The door?

WILLY: The washroom . . . the door . . . where's the door?

BIFF: [*Leading* WILLY *to the left.*] Just go straight down.

[WILLY *moves left.*]

THE WOMAN: Willy, Willy, are you going to get up, get up, get up, get up?

[WILLY *exits left.*]

LETTA: I think it's sweet you bring your daddy along.

MISS FORSYTHE: Oh, he isn't really your father!

BIFF: [*At left, turning to her resentfully.*] Miss Forsythe, you've just seen a prince walk by. A fine, troubled prince. A hardworking, unappreciated prince. A pal, you understand? A good companion. Always for his boys.

LETTA: That's so sweet.

HAPPY: Well, girls, what's the program? We're wasting time. Come on, Biff. Gather round. Where would you like to go?

BIFF: Why don't you do something for him?

HAPPY: Me!

BIFF: Don't you give a damn for him, Hap?

HAPPY: What're you talking about? I'm the one who—

BIFF: I sense it, you don't give a good goddam about him. [*He takes the rolled-up hose from his pocket and puts it on the table in front of* HAPPY.] Look what I found in the cellar, for Christ's sake. How can you bear to let it go on?

HAPPY: Me? Who goes away? Who runs off and—

BIFF: Yeah, but he doesn't mean anything to you. You could help him—I can't! Don't you understand what I'm talking about? He's going to kill himself, don't you know that?

HAPPY: Don't I know it! Me!

BIFF: Hap, help him! Jesus . . . help him . . . Help me, help me, I can't bear to look at his face! [*Ready to weep, he hurries out, up right.*]

HAPPY: [*Starting after him.*] Where are you going?

MISS FORSYTHE: What's he so mad about?

HAPPY: Come on, girls, we'll catch up with him.

MISS FORSYTHE: [*As* HAPPY *pushes her out.*] Say, I don't like that temper of his!

HAPPY: He's just a little overstrung, he'll be all right!

WILLY: [*Off left, as* THE WOMAN *laughs.*] Don't answer! Don't answer!

LETTA: Don't you want to tell your father—

HAPPY: No, that's not my father. He's just a guy. Come on, we'll catch Biff, and, honey, we're going to paint this town! Stanley, where's the check! Hey, Stanley!

[*They exit.* STANLEY *looks toward left.*]

STANLEY: [*Calling to* HAPPY *indignantly.*] Mr. Loman! Mr. Loman!

[STANLEY *picks up a chair and follows them off. Knocking is heard off left.* THE WOMAN *enters, laughing.* WILLY *follows her. She is in a black slip; he is buttoning his shirt. Raw, sensuous music accompanies their speech.*]

WILLY: Will you stop laughing? Will you stop?

THE WOMAN: Aren't you going to answer the door? He'll wake the whole hotel.

WILLY: I'm not expecting anybody.

THE WOMAN: Whyn't you have another drink, honey, and stop being so damn self-centered?

WILLY: I'm so lonely.

THE WOMAN: You know you ruined me, Willy? From now on, whenever you come to the office, I'll see that you go right through to the buyers. No waiting at my desk anymore, Willy. You ruined me.

WILLY: That's nice of you to say that.

THE WOMAN: Gee, you are self-centered! Why so sad? You are the saddest, self-centeredest soul I ever did see-saw. [*She laughs. He kisses her.*] Come on inside, drummer boy. It's silly to be dressing in the middle of the night. [*As knocking is heard.*] Aren't you going to answer the door?

WILLY: They're knocking on the wrong door.

THE WOMAN: But I felt the knocking. And he heard us talking in here. Maybe the hotel's on fire!

WILLY: [*His terror rising.*] It's a mistake.

THE WOMAN: Then tell them to go away!

WILLY: There's nobody there.

THE WOMAN: It's getting on my nerves, Willy. There's somebody standing out there and it's getting on my nerves!

WILLY: [*Pushing her away from him.*] All right, stay in the bathroom here, and don't come out. I think there's a law in Massachusetts about it, so don't come out. It may be that new room clerk. He looked very mean. So don't come out. It's a mistake, there's no fire.

[*The knocking is heard again. He takes a few steps away from her, and she vanishes into the wing. The light follows him, and now he is facing* YOUNG BIFF, *who carries a suitcase.* BIFF *steps toward him. The music is gone.*]

BIFF: Why didn't you answer?

WILLY: Biff! What are you doing in Boston?

BIFF: Why didn't you answer? I've been knocking for five minutes, I called you on the phone—

WILLY: I just heard you. I was in the bathroom and had the door shut. Did anything happen home?

BIFF: Dad—I let you down.

WILLY: What do you mean?

BIFF: Dad . . .

WILLY: Biffo, what's this about? [*Putting his arm around* BIFF.] Come on, let's go downstairs and get you a malted.

BIFF: Dad, I flunked math.

WILLY: Not for the term?

BIFF: The term. I haven't got enough credits to graduate.

WILLY: You mean to say Bernard wouldn't give you the answers?

BIFF: He did, he tried, but I only got a sixty-one.

WILLY: And they wouldn't give you four points?

BIFF: Birnbaum refused absolutely. I begged him, Pop, but he won't give me those points. You gotta talk to him before they close the school. Because if he saw the kind of man you are, and you just talked to him in your way, I'm sure he'd come through for me. The class came right before practice, see, and I didn't go enough. Would you talk to him? He'd like you, Pop. You know the way you could talk.

WILLY: You're on. We'll drive right back.

BIFF: Oh, Dad, good work! I'm sure he'll change for you!

WILLY: Go downstairs and tell the clerk I'm checkin' out. Go right down.

BIFF: Yes, sir! See, the reason he hates me, Pop—one day he was late for class so I got up at the blackboard and imitated him. I crossed my eyes and talked with a lithp.

WILLY: [*Laughing.*] You did? The kids like it?

BIFF: They nearly died laughing!

WILLY: Yeah? What'd you do?

BIFF: The thquare root of thixthy twee is . . . [WILLY *bursts out laughing;* BIFF *joins him.*] And in the middle of it he walked in!

[WILLY *laughs and* THE WOMAN *joins in offstage.*]

WILLY: [*Without hesitation.*] Hurry downstairs and—

BIFF: Somebody in there?

WILLY: No, that was next door.

[THE WOMAN *laughs offstage.*]

BIFF: Somebody got in your bathroom!

WILLY: No, it's the next room, there's a party—

THE WOMAN: [*Enters laughing. She lisps this.*] Can I come in? There's something in the bathtub, Willy, and it's moving!

> [WILLY *looks at* BIFF, *who is staring open-mouthed and horrified at* THE WOMAN.]

WILLY: Ah—you better go back to your room. They must be finished painting by now. They're painting her room so I let her take a shower here. Go back, go back . . . [*He pushes her.*]

THE WOMAN: [*Resisting.*] But I've got to get dressed, Willy, I can't—

WILLY: Get out of here! Go back, go back . . . [*Suddenly striving for the ordinary.*] This is Miss Francis, Biff, she's a buyer. They're painting her room. Go back, Miss Francis, go back . . .

THE WOMAN: But my clothes, I can't go out naked in the hall!

WILLY: [*Pushing her offstage.*] Get outa here! Go back, go back!

> [BIFF *slowly sits down on his suitcase as the argument continues offstage.*]

THE WOMAN: Where's my stockings? You promised me stockings, Willy!

WILLY: I have no stockings here!

THE WOMAN: You had two boxes of size nine sheers for me, and I want them!

WILLY: Here, for God's sake, will you get outa here!

THE WOMAN: [*Enters holding a box of stockings.*] I just hope there's nobody in the hall. That's all I hope. [*To* BIFF.] Are you football or baseball?

BIFF: Football.

THE WOMAN: [*Angry, humiliated.*] That's me too. G'night. [*She snatches her clothes from* WILLY, *and walks out.*]

WILLY: [*After a pause.*] Well, better get going. I want to get to the school first thing in the morning. Get my suits out of the closet. I'll get my valise. [BIFF *doesn't move.*] What's the matter? BIFF *remains motionless, tears falling.*] She's a buyer. Buys for J. H. Simmons. She lives down the hall—they're painting. You don't imagine—[*He breaks off. After a pause.*] Now listen, pal, she's just a buyer. She sees merchandise in her room and they have to keep it looking just so . . . [*Pause. Assuming command.*] All right, get my suits. [BIFF *doesn't move.*] Now stop crying and do as I say. I gave you an order. Biff, I gave you an order! Is that what you do when I give you an order? How dare you cry! [*Putting his arm around* BIFF.] Now look, Biff, when you grow up you'll understand about these things. You mustn't—you mustn't overemphasize a thing like this. I'll see Birnbaum first thing in the morning.

BIFF: Never mind.

WILLY: [*Getting down beside* BIFF.] Never mind! He's going to give you those points. I'll see to it.

BIFF: He wouldn't listen to you.

WILLY: He certainly will listen to me. You need those points for the U. of Virginia.

BIFF: I'm not going there.

WILLY: Heh? If I can't get him to change that mark you'll make it up in summer school. You've got all summer to—

BIFF: [*His weeping breaking from him.*] Dad . . .

WILLY: [*Infected by it.*] Oh, my boy . . .

BIFF: Dad . . .

WILLY: She's nothing to me, Biff. I was lonely, I was terribly lonely.

BIFF: You—you gave her Mama's stockings! [*His tears break through and he rises to go.*]

WILLY: [*Grabbing for* BIFF.] I gave you an order!

BIFF: Don't touch me, you—liar!

WILLY: Apologize for that!

BIFF: You fake! You phony little fake! You fake!

[*Overcome, he turns quickly and weeping fully goes out with his suitcase.* WILLY *is left on the floor on his knees.*]

WILLY: I gave you an order! Biff, come back here or I'll beat you! Come back here! I'll whip you! [STANLEY *comes quickly in from the right and stands in front of* WILLY. WILLY *shouts at* STANLEY.] I gave you an order . . .

STANLEY: Hey, let's pick it up, pick it up, Mr. Loman. [*He helps* WILLY *to his feet.*] Your boys left with the chippies. They said they'll see you home.

[*A* SECOND WAITER *watches some distance away.*]

WILLY: But we were supposed to have dinner together.

[*Music is heard,* WILLY*'s theme.*]

STANLEY: Can you make it?

WILLY: I'll—sure, I can make it. [*Suddenly concerned about his clothes.*] Do I—I look all right?

STANLEY: Sure, you look all right. [*He flicks a speck off* WILLY*'s lapel.*]

WILLY: Here—here's a dollar.

STANLEY: Oh, your son paid me. It's all right.

WILLY: [*Putting it in* STANLEY*'s hand.*] No, take it. You're a good boy.

STANLEY: Oh, no, you don't have to . . .

WILLY: Here—here's some more, I don't need it anymore. [*After a slight pause.*] Tell me—is there a seed store in the neighborhood?

STANLEY: Seeds? You mean like to plant?

[*As* WILLY *turns,* STANLEY *slips the money back into his jacket pocket.*]

WILLY: Yes. Carrots, peas . . .

STANLEY: Well, there's hardware stores on Sixth Avenue, but it may be too late now.

WILLY: [*Anxiously.*] Oh, I'd better hurry. I've got to get some seeds. [*He starts off to the right.*] I've got to get some seeds, right away. Nothing's planted. I don't have a thing in the ground.

[WILLY *hurries out as the light goes down.* STANLEY *moves over to the right after him, watches him off. The other* WAITER *has been staring at* WILLY.]

STANLEY: [*To the* WAITER.] Well, whatta you looking at?

[*The* WAITER *picks up the chairs and moves off right.* STANLEY *takes the table and follows him. The light fades on this area. There is a long pause, the sound of the flute coming over. The light gradually rises on the kitchen, which is empty.* HAPPY *appears at the door of the house, followed by* BIFF. HAPPY *is carrying a large bunch of long-stemmed roses. He enters the kitchen, looks around for* LINDA. *Not seeing her, he turns to* BIFF, *who is just outside the house door, and makes a gesture with his hands, indicating "Not here, I guess." He looks into the living-room and freezes. Inside,* LINDA, *unseen, is seated,* WILLY'*s coat on her lap. She rises ominously and quietly and moves toward* HAPPY, *who backs up into the kitchen, afraid.*]

HAPPY: Hey, what're you doing up? [LINDA *says nothing but moves toward him implacably.*] Where's Pop? [*He keeps backing to the right, and now* LINDA *is in full view in the doorway to the living-room.*] Is he sleeping?

LINDA: Where were you?

HAPPY: [*Trying to laugh it off.*] We met two girls, Mom, very fine types. Here, we brought you some flowers. [*Offering them to her.*] Put them in your room, Ma. [*She knocks them to the floor at* BIFF'*s feet. He has now come inside and closed the door behind him. She stares at* BIFF, *silent.*] Now what'd you do that for? Mom, I want you to have some flowers—

LINDA: [*Cutting* HAPPY *off, violently to* BIFF.] Don't you care whether he lives or dies?

HAPPY: [*Going to the stairs.*] Come upstairs, Biff.

BIFF: [*With a flare of disgust, to* HAPPY.] Go away from me! [*To* LINDA.] What do you mean, lives or dies? Nobody's dying around here, pal.

LINDA: Get out of my sight! Get out of here!

BIFF: I wanna see the boss.

LINDA: You're not going near him!

BIFF: Where is he? [*He moves into the living-room and* LINDA *follows.*]

LINDA: [*Shouting after* BIFF.] You invite him for dinner. He looks forward to it all day—[BIFF *appears in his parents' bedroom, looks around and exits.*]—and then you desert him there. There's no stranger you'd do that to!

HAPPY: Why? He had a swell time with us. Listen, when I—[LINDA *comes back into the kitchen.*]—desert him I hope I don't outlive the day!

LINDA: Get out of here!

HAPPY: Now look, Mom . . .

LINDA: Did you have to go to women tonight? You and your lousy rotten whores!

[BIFF *re-enters the kitchen.*]

HAPPY: Mom, all we did was follow Biff around trying to cheer him up! [*To* BIFF.] Boy, what a night you gave me!

LINDA: Get out of here, both of you, and don't come back! I don't want you tormenting him anymore. Go on now, get your things together! [*To* BIFF.] You can sleep in his apartment. [*She starts to pick up the flowers and stops herself.*] Pick up this stuff, I'm not your maid anymore. Pick it up, you bum, you! [HAPPY *turns his back to her in refusal.* BIFF *slowly moves over and gets down on his knees, picking up the flowers.*] You're a pair of animals! Not one, not another living soul would have had the cruelty to walk out on that man in a restaurant!

BIFF: [*Not looking at her.*] Is that what he said?

LINDA: He didn't have to say anything. He was so humiliated he nearly limped when he came in.

HAPPY: But, Mom, he had a great time with us—

BIFF: [*Cutting him off violently.*] Shut up!

[*Without another word,* HAPPY *goes upstairs.*]

LINDA: You! You didn't even go in to see if he was all right!

BIFF: [*Still on the floor in front of* LINDA, *the flowers in his hand; with self-loathing.*] No. Didn't. Didn't do a damned thing. How do you like that, heh? Left him babbling in a toilet.

LINDA: You louse. You . . .

BIFF: Now you hit it on the nose! [*He gets up, throws the flowers in the waste-basket.*] The scum of the earth, and you're looking at him!

LINDA: Get out of here!

BIFF: I gotta talk to the boss, Mom. Where is he?

LINDA: You're not going near him. Get out of this house!

BIFF: [*With absolute assurance, determination.*] No. We're gonna have an abrupt conversation, him and me.

LINDA: You're not talking to him! [*Hammering is heard from outside the house, off right.* BIFF *turns toward the noise. Suddenly pleading.*] Will you please leave him alone?

BIFF: What's he doing out there?

LINDA: He's planting the garden!

BIFF: [*Quietly.*] Now? Oh, my God!

[BIFF *moves outside,* LINDA *following. The light dies down on them and comes up on the center of the apron as* WILLY *walks into it. He is carrying a flashlight, a hoe, and a handful of seed packets. He raps the top of the hoe sharply to fix it firmly, and then moves to the left, measuring off the distance with his foot. He holds the flashlight to look at the seed packets, reading off the instructions. He is in the blue of night.*]

WILLY: Carrots . . . quarter-inch apart. Rows . . . one-foot rows. [*He measures it off.*] One foot. [*He puts down a package and measures off.*] Beets. [*He puts down another package and measures again.*] Lettuce. [*He reads the package, puts it down.*] One foot—[*He breaks off as* BEN *appears at the right and moves slowly down to him.*] What a proposition, ts, ts. Terrific, terrific. 'Cause she's suffered, Ben, the woman has suffered. You understand me? A man can't go out the way he came in, Ben, a man has got to add up to something. You can't, you can't—[BEN *moves toward him as though to interrupt.*] You gotta consider, now. Don't answer so quick. Remember, it's a guaranteed twenty-thousand-dollar proposition. Now look, Ben, I want you to go through the ins and outs of this thing with me. I've got nobody to talk to, Ben, and the woman has suffered, you hear me?

BEN: [*Standing still, considering.*] What's the proposition?

WILLY: It's twenty thousand dollars on the barrelhead. Guaranteed, gilt-edged, you understand?

BEN: You don't want to make a fool of yourself. They might not honor the policy.

WILLY: How can they dare refuse? Didn't I work like a coolie to meet every premium on the nose? And now they don't pay off! Impossible!

BEN: It's called a cowardly thing, William.

WILLY: Why? Does it take more guts to stand here the rest of my life ringing up a zero?

BEN: [*Yielding.*] That's a point, William. [*He moves, thinking, turns.*] And twenty thousand—that *is* something one can feel with the hand, it is there.

WILLY: [*Now assured, with rising power.*] Oh, Ben, that's the whole beauty of it! I see it like a diamond, shining in the dark, hard and rough, that I can pick up and touch in my hand. Not like—like an appointment! This would not be another damned-fool appointment, Ben, and it changes all the aspects. Because he thinks I'm nothing, see, and so he spites me. But the funeral—[*Straightening up.*] Ben, that funeral will be massive! They'll come from Maine, Massachusetts, Vermont, New Hampshire! All the old-timers with the strange license plates—that boy will be thunder-struck, Ben, because he never realized—I am known! Rhode Island, New York, New Jersey—I am known, Ben, and he'll see it with his eyes once and for all. He'll see what I am, Ben! He's in for a shock, that boy!

BEN: [*Coming down to the edge of the garden.*] He'll call you a coward.

WILLY: [*Suddenly fearful.*] No, that would be terrible.

BEN: Yes. And a damned fool.

WILLY: No, no, he mustn't, I won't have that! [*He is broken and desperate.*]

BEN: He'll hate you, William.

[*The gay music of the Boys is heard.*]

WILLY: Oh, Ben, how do we get back to all the great times? Used to be so full of light, and comradeship, the sleigh-riding in winter, and the ruddiness on his cheeks. And always some kind of good news coming up, always something nice coming up ahead. And never even let me carry the valises in the house, and simonizing, simonizing that little red car! Why, why can't I give him something and not have him hate me?

BEN: Let me think about it. [*He glances at his watch.*] I still have a little time. Remarkable proposition, but you've got to be sure you're not making a fool of yourself.

[BEN *drifts off upstage and goes out of sight.* BIFF *comes down from the left.*]

WILLY: [*Suddenly conscious of* BIFF, *turns and looks up at him, then begins picking up the packages of seeds in confusion.*] Where the hell is that seed? [*Indignantly.*] You can't see nothing out here! They boxed in the whole goddam neighborhood!

BIFF: There are people all around here. Don't you realize that?

WILLY: I'm busy. Don't bother me.

BIFF: [*Taking the hoe from* WILLY.] I'm saying good-bye to you, Pop. [WILLY *looks at him, silent, unable to move.*] I'm not coming back anymore.

WILLY: You're not going to see Oliver tomorrow?

BIFF: I've got no appointment, Dad.

WILLY: He put his arm around you, and you've got no appointment?

BIFF: Pop, get this now, will you? Everytime I've left it's been a fight that sent me out of here. Today I realized something about myself and I tried to explain it to you and I—I think I'm just not smart enough to make any sense out of it for you. To hell with whose fault it is or anything like that. [*He takes* WILLY's *arm.*] Let's just wrap it up, heh? Come on in, we'll tell Mom. [*He gently tries to pull* WILLY *to left.*]

WILLY: [*Frozen, immobile, with guilt in his voice.*] No, I don't want to see her.

BIFF: Come on! [*He pulls again, and* WILLY *tries to pull away.*]

WILLY: [*Highly nervous.*] No, no, I don't want to see her.

BIFF: [*Tries to look into* WILLY's *face, as if to find the answer there.*] Why don't you want to see her?

WILLY: [*More harshly now.*] Don't bother me, will you?

BIFF: What do you mean, you don't want to see her? You don't want them calling you yellow, do you? This isn't your fault; it's me, I'm a bum. Now come inside! [WILLY *strains to get away.*] Did you hear what I said to you?

[WILLY *pulls away and quickly goes by himself into the house.* BIFF *follows.*]

LINDA: [*To* WILLY.] Did you plant, dear?

BIFF: [*At the door, to* LINDA.] All right, we had it out. I'm going and I'm not writing anymore.

LINDA: [*Going to* WILLY *in the kitchen.*] I think that's the best way, dear. 'Cause there's no use drawing it out, you'll just never get along.

[WILLY *doesn't respond.*]

BIFF: People ask where I am and what I'm doing, you don't know, and you don't care. That way it'll be off your mind and you can start brightening up again. All right? That clears it, doesn't it? [WILLY *is silent, and* BIFF *goes to him.*] You gonna wish me luck, scout? [*He extends his hand.*] What do you say?

LINDA: Shake his hand, Willy.

WILLY: [*Turning to her, seething with hurt.*] There's no necessity to mention the pen at all, y'know.

BIFF: [*Gently.*] I've got no appointment, Dad.

WILLY: [*Erupting fiercely.*] He put his arm around . . . ?

BIFF: Dad, you're never going to see what I am, so what's the use of arguing? If I strike oil I'll send you a check. Meantime forget I'm alive.

WILLY: [*To* LINDA.] Spite, see?

BIFF: Shake hands, Dad.

WILLY: Not my hand.

BIFF: I was hoping not to go this way.

WILLY: Well, this is the way you're going. Good-bye. [BIFF *looks at him a moment, then turns sharply and goes to the stairs.* WILLY *stops him with.*] May you rot in hell if you leave this house!

BIFF: [*Turning.*] Exactly what is it that you want from me?

WILLY: I want you to know, on the train, in the mountains, in the valleys, wherever you go, that you cut down your life for spite!

BIFF: No, no.

WILLY: Spite, spite, is the word of your undoing! And when you're down and out, remember what did it. When you're rotting somewhere beside the railroad tracks, remember, and don't you dare blame it on me!

BIFF: I'm not blaming it on you!

WILLY: I won't take the rap for this, you hear?

[HAPPY *comes down the stairs and stands on the bottom step, watching.*]

BIFF: That's just what I'm telling you!

WILLY: [*Sinking into a chair at the table, with full accusation.*] You're trying to put a knife in me—don't think I don't know what you're doing!

BIFF: All right, phony! Then let's lay it on the line. [*He whips the rubber tube out of his pocket and puts it on the table.*]

HAPPY: You crazy—

LINDA: Biff!

[*She moves to grab the hose, but* BIFF *holds it down with his hand.*]

BIFF: Leave it there! Don't move it!

WILLY: [*Not looking at it.*] What is that?

BIFF: You know goddam well what that is.

WILLY: [*Caged, wanting to escape.*] I never saw that.

BIFF: You saw it. The mice didn't bring it into the cellar! What is this supposed to do, make a hero out of you? This supposed to make me sorry for you?

WILLY: Never heard of it.

BIFF: There'll be no pity for you, you hear it? No pity!

WILLY: [*To* LINDA.] You hear the spite!

BIFF: No, you're going to hear the truth—what you are and what I am!

LINDA: Stop it!

WILLY: Spite!

HAPPY: [*Coming down toward* BIFF.] You cut it now!

BIFF: [*To* HAPPY.] The man don't know who we are! The man is gonna know! [*To* WILLY.] We never told the truth for ten minutes in this house!

HAPPY: We always told the truth!

BIFF: [*Turning on him.*] You big blow, are you the assistant buyer? You're one of the two assistants to the assistant, aren't you?

HAPPY: Well, I'm practically—

BIFF: You're practically full of it! We all are! And I'm through with it. [*To* WILLY.] Now hear this, Willy, this is me.

WILLY: I know you!

BIFF: You know why I had no address for three months? I stole a suit in

Kansas City and I was in jail. [*To* LINDA, *who is sobbing.*] Stop crying. I'm through with it.

[LINDA *turns away from them, her hands covering her face.*]

WILLY: I suppose that's my fault!

BIFF: I stole myself out of every good job since high school!

WILLY: And whose fault is that?

BIFF: And I never got anywhere because you blew me so full of hot air I could never stand taking orders from anybody! That's whose fault it is!

WILLY: I hear that!

LINDA: Don't, Biff!

BIFF: It's goddam time you heard that! I had to be boss big shot in two weeks, and I'm through with it!

WILLY: Then hang yourself! For spite, hang yourself!

BIFF: No! Nobody's hanging himself, Willy! I ran down eleven flights with a pen in my hand today. And suddenly I stopped, you hear me? And in the middle of that office building, do you hear this? I stopped in the middle of that building and I saw—the sky. I saw the things that I love in this world. The work and the food and time to sit and smoke. And I looked at the pen and said to myself, what the hell am I grabbing this for? Why am I trying to become what I don't want to be? What am I doing in an office, making a contemptuous, begging fool of myself, when all I want is out there, waiting for me the minute I say I know who I am! Why can't I say that, Willy? [*He tries to make* WILLY *face him, but* WILLY *pulls away and moves to the left.*]

WILLY: [*With hatred, threateningly.*] The door of your life is wide open!

BIFF: Pop! I'm a dime a dozen, and so are you!

WILLY: [*Turning on him now in an uncontrolled outburst.*] I am not a dime a dozen! I am Willy Loman, and you are Biff Loman!

[BIFF *starts for* WILLY, *but is blocked by* HAPPY. *In his fury,* BIFF *seems on the verge of attacking his father.*]

BIFF: I am not a leader of men, Willy, and neither are you. You were never anything but a hard-working drummer who landed in the ash can like all the rest of them! I'm one dollar an hour, Willy! I tried seven states and couldn't raise it. A buck an hour! Do you gather my meaning? I'm not bringing home any prizes anymore, and you're going to stop waiting for me to bring them home!

WILLY: [*Directly to* BIFF.] You vengeful, spiteful mut!

[BIFF *breaks from* HAPPY. WILLY, *in fright, starts up the stairs.* BIFF *grabs him.*]

BIFF: [*At the peak of his fury.*] Pop, I'm nothing! I'm nothing, Pop. Can't you understand that? There's no spite in it anymore. I'm just what I am, that's all.

[BIFF's *fury has spent itself, and he breaks down, sobbing, holding on to* WILLY, *who dumbly fumbles for* BIFF's *face.*]

WILLY: [*Astonished.*] What're you doing? What're you doing? [*To* LINDA.] Why is he crying?

BIFF: [*Crying, broken.*] Will you let me go, for Christ's sake? Will you take that phony dream and burn it before something happens? [*Struggling to contain himself, he pulls away and moves to the stairs.*] I'll go in the morning. Put him—put him to bed. [*Exhausted,* BIFF *moves up the stairs to his room.*]

WILLY: [*After a long pause, astonished, elevated.*] Isn't that—isn't that remarkable? Biff—he likes me!

LINDA: He loves you, Willy!

HAPPY: [*Deeply moved.*] Always did, Pop.

WILLY: Oh, Biff! [*Staring wildly.*] He cried! Cried to me. [*He is choking with his love, and now cries out his promise.*] That boy—that boy is going to be magnificent!

[BEN *appears in the light just outside the kitchen.*]

BEN: Yes, outstanding, with twenty thousand behind him.

LINDA: [*Sensing the racing of his mind, fearfully, carefully.*] Now come to bed, Willy. It's all settled now.

WILLY: [*Finding it difficult not to rush out of the house.*] Yes, we'll sleep. Come on. Go to sleep, Hap.

BEN: And it does take a great kind of man to crack the jungle.

[*In accents of dread,* BEN'*s idyllic music starts up.*]

HAPPY: [*His arm around* LINDA.] I'm getting married, Pop, don't forget it. I'm changing everything. I'm gonna run that department before the year is up. You'll see, Mom. [*He kisses her.*]

BEN: The jungle is dark but full of diamonds, Willy.

[WILLY *turns, moves, listening to* BEN.]

LINDA: Be good. You're both good boys, just act that way, that's all.

HAPPY: 'Night, Pop. [*He goes upstairs.*]

LINDA: [*To* WILLY.] Come, dear.

BEN: [*With greater force.*] One must go in to fetch a diamond out.

WILLY: [*To* LINDA, *as he moves slowly along the edge of the kitchen, toward the door.*] I just want to get settled down, Linda. Let me sit alone for a little.

LINDA: [*Almost uttering her fear.*] I want you upstairs.

WILLY: [*Taking her in his arms.*] In a few minutes, Linda. I couldn't sleep right now. Go on, you look awful tired. [*He kisses her.*]

BEN: Not like an appointment at all. A diamond is rough and hard to the touch.

WILLY: Go on now. I'll be right up.

LINDA: I think this is the only way, Willy.

WILLY: Sure, it's the best thing.

BEN: Best thing!

WILLY: The only way. Everything is gonna be—go on, kid, get to bed. You look so tired.

LINDA: Come right up.

WILLY: Two minutes. [LINDA *goes into the living-room, then reappears in her bedroom.* WILLY *moves just outside the kitchen door.*] Loves me. [*Wonderingly.*] Always loved me. Isn't that a remarkable thing? Ben, he'll worship me for it!

BEN: [*With promise.*] It's dark there, but full of diamonds.

WILLY: Can you imagine that magnificence with twenty thousand dollars in his pocket?

LINDA: [*Calling from her room.*] Willy! Come up!

WILLY: [*Calling into the kitchen.*] Yes! Yes. Coming! It's very smart, you realize that, don't you, sweetheart? Even Ben sees it. I gotta go, baby. 'Bye! 'Bye! [*Going over to* BEN, *almost dancing.*] Imagine? When the mail comes he'll be ahead of Bernard again!

BEN: A perfect proposition all around.

WILLY: Did you see how he cried to me? Oh, if I could kiss him, Ben!

BEN: Time, William, time!

WILLY: Oh, Ben, I always knew one way or another we were gonna make it, Biff and I!

BEN: [*Looking at his watch.*] The boat. We'll be late. [*He moves slowly off into the darkness.*]

WILLY: [*Elegiacally, turning to the house.*] Now when you kick off, boy, I want a seventy-yard boot, and get right down the field under the ball, and when you hit, hit low and hit hard, because it's important, boy. [*He swings around and faces the audience.*] There's all kinds of important people in the stands, and the first thing you know . . . [*Suddenly realizing he is alone.*] Ben! Ben, where do I . . . ? [*He makes a sudden movement of search.*] Ben, how do I . . . ?

LINDA: [*Calling.*] Willy, you coming up?

WILLY: [*Uttering a gasp of fear, whirling about as if to quiet her.*] Sh! [*He turns around as if to find his way; sounds, faces, voices, seem to be swarming in upon him and he flicks at them, crying.*] Sh! Sh! [*Suddenly music, faint and high, stops him. It rises in intensity, almost to an unbearable scream. He goes up and down on his toes, and rushes off around the house.*] Shhh!

LINDA: Willy? [*There is no answer.* LINDA *waits.* BIFF *gets up off his bed. He is still in his clothes.* HAPPY *sits up.* BIFF *stands listening.*] [*With real fear.*] Willy, answer me! Willy! [*There is the sound of a car starting and moving away at full speed.*] No!

BIFF: [*Rushing down the stairs.*] Pop!

[*As the car speeds off, the music crashes down in a frenzy of sound, which becomes the soft pulsation of a single cello string.* BIFF *slowly returns to his bedroom. He and* HAPPY *gravely don their jackets.* LINDA *slowly walks out of her room. The music has developed into a dead march. The leaves of day are appearing over everything.* CHARLEY *and* BERNARD, *somberly dressed, appear and knock on the kitchen door.* BIFF *and* HAPPY *slowly descend the stairs to the kitchen as* CHARLEY *and* BERNARD *enter. All stop a moment when* LINDA, *in clothes of mourning, bearing a little bunch of roses, comes through the draped doorway into the kitchen. She goes to* CHARLEY *and takes his arm. Now all move toward the audience, through the wall-line of the kitchen. At the limit of the apron,* LINDA *lays down the flowers, kneels, and sits back on her heels. All stare down at the grave.*]

REQUIEM

CHARLEY: It's getting dark, Linda.

[LINDA *doesn't react. She stares at the grave.*]

BIFF: How about it, Mom? Better get some rest, heh? They'll be closing the gate soon.

[LINDA *makes no move. Pause.*]

HAPPY: [*Deeply angered.*] He had no right to do that. There was no necessity for it. We would've helped him.

CHARLEY: [*Grunting.*] Hmmm.

BIFF: Come along, Mom.

LINDA: Why didn't anybody come?

CHARLEY: It was a very nice funeral.

LINDA: But where are all the people he knew? Maybe they blame him.

CHARLEY: Naa. It's a rough world, Linda. They wouldn't blame him.

LINDA: I can't understand it. At this time especially. First time in thirty-five years we were just about free and clear. He only needed a little salary. He was even finished with the dentist.

CHARLEY: No man only needs a little salary.

LINDA: I can't understand it.

BIFF: There were a lot of nice days. When he'd come home from a trip; or on Sundays, making the stoop; finishing the cellar; putting on the new porch; when he built the extra bathroom; and put up the garage. You know something, Charley, there's more of him in that front stoop than in all the sales he ever made.

CHARLEY: Yeah. He was a happy man with a batch of cement.

LINDA: He was so wonderful with his hands.

BIFF: He had the wrong dreams. All, all, wrong.

HAPPY: [*Almost ready to fight* BIFF.] Don't say that!

BIFF: He never knew who he was.

CHARLEY: [*Stopping* HAPPY's *movement and reply. To* BIFF.] Nobody dast blame this man. You don't understand: Willy was a salesman. And for a salesman, there is no rock bottom to the life. He don't put a bolt to a nut, he don't tell you the law or give you medicine. He's a man way out there in the blue, riding on a smile and a shoeshine. And when they start not smiling back—that's an earthquake. And then you get yourself a couple of spots on your hat, and you're finished. Nobody dast blame this man. A salesman is got to dream, boy. It comes with the territory.

BIFF: Charley, the man didn't know who he was.

HAPPY: [*Infuriated.*] Don't say that!

BIFF: Why don't you come with me, Happy?

HAPPY: I'm not licked that easily. I'm staying right in this city, and I'm
gonna beat this racket! [*He looks at* BIFF, *his chin set.*] The Loman Brothers!
BIFF: I know who I am, kid.
HAPPY: All right, boy. I'm gonna show you and everybody else that Willy
Loman did not die in vain. He had a good dream. It's the only dream
you can have—to come out number-one-man. He fought it out here, and
this is where I'm gonna win it for him.
BIFF: [*With a hopeless glance at* HAPPY, *bends toward his mother.*] Let's go, Mom.
LINDA: I'll be with you in a minute. Go on, Charley. [*He hesitates.*] I want
to, just for a minute. I never had a chance to say good-bye. [CHARLEY
moves away, followed by HAPPY. BIFF *remains a slight distance up and left of*
LINDA. *She sits there, summoning herself. The flute begins, not far away, playing
behind her speech.*] Forgive me, dear. I can't cry. I don't know what it is,
but I can't cry. I don't understand it. Why did you ever do that? Help
me, Willy, I can't cry. It seems to me that you're just on another trip. I
keep expecting you. Willy, dear, I can't cry. Why did you do it? I search
and search and I search, and I can't understand it, Willy. I made the last
payment on the house today. Today, dear. And there'll be nobody home.
[*A sob rises in her throat.*] We're free and clear. [*Sobbing more fully, released.*]
We're free. [BIFF *comes slowly toward her.*] We're free . . . We're free . . .

[BIFF *lifts her to her feet and moves out up right with her in his arms.* LINDA
sobs quietly. BERNARD *and* CHARLEY *come together and follow them, followed by* HAPPY. *Only the music of the flute is left on the darkening stage as
over the house the hard towers of the apartment buildings rise into sharp focus.*]

CURTAIN

1949

HENRIK IBSEN
A Doll House[1]

CHARACTERS

TORVALD HELMER, *a lawyer*	THE HELMERS' THREE SMALL CHILDREN
NORA, *his wife*	ANNE-MARIE, *their nurse*
DR. RANK	HELENE, *a maid*
MRS. LINDE	A DELIVERY BOY
NILS KROGSTAD, *a bank clerk*	

The action takes place in HELMER'*s residence.*

ACT I

*A comfortable room, tastefully but not expensively furnished. A door to the right
in the back wall leads to the entryway; another to the left leads to* HELMER'*s study.*

1. Translated by Rolf Fjelde.

Between these doors, a piano. Midway in the left-hand wall a door, and further back a window. Near the window a round table with an armchair and a small sofa. In the right-hand wall, toward the rear, a door, and nearer the foreground a porcelain stove with two armchairs and a rocking chair beside it. Between the stove and the side door, a small table. Engravings on the walls. An etagère *with china figures and other small art objects; a small bookcase with richly bound books; the floor carpeted; a fire burning in the stove. It is a winter day.*

A bell rings in the entryway; shortly after we hear the door being unlocked. NORA *comes into the room, humming happily to herself; she is wearing street clothes and carries an armload of packages, which she puts down on the table to the right. She has left the hall door open; and through it a* DELIVERY BOY *is seen, holding a Christmas tree and a basket, which he gives to the* MAID *who let them in.*

NORA: Hide the tree well, Helene. The children mustn't get a glimpse of it till this evening, after it's trimmed. [*To the* DELIVERY BOY, *taking out her purse.*] How much?

DELIVERY BOY: Fifty, ma'am.

NORA: There's a crown. No, keep the change. [*The* BOY *thanks her and leaves.* NORA *shuts the door. She laughs softly to herself while taking off her street things. Drawing a bag of macaroons from her pocket, she eats a couple, then steals over and listens at her husband's study door.*] Yes, he's home. [*Hums again as she moves to the table right.*]

HELMER: [*From the study.*] Is that my little lark twittering out there?

NORA: [*Busy opening some packages.*] Yes, it is.

HELMER: Is that my squirrel rummaging around?

NORA: Yes!

HELMER: When did my squirrel get in?

NORA: Just now. [*Putting the macaroon bag in her pocket and wiping her mouth.*] Do come in, Torvald, and see what I've bought.

HELMER: Can't be disturbed. [*After a moment he opens the door and peers in, pen in hand.*] Bought, you say? All that there? Has the little spendthrift been out throwing money around again?

NORA: Oh, but Torvald, this year we really should let ourselves go a bit. It's the first Christmas we haven't had to economize.

HELMER: But you know we can't go squandering.

NORA: Oh yes, Torvald, we can squander a little now. Can't we? Just a tiny, wee bit. Now that you've got a big salary and are going to make piles and piles of money.

HELMER: Yes—starting New Year's. But then it's a full three months till the raise comes through.

NORA: Pooh! We can borrow that long.

HELMER: Nora! [*Goes over and playfully takes her by the ear.*] Are your scatterbrains off again? What if today I borrowed a thousand crowns, and you squandered them over Christmas week, and then on New Year's Eve a roof tile fell on my head, and I lay there—

NORA: [*Putting her hand on his mouth.*] Oh! Don't say such things!

HELMER. Yes, but what if it happened—then what?

NORA: If anything so awful happened, then it just wouldn't matter if I had debts or not.

HELMER: Well, but the people I'd borrowed from?

NORA: Them? Who cares about them! They're strangers.

HELMER: Nora, Nora, how like a woman! No, but seriously, Nora, you know what I think about that. No debts! Never borrow! Something of freedom's lost—and something of beauty, too—from a home that's founded on borrowing and debt. We've made a brave stand up to now, the two of us; and we'll go right on like that the little while we have to.

NORA: [*Going toward the stove.*] Yes, whatever you say, Torvald.

HELMER: [*Following her.*] Now, now, the little lark's wings mustn't droop. Come on, don't be a sulky squirrel. [*Taking out his wallet.*] Nora, guess what I have here.

NORA: [*Turning quickly.*] Money!

HELMER: There, see. [*Hands her some notes.*] Good grief, I know how costs go up in a house at Christmastime.

NORA: Ten—twenty—thirty—forty. Oh, thank you, Torvald; I can manage no end on this.

HELMER: You really will have to.

NORA: Oh yes, I promise I will. But come here so I can show you everything I bought. And so cheap! Look, new clothes for Ivar here—and a sword. Here a horse and a trumpet for Bob. And a doll and a doll's bed here for Emmy; they're nothing much, but she'll tear them to bits in no time anyway. And here I have dress material and handkerchiefs for the maids. Old Anne-Marie really deserves something more.

HELMER: And what's in that package there?

NORA: [*With a cry.*] Torvald, no! You can't see that till tonight!

HELMER: I see. But tell me now, you little prodigal, what have you thought of for yourself?

NORA: For myself? Oh, I don't want anything at all.

HELMER: Of course you do. Tell me just what—within reason—you'd most like to have.

NORA: I honestly don't know. Oh, listen, Torvald—

HELMER: Well?

NORA: [*Fumbling at his coat buttons, without looking at him.*] If you want to give me something, then maybe you could—you could—

HELMER: Come, on, out with it.

NORA: [*Hurriedly.*] You could give me money, Torvald. No more than you think you can spare; then one of these days I'll buy something with it.

HELMER: But Nora—

NORA: Oh, please, Torvald darling, do that! I beg you, please. Then I could hang the bills in pretty gilt paper on the Christmas tree. Wouldn't that be fun?

HELMER: What are those little birds called that always fly through their fortunes?

NORA: Oh yes, spendthrifts; I know all that. But let's do as I say, Torvald;

then I'll have time to decide what I really need most. That's very sensible, isn't it?

HELMER: [*Smiling.*] Yes, very—that is, if you actually hung onto the money I give you, and you actually used it to buy yourself something. But it goes for the house and for all sorts of foolish things, and then I only have to lay out some more.

NORA: Oh, but Torvald—

HELMER: Don't deny it, my dear little Nora. [*Putting his arm around her waist.*] Spendthrifts are sweet, but they use up a frightful amount of money. It's incredible what it costs a man to feed such birds.

NORA: Oh, how can you say that! Really, I save everything I can.

HELMER: [*Laughing.*] Yes, that's the truth. Everything you can. But that's nothing at all.

NORA: [*Humming, with a smile of quiet satisfaction.*] Hm, if you only knew what expenses we larks and squirrels have, Torvald.

HELMER: You're an odd little one. Exactly the way your father was. You're never at a loss for scaring up money; but the moment you have it, it runs right out through your fingers; you never know what you've done with it. Well, one takes you as you are. It's deep in your blood. Yes, these things are hereditary, Nora.

NORA: Ah, I could wish I'd inherited many of Papa's qualities.

HELMER: And I couldn't wish you anything but just what you are, my sweet little lark. But wait; it seems to me you have a very—what should I call it?—a very suspicious look today—

NORA: I do?

HELMER: You certainly do. Look me straight in the eye.

NORA: [*Looking at him.*] Well?

HELMER: [*Shaking an admonitory finger.*] Surely my sweet tooth hasn't been running riot in town today, has she?

NORA: No. Why do you imagine that?

HELMER: My sweet tooth really didn't make a little detour through the confectioner's?

NORA: No, I assure you, Torvald—

HELMER: Hasn't nibbled some pastry?

NORA: No, not at all.

HELMER: Not even munched a macaroon or two?

NORA: No, Torvald, I assure you, really—

HELMER: There, there now. Of course I'm only joking.

NORA: [*Going to the table, right.*] You know I could never think of going against you.

HELMER: No, I understand that; and you *have* given me your word. [*Going over to her.*] Well, you keep your little Christmas secrets to yourself, Nora darling. I expect they'll come to light this evening, when the tree is lit.

NORA: Did you remember to ask Dr. Rank?

HELMER: No. But there's no need for that; it's assumed he'll be dining with us. All the same, I'll ask him when he stops by here this morning. I've ordered some fine wine. Nora, you can't imagine how I'm looking forward to this evening.

NORA: So am I. And what fun for the children, Torvald!

HELMER: Ah, it's so gratifying to know that one's gotten a safe, secure job, and with a comfortable salary. It's a great satisfaction, isn't it?

NORA: Oh, it's wonderful!

HELMER: Remember last Christmas? Three whole weeks before, you shut yourself in every evening till long after midnight, making flowers for the Christmas tree, and all the other decorations to surprise us. Ugh, that was the dullest time I've ever lived through.

NORA: It wasn't at all dull for me.

HELMER: [*Smiling.*] But the outcome *was* pretty sorry, Nora.

NORA: Oh, don't tease me with that again. How could I help it that the cat came in and tore everything to shreds.

HELMER: No, poor thing, you certainly couldn't. You wanted so much to please us all, and that's what counts. But it's just as well that the hard times are past.

NORA: Yes, it's really wonderful.

HELMER: Now I don't have to sit here alone, boring myself, and you don't have to tire your precious eyes and your fair little delicate hands—

NORA: [*Clapping her hands.*] No, is it really true, Torvald, I don't have to? Oh, how wonderfully lovely to hear! [*Taking his arm.*] Now I'll tell you just how I've thought we should plan things. Right after Christmas— [*The doorbell rings.*] Oh, the bell. [*Straightening the room up a bit.*] Somebody would have to come. What a bore!

HELMER: I'm not at home to visitors, don't forget.

MAID: [*From the hall doorway.*] Ma'am, a lady to see you—

NORA: All right, let her come in.

MAID: [*To* HELMER.] And the doctor's just come too.

HELMER: Did he go right to my study?

MAID: Yes, he did.

[HELMER *goes into his room. The* MAID *shows in* MRS. LINDE, *dressed in traveling clothes, and shuts the door after her.*]

MRS. LINDE: [*In a dispirited and somewhat hesitant voice.*] Hello, Nora.

NORA: [*Uncertain.*] Hello—

MRS. LINDE: You don't recognize me.

NORA: No, I don't know—but wait, I think—[*Exclaiming.*] What! Kristine! Is it really you?

MRS. LINDE: Yes, it's me.

NORA: Kristine! To think I didn't recognize you. But then, how could I? [*More quietly.*] How you've changed, Kristine!

MRS. LINDE: Yes, no doubt I have. In nine—ten long years.

NORA: Is it so long since we met! Yes, it's all of that. Oh, these last eight years have been a happy time, believe me. And so now you've come in to town, too. Made the long trip in the winter. That took courage.

MRS. LINDE: I just got here by ship this morning.

NORA: To enjoy yourself over Christmas, of course. Oh, how lovely! Yes, enjoy ourselves, we'll do that. But take your coat off. You're not still cold? [*Helping her.*] There now, let's get cozy here by the stove. No, the easy chair there! I'll take the rocker here. [*Seizing her hands.*] Yes, now you have your old look again; it was only in that first moment. You're a bit more pale, Kristine—and maybe a bit thinner.

MRS. LINDE: And much, much older, Nora.

NORA: Yes, perhaps a bit older; a tiny, tiny bit; not much at all. [*Stopping short; suddenly serious.*] Oh, but thoughtless me, to sit here, chattering away. Sweet, good Kristine, can you forgive me?

MRS. LINDE: What do you mean, Nora?

NORA: [*Softly.*] Poor Kristine, you've become a widow.

MRS. LINDE: Yes, three years ago.

NORA: Oh, I knew it, of course; I read it in the papers. Oh, Kristine, you must believe me; I often thought of writing you then, but I kept postponing it, and something always interfered.

MRS. LINDE: Nora dear, I understand completely.

NORA: No, it was awful of me, Kristine. You poor thing, how much you must have gone through. And he left you nothing?

MRS. LINDE: No.

NORA: And no children?

MRS. LINDE: No.

NORA: Nothing at all, then?

MRS. LINDE: Not even a sense of loss to feed on.

NORA: [*Looking incredulously at her.*] But Kristine, how could that be?

MRS. LINDE: [*Smiling wearily and smoothing her hair.*] Oh, sometimes it happens, Nora.

NORA: So completely alone. How terribly hard that must be for you. I have three lovely children. You can't see them now; they're out with the maid. But now you must tell me everything—

MRS. LINDE: No, no, no, tell me about yourself.

NORA: No, you begin. Today I don't want to be selfish. I want to think only of you today. But there *is* something I must tell you. Did you hear of the wonderful luck we had recently?

MRS. LINDE: No, what's that?

NORA: My husband's been made manager in the bank, just think!

MRS. LINDE: Your husband? How marvelous!

NORA: Isn't it? Being a lawyer is such an uncertain living, you know, especially if one won't touch any cases that aren't clean and decent. And of course Torvald would never do that, and I'm with him completely there. Oh, we're simply delighted, believe me! He'll join the bank right after New Year's and start getting a huge salary and lots of commissions. From now on we can live quite differently—just as we want. Oh, Kristine, I feel so light and happy! Won't it be lovely to have stacks of money and not a care in the world?

MRS. LINDE: Well, anyway, it would be lovely to have enough for necessities.

NORA: No, not just for necessities, but stacks and stacks of money!

MRS. LINDE: [*Smiling.*] Nora, Nora, aren't you sensible yet? Back in school you were such a free spender.

NORA: [*With a quiet laugh.*] Yes, that's what Torvald still says. [*Shaking her finger.*] But "Nora, Nora" isn't as silly as you all think. Really, we've been in no position for me to go squandering. We've had to work, both of us.

MRS. LINDE: You too?

NORA: Yes, at odd jobs—needlework, crocheting, embroidery, and such— [*Casually.*] and other things too. You remember that Torvald left the department when we were married? There was no chance of promotion in his office, and of course he needed to earn more money. But that first year he drove himself terribly. He took on all kinds of extra work that kept him going morning and night. It wore him down, and then he fell deathly ill. The doctors said it was essential for him to travel south.

MRS. LINDE: Yes, didn't you spend a whole year in Italy?

NORA: That's right. It wasn't easy to get away, you know. Ivar had just been born. But of course we had to go. Oh, that was a beautiful trip, and it saved Torvald's life. But it cost a frightful sum, Kristine.

MRS. LINDE: I can well imagine.

NORA: Four thousand, eight hundred crowns it cost. That's really a lot of money.

MRS. LINDE: But it's lucky you had it when you needed it.

NORA: Well, as it was, we got it from Papa.

MRS. LINDE: I see. It was just about the time your father died.

NORA: Yes, just about then. And, you know, I couldn't make that trip out to nurse him. I had to stay here, expecting Ivar any moment, and with my poor sick Torvald to care for. Dearest Papa, I never saw him again, Kristine. Oh, that was the worst time I've known in all my marriage.

MRS. LINDE: I know how you loved him. And then you went off to Italy?

NORA: Yes. We had the means now, and the doctors urged us. So we left a month after.

MRS. LINDE: And your husband came back completely cured?

NORA: Sound as a drum!

MRS. LINDE: But—the doctor?

NORA: Who?

MRS. LINDE: I thought the maid said he was a doctor, the man who came in with me.

NORA: Yes, that was Dr. Rank—but he's not making a sick call. He's our closest friend, and he stops by at least once a day. No, Torvald hasn't had a sick moment since, and the children are fit and strong, and I am, too. [*Jumping up and clapping her hands.*] Oh, dear God, Kristine, what a lovely thing to live and be happy! But how disgusting of me—I'm talking of nothing but my own affairs. [*Sits on a stool close by* KRISTINE, *arms resting across her knees.*] Oh, don't be angry with me! Tell me, is it really true that you weren't in love with your husband? Why did you marry him, then?

MRS. LINDE: My mother was still alive, but bedridden and helpless—and I had my two younger brothers to look after. In all conscience, I didn't think I could turn him down.

NORA: No, you were right there. But was he rich at the time?

MRS. LINDE: He was very well off, I'd say. But the business was shaky, Nora. When he died, it all fell apart, and nothing was left.

NORA: And then—?

MRS. LINDE: Yes, so I had to scrape up a living with a little shop and a little teaching and whatever else I could find. The last three years have been like one endless workday without a rest for me. Now it's over, Nora. My poor mother doesn't need me, for she's passed on. Nor the boys, either; they're working now and can take care of themselves.

NORA: How free you must feel—

MRS. LINDE: No—only unspeakably empty. Nothing to live for now. [*Standing up anxiously.*] That's why I couldn't take it any longer out in that desolate hole. Maybe here it'll be easier to find something to do and keep my mind occupied. If I could only be lucky enough to get a steady job, some office work—

NORA: Oh, but Kristine, that's so dreadfully tiring, and you already look so tired. It would be much better for you if you could go off to a bathing resort.

MRS. LINDE: [*Going toward the window.*] I have no father to give me travel money, Nora.

NORA: [*Rising.*] Oh, don't be angry with me.

MRS. LINDE: [*Going to her.*] Nora dear, don't you be angry with me. The worst of my kind of situation is all the bitterness that's stored away. No one to work for, and yet you're always having to snap up your opportunities. You have to live; and so you grow selfish. When you told me the happy change in your lot, do you know I was delighted less for your sakes than for mine?

NORA: How so? Oh, I see. You think maybe Torvald could do something for you.

MRS. LINDE: Yes, that's what I thought.

NORA: And he will, Kristine! Just leave it to me; I'll bring it up so delicately— find something attractive to humor him with. Oh, I'm so eager to help you.

MRS. LINDE: How very kind of you, Nora, to be so concerned over me— doubly kind, considering you really know so little of life's burdens your-self.

NORA: I—? I know so little—?

MRS. LINDE: [*Smiling.*] Well, my heavens—a little needlework and such— Nora, you're just a child.

NORA: [*Tossing her head and pacing the floor.*] You don't have to act so superior.

MRS. LINDE: Oh?

NORA: You're just like the others. You all think I'm incapable of anything serious—

MRS. LINDE: Come now—

NORA: That I've never had to face the raw world.

MRS. LINDE: Nora dear, you've just been telling me all your troubles.

NORA: Hm! Trivia! [*Quietly.*] I haven't told you the big thing.

MRS. LINDE: Big thing? What do you mean?

NORA: You look down on me so, Kristine, but you shouldn't. You're proud that you worked so long and hard for your mother.

MRS. LINDE: I don't look down on a soul. But it *is* true: I'm proud—and happy, too—to think it was given to me to make my mother's last days almost free of care.

NORA: And you're also proud thinking of what you've done for your brothers.

MRS. LINDE: I feel I've a right to be.

NORA: I agree. But listen to this, Kristine—I've also got something to be proud and happy for.

MRS. LINDE: I don't doubt it. But whatever do you mean?

NORA: Not so loud. What if Torvald heard! He mustn't, not for anything in the world. Nobody must know, Kristine. No one but you.

MRS. LINDE: But what is it, then?

NORA: Come here. [*Drawing her down beside her on the sofa.*] It's true—I've also got something to be proud and happy for. I'm the one who saved Torvald's life.

MRS. LINDE: Saved—? Saved how?

NORA: I told you about the trip to Italy. Torvald never would have lived if he hadn't gone south—

MRS. LINDE: Of course; your father gave you the means—

NORA: [*Smiling.*] That's what Torvald and all the rest think, but—

MRS. LINDE: But—?

NORA: Papa didn't give us a pin. I was the one who raised the money.

MRS. LINDE: You? That whole amount?

NORA: Four thousand, eight hundred crowns. What do you say to that?

MRS. LINDE: But Nora, how was it possible? Did you win the lottery?

NORA: [*Disdainfully.*] The lottery? Pooh! No art to that.

MRS. LINDE: But where did you get it from then?

NORA: [*Humming, with a mysterious smile.*] Hmm, tra-la-la-la.

MRS. LINDE: Because you couldn't have borrowed it.

NORA: No? Why not?

MRS. LINDE: A wife can't borrow without her husband's consent.

NORA: [*Tossing her head.*] Oh, but a wife with a little business sense, a wife who knows how to manage—

MRS. LINDE: Nora, I simply don't understand—

NORA: You don't have to. Whoever said I *borrowed* the money? I could have gotten it other ways. [*Throwing herself back on the sofa.*] I could have gotten it from some admirer or other. After all, a girl with my ravishing appeal—

MRS. LINDE: You lunatic.

NORA: I'll bet you're eaten up with curiosity, Kristine.

MRS. LINDE: Now listen here, Nora—you haven't done something indiscreet?

NORA: [*Sitting up again.*] Is it indiscreet to save your husband's life?

MRS. LINDE: I think it's indiscreet that without his knowledge you—

NORA: But that's the point: he mustn't know! My Lord, can't you understand? He mustn't ever know the close call he had. It was to *me* the doctors came to say his life was in danger—that nothing could save him but a stay in the south. Didn't I try strategy then! I began talking about how lovely it would be for me to travel abroad like other young wives; I begged and I cried; I told him please to remember my condition, to be kind and indulge me; and then I dropped a hint that he could easily take out a loan. But at that, Kristine, he nearly exploded. He said I was frivolous, and it was his duty as man of the house not to indulge me in whims and fancies—as I think he called them. Aha, I thought, now you'll just have to be saved—and that's when I saw my chance.

MRS. LINDE: And your father never told Torvald the money wasn't from him?

NORA: No, never. Papa died right about then. I'd considered bringing him into my secret and begging him never to tell. But he was too sick at the time—and then, sadly, it didn't matter.

MRS. LINDE: And you've never confided in your husband since?

NORA: For heaven's sake, no! Are you serious? He's so strict on that subject. Besides—Torvald, with all his masculine pride—how painfully humiliating for him if he ever found out he was in debt to me. That would just ruin our relationship. Our beautiful, happy home would never be the same.

MRS. LINDE: Won't you ever tell him?

NORA: [*Thoughtfully.*] Yes—maybe sometime years from now, when I'm no longer so attractive. Don't laugh! I only mean when Torvald loves me less than now, when he stops enjoying my dancing and dressing up and reciting for him. Then it might be wise to have something in reserve— [*Breaking off.*] How ridiculous! That'll never happen—Well, Kristine, what do you think of my big secret? I'm capable of something too, hm? You can imagine, of course, how this thing hangs over me. It really hasn't been easy meeting the payments on time. In the business world there's what they call quarterly interest and what they call amortization, and these are always so terribly hard to manage. I've had to skimp a little here and there, wherever I could, you know. I could hardly spare anything from my house allowance, because Torvald has to live well. I couldn't let the children go poorly dressed; whatever I got for them, I felt I had to use up completely—the darlings!

MRS. LINDE: Poor Nora, so it had to come out of your own budget, then?

NORA: Yes, of course. But I was the one most responsible, too. Every time Torvald gave me money for new clothes and such, I never used more than half; always bought the simplest, cheapest outfits. It was a godsend that everything looks so well on me that Torvald never noticed. But it did weigh me down at times, Kristine. It *is* such a joy to wear fine things. You understand.

MRS. LINDE: Oh, of course.

NORA: And then I found other ways of making money. Last winter I was lucky enough to get a lot of copying to do. I locked myself in and sat writing every evening till late in the night. Ah, I was tired so often, dead tired. But still it was wonderful fun, sitting and working like that, earning money. It was almost like being a man.

MRS. LINDE: But how much have you paid off this way so far?

NORA: That's hard to say, exactly. These accounts, you know, aren't easy to figure. I only know that I've paid out all I could scrape together. Time and again I haven't known where to turn. [*Smiling.*] Then I'd sit here dreaming of a rich old gentleman who had fallen in love with me—

MRS. LINDE: What! Who is he?

NORA: Oh, really! And that he'd died, and when his will was opened, there in big letters it said, "All my fortune shall be paid over in cash, immediately, to that enchanting Mrs. Nora Helmer."

MRS. LINDE: But Nora dear—who *was* this gentleman?

NORA: Good grief, can't you understand? The old man never existed; that was only something I'd dream up time and again whenever I was at my wits' end for money. But it makes no difference now; the old fossil can go where he pleases for all I care; I don't need him or his will—because now I'm free. [*Jumping up.*] Oh, how lovely to think of that, Kristine! Carefree! To know you're carefree, utterly carefree; to be able to romp and play with the children, and to keep up a beautiful, charming home— everything just the way Torvald likes it! And think, spring is coming, with big blue skies. Maybe we can travel a little then. Maybe I'll see the ocean again. Oh yes, it *is* so marvelous to live and be happy!

[*The front doorbell rings.*]

MRS. LINDE: [*Rising.*] There's the bell. It's probably best that I go.

NORA: No, stay. No one's expected. It must be for Torvald.

MAID: [*From the hall doorway.*] Excuse me, ma'am—there's a gentleman here to see Mr. Helmer, but I didn't know—since the doctor's with him—

NORA: Who is the gentleman?

KROGSTAD: [*From the doorway.*] It's me, Mrs. Helmer.

[MRS. LINDE *starts and turns away toward the window.*]

NORA: [*Stepping toward him, tense, her voice a whisper.*] You? What is it? Why do you want to speak to my husband?

KROGSTAD: Bank business—after a fashion. I have a small job in the investment bank, and I hear now your husband is going to be our chief—

NORA: In other words, it's—

KROGSTAD: Just dry business, Mrs. Helmer. Nothing but that.

NORA: Yes, then please be good enough to step into the study. [*She nods indifferently as she sees him out by the hall door, then returns and begins stirring up the stove.*]

MRS. LINDE: Nora—who was that man?

NORA: That was a Mr. Krogstad—a lawyer.

MRS. LINDE: Then it really was him.

NORA: Do you know that person?

MRS. LINDE: I did once—many years ago. For a time he was a law clerk in our town.

NORA: Yes, he's been that.

MRS. LINDE: How he's changed.

NORA: I understand he had a very unhappy marriage.

MRS. LINDE: He's a widower now.

NORA: With a number of children. There now, it's burning. [*She closes the stove door and moves the rocker a bit to one side.*]

MRS. LINDE: They say he has a hand in all kinds of business.

NORA: Oh? That may be true; I wouldn't know. But let's not think about business. It's so dull.

[DR. RANK *enters from* HELMER'S *study.*]

RANK: [*Still in the doorway.*] No, no, really—I don't want to intrude, I'd just as soon talk a little while with your wife. [*Shuts the door, then notices* MRS. LINDE.] Oh, beg pardon. I'm intruding here too.

NORA: No, not at all. [*Introducing him.*] Dr. Rank, Mrs. Linde.

RANK: Well now, that's a name much heard in this house. I believe I passed the lady on the stairs as I came.

MRS. LINDE: Yes, I take the stairs very slowly. They're rather hard on me.

RANK: Uh-hm, some touch of internal weakness?

MRS. LINDE: More overexertion, I'd say.

RANK: Nothing else? Then you're probably here in town to rest up in a round of parties?

MRS. LINDE: I'm here to look for work.

RANK: Is that the best cure for overexertion?

MRS. LINDE: One has to live, Doctor.

RANK: Yes, there's a common prejudice to that effect.

NORA: Oh, come on, Dr. Rank—you really do want to live yourself.

RANK: Yes, I really do. Wretched as I am, I'll gladly prolong my torment indefinitely. All my patients feel like that. And it's quite the same, too, with the morally sick. Right at this moment there's one of those moral invalids in there with Helmer—

MRS. LINDE: [*Softly.*] Ah!

NORA: Who do you mean?

RANK: Oh, it's a lawyer, Krogstad, a type you wouldn't know. His character is rotten to the root—but even he began chattering all-importantly about how he had to *live.*

NORA: Oh? What did he want to talk to Torvald about?

RANK: I really don't know. I only heard something about the bank.

NORA: I didn't know that Krog—that this man Krogstad had anything to do with the bank.

RANK: Yes, he's gotten some kind of berth down there. [*To* MRS. LINDE.] I don't know if you also have, in your neck of the woods, a type of person who scuttles about breathlessly, sniffing out hints of moral corruption, and then maneuvers his victim into some sort of key position where he can keep an eye on him. It's the healthy these days that are out in the cold.

MRS. LINDE: All the same, it's the sick who most need to be taken in.

RANK: [*With a shrug.*] Yes, there we have it. That's the concept that's turning society into a sanatorium.

[NORA, *lost in her thoughts, breaks out into quiet laughter and claps her hands.*]

RANK: Why do you laugh at that? Do you have any real idea of what society is?

NORA: What do I care about dreary old society? I was laughing at something quite different—something terribly funny. Tell me, Doctor—is everyone who works in the bank dependent now on Torvald?

RANK: Is that what you find so terribly funny?

NORA: [*Smiling and humming.*] Never mind, never mind [*Pacing the floor.*] Yes, that's really immensely amusing: that we—that Torvald has so much power now over all those people. [*Taking the bag out of her pocket.*] Dr. Rank, a little macaroon on that?

RANK: See here, macaroons! I thought they were contraband here.

NORA: Yes, but these are some that Kristine gave me.

MRS. LINDE: What? I—?

NORA: Now, now, don't be afraid. You couldn't possibly know that Torvald had forbidden them. You see, he's worried they'll ruin my teeth. But hmp! Just this once! Isn't that so, Dr. Rank? Help yourself! [*Puts a macaroon in his mouth.*] And you too, Kristine. And I'll also have one, only a little one—or two, at the most. [*Walking about again.*] Now I'm really tremendously happy. Now there's just one last thing in the world that I have an enormous desire to do.

RANK: Well! And what's that?

NORA: It's something I have such a consuming desire to say so Torvald could hear.

RANK: And why can't you say it?

NORA: I don't dare. It's quite shocking.

MRS. LINDE: Shocking?

RANK: Well, then it isn't advisable. But in front of us you certainly can. What do you have such a desire to say so Torvald could hear?

NORA: I have such a huge desire to say—to hell and be damned!

RANK: Are you crazy?

MRS. LINDE: My goodness, Nora!

RANK: Go on, say it. Here he is.

NORA: [*Hiding the macaroon bag.*] Shh, shh, shh!

[HELMER *comes in from his study, hat in hand, overcoat over his arm.*]

NORA: [*Going toward him.*] Well, Torvald dear, are you through with him?

HELMER: Yes, he just left.

NORA: Let me introduce you—this is Kristine, who's arrived here in town.

HELMER: Kristine—? I'm sorry, but I don't know—

NORA: Mrs. Linde, Torvald dear. Mrs. Kristine Linde.

HELMER: Of course. A childhood friend of my wife's, no doubt?

MRS. LINDE: Yes, we knew each other in those days.

NORA: And just think, she made the long trip down here in order to talk with you.

HELMER: What's this?

MRS. LINDE: Well, not exactly—

NORA: You see, Kristine is remarkably clever in office work, and so she's terribly eager to come under a capable man's supervision and add more to what she already knows—

HELMER: Very wise, Mrs. Linde.

NORA: And then when she heard that you'd become a bank manager—the story was wired out to the papers—then she came in as fast as she could and—Really, Torvald, for my sake you can do a little something for Kristine, can't you?

HELMER: Yes, it's not at all impossible. Mrs. Linde, I suppose you're a widow?

MRS. LINDE: Yes.

HELMER: Any experience in office work?

MRS. LINDE: Yes, a good deal.

HELMER: Well, it's quite likely that I can make an opening for you—

NORA: [*Clapping her hands.*] You see, you see!

HELMER: You've come at a lucky moment, Mrs. Linde.

MRS. LINDE: Oh, how can I thank you?

HELMER: Not necessary. [*Putting his overcoat on.*] But today you'll have to excuse me—

RANK: Wait, I'll go with you. [*He fetches his coat from the hall and warms it at the stove.*]

NORA: Don't stay out long, dear.

HELMER: An hour; no more.

NORA: Are you going too, Kristine?

MRS. LINDE: [*Putting on her winter garments.*] Yes, I have to see about a room now.

HELMER: Then perhaps we can all walk together.

NORA: [*Helping her.*] What a shame we're so cramped here, but it's quite impossible for us to—

MRS. LINDE: Oh, don't even think of it! Good-bye, Nora dear, and thanks for everything.

NORA: Good-bye for now. Of course you'll be back this evening. And you too, Dr. Rank. What? If you're well enough? Oh, you've got to be! Wrap up tight now.

[*In a ripple of small talk the company moves out into the hall; children's voices are heard outside on the steps.*]

NORA: There they are! There they are! [*She runs to open the door. The children come in with their nurse,* ANNE-MARIE.] Come in, come in! [*Bends down and kisses them.*] Oh, you darlings—! Look at them, Kristine. Aren't they lovely!

RANK: No loitering in the draft here.

HELMER: Come, Mrs. Linde—this place is unbearable now for anyone but mothers.

[DR. RANK, HELMER, *and* MRS. LINDE *go down the stairs.* ANNE-MARIE *goes into the living room with the children.* NORA *follows, after closing the hall door.*]

NORA: How fresh and strong you look. Oh, such red cheeks you have! Like apples and roses. [*The children interrupt her throughout the following.*] And it was so much fun? That's wonderful. Really? You pulled both Emmy and Bob on the sled? Imagine, all together! Yes, you're a clever boy, Ivar. Oh, let me hold her a bit, Anne-Marie. My sweet little doll baby! [*Takes the smallest from the nurse and dances with her.*] Yes, yes, Mama will dance with Bob as well. What? Did you throw snowballs? Oh, if I'd only been there! No, don't bother, Anne-Marie—I'll undress them myself. Oh yes, let me. It's such fun. Go in and rest; you look half frozen. There's hot coffee waiting for you on the stove. [*The nurse goes into the room to the left.* NORA *takes the children's winter things off, throwing them about, while the children talk to her all at once.*] Is that so? A big dog chased you? But it didn't bite? No, dogs never bite little, lovely doll babies. Don't peek in the packages, Ivar! What is it? Yes, wouldn't you like to know. No, no, it's an ugly something. Well? Shall we play? What shall we play? Hide-and-seek? Yes, let's play hide-and-seek. Bob must hide first. I must? Yes, let me hide first. [*Laughing and shouting, she and the children play in and out of the living room and the adjoining room to the right. At last* NORA *hides under the table. The children come storming in, search, but cannot find her, then hear her muffled laughter, dash over to the table, lift the cloth up and find her. Wild shouting. She creeps forward as if to scare them. More shouts. Meanwhile, a knock at the hall door; no one has noticed it. Now the door half opens, and* KROGSTAD *appears. He waits a moment; the game goes on.*]

KROGSTAD: Beg pardon, Mrs. Helmer—

NORA: [*With a strangled cry, turning and scrambling to her knees.*] Oh! What do you want?

KROGSTAD: Excuse me. The outer door was ajar; it must be someone forgot to shut it—

NORA: [*Rising.*] My husband isn't home, Mr. Krogstad.

KROGSTAD: I know that.

NORA: Yes—then what do you want here?

KROGSTAD: A word with you.

NORA: With—? [*To the children, quietly.*] Go in to Anne-Marie. What? No, the strange man won't hurt Mama. When he's gone, we'll play some more. [*She leads the children into the room to the left and shuts the door after them. Then, tense and nervous:*] You want to speak to me?

KROGSTAD: Yes, I want to.

NORA: Today? But it's not yet the first of the month—

KROGSTAD: No, it's Christmas Eve. It's going to be up to you how merry a Christmas you have.

NORA: What is it you want? Today I absolutely can't—

KROGSTAD: We won't talk about that till later. This is something else. You do have a moment to spare, I suppose?

NORA: Oh yes, of course—I do, except—

KROGSTAD: Good. I was sitting over at Olsen's Restaurant when I saw your husband go down the street—

NORA: Yes?

KROGSTAD: With a lady.

NORA: Yes. So?

KROGSTAD: If you'll pardon my asking: wasn't that lady a Mrs. Linde?

NORA: Yes.

KROGSTAD: Just now come into town?

NORA: Yes, today.

KROGSTAD: She's a good friend of yours?

NORA: Yes, she is. But I don't see—

KROGSTAD: I also knew her once.

NORA: I'm aware of that.

KROGSTAD: Oh? You know all about it. I thought so. Well, then let me ask you short and sweet: is Mrs. Linde getting a job in the bank?

NORA: What makes you think you can cross-examine me, Mr. Krogstad—you, one of my husband's employees? But since you ask, you might as well know—yes, Mrs. Linde's going to be taken on at the bank. And I'm the one who spoke for her, Mr. Krogstad. Now you know.

KROGSTAD: So I guessed right.

NORA: [Pacing up and down.] Oh, one does have a tiny bit of influence, I should hope. Just because I am a woman, don't think it means that— When one has a subordinate position, Mr. Krogstad, one really ought to be careful about pushing somebody who—hm—

KROGSTAD: Who has influence?

NORA: That's right.

KROGSTAD: [In a different tone.] Mrs. Helmer, would you be good enough to use your influence on my behalf?

NORA: What? What do you mean?

KROGSTAD: Would you please make sure that I keep my subordinate position in the bank?

NORA: What does that mean? Who's thinking of taking away your position?

KROGSTAD: Oh, don't play the innocent with me. I'm quite aware that your friend would hardly relish the chance of running into me again; and I'm also aware now whom I can thank for being turned out.

NORA: But I promise you—

KROGSTAD: Yes, yes, yes, to the point: there's still time, and I'm advising you to use your influence to prevent it.

NORA: But Mr. Krogstad, I have absolutely no influence.

KROGSTAD: You haven't? I thought you were just saying—

NORA: You shouldn't take me so literally. I! How can you believe that I have any such influence over my husband?

KROGSTAD: Oh, I've known your husband from our student days. I don't think the great bank manager's more steadfast than any other married man.

NORA: You speak insolently about my husband, and I'll show you the door.

KROGSTAD: The lady has spirit.

NORA: I'm not afraid of you any longer. After New Year's, I'll soon be done with the whole business.

KROGSTAD: [*Restraining himself.*] Now listen to me, Mrs. Helmer. If necessary, I'll fight for my little job in the bank as if it were life itself.

NORA: Yes, so it seems.

KROGSTAD: It's not just a matter of income; that's the least of it. It's something else—All right, out with it! Look, this is the thing. You know, just like all the others, of course, that once, a good many years ago, I did something rather rash.

NORA: I've heard rumors to that effect.

KROGSTAD: The case never got into court; but all the same, every door was closed in my face from then on. So I took up those various activities you know about. I had to grab hold somewhere; and I dare say I haven't been among the worst. But now I want to drop all that. My boys are growing up. For their sakes, I'll have to win back as much respect as possible here in town. That job in the bank was like the first rung in my ladder. And now your husband wants to kick me right back down in the mud again.

NORA: But for heaven's sake, Mr. Krogstad, it's simply not in my power to help you.

KROGSTAD: That's because you haven't the will to—but I have the means to make you.

NORA: You certainly won't tell my husband that I owe you money?

KROGSTAD: Hm—what if I told him that?

NORA: That would be shameful of you. [*Nearly in tears.*] This secret—my joy and my pride—that he should learn it in such a crude and disgusting way—learn it from you. You'd expose me to the most horrible unpleasantness—

KROGSTAD: Only unpleasantness?

NORA: [*Vehemently.*] But go on and try. It'll turn out the worse for you, because then my husband will really see what a crook you are, and then you'll *never* be able to hold your job.

KROGSTAD: I asked if it was just domestic unpleasantness you were afraid of?

NORA: If my husband finds out, then of course he'll pay what I owe at once, and then we'd be through with you for good.

KROGSTAD: [*A step closer.*] Listen, Mrs. Helmer—you've either got a very bad memory, or else no head at all for business. I'd better put you a little more in touch with the facts.

NORA: What do you mean?

KROGSTAD: When your husband was sick, you came to me for a loan of four thousand, eight hundred crowns.

NORA: Where else could I go?

KROGSTAD: I promised to get you that sum—

NORA: And you got it.

KROGSTAD: I promised to get you that sum, on certain conditions. You were so involved in your husband's illness, and so eager to finance your trip, that I guess you didn't think out all the details. It might just be a good idea to remind you. I promised you the money on the strength of a note I drew up.

NORA: Yes, and that I signed.

KROGSTAD: Right. But at the bottom I added some lines for your father to guarantee the loan. He was supposed to sign down there.

NORA: Supposed to? He did sign.

KROGSTAD: I left the date blank. In other words, your father would have dated his signature himself. Do you remember that?

NORA: Yes, I think—

KROGSTAD: Then I gave you the note for you to mail to your father. Isn't that so?

NORA: Yes.

KROGSTAD: And naturally you sent it at once—because only some five, six days later you brought me the note, properly signed. And with that, the money was yours.

NORA: Well, then; I've made my payments regularly, haven't I?

KROGSTAD: More or less. But—getting back to the point—those were hard times for you then, Mrs. Helmer.

NORA: Yes, they were.

KROGSTAD: Your father was very ill, I believe.

NORA: He was near the end.

KROGSTAD: He died soon after?

NORA: Yes.

KROGSTAD: Tell me, Mrs. Helmer, do you happen to recall the date of your father's death? The day of the month, I mean.

NORA: Papa died the twenty-ninth of September.

KROGSTAD: That's quite correct; I've already looked into that. And now we come to a curious thing—[Taking out a paper.] which I simply cannot comprehend.

NORA: Curious thing? I don't know—

KROGSTAD: This is the curious thing: that your father co-signed the note for your loan three days after his death.

NORA: How—? I don't understand.

KROGSTAD: Your father died the twenty-ninth of September. But look. Here your father dated his signature October second. Isn't that curious, Mrs. Helmer? [NORA is silent.] Can you explain it to me? [NORA remains silent.] It's also remarkable that the words "October second" and the year aren't written in your father's hand, but rather in one that I think I know. Well, it's easy to understand. Your father forgot perhaps to date his signature, and then someone or other added it, a bit sloppily, before anyone knew of his death. There's nothing wrong in that. It all comes down to the signature. And there's no question about *that*, Mrs. Helmer. It really *was* your father who signed his own name here, wasn't it?

NORA: [After a short silence, throwing her head back and looking squarely at him.] No, it wasn't. *I* signed papa's name.

KROGSTAD: Wait, now—are you fully aware that this is a dangerous confession?

NORA: Why? You'll soon get your money.

KROGSTAD: Let me ask you a question—why didn't you send the paper to your father?

NORA: That was impossible. Papa was so sick. If I'd asked him for his signature, I also would have had to tell him what the money was for. But I couldn't tell him, sick as he was, that my husband's life was in danger. That was just impossible.

KROGSTAD: Then it would have been better if you'd given up the trip abroad.

NORA: I couldn't possibly. The trip was to save my husband's life. I couldn't give that up.

KROGSTAD: But didn't you ever consider that this was a fraud against me?

NORA: I couldn't let myself be bothered by that. You weren't any concern of mine. I couldn't stand you, with all those cold complications you made, even though you knew how badly off my husband was.

KROGSTAD: Mrs. Helmer, obviously you haven't the vaguest idea of what you've involved yourself in. But I can tell you this: it was nothing more and nothing worse that I once did—and it wrecked my whole reputation.

NORA: You? Do you expect me to believe that you ever acted bravely to save your wife's life?

KROGSTAD: Laws don't inquire into motives.

NORA: Then they must be very poor laws.

KROGSTAD: Poor or not—if I introduce this paper in court, you'll be judged according to law.

NORA: This I refuse to believe. A daughter hasn't a right to protect her dying father from anxiety and care? A wife hasn't a right to save her husband's life? I don't know much about laws, but I'm sure that somewhere in the books these things are allowed. And you don't know anything about it—you who practice the law? You must be an awful lawyer, Mr. Krogstad.

KROGSTAD: Could be. But business—the kind of business we two are mixed up in—don't you think I know about that? All right. Do what you want now. But I'm telling you *this:* if I get shoved down a second time, you're going to keep me company. [*He bows and goes out through the hall.*]

NORA: [*Pensive for a moment, then tossing her head.*] Oh, really! Trying to frighten me! I'm not so silly as all that. [*Begins gathering up the children's clothes, but soon stops.*] But—? No, but that's impossible! I did it out of love.

THE CHILDREN: [*In the doorway, left.*] Mama, that strange man's gone out the door.

NORA: Yes, yes, I know it. But don't tell anyone about the strange man. Do you hear? Not even Papa!

THE CHILDREN: No, Mama. But now will you play again?

NORA: No, not now.

THE CHILDREN: Oh, but Mama, you promised.

NORA: Yes, but I can't now. Go inside; I have too much to do. Go in, go in, my sweet darlings. [*She herds them gently back in the room and shuts the door after them. Settling on the sofa, she takes up a piece of embroidery and makes some stitches, but soon stops abruptly.*] No! [*Throws the work aside, rises, goes to the hall door and calls out.*] Helene! Let me have the tree in here. [*Goes to the table, left, opens the table drawer, and stops again.*] No, but that's utterly impossible!

MAID: [*With the Christmas tree.*] Where should I put it, ma'am?

NORA: There. The middle of the floor.

MAID: Should I bring anything else?

NORA: No, thanks. I have what I need.

[*The* MAID, *who has set the tree down, goes out.*]

NORA: [*Absorbed in trimming the tree.*] Candles here—and flowers here. That terrible creature! Talk, talk, talk! There's nothing to it at all. The tree's going to be lovely. I'll do anything to please you, Torvald. I'll sing for you, dance for you—

[HELMER *comes in from the hall, with a sheaf of papers under his arm.*]

NORA: Oh! You're back so soon?

HELMER: Yes. Has anyone been here?

NORA: Here? No.

HELMER: That's odd. I saw Krogstad leaving the front door.

NORA: So? Oh yes, that's true. Krogstad was here a moment.

HELMER: Nora, I can see by your face that he's been here, begging you to put in a good word for him.

NORA: Yes.

HELMER: And it was supposed to seem like your own idea? You were to hide it from me that he'd been here. He asked you that, too, didn't he?

NORA: Yes, Torvald, but—

HELMER: Nora, Nora, and you could fall for that? Talk with that sort of person and promise him anything? And then in the bargain, tell me an untruth.

NORA: An untruth—?

HELMER: Didn't you say that no one had been here? [*Wagging his finger.*] My little songbird must never do that again. A songbird needs a clean beak to warble with. No false notes. [*Putting his arm about her waist.*] That's the way it should be, isn't it? Yes, I'm sure of it. [*Releasing her.*] And so, enough of that. [*Sitting by the stove.*] Ah, how snug and cozy it is here. [*Leafing among his papers.*]

NORA: [*Busy with the tree, after a short pause.*] Torvald!

HELMER: Yes.

NORA: I'm so much looking forward to the Stenborgs' costume party, day after tomorrow.

HELMER: And I can't wait to see what you'll surprise me with.

NORA: Oh, that stupid business!

HELMER: What?

NORA: I can't find anything that's right. Everything seems so ridiculous, so inane.

HELMER: So my little Nora's come to *that* recognition?

NORA: [*Going behind his chair, her arms resting on its back.*] Are you very busy, Torvald?

HELMER: Oh—

NORA: What papers are those?

HELMER: Bank matters.

NORA: Already?

HELMER: I've gotten full authority from the retiring management to make all necessary changes in personnel and procedure. I'll need Christmas week for that. I want to have everything in order by New Year's.

NORA: So that was the reason this poor Krogstad—

HELMER: Hm.

NORA: [*Still leaning on the chair and slowly stroking the nape of his neck.*] If you weren't so very busy, I would have asked you an enormous favor, Torvald.

HELMER: Let's hear. What is it?

NORA: You know, there isn't anyone who has your good taste—and I want so much to look well at the costume party. Torvald, couldn't you take over and decide what I should be and plan my costume?

HELMER: Ah, is my stubborn little creature calling for a lifeguard?

NORA: Yes, Torvald, I can't get anywhere without your help.

HELMER: All right—I'll think it over. We'll hit on something.

NORA: Oh, how sweet of you. [*Goes to the tree again. Pause.*] Aren't the red flowers pretty—? But tell me, was it really such a crime that this Krogstad committed?

HELMER: Forgery. Do you have any idea what that means?

NORA: Couldn't he have done it out of need?

HELMER: Yes, or thoughtlessness, like so many others. I'm not so heartless that I'd condemn a man categorically for just one mistake.

NORA: No, of course not, Torvald!

HELMER: Plenty of men have redeemed themselves by openly confessing their crimes and taking their punishment.

NORA: Punishment—?

HELMER: But now Krogstad didn't go that way. He got himself out by sharp practices, and that's the real cause of his moral breakdown.

NORA: Do you really think that would—?

HELMER: Just imagine how a man with that sort of guilt in him has to lie and cheat and deceive on all sides, has to wear a mask even with the nearest and dearest he has, even with his own wife and children. And with the children, Nora—that's where it's most horrible.

NORA: Why?

HELMER: Because that kind of atmosphere of lies infects the whole life of a home. Every breath the children take in is filled with the germs of something degenerate.

NORA: [*Coming closer behind him.*] Are you sure of that?

HELMER: Oh, I've seen it often enough as a lawyer. Almost everyone who goes bad early in life has a mother who's a chronic liar.

NORA: Why just—the mother?

HELMER: It's usually the mother's influence that's dominant, but the father's works in the same way, of course. Every lawyer is quite familiar with it. And still this Krogstad's been going home year in, year out, poisoning his own children with lies and pretense; that's why I call him morally lost. [*Reaching his hands out toward her.*] So my sweet little Nora must promise me never to plead his cause. Your hand on it. Come, come, what's this? Give me your hand. There, now. All settled. I can tell you it'd be impossible for me to work alongside of him. I literally feel physically revolted when I'm anywhere near such a person.

NORA: [*Withdraws her hand and goes to the other side of the Christmas tree.*] How hot it is here! And I've got so much to do.

HELMER: [*Getting up and gathering his papers.*] Yes, and I have to think about getting some of these read through before dinner. I'll think about your costume, too. And something to hang on the tree in gilt paper, I may even see about that. [*Putting his hand on her head.*] Oh you, my darling little songbird. [*He goes into his study and closes the door after him.*]

NORA: [*Softly, after a silence.*] Oh, really! it isn't so. It's impossible. It must be impossible.

ANNE-MARIE: [*In the doorway, left.*] The children are begging so hard to come in to Mama.

NORA: No, no, no, don't let them in to me! You stay with them, Anne-Marie.

ANNE-MARIE: Of course, ma'am. [*Closes the door.*]

NORA: [*Pale with terror*]. Hurt my children—! Poison my home? [*A moment's pause; then she tosses her head.*] That's not true. Never. Never in all the world.

ACT II

Same room. Beside the piano the Christmas tree now stands stripped of ornament, burned-down candle stubs on its ragged branches. NORA's *street clothes lie on the sofa.* NORA, *alone in the room, moves restlessly about; at last she stops at the sofa and picks up her coat.*

NORA: [*Dropping the coat again.*] Someone's coming! [*Goes toward the door, listens.*] No—there's no one. Of course—nobody's coming today, Christmas Day—or tomorrow, either. But maybe—[*Opens the door and looks out.*] No, nothing in the mailbox. Quite empty. [*Coming forward.*] What nonsense! He won't do anything serious. Nothing terrible could happen. It's impossible. Why, I have three small children.

[ANNE-MARIE, *with a large carton, comes in from the room to the left.*]

ANNE-MARIE: Well, at last I found the box with the masquerade clothes.

NORA: Thanks. Put it on the table.

ANNE-MARIE: [*Does so.*] But they're all pretty much of a mess.

NORA: Ahh! I'd love to rip them in a million pieces!

ANNE-MARIE: Oh, mercy, they can be fixed right up. Just a little patience.

NORA: Yes, I'll go get Mrs. Linde to help me.

ANNE-MARIE: Out again now? In this nasty weather? Miss Nora will catch cold—get sick.

NORA: Oh, worse things could happen—How are the children?

ANNE-MARIE: The poor mites are playing with their Christmas presents, but—

NORA: Do they ask for me much?

ANNE-MARIE: They're so used to having Mama around, you know.

NORA: Yes, but Anne-Marie, I *can't* be together with them as much as I was.

ANNE-MARIE: Well, small children get used to anything.

NORA: You think so? Do you think they'd forget their mother if she was gone for good?

ANNE-MARIE: Oh, mercy—gone for good!

NORA: Wait, tell me, Anne-Marie—I've wondered so often—how could you ever have the heart to give your child over to strangers?

ANNE-MARIE: But I had to, you know, to become little Nora's nurse.

NORA: Yes, but how could you *do* it?

ANNE-MARIE: When I could get such a good place? A girl who's poor and who's gotten in trouble is glad enough for that. Because that slippery fish, he didn't do a thing for me, you know.

NORA: But your daughter's surely forgotten you.

ANNE-MARIE: Oh, she certainly has not. She's written to me, both when she was confirmed and when she was married.

NORA: [*Clasping her about the neck.*] You old Anne-Marie, you were a good mother for me when I was little.

ANNE-MARIE: Poor little Nora, with no other mother but me.

NORA: And if the babies didn't have one, then I know that you'd—What silly talk! [*Opening the carton.*] Go in to them. Now I'll have to—Tomorrow you can see how lovely I'll look.

ANNE-MARIE: Oh, there won't be anyone at the party as lovely as Miss Nora. [*She goes off into the room, left.*]

NORA: [*Begins unpacking the box, but soon throws it aside.*] Oh, if I dared to go out. If only nobody would come. If only nothing would happen here while I'm out. What craziness—nobody's coming. Just don't think. This muff—needs a brushing. Beautiful gloves, beautiful gloves. Let it go. Let it go! One, two, three, four, five, six—[*With a cry.*] Oh, there they are! [*Poises to move toward the door, but remains irresolutely standing.* MRS. LINDE *enters from the hall, where she has removed her street clothes.*]

NORA: Oh, it's you, Kristine. There's no one else out there? How good that you've come.

MRS. LINDE: I hear you were up asking for me.

NORA: Yes, I just stopped by. There's something you really can help me with. Let's get settled on the sofa. Look, there's going to be a costume party tomorrow evening at the Stenborgs' right above us, and now Tor-

vald wants me to go as a Neapolitan peasant girl and dance the tarantella[2] that I learned in Capri.

MRS. LINDE: Really, are you giving a whole performance?

NORA: Torvald says yes, I should. See, here's the dress. Torvald had it made
for me down there; but now it's all so tattered that I just don't know—

MRS. LINDE: Oh, we'll fix that up in no time. It's nothing more than the
trimmings—they're a bit loose here and there. Needle and thread? Good,
now we have what we need.

NORA: Oh, how sweet of you!

MRS. LINDE: [*Sewing.*] So you'll be in disguise tomorrow, Nora. You know
what? I'll stop by then for a moment and have a look at you all dressed
up. But listen, I've absolutely forgotten to thank you for that pleasant
evening yesterday.

NORA: [*Getting up and walking about.*] I don't think it was as pleasant as usual
yesterday. You should have come to town a bit sooner, Kristine—Yes,
Torvald really knows how to give a home elegance and charm.

MRS. LINDE: And you do, too, if you ask me. You're not your father's daughter for nothing. But tell me, is Dr. Rank always so down in the mouth
as yesterday?

NORA: No, that was quite an exception. But he goes around critically ill all
the time—tuberculosis of the spine, poor man. You know, his father was
a disgusting thing who kept mistresses and so on—and that's why the
son's been sickly from birth.

MRS. LINDE: [*Lets her sewing fall to her lap.*] But my dearest Nora, how do
you know about such things?

NORA: [*Walking more jauntily.*] Hmp! When you've had three children, then
you've had a few visits from—from women who know something of
medicine, and they tell you this and that.

MRS. LINDE: [*Resumes sewing; a short pause.*] Does Dr. Rank come here every
day?

NORA: Every blessed day. He's Torvald's best friend from childhood, and
my good friend, too. Dr. Rank almost belongs to this house.

MRS. LINDE: But tell me—is he quite sincere? I mean, doesn't he rather enjoy
flattering people?

NORA: Just the opposite. Why do you think that?

MRS. LINDE: When you introduced us yesterday, he was proclaiming that
he'd often heard my name in this house; but later I noticed that your
husband hadn't the slightest idea who I really was. So how could Dr.
Rank—?

NORA: But it's all true, Kristine. You see, Torvald loves me beyond words,
and, as he puts it, he'd like to keep me all to himself. For a long time
he'd almost be jealous if I even mentioned any of my old friends back
home. So of course I dropped that. But with Dr. Rank I talk a lot about
such things, because he likes hearing about them.

2. Lively folk dance of southern Italy, thought to cure the bite of the tarantula.

MRS. LINDE: Now listen, Nora; in many ways you're still like a child. I'm a good deal older than you, with a little more experience. I'll tell you something: you ought to put an end to all this with Dr. Rank.

NORA: What should I put an end to?

MRS. LINDE: Both parts of it, I think. Yesterday you said something about a rich admirer who'd provide you with money—

NORA: Yes, one who doesn't exist—worse luck. So?

MRS. LINDE: Is Dr. Rank well off?

NORA: Yes, he is.

MRS. LINDE: With no dependents?

NORA: No, no one. But—

MRS. LINDE: And he's over here every day?

NORA: Yes, I told you that.

MRS. LINDE: How can a man of such refinement be so grasping?

NORA: I don't follow you at all.

MRS. LINDE: Now don't try to hide it, Nora. You think I can't guess who loaned you the forty-eight hundred crowns?

NORA: Are you out of your mind? How could you think such a thing! A friend of ours, who comes here every single day. What an intolerable situation that would have been!

MRS. LINDE: Then it really wasn't him.

NORA: No, absolutely not. It never even crossed my mind for a moment— And he had nothing to lend in those days; his inheritance came later.

MRS. LINDE: Well, I think that was a stroke of luck for you, Nora dear.

NORA: No, it never would have occurred to me to ask Dr. Rank—Still, I'm quite sure that if I had asked him—

MRS. LINDE: Which you won't, of course.

NORA: No, of course not. I can't see that I'd ever need to. But I'm quite positive that if I talked to Dr. Rank—

MRS. LINDE: Behind your husband's back?

NORA: I've got to clear up this other thing; *that's* also behind his back. I've *got* to clear it all up.

MRS. LINDE: Yes, I was saying that yesterday, but—

NORA: [*Pacing up and down.*] A man handles these problems so much better than a woman—

MRS. LINDE: One's husband does, yes.

NORA: Nonsense. [*Stopping.*] When you pay everything you owe, then you get your note back, right?

MRS. LINDE: Yes, naturally.

NORA: And can rip it into a million pieces and burn it up—that filthy scrap of paper!

MRS. LINDE: [*Looking hard at her, laying her sewing aside, and rising slowly.*] Nora, you're hiding something from me.

NORA: You can see it in my face?

MRS. LINDE: Something's happened to you since yesterday morning. Nora, what is it?

NORA: [*Hurrying toward her.*] Kristine! [*Listening.*] Shh! Torvald's home.

Look, go in with the children a while. Torvald can't bear all this snipping and stitching. Let Anne-Marie help you.

MRS. LINDE: [*Gathering up some of the things.*] All right, but I'm not leaving here until we've talked this out. [*She disappears into the room, left, as* TORVALD *enters from the hall.*]

NORA: Oh, how I've been waiting for you, Torvald dear.

HELMER: Was that the dressmaker?

NORA: No, that was Kristine. She's helping me fix up my costume. You know, it's going to be quite attractive.

HELMER: Yes, wasn't that a bright idea I had?

NORA: Brilliant! But then wasn't I good as well to give in to you?

HELMER: Good—because you give in to your husband's judgment? All right, you little goose, I know you didn't mean it like that. But I won't disturb you. You'll want to have a fitting, I suppose.

NORA: And you'll be working?

HELMER: Yes. [*Indicating a bundle of papers.*] See. I've been down to the bank. [*Starts toward his study.*]

NORA: Torvald.

HELMER: [*Stops.*] Yes.

NORA: If your little squirrel begged you, with all her heart and soul, for something—?

HELMER: What's that?

NORA: Then would you do it?

HELMER: First, naturally, I'd have to know what it was.

NORA: Your squirrel would scamper about and do tricks, if you'd only be sweet and give in.

HELMER: Out with it.

NORA: Your lark would be singing high and low in every room—

HELMER: Come on, she does that anyway.

NORA: I'd be a wood nymph and dance for you in the moonlight.

HELMER: Nora—don't tell me it's that same business from this morning?

NORA: [*Coming closer.*] Yes, Torvald, I beg you, please!

HELMER: And you actually have the nerve to drag that up again?

NORA: Yes, yes, you've got to give in to me; you *have* to let Krogstad keep his job in the bank.

HELMER: My dear Nora, I've slated his job for Mrs. Linde.

NORA: That's awfully kind of you. But you could just fire another clerk instead of Krogstad.

HELMER: This is the most incredible stubbornness! Because you go and give an impulsive promise to speak up for him, I'm expected to—

NORA: That's not the reason, Torvald. It's for your own sake. That man does writing for the worst papers; you said it yourself. He could do you any amount of harm. I'm scared to death of him—

HELMER: Ah, I understand. It's the old memories haunting you.

NORA: What do you mean by that?

HELMER: Of course, you're thinking about your father.

NORA: Yes, all right. Just remember how those nasty gossips wrote in the papers about Papa and slandered him so cruelly. I think they'd have had him dismissed if the department hadn't sent you up to investigate, and if you hadn't been so kind and open-minded toward him.

HELMER: My dear Nora, there's a notable difference between your father and me. Your father's official career was hardly above reproach. But mine is; and I hope it'll stay that way as long as I hold my position.

NORA: Oh, who can ever tell what vicious minds can invent? We could be so snug and happy now in our quiet, carefree home—you and I and the children, Torvald! That's why I'm pleading with you so—

HELMER: And just by pleading for him you make it impossible for me to keep him on. It's already known at the bank that I'm firing Krogstad. What if it's rumored around now that the new bank manager was vetoed by his wife—

NORA: Yes, what then—?

HELMER: Oh yes—as long as our little bundle of stubbornness gets her way—! I should go and make myself ridiculous in front of the whole office— give people the idea I can be swayed by all kinds of outside pressure. Oh, you can bet I'd feel the effects of that soon enough! Besides—there's something that rules Krogstad right out at the bank as long as I'm the manager.

NORA: What's that?

HELMER: His moral failings I could maybe overlook if I had to—

NORA: Yes, Torvald, why not?

HELMER: And I hear he's quite efficient on the job. But he was a crony of mine back in my teens—one of those rash friendships that crop up again and again to embarrass you later in life. Well, I might as well say it straight out: we're on a first-name basis. And that tactless fool makes no effort at all to hide it in front of others. Quite the contrary—he thinks that entitles him to take a familiar air around me, and so every other second he comes booming out with his "Yes, Torvald!" and "Sure thing, Torvald!" I tell you, it's been excruciating for me. He's out to make my place in the bank unbearable.

NORA: Torvald, you can't be serious about all this.

HELMER: Oh no? Why not?

NORA: Because these are such petty considerations.

HELMER: What are you saying? Petty? You think I'm petty!

NORA: No, just the opposite, Torvald dear. That's exactly why—

HELMER: Never mind. You call my motives petty; then I might as well be just that. Petty! All right! We'll put a stop to this for good. [*Goes to the hall door and calls.*] Helene!

NORA: What do you want?

HELMER: [*Searching among his papers.*] A decision. [*The* MAID *comes in.*] Look here; take this letter; go out with it at once. Get hold of a messenger and have him deliver it. Quick now. It's already addressed. Wait, here's some money.

MAID: Yes, sir. [*She leaves with the letter.*]

HELMER: [*Straightening his papers.*] There, now, little Miss Willful.

NORA: [*Breathlessly.*] Torvald, what was that letter?

HELMER: Krogstad's notice.

NORA: Call it back, Torvald! There's still time. Oh, Torvald, call it back! Do it for my sake—for your sake, for the children's sake! Do you hear, Torvald; do it! You don't know how this can harm us.

HELMER: Too late.

NORA: Yes, too late.

HELMER: Nora dear, I can forgive you this panic, even though basically you're insulting me. Yes, you are! Or isn't it an insult to think that *I* should be afraid of a courtroom hack's revenge? But I forgive you anyway, because this shows so beautifully how much you love me. [*Takes her in his arms.*] This is the way it should be, my darling Nora. Whatever comes, you'll see: when it really counts, I have strength and courage enough as a man to take on the whole weight myself.

NORA: [*Terrified.*] What do you mean by that?

HELMER: The whole weight, I said.

NORA: [*Resolutely.*] No, never in all the world.

HELMER: Good. So we'll share it, Nora, as man and wife. That's as it should be. [*Fondling her.*] Are you happy now? There, there, there—not these frightened dove's eyes. It's nothing at all but empty fantasies—Now you should run through your tarantella and practice your tambourine. I'll go to the inner office and shut both doors, so I won't hear a thing; you can make all the noise you like. [*Turning in the doorway.*] And when Rank comes, just tell him where he can find me. [*He nods to her and goes with his papers into the study, closing the door.*]

NORA: [*Standing as though rooted, dazed with fright, in a whisper.*] He really could do it. He will do it. He'll do it in spite of everything. No, not that, never, never! Anything but that! Escape! A way out—[*The doorbell rings.*] Dr. Rank! Anything but that! *Anything,* whatever it is! [*Her hands pass over her face, smoothing it; she pulls herself together, goes over and opens the hall door. DR. RANK stands outside, hanging his fur coat up. During the following scene, it begins getting dark.*]

NORA: Hello, Dr. Rank. I recognized your ring. But you mustn't go in to Torvald yet; I believe he's working.

RANK: And you?

NORA: For you, I always have an hour to spare—you know that. [*He has entered, and she shuts the door after him.*]

RANK: Many thanks. I'll make use of these hours while I can.

NORA: What do you mean by that? While you can?

RANK: Does that disturb you?

NORA: Well, it's such an odd phrase. Is anything going to happen?

RANK: What's going to happen is what I've been expecting so long—but I honestly didn't think it would come so soon.

NORA: [*Gripping his arm.*] What is it you've found out? Dr. Rank, you have to tell me!

RANK: [*Sitting by the stove.*] It's all over with me. There's nothing to be done about it.

NORA: [*Breathing easier.*] Is it you—then—?

RANK: Who else? There's no point in lying to one's self. I'm the most miserable of all my patients, Mrs. Helmer. These past few days I've been auditing my internal accounts. Bankrupt! Within a month I'll probably be laid out and rotting in the churchyard.

NORA: Oh, what a horrible thing to say.

RANK: The thing itself is horrible. But the worst of it is all the other horror before it's over. There's only one final examination left; when I'm finished with that, I'll know about when my disintegration will begin. There's something I want to say. Helmer with his sensitivity has such a sharp distaste for anything ugly. I don't want him near my sickroom.

NORA: Oh, but Dr. Rank—

RANK: I won't have him in there. Under no condition. I'll lock my door to him—As soon as I'm completely sure of the worst, I'll send you my calling card marked with a black cross, and you'll know then the wreck has started to come apart.

NORA: No, today you're completely unreasonable. And I wanted you so much to be in a really good humor.

RANK: With death up my sleeve? And then to suffer this way for somebody else's sins. Is there any justice in that? And in every single family, in some way or another, this inevitable retribution of nature goes on—

NORA: [*Her hands pressed over her ears.*] Oh, stuff! Cheer up! Please—be gay!

RANK: Yes, I'd just as soon laugh at it all. My poor, innocent spine, serving time for my father's gay army days.

NORA: [*By the table, left.*] He was so infatuated with asparagus tips and *pâté de foie gras,* wasn't that it?

RANK: Yes—and with truffles.

NORA: Truffles, yes. And then with oysters, I suppose?

RANK: Yes, tons of oysters, naturally.

NORA: And then the port and champagne to go with it. It's so sad that all these delectable things have to strike at our bones.

RANK: Especially when they strike at the unhappy bones that never shared in the fun.

NORA: Ah, that's the saddest of all.

RANK: [*Looks searchingly at her.*] Hm.

NORA: [*After a moment.*] Why did you smile?

RANK: No, it was you who laughed.

NORA: No, it was you who smiled, Dr. Rank!

RANK: [*Getting up.*] You're even a bigger tease than I'd thought.

NORA: I'm full of wild ideas today.

RANK: That's obvious.

NORA: [*Putting both hands on his shoulders.*] Dear, dear Dr. Rank, you'll never die for Torvald and me.

RANK: Oh, that loss you'll easily get over. Those who go away are soon forgotten.

NORA: [*Looks fearfully at him.*] You believe that?

RANK: One makes new connections, and then—

NORA: Who makes new connections?

RANK: Both you and Torvald will when I'm gone. I'd say you're well under way already. What was that Mrs. Linde doing here last evening?

NORA: Oh, come—you can't be jealous of poor Kristine?

RANK: Oh yes, I am. She'll be my successor here in the house. When I'm down under, that woman will probably—

NORA: Shh! Not so loud. She's right in there.

RANK: Today as well. So you see.

NORA: Only to sew on my dress. Good gracious, how unreasonable you are. [*Sitting on the sofa.*] Be nice now, Dr. Rank. Tomorrow you'll see how beautifully I'll dance; and you can imagine then that I'm dancing only for you—yes, and of course for Torvald, too—that's understood. [*Takes various items out of the carton.*] Dr. Rank, sit over here and I'll show you something.

RANK: [*Sitting.*] What's that?

NORA: Look here. Look.

RANK: Silk stockings.

NORA: Flesh-colored. Aren't they lovely? Now it's so dark here, but tomorrow—No, no, no, just look at the feet. Oh well, you might as well look at the rest.

RANK: Hm—

NORA: Why do you look so critical? Don't you believe they'll fit?

RANK: I've never had any chance to form an opinion on that.

NORA: [*Glancing at him a moment.*] Shame on you. [*Hits him lightly on the ear with the stockings.*] That's for you. [*Puts them away again.*]

RANK: And what other splendors am I going to see now?

NORA: Not the least bit more, because you've been naughty. [*She hums a little and rummages among her things.*]

RANK: [*After a short silence.*] When I sit here together with you like this, completely easy and open, then I don't know—I simply can't imagine—whatever would have become of me if I'd never come into this house.

NORA: [*Smiling.*] Yes, I really think you feel completely at ease with us.

RANK: [*More quietly, staring straight ahead.*] And then to have to go away from it all—

NORA: Nonsense, you're not going away.

RANK: [*His voice unchanged.*]—and not even be able to leave some poor show of gratitude behind, scarcely a fleeting regret—no more than a vacant place that anyone can fill.

NORA: And if I asked you now for—? No—

RANK: For what?

NORA: For a great proof of your friendship—

RANK: Yes, yes?

NORA: No, I mean—for an exceptionally big favor—

RANK: Would you really, for once, make me so happy?

NORA: Oh, you haven't the vaguest idea what it is.

RANK: All right, then tell me.

NORA: No, but I can't, Dr. Rank—it's all out of reason. It's advice and help, too—and a favor—

RANK: So much the better. I can't fathom what you're hinting at. Just speak out. Don't you trust me?

NORA: Of course. More than anyone else. You're my best and truest friend, I'm sure. That's why I want to talk to you. All right, then, Dr. Rank: there's something you can help me prevent. You know how deeply, how inexpressibly dearly Torvald loves me; he'd never hesitate a second to give up his life for me.

RANK: [*Leaning close to her.*] Nora—do you think he's the only one—

NORA: [*With a slight start.*] Who—?

RANK: Who'd gladly give up his life for you.

NORA: [*Heavily.*] I see.

RANK: I swore to myself you should know this before I'm gone. I'll never find a better chance. Yes, Nora, now you know. And also you know now that you can trust me beyond anyone else.

NORA: [*Rising, natural and calm.*] Let me by.

RANK: [*Making room for her, but still sitting.*] Nora—

NORA: [*In the hall doorway.*] Helene, bring the lamp in. [*Goes over to the stove.*] Ah, dear Dr. Rank, that was really mean of you.

RANK: [*Getting up.*] That I've loved you just as deeply as somebody else? Was *that* mean?

NORA: No, but that you came out and told me. That was quite unnecessary—

RANK: What do you mean? Have you known—?

[*The* MAID *comes in with the lamp, sets it on the table, and goes out again.*]

RANK: Nora—Mrs. Helmer—I'm asking you: have you known about it?

NORA: Oh, how can I tell what I know or don't know? Really, I don't know what to say—Why did you have to be so clumsy, Dr. Rank! Everything was so good.

RANK: Well, in any case, you now have the knowledge that my body and soul are at your command. So won't you speak out?

NORA: [*Looking at him.*] After that?

RANK: Please, just let me know what it is.

NORA: You can't know anything now.

RANK: I have to. You mustn't punish me like this. Give me the chance to do whatever is humanly possible for you.

NORA: Now there's nothing you can do for me. Besides, actually, I don't need any help. You'll see—it's only my fantasies. That's what it is. Of course! [*Sits in the rocker, looks at him, and smiles.*] What a nice one you are, Dr. Rank. Aren't you a little bit ashamed, now that the lamp is here?

RANK: No, not exactly. But perhaps I'd better go—for good?

NORA: No, you certainly can't do that. You must come here just as you always have. You know Torvald can't do without you.

RANK: Yes, but *you?*

NORA: You know how much I enjoy it when you're here.

RANK: That's precisely what threw me off. You're a mystery to me. So many times I've felt you'd almost rather be with me than with Helmer.

NORA: Yes—you see, there are some people that one loves most and other people that one would almost prefer being with.

RANK: Yes, there's something to that.

NORA: When I was back home, of course I loved Papa most. But I always thought it was so much fun when I could sneak down to the maids' quarters, because they never tried to improve me, and it was always so amusing, the way they talked to each other.

RANK: Aha, so it's *their* place that I've filled.

NORA: [*Jumping up and going to him.*] Oh, dear, sweet Dr. Rank, that's not what I meant at all. But you can understand that with Torvald it's just the same as with Papa—

[*The MAID enters from the hall.*]

MAID: Ma'am—please! [*She whispers to NORA and hands her a calling card.*]

NORA: Ah [*Glancing at the card.*]! [*Slips it into her pocket.*]

RANK: Anything wrong?

NORA: No, no, not at all. It's only some—it's my new dress—

RANK: Really? But—there's your dress.

NORA: Oh, that. But this is another one—I ordered it—Torvald mustn't know—

RANK: Ah, now we have the big secret.

NORA: That's right. Just go in with him—he's back in the inner study. Keep him there as long as—

RANK: Don't worry. He won't get away. [*Goes into the study.*]

NORA: [*To the MAID.*]And he's standing waiting in the kitchen?

MAID: Yes, he came up by the back stairs.

NORA: But didn't you tell him somebody was here?

MAID: Yes, but that didn't do any good.

NORA: He won't leave?

MAID: No, he won't go till he's talked with you, ma'am.

NORA: Let him come in, then—but quietly. Helene, don't breathe a word about this. It's a surprise for my husband.

MAID: Yes, yes, I understand—[*Goes out.*]

NORA: This horror—it's going to happen. No, no, no, it can't happen, it mustn't.

[*She goes and bolts HELMER's door. The MAID opens the hall door for KROGSTAD and shuts it behind him. He is dressed for travel in a fur coat, boots, and a fur cap.*]

NORA: [*Going toward him.*] Talk softly. My husband's home.

KROGSTAD: Well, good for him.

NORA: What do you want?

KROGSTAD: Some information.

NORA: Hurry up, then. What is it?

KROGSTAD: You know, of course, that I got my notice.

NORA: I couldn't prevent it, Mr. Krogstad. I fought for you to the bitter end, but nothing worked.

KROGSTAD: Does your husband's love for you run so thin? He knows everything I can expose you to, and all the same he dares to—

NORA: How can you imagine he knows anything about this?

KROGSTAD: Ah, no—I can't imagine it either, now. It's not at all like my fine Torvald Helmer to have so much guts—

NORA: Mr. Krogstad, I demand respect for my husband!

KROGSTAD: Why, of course—all due respect. But since the lady's keeping it so carefully hidden, may I presume to ask if you've also a bit better informed than yesterday about what you've actually done?

NORA: More than you ever could teach me.

KROGSTAD: Yes, I *am* such an awful lawyer.

NORA: What is it you want from me?

KROGSTAD: Just a glimpse of how you are, Mrs. Helmer. I've been thinking about you all day long. A cashier, a night-court scribbler, a—well, a type like me also has a little of what they call a heart, you know.

NORA: Then show it. Think of my children.

KROGSTAD: Did you or your husband ever think of mine? But never mind. I simply wanted to tell you that you don't need to take this thing too seriously. For the present, I'm not proceeding with any action.

NORA: Oh no, really! Well—I knew that.

KROGSTAD: Everything can be settled in a friendly spirit. It doesn't have to get around town at all; it can stay just among us three.

NORA: My husband must never know anything of this.

KROGSTAD: How can you manage that? Perhaps you can pay me the balance?

NORA: No, not right now.

KROGSTAD: Or you know some way of raising the money in a day or two?

NORA: No way that I'm willing to use.

KROGSTAD: Well, it wouldn't have done you any good, anyway. If you stood in front of me with a fistful of bills, you still couldn't buy your signature back.

NORA: Then tell me what you're going to do with it.

KROGSTAD: I'll just hold onto it—keep it on file. There's no outsider who'll even get wind of it. So if you've been thinking of taking some desperate step—

NORA: I have.

KROGSTAD: Been thinking of running away from home—

NORA: I have!

KROGSTAD: Or even of something worse—

NORA: How could you guess that?

KROGSTAD: You can drop those thoughts.

NORA: How could you guess I was thinking of *that*?

KROGSTAD: Most of us think about *that* at first. I thought about it too, but I discovered I hadn't the courage—

NORA: [*Lifelessly.*] I don't either.

KROGSTAD: [*Relieved.*] That's true, you haven't the courage? You too?

NORA: I don't have it—I don't have it.

KROGSTAD: It would be terribly stupid, anyway. After that first storm at home blows out, why, then—I have here in my pocket a letter for your husband—

NORA: Telling everything?

KROGSTAD: As charitably as possible.

NORA: [*Quickly.*] He mustn't ever get that letter. Tear it up. I'll find some way to get money.

KROGSTAD: Beg pardon, Mrs. Helmer, but I think I just told you—

NORA: Oh, I don't mean the money I owe you. Let me know how much you want from my husband, and I'll manage it.

KROGSTAD: I don't want any money from your husband.

NORA: What do you want, then?

KROGSTAD: I'll tell you what. I want to recoup, Mrs. Helmer; I want to get on in the world—and there's where your husband can help me. For a year and a half I've kept myself clean of anything disreputable—all that time struggling with the worst conditions; but I was satisfied, working my way up step by step. Now I've been written right off, and I'm just not in the mood to come crawling back. I tell you, I want to move on. I want to get back in the bank—in a better position. Your husband can set up a job for me—

NORA: He'll never do that!

KROGSTAD: He'll do it. I know him. He won't dare breathe a word of protest. And once I'm in there together with him, you just wait and see! Inside of a year, I'll be the manager's right-hand man. It'll be Nils Krogstad, not Torvald Helmer, who runs the bank.

NORA: You'll never see the day!

KROGSTAD: Maybe you think you can—

NORA: I have the courage now—for *that.*

KROGSTAD: Oh, you don't scare me. A smart, spoiled lady like you—

NORA: You'll see; you'll see!

KROGSTAD: Under the ice, maybe? Down in the freezing, coal-black water? There, till you float up in the spring, ugly, unrecognizable, with your hair falling out—

NORA: You don't frighten me.

KROGSTAD: Nor do you frighten me. One doesn't do these things, Mrs. Helmer. Besides, what good would it be? I'd still have him safe in my pocket.

NORA: Afterwards? When I'm no longer—?

KROGSTAD: Are you forgetting that *I'll* be in control then over your final reputation? [NORA *stands speechless, staring at him.*] Good; now I've warned you. Don't do anything stupid. When Helmer's read my letter, I'll be waiting for his reply. And bear in mind that it's your husband himself who's forced me back to my old ways. I'll never forgive him for that. Good-bye, Mrs. Helmer. [*He goes out through the hall.*]

NORA: [*Goes to the hall door, opens it a crack, and listens.*] He's gone. Didn't leave the letter. Oh no, no, that's impossible too! [*Opening the door more and more.*] What's that? He's standing outside—not going downstairs. He's thinking it over? Maybe he'll—? [*A letter falls in the mailbox; then*

KROGSTAD's *footsteps are heard, dying away down a flight of stairs.* NORA *gives a muffled cry and runs over toward the sofa table. A short pause.*] In the mailbox. [*Slips warily over to the hall door.*] It's lying there. Torvald, Torvald—now we're lost!

MRS. LINDE: [*Entering with the costume from the room, left.*] There now, I can't see anything else to mend. Perhaps you'd like to try—

NORA: [*In a hoarse whisper.*] Kristine, come here.

MRS. LINDE: [*Tossing the dress on the sofa.*] What's wrong? You look upset.

NORA: Come here. See that letter? *There!* Look—through the glass in the mailbox.

MRS. LINDE: Yes, yes, I see it.

NORA: That letter's from Krogstad—

MRS. LINDE: Nora—it's Krogstad who loaned you the money!

NORA: Yes, and now Torvald will find out everything.

MRS. LINDE: Believe me, Nora, it's best for both of you.

NORA: There's more you don't know. I forged a name.

MRS. LINDE: But for heaven's sake—?

NORA: I only want to tell you that, Kristine, so that you can be my witness.

MRS. LINDE: Witness? Why should I—?

NORA: If I should go out of my mind—it could easily happen—

MRS. LINDE: Nora!

NORA: Or anything else occurred—so I couldn't be present here—

MRS. LINDE: Nora, Nora, you aren't yourself at all!

NORA: And someone should try to take on the whole weight, all of the guilt, you follow me—

MRS. LINDE: Yes, of course, but why do you think—?

NORA: Then you're the witness that it isn't true, Kristine. I'm very much myself; my mind right now is perfectly clear; and I'm telling you: nobody else has known about this; I alone did everything. Remember that.

MRS. LINDE: I will. But I don't understand all this.

NORA: Oh, how could you ever understand it? It's the miracle now that's going to take place.

MRS. LINDE: The miracle?

NORA: Yes, the miracle. But it's so awful, Kristine. It mustn't take place, not for anything in the world.

MRS. LINDE: I'm going right over and talk with Krogstad.

NORA: Don't go near him; he'll do you some terrible harm!

MRS. LINDE: There was a time once when he'd gladly have done anything for me.

NORA: He?

MRS. LINDE: Where does he live?

NORA: Oh, how do I know? Yes. [*Searches in her pocket.*] Here's his card. But the letter, the letter—!

HELMER: [*From the study, knocking on the door.*] Nora!

NORA: [*With a cry of fear.*] Oh! What is it? What do you want?

HELMER: Now, now, don't be so frightened. We're not coming in. You locked the door—are you trying on the dress?

NORA: Yes, I'm trying it. I'll look just beautiful, Torvald.

MRS. LINDE: [*Who has read the card.*] He's living right around the corner.

NORA: Yes, but what's the use? We're lost. The letter's in the box.

MRS. LINDE: And your husband has the key?

NORA: Yes, always.

MRS. LINDE: Krogstad can ask for his letter back unread; he can find some excuse—

NORA: But it's just this time that Torvald usually—

MRS. LINDE: Stall him. Keep him in there. I'll be back as quick as I can. [*She hurries out through the hall entrance.*]

NORA: [*Goes to HELMER's door, opens it, and peers in.*] Torvald!

HELMER: [*From the inner study.*] Well—does one dare set foot in one's own living room at last? Come on, Rank, now we'll get a look—[*In the doorway.*] But what's this?

NORA: What, Torvald dear?

HELMER: Rank had me expecting some grand masquerade.

RANK: [*In the doorway.*] That was my impression, but I must have been wrong.

NORA: No one can admire me in my splendor—not till tomorrow.

HELMER: But Nora dear, you look so exhausted. Have you practiced too hard?

NORA: No, I haven't practiced at all yet.

HELMER: You know, it's necessary—

NORA: Oh, it's absolutely necessary, Torvald. But I can't get anywhere without your help. I've forgotten the whole thing completely.

HELMER: Ah, we'll soon take care of that.

NORA: Yes, take care of me, Torvald, please! Promise me that? Oh, I'm so nervous. That big party—You must give up everything this evening for me. No business—don't even touch your pen. Yes? Dear Torvald, promise?

HELMER: It's a promise. Tonight I'm totally at your service—you little helpless thing. Hm—but first there's one thing I want to—[*Goes toward the hall door.*]

NORA: What are you looking for?

HELMER: Just to see if there's any mail.

NORA: No, no, don't do that, Torvald!

HELMER: Now what?

NORA: Torvald, please. There isn't any.

HELMER: Let me look, though. [*Starts out. NORA, at the piano, strikes the first notes of the tarantella. HELMER, at the door, stops.*] Aha!

NORA: I can't dance tomorrow if I don't practice with you.

HELMER: [*Going over to her.*] Nora dear, are you really so frightened?

NORA: Yes, so terribly frightened. Let me practice right now; there's still time before dinner. Oh, sit down and play for me, Torvald. Direct me. Teach me, the way you always have.

HELMER: Gladly, if it's what you want. [*Sits at the piano.*]

NORA: [*Snatches the tambourine up from the box, then a long, varicolored shawl, which she throws around herself, whereupon she springs forward and cries out:*] Play for me now! Now I'll dance!

[HELMER *plays and* NORA *dances.* RANK *stands behind* HELMER *at the piano and looks on.*]

HELMER: [*As he plays.*] Slower. Slow down.

NORA: Can't change it.

HELMER: Not so violent, Nora!

NORA: Has to be just like this.

HELMER: [*Stopping.*] No, no, that won't do at all.

NORA: [*Laughing and swinging her tambourine.*] Isn't that what I told you?

RANK: Let me play for her.

HELMER: [*Getting up.*] Yes, go on. I can teach her more easily then.

[RANK *sits at the piano and plays;* NORA *dances more and more wildly.* HELMER *has stationed himself by the stove and repeatedly gives her directions; she seems not to hear them; her hair loosens and falls over her shoulders; she does not notice, but goes on dancing.* MRS. LINDE *enters.*]

MRS. LINDE: [*Standing dumbfounded at the door.*] Ah—!

NORA: [*Still dancing.*] See what fun, Kristine!

HELMER: But Nora darling, you dance as if your life were at stake.

NORA: And it is.

HELMER: Rank, stop! This is pure madness. Stop it, I say!

[RANK *breaks off playing, and* NORA *halts abruptly.*]

HELMER: [*Going over to her.*] I never would have believed it. You've forgotten everything I taught you.

NORA: [*Throwing away the tambourine.*] You see for yourself.

HELMER: Well, there's certainly room for instruction here.

NORA: Yes, you see how important it is. You've got to teach me to the very last minute. Promise me that, Torvald?

HELMER: You can bet on it.

NORA: You mustn't, either today or tomorrow, think about anything else but me; you mustn't open any letters—or the mailbox—

HELMER: Ah, it's still the fear of that man—

NORA: Oh yes, yes, that too.

HELMER: Nora, it's written all over you—there's already a letter from him out there.

NORA: I don't know. I guess so. But you mustn't read such things now; there mustn't be anything ugly between us before it's all over.

RANK: [*Quietly to* HELMER.] You shouldn't deny her.

HELMER: [*Putting his arm around her.*] The child can have her way. But tomorrow night, after you've danced—

NORA: Then you'll be free.

MAID: [*In the doorway, right.*] Ma'am, dinner is served.

NORA: We'll be wanting champagne, Helene.

MAID: Very good, ma'am. [*Goes out.*]

HELMER: So—a regular banquet, hm?

NORA: Yes, a banquet—champagne till daybreak! [*Calling out.*] And some macaroons, Helene. Heaps of them—just this once.

HELMER: [*Taking her hands.*] Now, now, now—no hysterics. Be my own little lark again.

NORA: Oh, I will soon enough. But go on in—and you, Dr. Rank. Kristine, help me put up my hair.

RANK: [*Whispering, as they go.*] There's nothing wrong—really wrong, is there?

HELMER: Oh, of course not. It's nothing more than this childish anxiety I was telling you about. [*They go out, right.*]

NORA: Well?

MRS. LINDE: Left town.

NORA: I could see by your face.

MRS. LINDE: He'll be home tomorrow evening. I wrote him a note.

NORA: You shouldn't have. Don't try to stop anything now. After all, it's a wonderful joy, this waiting here for the miracle.

MRS. LINDE: What is it you're waiting for?

NORA: Oh, you can't understand that. Go in to them; I'll be along in a moment.

> [MRS. LINDE *goes into the dining room.* NORA *stands a short while as if composing herself; then she looks at her watch.*]

NORA: Five. Seven hours to midnight. Twenty-four hours to the midnight after, and then the tarantella's done. Seven and twenty-four? Thirty-one hours to live.

HELMER: [*In the doorway, right.*] What's become of the little lark?

NORA: [*Going toward him with open arms.*] Here's your lark!

ACT III

Same scene. The table, with chairs around it, has been moved to the center of the room. A lamp on the table is lit. The hall door stands open. Dance music drifts down from the floor above. MRS. LINDE *sits at the table, absently paging through a book, trying to read, but apparently unable to focus her thoughts. Once or twice she pauses, tensely listening for a sound at the outer entrance.*

MRS. LINDE: [*Glancing at her watch.*] Not yet—and there's hardly any time left. If only he's not—[*Listening again.*] Ah, there he is. [*She goes out in the hall and cautiously opens the outer door. Quiet footsteps are heard on the stairs. She whispers:*] Come in. Nobody's here.

KROGSTAD: [*In the doorway.*] I found a note from you at home. What's back of all this?

MRS. LINDE: I just *had* to talk to you.

KROGSTAD: Oh? And it just *had* to be here in this house?

MRS. LINDE: At my place it was impossible; my room hasn't a private entrance. Come in; we're all alone. The maid's asleep, and the Helmers are at the dance upstairs.

KROGSTAD: [*Entering the room.*] Well, well, the Helmers are dancing tonight? Really?

MRS. LINDE: Yes, why not?

KROGSTAD: How true—why not?

MRS. LINDE: All right, Krogstad, let's talk.

KROGSTAD: Do we two have anything more to talk about?

MRS. LINDE: We have a great deal to talk about.

KROGSTAD: I wouldn't have thought so.

MRS. LINDE: No, because you've never understood me, really.

KROGSTAD: Was there anything more to understand—except what's all too common in life? A calculating woman throws over a man the moment a better catch comes by.

MRS. LINDE: You think I'm so thoroughly calculating? You think I broke it off lightly?

KROGSTAD: Didn't you?

MRS. LINDE: Nils—is that what you really thought?

KROGSTAD: If you cared, then why did you write me the way you did?

MRS. LINDE: What else could I do? If I had to break off with you, then it was my job as well to root out everything you felt for me.

KROGSTAD: [*Wringing his hands.*] So that was it. And this—all this, simply for money!

MRS. LINDE: Don't forget I had a helpless mother and two small brothers. We couldn't wait for you, Nils; you had such a long road ahead of you then.

KROGSTAD: That may be; but you still hadn't the right to abandon me for somebody else's sake.

MRS. LINDE: Yes—I don't know. So many, many times I've asked myself if I did have that right.

KROGSTAD: [*More softly.*] When I lost you, it was as if all the solid ground dissolved from under my feet. Look at me; I'm a half-drowned man now, hanging onto a wreck.

MRS. LINDE: Help may be near.

KROGSTAD: It was near—but then you came and blocked it off.

MRS. LINDE: Without my knowing it, Nils. Today for the first time I learned that it's you I'm replacing at the bank.

KROGSTAD: All right—I believe you. But now that you know, will you step aside?

MRS. LINDE: No, because that wouldn't benefit you in the slightest.

KROGSTAD: Not "benefit" me, hm! I'd step aside anyway.

MRS. LINDE: I've learned to be realistic. Life and hard, bitter necessity have taught me that.

KROGSTAD: And life's taught me never to trust fine phrases.

MRS. LINDE: Then life's taught you a very sound thing. But you do have to trust in actions, don't you?

KROGSTAD: What does that mean?

MRS. LINDE: You said you were hanging on like a half-drowned man to a wreck.

KROGSTAD: I've good reason to say that.

MRS. LINDE: I'm also like a half-drowned woman on a wreck. No one to suffer with; no one to care for.

KROGSTAD: You made your choice

MRS. LINDE: There wasn't any choice then.

KROGSTAD: So—what of it?

MRS. LINDE: Nils, if only we two shipwrecked people could reach across to each other.

KROGSTAD: What are you saying?

MRS. LINDE: Two on one wreck are at least better off than each on his own.

KROGSTAD: Kristine!

MRS. LINDE: Why do you think I came into town?

KROGSTAD: Did you really have some thought of me?

MRS. LINDE: I have to work to go on living. All my born days, as long as I can remember, I've worked, and it's been my best and my only joy. But now I'm completely alone in the world; it frightens me to be so empty and lost. To work for yourself—there's no joy in that. Nils, give me something—someone to work for.

KROGSTAD: I don't believe all this. It's just some hysterical feminine urge to go out and make a noble sacrifice.

MRS. LINDE: Have you ever found me to be hysterical?

KROGSTAD: Can you honestly mean this? Tell me—do you know everything about my past?

MRS. LINDE: Yes.

KROGSTAD: And you know what they think I'm worth around here.

MRS. LINDE: From what you were saying before, it would seem that with me you could have been another person.

KROGSTAD: I'm positive of that.

MRS. LINDE: Couldn't it happen still?

KROGSTAD: Kristine—you're saying this in all seriousness? Yes, you are! I can see it in you. And do you really have the courage, then—?

MRS. LINDE: I need to have someone to care for; and your children need a mother. We both need each other. Nils, I have faith that you're good at heart—I'll risk everything together with you.

KROGSTAD: [*Gripping her hands.*] Kristine, thank you, thank you—Now I know I can win back a place in their eyes. Yes—but I forgot—

MRS. LINDE: [*Listening.*] Shh! The tarantella. Go now! Go on!

KROGSTAD: Why? What is it?

MRS. LINDE: Hear the dance up there? When that's over, they'll be coming down.

KROGSTAD: Oh, then I'll go. But—it's all pointless. Of course, you don't know the move I made against the Helmers.

MRS. LINDE: Yes, Nils, I know.

KROGSTAD: And all the same, you have the courage to—?

MRS. LINDE: I know how far despair can drive a man like you.

KROGSTAD: Oh, if I only could take it all back.

MRS. LINDE: You easily could—your letter's still lying in the mailbox.

KROGSTAD: Are you sure of that?

MRS. LINDE: Positive. But—

KROGSTAD: [*Looks at her searchingly.*] Is that the meaning of it, then? You'll save your friend at any price. Tell me straight out. Is that it?

MRS. LINDE: Nils—anyone who's sold herself for somebody else once isn't going to do it again.

KROGSTAD: I'll demand my letter back.

MRS. LINDE: No, no.

KROGSTAD: Yes, of course. I'll stay here till Helmer comes down; I'll tell him to give me my letter again—that it only involves my dismissal—that he shouldn't read it—

MRS. LINDE: No, Nils, don't call the letter back.

KROGSTAD: But wasn't that exactly why you wrote me to come here?

MRS. LINDE: Yes, in that first panic. But it's been a whole day and night since then, and in that time I've seen such incredible things in this house. Helmer's got to learn everything; this dreadful secret has to be aired; those two have to come to a full understanding; all these lies and evasions can't go on.

KROGSTAD: Well, then, if you want to chance it. But at least there's one thing I can do, and do right away—

MRS. LINDE: [*Listening.*] Go now, go, quick! The dance is over. We're not safe another second.

KROGSTAD: I'll wait for you downstairs.

MRS. LINDE: Yes, please do; take me home.

KROGSTAD: I can't believe it; I've never been so happy. [*He leaves by way of the outer door; the door between the room and the hall stays open.*]

MRS. LINDE: [*Straightening up a bit and getting together her street clothes.*] How different now! How different! Someone to work for, to live for—a home to build. Well, it is worth the try! Oh, if they'd only come! [*Listening.*] Ah, there they are. Bundle up. [*She picks up her hat and coat.* NORA*'s and* HELMER*'s voices can be heard outside; a key turns in the lock, and* HELMER *brings* NORA *into the hall almost by force. She is wearing the Italian costume with a large black shawl about her; he has on evening dress, with a black domino*[3] *open over it.*]

NORA: [*Struggling in the doorway.*] No, no, no, not inside! I'm going up again. I don't want to leave so soon.

HELMER: But Nora dear—

NORA: Oh, I beg you, please, Torvald. From the bottom of my heart, *please*—only an hour more!

HELMER: Not a single minute, Nora darling. You know our agreement. Come on, in we go; you'll catch cold out here. [*In spite of her resistance, he gently draws her into the room.*]

MRS. LINDE: Good evening.

NORA: Kristine!

HELMER: Why, Mrs. Linde—are you here so late?

MRS. LINDE: Yes, I'm sorry, but I did want to see Nora in costume.

NORA: Have you been sitting here, waiting for me?

MRS. LINDE: Yes. I didn't come early enough; you were all upstairs; and then I thought I really couldn't leave without seeing you.

---

3. Hood worn by members of some religious orders.

HELMER: [*Removing* NORA's *shawl.*] Yes, take a good look. She's worth looking at, I can tell you that, Mrs. Linde. Isn't she lovely?

MRS. LINDE: Yes, I should say—

HELMER: A dream of loveliness, isn't she? That's what everyone thought at
the party, too. But she's horribly stubborn—this sweet little thing.
What's to be done with her? Can you imagine, I almost had to use force
to pry her away.

NORA: Oh, Torvald, you're going to regret you didn't indulge me, even for
just a half hour more.

HELMER: There, you see. She danced her tarantella and got a tumultuous
hand—which was well earned, although the performance may have been
a bit too naturalistic—I mean it rather overstepped the proprieties of art.
But never mind—what's important is, she made a success, an overwhelming success. You think I could let her stay on after that and spoil the
effect? Oh no; I took my lovely little Capri girl—my capricious little Capri
girl, I should say—took her under my arm; one quick tour of the ballroom,
a curtsy to every side, and then—as they say in novels—the beautiful vision
disappeared. An exit should always be effective, Mrs. Linde, but that's
what I can't get Nora to grasp. Phew, it's hot in here. [*Flings the domino on a
chair and opens the door to his room.*] Why's it dark in here? Oh yes, of course.
Excuse me. [*He goes in and lights a couple of candles.*]

NORA: [*In a sharp, breathless whisper.*] So?

MRS. LINDE: [*Quietly.*] I talked with him.

NORA: And—?

MRS. LINDE: Nora—you must tell your husband everything.

NORA: [*Dully.*] I knew it.

MRS. LINDE: You've got nothing to fear from Krogstad, but you have to
speak out.

NORA: I won't tell.

MRS. LINDE: Then the letter will.

NORA: Thanks, Kristine. I know now what's to be done. Shh!

HELMER: [*Reentering.*] Well, then, Mrs. Linde—have you admired her?

MRS. LINDE: Yes, and now I'll say good night.

HELMER: Oh, come, so soon? Is this yours, this knitting?

MRS. LINDE: Yes, thanks. I nearly forgot it.

HELMER: Do you knit, then?

MRS. LINDE: Oh yes.

HELMER: You know what? You should embroider instead.

MRS. LINDE: Really? Why?

HELMER: Yes, because it's a lot prettier. See here, one holds the embroidery
so, in the left hand, and then one guides the needle with the right—so—
in an easy, sweeping curve—right?

MRS. LINDE: Yes, I guess that's—

HELMER: But, on the other hand, knitting—it can never be anything but
ugly. Look, see here, the arms tucked in, the knitting needles going up
and down—there's something Chinese about it. Ah, that was really a
glorious champagne they served.

MRS. LINDE: Yes, good night, Nora, and don't be stubborn anymore.

HELMER: Well put, Mrs. Linde!

MRS. LINDE: Good night, Mr. Helmer.

HELMER: [*Accompanying her to the door.*] Good night, good night. I hope you get home all right. I'd be very happy to—but you don't have far to go. Good night, good night. [*She leaves. He shuts the door after her and returns.*] There, now, at last we got her out the door. She's a deadly bore, that creature.

NORA: Aren't you pretty tired, Torvald?

HELMER: No, not a bit.

NORA: You're not sleepy?

HELMER: Not at all. On the contrary, I'm feeling quite exhilarated. But you? Yes, you really look tired and sleepy.

NORA: Yes, I'm very tired. Soon now I'll sleep.

HELMER: See! You see! I was right all along that we shouldn't stay longer.

NORA: Whatever you do is always right.

HELMER: [*Kissing her brow.*] Now my little lark talks sense. Say, did you notice what a time Rank was having tonight?

NORA: Oh, was he? I didn't get to speak with him.

HELMER: I scarcely did either, but it's a long time since I've seen him in such high spirits. [*Gazes at her a moment, then comes nearer her.*] Hm—it's marvelous, though, to be back home again—to be completely alone with you. Oh, you bewitchingly lovely young woman!

NORA: Torvald, don't look at me like that!

HELMER: Can't I look at my richest treasure? At all that beauty that's mine, mine alone—completely and utterly.

NORA: [*Moving around to the other side of the table.*] You mustn't talk to me that way tonight.

HELMER: [*Following her.*] The tarantella is still in your blood, I can see—and it makes you even more enticing. Listen. The guests are beginning to go. [*Dropping his voice.*] Nora—it'll soon be quiet through this whole house.

NORA: Yes, I hope so.

HELMER: You do, don't you, my love? Do you realize—when I'm out at a party like this with you—do you know why I talk to you so little, and keep such a distance away; just send you a stolen look now and then— you know why I do it? It's because I'm imagining then that you're my secret darling, my secret young bride-to-be, and that no one suspects there's anything between us.

NORA: Yes, yes; oh, yes, I know you're always thinking of me.

HELMER: And then when we leave and I place the shawl over those fine young rounded shoulders—over that wonderful curving neck—then I pretend that you're my young bride, that we're just coming from the wedding, that for the first time I'm bringing you into my house—that for the first time I'm alone with you—completely alone with you, your trembling young beauty! All this evening I've longed for nothing but you. When I saw you turn and sway in the tarantella—my blood was pounding till I couldn't stand it—that's why I brought you down here so early—

NORA: Go away, Torvald! Leave me alone. I don't want all this.

HELMER: What do you mean? Nora, you're teasing me. You will, won't you? Aren't I your husband—?

[*A knock at the outside door.*]

NORA: [*Startled.*] What's that?

HELMER: [*Going toward the half.*] Who is it?

RANK: [*Outside.*] It's me. May I come in a moment?

HELMER: [*With quiet irritation.*] Oh, what does he want now? [*Aloud.*] Hold on. [*Goes and opens the door.*] Oh, how nice that you didn't just pass us by!

RANK: I thought I heard your voice, and then I wanted so badly to have a look in. [*Lightly glancing about.*] Ah, me, these old familiar haunts. You have it snug and cozy in here, you two.

HELMER: You seemed to be having it pretty cozy upstairs, too.

RANK: Absolutely. Why shouldn't I? Why not take in everything in life? As much as you can, anyway, and as long as you can. The wine was superb—

HELMER: The champagne especially.

RANK: You noticed that too? It's amazing how much I could guzzle down.

NORA: Torvald also drank a lot of champagne this evening.

RANK: Oh?

NORA: Yes, and that always makes him so entertaining.

RANK: Well, why shouldn't one have a pleasant evening after a well-spent day?

HELMER: Well spent? I'm afraid I can't claim that.

RANK: [*Slapping him on the back.*] But I can, you see!

NORA: Dr. Rank, you must have done some scientific research today.

RANK: Quite so.

HELMER: Come now—little Nora talking about scientific research!

NORA: And can I congratulate you on the results?

RANK: Indeed you may.

NORA: Then they were good?

RANK: The best possible for both doctor and patient—certainty.

NORA: [*Quickly and searchingly.*] Certainty?

RANK: Complete certainty. So don't I owe myself a gay evening afterwards?

NORA: Yes, you're right, Dr. Rank.

HELMER: I'm with you—just so long as you don't have to suffer for it in the morning.

RANK: Well, one never gets something for nothing in life.

NORA: Dr. Rank—are you very fond of masquerade parties?

RANK: Yes, if there's a good array of odd disguises—

NORA: Tell me, what should we two go as at the next masquerade?

HELMER: You little featherhead—already thinking of the next!

RANK: We two? I'll tell you what: you must go as Charmed Life—

HELMER: Yes, but find a costume for *that*!

RANK: Your wife can appear just as she looks every day.

HELMER: That was nicely put. But don't you know what you're going to be?

RANK: Yes, Helmer, I've made up my mind.

HELMER: Well?

RANK: At the next masquerade I'm going to be invisible.

HELMER: That's a funny idea.

RANK: They say there's a hat—black, huge—have you never heard of the hat that makes you invisible? You put it on, and then no one on earth can see you.

HELMER: [*Suppressing a smile.*] Ah, of course.

RANK: But I'm quite forgetting what I came for. Helmer, give me a cigar, one of the dark Havanas.

HELMER: With the greatest pleasure. [*Holds out his case.*]

RANK: Thanks. [*Takes one and cuts off the tip.*]

NORA: [*Striking a match*] Let me give you a light.

RANK: Thank you. [*She holds the match for him; he lights the cigar.*] And now good-bye.

HELMER: Good-bye, good-bye, old friend.

NORA: Sleep well, Doctor.

RANK: Thanks for that wish.

NORA: Wish me the same.

RANK: You? All right, if you like—Sleep well. And thanks for the light. [*He nods to them both and leaves.*]

HELMER: [*His voice subdued.*] He's been drinking heavily.

NORA: [*Absently.*] Could be. [HELMER *takes his keys from his pocket and goes out in the hall.*] Torvald—what are you after?

HELMER: Got to empty the mailbox; it's nearly full. There won't be room for the morning papers.

NORA: Are you working tonight?

HELMER: You know I'm not. Why—what's this? Someone's been at the lock.

NORA: At the lock—?

HELMER: Yes, I'm positive. What do you suppose—? I can't imagine one of the maids—? Here's a broken hairpin. Nora, it's yours—

NORA: [*Quickly.*] Then it must be the children—

HELMER: You'd better break them of that. Hm, hm—well, opened it after all. [*Takes the contents out and calls into the kitchen.*] Helene! Helene, would you put out the lamp in the hall. [*He returns to the room, shutting the hall door, then displays the handful of mail.*] Look how it's piled up. [*Sorting through them.*] Now what's this?

NORA: [*At the window.*] The letter! Oh, Torvald, no!

HELMER: Two calling cards—from Rank.

NORA: From Dr. Rank?

HELMER: [*Examining them.*] "Dr. Rank, Consulting Physician." They were on top. He must have dropped them in as he left.

NORA: Is there anything on them?

HELMER: There's a black cross over the name. See? That's a gruesome notion. He could almost be announcing his own death.

NORA: That's just what he's doing.

HELMER: What! You've heard something? Something he's told you?

NORA: Yes. That when those cards came, he'd be taking his leave of us. He'll shut himself in now and die.

HELMER: Ah, my poor friend! Of course I knew he wouldn't be here much longer. But so soon—And then to hide himself away like a wounded animal.

NORA: If it has to happen, then it's best it happens in silence—don't you think so, Torvald?

HELMER: [*Pacing up and down.*] He'd grown right into our lives. I simply can't imagine him gone. He with his suffering and loneliness—like a dark cloud setting off our sunlit happiness. Well, maybe it's best this way. For him, at least. [*Standing still.*] And maybe for us too, Nora. Now we're thrown back on each other, completely. [*Embracing her.*] Oh you, my darling wife, how can I hold you close enough? You know what, Nora—time and again I've wished you were in some terrible danger, just so I could stake my life and soul and everything, for your sake.

NORA: [*Tearing herself away, her voice firm and decisive.*] Now you must read your mail, Torvald.

HELMER: No, no, not tonight. I want to stay with you, dearest.

NORA: With a dying friend on your mind?

HELMER: You're right. We've both had a shock. There's ugliness between us—these thoughts of death and corruption. We'll have to get free of them first. Until then—we'll stay apart.

NORA: [*Clinging about his neck.*] Torvald—good night! Good night!

HELMER: [*Kissing her on the cheek.*] Good night, little songbird. Sleep well, Nora. I'll be reading my mail now. [*He takes the letters into his room and shuts the door after him.*]

NORA: [*With bewildered glances, groping about, seizing* HELMER*'s domino, throwing it around her, and speaking in short, hoarse, broken whispers.*] Never see him again. Never, never. [*Putting her shawl over her head.*] Never see the children either—them, too. Never, never. Oh, the freezing black water! The depths—down—Oh, I wish it were over—He has it now; he's reading it—now. Oh no, no, not yet. Torvald, good-bye, you and the children—[*She starts for the hall; as she does,* HELMER *throws open his door and stands with an open letter in his hand.*]

HELMER: Nora!

NORA: [*Screams.*] Oh—!

HELMER: What is this? You know what's in this letter?

NORA: Yes, I know. Let me go! Let me out!

HELMER: [*Holding her back.*] Where are you going?

NORA: [*Struggling to break loose.*] You can't save me, Torvald!

HELMER: [*Slumping back.*] True! Then it's true what he writes? How horrible! No, no, it's impossible—it can't be true.

NORA: It *is* true. I've loved you more than all this world.

HELMER: Ah, none of your slippery tricks.

NORA: [*Taking one step toward him.*] Torvald—!

HELMER: What *is* this you've blundered into!

NORA: Just let me loose. You're not going to suffer for my sake. You're not going to take on my guilt.

HELMER: No more playacting. [*Locks the hall door.*] You stay right here and give me a reckoning. You understand what you've done? Answer! You understand?

NORA: [*Looking squarely at him, her face hardening.*] Yes. I'm beginning to understand everything now.

HELMER: [*Striding about.*] Oh, what an awful awakening! In all these eight years—she who was my pride and joy—a hypocrite, a liar—worse, worse— a criminal! How infinitely disgusting it all is! The shame! [NORA *says nothing and goes on looking straight at him. He stops in front of her.*] I should have suspected something of the kind. I should have known. All your father's flimsy values—Be still! All your father's flimsy values have come out in you. No religion, no morals, no sense of duty—Oh, how I'm punished for letting him off! I did it for your sake, and you repay me like this.

NORA: Yes, like this.

HELMER: Now you've wrecked all my happiness—ruined my whole future. Oh, it's awful to think of. I'm in a cheap little grafter's hands; he can do anything he wants with me, ask for anything, play with me like a puppet—and I can't breathe a word. I'll be swept down miserably into the depths on account of a featherbrained woman.

NORA: When I'm gone from this world, you'll be free.

HELMER: Oh, quit posing. Your father had a mess of those speeches too. What good would that ever do me if you were gone from this world, as you say? Not the slightest. He can still make the whole thing known; and if he does, I could be falsely suspected as your accomplice. They might even think that I was behind it—that I put you up to it. And all that I can thank you for—you that I've coddled the whole of our marriage. Can you see now what you've done to me?

NORA: [*Icily calm.*] Yes.

HELMER: It's so incredible, I just can't grasp it. But we'll have to patch up whatever we can. Take off the shawl. I said, take it off! I've got to appease him somehow or other. The thing has to be hushed up at any cost. And as for you and me, it's got to seem like everything between us is just as it was—to the outside world, that is. You'll go right on living in this house, of course. But you can't be allowed to bring up the children; I don't dare trust you with them—Oh, to have to say this to someone I've loved so much, and that I still—! Well, that's done with. From now on happiness doesn't matter; all that matters is saving the bits and pieces, the appearance—[*The doorbell rings.* HELMER *starts.*] What's that? And so late. Maybe the worst—? You think he'd—? Hide, Nora! Say you're sick.

[NORA *remains standing motionless.* HELMER *goes and opens the door.*]

MAID: [*Half dressed, in the hall.*] A letter for Mrs. Helmer.

HELMER: I'll take it. [*Snatches the letter and shuts the door.*] Yes, it's from him. You don't get it; I'm reading it myself.

NORA: Then read it.

HELMER: [*By the lamp.*] I hardly dare. We may be ruined, you and I. But—
I've got to know. [*Rips open the letter, skims through a few lines, glances at an enclosure, then cries out joyfully.*] Nora! [NORA *looks inquiringly at him.*] Nora! Wait—better check it again—Yes, yes, it's true. I'm saved. Nora, I'm saved!

NORA: And I?

HELMER: You too, of course. We're both saved, both of us. Look. He's sent back your note. He says he's sorry and ashamed—that a happy development in his life—oh, who cares what he says! Nora, we're saved! No one can hurt you. Oh, Nora, Nora—but first, this ugliness all has to go. Let me see—[*Takes a look at the note.*] No, I don't want to see it; I want the whole thing to fade like a dream. [*Tears the note and both letters to pieces, throws them into the stove and watches them burn.*] There—now there's nothing left—He wrote that since Christmas Eve you—Oh, they must have been three terrible days for you, Nora.

NORA: I fought a hard fight.

HELMER: And suffered pain and saw no escape but—No, we're not going to dwell on anything unpleasant. We'll just be grateful and keep on repeating: it's over now, it's over! You hear me, Nora? You don't seem to realize—it's over. What's it mean—that frozen look? Oh, poor little Nora, I understand. You can't believe I've forgiven you. But I have, Nora; I swear I have. I know that what you did, you did out of love for me.

NORA: That's true.

HELMER: You loved me the way a wife ought to love her husband. It's simply the means that you couldn't judge. But you think I love you any the less for not knowing how to handle your affairs? No, no—just lean on me; I'll guide you and teach you. I wouldn't be a man if this feminine helplessness didn't make you twice as attractive to me. You mustn't mind those sharp words I said—that was all in the first confusion of thinking my world had collapsed. I've forgiven you, Nora; I swear I've forgiven you.

NORA: My thanks for your forgiveness. [*She goes out through the door, right.*]

HELMER: No, wait—[*Peers in.*] What are you doing in there?

NORA: [*Inside.*] Getting out of my costume.

HELMER: [*By the open door.*] Yes, do that. Try to calm yourself and collect your thoughts again, my frightened little songbird. You can rest easy now; I've got wide wings to shelter you with. [*Walking about close by the door.*] How snug and nice our home is, Nora. You're safe here; I'll keep you like a hunted dove I've rescued out of a hawk's claws. I'll bring peace to your poor, shuddering heart. Gradually it'll happen, Nora; you'll see. Tomorrow all this will look different to you; then everything will be as it was. I won't have to go on repeating I forgive you; you'll feel it for yourself. How can you imagine I'd ever conceivably want to disown you— or even blame you in any way? Ah, you don't know a man's heart, Nora. For a man there's something indescribably sweet and satisfying in knowing he's forgiven his wife—and forgiven her out of a full and open heart. It's as if she belongs to him in two ways now: in a sense he's given her fresh into the world again, and she's become his wife and his child as well. From now on that's what you'll be to me—you little, bewildered, helpless thing. Don't be afraid of anything, Nora; just open your heart to me, and I'll be conscience and will to you both—[NORA *enters in her regular clothes.*] What's this? Not in bed? You've changed your dress?

NORA: Yes, Torvald, I've changed my dress.

HELMER: But why now, so late?

NORA: Tonight I'm not sleeping.

HELMER: But Nora dear—

NORA: [*Looking at her watch.*] It's still not so very late. Sit down, Torvald; we have a lot to talk over. [*She sits at one side of the table.*]

HELMER: Nora—what is this? That hard expression—

NORA: Sit down. This'll take some time. I have a lot to say.

HELMER: [*Sitting at the table directly opposite her.*] You worry me, Nora. And I don't understand you.

NORA: No, that's exactly it. You don't understand me. And I've never understood you either—until tonight. No, don't interrupt. You can just listen to what I say. We're closing out accounts, Torvald.

HELMER: How do you mean that?

NORA: [*After a short pause.*] Doesn't anything strike you about our sitting here like this?

HELMER: What's that?

NORA: We've been married now eight years. Doesn't it occur to you that this is the first time we two, you and I, man and wife, have ever talked seriously together?

HELMER: What do you mean—seriously?

NORA: In eight whole years—longer even—right from our first acquaintance, we've never exchanged a serious word on any serious thing.

HELMER: You mean I should constantly go and involve you in problems you couldn't possibly help me with?

NORA: I'm not talking of problems. I'm saying that we've never sat down seriously together and tried to get to the bottom of anything.

HELMER: But dearest, what good would that ever do you?

NORA: That's the point right there: you've never understood me. I've been wronged greatly, Torvald—first by Papa, and then by you.

HELMER: What! By us—the two people who've loved you more than anyone else?

NORA: [*Shaking her head.*] You never loved me. You've thought it fun to be in love with me, that's all.

HELMER: Nora, what a thing to say!

NORA: Yes, it's true now, Torvald. When I lived at home with Papa, he told me all his opinions, so I had the same ones too; or if they were different I hid them, since he wouldn't have cared for that. He used to call me his doll-child, and he played with me the way I played with my dolls. Then I came into your house—

HELMER: How can you speak of our marriage like that?

NORA: [*Unperturbed.*] I mean, then I went from Papa's hands into yours. You arranged everything to your own taste, and so I got the same taste as you—or I pretended to; I can't remember. I guess a little of both, first one, then the other. Now when I look back, it seems as if I'd lived here like a beggar—just from hand to mouth. I've lived by doing tricks for you, Torvald. But that's the way you wanted it. It's a great sin what you and Papa did to me. You're to blame that nothing's become of me.

HELMER: Nora, how unfair and ungrateful you are! Haven't you been happy here?

NORA: No, never. I thought so—but I never have.

HELMER: Not—not happy!

NORA: No, only lighthearted. And you've always been so kind to me. But our home's been nothing but a playpen. I've been your doll-wife here, just as at home I was Papa's doll-child. And in turn the children have been my dolls. I thought it was fun when you played with me, just as they thought it fun when I played with them. That's been our marriage, Torvald.

HELMER: There's some truth in what you're saying—under all the raving exaggeration. But it'll all be different after this. Playtime's over; now for the schooling.

NORA: Whose schooling—mine or the children's?

HELMER: Both yours and the children's, dearest.

NORA: Oh, Torvald, you're not the man to teach me to be a good wife to you.

HELMER: And you can say that?

NORA: And I—how am I equipped to bring up children?

HELMER: Nora!

NORA: Didn't you say a moment ago that that was no job to trust me with?

HELMER: In a flare of temper! Why fasten on that?

NORA: Yes, but you were so very right. I'm not up to the job. There's another job I have to do first. I have to try to educate myself. You can't help me with that. I've got to do it alone. And that's why I'm leaving you now.

HELMER: [*Jumping up.*] What's that?

NORA: I have to stand completely alone, if I'm ever going to discover myself and the world out there. So I can't go on living with you.

HELMER: Nora, Nora!

NORA: I want to leave right away. Kristine should put me up for the night—

HELMER: You're insane! You've no right! I forbid you!

NORA: From here on, there's no use forbidding me anything. I'll take with me whatever is mine. I don't want a thing from you, either now or later.

HELMER: What kind of madness is this!

NORA: Tomorrow I'm going home—I mean, home where I came from. It'll be easier up there to find something to do.

HELMER: Oh, you blind, incompetent child!

NORA: I must learn to be competent, Torvald.

HELMER: Abandon your home, your husband, your children! And you're not even thinking what people will say.

NORA: I can't be concerned about that. I only know how essential this is.

HELMER: Oh, it's outrageous. So you'll run out like this on your most sacred vows.

NORA: What do you think are my most sacred vows?

HELMER: And I have to tell you that! Aren't they your duties to your husband and children?

NORA: I have other duties equally sacred.

HELMER: That isn't true. What duties are they?

NORA: Duties to myself.

HELMER: Before all else, you're a wife and a mother.

NORA: I don't believe in that anymore. I believe that, before all else, I'm a human being, no less than you—or anyway, I ought to try to become one. I know the majority thinks you're right, Torvald, and plenty of books agree with you, too. But I can't go on believing what the majority says, or what's written in books. I have to think over these things myself and try to understand them.

HELMER: Why can't you understand your place in your own home? On a point like that, isn't there one everlasting guide you can turn to? Where's your religion?

NORA: Oh, Torvald, I'm really not sure what religion is.

HELMER: What—?

NORA: I only know what the minister said when I was confirmed. He told me religion was this thing and that. When I get clear and away by myself, I'll go into that problem too. I'll see if what the minister said was right, or, in any case, if it's right for me.

HELMER: A young woman your age shouldn't talk like that. If religion can't move you, I can try to rouse your conscience. You do have some moral feeling? Or, tell me—has that gone too?

NORA: It's not easy to answer that, Torvald. I simply don't know. I'm all confused about these things. I just know I see them so differently from you. I find out, for one thing, that the law's not at all what I'd thought—but I can't get it through my head that the law is fair. A woman hasn't a right to protect her dying father or save her husband's life! I can't believe that.

HELMER: You talk like a child. You don't know anything of the world you live in.

NORA: No, I don't. But now I'll begin to learn for myself. I'll try to discover who's right, the world or I.

HELMER: Nora, you're sick; you've got a fever. I almost think you're out of your head.

NORA: I've never felt more clearheaded and sure in my life.

HELMER: And—clearheaded and sure—you're leaving your husband and children?

NORA: Yes.

HELMER: Then there's only one possible reason.

NORA: What?

HELMER: You no longer love me.

NORA: No. That's exactly it.

HELMER: Nora! You can't be serious!

NORA: Oh, this is so hard, Torvald—you've been so kind to me always. But I can't help it. I don't love you anymore.

HELMER: [*Struggling for composure.*] Are you also clearheaded and sure about that?

NORA: Yes, completely. That's why I can't go on staying here.

HELMER: Can you tell me what I did to lose your love?

NORA: Yes, I can tell you. It was this evening when the miraculous thing didn't come—then I knew you weren't the man I'd imagined.

HELMER: Be more explicit; I don't follow you.

NORA: I've waited now so patiently eight long years—for, my Lord, I know miracles don't come every day. Then this crisis broke over me, and such a certainty filled me: *now* the miraculous event would occur. While Krogstad's letter was lying out there, I never for an instant dreamed that you could give in to his terms. I was so utterly sure you'd say to him: go on, tell your tale to the whole wide world. And when he'd done that—

HELMER: Yes, what then? When I'd delivered my own wife into shame and disgrace—!

NORA: When he'd done that, I was so utterly sure that you'd step forward, take the blame on yourself and say: I am the guilty one.

HELMER: Nora—!

NORA: You're thinking I'd never accept such a sacrifice from you? No, of course not. But what good would my protests be against you? That was the miracle I was waiting for, in terror and hope. And to stave that off, I would have taken my life.

HELMER: I'd gladly work for you day and night, Nora—and take on pain and deprivation. But there's no one who gives up honor for love.

NORA: Millions of women have done just that.

HELMER: Oh, you think and talk like a silly child.

NORA: Perhaps. But you neither think nor talk like the man I could join myself to. When your big fright was over—and it wasn't from any threat against me, only for what might damage you—when all the danger was past, for you it was just as if nothing had happened. I was exactly the same, your little lark, your doll, that you'd have to handle with double care now that I'd turned out so brittle and frail. [*Gets up.*] Torvald—in that instant it dawned on me that for eight years I've been living here with a stranger, and that I'd even conceived three children—oh, I can't stand the thought of it! I could tear myself to bits.

HELMER: [*Heavily.*] I see. There's a gulf that's opened between us—that's clear. Oh, but Nora, can't we bridge it somehow?

NORA: The way I am now, I'm no wife for you.

HELMER: I have the strength to make myself over.

NORA: Maybe—if your doll gets taken away.

HELMER: But to part! To part from you! No, Nora, no—I can't imagine it.

NORA: [*Going out, right.*] All the more reason why it has to be. [*She reenters with her coat and a small overnight bag, which she puts on a chair by the table.*]

HELMER: Nora, Nora, not now! Wait till tomorrow.

NORA: I can't spend the night in a strange man's room.

HELMER: But couldn't we live here like brother and sister—

NORA: You know very well how long that would last. [*Throws her shawl about her.*] Good-bye, Torvald. I won't look in on the children. I know they're in better hands than mine. The way I am now, I'm no use to them.

HELMER: But someday, Nora—someday—?

NORA: How can I tell? I haven't the least idea what'll become of me.

HELMER: But you're my wife, now and wherever you go.

NORA: Listen, Torvald—I've heard that when a wife deserts her husband's house just as I'm doing, then the law frees him from all responsibility. In any case, I'm freeing you from being responsible. Don't feel yourself bound, any more than I will. There has to be absolute freedom for us both. Here, take your ring back. Give me mine.

HELMER: That too?

NORA: That too.

HELMER: There it is.

NORA: Good. Well, now it's all over. I'm putting the keys here. The maids know all about keeping up the house—better than I do. Tomorrow, after I've left town, Kristine will stop by to pack up everything that's mine from home. I'd like those things shipped up to me.

HELMER: Over! All over! Nora, won't you ever think about me?

NORA: I'm sure I'll think of you often, and about the children and the house here.

HELMER: May I write you?

NORA: No—never. You're not to do that.

HELMER: Oh, but let me send you—

NORA: Nothing. Nothing.

HELMER: Or help you if you need it.

NORA: No. I accept nothing from strangers.

HELMER: Nora—can I never be more than a stranger to you?

NORA: [*Picking up the overnight bag.*] Ah, Torvald—it would take the greatest miracle of all—

HELMER: Tell me the greatest miracle!

NORA: You and I both would have to transform ourselves to the point that— Oh, Torvald, I've stopped believing in miracles.

HELMER: But I'll believe. Tell me! Transform ourselves to the point that—?

NORA: That our living together could be a true marriage. [*She goes out down the hall.*]

HELMER: [*Sinks down on a chair by the door, face buried in his hands.*] Nora! Nora! [*Looking about and rising.*] Empty. She's gone. [*A sudden hope leaps in him.*] The greatest miracle—?

[*From below, the sound of a door slamming shut.*]

1879

LORRAINE HANSBERRY

[WEB]   *A Raisin in the Sun*

> *What happens to a dream deferred?*
>
>> *Does it dry up*
>> *Like a raisin in the sun?*
>> *Or fester like a sore—*
>> *And then run?*
>> *Does it stink like rotten meat?*
>> *Or crust and sugar over—*
>> *Like a syrupy sweet?*
>>
>> *Maybe it just sags*
>> *Like a heavy load.*
>
> Or does it explode?
> —LANGSTON HUGHES[1]

CAST OF CHARACTERS

RUTH YOUNGER	JOSEPH ASAGAI
TRAVIS YOUNGER	GEORGE MURCHISON
WALTER LEE YOUNGER (BROTHER)	KARL LINDNER
BENEATHA YOUNGER	BOBO
LENA YOUNGER (MAMA)	MOVING MEN

The action of the play is set in Chicago's Southside, sometime between World War II and the present.

ACT I
Scene One

The Younger living room would be a comfortable and well-ordered room if it were not for a number of indestructible contradictions to this state of being. Its furnishings are typical and undistinguished and their primary feature now is that they have clearly had to accommodate the living of too many people for too many years—and they are tired. Still, we can see that at some time, a time probably no longer remembered by the family (except perhaps for MAMA), the furnishings of this room were actually selected with care and love and even hope—and brought to this apartment and arranged with taste and pride.

That was a long time ago. Now the once loved pattern of the couch upholstery has to fight to show itself from under acres of crocheted doilies and couch covers which have themselves finally come to be more important than the upholstery. And here a table or a chair has been moved to disguise the worn places in the carpet; but the carpet has fought back by showing its weariness, with depressing uniformity, elsewhere on its surface.

1. Hughes's poem, published in 1951, is entitled "Harlem (A Dream Deferred)."

Weariness has, in fact, won in this room. Everything has been polished, washed, sat on, used, scrubbed too often. All pretenses but living itself have long since vanished from the very atmosphere of this room.

Moreover, a section of this room, for it is not really a room unto itself, though the landlord's lease would make it seem so, slopes backward to provide a small kitchen area, where the family prepares the meals that are eaten in the living room proper, which must also serve as dining room. The single window that has been provided for these "two" rooms is located in this kitchen area. The sole natural light the family may enjoy in the course of a day is only that which fights its way through this little window.

At left, a door leads to a bedroom which is shared by MAMA *and her daughter,* BENEATHA. *At right, opposite, is a second room (which in the beginning of the life of this apartment was probably a breakfast room) which serves as a bedroom for* WALTER *and his wife,* RUTH.

Time: Sometime between World War II and the present.

Place: Chicago's Southside.

At Rise: It is morning dark in the living room. TRAVIS *is asleep on the make-down bed at center. An alarm clock sounds from within the bedroom at right, and presently* RUTH *enters from that room and closes the door behind her. She crosses sleepily toward the window. As she passes her sleeping son she reaches down and shakes him a little. At the window she raises the shade and a dusky Southside morning light comes in feebly. She fills a pot with water and puts it on to boil. She calls to the boy, between yawns, in a slightly muffled voice.*

RUTH *is about thirty. We can see that she was a pretty girl, even exceptionally so, but now it is apparent that life has been little that she expected, and disappointment has already begun to hang in her face. In a few years, before thirty-five even, she will be known among her people as a "settled woman."*

She crosses to her son and gives him a good, final, rousing shake.

RUTH: Come on now, boy, it's seven thirty! [*Her son sits up at last, in a stupor of sleepiness.*] I say hurry up, Travis! You ain't the only person in the world got to use a bathroom! [*The child, a sturdy, handsome little boy of ten or eleven, drags himself out of the bed and almost blindly takes his towels and "today's clothes" from drawers and a closet and goes out to the bathroom, which is in an outside hall and which is shared by another family or families on the same floor.* RUTH *crosses to the bedroom door at right and opens it and calls in to her husband.*] Walter Lee! . . . It's after seven thirty! Lemme see you do some waking up in there now! [*She waits.*] You better get up from there, man! It's after seven thirty I tell you. [*She waits again.*] All right, you just go ahead and lay there and next thing you know Travis be finished and Mr. Johnson'll be in there and you'll be fussing and cussing round here like a mad man! And be late too! [*She waits, at the end of patience.*] Walter Lee—it's time for you to get up!

[*She waits another second and then starts to go into the bedroom, but is apparently satisfied that her husband has begun to get up. She stops, pulls the door to, and returns to the kitchen area. She wipes her face with a moist cloth and runs her fingers through her sleep-disheveled hair in a vain effort and ties an apron around her housecoat. The bedroom door at right opens and her husband stands in the doorway in his pajamas, which are rumpled and mismated. He is a lean, intense young man in his middle thirties, inclined to quick nervous movements and erratic speech habits—and always in his voice there is a quality of indictment.*]

WALTER: Is he out yet?

RUTH: What you mean *out*? He ain't hardly got in there good yet.

WALTER: [*Wandering in, still more oriented to sleep than to a new day.*] Well, what was you doing all that yelling for if I can't even get in there yet? [*Stopping and thinking.*] Check coming today?

RUTH: They *said* Saturday and this is just Friday and I hopes to God you ain't going to get up here first thing this morning and start talking to me 'bout no money—'cause I 'bout don't want to hear it.

WALTER: Something the matter with you this morning?

RUTH: No—I'm just sleepy as the devil. What kind of eggs you want?

WALTER: Not scrambled. [RUTH *starts to scramble eggs.*] Paper come? [RUTH *points impatiently to the rolled up* Tribune *on the table, and he gets it and spreads it out and vaguely reads the front page.*] Set off another bomb yesterday.

RUTH: [*Maximum indifference.*] Did they?

WALTER: [*Looking up.*] What's the matter with you?

RUTH: Ain't nothing the matter with me. And don't keep asking me that this morning.

WALTER: Ain't nobody bothering you. [*Reading the news of the day absently again.*] Say Colonel McCormick[2] is sick.

RUTH: [*Affecting tea-party interest.*] Is he now? Poor thing.

WALTER: [*Sighing and looking at his watch.*] Oh, me. [*He waits.*] Now what is that boy doing in that bathroom all this time? He just going to have to start getting up earlier. I can't be late to work on account of him fooling around in there.

RUTH: [*Turning on him.*] Oh, no he ain't going to be getting up no earlier no such thing! It ain't his fault that he can't get to bed no earlier nights 'cause he got a bunch of crazy good-for-nothing clowns sitting up running their mouths in what is supposed to be his bedroom after ten o'clock at night . . .

WALTER: That's what you mad about, ain't it? The things I want to talk about with my friends just couldn't be important in your mind, could they?

[*He rises and finds a cigarette in her handbag on the table and crosses to the little window and looks out, smoking and deeply enjoying this first one.*]

RUTH: [*Almost matter of factly, a complaint too automatic to deserve emphasis.*] Why you always got to smoke before you eat in the morning?

WALTER: [*At the window.*] Just look at 'em down there . . . Running and racing

---

2. Robert Rutherford McCormick (1880–1955), owner-publisher of the *Chicago Tribune*.

to work . . . [*He turns and faces his wife and watches her a moment at the stove, and then, suddenly.*] You look young this morning, baby.

RUTH: [*Indifferently.*] Yeah?

WALTER: Just for a second—stirring them eggs. It's gone now—just for a second it was—you looked real young again. [*Then, drily.*] It's gone now— you look like yourself again.

RUTH: Man, if you don't shut up and leave me alone.

WALTER: [*Looking out to the street again.*] First thing a man ought to learn in life is not to make love to no colored woman first thing in the morning. You all some evil people at eight o'clock in the morning.

[TRAVIS *appears in the hall doorway, almost fully dressed and quite wide awake now, his towels and pajamas across his shoulders. He opens the door and signals for his father to make the bathroom in a hurry.*]

TRAVIS: [*Watching the bathroom.*] Daddy, come on!

[WALTER *gets his bathroom utensils and flies out to the bathroom.*]

RUTH: Sit down and have your breakfast, Travis.

TRAVIS: Mama, this is Friday. [*Gleefully.*] Check coming tomorrow, huh?

RUTH: You get your mind off money and eat your breakfast.

TRAVIS: [*Eating.*] This is the morning we supposed to bring the fifty cents to school.

RUTH: Well, I ain't got no fifty cents this morning.

TRAVIS: Teacher say we have to.

RUTH: I don't care what teacher say. I ain't got it. Eat your breakfast, Travis.

TRAVIS: I *am* eating.

RUTH: Hush up now and just eat!

[*The boy gives her an exasperated look for her lack of understanding, and eats grudgingly.*]

TRAVIS: You think Grandmama would have it?

RUTH: No! And I want you to stop asking your grandmother for money, you hear me?

TRAVIS: [*Outraged.*] Gaaaleee! I don't ask her, she just gimme it sometimes!

RUTH: Travis Willard Younger—I got too much on me this morning to be—

TRAVIS: Maybe Daddy—

RUTH: *Travis!*

[*The boy hushes abruptly. They are both quiet and tense for several seconds.*]

TRAVIS: [*Presently.*] Could I maybe go carry some groceries in front of the supermarket for a little while after school then?

RUTH: Just hush, I said. [TRAVIS *jabs his spoon into his cereal bowl viciously, and rests his head in anger upon his fists.*] If you through eating, you can get over there and make up your bed.

[*The boy obeys stiffly and crosses the room, almost mechanically, to the bed and more or less carefully folds the covering. He carries the bedding into his mother's room and returns with his books and cap.*]

TRAVIS: [*Sulking and standing apart from her unnaturally.*] I'm gone.

RUTH: [*Looking up from the stove to inspect him automatically.*] Come here. [*He crosses to her and she studies his head.*] If you don't take this comb and fix this here head, you better! [TRAVIS *puts down his books with a great sigh of oppression, and crosses to the mirror. His mother mutters under her breath about his "slubbornness."*] 'Bout to march out of here with that head looking just like chickens slept in it! I just don't know where you get your slubborn ways . . . And get your jacket, too. Looks chilly out this morning.

TRAVIS: [*With conspicuously brushed hair and jacket.*] I'm gone.

RUTH: Get carfare and milk money—[*Waving one finger.*]—and not a single penny for no caps, you hear me?

TRAVIS: [*With sullen politeness.*] Yes'm.

> [*He turns in outrage to leave. His mother watches after him as in his frustration he approaches the door almost comically. When she speaks to him, her voice has become a very gentle tease.*]

RUTH: [*Mocking; as she thinks he would say it.*] Oh, Mama makes me so mad sometimes, I don't know what to do! [*She waits and continues to his back as he stands stock-still in front of the door.*] I wouldn't kiss that woman good-bye for nothing in this world this morning! [*The boy finally turns around and rolls his eyes at her, knowing the mood has changed and he is vindicated; he does not, however, move toward her yet.*] Not for nothing in this world! [*She finally laughs aloud at him and holds out her arms to him and we see that it is a way between them, very old and practiced. He crosses to her and allows her to embrace him warmly but keeps his face fixed with masculine rigidity. She holds him back from her presently and looks at him and runs her fingers over the features of his face. With utter gentleness—*] Now—whose little old angry man are you?

TRAVIS: [*The masculinity and gruffness start to fade at last.*] Aw gaalee—Mama . . .

RUTH: [*Mimicking.*] Aw—gaaaaalleeeee, Mama! [*She pushes him, with rough playfulness and finality, toward the door.*] Get on out of here or you going to be late.

TRAVIS: [*In the face of love, new aggressiveness.*] Mama, could I *please* go carry groceries?

RUTH: Honey, it's starting to get so cold evenings.

WALTER: [*Coming in from the bathroom and drawing a make-believe gun from a make-believe holster and shooting at his son.*] What is it he wants to do?

RUTH: Go carry groceries after school at the supermarket.

WALTER: Well, let him go . . .

TRAVIS: [*Quickly, to the ally.*] I *have* to—she won't gimme the fifty cents . . .

WALTER: [*To his wife only.*] Why not?

RUTH: [*Simply, and with flavor.*] 'Cause we don't have it.

WALTER: [*To* RUTH *only.*] What you tell the boy things like that for? [*Reaching down into his pants with a rather important gesture.*] Here, son—

> [*He hands the boy the coin, but his eyes are directed to his wife's.* TRAVIS *takes the money happily.*]

TRAVIS: Thanks, Daddy.

[*He starts out.* RUTH *watches both of them with murder in her eyes.* WALTER *stands and stares back at her with defiance, and suddenly reaches into his pocket again on an afterthought.*]

WALTER: [*Without even looking at his son, still staring hard at his wife.*] In fact, here's another fifty cents... Buy yourself some fruit today—or take a taxicab to school or something!

TRAVIS: Whoopee—

[*He leaps up and clasps his father around the middle with his legs, and they face each other in mutual appreciation; slowly* WALTER LEE *peeks around the boy to catch the violent rays from his wife's eyes and draws his head back as if shot.*]

WALTER: You better get down now—and get to school, man.

TRAVIS: [*At the door.*] O.K. Good-bye.

[*He exits.*]

WALTER: [*After him, pointing with pride.*] That's my boy. [*She looks at him in disgust and turns back to her work.*] You know what I was thinking 'bout in the bathroom this morning?

RUTH: No.

WALTER: How come you always try to be so pleasant!

RUTH: What is there to be pleasant 'bout!

WALTER: You want to know what I was thinking 'bout in the bathroom or not!

RUTH: I know what you thinking 'bout.

WALTER: [*Ignoring her.*] 'Bout what me and Willy Harris was talking about last night.

RUTH: [*Immediately—a refrain.*] Willy Harris is a good-for-nothing loud mouth.

WALTER: Anybody who talks to me has got to be a good-for-nothing loud mouth, ain't he? And what you know about who is just a good-for-nothing loud mouth? Charlie Atkins was just a "good-for-nothing loud mouth" too, wasn't he! When he wanted me to go in the dry-cleaning business with him. And now—he's grossing a hundred thousand a year. A hundred thousand dollars a year! You still call *him* a loud mouth!

RUTH: [*Bitterly.*] Oh, Walter Lee ...

[*She folds her head on her arms over the table.*]

WALTER: [*Rising and coming to her and standing over her.*] You tired, ain't you? Tired of everything. Me, the boy, the way we live—this beat-up hole—everything. Ain't you? [*She doesn't look up, doesn't answer.*] So tired—moaning and groaning all the time, but you wouldn't do nothing to help, would you? You couldn't be on my side that long for nothing, could you?

RUTH: Walter, please leave me alone.

WALTER: A man needs for a woman to back him up . . .

RUTH: Walter—

WALTER: Mama would listen to you. You know she listen to you more than she do me and Bennie. She think more of you. All you have to do is just sit down with her when you drinking your coffee one morning and talking 'bout things like you do and— [*He sits down beside her and demonstrates graphically what he thinks her methods and tone should be.*] —you just sip your coffee, see, and say easy like that you been thinking 'bout that deal Walter Lee is so interested in, 'bout the store and all, and sip some more coffee, like what you saying ain't really that important to you— And the next thing you know, she be listening good and asking you questions and when I come home—I can tell her the details. This ain't no fly-by-night proposition, baby. I mean we figured it out, me and Willy and Bobo.

RUTH: [*With a frown.*] Bobo?

WALTER: Yeah. You see, this little liquor store we got in mind cost seventy-five thousand and we figured the initial investment on the place be 'bout thirty thousand, see. That be ten thousand each. Course, there's a couple of hundred you got to pay so's you don't spend your life just waiting for them clowns to let your license get approved—

RUTH: You mean graft?

WALTER: [*Frowning impatiently.*] Don't call it that. See there, that just goes to show you what women understand about the world. Baby, don't *nothing* happen for you in this world 'less you pay *somebody* off!

RUTH: Walter, leave me alone! [*She raises her head and stares at him vigorously—then says, more quietly.*] Eat your eggs, they gonna be cold.

WALTER: [*Straightening up from her and looking off.*] That's it. There you are. Man say to his woman: I got me a dream. His woman say: Eat your eggs. [*Sadly, but gaining in power.*] Man say: I got to take hold of this here world, baby! And a woman will say: Eat your eggs and go to work. [*Passionately now.*] Man say: I got to change my life, I'm choking to death, baby! And his woman say— [*In utter anguish as he brings his fists down on his thighs.*] — Your eggs is getting cold!

RUTH: [*Softly.*] Walter, that ain't none of our money.

WALTER: [*Not listening at all or even looking at her.*] This morning, I was lookin' in the mirror and thinking about it . . . I'm thirty-five years old; I been married eleven years and I got a boy who sleeps in the living room— [*Very, very quietly.*] —and all I got to give him is stories about how rich white people live . . .

RUTH: Eat your eggs, Walter.

WALTER: *Damn my eggs . . . damn all the eggs that ever was!*

RUTH: Then go to work.

WALTER: [*Looking up at her.*] See—I'm trying to talk to you 'bout myself— [*Shaking his head with the repetition.*] —and all you can say is eat them eggs and go to work.

RUTH: [*Wearily.*] Honey, you never say nothing new. I listen to you every day, every night and every morning, and you never say nothing new.

[*Shrugging.*] So you would rather *be* Mr. Arnold than be his chauffeur. So—I would *rather* be living in Buckingham Palace.[3]

WALTER: That is just what is wrong with the colored woman in this world . . . Don't understand about building their men up and making 'em feel like they somebody. Like they can do something.

RUTH: [*Drily, but to hurt.*] There *are* colored men who do things.

WALTER: No thanks to the colored woman.

RUTH: Well, being a colored woman, I guess I can't help myself none.

[*She rises and gets the ironing board and sets it up and attacks a huge pile of rough-dried clothes, sprinkling them in preparation for the ironing and then rolling them into tight fat balls.*]

WALTER: [*Mumbling.*] We one group of men tied to a race of women with small minds.

[*His sister* BENEATHA *enters. She is about twenty, as slim and intense as her brother. She is not as pretty as her sister-in-law, but her lean, almost intellectual face has a handsomeness of its own. She wears a bright-red flannel nightie, and her thick hair stands wildly about her head. Her speech is a mixture of many things; it is different from the rest of the family's insofar as education has permeated her sense of English—and perhaps the Midwest rather than the South has finally—at last—won out in her inflection; but not altogether, because over all of it is a soft slurring and transformed use of vowels which is the decided influence of the Southside. She passes through the room without looking at either* RUTH *or* WALTER *and goes to the outside door and looks, a little blindly, out to the bathroom. She sees that it has been lost to the Johnsons. She closes the door with a sleepy vengeance and crosses to the table and sits down a little defeated.*]

BENEATHA: I am going to start timing those people.

WALTER: You should get up earlier.

BENEATHA: [*Her face in her hands. She is still fighting the urge to go back to bed.*] Really—would you suggest dawn? Where's the paper?

WALTER: [*Pushing the paper across the table to her as he studies her almost clinically, as though he has never seen her before.*] You a horrible-looking chick at this hour.

BENEATHA: [*Drily.*] Good morning, everybody.

WALTER: [*Senselessly.*] How is school coming?

BENEATHA: [*In the same spirit.*] Lovely. Lovely. And you know, biology is the greatest. [*Looking up at him.*] I dissected something that looked just like you yesterday.

WALTER: I just wondered if you've made up your mind and everything.

BENEATHA: [*Gaining in sharpness and impatience.*] And what did I answer yesterday morning—and the day before that?

RUTH: [*From the ironing board, like someone disinterested and old.*] Don't be so nasty, Bennie.

---

3. Where the queen of Great Britain resides in London.

BENEATHA: [*Still to her brother.*] And the day before that and the day before that!

WALTER: [*Defensively.*] I'm interested in you. Something wrong with that? Ain't many girls who decide—

WALTER AND BENEATHA: [*In unison.*] —"to be a doctor."

[*Silence.*]

WALTER: Have we figured out yet just exactly how much medical school is going to cost?

RUTH: Walter Lee, why don't you leave that girl alone and get out of here to work?

BENEATHA: [*Exits to the bathroom and bangs on the door.*] Come on out of there, please!

[*She comes back into the room.*]

WALTER: [*Looking at his sister intently.*] You know the check is coming tomorrow.

BENEATHA: [*Turning on him with a sharpness all her own.*] That money belongs to Mama, Walter, and it's for her to decide how she wants to use it. I don't care if she wants to buy a house or a rocket ship or just nail it up somewhere and look at it. It's hers. Not ours—*hers.*

WALTER: [*Bitterly.*] Now ain't that fine! You just got your mother's interest at heart, ain't you, girl? You such a nice girl—but if Mama got that money she can always take a few thousand and help you through school too—can't she?

BENEATHA: I have never asked anyone around here to do anything for me.

WALTER: No! And the line between asking and just accepting when the time comes is big and wide—ain't it!

BENEATHA: [*With fury.*] What do you want from me, Brother—that I quit school or just drop dead, which!

WALTER: I don't want nothing but for you to stop acting holy 'round here. Me and Ruth done made some sacrifices for you—why can't you do something for the family?

RUTH: Walter, don't be dragging me in it.

WALTER: You are in it—Don't you get up and go work in somebody's kitchen for the last three years to help put clothes on her back?

RUTH: Oh, Walter—that's not fair . . .

WALTER: It ain't that nobody expects you to get on your knees and say thank you, Brother; thank you, Ruth; thank you, Mama—and thank you, Travis, for wearing the same pair of shoes for two semesters—

BENEATHA: [*Dropping to her knees.*] Well—I *do*—all right?—thank everybody . . . and forgive me for ever wanting to be anything at all . . . forgive me, forgive me!

RUTH: Please stop it! Your mama'll hear you.

WALTER: Who the hell told you you had to be a doctor? If you so crazy 'bout messing 'round with sick people—then go be a nurse like other women—or just get married and be quiet . . .

BENEATHA: Well—you finally got it said . . . it took you three years but you finally got it said. Walter, give up; leave me alone—it's Mama's money.

WALTER: *He was my father, too!*

BENEATHA: So what? He was mine, too—and Travis' grandfather—but the insurance money belongs to Mama. Picking on me is not going to make her give it to you to invest in any liquor stores— [*Underbreath, dropping into a chair.*] —and I for one say, God bless Mama for that!

WALTER: [*To* RUTH.] See—did you hear? Did you hear!

RUTH: Honey, please go to work.

WALTER: Nobody in this house is ever going to understand me.

BENEATHA: Because you're a nut.

WALTER: Who's a nut?

BENEATHA: You—you are a nut. Thee is mad, boy.

WALTER: [*Looking at his wife and his sister from the door, very sadly.*] The world's most backward race of people, and that's a fact.

BENEATHA: [*Turning slowly in her chair.*] And then there are all those prophets who would lead us out of the wilderness— [WALTER *slams out of the house.*] —into the swamps!

RUTH: Bennie, why you always gotta be pickin' on your brother? Can't you be a little sweeter sometimes? [*Door opens.* WALTER *walks in.*]

WALTER: [*To* RUTH.] I need some money for carfare.

RUTH: [*Looks at him, then warms; teasing, but tenderly.*] Fifty cents? [*She goes to her bag and gets money.*] Here, take a taxi.

[WALTER *exits.* MAMA *enters. She is a woman in her early sixties, full-bodied and strong. She is one of those women of a certain grace and beauty who wear it so unobtrusively that it takes a while to notice. Her dark-brown face is surrounded by the total whiteness of her hair, and, being a woman who has adjusted to many things in life and overcome many more, her face is full of strength. She has, we can see, wit and faith of a kind that keep her eyes lit and full of interest and expectancy. She is, in a word, a beautiful woman. Her bearing is perhaps most like the noble bearing of the women of the Hereros of Southwest Africa—rather as if she imagines that as she walks she still bears a basket or a vessel upon her head. Her speech, on the other hand, is as careless as her carriage is precise—she is inclined to slur everything—but her voice is perhaps not so much quiet as simply soft.*]

MAMA: Who that 'round here slamming doors at this hour?

[*She crosses through the room, goes to the window, opens it, and brings in a feeble little plant growing doggedly in a small pot on the window sill. She feels the dirt and puts it back out.*]

RUTH: That was Walter Lee. He and Bennie was at it again.

MAMA: My children and they tempers. Lord, if this little old plant don't get more sun than it's been getting it ain't never going to see spring again. [*She turns from the window.*] What's the matter with you this morning, Ruth? You looks right peaked. You aiming to iron all them things?

Leave some for me. I'll get to 'em this afternoon. Bennie honey, it's too drafty for you to be sitting 'round half dressed. Where's your robe?

BENEATHA: In the cleaners.

MAMA: Well, go get mine and put it on.

BENEATHA: I'm not cold, Mama, honest.

MAMA: I know—but you so thin . . .

BENEATHA: [*Irritably.*] Mama, I'm not cold.

MAMA: [*Seeing the make-down bed as* TRAVIS *has left it.*] Lord have mercy, look at that poor bed. Bless his heart—he tries, don't he?

[*She moves to the bed* TRAVIS *has sloppily made up.*]

RUTH: No—he don't half try at all 'cause he knows you going to come along behind him and fix everything. That's just how come he don't know how to do nothing right now—you done spoiled that boy so.

MAMA: Well—he's a little boy. Ain't supposed to know 'bout housekeeping. My baby, that's what he is. What you fix for his breakfast this morning?

RUTH: [*Angrily.*] I feed my son, Lena!

MAMA: I ain't meddling— [*Underbreath; busy-bodyish.*] I just noticed all last week he had cold cereal, and when it starts getting this chilly in the fall a child ought to have some hot grits or something when he goes out in the cold—

RUTH: [*Furious.*] I gave him hot oats—is that all right!

MAMA: I ain't meddling. [*Pause.*] Put a lot of nice butter on it? [RUTH *shoots her an angry look and does not reply.*] He likes lots of butter.

RUTH: [*Exasperated.*] Lena—

MAMA: [*To* BENEATHA. MAMA *is inclined to wander conversationally sometimes.*] What was you and your brother fussing 'bout this morning?

BENEATHA: It's not important, Mama.

[*She gets up and goes to look out at the bathroom, which is apparently free, and she picks up her towels and rushes out.*]

MAMA: What was they fighting about?

RUTH: Now you know as well as I do.

MAMA: [*Shaking her head.*] Brother still worrying hisself sick about that money?

RUTH: You know he is.

MAMA: You had breakfast?

RUTH: Some coffee.

MAMA: Girl, you better start eating and looking after yourself better. You almost thin as Travis.

RUTH: Lena—

MAMA: Un-hunh?

RUTH: What are you going to do with it?

MAMA: Now don't you start, child. It's too early in the morning to be talking about money. It ain't Christian.

RUTH: It's just that he got his heart set on that store—

MAMA: You mean that liquor store that Willy Harris want him to invest in?

RUTH: Yes—

MAMA: We ain't no business people, Ruth. We just plain working folks.

RUTH: Ain't nobody business people till they go into business. Walter Lee say colored people ain't never going to start getting ahead till they start gambling on some different kinds of things in the world—investments and things.

MAMA: What done got into you, girl? Walter Lee done finally sold you on investing.

RUTH: No. Mama, something is happening between Walter and me. I don't know what it is—but he needs something—something I can't give him anymore. He needs this chance, Lena.

MAMA: [*Frowning deeply.*] But liquor, honey—

RUTH: Well—like Walter say—I spec people going to always be drinking themselves some liquor.

MAMA: Well—whether they drinks it or not ain't none of my business. But whether I go into business selling it to 'em *is,* and I don't want that on my ledger this late in life. [*Stopping suddenly and studying her daughter-in-law.*] Ruth Younger, what's the matter with you today? You look like you could fall over right there.

RUTH: I'm tired.

MAMA: Then you better stay home from work today.

RUTH: I can't stay home. She'd be calling up the agency and screaming at them, "My girl didn't come in today—send me somebody! My girl didn't come in!" Oh, she just have a fit . . .

MAMA: Well, let her have it. I'll just call her up and say you got the flu—

RUTH: [*Laughing.*] Why the flu?

MAMA: 'Cause it sounds respectable to 'em. Something white people get, too. They know 'bout the flu. Otherwise they think you been cut up or something when you tell 'em you sick.

RUTH: I got to go in. We need the money.

MAMA: Somebody would of thought my children done all but starved to death the way they talk about money here late. Child, we got a great big old check coming tomorrow.

RUTH: [*Sincerely, but also self-righteously.*] Now that's your money. It ain't got nothing to do with me. We all feel like that—Walter and Bennie and me—even Travis.

MAMA: [*Thoughtfully, and suddenly very far away.*] Ten thousand dollars—

RUTH: Sure is wonderful.

MAMA: Ten thousand dollars.

RUTH: You know what you should do, Miss Lena? You should take yourself a trip somewhere. To Europe or South America or someplace—

MAMA: [*Throwing up her hands at the thought.*] Oh, child!

RUTH: I'm serious. Just pack up and leave! Go on away and enjoy yourself some. Forget about the family and have yourself a ball for once in your life—

MAMA: [*Drily.*] You sound like I'm just about ready to die. Who'd go with me? What I look like wandering 'round Europe by myself?

RUTH: Shoot—these here rich white women do it all the time. They don't think nothing of packing up they suitcases and piling on one of them big steamships and—swoosh!—they gone, child.

MAMA: Something always told me I wasn't no rich white woman.

RUTH: Well—what are you going to do with it then?

MAMA: I ain't rightly decided. [*Thinking. She speaks now with emphasis.*] Some of it got to be put away for Beneatha and her schoolin'—and ain't nothing going to touch that part of it. Nothing. [*She waits several seconds, trying to make up her mind about something, and looks at* RUTH *a little tentatively before going on.*] Been thinking that we maybe could meet the notes on a little old two-story somewhere, with a yard where Travis could play in the summertime, if we use part of the insurance for a down payment and everybody kind of pitch in. I could maybe take on a little day work again, few days a week—

RUTH: [*Studying her mother-in-law furtively and concentrating on her ironing, anxious to encourage without seeming to.*] Well, Lord knows, we've put enough rent into this here rat trap to pay for four houses by now . . .

MAMA: [*Looking up at the words "rat trap" and then looking around and leaning back and sighing—in a suddenly reflective mood—*] "Rat trap"—yes, that's all it is. [*Smiling.*] I remember just as well the day me and Big Walter moved in here. Hadn't been married but two weeks and wasn't planning on living here no more than a year. [*She shakes her head at the dissolved dream.*] We was going to set away, little by little, don't you know, and buy a little place out in Morgan Park. We had even picked out the house. [*Chuckling a little.*] Looks right dumpy today. But Lord, child, you should know all the dreams I had 'bout buying that house and fixing it up and making me a little garden in the back— [*She waits and stops smiling.*] And didn't none of it happen.

[*Dropping her hands in a futile gesture.*]

RUTH: [*Keeps her head down, ironing.*] Yes, life can be a barrel of disappointments, sometimes.

MAMA: Honey, Big Walter would come in here some nights back then and slump down on that couch there and just look at the rug, and look at me and look at the rug and then back at me—and I'd know he was down then . . . really down. [*After a second very long and thoughtful pause; she is seeing back to times that only she can see.*] And then, Lord, when I lost that baby—little Claude—I almost thought I was going to lose Big Walter too. Oh, that man grieved hisself! He was one man to love his children.

RUTH: Ain't nothin' can tear at you like losin' your baby.

MAMA: I guess that's how come that man finally worked hisself to death like he done. Like he was fighting his own war with this here world that took his baby from him.

RUTH: He sure was a fine man, all right. I always liked Mr. Younger.

MAMA: Crazy 'bout his children! God knows there was plenty wrong with Walter Younger—hard-headed, mean, kind of wild with women—plenty wrong with him. But he sure loved his children. Always wanted them to have something—be something. That's where Brother gets all these notions, I reckon. Big Walter used to say, he'd get right wet in the eyes sometimes, lean his head back with the water standing in his eyes and say, "Seem like God didn't see fit to give the black man nothing but dreams—but He did give us children to make them dreams seem worthwhile." [*She smiles.*] He could talk like that, don't you know.

RUTH: Yes, he sure could. He was a good man, Mr. Younger.

MAMA: Yes, a fine man—just couldn't never catch up with his dreams, that's all.

[BENEATHA *comes in, brushing her hair and looking up to the ceiling, where the sound of a vacuum cleaner has started up.*]

BENEATHA: What could be so dirty on that woman's rugs that she has to vacuum them every single day?

RUTH: I wish certain young women 'round here who I could name would take inspiration about certain rugs in a certain apartment I could also mention.

BENEATHA: [*Shrugging.*] How much cleaning can a house need, for Christ's sakes.

MAMA: [*Not liking the Lord's name used thus.*] Bennie!

RUTH: Just listen to her—just listen!

BENEATHA: Oh, God!

MAMA: If you use the Lord's name just one more time—

BENEATHA: [*A bit of a whine.*] Oh, Mama—

RUTH: Fresh—just fresh as salt, this girl!

BENEATHA: [*Drily.*] Well—if the salt loses its savor—[4]

MAMA: Now that will do. I just ain't going to have you 'round here reciting the scriptures in vain—you hear me?

BENEATHA: How did I manage to get on everybody's wrong side by just walking into a room?

RUTH: If you weren't so fresh—

BENEATHA: Ruth, I'm twenty years old.

MAMA: What time you be home from school today?

BENEATHA: Kind of late. [*With enthusiasm.*] Madeline is going to start my guitar lessons today.

[MAMA *and* RUTH *look up with the same expression.*]

MAMA: Your *what* kind of lessons?

BENEATHA: Guitar.

RUTH: Oh, Father!

MAMA: How come you done taken it in your mind to learn to play the guitar?

BENEATHA: I just want to, that's all.

MAMA: [*Smiling.*] Lord, child, don't you know what to do with yourself?

---

4. See Matthew 5.13: "You are the salt of the earth. But if the salt loses its taste, with what can it be seasoned? It is no longer good for anything but to be thrown out and trampled underfoot."

How long it going to be before you get tired of this now—like you got tired of that little play-acting group you joined last year? [*Looking at* RUTH.] And what was it the year before that?

RUTH: The horseback-riding club for which she bought that fifty-five-dollar riding habit that's been hanging in the closet ever since!

MAMA: [*To* BENEATHA.] Why you got to flit so from one thing to another, baby?

BENEATHA: [*Sharply.*] I just want to learn to play the guitar. Is there anything wrong with that?

MAMA: Ain't nobody trying to stop you. I just wonders sometimes why you has to flit so from one thing to another all the time. You ain't never done nothing with all that camera equipment you brought home—

BENEATHA: I don't flit! I—I experiment with different forms of expression—

RUTH: Like riding a horse?

BENEATHA: —People have to express themselves one way or another.

MAMA: What is it you want to express?

BENEATHA: [*Angrily.*] Me! [MAMA *and* RUTH *look at each other and burst into raucous laughter.*] Don't worry—I don't expect you to understand.

MAMA: [*To change the subject.*] Who you going out with tomorrow night?

BENEATHA: [*With displeasure.*] George Murchison again.

MAMA: [*Pleased.*] Oh—you getting a little sweet on him?

RUTH: You ask me, this child ain't sweet on nobody but herself— [*Under breath.*] Express herself!

[*They laugh.*]

BENEATHA: Oh—I like George all right, Mama. I mean I like him enough to go out with him and stuff, but—

RUTH: [*For devilment.*] What does *and stuff* mean?

BENEATHA: Mind your own business.

MAMA: Stop picking at her now, Ruth. [*A thoughtful pause, and then a suspicious sudden look at her daughter as she turns in her chair for emphasis.*] What *does* it mean?

BENEATHA: [*Wearily.*] Oh, I just mean I couldn't ever really be serious about George. He's—he's so shallow.

RUTH: Shallow—what do you mean he's shallow? He's *rich!*

MAMA: Hush, Ruth.

BENEATHA: I know he's rich. He knows he's rich, too.

RUTH: Well—what other qualities a man got to have to satisfy you, little girl?

BENEATHA: You wouldn't even begin to understand. Anybody who married Walter could not possibly understand.

MAMA: [*Outraged.*] What kind of way is that to talk about your brother?

BENEATHA: Brother is a flip—let's face it.

MAMA: [*To* RUTH, *helplessly.*] What's a flip?

RUTH: [*Glad to add kindling.*] She's saying he's crazy.

BENEATHA: Not crazy. Brother isn't really crazy yet—he—he's an elaborate neurotic.

MAMA: Hush your mouth!

BENEATHA: As for George. Well. George looks good—he's got a beautiful car and he takes me to nice places and, as my sister-in-law says, he is probably the richest boy I will ever get to know and I even like him sometimes—but if the Youngers are sitting around waiting to see if their little Bennie is going to tie up the family with the Murchisons, they are wasting their time.

RUTH: You mean you wouldn't marry George Murchison if he asked you someday? That pretty, rich thing? Honey, I knew you was odd—

BENEATHA: No I would not marry him if all I felt for him was what I feel now. Besides, George's family wouldn't really like it.

MAMA: Why not?

BENEATHA: Oh, Mama—The Murchisons are honest-to-God-real-*live*-rich colored people, and the only people in the world who are more snobbish than rich white people are rich colored people. I thought everybody knew that. I've met Mrs. Murchison. She's a scene!

MAMA: You must not dislike people 'cause they well off, honey.

BENEATHA: Why not? It makes just as much sense as disliking people 'cause they are poor, and lots of people do that.

RUTH: [*A wisdom-of-the-ages manner.* To MAMA.] Well, she'll get over some of this—

BENEATHA: Get over it? What are you talking about, Ruth? Listen, I'm going to be a doctor. I'm not worried about who I'm going to marry yet—if I ever get married.

MAMA AND RUTH: *If!*

MAMA: Now, Bennie—

BENEATHA: Oh, I probably will . . . but first I'm going to be a doctor, and George, for one, still thinks that's pretty funny. I couldn't be bothered with that. I am going to be a doctor and everybody around here better understand that!

MAMA: [*Kindly.*] 'Course you going to be a doctor, honey, God willing.

BENEATHA: [*Drily.*] God hasn't got a thing to do with it.

MAMA: Beneatha—that just wasn't necessary.

BENEATHA: Well—neither is God. I get sick of hearing about God.

MAMA: Beneatha!

BENEATHA: I mean it! I'm just tired of hearing about God all the time. What has He got to do with anything? Does He pay tuition?

MAMA: You 'bout to get your fresh little jaw slapped!

RUTH: That's just what she needs, all right!

BENEATHA: Why? Why can't I say what I want to around here, like everybody else?

MAMA: It don't sound nice for a young girl to say things like that—you wasn't brought up that way. Me and your father went to trouble to get you and Brother to church every Sunday.

BENEATHA: Mama, you don't understand. It's all a matter of ideas, and God is just one idea I don't accept. It's not important. I am not going out and be immoral or commit crimes because I don't believe in God. I don't even think about it. It's just that I get tired of Him getting credit for all the things the human race achieves through its own stubborn effort. There simply is no blasted God—there is only man and it is he who makes miracles!

[MAMA *absorbs this speech, studies her daughter and rises slowly and crosses to* BENEATHA *and slaps her powerfully across the face. After, there is only silence and the daughter drops her eyes from her mother's face, and* MAMA *is very tall before her.*]

MAMA: Now—you say after me, in my mother's house there is still God. [*There is a long pause and* BENEATHA *stares at the floor wordlessly.* MAMA *repeats the phrase with precision and cool emotion.*] In my mother's house there is still God.

BENEATHA: In my mother's house there is still God.

[*A long pause.*]

MAMA: [*Walking away from* BENEATHA, *too disturbed for triumphant posture. Stopping and turning back to her daughter.*] There are some ideas we ain't going to have in this house. Not long as I am at the head of this family.

BENEATHA: Yes, ma'am.

[MAMA *walks out of the room.*]

RUTH: [*Almost gently, with profound understanding.*] You think you a woman, Bennie—but you still a little girl. What you did was childish—so you got treated like a child.

BENEATHA: I see. [*Quietly.*] I also see that everybody thinks it's all right for Mama to be a tyrant. But all the tyranny in the world will never put a God in the heavens!

[*She picks up her books and goes out.*]

RUTH: [*Goes to* MAMA's *door.*] She said she was sorry.

MAMA: [*Coming out, going to her plant.*] They frightens me, Ruth. My children.

RUTH: You got good children, Lena. They just a little off sometimes—but they're good.

MAMA: No—there's something come down between me and them that don't let us understand each other and I don't know what it is. One done almost lost his mind thinking 'bout money all the time and the other done commence to talk about things I can't seem to understand in no form or fashion. What is it that's changing, Ruth?

RUTH: [*Soothingly, older than her years.*] Now . . . you taking it all too seriously. You just got strong-willed children and it takes a strong woman like you to keep 'em in hand.

MAMA: [*Looking at her plant and sprinkling a little water on it.*] They spirited all right, my children. Got to admit they got spirit—Bennie and Walter. Like this little old plant that ain't never had enough sunshine or nothing—and look at it . . .

[*She has her back to* RUTH, *who has had to stop ironing and lean against something and put the back of her hand to her forehead.*]

RUTH: [*Trying to keep* MAMA *from noticing.*] You . . . sure . . . loves that little old thing, don't you? . . .

MAMA: Well, I always wanted me a garden like I used to see sometimes at the back of the houses down home. This plant is close as I ever got to having one. [*She looks out of the window as she replaces the plant.*] Lord, ain't nothing as dreary as the view from this window on a dreary day, is there? Why ain't you singing this morning, Ruth? Sing that "No Ways Tired." That song always lifts me up so— [*She turns at last to see that* RUTH *has slipped quietly into a chair, in a state of semiconsciousness.*] Ruth! Ruth honey— what's the matter with you . . . Ruth!

[CURTAIN.]

Scene Two

It is the following morning; a Saturday morning, and house cleaning is in progress at the Youngers. Furniture has been shoved hither and yon and MAMA *is giving the kitchen-area walls a washing down.* BENEATHA, *in dungarees, with a handkerchief tied around her face, is spraying insecticide into the cracks in the walls. As they work, the radio is on and a Southside disk-jockey program is inappropriately filling the house with a rather exotic saxophone blues.* TRAVIS, *the sole idle one, is leaning on his arms, looking out of the window.*

TRAVIS: Grandmama, that stuff Bennie is using smells awful. Can I go downstairs, please?

MAMA: Did you get all them chores done already? I ain't seen you doing much.

TRAVIS: Yes'm—finished early. Where did Mama go this morning?

MAMA: [*Looking at* BENEATHA.] She had to go on a little errand.

TRAVIS: Where?

MAMA: To tend to her business.

TRAVIS: Can I go outside then?

MAMA: Oh, I guess so. You better stay right in front of the house, though . . . and keep a good lookout for the postman.

TRAVIS: Yes'm. [*He starts out and decides to give his aunt* BENEATHA *a good swat on the legs as he passes her.*] Leave them poor little old cockroaches alone, they ain't bothering you none.

[*He runs as she swings the spray gun at him both viciously and playfully.* WALTER *enters from the bedroom and goes to the phone.*]

MAMA: Look out there, girl, before you be spilling some of that stuff on that child!

TRAVIS: [*Teasing.*] That's right—look out now!

[*He exits.*]

BENEATHA: [*Drily.*] I can't imagine that it would hurt him—it has never hurt the roaches.

MAMA: Well, little boys' hides ain't as tough as Southside roaches.

WALTER: [*Into phone.*] Hello—Let me talk to Willy Harris.

MAMA: You better get over there behind the bureau. I seen one marching out of there like Napoleon yesterday.

WALTER: Hello, Willy? It ain't come yet. It'll be here in a few minutes. Did the lawyer give you the papers?

BENEATHA: There's really only one way to get rid of them, Mama—

MAMA: How?

BENEATHA: Set fire to this building.

WALTER: Good. Good. I'll be right over.

BENEATHA: Where did Ruth go, Walter?

WALTER: I don't know.

[*He exits abruptly.*]

BENEATHA: Mama, where did Ruth go?

MAMA: [*Looking at her with meaning.*] To the doctor, I think.

BENEATHA: The doctor? What's the matter? [*They exchange glances.*] You don't think—

MAMA: [*With her sense of drama.*] Now I ain't saying what I think. But I ain't never been wrong 'bout a woman neither.

[*The phone rings.*]

BENEATHA: [*At the phone.*] Hay-lo... [*Pause, and a moment of recognition.*] Well—when did you get back!... And how was it?... Of course I've missed you—in my way... This morning? No... house cleaning and all that and Mama hates it if I let people come over when the house is like this... You *have*? Well, that's different... What is it—Oh, what the hell, come on over... Right, see you then.

[*She hangs up.*]

MAMA: [*Who has listened vigorously, as is her habit.*] Who is that you inviting over here with this house looking like this? You ain't got the pride you was born with!

BENEATHA: Asagai doesn't care how houses look, Mama—he's an intellectual.

MAMA: *Who?*

BENEATHA: Asagai—Joseph Asagai. He's an African boy I met on campus. He's been studying in Canada all summer.

MAMA: What's his name?

BENEATHA: Asagai, Joseph. Ah-sah-guy... He's from Nigeria.

MAMA: Oh, that's the little country that was founded by slaves way back...

BENEATHA: No, Mama—that's Liberia.

MAMA: I don't think I never met no African before.

BENEATHA: Well, do me a favor and don't ask him a whole lot of ignorant questions about Africans. I mean, do they wear clothes and all that—

MAMA: Well, now, I guess if you think we so ignorant 'round here maybe you shouldn't bring your friends here—

BENEATHA: It's just that people ask such crazy things. All anyone seems to know about when it comes to Africa is Tarzan—

MAMA: [*Indignantly.*] Why should I know anything about Africa?

BENEATHA: Why do you give money at church for the missionary work?

MAMA: Well, that's to help save people.

BENEATHA: You mean save them from *heathenism*—

MAMA: [*Innocently.*] Yes.

BENEATHA: I'm afraid they need more salvation from the British and the French.

[RUTH *comes in forlornly and pulls off her coat with dejection. They both turn to look at her.*]

RUTH: [*Dispiritedly.*] Well, I guess from all the happy faces—everybody knows.

BENEATHA: You pregnant?

MAMA: Lord have mercy, I sure hope it's a little old girl. Travis ought to have a sister.

[BENEATHA *and* RUTH *give her a hopeless look for this grandmotherly enthusiasm.*]

BENEATHA: How far along are you?

RUTH: Two months.

BENEATHA: Did you mean to? I mean did you plan it or was it an accident?

MAMA: What do you know about planning or not planning?

BENEATHA: Oh, Mama.

RUTH: [*Wearily.*] She's twenty years old, Lena.

BENEATHA: Did you plan it, Ruth?

RUTH: Mind your own business.

BENEATHA: It is my business—where is he going to live, on the roof? [*There is silence following the remark as the three women react to the sense of it.*] Gee—I didn't mean that, Ruth, honest. Gee, I don't feel like that at all. I—I think it is wonderful.

RUTH: [*Dully.*] Wonderful.

BENEATHA: Yes—really.

MAMA: [*Looking at* RUTH, *worried.*] Doctor say everything going to be all right?

RUTH: [*Far away.*] Yes—she says everything is going to be fine . . .

MAMA: [*Immediately suspicious.*] "She"—What doctor you went to?

[RUTH *folds over, near hysteria.*]

MAMA: [*Worriedly hovering over* RUTH.] Ruth honey—what's the matter with you—you sick?

[RUTH *has her fists clenched on her thighs and is fighting hard to suppress a scream that seems to be rising in her.*]

BENEATHA: What's the matter with her, Mama?

MAMA: [*Working her fingers in* RUTH's *shoulder to relax her.*] She be all right. Women gets right depressed sometimes when they get her way. [*Speaking softly, expertly, rapidly.*] Now you just relax. That's right . . . just lean back, don't think 'bout nothing at all . . . nothing at all—

RUTH: I'm all right . . .

[*The glassy-eyed look melts and then she collapses into a fit of heavy sobbing. The bell rings.*]

BENEATHA: Oh, my God—that must be Asagai.

MAMA: [*To* RUTH.] Come on now, honey. You need to lie down and rest awhile . . . then have some nice hot food.

[*They exit,* RUTH's *weight on her mother-in-law.* BENEATHA, *herself profoundly disturbed, opens the door to admit a rather dramatic-looking young man with a large package.*]

ASAGAI: Hello, Alaiyo—

BENEATHA: [*Holding the door open and regarding him with pleasure.*] Hello . . . [*Long pause.*] Well—come in. And please excuse everything. My mother was very upset about my letting anyone come here with the place like this.

ASAGAI: [*Coming into the room.*] You look disturbed too . . . Is something wrong?

BENEATHA: [*Still at the door, absently.*] Yes . . . we've all got acute ghettoitus. [*She smiles and comes toward him, finding a cigarette and sitting.*] So—sit down! How was Canada?

ASAGAI: [*A sophisticate.*] Canadian.

BENEATHA: [*Looking at him.*] I'm very glad you are back.

ASAGAI: [*Looking back at her in turn.*] Are you really?

BENEATHA: Yes—very.

ASAGAI: Why—you were quite glad when I went away. What happened?

BENEATHA: You went away.

ASAGAI: Ahhhhhhhh.

BENEATHA: Before—you wanted to be so serious before there was time.

ASAGAI: How much time must there be before one knows what one feels?

BENEATHA: [*Stalling this particular conversation. Her hands pressed together, in a deliberately childish gesture.*] What did you bring me?

ASAGAI: [*Handing her the package.*] Open it and see.

BENEATHA: [*Eagerly opening the package and drawing out some records and the colorful robes of a Nigerian woman.*] Oh, Asagai! . . . You got them for me! . . . How beautiful . . . and the records too! [*She lifts out the robes and runs to the mirror with them and holds the drapery up in front of herself.*]

ASAGAI: [*Coming to her at the mirror.*] I shall have to teach you how to drape it properly. [*He flings the material about her for the moment and stands back to look at her.*] Ah—Oh-pay-gay-day, oh-gbah-mu-shay. [*A Yoruba exclamation for admiration.*] You wear it well . . . very well . . . mutilated hair and all.

BENEATHA: [*Turning suddenly.*] My hair—what's wrong with my hair?

ASAGAI: [*Shrugging.*] Were you born with it like that?

BENEATHA: [*Reaching up to touch it.*] No . . . of course not.

[*She looks back to the mirror, disturbed.*]

ASAGAI: [*Smiling.*] How then?

BENEATHA: You know perfectly well how . . . as crinkly as yours . . . that's how.

ASAGAI: And it is ugly to you that way?

BENEATHA: [*Quickly.*] Oh, no—not ugly . . . [*More slowly, apologetically.*] But it's so hard to manage when it's, well—raw.

ASAGAI: And so to accommodate that—you mutilate it every week?

BENEATHA: It's not mutilation!

ASAGAI: [*Laughing aloud at her seriousness.*] Oh . . . please! I am only teasing you because you are so very serious about these things. [*He stands back from her and folds his arms across his chest as he watches her pulling at her hair and frowning in the mirror.*] Do you remember the first time you met me at school? . . . [*He laughs.*] You came up to me and you said—and I thought you were the most serious little thing I had ever seen—you said: [*He imitates her.*] "Mr. Asagai—I want very much to talk with you. About Africa. You see, Mr. Asagai, I am looking for my *identity!*"

[*He laughs.*]

BENEATHA: [*Turning to him, not laughing.*] Yes—

[*Her face is quizzical, profoundly disturbed.*]

ASAGAI: [*Still teasing and reaching out and taking her face in his hands and turning her profile to him.*] Well . . . it is true that this is not so much a profile of a Hollywood queen as perhaps a queen of the Nile— [*A mock dismissal of the importance of the question.*] But what does it matter? Assimilationism is so popular in your country.

BENEATHA: [*Wheeling, passionately, sharply.*] I am not an assimilationist!

ASAGAI: [*The protest hangs in the room for a moment and* ASAGAI *studies her, his laughter fading.*] Such a serious one. [*There is a pause.*] So—you like the robes? You must take excellent care of them—they are from my sister's personal wardrobe.

BENEATHA: [*With incredulity.*] You—you sent all the way home—for me?

ASAGAI: [*With charm.*] For you—I would do much more . . . Well, that is what I came for. I must go.

BENEATHA: Will you call me Monday?

ASAGAI: Yes . . . We have a great deal to talk about. I mean about identity and time and all that.

BENEATHA: Time?

ASAGAI: Yes. About how much time one needs to know what one feels.

BENEATHA: You never understood that there is more than one kind of feeling which can exist between a man and a woman—or, at least, there should be.

ASAGAI: [*Shaking his head negatively but gently.*] No. Between a man and a

woman there need be only one kind of feeling. I have that for you . . .
Now even . . . right this moment . . .

BENEATHA: I know—and by itself—it won't do. I can find that anywhere.

ASAGAI: For a woman it should be enough.

BENEATHA: I know—because that's what it says in all the novels that men
write. But it isn't. Go ahead and laugh—but I'm not interested in being
someone's little episode in America or— [*With feminine vengeance.*] —one
of them! [ASAGAI *has burst into laughter again.*] That's funny as hell, huh!

ASAGAI: It's just that every American girl I have known has said that to me.
White—black—in this you are all the same. And the same speech, too!

BENEATHA: [*Angrily.*] Yuk, yuk, yuk!

ASAGAI: It's how you can be sure that the world's most liberated women
are not liberated at all. You all talk about it too much!

[MAMA *enters and is immediately all social charm because of the presence of
a guest.*]

BENEATHA: Oh—Mama—this is Mr. Asagai.

MAMA: How do you do?

ASAGAI: [*Total politeness to an elder.*] How do you do, Mrs. Younger. Please
forgive me for coming at such an outrageous hour on a Saturday.

MAMA: Well, you are quite welcome. I just hope you understand that our
house don't always look like this. [*Chatterish.*] You must come again. I
would love to hear all about— [*Not sure of the name.*] —your country. I
think it's so sad the way our American Negroes don't know nothing
about Africa 'cept Tarzan and all that. And all that money they pour
into these churches when they ought to be helping you people over there
drive out them French and Englishmen done taken away your land.

[*The mother flashes a slightly superior look at her daughter upon completion
of the recitation.*]

ASAGAI: [*Taken aback by this sudden and acutely unrelated expression of sympathy.*]
Yes . . . yes . . .

MAMA: [*Smiling at him suddenly and relaxing and looking him over.*] How many
miles is it from here to where you come from?

ASAGAI: Many thousands.

MAMA: [*Looking at him as she would* WALTER.] I bet you don't half look after
yourself, being away from your mama either. I spec you better come
'round here from time to time and get yourself some decent home-
cooked meals . . .

ASAGAI: [*Moved.*] Thank you. Thank you very much. [*They are all quiet, then—*]
Well . . . I must go. I will call you Monday, Alaiyo.

MAMA: What's that he call you?

ASAGAI: Oh—"Alaiyo." I hope you don't mind. It is what you would call a
nickname, I think. It is a Yoruba word. I am a Yoruba.

MAMA: [*Looking at* BENEATHA.] I—I thought he was from—

ASAGAI: [*Understanding.*] Nigeria is my country. Yoruba is my tribal origin—

BENEATHA: You didn't tell us what Alaiyo means . . . for all I know, you
might be calling me Little Idiot or something . . .

ASAGAI: Well . . . let me see . . . I do not know how just to explain it . . . The
sense of a thing can be so different when it changes languages.

BENEATHA: You're evading.

ASAGAI: No—really it is difficult . . . [*Thinking.*] It means . . . it means One for
Whom Bread—Food—Is Not Enough. [*He looks at her.*] Is that all right?

BENEATHA: [*Understanding, softly.*] Thank you.

MAMA: [*Looking from one to the other and not understanding any of it.*] Well . . .
that's nice . . . You must come see us again—Mr.—

ASAGAI: Ah-sah-guy . . .

MAMA: Yes . . . Do come again.

ASAGAI: Good-bye.

[*He exits.*]

MAMA: [*After him.*] Lord, that's a pretty thing just went out here! [*Insinu-
atingly, to her daughter.*] Yes, I guess I see why we done commence to get
so interested in Africa 'round here. Missionaries my aunt Jenny!

[*She exits.*]

BENEATHA: Oh, Mama! . . .

[*She picks up the Nigerian dress and holds it up to her in front of the mirror
again. She sets the headdress on haphazardly and then notices her hair again
and clutches at it and then replaces the headdress and frowns at herself. Then
she starts to wriggle in front of the mirror as she thinks a Nigerian woman
might.* TRAVIS *enters and regards her.*]

TRAVIS: You cracking up?

BENEATHA: Shut up.

[*She pulls the headdress off and looks at herself in the mirror and clutches at
her hair again and squinches her eyes as if trying to imagine something. Then,
suddenly, she gets her raincoat and kerchief and hurriedly prepares for going
out.*]

MAMA: [*Coming back into the room.*] She's resting now. Travis, baby, run next
door and ask Miss Johnson to please let me have a little kitchen cleanser.
This here can is empty as Jacob's kettle.

TRAVIS: I just came in.

MAMA: Do as you told. [*He exits and she looks at her daughter.*] Where you
going?

BENEATHA: [*Halting at the door.*] To become a queen of the Nile!

[*She exits in a breathless blaze of glory.* RUTH *appears in the bedroom doorway.*]

MAMA: Who told you to get up?

RUTH: Ain't nothing wrong with me to be lying in no bed for. Where did
Bennie go?

MAMA: [*Drumming her fingers.*] Far as I could make out—to Egypt. [RUTH *just looks at her.*] What time is it getting to?

RUTH: Ten twenty. And the mailman going to ring that bell this morning just like he done every morning for the last umpteen years.

[TRAVIS *comes in with the cleanser can.*]

TRAVIS: She say to tell you that she don't have much.

MAMA: [*Angrily.*] Lord, some people I could name sure is tight-fisted! [*Directing her grandson.*] Mark two cans of cleanser down on the list there. If she that hard up for kitchen cleanser, I sure don't want to forget to get her none!

RUTH: Lena—maybe the woman is just short on cleanser—

MAMA: [*Not listening.*] —Much baking powder as she done borrowed from me all these years, she could of done gone into the baking business!

[*The bell sounds suddenly and sharply and all three are stunned—serious and silent—mid-speech. In spite of all the other conversations and distractions of the morning, this is what they have been waiting for, even TRAVIS, who looks helplessly from his mother to his grandmother. RUTH is the first to come to life again.*]

RUTH: [*To TRAVIS.*] Get down them steps, boy!

[TRAVIS *snaps to life and flies out to get the mail.*]

MAMA: [*Her eyes wide, her hand to her breast.*] You mean it done really come?

RUTH: [*Excited.*] Oh, Miss Lena!

MAMA: [*Collecting herself.*] Well . . . I don't know what we all so excited about 'round here for. We known it was coming for months.

RUTH: That's a whole lot different from having it come and being able to hold it in your hands . . . a piece of paper worth ten thousand dollars . . . [TRAVIS *bursts back into the room. He holds the envelope high above his head, like a little dancer, his face is radiant and he is breathless. He moves to his grandmother with sudden slow ceremony and puts the envelope into her hands. She accepts it, and then merely holds it and looks at it.*] Come on! Open it . . . Lord have mercy, I wish Walter Lee was here!

TRAVIS: Open it, Grandmama!

MAMA: [*Staring at it.*] Now you all be quiet. It's just a check.

RUTH: Open it . . .

MAMA: [*Still staring at it.*] Now don't act silly . . . We ain't never been no people to act silly 'bout no money—

RUTH: [*Swiftly.*] We ain't never had none before—*open it!*

[MAMA *finally makes a good strong tear and pulls out the thin blue slice of paper and inspects it closely. The boy and his mother study it raptly over* MAMA's *shoulders.*]

MAMA: Travis! [*She is counting off with doubt.*] Is that the right number of zeros.

TRAVIS: Yes'm . . . ten thousand dollars. Gaalee, Grandmama, you rich.

MAMA: [*She holds the check away from her, still looking at it. Slowly her face sobers into a mask of unhappiness.*] Ten thousand dollars. [*She hands it to* RUTH.] Put it away somewhere, Ruth. [*She does not look at* RUTH; *her eyes seem to be seeing something somewhere very far off.*] Ten thousand dollars they give you. Ten thousand dollars.

TRAVIS: [*To his mother, sincerely.*] What's the matter with Grandmama—don't she want to be rich?

RUTH: [*Distractedly.*] You go on out and play now, baby. [TRAVIS *exits.* MAMA *starts wiping dishes absently, humming intently to herself.* RUTH *turns to her, with kind exasperation.*] You've gone and got yourself upset.

MAMA: [*Not looking at her.*] I spec if it wasn't for you all . . . I would just put that money away or give it to the church or something.

RUTH: Now what kind of talk is that. Mr. Younger would just be plain mad if he could hear you talking foolish like that.

MAMA: [*Stopping and staring off.*] Yes . . . he sure would. [*Sighing.*] We got enough to do with that money, all right. [*She halts then, and turns and looks at her daughter-in-law hard;* RUTH *avoids her eyes and* MAMA *wipes her hands with finality and starts to speak firmly to* RUTH.] Where did you go today, girl?

RUTH: To the doctor.

MAMA: [*Impatiently.*] Now, Ruth . . . you know better than that. Old Doctor Jones is strange enough in his way but there ain't nothing 'bout him make somebody slip and call him "she"—like you done this morning.

RUTH: Well, that's what happened—my tongue slipped.

MAMA: You went to see that woman, didn't you?

RUTH: [*Defensively, giving herself away.*] What woman you talking about?

MAMA: [*Angrily.*] That woman who—

[WALTER *enters in great excitement.*]

WALTER: Did it come?

MAMA: [*Quietly.*] Can't you give people a Christian greeting before you start asking about money?

WALTER: [*To* RUTH.] Did it come? [RUTH *unfolds the check and lays it quietly before him, watching him intently with thoughts of her own.* WALTER *sits down and grasps it close and counts off the zeros.*] Ten thousand dollars— [*He turns suddenly, frantically to his mother and draws some papers out of his breast pocket.*] Mama—look. Old Willy Harris put everything on paper—

MAMA: Son—I think you ought to talk to your wife . . . I'll go on out and leave you alone if you want—

WALTER: I can talk to her later—Mama, look—

MAMA: Son—

WALTER: WILL SOMEBODY PLEASE LISTEN TO ME TODAY!

MAMA: [*Quietly.*] I don't 'low no yellin' in this house, Walter Lee, and you know it— [WALTER *stares at them in frustration and starts to speak several times.*] And there ain't going to be no investing in no liquor stores. I don't aim to have to speak on that again.

[*A long pause.*]

WALTER: Oh—so you don't aim to have to speak on that again? So you have decided . . . [*Crumpling his papers.*] Well, *you* tell that to my boy tonight when you put him to sleep on the living-room couch . . . [*Turning to* MAMA *and speaking directly to her.*] Yeah—and tell it to my wife, Mama, tomorrow when she has to go out of here to look after somebody else's kids. And tell it to *me*, Mama, every time we need a new pair of curtains and I have to watch *you* go out and work in somebody's kitchen. Yeah, you tell me then!

[WALTER *starts out.*]

RUTH: Where you going?
WALTER: I'm going out!
RUTH: Where?
WALTER: Just out of this house somewhere—
RUTH: [*Getting her coat.*] I'll come too.
WALTER: I don't want you to come!
RUTH: I got something to talk to you about, Walter.
WALTER: That's too bad.
MAMA: [*Still quietly.*] Walter Lee— [*She waits and he finally turns and looks at her.*] Sit down.
WALTER: I'm a grown man, Mama.
MAMA: Ain't nobody said you wasn't grown. But you still in my house and my presence. And as long as you are—you'll talk to your wife civil. Now sit down.
RUTH: [*Suddenly.*] Oh, let him go on out and drink himself to death! He makes me sick to my stomach! [*She flings her coat against him.*]
WALTER: [*Violently.*] And you turn mine too, baby! [RUTH *goes into their bedroom and slams the door behind her.*] That was my greatest mistake—
MAMA: [*Still quietly.*] Walter, what is the matter with you?
WALTER: Matter with me? Ain't nothing the matter with *me*!
MAMA: Yes there is. Something eating you up like a crazy man. Something more than me not giving you this money. The past few years I been watching it happen to you. You get all nervous acting and kind of wild in the eyes—[WALTER *jumps up impatiently at her words.*] I said sit there now, I'm talking to you!
WALTER: Mama—I don't need no nagging at me today.
MAMA: Seem like you getting to a place where you always tied up in some kind of knot about something. But if anybody ask you 'bout it you just yell at 'em and bust out the house and go out and drink somewheres. Walter Lee, people can't live with that. Ruth's a good, patient girl in her way—but you getting to be too much. Boy, don't make the mistake of driving that girl away from you.
WALTER: Why—what she do for me?
MAMA: She loves you.
WALTER: Mama—I'm going out. I want to go off somewhere and be by myself for a while.

MAMA: I'm sorry 'bout your liquor store, son. It just wasn't the thing for us to do. That's what I want to tell you about—

WALTER: I got to go out, Mama—

[*He rises.*]

MAMA: It's dangerous, son.

WALTER: What's dangerous?

MAMA: When a man goes outside his home to look for peace.

WALTER: [*Beseechingly.*] Then why can't there never be no peace in this house then?

MAMA: You done found it in some other house?

WALTER: No—there ain't no woman! Why do women always think there's a woman somewhere when a man gets restless. [*Coming to her.*] Mama— Mama—I want so many things . . .

MAMA: Yes, son—

WALTER: I want so many things that they are driving me kind of crazy . . . Mama—look at me.

MAMA: I'm looking at you. You a good-looking boy. You got a job, a nice wife, a fine boy and—

WALTER: A job. [*Looks at her.*] Mama, a job? I open and close car doors all day long. I drive a man around in his limousine and I say, "Yes, sir; no, sir; very good, sir; shall I take the Drive, sir?" Mama, that ain't no kind of job . . . that ain't nothing at all. [*Very quietly.*] Mama, I don't know if I can make you understand.

MAMA: Understand what, baby?

WALTER: [*Quietly.*] Sometimes it's like I can see the future stretched out in front of me—just plain as day. The future, Mama. Hanging over there at the edge of my days. Just waiting for me—a big, looming blank space— full of *nothing*. Just waiting for *me*. [*Pause.*] Mama—sometimes when I'm downtown and I pass them cool, quiet-looking restaurants where them white boys are sitting back and talking 'bout things . . . sitting there turning deals worth millions of dollars . . . sometimes I see guys don't look much older than me—

MAMA: Son—how come you talk so much 'bout money?

WALTER: [*With immense passion.*] Because it is life, Mama!

MAMA: [*Quietly.*] Oh— [*Very quietly.*] So now it's life. Money is life. Once upon a time freedom used to be life—now it's money. I guess the world really do change . . .

WALTER: No—it was always money, Mama. We just didn't know about it.

MAMA: No . . . something has changed. [*She looks at him.*] You something new, boy. In my time we was worried about not being lynched and getting to the North if we could and how to stay alive and still have a pinch of dignity too . . . Now here come you and Beneatha—talking 'bout things we ain't never even thought about hardly, me and your daddy. You ain't satisfied or proud of nothing we done. I mean that you had a home; that we kept you out of trouble till you was grown; that you don't have to ride to work on the back of nobody's streetcar—You my children—but how different we done become.

WALTER: You just don't understand, Mama, you just don't understand.

MAMA: Son—do you know your wife is expecting another baby? [WALTER *stands, stunned, and absorbs what his mother has said.*] That's what she wanted to talk to you about. [WALTER *sinks down into a chair.*] This ain't for me to be telling—but you ought to know. [*She waits.*] I think Ruth is thinking 'bout getting rid of that child.[5]

WALTER: [*Slowly understanding.*] No—no—Ruth wouldn't do that.

MAMA: When the world gets ugly enough—a woman will do anything for her family. *The part that's already living.*

WALTER: You don't know Ruth, Mama, if you think she would do that.

[RUTH *opens the bedroom door and stands there a little limp.*]

RUTH: [*Beaten.*] Yes I would too, Walter. [*Pause.*] I gave her a five-dollar down payment.

[*There is total silence as the man stares at his wife and the mother stares at her son.*]

MAMA: [*Presently.*] Well— [*Tightly.*] Well—son, I'm waiting to hear you say something . . . I'm waiting to hear how you be your father's son. Be the man he was . . . [*Pause.*] Your wife say she going to destroy your child. And I'm waiting to hear you talk like him and say we a people who give children life, not who destroys them— [*She rises.*] I'm waiting to see you stand up and look like your daddy and say we done give up one baby to poverty and that we ain't going to give up nary another one . . . I'm waiting.

WALTER: Ruth—

MAMA: If you a son of mine, tell her! [WALTER *turns, looks at her and can say nothing. She continues, bitterly.*] You . . . you are a disgrace to your father's memory. Somebody get me my hat.

[CURTAIN.]

ACT II

Scene One

Time: Later the same day.

At rise: RUTH *is ironing again. She has the radio going. Presently* BENEATHA's *bedroom door opens and* RUTH's *mouth falls and she puts down the iron in fascination.*

RUTH: What have we got on tonight!

BENEATHA: [*Emerging grandly from the doorway so that we can see her thoroughly robed in the costume* ASAGAI *brought.*] You are looking at what a well-dressed Nigerian woman wears— [*She parades for* RUTH, *her hair completely hidden by the headdress; she is coquettishly fanning herself with an ornate oriental*

---

5. Abortions were illegal and dangerous in the United States at that time.

fan, mistakenly more like Butterfly⁶ than any Nigerian that ever was.] Isn't it beautiful? [*She promenades to the radio and, with an arrogant flourish, turns off the good loud blues that is playing.*] Enough of this assimilationist junk! [RUTH *follows her with her eyes as she goes to the phonograph and puts on a record and turns and waits ceremoniously for the music to come up. Then, with a shout—*] OCOMOGOSIAY!

[RUTH *jumps. The music comes up, a lovely Nigerian melody.* BENEATHA *listens, enraptured, her eyes far away—"back to the past." She begins to dance.* RUTH *is dumbfounded.*]

RUTH: What kind of dance is that?
BENEATHA: A folk dance.
RUTH: [*Pearl Bailey.*]⁷ What kind of folks do that, honey?
BENEATHA: It's from Nigeria. It's a dance of welcome.
RUTH: Who you welcoming?
BENEATHA: The men back to the village.
RUTH: Where they been?
BENEATHA: How should I know—out hunting or something. Anyway, they are coming back now . . .
RUTH: Well, that's good.
BENEATHA: [*With the record.*]

*Alundi, alundi
Alundi alunya
Jop pu a jeepua
Ang gu sooooooooooo*

*Ai yai yae . . .
Ayehaye—alundi . . .*

[WALTER *comes in during this performance; he has obviously been drinking. He leans against the door heavily and watches his sister, at first with distaste. Then his eyes look off—"back to the past"—as he lifts both his fists to the roof, screaming.*]

WALTER: YEAH . . . AND ETHIOPIA STRETCH FORTH HER HANDS AGAIN! . . .
RUTH: [*Drily, looking at him.*] Yes—and Africa sure is claiming her own tonight. [*She gives them both up and starts ironing again.*]
WALTER: [*All in a drunken, dramatic shout.*] Shut up! . . . I'm digging them drums . . . them drums move me! . . . [*He makes his weaving way to his wife's face and leans in close to her.*] In my heart of hearts— [*He thumps his chest.*] —I am much warrior!
RUTH: [*Without even looking up.*] In your heart of hearts you are much drunkard.
WALTER: [*Coming away from her and starting to wander around the room, shout-*

6. Butterfly McQueen (1911–1995), African American actor who appeared in *Gone with the Wind*.
7. That is, in the manner of the popular African American singer and entertainer (1918–1990).

ing.] Me and Jomo ... [*Intently, in his sister's face. She has stopped dancing to watch him in this unknown mood.*] That's my man, Kenyatta.[8] [*Shouting and thumping his chest.*] FLAMING SPEAR! HOT DAMN! [*He is suddenly in possession of an imaginary spear and actively spearing enemies all over the room.*] OCOMOGOSIAY ... THE LION IS WAKING ... OWIMOWEH! [*He pulls his shirt open and leaps up on a table and gestures with his spear. The bell rings.* RUTH *goes to answer.*]

BENEATHA: [*To encourage* WALTER, *thoroughly caught up with this side of him.*] OCOMOGOSIAY, FLAMING SPEAR!

WALTER: [*On the table, very far gone, his eyes pure glass sheets. He sees what we cannot, that he is a leader of his people, a great chief, a descendant of Chaka,[9] and that the hour to march has come.*] Listen, my black brothers—

BENEATHA: OCOMOGOSIAY!

WALTER: —Do you hear the waters rushing against the shores of the coast-lands—

BENEATHA: OCOMOGOSIAY!

WALTER: —Do you hear the screeching of the cocks in yonder hills beyond where the chiefs meet in council for the coming of the mighty war—

BENEATHA: OCOMOGOSIAY!

WALTER: —Do you hear the beating of the wings of the birds flying low over the mountains and the low places of our land—

[RUTH *opens the door.* GEORGE MURCHISON *enters.*]

BENEATHA: OCOMOGOSIAY!

WALTER: —Do you hear the singing of the women, singing the war songs of our fathers to the babies in the great houses ... singing the sweet war songs? OH, DO YOU HEAR, MY BLACK BROTHERS!

BENEATHA: [*Completely gone.*] We hear you, Flaming Spear—

WALTER: Telling us to prepare for the greatness of the time— [*To* GEORGE.] Black Brother!

[*He extends his hand for the fraternal clasp.*]

GEORGE: Black Brother, hell!

RUTH: [*Having had enough, and embarrassed for the family.*] Beneatha, you got company—what's the matter with you? Walter Lee Younger, get down off that table and stop acting like a fool ...

[WALTER *comes down off the table suddenly and makes a quick exit to the bathroom.*]

RUTH: He's had a little to drink ... I don't know what her excuse is.

GEORGE: [*To* BENEATHA.] Look honey, we're going *to* the theatre—we're not going to be *in* it ... so go change, huh?

RUTH: You expect this boy to go out with you looking like that?

---

8. Jomo Kenyatta (1893–1978), African political leader and first president of Kenya (1964–1978).
9. Zulu chief (1786–1828), also known as "Shaka" and called "The Black Napoleon" for his strategic and organizational genius.

BENEATHA: [*Looking at* GEORGE.] That's up to George. If he's ashamed of his heritage—

GEORGE: Oh, don't be so proud of yourself, Bennie—just because you look eccentric.

BENEATHA: How can something that's natural be eccentric?

GEORGE: That's what being eccentric means—being natural. Get dressed.

BENEATHA: I don't like that, George.

RUTH: Why must you and your brother make an argument out of everything people say?

BENEATHA: Because I hate assimilationist Negroes!

RUTH: Will somebody please tell me what assimila-who-ever means!

GEORGE: Oh, it's just a college girl's way of calling people Uncle Toms— but that isn't what it means at all.

RUTH: Well, what does it mean?

BENEATHA: [*Cutting* GEORGE *off and staring at him as she replies to* RUTH.] It means someone who is willing to give up his own culture and submerge himself completely in the dominant, and in this case, *oppressive* culture!

GEORGE: Oh, dear, dear, dear! Here we go! A lecture on the African past! On our Great West African Heritage! In one second we will hear all about the great Ashanti empires; the great Songhay civilizations; and the great sculpture of Bénin—and then some poetry in the Bantu—and the whole monologue will end with the word *heritage*! [*Nastily.*] Let's face it, baby, your heritage is nothing but a bunch of raggedy-assed spirituals and some grass huts!

BENEATHA: *Grass huts!* [RUTH *crosses to her and forcibly pushes her toward the bedroom.*] See there . . . you are standing there in your splendid ignorance talking about people who were the first to smelt iron on the face of the earth! [RUTH *is pushing her through the door.*] The Ashanti were performing surgical operations when the English— [RUTH *pulls the door to, with* BENEATHA *on the other side, and smiles graciously at* GEORGE. BENEATHA *opens the door and shouts the end of the sentence defiantly at* GEORGE.] —were still tattooing themselves with blue dragons . . . [*She goes back inside.*]

RUTH: Have a seat, George. [*They both sit.* RUTH *folds her hands rather primly on her lap, determined to demonstrate the civilization of the family.*] Warm, ain't it? I mean for September. [*Pause.*] Just like they always say about Chicago weather: If it's too hot or cold for you, just wait a minute and it'll change. [*She smiles happily at this cliché of clichés.*] Everybody say it's got to do with them bombs and things they keep setting off.[1] [*Pause.*] Would you like a nice cold beer?

GEORGE: No, thank you. I don't care for beer. [*He looks at his watch.*] I hope she hurries up.

RUTH: What time is the show?

GEORGE: It's an eight-thirty curtain. That's just Chicago, though. In New York standard curtain time is eight forty.

---

1. In the 1950s, people commonly blamed weather fluctuations on atomic testing.

[*He is rather proud of this knowledge.*]

RUTH: [*Properly appreciating it.*] You get to New York a lot?

GEORGE: [*Offhand.*] Few times a year.

RUTH: Oh—that's nice. I've never been to New York.

[WALTER *enters. We feel he has relieved himself, but the edge of unreality is still with him.*]

WALTER: New York ain't got nothing Chicago ain't. Just a bunch of hustling people all squeezed up together—being "Eastern."

[*He turns his face into a screw of displeasure.*]

GEORGE: Oh—you've been?

WALTER: *Plenty* of times.

RUTH: [*Shocked at the lie.*] Walter Lee Younger!

WALTER: [*Staring her down.*] Plenty! [*Pause.*] What we got to drink in this house? Why don't you offer this man some refreshment. [*To* GEORGE.] They don't know how to entertain people in this house, man.

GEORGE: Thank you—I don't really care for anything.

WALTER: [*Feeling his head; sobriety coming.*] Where's Mama?

RUTH: She ain't come back yet.

WALTER: [*Looking* MURCHISON *over from head to toe, scrutinizing his carefully casual tweed sports jacket over cashmere V-neck sweater over soft eyelet shirt and tie, and soft slacks, finished off with white buckskin shoes.*] Why all you college boys wear them fairyish-looking white shoes?

RUTH: Walter Lee!

[GEORGE MURCHISON *ignores the remark.*]

WALTER: [*To* RUTH.] Well, they look crazy as hell—white shoes, cold as it is.

RUTH: [*Crushed.*] You have to excuse him—

WALTER: No he don't! Excuse me for what? What you always excusing me for! I'll excuse myself when I needs to be excused! [*A pause.*] They look as funny as them black knee socks Beneatha wears out of here all the time.

RUTH: It's the college *style*, Walter.

WALTER: Style, hell, She looks like she got burnt legs or something!

RUTH: Oh, Walter—

WALTER: [*An irritable mimic.*] Oh, Walter! Oh, Walter! [*To* MURCHISON.] How's your old man making out? I understand you all going to buy that big hotel on the Drive?[2] [*He finds a beer in the refrigerator, wanders over to* MURCHISON, *sipping and wiping his lips with the back of his hand, and straddling a chair backwards to talk to the other man.*] Shrewd move. Your old man is all right, man. [*Tapping his head and half winking for emphasis.*] I mean he knows how to operate. I mean he thinks *big*, you know what I mean, I mean for a *home*, you know? But I think he's kind of running

---

2. Lake Shore Drive, a scenic thoroughfare along Lake Michigan.

out of ideas now. I'd like to talk to him. Listen, man, I got some plans that could turn this city upside down. I mean I think like he does. *Big.* Invest big, gamble big, hell, lose *big* if you have to, you know what I mean. It's hard to find a man on this whole Southside who understands my kind of thinking—you dig? [*He scrutinizes* MURCHISON *again, drinks his beer, squints his eyes and leans in close, confidential, man to man.*] Me and you ought to sit down and talk sometimes, man. Man, I got me some ideas . . .

GEORGE: [*With boredom.*] Yeah—sometimes we'll have to do that, Walter.

WALTER: [*Understanding the indifference, and offended.*] Yeah—well, when you get the time, man. I know you a busy little boy.

RUTH: Walter, please—

WALTER: [*Bitterly, hurt.*] I know ain't nothing in this world as busy as you colored college boys with your fraternity pins and white shoes . . .

RUTH: [*Covering her face with humiliation.*] Oh, Walter Lee—

WALTER: I see you all the time—with the books tucked under your arms—going to your [*British A—a mimic.*] "clahsses." And for what! What the hell you learning over there? Filling up your heads— [*Counting off on his fingers.*] —with the sociology and the psychology—but they teaching you how to be a man? How to take over and run the world? They teaching you how to run a rubber plantation or a steel mill? Naw—just to talk proper and read books and wear white shoes . . .

GEORGE: [*Looking at him with distaste, a little above it all.*] You're all wacked up with bitterness, man.

WALTER: [*Intently, almost quietly, between the teeth, glaring at the boy.*] And you—ain't you bitter, man? Ain't you just about had it yet? Don't you see no stars gleaming that you can't reach out and grab? You happy?—You contented son-of-a-bitch—you happy? You got it made? Bitter? Man, I'm a volcano. Bitter? Here I am a giant—surrounded by ants! Ants who can't even understand what it is the giant is talking about.

RUTH: [*Passionately and suddenly.*] Oh, Walter—ain't you with nobody!

WALTER: [*Violently.*] No! 'Cause ain't nobody with me! Not even my own mother!

RUTH: Walter, that's a terrible thing to say!

[BENEATHA *enters, dressed for the evening in a cocktail dress and earrings.*]

GEORGE: Well—hey, you look great.

BENEATHA: Let's go, George. See you all later.

RUTH: Have a nice time.

GEORGE: Thanks. Good night. [*To* WALTER, *sarcastically.*] Good night, Prometheus.[3]

[BENEATHA *and* GEORGE *exit.*]

---

3. In Greek mythology, Prometheus represented the bold creative spirit; he stole fire from Olympus (the locale of the gods) and gave it to humankind.

WALTER: [*To* RUTH.] Who is Prometheus?

RUTH: I don't know. Don't worry about it.

WALTER: [*In fury, pointing after* GEORGE.] See there—they get to a point where they can't insult you man to man—they got to go talk about something ain't nobody never heard of!

RUTH: How do you know it was an insult? [*To humor him.*] Maybe Prometheus is a nice fellow.

WALTER: Prometheus! I bet there ain't even no such thing! I bet that simpleminded clown—

RUTH: Walter—

[*She stops what she is doing and looks at him.*]

WALTER: [*Yelling.*] Don't start!

RUTH: Start what?

WALTER: Your nagging! Where was I? Who was I with? How much money did I spend?

RUTH: [*Plaintively.*] Walter Lee—why don't we just try to talk about it . . .

WALTER: [*Not listening.*] I been out talking with people who understand me. People who care about the things I got on my mind.

RUTH: [*Wearily.*] I guess that means people like Willy Harris.

WALTER: Yes, people like Willy Harris.

RUTH: [*With a sudden flash of impatience.*] Why don't you all just hurry up and go into the banking business and stop talking about it!

WALTER: Why? You want to know why? 'Cause we all tied up in a race of people that don't know how to do nothing but moan, pray and have babies!

[*The line is too bitter even for him and he looks at her and sits down.*]

RUTH: Oh, Walter . . . [*Softly.*] Honey, why can't you stop fighting me?

WALTER: [*Without thinking.*] Who's fighting you? Who even cares about you?

[*This line begins the retardation of his mood.*]

RUTH: Well— [*She waits a long time, and then with resignation starts to put away her things.*] I guess I might as well go on to bed . . . [*More or less to herself.*] I don't know where we lost it . . . but we have . . . [*Then, to him.*] I—I'm sorry about this new baby, Walter. I guess maybe I better go on and do what I started . . . I guess I just didn't realize how bad things was with us . . . I guess I just didn't really realize— [*She starts out to the bedroom and stops.*] You want some hot milk?

WALTER: Hot milk?

RUTH: Yes—hot milk.

WALTER: Why hot milk?

RUTH: 'Cause after all that liquor you come home with you ought to have something hot in your stomach.

WALTER: I don't want no milk.

RUTH: You want some coffee then?

WALTER: No, I don't want no coffee. I don't want nothing hot to drink. [*Almost plaintively.*] Why you always trying to give me something to eat?

RUTH: [*Standing and looking at him helplessly.*] What else can I give you, Walter Lee Younger?

[*She stands and looks at him and presently turns to go out again. He lifts his head and watches her going away from him in a new mood which began to emerge when he asked her "Who cares about you?"*]

WALTER: It's been rough, ain't it, baby? [*She hears and stops but does not turn around and he continues to her back.*] I guess between two people there ain't never as much understood as folks generally thinks there is. I mean like between me and you— [*She turns to face him.*] How we gets to the place where we scared to talk softness to each other. [*He waits, thinking hard himself.*] Why you think it got to be like that? [*He is thoughtful, almost as a child would be.*] Ruth, what is it gets into people ought to be close?

RUTH: I don't know, honey. I think about it a lot.

WALTER: On account of you and me, you mean? The way things are with us. The way something done come down between us.

RUTH: There ain't so much between us, Walter . . . Not when you come to me and try to talk to me. Try to be with me . . . a little even.

WALTER: [*Total honesty.*] Sometimes . . . sometimes . . . I don't even know how to try.

RUTH: Walter—

WALTER: Yes?

RUTH: [*Coming to him, gently and with misgiving, but coming to him.*] Honey . . . life don't have to be like this. I mean sometimes people can do things so that things are better . . . You remember how we used to talk when Travis was born . . . about the way we were going to live . . . the kind of house . . . [*She is stroking his head.*] Well, it's all starting to slip away from us . . .

[MAMA *enters, and* WALTER *jumps up and shouts at her.*]

WALTER: Mama, where have you been?

MAMA: My—them steps is longer than they used to be. Whew! [*She sits down and ignores him.*] How you feeling this evening, Ruth?

[RUTH *shrugs, disturbed some at having been prematurely interrupted and watching her husband knowingly.*]

WALTER: Mama, where have you been all day?

MAMA: [*Still ignoring him and leaning on the table and changing to more comfortable shoes.*] Where's Travis?

RUTH: I let him go out earlier and he ain't come back yet. Boy, is he going to get it!

WALTER: Mama!

MAMA: [*As if she has heard him for the first time.*] Yes, son?

WALTER: Where did you go this afternoon?

MAMA: I went downtown to tend to some business that I had to tend to.

WALTER: What kind of business?

MAMA: You know better than to question me like a child, Brother.

WALTER: [*Rising and bending over the table.*] Where were you, Mama? [*Bringing *his fists down and shouting.*] Mama, you didn't go do something with that insurance money, something crazy?

[*The front door opens slowly, interrupting him, and* TRAVIS *peeks his head in, less than hopefully.*]

TRAVIS: [*To his mother.*] Mama, I—
RUTH: "Mama I" nothing! You're going to get it, boy! Get on in that bedroom and get yourself ready!
TRAVIS: But I—
MAMA: Why don't you all never let the child explain hisself.
RUTH: Keep out of it now, Lena.

[MAMA *clamps her lips together, and* RUTH *advances toward her son menacingly.*]

RUTH: A thousand times I have told you not to go off like that—
MAMA: [*Holding out her arms to her grandson.*] Well—at least let me tell him something. I want him to be the first one to hear . . . Come here, Travis. [*The boy obeys, gladly.*] Travis— [*She takes him by the shoulder and looks into his face.*] —you know that money we got in the mail this morning?
TRAVIS: Yes'm—
MAMA: Well—what you think your grandmama gone and done with that money?
TRAVIS: I don't know, Grandmama.
MAMA: [*Putting her finger on his nose for emphasis.*] She went out and she bought you a house! [*The explosion comes from* WALTER *at the end of the revelation and he jumps up and turns away from all of them in a fury.* MAMA *continues, to* TRAVIS.] You glad about the house? It's going to be yours when you get to be a man.
TRAVIS: Yeah—I always wanted to live in a house.
MAMA: All right, gimme some sugar then— [TRAVIS *puts his arms around her neck as she watches her son over the boy's shoulder. Then, to* TRAVIS, *after the embrace.*] Now when you say your prayers tonight, you thank God and your grandfather—'cause it was him who give you the house—in his way.
RUTH: [*Taking the boy from* MAMA *and pushing him toward the bedroom.*] Now you get out of here and get ready for your beating.
TRAVIS: Aw, Mama—
RUTH: Get on in there— [*Closing the door behind him and turning radiantly to her mother-in-law.*] So you went and did it!
MAMA: [*Quietly, looking at her son with pain.*] Yes, I did.
RUTH: [*Raising both arms classically.*] Praise God! [*Looks at* WALTER *a moment, who says nothing. She crosses rapidly to her husband.*] Please, honey—let me be glad . . . you be glad too. [*She has laid her hands on his shoulders, but he shakes himself free of her roughly, without turning to face her.*] Oh, Walter . . . a home . . . a home. [*She comes back to* MAMA.] Well—where is it? How big is it? How much it going to cost?
MAMA: Well—
RUTH: When we moving?

MAMA: [*Smiling at her.*] First of the month.

RUTH: [*Throwing back her head with jubilance.*] Praise God!

MAMA: [*Tentatively, still looking at her son's back turned against her and* RUTH.] It's—it's a nice house too . . . [*She cannot help speaking directly to him. An imploring quality in her voice, her manner, makes her almost like a girl now.*] Three bedrooms—nice big one for you and Ruth . . . Me and Beneatha still have to share our room, but Travis have one of his own—and [*With difficulty.*] I figure if the—new baby—is a boy, we could get one of them double-decker outfits . . . And there's a yard with a little patch of dirt where I could maybe get to grow me a few flowers . . . And a nice big basement . . .

RUTH: Walter honey, be glad—

MAMA: [*Still to his back, fingering things on the table.*] 'Course I don't want to make it sound fancier than it is . . . It's just a plain little old house—but it's made good and solid—and it will be *ours*. Walter Lee—it makes a difference in a man when he can walk on floors that belong to *him* . . .

RUTH: Where is it?

MAMA: [*Frightened at this telling.*] Well—well—it's out there in Clybourne Park—[4]

[RUTH's *radiance fades abruptly, and* WALTER *finally turns slowly to face his mother with incredulity and hostility.*]

RUTH: Where?

MAMA: [*Matter-of-factly.*] Four o six Clybourne Street, Clybourne Park.

RUTH: Clybourne Park? Mama, there ain't no colored people living in Clybourne Park.

MAMA: [*Almost idiotically.*] Well, I guess there's going to be some now.

WALTER: [*Bitterly.*] So that's the peace and comfort you went out and bought for us today!

MAMA: [*Raising her eyes to meet his finally.*] Son—I just tried to find the nicest place for the least amount of money for my family.

RUTH: [*Trying to recover from the shock.*] Well—well—'course I ain't one never been 'fraid of no crackers[5] mind you—but—well, wasn't there no other houses nowhere?

MAMA: Them houses they put up for colored in them areas way out all seem to cost twice as much as other houses. I did the best I could.

RUTH: [*Struck senseless with the news, in its various degrees of goodness and trouble, she sits a moment, her fists propping her chin in thought, and then she starts to rise, bringing her fists down with vigor, the radiance spreading from cheek to cheek again.*] Well—well!—All I can say is—if this is my time in life—*my time*—to say good-bye— [*And she builds with momentum as she starts to circle the room with an exuberant, almost tearfully happy release.*] —to these God-damned cracking walls!— [*She pounds the walls.*] —and these marching roaches!— [*She wipes at an imaginary army of marching roaches.*] —and this cramped little closet which ain't now or never was no kitchen! . . . then

4. On Chicago's Near North Side. 5. Derogatory term for poor whites.

I say it loud and good, *Hallelujah! and good-bye misery . . . I don't never want to see your ugly face again!* [*She laughs joyously, having practically destroyed the apartment, and flings her arms up and lets them come down happily, slowly, reflectively, over her abdomen, aware for the first time perhaps that the life therein pulses with happiness and not despair.*] Lena?

MAMA: [*Moved, watching her happiness.*] Yes, honey?

RUTH: [*Looking off.*] Is there—is there a whole lot of sunlight?

MAMA: [*Understanding.*] Yes, child, there's a whole lot of sunlight.

[*Long pause.*]

RUTH: [*Collecting herself and going to the door of the room* TRAVIS *is in.*] Well—I guess I better see 'bout Travis. [*To* MAMA.] Lord, I sure don't feel like whipping nobody today!

[*She exits.*]

MAMA: [*The mother and son are left alone now and the mother waits a long time, considering deeply, before she speaks.*] Son—you—you understand what I done, don't you? [WALTER *is silent and sullen.*] I—I just seen my family falling apart today . . . just falling to pieces in front of my eyes . . . We couldn't of gone on like we was today. We was going backwards 'stead of forwards—talking 'bout killing babies and wishing each other was dead . . . When it gets like that in life—you just got to do something different, push on out and do something bigger . . . [*She waits.*] I wish you say something, son . . . I wish you'd say how deep inside you you think I done the right thing—

WALTER: [*Crossing slowly to his bedroom door and finally turning there and speaking measuredly.*] What you need me to say you done right for? *You* the head of this family. You run our lives like you want to. It was your money and you did what you wanted with it. So what you need for me to say it was all right for? [*Bitterly, to hurt her as deeply as he knows is possible.*] So you butchered up a dream of mine—you—who always talking 'bout your children's dreams . . .

MAMA: Walter Lee—

[*He just closes the door behind him.* MAMA *sits alone, thinking heavily.*]

[CURTAIN.]

Scene Two

Time: Friday night. A few weeks later.

At rise: Packing crates mark the intention of the family to move. BENEATHA *and* GEORGE *come in, presumably from an evening out again.*

GEORGE: O.K. . . . O.K., whatever you say . . . [*They both sit on the couch. He tries to kiss her. She moves away.*] Look, we've had a nice evening; let's not spoil it, huh? . . .

[*He again turns her head and tries to nuzzle in and she turns away from him, not with distaste but with momentary lack of interest; in a mood to pursue what they were talking about.*]

BENEATHA: I'm *trying* to talk to you.

GEORGE: We always talk.

BENEATHA: Yes—and I love to talk.

GEORGE: [*Exasperated; rising.*] I know it and I don't mind it sometimes . . . I want you to cut it out, see—The moody stuff, I mean. I don't like it. You're a nice-looking girl . . . all over. That's all you need, honey, forget the atmosphere. Guys aren't going to go for the atmosphere—they're going to go for what they see. Be glad for that. Drop the Garbo[6] routine. It doesn't go with you. As for myself, I want a nice— [*Groping.*] —simple [*Thoughtfully.*] —sophisticated girl . . . not a poet—O.K.?

[*She rebuffs him again and he starts to leave.*]

BENEATHA: Why are you angry?

GEORGE: Because this is stupid! I don't go out with you to discuss the nature of "quiet desperation"[7] or to hear all about your thoughts— because the world will go on thinking what it thinks regardless—

BENEATHA: Then why read books? Why go to school?

GEORGE: [*With artificial patience, counting on his fingers.*] It's simple. You read books—to learn facts—to get grades—to pass the course—to get a degree. That's all—it has nothing to do with thoughts.

[*A long pause.*]

BENEATHA: I see. [*A longer pause as she looks at him.*] Good night, George.

[GEORGE *looks at her a little oddly, and starts to exit. He meets* MAMA *coming in.*]

GEORGE: Oh—hello, Mrs. Younger.

MAMA: Hello, George, how you feeling?

GEORGE: Fine—fine, how are you?

MAMA: Oh, a little tired. You know them steps can get you after a day's work. You all have a nice time tonight?

GEORGE: Yes—a fine time. Well, good night.

MAMA: Good night. [*He exits.* MAMA *closes the door behind her.*] Hello, honey. What you sitting like that for?

BENEATHA: I'm just sitting.

MAMA: Didn't you have a nice time?

BENEATHA: No.

MAMA: No? What's the matter?

BENEATHA: Mama, George is a fool—honest. [*She rises.*]

6. Greta Garbo (1905–1990), Swedish-born American film star whose sultry, remote, and European femininity was widely imitated.

7. In *Walden* (1854), Henry Thoreau asserted that "the mass of men lead lives of quiet desperation."

MAMA: [*Hustling around unloading the packages she has entered with. She stops.*] Is he, baby?
BENEATHA: Yes.

[BENEATHA *makes up* TRAVIS' *bed as she talks.*]

MAMA: You sure?
BENEATHA: Yes.
MAMA: Well—I guess you better not waste your time with no fools.

[BENEATHA *looks up at her mother, watching her put groceries in the refrigerator. Finally she gathers up her things and starts into the bedroom. At the door she stops and looks back at her mother.*]

BENEATHA: Mama—
MAMA: Yes, baby—
BENEATHA: Thank you.
MAMA: For what?
BENEATHA: For understanding me this time.

[*She exits quickly and the mother stands, smiling a little, looking at the place where* BENEATHA *just stood.* RUTH *enters.*]

RUTH: Now don't you fool with any of this stuff, Lena—
MAMA: Oh, I just thought I'd sort a few things out.

[*The phone rings.* RUTH *answers.*]

RUTH: [*At the phone.*] Hello—Just a minute. [*Goes to door.*] Walter, it's Mrs. Arnold. [*Waits. Goes back to the phone. Tense.*] Hello. Yes, this is his wife speaking . . . He's lying down now. Yes . . . well, he'll be in tomorrow. He's been very sick. Yes—I know we should have called, but we were so sure he'd be able to come in today. Yes—yes, I'm very sorry. Yes . . . Thank you very much. [*She hangs up.* WALTER *is standing in the doorway of the bedroom behind her.*] That was Mrs. Arnold.
WALTER: [*Indifferently.*] Was it?
RUTH: She said if you don't come in tomorrow that they are getting a new man . . .
WALTER: Ain't that sad—ain't that crying sad.
RUTH: She said Mr. Arnold has had to take a cab for three days . . . Walter, you ain't been to work for three days! [*This is a revelation to her.*] Where you been, Walter Lee Younger? [WALTER *looks at her and starts to laugh.*] You're going to lose your job.
WALTER: That's right . . .
RUTH: Oh, Walter, and with your mother working like a dog every day—
WALTER: That's sad too—Everything is sad.
MAMA: What you been doing for these three days, son?
WALTER: Mama—you don't know all the things a man what got leisure can find to do in this city . . . What's this—Friday night? Well—Wednesday I borrowed Willy Harris' car and I went for a drive . . . just me and myself and I drove and drove . . . Way out . . . way past South Chicago, and I parked the car and I sat and looked at the steel mills all day long. I just

sat in the car and looked at them big black chimneys for hours. Then I drove back and I went to the Green Hat. [*Pause.*] And Thursday—Thursday I borrowed the car again and I got in it and I pointed it the other way and I drove the other way—for hours—way, way up to Wisconsin, and I looked at the farms. I just drove and looked at the farms. Then I drove back and I went to the Green Hat. [*Pause.*] And today—today I didn't get the car. Today I just walked. All over the Southside. And I looked at the Negroes and they looked at me and finally I just sat down on the curb at Thirty-ninth and South Parkway and I just sat there and watched the Negroes go by. And then I went to the Green Hat. You all sad? You all depressed? And you know where I am going right now—

[RUTH *goes out quietly.*]

MAMA: Oh, Big Walter, is this the harvest of our days?

WALTER: You know what I like about the Green Hat? [*He turns the radio on and a steamy, deep blues pours into the room.*] I like this little cat they got there who blows a sax . . . He blows. He talks to me. He ain't but 'bout five feet tall and he's got a conked head[8] and his eyes is always closed and he's all music—

MAMA: [*Rising and getting some papers out of her handbag.*] Walter—

WALTER: And there's this other guy who plays the piano . . . and they got a sound. I mean they can work on some music . . . They got the best little combo in the world in the Green Hat . . . You can just sit there and drink and listen to them three men play and you realize that don't nothing matter worth a damn, but just being there—

MAMA: I've helped do it to you, haven't I, son? Walter, I been wrong.

WALTER: Naw—you ain't never been wrong about nothing, Mama.

MAMA: Listen to me, now. I say I been wrong, son. That I been doing to you what the rest of the world been doing to you. [*She stops and he looks up slowly at her and she meets his eyes pleadingly.*] Walter—what you ain't never understood is that I ain't got nothing, don't own nothing, ain't never really wanted nothing that wasn't for you. There ain't nothing as precious to me . . . There ain't nothing worth holding on to, money, dreams, nothing else—if it means—if it means it's going to destroy my boy. [*She puts her papers in front of him and he watches her without speaking or moving.*] I paid the man thirty-five hundred dollars down on the house. That leaves sixty-five hundred dollars. Monday morning I want you to take this money and take three thousand dollars and put it in a savings account for Beneatha's medical schooling. The rest you put in a checking account—with your name on it. And from now on any penny that come out of it or that go in it is for you to look after. For you to decide. [*She drops her hands a little helplessly.*] It ain't much, but it's all I got in the world and I'm putting it in your hands. I'm telling you to be the head of this family from now on like you supposed to be.

8. Straightened hair.

WALTER: [*Stares at the money.*] You trust me like that, Mama?

MAMA: I ain't never stop trusting you. Like I ain't never stop loving you.

[*She goes out, and* WALTER *sits looking at the money on the table as the music continues in its idiom, pulsing in the room. Finally, in a decisive gesture, he gets up, and, in mingled joy and desperation, picks up the money. At the same moment,* TRAVIS *enters for bed.*]

TRAVIS: What's the matter, Daddy? You drunk?

WALTER: [*Sweetly, more sweetly than we have ever known him.*] No, Daddy ain't drunk. Daddy ain't going to never be drunk again. . . .

TRAVIS: Well, good night, Daddy.

[*The father has come from behind the couch and leans over, embracing his son.*]

WALTER: Son, I feel like talking to you tonight.

TRAVIS: About what?

WALTER: Oh, about a lot of things. About you and what kind of man you going to be when you grow up . . . Son—son, what do you want to be when you grow up?

TRAVIS: A bus driver.

WALTER: [*Laughing a little.*] A what? Man, that ain't nothing to want to be!

TRAVIS: Why not?

WALTER: 'Cause, man—it ain't big enough—you know what I mean.

TRAVIS: I don't know then. I can't make up my mind. Sometimes Mama asks me that too. And sometimes when I tell you I just want to be like you—she says she don't want me to be like that and sometimes she says she does . . .

WALTER: [*Gathering him up in his arms.*] You know what, Travis? In seven years you going to be seventeen years old. And things is going to be very different with us in seven years, Travis . . . One day when you are seventeen I'll come home—home from my office downtown somewhere—

TRAVIS: You don't work in no office, Daddy.

WALTER: No—but after tonight. After what your daddy gonna do tonight, there's going to be offices—a whole lot of offices . . .

TRAVIS: What you gonna do tonight, Daddy?

WALTER: You wouldn't understand yet, son, but your daddy's gonna make a transaction . . . a business transaction that's going to change our lives . . . That's how come one day when you 'bout seventeen years old I'll come home and I'll be pretty tired, you know what I mean, after a day of conferences and secretaries getting things wrong the way they do . . . 'cause an executive's life is hell, man— [*The more he talks the farther away he gets.*] And I'll pull the car up on the driveway . . . just a plain black Chrysler, I think, with white walls—no—black tires. More elegant. Rich people don't have to be flashy . . . though I'll have to get something a little sportier for Ruth—maybe a Cadillac convertible to do her shopping in . . . And I'll come up the steps to the house and the gardener will be clipping away at the hedges and he'll say, "Good evening, Mr. Younger."

And I'll say, "Hello, Jefferson, how are you this evening?" And I'll go inside and Ruth will come downstairs and meet me at the door and we'll kiss each other and she'll take my arm and we'll go up to your room to see you sitting on the floor with the catalogues of all the great schools in America around you . . . All the great schools in the world. And—and I'll say, all right son—it's your seventeenth birthday, what is it you've decided? . . . Just tell me where you want to go to school and you'll *go.* Just tell me, what it is you want to be—and you'll *be* it . . . Whatever you want to be—Yessir! [*He holds his arms open for* TRAVIS.] You just name it, son . . . [TRAVIS *leaps into them.*] and I hand you the world!

> [WALTER'*s voice has risen in pitch and hysterical promise and on the last line he lifts* TRAVIS *high.*]

[BLACKOUT.]

Scene Three

Time: Saturday, moving day, one week later.

Before the curtain rises, RUTH'*s voice, a strident, dramatic church alto, cuts through the silence.*

It is, in the darkness, a triumphant surge, a penetrating statement of expectation: "Oh, Lord, I don't feel no ways tired! Children, oh, glory hallelujah!"

As the curtain rises we see that RUTH *is alone in the living room, finishing up the family's packing. It is moving day. She is nailing crates and tying cartons.* BENEATHA *enters, carrying a guitar case, and watches her exuberant sister-in-law.*

RUTH: Hey!
BENEATHA: [*Putting away the case.*] Hi.
RUTH: [*Pointing at a package.*] Honey—look in that package there and see what I found on sale this morning at the South Center. [RUTH *gets up and moves to the package and draws out some curtains.*] Lookahere—hand-turned hems!
BENEATHA: How do you know the window size out there?
RUTH: [*Who hadn't thought of that.*] Oh—Well, they bound to fit something in the whole house. Anyhow, they was too good a bargain to pass up. [RUTH *slaps her head, suddenly remembering something.*] Oh, Bennie—I meant to put a special note on that carton over there. That's your mama's good china and she wants 'em to be very careful with it.
BENEATHA: I'll do it.

> [BENEATHA *finds a piece of paper and starts to draw large letters on it.*]

RUTH: You know what I'm going to do soon as I get in that new house?
BENEATHA: What?
RUTH: Honey—I'm going to run me a tub of water up to here . . . [*With her fingers practically up to her nostrils.*] And I'm going to get in it—and I am going to sit . . . and sit . . . and sit in that hot water and the first person who knocks to tell *me* to hurry up and come out—

BENEATHA: Gets shot at sunrise.

RUTH: [*Laughing happily.*] You said it, sister! [*Noticing how large* BENEATHA *is absent-mindedly making the note.*] Honey, they ain't going to read that from no airplane.

BENEATHA: [*Laughing herself.*] I guess I always think things have more emphasis if they are big, somehow.

RUTH: [*Looking up at her and smiling.*] You and your brother seem to have that as a philosophy of life. Lord, that man—done changed so 'round here. You know—you know what we did last night? Me and Walter Lee?

BENEATHA: What?

RUTH: [*Smiling to herself.*] We went to the movies. [*Looking at* BENEATHA *to see if she understands.*] We went to the movies. You know the last time me and Walter went to the movies together?

BENEATHA: No.

RUTH: Me neither. That's how long it been. [*Smiling again.*] But we went last night.

The picture wasn't much good, but that didn't seem to matter. We went—and we held hands.

BENEATHA: Oh, Lord!

RUTH: We held hands—and you know what?

BENEATHA: What?

RUTH: When we come out of the show it was late and dark and all the stores and things was closed up . . . and it was kind of chilly and there wasn't many people on the streets . . . and we was still holding hands, me and Walter.

BENEATHA: You're killing me.

[WALTER *enters with a large package. His happiness is deep in him; he cannot keep still with his new-found exuberance. He is singing and wiggling and snapping his fingers. He puts his package in a corner and puts a phonograph record, which he has brought in with him, on the record player. As the music comes up he dances over to* RUTH *and tries to get her to dance with him. She gives in at last to his raunchiness and in a fit of giggling allows herself to be drawn into his mood and together they deliberately burlesque an old social dance of their youth.*]

BENEATHA: [*Regarding them a long time as they dance, then drawing in her breath for a deeply exaggerated comment which she does not particularly mean.*] Talk about—oldddddddddd-fashionedddddddd—Negroes!

WALTER: [*Stopping momentarily.*] What kind of Negroes?

[*He says this in fun. He is not angry with her today, nor with anyone. He starts to dance with his wife again.*]

BENEATHA: Old-fashioned.

WALTER: [*As he dances with* RUTH.] You know, when these *New Negroes* have their convention— [*Pointing at his sister.*] —that is going to be the chairman of the Committee on Unending Agitation. [*He goes on dancing, then stops.*] Race, race, race! . . . Girl, I do believe you are the first person in the history of the entire human race to successfully brainwash yourself. [BENEATHA *breaks up and he goes on dancing. He stops again, enjoying his tease.*] Damn, even the N double A C P⁹ takes a holiday sometimes! [BENEATHA *and* RUTH *laugh. He dances with* RUTH *some more and starts to laugh and stops and pantomimes someone over an operating table.*] I can just see that chick someday looking down at some poor cat on an operating table before she starts to slice him, saying . . . [*Pulling his sleeves back maliciously.*] "By the way, what are your views on civil rights down there? . . ."

[*He laughs at her again and starts to dance happily. The bell sounds.*]

BENEATHA: Sticks and stones may break my bones but . . . words will never hurt me!

[BENEATHA *goes to the door and opens it as* WALTER *and* RUTH *go on with the clowning.* BENEATHA *is somewhat surprised to see a quiet-looking middle-aged white man in a business suit holding his hat and a briefcase in his hand and consulting a small piece of paper.*]

MAN: Uh—how do you do, miss. I am looking for a Mrs.— [*He looks at the slip of paper.*] Mrs. Lena Younger?

BENEATHA: [*Smoothing her hair with slight embarrassment.*] Oh—yes, that's my mother. Excuse me [*She closes the door and turns to quiet the other two.*] Ruth! Brother! Somebody's here. [*Then she opens the door. The* MAN *casts a curious quick glance at all of them.*] Uh—come in please.

MAN: [*Coming in.*] Thank you.

BENEATHA: My mother isn't here just now. Is it business?

MAN: Yes . . . well, of a sort.

WALTER: [*Freely, the Man of the House.*] Have a seat. I'm Mrs. Younger's son. I look after most of her business matters.

[RUTH *and* BENEATHA *exchange amused glances.*]

MAN: [*Regarding* WALTER, *and sitting.*] Well—My name is Karl Lindner . . .

WALTER: [*Stretching out his hand.*] Walter Younger. This is my wife— [RUTH *nods politely.*] —and my sister.

LINDNER: How do you do.

WALTER: [*Amiably, as he sits himself easily on a chair, leaning with interest forward on his knees and looking expectantly into the newcomer's face.*] What can we do for you, Mr. Lindner!

LINDNER: [*Some minor shuffling of the hat and briefcase on his knees.*] Well—I am a representative of the Clybourne Park Improvement Association—

WALTER: [*Pointing.*] Why don't you sit your things on the floor?

LINDNER: Oh—yes. Thank you. [*He slides the briefcase and hat under the chair.*] And as I was saying—I am from the Clybourne Park Improvement Association and we have had it brought to our attention at the last meeting that you people—or at least your mother—has bought a piece of resi-

---

9. National Association for the Advancement of Colored People, civil rights organization founded in 1909.

dential property at— [*He digs for the slip of paper again.*] —four o six Clybourne Street . . .

WALTER: That's right. Care for something to drink? Ruth, get Mr. Lindner
a beer.

LINDNER: [*Upset for some reason.*] Oh—no, really. I mean thank you very
much, but no thank you.

RUTH: [*Innocently.*] Some coffee?

LINDNER: Thank you, nothing at all.

[BENEATHA *is watching the man carefully.*]

LINDNER: Well, I don't know how much you folks know about our organization. [*He is a gentle man; thoughtful and somewhat labored in his manner.*]
It is one of these community organizations set up to look after—oh, you
know, things like block upkeep and special projects and we also have
what we call our New Neighbors Orientation Committee . . .

BENEATHA: [*Drily.*] Yes—and what do they do?

LINDNER: [*Turning a little to her and then returning the main force to* WALTER.]
Well—it's what you might call a sort of welcoming committee, I guess.
I mean they, we, I'm the chairman of the committee—go around and see
the new people who move into the neighborhood and sort of give them
the lowdown on the way we do things out in Clybourne Park.

BENEATHA: [*With appreciation of the two meanings, which escape* RUTH *and* WAL-
TER.] Un-huh.

LINDNER: And we also have the category of what the association calls— [*He
looks elsewhere.*] —uh—special community problems . . .

BENEATHA: Yes—and what are some of those?

WALTER: Girl, let the man talk.

LINDNER: [*With understated relief.*] Thank you. I would sort of like to explain
this thing in my own way. I mean I want to explain to you in a certain
way.

WALTER: Go ahead.

LINDNER: Yes. Well. I'm going to try to get right to the point. I'm sure we'll
all appreciate that in the long run.

BENEATHA: Yes.

WALTER: Be still now!

LINDNER: Well—

RUTH: [*Still innocently.*] Would you like another chair—you don't look comfortable.

LINDNER: [*More frustrated than annoyed.*] No, thank you very much. Please.
Well—to get right to the point I— [*A great breath, and he is off at last.*] I
am sure you people must be aware of some of the incidents which have
happened in various parts of the city when colored people have moved
into certain areas— [BENEATHA *exhales heavily and starts tossing a piece of
fruit up and down in the air.*] Well—because we have what I think is going
to be a unique type of organization in American community life—not
only do we deplore that kind of thing—but we are trying to do something about it. [BENEATHA *stops tossing and turns with a new and quizzical*

interest to the man.] We feel— [*Gaining confidence in his mission because of the interest in the faces of the people he is talking to.*] —we feel that most of the trouble in this world, when you come right down to it— [*He hits his knee for emphasis.*] —most of the trouble exists because people just don't sit down and talk to each other.

RUTH: [*Nodding as she might in church, pleased with the remark.*] You can say that again, mister.

LINDNER: [*More encouraged by such affirmation.*] That we don't try hard enough in this world to understand the other fellow's problem. The other guy's point of view.

RUTH: Now that's right.

[BENEATHA *and* WALTER *merely watch and listen with genuine interest.*]

LINDNER: Yes—that's the way we feel out in Clybourne Park. And that's why I was elected to come here this afternoon and talk to you people. Friendly like, you know, the way people should talk to each other and see if we couldn't find some way to work this thing out. As I say, the whole business is a matter of *caring* about the other fellow. Anybody can see that you are a nice family of folks, hard working and honest I'm sure. [BENEATHA *frowns slightly, quizzically, her head tilted regarding him.*] Today everybody knows what it means to be on the outside of something. And of course, there is always somebody who is out to take the advantage of people who don't always understand.

WALTER: What do you mean?

LINDNER: Well—you see our community is made up of people who've worked hard as the dickens for years to build up that little community. They're not rich and fancy people; just hard-working, honest people who don't really have much but those little homes and a dream of the kind of community they want to raise their children in. Now, I don't say we are perfect and there is a lot wrong in some of the things they want. But you've got to admit that a man, right or wrong, has the right to want to have the neighborhood he lives in a certain kind of way. And at the moment the overwhelming majority of our people out there feel that people get along better, take more of a common interest in the life of the community, when they share a common background. I want you to believe me when I tell you that race prejudice simply doesn't enter into it. It is a matter of the people of Clybourne Park believing, rightly or wrongly, as I say, that for the happiness of all concerned that our Negro families are happier when they live in their *own* communities.

BENEATHA: [*With a grand and bitter gesture.*] This, friends, is the Welcoming Committee!

WALTER: [*Dumfounded, looking at* LINDNER.] Is this what you came marching all the way over here to tell us?

LINDNER: Well, now we've been having a fine conversation. I hope you'll hear me all the way through.

WALTER: [*Tightly.*] Go ahead, man.

LINDNER: You see—in the face of all things I have said, we are prepared to make your family a very generous offer . . .
BENEATHA: Thirty pieces and not a coin less![1]
WALTER: Yeah?
LINDNER: [*Putting on his glasses and drawing a form out of the briefcase.*] Our association is prepared, through the collective effort of our people, to buy the house from you at a financial gain to your family.
RUTH: Lord have mercy, ain't this the living gall!
WALTER: All right, you through?
LINDNER: Well, I want to give you the exact terms of the financial arrangement—
WALTER: We don't want to hear no exact terms of no arrangements. I want to know if you got any more to tell us 'bout getting together?
LINDNER: [*Taking off his glasses.*] Well—I don't suppose that you feel . . .
WALTER: Never mind how I feel—you got any more to say 'bout how people ought to sit down and talk to each other? . . . Get out of my house, man.

   [*He turns his back and walks to the door.*]

LINDNER: [*Looking around at the hostile faces and reaching and assembling his hat and briefcase.*] Well—I don't understand why you people are reacting this way. What do you think you are going to gain by moving into a neighborhood where you just aren't wanted and where some elements—well—people can get awful worked up when they feel that their whole way of life and everything they've ever worked for is threatened.
WALTER: Get out.
LINDNER: [*At the door, holding a small card.*] Well—I'm sorry it went like this.
WALTER: Get out.
LINDNER: [*Almost sadly regarding* WALTER.] You just can't force people to change their hearts, son.

   [*He turns and put his card on a table and exits.* WALTER *pushes the door to with stinging hatred, and stands looking at it.* RUTH *just sits and* BENEATHA *just stands. They say nothing.* MAMA *and* TRAVIS *enter.*]

MAMA: Well—this all the packing got done since I left out of here this morning. I testify before God that my children got all the energy of the dead. What time the moving men due?
BENEATHA: Four o'clock. You had a caller, Mama.

   [*She is smiling, teasingly.*]

MAMA: Sure enough—who?
BENEATHA: [*Her arms folded saucily.*] The Welcoming Committee.

   [WALTER *and* RUTH *giggle.*]

---

1. See Matthew 26.15, in which Judas Iscariot is paid 30 pieces of silver to betray Jesus.

MAMA: [*Innocently.*] Who?

BENEATHA: The Welcoming Committee. They said they're sure going to be glad to see you when you get there.

WALTER: [*Devilishly.*] Yeah, they said they can't hardly wait to see your face.

[*Laughter.*]

MAMA: [*Sensing their facetiousness.*] What's the matter with you all?

WALTER: Ain't nothing the matter with us. We just telling you 'bout the gentleman who came to see you this afternoon. From the Clybourne Park Improvement Association.

MAMA: What he want?

RUTH: [*In the same mood as* BENEATHA *and* WALTER.] To welcome you, honey.

WALTER: He said they can't hardly wait. He said the one thing they don't have, that they just *dying* to have out there is a fine family of colored people! [*To* RUTH *and* BENEATHA.] Ain't that right!

RUTH *and* BENEATHA: [*Mockingly.*] Yeah! He left his card in case—

[*They indicate the card, and* MAMA *picks it up and throws it on the floor— understanding and looking off as she draws her chair up to the table on which she has put her plant and some sticks and some cord.*]

MAMA: Father, give us strength. [*Knowingly—and without fun.*] Did he threaten us?

BENEATHA: Oh—Mama—they don't do it like that anymore. He talked Brotherhood. He said everybody ought to learn how to sit down and hate each other with good Christian fellowship.

[*She and* WALTER *shake hands to ridicule the remark.*]

MAMA: [*Sadly.*] Lord, protect us . . .

RUTH: You should hear the money those folks raised to buy the house from us. All we paid and then some.

BENEATHA: What they think we going to do—eat 'em?

RUTH: No, honey, marry 'em.

MAMA: [*Shaking her head.*] Lord, Lord, Lord . . .

RUTH: Well—that's the way the crackers crumble. Joke.

BENEATHA: [*Laughingly noticing what her mother is doing.*] Mama, what are you doing?

MAMA: Fixing my plant so it won't get hurt none on the way . . .

BENEATHA: Mama, you going to take *that* to the new house?

MAMA: Un-huh—

BENEATHA: That raggedy-looking old thing?

MAMA: [*Stopping and looking at her.*] It expresses *me.*

RUTH: [*With delight, to* BENEATHA.] So there, Miss Thing!

[WALTER *comes to* MAMA *suddenly and bends down behind her and squeezes her in his arms with all his strength. She is overwhelmed by the suddenness of it and, though delighted, her manner is like that of* RUTH *with* TRAVIS.]

MAMA: Look out now, boy! You make me mess up my thing here!

WALTER: [*His face lit, he slips down on his knees beside her, his arms still about her.*] Mama . . . you know what it means to climb up in the chariot?

MAMA: [*Gruffly, very happy.*] Get on away from me now . . .

RUTH: [*Near the gift-wrapped package, trying to catch* WALTER's *eye.*] Psst—

WALTER: What the old song say, Mama . . .

RUTH: Walter—Now?

[*She is pointing at the package.*]

WALTER: [*Speaking the lines, sweetly, playfully, in his mother's face.*]

I got wings . . . you got wings . . .
All God's Children got wings[2] . . .

MAMA: Boy—get out of my face and do some work . . .

WALTER:
When I get to heaven gonna put on my wings,
Gonna fly all over God's heaven . . .

BENEATHA: [*Teasingly, from across the room.*] Everybody talking 'bout heaven ain't going there!

WALTER: [*To* RUTH, *who is carrying the box across to them.*] I don't know, you think we ought to give her that . . . Seems to me she ain't been very appreciative around here.

MAMA: [*Eying the box, which is obviously a gift.*] What is that?

WALTER: [*Taking it from* RUTH *and putting it on the table in front of* MAMA.] Well—what you all think? Should we give it to her?

RUTH: Oh—she was pretty good today.

MAMA: I'll good you—

[*She turns her eyes to the box again.*]

BENEATHA: Open it, Mama.

[*She stands up, looks at it, turns and looks at all of them, and then presses her hands together and does not open the package.*]

WALTER: [*Sweetly.*] Open it, Mama. It's for you. [MAMA *looks in his eyes. It is the first present in her life without its being Christmas. Slowly she opens her package and lifts out, one by one, a brand-new sparkling set of gardening tools.* WALTER *continues, prodding.*] Ruth made up the note—read it . . .

MAMA: [*Picking up the card and adjusting her glasses.*] "To our own Mrs. Miniver[3]—Love from Brother, Ruth and Beneatha." Ain't that lovely . . .

TRAVIS: [*Tugging at his father's sleeve.*] Daddy, can I give her mine now?

WALTER: All right, son. [TRAVIS *flies to get his gift.*] Travis didn't want to go

---

2. Lines from an African American spiritual. Walter's and Beneatha's next lines are also from the song.   3. The courageous, charismatic title character of a 1942 film starring Greer Garson.

in with the rest of us, Mama. He got his own. [*Somewhat amused.*] We don't know what it is . . .

TRAVIS: [*Racing back in the room with a large hatbox and putting it in front of his grandmother.*] Here!

MAMA: Lord have mercy, baby. You done gone and bought your grandmother a hat?

TRAVIS: [*Very proud.*] Open it!

[*She does and lifts out an elaborate, but very elaborate, wide gardening hat, and all the adults break up at the sight of it.*]

RUTH: Travis, honey, what is that?

TRAVIS: [*Who thinks it is beautiful and appropriate.*] It's a gardening hat! Like the ladies always have on in the magazines when they work in their gardens.

BENEATHA: [*Giggling fiercely.*] Travis—we were trying to make Mama Mrs. Miniver—not Scarlett O'Hara![4]

MAMA: [*Indignantly.*] What's the matter with you all! This here is a beautiful hat! [*Absurdly.*] I always wanted me one just like it!

[*She pops it on her head to prove it to her grandson, and the hat is ludicrous and considerably oversized.*]

RUTH: Hot dog! Go, Mama!

WALTER: [*Doubled over with laughter.*] I'm sorry, Mama—but you look like you ready to go out and chop you some cotton sure enough!

[*They all laugh except* MAMA, *out of deference to* TRAVIS' *feelings.*]

MAMA: [*Gathering the boy up to her.*] Bless your heart—this is the prettiest hat I ever owned— [WALTER, RUTH *and* BENEATHA *chime in—noisily, festively and insincerely congratulating* TRAVIS *on his gift.*] What are we all standing around here for? We ain't finished packin' yet. Bennie, you ain't packed one book.

[*The bell rings.*]

BENEATHA: That couldn't be the movers . . . it's not hardly two good yet—

[BENEATHA *goes into her room.* MAMA *starts for door.*]

WALTER: [*Turning, stiffening.*] Wait—wait—I'll get it.

[*He stands and looks at the door.*]

MAMA: You expecting company, son?

WALTER: [*Just looking at the door.*] Yeah—yeah . . .

[MAMA *looks at* RUTH, *and they exchange innocent and unfrightened glances.*]

---

4. The glamorous, headstrong heroine in *Gone with the Wind*.

MAMA: [*Not understanding.*] Well, let them in, son.

BENEATHA: [*From her room.*] We need some more string.

MAMA: Travis—you run to the hardware and get me some string cord.

[MAMA *goes out and* WALTER *turns and looks at* RUTH. TRAVIS *goes to a dish for money.*]

RUTH: Why don't you answer the door, man?

WALTER: [*Suddenly bounding across the floor to her.*] 'Cause sometimes it hard to let the future begin! [*Stooping down in her face.*]

I got wings! You got wings!
All God's children got wings!

[*He crosses to the door and throws it open. Standing there is a very slight little man in a not too prosperous business suit and with haunted frightened eyes and a hat pulled down tightly, brim up, around his forehead.* TRAVIS *passes between the men and exits.* WALTER *leans deep in the man's face, still in his jubilance.*]

When I get to heaven gonna put on my wings,
Gonna fly all over God's heaven . . .

[*The little man just stares at him.*]

Heaven—

[*Suddenly he stops and looks past the little man into the empty hallway.*] Where's Willy, man?

BOBO: He ain't with me.

WALTER: [*Not disturbed.*] Oh—come on in. You know my wife.

BOBO: [*Dumbly, taking off his hat.*] Yes—h'you, Miss Ruth.

RUTH: [*Quietly, a mood apart from her husband already, seeing* BOBO.] Hello, Bobo.

WALTER: You right on time today . . . Right on time. That's the way! [*He slaps* BOBO *on his back.*] Sit down . . . lemme hear.

[RUTH *stands stiffly and quietly in back of them, as though somehow she senses death, her eyes fixed on her husband.*]

BOBO: [*His frightened eyes on the floor, his hat in his hands.*] Could I please get a drink of water, before I tell you about it, Walter Lee?

[WALTER *does not take his eyes off the man.* RUTH *goes blindly to the tap and gets a glass of water and brings it to* BOBO.]

WALTER: There ain't nothing wrong, is there?

BOBO: Lemme tell you—

WALTER: Man—didn't nothing go wrong?

BOBO: Lemme tell you—Walter Lee. [*Looking at* RUTH *and talking to her more than to* WALTER.] You know how it was. I got to tell you how it was. I mean first I got to tell you how it was all the way . . . I mean about the money I put in, Walter Lee . . .

WALTER: [*With taut agitation now.*] What about the money you put in?

BOBO: Well—it wasn't much as we told you—me and Willy— [*He stops.*] I'm sorry, Walter. I got a bad feeling about it. I got a real bad feeling about it . . .

WALTER: Man, what you telling me about all this for? . . . Tell me what happened in Springfield . . .

BOBO: Springfield.

RUTH: [*Like a dead woman.*] What was supposed to happen in Springfield?

BOBO: [*To her.*] This deal that me and Walter went into with Willy—Me and Willy was going to go down to Springfield and spread some money 'round so's we wouldn't have to wait so long for the liquor license . . . That's what we were going to do. Everybody said that was the way you had to do, you understand, Miss Ruth?

WALTER: Man—what happened down there?

BOBO: [*A pitiful man, near tears.*] I'm trying to tell you, Walter.

WALTER: [*Screaming at him suddenly.*] THEN TELL ME, GODDAMMIT . . . WHAT'S THE MATTER WITH YOU?

BOBO: Man . . . I didn't go to no Springfield, yesterday.

WALTER: [*Halted, life hanging in the moment.*] Why not?

BOBO: [*The long way, the hard way to tell.*] 'Cause I didn't have no reasons to . . .

WALTER: Man, what are you talking about!

BOBO: I'm talking about the fact that when I got to the train station yesterday morning—eight o'clock like we planned . . . Man—*Willy didn't never show up.*

WALTER: Why . . . where was he . . . where is he?

BOBO: That's what I'm trying to tell you . . . I don't know . . . I waited six hours . . . I called his house . . . and I waited . . . six hours . . . I waited in that train station six hours . . . [*Breaking into tears.*] That was all the extra money I had in the world . . . [*Looking up at* WALTER *with the tears running down his face.*] Man, *Willy is gone.*

WALTER: Gone, what you mean Willy is gone? Gone where? You mean he went by himself. You mean he went off to Springfield by himself—to take care of getting the license— [*Turns and looks anxiously at* RUTH.] You mean maybe he didn't want too many people in on the business down there? [*Looks to* RUTH *again, as before.*] You know Willy got his own ways. [*Looks back to* BOBO.] Maybe you was late yesterday and he just went on down there without you. Maybe—maybe—he's been callin' you at home tryin' to tell you what happened or something. Maybe—maybe—he just got sick. He's somewhere—he's got to be somewhere. We just got to find him—me and you got to find him. [*Grabs* BOBO *senselessly by the collar and starts to shake him.*] We got to!

BOBO: [*In sudden angry, frightened agony.*] What's the matter with you, Walter! *When a cat take off with your money he don't leave you no maps!*

WALTER: [*Turning madly, as though he is looking for* WILLY *in the very room.*] Willy! . . . Willy . . . don't do it . . . Please don't do it . . . Man, not with that money . . . Man, please, not with that money . . . Oh, God . . . Don't let it be true . . . [*He is wandering around, crying out for* WILLY *and looking*

for him or perhaps for help from God.] Man ... I trusted you ... Man, I put
my life in your hands ... [*He starts to crumple down on the floor as* RUTH
just covers her face in horror. MAMA *opens the door and comes into the room,
with* BENEATHA *behind her.*] Man ... [*He starts to pound the floor with his fists,
sobbing wildly.*] *That money is made out of my father's flesh* ...

BOBO: [*Standing over him helplessly.*] I'm sorry, Walter ... [*Only* WALTER's *sobs
reply.* BOBO *puts on his hat.*] I had my life staked on this deal, too ...

    [*He exits.*]

MAMA: [*To* WALTER.] Son— [*She goes to him, bends down to him, talks to his bent
head.*] Son ... Is it gone? Son, I gave you sixty-five hundred dollars. Is it
gone? All of it? Beneatha's money too?

WALTER: [*Lifting his head slowly.*] Mama ... I never ... went to the bank at
all ...

MAMA: [*Not wanting to believe him.*] You mean ... your sister's school money
... you used that too ... Walter? ...

WALTER: Yessss! ... All of it ... It's all gone ... [*There is total silence.* RUTH
stands with her face covered with her hands; BENEATHA *leans forlornly against
a wall, fingering a piece of red ribbon from the mother's gift.* MAMA *stops and
looks at her son without recognition and then, quite without thinking about it,
starts to beat him senselessly in the face.* BENEATHA *goes to them and stops it.*]

BENEATHA: Mama!

    [MAMA *stops and looks at both of her children and rises slowly and wanders
    vaguely, aimlessly away from them.*]

MAMA: I seen ... him ... night after night ... come in ... and look at that
rug ... and then look at me ... the red showing in his eyes ... the veins
moving in his head ... I seen him grow thin and old before he was forty
... working and working and working like somebody's old horse ... killing himself ... and you—you give it all away in a day ...

BENEATHA: Mama—

MAMA: Oh, God ... [*She looks up to Him.*] Look down here—and show me
the strength.

BENEATHA: Mama—

MAMA: [*Folding over.*] Strength ...

BENEATHA: [*Plaintively.*] Mama ...

MAMA: Strength!

    [CURTAIN.]

ACT III

An hour later.

*At curtain, there is a sullen light of gloom in the living room, gray light not unlike
that which began the first scene of Act I. At left we can see* WALTER *within his room,
alone with himself. He is stretched out on the bed, his shirt out and open, his arms
under his head. He does not smoke, he does not cry out, he merely lies there, looking
up at the ceiling, much as if he were alone in the world.*

In the living room BENEATHA *sits at the table, still surrounded by the now almost ominous packing crates. She sits looking off. We feel that this is a mood struck perhaps an hour before, and it lingers now, full of the empty sound of profound disappointment. We see on a line from her brother's bedroom the sameness of their attitudes. Presently the bell rings and* BENEATHA *rises without ambition or interest in answering. It is* ASAGAI, *smiling broadly, striding into the room with energy and happy expectation and conversation.*

ASAGAI: I came over . . . I had some free time. I thought I might help with the packing. Ah, I like the look of packing crates! A household in preparation for a journey! It depresses some people . . . but for me . . . it is another feeling. Something full of the flow of life, do you understand? Movement, progress . . . It makes me think of Africa.

BENEATHA: Africa!

ASAGAI: What kind of a mood is this? Have I told you how deeply you move me?

BENEATHA: He gave away the money, Asagai . . .

ASAGAI: Who gave away what money?

BENEATHA: The insurance money. My brother gave it away.

ASAGAI: Gave it away?

BENEATHA: He made an investment! With a man even Travis wouldn't have trusted.

ASAGAI: And it's gone?

BENEATHA: Gone!

ASAGAI: I'm very sorry . . . And you, now?

BENEATHA: Me? . . . Me? . . . Me, I'm nothing . . . Me. When I was very small . . . we used to take our sleds out in the wintertime and the only hills we had were the ice-covered stone steps of some houses down the street. And we used to fill them in with snow and make them smooth and slide down them all day . . . and it was very dangerous you know . . . far too steep . . . and sure enough one day a kid named Rufus came down too fast and hit the sidewalk . . . and we saw his face just split open right there in front of us . . . And I remember standing there looking at his bloody open face thinking that was the end of Rufus. But the ambulance came and they took him to the hospital and they fixed the broken bones and they sewed it all up . . . and the next time I saw Rufus he just had a little line down the middle of his face . . . I never got over that . . .

> [WALTER *sits up, listening on the bed. Throughout this scene it is important that we feel his reaction at all times, that he visibly respond to the words of his sister and* ASAGAI.]

ASAGAI: What?

BENEATHA: That that was what one person could do for another, fix him up—sew up the problem, make him all right again. That was the most marvelous thing in the world . . . I wanted to do that. I always thought it was the one concrete thing in the world that a human being could do. Fix up the sick, you know—and make them whole again. This was truly being God . . .

ASAGAI: You wanted to be God?

BENEATHA: No—I wanted to cure. It used to be so important to me. I wanted to cure. It used to matter. I used to care. I mean about people and how their bodies hurt . . .

ASAGAI: And you've stopped caring?

BENEATHA: Yes—I think so.

ASAGAI: Why?

[WALTER *rises, goes to the door of his room and is about to open it, then stops and stands listening, leaning on the door jamb.*]

BENEATHA: Because it doesn't seem deep enough, close enough to what ails mankind—I mean this thing of sewing up bodies or administering drugs. Don't you understand? It was a child's reaction to the world. I thought that doctors had the secret to all the hurts . . . That's the way a child sees things—or an idealist.

ASAGAI: Children see things very well sometimes—and idealists even better.

BENEATHA: I know that's what you think. Because you are still where I left off—you still care. This is what you see for the world, for Africa. You with the dreams of the future will patch up all Africa—you are going to cure the Great Sore of colonialism with Independence—

ASAGAI: Yes!

BENEATHA: Yes—and you think that one word is the penicillin of the human spirit: "Independence!" But then what?

ASAGAI: That will be the problem for another time. First we must get there.

BENEATHA: And where does it end?

ASAGAI: End? Who even spoke of an end? To life? To living?

BENEATHA: An end to misery!

ASAGAI: [*Smiling.*] You sound like a French intellectual.

BENEATHA: No! I sound like a human being who just had her future taken right out of her hands! While I was sleeping in my bed in there, things were happening in this world that directly concerned me—and nobody asked me, consulted me—they just went out and did things—and changed my life. Don't you see there isn't any real progress, Asagai, there is only one large circle that we march in, around and around, each of us with our own little picture—in front of us—our own little mirage that we think is the future.

ASAGAI: That is the mistake.

BENEATHA: What?

ASAGAI: What you just said—about the circle. It isn't a circle—it is simply a long line—as in geometry, you know, one that reaches into infinity. And because we cannot see the end—we also cannot see how it changes. And it is very odd but those who see the changes are called "idealists"— and those who cannot, or refuse to think, they are the "realists." It is very strange, and amusing too, I think.

BENEATHA: You—you are almost religious.

ASAGAI: Yes . . . I think I have the religion of doing what is necessary in the world—and of worshipping man—because he is so marvelous, you see.

BENEATHA: Man is foul! And the human race deserves its misery!

ASAGAI: You see: *you* have become the religious one in the old sense. Already, and after such a small defeat, you are worshipping despair.

BENEATHA: From now on, I worship the truth—and the truth is that people are puny, small and selfish . . .

ASAGAI: Truth? Why is it that you despairing ones always think that only you have the truth? I never thought to see *you* like that. You! Your brother made a stupid, childish mistake—and you are grateful to him. So that now you can give up the ailing human race on account of it. You talk about what good is struggle; what good is anything? Where are we all going? And why are we bothering?

BENEATHA: *And you cannot answer it!* All your talk and dreams about Africa and Independence. Independence and then what? What about all the crooks and petty thieves and just plain idiots who will come into power to steal and plunder the same as before—only now they will be black and do it in the name of the new Independence—You cannot answer that.

ASAGAI: [*Shouting over her.*] *I live the answer!* [*Pause.*] In my village at home it is the exceptional man who can even read a newspaper . . . or who ever *sees* a book at all. I will go home and much of what I will have to say will seem strange to the people of my village . . . But I will teach and work and things will happen, slowly and swiftly. At times it will seem that nothing changes at all . . . and then again . . . the sudden dramatic events which make history leap into the future. And then quiet again. Retrogression even. Guns, murder, revolution. And I even will have moments when I wonder if the quiet was not better than all that death and hatred. But I will look about my village at the illiteracy and disease and ignorance and I will not wonder long. And perhaps . . . perhaps I will be a great man . . . I mean perhaps I will hold on to the substance of truth and find my way always with the right course . . . and perhaps for it I will be butchered in my bed some night by the servants of empire . . .

BENEATHA: *The martyr!*

ASAGAI: . . . or perhaps I shall live to be a very old man, respected and esteemed in my new nation . . . And perhaps I shall hold office and this is what I'm trying to tell you, Alaiyo; perhaps the things I believe now for my country will be wrong and outmoded, and I will not understand and do terrible things to have things my way or merely to keep my power. Don't you see that there will be young men and women, not British soldiers then, but my own black countrymen . . . to step out of the shadows some evening and slit my then useless throat? Don't you see they have always been there . . . that they always will be. And that such a thing as my own death will be an advance? They who might kill me even . . . actually replenish me!

BENEATHA: Oh, Asagai, I know all that.

ASAGAI: Good! Then stop moaning and groaning and tell me what you plan to do.

BENEATHA: Do?

ASAGAI: I have a bit of a suggestion.

BENEATHA: What?

ASAGAI: [*Rather quietly for him.*] That when it is all over—that you come home with me—

BENEATHA: [*Slapping herself on the forehead with exasperation born of misunderstanding.*] Oh—Asagai—at this moment you decide to be romantic!

ASAGAI: [*Quickly understanding the misunderstanding.*] My dear, young creature of the New World—I do not mean across the city—I mean across the ocean; home—to Africa.

BENEATHA: [*Slowly understanding and turning to him with murmured amazement.*] To—to Nigeria?

ASAGAI: Yes! . . . [*Smiling and lifting his arms playfully.*] Three hundred years later the African Prince rose up out of the seas and swept the maiden back across the middle passage over which her ancestors had come—

BENEATHA: [*Unable to play.*] Nigeria?

ASAGAI: Nigeria. Home. [*Coming to her with genuine romantic flippancy.*] I will show you our mountains and our stars; and give you cool drinks from gourds and teach you the old songs and the ways of our people—and, in time, we will pretend that— [*Very softly.*] —you have only been away for a day—

[*She turns her back to him, thinking. He swings her around and takes her full in his arms in a long embrace which proceeds to passion.*]

BENEATHA: [*Pulling away.*] You're getting me all mixed up—

ASAGAI: Why?

BENEATHA: Too many things—too many things have happened today. I must sit down and think. I don't know what I feel about anything right this minute.

[*She promptly sits down and props her chin on her fist.*]

ASAGAI: [*Charmed.*] All right, I shall leave you. No—don't get up. [*Touching her, gently, sweetly.*] Just sit awhile and think . . . Never be afraid to sit awhile and think. [*He goes to door and looks at her.*] How often I have looked at you and said, "Ah—so this is what the New World hath finally wrought . . ."

[*He exits.* BENEATHA *sits on alone. Presently* WALTER *enters from his room and starts to rummage through things, feverishly looking for something. She looks up and turns in her seat.*]

BENEATHA: [*Hissingly.*] Yes—just look at what the New World hath wrought! . . . Just look! [*She gestures with bitter disgust.*] There he is! *Monsieur le petit bourgeois noir*—himself! There he is—Symbol of a Rising Class! Entrepreneur! Titan of the system! [WALTER *ignores her completely and continues frantically and destructively looking for something and hurling things to the floor and tearing things out of their place in his search.* BENEATHA *ignores the eccentricity of his actions and goes on with the monologue of insult.*] Did you dream of yachts on Lake Michigan, Brother? Did you see yourself on that Great

Day sitting down at the Conference Table, surrounded by all the mighty bald-headed men in America? All halted, waiting, breathless, waiting for your pronouncements on industry? Waiting for you—Chairman of the Board? [WALTER *finds what he is looking for—a small piece of white paper— and pushes it in his pocket and puts on his coat and rushes out without ever having looked at her. She shouts after him.*] I look at you and I see the final triumph of stupidity in the world!

[*The door slams and she returns to just sitting again.* RUTH *comes quickly out of* MAMA's *room.*]

RUTH: Who was that?

BENEATHA: Your husband.

RUTH: Where did he go?

BENEATHA: Who knows—maybe he has an appointment at U.S. Steel.

RUTH: [*Anxiously, with frightened eyes.*] You didn't say nothing bad to him, did you?

BENEATHA: Bad? Say anything bad to him? No—I told him he was a sweet boy and full of dreams and everything is strictly peachy keen, as the ofay[5] kids say!

[MAMA *enters from her bedroom. She is lost, vague, trying to catch hold, to make some sense of her former command of the world, but it still eludes her. A sense of waste overwhelms her gait; a measure of apology rides on her shoulders. She goes to her plant, which has remained on the table, looks at it, picks it up and takes it to the window sill and sits it outside, and she stands and looks at it a long moment. Then she closes the window, straightens her body with effort and turns around to her children.*]

MAMA: Well—ain't it a mess in here, though? [*A false cheerfulness, a beginning of something.*] I guess we all better stop moping around and get some work done. All this unpacking and everything we got to do. [RUTH *raises her head slowly in response to the sense of the line; and* BENEATHA *in similar manner turns very slowly to look at her mother.*] One of you all better call the moving people and tell 'em not to come.

RUTH: Tell 'em not to come?

MAMA: Of course, baby. Ain't no need in 'em coming all the way here and having to go back. They charges for that too. [*She sits down, fingers to her brow, thinking.*] Lord, ever since I was a little girl, I always remembers people saying, "Lena—Lena Eggleston, you aims too high all the time. You needs to slow down and see life a little more like it is. Just slow down some." That's what they always used to say down home—"Lord, that Lena Eggleston is a high-minded thing. She'll get her due one day!"

RUTH: No, Lena . . .

MAMA: Me and Big Walter just didn't never learn right.

RUTH: Lena, no! We gotta go. Bennie—tell her . . . [*She rises and crosses to* BENEATHA *with her arms outstretched.* BENEATHA *doesn't respond.*] Tell her

5. White.

we can still move...the notes ain't but a hundred and twenty-five a month. We got four grown people in this house—we can work...

MAMA: [*To herself.*] Just aimed too high all the time—

RUTH: [*Turning and going to* MAMA *fast—the words pouring out with urgency and desperation.*] Lena—I'll work...I'll work twenty hours a day in all the kitchens in Chicago...I'll strap my baby on my back if I have to and scrub all the floors in America and wash all the sheets in America if I have to—but we got to move...We got to get out of here...

[MAMA *reaches out absently and pats* RUTH's *hand.*]

MAMA: No—I sees things differently now. Been thinking 'bout some of the things we could do to fix this place up some. I seen a second-hand bureau over on Maxwell Street[6] just the other day that could fit right there. [*She points to where the new furniture might go.* RUTH *wanders away from her.*] Would need some new handles on it and then a little varnish and then it look like something brand-new. And—we can put up them new curtains in the kitchen...Why this place be looking fine. Cheer us all up so that we forget trouble ever came...[*To* RUTH.] And you could get some nice screens to put up in your room round the baby's bassinet ...[*She looks at both of them, pleadingly.*] Sometimes you just got to know when to give up some things...and hold on to what you got.

[WALTER *enters from the outside, looking spent and leaning against the door, his coat hanging from him.*]

MAMA: Where you been, son?

WALTER: [*Breathing hard.*] Made a call.

MAMA: To who, son?

WALTER: To The Man.

MAMA: What man, baby?

WALTER: The Man, Mama. Don't you know who The Man is?

RUTH: Walter Lee?

WALTER: *The Man.* Like the guys in the streets say—The Man. Captain Boss— Mistuh Charley...Old Captain Please Mr. Bossman...

BENEATHA: [*Suddenly.*] Lindner!

WALTER: That's right! That's good. I told him to come right over.

BENEATHA: [*Fiercely, understanding.*] For what? What do you want to see him for!

WALTER: [*Looking at his sister.*] We going to do business with him.

MAMA: What you talking 'bout, son?

WALTER: Talking 'bout life, Mama. You all always telling me to see life like it is. Well—I laid in there on my back today...and I figured it out. Life just like it is. Who gets and who don't get. [*He sits down with his coat on and laughs.*] Mama, you know it's all divided up. Life is. Sure enough. Between the takers and the "tooken." [*He laughs.*] I've figured it out finally. [*He looks around at them.*] Yeah. Some of us always getting

6. A street market southwest of the Loop.

"tooken." [*He laughs.*] People like Willy Harris, they don't never get "tooken." And you know why the rest of us do? 'Cause we all mixed up. Mixed up bad. We get to looking 'round for the right and the wrong, and we worry about it and cry about it and stay up nights trying to figure out 'bout the wrong and the right of things all the time . . . And all the time, man, them takers is out there operating, just taking and taking. Willy Harris? Shoot—Willy Harris don't even count. He don't even count in the big scheme of things. But I'll say one thing for old Willy Harris . . . he's taught me something. He's taught me to keep my eye on what counts in this world. Yeah— [*Shouting out a little.*] Thanks, Willy!

RUTH: What did you call that man for, Walter Lee?

WALTER: Called him to tell him to come on over to the show. Gonna put on a show for the man. Just what he wants to see. You see, Mama, the man came here today and he told us that them people out there where you want us to move—well they so upset they willing to pay us not to move out there. [*He laughs again.*] And—and oh, Mama—you would of been proud of the way me and Ruth and Bennie acted. We told him to get out . . . Lord have mercy! We told the man to get out. Oh, we was some proud folks this afternoon, yeah. [*He lights a cigarette.*] We were still full of that old-time stuff . . .

RUTH: [*Coming toward him slowly.*] You talking 'bout taking them people's money to keep us from moving in that house?

WALTER: I ain't just talking 'bout it, baby—I'm telling you that's what's going to happen.

BENEATHA: Oh, God! Where is the bottom! Where is the real honest-to-God bottom so he can't go any farther!

WALTER: See—that's the old stuff. You and that boy that was here today. You all want everybody to carry a flag and a spear and sing some marching songs, huh? You wanna spend your life looking into things and trying to find the right and the wrong part, huh? Yeah. You know what's going to happen to that boy someday—he'll find himself sitting in a dungeon, locked in forever—and the takers will have the key! Forget it, baby! There ain't no causes—there ain't nothing but taking in this world, and he who takes most is smartest—and it don't make a damn bit of difference *how*.

MAMA: You making something inside me cry, son. Some awful pain inside me.

WALTER: Don't cry, Mama. Understand. That white man is going to walk in that door able to write checks for more money than we ever had. It's important to him and I'm going to help him . . . I'm going to put on the show, Mama.

MAMA: Son—I come from five generations of people who was slaves and sharecroppers—but ain't nobody in my family never let nobody pay 'em no money that was a way of telling us we wasn't fit to walk the earth. We ain't never been that poor. [*Raising her eyes and looking at him.*] We ain't never been that dead inside.

BENEATHA: Well—we are dead now. All the talk about dreams and sunlight that goes on in this house. All dead.

WALTER: What's the matter with you all! I didn't make this world! It was give to me this way! Hell, yes, I want me some yachts someday! Yes, I want to hang some real pearls 'round my wife's neck. Ain't she supposed to wear no pearls? Somebody tell me—tell me, who decides which women is suppose to wear pearls in this world. I tell you I am a *man*—and I think my wife should wear some pearls in this world!

[*This last line hangs a good while and* WALTER *begins to move about the room. The word "Man" has penetrated his consciousness; he mumbles it to himself repeatedly between strange agitated pauses as he moves about.*]

MAMA: Baby, how you going to feel on the inside?

WALTER: Fine! . . . Going to feel fine . . . a man . . .

MAMA: You won't have nothing left then, Walter Lee.

WALTER: [*Coming to her.*] I'm going to feel fine, Mama. I'm going to look that son-of-a-bitch in the eyes and say— [*He falters.*] —and say, "All right, Mr. Lindner— [*He falters even more.*] —that's your neighborhood out there. You got the right to keep it like you want. You got the right to have it like you want. Just write the check and—the house is yours." And, and I am going to say— [*His voice almost breaks.*] And you—you people just put the money in my hand and you won't have to live next to this bunch of stinking niggers! . . . [*He straightens up and moves away from his mother, walking around the room.*] Maybe—maybe I'll just get down on my black knees . . . [*He does so;* RUTH *and* BENNIE *and* MAMA *watch him in frozen horror.*] Captain, Mistuh, Bossman. [*He starts crying.*] A-hee-hee-hee! [*Wringing his hands in profoundly anguished imitation.*] Yassss-suh! Great White Father, just gi' ussen de money, fo' God's sake, and we's ain't gwine come out deh and dirty up yo' white folks neighborhood . . .

[*He breaks down completely, then gets up and goes into the bedroom.*]

BENEATHA: That is not a man. That is nothing but a toothless rat.

MAMA: Yes—death done come in this here house. [*She is nodding, slowly, reflectively.*] Done come walking in my house. On the lips of my children. You what supposed to be my beginning again. You—what supposed to be my harvest. [*To* BENEATHA.] You—you mourning your brother?

BENEATHA: He's no brother of mine.

MAMA: What you say?

BENEATHA: I said that that individual in that room is no brother of mine.

MAMA: That's what I thought you said. You feeling like you better than he is today? [BENEATHA *does not answer.*] Yes? What you tell him a minute ago? That he wasn't a man? Yes? You give him up for me? You done wrote his epitaph too—like the rest of the world? Well, who give you the privilege?

BENEATHA: Be on my side for once! You saw what he just did, Mama! You saw him—down on his knees. Wasn't it you who taught me—to despise any man who would do that. Do what he's going to do.

MAMA: Yes—I taught you that. Me and your daddy. But I thought I taught you something else too . . . I thought I taught you to love him.

BENEATHA: Love him? There is nothing left to love.

MAMA: There is always something left to love. And if you ain't learned that, you ain't learned nothing. [*Looking at her.*] Have you cried for that boy today? I don't mean for yourself and for the family 'cause we lost the money. I mean for him; what he been through and what it done to him. Child, when do you think is the time to love somebody the most; when they done good and made things easy for everybody? Well then, you ain't through learning—because that ain't the time at all. It's when he's at his lowest and can't believe in hisself 'cause the world done whipped him so. When you starts measuring somebody, measure him right, child, measure him right. Make sure you done taken into account what hills and valleys he come through before he got to wherever he is.

[TRAVIS *bursts into the room at the end of the speech, leaving the door open.*]

TRAVIS: Grandmama—the moving men are downstairs! The truck just pulled up.

MAMA: [*Turning and looking at him.*] Are they, baby? They downstairs?

[*She sighs and sits.* LINDNER *appears in the doorway. He peers in and knocks lightly, to gain attention, and comes in. All turn to look at him.*]

LINDNER: [*Hat and briefcase in hand.*] Uh—hello . . . [RUTH *crosses mechanically to the bedroom door and opens it and lets it swing open freely and slowly as the lights come up on* WALTER *within, still in his coat, sitting at the far corner of the room. He looks up and out through the room to* LINDNER.]

RUTH: He's here.

[*A long minute passes and* WALTER *slowly gets up.*]

LINDNER: [*Coming to the table with efficiency, putting his briefcase on the table and starting to unfold papers and unscrew fountain pens.*] Well, I certainly was glad to hear from you people. [WALTER *has begun the trek out of the room, slowly and awkwardly, rather like a small boy, passing the back of his sleeve across his mouth from time to time.*] Life can really be so much simpler than people let it be most of the time. Well—with whom do I negotiate? You, Mrs. Younger, or your son here? [MAMA *sits with her hands folded on her lap and her eyes closed as* WALTER *advances.* TRAVIS *goes close to* LINDNER *and looks at the papers curiously.*] Just some official papers, sonny.

RUTH: Travis, you go downstairs.

MAMA: [*Opening her eyes and looking into* WALTER'*s.*] No. Travis, you stay right here. And you make him understand what you doing, Walter Lee. You teach him good. Like Willy Harris taught you. You show where our five generations done come to. Go ahead, son—

WALTER: [*Looks down into his boy's eyes.* TRAVIS *grins at him merrily and* WALTER *draws him beside him with his arm lightly around his shoulders.*] Well, Mr. Lindner. [BENEATHA *turns away.*] We called you— [*There is a profound, simple groping quality in his speech.*] —because, well, me and my family [*He*

looks around and shifts from one foot to the other.] Well—we are very plain
people . . .

LINDNER: Yes—

WALTER: I mean—I have worked as a chauffeur most of my life—and my
wife here, she does domestic work in people's kitchens. So does my
mother. I mean—we are plain people . . .

LINDNER: Yes, Mr. Younger—

WALTER: [*Really like a small boy, looking down at his shoes and then up at the
man.*] And—uh—well, my father, well, he was a laborer most of his life.

LINDNER: [*Absolutely confused.*] Uh, yes—

WALTER: [*Looking down at his toes once again.*] My father almost beat a man
to death once because this man called him a bad name or something,
you know what I mean?

LINDNER: No, I'm afraid I don't.

WALTER: [*Finally straightening up.*] Well, what I mean is that we come from
people who had a lot of pride. I mean—we are very proud people. And
that's my sister over there and she's going to be a doctor—and we are
very proud—

LINDNER: Well—I am sure that is very nice, but—

WALTER: [*Starting to cry and facing the man eye to eye.*] What I am telling you
is that we called you over here to tell you that we are very proud and
that this is—this is my son, who makes the sixth generation of our family
in this country, and that we have all thought about your offer and we
have decided to move into our house because my father—my father—he
earned it. [MAMA *has her eyes closed and is rocking back and forth as though
she were in church, with her head nodding the amen yes.*] We don't want to
make no trouble for nobody or fight no causes—but we will try to be
good neighbors. That's all we got to say. [*He looks the man absolutely in
the eyes.*] We don't want your money.

[*He turns and walks away from the man.*]

LINDNER: [*Looking around at all of them.*] I take it then that you have decided
to occupy.

BENEATHA: That's what the man said.

LINDNER: [*To* MAMA *in her reverie.*] Then I would like to appeal to you, Mrs.
Younger. You are older and wiser and understand things better I am
sure . . .

MAMA: [*Rising.*] I am afraid you don't understand. My son said we was going
to move and there ain't nothing left for me to say. [*Shaking her head with
double meaning.*] You know how these young folks is nowadays, mister.
Can't do a thing with 'em. Good-bye.

LINDNER: [*Folding up his materials.*] Well—if you are that final about it . . .
There is nothing left for me to say. [*He finishes. He is almost ignored by the
family, who are concentrating on* WALTER LEE. *At the door* LINDNER *halts and
looks around.*] I sure hope you people know what you're doing.

[*He shakes his head and exits.*]

RUTH: [*Looking around and coming to life.*] Well, for God's sake—if the moving men are here—LET'S GET THE HELL OUT OF HERE!

MAMA: [*Into action.*] Ain't it the truth! Look at all this here mess. Ruth, put Travis' good jacket on him . . . Walter Lee, fix your tie and tuck your shirt in, you look just like somebody's hoodlum. Lord have mercy, where is my plant? [*She flies to get it amid the general bustling of the family, who are deliberately trying to ignore the nobility of the past moment.*] You all start on down . . . Travis child, don't go empty-handed . . . Ruth, where did I put that box with my skillets in it? I want to be in charge of it myself . . . I'm going to make us the biggest dinner we ever ate tonight . . . Beneatha, what's the matter with them stockings? Pull them things up, girl . . .

[*The family starts to file out as two moving men appear and begin to carry out the heavier pieces of furniture, bumping into the family as they move about.*]

BENEATHA: Mama, Asagai—asked me to marry him today and go to Africa—

MAMA: [*In the middle of her getting-ready activity.*] He did? You ain't old enough to marry nobody— [*Seeing the moving men lifting one of her chairs precariously.*] Darling, that ain't no bale of cotton, please handle it so we can sit in it again. I had that chair twenty-five years . . .

[*The movers sigh with exasperation and go on with their work.*]

BENEATHA: [*Girlishly and unreasonably trying to pursue the conversation.*] To go to Africa, Mama—be a doctor in Africa . . .

MAMA: [*Distracted.*] Yes, baby—

WALTER: Africa! What he want you to go to Africa for?

BENEATHA: To practice there . . .

WALTER: Girl, if you don't get all them silly ideas out your head! You better marry yourself a man with some loot . . .

BENEATHA: [*Angrily, precisely as in the first scene of the play.*] What have you got to do with who I marry!

WALTER: Plenty. Now I think George Murchison—

[*He and* BENEATHA *go out yelling at each other vigorously;* BENEATHA *is heard saying that she would not marry* GEORGE MURCHISON *if he were Adam and she were Eve, etc. The anger is loud and real till their voices diminish.* RUTH *stands at the door and turns to* MAMA *and smiles knowingly.*]

MAMA: [*Fixing her hat at last.*] Yeah—they something all right, my children . . .

RUTH: Yeah—they're something. Let's go, Lena.

MAMA: [*Stalling, starting to look around at the house.*] Yes—I'm coming. Ruth—

RUTH: Yes?

MAMA: [*Quietly, woman to woman.*] He finally come into his manhood today, didn't he? Kind of like a rainbow after the rain . . .

RUTH: [*Biting her lip lest her own pride explode in front of* MAMA.] Yes, Lena.

[WALTER'S *voice calls for them raucously.*]

MAMA: [*Waving* RUTH *out vaguely.*] All right, honey—go on down. I be down directly.

[RUTH *hesitates, then exits.* MAMA *stands, at last alone in the living room, her plant on the table before her as the lights start to come down. She looks around at all the walls and ceilings and suddenly, despite herself, while the children call below, a great heaving thing rises in her and she puts her fist to her mouth, takes a final desperate look, pulls her coat about her, pats her hat and goes out. The lights dim down. The door opens and she comes back in, grabs her plant, and goes out for the last time.*]

[CURTAIN.]

1959

Biographical Sketches: Playwrights

ANTON CHEKHOV
(1860–1904)

The son of a grocer and the grandson of an emancipated serf, Anton Pavlovich Chekhov was born in the Russian town of Taganrog. In 1875, his father, facing bankruptcy and imprisonment, fled to Moscow; shortly after, the rest of the family lost their house to a former friend and lodger, a misfortune that Chekhov would revisit in *The Cherry Orchard*. In 1884, Chekhov received his M.D. from the University of Moscow; in the early 1890s, he purchased an estate near Moscow and became both an industrious landowner and a doctor to the local peasants. Throughout the 1880s, he supported his family and financed his medical studies by writing the sketches and stories that would eventually win him enduring international acclaim. Chekhov began writing for the stage in 1887. Early productions of his plays were poorly received: *The Wood Demon* (later rewritten as *Uncle Vanya*) was performed only a few times in 1889 before closing; the 1896 premiere of *The Seagull* turned into a riot when an audience expecting comedy found themselves watching an experimental tragedy. Konstantin Stanislavsky, director at the Moscow Art Theater, helped restore Chekhov's reputation with successful productions of *The Seagull* and *Uncle Vanya* in 1899, *The Three Sisters* in 1901, and *The Cherry Orchard* in 1904.

SUSAN GLASPELL
(1876–1948)

Born and raised in Davenport, Iowa, Susan Glaspell graduated from Drake University and worked on the staff of the Des Moines *Daily News* until her stories began appearing in magazines such as *Harper's* and *Ladies' Home Journal*. In 1911, Glaspell moved to New York City, where, two years later, she married the theater director George Cram Cook. In 1915 they founded the Provincetown Playhouse (later the Playwright's Theater), an extraordinary Cape Cod gathering of actors, directors, and playwrights, including Eugene O'Neill, Edna St. Vincent Millay, and John Reed. The Provincetown Players produced several of Glaspell's early plays, including *Trifles* (1916); her later plays include *The Inheritors* (1921), *The Verge* (1921), *Bernice* (1924), and *Alison's House* (1930), for which she won the Pulitzer Prize. Glaspell spent the last part of her life writing fiction in Provincetown; among her many books are *Visioning* (1911), *Lifted Masks: Stories* (1912), *Fidelity* (1915), *The Road to the Temple* (1926), and *The Morning Is Near Us* (1940).

LORRAINE HANSBERRY (1930–1965)

The first African American woman to have a play produced on Broadway, Lorraine Hansberry was born in Chicago to a prominent family and even at a young age showed an interest in writing. She attended the University of Wisconsin, the

Art Institute of Chicago, and Roosevelt University, then moved to New York City in order to concentrate on writing for the stage. After extensive fund-raising, Hansberry's play *A Raisin in the Sun* (loosely based on events involving her own family) opened in 1959 at the Ethel Barrymore Theatre on Broadway, received critical acclaim, and won the New York Drama Critics' Circle Award for Best Play. Hansberry's second production, *The Sign in Sidney Brustein's Window,* had a short run on Broadway in 1964. Shortly after, Hansberry died of cancer. *To Be Young, Gifted, and Black,* adapted from her writing, was produced off-Broadway in 1969 and published the next year, when her drama *Les Blancs* was also produced.

HENRIK IBSEN
(1828–1906)

Born in Skien, Norway, Henrik Ibsen was apprenticed to an apothecary until 1850, when he left for Oslo and published his first play, *Catilina,* a verse tragedy. By 1857 Ibsen was director of Oslo's Norwegian Theater, but his early plays, such as *Love's Comedy* (1862), were poorly received. Disgusted with what he saw as Norway's backwardness, Ibsen left in 1864 for Rome, where he wrote two more verse plays, *Brand* (1866) and *Peer Gynt* (1867), before turning to the realistic style and harsh criticism of traditional social mores for which he is best known. *The League of Youth* (1869), *Pillars of Society* (1877), *A Doll House* (1879), *Ghosts* (1881), *An Enemy of the People* (1882), *The Wild Duck* (1884), and *Hedda Gabler* (1890) won him a reputation throughout Europe as a controversial and outspoken advocate of moral and social reform. Near the end of his life, Ibsen explored the human condition in the explicitly symbolic terms of *The Master Builder* (1892) and *When We Dead Awaken* (1899). Ibsen's works had enormous influence over the drama of the twentieth century.

ARTHUR MILLER
(1915–2005)

Arthur Miller was born in New York City to a prosperous family whose fortunes were ruined by the Depression, a circumstance that would shape his political outlook and imbue him with a deep sense of social responsibility. Miller studied history, economics, and journalism at the University of Michigan, began writing plays, and joined the Federal Theater Project, a proving ground for some of the best playwrights of the period. He had his first Broadway success, *All My Sons,* in 1947, followed two years later by his Pulitzer Prize–winning masterpiece, *Death of a Salesman,* a starkly poetic depiction of the American dream as a hollow sham. In 1953, against the backdrop of Senator Joseph McCarthy's anti-Communist "witch-hunts," Miller fashioned another modern parable, his Tony Award–winning *The Crucible,* based on the seventeenth-century Salem witch trials. Among his other works for the stage are the Pulitzer Prize–winner *A View from the Bridge* (1955), *After the Fall* (1964), *Incident at Vichy* (1965), *The Price* (1968), *The Ride Down Mt. Morgan* (1991), *Broken Glass* (1994), and *Resurrection Blues* (2004). In addition, Miller wrote a novel, *Focus* (1945); the screenplay for the film *The Misfits* (1961), which starred his second wife, Marilyn Monroe; *The Theater Essays* (1971), a collection of his writings about dramatic literature; and *Timebends* (1987), his autobiography.

WILLIAM SHAKE-SPEARE (1554–1616)

Considering the great and well-deserved fame of his work, surprisingly little is known of William Shakespeare's life. Between 1585 and 1592, he left his birthplace of Stratford-upon-Avon for London to begin a career as playwright and actor. No dates of his professional career are recorded, however, nor can the order in which he composed his plays and poetry be determined with certainty. By 1594, he had established himself as a poet with two long works—*Venus and Adonis* and *The Rape of Lucrece;* his more than 150 sonnets are supreme expressions of the form. His matchless reputation, though, rests on his works for the theater. Shakespeare produced perhaps thirty-five plays in twenty-five years, proving himself a master of every dramatic genre: tragedy (in works such as *Macbeth, Hamlet, King Lear,* and *Othello*); historical drama (for example, *Richard III* and *Henry IV*); comedy (*A Midsummer Night's Dream, Twelfth Night, As You Like It,* and many more); and romance or "tragicomedy" (in plays such as *The Tempest* and *Cymbeline*). Without question, Shakespeare is the most quoted, discussed, and beloved writer in English literature.

SOPHOCLES

(496?–406 B.C.E.)
Sophocles lived at a time when Athens and Greek civilization were at the peak of their power and influence. He not only served as a general under Pericles and played a prominent role in the city's affairs but also was arguably the greatest of the Greek tragic playwrights, winning the annual dramatic competition about twenty times, a feat unmatched by even his great contemporaries, Aeschylus and Euripides. An innovator, Sophocles fundamentally changed the nature of dramatic performance by adding a third actor, enlarging the chorus, and introducing the use of painted scenery. Aristotle held that Sophocles' *Oedipus the King* (c. 429 B.C.E.) was the perfect tragedy and used it as his model when he dis-

cussed the nature of tragedy in his *Poetics.* Today only seven of Sophocles' tragedies survive—the Oedipus trilogy (*Oedipus the King, Oedipus at Colonus,* and *Antigone*), *Philoctetes, Ajax, Trachiniae,* and *Electra*—though he is believed to have written as many as 123 plays.

AUGUST WILSON

(1945–2005)
Frederick August Kittel was born in a lower-class black neighborhood of Pittsburgh, Pennsylvania. At fifteen, disgusted by treatment he considered racist, he left school and sought to educate himself at the local library. A black nationalist and participant in the Black Arts Movement during the 1960s and '70s, Wilson disavowed his white father and adopted his black mother's surname. In 1968 he cofounded the Black Horizons Theater Company, in St. Paul, Minnesota; he later founded the Playwrights Center in Minneapolis. The 1984 Broadway production of *Ma Rainey's Black Bottom* established his theatrical reputation, and after that he wrote a series of plays dealing with the black experience in America, each one set during a different decade of the twentieth century. Among his plays are *Jitney* (1982); *Fences* (1985), winner of the 1987 Pulitzer Prize; *Joe Turner's Come and Gone* (1986); *The Piano Lesson* (1987), which won a Tony Award, the Drama Critics Circle Award, the American Theater Critics Outstanding Play Award, and the 1990 Pulitzer Prize; *Two Trains Running* (1992); *Seven Guitars* (1995); *King Hedley II* (2001); and *Gem of the Ocean* (2003).

Writing about Literature

When it comes to the study of literature, reading and writing are closely interrelated—even mutually dependent—activities. On the one hand, the quality of whatever we write about a literary text depends entirely upon the quality of our work as readers. On the other hand, our reading isn't truly complete until we've tried to capture our sense of a text in writing. Indeed, we often read a literary work much more actively and attentively when we integrate informal writing into the reading process—pausing periodically to mark especially important or confusing passages, to jot down significant facts, to describe the impressions and responses the text provokes—or when we imagine our reading (and our informal writing) as preparation for writing about the work in a more sustained and formal way.

Writing about literature can take any number of forms, ranging from the very informal and personal to the very formal and public. In fact, your instructor may well ask you to try your hand at more than one form. However, the essay is by far the most common and complex form that writing about literature takes. As a result, the following chapters will focus on the essay. A first, short chapter covers three basic ways of writing about literature. The second chapter, "The Elements of the Essay," seeks to answer a very basic set of questions: *When an instructor says, "Write an essay," what precisely does that mean? What is the purpose of an essay, and what form does it need to take in order to achieve that purpose?* The third chapter, "The Writing Process," addresses questions about how an essay is produced, while the fourth chapter explores the special steps and strategies involved in writing a research essay—a type of essay about literature that draws on secondary sources. "Quotation, Citation, and Documentation" explains the rules and strategies involved in quoting and citing both literary texts and secondary sources using the documentation system recommended by the Modern Language Association (MLA). And, finally, we present a sample research essay, annotated to point out some its most important features.

18   PARAPHRASE, SUMMARY, DESCRIPTION

Before turning to the essay, let's briefly consider three other basic ways of writing about literature: *paraphrase, summary*, and *description*. Each of these can be useful both as an exercise to prepare for writing an essay and as part of a completed essay. That is, an essay about a literary text must do more than paraphrase, summarize, or describe the text; yet a good essay about a literary text almost always incorporates some paraphrase, summary, and description of the literature and, in the case of a research essay, of secondary sources as well.

18.1 PARAPHRASE

To paraphrase a statement is to restate it in your own words. Since the goal of paraphrase is to represent a statement fully and faithfully, paraphrases tend to be at least as long as the original, and one usually wouldn't try to paraphrase an entire work of any length. The following examples offer paraphrases of sentences from a work of fiction (Jane Austen's *Pride and Prejudice*), a poem (W. B. Yeats's "All Things Can Tempt Me"), and an essay (George L. Dillon's "Styles of Reading").

ORIGINAL SENTENCE	PARAPHRASE
It is a truth universally acknowledged that a single man in possession of a good fortune must be in want of a wife.	Everyone agrees that a propertied bachelor needs (or wants) to find a woman to marry.
All things can tempt me from this craft of verse: One time it was a woman's face, or worse— The seeming needs of my fool-driven land; Now nothing but comes readier to the hand Than this accustomed toil....	Anything can distract me from writing poetry: One time I was distracted by a woman's face, but I was even more distracted by (or I found an even less worthy distraction in) the attempt to fulfill what I imagined to be the needs of a country governed by idiots. At this point in my life I find any task easier than the work I'm used to doing (writing poetry).
... making order out of Emily's life is a complicated matter, since the narrator recalls the details through a nonlinear filter.	It's difficult to figure out the order in which events in Emily's life occurred because the narrator doesn't relate them chronologically.

Paraphrase resembles translation. Indeed, the paraphrase of Yeats is essentially a "translation" of poetry into prose, and the paraphrases of Austen and of Dillon are "translations" of one kind of prose (formal nineteenth-century British prose, the equally formal but quite different prose of a twentieth-century literary critic) into another kind (colloquial twentieth-century American prose).

But what good is that? First, paraphrasing tests that you truly understand what you've read; it can be especially helpful when an author's diction and syntax seem difficult, complex, or "foreign" to you. Second, paraphrasing can direct your attention to nuances of tone or potentially significant details. For example, paraphrasing Austen's sentence might highlight its irony and call attention to the multiple meanings of phrases such as *a good fortune* and *in want of.* Similarly, paraphrasing Yeats might help you to think about all that he gains by making himself the object rather than the subject of his sentence. Third, paraphrase can help you begin generating the kind of interpretive questions that can drive an essay. For example, the Austen paraphrase might suggest the following questions: *What competing definitions of "a good fortune" are set out in* Pride and Prejudice? *Which definition, if any, does the novel as a whole seem to endorse?*

18.2 SUMMARY

A summary is a fairly succinct restatement or overview of the content of an entire text or source (or a significant portion thereof). Like paraphrases, summaries should always be stated in your own words.

A summary of a literary text is generally called a *plot summary* because it focuses on the action or plot. Here, for example, is a summary of Edgar Allan Poe's "The Raven":

> The speaker of Poe's "The Raven" is sitting in his room late at night reading in order to forget the death of his beloved Lenore. There's a tap at the door; after some hesitation he opens it and calls Lenore's name, but there is only an echo. When he goes back into his room he hears the rapping again, this time at his window, and when he opens it a raven enters. He asks the raven its name, and it answers very clearly, "Nevermore." As the speaker's thoughts run back to Lenore, he realizes the aptness of the raven's word: she shall sit there nevermore. But, he says, sooner or later he will forget her, and the grief will lessen. "Nevermore," the raven says again, too aptly. Now the speaker wants the bird to leave, but "Nevermore," the raven says once again. At the end, the speaker knows he'll never escape the raven or its dark message.

Though a summary should be significantly shorter than the original, it can be any length you need it to be. Above, the 108 lines of Poe's poem have been reduced to about 160 words. But one could summarize this or any other work in as little as one sentence. Here, for example, are three viable one-sentence summaries of *Hamlet*:

> A young man seeking to avenge his uncle's murder of his father kills his uncle, while also bringing about his own and many others' deaths.

> A young Danish prince avenges the murder of his father, the king, by his uncle, who had usurped the throne, but the prince himself is killed, as are others, and a well-led foreign army has no trouble successfully invading the decayed and troubled state.

> When, from the ghost of his murdered father, a young prince learns that his uncle, who has married the prince's mother, is the father's murderer, the prince plots revenge, feigning madness, acting erratically—even insulting the

woman he loves—and, though gaining his revenge, causes the suicide of his
beloved and the deaths of others and, finally, of himself.

As these *Hamlet* examples suggest, different readers—or even the same
reader on different occasions—will almost certainly summarize the same text
in dramatically different ways. Summarizing entails selection and emphasis.
As a result, any summary reflects a particular point of view and may even
imply a particular interpretation or argument. When writing a summary,
you should try to be as objective as possible; nevertheless, your summary
will reflect your own understanding and attitudes. For this reason, summarizing a literary text may help you to begin figuring out just what your
particular understanding of a text is, especially if you then compare your
summary to those of other readers.

18.3 DESCRIPTION

Whereas both summary and paraphrase focus on content, a description of
a literary text focuses on its overall form or structure or some particular
aspect thereof. Here, for example, is a description (rather than a summary)
of the rhyme scheme of "The Raven":

> Poe's "The Raven" is a poem of 108 lines divided into eighteen six-line stan-
> zas. If you were to look just at the ends of the lines, you would notice only one
> or two unusual features: not only is there only one rhyme sound per stanza—
> lines 2, 4, 5, and 6 rhyming—but one rhyme sound is the same in all eighteen
> stanzas, so that seventy-two lines end with the sound "ore." In addition, the
> fourth and fifth lines of each stanza end with an identical word; in six of the
> stanzas that word is "door" and in four others "Lenore." There is even more
> repetition: the last line of six of the first seven stanzas ends with the words
> "nothing more," and the last eleven stanzas end with the word "Nevermore."
> The rhyming lines—other than the last, which is very short—in each stanza are
> fifteen syllables long, the rhymed line sixteen. The longer lines give the effect
> of shorter ones, however, and add still further to the frequency of repeated
> sounds, for the first half of each opening line rhymes with the second half of
> the line, and so do the halves of line 3. There is still more: the first half of line
> 4 rhymes with the halves of line 3 (in the first stanza the rhymes are "dreary" /
> "weary" and "napping" / "tapping" / "rapping"). So at least nine words in
> each six-line stanza are involved in the regular rhyme scheme, and many stan-
> zas have added instances of rhyme or repetition. As if this were not enough,
> all the half-line rhymes are rich feminine rhymes, where both the accented and
> the following unaccented syllables rhyme—"dreary" / "wary."

You could similarly describe many other formal elements of the poem—
images and symbols, for example. You can describe a play in comparable
terms—acts, scenes, settings, time lapses, perhaps—and you might describe
a novel in terms of chapters, books, summary narration, dramatized scenes.
In addition to describing the narrative structure or focus and voice of a short
story, you might describe the diction (word choice), the sentence structure,
the amount and kind of description of characters or landscape, and so on.

19 THE ELEMENTS OF THE ESSAY

As you move from reading literary works to writing essays about them, remember that the essay—like the short story, poem, or play—is a distinctive subgenre with unique elements and conventions. Just as you come to a poem or play with a certain set of expectations, so will readers approach your essay. They will be looking for particular elements, anticipating that the work will unfold in a specific way. This chapter explains and explores those elements so that you can develop a clear sense of what makes a piece of writing an essay and why some essays are more effective than others.

An essay has particular elements and a particular form because it serves a specific purpose. Keeping this in mind, consider what an essay is and what it does. An essay is a relatively short written composition that articulates, supports, and develops an idea or claim. Like any work of expository prose, it aims to explain something complex. Explaining in this case entails both *analysis* (breaking the complex "thing" down into its constituent parts and showing how they work together to form a meaningful whole) and *argument* (working to convince someone that the analysis is valid). In an essay about literature, the literary work is the complex thing that you are helping a reader to better understand. The essay needs to show the reader a particular way to understand the work, to interpret or read it. That interpretation or reading starts with the essayist's own personal response. But an essay also needs to persuade the reader that this interpretation is reasonable and enlightening—that it is, though it is distinctive and new, it is more than merely idiosyncratic or subjective.

To achieve these ends, an essay must incorporate four elements: an appropriate *tone*, a clear *thesis*, a coherent *structure*, and ample, appropriate *evidence*.

19.1 TONE (AND AUDIENCE)

Although your reader or audience isn't an element *in* your essay, tone is. And tone and audience are closely interrelated. In everyday life, the tone we adopt has everything to do with whom we are talking to and what situation we're in. For example, we talk very differently to our parents than to our best friends. And in different situations we talk to the same person in different ways. What tone do you adopt with your best friends when you want to borrow money? when you need advice? when you're giving advice? when you're deciding whether to eat pizza or sushi? In each case you act on your knowledge of who your friends are, what information they already have, and what their response is likely to be. But you also try to adopt a tone that will encourage them to respond in a certain way.

In writing, as in everyday life, your audience, situation, and purpose should shape your tone. Conversely, your tone will shape your audience's response.

You need to figure out both who your readers are and what response you want to elicit. Who is your audience? When you write an essay for class, the obvious answer is your instructor. But in an important sense, that is the wrong answer. Although your instructor could literally be the only person besides you who will ever read your essay, you write about literature to learn how to write for an audience of peers—people a lot like you who are sensible and educated and who will appreciate having a literary work explained so that they can understand it more fully. Picture your reader as someone about your own age with roughly the same educational background. Assume the person has some experience in reading literature, but that he or she has read this particular work only once and has not yet closely analyzed it. You should neither be insulting and explain the obvious nor assume that your reader has noticed, considered, and remembered every detail.

Should you, then, altogether ignore the obvious fact that an instructor—who probably has a master's degree or doctorate in literature—is your actual reader? Not altogether: you don't want to get so carried away with speaking to people of your own age and interests that you slip into slang, or feel the need to explain what a stanza is, or leave unexplained an allusion to your favorite movie. Even though you do want to learn from the advice and guidelines your instructor has given, try not to be preoccupied with the idea that you are writing for someone "in authority" or someone utterly different from yourself.

Above all, don't think of yourself as writing for a captive audience, for readers who have to read what you write or who already see the text as you do. (If that were the case, there wouldn't be much point in writing at all.) It is not always easy to know how interested your readers will be or how their views might differ from yours, so you must make the most of every word. Remember that the purpose of your essay is to persuade readers to see the text your way. That process begins with persuading them that you deserve their attention and respect. The tone of your paper should be serious and straightforward, respectful toward your readers and the literary work. But its approach and vocabulary, while formal enough for academic writing, should be lively enough to interest someone like you. Try to imagine, as your ideal reader, the person in class whom you most respect but who often seems to see things differently from you. Write to capture and hold that person's attention and respect. Encourage your reader to adopt a desirable stance *toward* your essay by adopting that same stance *in* your essay. Engage and convince your reader by demonstrating your engagement and conviction. Encourage your reader to keep an open mind by showing that you have done the same.

19.2 THESIS

A thesis is to an essay what a theme is to a short story, play, or poem: it's the governing idea, proposition, claim, or point. Good theses come in many shapes and sizes. A thesis cannot always be conveyed in one sentence, nor will it always appear in the same place in every essay. But you will risk both appearing confused and confusing the reader if you can't state the thesis in one to three sentences or if the thesis doesn't appear somewhere in your introduction, usually near its end.

Regardless of its length or location, a thesis must be debatable—a claim that all readers won't automatically accept. It's a proposition that *can* be proven with evidence from the text. Yet it's one that *has* to be proven, that isn't obviously true or factual, that must be supported with evidence in order to be fully understood or accepted by the reader. The following examples juxtapose a series of inarguable topics or fact statements—ones that are merely factual or descriptive—with thesis statements, each of which makes a debatable claim about the topic or fact:

TOPIC OR FACT STATEMENTS	THESIS STATEMENTS
"The Story of an Hour" explores the topic of marriage.	In "The Story of an Hour," Chopin poses a troubling question: Does marriage inevitably encourage people to "impose [their] private will upon a fellow-creature" (315)?
"The Blind Man," "Cathedral," and "The Lame Shall Enter First" all feature characters with physical handicaps.	"The Blind Man," "Cathedral," and "The Lame Shall Enter First" feature protagonists who learn about their own emotional or spiritual shortcomings through an encounter with a physically handicapped person. In this way, all three stories invite us to question traditional definitions of "disability."
The experience of the speaker in "How I Discovered Poetry" is very ambiguous.	In "How I Discovered Poetry," what the speaker discovers is the ambiguous power of words—their capacity both to inspire and unite and to denigrate and divide.
"London" consists of three discrete stanzas that each end with a period; two-thirds of the lines are end-stopped.	In "London," William Blake uses a variety of formal techniques to suggest the unnatural rigidity and constraints of urban life.
A Streetcar Named Desire uses a lot of Darwinian language.	*A Streetcar Named Desire* asks whether or not it is truly the "fittest" who "survive" in contemporary America.
Creon and Antigone are both similar and different.	Creon and Antigone are alike in several ways, especially the inconsistency of their values and the way they are driven by passion below the surface of rational argument. Both are also one-sided in their commitments. . . . This does not mean, however, that they are equally limited in the values to which they adhere. —Mary Whitlock Blundell, "Helping Friends . . ."

All of the thesis statements above are arguable, but they share other traits as well. All are clear and emphatic. Each implicitly answers a compelling interpretive question—for instance, *What do Antigone and Creon stand for? Which character and worldview, if any, does the play as a whole ultimately champion?*

Yet each statement entices us to read further by generating more questions in our minds—*How and why do Creon and Antigone demonstrate "inconsistency" and "one-sidedness"? If these two characters are not equally limited, which of them is more limited?* An effective thesis enables the reader to enter the essay with a clear sense of what its writer will try to prove, and it inspires the reader with the desire to see the writer do it. We want to understand how the writer arrived at this view, to test whether it's valid, and to see how the writer will answer the other questions the thesis has generated in our minds. A good thesis captures the reader's interest and shapes his or her expectations. It also makes promises that the rest of the essay should fulfill.

At the same time, an arguable claim is not one-sided or narrow-minded. A thesis needs to stake out a position, but a position can and should admit complexity. Literary texts tend to focus more on exploring problems, conflicts, and questions than on offering solutions, resolutions, and answers. Their goal is to complicate, not simplify, our way of looking at the world. The best essays about literature and the theses that drive them often share a similar quality.

19.2.1 Interpretive versus Evaluative Claims

All the theses in the previous examples involve *interpretive* claims—claims about how a literary text works, what it says, how one should understand it. And interpretive claims generally work best as theses.

Yet it's useful to remember that in reading and writing about literature we often make (and debate) a different type of claim—the *evaluative.* Evaluation entails judging or assessing. Evaluative claims about literature tend to be of two kinds. The first involves aesthetic judgment, the question being whether a text (or a part or element thereof) succeeds in artistic terms. (This kind of claim features prominently in book reviews, for example.) The second involves philosophical, ethical, or even socially or politically based judgment, the question being whether an idea or action is wise or good, valid or admirable. All interpretive and evaluative claims involve informed opinion (which is why they are debatable). But whereas interpretive claims aim to elucidate the opinions expressed *in* and *by* the text, the second kind of evaluative claim assesses the value or validity of those opinions, often by comparing them with the writer's own.

The following examples juxtapose a series of interpretive claims with evaluative claims of both types:

INTERPRETIVE CLAIMS	EVALUATIVE CLAIMS
"A Conversation with My Father" explores the relative values of realistic and fantastic fiction. Rather than advocating one type of fiction, however, the story ends up affirming just how much we need stories of any and every kind.	"A Conversation with My Father" fails because it ends up being more a stilted Platonic dialogue about works of fiction than a true work of fiction in its own right.
	The father in "A Conversation with My Father" is absolutely right: realistic stories are more effective and satisfying than fantastic ones.

The speaker of John Donne's "Song" is an angry and disillusioned man obsessed with the infidelity of women.	In "Song," John Donne does a very effective job of characterizing the speaker, an angry and disillusioned man obsessed with the infidelity of women.
	John Donne's "Song" is a horribly misogynistic poem because it ends up endorsing the idea that women are incapable of fidelity.
"How I Learned to Drive" demonstrates that, in Paula Vogel's words, "it takes a whole village to molest a child."	"How I Learned to Drive" is at once too preachy and too self-consciously theatrical to be dramatically effective.
	By insisting that sexual abuse is a crime perpetrated by a "whole village" rather than by an individual, Paula Vogel lets individual abusers off the hook, encouraging us to see them as victims rather than as the villains they really are.

In practice, the line between these different types of claims can become very thin. For instance, an essay claiming that Paula Vogel's play conveys a socially dangerous or morally bad message about abuse may also claim that it is, as a result, an aesthetically flawed play. Further, an essay defending an interpretive claim about a text implies that it is at least aesthetically or philosophically worthy enough to merit interpretation. Conversely, defending and developing an evaluative claim about a text always requires a certain amount of interpretation. (You have to figure out what the text says in order to figure out whether the text says it well or says something worthwhile.)

To some extent, then, the distinctions are ones of emphasis. But they are important nonetheless. And unless instructed otherwise, you should generally make your thesis an interpretive claim, reserving evaluative claims for conclusions. (On conclusions, see 19.3.3.)

19.3 STRUCTURE

Like any literary text, an essay needs to have a beginning (or introduction), a middle (or body), and an ending (or conclusion). Each of these parts has a distinct function.

19.3.1 Beginning: The Introduction

Your essay's beginning, or introduction, should draw readers in and prepare them for what's to come by:

- articulating the thesis;
- providing whatever basic information—about the text, the author, and/or the topic—readers will need to follow the argument; and
- creating interest in the thesis by demonstrating that there is a problem or question that it resolves or answers.

This final task involves showing readers why your thesis isn't dull or obvious, establishing a specific *motive* for the essay and its readers. There are numerous possible motives, but writing expert Gordon Harvey has identified three especially common ones:

1. The truth isn't what one would expect or what it might appear to be on a first reading.
2. There's an interesting wrinkle in the text—a paradox, a contradiction, a tension.
3. A seemingly tangential or insignificant matter is actually important or interesting.

(On motives specific to research essays, see 21.1.1.)

19.3.2 Middle: The Body

The middle, or body, of your essay is its beating heart, the place where you do the essential work of supporting and developing the thesis by presenting and analyzing evidence. Each of the body paragraphs needs to articulate, support, and develop one specific claim—a debatable idea directly related to, but smaller and more specific than, the thesis. This claim should be stated fairly early in the paragraph in a *topic sentence*. And every sentence in the paragraph should help prove, or elaborate on, that claim. Indeed, each paragraph ideally should build from an initial, general statement of the claim to the more complex form of it that you develop by presenting and analyzing evidence. In this way, each paragraph functions like a miniature essay with its own thesis, body, and conclusion.

Your essay as a whole should develop logically just as each paragraph does. To ensure that that happens, you need to:

- order your paragraphs so that each builds on the last, with one idea following another in a logical sequence. The goal is to lay out a clear path for the reader. Like any path, it should go somewhere. Don't just prove your point; develop it.
- present each idea/paragraph so that the logic behind the sequential order is clear. Try to start each paragraph with a sentence that functions as a bridge, carrying the reader from one point to the next. Don't make the reader have to leap.

19.3.3 Ending: The Conclusion

In terms of their purpose (not their content), conclusions are introductions in reverse. Whereas introductions draw readers away from their world and into your essay, conclusions send them back. Introductions work to convince readers that they should read the essay. Conclusions work to show them why and how the experience was worthwhile. You should approach conclusions, then, by thinking about what sort of lasting impression you want to create. What precisely do you want readers to take with them as they journey back into the "real world"?

Effective conclusions often consider three things:

1. *Implications*—What picture of your author's work or worldview does your argument imply or suggest? Alternatively, what might your argument imply about some real-world issue or situation? Implications don't have to be earth-shattering. For example, it's unlikely that your reading of Flannery O'Connor's "Everything That Rises Must Converge" will rock your readers' world. Moreover, trying to convince readers that it can may well have the opposite effect. Yet your argument should in some small but significant way change the way readers see O'Connor's work; alternatively, it might give them new insight into how racism works, or how difficult it is for human beings to adjust to changes in the world around us, or how mistaken it can be to see ourselves as more enlightened than our elders, and so on.

2. *Evaluation*—What might your argument about the text reveal about the literary quality or effectiveness of the text as a whole or of some specific element? Alternatively, to what extent and how do you agree and/or disagree with the author's conclusions about a particular issue? How, for example, does your own view of how racism works compare to the viewpoint implied in "Everything That Rises Must Converge"? (For more on evaluative claims, see 19.2.1.)

3. *Areas of ambiguity or unresolved questions*—Are there any remaining puzzles or questions that your argument and/or the text itself doesn't resolve or answer? Alternatively, might your argument suggest a new question or puzzle worth investigating?

Above all, don't repeat what you've already said. If the essay has done its job to this point, and especially if the essay is relatively short, your readers may feel bored and insulted if they get a mere summary. You should clarify anything that needs clarifying, but go a little beyond that. The best essays are rounded wholes in which conclusions do, in a sense, circle back to the place where they started. However, the best essays remind readers of where they began only in order to give them a more palpable sense of how far they've come.

19.4 EVIDENCE

In terms of convincing readers that your claims are valid, both the amount and the quality of your evidence count. And the quality of your evidence will depend, in great part, on how you prepare and present it. Each of the ideas that makes up the body of your essay must be supported and developed with ample, appropriate evidence. Colloquially speaking, the term *evidence* simply refers to facts. But it's helpful to remember that a fact by itself isn't really evidence for anything, or rather that—as lawyers well know—any one fact can be evidence for many things. Like lawyers, essayists turn a fact into evidence by interpreting it; drawing an inference from it; giving the reader a vivid sense of why and how the fact supports a specific claim. You need, then, both to present specific facts and to actively interpret them. *Show* readers why and how each fact matters.

Quotations are an especially important form of evidence in essays about literature; indeed, an essay about literature that contains no quotations will likely be relatively weak. The reader of such an essay may doubt whether its argument emerges out of a thorough knowledge of the work. However, quotations are by no means the only facts on which you should draw. Indeed, a quotation will lead your reader to expect commentary on, and interpretation of, its language. As a general rule, you should quote directly from the text only when its wording is significant. Otherwise, simply paraphrase, describe, or summarize. The following example demonstrates the use of both summary and quotation. (On effective quotation, see 22.1; on paraphrase, summary, and description, see ch. 18.)

> At many points in the novel, religion is represented as having degenerated into a system of social control by farmers over workers. Only respectable young men can come courting at Upper Weatherbury farm, and no swearing is allowed (ch. 8). Similarly, the atmosphere in Boldwood's farm kitchen is "like a Puritan Sunday lasting all the week." Bathsheba tries to restrict her workers to drinking mild liquor, and church attendance is taken as the mark of respectability.
> —Fred Reid, "Art and Ideology in *Far from the Madding Crowd*,"
> *Thomas Hardy Annual 4* (London: Macmillan, 1986)

> NOTE: Pay special attention to the way this writer uses paraphrase, summary, and quotation. At the beginning of the paragraph, he simply paraphrases certain rules; at its end, he summarizes or describes one character's action. Here, he can use his own words because it's the rules and actions that illustrate his point, not the words that the novelist uses to describe them. However, Reid does quote the text when its (religious) language is the crucial, evidentiary element.

19.5 CONVENTIONS THAT CAN CAUSE PROBLEMS

A mastery of basic mechanics and writing conventions is essential to convincing your readers that you are a knowledgeable and careful writer whose ideas they should respect. This section explores three conventions that are especially crucial to essays about literature.

19.5.1 Tenses

Essays about literature tend to function almost wholly in the present tense, a practice that can take some getting used to. The rationale is that the action within any literary work never stops: a text simply, always *is*. Thus yesterday, today, and tomorrow, Ophelia *goes* mad; "The Lost World" *asks* what it means to grow up; Wordsworth *sees* nature as an avenue to God; and so on. When in doubt, stick to the present tense when writing about literature.

An important exception to this general rule is demonstrated in the following example. As you read the excerpt, pay attention to the way the writer shifts between tenses, using various past tenses to refer to completed actions that took place in the actual past, and using the present tense to refer to actions that occur within, or are performed by, the text.

> In 1959 Plath **did not** consciously **attempt** to write in the domestic poem genre, perhaps because she **was not** yet ready to assume her majority. Her journal entries of that period **bristle** with an impatience at herself that **may derive** from this reluctance.... But by fall 1962, when she **had** already **lost** so much, she **was** ready.... In "Daddy" she **achieved** her victory in two ways. First, ... she symbolically **assaults** a father figure who **is identified** with male control of language.
>
> —Steven Gould Axelrod, "Jealous Gods"

19.5.2 Titles

Underline or italicize the titles of all books and works published independently, including:

- long poems (*Endymion; Paradise Lost*)
- plays (*A Midsummer Night's Dream; Death and the King's Horseman*)
- periodicals: newspapers, magazines, scholarly journals, and the like (*New York Times; College English*)

Use quotation marks for the titles of works that have been published as part of longer works, including:

- short stories ("A Rose for Emily"; "Happy Endings")
- essays and periodical articles ("A Rose for 'A Rose for Emily' "; "Art and Ideology in *Far from the Madding Crowd*")
- poems ("Daddy"; "Ode to a Nightingale")

Generally speaking, you should capitalize the first word of every title, as well as all the other words that aren't either articles (e.g., *the, a*); prepositions (e.g., *among, in, through*); or conjunctions (e.g., *and, but*). One exception to this rule is the poem in which the first line substitutes for a missing title (a category that includes everything by Emily Dickinson, as well as the sonnets of Shakespeare and Edna St. Vincent Millay). In such cases, only the first word is capitalized. Often, the entire phrase is placed in brackets—as in "[Let me not to the marriage of true minds]"—but you will just as often see such titles without brackets.

19.5.3 Names

When first referring to an author, use his or her full name; thereafter, use the last name. (For example, although you may feel a real kinship with Robert Frost, you will appear disrespectful if you refer to him as Robert.)

With characters' names, use the literary work as a guide. Because "Bartleby, the Scrivener" always refers to its characters as *Bartleby, Turkey,* and *Nippers,* so should you. But because "The Management of Grief" refers to Judith Templeton either by her full name or by her first name, it would be odd and confusing to call her *Templeton.*

20 THE WRITING PROCESS

It's fairly easy to describe the purpose and formal elements of an essay. Actually writing one is more difficult. So, too, is prescribing a precise formula for how to do so. In practice, the writing process will vary from writer to writer and from assignment to assignment. No one can give you a recipe. However, this chapter presents a menu of possible approaches and exercises, which you should test out and refine for yourself.

As you do so, keep in mind that writing needn't be a solitary enterprise. Most writers—working in every genre, at every level—get inspiration, guidance, help, and feedback from other people throughout the writing process, and so can you. Your instructor may well create opportunities for collaboration, having you and your colleagues work together to plan essays, critique drafts, and so on. Even if that isn't the case, you can always reach out to others on your own. Since every essay will ultimately have to engage readers, why not bring some actual readers and fellow writers into the writing process? Use class discussions to generate and test out essay topics and theses. Ask the instructor to clarify assignments or to talk with you about your plans. Have classmates, friends, or roommates read your drafts.

Of course, your essay ultimately needs to be your own work. You, the individual writer, must be the ultimate arbiter, critically scrutinizing the advice you receive, differentiating valid reader responses from idiosyncratic ones. But in writing about literature, as in reading it, we all can get a much better sense of what we think by considering others' views.

20.1 GETTING STARTED

20.1.1 Scrutinizing the Assignment

For student essayists, as for most professional ones, the writing process usually begins with an assignment. Though assignments vary greatly, all impose certain restrictions. These are designed not to hinder your creativity but to direct it into productive channels, ensuring that you hone certain skills, try out various approaches, and avoid common pitfalls. Your first task as a writer is thus to scrutinize the assignment. Make sure that you fully understand what you are being asked to do (and not do), and ask questions about anything unclear or puzzling.

Almost all assignments restrict the length of the essay by giving word or page limits. Keep those limits in mind as you generate and evaluate potential essay topics, making sure that you choose a topic you can handle in the space allowed. Many assignments impose further restrictions, often indicating the texts and/or topics to be explored. As a result, any given assignment will significantly shape the rest of the writing process—determining, for example, whether and how you should tackle a step such as "Choosing a Text" or "Identifying Topics."

Here are three representative essay assignments, each of which imposes a different set of restrictions:

1. Choose any story in this anthology and write an essay analyzing the way in which its protagonist changes.

2. Write an essay analyzing one of the following sonnets: "The New Colossus," "Range-Finding," or "London, 1802." Be sure to consider how the poem's form contributes to its meaning.

3. Write an essay exploring the significance of references to eyes and vision in *A Midsummer Night's Dream*. What, through them, does the play suggest about both the power and the limitations of human vision?

The first assignment dictates the topic and main question. It also provides the kernel of a thesis: *In [story title], [protagonist's name] goes from being a _____ to a _____ OR By the end of [story title], [protagonist's name] has learned that _____*. The assignment leaves you free to choose which story you will write about, although it limits you to those in which the protagonist clearly changes or learns a lesson of some kind. The second assignment limits your choice of texts to three. Though it also requires that your essay address the effects of the poet's choice to use the sonnet form, it doesn't require this to be the main topic of the essay. Rather, it leaves you free to pursue any topic that focuses on the poem's meaning. The third assignment is the most restrictive. It indicates both the text and the general topic to be explored, while requiring you to narrow the topic and formulate a specific thesis.

20.1.2 Choosing a Text

If the assignment allows you to choose which text to write about, try letting your initial impressions or "gut reactions" guide you. If you do so, your first impulse may be to choose a text that you like or "get" right away. Perhaps its language resembles your own; it depicts speakers, characters, or situations that you easily relate to; or it explores issues that you care deeply about. Following that first impulse can be a great idea. Writing an engaging essay requires being engaged with whatever we're writing about, and we all find it easier to engage with texts, authors, and/or characters that we like immediately.

You may discover, however, that you have little interesting or new to say about such a text. Perhaps you're too emotionally invested to analyze it closely, or maybe its meaning seems so obvious that there's no puzzle or problem to drive an argument. You might, then, find it more productive to choose a work that provokes the opposite reaction—one that initially puzzles or angers you, one whose characters or situations seem alien, one that investigates an issue you haven't previously thought much about or that articulates a theme you don't agree with. Sometimes such negative responses can have surprisingly positive results when it comes to writing. One student writer, for example, summed up her basic response to William Blake's *The Marriage of Heaven and Hell* with the words "He's crazy." Initially, the poem made no sense to her. And that's precisely why she decided to write about it: she needed to do so, to make sense of it for other readers, in order to make sense of it for herself. In the end, she wrote a powerful essay exploring how the poem defined, and why it celebrated, seeming insanity.

When writing about a text that you've discussed in class, you might make similar use of your "gut responses" to that conversation. Did you strongly agree or disagree with one of your classmate's interpretations of a particular text? If so, why not write about it?

20.1.3 Identifying Topics

When an assignment allows you to create your own topic, you will much more likely build a lively and engaging essay from a particular insight or question that captures your attention and makes you want to say something, solve a problem, or stake out a position. The best papers originate in an individual response to a text and focus on a genuine question about it. Even when an instructor assigns a topic, the effectiveness of your essay will largely depend on whether or not you have made the topic your own, turning it into a question to which you discover your own answer.

Often we refer to "finding" a topic, as if there are a bevy of topics "out there" just waiting to be plucked like ripe fruit off the topic-tree. In at least two ways, that's true. For one thing, as we read a literary work, certain topics often do jump out and say, "Hey, look at me! I'm a topic!" A title alone may have that effect: What rises and converges in "Everything That Rises Must Converge"? Why is Keats so keen on that darn nightingale; what does it symbolize for him? Why does Wilde think it's important *not* to be earnest?

For another thing, certain general topics can be adapted to fit almost any literary work. In fact, that's just another way of saying that there are certain common types (or subgenres) of literary essays, just as there are of short stories, plays, and poems. For example, one very common kind of literary essay explores the significance of a seemingly insignificant aspect or element of a work—a word or group of related words, an image or image-cluster, a minor character, an incident or action, and so on. Equally common are character-focused essays of three types. The first explores the outlook or worldview of a character and its consequences. The second considers the way a major character develops from the beginning of a literary work to its end. The third analyzes the nature and significance of a conflict between two characters (or two groups of characters) and the way this conflict is ultimately resolved. Especially when you're utterly befuddled about where to begin, it can be very useful to keep in mind these generic topics and essay types and to use them as starting points. But remember that they are just starting points. One always has to adapt and narrow a generic topic such as "imagery" or "character change" in order to produce an effective essay. In practice, then, no writer simply "finds" a topic; he or she *makes* one.

Similarly, though the topic that leaps out at you immediately might end up being the one you find most interesting, you can only discover that by giving yourself some options. It's always a good idea to initially come up with as many topics as you can. Test out various topics to see which one will work best. Making yourself identify multiple topics will lead you to think harder, look more closely, and reach deeper into yourself and the work.

Here are some additional techniques to identify potential topics. In each case, write your thoughts down. Don't worry at this point about what form your writing takes or how good it is.

- *Analyze your initial response.*

  If you've chosen a text that you feel strongly about, start with those responses. Try to describe your feelings and trace them to their source. Be as specific as possible. What moments, aspects, or elements of the text most affected you? Exactly how and why did they affect you? What was most puzzling? amusing? annoying? intriguing? Try to articulate the question behind your feelings. Often, strong responses result when a work either challenges or affirms an expectation, assumption, or conviction that you, the reader, bring to the work. Think about whether and how that's true here. Define the specific expectation, assumption, or conviction. How, where, and why does the text challenge it? fulfill and affirm it? Which of your responses and expectations are objectively valid, likely to be shared by other readers?

- *Think through the elements.*

  Start with a list of elements and work your way through them, thinking about what's unique or interesting or puzzling about the text in terms of each. When it comes to tone, what stands out? What about the speaker? the situation? other elements? Come up with a statement about each. Look for patterns among your statements. Also, think about the questions implied or overlooked by your statements.

- *Pose motive questions.*

  In articulating a motive in your essay's introduction, your concern is primarily with the readers, your goal being to give them a solid reason to keep on reading. But you can often work your way toward a topic (or topics) by considering motive. As suggested earlier (19.3.1), there are three common motives. Turn each one into a question in order to identify potential topics:

  1. What element(s) or aspect(s) of this work might a casual reader misinterpret?
  2. What interesting paradox(es), contradiction(s), or tension(s) do you see in this text?

3. What seemingly minor, insignificant, easily ignored element(s) or aspect(s) of this text might in fact have major significance?

20.1.4 Formulating a Question and a Thesis

Almost any element, aspect, or point of interest in a text can become a topic for a short essay. Before you can begin writing an essay on that topic, however, you need to come up with a thesis or hypothesis—an arguable statement about the topic. Quite often, one comes up with topic and thesis simultaneously: you might well decide to write about a topic precisely because you've got a specific claim to make about it. At other times, that's not the case: the topic comes much more easily than the thesis. In those cases, it helps to formulate a specific question about the topic and to develop a specific answer. That answer will be your thesis.

Again, remember that your question and thesis should focus on something specific, yet they need to be generally valid, involving more than your personal feelings. Who, after all, can really argue with you about how you feel? The following example demonstrates the way you might freewrite your way from an initial, subjective response to an arguable thesis:

> *I really admire Bartleby.*
> *But why? What in the story encourages me to respond that way to him? Well, he sticks to his guns and insists on doing only what he "prefers" to do. He doesn't just follow orders. That makes him really different from all the other characters in the story (especially the narrator). And also from a lot of people I know, even me. He's a nonconformist.*
> *Do I think other readers should feel the same way? Maybe, but maybe not. After all, his refusal to conform does cause problems for everyone around him. And actually it doesn't do him a lot of good either. Plus, he would be really annoying in real life. And, even if you admire him, you can't really care about him because he doesn't seem to care about anybody else.*
> *Maybe that's the point. Through Bartleby, Melville explores both how rare and important, and how dangerous, nonconformity can be.*

Regardless of how you arrive at your thesis or how strongly you believe in it, it's still helpful at this early stage to think of it as a working hypothesis—a claim that's provisional, still open to rethinking and revision.

20.2 PLANNING

Once you've formulated a tentative thesis, you need to (1) identify the relevant evidence, and (2) figure out how to structure your argument, articulating and ordering your claims or sub-ideas. Generally speaking, it works best to tackle structure first—that is, to first figure out your claims and create an outline—because doing so will help you get a sense of what kind of evidence you need. However, you may sometimes get stuck and need to reverse this process, gathering evidence first in order to then formulate and order your claims.

20.2.1 Moving from Claims to Evidence

If you want to focus first on structure, start by looking closely at your thesis. As in many other aspects of writing, it helps to temporarily fill your readers' shoes, trying to see your thesis and the promises it makes from the readers' point of view. What will they need to be shown, and in what order?

If a good thesis shapes readers' expectations, it can also guide you, as a writer. A good thesis often implies what the essay's claims should be and how they should be ordered. For instance, a thesis that focuses on the development of a character implies both that the first body paragraphs will explain what the character is initially like and that later paragraphs will explore how and why that character changes over the course of the story, poem, or play. Similarly, the Bartleby thesis developed in the previous example—*Through Bartleby, Melville explores both how rare and important, and how dangerous, nonconformity can be.*—implies that the writer's essay will address four major issues and will thus have four major parts. The first part must show that Bartleby is a nonconformist. The second part should establish that this nonconformity is rare, a quality that isn't shared by the other characters in the story. Finally, the third and fourth parts should explore, respectively, the positive and negative aspects or consequences of Bartleby's nonconformist behavior. Some or all of these parts may need to include multiple paragraphs, each devoted to a more specific claim.

At this stage, it's very helpful to create an outline. Write down or type out your thesis, and then list each claim (to create a *sentence outline*) or each of the topics to be covered (to create a *topic outline*). Now you can return to the text, rereading it in order to gather evidence for each claim. In the process, you might discover facts that seem relevant to the thesis but that don't relate directly to any of the claims you've articulated. In that case, you may need to insert a new claim into the outline. Additionally, you may find (and should actively look for) facts that challenge your argument. Test and reassess your claims against those facts.

20.2.2 Moving From Evidence to Claims

If you are focusing first on evidence, start by rereading the literary work in a more strategic way, searching for everything relevant to your topic— words, phrases, structural devices, changes of tone, and so forth. As you read (slowly and single-mindedly, with your thesis in mind), keep your pen constantly poised to mark or note down useful facts. Be ready to say something about the facts as you come upon them; immediately write down any ideas that occur to you. Some of these will appear in your essay; some won't. Just like most of the footage shot in making a film, many of your notes will end up on the cutting-room floor. As in filmmaking, however, having too much raw material is preferable to not having enough.

No one can tell you exactly how to take notes. But here is one process that you might try. Be forewarned: this process involves using notecards or uniform sheets of paper. Having your notes on individual cards makes it easier to separate and sort them, a concrete, physical process that can aid the mental process of organizing thoughts and facts. If you are working on a computer, create notecards by putting page breaks between each note or by leaving enough space so that you can cut each page down to a uniform size.

1. Keep your thesis constantly in mind as you reread and take notes. Mark all the passages in the text that bear on your thesis. For each, create a notecard that contains both (a) a single sentence describing how the passage relates to your thesis, and (b) the specific information about the passage's location that you will need to create a parenthetical citation. (The information you need will depend on the kind of text you're working with; for specifics, see 22.2.1.) Also, make cards for other relevant, evidentiary facts—like aspects of a poem's rhyme scheme.

2. Keep reading and taking notes until you experience any of the following:
   - get too tired and lose your concentration. (Stop, take a break, come back later.)
   - stop finding relevant evidence or perceive a noticeable drying up of your ideas. (Again, it's time to pause. Later, when your mind is fresh, read the text one more time to ensure that you didn't miss anything.)
   - find yourself annotating every sentence or line, with the evidence all running together into a single blob. (If this happens, your thesis is probably too broad. Simplify and narrow it. Then continue notetaking.)
   - become impatient with your notetaking and can't wait to get started writing. (Start drafting immediately. But be prepared to go back to systematic notetaking if your ideas stop coming or your energy fades.)
   - find that the evidence is insufficient for your thesis, that it points in another direction, or that it contradicts your thesis. (Revise your thesis to accommodate the evidence, and begin rereading once more.)

3. When you think you have finished notetaking, read all your note-cards over slowly, one by one, and jot down any further ideas as they occur to you, each one on a separate notecard.

Use your notecards to work toward an outline. Again, there are many ways to go about doing this. Here's one process:

1. Sort your cards into logical groups or clusters. Come up with a keyword for that group, and write that word at the top of each card in the group.

2. Set your notecards aside. On a fresh sheet of paper or in a separate document on your computer, write all the major points you want to make. Write them randomly, as they occur to you. Then read quickly through your notecards, and add to your list any important points you have left out.

3. Now it's time to order your points. Putting your points in order is something of a guess at this point, and you may well want to re-order later. For now, take your best guess. Taking your random list, put a "1" in front of the point you will probably begin with, a "2" before the probable second point, and so on.

4. Copy the list in numerical order, revising (if necessary) as you go.

5. Match up your notes (and examples) with the points on your outline. Prepare a title card for each point in the outline, writing on it the point and its probable place in the essay. Then line them up in order before you begin writing. If you're working on a computer, use the search function to find each instance of a keyword, phrase, or name. Then cut and paste in order to arrange your electronic "cards" under the headings you've identified.

6. At this point, you may discover cards that resist classification, cards that belong in two or more places, and/or cards that don't belong anywhere at all. If a card relates to more than one point, put it in the pile with the lowest number, but write on it the number or numbers of other possible locations. Try to find a place for the cards that don't seem to fit, and then put any that remain unsorted into a special file marked "?" or "use in revision."

Before you begin drafting, you may want to develop a more elaborate outline, incorporating examples and including topic sentences for each paragraph; or you may wish to work directly from your sketchy outline and cards.

20.3 DRAFTING

If you've taken enough time with the planning process, you may already be quite close to a first draft. If you've instead jumped straight into writing, you may have to move back and forth between composing and taking some of the steps described in the last section. Either way, remember that first drafts are often called *rough drafts* for a reason. Think of yourself as a painter "roughing out" a sketch in preparation for the more detailed painting to come. The most important thing is to start writing and keep at it.

Try to start with your thesis and work your way step by step through the entire body of the essay at one sitting. (However, you don't actually have to sit the whole time; if you get stuck, jump up and down, walk around the room, water your plants. Then get back to work.) You will almost certainly feel frustrated at times—as you search for the right word, struggle to decide how the next sentence should begin, or discover that you need to tackle ideas in a different order from what you originally had planned.

Stick to it. If you become truly stuck, try to explain your point to another person, or get out a piece of paper or open a new computer file and try working out your ideas or freewriting for a few minutes before returning to your draft. Or, if you get to a section you simply can't write at the moment, make a note about what needs to go in that spot. Then move on and come back to that point later.

Whatever it takes, stay with your draft until you've at least got a middle, or body, that you're relatively satisfied with. Then take a break. Later or even tomorrow come back and take another shot, attaching an introduction and conclusion to the body, filling in any gaps, doing your utmost to create a relatively satisfying whole. Now pat yourself on the back and take another break.

20.4 REVISING

Revision is one of the most important and difficult tasks for any writer. It's a crucial stage in the writing process, yet one that is all too easy to ignore or mismanage. The difference between a so-so essay and a good one, between a good essay and a great one, often depends entirely on effective revision. Give yourself time to revise and develop revision strategies that work for you; the investment in time and effort will pay rich dividends.

Ideally, the process of revision should involve three distinct tasks: assessing the elements, improving the argument, and editing and proofreading. Each of these may require a separate draft. Before considering those three tasks, however, you should be aware of the following three general tips.

First, effective revision requires you to temporarily play the role of reader, as well as writer, of your essay. Take a step back from your draft, doing your utmost to look at it from a more objective point of view. Revision demands re-vision—looking again, seeing anew. As a result, this is an especially good time to involve other people. Have a classmate or friend read and critique your draft.

Second, at this stage it helps to think less in absolute terms (right and wrong, good and bad) than in terms of strengths and weaknesses (elements and aspects of the draft that work well and those that can be improved through revision). If you can understand what's making your essay work as well as what's detracting from it, then you're better able to improve it. Don't get distracted from this important work by grammatical errors, spelling mistakes, or other minutiae; there will be time to correct them later.

Third, learn to take full advantage of all the capabilities of the computer, but also recognize its limitations. Cutting and pasting make experimenting with different organizational strategies a breeze; word-processing programs identify problems with grammar, spelling, and syntax; the search function can locate repetitive or problematic wording; and so on. You should familiarize yourself with, and use, all of the tools your computer provides and be thankful that you barely know the meaning of the word *white-out*. But you should also remember that the computer is just a tool with limits and that you must be its master. Like any tool, it can create new problems in the process of solving old ones. When it comes to grammar, syntax, and spelling, for instance, you should always pay attention to your program's queries and suggestions. But if you let it make all the decisions, you may end up with an essay full of malapropisms at once hilarious and tragic (one student essay consistently referred to human beings as *human beans*!) or of sentences that are all exactly the same size and shape—all perfectly correct, and all perfectly boring. Also, because the computer makes cutting and pasting so easy and only shows an essay one screen at a time, it's much easier to reorganize but much harder to recognize the effects of doing so. During revision, then, you should at times move away from the computer screen. Print out a hard copy periodically so that you can assess your essay as a whole, identifying problems that you can return to the computer to fix.

20.4.1 Assessing the Elements

The first step in revision is to make sure that all the elements or working parts of the essay are indeed working. To help with that process, run through the following checklist in order to identify the strengths and weaknesses of your draft. Try to answer each question honestly.

Thesis
- [ ] Is there *one* claim that effectively controls the essay?
- [ ] Is the claim debatable?
- [ ] Does the claim demonstrate real thought? Does it truly illuminate the text and the topic?

Structure

BEGINNING
- [ ] Does the introduction establish a clear motive for readers, effectively convincing them that there's something worth thinking, reading, and writing about here?
- [ ] Does it give readers all (and only) the basic information they need about the text, author, and/or topic?
- [ ] Does the introduction clearly state the central claim or thesis? Is it obvious which claim is the thesis?

MIDDLE
- [ ] Does each paragraph state one debatable claim? Is the main claim always obvious? Does everything in the paragraph relate to, and help to support and develop, that claim?
- [ ] Is each of those claims clearly related to (but different from) the thesis?

☐ Are the claims/paragraphs logically ordered?

☐ Is that logic clear? Is each claim clearly linked to those that come before and after? Are there any logical "leaps" that readers might have trouble taking?

☐ Does each claim/paragraph clearly build on the last one? Does the argument move forward, or does it seem more like a list or a tour through a museum of interesting observations?

☐ Do any key claims or steps in the argument seem to be missing?

TIP: You may be better able to discover structural weaknesses if you:
1. re-outline your draft as it is. Copy your thesis statement and each of your topic sentences into a separate document. Then pose the above questions. OR
2. read through the essay with highlighters of various colors in hand. As you read, color-code parts that could be restatements of the same or closely related ideas. Then reorganize to match up the colors.

ENDING

☐ Does the conclusion give readers the sense that they've gotten somewhere and that the journey has been worthwhile?

☐ Does it indicate the implications of the argument, consider relevant evaluative questions, and/or discuss questions that remain unanswered?

Evidence

☐ Is there ample, appropriate evidence for each claim?

☐ Are the appropriateness and significance of each fact—its relevance to the claim—perfectly clear?

☐ Are there any weak examples or inferences that aren't reasonable? Are there moments when readers might ask, "But couldn't that fact instead mean this?"

☐ Is all the evidence considered? What about facts that might complicate or contradict the argument? Are there moments when readers might think, "But what about this other fact?"

☐ Is each piece of evidence clearly presented? Do readers have all the contextual information they need to understand a quotation?

☐ Is each piece of evidence gracefully presented? Are quotations varied by length and presentation? Are they ever too long? Are there any unnecessary block quotations, or block quotations that require additional analysis? (For more specific explanations and advice on effective quotation, see 22.1.)

Though you want to pay attention to all of the elements, first drafts often have similar weaknesses. There are three especially common ones:

• *Mismatch between thesis and argument or between introduction and body* Sometimes a first or second draft ends up being a tool for discovering what your thesis really is. As a result, you may find that the thesis of your draft (or your entire introduction) doesn't fit the argument you've ended up making. You thus need to start your revision by reworking the thesis and introduction. Then work your way back through the essay, making sure that each claim or topic sentence fits the new thesis.

- *The list, or "museum tour," structure*
  In a draft, writers sometimes present each claim as if it were just an item on a list (*First, second,* and so on) or as a stop on a tour of ideas (*And this is also important . . .*). But presenting your ideas in this way keeps you and your readers from making logical connections between ideas. It may also prevent your argument from developing. Sometimes it can even be a symptom of the fact that you've ceased arguing entirely, falling into mere plot summary or description. Check to see if number-like words or phrases appear prominently at the beginning of your paragraphs or if your paragraphs could be put into a different order without fundamentally changing what you're saying. At times, solving this problem will require wholesale rethinking and reorganizing. But at other times, you will just need to add or rework topic sentences. Make sure that there's a clearly stated, debatable claim upfront and in charge of each paragraph and that each claim relates to, but differs from, the thesis.

- *Missing sub-ideas*
  You may find that you've skipped a logical step in your argument—that the claim you make in, say, body paragraph 3 actually depends on, or makes sense only in light of, a more basic claim that you took for granted in your draft. In that case, you'll need to create and insert a new paragraph that articulates, supports, and develops this key claim.

20.4.2 Enriching the Argument

Step 1 of the revision process aims to ensure that your essay does the best possible job of making your argument. But revision is also an opportunity to go beyond that—to think about ways in which your overall argument might be made more thorough and complex. In drafting an essay our attention is often and rightly focused on emphatically staking out a particular position and proving its validity. This is the fundamental task of any essay, and you certainly don't want to do anything at this stage to compromise that. At the same time, you do want to make sure that you haven't purchased clarity at the cost of oversimplification by, for example, ignoring evidence that might undermine or complicate your claims, alternative interpretations of the evidence you do present, or alternative claims or points of view. Remember, you have a better chance of persuading readers to accept your point of view if you show them that it's based on a thorough, open-minded exploration of the text and topic. Don't invent unreasonable or irrelevant complications or counterarguments. Do try to assess your argument objectively and honestly, perhaps testing it against the text one more time. Think like a reader rather than a writer: Are there points where a reasonable reader might object to, or disagree with, the argument? Have you ignored or glossed over any questions or issues that a reasonable reader might expect an essay on this topic to address?

20.4.3 Editing and Proofreading

Once you've gotten the overall argument in good shape, it's time to focus on the small but important stuff—words and sentences. Your prose should not only convey your ideas to your readers but also demonstrate how much you care about your essay. Flawless prose can't disguise a vapid or illogical argument, but faulty, flabby prose can destroy a potentially persuasive and thoughtful one. Don't sabotage all your hard work by failing to correct misspelled words, grammatical problems, misquotations, incorrect citations, or typographical errors. Little oversights make all the difference when it comes to clarity and credibility.

Though you will want to check all of the following aspects of your essay, it will probably be easier to spot mistakes and weaknesses if you read through the essay several times, concentrating each time on one specific aspect.

Every writer has individual weaknesses and strengths, and every writer tends to be overly fond of certain phrases and sentence structures. With practice, you will learn to watch out for the kinds of mistakes to which you are most prone. Eventually, you can and should develop your own *personalized* editing checklist.

Sentences

☐ Does each one read clearly and crisply?
☐ Are they varied in length, structure, and word order?
☐ Is my phrasing direct rather than roundabout?

TIPS:

1. Try circling, or using your computer to search for, every preposition and *to be* verb. Since these can lead to confusion or roundabout phrasing, weed out as many as you can.
2. Try reading your paper aloud or having your roommate read it to you. Note places where you stumble, and listen for sentences that are hard to get through or understand.

Words

☐ Have I used any words whose meaning I'm not sure of?
☐ Are the idioms used correctly? Is my terminology correct?
☐ Do my key words always mean *exactly* the same thing?
☐ Do I ever use a fancy word or phrase where a simpler one might do?

☐ Are there any unnecessary words or phrases?
☐ Do my metaphors and figures of speech make literal sense?
☐ Are my verbs active and precise?
☐ Are my pronoun references clear and correct?
☐ Do my subjects and verbs always agree?

Mechanics

☐ Is every quotation correctly worded and punctuated?
☐ Is the source of each quotation clearly indicated through parenthetical citation?
☐ Have I checked the spelling of words I'm not sure of? (Remember that spell-checks won't indicate how to spell every word and that they sometimes create mistakes by substituting the wrong word for the misspelled one.)
☐ Are my pages numbered?
☐ Does the first page of my essay clearly indicate my name (and any other required identifying information), as well as my essay's title?

20.5 CRAFTING A TITLE

Complete your essay by giving it a title. As any researcher trying to locate and assess sources by browsing titles will tell you, titles are extremely important. They're the first thing readers encounter and a writer's first opportunity to create a good impression and to shape readers' expectations. Every good essay deserves a good title. And a good title is one that both *informs* and *interests*. Inform readers by telling them both the work(s) your essay will analyze and something about your topic. Interest them with an especially vivid and telling word or a short phrase from the literary work (" 'We all said, "she will kill herself" ': The Narrator/Detective in William Faulkner's 'A Rose for Emily' "), with a bit of wordplay (" 'Tintern Abbey' and the Art of Artlessness"), or with a little of both ("A Rose for 'A Rose for Emily' ").

21 THE RESEARCH ESSAY

Writing a research essay may seem like a daunting task that requires specialized skills and considerable time and effort. Research does add a few more steps to the writing process, so that process will take more time. And those steps require you to draw upon, and develop, skills somewhat different from those involved in creating other kinds of essays. But a research essay is, after all, an essay. Its core elements are those of any essay, its basic purpose exactly the same—to articulate and develop a debatable claim about a literary text. As a result, this kind of essay draws upon many of the same skills and strategies you've already begun to develop. Similarly, though you will need to add a few new steps, the writing process still involves getting started, planning, drafting, and revising—exactly the same dance whose rhythms you've already begun to master.

Indeed, the only distinctive thing about a research essay is that it requires the use of secondary sources. Though that adds to your burden in some ways, it can lighten it in others. Think of secondary sources not as another ball you have to juggle but as another tool you get to add to your toolbelt: you're still being asked to build a cabinet, but now you get to use a hammer *and* a screwdriver. This chapter will help you make the best use of this powerful tool.

21.1 TYPES AND FUNCTIONS OF SECONDARY SOURCES

Whenever we write an essay about literature, we engage in a conversation with other readers about the meaning and significance of a particular work (or works). Effective argumentation always depends on imagining how other readers are likely to respond to, and interpret, the literary text. And almost all texts and authors are the subject of actual public conversations, often extending over many years and involving numerous scholarly readers. A research essay can be an opportunity to investigate this conversation and to contribute to it. In this case, your secondary sources will be works in which literary scholars analyze a specific text or an author's body of work.

Not surprisingly, each literary work is significantly shaped by, and speaks to, its author's unique experience and outlook, as well as the events and debates of the era in which the author lived. So a research assignment can be an opportunity to learn more about a particular author, about that author's canon, or about the place and time in which the author lived and worked. The goal of the essay will be to show how context informs text or vice versa. Secondary sources for this sort of research essay will be biographies of the author, essays or letters by the author, and/or historical works of some kind.

Generally speaking, three types of secondary sources are used in essays about literature: *literary criticism, biography,* and *history*. The goal of a particular essay and the kinds of questions it raises will determine which kind of sources you use.

In practice, however, many secondary sources cross these boundaries. Biographies of a particular author often offer literary critical interpretations of that author's work; works of literary criticism sometimes make use of historical or biographical information; and so on. And you, too, may want or need to draw on more than one kind of source in a single essay. Your instructor will probably give you guidance about what kinds of sources and research topics or questions are appropriate. So make sure that you have a clear sense of the assignment before you get started.

Unless your instructor indicates otherwise, *your* argument should be the focus of your essay, and secondary sources should be just that—secondary. They should merely serve as tools that you use to deepen and enrich your argument about the literary text. They shouldn't substitute for it. Your essay should never simply repeat or report on what other people have already said.

Thus even though secondary sources are important to the development of your research essay, they should not be the source of your ideas. Instead, as one popular guide to writing suggests,* they are sources of:

- *opinion* (or *debatable claims*)—other readers' views and interpretations of the text, author, or topic, which "you support, criticize, or develop";
- *information*—facts (which "you interpret") about the author's life; the text's composition, publication, or reception; the era during, or about which, the author wrote; or the literary movement of which the author was a part;
- *concept*—general terms or theoretical frameworks that you borrow and apply to your author or text.

Again, any one source will likely offer more than one of these things. Nonetheless, the distinction between opinion (debatable claim) and information (factual statement) is crucial. As you read a source, you must discriminate between the two. And when drawing upon sources in your essay, remember that an opinion about a text, no matter how well informed, isn't the same as evidence. Only facts can serve that function. Suppose, for example, that you are writing an essay on Sylvia Plath's poem "Daddy." You claim that the speaker adopts two voices, that of her child self and that of her adult self—an opinion also set forth in Stephen Gould Axelrod's essay "Jealous Gods." You cannot prove this claim to be true by merely saying that Axelrod makes the same claim. Like any debatable claim, this one must be backed up with evidence from the primary text.

---

* Gordon Harvey, *Writing with Sources* (Indianapolis: Hackett, 1998) 1.

In this situation, however, you must indicate that a source has made the same claim that you do in order to:

- give the source credit for having this idea or stating this opinion before you did (see 21.4.1);
- encourage readers to see you as a knowledgeable and trustworthy writer, one who has taken the time to explore, digest, and fairly represent others' opinions;
- demonstrate that your opinion isn't merely idiosyncratic because another informed, even "expert," reader agrees with you.

Were you to disagree with the source's opinion, you would need to acknowledge that disagreement in order to demonstrate the originality of your own interpretation, while also (again) encouraging readers to see you as a knowledgeable, careful, trustworthy writer.

You will need to cite sources throughout your essay whenever you make (1) a claim that complements or contradicts the opinion-claim of a source, or (2) a claim that requires secondary-source information or concepts. In essays that draw upon literary critical sources, those sources may prove especially helpful when articulating motive (see 35.1.1).

21.1.1 Source-Related Motives

Not all research essays use sources to establish motive. However, this is one technique you can use to ensure that your own ideas are the focus of your essay and to demonstrate that (and how) your essay contributes to a literary critical conversation rather than just reporting on it or repeating what others have already said.

In addition to the general motives described above (19.3.1), writing expert Gordon Harvey has identified three common source-related motives:

1. Sources offer different opinions about a particular issue, thus suggesting that there is still a problem or a puzzle worth investigating.

> [A]lmost all interpreters of [*Antigone*] have agreed that the play shows Creon to be morally defective, though they might not agree about the particular nature of his defect. [examples] . . . I want to suggest [instead] that. . . .
> —Martha Nussbaum, "The Fragility of Goodness . . . "

2. A source (or sources) makes a faulty claim that needs to be challenged or clarified.

> Modern critics who do not share Sophocles' conviction about the paramount duty of burying the dead and who attach more importance than he did to the claims of political authority have tended to underestimate the way in which he justifies Antigone against Creon. [examples]
> —Maurice Bowra, "Sophoclean Tragedy"

3. Sources neglect a significant aspect or element of the text, or they make a claim that needs to be further developed or applied in a new way.

> At first sight, there appears little need for further study of the lovers in *Far from the Madding Crowd*, and even less of their environment. To cite but a few critics, David Cecil has considered the courtship of Bathsheba, Virginia Hyman her moral development through her varied experience in love, George Wing her suitors, Douglas Brown her relation to the natural environment, Merryn Williams that of Gabriel Oak in contrast to Sergeant Troy's aliena- tion from nature, and, most recently, Peter Casagrande Bathsheba's refor- mation through her communion with both Gabriel and the environment. To my knowledge, none has considered the modes or styles in which those and other characters express love and how far these may result from or determine their attitude to the land and its dependents, nor the tragic import in the Wessex novels of incompatibility in this sense between human beings, as distinct from that between the human psyche and the cosmos.
> —Lionel Adey, "Styles of Love in *Far from the Madding Crowd*," *Thomas Hardy Annual 5* (London: Macmillan, 1987)

21.2 RESEARCH AND THE WRITING PROCESS

Keeping in mind the overall goal of making secondary sources secondary, you have two options about when and how to integrate research into the writing process: (1) you may consult sources in the exploratory phase, using them to generate potential topics and theses for your essay, or (2) you may consult sources during (or even after) the planning or drafting phases, using them to refine and test a tentative thesis. Each approach has advantages and disadvantages.

21.2.1 Using Research to Generate Topic and Thesis

You may consult secondary sources very early in the writing process, using them to help generate your essay topic and thesis (or several potential ones from which you will need to choose). This approach has three advantages. First, you approach the research with a thoroughly open mind and formulate your own opinion about the text(s) only after having considered the range of opinions and information that the sources offer. Second, as you investi- gate others' opinions, you may find yourself disagreeing, thereby discovering that your mind isn't nearly as open as you'd thought—that you do, indeed, have an opinion of which you weren't fully aware. (Since you've discovered this by disagreeing with a published opinion, you're well on your way to having a motive as well as a thesis.) Third, because you begin by informing yourself about what others have already said, you may be in less danger of simply repeating or reporting.

The potential disadvantage is that you may become overwhelmed by the sheer number of sources or by the amount and diversity of information and opinion they offer. You may agree with everyone, being unable to discriminate among others' opinions or to formulate your own. Or you may find that the conversation seems so exhaustive that you despair of finding anything new to add. If you take this approach, you should maximize the advantages and minimize the disadvantages by keeping in mind a set of clearly defined motive-related questions.

If your sources are works of literary criticism, your goal is to answer two general questions: *What's the conversation about? How can I contribute to it?* To answer those questions, it helps to recall the various motives described in section 21.1.1. Turn them into questions that you can pose about each source:

- ☐ Do the critics tend to disagree about a particular issue? Might I take one side or another in this debate? Might I offer an alternative?
- ☐ Do any critics make a claim that I think deserves to be challenged or clarified?
- ☐ Do the critics ignore a particular element or aspect of the text that I think needs to be investigated? Do any of the critics make a claim that they don't really develop? Or do they make a claim about one text that I might apply to another?

If your sources are historical or biographical, you will instead need to ask questions such as:

- ☐ Is there information here that might help readers understand some aspect of the literary work in a new way?
- ☐ Does any of this information challenge or complicate my previous interpretation of the text, or an interpretation that I think other readers might adopt if they weren't aware of these facts?

21.2.2 Using Research to Refine and Test a Thesis

Because of the potential problems of consulting secondary sources in the exploratory phase of the writing process (21.2.1), your instructor may urge you to delay research until later—after you've formulated a tentative thesis, gathered evidence, or written a complete rough draft. This approach may be especially appealing when you begin an assignment with a firm sense of what you want to write. The chief advantage of this approach is that you can look at secondary sources more selectively and critically, seeking information and opinions that will deepen, confirm, or challenge your argument. And since you've already formulated your opinion, you may be in less danger of becoming overwhelmed by others'.

There are, however, several things to watch out for if you take this approach. First, you must be especially careful not to ignore, distort, or misrepresent any source's argument in the interest of maintaining your own. Second, you must strive to keep your mind open, remembering that the goal of your research is to *test* and *refine* your opinion, not just to *confirm* it. A compelling argument or new piece of information may well require you to modify or broaden your original argument. Third, you still need to pose the general questions outlined above (21.2.1).

21.3 THE RESEARCH PROCESS

Regardless of when you begin your research, the process will involve four tasks:

- creating and maintaining a working bibliography;
- identifying and locating potentially useful secondary sources;
- evaluating the credibility of sources;
- taking notes.

21.3.1 Creating a Working Bibliography

A working bibliography lists all the sources that you *might* use in your research essay. It is a "working" document in two ways. For one thing, it will change throughout the research process—expanding each time you add a potentially useful source and contracting when you omit sources that turn out to be less relevant than you anticipated. Also, once you have written your essay, your working bibliography will evolve one last time, becoming your list of works cited. For another thing, you can use your bibliography to organize and keep track of your research "work." To this end, some research-ers divide the bibliography into three parts: (1) sources that they need to locate, (2) sources that they have located and think they will use, and (3) sources that they have located but think they probably won't use. (Keeping track of "rejects" ensures, first, that you won't have to start from scratch if you later change your mind; second, that you won't forget that you've already located and rejected a source if you come across another reference to it.)

Because you will need to update your bibliography regularly and because it will ultimately become the kernel of your list of works cited, you should consider using a computer. In that case, you'll need to print a copy or take your laptop along each time you head to the library. However, some research-ers find it helpful to also or instead use notecards, creating a separate card for each source. You can then physically separate cards dedicated to sources to be located, sources already located, and "rejected" sources. Just in case your cards get mixed up, however, you should also always note the status of the source on the card (by writing at the top "find," "located," or "rejected").

Regardless of the format you use, your record for each source should include all the information you will need in order both to locate the source and to cite it in your essay. Helpful location information might include the library in which it's found (if you're using multiple libraries), the section of the library in which it's held (e.g., "Reference," "Stacks"), and its call number. As for citation or publication information, it's tempting to ignore this until the very end of the writing process, and some writers do. But if you give in to that temptation, you will, at best, create much more work for yourself down the road. At worst, you'll find yourself unable to use a great source in your essay because you can't relocate the necessary information about it. To avoid these fates, note down all facts you will need for a works cited entry (see 22.2.2). Finally, consider noting where you first discovered each source, just in case you later need to double-check citation information or to remind yourself why you considered a source potentially useful or authoritative. (Though you can use abbreviations, make sure they're ones you'll recognize later.)

Here are two sample entries from the working bibliography of a student researching Adrienne Rich's poetry. Each entry includes all the required citation information, as well as notes on where the student discovered the source and where it is located.

Sample Working Bibliography Entries

Boyers, Robert. "On Adrienne Rich: Intelligence and Will." Salmagundi 22–23 (Spring–Summer 1973): 132–48. Source: *DLB* 5. Loc.: UNLV LASR AS30.S33

Martin, Wendy. American Triptych: Anne Bradstreet, Emily Dickinson, Adrienne Rich. U of North Carolina P, 1984. Source: *LRC/CLC*. UNLV Stacks PS310.F45 M3 1984

Once you locate a source, double-check the accuracy and thoroughness of your citation information and update your working bibliography. (Notice, for example, that this student will need to check *American Triptych* to find out the city where it was published and then add this information to her bibliography.)

21.3.2 Identifying and Locating Sources

Regardless of your author, text, or topic, you will almost certainly find a wealth of sources to consult. Your first impulse may be to head straight for the library catalog. But the conversation about literature occurs in periodicals as well as books, and not all contributions to that conversation are equally credible or relevant. For all these reasons, consider starting with one of the reference works or bibliographies described in this section. Then you can head to the catalog armed with a clear sense of what you're looking for.

Once you find one good secondary source, you can use its bibliography to refine your own. Checking the footnotes and bibliographies of several (especially recent) sources will give you a good sense of what other sources are available and which ones experts consider the most significant.

REFERENCE WORKS

Your library will contain many reference works that can be helpful starting points, and some may be accessible via the library's Web page. Here are six especially useful ones.

Literature Resource Center (LRC)

One online source to which your library may subscribe is Gale's *Literature Resource Center*. Designed with undergraduate researchers in mind, it's an excellent place to start. Here you can access and search:

- all the material in two of the reference works described below (*Dictionary of Literary Biography* and *Contemporary Authors*) and in both Merriam-Webster's *Encyclopedia of Literature* and Gale's For Students series (*Novels for Students, Literature of Developing Nations for Students,* etc.);
- much (though not all) of the material contained in Gale's Literary Criticism series (another of the reference works described below);
- selected full-text critical essays (or articles) from more than 250 literary journals.

Depending upon your library's subscription arrangement, *LRC* may also give you access to the *MLA Bibliography* (from 1963) and/or to the Twayne's Authors series (both described below).

You can search the database in numerous ways, but you should probably start with an author search. Results will appear as a list of sources divided into four files: Biographies; Literary Criticism, Articles, and Work Overviews; Bibliographies (of works by and about the author); Additional Resources (such as author-focused Web sites). You can access each file or list by simply clicking on the appropriate tab. (There will be a good deal of overlap among the files.) You can then click any item on the list in order to open and read it. Once an item is open, you can also print or e-mail it by clicking on the appropriate icons and following the directions.

If your library doesn't subscribe to *LRC*, consider starting with the printed reference works listed below. Because each is a multivolume work, you will need to consult its cumulative index to find out which volumes contain entries on your author. None of these series can keep up to the minute with the literary critical conversation about a particular author or work, and all offer only selective bibliographies. Such selectivity is both the greatest strength and the greatest limitation of these reference works.

Dictionary of Literary Biography (DLB)

One of the most important and authoritative reference works for students of literature, the *Dictionary of Literary Biography* covers primarily British and American authors, both living and dead. Each volume focuses on writers working in a particular genre and period. (Volume 152, 4th series, for example, covers *American Novelists since World War II.*) Written by a scholar in the field, each entry includes a photo or sketch of the author, a list of his or her publications, a bibliography of selected secondary sources, and an overview of the author's life and work. The overviews are often very thorough, incorporating brief quotations from letters, interviews, reviews, and so on. You will find multiple entries on any major author, each focusing on a particular portion of his or her canon. The volume titles will give you a good sense of which entry will be most relevant to you. Entries on W. B. Yeats, for example, appear in volume 10, *Modern British Dramatists, 1900–1945;* volume 19, *British Poets, 1880–1914;* volume 98, *Modern British Essayists,* First Series; and volume 156, *British Short-Fiction Writers, 1880–1914: The Romantic Tradition.*

Contemporary Authors: A Biobibliographical Guide to Current Authors and Their Works (CA)

Gale's *Contemporary Authors* focuses on twentieth- and twenty-first-century writers from around the world and in a range of fields (including the social and natural sciences). In terms of content, its entries closely resemble those in the *DLB* (see above). But *CA* entries tend to be much shorter.

Literary Criticism (LC)

Also published by Gale, the Literary Criticism series is, in effect, a series of series, each of which covers a particular historical period. (See below for individual series titles, as well as information about the periods covered by each one.) Each entry includes a very brief overview of the author's life and work. (There is often overlap between these overviews and those in *CA*.) But there are two key differences between the *LC* series and both the *DLB* and *CA*. First, the *LC* series includes entries devoted entirely to some individual works, as well as entries on an author's entire canon. (For example, Nineteenth-Century Literature Criticism contains both a general entry on Charlotte Brontë and one devoted exclusively to *Jane Eyre.*) Second, the bulk of each entry is devoted to excerpts (often lengthy) from some of the most important reviews and literary criticism on an author and/or work, and coverage extends from the author's day up to the time when the *LC* entry was written. Each entry concludes with a bibliography of additional secondary sources. The *LC* series will thus give a lot of guidance in identifying authoritative sources, as well as access to excerpts from sources that your library doesn't own.

Here are the titles of the five series, along with information about the period each one covers. To identify the appropriate series, you will need to know the year in which your author died.

- Contemporary Literary Criticism (living authors and those who died from 1960 on)
- Twentieth-Century Literary Criticism (authors who died 1900–1959)
- Nineteenth-Century Literature Criticism (authors who died 1800–1899)
- Literature Criticism from 1400 to 1800 (authors [except Shakespeare] who died 1400–1799)
- Shakespearean Criticism

The Critical Heritage

For some major authors, you can find information and excerpts like those offered by *LC* within the individual volumes of the Critical Heritage series. Unlike the reference works described above, this series is a collection of discrete publications such as *The Brontës: The Critical Heritage*. Each will be held not in the reference department, but in the section of the stacks devoted to scholarship on a specific author. You will thus need to search your library's catalog to find it. These volumes are not regularly updated, so each will give a good sense of your author's reception only up to the time it was published.

Twayne's Authors

The Twayne's Authors series incorporates three distinct series: Twayne's United States Authors, Twayne's English Authors, and Twayne's World Authors. Each volume in each series is a distinct book focusing on one author and typically offering both biographical information and interpretation of major works. All aim to be generally accessible and introductory. (As the publishers themselves put it, "The intent of each volume in these series is to present a critical-analytical study of the works of the writer; to include biographical and historical material that may be necessary for understanding, appreciation, and critical appraisal of the writer; and to present all material in clear, concise English.") Yet because each volume is the work of an individual specialist, it represents that scholar's particular point of view (or opinion), and volumes differ a good deal in terms of organization, approach, and level of difficulty.

Each volume will be held not in the reference department, but in the section of the stacks devoted to scholarship on a specific author. To find it, you will need to search the catalog.

MLA INTERNATIONAL BIBLIOGRAPHY

For much more thorough, up-to-date lists of secondary sources—especially periodical articles—you should consult scholarly bibliographies. In terms of literary criticism, the most comprehensive and useful general bibliography is *The MLA International Bibliography of Books and Articles on the Modern Languages and Literatures*. Since 1969, the *MLA Bibliography* has aimed to provide a comprehensive list of all scholarship published anywhere in the world on literature and modern languages, including books, dissertations, book chapters, and articles in over two thousand periodicals. Though it doesn't quite live up to that aim, it comes closer than any other reference work. (The *Bibliography* in fact began in 1922 but initially included only American scholarship; international coverage began in 1956, but the range of publications remained limited until 1969.) Updated annually, the bibliography is available in print, CD-ROM, and online versions, so what the bibliography encompasses, how many years it covers, and how you use it will depend on the version you consult.

In the print version, each volume lists articles and books published in a specific year, so you should start with the most recent volume and then work your way backward through earlier volumes. Each volume is arranged by nationality or language, then by period, then by author and title.

The CD-ROM and online versions allow you to do topic or keyword searches to find all relevant publications, regardless of the year of publication. Ask a librarian for help with accessing and searching the database.

ONLINE AND CARD CATALOGS

Your library's catalog will guide you to books about the author's work. However, the title of a potentially useful book may be too general to indicate whether it covers the text and topic in which you're interested. If your library's catalog is online, use keyword searches to limit the number and range of books that the computer finds. For example, if you're writing about William Faulkner's "A Rose for Emily," first limit the search to items that include both "Faulkner" and "A Rose for Emily." If you find few matches or none, broaden the search to include all books about William Faulkner.

The books that you find through a catalog search will lead you to a section of the library where other books on your subject are held (because each will have a similar Library of Congress call number). Even if you locate the books you were looking for right away, take a moment to browse. Books shelved nearby probably cover similar topics, and they may prove even more useful than the ones you originally sought. You can also do this kind of browsing online because most online catalogs offer the option of moving from the record of one book to the records of those that appear just before and after it in the catalog.

THE INTERNET

With its innumerable links and pathways, the Internet seems the perfect resource for research of any kind. And in fact some excellent online resources are available to students of literature. *Bartleby.com* is a good, general information site. Here you can access and search several reference works, including the *Columbia Encyclopedia,* the *American Heritage Dictionary of the English Language,* and the eighteen-volume *Cambridge History of English and American Literature,* as well as full-text versions of numerous poems and works of fiction and nonfiction.

There are also many scholarly sites dedicated to specific authors, works, and literary periods. Most sites provide links to others. One site especially useful as a gateway to thousands of more specific sites is *The Voice of the Shuttle* <http://vos.ucsb.edu/>.

If you don't find an appropriate link on *The Voice of the Shuttle,* you will probably want to conduct a search using one of the commonly available search engines. Searches using keywords such as "Chekhov" or "poetry" will lead you to thousands of possible matches, however, so you should limit your search by creating search strings longer than one word. Read onscreen directions carefully to make sure that the search engine treats the search string as a unit and doesn't find every mention of each individual word.

Despite the obvious benefits of the Internet, you should be cautious in your use of online sources for two reasons. First, although many sites provide solid information and informed opinion, many more offer misinformation or unsubstantiated opinion. Unlike journal articles and books, which are rigorously reviewed by experts before they are accepted for publication, many Internet sources are posted without any sort of review process, and authorship is often difficult to pin down. As a result, you need to be especially careful to identify and evaluate the ultimate source of the information and opinions you find in cyberspace. (For more on evaluating sources, see 21.3.3.)

Second, because the Internet enables you to jump easily from one site to another and to copy whole pages of text merely by cutting and pasting, you may lose your place and be unable to provide readers with precise citations. More serious, you may lose track of where your own words end and those of your source begin, thereby putting yourself at risk of plagiarizing (see 21.4.1). In addition, the Internet is itself constantly mutating; what's there today may not be there tomorrow. All this makes it difficult to achieve the goal of all citation: to enable readers to retrace your steps and check your sources. When you find sites that seem potentially useful, bookmark them if you can. If not, make sure that you accurately write down (or, better, copy directly into a document) the URL of each, as well as the other information you will need for your list of works cited: the author's name, if available; the site or page title; the date the site was last revised or originally published; and the date you accessed it. If the material on the site has been taken from a printed source, note all of the particulars about this source as well.

As a general rule, Internet sources should supplement print sources, not substitute for them.

21.3.3 Evaluating Sources

Not all sources are equally reliable or credible. The credibility and persuasiveness of your essay will depend, in part, on the credibility of the sources you draw on. This is a good reason to start with reference works that will guide you to credible sources.

Nonetheless, it is very important to learn how to gauge for yourself the credibility of sources. As you do so, keep in mind that finding a source to be credible isn't the same as agreeing with everything it says. At this stage, concentrate on whether the opinions expressed in a source are worthy of serious consideration, not on whether you agree with them. Here are some especially important questions to consider:

1. *How credible is the publisher (in the case of books), the periodical (in the case of essays, articles, and reviews), or the sponsoring organization (in the case of Internet sources)?*

   Generally speaking, academics give most credence to books published by academic and university presses and to articles published in scholarly or professional journals because all such publications undergo a rigorous peer-review process. As a result, you can trust that these publications have been judged credible by more than one recognized expert. For periodicals aimed at a more general audience, you should prefer prominent, highly respected publications such as the *Los Angeles Times* or the *New Yorker* to, say, the *National Enquirer* or *People* magazine.

Internet sources are not subjected to rigorous review processes, but many sites are created and sponsored by organizations. Be sure to identify the sponsoring organization and carefully consider its nature, status, and purpose. The last part of the domain name will indicate the kind of organization it is: the suffix *.com* indicates that the ultimate source is a *company* or commercial, for-profit enterprise; *.org*, a nonprofit or charitable *organization*; *.gov*, a *government* agency; and *.edu*, an *educational* institution. Though you will often find more reliable information via *.gov* or *.edu* sites, this won't always be the case. *Bartleby.com* is, for example, only one of many extremely useful commercial sites, whereas many *.edu* sites feature the work of students who may have much less expertise than you do.

2. *How credible is the author? Is he or she a recognized expert in the relevant field or on the relevant subject?*

Again, publication by a reputable press or in a reputable periodical generally indicates that its author is considered an expert. But you can also investigate further by checking the thumbnail biographies that usually appear within the book or journal (typically near the beginning or end). Has this person been trained or held positions at respected institutions? What else has he or she published?

3. *How credible is the actual argument?*

Assess the source's argument by applying all that you've learned about what makes an argument effective. Does it draw on ample, appropriate, convincing evidence? Does it consider all the relevant evidence? Are its inferences reasonable? Are its claims sound? Does the whole seem fair, balanced, and thorough? Has the author considered possible counterarguments or alternative points of view?

Finally, researchers in many fields would encourage you to consider the source's publication date and the currency of the information it contains. In the sciences, for example, preference is almost always given to the most recently published work on a given topic because new scholarly works tend to render older ones obsolete. In the humanities, too, new scholarly works build on old ones. You should consult recently published sources in order to get a sense of what today's scholars consider the most significant, debatable questions and what answers they offer. Though originality is as important in the humanities as in other scholarly fields, new work in the humanities doesn't necessarily render older work utterly obsolete. For example, a 1922 article on Shakespeare's *Hamlet* may still be as valid and influential as one published in 2002. As a result, you should consider the date of publication in evaluating a source, but don't let age alone determine its credibility or value.

21.3.4 Taking Notes

Once you've acquired the books and articles you determine to be most credible and potentially useful, it's a good idea to skim each one. (In the case of a book, concentrate on the introduction and on the chapter that seems most relevant.) Focus at this point on assessing the relevance of each source to your topic. Or, if you're working your way toward a topic, look for things that spark your interest. Either way, try to get a rough sense of the overall conversation—of the issues and topics that come up again and again across the various sources.

After identifying the sources most pertinent to your argument, begin reading more carefully and taking notes. Again, some researchers find it easier to organize (and reorganize) notes by using notecards, creating one card for each key point. (If you use this method, make sure that each card clearly indicates the source author and short title because cards have a tendency to get jumbled.) Today, however, most researchers take notes on the computer, creating a separate document or file for each source.

Regardless of their form, your notes should be as thorough and accurate as possible. Be thorough because memory is a treacherous thing; it's best not to rely too heavily on it. Be accurate to avoid a range of serious problems, including plagiarism (see 21.4.1).

Your notes for each source should include four things: summary, paraphrase, and quotation, as well as your own comments and thoughts. It's crucial to visually discriminate among these by, for instance, always recording your own comments and thoughts in a separate computer document or file or on a separate set of clearly labeled or differently colored notecards.

Whenever you write down, type out, or paste in more than two consecutive words from a source, you should:

- place these words in quotation marks so that you will later recognize them as quotations;
- make sure to quote with absolute accuracy every word and punctuation mark;
- record the page where the quotation is found (in the case of print sources).

Keep such quotations to a minimum, recording only the most vivid or telling.

In lieu of extensive quotations, try to summarize and paraphrase as much as possible. You can't decide how to use the source or whether you agree with its argument unless you've first understood it, and you can best understand and test your understanding through summary and paraphrase. Start with a two- or three-sentence summary of the author's overall argument. Then summarize each of the relevant major subsections of the argument. Paraphrase especially important points, making sure to note the page on which each appears.

You may want to try putting your notes in the form of an outline. Again, start with a brief general summary. Then paraphrase each of the major relevant subclaims, incorporating summaries and quotations where appropriate.

Especially if you're dealing with literary criticism, it can be useful to complete the note-taking process by writing a summary that covers all of your sources. Your goal is to show how all the arguments fit together to form one coherent conversation. Doing so will require that you both define the main questions at issue in the conversation and indicate what stance each source takes on each question—where and how their opinions coincide and differ. One might say, for example, that the main questions about Sophocles' play *Antigone* that preoccupy most scholars are (1) *What is the exact nature of the conflict between Creon and Antigone, or what two conflicting worldviews do they represent?* and (2) *How is that conflict resolved? Which, if any, character and worldview does the play as a whole endorse?* A synthetic summary of your sources would explain how each critic answers each question. This kind of summary can be especially helpful when you haven't yet identified a specific essay topic or crafted a thesis because it may help you to see gaps in the conversation, places where you can enter and contribute.

21.4 INTEGRATING SOURCE MATERIAL INTO THE ESSAY

In research essays, you can refer to sources in a number of ways. You can

briefly allude to them:

> Many critics, including Maurice Bowra and Bernard Knox, see Creon as morally inferior to Antigone.

summarize or paraphrase their contents:

> According to Maurice Bowra, Creon's arrogance is his downfall. However prideful Antigone may occasionally seem, Bowra insists that Creon is genuinely, deeply, and consistently so (2108).

quote them directly:

> For Bowra, Creon is the prototypical "proud man" (2107); where Antigone's arrogance is only "apparent," Creon's is all too "real" (2108).

With secondary sources, be very careful about how often you quote and when and how you do so. Keep the number and length of quotations to a minimum. After all, this is *your* essay, and you should use your own words whenever possible, even to describe someone else's ideas. Save quotations for when you really need them: when the source's author has expressed an idea with such precision, clarity, or vividness that you simply can't say it any better; or when a key passage from your source is so rich or difficult that you need to analyze its ideas and language closely. As with primary texts, lengthy quotation will lead the reader to expect sustained analysis. And only rarely will you want to devote a large amount of your limited time and space to thoroughly analyzing the language of a source (as opposed to a primary text). (For more on responsible and effective quotation, see 22.1.)

One advantage of direct quotation is that it's an easy way to indicate that ideas derive from a source rather than from you. But whether you are quoting, summarizing, or paraphrasing a source, use other techniques as well to ensure that there's no doubt about where your ideas and words leave off and those of a source begin (see 21.4.1). A parenthetical citation within a sentence indicates that something in it comes from a specific source, but unless you indicate otherwise, it will also imply that the entire sentence is a paraphrase of the source. For clarity's sake, then, you should also mention the source or its author in your text, using signal phrases (*According to X*; *As X argues*; *X notes that*, etc.) to announce that you are about to introduce someone else's ideas. If your summary of a source goes on for more than a sentence or two, keep on using signal phrases to remind readers that you're still summarizing someone else's ideas rather than stating your own, as Lawrence Rodgers does in the example below.

> The ways of interpreting Emily's decision to murder Homer are numerous. . . . For simple clarification, they can be summarized along two lines. One group finds the murder growing out of Emily's demented attempt to forestall the inevitable passage of time—toward her abandonment by Homer, toward her own death, and toward the steady encroachment of the North and the New South on something loosely defined as the "tradition" of the Old South. Another view sees the murder in more psychological terms. It grows out of Emily's complex relationship to her father, who, by elevating her above all of the eligible men of Jefferson, insured that to yield what one commentator called the "normal emotions" associated with desire, his daughter had to "retreat into a marginal world, into fantasy" (O'Connor 184).
>
> These lines of interpretation complement more than critique each other. . . . Together, they de-emphasize the element of detection, viewing the murder and its solution not as the central action but as manifestations of the principal element, the decline of the Grierson lineage and all it represents. Recognizing the way in which the story makes use of the detective genre, however, adds another interpretive layer to the story by making the narrator . . . a central player in the pattern of action.
>
> —Lawrence R. Rodgers, " 'We All Said . . .'"

> NOTE: In the first paragraph, Rodgers summarizes other critics' arguments in his own words, briefly but clearly. To ensure that we know he's about to summarize, he actually announces this intention ("*For simple clarification, they can be summarized* . . . "). As he begins summarizing each view, he reminds us that it is a "view," that he's still not describing his own thoughts. Finally, he uses this unusually long summary to make a very clear and important point: *everyone except me has ignored this element!*

21.4.1 Using Sources Responsibly

Both the clarity and the credibility of any research essay depend upon the responsible use of sources. And using sources responsibly entails accurately representing them and clearly discriminating between your own words and ideas and those that come from sources. Since ideas, words, information, and concepts not directly and clearly attributed to a source will be taken as your own, any lack of clarity on this score amounts to *plagiarism*. Representing anyone else's ideas or data as your own, even if you state them in your own words, is plagiarism—whether you do so intentionally or unintentionally; whether ideas are taken from a published book or article, another student's paper, the Internet, or any other source. Plagiarism is the most serious of offenses within academe because it amounts to stealing ideas, the resource most precious to this community and its members. As a result, the punishments for plagiarism are severe—including failure, suspension, and expulsion.

To avoid both the offense and its consequences, you must always:

- put quotation marks around any quotation from a source (a quotation being any two or more consecutive words or any one especially distinctive word, label, or concept);

- credit a source whenever you take from it any of the following:
  —a quotation (as described above);
  —a nonfactual or debatable claim (an idea, opinion, interpretation, evaluation, or conclusion) stated in your own words;
  —a fact or piece of data that isn't common knowledge; or
  —a distinctive way of organizing factual information.

To clarify, a fact counts as common knowledge—and therefore doesn't need to be credited to a source—whenever you can find it in multiple, readily available sources, none of which seriously question its validity. For example, it is common knowledge that Sherman Alexie is Native American, that he was born in 1966, and that he published a collection of short stories entitled *Ten Little Indians*. No source can "own" or get credit for these facts. However, a source can still "own" a particular way of arranging or presenting such facts. If, for example, you begin your essay by stating—in your own words—a series of facts about Alexie's life in exactly the same order they appear in, say, the *Dictionary of Literary Biography*, then you would need to acknowledge that by citing the *Dictionary*. When in doubt, cite. (For guidance about *how* to do so, see 22.2.)

22

QUOTATION, CITATION, AND DOCUMENTATION

The bulk of any essay you write should consist of your own ideas expressed in your own words. Yet you can develop your ideas and persuade readers to accept them only if you present and analyze evidence. In essays about literature, quotations are an especially privileged kind of evidence. If your essay also makes use of secondary sources, you will need to quote (selectively) from some of these as well. In either case, your clarity and credibility will depend on how responsibly, effectively, and gracefully you move between others' words and your own. Clarity and credibility will also depend on letting your readers know—through precise citation and documentation—exactly where they can find each quotation and each fact or idea that you paraphrase. This chapter addresses the issue of *how* to quote, cite, and document texts and sources. (For a discussion of *when* to do so, see 19.4 and 21.4.)

22.1 EFFECTIVE QUOTATION

When it comes to quoting, there are certain rules that you must follow and certain strategies that, though not required, will help to make your argument more clear and effective.

22.1.1 Rules You Must Follow

1. Generally speaking, you should reproduce a quotation exactly as it appears in the original: include every word and preserve original spelling, capitalization, italics, and so on. However, there are a few exceptions:

   - When absolutely necessary, you may make minor changes to the quotation as long as (a) they do not distort the sense of the quotation, and (b) you clearly acknowledge them. For instance:

     —Additions and substitutions (e.g., of verb endings or pronouns) may be necessary in order to reconcile the quotation's grammar and syntax with your own or to ensure that the quotation makes sense out of its original context. Enclose these additions and changes in brackets.

     —Omit material from quotations to ensure you stay focused only on what's truly essential. Indicate omissions with ellipsis points unless the quotation is obviously a sentence fragment.

Notice how these rules are followed in the two examples below:

> Sethe, like Jacobs, experiences the wish to give up the fight for survival and die, but while Jacobs says she was "willing to bear on" "for the children's sakes" (127), the reason that Sethe gives for enduring is the physical presence of the baby in her womb: "[I]t didn't seem such a bad idea [to die], . . . but the thought of herself stretched out dead while the little antelope lived on . . . in her lifeless body grieved her so" that she persevered (31).

> When Denver tries to leave the haunted house to get food for her mother and Beloved, she finds herself imprisoned within her mother's time—a time that, clinging to places, is always happening again: "Out there . . . were places in which things so bad had happened that when you went near them it would happen again. . . ."
>
> —Jean Wyatt, "Giving Body to the Word: The Maternal Symbolic in Toni Morrison's *Beloved*," *PMLA* 108 (May 1993): 474–88

NOTE: In the first example, Wyatt uses brackets to indicate two changes, the capitalization of "it" and the addition of the words "to die." Ellipses indicate that she's omitted a word or words within the sentence that follows the colon. However, she doesn't need to begin or end the phrases *"willing to bear on"* and *"for the children's sake"* with ellipses because both are obviously sentence fragments. In the second example, notice that Wyatt does need to end the quotation with ellipsis points. Even though it reads like a complete sentence, this isn't the case; the sentence continues in the original text.

—Occasionally, you may want to draw your readers' attention to a particular word or phrase within the quotation by using italics. Indicate this change by putting the words "emphasis added" (not underlined or in italics) into your parenthetical citation.

> Like his constant references to "Tragedy," the wording of the father's question demonstrates that he is almost as hesitant as his daughter to confront death head-on: "When will you look *it* in the face?" he asks her (36; emphasis added).

• Although you should also accurately reproduce original punctuation, there is one exception to this rule: when incorporating a quotation into a sentence, you may *end* it with whatever punctuation mark your sentence requires. You do not need to indicate this particular change with brackets.

> Whether portrayed as "queen," "saint," or "angel," the same "nameless girl" "looks out from all his canvases" (Rossetti, lines 5–7, 1).

NOTE: In the poem quoted ("In an Artist's Studio"), the words *queen* and *angel* are not followed by commas. Yet the syntax of this sentence requires that commas be added. Similarly, the word *canvases* is followed by a comma in the poem, but the sentence requires that this comma be changed to a period.

2. When incorporating short quotations into a sentence, put them in quotation marks and make sure that they fit into the sentence grammatically and syntactically. If necessary, you may make changes to the quotation (e.g., altering verb endings or pronouns) in order to reconcile its grammar and syntax with your own. But you should—again—always indicate changes with brackets.

> It isn't until Mr. Kapasi sees the "topless women" carved on the temple that it "occur[s] to him . . . that he had never seen his own wife fully naked" (333).

3. When quoting fewer than three lines of poetry, indicate any line break with a slash mark, any stanza break with a double slash mark.

> Before Milton's speaker can question his "Maker" for allowing him to go blind, "Patience" intervenes "to prevent / That murmur" (lines 8–9), urging him to see that "God doth not need / Either man's work or his own gifts . . ." (lines 9–10).

> "The cane appears // in our dreams," the speaker explains (Dove, lines 15–16).

4. Long quotations—four or more lines of prose, three of poetry—should be indented and presented without quotation marks to create a *block quotation*. In the case of poetry, reproduce original line and stanza breaks.

> Whereas the second stanza individualizes the dead martyrs, the third considers the characteristics they shared with each other and with all those who dedicate themselves utterly to any one cause:
>
>> Hearts with one purpose alone
>> Through summer and winter seem
>> Enchanted to a stone
>> To trouble the living stream. (lines 41–44)
>
> Whereas all other "living" people and things are caught up in the "stream" of change represented by the shift of seasons, those who fill their "Hearts with one purpose alone" become as hard, unchanging, and immoveable as stones.

5. Unless they are indented, quotations belong in double quotation marks; quotations within quotations get single quotation marks. However, if everything in your quotation appears in quotation marks in the original, you do not need to reproduce the single quotation marks.

> The words of Rufus Johnson come ringing back to the reader: " 'Listen here,' he hissed, 'I don't care if he's good or not. He ain't *right!*' " (468).

> As Rufus Johnson says of Sheppard, "I don't care if he's good or not. He ain't *right!*" (468).

6. Follow a word-group introducing a quotation with whatever punctuation is appropriate to your sentence. For instance:

—If you introduce a quotation with a full independent clause (other than something like *She says*), separate the two with a colon.

Ironically, Mr. Lindner's description of the neighborhood's white residents makes them sound exactly like the Youngers, the very family he's trying to exclude: "They're not rich and fancy people; just hard-working, honest people who don't really have much but . . . a dream of the kind of community they want to raise their children in" (1093).

—If you introduce or interrupt a quotation with an expression such as *she says* or *he writes,* use a comma (or commas) or add a *that.* Likewise, use a comma if you end a quotation with an expression such as *he says,* unless the quotation ends with a question mark or exclamation point.

Alvarez claims, "The whole poem works on one single, returning note and rhyme . . ." (1214).

Alvarez suggests that "The whole poem works on one single, returning note and rhyme . . ." (1214).

"The whole poem," Alvarez argues, "works on one single, returning note and rhyme . . ." (1214).

"Here comes one," says Puck. "Where art thou, proud Demetrius?" asks Lysander (Shakespeare 3.2.400–401).

—If quoted words are blended into your sentence, use the same punctuation (or lack thereof) that you would if the words *were not* quoted.

Miriam Allott suggests that the odes, like "all Keats's major poetry," trace the same one "movement of thought and feeling," which "at first carries the poet . . . into an ideal world of beauty and permanence, and finally returns him to what is actual and inescapable."

Keats's poetry just as powerfully evokes the beauty of ordinary, natural things— of "the sun, the moon, / Trees," and "simple sheep"; of "daffodils" and "musk-rose blooms" (*Endymion,* lines 13–14, 15, 19); of nightingales, grasshoppers, and crickets; of "the stubble-plains" and "barred clouds" of a "soft-dying" autumn day ("To Autumn," lines 25–26).

When the narrator's eighty-six-year-old father asks her to tell him a "simple story" with "recognizable people" and a plot that explains "what happened to them next" (33), he gets "an unadorned and miserable tale" whose protagonist ends up "Hopeless and alone" (33).

7. Commas and periods belong inside quotation marks, semicolons outside. Question marks and exclamation points go inside quota-

tion marks if they are part of the quotation, outside if they aren't. (Since parenthetical citations will often alter your punctuation, they have been omitted in the following examples. On the placement and punctuation of parenthetical citations, see 22.2.1.)

"You have a nice sense of humor," the narrator's father notes, but "you can't tell a plain story."

Wordsworth calls nature a "homely Nurse"; she has "something of a Mother's Mind."

What does Johnson mean when he says, "I don't care if he's good or not. He ain't *right!*"?

Bobby Lee speaks volumes about the grandmother when he says, "She was a talker, wasn't she?"

22.1.2 Useful Strategies

1. Make the connection between quotations and inferences as seamless as possible. Try to put them next to each other (in one sentence, if possible). Avoid drawing attention to your evidence as evidence. Don't waste time with phrases such as *This statement is proof that . . . ; This phrase is significant because . . . ; This idea is illustrated by . . . ; There is good evidence for this . . . ;* and the like. Show why facts are meaningful or interesting rather than simply saying that they are.

INEFFECTIVE QUOTING	EFFECTIVE QUOTING
Wordsworth calls nature a "homely Nurse" and says she has "something of a Mother's mind" (lines 81, 79). This diction supports the idea that he sees nature as a beneficent, maternal force. He is saying that nature is an educator and a healer.	Wordsworth describes nature as a beneficent, maternal force. A "homely Nurse" with "something of a Mother's Mind," nature both heals and educates (lines 81, 79).
Tennyson advocates decisive action, even as he highlights the forces that often prohibited his contemporaries from taking it. This is suggested by the lines "Made weak by time and fate, but strong in will, / To strive, to seek, to find, and not to yield" (lines 69-70).	Tennyson advocates forceful action, encouraging his contemporaries "To strive, to seek, to find, and not to yield" (line 70). Yet he recognizes that his generation is more tempted to "yield" than earlier ones because they have been "Made weak by time and fate" (line 69).

2. Introduce or follow a quotation from a source (as well as a paraphrase or summary) with a *signal phrase* that includes the source author's name; you might also include the author's title and/or a bit of information about his or her status, if that information helps to establish credibility.

In his study of the Frankenstein myth, Chris Baldick claims that "[m]ost myths, in literate societies at least, prolong their lives not by being retold at great length, but by being alluded to" (3)—a claim that definitely applies to the Hamlet myth.

Oyin Ogunba, himself a scholar of Yoruban descent, suggests that many of Soyinka's plays attempt to capture the mood and rhythm of traditional Yoruban festivals (8).

As historian R. K. Webb observes, "Britain is a country in miniature" (1).

To avoid boring your readers, vary the content and placement of these phrases while always choosing the most accurate verb. (*Says,* for example, implies that words are spoken, not written.) You may find it useful to consult the following list of verbs that describe what sources do.

Verbs to Use in Signal Phrases

affirms	considers	explains	insists	shows
argues	contends	explores	investigates	sees
asks	demonstrates	finds	maintains	speculates
asserts	describes	focuses on	notes	states
believes	discusses	identifies	observes	stresses
claims	draws atten-	illustrates	points out	suggests
comments	tion to	implies	remarks	surmises
concludes	emphasizes	indicates	reports	writes

3. Lead your readers into fairly long quotations by giving them:

- a clear sense of what to look for in the quotation;
- any information they need to understand the quotation and to appreciate its significance. Quite often, contextual information— for instance, about who's speaking to whom and in what situation—is crucial to a quotation's meaning; this is especially true when quoting dialogue. Also pay attention to pronouns: if the quotation contains a pronoun without an obvious referent, either indicate the specific referent in advance or add the appropriate noun into the quotation. (Again, place added words in brackets.)

INEFFECTIVE QUOTING	EFFECTIVE QUOTING
A Raisin in the Sun seems to endorse traditional gender roles: "I'm telling you to be the head of this family . . . like you supposed to be" (1087); "the colored woman" should be "building their men up and making 'em feel like they somebody" (1087).	*A Raisin in the Sun* seems to endorse traditional gender roles. When Mama tells Walter "to be the head of this family from now on like you supposed to be" (1053), she affirms that Walter, rather than she or Ruth or Beneatha, is the rightful leader of the family. Implicitly she's also doing what Walter elsewhere says "the colored woman" should do—"building their men up and making 'em feel like they somebody" (1053).

Julian expresses disgust for the class distinctions so precious to his mother: "Rolling his eyes upward, he put his tie back on. 'Restored to my class,' he muttered" (490).	Julian professes disgust for the class distinctions so precious to his mother. At her request, he puts back on his tie, but he can't do so without "[r]olling his eyes" and making fun of the idea that he is thereby "[r]estored to [his] class" (490).

NOTE: Here, the more effective examples offer crucial information about who is speaking (*"When Lena tells Walter"*) or what is happening (*"At her request, he puts back on his tie"*). They also include statements about the implications of the quoted words (*"she affirms that Walter . . . is the rightful leader of the family"*). At the same time, background facts are subordinated to the truly important, evidentiary ones.

4. Follow each block quotation with a sentence or more of analysis. It often helps to incorporate into that analysis certain key words and phrases from the quotation.

The second stanza of the poem refers back to the title poem of *The Colossus*, where the speaker's father, representative of the gigantic male other, so dominated her world that her horizon was bounded by his scattered pieces. In "Daddy," she describes him as

> Marble-heavy, a bag full of God,
> Ghastly statue with one grey toe
> Big as a Frisco seal
>
> And a head in the freakish Atlantic
> Where it pours bean green over blue
> In the waters off beautiful Nanset.

. . . Here the image of her father, grown larger than the earlier Colossus of Rhodes, stretches across and subsumes the whole of the United States, from the Pacific to the Atlantic ocean.
—Pamela J. Annas, *"A Disturbance of Mirrors"*

5. Be aware that even though long (especially block) quotations can be effective, they should be used sparingly. Long quotations can create information overload or confusion for readers, making it hard for them to see what is most significant. When you quote only individual words or short phrases, weaving them into your sentences, readers stay focused on what's significant, and it's easier to show them why it's significant, to get inferences and facts right next to each other.

6. Vary the length of quotations and the way you present them, using a variety of strategies. Choose the strategy that best suits your purpose at a specific moment in your essay, while fairly and fully representing the text. It can be very tempting to fall into a pattern— always, for example, choosing quotations that are at least a sentence long and introducing each with an independent clause and a colon. But overusing any one technique can easily render your essay

monotonous. It might even prompt readers to focus more on the (inelegant) way you present evidence than on its appropriateness and significance.

22.2 CITATION AND DOCUMENTATION

In addition to indicating which facts, ideas, or words derive from someone else, always let your readers know where each can be found. You want to enable readers not only to "check up" on you, but also to follow in your footsteps and build on your work. After all, you hope that your analysis of a text will entice readers to reread certain passages from a different point of view.

At the same time, you don't want information about how to find others' work to interfere with readers' engagement with your work. Who, after all, could really make sense of an essay full of sentences such as these: (1) *"I know not 'seems,' " Hamlet claims in line 76 of Act 1, Scene 2*, and (2) *On the fourth page of her 1993* PMLA *article (which was that journal's 108th volume), Jean Wyatt insists that Morrison's "plot . . . cannot move forward because Sethe's space is crammed with the past."*

To ensure that doesn't happen, it is important to have a system for conveying this information in a concise, unobtrusive way. There are, in fact, many such systems currently in use. Different disciplines, publications, and even instructors prefer or require different systems. In literary studies (and the humanities generally), the preferred system is that developed by the Modern Language Association (MLA).

In this system, parenthetical citations embedded in an essay are keyed to an alphabetized list of works cited that appears at its end. Parenthetical citations allow the writer to briefly indicate where an idea, fact, or quotation appears, while the list of works cited gives readers all the information they need to find that source. Here is a typical sentence with parenthetical citation, as well as the works cited entry to which it refers.

Sample Parenthetical Citation

In one critic's view, "Ode on a Grecian Urn" explores "what great art means" not to the ordinary person, but only "to those who create it" (Bowra 148).

NOTE: Here, the parenthetical citation indicates that readers can find this quotation on page 148 of some work by an author named Bowra. To find out more, readers must turn to the list of works cited and scan it for an entry, like the following, that begins with the name "Bowra."

Sample Works Cited Entry

Bowra, C. M. <u>The Romantic Imagination</u>. Oxford: Oxford UP, 1950.

This example gives a basic sense of how parenthetical citations and the list of works cited work together in the MLA system. Note that each parenthetical citation must "match up" with one (and only one) works cited entry.

The exact content of each parenthetical citation and works cited entry will depend upon a host of factors. The next two sections focus on these factors.

22.2.1 Parenthetical Citation

THE GENERIC PARENTHETICAL CITATION: AUTHOR(S) AND PAGE NUMBER(S)

The generic MLA parenthetical citation includes an author's name and a page number (or numbers). If the source has two or three authors, include all last names, as in (Gilbert and Gubar 57). If it has four or more, use the first author's name followed by *et al.* (Latin for "and others") in roman type, as in the second example below. In all cases, nothing but a space separates author's name(s) from page number(s).

> Most domestic poems of the 1950s foreground the parent-child relationship (Axelrod 1230).
>
> Given their rigid structure, it is perhaps "[n]ot surprisin[g]" that many sonnets explore the topic of "confinement" (Booth et al. 1022).

Notice the placement of the parenthetical citations in these examples. In each one the citation comes at the end of the sentence, yet it appears *inside* the period (because it is part of the sentence) and *outside* the quotation marks (because it isn't part of the quotation). Such placement of parenthetical citations should be your practice in all but two situations (both described in the next section).

VARIATIONS IN PLACEMENT

In terms of placement, the first exception is the block quotation. In this case, the parenthetical citation should immediately *follow* (not precede) the punctuation mark that ends the quotation.

> As historian Michael Crowder insists, Western-style education was the single "most radical influence on Nigeria introduced by the British" because it
>> came to be seen as a means not only of economic betterment but of social elevation. It opened doors to an entirely new world, the world of the white man. Since missionaries had a virtual monopoly on schools, they were able to use them as a means of further proselyti-zation, and continued to warn their pupils of the evils of their former way of life. (195)

The second exception is the sentence that either incorporates material from multiple sources or texts (as in the first example below) or refers both to something from a source or text and to your own idea (as in the second example below). In either situation, you will need to put the appropriate parenthetical citation in mid-sentence right next to the material to which it refers, even at the risk of interrupting the flow of the sentence.

> Critics describe Caliban as a creature with an essentially "unalterable natur[e]" (Garner 458), "incapable of comprehending the good or of learning from the past" (Peterson 442), "impervious to genuine moral improvement" (Wright 451).

> If Caliban is "incapable of . . . learning from the past" (Peterson 442), then how do we explain the changed attitude he seems to demonstrate at the end of the play?

VARIATIONS IN CONTENT

The generic MLA citation may contain the author's name(s) and the relevant page number(s), but variations are the rule when it comes to content. The six most common variations occur when you do the following:

1. *Name the author in a signal phrase*
   Parenthetical citations should include only information that isn't crucial to the sense and credibility of your argument. Yet in nine cases out of ten, information about *whose* ideas, data, or words you are referring to is crucial in precisely this way. As a result, it is usually a good idea to indicate this in your text. When you do so, the parenthetical citation need only include the relevant page number(s).

   > Jefferson's "new generation" are, in Judith Fetterley's words, just "as much bound by the code of gentlemanly behavior as their fathers were" (619).

   > According to Steven Gould Axelrod, most domestic poems of the 1950s foreground the parent-child relationship (1230).

2. *Cite a poem or play*
   In the case of most poetry, refer to line (not page) numbers.

   > Ulysses encourages his men "To strive, to seek, to find, and not to yield" (line 70).

   In the case of classic plays, indicate act, scene, and line numbers, and separate them with periods.

   > "I know not 'seems,' " Hamlet claims (1.2.76).

3. *Cite multiple works by the same author or a work whose author is unknown*
   When citing multiple works by the same author or an anonymous work, you will need to indicate the title of the specific work to which you refer. Either indicate the title in your text, putting only the page number(s) in a parenthetical citation (as in the first example below),

or create a parenthetical citation in which the first word or two of the title is followed by the page number(s) (as in the third example below). In the latter case, you should format the title words exactly as you would the full title, using quotation marks for essays, short stories, and short poems, and using italics or underlining for books.

As Judith Fetterley argues in "A Rose for 'A Rose for Emily,' " Jefferson's younger generation is just "as much bound by the code of gentlemanly behavior as their fathers were" (619).

Jefferson's "new generation" is, in Judith Fetterley's words, just "as much bound by the code of gentlemanly behavior as their fathers were" ("A Rose" 562).

Arguably, Jefferson's "new generation" is just "as much bound by the code of gentlemanly behavior as their fathers were" (Fetterley, "A Rose" 619).

4. *Cite a source quoted in another source*
When quoting the words of one person as they appear in another author's work, mention the person's name in a signal phrase. Then create a parenthetical citation in which the abbreviation "qtd. in" is followed by the author's name and the relevant page number(s).

Hegel describes Creon as "a moral power," "not a tyrant" (qtd. in Knox 2108).

5. *Cite multiple authors with the same last name*
In this case, you should either use the author's full name in a signal phrase (as above) or add the author's first initial to the parenthetical citation (as below).

Beloved depicts a "a specifically female quest powered by the desire to get one's milk to one's baby" (J. Wyatt 475).

6. *Cite multiple sources for the same idea or fact*
In this case, put both citations within a single set of parentheses and separate them with a semicolon.

Though many scholars attribute Caliban's bestiality to a seemingly innate inability to learn or change (Garner 458; Peterson 442; Wright 451), others highlight how inefficient or problematic Prospero's teaching methods are (Willis 443) and how invested Prospero might be in keeping Caliban ignorant (Taylor 384).

7. *Cite a work without numbered pages*
Omit page numbers from parenthetical citations if you cite:

- an electronic work that isn't paginated;
- a print work whose pages aren't numbered;

- a print work that is only one page long;
- a print work, such as an encyclopedia, that is organized alphabetically.

If at all possible, mention the author's name and/or the work's title in your text (so that you don't need any parenthetical citation). Otherwise, create a parenthetical citation that contains, as appropriate, the author's name and/or the first word(s) of the title.

8. *Italicize words that aren't italicized in the original*
   If you draw your readers' attention to a particular word or phrase within a quotation by using italics or underlining, your parenthetical citation must include the words "emphasis added."

   > Like his constant references to "Tragedy," the wording of the father's question demonstrates that he is almost as hesitant as his daughter to confront death head-on: "When will you look *it* in the face?" he asks her (36; emphasis added).

22.2.2 The List of Works Cited

The alphabetized list of works cited should appear at the end of your completed essay. It must include all, and only, the texts and sources that you cite in your essay; it also must provide full publication information about each one.

If you're writing a research essay and have created and maintained a working bibliography (see 21.3.1), that bibliography will become the core of your works cited list. To turn the former into the latter, you will need to:

- delete sources that you did not ultimately cite in your essay;
- add an entry for each primary text you did cite;
- delete notes about where you found sources (call numbers, etc.).

FORMATTING THE LIST OF WORKS CITED

The list of works cited should appear on a separate page (or pages) at the end of your essay. (If you conclude your essay on page 5, for example, you would start the list of works cited on page 6.) Center the heading "Works Cited" (without quotation marks) at the top of the first page, and double-space throughout.

The first line of each entry should begin at the left margin; the second and subsequent lines should be indented 5 spaces or ½ inch.

Alphabetize your list by the last names of the authors or editors. In the case of anonymous works, alphabetize by the first word of the title other than *A, An,* or *The.*

If your list includes multiple works by the same author, begin the first entry with the author's name and each subsequent entry with three hyphens followed by a period. Alphabetize these listings by the first word of the title, again ignoring the words *A, An,* or *The.*

FORMATTING WORKS CITED ENTRIES

The exact content and style of each entry in your list of works cited will depend upon the type of source it is. Following are examples of some of the most frequently used types of entries in lists of works cited. For all other types, consult the sixth edition of the *MLA Handbook.*

Book by a single author or editor

> Webb, R. K. Modern England: From the Eighteenth Century to the Present. New York: Columbia UP, 1969.
>
> Wu, Duncan, ed. A Companion to Romanticism. Oxford: Blackwell, 1998.

Book with an author and an editor

> Keats, John. Complete Poems. Ed. Jack Stillinger. Cambridge: Belknap-Harvard UP, 1982.

Book by two or three authors or editors

> Gallagher, Catherine, and Thomas Laqueur, eds. The Making of the Modern Body: Sexuality and Society in the Nineteenth Century. Berkeley: U of California P, 1987.

Book by more than three authors or editors

> Zipes, Jack, et al. The Norton Anthology of Children's Literature. New York: Norton, 2005.

Introduction, preface, or foreword

> O'Prey, Paul. Introduction. Heart of Darkness. By Joseph Conrad. New York: Viking, 1983. 7-24.

Essay, poem, or any other work in an edited collection or anthology

> Shaw, Philip. "Britain at War: The Historical Context." A Companion to Romanticism. Ed. Duncan Wu. Oxford: Blackwell, 1998. 48-60.
>
> Yeats, W. B. "The Lake Isle of Innisfree." The Norton Introduction to Literature. 9th ed. Ed. Alison Booth, J. Paul Hunter, and Kelly J. Mays. New York: Norton, 2005. 1285.

Multiple short works from one collection or anthology

> Booth, Alison, J. Paul Hunter, and Kelly J. Mays, eds. The Norton Introduction to Literature. Portable ed. New York: Norton, 2006.
>
> Frost, Robert. "The Road Not Taken." Booth, Hunter, and Mays. 584.
>
> Keats, John. "Ode to a Nightingale." Booth, Hunter, and Mays. 595.

Article in a reference work

> "Magna Carta." Encyclopaedia Britannica. 14th ed. 630–35.

Article in a scholarly journal

> Wyatt, Jean. "Giving Body to the Word: The Maternal Symbolic in Toni Morrison's Beloved." *PMLA* 108 (May 1993): 474-88.

Article in a newspaper or magazine

> McNulty, Charles. "All the World's a Stage Door." Village Voice 13 Feb. 2001: 69.

Review or editorial

> Leys, Simon. "Balzac's Genius and Other Paradoxes." Rev. of Balzac: A Life, by Graham Robb. New Republic 20 Dec. 1994: 26-27.

NOTE: The first name here is that of the reviewer, the second that of the author whose book is being reviewed.

Internet site

> U.S. Department of Education (ED) Home Page. US Dept. of Education. 12 Aug. 2004 <http://www.ed.gov/index.jhtml>.
> Yeats Society Sligo Home Page. Yeats Society Sligo. 12 Nov. 2004 <http://www.yeats-sligo.com/>.

Article on a Web site

> Padgett, John B. "William Faulkner." The Mississippi Writers Page. 29 Mar. 1999. 8 Feb. 2004 <http://www.olemiss.edu/depts/english/ms-writers/dir/faulkner_william/>.

NOTE: The first date indicates when material was published or last updated. The second date indicates when you accessed the site.

23 SAMPLE RESEARCH PAPER

The student essay below was written in response to the following assignment:

> Write an essay of 10–15 pages that analyzes at least two poems by any one author in your text and draws upon three or more secondary sources. At least one of these sources must be a work of literary criticism (a book or article in which a scholar interprets your author's work).

Richard Gibson's response to this assignment is an essay that explores the treatment of religion in four poems by Emily Dickinson; Gibson asks how conventional that treatment was in its original historical and social context. Notice that Gibson uses a variety of sources: literary critical studies of Dickinson's poetry; Dickinson biographies; historical studies of nineteenth-century American religious beliefs and practices; letters written by and to Dickinson; and a dictionary. At the same time, notice that Gibson's thesis is an original, debatable interpretive claim about Dickinson's poetry and that he supports and develops that claim by carefully analyzing four poems.

Gibson 1

Richard Gibson
Professor William Barksdale
English 301
4 March 2004

Keeping the Sabbath Separately:
Emily Dickinson's Rebellious Faith

When cataloguing Christian poets, it might be tempting to place Emily Dickinson between Dante and John Donne. She built many poems around biblical quotations, locations, and characters. She meditated often on the afterlife, prayer, and trust in God. Yet Dickinson was also intensely doubtful of the strand of Christianity that she inherited; in fact, she never became a Christian by the standards of her community in nineteenth-century Amherst, Massachusetts. Rather, like many of her contemporaries in Boston, Dickinson recognized the tension between traditional religious teaching and modern ideas. And these tensions,

Gibson establishes a motive for his essay by first stating a claim about Dickinson's poetry that a casual reader might be tempted to adopt and then pointing out the problems with that claim in order to set up the more subtle and complex claim that is his thesis.

Gibson does a great job of establishing key terms—"traditional religious teaching," "modern ideas," and "unorthodox beliefs." Notice how he repeats these terms and variations on them throughout the essay in order to link his various subideas.

between hope and doubt, between tradition and modernity, animate her poetry. In "Some keep the Sabbath going to church—," "The Brain—is wider than the Sky—," "Because I could not stop for Death—," and "The Bible is an antique Volume," the poet uses traditional religious terms and biblical allusions. But she does so in order both to criticize traditional doctrines and practices and to articulate her own unorthodox beliefs.

In some ways, Emily Dickinson seemed destined by birth and upbringing to be a creature of tradition. After all, her ancestry stretched back to the origin of the Massachusetts Bay Colony; her ancestor Nathaniel Dickinson "was among the four hundred or so settlers who accompanied John Winthrop in the migration that began in 1630" (Lundin 8). Winthrop and his followers were Puritans, a group of zealous Christians who believed in the literal truth and authority of the Bible; the innate corruption of humanity; the doctrine of salvation by faith, not works; and the idea that only certain people were "predestined" for heaven (Noll 21). A few decades after his immigration, Nathaniel Dickinson moved to western Massachusetts, where he and his descendants would become farmers and stalwarts in local churches (Lundin 9). Although Emily Dickinson's grandfather, Samuel Fowler Dickinson, and her father, Edward Dickinson, would give up farming to become lawyers, they, too, subscribed to the articles of their inherited religion (9). In short, for more than three hundred years prior to her birth, Emily Dickinson's family faithfully adhered to the Puritan tradition.

Gibson simply paraphrases because his focus is the information in the source, not its words. Nonetheless, Gibson uses parenthetical citations to indicate where in the source one can find this information.

Gibson omits the author's name in this parenthetical citation because he is referring to the source indicated in the preceding parenthetical citation.

From early life to her year at college, Dickinson received an education that was "overwhelmingly religious" and traditional (Jones 295). The daily routine of the Dickinson household included prayer and readings from the Bible (296). She also received religious teaching regularly at the First Congregational Church and its "Sabbath [Sunday] school" (296). In her weekday schooling, Dickinson read textbooks such as The New England Primer and Amherst resident Noah Webster's spelling book that included "catechisms," or methodical teachings in religious doctrine and morality (296).

In the early nineteenth century, though, traditional churchgoers in western Massachusetts began to look warily to the east, especially to Boston, where nontraditional religious thinking had developed among both the "liberal Congregationalists" and the "free-thinking rationalists," or "deists" (Noll 138–42, 143–45). Because these theologies were distinctly European and philosophical, they won few converts outside Boston (143, 145). The greater threat was Unitarianism, which had sprung up in Congregational churches. The Unitarians rejected many of the foundational beliefs of the Puritans and instead "promoted a benevolent God, a balanced universe, and a sublime human potential" (284). Former Unitarian minister and transcendentalist philosopher Ralph Waldo Emerson, an author whom Dickinson admired, gained national attention through his writings and speeches on self-reliance and the individual's "direct access" to the "divine spirit" that is behind all "religious systems" (Doriani 18; Norberg xiii–xv). Binding these Bostonian theologies together is an agreement that reason should be applied to religious beliefs. Each then concluded that some—or, in a few minds, most—of the traditional Christian doctrines (to which Amherst adhered) should be abandoned or revised.

Many Bostonian thinkers were influenced by recent developments in science and philosophy that contested the traditional Christian conception of the universe and of the Bible's literal truth. Earlier generations of scientists and philosophers had postulated that the universe obeys fixed laws, which led to ongoing debates about whether the miracles described in the Bible were plausible, even possible (Noll 108). The new astronomy discredited biblical

Gibson refers readers to all the pages in the source that discuss the debate to which he refers—not just to those pages where the quoted phrases appear.

Gibson 4

passages describing irregular movements of the sun and the stars. The foremost contemporary dispute, though, concerned the age of the universe. The traditional Christian interpretation of the Bible stated that the universe had existed for about six thousand years (Lundin 32). Early-nineteenth-century geologists, though, had discovered fossils and rock formations that suggested that the Earth was significantly older. Some Christians dug in their heels, while others, like Amherst College professor Edward Hitchcock, attempted to "reconcile orthodoxy and the new geology"—an effort in which the young Dickinson "took comfort" (32). The intellectual scene of Massachusetts at the time of Dickinson's youth thus offered many competing answers to questions about divinity, the historicity of the Bible, and the cosmos. The reign of the old Puritan beliefs over the minds of New England was beginning to wane.

Gibson uses double quotation marks to enclose words he's taken from a source, single quotation marks to enclose words quoted in that source.

The term *sic* indicates that a spelling or grammar problem within the quotation is present in the original. Gibson encloses the term in brackets to indicate that it is his addition.

Dickinson herself began to confess doubts about her ability to join the First Congregational Church while still a teenager. In nineteenth-century Amherst, "to 'become a Christian' and join the church" required "only" that one "subscribe to the articles of faith and offer the briefest of assurance [sic] of belief in Christ" (Lundin 51). At age fifteen, though, Dickinson felt unable to do even this much, writing to her friend Abiah Root that she "had not yet made [her] peace with God." Unable to "feel that [she] could give up all for Christ, were [she] called to die," she asked her friend to pray for her, "that [she] may yet enter into the kingdom [of God], that there may be room left for [her] in the shining courts above" (8 Sept. 1846).

During her stay at Mount Holyoke Women's Seminary, from September 1847 to May 1848, Dickinson was frequently invited, even pressured, to become a Christian. Mary Lyon, headmistress of the college, "laid stress on the salvation of souls" and asked her "students to classify themselves according to their religious condition at the beginning of the year" (Jones 314). Asked to identify herself as a "No-Hoper," "Hoper," or "Christian," Dickinson chose the first of these options (Lundin 40–41). A few months into the school year, she informed Root that "there is a great deal of [religious] interest here and many are flocking to the ark of safety." Dickinson confessed, though, that she "[had] not yet given up to the claims of Christ," but was "not entirely thoughtless on so important & serious a subject" (17 Jan. 1848). In her final letter to Root from Mount Holyoke, Dickinson describes herself as "filled with self-recrimination about the opportunities [for salvation] [she had] missed," fearful that she might never "cast her burden on Christ" (16 May 1848). She thus left Mount Holyoke just as she came to it—a "No-Hoper."

In order to make quoted material fit grammatically and syntactically into his sentences, Gibson changes pronouns and adds explanatory words, enclosing all changed or added words in brackets.

Many critics, including recent biographer Roger Lundin, see the year at Mount Holyoke as a turning point in Emily Dickinson's life, the time when it became clear that she would never "become a Christian" according to Amherst's standards (47–48). Dickinson would never join the First Congregationalist Church and, by the age of thirty, stopped going to services altogether (99). She would likewise never join the Unitarians. Many of her spiritual ideas would resemble those of the transcendentalist Emerson, yet important distinctions remained (171). Throughout her life, she wrote to Christian friends, including ministers, on spiritual topics, despite their doctrinal differences (Lease 50–51). Dickinson thus eschewed New England's religious congregations and asserted her independence in spiritual matters. Yet she always remained interested in the traditional perspective, and, as a poet, she relied on the traditional terminology in order to relate her new thinking.

The author's name is omitted from this parenthetical citation because it is included in the sentence.

Dickinson's well-known poem "Some keep the Sabbath going to church—," which she wrote around 1860, demonstrates this tendency. The opening line places the poem's events on the "Sabbath," the day

of worship in Judeo-Christian traditions (<u>Oxford</u>).
Thus, while the speaker does not follow her
traditional peers "to Church," she nonetheless
observes the traditional day (line 1). The speaker
finds a "Bobolink," a native bird, to be the service's
"Chorister" (line 3), the official term for the leader of
a church choir (<u>Oxford</u>). A few lines later, the speaker
calls this bird "Our little Sexton," the title of the
manager of the church grounds. Normally, the sexton
"[tolls] the Bell, for Church" (line 7), yet this sexton
"sings" (line 8). The "Orchard" where she sits
resembles an important part of church architecture,
"a Dome." In this intimate setting, "God preaches, a
noted Clergyman— / and the sermon is never long"
(lines 9–10). The sermon satisfies two desires that
most people have at church: first, to encounter God,
and, second, not to be bored. In this natural scene
"instead of getting to Heaven, at last— / [She's]
going, all along" (lines 11–12).

The poem is so pleasant that it is easy to overlook
the fact that its central message, that staying at home
can be a spiritual experience, is subversive, for
church attendance was important in traditional
Congregationalist towns like Amherst (Rabinowitz 64–
77). In fact, the word "some" might be an
understatement, as, in 1860, most citizens in Amherst
probably attended a church on Sunday. The
speaker's situation instead resembles Emerson's 1842
description of the transcendentalists, those "lonely"
and "sincere and religious" people who "repel
influences" and "shun general society" (104–05).
Furthermore, the speaker claims access to God
without the aid of a religious community, a pastor, or
a sacred text, all of which, as seen above, were
essential to Puritan religious experience. In this
poem, then, the speaker frames her spiritual
experience in traditional terms and even keeps a few
of the traditional practices, yet she simultaneously
describes the benefits of departing from traditional
practice.

This citation refers to a line in the poem, not to a page number. The page number is indicated in the list of works cited.

A slash mark indicates a line break.

Gibson 7

While "Some keep the Sabbath going to church—" reveals Dickinson's changes in practice, "The Brain— is wider than the Sky—," composed perhaps two years later, shows her shift in theology. The speaker asserts a confidence in the power of the human intellect that resembles that of Boston's nontraditional thinkers. In each stanza, she invites the reader to measure the brain by comparing it to some other enormous entity. First, she finds that the brain "is wider than the Sky" and urges the reader to "put them side by side" and see that "the one the other will contain / with ease" and the reader "beside" (lines 1–4). Second, she observes that the brain "is deeper than the sea" and, again, urges the reader to "hold them" and see that "the one the other will absorb / as Sponges—Buckets—do" (lines 5–8). The speaker has a complicated imaginative method: her materials thus far are all physical—brain, sky, sea— but the qualities that she compares are mixed— physical length and depth versus metaphysical length and depth.

> Gibson carefully leads the reader from one section of his essay to another with a transitional sentence that first summarizes the claim developed in the last section and then articulates the claim that he will develop in the next section.

In the third stanza, when the speaker observes that the brain "is just the weight of God" (line 9), she introduces theological material into her experiment. She asks the reader to "Heft," or weigh (<u>Oxford</u>), the two "Pound for Pound" and forecasts that "they will differ—if they do— / as Syllable from Sound" (lines 10–12). The poet switches from physical science to linguistics in this closing simile, the meaning of which divides scholars. William Sherwood argues that "each syllable is . . . finite" and "includes only a fraction of the total range of sound," yet "at the same time the syllable is the instrument by which sound is articulated" (127–28). Robert Weisbuch tries to take into account the context of the simile, arguing,

> Gibson's reference to "scholars" tells the reader that he's about to describe and consider other interpretations.

> We must take the qualifying "if they do" ironi-
> cally. The difference of weight between "Sylla-
> ble" and "Sound" is at once minute and
> absolute, the difference of a hair. It is the differ-
> ence between the thing itself and its imperfect,

itemized explanation. It is the difference, say, between paraphrase and poetry, poetry and thought. The brain is not quite and not at all the weightless weight of God. (84)

Weisbuch is right to note that the phrase "if they do" is ironic, as "Syllable" and "Sound" undeniably differ. Sherwood helpfully argues that these are differences in quantity and clarity. Thus, though the brain "As Syllable" is, ultimately, less than "the weight of God," it is more intelligible, perhaps more intelligent, than "the total range of sound."

The speaker of this poem is of a scientific bent; her measurements of length, depth, and weight recall the instruction in science that Dickinson received throughout her schooling (Jones 309; Lundin 30). Yet the speaker also believes that there are things beyond or outside the physical world of science and is just as eager to apply her scientific method to them. She perceives both that the human intellect is enormously expansive and that there is a God behind the cosmos. The divinity that she describes, though, is not the one her ancestors worshipped in Amherst: the speaker's God is more like a force than a person, more like the spirit of the universe than its sovereign. In "Some keep the Sabbath going to church—" Dickinson's orchard still seemed planted in Amherst. In "The Brain—is wider than the Sky," it becomes conspicuously a satellite of Boston.

This departure from traditional theology caused Dickinson to revise her vision of the afterlife, as suggested by her 1863 "Because I could not stop for Death—." The poem begins by personifying Death as a carriage-driver (lines 1–3). This personification of death echoes several biblical passages; Dickinson's Death "may," for example, "represent one of the Four Horsemen of the Apocalypse" (Bennett 208). The poet's "kindly" personification is, of course, both more benevolent than the destructive biblical figure and, with his carriage, more modern (line 2). The carriage ride takes the speaker past a school, "Fields of Gazing Grain," the "Setting Sun," and then "[pauses]" at a

"House," before proceeding "toward Eternity" (lines 9, 11, 12, 17, 24). The "House" "[seems] / a Swelling of the Ground," and is, in fact, a grave (lines 10–11). Thus, the carriage drives the speaker through the stages of life—from youth to maturity, decline, death, and, ultimately, the afterlife.

Although Dickinson may draw her image of Death from the Christian tradition, her Death drives the speaker into a distinctly nontraditional afterlife. The speaker tells the reader early on that Death's carriage "[holds]" "Immortality" and then, in the closing stanza, that she has "surmised" that the carriage's direction is "toward Eternity" (lines 3, 4, 23, 24). In the Puritan theological tradition, death leads to Heaven or Hell, paradise or perdition. Yet Dickinson's carriage does not drive toward either destination; rather, the afterlife is just a continuous movement, a continuation of consciousness. "Some keep the Sabbath going to church—" prepared us, quite subtly, for this conception of the afterlife; there, too, Heaven is not a not place one "[gets] to," "at last," but a state to which one can be "going all along" (lines 11–12). In "Because I could not stop for Death—," the speaker sounds neither blissful nor pessimistic about this state. Her consciousness has adapted to her new existence: "centuries" pass now, "and yet / [it] feels shorter than the Day" when she "first surmised" the carriage's direction (lines 21–23). The word "surmised," though, signals that she is not entirely certain about what, if anything, is to come.

Uncertainty about the afterlife would remain with Dickinson throughout her life and, in 1882, would result in her asking the Reverend Washington Gladden, a somewhat unorthodox Congregationalist, "Is immortality true?" (Lease 50; Gladden). At this time, one of Dickinson's friends, a pastor, had recently died and another friend had become seriously ill (Gladden). Gladden's attempt to reassure her of the truth of immortality draws mostly from his argument that the authoritative figure "Jesus Christ

No page number is needed in the parenthetical citations for Gladden because the source is only one page long (see Works Cited).

taught" immortality. At the same time, he admits that "absolute demonstration there can be none of this truth."

In perhaps the same year, Dickinson wrote "The Bible is an antique Volume," which shows a mix of skepticism and optimism about the source of Gladden's arguments. The first three lines undermine the Bible's authority; it is an "antique Volume," authored by "faded Men / at the suggestion of Holy Spectres." The poet then provides a list of biblical "Subjects" that "reads like the playbill of a cheap traveling show" (Lundin 203): Eden is "the ancient Homestead"; Satan "the brigadier"; Judas "the Great Defaulter"; David "the Troubadour"; and sin "a distinguished Precipice / others must resist" (lines 4–10). The speaker then uses quotation marks to show her dissatisfaction with religious categories, saying, "Boys that 'believe' are very lonesome / other boys are 'lost' " (lines 11–12). Thus far, the speaker has given us every reason to abandon the Bible—she has discredited its authors, shown the silliness of its subjects, and revealed the tragic culture that surrounds it.

Yet the speaker believes that "had but the Tale [the Bible] a warbling Teller— / all the Boys would come" (lines 13–14). A "warbling Teller" is one whose voice is "thrilling," "ardent," or "friendly" (Bennett 430). For an example, she borrows the poet Orpheus from Greek mythology. His "Sermon," unlike the one the "believing" and "lost" boys now hear, "captivated— / it did not condemn" (lines 15–16). In addition to drawing distinct lines between the saved and the damned, like headmistress Mary Lyon, Puritans often used condemnation, in the now-infamous "fire and brimstone" style, to rouse the immoral to seek salvation (Lundin 11–12; Rabinowitz 5). Instead Dickinson here favors a passionate or intellectual response to a captivating speech over a moral response to a condemning one. She remains a believer in "the emotional force of the Scriptures and

Notice how Gibson leads the reader from one idea/paragraph to the next with a transition sentence that states the coming paragraph's main idea (This poem "shows a mix of skepticism and optimism about the" Bible) by referring back to the concerns of the last paragraph ("Gladden's arguments").

Gibson 11

[their] expositors," even if she doubts the Bible's historical accuracy and rejects the claims of traditionalist preachers (Doriani 198). The implication of these closing lines, then, is that the Bible is—when read in the right spirit—still a valuable "Volume" for building a community. The Bible has reduced religious authority, but, when performed properly, retains inspirational power. The subtle magic of the poem is that Dickinson herself, in her parodies of biblical "Subjects," enlivens the Bible, "captivates" readers with the old "Tale" through her "warbling" poem.

Though Emily Dickinson might not be a "Christian poet" in the traditional sense of the term, she does beautify and hand down a few beloved pieces of her inheritance, New England Puritanism. She "[keeps] the Sabbath," but at home. She imagines eternity, but without a Heaven or a Hell. She calls the Bible's authors "faded men," but frequently enlivens their "antique" passages in her poems. Over the years, her ideas about God, the universe, and the afterlife changed, but her yearnings to encounter the divine and to experience immortality remained. Emily Dickinson may have physically withdrawn from Amherst society, yet her mind did not withdraw from the intellectual struggles between traditional Amherst and modern Boston. Her spiritual questions and insights are distinctively personal and deeply honest; she is neither a purely skeptical nor a purely religious poet. Her intellect kept her, to her death in 1886, a "No-Hoper" by Mary Lyon's standards, yet, for modern readers, who understand her doubts and share her longings, she is a refreshingly hopeful poet.

Gibson begins his conclusion by returning to the issue he raised in his introduction (Dickinson's status as a "Christian poet"). He then summarizes his argument by briefly reiterating his key points and using a few key words from Dickinson to do so, thus reminding us of how grounded his argument is in textual evidence. Finally, he moves from summarizing his argument to considering its implications for our overall view of Dickinson's poetry.

Works Cited

Bennett, Fordyce R. A Reference Guide to the Bible in Emily Dickinson's Poetry. Lanham: Scarecrow, 1997.

Dickinson, Emily. "Because I could not stop for Death." Dickinson, Complete Poems 350.

- - -. "The Bible is an antique Volume." Dickinson, Complete Poems 644.

- - -. "The Brain—is wider than the Sky—." Dickinson, Complete Poems 312.

- - -. The Complete Poems of Emily Dickinson. Ed. Thomas H. Johnson. Boston: Little, 1960.

- - -. Letters. Ed. Thomas H. Johnson. Vol. 1. Cambridge: Belknap, 1958.

- - -. "Some keep the Sabbath going to church." Dickinson, Complete Poems 153–54.

- - -. "To Abiah Root." 8 Sept. 1846. Dickinson, Letters 36.

- - -. "To Abiah Root." 17 Jan. 1848. Dickinson, Letters 60.

- - -. "To Abiah Root." 16 May 1848. Dickinson, Letters 67–68.

Doriani, Beth M. Emily Dickinson: Daughter of Prophecy. Amherst: U of Massachusetts P, 1996.

Gladden, Washington. "To Emily Dickinson." 27 May 1882. Letter 752a of Emily Dickinson: Selected Letters. Ed. Thomas H. Johnson. Cambridge: Belknap, 1971. 282.

Jones, Rowena Revis. "The Preparation of a Poet: Puritan Directions in Emily Dickinson's Education." Studies in the American Renaissance, 1982. Boston: Twayne, 1982.

Lease, Benjamin. " 'This World is not Conclusion': Dickinson, Amherst, and 'the local conditions of the soul.' " Emily Dickinson Journal 3.2 (1994): 38–55.

Lundin, Roger. Emily Dickinson and the Art of Belief. 2nd ed. Grand Rapids: Eerdmans, 2004.

Noll, Mark A. America's God: From Jonathan Edwards to Abraham Lincoln. New York: Oxford UP, 2002.

Norberg, Peter. Introduction. Essays and Poems by Ralph Waldo Emerson. New York: Barnes and Noble, 2004. xiii–xxxiii.

The Oxford English Dictionary. 2nd ed. 1989.

Rabinowitz, Richard. The Spiritual Self in Everyday Life: The Transformation of Personal Religious Experience in Nineteenth-Century New England. Boston: Northeastern UP, 1989.

Sherwood, William R. Circumference and Circumstance: Stages in the Mind and Art of Emily Dickinson. New York: Columbia UP, 1968.

Weisbuch, Robert. "The Necessary Veil: A Quest Fiction." Emily Dickinson. Ed. Harold Bloom. New York: Chelsea, 1985.

Critical Approaches

Few human abilities are more remarkable than the ability to read and interpret literature. A computer program or a database can't perform the complex process of reading and interpreting—not to mention writing about—a literary text, although computers can easily exceed human powers of processing codes and information. Readers follow the sequence of printed words and as if by magic re-create a scene between characters in a novel or play, or they respond to the almost inexpressible emotional effect of a poem's figurative language. Experienced readers can pick up on a multitude of literary signals all at once. With rereading and some research, readers can draw on information such as the author's life or the time period when this work and others like it were first published. Varied and complex as the approaches to literary criticism may be, they are not difficult to learn. For the most part schools of criticism and theory have developed to address questions that any reader can begin to answer.

As we noted in the introduction, there are essentially three participants in what could be called the literary exchange or interaction: the *text,* the *source* (the *author* and other factors that produce the text), and the *receiver* (the *reader* and other aspects of *reception*). All the varieties of literary analysis concern themselves with these aspects of the literary exchange in varying degrees and with varying emphases. Although each of these elements has a role in any form of literary analysis, systematic studies of literature and its history have defined approaches or methods that focus on the different elements and circumstances of the literary interaction. The first three sections below—"Emphasis on the Text," "Emphasis on the Source," and "Emphasis on the Receiver"—describe briefly those schools or modes of literary analysis that have concentrated on one of the three elements while de-emphasizing the others. These different emphases, plainly speaking, are habits of asking different kinds of questions. Answers or interpretations will vary according to the questions we ask of a literary work. In practice the range of questions can be—to some extent *should* be—combined whenever we develop a literary interpretation. Such questions can always generate the thesis or argument of a critical essay.

Although some approaches to literary analysis treat the literary exchange (text, source, receiver) in isolation from the world surrounding that exchange (the world of economics, politics, religion, cultural tradition, and sexuality— in other words, the world in which we live), most contemporary modes of analysis acknowledge the importance of that world to the literary exchange. These days, even if a literary scholar wants to focus primarily on the text or its source or receiver, she or he will often incorporate some of the observations and methods developed by theorists and critics who have turned their attention toward the changing world surrounding the formal conventions of literature, the writing process and writer's career, and the reception or response to literature. We describe the work of such theorists and critics in the fourth section below, "Historical and Ideological Criticism."

Before expanding on the kinds of critical approaches within these four categories, let's consider one example in which questions concerning the text, source, and receiver, as well as a consideration of historical and ideological questions, would contribute to a richer interpretation of a text. To begin as usual with preliminary questions about the *text: What* is "First Fight. Then Fiddle." (see p. 548)? Printed correctly on a separate piece of paper, the text would tell us at once that it is a poem because of its form: rhythm, repeating word sounds, lines that leave very wide margins on the page. Because you are reading this poem in this book, you know even more about its form (in this way, the publication *source* gives clues about the *text*). By putting it in a section with other poetry, we have told you it is a poem worth reading, rereading, and thinking about. (What other ways do you encounter poems, and what does the medium of presenting a poem tell you about it?)

You should pursue other questions focused on the text. What *kind* of poem is it? Here we have helped you, especially if you are not already familiar with the sonnet form, by grouping this poem with other sonnets. Classifying "First Fight. Then Fiddle." as a sonnet might then prompt you to interpret the ways that this poem is or is not like other sonnets. Well and good: you can check off its fourteen lines of (basically) iambic pentameter, and note its somewhat unusual rhyme scheme and meter, in relation to the rules of **Italian** and **English sonnets**. *Why* does this experiment with the sonnet form matter?

To answer questions about the purpose of form, you need to answer some basic questions about *source,* such as: *When* was this sonnet written and published? *Who* wrote it? What do you know about Gwendolyn Brooks, about 1949, about African American women and/or poets in the United States at that time? A short historical and biographical essay answering such questions might help put the sonnetness of "First Fight. Then Fiddle." in context. But assembling all the available information about the source and original context of the poem, even some sort of documented testimony from Brooks about her intentions or interpretation of it, would still leave room for other questions leading to new interpretations.

What about the *receiver* of "First Fight. Then Fiddle."? Even within the poem a kind of audience exists. This sonnet seems to be a set of instructions addressed to "you." (Although many sonnets are addressed by a speaker, "I," to an auditor, "you," such address rarely sounds like military commands, as it does here.) This internal audience is not of course to be confused with real people responding to the poem. How did readers respond to it when it was first published? Can you find any published reviews, or any criticism of this sonnet published in studies of Gwendolyn Brooks?

Questions about the receiver, like those about the author and other sources, readily connect with historical questions. Would a reader or someone listening to this poem read aloud respond differently in the years after World War II than in an age of global terrorism? Does it make a difference if the audience addressed by the speaker *inside* the poem is imagined as a group of African American men and women or as a group of European American male commanders? (The latter question could be regarded as involving questions about the text and the source as well as about the receiver.) Does a reader need to identify with any of the particular groups the poem fictitiously addresses, or would any reader, from any background, respond to it the same way? Even the formal qualities of the text could be examined through historical lenses: the sonnet form has been associated with prestigious European literature, and with themes of love and mortality, since the Renaissance. It is significant that a twentieth-century African American poet chose *this* traditional form to twist "threadwise" into an antiwar protest.

The above are only some of the worthwhile questions concerning this short, intricate poem. (We will develop a few more thoughts about it in illustrating different approaches to the text and to the source.) Similarly, the complexity of critical approaches far exceeds our four categories. While a great deal of worthwhile scholarship and criticism borrows from a range of theories and methods, below we give necessarily simplified descriptions of various critical approaches that have continuing influence. We cannot trace a history of the issues involved, or the complexity and controversies within these movements. Instead think of what follows as a road map to the terrain of literary analysis. Many available resources describe the entire landscape of literary analysis in more precise detail. If you are interested in learning more about these or any other analytical approaches, consult the works listed in the bibliography at the end of this chapter.

EMPHASIS ON THE TEXT

This broad category encompasses approaches that minimize the elements associated with the author/source or the reader/reception to focus on the work. In a sense any writing about literature presupposes recognition of form, in that it deems the object of study to *be* a literary work, and to belong to a type or genre of literature, as Brooks's poem belongs with sonnets. Moreover, almost all literary criticism notes some details of style or structure, some *intrinsic* features such as the relation between dialogue or narrated summary, or the pattern of rhyme and meter. But *formalist* approaches go further by foregrounding the design of the text as inherent to the meaning of the whole work.

Some formalists, reasonably denying the division of content from form (since the form is part of the content or meaning), have more controversially excluded any discussion of *extrinsic* matters such as the author's biography or questions of psychology, sociology, or history. This has led to accusations that formalism, in avoiding relevance to actual authors and readers or to the world of economic power or social change, also avoids political issues or commitments. Some historical or ideological critics have therefore argued that formalism supports the powers that be, since it precludes protest. Conversely, some formalists charge that any extrinsic—that is, historical, political, ideological, as well as biographical or psychological—interpretations of literature reduce the text to a set of more or less cleverly encoded messages or propaganda. A formalist might maintain that the inventive wonders of art exceed any practical function it serves. In practice influential formalisms have generated modes of *close reading* that balance attention to form, significance, and social context, with some acknowledgment of the political implications of literature. In the early twenty-first century the formalist methods of close reading remain influential, especially in classrooms. Indeed, *The Norton Introduction to Literature* adheres to these methods in its presentation of elements and interpretation of form.

New Criticism

One strain of formalism, loosely identified as the New Criticism, dominated literary studies from approximately the 1920s to the 1970s. New Critics rejected both of the approaches that prevailed then in the relatively new field of English studies: the dry analysis of the development of the English language, and the misty appreciation and evaluation of great works. Generally, New Criticism minimizes consideration of both the source and the receiver, favoring the intrinsic qualities of a unified literary work. Psychological or historical information about the author, the intentions or feelings of authors or readers, and any philosophical or socially relevant "messages" derived from the work all are out of bounds in a New Critical reading. The text in a fundamental way refers to itself: its medium is its message. Although interested in ambiguity and irony as well as figurative language, a New Critical reader establishes the organic unity of the unique work. Like an organism, the work develops in a synergetic relation of parts to whole.

A New Critic might, for example, publish an article titled "A Reading of 'First Fight. Then Fiddle.' " (The method works best with lyric or other short forms because it requires painstaking attention to details such as metaphors or alliteration.) Little if anything would be said of Gwendolyn Brooks or the poem's relation to modernist poetry. The critic's task is to give credit to the poem, not the poet or the period, and if it is a good poem, implicitly, it can't be merely "about" World War II or civil rights. New Criticism presumes that a good literary work symbolically embodies universal human themes and may be interpreted objectively on many levels. These levels may be related more by tension and contradiction than harmony, yet that relation demonstrates the coherence of the whole poem.

Thus the New Critic's essay might include some of the following observations. The title—which reappears as half of the first line—consists of a pair of two-word imperative sentences, and most statements in the poem paraphrase these two sentences, especially the first of them, "First fight." Thus an alliterative two-word command, "Win war" (line 12), follows a longer version of such a command: "But first to arms, to armor" (line 9). Echoes of this sort of exhortation appear throughout. We, as audience, begin to feel "bewitch[ed], bewilder[ed]" (line 4) by a buildup of undesirable urgings, whether at the beginning of a line ("Be deaf," line 11) or the end of a line ("Be remote," line 7; "Carry hate," line 9) or in the middle of a line ("Rise bloody," line 12). It's hardly what we would want to do. Yet the speaker makes a strong case for the practical view that a society needs to take care of defense before it can "devote" itself to "silks and honey" (lines 6–7), that is, the soft and sweet pleasures of art. But what kind of culture would place "hate / In front of . . . harmony" and try to ignore "music" and "beauty" (lines 9–11)? What kind of people are only "remote / A while from malice and from murdering" (lines 6–7)? A society of warlike heroes would rally to this speech. Yet on rereading, many of the words jar with the tone of heroic battle cry.

The New Critic examines not only the speaker's style and words but the order of ideas and lines in the poem. Ironically, the poem defies the speaker's command; it fiddles first, and then fights, as the **octave** (first eight lines) concern art, and the **sestet** (last six) concern war. The New Critic might be delighted by the irony that the two segments of the poem in fact unite, in that their topics—octave on how to fiddle, sestet on how to fight—mirror each other. The beginning of the poem plays with metaphors for music and art as means of inflicting "hurting love" (line 3) or emotional conquest, that is, ways to "fight." War and art are both, as far as we know, universal in all human societies. The poem, then, is an organic whole that restates ancient themes.

Later critics have pointed out that New Criticism, despite its avoidance of extrinsic questions, had a political context of its own. The affirmation of unity for the artwork and humanities in general should be regarded as a strategy adapted during the Cold War as a counterbalance to the politicization of art in fascist and communist regimes. New Criticism also provided a program for literary reading that is accessible to beginners regardless of their social background, in keeping with the opening of college-level English studies to more women, minorities, and members of the working class. By the 1970s these same groups had helped generate two sources of opposition to New Criticism's ostensible neutrality and transparency: critical studies that emphasized the politics of social differences (e.g., feminist criticism); and theoretical approaches, based on linguistics, philosophy, and political theory, that effectively distanced nonspecialists once more.

Structuralism

Whereas New Criticism was largely a British and American phenomenon, structuralism and its successor, poststructuralism, derive primarily from French theorists. Strains of structuralism also emerged in the Soviet Union and in Prague, influenced by the demand for a science of criticism that would avoid direct political confrontation. Each of these movements was drawn to scientific objectivity—difficult to attain in literature, arts, and other "humanities"—and at the same time wary of political commitment. Politics, after all, had been the rallying cry for censorship of science, art, and inquiry throughout centuries and in recent memory.

Structuralist philosophy, however, was something rather new. Influenced by the French linguist Ferdinand de Saussure (1857–1913), structuralists sought an objective system for studying the principles of language. Saussure distinguished between individual uses of language, such as the sentences you or I just spoke or wrote (*parole*), and the sets of rules of English or any language (*langue*). Just as a structuralist linguist would study the interrelations of signs in the *langue* rather than the variations in specific utterances in *parole*, a structuralist critic of literature or culture would study shared systems of meaning, such as genres or myths that pass from one country or period to another, rather than a certain poem in isolation (the favored subject of New Criticism).

Another structuralist principle derived from Saussure is the emphasis on the arbitrary association between a word and what it is said to signify, the *signifier* and the *signified*. The word "horse," for example, has no divine, natural, or necessary connection to that four-legged, domesticated mammal, which is named by other combinations of sounds and letters in other languages. Any language is a network of relations among such arbitrary signifiers, just as each word in the dictionary must be defined using other words in that dictionary. Structuralists largely attribute the meanings of words to rules of differentiation from other words. Such differences may be phonetic (as among the words "cat" and "bat" and "hat") or they may belong to conceptual associations (as among the words "dinky," "puny," "tiny," "small," "miniature," "petite," "compact"). Structuralist thought has particularly called attention to the way that opposites or dualisms such as "night" and "day" or "feminine" and "masculine" define each other through their differences rather than in direct reference to objective reality. For example, the earth's motion around the sun produces changing exposure to sunlight daily and seasonally, but by linguistic convention we call it "night" between, let's say, 8 p.m. and 5 a.m., no matter how light it is. (We may differ in opinions about "evening" or "dawn." But our "day" at work may begin or end in the dark.) The point is that arbitrary labels divide what in fact is continuous.

Structuralism's linguistic insights have greatly influenced literary studies. Like New Criticism, structuralism shows little interest in the creative process or in authors, their intentions, or their circumstances. Similarly, structuralism discounts the idiosyncrasies of particular readings; it takes texts to represent interactions of words and ideas that stand apart from individual human identities or sociopolitical commitments. Structuralist approaches have applied less to lyric poetry than to myths, narratives, and cultural practices, such as sports or fashion. Although structuralism tends to affirm a universal humanity as the New Critics might do, its work in comparative mythology and anthropology challenged the absolute value that New Criticism tended to grant to time-honored canons of great literature.

The structuralist would regard a text not as a self-sufficient icon but as part of a network of conventions. A structuralist essay on "First Fight. Then Fiddle." might ask why the string is plied with the "feathery sorcery" (line 2) of the "bow" (line 7). These words suggest the art of a Native American trickster or primitive sorcerer, while at the same time the instrument is a disguised weapon: a stringed bow with feathered arrows (the term "muzzle" is a similar pun, suggesting an animal's snout and the discharging end of a gun). Or is the fiddle—a violin played in musical forms such as bluegrass— a metaphor for popular art or folk resistance to official culture? In many folk tales a hero is taught to play the fiddle by the devil or tricks the devil with a fiddle or similar instrument. Further, a structuralist reading might attach great significance to the sonnet form as a paradigm that has shaped poetic expression for centuries. The classic "turn" or reversal of thought in a sonnet may imitate the form of many narratives of departure and return, separation and reconciliation. Brooks's poem repeats in the numerous short reversing imperatives, as well as in the structure of octave versus sestet, the eternal oscillation between love and death, creation and destruction.

Poststructuralism

By emphasizing the paradoxes of dualisms and the ways that language constructs our awareness, structuralism planted the seeds of its own destruction or, rather, deconstruction. Dualisms (e.g., masculine/feminine, mind/ body, culture/nature) cannot be separate-but-equal; rather they take effect as differences of power in which one dominates the other. Yet as the German philosopher of history Georg Wilhelm Friedrich Hegel (1770–1831) insisted, the relations of the dominant and subordinate, of master and slave readily invert themselves. The master is dominated by his need for the slave's subordination; the possession of subordinates defines his mastery. As Brooks's poem implies, each society reflects its own identity through an opposing "they," in a dualism of civilized/barbaric. The instability of the speaker's position in this poem (is he or she among the conquerors or the conquered?) is a model of the instability of roles throughout the human world. There is no transcendent ground—except on another planet, perhaps—from which to measure the relative positions of the polar opposites on Earth. Roland Barthes (1915–1980) and others, influenced by the radical movements of the 1960s and the increasing complexity of culture in an era of mass consumerism and global media, extended structuralism into more profoundly relativist perspectives.

Poststructuralism is the broad term used to designate the philosophical position that attacks the objective, universalizing claims of most fields of knowledge since the eighteenth century. Poststructuralists, distrusting the optimism of a positivist philosophy that suggests the world is knowable and explainable, ultimately doubt the possibility of certainties of any kind, since language signifies only through a chain of other words rather than through any fundamental link to reality. This argument derives from structuralism, yet it also criticizes structuralist universalism and avoidance of political issues. *Ideology* is a key conceptual ingredient in the poststructuralist argument against structuralism. Ideology is a slippery term that can broadly be defined as a socially shared set of ideas that shape behavior; often it refers to the values that legitimate the ruling interests in a society, and in many accounts it is the hidden code that is officially denied. (We discuss kinds of "ideological" criticism later.) Poststructuralist theory has played a part in a number of critical schools introduced below, not all of them focused on the text. But in literary criticism, poststructuralism has marshaled most forces under the banner of deconstruction.

Deconstruction

Deconstruction insists on the logical impossibility of knowledge that is not influenced or biased by the words used to express it. Deconstruction also claims that language is incapable of representing any sort of reality directly. As practiced by its most famous proponent, the French philosopher Jacques Derrida (1930–2004), deconstruction endeavors to trace the way texts imply the contradiction of their explicit meanings. The deconstructionist delights in the sense of dizziness as the grounds of conviction crumble away; *aporia*, or irresolvable doubt, is the desired, if fleeting, end of an encounter with a text. Deconstruction threatens *humanism*, or the worldview that is centered on human values and the self-sufficient individual, because it denies that there is an ultimate, solid reality on which to base truth or the identity of the self. All values and identities are constructed by the competing systems of meaning, or *discourses*. This is a remarkably influential set of ideas that you will meet again as we discuss other approaches.

The traditional concept of the author as creative origin of the text comes under fire in deconstructionist criticism, which emphasizes instead the creative power of language or the text, and the ingenious work of the critic in detecting gaps and contradictions in writing. Thus like New Criticism, deconstruction disregards the author and concentrates on textual close reading, but unlike New Criticism, it features the role of the reader as well. Moreover, the text need not be respected as a pure and coherent icon. Deconstructionists might "read" many kinds of writing and representation in other media in much the same way that they might read Milton's *Paradise Lost*, that is, irreverently. Indeed, when deconstruction erupted in university departments of literature, traditional critics and scholars feared the breakdown of the distinctions between literature and criticism and between literature and many other kinds of text. Many attacks on literary theory have particularly lambasted deconstructionists for apparently rejecting all the reasons to care about literature in the first place and for writing in a style so flamboyantly obscure that no one but specialists can understand. Yet in practice Derrida and others have carried harmony before them, to paraphrase Brooks; their readings can delight in the play of figurative language, thereby enhancing rather than debunking the value of literature.

A deconstructionist might read "First Fight. Then Fiddle." in a manner somewhat similar to the New Critic's, but with even more focus on puns and paradoxes and with resistance to organic unity. For instance, the two alliterative commands, "fight" and "fiddle," might be opposites, twins, or inseparable consequences of each other. The word "fiddle" is tricky. Does it suggest that art is trivial? Does it allude to a dictator who "fiddles while Rome burns," as the saying goes? Someone who "fiddles" is not performing a grand, honest, or even competent act: one fiddles with a hobby, with the books, with car keys in the dark. The artist in this poem defies the orthodoxy of the sonnet form, instead making a kind of harlequin patchwork out of different traditions, breaking the rhythm, intermixing endearments and assaults.

To the deconstructionist the recurring broken antitheses of war and art, art and war cancel each other out. The very metaphors undermine the speaker's summons to war. The command "Be deaf to music and to beauty blind," which takes the form of a *chiasmus,* or X-shaped sequence (adjective, noun; noun, adjective), is a kind of miniature version of this chiasmic poem. (We are supposed to follow a sequence, fight then fiddle, but instead reverse that by imagining ways to do violence with art or to create beauty through destruction.) The poem, a lyric written but imagined as spoken or sung, puts the senses and the arts under erasure; we are somehow not to hear music (by definition audible), not to see beauty (here a visual attribute). "Maybe not too late" comes rather too late: at the end of the poem it will be too late to start over, although "having first to civilize a space / Wherein to play your violin with grace" (lines 12–14) comes across as a kind of beginning. These comforting lines form the only heroic couplet in the poem, the only two lines that run smoothly from end to end. (All the other lines have **caesuras, enjambments,** or balanced pairs of concepts, as in "from malice and from murdering" [line 8].) But the violence behind "civilize," the switch to the high-art term "violin," and the use of the Christian term "grace" suggest that the pagan erotic art promised at the outset, the "sorcery" of "hurting love" that can "bewitch," will be suppressed.

Like other formalisms, deconstruction can appear apolitical or conservative because of its skepticism about the referential connection between literature and the world of economics, politics, and other social forms. Yet poststructuralist linguistics provides a theory of *difference* that clearly pertains to the rankings of status and power in society, as in earlier examples of masculine/feminine, master/slave. The *Other,* the negative of the norm, is always less than an equal counterpart. Deconstruction has been a tool for various poststructuralist thinkers—including the historian Michel Foucault (1926–1984), the feminist theorist and psychoanalyst Julia Kristeva (b. 1941), and the psychoanalytic theorist Jacques Lacan (1901–1981).

Narrative Theory

Before concluding the discussion of text-centered approaches, we should mention the schools of narratology and narrative theory that have shaped study of the novel and other kinds of narrative. Criticism of fiction has been in a boom period since the 1950s, but the varieties of narrative theory per se have had more limited effect than the approaches we have discussed above. Since the 1960s different analysts of the forms and techniques of narrative, most notably the Chicago formalists and the structuralist narratologists, have developed terminology for the various interactions of author, implied author, narrator, and characters; of plot and the treatment of time in the selection and sequence of scenes; of voice, point of view, or focus and other aspects of fiction. As formalisms, narrative theories tend to exclude the author's biography, individual reader response, and the historical context of the work or its actual reception.

Narratology began by presenting itself as a structuralist science; its branches have grown from psychoanalytic theory or extended to reader-response criticism. In recent decades studies of narrative technique and form have responded to Marxist, feminist, and other ideological criticism that insists on the political contexts of literature. One important influence on this shift has been the revival of the work of Mikhail Bakhtin (1895–1975), which features the novel as a *dialogic* form that pulls together the many discourses and voices of a culture and its history. Part of the appeal of Bakhtin's work has been the fusion of textual close reading with comprehension of material factors such as economics and class, and a sense of the open-endedness and contradictoriness of writing (in the spirit of deconstruction more than of New Criticism). Like other Marxist-trained European formalists, Bakhtin sought to place the complex literary modes of communication in the light of politics and history.

EMPHASIS ON THE SOURCE

As the above examples suggest, a great deal can be drawn from a text without any reference to its source or author. For millennia many anonymous works were shared in oral or manuscript form, and even after printing spread in Europe it was not necessary to know the author's name or anything about him or her. Yet criticism from its beginnings in ancient Greece has been interested in the designing intention "behind" the text. Even when no evidence remained about the author, a legendary personality has been invented to satisfy readers' curiosity. From the legend of blind Homer to the latest debates about biographical evidence and portraits of William Shakespeare, literary criticism has been accompanied by interest in the author's life.

Biographical Criticism

This approach reached its height in an era when humanism prevailed in literary studies (roughly 1750s to 1960s). At this time there was widely shared confidence in the ideas that art and literature were the direct expressions of the artist's or writer's genius and that criticism of great works supported veneration of the great persons who created them. The lives of some famous writers became the models that aspiring writers emulated. Criticism at times was skewed by social judgments of personalities, as when Keats was put down as a "Cockney" poet, that is, London-bred and lower-class. Many writers have struggled to get their work taken seriously because of mistaken biographical criticism. Women or minorities have at times used pseudonyms or published anonymously to avoid having their work put down or having it read only through the expectations, negative or positive, of what a woman or person of color might write. Biographical criticism can be diminishing in this respect. Others have objected to reading literature as a reflection of the author's personality. Such critics have supported the idea that the highest literary art is pure form, untouched by gossip or personal emotion. In this spirit some early twentieth-century critics as well as modernist writers such as T. S. Eliot, James Joyce, and Virginia Woolf tried to dissociate the text from the personality or political commitments of the author. (The theories of these writers and their actual practices did not quite coincide.)

In the early twentieth century, psychoanalytic interpretations placed the text in light of the author's emotional conflicts, and other interpretations relied heavily on the author's stated intentions. (Although psychoanalytic criticism entails more than analysis of the author, we will introduce it as an approach that primarily concerns the human source[s] of literature; it usually has less to say about the form and receiver of the text.) Author-based readings can be reductive. All the accessible information about a writer's life cannot explain the writings. As a young man D. H. Lawrence might have hated his father and loved his mother, but all men who hate their fathers and love their mothers do not write fiction as powerful as Lawrence's. Indeed, Lawrence cautioned that we should "trust the tale, not the teller."

Any kind of criticism benefits, however, from being informed by the writer's life and career to some extent. Certain critical approaches, devoted to recognition of separate literary traditions, make sense only in light of supporting biographical evidence. Studies that concern traditions such as Irish literature, Asian American literature, or literature by Southern women require reliable information about the writers' birth and upbringing and even some judgment of the writers' intentions to write *as* members of such traditions. (We discuss feminist, African American, and other studies of distinct literatures in the "Historical and Ideological Criticism" section, although such studies recognize the biographical "source" as a starting point.)

A reading of "First Fight. Then Fiddle." becomes rather different when we know more about Gwendolyn Brooks. An African American, she was raised in Chicago in the 1920s. These facts begin to provide a context for her work. Some of the biographical information has more to do with her time and place than with her race and sex. Brooks began in the 1940s to associate with Harriet Monroe's magazine, *Poetry,* which had been influential in promoting modernist poetry. Brooks early received acclaim for books of poetry that depict the everyday lives of poor, urban African Americans; in 1950 she was the first African American to win a Pulitzer Prize. In 1967 she became an outspoken advocate for the Black Arts movement, which promoted a separate tradition rather than integration into the aesthetic mainstream. But even before this political commitment, her work never sought to "pass" or to distance itself from racial difference, nor did it become any less concerned with poetic tradition and form when she published it through small, independent black presses in her "political" phase.

It is reasonable, then, to read "First Fight. Then Fiddle.," published in 1949, in relation to the role of a racial outsider mastering and adapting the forms of a dominant tradition. Perhaps Brooks's speaker addresses an African American audience in the voice of a revolutionary, calling for violence to gain the right to express African American culture. Perhaps the lines "the music that they wrote / Bewitch, bewilder. Qualify to sing / Threadwise" (lines 3–5) suggest the way that the colonized may transform the empire's music rather than the other way around. Ten years before the poem was published, a famous African American singer, Marian Anderson, had more than "qualif[ied] to sing" opera and classical concert music, but had still encountered the color barrier in the United States. Honored throughout Europe as the greatest living contralto, Anderson was barred in 1939 from performing at Constitution Hall in Washington, D.C., because of her race. Instead she performed at the Lincoln Memorial on Easter Sunday to an audience of seventy-five thousand people. It was not easy to find a "space" in which to practice her art. Such a contextual reference, whether or not intended, relates biographically to Brooks's role as an African American woman wisely reweaving classical traditions "threadwise" rather than straining them into "hempen" (line 5) ropes. Beneath the manifest reference to the recent world war, this poem refers to the segregation of the arts in America. (Questions of source and historical context often interrelate.)

Besides readings that derive from biographical and historical information, there are still other ways to read aspects of the *source* rather than the *text* or the *receiver*. The source of the work extends beyond the life of the person who wrote it to include not only the writer's other works but also the circumstances of contemporary publishing; contemporary literary movements; the history of the composition and publication of this particular text, with all the variations; and other contributing factors. While entire schools of literary scholarship have been devoted to each of these matters, any analyst of a particular work should bear in mind what is known about the circumstances of writers at that time, the material conditions of the work's first publication, and the means of dissemination ever since. It makes a difference in our interpretation to know that a certain sonnet circulated in manuscript in a small courtly audience or that a particular novel was serialized in a weekly journal.

Psychoanalytic Criticism

With the development of psychology and psychoanalysis toward the end of the nineteenth century, many critics were tempted to apply psychological theories to literary analysis. Symbolism, dreamlike imagery, emotional rather than rational logic, a pleasure in language all suggested that literature profoundly evoked a mental and emotional landscape, often one of disorder or abnormality. From mad poets to patients speaking in verse, imaginative literature might be regarded as a representation of shared irrational structures within all *psyches* (i.e., souls) or selves. While psychoanalytic approaches have developed along with structuralism and poststructuralist linguistics and philosophy, they rarely focus on textual form. Rather, they attribute latent or hidden meaning to unacknowledged desires in some person, usually the author or source behind the character in a narrative or drama. A psychoanalytic critic could focus on the response of readers and, in recent decades, usually accepts the influence of changing social history on the structures of sexual desire represented in the work. Nevertheless, psychoanalysis has typically aspired to a universal, unchanging theory of the mind and personality, and criticism that applies it has tended to emphasize the authorial source.

FREUDIAN CRITICISM

For most of the twentieth century, the dominant school of psychoanalytic critics was the Freudian, based on the work of Sigmund Freud (1856–1939). Many of its practitioners assert that the meaning of a literary work exists not on its surface but in the psyche (some would even claim, in the neuroses) of the author. Classic psychoanalytic criticism read works as though they were the recorded dreams of patients; interpreted the life histories of authors as keys to the works; or analyzed characters as though like real people they have a set of repressed childhood memories. (In fact, many novels and most plays leave out information about characters' development from infancy through adolescence, the period that psychoanalysis especially strives to reconstruct.)

A well-known Freudian reading of *Hamlet,* for example, insists that Hamlet suffers from an Oedipus complex, a Freudian term for a group of repressed desires and memories that corresponds with the Greek myth that is the basis of Sophocles' play *Oedipus the King.* In this view Hamlet envies his uncle because the son unconsciously wants to sleep with his mother, who was the first object of his desire as a baby. The ghost of Hamlet Sr. may then be a manifestation of Hamlet's unconscious desire or a figure for his guilt for wanting to kill his father, the person who has a right to the desired mother's body. Hamlet's madness is not just acting but the result of this frustrated desire; his cruel mistreatment of Ophelia is a deflection of his disgust at his mother's being "unfaithful" in her love for him. Some Freudian critics stress the author's psyche and so might read *Hamlet* as the expression of Shakespeare's own Oedipus complex. In another mode psychoanalytic critics, reading imaginative literature as symbolic fulfillment of unconscious wishes much as an analyst would interpret a dream, decipher objects, spaces, or actions that appear to relate to sexual anatomy or activity. Much as if tracing out the extended metaphors of an erotic poem by Donne or a blues or Motown lyric, the Freudian reads containers, empty spaces, or bodies of water as female; tools, weapons, towers or trees, trains or planes as male.

Psychoanalytic criticism, learning from Freud's ventures in literary criticism, has favored narrative fiction with uncanny, supernatural, or detective elements. Plots with excessive, inexplicable fatalities seem to express wishes unconsciously shared by all readers as well as the writer. The method has often been applied to writers of such stories whose biographies are well documented. The life and works of Edgar Allan Poe (1809–1849) therefore have attracted psychoanalytic readings. An orphan who quarreled with the surrogate father who raised him, Poe seems to have been tormented by an unresolved desire for a mother figure. A series of beloved mother figures died prematurely, including his mother and Mrs. Allan, the woman who raised him. He became attached to his aunt and fell in love with her daughter, Virginia Clemm, whom he married in 1836 when she was thirteen, and who died of tuberculosis in 1847. He famously asserted that the most apt subject of poetry is the death of a beautiful woman. In Poe's "The Raven" a macabre talking bird intrudes in the speaker's room and induces an obsession with the dead beloved, a woman named Lenore. In a Freudian reading Poe's "The Cask of Amontillado" appears to transpose a fantasy of return to the womb—an enclosed space holding liquids—into a fulfilled desire to kill a male rival.

JUNGIAN AND MYTH CRITICISM

Just as a Freudian assumes that all human psyches have similar histories and structures, the Jungian critic assumes that we all share a universal or collective unconscious (as well as having a racial and individual unconscious). According to Carl Gustav Jung (1875–1961) and his followers, the unconscious harbors universal patterns and forms of human experiences, or archetypes. We can never know these archetypes directly, but they surface in art in an imperfect, shadowy way, taking the form of archetypal images—the snake with its tail in its mouth, rebirth, mother, the double, the descent into hell. In the classic quest narrative, the hero struggles to free himself (the gender of the pronoun is significant) from the Great Mother, to become a separate, self-sufficient being (combating a demonic antagonist), surviving trials to gain the reward of union with his ideal other, the feminine anima. In a related school of *archetypal criticism*, influenced by Northrop Frye (1912–1991), the prevailing myth follows a seasonal cycle of death and rebirth. Frye proposed a system for literary criticism that classified all literary forms in all ages according to a cycle of genres associated with the phases of human experience from birth to death and the natural cycle of seasons (e.g., Spring/Romance).

These approaches have been useful in the study of folklore and early literatures as well as in comparative studies of various national literatures. While most myth critics focus on the hero's quest, there have been forays into feminist archetypal criticism. These emphasize variations on the myths of Isis and Demeter, goddesses of fertility or seasonal renewal, who take different forms to restore either the sacrificed woman (Persephone's season in the underworld) or the sacrificed man (Isis's search for Osiris and her rescue of their son, Horus). Many twentieth-century poets were drawn to the heritage of archetypes and myths. Adrienne Rich's "Diving into the Wreck," for example, self-consciously rewrites a number of gendered archetypes, with a female protagonist on a quest into a submerged world. Most critics today, influenced by poststructuralism, have become wary of universal patterns. Like structuralists, Jungians and archetypal critics strive to compare and unite the ages and peoples of the world and to reveal fundamental truths. Rich, as a feminist poet, suggests that the "book of myths" is an eclectic anthology that needs to be revised. Claims of universality tend to obscure the detailed differences between cultures and often appeal to some idea of *biological determinism*. Such determinism diminishes the power of individuals to design alternative life patterns and even implies that no literature can really surprise us.

LACANIAN CRITICISM

As it has absorbed the indeterminacies of poststructuralism under the influence of thinkers such as Jacques Lacan and Julia Kristeva, psychological criticism has become increasingly complex. Few critics today are direct Freudian analysts of authors or texts, and few maintain that universal archetypes explain the meaning of a tree or water in a text. Yet psychoanalytic theory continues to inform many varieties of criticism, and most new work in this field is affiliated with Lacanian psychoanalysis. Lacan's theory unites poststructuralist linguistics with Freudian theory. The Lacanian critic, like a deconstructionist, focuses on the text that defies conscious authorial control, foregrounding the powerful interpretation of the critic rather than the author or any other reader. Accepting the Oedipal paradigm and the unconscious as the realm of repressed desire, Lacanian theory aligns the development and structure of the individual human *subject* with the development and structure of language. To simplify a purposefully dense theory: The very young infant inhabits the Imaginary, in a preverbal, undifferentiated phase dominated by a sense of union with Mother. Recognition of identity begins with the Mirror Stage, ironically with a disruption of a sense of oneness. For when one first looks into a mirror, one begins to recognize a split or difference between one's body and the image in the mirror. This splitting prefigures a sense that the *object* of desire is Other and distinct from the subject. With difference or the splitting of subject and object comes language and entry into the Symbolic Order, since we use words to summon the absent object of desire (as a child would cry "Mama" to bring her back). But what language signifies most is the lack of that object. The imaginary, perfectly nurturing Mother would never need to be called.

As in the biblical Genesis, the Lacanian "genesis" of the subject tells of a loss of paradise through knowledge of the difference between subject and object or Man and Woman (eating of the Tree of the Knowledge of Good and Evil leads to the sense of shame that teaches Adam and Eve to hide their nakedness). In Lacanian theory the Father governs language or the Symbolic Order; the Word spells the end of a child's sense of oneness with the Mother. Further, the Father's power claims omnipotence, the possession of male prerogative symbolized by the Phallus, which is not the anatomical difference between men and women but the idea or construction of that difference. Thus it is language or culture rather than nature that generates the difference and inequality between the sexes. Some feminist theorists have adopted aspects of Lacanian psychoanalytic theory, particularly the concept of *the gaze*. This concept notes that the masculine subject is the one who looks, whereas the feminine object is to be looked at.

Another influential concept is *abjection*. Julia Kristeva's theory of abjection most simply reimagines the infant's blissful sense of union with the mother and the darker side of such possible union. To return to the mother's body would be death, as metaphorically we are buried in Mother Earth. Yet according to the theory, people both desire and dread such loss of boundaries. A sense of self or *subjectivity* and hence of independence and power depends on resisting abjection. The association of the maternal body with abjection or with the powerlessness symbolized by the female's Lack of the Phallus can help explain negative cultural images of women. Many narrative genres seem to split the images of women between an angelic and a witchlike type. Lacanian or Kristevan theory has been well adapted to film and to the fantasy and other popular forms favored by structuralism or archetypal criticism.

Psychoanalytic literary criticism today—as distinct from specialized discussion of Lacanian theory, for example—treads more lightly than in the past. In James Joyce's "Araby" a young Dublin boy, orphaned and raised by an aunt and uncle, likes to haunt a back room in the house; there the "former tenant, . . . a priest, had died" (paragraph 2). (Disused rooms at the margins of houses resemble the unconscious, and a dead celibate "father" suggests a kind of failure of the Law, conscience, or in Freudian terms, superego.) The priest had left behind a "rusty bicycle-pump" in the "wild garden" with "a central apple tree" (these echoes of the garden of Eden suggesting the impotence of Catholic religious symbolism). The boy seems to gain consciousness of a separate self—or his subjectivity is constructed—through his gaze upon an idealized female object, Mangan's sister, whose "name was like a summons to all my foolish blood" (paragraph 4). Though he secretly watches and follows her, she is not so much a sexual fantasy as a beautiful art object (paragraph 9). He retreats to the back room to think of her in a kind of ecstasy that resembles masturbation. Yet it is not masturbation: it is preadolescent, dispersed through all orifices—the rain feels like "incessant needles . . . playing in the sodden beds"; and it is sublimated, that is, repressed and redirected into artistic or religious forms rather than directly expressed by bodily pleasure: "All my senses seemed to desire to veil themselves" (paragraph 6).

It is not in the back room but on the street that the girl finally speaks to the hero, charging him to go on a quest to *Araby*. After several trials the hero carrying the talisman arrives in a darkened hall "girdled at half its height by a gallery," an underworld or maternal space that is also a deserted temple (paragraph 25). The story ends without his grasping the prize to carry back, the "chalice" or holy grail (symbolic of female sexuality) that he had once thought to bear "safely through a throng of foes" (paragraph 5).

Such a reading seems likely to raise objections that it is overreading: *you're seeing too much in it; the author didn't mean that.* This has been a popular reaction to psychoanalysis for over a hundred years, but it is only a heightened version of a response to many kinds of criticism. This sample reading pays close attention to the text, but does not really follow a formal approach because its goal is to explain the psychological motivations or sources of the story's details. We have mentioned nothing about the author, though we could have placed the above reading within a psychoanalytic reading of Joyce's biography.

EMPHASIS ON THE RECEIVER

In some sense critical schools develop in reaction to the excesses of other critical schools. By the 1970s, in a time of political upheaval that placed a value on individual expression, a number of critics felt that the various routes toward objective criticism had proven dead ends. New Critics, structuralists, and psychoanalytic or myth critics had sought objective, scientific systems that disregarded changing times, political issues, or the reader's personal response. New Critics and other formalists tended to value a literary canon made up of works that were regarded as complete, unchanging objects to be comprehended as if spatially in a photograph according to timeless standards.

Reader-Response Criticism

Among critics who challenged New Critical assumptions, the reader-response critics regarded the work not as what is printed on the page but as what is experienced temporally through each act of reading. In effect the reader performs the poem into existence the way a musician performs a score. Reader-response critics ask not what a work means but what a work does or, rather, what it makes a reader do. Literary texts especially leave gaps that experienced readers fill according to expectations or conventions. Individual readers differ, of course, and gaps in a text provide space for different readings or interpretations. Some of these lacunae are temporary—such as the withholding of the murderer's name until the end of a mystery novel— and are closed by the text sooner or later, though each reader will in the meantime fill them differently. But other lacunae are permanent and can never be filled with certainty; they result in a degree of uncertainty or indeterminacy in the text.

The reader-response critic observes the expectations aroused by a text, how they are satisfied or modified, and how the reader projects a comprehension of the work when all of it has been read, and when it is reread in whole or in part. Such criticism attends to the reading habits associated with different genres and to the shared assumptions of a cultural context that seem to furnish what is left unsaid in the text. Margaret Atwood's story "Happy Endings" could almost be an essay on reader response in the guise of do-it-yourself instructions to a simpleminded reader: "John and Mary meet. What happens next? If you want a happy ending, try A" (paragraphs 1–3). This beginning seems to steer the reader to follow alphabetized instructions to assist in designing the narrative. It also satirizes romance plot conventions. Every romance fan knows that if a male and a female character meet, they will fall in love, and that some conflict will delay their marriage until it is resolved—unless the conflict proves insurmountable. As Atwood humorously shows, various love triangles or death will change the outcome. In spite of the scanty details given in the text, each reader will fill in the gaps and imagine "How and Why" (paragraph 23), the realistic details and rounded characterization that he or she has learned to imagine from reading other fiction.

Beyond theoretical formulations about reading, there are other approaches to literary study that concern the receiver rather than the text or source. A critic might examine specific documents of a work's reception, from contemporary reviews to critical essays written across the generations since the work was first published. Sometimes we have available diaries or autobiographical evidence about readers' encounters with particular works. Just as there are histories of publishing and of the book, there are histories of literacy and reading practices. Poetry, fiction, and drama often directly represent the theme of reading as well as writing. Many published works over the centuries have debated the benefits and perils of reading works such as sermons or novels. Different genres and particular works construct different classes or kinds of readers in the way they address them or supply what they are supposed to want. Some scholars have found quantitative measures for reading, from sales and library lending rates to questionnaires.

Finally, the role of the reader or receiver in literary exchange has been portrayed from a political perspective. Literature helps shape social identity, and social status shapes access to different kinds of literature. Feminist critics adapted reader-response criticism, for example, to note that girls often do not identify with many American literary classics as boys do, and thus girls do not simply accept the idea of women as angels, temptresses, or scolds who should be abandoned for the sake of all-male adventures. Studies of African American literature and other ethnic literatures have often featured discussion of literacy and of the obstacles for readers who cannot find their counterparts within the texts or who encounter negative stereotypes of their group. Thus, as we will discuss below, most forms of historical and ideological criticism include some consideration of the reader.

HISTORICAL AND IDEOLOGICAL CRITICISM

Approaches to the text, the author, and the reader, outlined above, each may take some note of historical contexts, including changes in formal conventions, the writer's milieu, or audience expectations. In the nineteenth century, historical criticism took the obvious facts that a work is created in a specific historical and cultural context and that the author is a part of that context as reasons to treat literature as a reflection of society. Twentieth-century formalists rejected the *reflectivist* model of art in the old historical criticism, that is, the assumption that literature and other arts straightforwardly express the collective spirit of the society at that time. But as we have remarked, formalist rules for isolating the work of art from social and historical context met resistance in the last decades of the twentieth century. In a revival of historical approaches, critics have replaced the reflectivist model with a *constructivist* model, whereby literature and other cultural discourses help construct social relations and roles rather than merely reflecting them. In other words, art is not just the frosting on the cake but an integral part of the recipe's ingredients and instructions. A society's ideology, its inherent system of representations (ideas, myths, images), is inscribed in and by literature and other cultural forms, which in turn help shape identities and social practices.

Since the 1980s historical approaches have regained great influence in literary studies. Some critical schools have been insistently *materialist,* that is, seeking causes more in concrete conditions such as technology, production, and distribution of wealth, or the exploitation of markets and labor in and beyond Western countries. Such criticism usually owes an acknowledged debt to Marxism. Other historical approaches have been influenced to a degree by Marxist critics and cultural theorists, but work within the realm of ideology, textual production, and interpretation, using some of the methods and concerns of traditional literary history. Still others emerge from the civil rights movement and the struggles for recognition of women and racial, ethnic, and sexual constituencies.

Feminist studies, African American studies, gay and lesbian studies, and studies of the cultures of different immigrant and ethnic populations within the United States have each developed along similar theoretical lines. These schools, like Marxist criticism, adopt a constructivist position; literature is not simply a reflection of prejudices and norms, but helps define as well as reshape social identities, such as what it means to be an African American woman. Each of these schools has moved through stages of first claiming *equality* with the literature dominated by white Anglo American men, then affirming the *difference* of their own separate culture, and then theoretically *questioning the terms and standards* of such comparisons. At a certain point in the thought process, each group rejects *essentialism,* the notion of innate or biological bases for the differences between the sexes, races, or other groups. This rejection of essentialism is usually called the constructivist position, in a somewhat different but related sense to our definition above. Constructivism maintains that identity is socially formed rather than biologically determined. Differences of anatomical sex, skin color, first language, parental ethnicity, and eventual sexual practices have great impact on how one is classified, brought up, and treated socially, and on one's subjectivity or conception of identity. These differences are, however, more constructed by ideology and the resulting behaviors than by any natural programming.

Marxist Criticism

The most insistent and vigorous historical approach through the twentieth century to the present has been Marxism, based on the work of Karl Marx (1818–1883). With roots in nineteenth-century historicism, Marxist criticism was initially reflectivist. Economics, the underlying cause of history, was thus the *base,* and culture, including literature and the other arts, was the *superstructure,* an outcome or reflection of the base. Viewed from the Marxist perspective, the literary works of a period were economically determined; they would *reflect* the state of the struggle between classes in any place and time. History enacted recurrent three-step cycles, a pattern that Hegel had defined as *dialectic* (Hegel was cited above on the interdependence of master and slave). Each socioeconomic phase, or *thesis*, is counteracted by its *antithesis*, and the resulting conflict yields a *synthesis*, which becomes the ensuing *thesis*, and so on. As with early Freudian criticism, early Marxist criticism was often overly concerned with labeling and exposing illusions or deceptions. A novel might be read as thinly disguised defense of the power of bourgeois industrial capital; its appeal on behalf of the suffering poor might be dismissed as an effort to fend off a class rebellion.

As a rationale for state control of the arts, Marxism was abused in the Soviet Union and in other totalitarian states. In the hands of sophisticated critics, however, Marxism has been richly rewarding. Various schools that unite formal close reading and political analysis developed in the early twentieth century under Soviet communism and under fascism in Europe, often in covert resistance. These schools in turn have influenced critical movements in North American universities through translations or through members who came to the United States; New Criticism, structuralist linguistics, deconstruction, and narrative theory have each borrowed from European Marxist critics.

Most recently, a new mode of Marxist theory has developed, largely guided by the thinking of Walter Benjamin (1892–1940) and Theodor Adorno (1903–1969) of the Frankfurt School in Germany, Louis Althusser (1918–1990) in France, and Raymond Williams (1921–1998) in Britain. This work has generally tended to modify the base/superstructure distinction and to interrelate public and private life, economics and culture. Newer Marxist interpretation assumes that the relation of a literary work to its historical context is *overdetermined*—the relation has multiple determining factors rather than a sole cause or aim. This thinking similarly acknowledges that neither the source nor the receiver of the literary interaction is a mere tool or victim of the ruling powers or state. Representation of all kinds, including literature, always has a political dimension, according to this approach; conversely, political and material conditions such as work, money, or institutions depend on representation.

Showing some influence of psychoanalytic and poststructuralist theories, recent Marxist literary studies examine the effects of ideology by focusing on the works' gaps and silences: ideology may be conveyed in what is repressed or contradicted. In many ways Marxist criticism has adapted to the conditions of consumer rather than industrial capitalism and to global rather than national economies. The revolution that was to come when the proletariat or working classes overthrew the capitalists has never taken place; in many countries industrial labor has been swallowed up by the service sector, and workers reject the political Left that would seem their most likely ally. Increasingly, Marxist criticism has acknowledged that the audience of literature may be active rather than passive, just as the text and source may be more than straightforward instructions for toeing the political line. Marxist criticism has been especially successful with the novel, since that genre more than drama or short fiction is capable of representing numerous people from different classes as they develop over a significant amount of time.

Feminist Criticism

Like Marxist criticism and the schools discussed below, feminist criticism derives from a critique of a history of oppression, in this case the history of women's inequality. Feminist criticism has no single founder like Freud or Marx; it has been practiced to some extent since the 1790s, when praise of women's cultural achievements went hand in hand with arguments that women were rational beings deserving equal rights and education. Contemporary feminist criticism emerged from a "second wave" of feminist activism, in the 1960s and 1970s, associated with the civil rights and antiwar movements. One of the first disciplines in which women's activism took root was literary criticism, but feminist theory and women's studies quickly became recognized methods across the disciplines.

Feminist literary studies began by denouncing the misrepresentation of women in literature and affirming women's writings, before quickly adopting the insights of poststructuralist theory; yet the early strategies continue to have their use. At first, feminist criticism in the 1970s, like early Marxist criticism, regarded literature as a reflection of patriarchal society's sexist base; the demeaning images of women in literature were symptoms of a system that had to be overthrown. Feminist literary studies soon began, however, to claim the *equal* worth if distinctive themes of writings by women and men. Critics such as Elaine Showalter (b. 1941), Sandra M. Gilbert (b. 1936), and Susan Gubar (b. 1944) featured the canonical works by women, relying on close reading with some aid from historical and psychoanalytic methods. Yet by the 1980s it was widely recognized that a New Critical method would leave most of the male-dominated canon intact and most women writers still in obscurity, because many women had written in different genres and styles, on different themes, and for different audiences than had male writers.

To affirm the *difference* of female literary traditions, some feminist studies claimed women's innate or universal affinity for fluidity and cycle rather than solidity and linear progress. Others concentrated on the role of the mother in human psychological development. According to this argument, girls, not having to adopt a gender role different from that of their first object of desire, the mother, grow up with less rigid boundaries of self and a relational rather than judgmental ethic. The dangers of these intriguing generalizations soon became apparent. If the reasons for women's differences from men were biologically based or were due to universal archetypes, there was no solution to women's oppression, which many cultures worldwide had justified in terms of biological reproduction or archetypes of nature.

At this point in the debate, feminist literary studies intersected with poststructuralist linguistic theory in *questioning the terms and standards* of comparison. French feminist theory, articulated most prominently by Hélène Cixous (b. 1935) and Luce Irigaray (b. 1932), deconstructed the supposed archetypes of gender written into the founding discourses of Western culture. We have seen that deconstruction helps expose the power imbalance in every dualism. Thus man is to woman as culture is to nature or mind is to body, and in each case the second term is held to be inferior or Other. The language and hence the worldview and social formations of our culture, not nature or eternal archetypes, constructed woman as Other. This insight was helpful in avoiding essentialism or biological determinism.

Having reached a theoretical criticism of the terms on which women might claim equality or difference from men in the field of literature, feminist studies also confronted other issues in the 1980s. Deconstructionist readings of gender difference in texts by men as well as women could lose sight of the real world, in which women are paid less and are more likely to be victims of sexual violence. Some feminist critics with this in mind pursued links with Marxist or African American studies; gender roles, like those of class and race, were interdependent systems for registering the material consequences of people's differences. It no longer seemed so easy to say what the term "women" referred to, when the interests of different kinds of women had been opposed to each other. African American women asked if feminism was really their cause, when white women had so long enjoyed power over both men and women of their race. In a classic Marxist view, women allied with men of their class rather than with women of other classes. It became more difficult to make universal claims about women's literature, as the horizon of the college-educated North American feminists expanded to recognize the range of conditions of women and literature worldwide. Feminist literary studies have continued to consider famous and obscure women writers; the way women and gender are portrayed in writings by men as well as women; feminist issues concerning the text, source, or receiver in any national literature; theoretical and historical questions about the representation of differences such as gender, race, class, and nationality, and the way these differences shape each other.

Gender Studies and Queer Theory

From the 1970s, feminists sought recognition for lesbian writers and lesbian culture, which they felt had been even less visible than male homosexual writers and gay culture. Concurrently, feminist studies abandoned the simple dualism of male/female, part of the very binary logic of patriarchy that seemed to cause the oppression of women. Thus feminists recognized a zone of inquiry, the study of gender, as distinct from historical studies of women, and increasingly they included masculinity as a subject of investigation. As gender studies turned to interpretation of the text in ideological context regardless of the sex or intention of the author, it incorporated the ideas of Michel Foucault's *History of Sexuality* (1976). Foucault helped show that there was nothing natural, universal, or timeless in the constructions of sexual difference or sexual practices. Foucault also introduced a history of the concept of homosexuality, which had once been regarded in terms of taboo acts and in the later nineteenth century became defined as a disease associated with a personality type. Literary scholars began to study the history of sexuality as a key to the shifts in modern culture that had also shaped literature.

In the 1980s, gender had come to be widely regarded as a discourse that imposed binary social norms on human beings' diversity. Theorists such as Donna Haraway (b. 1944) and Judith Butler (b. 1956) insisted further that sex and sexuality have no natural basis; even the anatomical differences are representations from the moment the newborn is put in a pink or blue blanket. Moreover, these theorists claimed that gender and sexuality are *performative* and malleable positions, enacted in many more than two varieties. From cross-dressing to surgical sex changes, the alternatives chosen by real people have collaborated with the critical theories and generated both writings and literary criticism about those writings. Perhaps biographical and feminist studies face new challenges when identity seems subject to radical change and it is less easy to determine the sex of an author.

Gay and lesbian literary studies have included practices that parallel feminist criticism. At times critics identify oppressive or positive representations of homosexuality in works by men or women, gay, lesbian, or straight. At other times critics seek to establish the equivalent stature of a work by a gay or lesbian writer or, because these identities tended to be hidden in the past, to reveal that a writer *was* gay or lesbian. Again stages of *equality* and *difference* have yielded to a *questioning of the terms of difference*, in this case what has been called queer theory (the stages have not superseded each other). The field of queer theory hopes to leave everyone guessing rather than to identify gay or lesbian writers, characters, or themes. One of its founding texts, *Between Men* (1985), by Eve Kosofsky Sedgwick (b. 1950), drew upon structuralist insight into desire as well as anthropological models of kinship to show that, in canonical works of English literature, male characters bond together through their rivalry for and exchange of a woman. Queer theory, because it rejects the idea of a fixed identity or innate or essential gender, likes to discover resistance to heterosexuality in unexpected places. Queer theorists value gay writers such as Oscar Wilde, but they also find queer implications regardless of the author's acknowledged identity. This approach emphasizes not the surface signals of the text but what the audience or receiver might detect. It encompasses elaborate close reading of varieties of work; characteristically, a leading queer theorist, D. A. Miller (b. 1948), has written in loving detail about Jane Austen and about Broadway musicals.

African American and Ethnic Literary Studies

Critics sought to define an African American literary tradition as early as the turn of the twentieth century. A period of literary success in the 1920s, known as the Harlem Renaissance, produced some of the first classic essays on writings by African Americans. Criticism and histories of African American literature tended to ignore and dismiss women writers, while feminist literary histories, guided by the Virginia Woolf's classic *A Room of One's Own* (1929), neglected women writers of color. Only after feminist critics began to succeed in the academy and African American studies programs were established did the whiteness of feminist studies and masculinity of African

American studies became glaring; both fields have for some time corrected this problem of vision. The study of African American literature followed the general pattern that we have noted, first striving to claim equality, on established aesthetic grounds, of works such as Ralph Ellison's magnificent *Invisible Man* (1952). Then in the 1960s the Black Arts or Black Aesthetic emerged. Once launched in the academy, however, African American studies has been devoted less to celebrating an essential racial difference than to tracing the historical construction of a racial Other and a subordinated literature. The field sought to recover genres in which African Americans have written, such as slave narratives, and traced common elements in fiction or poetry to the conditions of slavery and segregation. By the 1980s feminist and poststructuralist theory had an impact in the work of some African American critics such as Henry Louis Gates Jr. (b. 1950), Houston A. Baker Jr. (b. 1943), Hazel V. Carby (b. 1948), and Deborah E. McDowell (b. 1951), while others objected that the doubts raised by "theory" stood in the way of political commitment. African Americans' cultural contributions to America have gained much more recognition than before. New histories of American culture have been written with the view that racism is not an aberration but inherent to the guiding narratives of national progress. Many critics now regard race as a discourse with only slight basis in genetics but with weighty investments in ideology. This poststructuralist position coexists with scholarship that takes into account the race of the author or reader or that focuses on African American characters or themes.

In recent years a series of fields has arisen in recognition of the literatures of other American ethnic groups, large and small: Asian Americans, Native Americans, and Chicano/as. Increasingly, such studies avoid romanticizing an original, pure culture or assuming that these literatures by their very nature undermine the values and power of the dominant culture. Instead, critics emphasize the *hybridity* of all cultures in a global economy. The contact and intermixture of cultures across geographical borders and languages (translations, the "creole" speech made up of native and acquired languages, dialects) may be read as enriching themes for literature and art, albeit they are caused by economic exploitation. In method and in aim these fields have much in common with African American studies, though each cultural and historical context is very different. Each field deserves the separate study that we cannot offer here.

Not so very long ago, critics might have been charged with a fundamental misunderstanding of the nature of literature if they pursued matters considered the business of sociologists, matters—such as class, race, and gender—that seemed extrinsic to the text. The rise of the above fields has made it expected that a critic will address questions about class, race, and gender to place a text, its source, and its reception in historical and ideological context. One brief example might illustrate the way Marxist, feminist, queer, and African American criticism can contribute to a literary reading.

Tennessee Williams's *A Streetcar Named Desire* was first produced in 1947 and won the Pulitzer Prize in 1948. Part of its acclaim was likely due to its fashionable blend of naturalism and symbolism: the action takes place in a shabby tenement on an otherworldly street, Elysian Fields—in an "atmosphere of decay" laced with "lyricism," as Williams's stage directions put it. After the Depression and World War II, American audiences welcomed a turn away from world politics into the psychological core of human sexuality. This turn to ostensibly individual conflict was a kind of alibi for at least two sets of issues that Williams and the middle-class theatergoers in New York and elsewhere sought to avoid. First, the racial questions that relate to questions of gender and class: what is the play's attitude to race, and what is Williams's attitude? Biography seems relevant, though not the last word on what the play means. Williams's family had included slave-holding cotton growers, and he chose to spend much of his adult life in the South, which he saw as representing a beautiful but dying way of life. He was deeply attached to women in his family who might be models for the brilliant, fragile, cultivated Southern white woman, Blanche DuBois. Blanche ("white" in French), representative of a genteel, feminine past that has gambled, prostituted, dissipated itself, speaks some of the most eloquent lines in the play when she mourns the faded Delta plantation society. Neither the playwright nor his audience wished to deal with segregation in the South, a region that since the Civil War had festered as a kind of agricultural working class in relation to the dominant North—which had its racism, too.

The play scarcely notices race. The main characters are white. The cast includes a "Negro Woman" as servant, and a blind Mexican woman who offers artificial flowers to remember the dead, but these figures seem either stage business or symbolism. Instead, racial difference is transposed as ethnic and class difference, in the story of a working-class Pole intruding into a family clinging to French gentility. Stella warns Blanche that she lives among "heterogeneous types" and that Stanley is "a different species." The play thus transfigures of contemporary anxieties about miscegenation, as the virile (black) man dominates the ideal white woman and rapes the spirit of the plantation South. A former army man who works in a factory, Stanley represents as well the defeat of the old, agricultural economy by industrialization.

The second set of issues that neither the playwright nor his audience confronts directly is the disturbance of sexual and gender roles that would in later decades lead to movements for women's and gay rights. It was well known in New Orleans at least that Williams was gay. In the 1940s he lived with his lover, Pancho Rodriguez y Gonzales, in the French Quarter. Like many homosexual writers in different eras, Williams recasts homosexual desire in heterosexual costume. Blanche, performing femininity with a kind of camp excess, might be a fading queen pursuing and failing to capture younger men. Stanley, hypermasculine, might caricature the object of desire of both men and women as well as the anti-intellectual, brute force in postwar America. His conquest of women (he had "the power and pride of a richly feathered male bird among hens") appears to be biologically determined. By the same token it seems natural that Stanley and his buddies go out to work and their wives become homemakers in the way now seen as typical of the 1950s. In this world, artists, homosexuals, or unmarried working women like Blanche would be both vulnerable and threatening. Blanche after all has secret pleasures—drinking and sex—that Stanley indulges in openly. Blanche is the one who is taken into custody by the medical establishment, which in this period diagnosed homosexuality as a form of insanity.

New Historicism

Three interrelated schools of historical and ideological criticism have been important innovations in the past two decades. These are part of the swing of the pendulum away from formal analysis of the text and toward historical analysis of context. New historicism has less obvious political commitments than Marxism, feminism, or queer theory, but it shares their interest in the power of discourse to shape ideology. Old historicism, in the 1850s–1950s, confidently told a story of civilization's progress from the point of view of a Western nation; a historicist critic would offer a close reading of the plays of Shakespeare and then locate them within the prevailing Elizabethan "worldview." "New Historicism," labeled in 1982 by Stephen Greenblatt (b. 1943), rejected the technique of plugging samples of a culture into a history of ideas. Influenced by poststructuralist anthropology, New Historicism tried to take a multilayered impression or "thick description" of a culture at one moment in time, including popular as well as elite forms of representation. As a method, New Historicism belongs with those that deny the unity of the text, defy the authority of the source, and license the receiver—much like deconstructionism. Accordingly, New Historicism doubts the accessibility of the past; all we have is discourse. One model for New Historicism was the historiography of Michel Foucault, who as we have said insisted on the power of discourses, that is, not only writing but all structuring myths or ideologies that underlie social relations. The New Historicist, like Foucault, is interested in the transition from the external powers of the state and church in the feudal order to modern forms of power. The rule of the modern state and middle-class ideology is enforced insidiously by systems of surveillance and by each individual's internalization of discipline (not unlike Freud's idea of the superego).

No longer so "new," the New Historicists have had a lasting influence on a more narrative and concrete style of criticism even among those who espouse poststructuralist and Marxist theories. A New Historicist article begins with an anecdote, often a description of a public spectacle, and teases out the many contributing causes that brought disparate social elements together in that way. It usually applies techniques of close reading to forms that would not traditionally have received such attention. Although it often concentrates on events several hundred years ago, in some ways it defies historicity, flouting the idea that a complete objective impression of the entire context could ever be achieved.

Cultural Studies

Popular culture often gets major attention in the work of New Historicists. Yet today most studies of popular culture would acknowledge their debt instead to cultural studies, as filtered through the now-defunct Center for Contemporary Cultural Studies, founded in 1964 by Stuart Hall (b. 1932) and others at the University of Birmingham in England. Method, style, and subject matter may be similar in New Historicism and cultural studies: both attend to historical context, theoretical method, political commitment, and textual analysis. But whereas the American movement shares Foucault's paranoid view of state domination through discourse, the British school, influenced by Raymond Williams and his concept of "structures of feeling," emphasizes the possibility that ordinary people, the receivers of cultural forms, may resist dominant ideology. The documents examined in a cultural-studies essay may be recent, such as artifacts of tourism at Shakespeare's birthplace rather than sixteenth-century maps. Cultural studies today influences history, sociology, communications and media, and literature departments; its studies may focus on television, film, romance novels, advertising, or on museums and the art market, sports and stadiums, New Age religious groups, or other forms and practices.

The questions raised by cultural studies would encourage a critic to place a poem like Marge Piercy's "Barbie Doll" in the context of the history of that toy, a doll whose slender, impossibly long legs, tiptoe feet (not unlike the bound feet of Chinese women of an earlier era), small nose, and torpedo breasts enforced a 1950s ideal for the female body. A critic influenced by cultural studies might align the poem with other works published around 1973 that express feminist protest concerning cosmetics, body image, consumption, and the objectification of women, while she or he would draw on research into the founding and marketing of Mattel toys. The poem reverses the Sleep- ing Beauty story: this heroine puts herself into the coffin rather than waking up. The poem omits any hero—Ken?—who would rescue her. "Barbie Doll" protests the pressure a girl feels to fit into a heterosexual plot of romance and marriage; no one will buy her if she is not the right toy or accessory.

Indeed, accessories such as "GE stoves and irons" (line 3) taught girls to plan their lives as domestic consumers, and Barbie's lifestyle is decidedly middle-class and suburban (everyone has a house, car, pool, and lots of handbags). The whiteness of the typical "girlchild" (line 1) goes without saying. Although Mattel produced Barbie's African American friend, Christie, in 1968, Piercy's title makes the reader imagine Barbie, not Christie. In 1997 Mattel issued Share a Smile Becky, a friend in a wheelchair, as though in answer to the humiliation of the girl in Piercy's poem, who feels so deformed, in spite of her "strong arms and back, / abundant sexual drive and manual dexterity" (lines 8-9), that she finally cripples herself. The icon, in short, responds to changing ideology. Perhaps responding to generations of objections like Piercy's, Barbies over the years have had feminist career goals, yet women's lives are still plotted according to physical image.

In this manner a popular product might be "read" alongside a literary work. The approach would be influenced by Marxist, feminist, gender, and racial studies, but it would not be driven by a desire to destroy Barbie as sinister, misogynist propaganda. Piercy's kind of protest against indoctrination has gone out of style. Girls have found ways to respond to such messages and divert them into stories of empowerment. Such at least is the outlook of cultural studies, which usually affirms popular culture. A researcher could gather data on Barbie sales and could interview girls or videotape their play, to establish the actual effects of the dolls. Whereas traditional anthropology examined non-European or preindustrial cultures, cultural studies may direct its "field work," or ethnographic research, inward, at home. Nevertheless, many contributions to cultural studies rely on methods of textual close reading or Marxist and Freudian literary criticism developed in the mid-twentieth century.

Postcolonial Criticism and Studies of World Literature

A Web site on the invention of the Barbie doll says that Barbies are sold in over 150 countries around the world and that "more than one billion Barbie dolls (and family members) have been sold since 1959, and placed head-to-toe, the dolls would circle the earth more than seven times" <http://www.ideafinder.com/history/inventions/story081.htm>. Such a global reach for an American toy begins to seem less like play and more like imperial domination. In the middle of the twentieth century, meanwhile, the remaining colonies of the European nations struggled toward independence. French-speaking Frantz Fanon (1925–1961) of Martinique was one of the most compelling voices for the point of view of the colonized or exploited countries, which like the feminine Other had been objectified and denied the right to look and talk back. Edward Said (1935–2003), in *Orientalism* (1978), brought a poststructuralist analysis to bear on the history of colonization, illustrating the ways that Western culture feminized and objectified the East. Postcolonial literary studies developed into a distinct field in the 1990s in light of globalization and the replacement of direct colonial power with international corporations. In general this field cannot share the optimism of some cultural studies, given the histories of slavery and economic exploitation of colonies and the violence committed in the name of civilization's progress. Studies by Gayatri Chakravorty Spivak (b. 1942) and Homi K. Bhabha (b. 1949) have further mingled Marxist, feminist, and poststructuralist theory to reread both canonical Western works and the writings of people from beyond centers of dominant culture. Colonial or postcolonial literatures may include works set or published in countries during colonial rule or after independence, or they may feature texts produced in the context of international cultural exchange, such as a novel in English by a woman of Chinese descent writing in Malaysia.

Like feminist studies and studies of African American or other literatures, the field is inspired by recovery of neglected works, redress of a systematic denial of rights and recognition, and increasing realization that the dualisms of opposing groups reveal interdependence. In this field the stage of difference came early, with the celebrations of African heritage known as *Négritude*, but the danger of that essentialist claim was soon apparent: the Dark Continent or wild island might be romanticized and idealized as a source of innate qualities of vitality long repressed in Enlightened Europe. Currently, most critics accept that the context for literature in all countries is hybrid, with immigration and educational intermixing. Close readings of texts are always linked to the author's biography and literary influences and placed within the context of contemporary international politics as well as colonial history. Many fiction writers, from Salman Rushdie to Jhumpa Lahiri, make the theme of cultural mixture or hybridity part of their work, whether in a pastiche of Charles Dickens or a story of an Indian family growing up in New Jersey and returning as tourists to the supposed "native" land. Poststructuralist theories of trauma, and theories of the interrelation of narrative and memory, provide explanatory frames for interpreting writings from Afghanistan to the former Zaire.

Studies of postcolonial culture retain a clear political mission that feminist and Marxist criticism have found difficult to sustain. Perhaps this is because the scale of the power relations is so vast, between nations rather than the sexes or classes within those nations. Imperialism can be called an absolute evil, and the destruction of local cultures a crime against humanity. Today some of the most exciting literature in English emerges from countries once under the British Empire, and all the techniques of criticism will be brought to bear on it. If history is any guide, in later decades some critical school will attempt to read the diverse literatures of the early twenty-first century in pure isolation from authorship and national origin, as self-enclosed form. The themes of hybridity, indeterminacy, trauma, and memory will be praised as universal. It is even possible that readers' continuing desire to revere authors as creative geniuses in control of their meanings will regain respectability among specialists. For the elements of the literary exchange— text, source, and receiver—are always there to provoke questions that generate criticism, which in turn produces articulations of the methods of that criticism. It is an ongoing discussion worth participating in.

BIBLIOGRAPHY

For good introductions to the issues discussed here, see the following books, from which we have drawn in our discussion and definitions. Some of these provide bibliographies of the works of critics and schools mentioned above.

Alter, Robert. *The Pleasure of Reading in an Ideological Age.* New York: Norton, 1996. Rpt. of *The Pleasures of Reading: Thinking about Literature in an Ideological Age.* 1989.

Barnet, Sylvan, and William E. Cain. *A Short Guide to Writing about Literature.* 10th ed. New York: Longman, 2005.

Barry, Peter. *Beginning Theory: An Introduction to Literary and Cultural Theory.* 2nd ed. Manchester: Manchester UP, 2002.

Bressler, Charles E. *Literary Criticism: An Introduction to Theory and Practice.* 3rd ed. Upper Saddle River: Prentice, 2003.

Culler, Jonathan. *Literary Theory: A Very Short Introduction.* Oxford: Oxford UP, 1997.

Davis, Robert Con, and Ronald Schleifer. *Contemporary Literary Criticism: Literary and Cultural Studies.* 4th ed. New York: Addison, 1999.

During, Simon. *Cultural Studies: A Critical Introduction.* New York: Routledge, 2005.

——. *The Cultural Studies Reader.* New York: Routledge, 1999.

Eagleton, Mary, ed. *Feminist Literary Theory: A Reader.* 2nd ed. Malden: Blackwell, 1996.

Eagleton, Terry. *Literary Theory: An Introduction.* 2nd rev. ed. Minneapolis: U of Minnesota P, 1996.

Groden, Michael, and Martin Kreiswirth. *The Johns Hopkins Guide to Literary Theory and Criticism.* Baltimore: Johns Hopkins UP, 1994.

Hawthorn, Jeremy. *A Glossary of Contemporary Literary Theory.* 3rd ed. London: Arnold, 1998.

Leitch, Vincent B. *American Literary Criticism from the Thirties to the Eighties.* New York: Columbia UP, 1989.

——, et al. *The Norton Anthology of Theory and Criticism.* New York: Norton, 2001.

Lentricchia, Frank. *After the New Criticism.* Chicago: U of Chicago P, 1981.

Macksey, Richard, and Eugenio Donato, eds. *The Structuralist Controversy: The Languages of Criticism and the Sciences of Man.* 1972. Ann Arbor: Books on Demand, n.d.

Moi, Toril. *Sexual-Textual Politics.* New York: Routledge, 1985.

Murfin, Ross, and Supryia M. Ray. *The Bedford Glossary of Critical and Literary Terms.* Boston: Bedford, 1997.

Piaget, Jean. *Structuralism.* Trans. and ed. Chaninah Maschler. New York: Basic, 1970.

Selden, Raman, and Peter Widdowson. *A Reader's Guide to Contemporary Literary Theory.* 3rd ed. Lexington: U of Kentucky P, 1993.

Todorov, Tzvetan. *Mikhail Bakhtin: The Dialogic Principle.* Trans. Wlad Godzich. Minneapolis: U of Minnesota P, 1984.

Turco, Lewis. *The Book of Literary Terms.* Hanover: UP of New England, 1999.

Veeser, Harold, ed. *The New Historicism.* New York: Routledge, 1989.

——. *The New Historicism Reader.* New York: Routledge, 1994.

Warhol, Robyn R., and Diane Price Herndl. *Feminisms.* 2nd ed. New Brunswick: Rutgers UP, 1997.

Wolfreys, Julian. *Literary Theories: A Reader and Guide.* Edinburgh: Edinburgh UP, 1999.

Glossary

Boldface words within definitions are themselves defined in the glossary.

acting the last of the four steps of characterization in a performed play.

action an imagined event or series of events; an event may be verbal as well as physical, so that saying something or telling a story within the story may be an event.

allegory as in **metaphor**, one thing (usually nonrational, abstract, religious) is implicitly spoken of in terms of something concrete, but in an allegory the comparison is extended to include an entire work or large portion of a work.

alliteration the repetition of initial consonant sounds through a sequence of words—for example, "While I nodded, nearly napping" in Edgar Allan Poe's "The Raven."

allusion a reference—whether explicit or implicit, to history, the Bible, myth, literature, painting, music, and so on—that suggests the meaning or generalized implication of details in the story, poem, or play.

ambiguity the use of a word or expression to mean more than one thing.

amphitheater the design of classical Greek theaters, consisting of a stage area surrounded by a semicircle of tiered seats.

analogy a comparison based on certain resemblances between things that are otherwise unlike.

anapestic a metrical form in which each foot consists of two unstressed syllables followed by a stressed one.

antagonist a neutral term for a **character** who opposes the leading male or female character. *See* **hero/heroine** and **protagonist**.

antihero a leading **character** who is not, like a **hero**, perfect or even outstanding, but is rather ordinary and representative of the more or less average person.

archetype a **plot** or **character** element that recurs in cultural or cross-cultural **myths**, such as "the quest" or "descent into the underworld" or "scapegoat."

arena stage a stage design in which the audience is seated all the way around the acting area; actors make their entrances and exits through the auditorium.

assonance the repetition of vowel sounds in a sequence of words with different endings—for example, "The death of the poet was kept from his poems" in W. H. Auden's "In Memory of W. B. Yeats."

aubade a morning song in which the coming of dawn is either celebrated or denounced as a nuisance.

auditor someone other than the reader—a **character** within the fiction—to whom the story or "speech" is addressed.

authorial time distinct from **plot time** and **reader time**, authorial time denotes the influence that the time in which the author was writing had upon the **conception** and **style** of the text.

ballad a narrative poem that is, or originally was, meant to be sung. Characterized by repetition and often by a repeated refrain (recurrent phrase or series of phrases), ballads were originally a folk creation, transmitted orally from person to person and age to age.

ballad stanza a common **stanza** form, consisting of a quatrain that alternates four-beat and three-beat lines; lines 1 and 3 are unrhymed iambic tetrameter (four beats), and lines 2 and 4 are rhymed iambic trimeter (three beats).

blank verse the verse form most like everyday human speech; blank verse consists of unrhymed lines in **iambic pentameter**. Many of Shakespeare's plays are in blank verse.

caesura a short pause within a line of poetry; often but not always signaled by punctuation. Note the two caesuras in this line from Poe's "The Raven": "Once upon a midnight dreary, while I pondered, weak and weary."

canon when applied to an individual author, *canon* (like **oeuvre**) means the sum total of works written by that author. When used generally, it means the range of works that a consensus of scholars, teachers, and readers of a particular time and culture consider "great" or "major." This second sense of the word is a matter of debate since the literary canon in Europe and America has long been dominated by the works of white men. During the last several decades, the canon in the United States has expanded considerably to include more works by women and writers from various ethnic and racial backgrounds.

casting the third step in the creation of a **character** on the stage; deciding which actors are to play which parts.

centered (central) consciousness a limited third-person **point of view**, one tied to a single **character** throughout the story; this character often reveals his or her inner thoughts but is unable to read the thoughts of others.

character (1) a fictional personage who acts, appears, or is referred to in a work; (2) a combination of a person's qualities, especially moral qualities, so that such terms as "good" and "bad," "strong" and "weak," often apply. *See* **nature** and **personality**.

characterization the fictional or artistic presentation of a fictional personage. A term like "a good character" can, then, be ambiguous—it may mean that the personage is virtuous or that he or she is well presented regardless of his or her characteristics or moral qualities.

chorus in classical Greek plays, a group of actors who commented on and described the **action** of a play. Members of the chorus were often masked and relied on song, dance, and recitation to make their commentary.

classical unities as derived from Aristotle's *Poetics,* the principles of structure that require a play to have one action that occurs in one place and within one day.

climax also called the **turning point,** the third part of **plot structure,** the point at which the **action** stops rising and begins falling or reversing.

colloquial diction a level of language in a work that approximates the speech of ordinary people. The language used by characters in Toni Cade Bambara's "Gorilla, My Love" is a good example.

comedy a broad category of dramatic works that are intended primarily to entertain and amuse an audience. Comedies take many different forms, but they share three basic characteristics: (1) the values that are expressed and that typically present the conflict within the play are social and determined by the general opinion of society (as opposed to being universal and beyond the control of humankind, as in **tragedy**); (2) **characters** in comedies are often defined primarily in terms of their society and their role within it; (3) comedies often end with a restoration of social order in which one or more characters take a proper social role.

conception the first step in the creation of any work of art, but especially used to indicate the first step in the creation of a dramatic **character,** whether for written text or performed play; the original idea, when the playwright first begins to construct (or even dream about) a **plot,** the **characters,** the **structure,** or a **theme.**

conclusion the fifth part of **plot structure,** the point at which the situation that was destabilized at the beginning of the story becomes stable once more.

concrete poetry poetry shaped to look like an object. Robert Herrick's "Pillar of Fame," for example, is arranged to look like a pillar. Also called **shaped verse.**

confessional poem a relatively recent (or recently defined) **kind** in which the speaker describes a state of mind, which becomes a **metaphor** for the larger world.

conflict a struggle between opposing forces, such as between two people, between a person and something in nature or society, or even between two drives, impulses, or parts of the self.

connotation what is suggested by a word,

apart from what it explicitly describes. *See* denotation.

controlling metaphors metaphors that dominate or organize an entire poem. In Linda Pastan's "Marks," for example, the controlling metaphor is of marks (grades) as a way of talking about the speaker's performance of roles within her family.

conventions standard or traditional ways of saying things in literary works, employed to achieve certain expected effects.

cosmic irony a type of irony that arises out of the difference between what a character aspires to and what so-called universal forces deal him or her; such irony implies that a god or fate controls and toys with human actions, feelings, lives, outcomes.

criticism *See* literary criticism.

culture a broad and relatively indistinct term that implies a commonality of history and some cohesiveness of purpose within a group. One can speak of southern culture, for example, or urban culture, or American culture, or rock culture; at any one time, each of us belongs to a number of these cultures.

dactylic the metrical pattern in which each foot consists of a stressed syllable followed by two unstressed ones.

denotation a direct and specific meaning. *See* connotation.

descriptive structure a textual organization determined by the requirements of describing someone or something.

diction an author's choice of words.

discriminated occasion the first specific event in a story, usually in the form of a specific scene.

discursive structure a textual organization based on the form of a treatise, argument, or essay.

dramatic irony a plot device in which a character holds a position or has an expectation that is reversed or fulfilled in a way that the character did not expect but that we, as readers or as audience members, have anticipated because our knowledge of events or individuals is more complete than the character's.

dramatic monologue a monologue set in a specific situation and spoken to an imaginary audience.

dramatic structure a textual organization based on a series of scenes, each of which is presented vividly and in detail.

dramatis personae the list of characters that appears either in the play's program or at the top of the first page of the written play.

echo a verbal reference that recalls a word, phrase, or sound in another text.

elegy in classical times, any poem on any subject written in "elegiac" meter; since the Renaissance, usually a formal lament on the death of a particular person.

English sonnet *see* Shakespearean sonnet.

enjambment running over from one line of poetry to the next without stop, as in the following lines by Wordsworth: "My heart leaps up when I behold / A rainbow in the sky."

epic a poem that celebrates, in a continuous narrative, the achievements of mighty heroes and heroines, usually in founding a nation or developing a culture, and uses elevated language and a grand, high style.

epigram originally any poem carved in stone (on tombstones, buildings, gates, and so forth), but in modern usage a very short, usually witty verse with a quick turn at the end.

expectation the anticipation of what is to happen next (*see* curiosity and suspense), what a character is like or how he or she will develop, what the theme or meaning of the story will prove to be, and so on.

exposition that part of the structure that sets the scene, introduces and identifies characters, and establishes the situation at the beginning of a story or play. Additional exposition is often scattered throughout the work.

extended metaphor a detailed and complex metaphor that stretches through a long section of a work.

falling action the fourth part of plot structure, in which the complications of the rising action are untangled.

farce a play characterized by broad humor, wild antics, and often slapstick, pratfalls, or other physical humor.

figurative usually applied to language that uses **figures of speech**. Figurative language heightens meaning by implicitly or explicitly representing something in terms of some other thing, the assumption being that the "other thing" will be more familiar to the reader.

figures of speech comparisons in which something is pictured or figured in other, more familiar terms.

first-person narrator a character, "I," who tells the story and necessarily has a limited point of view; may also be an unreliable narrator.

flashback a plot-structuring device whereby a scene from the fictional past is inserted into the fictional present or dramatized out of order.

flat character a fictional character, often but not always a minor character, who is relatively simple; who is presented as having few, though sometimes dominant, traits; and who thus does not change much in the course of a story. See **round character**.

focus the point from which people, events, and other details in a story are viewed. See **point of view**.

foil one character that serves as a contrast to another.

formal diction language that is lofty, dignified, and impersonal. See **colloquial diction** and **informal diction**.

free verse poetry characterized by varying line lengths, lack of traditional **meter**, and nonrhyming lines.

genre the largest category for classifying literature—fiction, poetry, drama. See **kind** and **subgenre**.

haiku an unrhymed poetic form, Japanese in origin, that contains seventeen syllables arranged in three lines of five, seven, and five syllables, respectively.

hero/heroine the leading male/female character, usually larger than life, sometimes almost godlike. See **antihero**, **protagonist**, and **villain**.

heroic couplet rhymed pairs of lines in iambic pentameter.

hexameter a line of poetry with six feet: "She comes, | she comes | again, | like ring | dove frayed | and fled" (Keats, *The Eve of St. Agnes*).

high (verbal) comedy humor that employs subtlety, wit, or the representation of refined life. See **low (physical) comedy**.

hyperbole overstatement characterized by exaggerated language.

iamb a metrical foot consisting of an unstressed syllable followed by a stressed one.

iambic pentameter a metrical form in which the basic foot is an **iamb** and most lines consist of five iambs; iambic pentameter is the most common poetic meter in English: "One com | mon note | on ei | ther lyre | did strike" (Dryden, "To the Memory of Mr. Oldham")

imagery broadly defined, any sensory detail or evocation in a work; more narrowly, the use of figurative language to evoke a feeling, to call to mind an idea, or to describe an object.

imitative structure a textual organization that mirrors as exactly as possible the structure of something that already exists as an object and can be seen.

implied author the guiding personality or value system behind a text; the implied author is not necessarily synonymous with the actual author.

informal diction language that is not as lofty or impersonal as **formal diction**; similar to everyday speech. See **colloquial diction**, which is one variety of informal diction.

initiation story a kind of short story in which a character—often but not always a child or young person—first learns a significant, usually life-changing truth about the universe, society, people, himself or herself.

in medias res "in the midst of things"; refers to opening a story in the middle of the **action**, necessitating filling in past details by **exposition** or **flashback**.

irony a situation or statement characterized by a significant difference between what is expected or understood and what actually happens or is meant. See **cosmic irony**, **dramatic irony**, and **situational irony**.

Italian sonnet *see* **Petrarchan sonnet**.

limerick a light or humorous verse form of mainly **anapestic** verses of which the first, second, and fifth lines are of three feet; the third and fourth lines are of two feet; and the rhyme scheme is *aabba*.

limited point of view or **limited focus** a perspective pinned to a single **character**, whether a first-person- or a third-person-centered consciousness, so that we cannot know for sure what is going on in the minds of other characters; thus, when the focal character leaves the room in a story we must go, too, and cannot know what is going on while our "eyes" or "camera" is gone. A variation on this, which generally has no name and is often lumped with the **omniscient point of view**, is the **point of view** that can wander like a camera from one character to another and close in or move back but cannot (or at least does not) get inside anyone's head and does not present from the inside any character's thoughts.

literary criticism the evaluative or interpretive work written by professional interpreters of texts. It is "criticism" not because it is negative or corrective, but rather because those who write criticism ask hard, analytical, crucial, or "critical" questions about the works they read.

litotes a figure of speech that emphasizes its subject by conscious **understatement**. An example from common speech is to say "Not bad" as a form of high praise.

low (physical) comedy humor that employs burlesque, horseplay, or the representation of unrefined life. *See* **high (verbal) comedy**.

lyric originally, a poem meant to be sung to the accompaniment of a lyre; now, any short poem in which the **speaker** expresses intense personal emotion rather than describing a narrative or dramatic situation.

major (main) characters those characters whom we see and learn about the most.

meditation a contemplation of some physical object as a way of reflecting upon some larger truth, often (but not necessarily) a spiritual one.

memory devices also called *mnemonic devices;* these devices—including rhyme, repetitive phrasing, and **meter**—when part of the structure of a longer work, make that work easier to memorize.

metaphor (1) one thing pictured as if it were something else, suggesting a likeness or **analogy** between them; (2) an implicit comparison or identification of one thing with another unlike itself without the use of a verbal signal. Sometimes used as a general term for **figure of speech**.

meter the more or less regular pattern of stressed and unstressed syllables in a line of poetry. This is determined by the kind of "foot" (**iambic** and **dactylic**, for example) and by the number of feet per line (five feet = pentameter, six feet = hexameter, for example).

minor characters those figures who fill out the story but who do not figure prominently in it.

mode style, manner, way of proceeding, as in "tragic mode"; often used synonymously with **genre, kind,** and **subgenre**.

monologue a speech of more than a few sentences, usually in a play but also in other genres, spoken by one person and uninterrupted by the speech of anyone else. *See* **soliloquy**.

motif a recurrent device, formula, or situation that deliberately connects a poem with common patterns of existing thought.

myth like **allegory**, myth usually is symbolic and extensive, including an entire work or story. Though it no longer is necessarily specific to or pervasive in a single **culture**—individual authors may now be said to create myths—myth still seems communal or cultural, while the symbolic can often involve private or personal myths. Thus stories more or less universally shared within a culture to explain its history and traditions are frequently called myths.

narrative structure a textual organization based on sequences of connected events usually presented in a straightforward chronological framework.

narrator the **character** who "tells" the story.

occasional poem a poem written about or for a specific occasion, public or private.

octameter a line of poetry with eight feet: "Once u | pon a | midnight | dreary | while I | pondered, | weak and | weary" (Poe, "The Raven").

octave the first eight lines of the Italian, or Petrarchan, sonnet. See also sestet.

ode a lyric poem characterized by a serious topic and formal tone but no prescribed formal pattern. See Keats's odes and Shelley's "Ode to the West Wind."

oeuvre the sum total of works verifiably written by an author. See canon.

omniscient point of view also called unlimited point of view; a perspective that can be seen from one character's view, then another's, then another's, or can be moved in or out of any character's mind at any time. Organization in which the reader has access to the perceptions and thoughts of all the characters in the story.

onomatopoeia a word capturing or approximating the sound of what it describes; *buzz* is a good example.

orchestra in classical Greek theater, a semicircular area used mostly for dancing by the chorus.

overplot a main plot in fiction or drama.

overstatement exaggerated language; also called hyperbole.

oxymoron a figure of speech that combines two apparently contradictory elements, as in *wise fool (sophomore)*.

parable a short fiction that illustrates an explicit moral lesson.

paradox a statement that seems contradictory but may actually be true, such as "That I may rise and stand, o'erthrow me" in Donne's "Batter My Heart."

parody a work that imitates another work for comic effect by exaggerating the style and changing the content of the original.

pastoral a poem (also called an eclogue, a bucolic, or an idyll) that describes the simple life of country folk, usually shepherds who live a timeless, painless (and sheepless) life in a world full of beauty, music, and love.

pastoral play a play that features the sort of idyllic world described in the definition for pastoral.

pentameter a line of poetry with five feet: "Nuns fret | not at | their con | vent's nar | row room" (Wordsworth).

persona the voice or figure of the author who tells and structures the story and who may or may not share the values of the actual author.

personification (or *prosopopeia*) treating an abstraction as if it were a person by endowing it with humanlike qualities.

Petrarchan sonnet also called Italian sonnet; a sonnet form that divides the poem into one section of eight lines (octave) and a second section of six lines (sestet), usually following the *abbaabba cdecde* rhyme scheme or, more loosely, an *abbacddc* pattern.

plot/plot structure the arrangement of the action.

plot summary a description of the arrangement of the action in the order in which it actually appears in a story. The term is popularly used to mean the description of the history, or chronological order, of the action as it would have appeared in reality. It is important to indicate exactly in which sense you are using the term.

plot time the temporal setting in which the action takes place in a story or play.

point of view also called focus; the point from which people, events, and other details in a story are viewed. This term is sometimes used to include both focus and voice.

precision exactness, accuracy of language or description.

presentation the second step in the creation of a character for the written text and the performed play; the representation of the character by the playwright in the words and actions specified in the text.

props articles and objects used on the stage.

proscenium arch an arch over the front of a stage; the proscenium serves as a "frame" for the action on stage.

protagonist the main character in a work, who may be male or female, heroic or not heroic. See antagonist, antihero, and hero/heroine. *Protagonist* is the most neutral term.

protest poem a poetic attack, usually quite direct, on allegedly unjust institutions or social injustices.

psychological realism a modification of the concept of realism, or telling it like it is, which recognizes that what is real to the individual is that which he or she perceives. It is the ground for the use of the **centered consciousness**, or the first-person narrator, since both of these present reality only as something perceived by the focal **character**.

reader time the actual time it takes a reader to read a work.

realism the practice in literature of attempting to describe nature and life without idealization and with attention to detail.

red herring a false lead, something that misdirects expectations.

referential when used to describe a poem, play, or story, *referential* means making textual use of a specific historical moment or event or, more broadly, making use of external, "natural," or "actual" detail.

reflective (meditative) structure a textual organization based on the pondering of a **subject**, **theme**, or event, and letting the mind play with it, skipping from one sound to another or to related thoughts or objects as the mind receives them.

represent to verbally depict an image so that readers can "see" it.

rhetorical trope traditional **figure of speech**, used for specific persuasive effects.

rhyme scheme the pattern of end rhymes in a poem, often noted by small letters, e.g., *abab* or *abba*, etc.

rhythm the modulation of weak and strong (or stressed and unstressed) elements in the flow of speech. In most poetry written before the twentieth century, rhythm was often expressed in regular, metrical forms; in prose and in **free verse**, rhythm is present but in a much less predictable and regular manner.

rising action the second of the five parts of **plot structure**, in which events complicate the situation that existed at the beginning of a work, intensifying the **conflict** or introducing new conflict.

rite of passage a ritual or ceremony marking an individual's passing from one stage or state to a more advanced one, or an event in one's life that seems to have such significance; a formal initiation. Rites of passage are common in initiation stories.

round characters complex characters,

often **major characters**, who can grow and change and "surprise convincingly"— that is, act in a way that you did not expect from what had gone before but now accept as possible, even probable, and "realistic."

sarcasm a form of **verbal irony** in which apparent praise is actually harshly or bitterly critical.

satire a literary work that holds up human failings to ridicule and censure.

scanning/scansion *Scansion* is the process of *scanning* a poem, analyzing the verse to show its **meter**, line by line.

second-person narrator a character, "you," who tells the story and necessarily has a **limited point of view**; may be seen as an extension of the reader, an external figure acting out a story, or an **auditor**; may also be an **unreliable narrator**.

sestet the last six lines of the Italian, or Petrarchan, **sonnet**. See also **octave**.

sestina an elaborate verse **structure** written in **blank verse** that consists of six stanzas of six lines each followed by a three-line stanza. The final words of each line in the first stanza appear in variable order in the next five stanzas, and are repeated in the middle and at the end of the three lines in the final stanza, as in Elizabeth Bishop's "Sestina."

set the design, decoration, and scenery of the stage during a play.

setting the time and place of the **action** in a story, poem, or play.

Shakespearean sonnet also called an English sonnet; a sonnet form that divides the poem into three units of four lines each and a final unit of two lines (4+4+4+2 structure). Its classic rhyme scheme is *abab cdcd efef gg*, but there are variations.

shaped verse another name for **concrete poetry**; poetry that is shaped to look like an object.

simile a direct, explicit comparison of one thing to another, usually using the words *like* or *as* to draw the connection. *See* **metaphor**.

situation the context of the literary work's **action**, what is happening when the story, poem, or play begins.

situational irony in a narrative, the incongruity between what the reader and/or character expects to happen and what actually does happen.

skene a low building in the back of the stage area in classical Greek theaters. It represented the palace or temple in front of which the **action** took place.

soliloquy a monologue in which the **character** in a play is alone and speaking only to him- or herself.

sonnet a fixed verse form consisting of fourteen lines usually in **iambic pentameter**. *See* **Italian sonnet** and **Shakespearean sonnet**.

spatial setting the place of a poem, story, or play.

speaker the person, not necessarily the author, who is the voice of a poem.

Spenserian stanza a **stanza** that consists of eight lines of **iambic pentameter** (five feet) followed by a ninth line of iambic **hexameter** (six feet). The rhyme scheme is *ababbcbcc*.

spondee a metrical foot consisting of a pair of stressed syllables ("Dead set").

stage directions The words in the printed text of a play that inform the director, crew, actors, and readers how to stage, perform, or imagine the play. Stage directions are not spoken aloud and may appear at the beginning of a play, before any scene, or attached to a line of dialogue. The place and time of the action, the design of the set itself, and at times the characters' actions or tone of voice are dictated through stage directions and interpreted by the group of people that put on a performance.

stanza a section of a poem demarcated by extra line spacing. Some distinguish between a stanza, a division marked by a single pattern of **meter** or rhyme, and a verse paragraph, a division governed by thought rather than sound pattern.

stereotype a **characterization** based on conscious or unconscious assumptions that some one aspect—such as gender, age, ethnic or national identity, religion, occupation, marital status, and so on—is predictably accompanied by certain **character** traits, actions, even values.

stock character a **character** that appears in a number of stories or plays, such as the cruel stepmother, the braggart, and so forth.

structure the organization or arrangement of the various elements in a work.

style a distinctive manner of expression; each author's style is expressed through his/her **diction, rhythm, imagery**, and so on.

subgenre a division within the category of a **genre**; *novel, novella*, and *short story* are subgenres of the genre *fiction*.

subject (1) the concrete and literal description of what a story is about; (2) the general or specific area of concern of a poem—also called **topic**; (3) also used in fiction commentary to denote a **character** whose inner thoughts and feelings are recounted.

subplot another name for an **underplot**; a subordinate **plot** in fiction or drama.

suspense the expectation of and doubt about what is going to happen next.

syllabic verse a form in which the poet establishes a precise number of syllables to a line and repeats it in subsequent stanzas.

symbol a person, place, thing, event, or pattern in a literary work that designates itself and at the same time figuratively represents or "stands for" something else. Often the thing or idea represented is more abstract, general, non- or superrational; the symbol, more concrete and particular.

symbolic poem a poem in which the use of **symbols** is so pervasive and internally consistent that the larger referential world is distanced, if not forgotten.

syntax the way words are put together to form phrases, clauses, and sentences.

technopaegnia the art of "shaped" poems in which the visual force is supposed to work spiritually or magically.

temporal setting the time of a story, poem, or play.

terza rima a verse form consisting of three-line **stanzas** in which the second line of each stanza rhymes with the first and third of the next.

tetrameter a line of poetry with four feet: "The Grass | divides | as with | a comb" (Dickinson).

tetrameter couplet rhymed pairs of lines that contain (in classical **iambic, trochaic**, and **anapestic** verse) four measures of two feet or (in modern English verse) four metrical feet.

theme (1) a generalized, abstract paraphrase of the inferred central or dominant idea or concern of a work; (2) the statement a poem makes about its subject.

third-person narrator a character, "he" or "she," who "tells" the story; may have either a limited point of view or an omniscient point of view; may also be an unreliable narrator.

thrust stage a stage design that allows the audience to sit around three sides of the major acting area.

tone the attitude a literary work takes toward its subject and theme.

topic (1) the concrete and literal description of what a story is about; (2) a poem's general or specific area of concern. Also called subject.

tradition an inherited, established, or customary practice.

traditional symbols symbols that, through years of usage, have acquired an agreed-upon significance, an accepted meaning. See archetype.

tragedy a drama in which a character (usually a good and noble person of high rank) is brought to a disastrous end in his or her confrontation with a superior force (fortune, the gods, social forces, universal values), but also comes to understand the meaning of his or her deeds and to accept an appropriate punishment. Often the protagonist's downfall is a direct result of a fatal flaw in his or her character.

trochaic a metrical form in which the basic foot is a trochee.

trochee a metrical foot consisting of a stressed syllable followed by an unstressed one ("Homer").

turning point the third part of plot structure, the point at which the action stops rising and begins falling or reversing. Also called climax.

underplot a subordinate plot in fiction or drama. Also called a subplot.

understatement language that avoids obvious emphasis or embellishment; litotes is one form of it.

unity of time one of the three unities of drama as described by Aristotle in his *Poetics*. Unity of time refers to the limitation of a play's action to a short period—usually the time it takes to present the play or, at any rate, no longer than a day. See classical unities.

unlimited point of view also called omniscient point of view; a perspective that can be seen from one character's view, then another's, then another's, or can be moved in or out of any character's mind at any time. Organization in which the reader has access to the perceptions and thoughts of all the characters in the story.

unreliable narrator a speaker or voice whose vision or version of the details of a story are consciously or unconsciously deceiving; such a narrator's version is usually subtly undermined by details in the story or the reader's general knowledge of facts outside the story. If, for example, the narrator were to tell you that Columbus was Spanish and that he discovered America in the fourteenth century when his ship the *Golden Hind* landed on the coast of Florida near present-day Gainesville, you might not trust other things he tells you.

verbal irony a statement in which the literal meaning differs from the implicit meaning. See dramatic irony and situational irony.

verse paragraph see stanza.

villain the one who opposes the hero and heroine—that is, the "bad guy." See antagonist and hero/heroine.

villanelle a verse form consisting of nineteen lines divided into six stanzas—five tercets (three-line stanzas) and one quatrain (four-line stanza). The first and third lines of the first tercet rhyme, and this rhyme is repeated through each of the next four tercets and in the last two lines of the concluding quatrain. The villanelle is also known for its repetition of select lines. A good example of a twentieth-century villanelle is Dylan Thomas's "Do Not Go Gentle into That Good Night."

voice the acknowledged or unacknowledged source of a story's words; the speaker; the "person" telling the story.

word order the positioning of words in relation to one another.

Permissions Acknowledgments

Texts

FICTION

JAMES BALDWIN: "Sonny's Blues." Originally published in *Partisan Review*. Collected in *Going to Meet the Man* by James Baldwin. Copyright © 1965 by James Baldwin. Copyright renewed. Published by Vintage Books. Reprinted by arrangement with the James Baldwin Estate.

TONI CADE BAMBARA: "Gorilla, My Love" from *Gorilla, My Love* by Toni Cade Bambara. Copyright © 1971 by Toni Cade Bambara. Reprinted by permission of Random House, Inc.

LINDA BREWER: "20/20" from *Micro Fiction: An Anthology of Really Short Stories* edited by Jerome Stern. Reprinted with the permission of the author.

ANGELA CARTER: "A Souvenir from Japan." Originally published in *Fireworks*. Copyright © 1995 by the Estate of Angela Carter. Reprinted by permission of the Estate of Angela Carter, c/o Rogers, Coleridge and White Ltd., 20 Powis Mews, London W11 1JN.

RAYMOND CARVER: "Cathedral" from *Cathedral* by Raymond Carver. Copyright © 1981, 1982, 1983 by Raymond Carver. Reprinted by permission of Alfred A. Knopf, Inc.

JOHN CHEEVER: "The Country Husband" from *The Short Stories of John Cheever* by John Cheever. Copyright © 1978 by John Cheever. Reprinted by permission of Alfred A. Knopf, Inc., a division of Random House, Inc.

LOUISE ERDRICH: "Love Medicine" from *Love Medicine* by Louise Erdrich. Copyright © 1984, 1993 by Louise Erdrich. Reprinted by permission of Henry Holt & Company, LLC.

WILLIAM FAULKNER: "A Rose for Emily" from *Collected Stories of William Faulkner* (New York: Random House, 1950). Reprinted by permission.

ERNEST HEMINGWAY: "Hills Like White Elephants" from *Men Without Women* by Ernest Hemingway. Copyright © 1927 by Charles Scribner's Sons. Copyright renewed 1955 by Ernest Hemingway. Reprinted by permission of Scribner, a division of Simon & Schuster, and the Hemingway Foreign Rights Trust.

JAMES JOYCE: "Araby" from *Dubliners* by James Joyce, copyright 1916 by B.W. Heubsch. Definitive text copyright © 1967 by the Estate of James Joyce. Used by permission of Viking Penguin, a division of Penguin Group (USA), Inc.

FRANZ KAFKA: "A Hunger Artist" from *Franz Kafka: The Complete Stories* by Nahum N. Glatzer, Editor. Copyright © 1946, 1947, 1948, 1949, 1954, 1958, 1971 by Schocken Books, Inc. Reprinted by permission of Schocken Books, published by Pantheon Books, a division of Random House, Inc.

YASUNARI KAWABATA: "The Grasshopper and the Bell Cricket" from *Palm-of-the-Hand Stories* by Yasunari Kawabata. Translated by Lane Dunlop and J. Martin Holman. Translation copyright © 1988 by Lane Dunlop and J. Martin Holman. Reprinted by permission of North Point Press, a division of Farrar, Straus & Giroux, Inc.

JAMAICA KINCAID: "Girl" from *At the Bottom of the River* by Jamaica Kincaid. Copyright © 1983 by Jamaica Kincaid. Reprinted by permission of Farrar, Straus & Giroux, Inc.

POETRY

Illustrations

Yasunari Kawabata. Bettmann/Corbis.

Jamaica Kincaid. Jeremy Bembara/Corbis.

D. H. Lawrence. University of Nottingham Library, D. H. Lawrence Collection. Reprinted by permission of the University of Nottingham.

Herman Melville. Bettmann/Corbis.

Bharati Mukherjee. Courtesy of Hyperion.

Flannery O'Connor. Photo by Ralph Morrissey. Reprinted by the courtesy of the Morrissey Collection and the photographic archives, Vanderbilt University, Nashville, Tennessee.

Grace Paley. Christopher Felver/Corbis.

Edgar Allan Poe. Bettmann/Corbis.

Katherine Anne Porter. Bettmann/Corbis.

Amy Tan. Christopher Felver/Corbis.

Eudora Welty. Bettmann/Corbis.

William Carlos Williams. Pach Brothers/Corbis.

Poetry

W. H. Auden. Corbis.

Elizabeth Bishop. Bettmann/Corbis.

William Blake. Bettmann/Corbis.

Gwendolyn Brooks. AP/Wide World Photos.

Elizabeth Barrett Browning. Bettmann/Corbis.

Robert Browning. Bettmann/Corbis.

Robert Burns. Bettmann/Corbis.

Samuel Taylor Coleridge. Bettmann/Corbis.

Emily Dickinson. Bettmann/Corbis.

John Donne. Bettmann/Corbis.

Paul Laurence Dunbar. Corbis.

T. S. Eliot. Hulton-Deutsch Collection/Corbis.

Robert Frost. E. O. Hoppé/Corbis.

Thomas Gunn. Christopher Felver/Corbis.

Thomas Hardy. Bettmann/Corbis.

Seamus Heaney. Christopher Felver/Corbis.

Robert Herrick. Hulton-Deutsch Collection/Corbis.

Gerard Manley Hopkins. The Granger Collection, New York.

Ben Jonson. Corbis.

John Keats. Bettmann/Corbis.

Galway Kinnell. Christopher Felver/Corbis.

Andrew Marvell. Mary Evans Picture Library.

Claude McKay. Corbis.

Edna St. Vincent Millay. Underwood & Underwood/Corbis.

John Milton. Stefano Bianchetti/Corbis.

Howard Nemerov. Bettmann/Corbis.

Sharon Olds. Christopher Felver/Corbis.

Dorothy Parker. AP/Wide World Photos.

Sylvia Plath. Courtesy of the Sylvia Plath Collection, Mortimer Rare Book Room, Smith College.

Ezra Pound. E. O. Hoppé/Corbis.

Adrienne Rich. Courtesy of Lilian Kemp.

William Shakespeare. Droeshout engraving. Chris Hellier/Corbis.

Wallace Stevens. Bettmann/Corbis.

Lord Alfred Tennyson. Bettmann/Corbis.

Index of Authors

Index of Titles and First Lines